# SPACE MARINES

Dissolution comes from the walls. For a moment, they lose all definition. Chaos itself billows and writhes. And the ship can also sing. The corridor resounds with a fanfare of screaming human voices and a drum-beat that is the march of wrath itself. Then the walls give birth. Their offspring have hides the colour of blood. Their limbs are long, grasping, with muscles of steel stretched over deformed bones. Their skulls are mocking, predatory fusions of the horned goat and the armoured helm. Their eyes are blank with glowing, pus-yellow hatred. They are bloodletters, daemons of Khorne, and the sight of their arrival has condemned mortal humans beyond counting to a madness of terror.

As for my brothers and myself, at last we have a foe to fight. We form a circle of might and faith. 'Now, brothers,' Dantalion says. 'Now this vessel of the damned shows its true nature. Strike hard, steadfast in the light of Sanguinius and the Emperor!'

'These creatures, sergeant,' I tell Gamigin, 'you are at full liberty to kill.'

WARHAMMER
40,000
SPACE MARINE BATTLES

A WARHAMMER 40,000 OMNIBUS

# SPACE MARINES

EDITED BY
CHRISTIAN DUNN
NICK KYME
LINDSEY PRIESTLEY

BLACK LIBRARY

**A Black Library Publication**

*Heroes of the Space Marines* copyright © 2009, Games Workshop Ltd.
*Legends of the Space Marines* copyright © 2010, Games Workshop Ltd.
*Victories of the Space Marines* copyright © 2011, Games Workshop Ltd.
'Eclipse of Hope' & 'Torturer's Thirst' copyright © 2012, Games Workshop Ltd.
'Tower of Blood' was first published in *Hammer and Bolter magazine*,
copyright © 2011, Games Workshop Ltd.
'Last Man Standing', 'The Chosen' & 'The Pilgrim' first published in *Warhammer Monthly*
magazine, copyright © 1998-2004, Games Workshop Ltd.
All rights reserved.

This omnibus edition published in Great Britain in 2013 by
Black Library,
Games Workshop Ltd.,
Willow Road,
Nottingham, NG7 2WS, UK.

10 9 8 7 6 5 4 3 2 1

Cover illustration by Marek Okon.

© Games Workshop Limited 1998, 2013. All rights reserved.

Black Library, the Black Library logo, The Horus Heresy, The Horus Heresy logo, The
Horus Heresy eye device, Space Marine Battles, the Space Marine Battles logo, Warhammer
40,000, the Warhammer 40,000 logo, Games Workshop, the Games Workshop logo and
all associated brands, names, characters, illustrations and images from the Warhammer
40,000 universe are either ®, ™ and/or © Games Workshop Ltd 2000-2013, variably
registered in the UK and other countries around the world. All rights reserved.

A CIP record for this book is available from the British Library.

UK ISBN 13: 978 1 84970 484 7
US ISBN 13: 978 1 84970 485 4

No part of this publication may be reproduced, stored in a retrieval system, or transmitted
in any form or by any means, electronic, mechanical, photocopying, recording or
otherwise, without the prior permission of the publishers.

This is a work of fiction. All the characters and events portrayed in this book are fictional,
and any resemblance to real people or incidents is purely coincidental.

See Black Library on the internet at

# www.blacklibrary.com

Find out more about Games Workshop
and the world of Warhammer 40,000 at

# www.games-workshop.com

Printed and bound by CPI Group (UK) Ltd, Croydon, CR0 4YY

It is the 41st millennium. For more than a hundred centuries the Emperor has sat immobile on the Golden Throne of Earth. He is the master of mankind by the will of the gods, and master of a million worlds by the might of his inexhaustible armies. He is a rotting carcass writhing invisibly with power from the Dark Age of Technology. He is the Carrion Lord of the Imperium for whom a thousand souls are sacrificed every day, so that he may never truly die.

Yet even in his deathless state, the Emperor continues his eternal vigilance. Mighty battlefleets cross the daemon-infested miasma of the warp, the only route between distant stars, their way lit by the Astronomican, the psychic manifestation of the Emperor's will. Vast armies give battle in His name on uncounted worlds. Greatest amongst his soldiers are the Adeptus Astartes, the Space Marines, bio-engineered super-warriors. Their comrades in arms are legion: the Imperial Guard and countless Planetary Defence Forces, the ever-vigilant Inquisition and the tech-priests of the Adeptus Mechanicus to name only a few. But for all their multitudes, they are barely enough to hold off the ever-present threat from aliens, heretics, mutants - and worse.

To be a man in such times is to be one amongst untold billions. It is to live in the cruellest and most bloody regime imaginable. These are the tales of those times. Forget the power of technology and science, for so much has been forgotten, never to be re-learned. Forget the promise of progress and understanding, for in the grim dark future there is only war. There is no peace amongst the stars, only an eternity of carnage and slaughter, and the laughter of thirsting gods.

# CONTENTS

## Legends of the Space Marines

## Victories of the Space Marines

# POWER OF THE SPACE MARINES

For more than a generation now, the term Space Marine has been synonymous with the genetically enhanced giants of the Warhammer 40,000 universe. Millions of 28mm scale simulacra of these superhuman killing machines sit in the collections of hobbyists worldwide, lovingly painted in the colours of the Ultramarines, Dark Angels, Space Wolves or other Chapters of the Adeptus Astartes, often of the hobbyist's own creation. So pervasive and persuasive has the concept of the Space Marine become that it is almost at the point of being used as shorthand for Warhammer 40,000 as a whole. No coincidence then that when one of the world's largest software publishers wanted to create a first-person shooter based upon the Warhammer 40,000 universe, not only did they opt for a Space Marine as a protagonist, they also called it that.

Just as the notion of the Warhammer 40,000 Space Marine has entered the consciousness of that sub-strata of society we lovingly refer to as 'geeks', so too has it become ingrained into science fiction literature. Millions of words have been published in dozens of languages of their adventures, hundreds of novels and short stories that bring to life the toy soldier on the shelf or marching across the table in their local Games Workshop store.

The appetite for these stories is enormous. Each month, new tales are published in digital and printed form, in prose, audio and even graphic form (some of which are included in this volume) and still the reader hungers for more. Again, it's no coincidence that the first of Black Library's *New York Times* bestsellers were drawn from the Horus Heresy series, the ultimate Space Marine story of brother versus brother, Legion against Legion.

Like the aforementioned hobbyists, the authors of these tales carefully paint their Space Marines, words their medium, the page their canvas. Whereas the Space Marines on the tabletop are brought to life by the brush strokes of their owner, their fictional analogues breathe through the skill of the author, transporting the reader 38,000 years into the future amid battlefields torn asunder by the heretic and the alien, the enemy within and the enemy without. In all corners of the globe, readers eagerly await the next instalment of the adventures of their favourite heroes and anti-heroes (no simple black and white morality in the grim darkness of the far future) or long for the day that their favourite Chapter or character will come alive on the page.

There are a thousand Space Marines in each individual Chapter, a thousand Chapters that make up the Adeptus Astartes. One million characters, over a million potential stories.

Here are just some of them.

*Christian Dunn*
*Nottingham, England*
*May 2013*

# HEROES OF THE
# SPACE MARINES

# THE SKULL HARVEST

*Graham McNeill*

Dead, glassy eyes stared up at the bar patrons from the floor as the rolling head finally came to a halt. It had been a swift blow, the edge of the killer's palm like a blade, and the snarling warrior's head was ripped from his neck before the last words of his challenge were out of his mouth.

The body still stood, its murderer grasping the edge of its crimson-stained breastplate in one gnarled grey fist. Blood pooled beneath the head and squirted upwards from the stump of neck. The body's legs began to twitch, as though it sought to escape its fate even in death. The killer released his grip and turned away as the body crashed to the dirty, ash- and dust-streaked floor in a clatter of steel and dead meat.

The excitement over, the patrons of the darkened bar returned to their drinks and plotting, for no one came to a place like this without schemes of revenge, murder, pillage and destruction in mind.

Honsou of the Iron Warriors was no exception, and his champion's bloody display of lethal prowess was just the first step in his own grand design.

The air was thick with intrigue, grease and smoke, the latter curling around heavy rafters that looked as though they had once been part of a spaceship. Irregular clay bricks supported a roof formed from sheets of corrugated iron, and thin slats of harsh light, like the burning white sky of Medrengard, shone through bullet holes and gaps in the construction.

The killer of the now headless body licked the blood from the edge of its hand, and Honsou grinned as he saw the urge to continue killing in

15

his champion's all too familiar grey eyes and taut posture. It called itself the Newborn, and was clad in tarnished power armour the colour of wrought iron. Its shoulder guards were edged in yellow and black, and a rough cloak of ochre was draped around its wide shoulders. It was every inch an Iron Warrior but for its face: a slack fleshmask of stolen skin that was the image of a man Honsou would one day kill. Stitched together from the skins of dead prisoners, the Newborn's face was that of the killer in the dark, the terror of the night and the lurker in the shadows that haunts the dreams of the fearful.

It turned towards Honsou and he felt a delicious shiver of vicarious excitement as he glanced at the dead body on the floor.

'Nicely done,' said Honsou. 'Poor bastard didn't even get to finish insulting me.'

The Newborn shrugged as it sat across the table from him. 'He was nothing, just a slave warrior.'

'True, but he died just as bloodily as the next man.'

'Killing this one might make you the "next man" to his master,' said the Newborn.

'Better he dies now than we end up recruiting him and he fails in battle,' said Cadaras Grendel from across the table as he finished a tin mug of harsh liquor. 'Don't want any damn wasters next to me if we have to fight anything tough in the next few days.'

Grendel was a brute, an armoured killer who delighted in slaughter and the misery of others. Once, he had fought for a rival Warsmith on Medrengard, though in defeat he had transferred his allegiance to Honsou. Despite that switch, Honsou knew Grendel's continued service was bought with the promise of carnage and that his loyalty was that of a starving wolf on a short leash. The warrior's face was a scarred and pitted nightmare of battered flesh, his cruel features topped with a close-cropped mohican.

'Trust me,' said the warrior next to Grendel, 'the Skull Harvest weeds out the chaff early on. Only the strongest and most vicious will survive to the end.'

Honsou nodded and said, 'You should know, Vaanes. You've been here before.'

Clad in the midnight-black armour of the Raven Guard, Ardaric Vaanes was the polar opposite of Cadaras Grendel; lithe, elegant and handsome. His long dark hair was bound in a tight scalp-lock and his hooded eyes were set in a face that was aquiline and which bore ritual scars on each cheek.

The former Raven Guard had changed since Honsou had first recruited him to train the Newborn. Honsou had never fully believed that a warrior once loyal to the False Emperor could completely throw off the shackles of his former master, but from what Cadaras Grendel had told him of Vaanes's actions on the orbital battery above

Tarsis Ultra, it seemed such concerns were groundless.

'Indeed,' agreed Vaanes. 'And I can't say I'm happy to be back. This isn't a place to come to unless you're prepared for the worst. Especially during the Skull Harvest.'

'We're prepared for the worst,' said Honsou, leaning over and lifting the severed head from the floor and depositing it on their table. The dead man's expression was frozen in surprise, and Honsou wondered if he'd lived long enough to see the bar spinning around as his head rolled across the floor. The skin was waxy and moist, the iconic mark of a red skull branded into its forehead over a tattoo of an eight-pointed star. 'After all, that's why we're here and why I had the Newborn kill this one.'

Like his warriors, Honsou had changed a great deal since his rise to prominence had begun on Hydra Cordatus. His unique silver arm was new and a bolt-round had pulverised the left side of his face, leaving it a burned and bloody ruin and making a glutinous, fused mess of his eye. That eye had been replaced with an augmetic implant and as much as he had changed physically, Honsou knew that it was nothing compared to the changes wrought within him.

Vaanes reached over and lifted the head, turning it over and allowing the blood to drip down his gauntlets. Honsou saw Vaanes's eyes widen as he touched the head, his nostrils flaring as he took in the scents of the dead man, while running his fingers over the cold flesh.

'This was one of Pashtoq Uluvent's fighters,' said Vaanes.

'Who?'

'A follower of the Blood God,' said Vaanes, turning the head around and tapping the sigil branded on its forehead. 'That's his mark.'

'Is he powerful?' asked Grendel.

'Very powerful,' said Vaanes. 'He has come to the Skull Harvest many times to recruit fighters for his warband.'

'And he's won?'

'Champions that don't win the Skull Harvest end up dead,' said Vaanes.

'Killing one of his men ought to get his attention,' said Honsou.

'I think it just did,' said Grendel, nodding towards the bar's door with a wide grin of anticipation.

A towering warrior in armour that had once been black and yellow, but which was now so stained with blood that it resembled a deep, rusted burgundy, marched towards their table.

Grendel reached for his weapon, but Honsou shook his head.

The warrior's helm was horned and two long tusks sprouted from beneath the visor of his helmet. Honsou couldn't tell whether they were part of his armour or his flesh. The same symbol branded into the head was cut into the warrior's breastplate, and his breath was a rasping growl, like that of a ravenous beast. He carried an axe with a bronze blade that dripped blood and shone with the dull fire of a smouldering forge.

The warrior planted his axe, blade down, on the floor and banged his fist against his breastplate. 'I am Vosok Dall, servant of the Skull Throne, and I have come to take your life.'

Honsou took the measure of the warrior in a heartbeat.

Vosok Dall was a renegade, from the Scythes of the Emperor by the crossed-scythe heraldry on his shoulder guard, but a warrior who now killed in the name of a blood-drenched god that revelled in murder and battle. He would be strong and capable, with a hunger for glory and martial honour unmatched even by those who still fought for the Imperium.

'I thought your Chapter was dead,' said Honsou, pushing himself to his feet. 'Didn't the swarm fleets turn your world into an airless rock?'

'You speak of events that do not concern you, maggot,' barked Dall. 'I am here to kill you, so ready your weapon.'

'You see,' said Honsou, shaking his head. 'That's what you followers of the Blood God always get wrong. You always talk too much.'

'No more talk then,' said Dall. 'Fight.'

Honsou didn't answer, simply sweeping his axe from beside the table. The blade of the weapon was glossy and black, its sheened surface featureless and seeming to swallow any light unfortunate enough to touch it.

Honsou was fast, but Dall was faster and brought his own axe up to block the strike. The warrior spun the axe and slashed it around in a bifurcating sweep. Honsou ducked and rammed the haft of his weapon into Dall's gut, spinning away from his opponent's reverse stroke. The blade passed millimetres from his head and he felt the angry heat that burned within the warp-forged weapon.

He took a double-handed grip on his axe and widened his stance as Dall came at him. The warrior of the Blood God was fast and his roar of hatred shook the very walls, but Honsou had faced down more terrifying foes than Vosok Dall and lived.

Honsou stepped to meet the attack, throwing his arm up to block the blow. The axe slashed down and bit deeply, the blade stuck fast into Honsou's forearm. Like the Newborn and Cadaras Grendel, Honsou wore the dull metal colours of the Iron Warriors, but the arm struck by Vosok Dall's axe appeared to be incongruously fashioned from the purest, gleaming silver.

Dall grunted in shock, and Honsou knew this warrior would expect anything he hit with his axe to go down and stay down.

That shock cost him his life.

The warrior tugged at his weapon, but the blade was stuck fast and Honsou swung his axe in a mighty downward arc, hammering the glossy black blade through the top of his foe's skull. The axe smashed through Dall's helmet, skull and neck before finally lodging in the centre of his sternum.

Vosok Dall dropped to his knees and toppled onto his side, his dead weight dragging Honsou with him. Dall's entire body convulsed as the malevolent warp beast bound to Honsou's axe ripped his soul apart for sport.

Blood fanned from the cloven skull in a flood of crimson, and even as Dall's soul was devoured, his grip remained strong on his weapon.

A bright orange line, like that of a welder's acetylene torch, hissed around the edge of where Dall's axe was buried in Honsou's arm and the weapon fell free with a crescent-shaped bite taken from it. Even as Honsou watched, the fiery lustre of the blade faded as its power passed away.

Where Dall's blade had penetrated Honsou's arm was unblemished and smooth, as though it had come straight from the silversmith's workbench. Honsou neither knew nor cared about the source of the arm's power to heal itself, it was enough that it had saved him once again.

He rose to his full height, standing triumphant over the dead body of Vosok Dall as the patrons of the bar stared in amazement at him.

'I am Honsou of the Iron Warriors!' he bellowed, lifting his axe high over his head. 'I am here for the Skull Harvest and I am afraid of no man. Any warrior who thinks he is worthy of joining me should make himself known at my camp. Look for the banner of the Iron Skull on the northern promontory.'

A man in a battered flak vest with a long rifle slung over his shoulder and a battered Guardsman's helmet jammed onto his rugged features stood up as Honsou made his way to the door.

'Every warlord that comes in here thinks he's got a big plan,' said the man. 'What's so special about yours? Most of them never come back, so why should I fight for you?'

'What's your name?'

'Pettar. Hain Pettar.'

'Because I'm going to win, Hain Pettar.'

'They all say that,' said Pettar.

Honsou shouldered his axe and said, 'The difference is I mean it.'

'So, who you planning to fight if you live through the Skull Harvest?'

Honsou grinned. 'The worlds of Ultramar are going to burn in the fires of my crusade.'

'Ultramar?' said Pettar. 'Now I know you're crazy; that fight's suicide.'

'Maybe,' said Honsou. 'But maybe not, and if it's not a fight worth making, then this galaxy has run out of things to live for.'

The mountain city simmered with tension and threat. Warriors of every size and description thronged the paths, squares and narrow alleys that twisted between the city's ramshackle structures of brick and junk. This close to the Skull Harvest, the city's inhabitants were on edge, hands hovering near the contoured handles of pistols and skin-wrapped sword grips. Honsou could read the currents of threat as clearly as the transformed magos, Adept Cycerin, could read the currents of the empyrean and knew violence was ready to erupt at any second.

Which was just as it should be.

The sky was the colour of a smeared borealis, swirling with unnatural hues known only to the insane. Lightning flashed in aerial whirlpools and Honsou tore his gaze from the pleasing spectacle. Only the unwary dared stare into the abyss of such skies and he grinned as he remembered his flesh playing host to one of the creatures that dwelled beyond the lurid colours.

The streets were sloping thoroughfares of hard-packed earth, and Honsou scanned the crowds around them for an old enemy, a new rival or simply a warrior looking to make a name for himself by killing someone like him.

Hawkers and charlatans lined the streets, filling the air with strange aromas, chants and promises, each offering pleasures and wares that could only be found in a place this deep in the Maelstrom; nightmare-flects, blades of daemon-forged steel, carnal delights with warp-altered courtesans, opiates concocted from the immaterial substance of void-creatures and promises of eternal youth.

In addition to the swaggering pirate bands, mercenary kin-broods and random outcasts, lone warriors stood at street corners, boasting of their prowess while demonstrating their skills. A grey-skinned loxatl climbed the brickwork of a dark tower, its armature weapons flexing and aiming without apparent need for hands. A robed Scythian distilled venom before a gathered audience, while a band of men and women in heavy armour demonstrated sword and axe skills. Others spun firearms, took shots at hurled targets and displayed yet more impressive feats of exceptional marksmanship.

'Any of them taking your fancy?' asked Cadaras Grendel, nodding towards the martial displays.

Honsou shook his head. 'No, these are the chaff. The real warriors of skill won't show their hand so early.'

'Like we just did?' said Vaanes.

'We're new here,' explained Honsou. 'I needed to get my name into circulation, but I'll let Pashtoq Uluvent build it for me when he comes against us.'

'You had me kill that man to provoke an attack on us?' queried the Newborn.

'Absolutely,' said Honsou. 'I need the warriors gathered here to know me and respect me, but I can't go around like these fools telling people how powerful I am. I'll get others to do that for me.'

'Assuming we survive Uluvent's retaliation.'

'There's always that,' agreed Honsou. 'But I never said this venture wouldn't be without some risk.'

* * *

They made their way through the streets of the city, following a path that took them through areas of bleak night, searing sunlight and voids of deadened sound where every step seemed to take a lifetime. Coming from Medrengard, a world deep in the Eye of Terror, Honsou was no stranger to the chaotic flux of worlds touched by the warp, but the capricious nature of the environment around the mountain was unsettling.

He looked towards the mountain's summit, where the mighty citadel of this world's ruler squatted like a vast crown of black stone. Hewn from the rock of the mountain, the entire peak had been hollowed out and reshaped into a colossal fortress from which its master plotted his sector-wide carnage.

Curved redoubts and precisely angled bastions cut into the rock dominated the upper reaches of the mountain and coils of razor wire, like an endless field of thorns, carpeted every approach to its great, iron-spiked barbican.

Honsou's Iron Warrior soul swelled with pleasure at the sight of so formidable a fortress.

Mighty defensive turrets protected the fortress, armed with guns capable of bringing down the heaviest spaceship and smashing any armada that dared come against this place.

Even in its prime, Khalan-Ghol could not have boasted so fearsome an array of weapons.

Ardaric Vaanes leaned in close and pointed to a nearby gun emplacement aimed at the heavens. 'Big guns never tire, isn't that what he always says?'

'So it's said,' agreed Honsou, 'but if what happened on Medrengard taught me anything, it's that fortresses are static and it's only a matter of time until someone attacks you. This place is impressive, right enough, but my days of fortress building are over.'

'I never thought I'd hear an Iron Warrior say he was tired of fortresses.'

'I'm not tired of fortresses, Vaanes,' said Honsou with a grin. 'I'm just directing my energies towards bringing them to ruin.'

Honsou had based his warriors on a northern promontory of the mountain, a site that offered natural protection in the form of sheer cliffs on three sides that dropped thousands of metres to the valley floor. Under normal circumstances, it would have been a poor site for a fortress, as it could easily be blockaded, but Honsou had no intention of staying for any length of time. His warband had cleared the promontory of its former occupants in a brutal firefight that had seen them hurling their captives to their doom as an offering to the gods.

The Iron Skull flew over Honsou's temporary fortress, a graceless collection of gabions fashioned from linked sections of thick wire mesh lined with heavy-duty fabric and filled with sand, earth, rocks and gravel. A line of these blocky gabions stretched across the width of the promontory, and yet more had been stacked to form towers where heavy weapons could be mounted.

In truth, it was more of a defensive wall than a fortress and wasn't a patch on even the lowliest Warsmith's citadel on Medrengard, but it was as strong as he could make it and should suffice for the length of the Skull Harvest.

An adamantine gate swung outwards as Honsou and the others approached, the guns mounted on the blocky towers either side of it tracking them until they passed inside. Two dozen Iron Warriors manned the walls, their armour dusty and scored by the planet's harshly unpredictable climate. The remainder of Honsou's force was spread throughout the camp or aboard the *Warbreed*, the venerable ship that had brought them here and which now moored uneasily among the fleets in orbit around this world.

Honsou marched directly to an iron-sheeted pavilion at the centre of his camp, itself protected by more of the blocky, earth-filled gabions. His banner snapped and fluttered in the wind, the Iron Skull seeming to grin with a mocking sneer, as though daring the world to attack. Grendel, Vaanes and the Newborn followed him past the two hulking warriors in Terminator armour guarding the entrance to the pavilion. Each of the giant praetorians was armed with a long, hook-bladed pike and looked like graven metal statues, their bodies as inflexible as their hearts.

Inside the pavilion, the walls were hung with maps depicting arcs of the galaxy, planetary orbits, system diagrams and a variety of mystical sigils scrawled on pale sheets of skin, both human and alien. An iron-framed bed sat in the centre of the space, surrounded by bare metal footlockers filled with books and scrolls. A trio of smoking braziers filled the pavilion with the heady scent of burning oils said to draw the eyes of the gods.

Honsou set his axe upon a rack of weapons and poured himself a goblet of water from a copper ewer. He didn't offer any to his champions and took a long draught before turning to face them.

'So,' he began, 'What do you make of our first foray?'

Grendel helped himself to a goblet of water and said, 'Not bad, though I didn't get to kill anything. If this Pashtoq Uluvent is as mad as all the other followers of the Blood God I've met, then we shouldn't have to wait too long for his response.'

'Vaanes? What do you think? You've fought in one of these before, what happens next?'

'First you'll be summoned to the citadel to pay homage,' said Vaanes, idly lifting a book from the footlocker nearest the bed. 'Then there will be a day of sacrifices before the contests begin.'

'Homage,' spat Honsou. 'I detest the word. I give homage to no man.'

'That's as may be,' said Vaanes. 'But you're not so powerful you can break the rules.'

Honsou nodded, though it sat ill with him to bow and scrape before another, even one as infamous as the master of this world. He snatched the book Vaanes held and set it down on the bed.

'And after all this homage and sacrifice, what happens after that?'

'Then the killings begin,' said Vaanes, looking in puzzlement at him. 'The leaders of the various warbands challenge one another for the right to take their warriors. Mostly their champions answer these challenges, for only when the stakes are highest do the leaders enter the fray.'

'These challenges, are they straight up fights?' asked Honsou.

'Sometimes,' said Vaanes. 'The last one usually is, but they can take any form before that. You almost never know until you set foot in the arena what you'll be up against. I've seen clashes of tanks, bare-knuckle fights to the death, battles with xenos monsters and psychic duels. You never know.'

'That mean I'll maybe get to kill something?' said Grendel with undisguised relish.

'I can as good as guarantee it,' replied Vaanes.

'Then we need to know what we're up against,' said Honsou. 'If we're going to get ourselves an army, we need to know who we're taking it from.'

'How do you propose we do that?' said Grendel.

'Go through the city. Explore it and find out who's here. Learn their strengths and weaknesses. Make no secret of where your allegiance lies and if you need to crack some heads open, then that's fine too. Grendel, you know what to do?'

'Aye,' agreed Grendel, with a gleam of anticipation in his eye. 'I do indeed.'

Honsou caught the look that passed between the Newborn and Ardaric Vaanes, relishing their confusion. It never did to have your underlings *too* familiar with your plans.

'Now get out, I have research to do,' said Honsou, lifting the book he had taken off Vaanes from the bed. 'Amuse yourselves as you see fit until morning.'

'Sounds like a plan to me,' said Grendel, drawing a long-bladed knife.

Honsou was about to turn away from his subordinates when he saw the Newborn cock its head to one side and the inner light that lurked just beneath its borrowed skin pulse with a shimmering heartbeat. In the months they had fought together, Honsou recognised the warning.

'Enemies are approaching,' said the Newborn, answering Honsou's unasked question.

'What? How do you know?' demanded Grendel.

'I can smell the blood,' said the Newborn.

The ground before Honsou's defensive wall was littered with bodies. Gunfire flashed from the towers and ramparts, a brutal curtain of fire that sawed through the ranks of flak-armoured warriors who hurled themselves without fear at the gates. Sudden darkness had fallen, as though a shroud of night had been cast over the promontory, and stuttering tongues of flame lit the night as the two forces tore at one another.

The Newborn's warning had come not a second too soon and Honsou had massed his warriors on the crude walls in time to see a host of screaming men emerge from the darkness towards them. They were an unlikely storming force, a ragged mix of human renegades of all shapes and sizes. Most wore iron masks or skull-faced helmets and their uniforms – such as they were – were little more than bloodstained rags stitched together like the Newborn's skin.

They came on in a howling mass, firing a bizarre mix of weapons at the defenders. Las-bolts and solid rounds smacked into the walls or from the ceramite plate of the Iron Warriors. What the attackers lacked in skill and tactical acumen, they made up for in sheer, visceral ferocity.

It wasn't nearly enough.

Disciplined volleys barked again and again from the Iron Warriors and line after line of attackers was cut down. Their primitive armour was no match for the mass-reactive bolts of the defenders, each a miniature rocket that exploded within the chest cavity of its target.

Heavy weapons on the towers carved bloody gouges in the attacking horde, but the carnage only seemed to spur them to new heights of fanaticism, as though the bloodshed were an end in itself.

'Don't these fools realise they'll never get in?' said Ardaric Vaanes as he calmly snapped off a shot that detonated within the bronze mask of a flag-waving maniac as he ran at the gate without even a weapon unsheathed.

'They don't seem to care,' said Honsou, reloading his bolter. 'This isn't about getting in, it's about letting us know that we're being challenged.'

'You reckon these are Uluvent's men?' said Grendel, clearly enjoying this one-sided slaughter. Grendel had allowed the enemy to reach his section of the walls before ordering his men to open fire, and Honsou saw the relish he took in such close-range killing.

'Without a doubt,' said Honsou.

'He must have known they'd all get killed,' pointed out Vaanes.

'He didn't care,' said the Newborn, standing just behind Honsou's right shoulder. Its unnatural flesh was still glowing and there was a hungry light in its eyes. 'His god cares not from where the blood flows and neither does he. By throwing away the lives of these men, Pashtoq Uluvent is showing us how powerful he is. That he can afford to lose so many men and not care.'

'Getting clever in your old age,' said Grendel with a grin and slapped the arm of the Newborn. His champion flinched at Grendel's touch and Honsou knew it detested the mohicaned warrior. Something to bear in mind if Grendel became a problem.

The slaughter – it could not be called a battle – continued for another hour before the last shots faded. The attackers had not retreated and had fought to the last, their bodies spread like a carpet of ruptured flesh and blood before the Iron Warriors compound.

The strange darkness that had come with the attack now lifted like the dawn and Honsou saw a lone figure threading his way through the field of corpses towards the fortress.

Cadaras Grendel raised his bolter, but Vaanes reached out and lowered the weapon's barrel.

'What the hell do you think you're doing, Vaanes?' snarled Grendel.

'That's not one of Uluvent's men,' said Vaanes. 'You don't want to kill this one.'

'Shows what *you* know,' said the scarred warrior, turning to Honsou for acknowledgement. Honsou gave a brief nod and turned to watch as the newcomer approached the gate without apparent fear of the many guns aimed at him.

'Who is he?' said Honsou. 'Do you recognise him?'

'No, but I know who he represents,' said Vaanes, gesturing to the looming citadel that dominated the skyline.

'Open the gates,' ordered Honsou. 'Let's hear what he has to say.'

Despite his earlier confidence, Honsou couldn't help but feel apprehensive as he climbed the twisting, corkscrew stairs carved into the sheer sides of the rock face that led towards the mountainous citadel. The emissary led them, his sandaled feet seeking out the steps as surely as if he had trod them daily for a thousand years. For all Honsou knew, perhaps he had.

Honsou had met the emissary, a nameless peon in the robes of a scribe, at the gate of his makeshift fortress where he was handed a scroll case of ebony inlaid with golden thorns. He removed the scroll, a single sheet of cartridge paper instead of the more melodramatic human skin he'd expected, and read the tight, mechanical-looking script written upon it before passing the scroll to Ardaric Vaanes.

'Well?' he'd said when Vaanes had read its contents.

'We go,' said Vaanes instantly. 'When this world's master summons you, it is death to refuse.'

His message delivered, the emissary turned and led them through the squalid streets of the city towards the tallest peak, climbing steep stairs cut into the rocky flanks of the mountain. Honsou had brought Vaanes and the Newborn with him, leaving Grendel to finish the execution of the wounded attackers and keep the compound safe against further assaults.

The climb was arduous, even to one whose muscles were enhanced with power armour, and many times Honsou thought he was set to plummet to his death until the Newborn helped steady him. Their route took them across treacherous chain bridges, along narrow ledges and though snaking tunnels that wound a labyrinthine passage through the depths of the mountain and avoided the fields of razor wire. Though he tried to memorise the route, Honsou soon found himself confounded by occluded passageways, switchbacks and the strange angles within the bowels of the fortress.

On the few occasions they emerged onto the side of the mountain, Honsou saw how high they had climbed. Below them, the city shone like a bruised diamond, torches and cookfires dotting the mountainside like sunlight on quartz as the skies darkened to a sickly purple. Thousands upon thousands of warriors were gathered in makeshift camps throughout the city and Honsou knew that if he made the right moves, they could be his.

Any army gathered from this place would be a patchwork force of differing fighting styles, races and temperaments, but it would be large and, above all, it would be powerful enough to achieve its objective. And if the books he had taken from the chained libraries of Khalan-Ghol gave up their secrets, he would have something of even greater value than mere warriors to drown the worlds of Ultramar in blood.

The higher they climbed, the more Honsou felt his appreciation for the design of this fortress shift from grudging admiration to awe. It was constructed with all the cunning of the most devious military architect, yet eschewed the brutal functionality common to the Iron Warriors for a malicious spite in some of the more deadly traps.

At last, they emerged within an enclosed esplanade lined with pillars and crowned with what could only be the outer hull plates of a spaceship. The metal was buckled and scored from multiple impacts, the sheeting blackened and curved where the intense heat of laser batteries had pounded the armour to destruction.

A great, thorn-patterned gate stood open at the end of the esplanade and a hundred warriors in power armour lined the route they must take through it. Each of the warriors was armoured differently, a multitude of colours and designs, some so old they were the image of that worn by Honsou. Only one thing unified these warriors, a jagged red cross painted through the Chapter insignia worn on their left shoulder guard.

The emissary led them down this gauntlet of warriors, and Honsou saw Salamanders, Night Lords, Space Wolves, Dark Angels, Flesh Tearers, Iron Hands and a dozen other Chapters. He noted with grim amusement that no Ultramarines made up these warriors' numbers and doubted that any of Macragge's finest would be found in this garrison.

Beyond the gateway, the fortress became a gaudy palace, a golden wonder of fabulous, soaring design that was completely at odds with the external solemnity of its design. Honsou found the interior garish and vulgar, its ostentation the antithesis of his tastes, such as they were. This was not the palace of a warlord; it was the domain of a decadent egotist. Then again, he should not have been surprised, after all, wasn't it his monstrous ego and megalomania that had brought the citadel's builder low in the first place?

At last they came to a set of gilded doors, taller than a Warlord Titan, which swung open in a smooth arc to reveal a grand throne room of milky white marble and gold. The sounds of voices and armoured bodies came from beyond and, as Honsou and his retinue followed the emissary through, they saw the towering form of a daemonic Battle Titan serving as the backdrop to a tall throne that sat on a raised dais at the far end of the chamber.

A hundred captured battle flags hung from the vaulted ceiling and the chamber was thick with warriors of all sizes and descriptions.

'I thought this summons was just for us,' said Honsou.

'What made you think that?' replied Vaanes. 'Did you think you were a special case?'

Honsou ignored the venomous relish in Vaanes's words and didn't reply. He *had* thought the summons was for him and him alone, but saw how foolish that belief had been. This was the Skull Harvest and every warrior gathered here would be thinking that he alone would be the victor.

He saw a profusion of horns, crimson helms, glittering axes and swords, alien creatures in segmented armour and a riotous profusion of standards, many depicting one of the glorious sigils of the Dark Gods.

'Should we have brought a standard?' hissed Honsou, leaning close to Ardaric Vaanes.

'We could have, but it wouldn't have impressed him.'

'There is fear in this room,' said the Newborn. 'I can sense it flowing through this place like the currents of the warp.'

Honsou nodded. Even he could sense the lurking undercurrent of unease that permeated the throne room. The throne itself was empty, a carved block of thorn-wrapped onyx that would surely dwarf any man who sat upon it, even a Space Marine.

He turned as his instincts for danger warned him of threat and his hand snatched to his sword hilt as a looming shadow enveloped him.

'You are Honsou?' said a booming voice like the sound of tombstones colliding.

'I am,' he said, looking up into the furnace eyes of a warrior clad in vivid red battle plate that was scarred and burned with the fires of battle and which resembled the lined texture of exposed muscle. His shoulder guards were formed from an agglomerated mass of bones, upon which was carved the icon of a planet being devoured between a set of fanged jaws.

Upon a heavily scored breastplate of fused ribs, Honsou saw a red skull branded over the insignia of an eight-pointed star and knew who stood before him. The warrior's blazing eyes were set deep within a helmet fashioned from a skull surely taken from the largest greenskin imaginable, and they were fixed on Honsou in an expression of controlled rage.

'Pashtoq Uluvent, I presume,' said Honsou.

'I am the Butcher of Formund, the bloodstorm of the night that takes the skulls of the blessed ones for the Master of the Brazen Throne,' said the giant and Honsou smelled the odour of spoiled blood upon Uluvent's armour.

'What do you want?' said Honsou. 'Didn't you lose enough men attacking my compound?'

'Simple blood sacrifices,' said Uluvent. 'A statement of challenge.'

'You let your men die just to issue a challenge?' said Honsou, impressed despite himself.

'They were nothing, fodder to show my displeasure. But Vosok Dall was a chosen warrior of my warband and his death must be avenged with yours.'

'Many have tried to kill me,' said Honsou, squaring his shoulders before the champion of the Blood God, 'but none have succeeded, and they were a lot tougher than you.'

Uluvent chuckled, the mirthless noise sounding as though it issued from a benighted cavern at the end of the world, and reached up to tap Honsou's forehead. 'When the Harvest begins, you and I shall meet on the field of battle and your mongrel skull will be mounted on my armour.'

Before Honsou could reply, Pashtoq Uluvent turned and marched away. Honsou felt his anger threaten to get the better of him, and only quelled the urge to shoot Uluvent in the back with conscious effort.

'It'll be a cold day in the warp before *that* happens,' he hissed as the Battle Titan's warhorn let out a discordant bray of noise; part fanfare, part roar of belligerence. The harsh wall of noise echoed around the chamber, reverberating from the pillars and reaching into every warrior's bones with its static-laced scrapcode.

Honsou blinked as he saw that the throne at the foot of the Battle Titan was now occupied. Had it been occupied a moment ago? He would have sworn that it had been empty, but sat like a great king of old upon the onyx throne was a towering warrior in crimson armour edged in gold. A halo of blades wreathed his pallid, ashen face and his right arm was a monstrous claw with unsheathed blades that shimmered with dark energies.

A great axe was clasped in this mighty king's other hand and his merciless eyes swept the warriors assembled before him with a searching gaze that left no secret unknown to him. At his shoulder squatted a chittering, reptilian beast that wrapped its slimy flesh around the vents of the warrior's backpack.

The howl of the titan's warhorn ceased abruptly and all eyes turned to the warrior king upon the onyx throne. Every champion in the room dropped to one knee at the sight of so mighty a warlord.

Huron Blackheart.

The Tyrant of Badab.

At length the Tyrant spoke, his voice booming and powerful. A voice used to command. A voice that had convinced three Chapters of the Adeptus Astartes to side with him against their brothers. A voice belonging to a warrior who had survived the death of half his body and not only lived, but returned stronger and more deadly than ever.

Though he tried not to be, Honsou couldn't help but be impressed.

'I see many hungry faces before me,' said the Tyrant. 'I see warlords and corsairs, mercenaries and outcasts, renegades and traitors. What you were before you came here does not interest me, all that matters in the Skull Harvest is who is the strongest.'

Huron Blackheart rose to his feet and stepped from the dais to move amongst those who came before him. The loathsome creature at his shoulder hissed and spat, the pigments of its mottled hide running from spotted to scaled and back again in a heartbeat. Its eyes were black gems, devoid of expression, yet Honsou sensed malignant intelligence behind them.

A warrior in the armour of the Astral Claws, the Tyrant's former Chapter, followed behind Huron Blackheart and Honsou sensed a darkly radiant power within him, as though what lurked beneath the ceramite plates was something no longer wholly human.

Accompanying this warrior was a tall woman of startling appearance, with features so thin as to be emaciated. Her dark hair was pulled severely back from her face and cascaded to her ankles. Golden flecks danced in her eyes and her emerald robes hung from her thin frame as though intended for someone more generously proportioned. She carried a heavy ebony staff topped with a horned skull. Honsou recognised a sorceress when he saw one.

As Huron Blackheart made his way through the crowds of warriors, Honsou saw that the size of the man's throne was not simply an exercise in vanity; he dwarfed even the mightiest of his supplicants.

No wonder the piratical fleets that raided the shipping lanes around New Badab were the terror of the Imperium's shipmasters. Blackheart's reavers plagued the worlds of the Corpse-Emperor from the Tyrant's bases scattered around the Maelstrom, bringing him plunder, slaves, weapons and, most importantly, ships.

The Tyrant and his bodyguards moved through his throne room and the warriors gathered before him bowed and scraped. Honsou felt his lip curl in distaste.

'They worship him like he was a god,' he said.

'On New Badab he might as well be,' said Vaanes. 'He has the power of life and death over everyone here.'

'Not me, he doesn't.'

'Even you,' promised Vaanes.

'Then I'll be sure to keep my thoughts to myself.'

Vaanes chuckled. 'That'll be a first, but it doesn't matter. That creature on his shoulder, the Hamadrya, is said to be able to see into the hearts of men and whisper their darkest thoughts in the Tyrant's ear. Imperial assassins have tried to slay Blackheart for decades, but none have ever come close, the Hamadrya senses their thoughts long before they get near.'

Honsou nodded at Vaanes's words, watching the unseemly displays of fealty and obeisance made by the various warlords and corsair chieftains. He looked across the throne room and saw that Pashtoq Uluvent also kept himself aloof from such toadying, and his respect for the warrior went up a notch.

Then the Tyrant turned his gaze on Honsou and he felt the blood drain from his face and a chill touch of fear run the length of his spine. It was a sensation new to Honsou and he liked it not at all. The Tyrant of Badab's thin, lipless mouth smiled, exposing teeth sharpened to razor points, and Honsou found himself helpless before the warrior's gimlet gaze.

The warriors parted before the Tyrant as he strode towards Honsou, the claws of his huge gauntlet alive with baleful energies and the Hamadrya hissing in animal rage.

Huron Blackheart was a giant of a warrior, his already formidable physique boosted by cybernetic augmentation and the blessings of the Dark Gods. Honsou's head came to the centre of the Tyrant's chest plate and though it galled him to do so, he was forced to look up to the lord of New Badab.

He felt as though he were a morsel held helpless before some enormous predator or a particularly rare specimen about to be pinned to the board of a collector. The Tyrant stared at him until Honsou felt he could stand no more, then transferred his gaze to the Newborn and Ardaric Vaanes.

'This one is touched by the raw power of the warp,' said the Tyrant, lifting the Newborn's head with the tips of his claws. 'Powerful and unpredictable, but very dangerous. And you...'

This last comment was addressed to Ardaric Vaanes and with the Newborn forgotten, the Tyrant turned Vaanes's shoulder guard with the blade of his axe, nodding as he saw the red cross of the Red Corsairs.

'I know you,' said the Tyrant. 'Vaanes. Late of the Raven Guard. You fight for another now?'

'I do, my lord,' said Vaanes, bowing before his former master.

'This half-breed?'

'The last person who called me that ended up dead,' snarled Honsou.

Without seeming to move, the Tyrant's claw shot out and punched into Honsou's breastplate, lifting him from his feet. Honsou could feel the cold, dark metal of the claws digging at the flesh of his chest, the force of the Tyrant's blow precisely measured.

'And the last person who failed to show me respect in my own throne room suffers now at the hands of my most skilled daemonic torturers. They tear his soul apart each day then reclaim its soiled fragments from the warp and the process begins anew. He has suffered this agony for eight decades and I have no inclination to end his torments. You wish a similar fate?'

Honsou's life hung by a thread, yet he still managed defiance in his tone. 'No, my lord, I do not, but I am no longer the half-breed. I am a Warsmith of the Iron Warriors.'

'I know who you are, warrior,' said the Tyrant. 'The immaterium gibbers with your slaughters and the corruption you have wrought. I know why you are here and have seen the path of your fate. You will wreak havoc in the realm of the Corpse-Emperor's worshippers, but those you have wronged will shake the heavens to see you dead. Yet for all your arrogance and bitterness, you have something most others lack.'

'And what's that?' spat Honsou.

'You have a grand vision of revenge and the chance that you might succeed is all that stays my hand.'

Huron Blackheart then turned his attention back to Vaanes and said, 'You wear my marking upon your armour, Ardaric Vaanes, but I sense that you serve a power greater than this half-breed. Just remember that the Dark Prince is a jealous lord and suffers no other masters but he.'

Blackheart sheathed his blades and Honsou dropped to the floor of the throne room, breathless and chilled to the bone from the touch of the Tyrant's claws. The breath heaved in his chest and he felt the nearness of death as a cold shroud upon his heart. He looked up, but the Tyrant had already moved away.

As Honsou picked himself up, he saw the Tyrant's sorceress stare with naked interest at the Newborn, her eyes lingering long over the stitched nightmare of its dead fleshmask. Blackheart climbed the dais to his throne and turned to address the gathered champions with his axe and claw raised above his head.

'Any warrior who dares to bare his neck in the Skull Harvest should present his blade upon the Arena of Thorns when the Great Eye opens. Blood will be spilled, the weak will die and the victor shall benefit greatly from my patronage.'

The Tyrant lowered his voice, yet its power was still palpable and Honsou felt as though the words were spoken just for him. 'But know this: the gods are watching and they will rend the souls of the unworthy for all eternity.'

* * *

In days that followed, Honsou's warriors explored the city on the flanks of the Tyrant's mountain, learning all they could in preparation for the violence to come. Warbands were identified and their warriors observed, for each warlord was keen to display the prowess of his fighters and champions.

Ardaric Vaanes watched the sensual slaughters of Notha Etassay's blade dancers, a troupe of decadent warrior priests to whom no sensation of the blade was unknown and whose every kill was performed with the utmost grace and enjoyment. Notha Etassay, an androgynous beauty of uncertain sex, bade Vaanes spar with them and, upon tasting his blood, immediately offered him a place within the troupe.

With every battle he fought, Vaanes felt the vicarious thrill of the kill as every sensation of the graceful ballet of blades was channelled through every warrior priest. It was only with great regret that Vaanes declined Etassay's offer of a bond ritual with the troupe.

Unimpressed with the delicate bladework of Notha Etassay, Cadaras Grendel left Vaanes and the Newborn to their sport and spent his days watching the blood games of Pashtoq Uluvent's warriors as they hacked their way through naked slave gangs. Their victims were armed with little more than knives and raw terror, and such brutal murders were more to Grendel's liking. Soon he found himself wetting his blades with blood in Uluvent's arena. Such was his bloodlust that within the hour he was granted an audience upon the killing floor by Pashtoq Uluvent himself.

Those battle machines of Votheer Tark that could be brought up the mountain roared and rampaged, their engines howling like trapped souls as they crushed prisoners beneath their tracks or tore them limb from limb with clawed pincer arms. Kaarja Salombar's corsairs staged flamboyant displays of marksmanship and sword mastery, but Vaanes was unimpressed, having seen the exquisite bladework of Notha Etassay's devotees.

Honsou himself ventured little from behind his walls, his every waking moment spent in contemplation of the ancient tomes he had brought from Khalan-Ghol. What he sought within their damned pages he would not reveal, but as the days passed, his obsession with the secrets contained in the mad ravings committed to the page grew ever deeper.

The Newborn stayed close to Ardaric Vaanes, watching the killings and displays of martial ability with a dispassionate eye. It was stronger and more skilful than the majority of the warriors here, yet only recently had it begun to take pleasure in the infliction of pain and death. Differing angels warred within its mind; the teachings of its creator and the buried instincts and memories of the gene-heritage bequeathed to it by Uriel Ventris.

Of all the warrior bands gathered for the Skull Harvest, the Newborn was most fascinated by the loxatl, a band of alien mercenaries that laired in burrows hollowed from the sides of the mountain. Vaanes and the Newborn watched the fighting drills of the loxatl on a patch of open ground before these caves.

The leader of this brood-group was a kin leader who went by the name of Xaneant. Whether this was the creature's true name or one foisted upon it by human tongues was unclear, but the Newborn was impressed by the alien mercenaries, liking their fluid, sinuous movements and utter devotion to the members of their brood.

Something in that kin-bond was achingly familiar and the Newborn wondered where the sense of belonging it felt came from. Was it responding to a memory buried deep within its altered brain or was this a fragment of the psyche the Daemonculaba had stamped upon it?

'They are all related,' said the Newborn, watching as the loxatl spun like fireflies through a series of lightning fast manoeuvres designed to showcase their speed and agility. 'Would that not hinder them in battle?'

'In what way?' asked Vaanes.

'Would there not be grief or horror if a kin-member died?'

'I don't think the loxatl think that way,' said Vaanes. 'It sounds obvious, but they're not like humans. It's a good observation though. I remember reading that in ancient wars, kings would sometimes raise regiments formed by men and women from the same towns, thinking it would create a bond of loyalty that would make them stronger.'

'And did it?'

'Before the killing started, yes, but when battle was joined and people began to die, the sight of friends and loved ones torn up by shellfire or cut to pieces by swords and axes destroyed any fighting spirit they might have had.'

'So why do the loxatl do it?' asked the Newborn. 'If such groupings are so brittle, why do it? Surely it is better to fight alone or alongside those you do not care about.'

'Yes and no,' said Vaanes, slipping back into the role of mentor and instructor. 'What keeps many fighting units together is the warrior next to him and the desire not to let your battle-brothers down. Shared camaraderie gives a fighting unit cohesion, but that needs to be alloyed to an unbreakable fighting spirit in order to avoid being broken when the killing starts.'

'Like the Adeptus Astartes?'

'Not all of them,' said Vaanes bitterly.

'The Ultramarines?'

'Yes, the Ultramarines,' sighed Vaanes. 'You get that from Ventris?'

'I think so,' said the Newborn. 'I have a desire for brotherhood with those I fight alongside, but I don't feel it.'

Vaanes laughed. 'No, you won't in Honsou's warband. It's said the Iron Warriors were never ones for easy camaraderie, even before they followed Horus into rebellion.'

'Is that a weakness?'

'I don't know yet. Time will tell, I suppose,' said Vaanes. 'Some war-bands fight for money, some for revenge, some for honour and some for the slaughter, but it all ends up the same way.'

'What way is that?'

'In death,' said a voice behind them and both the Newborn and Vaanes turned to see Huron Blackheart's emaciated sorceress. The woman's gaunt features were even more skeletal in the daylight, the brightness of the sky imparting an unhealthy translucence to her skin and reflecting from the gold in her eyes. Her robes shimmered and her hair whipped and twisted like a dark snake with the motion of her head.

'Yes,' said Vaanes. 'In death.'

The sorceress smiled, exposing stumps of yellowed teeth, and Vaanes grimaced. The woman appeared young, yet the price she had paid for her powers was rotting her away from the inside out. 'The Lost Child and the Blind Warrior; fitting that I should find you observing the dis-plays of an alien species whose thought processes are utterly inimical to humanity.'

Vaanes felt his skin crawl at the nearness of the sorceress. Within the seething cauldron of the Maelstrom, the terrifying power of the imma-terium was a constant, gnawing presence on the edge of perception, but her proximity seemed to act as a locus for warp entities gathering like vultures around a corpse. Vaanes could feel their astral claws scratching at the lid of his mind.

He glanced over at the Newborn, seeing it twitch and flinch as though there was an invisible host of buzzing, stinging insects swarming around its face, but which it was trying to ignore.

'What do you want?' said Vaanes, gripping the Newborn's arm and dragging it away from her loathsome presence. 'I detest your kind and wish to hear nothing you have to say.'

'Do not be so quick to dismiss what I have to offer, warrior of Corax,' hissed the sorceress, reaching out and placing a hand on the Newborn's chest.

'Never speak that name again,' snarled Vaanes. 'It means nothing to me now.'

'Not now, but one day it will again,' promised the sorceress.

'You see the future?' asked the Newborn. 'You know what is to hap-pen? All of it?'

'Not all of it,' admitted the sorceress, 'but those whose lives stir the currents of the warp are bright lights in the darkness. A measure of their path is illuminated for those with the sight to see it.'

'Do you see mine?' said the Newborn.

The sorceress laughed, a shrill bite on the air that caused the loxatl to halt their martial display and screech in rage. Shimmering patterns danced over their glistening hides and they vanished in a blur of motion, slithering and skittering across the mountainside to boltholes carved in the rocks.

'The destiny of the Lost Child cleaves into the future like a fiery spear-tip,' said the sorceress. 'His destiny is woven into the tapestry of a great hero's death, the fall of a star and the rise of an evil thought long dead.'

'You speak in meaningless riddles,' said Vaanes, dragging the New-born away.

'Wait!' cried the Newborn. 'I want more.'

'Trust me, you don't,' warned Vaanes, seeing Cadaras Grendel marching towards them, his armour splashed with blood. 'Nothing good can come of it.'

'The Lost Child wishes to hear what I have to say,' screeched the sorceress, barring their way with her skull-topped staff.

Vaanes unsheathed the caged lightning of his gauntlet-mounted claws and rammed the foot-long blades up into the sorceress's chest, tearing up through her heart and lungs. She died without a sound, the breath ghosting from her lips in a sparkling, iridescent cloud and the golden light fading from her eyes. Vaanes sucked in her dying breath, revelling in the sensations of fear, horror and pain it contained. His entire body shook with the deliciousness of her soul and all thought of consequence fled from his thoughts at the ecstasy of the kill.

Vaanes lowered his arm and let her skeletal frame slide from the blades of his gauntlet. Her corpse flopped to the ground and he set off towards Cadaras Grendel with the Newborn in tow.

'What was that about?' said Grendel, looking over at the shrivelled body of the sorceress. Whatever force had animated her wasted frame had fled her body, leaving a desiccated husk of shrivelled flesh and dried bone.

'Nothing,' replied Vaanes, drawing a deep breath. 'Forget it.'

'Fine,' said Grendel, gesturing towards the sky. 'Honsou wants you back at the compound. The Skull Harvest is about to begin.'

Vaanes looked up, seeing the swirling colours gathering around a toxic swirl of amber, like the cancerous epicentre of a diseased whirlpool.

'The Great Eye...it's opening,' he whispered as Grendel made his way past him in the opposite direction. 'Are you coming back too?'

Grendel nodded, grinning with feral anticipation. 'Don't worry about it. I'll see you in the arena.'

Vaanes didn't like the sound of that, but let it go, wondering whose blood stained Grendel's breastplate. The Iron Warrior looked down at the withered remains of the sorceress.

'Did she try and tell your fortune?' said Grendel, kneeling beside the sagging cloth of the sorceress's robes.

'Something like that,' agreed Vaanes.

'And you killed her for it?'

'Yes.'

'Too bad for her she didn't see *that* coming.'

The Skull Harvest got underway, as all such gatherings do, with sacrifice. Framed by the towering majesty of a growling Battle Titan, the Tyrant of Badab tore the hearts from a captured warrior of the Howling Griffons and hurled them into the arena, where they pulsed bright arterial blood onto the gritty sand until they were emptied.

The first day was taken up with the various champions' warbands announcing themselves to the Tyrant, who sat upon a grand throne of bronze and amber, and the allocation of challenges. Blood feuds would be settled first and a number of champions bellowed the names of those they wished to fight in the name of avenging an insult to their honour.

Honsou expected Pashtoq Uluvent to issue such a challenge, but the red-armoured warrior had yet to appear.

'I expected Uluvent to be here,' noted Vaanes, as though reading his mind. 'Champions of the Blood God are usually the first to arrive and begin the killing.'

'No, Uluvent's smarter than that,' said Honsou.

'What do you mean?'

'I think he wants to wait until further into the Harvest before trying to kill me. It'll be more of a triumph for him if he slays me after we've taken other warbands with our own killings. He'll have his blood feud resolved *and* he'll take all my warriors.'

'Then he's more cunning than most champions of the Blood God.'

'Maybe,' agreed Honsou with a smile. 'We'll see how that works out for him.'

'And Grendel, where's he?' asked Vaanes. 'I haven't seen him since yesterday. He said he'd be here. The other champions will know that one of our inner circle hasn't appeared for the beginning of the death games.'

'Forget Grendel,' said Honsou. 'We don't need him.'

'I see him,' said the Newborn, gesturing with a nod of his helmet to the opposite side of the arena. 'Over there.'

Honsou looked over and saw the ranks of gathered champions part as Pashtoq Uluvent took his place on the circumference of the arena. The red-armoured warrior with the ork-skull helmet raised his red-bladed sword and a raucous cheer was torn from thousands of throats as his skull rune banner was unfurled.

Standing beside Uluvent was Cadaras Grendel, his armour streaked with fresh blood and his chainsword unsheathed. The Iron Warrior shrugged and raised his sword to lick wet blood from the blade.

'Grendel's betrayed us?' said Vaanes, his voice thick with anger.

'It was only a matter of time,' said Honsou. 'To be honest I expected it sooner.'

'I'll kill him,' snarled Vaanes.

'No,' said Honsou. 'Grendel and I will have a reckoning, but it won't be here. Do you understand me?'

Vaanes said nothing, but Honsou could see the anger in the warrior's eyes and just hoped the former Raven Guard would be able to restrain the urge to strike down Grendel for now.

'I don't understand you, Honsou,' said Vaanes eventually.

'Not many people do,' replied Honsou. 'And that's the way I like it.'

A warrior in bronze armour emblazoned with the skull rune of the Blood God made the first kill of the day, disembowelling a champion in spiked armour who Honsou saw was hopelessly outmatched in the first moments of the duel. The slain warrior's head was mounted upon a spike of black iron beneath the Tyrant's throne.

The warband of the defeated warrior now belonged to his killer, their loyalty won through the display of greater strength and skill. Such loyalty could be a fragile thing, but few gathered here cared for whom they fought, simply that they fought for the strongest, most powerful champion of the Skull Harvest.

Ranebra Corr's sword-champion slew the hearthguard of Yeruel Mzax, a clan warrior of the Cothax stars. The clan-laws forbade Mzax to fight under the leadership of another and he hacked his own head off with an energised claw attached to the upper edge of his gauntlet.

Votheer Tark's battle engine was a hulking monster that had once been a Dreadnought, but which had been altered by Tark's Dark Mechanicum adepts into the housing for a shrieking entity brought forth from the warp. It tore through the warbands of three champions before finally being brought low by one of Pashtoq Uluvent's berserk warriors who fought through the loss of an arm to detonate a melta bomb against its sarcophagus.

The daemon was torn screaming back to the warp and the lower half of the berserker was immolated in the blast. Even with his legs vaporised, the berserker crawled towards Huron Blackheart's throne to deposit the defeated engine's skull-mount.

The Newborn won two duels on the first day of killing; crushing the skull of Kaarja Salombar's corsair pistolier before he could loose a single shot, and eventually defeating the loxatl kin-champion of Xaneant's brood group. This last battle was fought for nearly an hour, with the loxatl unable to put the Newborn down, despite exhausting its supply of flechettes into its opponent.

A daemonic creation of Khalan-Ghol's birth chambers, the Newborn's powers of regeneration were stronger in the warp-saturated Maelstrom and each wound, though agonising, was healed within moments of its infliction.

Exhausted and without ammunition, the loxatl eventually pounced on the Newborn, using its dewclaws to tear at its armour, but even its speed was no match for the Newborn's resilience. At last, the hissing, panting beast was defeated, drained and unable to defend itself when the Newborn crushed its neck and tore its head from its shoulders.

As the fighting and killing went on, warbands began to agglomerate as their champions were slain and armies formed as the most powerful warlords drew more and more fighters to their banner.

Cadaras Grendel fought with his customary brutal remorselessness, winning several bouts for Pashtoq Uluvent, and Honsou could see Ardaric Vaanes's fury at this betrayal simmering ever closer to the surface. To dilute that anger, Honsou sent the former Raven Guard into the arena while the Newborn healed and Vaanes eagerly slaughtered warriors from three warbands, one after the other, bringing yet more blood-bonded fighters into Honsou's growing army.

Honsou himself took to the field of battle twice; once to slay a pirate chieftain armed with two razor-edged tulwars, and once to break a kroot warrior leader who fought with a long, twin-bladed stave he wielded with preternatural speed and precision.

As the Newborn strangled a towering ogre-creature with its own energy whip, winning a hundred of the brutish monsters to Honsou's banner, the fourth day of killing drew to an end.

The armies of three champions were all that remained.

Pashtoq Uluvent's force of blood-hungry skull-takers, Notha Etassay's blade-dancers.

And Honsou's Iron Warriors.

With the victories he and his champions had won, Honsou's force had grown exponentially in size, numbering somewhere in the region of five thousand soldiers. Scores of armoured units and fighting machines, as well as all manner of xenos and corsair warbands were now his to command. The swords of seventeen warbands now belonged to Honsou and, by any measure of reckoning, he had a fearsome force with which to wreak havoc on his enemies.

Pashtoq Uluvent had amassed a force in the region of six thousand fighters, while Notha Etassay had procured five thousand through his exquisite slaughters. Any one of these forces was powerful enough to carve itself a fearsome slice of Imperial space and enjoy a period of slaughter unmatched in its previous history.

But the Skull Harvest was not yet over and the Tyrant's rule decreed that there could be only one champion left standing at its end.

Darkness closed in as the three warriors stepped into the arena, clad in their armour and each armed with their weapon of choice. Honsou's arm glittered in the torchlight that surrounded the arena as baying crowds of warriors cheered for their respective champions.

The three warriors marched to stand facing one another in the centre of the arena and Honsou took the opportunity to study his opponents, knowing his life would depend on knowing them better than they knew themselves.

Notha Etassay wore a light, form-fitting bodyglove of rippling black leather with buckled straps holding strategically situated elements of flexible plate. The androgynous champion sashayed into the arena and performed a scintillating pre-battle ritual of acrobatic twists and leaps while spinning twin swords of velvety darkness through the air. Etassay's face was concealed by a studded leather mask with scar-like zippers and tinted glass orbs that glittered with wry amusement, as though this were a meeting of comrades instead of a duel to the death.

Pashtoq Uluvent planted his sword in the bloody earth of the arena and roared a wordless, inchoate bellow of ferocity to the heavens. His armour dripped with the blood of sacrifices and the flesh-texture of his armour seemed to swell and pulse with the beat of his heart. His eyes were like smouldering pools of blood within his helmet and he reached up with a serrated dagger to cut into the meat of his neck.

The champion of the brazen god of battle hurled the dagger away as blood began leaking from the open wound.

Honsou narrowed his eyes. 'Giving up already, Uluvent?'

'If I cannot kill you before my life bleeds out, then I am not worthy of victory and my death will honour the Skull Throne,' said Uluvent.

'Don't expect me to do anything like that,' said Honsou.

'I don't,' replied Uluvent. 'You are the mongrel by-blow of melded genes wrought in desperate times. You are a creature without honour that should never have been brought into existence.'

Honsou controlled his anger as Uluvent continued. 'One of your champions has already sworn himself to me, but I will kill you quickly if you submit to my dominance.'

'I don't submit to anyone,' Honsou warned his enemy.

Notha Etassay laughed, a high, musical sound of rich amusement. 'Whereas it's something I do rather well, though I prefer to be the dominant one in any intercourse.'

'You both disgust me,' snarled Uluvent. 'It insults my honour that I must fight you.'

The howl of the Battle Titan's warhorn echoed across the arena and the cheering warriors fell silent as the Tyrant of Badab rose from his throne to address the gathered champions, the Hamadrya curled around his thigh like a vile leech.

'Tonight the Skull Harvest ends!' said Huron Blackheart, his voice carried around the arena to the furthest reaches of the mountain. 'One champion will be victorious and his enemies will be broken upon the sands of this arena. Fight well and you will go forth to bring terror and death to those who betrayed our trust in them.'

The Tyrant of Badab locked eyes with each of the three champions in turn and raised his mighty clawed gauntlet. 'Now fight!'

Honsou sprang back from a decapitating sweep of Pashtoq Uluvent's axe, swaying aside as Etassay's black sword licked out and sliced into his shoulder guard. Honsou's black-bladed axe lashed out in a wide arc, forcing both opponents back and the three champions broke from the centre of the arena.

Etassay danced away from Honsou, swords twirling and face unreadable behind the leather mask, while Uluvent hefted his sword in a tight grip, watching warily for any movement from his opponents. Honsou knew Uluvent was the stronger of his foes, but Etassay's speed was ferocious, and who knew what power rested in his dark blades.

Honsou's axe was hungry for killing and he felt its insatiable lust to wreak harm running along the length of its haft and into his limbs. Or at least one of them. The power residing in the silver arm he had taken from the Ultramarines sergeant was anathema to the creature bound to his weapon.

This stage of a battle would be where each warrior sought to gauge the measure of the other, searching for signs of weakness or fear to be exploited. Honsou knew he would find neither in these two opponents, warriors hardened by decades of war and devotion to their gods.

Every fibre of Uluvent's being would be dedicated to killing in the Blood God's name, while Etassay would seek to wring every sensation from this bout. Winning would be secondary to the desire to experience the furthest excesses of violence, pain and pleasure.

Honsou cared nothing for the thrill of the fight, nor the honour of the kill. This entire endeavour was a means to an end. He cared nothing for the piratical schemes of the Tyrant, nor honouring any one of the ancient gods of the warp.

Etassay made the first move, leaping in close to Uluvent, his dark swords singing for the red-armoured champion. Uluvent moved swiftly, swinging his own sword up to block the blows and spinning on his heel to slash at Etassay's back. But the champion of the Dark Prince was no longer there, vaulting up and over the blade in a looping backwards somersault.

Honsou charged in, swinging his axe for Etassay, but the warrior dropped beneath the blow and smoothly pivoted onto his elbow, swinging his body out like a blade to take Honsou's legs out from under him.

Uluvent leapt towards Honsou as he fell, the red-bladed sword thrust downwards at his chest, but Honsou scrambled aside and the weapon plunged into the earth. Etassay's boot thundered against Uluvent's helmet and the roaring champion of the Blood God fell back, leaving his sword jammed in the ground.

Honsou pushed himself to his feet and furiously blocked and parried as Etassay spun away from his attack on Uluvent and came at him with a dizzying series of sword strikes. The champion of the Dark Prince was unimaginably fast and it was all Honsou could do to keep himself from being sliced into ribbons. His armour was scored and sliced numerous times and he realised that Etassay was playing with him, prolonging the battle to better enjoy the sense of superiority.

Honsou's bitterness flared, but he fought against it, knowing that Etassay would punish him for even the smallest lapse in concentration. Instead he forced himself to concentrate on exploiting the warrior's arrogance. Etassay thought he was better than Honsou and that would be his downfall.

Out of the corner of his eye, Honsou saw Uluvent circling them, waiting on a chance to reclaim his sword with a patience the Blood God's warriors were not known for. Honsou kept himself close to the weapon, forcing Uluvent to keep his distance. One opponent he could handle. Two? Probably not.

At last Etassay seemed to tire of Honsou and said, 'Let the other one have his blade. This contest is tiresome without his colourful rages.'

Honsou did not reply, instead turning towards the sword embedded in the sand and hacking his daemon axe through the blade. Uluvent's sword shattered into a thousand fragments and Honsou sensed Etassay's petulant displeasure through the studded mask.

Etassay leapt towards him, but Honsou had banked on such a manoeuvre and was ready for it. He hammered the pommel of his axe into Etassay's sternum and the champion dropped to the ground with a strangled, breathless cry.

Honsou heard Uluvent make his move and turned as he stamped down hard on Etassay's chest, hearing a brittle crack of bone. Uluvent slammed into Honsou and they tumbled to the sand. Honsou lost his grip on his axe as Uluvent's gauntlets fastened on his throat. The two warriors grappled in the bloody sand, pummelling one another with iron-hard fists.

Uluvent spat into Honsou's face. 'Now you die!'

Honsou rammed his knee into Uluvent's stomach, but the warrior's grip was unbreakable. Again and again he slammed his knee upwards until at last he felt the grip on his throat loosen. He managed to free one arm and slammed the heel of his palm into Uluvent's skull-faced helmet. Bone shattered and the bleeding wound in Uluvent's neck was exposed, spattering Honsou's helmet in blood.

Honsou slammed his fist into the wound, digging his fingers into Uluvent's neck and tearing the cut wider. His foe bellowed in pain and rolled off Honsou, rising unsteadily to his feet and lurching over to his followers to retrieve another weapon with one hand pressed to the ruin of his neck.

Honsou stood, groggy and battered, and set off after Uluvent, snatching his axe up from the ground next to the groaning figure of Etassay. He ignored the Dark Prince's champion, the warrior was beaten and probably in throes of ecstasy at the pain coursing along every nerve ending.

Honsou felt new strength in his limbs as he followed Uluvent. The warrior had torn off his shattered helmet and Honsou saw his face was hideously scarred and burned. Blood squirted from where Honsou had torn his neck wound further open, but the pain only seemed to galvanise Uluvent as he bellowed for a fresh blade.

Neck wound or no, Uluvent was still a fearsome opponent and armed with a fresh weapon, could still easily kill Honsou.

Cadaras Grendel held a wide-bladed sword out towards Pashtoq Uluvent and Honsou held his breath...

Pashtoq Uluvent reached for the weapon, but at the last moment, Cadaras Grendel reversed his grip and rammed the blade into the champion's chest. The tip of the weapon ripped out through the back of Uluvent's armour and the mighty warrior staggered as Grendel twisted the blade deeper into his chest.

Uluvent roared in pain and spun away from Grendel, wrenching the sword from his grip and dropped to his knees. Honsou gave him no chance to recover from his shock and pain, and brought his axe down upon the warrior's shoulder. The dark blade smashed Uluvent's shoulder guard to splinters and clove the champion of the Blood God from collarbone to pelvis.

Stunned silence swept over the gathered crowds, for none had ever expected to see Pashtoq Uluvent brought low. Cadaras Grendel stepped from the ranks of the Blood God's warriors to stand next to Honsou as the blazing fire of Pashtoq Uluvent's eyes began to fade.

'Sorry,' said Grendel with a grin. 'Honsou may be a mongrel half-breed, and even though I know you'll lead me to a bloodier fight, I think he'll lead me to one I'll live through.'

Uluvent looked up at Honsou with hate and pain misting his vision. 'Give... me... a blade.'

Honsou was loath to indulge the champion's request, but knew he would need to if there were to be any shred of loyalty in the warriors he would win from Uluvent.

'Give it to him,' ordered Honsou.

Grendel nodded and reached down to drag the sword from the defeated champion's chest in a froth of bright blood. He held the weapon towards Uluvent, who took the proffered sword in a slack grip.

'And... my skull,' gasped Uluvent with the last of his strength. 'You... have... to take... it.'

'My pleasure,' said Honsou, raising his axe and honouring Pashtoq Uluvent's last request.

With Pashtoq Uluvent's head mounted on the spikes below Huron Blackheart's throne, the Skull Harvest was over. Hundreds had died upon the sands of the Tyrant's arena, but such deaths were meaningless in the grand scheme of things, serving only to feed Blackheart's ego and amuse the Dark Gods of the warp.

At the final tally, Honsou left New Badab with close to seventeen thousand warriors sworn in blood to his cause. Pashtoq Uluvent's warriors, and those he had won, were now Honsou's, their banners now bearing the Iron Skull device.

Notha Etassay had survived the final battle and had willingly sworn allegiance to Honsou after hoarsely thanking him for the exquisite sensation of bone shards through the lungs.

Huron Blackheart had been true to his word, and the victor of the Skull Harvest had indeed benefited greatly from his patronage. As the *Warbreed* broke orbit, numerous other vessels accompanied it, gifts from the Tyrant of Badab to be used for the express purpose of dealing death to the forces of the Imperium. In addition to these vessels, the ships of the defeated champions formed up around Honsou's flagship to form a ragtag, yet powerful, fleet of corsairs and renegades.

Battered warships, ugly bulk carriers, planetary gunboats, warp-capable system monitors and captured cruisers followed the *Warbreed* as it plotted a careful route through the Maelstrom, away from the domain of Huron Blackheart.

The sickly yellow orb of New Badab was swallowed in striated clouds of nebulous dust and polluted immaterial effluent vomited from the wound in real space as the fleet pulled away, and Honsou recalled the final words the mighty Tyrant had said to him.

Blackheart had pointed his dark-bladed claw towards Ardaric Vaanes, Cadaras Grendel and the Newborn as they boarded the battered Stormbirds ahead of Honsou.

'Kill them when they are of no more use to you,' said the Tyrant. 'Otherwise they will only betray you.'

'They wouldn't dare,' Honsou had said, though a seed of doubt had been planted.

'Always remember,' said Huron Blackheart. 'The strong are strongest alone.'

# GAUNTLET RUN

### Chris Roberson

The rising sun was just cresting the mountaintops, barely visible on the eastern horizon, fat and red like an overripe fruit. The morning sunlight lanced across the alkaline flats, every stone and promontory casting long shadows that stretched over the bone-dry remains of an ancient seabed that had dried up long before man's ancestors on Terra had first descended from the trees. Nothing lived in that dead and dry place, the only movement the dust devils kicked up by the hot winds that blew from north to south and back again. These tiny brief-lived tornadoes fed on the thin layer of dust atop the salt flats dried hard as rockcrete, with no sound to be heard but the plaintive whistle of the winds.

Then the Scout bike squadron thundered in from the west, their mighty engines deafening, the treads of their fat tyres tearing up the dry ground, sending up great plumes of dust churning in their wake.

The Imperial Fists had arrived.

The squad of bike Scouts raced east across the desert in a tight vanguard formation. At the forward point of their chevron was Veteran Sergeant Hilts, on his left flank Scouts Zatori and s'Tonan, on his right flank Scouts du Queste and Kelso.

Zatori continued to glance behind. As left flank outrider, it fell to him to watch their left rear, just as Kelso covered their right rear as right flank outrider, while s'Tonan and du Queste scanned the approaches before them, and Hilts set the pace and marked their course.

They had been running through the night, zigzagging north-east and south-east, but while they had yet to unsheathe their blades and the barrels of their bikes' twin-linked bolters were idling and cool, this was no pleasure drive. The stakes for their current mission were dire, with the life of every human on Tunis in the balance. If they were not able to locate enemy forces – and enemy forces of a very particular kind – then they would fail in their duty, and millions would pay the price. But as the morning dawned, they had still found no sign of the enemy.

Until now.

'Sergeant,' Zatori voxed over the shared channel, for all the squad to hear, 'we have picked up a tail.'

Zatori concentrated, employing the enhanced vision of the Astartes to peer farther than an unaugmented human would have dreamed possible.

'It's the greenskins,' he added in confirmation. 'And they've spotted us.'

'Acknowledged,' Veteran Sergeant Hilts voxed in reply, gunning his engine and putting on speed. He motioned forward with his massive power fist. 'Throttle up, squad. The race is on.'

It had been only a few weeks since an ork space hulk had appeared in orbit above the planet Tunis without warning, spat out by a random rift in the fabric of space itself. The human inhabitants below had scarcely noticed the hulk overhead before countless landers began dropping from the skies, disgorging warriors and war-machines alike.

The first encounters between the human inhabitants and the ork invaders had been brutal and short. The easternmost settlements, ringing the western edge of the salt flats, had been obliterated by orks mounted on bikes, buggies, and battlewagons, gangs of greenskins addicted to movement and murder, ranging as outriders while the main force of the orks entrenched somewhere in the endless caverns and subterranean passages that burrowed under the mountains to the east. The Space Marines knew the orks had a hidden base somewhere beneath those peaks, and if the Fists were unable to locate it, they had little chance of preventing a full-scale invasion. It was only a matter of time before the main body of the ork invaders completed work on their siege-machines and attacked the human inhabitants en masse, but until that time the ork outriders would find their entertainment and excitement where they could.

A speed freek never stops, never sleeps, never hesitates. For him, there is only motion.

Rotgrim Skab knew that better than anyone. Since the moment the landers had touched down on the surface of this world, he and his crew had been up and running. As Nob of a speed freek warband of the Evil Sunz clan, it was Rotgrim's responsibility to get the bikeboyz fired up and rolling, to pick a point on the horizon and head out, and then kill every living thing they encountered along the way.

He raced at the head of the pack, massive legs wrapped around the casing of his warbike's supercharged engine, its throaty roar the only sound in his ears, exhaust and dust filling his flaring nostrils. Behind him ranged supercharged trucks and battlewagons, bikes and buggies, more than a dozen in all; bikeboyz of the Evil Sunz clan, decked out in leathers, chains and harnesses, with massive steel-toed boots on their feet and metal studs screwed directly into the bones of their foreheads. And all of them had red somewhere on them, whether cloth or armour, paint or spattered blood.

As leader of the warband, the Nob himself, Rotgrim was decked out in red from head to toe, with an axe in one hand and a dakkagun holstered at his side. His ride was painted blood red from grille to ground, as was only fitting – as the old ork adage went, the colour red makes things go faster. On a stanchion mounted behind him hung the banner of the Evil Sunz, a blood-red ork face grimacing from the heart of a starburst.

Rotgrim's warband had been going on raiding forays ever since they touched down on this dry, dusty world, impatient with the preparations being carried out in the tunnels and caverns below the mountains to the east. When the word was given, the full body of the ork army would be unleashed on the humans cowering in their settlements across the desert, and when the army moved out, the Evil Sunz would be in the vanguard.

There'd be work enough for them all to do, when the word was given, but there was no point in sitting around on their thumbs, just waiting, while they could be out and moving.

When Rotgrim spotted the five humans tooling across the desert on their little bikes, he decided to have a little fun before taking them down. It had been too long since he and the rest of the boyz'd had moving targets to practice on.

It had been lucky for the locals that the Imperial Fists transport had been in the area at all, Scout Zatori knew. When the planetary governor of Tunis had sent out his distress call, just as the ork landers first started dropping from the sky on the far side of the planet, the Imperial Fists had been near the system, returning from a previous undertaking to the *Phalanx*, the Chapter's fortress-monastery, currently at anchor at a few weeks' distance.

Of course, the transport had been a Gladius-class frigate, carrying only a single squad of Veterans for the First Company, accompanied by a Scout squad of the Tenth. But the planetary governor had not been in any position to complain about the size of the force that responded to his desperate calls for aid.

Like the others in the bike squad commanded by Veteran Sergeant Hilts, Zatori was just a novice, not yet a full battle-brother of the Imperial Fists, lacking the black carapace that would allow him to wear and control the powered ceramite armour of a full-fledged Adeptus Astartes. But the years he had spent on the *Phalanx* being transformed from a boy into a post-human son of Dorn had already set him apart from the rank and file of humanity. When the landing party had quit their drop-pods and been received by the planetary governor, Zatori and his fellow Scouts had towered over the locals, who quavered in their shadows, nearly as frightened of the Imperial Fists – Space Marine and Scout alike – as they were of the greenskins who threatened to overrun them from the east.

Aside from Chapter serfs, like those who crewed the Gladius frigate in orbit overhead, or those who served onboard the *Phalanx*, Zatori had had precious little dealing with normal humans these last few years. But looking into the faces of the planetary governor and those who sheltered with him in the strongholds to the west, Zatori could not help but be reminded of the first time he'd seen a Space Marine himself, on the battlefields of Eokaroe, on his far distant home of Triandr. They had seemed the legends of his ancestors given flesh, giant warrior-knights stepping from the realm of myths into the world of men.

Now, years later, Zatori was one of them, at least in the eyes of normal men and women. Though still only a Scout, he was a proud Son of Dorn all the same, an Imperial Fist. He would strike with the Emperor's own righteous fury. That was his duty. That was his honour.

The five Imperial Fists thundered east across the desert, maintaining their vanguard formation with rigid discipline. The greenskins were closing fast, coming right up behind.

In contrast with the regimented formation of the Fists, the morning sun glinting on the golden yellow and jet-black of their armour and bikes, the greenskins were a ragtag assortment of monsters, their vehicles belching exhaust and rumbling like unending death-rattles. But they were no slower, for all of that, thundering after the Fists like a fast approaching storm front.

Glancing back, Scout Zatori steeled his nerves as he saw an ork warbike roaring up behind, tantalisingly close to his own back tyre. Bike and rider were both covered in red, the colour of new-spilt arterial blood, with a banner fluttering madly from a rear-mounted stanchion, marking the rider as the warband's leader.

The ork leader waved an axe overhead, his wide-mouthed howls lost to the wind. Then he fired a prolonged burst from the twin-linked guns forward mounted before him. Zatori might have fallen there and then if not for the fact that the warbike bucked and spun wildly out of control as soon as the poorly balanced guns were fired, sending the shots wide of the mark. As it was, the explosive shells passed so near Zatori's left shoulder as they flew by that the Scout fancied he could feel the heat of their passage.

Zatori glanced to the right, and caught a glimpse of a pair of war-buggies approaching du Queste and Kelso's flank. On the back of each of the two-man attack vehicles stood gunners on weapons plat-forms, and in the brief instant that Zatori's gaze took in the scene, he saw one of the gunners fire off a pair of rockets. As the rockets dug into the ground only metres from Kelso's back tyre, sending up a gout of dust and rock, Zatori turned his attention back to the ground before his own wheels.

Like the rest of the Scouts, Zatori was waiting for Veteran Sergeant Hilts to give the signal. Their orders called for them to maintain close formation after first enemy contact, right up until the sergeant gave the word, and then the next stage of their mission plan would be put into motion.

Zatori just hoped he survived long enough to follow the order.

'Squad,' Veteran Sergeant Hilts voxed at last. 'Evasive pattern alpha.'

'Confirmed,' Zatori chorused back with the others, and then as one they broke formation, the left flank jinking right and the right flank jink-ing left, their paths twisting like DNA helixes as they gunned forward, leaving the disorderly orks in pursuit to compensate.

Now the Scouts would have to remain mobile long enough to see how the greenskins would respond.

Dust gritted in Rotgrim's eyes, the carcasses of countless insects entombed between his teeth. He whirled his axe overhead, urging the rest of the warband to greater speeds.

A dozen metres to his right, a skorcha let loose a gout of flame at the nearest of the humans, the huge vats of promethium mounted on the rear of the buggy fuelling the heavy-duty flamethrowers operated by a pair of Evil Sunz. The flame was all but spent by the time the last flicker-ing tongues of the stream lapped the back of one of the human riders, doing little more than scorching his armour, but it was a start, at least.

Rotgrim fired off another burst from the twin dakkaguns on the front of his ride, the irregular percussive sound music in his ears. The shots went wide of the human he was tailing, and Rotgrim found little satis-faction in the puffs of dust and rock kicked up where the explosive shells finally struck the ground, far ahead.

A warbiker off to Rotgrim's left kept firing off shots from his rifle, laying down cover to keep the humans off balance while Rotgrim and the others narrowed the distance. Another warbuggy fired off a few shots with a mega-blaster, and another loosed a pair of rockets from its launcher. None of the shots, large or small, did much more than kick up dust, like Rotgrim's had done, but the humans were forced to jag back and forth to avoid the orks' fire, which served to slow them down.

And then, seemingly all at once, the distance had shrunk to nothing. Instead of just pursuing the humans, Rotgrim's crew was right in with them. Close enough for melee action, for close combat weapons rather than unreliable ranged fire.

This was where the fun really started. Not in lobbing shots at distant targets, hoping against hope that something hit home. But instead in taking the fight right to the enemy, dive-bombing them head on like a bomber coming in for the kill, speed against speed, motion against motion.

An evil grin curled Rotgrim's rubbery lips, exposing vicious, yellowed teeth, dotted with insect carcasses like sunspots on a jaundiced star. This *was* going to be fun.

Scout Zatori couldn't help but be reminded of the words of Rhetoricus, who long centuries before had codified the Rites of Battle by which the Imperial Fists guided their actions. In the estimation of the Chapter, Rhetoricus was surpassed only by the Primarch Rogal Dorn himself. Rhetoricus had penned any number of tracts, codices, and lexicons, but principal among them was *The Book of Five Spheres*, the catechism of the sword. In it, Rhetoricus had stressed the importance of knowing the advantages and shortcomings of each weapon in a warrior's arsenal. He had spoken of the importance of ranged weapons in the open field, of flame weapons and meltas in entrenched defence, of heavy ordnance for bombardment and of blast weapons for barrage. But more than any other, he had sung the praises of the sword in close combat.

It was seldom, if ever, that a battle-brother of the Imperial Fists Chapter went into the field of battle without a sword in his fist or at his hip, and not uncommon for Fists to enter the fray with no weapon save his trusted blade. Some, like Captain Eshara of the Third Company, even went into battle with a sword in each hand, testing his skill with the blade against all enemies of the Golden Throne. Even the Master of the First Company – to say nothing of being First Captain, Overseer of the Armoury, and Watch Commander of the *Phalanx* – the legendary Captain Lysander had wielded nothing but a sword in the undertaking on Malodrax, scouring the Iron Warriors from the planet and reclaiming his master-crafted thunder hammer, the Fist of Dorn, which had been first given to him by the martyred Captain Kleitus more than a millennium before Zatori was born.

In *The Book of Five Spheres*, Rhetoricus wrote, 'The sword is at its most advantageous in confined places, or in the melee, or in close quarters – any situation in which you can close with an opponent.' And later, 'The soul of the Imperial Fist can be found in his sword.' Also, 'When the odds are innumerable against you, and there is little hope for victory, still a holy warrior with a sword in his hand can prevail, if his intent is righteous and pure.'

So as the greenskin warbiker with the massive axe barrelled towards him, Zatori tightened his grip on his sword, his other hand gripping his bike's handlebars, and silently repeated the *Litany of the Blade*. As the ork swung his axe overhand at Zatori's bare head, just as their two bikes were about to career into one another, the Scout muttered a prayer to Dorn and the Emperor that his parry would be sufficient to the task.

Rotgrim brought his axe down in a one-handed swing, right at the human's naked head. But before the blade bit into skin and skull, the human managed to turn the axe away with his sword, sending up a shower of sparks. Just as their blades struck, their two bikes collided off one another with a bone-crunching jar. As the two riders fought to maintain their balance, offsetting the force of the impact, they veered away from one another once more, each readying for another blow.

Teeth bared, Rotgrim hurled abuse at the human, who suddenly let go of his handlebars. It would have been funny, seeing a human riding a little bike hands free, if that hand hadn't come back up another moment later with a big gun in it.

Rotgrim yanked his forks to the right just in time to miss the torrent of heat that poured out of the gun, hot enough to fuse the sand on the ground into glass.

With a grim snarl, Rotgrim couldn't help but chuckle. The human wasn't the only one with a holdout.

Steadying his bike's forks with his knees, he let go of the handle and then yanked his dakkagun out of its holster.

The melta gun was a temporary deterrent at best, Zatori knew. It was only useful anyway over the shortest of distances, the promethium it excited into a sub-molecular state impossible to aim more than a few metres; but it was difficult to use any ranged weapons at high speed, anyway, so the trade-off between range and firepower for the Bike Scouts was deemed well worth it. As it was, between the melta guns for ranged firing and their swords for close combat, Veteran Sergeant Hilts had told the Scouts not to expect much opportunity to use their twin-linked bolters. After all, the bolters were designed to be fired at a target the bike was heading *towards*, and this mission would require them to head *away* from the enemy until the race was over. There would be enemies aplenty when – and if – they reached their goal, but even then the bike's bolters would be of little use, if all went to plan.

When he'd parried the greenskin's first blow, Zatori had known he'd need to reposition before he took another, or he'd be off his seat and sprawled in the dust. Though he'd trained to use the blade in either hand, still he was far less proficient with his left, and with the ork approaching from the left rear, he didn't have the option of switching the sword to his right. His defensive options would be limited, perhaps fatally so, if he had to cross his body to parry and block, and offensive options would be reduced to virtually nil, and so the sword in his left hand was the only option. But while his left arm was no less strong than his right, the level of skill was simply not the same in both, as he'd learned to his shame in duels on board the *Phalanx*.

After deflecting the ork's first blow, their bikes collided and then spun slightly apart, with the greenskin a short distance behind Zatori's bike. The next attack, Zatori knew, would be coming from that angle. Poorly braced as he was, there was simply too great a chance that the greenskin would unseat him, and then Zatori's race would be at an end, far too soon.

It was necessary, then, to change the parameters of the engagement. Or, as Rhetoricus put it in *The Book of Five Spheres*, 'When facing defeat or deadlock, seize the advantage by ascertaining the opponent's state and changing your approach.'

So as the greenskin readied for his next attack, Zatori risked letting go of his handlebars, pulled out his melta gun, and sent a blast of superheated gas shooting over. Then, when the ork responded as Zatori anticipated he would, by drawing his own firearm and returning fire, Zatori slammed the melta gun back into his holster, and yanked hard left on his handlebars, sending his bike careering towards the greenskin's. Damning the imprecise but no less deadly fire of the ork, Zatori's path took him barrelling right past the greenskin's, the Scout's forward tyre just missing the ork's rear wheel as they zoomed past, Zatori's sword swinging across his body as they drew near.

When Zatori felt the sword tug in his hand as he whizzed past the ork's rear, he hoped for a moment that he might have scored a hit against the greenskin, who'd been unable to raise his axe in time to parry. Glancing back Zatori now saw that the ork was unharmed, but that the stanchion that had held the banner aloft had been cut clean through, the grimacing red ork emblazoned on it now fluttering down to the churned earth.

In that instant Zatori's gaze locked with the greenskin's, and he saw murder in the ork's flashing eyes.

Fun was one thing. Rotgrim couldn't blame a human for taking a few potshots in battle, or for trying to stick Rotgrim with his pointy blade. It was only fair, after all. Rotgrim'd kill him, sooner or later, but the little guy had a right to fight back. Wouldn't be any fun, otherwise.

But knocking the Evil Sunz standard down into the dirt? Now *that*, that just wasn't right.

Rotgrim jammed his dakkagun back into its holster. He wasn't going to use bullets or shells for this one. He was going to take care of this one with his *hands*.

Zatori was steering back around so that his front forks were aiming towards the mountains when he heard a voice buzzing over the vox.

'Zatori, on your right!'

The next instant, Scout Kelso rammed by at top speed, crossing Zatori's path from right to left, barely avoiding a collision.

'Want to trade?' Kelso voxed as he slewed around, dust flying in a wide arc. He jerked a thumb back the way he'd come, at the flame-belching warbuggy following a short distance behind him.

Zatori glanced over his own shoulder at the ork warbiker following in his wake, a murderous scowl on his green face.

Before he could answer, though, Kelso gunned his engine and went racing right at the warbiker. 'My thanks, Zatori. I was getting bored.'

In the next moment, the warbuggy that previously had been pursuing Kelso roared behind Zatori, between him and the warbiker, the flamethrowers' attention now turned to their new target. In the dance of death between the Scouts and the orks, Zatori and Kelso appeared to have traded partners.

Zatori still found Kelso's manner difficult to understand. All Imperial Fists found some measure of satisfaction in carrying out their holy duty, but Kelso seemed to find some strangely manic *joy* in battle, and often conducted himself in a way that the more choleric Zatori found all but impossible to understand. It was perhaps not as noxious to him as the laconic attitude of du Queste, nor the seemingly emotionless reserve of s'Tonan, but still and above all Zatori found Kelso's joyous abandon in battle difficult to reconcile with the sombre duties of an Astartes.

Blistering tongues of flame lapped at the ceramite of Zatori's armour as the warbuggy veered in pursuit, and the Scout poured on speed to keep from getting roasted alive.

Rotgrim roared in annoyance as the skorcha trundled between him and his prey, but when the other human biker came racing towards him, sword swinging overhead and a joyous smile on his face, the Nob figured this new human would serve as an adequate appetiser. If he could not take vengeance on the one that had dishonoured the Evil Sunz standard just yet, he could first colour his axe with the blood of this one.

The human was riding straight at Rotgrim, and the ork wasn't sure if it was playing dare, to see which of them would veer away first, or else wanted to joust like horseback warriors on some feral world. The strange thing was that the human almost looked like he was *laughing*.

Well, if it was the speed that was tickling him, Rotgrim could almost understand it.

Of course, in another second or two, it would be Rotgrim's axe that would be tickling the inside of the human's brainpan, and he wouldn't be laughing so much after that.

The ground beneath Zatori's tyres was getting rougher the farther east they raced. Where there had been only scattered rocks and small promontories breaking the level horizon of the salt flats to the west, as they moved eastward there were increasing numbers of larger rocks rising like the tips of icebergs above the salty ground, some almost as large as Zatori's bike. With these obstacles in his path, he was no longer able simply to open up the throttle and thunder ahead, but was forced to zig-zag to keep from colliding with stones large enough to arrest his forward motion in a bone-smashing crash.

The warbuggy pursuing him, unfortunately, was raised on four fat tyres, its supercharged engine powerful enough to push it up and over the smaller rocks with scarcely any loss of forward momentum. So while Zatori was forced to bleed off speed as he zigged and zagged back and forth, the warbuggy ploughed on ahead at full tilt, closing the gap between them.

The promethium-fuelled torches at the back of the warbuggy bathed Zatori in a cascade of flame, and he grit his teeth against the searing pain. He could feel the skin at the back of his neck blistering and cracking, the close-cropped hair on his scalp singing off, and while he knew his blood would already be flooding with Larraman cells from the implant in his chest, creating instant scar tissue and staunching the flow of blood to the affected area, that knowledge did little to lessen the agony itself.

Fortunately, Zatori had spent his time in the Pain Glove, as Initiate, Neophyte, and Scout, and had cleaved to the sacred words of Rhetoricus: 'Pain is the wine of communion with heroes.' If he could learn to endure prolonged periods with that tunic of electrofibres, suspended for what seemed an eternity within the steel gibbet deep within the *Phalanx*, meditating on the image of Rogal Dorn and learning to focus past the pain, remaining fully conscious throughout – if Zatori could do that, then he could endure the mere *discomfort* of having his flesh cooked off the bone by burning promethium.

He knew that, if the greenskins were in close enough proximity for their flamethrowers to paint him, then they were also close enough for Zatori's own melta gun to return the compliment.

With a silent prayer for forgiveness to the spirit of his blade, Zatori slammed his sword into the sheath on his back in one smooth motion, and then whipped his melta gun out of its holster on the side of his bike. Without wasting a moment, he twisted at the waist as far as he was able, swung the melta gun around and sent a blast of superheated gas back at the pursuing warbuggy.

Rotgrim and his human prey were less than an eye blink apart now, each with their blades on high. At the last possible instant, the human jinked to the left, swinging his sword at Rotgrim's broad chest. But Rotgrim had seen the swing coming, and just as the human pulled to the left, the ork slammed on the brakes for the briefest instant, arresting his speed just long enough for the swing to whistle by harmlessly, while at the same time whirling his axe in a wide arc aimed at the soft meat of the human neck rising above the neck of his armour.

Rotgrim punched his bike to speed almost immediately after braking, and so could scarcely feel the tug of resistance as his axe sliced through the human's neck. But glancing back he saw the human's bike careening off, veering wildly left and right, as the headless rider flopped back on the seat, sword still held in his lifeless hand, the head bouncing and skipping along on the ground behind.

Rotgrim noted the incarnadined edge of his axe with satisfaction. It was a nice shade of red now. But it needed to get redder.

Zatori's melta blast struck the greenskin driver head on, all but vaporising him instantly from the abdomen up, leaving only a pair of dismembered hands dangling lifeless from the steering wheel and an oozing puddle of viscera pooling atop the burnt remains of his hips and legs.

The flamethrower operators on the rear platform tried to direct another stream of incendiary his way, but their attempt was stymied by the warbuggy careering wildly out of control, driverless, into one of the larger rocks. With a squeal of metal on stone, the warbuggy came to an abrupt halt, and the pair of greenskins were sent hurtling through the air, tumbling end over end. The vat of promethium, jarred by the impact, spilled over, and as the liquid sloshed into the open flames of the throwers it caught fire, the resultant blast engulfing the warbuggy in a crumping black cloud of smoke and heat.

It was only as he turned his attention back to the ground ahead that he saw the headless body of Scout Kelso crashing into the dust a hundred or so metres off. Kelso's head, bouncing along the dead seabed far behind his body, wasn't smiling anymore.

Rotgrim saw the skorcha explode, a mushroom of black smoke rising into the air as the thunderclap of the explosion rumbled through the dry air, just audible above the throaty roar of his warbike's engine. The humans were down a rider, with only four left in the saddle, and even with the loss of the skorcha the Evil Sunz still had nearly a dozen vehicles on the move.

Scanning the horizon, Rotgrim could just glimpse the human who'd defiled the Evil Sunz standard, zipping off to the east. There were too many obstacles in between for Rotgrim to catch up quickly, and there were easier targets closer anyway, that deserved the attention of his axe first.

It was getting high time to bring this particular race to a close, though.

Drawing his dakkagun, he fired a few quick bursts into the air in a set pattern, two long, four short, one long. The noise of the shots would carry over the growl of even supercharged engines, and every biker boy of the warband would recognize the sequence, and what it meant.

Rotgrim's orders were clear – it was time to stop racing for the sake of racing, and to start driving their quarry into the endgame.

'Hilts to Zatori,' came the voice of the Veteran Sergeant over the vox. 'What's your status?'

'Kelso is down, sir,' Zatori voxed back in clipped tones. 'I'm still up and running towards the east' – he glanced back, and saw the attack bike now coursing after him – 'and am pursued by a greenskin biker. I had a clash with their leader, but I've lost sight of him.'

'Acknowledged.' Then, after a pause, 'I think I've picked up the leader. Big monster in red gear on a red bike. But I don't see the clan standard...'

Zatori could not suppress a small grin as he made a tight swerve around a waist-high rock in his path. 'That would be my fault, sergeant. I cut it down and left it in the dust.'

The Scout could hear Veteran Sergeant Hilts's short, dry chuckle buzzing through the comm-bead he wore in his ear. 'No wonder he looks so displeased.'

'I didn't intend to win his approval.'

A small-arms round pinged off the gold and jet ceramite of Zatori's armour, the shot thudding into his left shoulder as the pursuing attack bike attempted to pick him off with a firearm. A second shot followed, also on his left but further down, nearer his waist. Each time, he reflexively leaned to the right, pulling away from the shot.

'Their tactics have changed,' Veteran Sergeant Hilts voxed, after a moment's silence. 'They're stopped going for kill shots, and are using nuisance tactics, instead.'

Zatori glanced to his right, and could see the sergeant angling towards him, their trajectories meeting somewhere ahead of them, and behind the sergeant the red-clad leader of the warband.

When Hilts remained silent, Zatori realized that the veteran sergeant was giving him the opportunity to divine the significance of his words. Hilts had trained Scouts of the Imperial Fists for longer than Zatori had been alive, and was always looking for a teachable moment, whether in the sparring ring or in the battlefield, an opportunity for the novices under his command to learn an essential combat lesson.

'They are herding us,' Zatori said at last, as confidently as he was able.

'Yes,' Hilts allowed. 'Exactly as we'd hoped.'

'Your orders, sir?'

'Allow yourself to be herded,' Hilts replied. 'And try not to get killed doing it.'

Rotgrim watched as the power fist-wearing human biker he was pursuing pulled alongside another, and a single glance was enough to tell him that this second human was the one who had cut down the banner stanchion and disgraced the Evil Sunz. Trailing the human was another biker boy, a pistol in his fist, planting careful shots on the human's back, steering his quarry just as Rotgrim's signal had ordered.

The plan was to allow all of the humans still upright to stay moving until they got to the wall, where they'd stop and have a final bit of fun. But seeing the bare head of the human bastard who'd knocked the standard in the dirt convinced Rotgrim that maybe one or two of them could still fall along the way. The few who reached the wall would have to be enough fun for the others.

Rotgrim whirled his axe overhead, signalling the other biker boy. A quick jab of his finger, first at the pair of humans, then at his own massive chest, was a simple enough message to carry even over the dust-filled air: These humans were *his*.

Zatori caught a glimpse of Scouts du Queste and s'Tonan veering in from the right, pursued by a trio of warbuggies. It was clear he'd been right, and that the greenskins were herding them, steering their advance towards the west. He just hoped the orks were driving them where Hilts *thought* they were heading.

He and Hilts were riding side by side now, jinking back and forth to dodge the ever-growing number of rocky protuberances and outcroppings, ever larger as they continued eastward, the largest of them now taller than Zatori when astride his bike.

There had been two greenskin bikes in their wake, but when Zatori chanced a glance back to see how close they had come, one of the orks was peeling off to cover their left flank. Only the warband's leader, the red of Kelso's blood still staining his axe blade the same shade as his leathers and ride, was still in pursuit, and closing fast.

'Zatori to Hilts,' he voxed. 'The leader is gaining.'

Hilts spared an instant to look back over his shoulder, then turned back to face forward. 'Tighten up, Zatori. This may get bumpy.'

The mountains on the eastern edge of the salt flats now towered before them. The sun was nearing its zenith, and the shadows had shrunk almost to nothing, making it more difficult to spot some of the smaller rocks in their path.

As they headed into the maze-like network of rocks and ridges that stretched out from the base of the mountains, Rotgrim gauged it impossible to pull up between the two humans, as he'd intended, laying about him on both sides with his axe. And since the human who'd disgraced the standard was now riding slightly ahead of the other one with the power fist, it meant that Rotgrim would have to get through him first before taking out his vengeance on the human bastard.

An evil grin tugged up the corners of Rotgrim's wide mouth as an idea struck. He hung his axe on his belt, then reached behind him and

snapped off the broken spar which was all that remained of the stanchion that had once held the Evil Sunz banner aloft.

As the two humans pulled into a relatively open stretch of ground,
Rotgrim punched his warbike into a sudden burst of speed, pulling up
alongside them on the right. As the human on the right turned to grab
at Rotgrim with his power fist, the ork leaned over as far over to the left
as he could go without tipping his bike over, and drove the broken spar
like a lance between the spokes of the human's front wheel.

The power fist closed on empty air as the front wheel pegged, and
with a squeal of metal on metal the human's bike flipped end over end.

Before Rotgrim even had a chance to savour the destruction, though, a
blast of superheated air shot right across his path, and he was forced to
veer off hard to the right to avoid the next shot from the twice-damned
human's heat gun.

'Squad! Cover needed!' Zatori voxed urgently, as he watched Veteran
Sergeant Hilts tumbling through the air. A melta blast had been enough
to drive the ork leader away, if only for a moment, but it wouldn't keep
him off Zatori's back for long. And if their mission had any hope for
success, Zatori couldn't let Hilts lie wherever he fell.

In response to Zatori's call, the other two Scouts, du Queste and
s'Tonan, came roaring over at speed, swords swinging and bolts flashing
from their twin-linked bolters. They threw themselves at the ork leader,
slewing in between him and Zatori, giving the latter a few moments
grace to act.

While the ork leader was occupied with du Queste and s'Tonan, Zatori
ground to a halt where Hilts had come to rest. The sergeant was pinned
between the massive rock that had arrested his forward motion and
the heavy bike that had arrived a split second after. The bike itself was
a mangled mess, bent out of its true shape, the forward forks snapped
off and the tyre still trundling away in the dust. Hilts was in little better
shape. At the speeds they'd been travelling, the force of the impact with
the massive rock outcropping had been enough to dent his ceramite
armour in several places, and he was bleeding generously from wounds
that his Larraman cells had not yet been able to staunch. One leg was
bent forwards at an obscene angle, and his left arm appeared to be
pulled completely from its socket. The impact of the bike had only
worsened the damage.

'Take... take it...' Zatori heard Hilts say, not over the vox – the sergeant's ability to transmit no doubt compromised by the crash – but the
words instead rasping out through Hilts's damaged visor.

The sergeant raised his power fist, and Zatori could see the small
device affixed to the gauntlet's cuff.

'Sorry, sir,' Zatori said, leaping off his bike and rushing to Hilts's side.
With a grunt of effort, he heaved the mangled bike off of the sergeant.

'We're already a rider down, and I can't conscience leaving another behind.'

Slipping both hands beneath the sergeant's battered form, Zatori straightened and lifted Hilts into the air. Hurrying to his bike, Zatori draped the sergeant over the back like saddlebags, and after securing him in place jumped back into the seat.

'Scout...' Hilts said, as Zatori gunned the engine, his voice scarcely audible. Zatori knew that, in the face of such massive injuries, Hilts would be going into a fugue state as his body attempted to repair itself. 'Press on... No matter what... Press...'

The sergeant slipped into unconsciousness, his body's full attention on its injuries.

'Squad!' Zatori voxed, as he kicked his bike into motion, driving towards the mountains which now loomed before them. 'The sergeant's with me. Now let's end this race!'

They thundered to the east, the Scouts pulling just ahead of the Evil Sunz, and as they neared the foothills of the mountains, the rocky protuberances and outcroppings grew larger and more numerous, rising like ghost ships above the dead seabed. The way forward was difficult, and Scouts and orks alike were forced to jink constantly back and forth to avoid running aground.

And with each passing instant the mountains grew ever closer, ever larger, swelling to fill the horizon as far as the eye could see.

Rotgrim rumbled in grim satisfaction as he saw the three human bikers approach the end of the race.

There was nowhere for them to run. Just as Rotgrim had ordered, the warband had herded the humans across the salt flats, through the maze of stones, to a defile that ran a hundred or so metres deep into the living rock of a mountain before ending at a solid rock face. And it was to this wall of stone that the humans had run their bikes.

Rotgrim ground his bike to a halt, and the rest of the warband skidded in behind him. He snarled, hefting his axe.

The three humans were on their feet now, swords and guns in hand, ringed protectively around the fallen human draped over one of the bikes.

It was almost funny, Rotgrim thought. The humans acted like they even had a *chance*. And who knows, against Rotgrim and his crew of biker boyz, maybe they might have.

But what the humans didn't know was that it *wasn't* just Rotgrim and his crew they had to worry about.

Now the fun would start, Rotgrim thought, climbing off his warbike. He hit the transmitter on his belt, signalling that they had arrived.

The humans turned at the sound of the hidden hatch opening in the

*Space Marines*

rock face behind them. Even before the hatch was clear a dozen orks were spilling through, axes, guns, and pistols armed and ready.

There were dozens at first, then hundreds, pouring out of the hatch that led to the passages and caverns hidden beneath the mountain.

Zatori kept close to his bike, with Veteran Sergeant Hilts still draped over the back like saddlebags, his massive power fist dangling just centimetres above the hard packed dirt.

The Scout could hear the hideous laughter of the green-skinned monsters, and knew that they must find some humour in the fact that the squad had failed to outrun them.

But what the orks did not know was that Zatori and the others never *meant* to outrun them, but merely outpace them. And now they had reached the end of the run.

Zatori smiled as he reached down and detached the small device attached to the power fist's cuff. He held it aloft, and as he thumbed the switch the miniature teleport homer began to hum faintly.

There was a flash of light and a sudden, deafening boom, and before Zatori stood a towering Space Marine, his ceramite armour finished golden yellow and jet black, a storm shield on one arm and a massive thunder hammer in his other hand. A cloak fluttered behind him in the dry, hot wind, and above the Space Marine's shoulders rose a stanchion surmounted by a wreathed death's-head, bearing a scroll-shaped crossbar on which was emblazoned his name: LYSANDER.

'Primarch!' Captain Lysander shouted, swinging his thunder hammer, the Fist of Dorn, overhead. 'To your glory and the glory of Him on Terra!'

With a snarl on his lips, Captain Lysander charged towards the orks massed before the open hatch, without hesitation, without pause. Just as the captain cleared the patch of dirt upon which he had appeared, another Space Marine flashed into existence, and then another, and another, all with thundering war cries on their lips, all with their swords drawn and ready for blood. An entire squad of Veterans of the Imperial Fists, each of them in Terminator armour, each of them rushing to close with the ork invaders.

The Veterans of the First Company tore into the massed greenskins, swords biting. Already Captain Lysander was plunging into the hidden underground complex beyond the open hatch, laying waste to all he found.

Rotgrim stood dumbly for a moment, watching the armoured humans smashing into his fellow orks. And all he could think was that this was all the fault of the humans he'd been chasing, and of that twice-damned human in particular. He could picture the standard of the Evil Sunz lying somewhere out there in the salty dust.

He tightened his grip on his axe, rubbery lips curling in a snarl.

This race wasn't over yet, he realised.

Not until he'd got his vengeance.

Zatori and the other two Scouts gathered around the supine form of Veteran Sergeant Hilts at the extraction point, waiting for the gunship that was thundering in to extract them. From where they stood, some distance from the base of the mountain, they could hear the sound of battle as the Veteran squad clashed with the orks, the greenskins ill-prepared for such an assault.

'I would have liked to stay and watch the Veterans in action,' s'Tonan said, eyeing the horizon.

The bike squad's run across the desert had been a subterfuge all along, to get the homer deep enough into the enemy ranks for the Terminators to take them out from within, in one fell swoop.

'And I would like to get clear of the greenskins' stench,' answered du Queste, picking bugs from his teeth.

Zatori didn't have a chance to say just what he would like, as they were interrupted by a bellowing roar coming from the direction of the mountains.

It was the red-clad leader of the warband, rushing towards them at full tilt, his enormous axe held high overhead. He was driving straight at Zatori with murder in his eyes, an animalistic howl reverberating from between his cracked and massive teeth.

Zatori didn't waste an instant by dropping into a defensive posture, or by reciting the abbreviated *Litany of the Blade*, or by raising his sword into the en garde position. Instead, he simply drew his melta gun, squeezed the trigger, and melted the oncoming ork into a puddle of ooze and charred bone with a single prolonged blast.

'And what would Rhetoricus say about *that* manoeuvre?' du Queste asked, eyes narrowed and a slight smile tugging the corners of his lips.

'Simple,' Zatori answered. 'I ascertained the opponent's state,' he hefted his melta gun, 'and seized the advantage by changing my approach.'

# RENEGADES

### *Gav Thorpe*

The growling of engines and the roar of battle cannons reverberated around the massive hall, the echoes overlapping into a constant thunder of destruction. Intricately designed mosaics upon the wall shattered into thousands of multi-coloured shards under the impact of shells and las-fire. The marble tiles of the flooring cracked and heaved under iron treads as battle tanks lumbered forwards. Soldiers garbed in long black overcoats hurried from cover to cover; sheltering behind the immense pillars supporting the ceiling, scurrying to and fro behind mounds of rubble and leaping into craters gouged into the once-gleaming floor.

The tumult of war drowned out the shouted commands of the rebels' leaders, who waved forward their men from atop the blasted remains of armoured transports and the plinths of ravaged statues of former Imperial commanders. Their men chanted new slogans in defiance of their ousted commanders; battle cries filled with hate and calls for justice.

All along the mile-long hall the forces of the insurrectionists surged forwards under the cover of their tanks' guns.

Ahead of them the Astartes of the Avenging Sons Chapter stood defiant, their blue armour covered in dust and grime. They had come to quell a rebellion, only to find a world gripped by civil war. They had arrived to execute the rebel leaders and restore the rule of the Imperial commander, now they defended the same man against a whole world risen up against the tyranny of their ruler. The fighting had taken a bloody toll. There were thirty of them left; thirty Space Marines of the one hundred and three who had first come to Helmabad.

From behind makeshift barricades of twisted metal, heaps of lumpen rockcrete and barriers of piled bodies the Astartes poured fire into their attackers. The air was alight with the flickering rocket trails of bolter rounds, while blinding lascannon blasts blazed out to sear through armoured hulls and flesh alike. The crunch of heavy bolter fire and the crackling roar of plasma howled the Space Marines' fury.

Behind the wall of armoured giants cowered the relatively few men that still remained loyal to Commander Mu'shan, snapping off shots from their lasguns in scattered moments of bravery. Once they had been the elite, the lauded Sepulchre Guard of Helmabad. Now the ire of those they had once sworn to protect had humbled them. Their death's head masks seemed comical rather than grim. Their gold brocade and epaulettes were tattered and their black carapace armour pitted, scarred and filthy.

Amidst the fire and devastation strode Brother-Captain Gessart of the Avenging Sons. Like his battle-brothers he wore armour marked from much fighting. Its blue paint was burnt and cracked ceramite showed through his livery in dozens of places. His left shoulder pad was a plain, dull white; a hasty replacement for the one he had lost two days ago. His golden helmet was slicked with a layer of dust, and blood stained the silver eagle upon his chest; the blood of enemies a better badge of honour than the symbol it obscured.

Gessart barked commands as he led the defenders, each order punctuated by a salvo of shots from the storm bolter in his hands.

'Dispersive fire on the left,' he growled, loosing off three rounds that tore through a junior officer half-hidden behind the tangled remains of an iron bench. The men the dead officer had been attempting to rally melted away into the dust clouds and smoke.

Just behind the captain stood Librarian Zacherys, a nimbus of energy glowing from the Librarian's psychic hood, the force sword in his right fist blazing with power. Helmetless, Zacherys's face was a mask of strain as he projected an invisible wall of force around the Space Marines. With sparks of warp energy, las-bolts and autogun rounds crackled into oblivion around the psyker.

'Show them no mercy!' bellowed Herdain, the Company Chaplain, as he stepped up onto a pile of rubble and loosed a succession of plasma bolts from his pistol. The conversion field hidden within the Chaplain's rosarius intermittently blazed into blinding life as enemy fire converged on the grim custodian.

'How can so many be so misguided?' said Rykhel, his bolter raised to his shoulder, his shots controlled and precise. 'They are blind to their doom.'

'Pick your targets,' said Gessart. 'Make every shot count.'

'It's hard to miss,' laughed Lehenhart, his bolter spewing rounds that chewed through a rebel squad dashing across the open area directly in front of the Space Marines. 'We haven't had such easy targets since those orks charged us on Caraphis.'

'You'll lead us to victory, captain,' said Willusch. 'The primarch favours you.'

'Just stay focused,' said Gessart as he loosed off another burst of fire.

The firefight continued for several more minutes, the Space Marines manoeuvring and concentrating their fire wherever the rebels looked to be gathering in numbers.

'Recon walkers on the right flank. Three, possibly four,' warned Willusch. He swung his heavy bolter in a slow arc, his volley hammering through plasteel and rockcrete at the rebels cowering behind. 'I can't draw on them from here.'

'Lehenhart, Herdain, Nicz and Rykhel with me,' Gessart snapped. 'Ready grenades for counterattack.'

The five Space Marines pounded to the right along the barricade line. A long gallery ran alongside this side of the hall, the wall between cracked and holed in places, through which the captain saw the gawky forms of Sentinel walkers advancing. If they were allowed to continue they would reach the end of the line and would be able to pour fire from behind the defence works.

'Breach on my signal,' Gessart called out.

They were less than a dozen paces from the wall when Gessart unleashed a long burst from his storm bolter, the rounds punching into the rockcrete and gouging great holes with their detonations. The others did the same, ripping up the wall with their fire.

'Breach!' shouted Gessart, lowering his left shoulder and charging full speed at the damaged rockcrete. The blasted wall shattered under the impact of the massive Space Marine and the captain smashed through into the gallery beyond amidst a cloud of stone splinters and crumbling plaster. To his left and right the others made similarly dramatic entrances.

The Avenging Sons had breached just behind four Sentinel walkers. The rearmost turned awkwardly, its double-jointed legs buckling as it struggled over a mound of rubble. The pilot's eyes widened with horror inside the open cockpit as Rykhel's frag grenade landed in his lap. He reached up to slap the release buckle on his restraining belt. A moment later the grenade detonated, spraying the inside of the walker with lethal shrapnel. The pilot was shredded, his bloodied, ragged form disembowelled. Its controls destroyed, the walker swayed to the left and then nose-dived to the right, the impact buckling its chin-mounted multilaser.

The three others were beginning to turn, but not quickly enough to bring their weapons to bear. Nicz had a krak grenade in his hand. He leapt forwards and slammed the magnetic explosive onto the lower joint of the closest Sentinel's left leg before jumping back. The grenade detonated, shearing away the walker's steel limb. The Sentinel toppled backwards and Nicz punched his gauntleted fist through its exposed underside, tearing free a handful of wires and hydraulics. Red fluid spurted from the severed lines, spraying like arterial blood from the critically wounded Sentinel.

Gessart jumped up towards the next Sentinel, his free hand grabbing hold of the edge of the cockpit. The pilot pulled out a laspistol and fired it point blank into Gessart's chest as the captain heaved himself up, the shots flickering harmless from the solid plastron of his armour. Gessart swung his storm bolter around and fired two shots; the first round ripped apart the pilot's chest, the second disintegrated his head in a shower of gore; blood and brain matter spattered across Gessart's golden helm. The Sentinel jerked spasmodically as the dead man's muscles contracted at the controls, throwing Gessart to the ground in its mechanical death throes.

The last pilot fired his multilaser, the shots falling well wide, as he tried to steer his walker to face his attackers. Lehenhart reached up and grabbed the swivelling weapon with his right hand. The creak of hydraulics competed with the whine of servos as the Sentinel's systems battled against the artificial muscles of Lehenhart's bionic arm and power armour. With a screech and a shower of sparks the Sentinel's actuators lost the fight and Lehenhart ripped the multilaser from its housing. Herdain's plasma pistol tore a glowing hole through the walker's engine block which exploded in a ball of blue flame, sending Lehenhart and the Chaplain crunching into the rubble littering the gallery floor.

The pilot of the walker crippled by Nicz pulled himself free of the cockpit and dragged himself a few paces across the grit of the floor, his leg shattered by the same blow that had destroyed his machine. Lehenhart picked himself up and grabbed the back of the man's flak jacket. Casually lifting the soldier into the air, the Space Marine turned to Gessart.

'Anyone want a new pet?' Lehenhart asked.

'Perhaps we can interrogate him for intelligence,' said Nicz.

Gessart glanced at the wounded man. Tears made tracks through the filth on his smoke-grimed face beneath the peak of his skewed leather helmet. The man's distress meant nothing to the captain. He was the enemy, that was all that mattered.

'There's nothing he can tell us that we don't know already,' said the captain with a dismissive shake of the head.

Lehenhart shrugged, the actuators beneath his shoulder pads whining in protest as they tried to replicate the expressive gesture. With a swing of his arm, the Space Marine smashed the pilot against the wreckage of his walker, dashing in his skull and snapping his spine with one blow. Lehenhart let the limp corpse drop from his fingers.

Gessart checked down the gallery to see if any other rebels had been following the walkers. He could see nothing and guessed they had been waiting until the sentinels secured a forward position. Still, he could not defend the gallery and the hallway at the same time; not if the rebels made a determined push along both. He was thankful that the rebel commanders, whoever they now were after overthrowing the Imperial commander's regime, seemed to place a tactically-limiting value on their follower's lives. An enemy with a more detached attitude would have overrun the hall on the first attack.

'Back to the line,' Gessart ordered.

For another six hours the battle for the audience hall raged. There had been little let-up in the fighting and even Gessart was beginning to feel the strain of the constant vigilance required; not just on the line here but from more than forty days of continuous war since they had arrived on Helmabad.

Smoke billowing from four wrecked tanks hung heavily in the still air, obscuring growing numbers of shadowy figures beyond. The rebels were clearly massing for another attack, as they had done three times before in the last twenty hours.

'Ammunition check,' said Gessart, ejecting his own empty magazine and slamming another drum into place on the side of the storm bolter.

'Last belt, captain,' Brother Willusch reported on the comm.

'Seven rounds left, captain,' warned Brother Rykhel.

'Power pack at thirty-five per cent,' said Brother Heynke.

As the rest gave their reports it was quickly apparent that every Space Marine was running low. Gessart looked out at the hundreds of soldiers now creeping closer and closer to their line. Some were less than fifty metres away, firing blind from their hiding places to cover the advance of their comrades. Gessart knew that they would be moving up heavier weaponry and the Space Marines would feel the full wrath of the rebels' attack soon.

Another Leman Russ tank rumbled into view. It foolishly shouldered aside the wreckage of a transport and crawled forwards, its cannon swinging towards Gessart's position. Obviously the men inside had not learnt from the mistakes of their fellow tank crews. The captain fearlessly stared down the bore of the gun for a moment.

'Heynke!' Gessart called out, but his warning was unnecessary; even as the name left his lips Heynke's lascannon spat out a blast of energy that slammed into the turret of the tank. The shot ignited the shells stored inside and the whole of the turret erupted into a blossom of fire and smoke, hurling a burning body out onto the blood-soaked marble.

'Power pack at thirty per cent,' warned Heynke. 'No more than half a dozen shots left, brother-captain. What are your orders, captain?'

'We are outgunned,' said Rykhel. 'We need to defend a more enclosed area.'

'It is our duty to press forward and drive these scum from the palace, captain,' snapped Herdain. 'Remember the teachings of Guilliman!'

Las- and heavy weapons fire intensified around the knot of Space Marines as more and more rebels got into position. Las-bolts, shrapnel and splinters of rockcrete pattered from their armour. Gessart could see only two options: retreat to the next position or counterattack and drive back the soldiers with hand to hand combat. He chose the former.

'Colonel, fall back to the access way,' Gessart directed his order to Colonel Akhaim, the leader of the Sepulchre Guard.

The Guardsmen needed no further encouragement and were soon scrambling and scrabbling over the wreckage towards the corridor behind them. A few minutes later Gessart signalled his own squads to withdraw. The Avenging Sons pulled back from the line, facing their foes all the while. No shots were fired to cover their retreat; the Space Marines were contemptuous of the rebels' weapons, and they needed to save every last shred of ammunition if they were to continue the war.

As they passed into the corridor the Space Marines retreated past a ring of melta-bombs secured to the walls and ceiling. When they were clear of the area Gessart sent the detonation signal. The ground underfoot shuddered as the captain watched the gateway into the audience hall disappear under tons of rockcrete and twisted steel. Now there was only one way in to and out of the central sepulchre where the Imperial commander was hidden.

'Reminds me of Archimedon,' said Nicz from behind the captain.

Gessart turned to look at the Space Marine, unable to see Nicz's expression hidden inside his helmet.

'Keep that thought to yourself,' snarled Gessart.

The sepulchre was the inner reaches of the Imperial commander's palace; a maze of corridors and chambers dug into the heartrock that were the foundations of the citadel. Before the uprising they had been home to functionaries and courtiers, now they were a makeshift hospital, communications station and headquarters. The brick tunnels were now choked with storage crates and wounded men on bloodstained bedding. The ghostly echoes of the dying resounded along the long, low tunnels.

Having left some of his warriors to defend the last gateway to the surface, Gessart led the remnants of his company through the winding subterranean passages. He ignored the moans of the wounded and the scared chatter of the Sepulchre Guard. Here and there a radio squawked out tinny propaganda transmitted by the rebels – a crude but effective jamming of the loyalists' communications.

Passing an archway the captain heard laughter and swearing from the chamber beyond. He stooped under the low arch into the room. Inside were a handful of Guardsmen clustered around a battered vox-caster.

'You'll be getting the same as your dog-faced friends,' their sergeant was saying into the pick-up. 'Just try to come through the east gate and the Avenging Sons will send you crying to your mothers.'

Gessart's massive armoured boot crushed the vox-caster, which died with a piercing screech.

'No communication with the enemy!' bellowed the captain.

The Guardsmen cowered before Gessart's anger as he loomed over them.

'This endless chatter gives the enemy vital information,' the captain told them. It was not the first time that he had been forced to explain his edict for radio silence. 'Fools such as you tell them where we keep our supplies, where our defences are strongest, where we intend to strike. If you wish to help the rebels at least have the courage to do it with your guns.'

Suitably cowed the Guardsmen muttered their apologies, avoiding the disconcerting gaze of the captain's blank eye lenses.

'Hopeless,' muttered Gessart as he turned back into the corridor.

The captain soon led the others into the central chamber; an octagonal meeting place of the main thoroughfares that radiated outwards to the far reaches of the sepulchre. Rykhel was already waiting; his helmet removed to reveal a lean face and agitated grey eyes.

'We have less than two hundred bolter rounds left,' the Space Marine explained with a grim expression. 'Less than fifty heavy shells for Willusch. Power packs are still plentiful.'

'One engagement,' said Heynke.

'A short one, perhaps,' said Lehenhart, his mood unusually subdued. 'It'll be short for the wrong reasons.'

'It's only through good fire discipline we've made our supplies last this long,' said Rykhel. 'We weren't equipped for an elongated campaign. We're already seventy days over our predicted combat threshold.'

'Tell me something I don't already know,' said Gessart. 'Other weapons?'

Rykhel strode across the chamber and picked up one of the many Guard-issue lasguns stacked against the walls. Its barrel crumpled in the augmented grip of his hand.

'Useless for our purposes,' said Rykhel, tossing the remnants of the lasgun aside. 'Simply not durable enough. We would be better using our fists.'

'If that is what we must do, that is what we shall do,' said Herdain. His skull helm turned slowly as the Chaplain looked at the assembled Space Marines. 'We fight to the last breath.'

Gessart did not reply, for his own thoughts were very different. Instead he looked towards Zacherys. The Librarian had pulled off his helmet, his black hair plastered with waxy sweat across his face. He leaned against the wall, the bricks behind him cracking under the strain as if in sympathy for the laboured psyker.

'Have you detected any sign of relief or reinforcement?' Gessart asked. 'Any vision or message?'

The Librarian shook his head silently.

'Nothing at all?' Gessart continued. 'No warp-chatter? No ship wakes?'

'Nothing,' said Zacherys in a cracked whisper. 'There is a veil upon Helmabad that I cannot pierce. I cannot see beyond the curtain of blood.'

'Rest,' said Gessart, crossing the chamber to lay a hand upon the Librarian's head. 'Regather your strength.'

Zacherys nodded and pushed himself upright.

'I do not wish to bring woe, but this does not augur well,' croaked the Librarian. The others watched as he straightened and walked from the vault with as much dignity as he could muster.

'His reticence worries me,' said Herdain once Zacherys was out of earshot.

'I trust no one more than Zacherys,' said Gessart. 'He guided us here. I trust he will lead us on the right path.'

'As he did on Archimedon?' asked Nicz. 'You followed his prophecy then and what did we get? A penitence patrol that has brought us to this Emperor-forsaken war.'

'I said not to speak of that place,' said Gessart, squaring off to Nicz. 'Your indiscipline borders on insubordination.'

'If I have my doubts it is not wise to keep them hidden,' said Nicz, looking at Herdain. 'Is it not true that the doubt that is buried festers into heresy, Brother-Chaplain?'

'There is a time and a place for voicing concerns,' Herdain replied evenly. 'This is neither. Respect your superiors or there will be consequences.'

'All I am saying is that we were never prepared for this fight,' said Nicz. 'You brought us here to put down a… What was it? A "small uprising", wasn't it? This world has been wracked in civil war for eight years. We should not have stayed.'

'The Chapter will respond,' said Herdain. 'More will come, either to aid us, or to avenge us.'

'Zacherys did not seem so certain,' said Heynke. 'All he talks about is the "curtain of blood" that surrounds this place. His messages have gone nowhere.'

'Then here we will make our last stand,' said Herdain. 'We live for battle and we shall die for battle.'

'We lay down our lives for victory,' said Gessart. 'I am not convinced there is any victory to be won here.'

Gessart was alone in one of the many chambers of the sepulchre, performing the rituals of maintenance on his storm bolter. The captain sat with his back to a crumbling vault wall, the storm bolter cradled delicately in his hands. He had removed his helm to see better and his craggy features were illuminated by the flicker of candles in small alcoves around the chamber. By the dim light he worked a cloth over the exposed innards of the weapon, inspecting each piece carefully before replacing it.

Now and then a detonation would set the whole network of corridors trembling, showering mortar dust from the walls and ceiling. The rebels' bombardment had been continuous, trying to force a breach through the gateways since the Space Marines had withdrawn from the upper levels. Though the defences were strong, the men who defended the catacombs were weary and disillusioned. Once the gates collapsed – perhaps two days, perhaps three or four – there would be nothing left but a last stand against an unstoppable army.

'Captain?' said Willusch from the doorway. He had stripped his armour of backpack, helm and shoulder pads. It made Willusch look strangely thin and weak, something Gessart knew to be utterly wrong. 'May I speak with you?'

Gessart looked up and waved in the Space Marine, placing his storm bolter to one side. Willusch did not sit.

'I have concerns, captain,' said Willusch.

'Our Brother-Chaplain is always ready to listen,' said Gessart.

'It is with Herdain that I have an issue,' Willusch said, his hands clasped at his waist.

'How so?' asked Gessart.

'I know that you forbade us from speaking of Archimedon, but I must,' said Willusch.

'Say what you must, brother,' said Gessart with a sigh.

'Thank you, captain,' Willusch said. He remained absolutely still as he spoke, his scarred face a picture of intense sincerity. 'We were right to do what we did on Archimedon. It is not in the teachings of the primarch to throw our lives away in needless sacrifice. We could not defend the space port any longer against the enemy. It had to be destroyed.'

'I do not need to justify my actions,' Gessart said angrily. 'As I told you all at the time, thousands would die, but not in vain. If the renegades had captured the port they would have been able to wreak unknown terror and destruction.'

'Yet the masters of the Chapter felt that you were in error,' said Willusch. 'They have punished us for that decision; a punishment that has led us to this place.'

'A chance of fate, perhaps,' said Gessart with a shake of the head. 'There is no divine justice in our coming here, merely the happenstance of location and the vagaries of astrotelepathy.'

'I concur, captain,' said Willusch. 'Yet Herdain lectured us when you departed. He told us that we were about to lay our lives upon the altar of battle for the glory of the Chapter.'

'And perhaps we will,' said Gessart. 'I see no way for us to break out of our predicament. The enemy number in their billions. Billions, Willusch! In all likelihood it is well that Herdain resigns us to our doom.'

'He not only expects it, he craves it,' said Willusch, now growing more animated. 'He would have us throw away our lives as a gesture of penance for Archimedon. He was not there yet he attributes us with a great shame for the judgement of the Chapter upon us. He does not seek victory, he seeks to absolve us with our deaths!'

Before Gessart replied a wailing shout echoed along the stone labyrinth; the cry of Zacherys. The captain pushed himself to his feet and strode out of the chamber, Willusch close on his heels. The pair marched quickly through the winding corridors, following the source of the shouts that continued to cry out. When they arrived at Zacherys's quarters Gessart saw that many of his warriors were already there.

The chamber was dark, lit by a single guttering lantern overhead. In the centre of the circle of Space Marines, Nicz was on one knee, the Librarian's head cradled in his armoured lap. Motes of energy danced around the psyker's lips as he shouted wordlessly, but the Librarian was otherwise utterly inert. Gessart noticed thick blood oozing from Zacherys's gums as he wailed.

'What is happening?' demanded Herdain as he entered from the opposite doorway.

'I just found–' began Nicz.

Zacherys's eyes snapped open and a blast of power exploded from him, hurling the Space Marines to the ground. Nicz was flung against the wall and flopped to the ground, dazed. The others groped their way back to their feet as the Librarian stood. His eyes were a liquid crimson and his teeth stained with blood.

'The curtain of blood is parting,' Zacherys whispered. 'The realm beyond breaks through. The legion across the divide awaits. The clarions of Chaos call loud.'

'What do you see?' demanded Gessart, striding across the small chamber. He reached out to touch the Librarian but held back his hand at the last moment.

'Death is coming!' hissed Zacherys. He turned his otherworldly eyes on Gessart. 'Yet, you are not destined to die here.'

With a shuddering gasp, the psyker fell to his knees and slumped forwards onto all fours. When he raised his head again, his eyes were once more the pale blue they had always been. Gessart crouched beside his friend and laid a comforting hand on his left shoulder pad.

'What did you see?' he asked again, his voice now gentle, barely audible.

'The warp opens,' said Zacherys.

There was a moment of murmuring discontent from the other Space Marines and Gessart shot them a fierce glance to quell it.

'Traitors?' asked Herdain.

'Worse,' said Zacherys, getting to his feet with the aid of Gessart. 'Chaos Incarnate. The Evil Given Life. A Nightmare Host.'

'Daemons,' muttered Rykhel.

'The rebels,' the Librarian continued. 'They know not what they do, but their fear and their loathing beckons the apparitions. They idly whisper the names of ancient powers lost in antiquity and draw the gaze of them to this world.'

'How long do we have to get ready for the festivities?' asked Lehenhart.

'Less than a day,' the Librarian replied. 'Hours, more likely. I can feel the rift opening, out in the stars above the city. They will come here first. Everything will die.'

'Not us,' said Herdain. 'We shall fight on gloriously. You said yourself that we will not die here.'

'He said that I would not die here,' said Gessart. 'I didn't hear him mention your name.'

'Yet how would you survive while we perish?' said Nicz, who had recovered and was pushing himself to his feet, using the wall to keep his balance.

'None need to die here,' said Gessart. He turned his dark gaze upon his Space Marines. 'This world is lost; to the rebels or the daemons. It matters not which darkness devours Helmabad, only that we survive to warn of its fall.'

'So we cut and run again?' said Nicz.

'That would not be my choice of phrase,' said Gessart.

'There is no honour in empty sacrifice,' said Willusch, taking a step to stand beside his captain.

'Sacrifice is the honour,' snapped Herdain. 'The Astartes were created to lay down their lives in battle. This cowardice will not be tolerated.'

'It's not cowardice, it's survival,' said Lehenhart. 'Humanity will not be guarded by our corpses.'

'I will not let you repeat the sins of Archimedon,' said Herdain, rounding on Gessart. 'You failed in your leadership then and you are failing now. You are no longer fit to lead this company.'

'Company?' laughed Nicz. 'There is no company here. No Chapter. We are all that remain. I will not die here in a vain gesture.'

'Heresy!' roared Herdain, snatching his plasma pistol from its holster and pointing it at Nicz. 'Pay no heed to this treachery, brothers.'

Rykhel held up his hands and stepped forwards.

'I swore an oath to the Chapter,' he said. 'I am Astartes, of the Avenging Sons. My life was forfeit the day I took that oath, as were all of yours. It is not our place to pick and choose our fates, but to fight until we can fight no more.'

There was a chorus of assent from several of the Space Marines, most of them newer recruits to the company, brought in to replace the losses of Archimedon. Gessart looked at the assembly and saw a mixture of hope and doubt in their eyes. Willusch gave him a reassuring nod.

'We cannot stand divided,' said Gessart. 'I am your captain, your commander. I alone lead this company, what remains of it.'

'I still follow where you lead,' said Willusch.

'And I,' said Zacherys. 'There is no defeating this foe.'

'I was taught to fight, not commit suicide,' said Lehenhart. 'Staying here would be suicide, by my reckoning.'

Herdain's face was a mask of hatred as he stared at Gessart and his companions. He turned his fell look upon Heynke.

'You, brother, what do you say?' the Chaplain demanded.

Heynke stood transfixed for a moment, his eyes shifting between Gessart and Herdain before straying around the room to look at his battle-brothers. He opened his mouth to speak and then closed it again.

'Is this the bravery of the Avenging Sons?' shouted Herdain, grabbing the rim of the breastplate at Heynke's throat and pulling him forward. 'Make your loyalties known! Show your purity!'

'I will fight!' declared Ruphen, drawing up his bolter to his shoulder and aiming at the group clustered around Gessart.

'This is insanity,' muttered Tylo, the company's Apothecary. His white armour stood out amongst the deep blue of his battle-brothers as he pushed his way forward. 'We cannot fail here and allow our gene-seed to fall into the clutches of traitors. We must seek to preserve the future.'

'What future is there without honour?' said Herdain, lowering his pistol, his eyes imploring.

The crack of a bolt-round rang out around the chamber and the Chaplain's head exploded in a blossom of blood and fragments of bone. Gessart stood with Zacherys's smoking pistol in his fist; the captain had not brought his own weapon with him.

'More future than death holds,' Gessart declared.

Ruphen opened fire with his bolter and anarchy filled the chamber. Gessart lunged to his left, pushing Zacherys clear of the Space Marine's fire. Nicz and Lehenhart opened up with their bolters. Within a second, the two camps were locked in bitter combat, blazing away with bolters and pounding each other with fists and chainswords, their harsh shouts accompanying the roar of weapons.

In a matter of moments four Space Marines lay dead on the rocky floor and six more were sorely wounded. Nicz loomed over brother Karlrech, one of those who had sided with Herdain. His bolter was inches from the bleeding Space Marine's face. Lehenhart was holding down Rykhel with the aid of two more battle-brothers. Heynke and a few others looked on with expressions of horror.

Gessart handed back the pistol to Zacherys and walked towards the subdued followers of the Chaplain.

'If you wish to die on Helmabad, I will grant you that fate,' he said calmly, looking not only at those who had spoken against him but those who had remained silent. 'I hold no ill will against you, for we must each make a choice now. It will be quick for those who wish to preserve their honour. For those who swear anew to follow me, there will be no judgement on what has just passed.'

'I will follow the will of my brothers,' said Heynke. 'If it is their choice that we leave, then I shall be with them.'

'Death before dishonour!' spat Karlrech.

Gessart gave Nicz a nod, who pulled the trigger and ended Karlrech's protests with the angry retort of his bolter.

'Anybody else?' Nicz asked, straightening, his face a crimson mask of the dead Space Marine's blood.

Brother Hechsen stepped forwards and grabbed the muzzle of Nicz's bolter and placed it under his chin. He stared defiantly at Gessart.

'This is treachery,' said Hechsen. 'I name you all renegades, and I will not be numbered amongst you in the annals of shame. I am an Avenging Son and proud to die as such. You are less than cowards, for you are traitors.'

Gessart noticed a few of his warriors wince as Nicz fired again, but he kept his own eyes firmly fixed on those of Hechsen. He felt nothing. Inside he was empty, as he had been for several years; ever since Archimedon. He had not wished events to turn in this way, but he was accepting of whatever fate had dealt him.

No more Space Marines stepped forwards at Nicz's next inquiry and Gessart nodded approvingly. Lehenhart pulled Rykhel to his feet and patted him on the head. Tylo moved to the dead warriors and began the bloody process of removing their gene-seed as Gessart turned to Zacherys.

'We shall not die on Helmabad,' the captain said.

'Aye, captain,' said the Librarian with a weak smile.

'I hope you have a plan for how you're going to make that happen,' said Lehenhart. 'There's still millions of rebels camped outside, and we need to get off this world.'

'Captain!' Nicz called out and pointed towards one of the chamber doors.

Clustered outside was a handful of the Sepulchre Guard, who looked upon the awful scene with wide eyes and trembling lips.

'Nicz, Lehenhart, Heynke, Willusch,' Gessart snapped. 'Deal with them.'

As the Space Marines turned towards the doorway the Guardsmen bolted.

'Fists and knives,' Gessart added. 'Save what ammunition you can.'

The central chamber of the sepulchre was deathly quiet, disturbed only by moans and whispers of dying Sepulchre Guards echoing from the corridors surrounding it. It was a large space, its wide floor decorated with tiles carved with the Imperial aquila, thirty pillars inscribed with the names of faithful Imperial servants supported the vaulted ceiling. At one end Imperial Commander Mu'shan sat upon a high-backed chair of dark red wood, his wizened face hidden by the cowl of his golden robe. Nicz stood to his left, bolter in hand, while Hurstreich loomed on the governor's right. Gessart leant against one of the pillars not far from the throne, talking to Lehenhart and Zacherys. Some of the other Space Marines stood guard at the entrance hall, others stood sentry behind the sealed east gate, whilst five had been despatched on a mission beyond the sepulchre by their captain.

'The breach is coming closer,' warned the Librarian, his voice low. 'I can feel the curtain of blood thinning. I hear the voices of the beasts that dwell on the other side. They are hungry, I can feel it. They sense the terror of this world and they thirst for it.'

'We could probably fight our way back to the Thunderhawk,' said Lehenhart. 'It's less than a mile from the north-west gate.'

'As a last resort, yes,' Gessart replied. 'I would rather not use up the remaining supplies fighting the rebels only to be unarmed when the daemons arrive. There is another way; one that carries less risk.'

'What do you have in mind?' asked Lehenhart.

'That is not your concern,' snapped Gessart. 'Be ready to move out on my word.'

'Of course,' said Lehenhart. 'You know, a little trust goes a long way.'

Gessart darted the Space Marine a scowl in reply and Lehenhart swiftly retreated, joining his comrades at the main door.

'What is your intent, renegade?' Mu'shan's high-pitched voice floated across the hall.

Gessart strode to the Imperial commander and stood in front of him, swathing the aging ruler with his shadow. He looked down at the shrivelled dignitary and wondered how such a decrepit specimen could ever have been trusted with the sovereign rule of Helmabad.

'It was not I that surrendered his world to the rebels,' said Gessart. 'The blame for all that has befallen you lies at your own feet. Your laxness in prosecuting the Emperor's will has been your undoing.'

'And so in hindsight you would hold me guilty of this, when it is you who are supposed to be our saviours?' Mu'shan spoke quietly but with defiance. 'What hope is there for mankind if our greatest defenders forget their oaths and put their survival ahead of their duty?'

'You speak to me of duties?' said Gessart with a sneer. 'How is it that three-quarters of your citizens rose up in revolt against your command? Explain to me why the Astartes should shed their blood to save the rulership of a man who did not defend it himself?'

'If I am weak, then it is beholden to you and your kind to remain strong,' said Mu'shan, pulling back his hood to reveal a thin, wrinkled face with alabaster-white skin. His eyes were dark blue and intent as he stared at Gessart. 'If I failed, it is because of my human weakness. You were created to be better than human; stronger, more devoted, dependable and unflinching. Has so much been lost these ten thousand years that the war-angels of the Astartes consider the protection of mankind beneath their dignity?'

'Has man fallen so low that he must always look to the Astartes to cure every ill it suffers?' countered Gessart. 'We wage war for the protection of humankind, of the race, not in the defence of individuals. Did the Emperor grant you such a greater lot in your life, that it is worth our lives to defend you for a few hours more when we could live and save a billion others?'

Mu'shan stood slowly, awkwardly, lips pursed, his head barely reaching the chest of Gessart. His back was bent and as he reached forward a hand to lay it upon the eagle of Gessart's armour his skeletal limbs were plain to see.

'If you judge the worth of your battles by numbers alone, then you have already lost,' said Mu'shan. 'Beneath this breast of muscle and fused bone beats the heart of a man. Does it not tell you that what you do is wrong?'

Gessart gently brushed aside the commander's hand, fearful that so frail was Mu'shan that even this light touch might break his weak bones.

'I have read the *Tactica Imperialis* too,' said Gessart. 'It also says, "The mere slaughter of your foe is no substitute for true victory." A man's heart may beat in my chest, but beside it beats the secondary heart of the Space Marine. We are not alike. We share no common bond. You ask that I be human and sacrifice myself for you. The nature of the galaxy demands that I be more than human and live to fight further battles. To accept defeat, for our deaths will not prevent it here, is no courage at all. To accept death, no matter the circumstance, is the counsel of despair. I will listen to it no longer.'

Gessart turned away and heard Mu'shan wheeze as he sat down again. His ears also detected the tramp of heavy boots outside and a moment later the guards at the door parted to allow Willusch, Heynke and three other Space Marines to enter. Between them they carried the limp forms of four men, their greatcoats torn, insignias cut out. Rebels.

'Tylo!' Gessart called as the prisoners were dropped unceremoniously in the middle of the chamber.

The Apothecary walked over to the captives and, after giving them a brief inspection, nodded to confirm that they were still alive.

'Wake them up,' said Gessart.

Willusch strode across the chamber to the pile of crates and barrels in one corner, returning quickly with a glass demijohn of water. He tipped its contents over the faces of the men, who rose to wakefulness with splutters and coughs. They gazed at the Space Marines towering over them, their eyes full of fear, and their mouths aghast.

'Listen, do not speak,' snapped Gessart. 'Do as I say and you will live. Any defiance and you will be slain.'

The men nodded dumbly in understanding.

'That is well,' said Gessart, crouching down beside the prisoners, the joints of his armour creaking as he did so. He turned his gaze to Heynke. 'Fetch a vox-caster.'

Heynke headed back into the recesses of the hall without question and returned promptly carrying a comms unit under one arm. He placed it on the floor next to Gessart and knelt on one knee beside it.

'Who are we contacting?' Heynke said.

Gessart looked at the prisoners with a vicious smile.

'The enemy,' he said.

Gessart's captives were more than willing to give up the command frequencies of their superiors, and after several messages, the Space Marines worked their way up the chain to speak to those in charge.

'Who am I addressing?' asked Gessart, the vox-caster's pick-up dwarfed by his huge fist.

'Serain Am'hep, Third Apostle of the Awakening,' a tinny voice crackled back.

'Third what?' snorted Lehenhart. 'Unbelievable!'

Gessart waved him into silence and pressed the transmit stud.

'Do you have the authority to discuss terms?' the captain asked.

'I am a member of the Revolutionary Council,' Serain Am'hep replied. 'I have with me the fourth and eighth Apostles and we speak for all members.'

'Finally!' said Gessart. He began to pace around the prisoners as he spoke. 'It is my desire to end this conflict.'

'You wish to discuss surrender?' Am'hep's incredulity was clear in the tone of his voice.

'Of course not,' said Gessart.

'There's no way we could possibly take you all prisoner!' Lehenhart called from behind his leader.

Gessart turned with a frown and wordlessly pointed towards the guards at the door. Lehenhart gave a sullen nod and departed to join them.

'Let me be direct with you,' said Gessart. 'I wish to arrange our safe departure in return for the delivery of Imperial Commander Mu'shan.'

'What?' came Mu'shan's choked cry from the end of the hall.

Surprise was written across the faces of many of the Space Marines. Nicz simply nodded with a grim smile.

'You will turn over the faithless Mu'shan to our justice?' asked Am'hep.

'Once we have departed, you will be free to enter the sepulchre without resistance and claim him for yourselves,' said Gessart.

'Why would we allow you to walk free?' said Am'hep. 'We have the manpower to storm the sepulchre any time that we wish.'

'You are welcome to expend the lives of thousands of your followers in the attempt,' said Gessart. 'I'm sure their deaths will not discourage the rest.'

There was a long pause as Am'hep undoubtedly conferred with his companions. Gessart glanced towards the throne, where Mu'shan was sat trembling, his eyes boring holes of hatred into the Space Marine captain. Gessart ignored him and looked away.

'What guarantee can we be given that you have not spirited Mu'shan away by some means?' said Am'hep.

'None,' replied Gessart. 'However, should you try to double-cross me, my strike cruiser in orbit has locked onto your comms-signal and is even now aiming its cannons at your position. If I fail to report to them once we leave the sepulchre they will reduce your camp to ashes, and you along with it.'

'Really?' whispered Willusch with a smile. 'I never knew we could do that.'

'He's lying, you idiot,' snapped Nicz. 'Even if we were actually in contact with the *Vengeful* they can't track a solitary carrier wave signal from orbit. We would have blasted their commanders to oblivion by now if we could.'

Gessart shook his head despairingly and clicked the transmit stud once more.

'I expect your reply within five minutes,' he told the rebel leaders. 'If I have not had confirmation by then, I will assume you wish the war to continue.'

He tossed the pick-up to the floor and walked away.

'What if they refuse?' asked Tylo. 'They could bombard us for days and reduce the sepulchre to rubble and trap us in here.'

'No,' Mu'shan called out. 'They're revolutionaries. They need to show their pawns that I have been truly overthrown. It is, however, a grave mistake to trust them. To defeat the Astartes will be a powerful symbol for them also.'

Gessart stalked along the hallway, his eyes fixed upon the Imperial commander.

'You try to goad me by speaking of defeat?' Gessart said as he walked. 'Your crude manipulations may have been sufficient to fool and subdue your council, but they do not work on me. You forget that we are trained to believe in the right of our cause. We do not flinch from the harsh truths that ordinary men would shy away from. Once committed to a cause we are indefatigable; swayed not by propaganda or deception.'

'You believe your actions here are justified?' croaked Mu'shan. 'You have made your decision and will no longer listen to reason?'

'The reason of men is filled with doubt and fear,' said Gessart as he stopped in front of the governor. 'Their logic is tainted by affection, compassion and mercy. They believe that life should be fair, rather than just.'

'I did not realise that the argument of semantics was part of your training,' said Mu'shan with a dismissive shake of the head. 'It has bred arrogance.'

'The insecure see self-assurance and call it hubris,' said Gessart. 'You call it semantics. In training it was called the shield of righteousness and the armour of contempt. We indeed learn of the trickery of words, so that we might spot the falsehoods presented as facts by our foes. Our minds are as hardened to doubt as our bodies are to injury. Your self-interest is plain, and so easily ignored.'

'My self-interest?' laughed Mu'shan bitterly. 'You flee this battle to save yourself!'

'It does not matter which course of action I have chosen,' said Gessart. 'Label it as you will. The fact remains that I am decided on it, and your so-called arguments are nothing more than a petty, irritating distraction. If you continue, I shall be forced to silence you.'

Mu'shan looked into Gessart's eyes and saw nothing but harsh sincerity. He shook his head once more and lifted up his cowl to hide his leathery face.

Gessart was halfway back to the vox-caster when it crackled into life.

'We have contacted our fellow Apostles and we have reached a decision,' said Am'hep. 'In two hours from now you shall assemble at the east gate and open it. You will be allowed to depart and will be given clear passage to your transport. You will not be hindered. When you have left we shall enter the sepulchre and arrest the treacherous Mu'shan. Are you agreed with this plan?'

Gessart took the proffered pick-up from Willusch and squeezed the transmit stud.

'The east gate, in two hours,' Gessart repeated. 'It is agreed.'

Dropping the handset to the floor he turned to his warriors.

'Scout the sepulchre for power packs, ammunition and any other supplies of use to us,' said Gessart. 'Armour up and be ready for action in ninety minutes. Tylo, prepare your gene-seed extractions for transit. Brothers, we are leaving Helmabad.'

Gessart's Space Marines were a peculiar sight as they gathered just inside the massive bastion of the east gateway. Helmeted once more, they assumed the appearance of faceless angels of death, but now tempered with the baggage of their war on Helmabad. Their armour was rent and pitted with damage from the long fighting, patched here and there with battlefield repairs. They carried kitbags from the slain Guardsmen stuffed with power packs and water canteens. Nicz had an ornate power sword looted from the body of Colonel Akhaim; it looked small in his armoured fist, but was still a valuable prize.

Some of them had promethium containers hung from their belts, and the small fragmentation grenades used by the Imperial commander's forces. Lehenhart had supplemented his bolter with an autocannon taken from its tripod, which he now carried over his shoulder, belts of shells hooked over one of the exhaust vents of his backpack.

They had been busy this last hour and a half, that was for sure.

'Ready?' asked Gessart. He received nods and affirmatives in response. He gave the signal to Heynke to start the gate-opening sequence.

He was stood at a rune panel set atop a lectern facing the huge armoured doors. Heynke's gauntleted hands moved quickly over the glowing screen. Gears hidden in the floor far below the sepulchre started to turn slowly, their rumbling causing the floor to shudder. A warning klaxon sounded and red lights flashed on and off in the mass of machinery above the Space Marines.

The inner gate creaked and squealed as it opened outwards, driven by massive pistons. Amber lights flickered into life in the high, narrow hallway beyond.

'Move out,' snapped Gessart.

With the four captured rebels in front of them, the Space Marines strode into the antechamber. Gessart gave Heynke the nod, who activated the outer door locks and then followed his leader into the gatehouse.

There was more grinding of huge engines beneath them and then a sliver of bright light appeared in the plasteel door ahead. The sliver became a crack and then widened into a shaft of blinding sunlight. It was sunset and Helmabad's star was low on the horizon, almost directly opposite the east gate. Gessart's visor darkened immediately as the auto-senses filtered out the sudden brightness.

Through the tint, Gessart could see a massive ruined hallway, with tall windows all along its length through which the light was streaming. A long colonnade, its columns broken in places, ran down the centre, lined with troops and vehicles. Hundreds of weapons from lasguns to battle cannons were directed towards the Space Marines as they emerged. Most of the roof had collapsed and the dusk sky provided a ruddy ceiling.

A shimmering aurora hung to the north, making the sky look like a curtain of blood. At the realisation, Gessart hurriedly glanced at Zacherys. The Librarian nodded meaningfully.

Ahead, and to the left, stood a knot of serious-looking men in grey robes. There were eight of them, each with his head shaven, his face and scalp painted black. Their white eyes stood out like pearls floating upon ink. Gessart looked at the Apostles of the Awakening but they all cast their gaze upon the rubble-strewn floor; out of disdain, fear or shame, Gessart could not tell.

The shattered plascrete crunched underfoot in the quiet, joined only by the throbbing of combustion engines. Gessart turned his eyes directly ahead and walked without fear down the steps of the eastern gatehouse and into the hall.

'Go,' he said to the captured rebels, waving them away. They gave grateful smiles and grins as they scurried across the debris to rejoin their insurrectionist comrades.

The Space Marines' advance along the hall was not hurried, but nor was it slow. Gessart was keen not to show any fear, but he was very aware that it was more than a mile to the Thunderhawk's landing pad up on the roof of the palace, and time was a resource that was rapidly running out.

The tramp of booted feet signalled an escort falling into place behind the Space Marines. Gessart glanced back and saw the fear etched into the faces of those that followed. If the Astartes chose to fight, the men closest to the Space Marines knew they would be the first to die.

Further on, tank engines belched into fuming life and the crunch and clatter of treads announced the armoured element of their guard was now getting underway. Gessart was not worried. At this close range, the presence of the tanks was for show rather than any real protection. With another glance towards the darkening red sky, he began to slowly increase his pace.

As the small group reached the end of the hall, Gessart turned back towards the sepulchre. Already squads of troops were streaming up the steps to search for the Imperial commander. Mu'shan wouldn't be hard to find; Gessart had manacled him to his chair of office and transmitted the location of the inner chamber just before he'd left for the gatehouse.

Assured that there would be no treachery, Gessart lead his Space Marines onwards.

The Avenging Sons' last remaining Thunderhawk gunship sat atop one of the landing platforms of the palace's east wing, surrounded by a cordon of guards. The Avenging Sons had lost their other craft one by one during the course of many missions against the rebels, and Gessart had wisely decided to keep one of the gunships intact. Fearing the vessel to be booby-trapped the rebels had not interfered with the Thunderhawk or tried to gain entry; early in the campaign the traitors had tried to capture a damaged Rhino personnel carrier and the transport's machine-spirit had detonated its engines, slaying several dozen looters.

The Helmabadians guarding the craft withdrew into the palace as Gessart and his warriors approached, giving the Space Marines unimpeded access. Nicz moved to the assault ramp at the front of the slab-sided craft and opened the access controls while Gessart and the others scanned the surrounding gantries and rooftops for signs of heavy weapons ready to bring them down once they were airborne. Gessart could see nothing with enough firepower to down the Thunderhawk and gave Nicz the signal to open the ramp.

The ring of Space Marines collapsed back towards the gunship as the ramp growled down from the hull of the Thunderhawk. They were as alert now as they had been throughout the march from the sepulchre, expecting treachery but careful not to provoke a response from the rebels that had shadowed them. Gessart was the last to board, and gave a look towards the heavens where the night sky was dominated by the rippling waves of the red aurora. He slammed a hand onto the button that would close the ramp as he strode into the Thunderhawk's interior.

Nicz was already in the cockpit at the pilot's controls, Vanghort beside him in the navigator's position. Gessart stepped backwards into one of the flight alcoves along the flanks of the hull. Mechanics hissed as servo arms came down from the ceiling and detached the Space Marine's backpack and plugged it into the Thunderhawk's system to recharge. Even the compensating muscle-like fibre bundles of his power armour felt lighter without the backpack's reactor weighing him down. A quick check of the suit's systems in his visor display confirmed that his armour had internal power for several hours; more than enough for them to reach the strike cruiser in orbit. Thus freed of the bulky backpack, Gessart was able to work his way between the rows of benches into the control chamber and climb up into the command chair behind Nicz. He activated the comm-link and punched in the frequency of the strike cruiser's bridge.

'*Vengeful*, this is Gessart,' he said, the Thunderhawk's own communications system picking up his helmet's signal and amplifying it into orbit. 'Confirm extraction by Thunderhawk imminent. Stand in to low orbit above our position and beat to quarters. Be ready to leave at flank speed upon our arrival.'

'Captain!' came the surprised voice of Kholich Beyne, Gessart's chief functionary aboard the *Vengeful*. 'We thought you might be dead.'

'I still might be if you don't get ready to leave right now,' Gessart snarled. 'You can leave the celebrations until we're out-system.'

'Understood, captain,' said Beyne, his tone controlled once more. 'Will rendezvous over your position in one-eight standard minutes. Confirm.'

'Confirmed,' said Gessart before he closed the contact. He reached up and pulled down the restraint harness above his head, fixing its locking bolts into position on his shoulder pads. 'Everybody get secure for rapid departure!'

When the other Space Marines confirmed that they were in their positions Gessart reached out and patted Nicz on the back of the head. Without a word, Nicz gunned the engines into life, which kicked in with a throaty roar that set the whole gunship to juddering.

'Goodbye, Helmabad,' said Lehenhart over the comm-net. As Nicz opened up the launch thrusters the Thunderhawk surged into the air upon columns of fire. Gessart felt the gravitational forces pushing at him even through the pressurised balance of his armour and he gritted his teeth against the sickening sensation in his stomach.

Nicz rolled the Thunderhawk to the right as they pulled up into a steep climb, taking them over the ruins of the palace.

'Come take a look at this, captain,' said Heynke from his position at the starboard lascannon array.

Gessart glanced at the launch chronometer and saw that they were still over a hundred seconds from orbital thrust. Plenty of time to investigate. He punched the harness release and levered it back over his head. The Thunderhawk shaking under the tread of his magno-grip boots, Gessart made his way down the steeply inclined hull towards Heynke. The Space Marine pointed to the monitor displaying the image from the external gun camera. He had the magnification set at thirty times normal Space Marine vision and it showed the steps of the sepulchre eastern gate. Gessart could see thousands of rebels were crowded into the outer hall and tens of thousands more could be seen outside the palace and crushing into the galleries and on balconies. Through the remnants of the hall's roof the scene playing out upon the steps was clear to see.

The eight Apostles of the Awakening stood in a circle around a golden-robed figure: unmistakeably Mu'shan. The dwindling light of the dusk glittered on blades as they struck him down and the surrounding rebels threw up their arms and cast their hats and helmets into the air in celebration. Lasrifle shots flashed into the sky as they fired victory volleys.

Heynke looked over his shoulder but said nothing. Gessart nodded in understanding and patted Heynke hard on the shoulder pad.

'It would have happened even if we had stayed,' said Gessart. 'He was slain swiftly. Perhaps it is better that he died at the hands of those who despised him than he survived to be taken by the daemons.'

Gessart clambered his way back to the control cabin and locked himself in once more. By now the Thunderhawk was shaking violently as its thrusters accelerated the gunship to hypersonic speeds. The external pick-ups of his helm relayed the creaks and groans of straining metal and ceramite as the Thunderhawk fought against gravity and friction. Looking out of the armoured canopy, Gessart could see the stubby nose of the craft beginning to glow with heat, and beyond that the great wound in reality like a pulsing red sheet of energy.

'Check seals for depressurisation,' Nicz said over the link. 'Orbital velocity in thirty seconds.'

Gessart hoped fervently that they reached the safety of the strike cruiser before the rift opened and the hellish legions that waited beyond were unleashed. He didn't need Zacherys's psychic insight to know that it would be close. Very close.

Even as Nicz switched power to the landing thrusters and the Thunder-hawk screamed into the docking bay of the *Vengeful* Gessart was already out of his seat. He tapped into the internal ship link to the bridge.

'Kholich, full power to engines, maximum acceleration!' he snapped.

'Understood, captain,' came Beyne's reply.

The roar of plasma was joined by the screech of metal as the Thunderhawk touched down onto the docking platform. Gessart leapt down into the main compartment and activated the assault ramp.

'Zacherys, with me,' he ordered as he thundered onto the lowering ramp. 'The rest of you get to battle stations and prepare the gun crews.'

Gessart was off the Thunderhawk before the ramp had finished lowering, leaping the last few metres to the decking, Zacherys a few strides behind him. The *Vengeful* was awash with tremors as her powerful engines burned into life. Stunned serfs looked up from their consoles and cranes as the Space Marines dashed past. Gessart exited the hangar into the main dorsal corridor at a run. Turning left he headed towards the nearest conveyor and punched in the code for the bridge.

'Report on the warp breach,' Gessart demanded as he waited for the conveyor to arrive.

'Activity increasing, captain,' said Beyne.

'It's opening,' whispered Zacherys. 'It's almost time.'

The conveyor arrived with a hiss of brakes and a clang. The doors squealed open at a touch of the runepad. Gessart stepped inside and almost dragged Zacherys with him. Closing the door, Gessart set the transporter into motion and forced himself to calm down. In the three minutes it took for the conveyor to arrive at the main bridge station he was back in control, his rising sense of urgency brutally quashed.

The armoured doors to the bridge grumbled open at his approach to reveal a scene of frenzied activity. The warp breach was front and centre of the main display, algorithms and symbols scrolling past as its energies were detected and measured.

Gessart was no more than a pace inside the bridge when Zacherys gave a cry of pain. Turning, Gessart saw the Librarian fall to one knee, his hands clasped to his head.

'The curtain of blood falls away!' he shouted. 'The rift opens!'

Gessart looked back at the screen and saw that the waving red energy seemed to part, unveiling a swirling maelstrom of colours. Though he had no psychic power at all even he could hear the screams and shouts of the daemonic host, like distant cries within his skull.

'Immediate warp jump,' snapped Gessart, focusing his attention back on the bridge.

Beyne stood to one side of the command chair; a young, bright-eyed retainer with long hair. He was dressed in blue service robes like the other serfs, though his rank was signified by the silver rope at his waist. He held a dataslab in one hand, forgotten now, his gaze distant as he listened to the inner voices now assailing everybody aboard.

'Activate warp shields,' shouted Gessart. 'Prepare for immediate jump.'

There was no reaction from the crew.

'Beyne!' Gessart yelled, grabbing the man by his arm, careful not to squeeze too tightly and shatter the bone. The pain brought Beyne out of his trance and he looked at Gessart with panicked eyes.

'Warp jump?' he stuttered. 'If we open a gate here the gravitational forces will pull us apart.'

'There's already a gate open, you imbecile!' said Gessart, thrusting a finger towards the pulsing daemonic rift.

'Enter that?' replied Beyne, the fear written across his youthful face.

'Heading zero-zero-eight by zero-seventeen by thirteen degrees,' Gessart bellowed, turning his attention to the helmsmen to his left. They nodded and their fingers danced across their control panels as they laid in the course that would take the *Vengeful* directly into the warp breach.

Satisfied that they were at least headed in the correct direction, Gessart turn to Zacherys, who was back on his feet, staring intently at the main screen.

'I need you to navigate, Zacherys,' Gessart said, stepping towards the Librarian. 'Can you do that?'

The Librarian nodded.

'Where are we heading?' he asked.

'Anywhere away from here,' said Gessart.

Zacherys turned on his heel and made his way back into the main corridor, heading towards the navigational pilaster above the bridge. The doors closed behind him with a resounding crash.

Gessart fixed his attention back to the main screen and the warp rift displayed upon it. It looked like a writhing miasma, interchanging between strangely-coloured flames, bright spirals of light and a seething ring of boiling reality. Faces appeared briefly and then faded from view. Swirls and counter-swirls of different hues rippled across its surface.

The sound of an alarm pinging from a console broke Gessart's fixation.

'Saviour pod launched from the third battery, captain,' announced one of the bridge attendants.

'What?' said Gessart. 'Who launched it?'

He strode across the bridge and shoved the serf out of his way. A schematic of the foremost starboard battery was on the screen, the saviour pod channel flashing green. A circular sensor display showed the evacuation craft on a trajectory towards the planet below. Gessart activated his ship-wide address.

'All Astartes, report in!' he barked.

As his warriors called in their locations, it became clear that Rykhel was missing. Gessart recalled that he had only been a reluctant convert to the departure from Helmabad.

'Get me a hail frequency for that pod,' Gessart demanded, rounding on the attendant who was nursing his arm from where Gessart had shoved him.

'Linking in to your helm comms, captain,' a serf at the communications bench told him.

'Rykhel?' Gessart said.

There was a hiss of static for a moment before the Space Marine replied.

'This is wrong, Gessart,' said Rykhel. 'I cannot be a part of this.'

'Coward,' snarled Gessart. 'At least the others faced me and took their fate as warriors.'

'The Chapter must hear of this treachery,' said Rykhel. 'You murdered Herdain and fled your duty. You cannot be allowed to go unpunished for this. You talked your way out of the recriminations for Archimedon; I cannot let you do that again. You have taken the first steps on a dark path and you have damned yourself and those that follow you.'

Gessart heard the snick of the connection cutting before he could reply. Thankfully Rykhel's accusations had been made on his command line, heard only by Gessart. He looked around the bridge and saw the serfs going about their work, ignorant of the exchange.

'Continue on course,' Gessart said, focusing on the screen once more.

He wasn't afraid of the consequences. Rykhel would die; at the hands of the rebels or the daemons. It was not important, for Gessart had resigned himself to his fate the moment he shot Herdain. The others had not yet realised that they were truly renegades now.

The warp breach was expanding even as the *Vengeful* hurtled towards it. It swelled in size until the main screen could not contain it even without magnification.

'I'm in position,' Zacherys reported in Gessart's ear.

A few minutes later Gessart felt the lurch in his body and mind that signified a jump into warp space. Dislocation throbbed through his being as the *Vengeful* burst into the immaterium. His nerves buzzed with energy and shadows played across his vision. The constant murmuring of the daemons became louder and for a moment Gessart was sure that insubstantial hands were clawing at him. He knew the sensations to be false; the psychic shields of the strike cruiser were operating normally. Controlling the unnatural dread that seeped into the corners of his mind, Gessart switched off the screen and turned away.

There was now no sensation of movement. All was calm as the *Vengeful* drifted upon the psychic tides, the raging tempest of energy held at bay by her warp screens.

'Can you plot a course?' Gessart asked as he hailed Zacherys.

The Librarian's reply was halting and suffused with strain.

'No fix on Astronomican,' he said. 'Heading for eye of storm. Need to concentrate.'

'Stand down from general quarters,' Gessart announced. 'Follow warp security rituals.'

Unseen and out of mind, the world of Helmabad descended into nightmare.

* * *

Once the *Vengeful* was well clear of the Helmabad system and the roiling warp storm unleashed by the daemons, Gessart called his surviving Space Marines together. They gathered in the strike cruiser's chapel; a carefully considered choice by Gessart in relation to what he had to say.

The others entered to find Gessart already awaiting them, stripped of his armour, which was stowed on a frame to one side of the Chapter shrine. The small altar was bare of the ornaments and relics usually displayed. They had been the artifices of Herdain, and Gessart had already disposed of them. In a similar vein, the company banner, which had remained on the ship for its safety, had been taken down and stowed away. Now the only reminder of the Space Marines' allegiance was the Chapter symbol engraved into the metal of the bulkhead. Gessart had already arranged for some of the serfs to etch it out with acid once he was finished here.

He stood with his arms folded across his broad chest as his battle-brothers attended him. Some looked at the bare wall and empty altar with confusion. Others were impassive, perhaps having already guessed the nature of Gessart's announcement. Nicz stood apart from the rest, his eyes narrowed as he hawkishly watched Gessart.

The last to enter was Zacherys. The Librarian still wore his armour, though within the confines of the ship's warp shield he had removed his psychic hood to allow him to better see the currents of the immaterium and guide the ship. He did not look at Gessart, but instead stayed at the door, perhaps having already seen what was unfolding.

Gessart said nothing. Instead he crossed the chapel to where his armour stood. Leaning down, he picked up a container of paint used by the serfs. Wordlessly, he dipped a thick brush into the black liquid within and drew the brush across the symbol upon his armour's shoulder pad. A few of the Space Marines gasped at this obvious affront to the armour's spirit and the obliteration of his rank insignia.

'I am no longer a captain,' Gessart intoned. He painted out the chest eagle. 'The Third Company is no more.'

Gessart continued to daub the black onto his armour, his rough strokes eradicating the heraldry, campaign badges and honours displayed upon it.

'We cannot return to the Chapter,' Gessart said, putting down the paint and turning to face his men. 'They will not understand what it is that we have done. We have killed our battle-brothers, and to our former masters there is no greater heresy. Rykhel deserted us for fear of their vengeance and he was right to do so. Think with your hearts and remember the hatred you felt for the traitors we have faced before. We are now those traitors. We willingly stepped over a boundary that kept us in check. If ever the Chapter learns that we have survived, they will hunt us down without pity or remorse.'

Gessart picked up the paint once more and walked forwards. He proffered the container to Lehenhart who stood at one end of the group.

'You are an Avenging Son no longer,' Gessart said.

Lehenhart looked grim, in stark contrast to his usual ready laugh and lively eyes. He nodded, turning his gaze towards the deck. With a brushstroke Gessart covered up Lehenhart's Chapter symbol. Next in line was Gundar. He took the brush from Gessart and painted out the symbol himself.

Some of the Space Marines were eager to break the last of their ties, hoping that perhaps the guilt they felt would be destroyed along with the blazen of the Avenging Sons. Others hesitated, seeking some remorse in Gessart's eyes. They saw nothing but his iron-hard will to survive and realised that they were not being presented with a choice; they had made their decision back in the inner sepulchre of Helmabad. One by one the Space Marines destroyed that which had been most precious to them. A few had tears in their eyes, the first emotion they had felt since being brought to the Chapter as youths many war-torn years ago.

Nicz was the last, his eyes boring holes into Gessart as he took the brush from his former captain and splashed the dark paint across his shoulder.

'If you are captain no more, why do you still remain in command?' Nicz asked, handing the brush back to Gessart. 'By what authority do you give us orders?'

Gessart did not say anything immediately but instead met Nicz's cold stare with his own. Neither was willing to look away and they stood like that for several minutes.

'If you think you can kill me, take your shot,' Gessart eventually hissed, his eyes unwavering. 'When you do, make it count. I won't give you a second chance.'

Confident that his message was clear, Gessart stepped back, still eying Nicz, and then eventually broke contact to look at the others.

'What do we do now?' asked Willusch.

Gessart grinned. 'Whatever we want,' he replied.

'Where should we go?' said Tyrol.

'Where all the renegades go,' Gessart told them. 'The Eye of Terror.'

# HONOUR AMONG FIENDS

*Dylan Owen*

'Contact zero-thirty!'

'You sure, Scaevolla? I see nothing.'

'Trust me, Larsus!'

Scaevolla stroked the trigger of his bolter. A dozen rounds barked into the obscuring green fog, and screams wailed from the soupy atmosphere ahead. He and his men pounded towards the cries, eight hulking warriors in black power armour trimmed with gold. A blazing eye was superimposed on the eight-pronged star of Chaos emblazoned on their right shoulder pads: the heraldry of the Black Legion.

The warriors whooped feral cries of joy. It had been a long journey through the void to this barren, mist-swathed planet, but now they could let off steam against the minions of the False Emperor ahead. Scaevolla almost felt sorry for the enemy. He needed one alive, to learn where fate had directed him, and to discover the name of the man he had sought since the visions made him leave the Eye of Terror a year ago.

It was always a nightmare that would inspire Scaevolla to lead his men on another hunt. A year ago he had woken screaming from such a dream: silver, unblinking eyes penetrating his sleep. Instinct had led him to navigate his battle frigate, *Talon of the Ezzelite*, out of the shifting spheres of the Eye of Terror into the reality of Imperial space. A series of portents had led him to this world of lethal mists. Dozens of battleships emblazoned with symbols of the Ruinous Powers blockaded the planet, the wreckage of Imperial vessels drifting amongst them. The *Talon* had evaded these and landed undetected among low, mist-shrouded hills on a continent wracked by war. A kilometre away was a sprawling city under siege, towards which Scaevolla's esoteric senses tugged. Whenever he closed his eyes, the image of a crowned skull seared his mind's vision, and he knew that the man he had to kill commanded the defenders here.

Las-rounds whined past or pattered harmlessly off the warriors' armour. Scaevolla felt one brush his temple, but felt no pain. He pumped off another dozen rounds into the fog, each shot followed by a scream, closer this time. At his left, Opus, the bull of the squad, howled a tuneless battle-dirge accompanied by the roar of his autocannon.

Lines of men in grey battle uniform emerged wraith-like from the mist, their masked helmets lending them an alien appearance – wide black eyes and metal snouts. The troopers' helmets depicted a silver double-headed eagle, the insignia of the Imperial Guard. The front rank of the platoon knelt and the second rank stood upright, lasguns at the ready while the fallen curled on the floor. Ethereal green tentacles probed the living and caressed the dead. A sergeant bellowed and another volley was unleashed, but the shrill hail washed over the attackers' power armour with no effect. Scaevolla calmly loosed a bolt and watched as the sergeant's head exploded into meat and bone. He had not expected to encounter any of the planet's defenders so soon after leaving the *Talon*. Perhaps this platoon of troopers was as lost in the mists as his squad was.

Scaevolla and his men smashed into the enemy lines. When a man enters combat, his experience of time slows. For Scaevolla, the first second of the skirmish froze completely. He observed the tableau of impending destruction. Opus was mouthing a song, no doubt accompanying the infernal choir that sang ceaselessly inside his skull, his eyes rolled up into the sockets of his bald head, the death spitting from his autocannon hanging in mid-air. To Opus's left was Sharn, his helmet featureless, devoid even of eye-slits, his flamer bathing the troopers with liquid fire. Further away was Ferox, head flipped back at an unnatural angle as a smooth shaft of glistening muscle with a muzzle of snapping teeth began to emerge from his mouth. Ahead was Icaris, his face contorted with anguish, tears of blood frozen on his cheeks, the air patterned crimson where his chainaxe lopped his opponents' limbs. Icaris wept for his victims, who would never know the joys of serving the true gods.

Scaevolla glanced right. Lieutenant Larsus had bisected a Guardsman with his chainsword, and was caught in mid-laughter savouring the gore splashing his face. Beyond him was Surgit, towering over his foes, power sword scabbarded, pistol holstered, his horned helm scanning the platoon for a worthy foe. Finally came Manex, emptying a stream of ammunition from his two bolt pistols into the enemy line, mouth frothing and eyes bulging from the poisons that fed into his brain from the tubes within his armour. Pride swelled in Scaevolla's chest as he regarded his squad. Countless warzones had honed their battle skills, and none had ever failed him.

The frozen scene melted, the motionless fighters slamming back to life. Bodies piled around the feet of Icaris and Larsus, both a blur of whirring chainblades, and Ferox's monstrous tongue lashed among the troopers, flensing flesh, his hands erupting into vicious, slashing claws. Manex ripped torsos apart with the ferocity of his gunfire, and Opus howled aloud an incomprehensible opera, chorused by the deadly riff of his autocannon, while Sharn burned a hole in the enemy lines. Although outnumbered, the warriors of the Black Legion were carving bloody chunks in the ranks of the Imperial Guard, whose bayonets stabbed feebly at their power armour. The troopers' attempts at swamping their attackers through sheer weight of numbers were like the ocean lashing in vain at a tidal wall.

A commissar in a leering skull mask rushed into the fray, power sword raised, haranguing the troopers to fight to the bitter end, cutting down those who dared take a step backwards. Surgit, ignoring the las-fire zipping around him, cackled in triumph, drew his power sword and ploughed through the troopers to meet the officer blow for blow.

A bayonet stabbed at Scaevolla, who opened a hole in its owner's skull with a shot from his boltgun. More bayonets bit into his armour. Scaevolla stepped back, firing indiscriminately, and the bayonets fell away into the fog. A single trooper stood his ground, clutching his ruined arm. Scaevolla reached out with his left hand and gently traced the leather of the man's mask with a claw of his armoured glove. He spoke softly. 'What year is this? What planet? Who leads your foes?'

The words choked weakly from behind the gas mask.

'Pl... planet? Zincali VI. We fight the Traitor-Lord H'raxor. The year? W... why...?'

'Who commands your defences?'

'Captain Demetros... of the Imperial Fists... he will cleanse your filth. The Emperor protects...'

With a flick of Scaevolla's clawed fingers, the material of the gas mask fell away, revealing a pale face, eyes dazed. The soldier took a deep breath and winced. He clamped his uninjured hand to his neck, his mouth gaping wide, throat gurgling, and as Scaevolla watched, dark green, fleshy shoots pushed their way out of the soldier's mouth, bulging his neck. The man sank to his knees, tiny vines growing from his nostrils. With a strangled groan, he toppled to his side, eyes glazed, and within seconds his corpse was wrapped in a vegetal embrace, roots snaking into the black earth, pinning the body to the ground.

Scaevolla breathed deeply, the spore-rich air bitter to the taste. He smiled at the frailty of lesser men.

The sounds of battle trailed away. The few Imperial Guard who had survived the onslaught had vanished like ghosts into the green mist. Where once had stood an ordered line of determined soldiers there now lay piles of broken corpses, green shoots sprouting from bloody wounds where the minute spores in the mist had seeded in flesh. The ground flared where Sharn's flamer incinerated the bodies of the half-dead, and in the fire's glow, Icaris mumbled the Litany of Execration over the corpses. Manex struggled in Opus's iron grip, pinned down until his frenzy subsided. Ferox was metamorphosing back, his hands already human, his eel-like appendage vomiting gobbets of half-digested meat as it shrank back into his distended mouth. For his outstanding valour, Ferox had been blessed by the gods with these mutations, which burst forth from his flesh under duress. While his comrades regarded Ferox with awe, Scaevolla did not share their admiration. He remembered the old Ferox that these gifts had consumed, who had bolstered the squad's morale with his easy manner and ready wit, now long disappeared.

There was no sign of Surgit. Scaevolla called out his name.

'Here!' The horns of the warrior's helmet lent him a daemonic appearance as he emerged from the clinging fog carrying the commissar's head. He sniffed. 'A disappointing match. His hatred made him clumsy. My blade feels sullied.'

'A fine fight you've led us to, captain.' Larsus approached, grinning through a mask of drying blood at Scaevolla. 'You never disappoint. Is our quarry here?'

'His name is Demetros. The visions were true. He commands the Corpse-Emperor's forces.' Scaevolla's voice became heavy. 'Lieutenant, do you ever tire of the chase?'

Larsus rapped the image of the Eye of Horus on Scaevolla's right shoulder pad. 'Never. So long as we fight, the legacy of the Warmaster lives on.'

It had been during the false Emperor's Great Crusade that Scaevolla and his men had learned their battlecraft, and bonded in blood and violence. In those days they had been Luna Wolves, their armour white; innocents blind to the Emperor's weakness. Then Horus, beloved Warmaster, had cast the scales from their eyes, and they had fought as his devoted Sons to free themselves from the false Emperor's coils. At the edge of victory, the Warmaster fell, and his Legion had fled to the protective shadows of the warp, where it became known as the Black Legion. To mark the Legion's sorrow and disgrace, its warriors' power armour was lacquered black, although the edges of the armour gleamed with gold, for even the darkest night is banished by the gleam of a new dawn. Scaevolla's men believed that every minion of the Corpse-Emperor they slew brought closer a new golden age for their Legion.

Scaevolla's memory of those days was scarred by rage and betrayal. The past haunted him with the face of a murdered comrade. The pain had not dulled in... how many years? A hundred, a thousand... *ten thousand*? Time was exiled from the Eye of Terror, Scaevolla's life one long dream-like existence until he was spat out into reality to honour his oath.

Larsus broke Scaevolla's reverie. 'Captain, why the grim face? Is our small victory not sweet enough?'

'It's nothing,' Scaevolla shook his head to clear his mind. 'Gather the hounds, lieutenant. Let's see where the scent has led us to.'

Scaevolla hugged the brow of the hill. Piercing the sea of green fog that roiled in the valley below were uncountable battle standards, laden with gory trophies. The valley seemed to rumble under the advance of the obscured army. The bronze turrets of assault tanks and upper hulls of troop transports, crested with spikes, resembled an innumerable fleet of sea craft ploughing through ethereal waves. A score of monstrous war machines waded among them, each clanking on six steel legs like nightmarish metal spiders. The horde swept towards the horizon where a termites' nest of cyclopean buildings rose from the mist like an island. The city's ziggurats glittered with a million dots of light, their heights vanishing into red nimbus, and a thousand chimneys belched smoke into the sky. Circling the factory-city was a wall that dwarfed even the clanking war machines. Titanic bastions guarded the circuit, their cannons spitting plasma onto the advancing horde. Among the serried grey ranks of troopers manning the defences were phalanxes of power-armoured warriors, distinct in brilliant yellow, proud standards depicting a black-clenched fist on a white field; Space Marines of the Imperial Fists Chapter defended in force.

Larsus, crouched next to Scaevolla, gave a low whistle. 'A city of ten billion souls. H'raxor wants to build a mountain of skulls.'

'No,' whispered Scaevolla. 'If he only desired trophies, he would have attacked a less well-defended target.'

Blasts smacked the valley, yellow blossoms briefly parting the mists to reveal a circle of torn corpses, and a tank was hurled into the air ablaze, to land with a ripping explosion.

Scaevolla licked the air. 'These mists are rich in protein. Perhaps this planet's manufactorums process the atmosphere into food. The destruction of this world may mean famine for those Imperial outposts it feeds. This is the opening gambit of a major invasion. H'raxor has great ambition. We'll let him enjoy his petty conquest, as long as he doesn't interfere with our mission. Our quarry is in the city. I feel it. We must reach him quickly, before the defenders are overrun.'

'There.' Larsus pointed at a bronze-plated Land Raider battle tank, festooned with hooks and barbs, advancing at the foot of their hill in support of the army's reserve. 'We steal a ride.'

Scaevolla nodded. 'Get to work, lieutenant.'

While Larsus signalled orders to the squad waiting behind him,

Scaevolla removed a small silver discus from his grenade belt and fingered a switch on its ornate shell. Raising the discus to his lips, he kissed it once then spun it at the vehicle below. There was a flash and the tank came to a halt with a squeal of engines, blue sparks rippling across its hull. Scaevolla and his squad pelted down the hill, penetrating the mist. The mutant soldiers hugging the vehicle for cover milled around in confusion, muffled curses escaping the crude respirators clamped around their mouths.

'Out of the way, scum!' roared Larsus, felling soldiers who failed to yield. The mutants gibbered as they pushed each other to escape.

Ferox and Icaris vaulted to the top of the vehicle, while the rest of the squad surrounded it. A crewman emerged from a hatch on the tank's upper hull, blue sparks playing across his brassy power armour. Icaris yanked him out and silenced him with a bolt. Ferox slid through the opening. There followed a muffled roar, then the portal closest to Manex slid open and another crewman toppled out, his bronze armour rent with gashes. Manex peppered him with bolts.

'Good work, brothers.' Larsus peered through the open portal. Inside the gore-splattered interior of the tank, Ferox straddled a third crewman, his head snapped back and the fleshy eel extended from his mouth, sucking at the innards of his victim.

'Inside,' urged Scaevolla. He followed his squad into the vehicle and pointed at the feeding Ferox. 'Calm him.' Larsus eased Ferox from his kill with gentle movements and a soft voice. Already, the eel was shrinking back into Ferox's throat, its recent meal sloshing onto the floor.

Icaris positioned himself at the controls, the blue sparks that danced across the console sputtering like dying flames. He caressed the array of switches as they flashed back to life. 'Power returning. Yes, here she comes. I think she likes us; she finds our antics… amusing.'

The portal and hatch clanged shut, the cabin shuddered as the engines roared, and the Land Raider lurched forward. Inside, its inner walls purred and blinked with myriad eyes at the new crew.

The Land Raider careened across the battlefield, crushing mutant soldiers beneath its treads. Fog clouded the viewports, but the intelligence fettered within the vehicle's shell guided it towards its destination, a heavily defended gate in the city wall. Halfway across, a missile rocketed into the Land Raider's hull, and the daemon-spirit keened in agony, but the damage was superficial. Soon the gateway loomed out of the mist, its portcullis buckled and scorched. A semi-circle of twisted mutant corpses defined the killing ground around the base of the gate, into which H'raxor's soldiers marched, chanting defiantly as they soaked up the defenders' precious ammunition.

As the Land Raider came into range of the gate's barbican it suffered sustained fire. Opus emerged head and shoulders from the vehicle's hatch to rake defenders off the battlements with the pintle-mounted gun, indifferent to the las-fire whining inches from his face and the explosions impacting off the hull. The Land Raider's lascannons strobed at the weakened gate, but the portal absorbed the laser fire intact.

'Ram the gates!' ordered Scaevolla desperately. Everyone in the troop compartment tensed. Manex inhaled deeply from his tox-tubes and Ferox began coughing strings of drool. Scaevolla knew they had to evacuate before the blood lust and the Dark Gods' gift took hold.

'Ram them now!'

The Land Raider rattled from a violent explosion and Opus dropped from the firing hatch, a face of burnt flesh, power armour embedded with shrapnel, his ruined lips mouthing demented lyrics.

Icaris screamed from the controls, 'The gates are not going to give!'

'Continue, Brother Icaris,' yelled Scaevolla. He braced himself. There was a crashing rip of torn metal, and every bone in his body seemed to jar from the impact. The keening of the daemon-spirit raked his eardrums. With a sharp crack, Ferox's head snapped back, his mutation probing from his throat.

'We're through!' shouted Icaris. 'Seventy per cent damage to auxiliary reactor, firing systems all down–'

'Open the hatches!'

'Impossible... locking rune overridden... she doesn't like us anymore!'

The eel snaked from Ferox's gullet. Then, with a feral roar, Manex gripped the hatch with both hands and wrenched it open. Green fronds of mist wisped into the cabin. With a single cry, Scaevolla and his squad bounded out of the vehicle.

Scaevolla felt the flow of time cease once again. Manex was down, a shield for his companions, his armour punctured a dozen times. Larsus and Surgit were behind him, their bolters loosing a ribbon of shots as they charged the phalanx of Imperial Fists that opposed them. Sharn was licking the enemy with flesh-melting heat, while Ferox, fully deformed, stretched towards the enemy, yellow gore spurting from a hit to his pulsing eel-muscle.

Scaevolla's sword was already in his hand, its blade long and slender, a single rune engraved at its tip. Scaevolla had been rewarded with the runeblade *Fornax* when he had laid the first skull before the floating Altar of the Four Gods on the daemon-world Sebaket. How long ago had that been? Now a pyramid of five hundred skulls marked his success in the hunt. He wondered what divine favour victory would win him this time?

There was only one reward which Scaevolla desired: an end to this eternal chase. The gods drove him without rest to fulfil his vow. While his men fought for the sheer joy of killing, Scaevolla could no longer share their enthusiasm. The deaths blurred into one, dulling the emotion of the kill. His swordplay failed to thrill him, no longer a display of skill but mechanistic rote. He felt hollow. He had prayed to his masters for clemency, for release from his oath, which he had fulfilled five hundred times, but they would never grant him manumission. The only way out was escape.

A bolt-round rebounded off Scaevolla's chest guard with a bang. The world slipped back into motion, and the wild charge of Scaevolla's warriors met the stoic wall of yellow power armour. Surgit rejoiced. 'At last! A foe worthy of my wrath!'

With a juddering retort, the heavy bolter atop the crippled Land Raider came to life as Icaris, who had manoeuvred himself to the gun-turret, pinned down reinforcements trying to enter the fight.

'Dreadnought!' Icaris's heavy bolter shells pattered uselessly against the walker striding powerfully towards the combat, its crushing claws poised to strike.

Scaevolla stepped in front of the war-hulk, sword pointed in challenge. For how long had the withered corpse inside this walking coffin been compelled to cheat death?

'By the four gods,' shouted Scaevolla, 'I will end your misery.'

The Dreadnought, liveried in the heraldry of the Imperial Fists, overshadowed Scaevolla, but the prayer scrolls and relic bones decorating the walker's hulk would be no ward against his runesword, which could penetrate any earthly metal.

A stray mortar exploded between them.

White light consumed Scaevolla's vision, then darkness. He was flying. He felt no pain. He panicked. It was not yet time to die! Scaevolla had chosen the manner of his death, and it was not this way.

Scaevolla landed with a crash and fought for breath. His vision cleared to reveal the Dreadnought, unscratched by the explosion, looming over him, fists crackling with energy. The fingers of Scaevolla's outstretched left hand brushed the hilt of his runesword.

With a bestial snarl, a giant lurched from the wreckage of the Land Raider. Opus, his head in tatters, pounded the Dreadnought's hull with tactical artillery from his autocannon.

Scaevolla's grip folded around the handle of his sword and he lunged at the reeling Dreadnought, its armour scorching where the glowing runesword penetrated. Scaevolla slid the blade out and leapt back. The Dreadnought's oculus flashed green then faded to black, and the metal behemoth crashed forward.

Scaevolla raised his blade in salute. Something ancient had just perished. Scaevolla swallowed his envy.

The warriors of the Black Legion had decimated the line of Imperial Fists, though a few persevered despite severed limbs and mortal wounds. One Space Marine lay prone, his legs a crimson ruin, loosing shots from his bolt pistol until silenced by Icaris's stamping boot. Another, his helmet cloven, his eyes dashed from his face, fought blind, almost decapitating Larsus with his blade until finished by the lieutenant's chainsword.

Surgit ran up to the wrecked Dreadnought, shaking his fist in Scaevolla's face. 'Whoreson! That should have been mine!'

Larsus pushed Surgit aside. 'Scaevolla, we have to go. Lord H'raxor's army has broken through.'

The gateway was choked with masked mutants fighting each other to be first through the breach. The defenders in the bastions concentrated their fire on the horde, but for every abomination they felled, two more stepped over the corpse. Behind the seething, dying mass, scarlet-armoured berserk warriors wearing rictus helms chopped through the scum with chainswords, chanting paeans to their bloody god.

Scaevolla's squad stood in a wide bailey that stretched between the defensive wall and the soaring buildings of the city. From the right clanked a wall of battle tanks to plug the breach. From the left marched lines of gas-masked troopers. Ahead, across the bailey, barely discernable through the fog, yawned the entrance to a manufactorum, the heights of the complex disappearing into red clouds. There was only one way forward before the jaws of flesh and metal closed.

'Follow me, men!' Scaevolla sprinted through the obscuring mist for the huge doors.

The manufactorum was a cathedral of industry. Furnaces burned – altars of hungry flames – and huge vats steamed stinking vapours like sacred censers. Machinery hissed, impatient to be reanimated, and ducts and gantries spiralled up into echoing blackness. Holed by a single melta charge, the doors had proved no obstacle, and neither had the desultory force of factory guards; the innards of forty men decorated the floor.

Surgit spat at the corpses. 'We ran from an army to face mere factotums.'

'We did not run, brother,' retorted Larsus. 'We are on the hunt, remember. The chaff outside is not worth our while.'

'Calm,' snapped Scaevolla, and Surgit and Larsus backed away from each other. 'How is Manex?'

'Fit to shatter more skulls.' Manex had been dragged to safety by Opus. His armour was pitted with holes and half his face was fleshy pulp. 'I've suffered worse.'

'Ferox?'

Larsus shrugged. 'He'll find us when he's had his fill.'

'Sharn, Icaris, ready for battle?'

Sharn bowed, then returned to caressing the white flames of a nearby kiln. Icaris had sunk to his knees, cradling the severed head of a factory-drudge.

'Why do they fight us? We show them our might, yet they refuse to follow our path. We evangelise with sword and fire, but to what end? They

perish in their millions for their faith in a dead God-Emperor. We offer
the secret knowledge of the stars, yet they prefer to die ignorant. Why,
my captain?' Icaris's cheeks were streaked with bloody tears.

Scaevolla softly cupped his battle-brother's chin with his armoured
glove. The scars on the young face were testament to his many victories.

'The gods demand sacrifice, boy. We are the reapers who sate their
eternal hunger. These men are mere animals, fit only for the holy pyre;
don't weep for the fate of the weak.'

'But I must, captain. I will weep until the entire universe bends its
knee to the gods.'

Scaevolla admired Icaris's devotion, but said nothing more. Let him
enjoy the lie. Once Scaevolla too had believed it was his vocation to
shatter the shackles of order that chained the galaxy, but he knew from
bitter experience that the gods demanded war only for the sake of petty
entertainment. Lord H'raxor fought in vain to win glory, for when
the gods tired of him, he would be cast down and forgotten. Perhaps
Horus's rebellion, too, had been nothing more than a brief diversion
for the gods. Perhaps, at the brink of victory, it had delighted them to
see their servant fall and watch his armies collapse into animosity. It was
for their amusement that Scaevolla scoured the galaxy on an unending
bloodhunt.

As he contemplated the will of his divine masters, unwelcome memories invaded his mind...

...*Scaevolla cradled the dying Space Marine, whose yellow power armour
was spattered with the filth of battle. Scaevolla's pale armour was similarly
grimed. The surrounding storm of war felt ten thousand years away. Scaevolla
looked down at his battle-brother's face: a patrician nose, a powerful chin, the
well-defined skull of a noble warrior, defiant even at the approach of death. Silver eyes dimmed as the life drained away, their glassy stare haunting Scaevolla.*

'*Aleph, my friend, you could have saved yourself!*' *Scaevolla choked on the
words.* '*Why did you follow the lies of the False Emperor? Your liege-lord is
Horus. You know it, brother. Say it!*'

*Life beat weakly within the Space Marine, but Aleph's lips did not move. The
silence stoked Scaevolla's anger.*

'*Damn you, Aleph! We swore to conquer galaxies together, unstoppable,
our crusade unending. Remember how we cleansed the Haruspex of Crore?
How we defended the monastery of Satrapos alone against the ork hordes of
the Starbiter?*'

*During the Great Crusades, when Scaevolla's Legion had been called the
Luna Wolves, the Imperial Fists had fought alongside them in many battles. It
was common lore that Horus, primarch of the Luna Wolves, had, as a mark
of respect, joked that a war between his Legion and the Imperial Fists would
last for eternity.*

*At the battle of Thrael Falls on Cestus II, Scaevolla had rescued Captain
Aleph of the Imperial Fists from the anak, the planet's monstrous aboriginals.*

*The two Space Marines bonded in friendship and fought together in many battles when the paths of their Legions crossed. But when Horus declared his true colours, Scaevolla failed to convince his friend that the road to glory lay with the Warmaster. The rebellion parted them and they would not meet again until the siege of the Emperor's palace on Terra, when the Sons of Horus assaulted the Eternity Gate, guarded by the Imperial Fists. Across the carnage of the battlefield, Scaevolla had sought out his former battle-brother. They had fought, and Aleph had fallen, pierced by Scaevolla's sword.*

Scaevolla remembered his final words to the dying Space Marine. 'All the glory we fought for, my brother, gone to dust.'

It was only then that Aleph's lips moved. 'It was not our glory, brother,' he spat out the word with a phlegm of blood. 'The glory was the Emperor's.'

Scaevolla sneered. 'Your Emperor fights to defend dishonourable men, weaklings, slaves, who cower while we, men of virtue, spill our sacred blood on their behalf. Your Emperor could have been a god, and we his angels, but instead he chose servitude to protect his bleating flock.' Urgency touched Scaevolla's words. 'Look into your heart. You know I am right.'

Aleph shook his head.

Hot tears coursed Scaevolla's cheeks. 'I offer you freedom, brother, and you choose death.'

A hundred wounds Scaevolla had suffered, but none had bitten as deep as this. Aleph had rebuked the Warmaster, and had forced Scaevolla's hand to fratricide. Aleph had betrayed his battle-brother.

'Fool!' snarled Scaevolla. 'I rescued you. You owe me your life. Listen to me. I can save you again: disown the false Emperor and join me.'

Aleph chuckled hoarsely. 'Had the Emperor granted me foresight, I would have preferred to have been torn alive by the anak than rescued by the whelp of an insane blackguard.'

Rage conquered Scaevolla. His bitter agony turned to anger, sweet to taste.

'You dare mock the Warmaster! I swear, with the four gods as my witness, I shall avenge your insults a thousandfold.'

Laughter echoed madly in Scaevolla's head.

'I shall hunt down and kill your progeny, to the end of time. Your sons will suffer by my blade for your devotion to your weakling Emperor.'

Scaevolla tore Aleph's armour from his chest and dug deep into the flesh. With a sickening squelch, he removed a gland from the mess, his armoured gloves wet and red. As the light in Aleph's eyes vanished, Scaevolla taunted him with the bloody trophy. 'I shall replay this moment of victory over you again and again.'

With reverence, he nestled the organ in Aleph's dead hands. The progenoid gland contained the gene-seed necessary to cultivate Aleph's successor. Apothecaries scoured the battlefield under fire, collecting the precious material. When they recovered Aleph's progenoid gland, his essence would live on in a new recruit implanted with his gene-seed. Scaevolla would pursue each of Aleph's genetic heirs and make them suffer the same fate as their progenitor.

*In invoking the four gods, he had bound himself to this oath.*

*Scaevolla stood and addressed the corpse. 'I shall build a monument to the gods you spurned with the skulls of your descendants. Yours shall be the foundation stone.'*

*With a swift swipe of his blade he decapitated his former battle-brother. As he stooped to pick up the fallen head, Larsus appeared, stumbling on the wreckage of the battlefield, panic on his bloodied face. Scaevolla paled as he heard his words.*

*'Captain, all hope is lost. The Warmaster is dead! We must go!'*

*'What did you say?'*

*Larsus repeated himself, louder…*

…The past faded. Scaevolla gathered his wits back to the present. Larsus was shaking his shoulder.

'Captain, we must go. H'raxor's army has broken the outer defences.'

Outside, the triumphant battle cries of the invading horde were drowning out the defenders' screams. Scaevolla paused, inhaling deeply. His quarry was close. His senses were drawn to the factory's heights.

'We go up.'

Scaevolla watched the trooper pirouette towards a gaping vat far below and vanish with a splash into the volcanic brew, the last of those who had engaged his squad as they clambered up ladders and along gantries to the higher levels of the factory, led by their leader's instinct.

The squad stood before a set of sturdy doors. Scaevolla could almost taste his quarry's presence beyond them. Quietly, he took Larsus to one side. 'Lieutenant, whatever happens, do not intervene to save me. If I should fall, it is the will of the gods. Bear my head to Sebaket and top the altar with my skull as a mark of my failure.'

Larsus looked stunned. 'What do you mean, captain? There is no soul in this galaxy who could best you.'

Scaevolla turned away from his lieutenant. He pointed at the doors. 'Opus?'

The bull ran at the doors and shouldered them open. Daylight spilled from the breach. Scaevolla followed, the rest of his men close behind.

Outside was a wide plaza, open to the gusting wind, with a view across the mist-wreathed killing fields far below. Low clouds, an angry red, obscured the sky. A platoon of Imperial Fists ranged across the plaza. The tallest was cloaked in sweeping blue, crowned with the golden laurels of an officer. An ornate sword hissed with energy in his hands.

Scaevolla thrilled. Aleph's features were etched on Captain Demetros's noble face. He barked his orders. 'The captain is mine. Destroy the others.'

The bark of bolters greeted the warriors' charge, their black armour soaking up the deadly hail. Scaevolla watched his squad advance.

'Farewell,' he whispered sadly, then muttered a pledge to the gods.

'Now it's time to end your sport. I will lay no more skulls before your altar.'

Scaevolla walked forward, singling out the captain with his runesword. Five hundred times he had re-enacted this scene. Five hundred times he had vanquished his silver-eyed opponent, heir of Aleph, and removed his head as a trophy. His rage had been satisfied long ago. He'd had to endure the pain of murdering his comrade over and over again, but he could endure it no longer.

Scaevolla circled, a black wolf stalking its prey. His rival adopted a duelling posture, power sword balanced to parry or bite. As he closed, Scaevolla saw Demetros's silver eyes narrow with faint recognition. That silver stare pinned Scaevolla's gaze, transporting him to another time, another place...

...*The sounds of battle roared, explosions and gunfire and the screams of the dying. The ground shuddered to the tread of a Titan's foot, scattering squads of Imperial Fists before it. The magnificent Eternity Gate, glowering over the battlefield, shook to the fiery kiss of a hundred missiles. A gunship screeched overhead, spitting death, and a dozen advancing green-armoured Sons of Horus fell in a shower of flame. Mud from the explosions spattered Scaevolla's pale armour, but he did not flinch. The cacophony of battle was a mere murmur to him as he circled his opponent, the surrounding blur of violence an illusion.*

'*Brother Scaevolla.*' *Scaevolla's silver-eyed adversary broke the silence.* '*I have missed you.*'

'*And I you, Brother Aleph.*' *Scaevolla smiled ruefully.* '*Surrender your sword. You've laid low many of the Warmaster's servants but I will vouch for you before him. He will forgive.*'

'*Why should I give my heart to a traitor?*' *spat Aleph. His eyes steeled.* '*His madness has destroyed everything the Emperor has fought for. Your Warmaster has stolen your reason, Scaevolla. You may live your lie for ten millennia, but your heart will weary of your lusts, and you'll be left an empty husk.*' *Aleph breathed deeply, his features pulled with sorrow.* '*Let me end it here, my friend. On the point of my blade. I cannot save you from your past, but I can save you from the future.*'

*Their eyes continued to lock.*

*Aleph nodded slowly.* '*So be it. We fight...*'

...Scaevolla was jolted back into the present as Demetros's blade sprang from nowhere. He blocked with a rapid parry, his runesword sparking as it slid down his rival's power weapon. With a flick of his blade, Demetros tried to disarm him, but Scaevolla was too nimble and returned with a counter-blow. Demetros inclined his head slightly, and the runesword's sweep skimmed his cheek.

A hideous ululation broke the duellist's concentration. Fury burst from the plaza doors, clad in baroque armour slick with gore. Odes to the Blood God howled from rictus battle-helms as the berserkers fell on the Imperial Fists, chainaxes chopping. One of the crazed attackers sliced apart a Space Marine, but was in turn disembowelled by Surgit, whose kill he had stolen. Soon the plaza was a confused melee: black, yellow and crimson power armour battling each other.

Five berserkers converged on Captain Demetros.

'No!' screamed Scaevolla, decapitating one with a swing of his blade.

The headless corpse tottered forward, flailing past the startled Space Marine. Scaevolla turned to engage two of the surviving berserkers. Demetros was forced to defend against the other pair. Together they stood almost side by side, blocking every frenzied attack. Though their assailants' blows were everywhere, their defences blurred in reply. A chainaxe buzzed past Demetros's head, who ducked and rammed his blade deep into its wielder's chest. Another berserker lunged enthusiastically at Scaevolla, who cut his legs from under him, the severed stumps smoking where the runesword had bitten.

With a crunch, a chainaxe penetrated Demetros's shoulder guard. He shrugged off the wound, but tottered back, unbalanced. Howling, the devotee of the Blood God raised his weapon to deal the death blow, but the axe stopped centimetres from Demetros's skull, met by Scaevolla's sword. Scaevolla raked his blade down the weapon's shaft, slicing through its guard and ruining the fingers clutching the hilt, before decapitating its wielder with a whirling blow. Demetros rolled to a kneeling position to gut the final attacker. Scaevolla spun to face the Imperial Fist, who rose to his feet, the berserker's corpse slipping from his blade.

Scaevolla gave a slight bow. 'Just like old times.'

Demetros frowned. 'I have seen you fight before.'

'We have never met,' Scaevolla smiled slyly. 'But I have spilled your blood many, many times.'

Demetros shook his head slowly. 'You are insane.'

Around the duellists, Scaevolla's warriors had formed a defensive ring. Berserkers and Space Marines lay in a crimson circle at their feet.

'Shield the captain!' yelled Larsus as a howling tide of berserkers and mutants flowed into the plaza.

'Fresh meat!' cried Surgit with satisfaction, swinging his power sword above his head.

The fighting was chaotic, Imperial Fists and berserkers hacking at each other, and mutants caught in the melee, chopped into a crimson spray. Amidst this tumult, Scaevolla's warriors cut down any that attempted to breach their circle. As they fought, Opus sang, Icaris wept, Manex roared and Sharn slew silently.

Scaevolla and Demetros stood undisturbed in their arena.

Demetros frowned. 'You defend me against your own kind. You are jealous for my death. Why?'

'For the sins of your father,' replied Scaevolla. 'He did my liege lord a great disservice once. But fortune smiles on you, Demetros. You are the one who will win back your father's honour. Let us finish this. My men are strong, but they cannot hold out against two armies.'

Scaevolla tipped his runesword to his forehead in salute. Demetros stood motionless. Blades blurred, then the two were statues. Neither betrayed exertion. A feint from the Space Marine, a retort from Scaevolla, swift attack and counterattack blocked and blocked again. Scaevolla twisted his blade and his opponent's sword flew from his grasp, to land with a clatter between them. Scaevolla's runesword glowed, as though excited by the impending kill, but Scaevolla dipped his blade and flipped the fallen power sword back at Demetros, who deftly caught it.

'A hero should never be defenceless,' said Scaevolla.

Demetros replied with a lightning thrust, but Scaevolla parried. Then Demetros executed a brilliant side step, and his sword was beyond Scaevolla's guard.

The world stilled around Scaevolla, the blade hovering a second away from his heart. At this, the final moment, he felt alive; fear and elation mingled in one delicious cocktail. His vow was broken; at last he would sleep.

But if Scaevolla shifted his torso a fraction to the right, the blade would slide parallel to his armour, cutting a flesh wound, deep but not mortal.

Scaevolla remained still.

Reality surged back with a sucking roar, and the blade plunged through black power armour. Scaevolla smiled. The power sword had punctured his heart and split the back of his armour. When the blade slid free, Scaevolla was still standing.

'A fine blow, my friend. A blow worthy of my death.'

Scaevolla wondered how a dead man could speak. There was no pain. The tumult of the surrounding battle did not ebb away.

Demetros backed off, enraged. 'How can this be? Daemon!'

Scaevolla looked down at the gash in his chest. Where there should have been spilling gore, there was instead a hole. As though torn through the fabric of space, a thousand stars swirled like gloating eyes within the wound. Laughter echoed madly in Scaevolla's head: four terrible voices. He opened his mouth, but it was their voice which spoke.

'You think a scratch can fell a champion of the Dark Gods? It will take more than a cur of the Dog-Emperor to cut this puppet's strings!'

Scaevolla struggled to control his tongue. 'You cannot kill me. Run, brother. Save yourself!'

Demetros scoffed. 'Run? I am a Space Marine of the Imperial Fists. I do not run.'

Scaevolla's runesword glowed hungrily. He cried out to the sky. 'I will not slay him! There is no honour in this fight!'

As Demetros closed in for the kill again, Scaevolla tried to bare his neck to the oncoming blade, but his runesword wrestled his will, and it blocked the strike with a clash. Scaevolla swiped again, his limbs not his own, and Demetros shuffled backwards, a thread of scorched flesh lining his throat. The Space Marine fell to his knees, expressionless, his power sword clattering to the ground.

Over the noise of the Imperial Fists' battle hymns, the wild canticles of the berserkers and screams of dying mutants, Larsus cried out to his captain. 'It is finished. We must leave – now!'

Scaevolla gazed at the corpse of Demetros. He would order Sharn to incinerate the body, destroying the progenoid glands, ending the hunt here.

Suddenly, onto the plaza tore a mass of pulsing muscle straining within a black carapace fused to flesh. A voracious eel-like member gnashed and swallowed. Ferox had been rewarded with the warp's ultimate boon: the gift of spawnhood. He would slaughter mindlessly for the pleasure of the gods.

Scaevolla's order died on his lips. Watching what once had been Ferox whine and gibber as it slew, Scaevolla realised what fate awaited him should he attempt to renege on his oath. He chilled. The gods would never allow the chase to end. Sullenly, he bowed to his dead foe. It was better to embrace enslavement than have the remnants of his humanity eaten away. 'Until next we meet, my friend.' The words left a bitter taste.

With his sword, he sheared off Demetros's head and picked up the trophy by the hair: one more skull for the floating altar.

Larsus yelled an order. 'Squad, converge! We return to the *Talon*.'

The defensive circle tightened to a knot around Scaevolla, who flicked a device on his belt, and the squad shimmered and disappeared, the maelstrom of battle flooding into the space they left.

The apothecary darted among the corpses of his fallen battle-brothers, ignoring the violence swirling around him as he harvested their precious gene-seed. He knelt over the body of Captain Demetros.

'Emperor's tears,' he exclaimed. 'They've taken his head!' With a heavy heart, he muttered the orison of passing and extracted the vital fluid from the progenoid gland in the corpse's chest with his reductor. 'Your line will live on to avenge this atrocity, my captain.'

Somewhere in the aether, laughter rippled. The game would continue.

# FIRES OF WAR

*Nick Kyme*

'Give me some good news, Helliman,' growled Colonel Tonnhauser. The old soldier spoke out the side of his mouth, a cigar smouldering between his lips.

He ducked instinctively as another explosion rocked the walls of the workshop, sending violent tremors through the floor and chips of rock-crete spitting from the ceiling onto the map-strewn bench below.

'That was closer...' Tonnhauser muttered, blowing smoke as he brushed away the dislodged dust and debris for the umpteenth time.

It's a hard thing for a man to lose his own city to an enemy. When that enemy comes from within, it's even more repugnant. But that was the stark reality facing Abel Tonnhauser of the 13th Stratosan Aircorps. He'd given too much ground already to the endless hordes of insurgent cultists, and still they pushed for more. Soon there'd be nothing left. The defence of the three primary cities of Stratos was on the brink of failure. The cloud-and-bolt badge he wore, though tarnished by weeks of fighting, was pinned proudly to a double-breasted tan leather jacket. It was only made of brass, but felt about as heavy as an anvil.

The workshop structure in which he'd made his command post was full of disused aeronautical equipment and machinery, more or less a refit and repair yard for dirigibles and other flying craft that were a necessary part of life on Stratos. Air tanks, pressure dials and coils of ribbed hosing were strewn throughout the building. The one in which Tonnhauser conferred with Sergeant Helliman, while Corpsman Aiker monitored the vox-traffic, was broad and long with vast angular arches and tall support columns, all chrome and polished plasteel.

Typical of the Stratosan architectural style, it had been beautiful once but was now riddled with bullet holes and crumbling from shell damage. A demo-charge rigged by insurgents to a ballast tractor had taken out most of the south-facing wall, the bulk of the colonel's command staff with it. With no time to effect repairs, a sheet of plastek had been piston-drilled to cover the hole.

This largely pointless measure did little to keep out the stutter of sporadic gunfire and incessant explosions from tripped booby traps and purloined grenade launchers. Sergeant Helliman had to raise his voice to be heard.

'Three loft-cities remain under the control of the insurgents, sir: Cumulon, here in Nimbaros, and Cirrion. They have also collapsed all except the three major sky-bridges into these areas.'

'What of our ground forces, any progress there?' asked Tonnhauser, lifting his peaked cap to run a hand across his receding hairline and wishing dearly that the expulsion of the insurgents was someone else's job.

Helliman looked resigned, the young officer grown thinner over the passing weeks, and pale as a wraith.

'Heavy resistance is dogging our efforts to make any inroads into the cities. The insurgents are dug in and well organised.'

Helliman paused to clear his dry throat.

'There must be at least ninety thousand of the cities' total populations corrupted by cult activity. They hold all of the materiel factorums and are equipping themselves with our stockpiles. Armour too.'

Tonnhauser surveyed the city maps on the bench, looking for potential avenues of assault he might have missed. He saw only bottlenecks and kill-zones in which the Aircorps would be snared.

Helliman waited anxiously for Tonnhauser's response, and the void in conversation was filled by the frantic chatter coming from the command vox. Corpsman Aiker, crouched by the boxy unit in one corner of the workshop, tried his best to get a clear signal but static ran riot over all channels in the wake of the destruction of the antenna towers. Tonnhauser didn't need to hear the substance of the vox-reports to know it was bad.

'What *do* we hold then?' he asked at last, looking up into the sergeant's tired eyes.

'Our safe zones are–'

A shuddering explosion slapped against the workshop, cutting Helliman off. Fire spilled through the plastek towards the sergeant in a tide. It funnelled outwards, the plastek becoming fluid in the intense heat wave, and melted around the hapless Helliman.

Tonnhauser swore loudly as he was dumped on his arse, but had enough presence of mind to pull out his service pistol and shoot the screaming sergeant through the head to spare him further agony.

Ears still ringing from the blast, Tonnhauser saw a figure scuttle through the fire-limned gouge in the plastek. It was a man, or at least a dishevelled interpretation of one, clad in rags and flak armour. His hair was sheared roughly all the way down to the skull. Hate-filled eyes caught sight of Tonnhauser as the wretch cast about the room. But it was the mouth of the thing that gave the loyal Stratosan pause. It was sewn shut with thick black wire, the lips and cheeks shot through with purple-blue veins.

At first, Tonnhauser thought the insurgent was unarmed. Then he saw the grenade clutched in his left hand...

'Holy Emperor...'

Tonnhauser shot him through the forehead. As the cultist fell back there was an almighty thunderclap as the grenade went off, blasting the bodily remains of the insurgent to steaming chunks of meat.

The metal workbench spared Tonnhauser from the explosion, but he had little time to offer up his thanks to the Throne. Through the smoke and falling debris three more insurgents emerged, mouths sewn shut just like the first. Two carried autoguns; one had a crude-looking heavy stubber.

Squeezing off a desultory burst of fire, Tonnhauser went to ground behind the solid bench just as metal rain ripped into the workshop. It chewed up the room with an angry roar, tearing up the walls and disused machinery, perforating Corpsman Aiker where he crouched.

Crawling on his hands and knees, Tonnhauser pressed himself tighter into cover, discharging the spent clip from his pistol before reaching for another with trembling fingers.

*No way could he kill them all...*

Through the incessant barrage of gunfire, Tonn-hauser first heard the *plink-plink* of a small metal object nearby, then saw the tossed grenade land and roll to within a metre of his foot. Survival instinct taking over, he lurched towards the grenade and kicked. It went off seconds later, heat, noise and pressure crashing over Tonnhauser in a violent wave, close enough for a shard of shrapnel to embed itself in his outstretched leg.

The colonel bit down so he wouldn't cry out.

Won't give this scum the satisfaction, he thought.

A sudden rash of las-fire spat overhead and abruptly the shooting ceased.

'Colonel,' an urgent voice called out from across the workbench a few moments later.

'Behind here,' Tonnhauser growled, wincing in pain as he saw the jagged metal sticking out of his leg.

Five Stratosan Aircorpsmen ran around the side of the bench, lasguns hot.

Tonnhauser read the first man's rank pins.

'Impeccable timing, Sergeant Rucka, but aren't you supposed to be with Colonel Yonn and the 18th at the Cirrion border?'

A second corpsman carried a portable vox. Reports were drumming out on all frequencies, accompanied by a throbbing chorus of explosions and muted gunfire from across the length and breadth of Nimbaros.

'Colonel Yonn is dead, sir. And the 18th are pulling out of Cirrion. The city is totally lost, all safe zones are compromised,' Rucka told him. 'We've got to get you out.'

Tonnhauser grimaced as two of the other corpsmen helped him to his feet.

'What about Cumulon? Has that fallen too?' he asked, passing the dead bodies of the three cultists, and staggering out of the back entrance to the workshop.

The sergeant's tone was hollow but pragmatic.

'We've lost them all, sir. We're in full retreat, back beyond the city limits and across the sky-bridge to Pileon.'

Once out into the city streets the noise of the encroaching gun battle grew exponentially louder. Tonnhauser looked up to the dome roof of the city and saw a stormy sky through the reinforced plastek above him. Scudding smoke clouded his view as the upper atmosphere of the loft-city was lost from sight. As he fell back with Sergeant Rucka and his squad, Tonnhauser risked a glance over his shoulder. A mass retreat was in effect. Distant insurgents closed on their position en masse, clutching various guns and improvised weapons. Their battle cries were muted by the wire lacing their lips together – the effect was unnerving. Tonnhauser didn't need to hear them to tell the enemy was pressing a large-scale attack.

A gas-propelled rocket roared close by overhead, forcing Tonnhauser and the others to duck. It struck the side of a mag-tram depot and exploded outwards, engulfing an entrenched Aircorps gunnery position. The three-man team died screaming amidst brick and fire.

Rucka altered course abruptly, taking Tonnhauser and his men away from the destruction of the depot and down a side alley.

'Throne, how did this happen?' Tonnhauser asked when Rucka had them stop in the alley to wait for the all-clear to proceed. 'We were pressing them back, weren't we?'

'Took us by surprise,' said Rucka, ducking back into the alley as a bomb blast lit up the road beyond. 'Set off a chain of booby traps that decimated our troops then launched a mass ground offensive. They're using advanced military tactics. No way can we retake the cities like this. We'll have to regroup. Maybe then we can get Nimbaros and Cumulon back, but Cirrion…' The sergeant's words trailed away, telling Tonnhauser everything he needed to know about the capital's fate.

'What about Governor Varkoff?'

'He's alive, bunkered down in Pileon. It's the nearest of the minor sky-cities that's still under our control. That's where we are headed now. He's enacted official distress protocols on all Imperial astropathic and comm-range frequencies, requesting immediate aid.'

'Do something for me will you, corpsman,' said Tonnhauser. The colonel had moved to the end of the alley and watched as another explosion took out a statue of the first Stratosan governor. It was a symbol of Imperial rule and order. It shattered as it struck the ground wrapped in fire.

'What's that, sir?'

'Get on your knees and pray,' Tonnhauser said. 'Pray for a bloody miracle…'

*For the last forty years, the dream hadn't changed.*

*At first there was only a vague sensation of heat, and then Dak'ir was back in the hot dark of the caves of Ignea on Nocturne. In his dream he was only a boy, the rock wall of that hostile place coarse and sharp against his pre-adolescent skin as he touched it. Mineral seams glinted in the glow of lava pools fed by the river of fire that was the lifeblood of the mountain above him. Ignea then faded, and the light from the river of fire died with it, resolving into a new vista…*

*The Cindara Plateau stretched before Dak'ir's sandaled feet, its edge delineated by rock-totems, its surface the colour of rust and umber. Ash scudded in drifts across the Pyre Desert below, obscuring scaled saurochs as they hunted for sustenance amongst the crags. Above there came the sound of thunder, as if Mount Deathfire was about to erupt flame and smoke to blot out the heavens. But the great mountain of Nocturne slumbered still. Instead, Dak'ir looked up and saw a fiery blaze of a different kind, the engines of a vast ship slowly coming to land.*

*A ramp opened in the side of the vessel as it came to rest at last, and a warrior stepped out, tall and powerful, clad in armour of green plate and emblazoned with the symbol of the salamander, the noble creatures that lived in the heart of the earth. Others joined the warrior, Dak'ir knew some of them; he had worked beside them rebuilding and rock-harvesting after the Time of Trial. His heart quailed at the sight of these giants, though. For he knew they had come for him…*

*The image changed again, and this time Dak'ir had changed too. He now wore the mantle of warrior, carried the tools of war. His body was armoured in carapace, a holy bolt pistol gripped in his Astartes fist, his onyx flesh a stark reminder of his superhuman apotheosis. Monoliths of stone and marble loomed above Dak'ir like grey sentinels, ossuary roads paved the streets and the acrid stench of grave dust filled the air. This was not Nocturne; this was Moribar, and here the skies were wreathed in death.*

*Somewhere on the horizon of that grey and terrible world Dak'ir heard screaming and the vision in his mind's eye bled away to be filled by a face on fire. He had seen it so many times, 'the burning face', agonised and accusing, never letting him truly rest. It burned and burned, and soon Dak'ir was burning too, and the screams that filled his ears became his own...*

*'We were only meant to bring them back...'*

Dak'ir's eyes snapped open as he came out of battle-meditation. Acutely aware of his accelerated breathing and high blood pressure, he went through the mental calming routines as taught to him when he had first joined the superhuman ranks of the Space Marines.

With serenity came realisation. Dak'ir was standing in the half-darkness of his isolation chamber, a solitorium, one of many aboard the strike cruiser *Vulkan's Wrath*. It was little more than a dungeon: sparse, austere and surrounded on all sides by cold, black walls.

More detailed recollection came swiftly.

An urgent communication had been picked up weeks ago via astro-pathic messenger and interpreted by the Company Librarian, Pyriel. The Salamanders were heading to the Imperial world of Stratos.

A prolific mining colony, one of many along the Hadron Belt in the Reductus Sector of Segmentum Tempestus, Stratos had great value to the Imperium for its oceanic minerals as well as its regular tithe of inductees to the Imperial Guard. Rescue of Stratos, liberation for its inhabitants from the internecine enemies that plagued it, was of paramount importance.

Hours from breaking orbit, Captain Ko'tan Kadai had already assigned six squads, including his own *Inferno Guard*, to be the task force that would make planetfall on Stratos and free the world from anarchy. As Promethean belief dictated, all Salamanders about to embark on battle must first be cleansed by fire and endure a period of extended meditation to focus their minds on self-reliance and inner fortitude.

All but Dak'ir had been untroubled in their preparations.

Such a fact would not go unnoticed.

'My lord?' a deep and sonorous voice asked.

Dak'ir looked in its direction and saw the hooded form of Tsek. His brander-priest was dressed in emerald green robes with the Chapter icon, a snarling salamander head inside a ring of fire, stitched in amber-coloured wire across his breast. Half-concealed augmetics were just visible beneath the serf's attire in the flickering torchlight.

The chamber was small, but had enough room for an Adeptus Astartes' attendants.

'Are you ready for the honour-scarring, my lord?' asked Tsek.

Dak'ir nodded, still a little disoriented from his dream. He watched as Tsek brought forth a glowing rod, white-hot from the embers of the brazier-cauldron that Dak'ir was standing in barefooted. The Astartes barely registered the pain from the fire-wrapped coals beneath him. There was not so much as a globule of sweat across his bald head or onyx-black body, naked but for a tribal sash clothing his loins.

The ritual was part of the teachings of the Promethean Cult, to which all warriors of the Salamanders stoically adhered.

As Tsek applied the branding rod to Dak'ir's exposed skin he embraced the pain it brought. His fiery eyes, like red-hot coals themselves, watched approvingly. First, Tsek burned three bars and then a swirl bisecting them. It conjoined the many marks he and other brander-priests had made upon Dak'ir's body where they'd healed and scarred into a living history of the Salamander's many conflicts. Each was a battle won, a foe vanquished. No Salamander went into battle without first being marked to honour it and then again at battle's end to commemorate it.

Dak'ir's own marks wreathed his legs, arms and some of his torso and back. They were intricate, becoming more detailed as each new honour scar was added. Only a veteran of many campaigns, a Salamander of centuries' service, ever bore such markings on his face.

Tsek bowed his head and stepped back into shadow. A votive-servitor shambled forward in his wake on reverse-jointed metal limbs, bent-backed beneath the weight of a vast brazier fused to its spine. Dak'ir reached out and plunged both hands into the iron caldera of the brazier, scooping up the fragments of ash from the burned matter collected at its edges.

Dak'ir smeared the white ash over his face and chest, inscribing the Promethean symbols of the hammer and the anvil. They were potent icons in Promethean lore, believed to garner endurance and strength.

'Vulkan's fire beats in my breast...' he intoned, making a long sweep with his palm to draw the hammer's haft.

'With it I shall smite the foes of the Emperor,' another voice concluded, letting Dak'ir cross the top of the haft with his palm to form the hammer's head before revealing himself.

Brother Fugis stepped into the brazier's light, clanking loudly as he moved. He was already clad in his green power armour, but went unhooded. His blood-red eyes blazed vibrantly in the half-dark. As befitted a Space Marine of his position, Fugis bore the ash-white of the Apothecaries on his right shoulder pad, though the left still carried the insignia of his Chapter on a jet-black field, the snarling salamander head there a blazing orange to match the pauldrons of his Third Company battle-brothers.

Thin-faced and intimidating, some in the company had suggested Fugis might be better served in a more spiritual profession than the art of healing. Such 'suggestions' were never voiced out loud, however, or given in front of the Apothecary, for fear of reprisal.

Dak'ir's response to the Apothecary's sudden presence was less than genial.

'What are you doing here, brother?'

Fugis did not answer straight away. Instead, he scanned a bio-reader over Dak'ir's body.

'Captain Kadai asked me to visit. Examinations are best conducted before you're armoured.'

Fugis paused as he waited for the results of the bio-scan, his blade-thin face taut like wire.

'Your arm, Astartes,' he added without looking up, but gesturing for Dak'ir's limb.

Dak'ir held his arm out for the Apothecary, who took it by the wrist and syringed off a portion of blood into a vial. A chamber in his gauntlet then performed a bio-chemical analysis after the vial was inserted into its miniature centrifuge.

'Are all of my brothers undergoing such rigorous conditioning?' asked Dak'ir, keeping the annoyance from his voice.

Fugis was evidently satisfied with the serology results, but his tone was still matter of fact.

'No, just you.'

'If my brother-captain doubts my will, he should have Chaplain Elysius appraise me.'

The Apothecary seized Dak'ir's jaw suddenly in a gauntleted fist and carefully examined his face. 'Elysius is not aboard the *Vulkan's Wrath*, as you well know, so you will have to endure my *appraisal* instead.'

With the index finger of his other hand Fugis pulled down the black skin beneath Dak'ir's left eye, diffusing its blood-red glow across his cheek.

'You are still experiencing somnambulant visions during battle-meditation?' he asked. Then, apparently satisfied, he let Dak'ir go.

The brother-sergeant rubbed his jaw where the Apothecary had pinched it.

'If you mean, am I dreaming, then yes. It happens sometimes.'

The Apothecary looked at the instrument panel on his glove, his expression inscrutable.

'What do you dream about?'

'I am a boy again, back on Nocturne in the caves of Ignea. I see the day I passed the trials on the Cindara Plateau and became an Adeptus Astartes, my first mission as a neophyte...' The Salamander's voice trailed away, as his expression darkened in remembrance.

*The burning face...*

'You are the only one of us, the only Fire-born, ever to be chosen from Ignea,' Fugis told him, eyes penetrating as he looked at Dak'ir.

'What does that matter?'

Fugis ignored him and went back to his analysis.

'You said, "We were only meant to bring them back". Who did you mean?' he asked after a moment.

'You were there on Moribar,' Dak'ir uttered and stepped off the brazier-cauldron, hot skin steaming as it touched the cold metal floor of his isolation cell. 'You know.'

Fugis looked up from his instruments and his data. His eyes softened fleetingly with regret. They quickly narrowed, however, sheathed behind cold indifference.

He laughed mirthlessly, his lip curling in more of a sneer than a smile.

'You are fit for combat, brother-sergeant,' he said. 'Planetfall on Stratos is in less than two hours. I'll see you on assembly deck six before then.'

Fugis then saluted, more by rote than meaning, and turned his back on his fellow Salamander.

Dak'ir felt relief as the Apothecary departed.

'And Brother Dak'ir... Not all of us *want* to be brought back. Not all of us *can* be brought back,' said Fugis, swallowed by the dark.

The surface of Stratos writhed with perpetual storms. Lightning streaked the boiling tumult and thunderheads collided in violent flashes, only to break apart moments later. Through these ephemeral gaps in the clouds tiny nubs of chlorine-bleached rock and bare earth were revealed, surrounded by a swirling maelstrom sea.

The Thunderhawk gunships *Fire-wyvern* and *Spear of Prometheus* tore above the storm's fury, turbofans screaming. They were headed for the conglomeration of floating cities in Stratos's upper atmosphere. Named 'loft-cities' by the Stratosan natives, these great domed metropolises of chrome and plascrete were home to some four-point-three million souls and linked together by a series of massive sky-bridges. Due to the concentrated chlorine emissions from their oceans the Stratosans had been forced to elevate their cities with massive plasma-fuelled gravitic engines; so high, in fact, that each required its own atmosphere in order for the inhabitants to breathe.

The words of Fugis were still on Dak'ir's mind and he willed the furore inside the Chamber Sanctuarine of the *Fire-wyvern* to smother his thoughts. The gunship's troop hold was almost at capacity – twenty-five Astartes secured in standing grav-harness as the Thunderhawk made its final descent.

Brother-Captain Kadai was closest to the exit ramp, his gaze burning with courage and conviction. He was clad in saurian-styled artificer armour and, like his charges, had yet to don his helmet. Instead, he had it clasped to his armour belt, a simulacrum of a snarling fire drake fashioned in metal. His close-cropped hair was white and shaven into a strip that bisected his head down the middle. Alongside him was his command squad, the Inferno Guard: N'keln, Kadai's second in command, a steady if uncharismatic officer; Company Champion Vek'shen, who had bested countless foes in the Chapter's name, and gripped his fire-glaive; Honoured Brother Malicant who bore the company's banner into battle, and Honoured Brother Shen'kar, clasping a flamer to his chest. Fugis was the last of them. The Apothecary nodded discreetly in Dak'ir's direction when he saw him.

It was dark in the chamber. Tiny ovals of light came from the Sala-manders, their red eyes aglow. As Dak'ir's gaze left Fugis it settled on another's, one that burned coldly.

Brother-Sergeant Tsu'gan glared from across the hold.

Dak'ir felt his fists clench.

Tsu'gan was the epitome of Promethean ideal. Strong, tenacious, self-sacrificing – he was everything a Salamander should aspire to be. But there was a vein of arrogance and superiority hidden deep within him. He was born in Hesiod, one of the seven Sanctuary Cities of Nocturne, and the principal recruiting grounds for the Chapter. Unlike most on the volcanic death world, Tsu'gan was raised into relative affluence. His family were nobles, tribal kings at the tenuous apex of Nocturnean wealth and influence.

Dak'ir, as an itinerant cave-dwelling Ignean, was at its nadir. The fact that he became Astartes at all was unprecedented. So few from the nomadic tribes ever reached the sacred places where initiates under-went the trials, let alone competed and succeeded in them. Dak'ir was, in many ways, unique. To Tsu'gan, he was an aberration. Both should have left their human pasts behind when they were elevated to Astartes, but centuries of ingrained prejudice were impossible to suppress.

The Thunderhawk banked sharply as it made for the landing zone adjacent to the loft-city of Nimbaros, breaking the tension between the two sergeants. The exterior armour plate shrieked in protest with the sudden exertion, the sound transmitting internally as a dull metal moan.

'A portent of the storm to come?' offered Ba'ken in a bellow.

The bald-headed Astartes was Dak'ir's heavy weapons trooper, his broad shoulders and thick neck making him ideally equipped for the task. Ba'ken, like many of his Chapter, was also a gifted artisan and craftsman. The heavy flamer he had slung on his back was unique amongst Tactical squads, and he had manufactured the weapon himself in the blazing forges of Nocturne.

'According to the Stratosan's reports, the traitors are dug in and have numbers. It will not be–'

'*We* are the storm, brother,' Tsu'gan interjected, shouting loudly above the engine din before Dak'ir could finish. 'We'll cleanse this place with fire and flame,' he snarled zealously, 'and purge the impure.'

Ba'ken nodded solemnly to the other sergeant, but Dak'ir felt his skin flush with anger at such blatant disrespect for his command.

An amber warning light winked into existence above them and Brother-Captain Kadai's voice rang out, preventing any reprisal.

'Helmets on, brothers!'

There was a collective *clank* of metal on metal as the Astartes donned battle-helms.

Dak'ir and Tsu'gan fitted theirs last of all, unwilling to break eye contact for even a moment. In the end Tsu'gan relented, smiling darkly as he mouthed a phrase.

'*Purge the impure.*'

'Cumulon in the east and Nimbaros in the south are still contested, but my troops are taking more ground by the hour and have managed to secure the sky-bridges that link the three cities,' explained a sweating Colonel Tonnhauser over the crackling pict-link of Kadai's Land Raider Redeemer, *Fire Anvil.* 'We're using them to siphon out civilian survivors. There are still thousands trapped behind enemy lines though, my men amongst them.'

'You have done the Emperor's work here, and have my oath as a Salamander of Vulkan that if those men can be saved, I will save them,' Kadai replied, standing inside the hold of his war machine as it shuddered over the sky-bridge to Cirrion. Four armoured Rhinos rumbled behind it in convoy, transporting the rest of the battlegroup.

Once the Salamanders had made planetfall outside Nimbaros, Kadai had ordered Brother Argos, Master of the Forge, to make a structural assessment of the approach road to Cirrion. Using building schematics from the Stratosan cities inloaded to the *Vulkan's Wrath*'s cogitators and then exloaded back to a display screen on the *Fire-wyvern*, the Techmarine had determined the sky-bridges were unfeasible locations for the gunships to land and redeploy the Astartes.

Less than twenty minutes later, three Thunderhawk transporters had descended from orbit and deployed the Salamanders' dedicated transport vehicles.

Kadai had held his Salamanders at the landing zone in squad formation, ready for the arrival of the transports. There had been no time for a tactical appraisal with the Stratosan natives. That would have to be conducted en route to Cirrion.

'I pray to the Emperor that some yet live,' Tonn-hauser continued over the pict-link, network-fed to all of the Astartes transports. 'But I fear Cirrion is lost to us, lord Astartes,' he added, lighting up a fresh cigar with shaking fingers. 'There's nothing left there but death and terror now.' He seemed to be avoiding eye contact with the screen. Kadai had taken off his helmet during the ride over the sky-bridge and the human clearly found his appearance unsettling.

'*Wars have been won on the strength of that alone,*' he remembered the old Master of Recruits telling him almost three hundred years ago when he had first been given the black carapace.

'Tell me of the enemy,' Kadai said, face hardening at the thought of such suffering.

'They call themselves the Cult of Truth,' said Tonnhauser, the pict-link breaking up for a moment with the static interference. 'Until roughly three months ago, they were merely a small group of disaffected

Imperial citizens adept at dodging the mauls of the city proctors. Now they are at least fifty thousand strong, and dug in all throughout Cirrion. They're heavily armed. Most of the Stratosan war-smiths are based in the capital, as are our dirigible fleets, our airships. They carry a mark on their bodies, usually hidden, like a tattoo in the shape of a screaming mouth. And their mouths...' he said, taking a shuddering breath, 'their mouths are sewn shut with wire. We think they might remove their tongues, too.'

'What makes you say that?'

Tonnhauser met the captain's burning gaze in spite of his fear.

'Because no one has ever heard them speak.' Tonnhauser paled further. 'To fight an enemy that does not cry out, that does not shout orders. It's not natural.'

'Do they have a leader, this *cult*?' said Kadai, showing his distaste at such depravity.

Tonnhauser took a long drag on his cigar, before crushing it in an ash tray and lighting another.

'Our gathered intelligence is limited,' he admitted. 'But we believe there is a hierophant of sorts. Again, this is unconfirmed, but we think he's in the temple district. What we do know is that they call him the *Speaker*.'

'An ironic appellation,' Kadai muttered. 'How many troops do you have left, colonel?'

Tonnhauser licked his lips.

'Enough to hold the two satellite cities. The rest of my men in Cirrion are being pulled out as we speak. Civilians too. I've lost so many...' Tonnhauser's face fell. He looked like a man with nothing more to give.

'Hold those cities, colonel,' Kadai told him. 'The Salamanders will deal with Cirrion, now. You've done your duty as a servant of the Imperium and will be honoured for it.'

'Thank you, my lord.'

The pict-link crackled into static as Kadai severed the connection.

The captain turned from the blank display screen to find Apothecary Fugis at his shoulder.

'Their courage hangs by a thread,' he muttered. 'I have never seen such despair.'

'Our intervention is timely then.' Kadai glanced over Fugis's shoulder and saw the rest of his command squad.

N'keln was readying them for battle, leading them in the rites of the Promethean Cult.

'Upon the anvil are we tempered, into warriors forged...' he intoned, the others solemnly following his lead. They surrounded a small brazier set into the floor of the troop hold. Offerings to Vulkan and the Emperor burned within the crucible, scraps of banners or powdered bone, and one by one the Inferno Guard took a fistful of the ash and marked their armour with it.

'Guerrilla warfare is one thing, but to defeat an entire Imperial Guard regiment... Do you think we face more than a cult uprising here?' asked Fugis, averting his gaze from the ritual and resolving to make his own observances later.

Kadai brought his gaze inward as he considered the Apothecary's question.

'I don't know yet. But something plagues this place. This so-called Cult of Truth certainly has many followers.'

'Its spread is endemic, suggesting its root is psychological, rather than ideological,' said the Apothecary.

Kadai left the implication unspoken.

'I can't base a strategy on supposition, brother. Once we breach the city, then we'll find out what we're facing.' The captain paused a moment before asking, 'What of Dak'ir?'

Fugis lowered his voice, so the others could not hear him.

'Physically, our brother is fine. But he is still troubled. Remembrances of his human childhood on Nocturne and his first mission...'

Kadai scowled, 'Moribar... Over four decades of battles, yet still this one clings to us like a dark shroud.'

'His memory retention is... *unusual*. And I think he feels guilt for what happened to Nihilan,' offered Fugis.

Kadai's expression darkened further.

'He is not alone in that,' he muttered.

'Ushorak, too.'

'Vai'tan Ushorak was a traitor. He deserved his fate,' Kadai answered flatly, before changing the subject. 'Dak'ir's spirit will be cleansed in the crucible of battle; that is the Salamanders way. Failing that I will submit him to the Reclusiam and Chaplain Elysius for conditioning.'

Kadai reactivated the open vox-channel, indicating that the conversation was over.

It was time to address the troops.

'Brothers.' Dak'ir heard the voice of his captain over the vox. 'Our task here is simple. Liberate the city, protect its citizens and destroy the heretics. Three assault groups will enter Cirrion on a sector by sector cleanse and burn – *Hammer*, *Anvil* and *Flame*. Sergeants Tsu'gan and Dak'ir will lead *Anvil* and *Flame*, into the east and west sectors of the city respectively. Devastator heavy support is Sergeant Ul'shan's Hellfire Squad for *Anvil* and Sergeant Lok's Incinerators for *Flame*. I lead *Hammer* to the north with Sergeant Omkar. Flamers with all units. Let nothing stay your wrath. This is the kind of fight we were born for. In the name of Vulkan. Kadai out.'

Static reigned once more. Dak'ir cut the link completely as the convoy rumbled on slowly past sandbagged outposts crested with razor wire. Weary troops with hollow eyes manned those stations, too tired or inured by weeks of fighting to react to the sight of the Astartes.

'This is a broken force,' muttered Ba'ken, breaking the silence as he peered out of one of the Rhino's vision slits.

Dak'ir followed his trooper's gaze. 'They are not like the natives of Nocturne, Ba'ken. They are unused to hardship like this.'

A lone file of Stratosan Aircorps passed the convoy, marching in the opposite direction. They trudged like automatons, nursing wounds, hobbling on sticks, lasguns slung loose over their shoulders. Every man wore a respirator, and a tan stormcoat to ward off the chill of the open atmosphere. Only the cities were domed, the sky-bridges open to the elements, though they had high walls and were suspended from rugged-looking towers by thick cables.

The gate of Cirrion loomed at the end of the blasted road. The way into the capital city was huge, all bare black metal, and hermetically sealed to maintain its atmospheric integrity.

'I heard a group of corpsmen talking before we mustered out,' offered Ba'ken as they approached the gate. 'One of them said that Cirrion was how he imagined hell.'

Dak'ir was checking the power load of his plasma pistol before slamming it back into its holster. 'We were born in hell, Ba'ken. What do we have to fear from a little fire?'

Ba'ken's booming laughter thundered in the Rhino all the way up to the gate.

Deep within the bowels of Cirrion the shadows were alive with monsters.

Sergeant Rucka fled through shattered streets, his pursuers at his heels. His heart was pounding. Cirrion's principal power grid had collapsed, leaving failing back-up generators to provide intermittent illumination for the city via its lume-lamps. With every sporadic blackout, the shadows seemed to fill with new threats and fresh enemies. It didn't help matters.

Rucka had been at the front of the second push in the capital city. The attack had failed utterly. Something else was stalking the darkened corridors of Cirrion, and it had fallen upon his battalion with furious wrath. It was totally unexpected. In strategising his battalion's assault Rucka had deliberately taken an oblique route, circumventing the main battle zones, to come through the northern sector of the city.

All Stratosan-gathered intelligence had suggested that insurgent resistance would be light. It wasn't insurgents that had wiped out five hundred men.

Rucka was the last of them, having somehow escaped the carnage, but now the cultists had found him. They were gaining too. His once proud city was in ruins. He didn't know this dystopian version of it. Where there should have been avenues there were rubble blockades. Where there should be plazas of chrome there were charred pits falling away into stygian darkness. Hell had come here. There was no other word to describe it.

Rounding another corner, Rucka came to an abrupt halt. He was standing at the mouth to a mag-tram station; on one side a stack of industrial warehouses, on the other a high wall and an overpass. The trams themselves littered the way ahead, just burnt out wrecks, daubed in crude slogans. But it was the tunnel itself that caught the sergeant's attention. Something skittered there in the abject darkness.

Behind him, Rucka heard the pack. They'd slowed. He realised then he'd been steered to this place.

Slowly the skittering from the tunnel became louder and the pack from behind him closer. The cultists scuttled into view. Rucka counted at least fifty men and women, their mouths sewn shut, blue veins threading from their puckered lips. They carried picks and shards of metal and glass.

It wasn't the end that Rucka had envisaged for himself.

The sergeant had picked out his first opponent and was about to take aim with his lasgun when a piece of rockcrete clattered down onto the street. Rucka traced its trajectory back to the overpass and saw the silhouettes of three armoured giants in the ambient light.

The brief spark of salvation given life in Rucka's mind was quickly crushed when he realised that these creatures were not here to save him.

Thunder roared and muzzle flares tore away the darkness a second later.

Rucka read what was about to happen and went to ground just before the onslaught. The deadly salvo lasted heartbeats, but it was enough. The cultists were utterly annihilated – their broken, blasted bodies littered the street like visceral trash.

Rucka was on his back, still dazed from the sudden attack. When he couldn't feel his legs, he realised he'd been hit. Heat blazed down his side like an angry knife ripping at his skin. His fatigues were wet, probably with his own blood. A sudden earth tremor shook the rockcrete where Rucka lay prone, sending fresh daggers of pain through his body, as something large and dense smashed into the ground. More impacts followed, landing swift and heavy like mortar strikes.

Vision fogging, the sergeant managed to turn his head... His blood-rimed eyes widened. Crouched in gory armour, two bloody horns curling from its snarling dragon helm, was a terrible giant. It rose to its feet, like some primordial beast uncurling from the abyss, to reveal an immense plastron swathed in red scales. Heat haze seemed to emanate from its armoured form as if it had been fresh-forged from the mantle of a volcano.

'The vault, where is it?' the dragon giant asked, fiery embers rasping through its fanged mouth-grille as if it breathed ash and cinder.

'Close...' said another. Its voice was like cracked parchment but carried the resonance of power.

Though he couldn't see them in his eye-line, Rucka realised the secondary impacts had been the giant warrior's companions.

'We are not alone,' said a third, deep and throaty like crackling magma.

'Salamanders,' said the dragon giant, his vitriol obvious.

'Then we had best be swift,' returned the second voice. 'I do not want
to miss them.'

Rucka heard heavy footfalls approaching and felt the ominous gaze of
one of the armoured giants upon him.

'This one still lives,' it barked.

Rucka's vision was fading, but the sergeant could still smell copper
coming off its armour, mangled with the acrid stench of gun smoke.

'No survivors,' said the second voice. 'Kill it quickly. We have no time
for *amusement*, Ramlek.'

'A pity…'

Rucka tried to speak.

'The Empe–'

Then his world ended in fire.

The black iron gates of Cirrion parted with slow inevitability.

The armoured Astartes convoy rumbled through into the waiting darkness. After a few moments the gates shut behind them. Halogen strip
lights flickered into life on the flanking walls revealing a large metal
chamber, wide enough for the transports to travel abreast.

Abandoned Stratosan vehicles lay abutting the walls, dragged aside by
clearance crews. Caches of discarded equipment were strewn nearby the
forlorn AFVs. Webbing, luminator rigs and other ancillary kit had been
left behind, but no weapons – all the guns were needed by the human
defenders.

Hermetically sealed from the outside to preserve atmospheric integrity, the holding area had another gate on the opposite side. This second
gate opened when the Salamanders were halfway across the vast corridor
with a hiss of pressure, and led into Cirrion itself.

The outskirts of the benighted city beckoned.

Deserted avenues bled away into blackness and buildings lay in ruins
like open wounds. Fire seared the walls and blood washed the streets.
Despair hung thick in the air like a tangible fug. Death had come to Cirrion, and held it tightly in its bony grasp.

Akin to a hive, Cirrion was stacked with honey-comb levels in
the most densely packed areas. Grav-lifts linked these plateau-
conurbations of chrome and blue. Sub-levels plunged in other places,
allowing access to inverted maintenance spires or vast subterranean
freight yards. Above, a dense pall of smoke layered the ceiling in a
roiling mass. Breaks in the grey-black smog revealed thick squalls
of cloud and the flash of lightning arcs from the atmospheric storm
outside and beyond the dome.

Tactically, the city was a nightmarish labyrinth of hidden pitfalls, artificial bottlenecks and kill-zones. Tank traps riddled the roads. Spools of razor wire wreathed every alleyway. Piled rubble and wreckage created makeshift walls and impassable blockades.

The Salamanders reached as far as Aereon Square, one of Cirrion's communal plazas, when the wreckage-clogged, wire-choked streets prevented the transports from going any further.

It was to be the first of many setbacks.

'Salamanders, disembark,' Kadai voiced sternly over the vox. 'Three groups, quadrant by quadrant search. Vehicles stay here. We approach on foot.'

'Nothing,' Ba'ken's voice was tinny through his battle-helm as he stood facing the doorway to one of Cirrion's municipal temples. It yawned like a hungry maw, the shadows within filled with menace.

From behind him, Dak'ir's order was emphatic.

'Burn it.'

Ba'ken hefted his heavy flamer and doused the room beyond with liquid promethium. The sudden burst of incendiary lit up a broad hallway like a flare, hinting at a larger space in the distance, before dying back down to flickering embers.

'Clear,' he shouted, stepping aside heavily with the immense weapon, allowing the sergeant and his battle-brothers through.

Sergeant Lok and his Devastators were assigned to the rearguard and took up positions to secure the entrance as Ba'ken followed the Tactical squad inside.

Dak'ir entered quickly, his squad fanning out from his lead to cover potential avenues of attack.

They'd been travelling through the city for almost an hour, through three residential districts filled with debris, and still no contact with friend or foe. Regular reports networked through the Astartes' commfeeds in their helmets revealed the same from the other two assault groups.

Cirrion was dead.

Yet, there were signs of recent abandonment: lume-globes flickering in the blasted windows of tenements, sonophones playing grainy melodies in communal refectories, the slow-running engines of dormant grav-cars and the interior lamps of mag-trams come to an all-stop on the rails. Life here had ended abruptly and violently.

Numerous roads and more conventional routes were blocked by pitfalls or rubble. According to Brother Argos, the municipal temple was the most expedient way to penetrate deeper into the east sector. It was also postulated that it was a likely location for survivors to congregate. The Techmarine was back in Nimbaros with Colonel Tonnhauser, guiding the three assault groups via a hololithic schematic, adjusting the image as he was fed reports of blockades, street collapses or structural levelling by Salamanders in the field.

'Brother Argos, this is *Flame*. We've reached the municipal temple and need a route through,' said Dak'ir. Even through his power armour, he was aware of the dulcet hum of the plasma engines keeping the massive city aloft and reminding him of the precariousness of their battlefield.

Putting the thoughts out of his mind, he swept the luminator attached to his battle-helm around the vast hall. Within its glare a lozenge-shaped chamber with racks of desks on both flanking walls was revealed. Overhead, exterior light from the city's lume-lamps spilled through a glass-domed ceiling in grainy shafts illuminating patches on the ground. Lightning flashes from Stratos's high atmosphere outside augmented it.

Parchments and scraps of vellum set ablaze by Ba'ken's flamer skittered soundlessly across a polished floor, or twisted like fireflies on an unseen breeze. More of the papers were fixed to pillars that supported the vaulted roof above, fluttering fitfully – some stuck with votive wax, others hammered fast with nails and stakes. The messages were doubtless pinned up by grieving families long since given in to despair.

'These are death notices, prayers for the missing,' intoned Brother Emek, using the muzzle of his bolter to hold one still so he could read it.

'More here,' added Brother Zo'tan. He panned the light from his luminator up a chrome-plated staircase at the back of the room to reveal the suited bodies of clerks and administrators entangled in the balustrade. Torn scrolls were pinned to the banister, and gathered over the corpses on the steps like a paper shroud.

'There must be thousands...' uttered Sergeant Lok, who had entered the lobby. The hard-faced veteran looked grimmer than ever as he surveyed the records of the dead with his bionic eye.

'Advance to the north end of the hall,' the Techmarine's voice returned, cracked with interference as it called the Salamanders back. 'A stairway leads to a second level. Proceed north through the next chamber then east across a gallery until you find a gate. That's your exit.'

Dak'ir killed the comm-feed. In the sudden silence he became aware of the atmospheric processors droning loudly in the barrier wall around the city, purifying, recycling, regulating. He was about to give the order to move out when the sound changed abruptly. The pitch became higher, as if the processing engine were switched to a faster setting.

Dak'ir re-opened the comm-feed in his battle-helm.

'Tsu'gan, are you detecting any variance in the atmospheric processors in your sector?'

Crackling static returned for a full thirty seconds before the sergeant replied.

'It's nothing. Maintain your vigilance, Ignean. I have no desire to haul your squad out of trouble when you let your guard slip.'

Tsu'gan cut the feed.

Dak'ir swore under his breath.

'Move out,' he told his squad. He hoped they'd find the enemy soon.

'He should never have been chosen to lead,' muttered Tsu'gan to his second, Iagon.

'Our brother-captain must have his reasons,' he replied, his tone ever sinuous but carefully neutral.

Iagon was never far from his sergeant's side, and was ever ready with his counsel. His body was slight compared to most of his brethren, but he made up for sheer bulk with guile and cunning. Iagon gravitated towards power, and right now that was Tsu'gan, Captain Kadai's star ascendant. He also carried the squad's auspex, maintaining a watch for unusual spikes of activity that might prelude an ambush, walking just two paces behind his sergeant as they stalked through the shadows of a hydroponics farm.

Tiny reservoirs of nutrient solution encased in chrome tanks extended across an expansive domed chamber. The chemical repositories were set in serried ranks and replete with various edible plant life and other flora. The foliage inside the vast gazebo of chrome and glass was overgrown, resembling more an artificial jungle than an Imperial facility for the sector-wide provision of nutrition.

'Then that is his folly,' Tsu'gan replied, and signalled a sudden halt.

He crouched, peering into the arboreal gloom ahead. His squad, well-drilled by their sergeant, adopted overwatch positions.

'Flamer,' he growled into the comm-feed.

Brother Honorious moved forwards, the igniter of his weapon burning quietly. The Salamander noticed the blue flame flicker for just a moment as if reacting to something in the air. Slapping the barrel, Honorious muttered a litany to the machine-spirits and the igniter returned to normal.

'On your order, sergeant.'

Tsu'gan held up his hand.

'Hold a moment.'

Iagon low-slung his bolter to consult the auspex.

'No life form readings.'

Tsu'gan's face was fixed in a grimace.

'Cleanse and burn.'

'We would be destroying the food supply for an entire city sector,' said Iagon.

'Believe me, Iagon, the Stratosans are long past caring. I'll take no chances. Now,' he said, turning back to Honorious, 'cleanse and burn.'

The roar of the flamer filled the hydroponics dome as the sustenance of Cirrion was burned to ash.

* * *

'They are drawing us in,' said Veteran Sergeant N'keln over the comm-feed. He was in the lead, tracking his bolter left and right for any sign of the enemy.

'I know,' Kadai agreed, trusting his and N'keln's warrior instincts. The captain held his inferno pistol by his side, thunder hammer crackling quietly in his other hand. 'Remain vigilant,' he hissed through his battle-helm, his squad treading warily with bolters ready.

The city loomed tall and imposing as the Salamanders advanced slowly down a narrow road choked with wreckage and Stratosan corpses – 'remnants' of the battalions Tonnhauser had mentioned. The hapless human troopers had erected sandbagged emplacements and makeshift barricades. Habs had been turned into bunkers, and bodies hung forlornly from their windows like rags. The defences had not availed them. The Stratosan infantry had been crushed.

Fugis was crouched over the blasted remains of a lieutenant, scowling.

'Massive physical trauma,' muttered the Apothecary as Captain Kadai approached him.

'Colonel Tonnhauser said the cultists were heavily armed,' offered N'keln alongside him.

Fugis regarded the corpse further. 'Ribcage is completely eviscerated, chest organs all but liquefied.' Looking up at his fellow Salamanders, his red eyes flared behind his helmet lenses. 'This is a bolter wound.'

Kadai was about to respond when Brother Shen'kar called from up ahead.

'I have movement!'

'Keep it tight,' warned Dak'ir as he advanced up the lobby stairs towards a large chrome archway leading to the second level of the municipal temple.

The igniter on Ba'ken's heavy flamer spat and flickered furiously until he reduced the fuel supply down the hose.

'Problem?'

'It's nothing sergeant,' he replied.

Dak'ir continued up the stairway, battle-brothers on either side of him, the Devastators still in the lobby below, ready to move up if needed. When he reached the summit he saw another long hallway beyond, just as Brother Argos had described. The room was filled with disused cogitators and other extant machinery. Sweeping his gaze across the junk, Dak'ir stopped abruptly.

In the centre of the hall, surrounded by more dead Administratum workers, was a boy. An infant, no more than eight years old, he was barefoot and clad in rags. Dirt and dried blood encrusted his body like a second skin. The boy was staring right at Dak'ir.

'Don't move,' he whispered to his battle-brothers through the comm-feed. 'We have a survivor.'

'Mercy of Vulkan…' breathed Ba'ken, alongside him.

'Stay back,' warned Dak'ir, taking a step.

The boy flinched, but didn't run. Tears were streaming down his face, cutting through the grime and leaving pale channels in their wake.

Dak'ir scanned the hall furtively for any potential threats, before deeming the way was clear. Holstering his plasma pistol and sheathing his chainsword, he then showed his armoured palms to the boy.

'You have nothing to fear…' he began, and slowly removed his battle-helm. Dak'ir realised his mistake too late.

This infant was no native of Nocturne. One look at the Salamander's onyx-black skin and burning eyes and the child yelped and fled for his life back across the hall.

'Damn it!' Dak'ir hissed, ramming his battle-helm back on and re-arming himself. 'Sergeant Lok, you and your squad secure the room and await our return,' he ordered through the comm-feed. 'Brothers, the rest of you with me – there may be survivors, and the boy will lead us to them.'

The Salamanders gave chase, whilst the Devastators moved up the stairs behind them. Dak'ir was halfway across the hall with his squad when he felt the tiny pressure of a wire snapping against his greave. He turned, about to shout a warning, when the entire room exploded.

'Dead end,' stated Brother Honorious, standing before the towering barricade of heaped grav-cars and mag-trams.

Tsu'gan and *Anvil* had left the hydroponics farm a smouldering ruin and had advanced into the city. Directed by Brother Argos, they'd passed through myriad avenues in the urban labyrinth until reaching a narrow defile created by tall tenement blocks and overhanging tower-levels. A hundred metres in and they'd rounded a corner only to find it blocked.

'We'll burn through it,' said Tsu'gan, about to order Sergeant Ul'shan's Devastators forwards. The multi-meltas would soon–

'Wait,' said Tsu'gan, surveying the tall buildings reaching over them. 'Double back, we'll find another way.'

At the opposite end of the alleyway a huge trans-loader rolled into view, cutting off their exit. Slowly at first, but with growing momentum it rumbled towards the Salamanders.

'Multi-meltas now! Destroy it!'

Sergeant Ul'shan swung his squad around to face the charging vehicle just as the cultist heavy weapon crews emerged from their hiding places in the tenements above and filled the alleyway with gunfire.

'Eyes open,' hissed Captain Kadai.

The Inferno Guard, together with Omkar's Devastators, were crouched in ready positions spread across the street. The dangers were manifold – every window, every alcove or shadowed corner could contain an enemy.

Kadai's gaze flicked back to Fugis as the Apothecary hurried, head low, towards a distant gun emplacement. A Stratosan lay slumped next to its sandbagged wall, alive but barely moving. Kadai watched the trooper's hand flick up for the third time as he signalled for aid.

Something didn't feel right.

The trooper's movements were limp, but somehow forced.

Sudden unease creeping into the pit of his stomach, Kadai realised it was a trap.

'Fugis, stop!' he yelled into the comm-feed.

'I'm almost there, captain...'

'Apothecary, obey my ord–'

The roar of a huge fireball billowing out from the emplacement cut Kadai off. Fugis was lifted off his feet by the blast wave, the slain Stratosans buoyed up with him like broken dolls. Chained detonations ripped up the road, rupturing rockcrete, as an entire section of it broke apart and fell away creating a huge chasm.

Flattened by the immense explosion, Captain Kadai was still struggling to his feet, shaking off the blast disorientation, when he saw Fugis lying on his chest, armour blackened by fire, gripping the edge of the artificial crater made during the explosion. Kadai cried out as the Apothecary lost his hold and slipped down into the gaping black abyss of Cirrion's underbelly, vanishing from sight.

From the hidden darkness of the city, the depraved cultists swarmed into the night and the shooting began.

Shrugging off the effects of the explosion, Dak'ir saw figures moving through the settling dust and smoke.

One loomed over him. Its mouth was stitched with black wire; blue veins infected its cheeks. Eyes filled with fervour, the cultist drove a pickaxe against the Space Marine's armour. The puny weapon broke apart on impact.

'Salamanders,' roared Dak'ir, rallying his squad as he pulverised the cultist's face with an armoured fist. He took up his chainsword, which had spilled from his grip in the blast, eviscerating three more insurgents as they came at him with cudgels and blades.

Reaching for his plasma pistol, he stopped short. The atmospheric readings in his battle-helm were showing a massive concentration of hydrogen; the air inside the dome was saturated with it.

To Dak'ir's left flank, Ba'ken was levelling his heavy flamer as a massive surge of cultists spilled into the hall...

'Wai–'

'Cleanse and burn!'

As soon as the incendiary hit the air, the weapon exploded. Ba'ken was engulfed in white fire then smashed sideways, through the rockcrete wall and into an adjoining chamber where he lay unmoving.

'Brother down!' bellowed Dak'ir, Emek offering suppressing fire with his bolter as he came forwards, chewing up cultists like meat sacks.

More were piling through in a steady stream, seemingly unaffected by the bolt storm. Picks and blades gave way to heavy stubbers and auto-cannons, and Dak'ir saw the first wave for what it was: a flesh shield.

Another Salamander came up on the sergeant's other flank, Brother Ak'sor. He was readying his flamer when Dak'ir shouted into the comm-feed.

'Stow all flamers and meltas. The air is thick with a gaseous hydrogen amalgam. Bolters and secondary weapons only.'

The Salamanders obeyed at once.

The press of cultists came on thickly now, small-arms fire whickering from their ranks as the heavy weapons were prepared to shoot. Dak'ir severed the head from one insurgent and punched through the sternum of another.

'Hold them,' he snapped, withdrawing a bloody fist.

Ak'sor had pulled out a bolt pistol. Bullets pattered against his armour as he let rip, chewing up a bunch of cultists with autoguns. The dull *thump-thud* of the heavier cannons starting up filled the room and Ak'sor staggered as multiple rounds struck him. From somewhere in the melee, a gas-propelled grenade whined and Ak'sor disappeared behind exploding shrapnel. When the smoke had cleared, the Salamander was down.

'Retreat to the lobby, all Salamanders,' shouted Dak'ir, solid shot rebounding off his armour as he hacked down another cultist that came within his death arc.

The Astartes fell back as one, two battle-brothers coming forward to drag Ba'ken and Ak'sor from the battle. As Dak'ir's squad reached the stairs and started to climb down, Sergeant Lok rushed in. Due to the presence of the explosive hydrogen gas the Incinerators were down to a single heavy bolter, strafing the doorway and ripping up cultists with a punishing salvo.

There was scant respite as the enemy pressed its advantage, wired-mouthed maniacs hurling themselves into the furious bolter fire in their droves. Brother Ionnes was chewing through the belt feed of his heavy bolter with abandon, his fellow Salamanders adding their own weapons to the barrage, but the cultists came on still. Like automatons, they refused to yield to panic, the fates of their shattered brethren failing to stall, let alone rout them.

'They're unbreakable!' bellowed Lok, smashing an insurgent to pulp with his power fist, whilst firing his bolter one-handed. A chainsaw struck his outstretched arm seemingly from nowhere and he grimaced, his weapon falling from nerveless fingers. Red-eyed eviscerator priests were moving through the throng, wielding immense double-handed chainblades. Dak'ir crushed the zealot's skull with a punch, but realised they were slowly being enveloped.

'Back to the entrance,' he cried, taking up Lok's fallen bolter and spraying an arc of fire across his left flank. The ones he killed didn't even scream. Step by agonising step, the Salamanders withdrew. There was a veritable bullet hail coming from the enemy now, whose numbers seemed limitless and came from every direction at once.

Inside the comm-feed it was chaos. Fragmented reports came in, plagued by static interference, from both *Anvil* and *Hammer*.

'*Heavy casualties… enemy armour moving in… thousands everywhere… brother down!*'

'Captain Kadai,' Dak'ir yelled into the vox. 'Brother-captain, this is *Flame*. Please respond.'

After a long minute, Kadai's broken reply came back.

'*Kadai… here… Fall… back… regroup… Aereon Square…*'

'Captain, I have two battle-brothers badly injured and in need of medical attention.'

Another thirty seconds passed, before another stuttering response.

'*Apothecary… lost… Repeat… Fugis is gone…*'

*Gone.* Not wounded or down, just gone. Dak'ir felt a ball of hot pain develop in his chest. Stoic resolve outweighed his anger – he gave the order for a fighting withdrawal to Aereon Square, and then raised Tsu'gan on the comm-feed.


'Vulkan's blood! I will not retreat in the face of this rabble,' Tsu'gan snarled at Iagon. 'Tell the Ignean I have received no such order.'

*Anvil* had, under Tsu'gan's steely leadership, broken free of the ambush without casualties, though Brother Honorious was limping badly and Sergeant Ul'shan had lost an eye when the trans-loader hit and the drums of incendiary heaped onboard had exploded.

Without use of their multi-meltas, Tsu'gan had torn through the vehicle wreckage himself, scything cultists down on the other side with his combi-bolter. They were falling back to defended positions in the wider street beyond when Dak'ir's message came through.

At some point during the fighting, Tsu'gan had damaged his battle-helm and he'd torn it off. Since then he'd been relying on Iagon for communication with the other assault groups.

'We are Salamanders, born in fire,' he raged zealously, 'the anvil upon which our enemies are broken. We do not yield. *Ever!*'

Iagon dutifully relayed the message, indicating his sergeant's refusal to comply.

Further up the street, something loud and heavy was rumbling towards them. It broke Tsu'gan's stride for just a moment as a tank, festooned with armour plates and daubed with the gaping maw symbol of the Cult of Truth, came into view. Swinging around its fat metal turret, the tank's battle cannon fired, jetting smoke and rocking the vehicle back on its tracks.

Tsu'gan had his warriors in a defensive battle line, strafing the oncoming cultist hordes with controlled bursts of bolter fire. The tank shell hit with all the force of a thunderbolt, and tore the ragged line apart.

Salamanders were tossed into the air with chunks of rockcrete chewed out of the road, and fell like debris.

'Close ranks. Hold positions,' Tsu'gan snarled, crouching down next to a partially destroyed barricade once occupied by Stratosan Aircorps.

Iagon shoved one of the bodies out of the way, so he could rest his bolter in a makeshift firing lip.

'Still nothing from the captain,' he said between bursts.

Tsu'gan's reaction to the news was guarded, his face fixed in a perpetual scowl.

'Ul'shan,' he barked to the sergeant of the Devastators, 'all fire on that tank. In the name of Vulkan, destroy it.'

Bolter fire *pranged* against the implacable vehicle, grinding forwards as it readied for another shot with its battle cannon. In the turret, a crazed cultist took up the heavy stubber and started hosing the Salamanders with solid shot.

'You others,' bellowed Tsu'gan, standing up and unhitching something from his belt, 'grenades on my lead.' He launched a krak grenade overarm. It soared through the air at speed, impelled by Tsu'gan's strength, and rolled into the tank's path. Several more followed, *thunking* to earth like metal hail.

At the same time, Iagon's bolter fire shredded the cultist in the stubber nest, whilst Sergeant Ul'shan's heavy bolters hammered the tank's front armour and tracks. An explosive round from the salvo clipped one of the krak grenades just as the armoured vehicle was driving over it. A chained detonation tore through the tank as the incendiaries exploded, ripping it wide open.

'Glory to Prometheus!' roared Tsu'gan, punching the air as his warriors chorused after him.

His fervour was dampened when he saw shadows moving through the smoke and falling shrapnel. Three more tanks trundled into view.

Tsu'gan shook his head in disbelief.

'*Mercy of Vulkan...*' he breathed, just as the comm-link with Captain Kadai was restored. The sergeant glared at Iagon with iron-hard eyes.

They were falling back to Aereon Square.

Dak'ir had been right. Tsu'gan felt his jaw tighten.

'Hold the line!' Kadai bellowed into the comm-feed. 'We make our stand here.'

The Salamanders held position stoically, strung out across the chewed-up defences, controlled bursts thundering from their bolters. Behind them were the armoured transports. Storm bolters shuddered from turret mounts on the Rhinos and *Fire Anvil's* twin-linked assault cannon whirred in a frenzy of heavy fire, though the Land Raider's flamestorm side sponsons were powered down.

The Salamanders had converged quickly on Aereon Square, the fighting withdrawal of the three assault groups less cautious than their original attack.

The slab floor of the square was cratered by bomb blasts and fire-blackened. Fallen pillars from adjacent buildings intruded on its perimeter. The centre of the broad plaza was dominated by a felled statue of one of Stratos's Imperial leaders, encircled by a damaged perimeter wall. It was here that Kadai and his warriors made their stand.

The cultists came on in the face of heavy fire, swarming from every avenue, every alcove, like hell-born ants. Hundreds were slain in minutes. But despite the horrendous casualties, they were undeterred and made slow progress across the killing ground. The corpses piled up like sandbags at the edge of the square.

'None shall pass, Fire-born!' raged Kadai, the furious zeal of Vulkan, his progenitor, filling him with righteous purpose. *Endure* – it was one of the central tenets of the Promethean Cult, *endure and conquer*.

The bullet storms crossed each other over a shortening distance as the cultist thousands poured intense fire into the Salamanders' defensive positions. Chunks of perimeter wall, and massive sections of the fallen statue, were chipped apart in the maelstrom.

Brother Zo'tan took a round in the left pauldron, then another in the neck, grunted and fell to his knees. Dak'ir moved to cover him, armour shuddering as he let rip with a borrowed bolter. Insurgent bodies were destroyed in the furious barrage, torn apart by explosive rounds, sundered by salvos from heavy bolters, shredded by the withering hail from assault cannons whining red-hot.

Still the cultists came.

Dak'ir gritted his teeth and roared.

'No retreat!'

Slowly, inevitably, the hordes began to thin. Kadai ordered a halt to the sustained barrage. Like smoke dispersing from a doused pyre, the insurgents were drifting away, backing off silently into the gloom until they were at last gone from sight.

The tenacity of the Salamanders had kept the foe at bay this time. Aereon Square was held.

'Are they giving up?' asked Dak'ir, breathing hard underneath his power armour as he tried to slow his body down from its ultra-heightened battle-state.

'They crawl back to their nests,' Kadai growled. His jaw clenched with impotent anger. 'The city is theirs... for now.'

Stalking from the defence line, Kadai quickly set up sentries to watch the approaches to the square, whilst at the same time contacting Techmarine Argos to send reinforcements from *Vulkan's Wrath*, and a Thunderhawk to extract the dead and wounded. The toll was much heavier than he had expected. Fourteen wounded and six dead. Most keenly felt of all, though, was the loss of Fugis.

The Salamanders were a small Chapter, their near-annihilation during one of the worst atrocities of the Heresy, when they were betrayed by their erstwhile brothers, still felt some ten thousand years later. They had been Legion then, but now they were merely some eight hundred Astartes. Induction of new recruits was slow and only compounded their low fighting strength.

Without their Apothecary and his prodigious medical skills, the most severe injuries suffered by Kadai's Third Company would remain untended and further debilitate their combat effectiveness. Worse still, the gene-seeds of those killed in action would be unharvested, for only Fugis possessed the knowledge and ability to remove these progenoids safely. And it was through these precious organs that future Space Marines were engineered, allowing even the slain to serve their Chapter in death. The losses suffered by Third Company, then, became permanent with the loss of their Apothecary, a solemn fact that put Kadai in a black mood.

'We will re-assault the city proper as soon as we're reinforced,' he raged.

'We should level the full weight of the company against them. Then these heretics will break,' asserted Tsu'gan, clenching a fist to emphasise his vehemence.

Both he and Dak'ir accompanied Kadai as he walked from the battle line, leaving Veteran Sergeant N'keln to organise the troops. The captain unclasped his battle-helm to remove it. His white crest of hair was damp with sweat. His eyes glowed hotly, emanating anger.

'Yes, they will learn that the Salamanders do not yield easily.'

Tsu'gan grinned ferally at that.

Dak'ir thought only of the brothers they had already lost, and the others that would fall in another hard-headed assault. The traitors were dug-in and had numbers – without flamers to flush out ambushers and other traps, breaking Cirrion would be tough.

Then something happened that forestalled the captain's belligerent plan for vengeance. Far across Aereon Square, figures were emerging through the smoke and dust. They crept from their hiding places and shambled towards the Salamanders, shoulders slumped in despair.

Dak'ir's eyes widened when he saw how many there were, 'Survivors… the civilians of Cirrion.'

'Open it,' rasped the dragon giant. His scaled armour coursed with eldritch energy, throwing sharp flashes of light into the gloom. He and his warriors had reached a subterranean metal chamber that ended in an immense portal of heavy plasteel.

Another giant wearing the red-scaled plate came forward. Tendrils of smoke emanated from the grille in his horned helmet. The silence of the outer vault was broken by the hissing, crackling intake of breath before the horned one unleashed a furious plume of flame. It surged hungrily through the grille-plate in a roar, smashing against the vault door and devouring it.

Reinforced plasteel bars blackened and corroded in seconds, layers of ablative ceramite melted away before the adamantium plate of the door itself glowed white-hot and sloughed into molten slag.

The warriors had travelled swiftly through the mag-tram tunnel, forging deep into the lesser known corridors of Cirrion. None had seen them approach. Their leader had made certain that the earlier massacre left no witnesses. After almost an hour, they had reached their destination. Here, in the catacombs of the city, the hydrogen gas clouds could not penetrate. They were far from the fighting; the battles going on in the distant districts of Cirrion sounded dull and faraway through many layers of rockcrete and metal.

'Is it here?' asked a third warrior as the ragged portal into the vault cooled, his voice like crackling magma. Inside were hundreds of tiny strongboxes, held here for the aristocracy of Stratos so they could secure that which they held most precious. No one could have known of the artefact that dwelled innocuously in one of those boxes. Even upon seeing it, few would have realised its significance, the terrible destructive forces it could unleash.

'Oh yes...' replied the eldritch warrior, closing crimson-lidded eyes as he drew upon his power. 'It is exactly where he said it would be.'

Desperate and dishevelled, the Stratosan masses tramped into Aereon Square.

Most wore little more than rags, the scraps of whatever clothed them when the cultists had taken over the city. Some clutched the tattered remnants of scorched belongings, the last vestiges of whatever life they once had in Cirrion now little more than ashen remains. Many had strips of dirty cloth or ragged scarves tied around their noses and mouths to keep out the worst of the suffocating hydrogen gas. A few wore battered respirators, and shared them with others; small groups taking turns with the rebreather cups. The hydrogen had no such ill-effects on the Salamanders, their Astartes multi-lung and oolitic kidney acting in concert to portion off and siphon out any toxins, thus enabling them to breathe normally.

'An entire city paralysed by terror...' said Ba'ken as another piece of shrapnel was removed from his face.

The burly Salamander was sat up against the perimeter wall, and being tended to by Brother Emek who had some rudimentary knowledge of field surgery. Ba'ken's battle-helm had all but shattered in the explosion that destroyed his beloved heavy flamer and, after being propelled through the wall, fragments of it were still embedded in his flesh.

'This is but the first of them, brother,' replied Dak'ir, regarding the weary passage of the survivors with pity as they passed the Salamanders sentries.

Aereon Square was slowly filling. Dak'ir followed the trail of pitiful wretches being led away in huddled throngs by Stratosan Aircorps to the Cirrion gate. From there, he knew, an armoured battalion idled, ready to escort the survivors across the sky-bridge and into the relative safety of Nimbaros. Almost a hundred had already been moved and more still were massing in the square as the Aircorps struggled to cope with them all.

'Why show themselves now?' asked Ba'ken, with a nod to Emek who took his leave having finally excised all the jutting shrapnel. The wounds were already healing; the Larraman cells in Ba'ken's Astartes blood accelerating clotting and scarring, the ossmodula implanted in his brain encouraging rapid bone growth and regeneration.

Dak'ir shrugged. 'The enemy's withdrawal to consolidate whatever ground they hold, together with our arrival must have galvanised them, I suppose. Made them reach out for salvation.'

'It is a grim sight.'

'Yes...' Dak'ir agreed, suddenly lost in thought. The war on Stratos had suddenly adopted a different face entirely now: not one bound by wire or infected by taint, but one that pleaded for deliverance, that had given all there was to give, a face that was ordinary and innocent, and afraid. As he watched the human detritus tramp by, the sergeant took in the rest of the encampment.

The perimeter wall formed a kind of demarcation line, dividing the territory of the Salamanders and that held by the Cult of Truth. Kadai was adamant they would hold onto it. A pair of Thunderfire cannons patrolled the area on grinding tracks, servos whirring as their Tech-marines cycled the cannons through various firing routines.

Brother Argos had arrived in Aereon Square within the hour, bringing the artillery and his fellow Techmarines with him.

There would be no further reinforcements.

Ferocious lightning storms were wreaking havoc in the upper atmosphere of Stratos, caused by a blanketing of thermal low pressure emanating off the chlorine-rich oceans. Any descent by Thunderhawks was impossible, and all off-planet communication was hindered massively. Kadai and the Salamanders who had made the initial planetfall were alone – a fact they bore stoically. It would have to be enough.

'How many of our fallen brothers will be for the long dark?' Ba'ken's voice called Dak'ir back. The burly Salamander was staring at the medi-caskets of the dead and severely wounded, aligned together on the far side of the perimeter wall. 'I hope I will never suffer that fate...' he confessed in a whisper. 'Entombed within a Dreadnought. An existence without sensation, as the world dims around me, enduring forever in a cold sarcophagus. I would rather the fires of battle claim me first.'

'It is an honour to serve the Chapter eternally, Ba'ken,' Dak'ir admonished, though his reproach was mild. 'In any case, we don't know what their fates will be,' he added, 'save for that of the dead...'

The fallen warriors of Third Company were awaiting transit to Nimbaros. Here, they would be kept secure aboard *Fire-wyvern* until the storms abated and the Thunderhawk could return them to the *Vulkan's Wrath* where they would be interred in the strike cruiser's *pyreum*.

All Salamanders, once their progenoids had been removed, were incinerated in the pyreum, still wearing their armour, their ashes offered in Promethean ritual to honour the heroic dead and empower the spirits of the living. Such practices were only ever conducted by a Chaplain, and since Elysius was not with the company at this time, the ashen remains would be stored in the strike cruiser's crematoria until he rejoined them or they returned to Nocturne.

Such morbid thoughts inevitably led to Fugis, and the Apothecary's untimely demise.

'I spoke to him before the mission, before he died,' said Dak'ir, his eyes far away.

'Who?'

'Fugis. In the isolation chamber aboard the *Vulkan's Wrath*.'

Ba'ken stood up and reached for his pauldron, easing the stiffness from his back and shoulders. The left one had been dislocated before Brother Emek had righted it, and Ba'ken's pauldron had been removed to do it.

'What did he say?' he asked, affixing the armour expertly.

*Not all of us* want *to be brought back. Not all of us* can *be brought back.*

'Something I will not forget...'

Dak'ir shook his head slowly, his gaze fixed on the darkness beyond Aereon Square. 'I do not think we are alone here, Ba'ken,' he said at length.

'Clearly not – we fight a horde of thousands.'

'No... There is something else, too.'

Ba'ken frowned. 'And what is that, brother?'

Dak'ir voice was hard as stone. 'Something worse.'

The interior of the *Fire Anvil*'s troop hold was aglow as Dak'ir entered the Land Raider. A revolving schematic in the middle of the hold threw off harsh blue light, bathing the metal chamber and the Astartes gathered within. The four Salamanders present had already removed battle-helms. Their eyes burned warmly in the semi-darkness, at odds with the cold light of the hololith depicting Cirrion.

Summoned at Kadai's request, Dak'ir had left Ba'ken at the perimeter wall to rearm himself, ready for the next assault on Cirrion.

'Without flamers and meltas we face a much sterner test here,' Kadai said, nodding to acknowledge Dak'ir's arrival, as did N'keln.

Tsu'gan offered no such geniality, and merely scowled.

'Tactically, we can hold Aereon Square almost indefinitely,' Kadai continued. 'Thunderfire cannons will bulwark our defensive line, even without reinforcement from the *Vulkan's Wrath* to compensate for our losses. Deeper penetration into the city, however, will not be easy.'

The denial of reinforcements was a bitter blow, and Kadai had been incensed at the news. But the granite-hard pragmatist in him, the Salamanders spirit of self-reliance and self-sacrifice, proved the stronger and so he had put his mind to the task at hand using the forces he did possess. In response to the casualties, Kadai had combined the three groups of Devastators into two squads under Lok and Omkar, Ul'shan with his injury deferring to the other two sergeants. Without reinforcements, the Tactical squads would simply have to soak up their losses.

'With Fugis gone, I'm reluctant to risk more of our battle-brothers heading into the unknown,' Kadai said, the shadows in his face making him look haunted. 'The heretics are entrenched and well-armed. We are few. This would present little impediment should we have the use of our flamers, but we do not.'

'Is there a way to purify the atmosphere?' asked N'keln. He wheezed from a chest wound he'd sustained during the withdrawal to Aereon Square. N'keln was a solid, dependable warrior, but leader-ship did not come easily to him and he lacked the guile for higher command. Still, his bravery had been proven time and again, and was above reproach. It was an obvious but necessary question.

Brother Argos stepped forward into the reflected light of the schematic.

The Techmarine went unhooded. The left portion of his face was framed with a steel plate, the snarling image of a salamander seared into it as an honour marking. Burn scars from the brander-priests wreathed his skin in whorls and bands. A bionic eye gleamed coldly in contrast to the burning red of his own. Forked plugs bulged from a glabrous scalp like steel tumours, and wires snaked around the side of his neck and fed into his nose.

When he spoke, his voice was deep and metallic.

'The hydrogen emissions being controlled by Cirrion's atmospheric processors are a gaseous amalgam used to inflate the Stratosan dirigibles – a less volatile compound, and the reason why bolters are still functioning normally. Though I have managed to access some of the city's internal systems, the processors are beyond my knowledge to affect. It would require a local engineer, someone who maintained the system originally. Unfortunately, there is simply no way to find anyone with the proper skills, either alive amongst the survivors or amongst those still trapped in the city.' Argos paused. 'I am sorry, brothers, but any use of incendiary weapons in the city at this time would be catastrophic.'

'One thing is certain,' Kadai continued, 'the appearance of civilian survivors effectively prevents any massed assault. I won't jeopardise innocent lives needlessly.'

Tsu'gan shook his head.

'Brother-captain, with respect, if we do not act the collateral damage will be much worse. Our only recourse is to lead a single full-strength force into Cirrion, and sack it. The insurgents will not expect such a bold move.'

'We are not inviolable against their weapons,' Dak'ir countered. 'It is not only the Stratosans you risk with such a plan. What of my battle-brothers? Their duty ended in death. You would add more to that tally? Our resources are stretched thin enough as it is.'

Tsu'gan's face contorted with anger.

'Sons of Vulkan,' he cried, smacking the plastron of his power armour with his palms. 'Fire-born,' he added, clenching a fist, '*that* is what we are. Unto the Anvil of War, that is our creed. I do not fear battle and death, even if you do, Ignean.'

'I fear nothing,' snarled Dak'ir. 'But I won't cast my brothers into the furnace for no reason, either.'

'Enough!' The captain's voice demanded the attention of the bickering sergeants at once. Kadai glared at them both, eyes burning with fury at such disrespect for a fellow battle-brother. 'Dispense with this enmity,' he warned, exhaling his anger. 'It will not be tolerated. We have our enemy.'

The sergeants bowed apologetically, but stared daggers at each other before they stood down.

'There will be no massed assault,' Kadai reasserted. 'But that is not to say we will not act, either. These heretics are single-minded to the point of insanity, driven by some external force. No ideology, however fanatical, could impel such… madness,' he added, echoing Fugis's earlier theory. The corner of Kadai's mouth twinged in a brief moment of remembrance. 'The hierophant of the cult, this Speaker, is the key to victory on Stratos.'

'An assassination,' stated Tsu'gan, folding his arms in approval.

Kadai nodded.

'Brother Argos has discovered a structure at the heart of the temple district called Aura Hieron. Colonel Tonnhauser's intelligence has this demagogue there. We will make for it.' The captain's gaze encompassed the entire room. 'Two combat squads made up from the Devastators will be left behind with Brother Argos, who will be guiding us as before. This small force, together with the Thunderfire cannons, will hold Aereon Square and protect the emerging survivors.'

Tsu'gan scowled at this.

'Aereon Square is like a refugee camp as it is. The Aircorps cannot move the survivors fast enough. All they are doing is getting in our way. Our mission is to crush this horde, and free this place from terror. How can we do that if we split our forces protecting the humans? We should take every battle-brother we have.'

Kadai leaned forwards. His eyes were like fiery coals and seemed to chase away the cold light of the hololith.

'I will not abandon them, Tsu'gan. We are not the Marines Malevolent, nor the Flesh Tearers nor any of our other bloodthirsty brothers. Ours is a different creed, one of which we Salamanders are rightly proud. We will protect the innocent if–'

The *Fire Anvil* was rocked by a sudden tremor, and the dull *crump* of an explosion came through its armoured hull from the outside.

Brother Argos lowered the ramp at once and the Salamanders rushed outside to find out what had happened.

Fire and smoke lined a blackened crater in the centre of Aereon Square. The mangled corpses of several Stratosan civilians, together with a number of Aircorps were strewn within it, their bodies broken by a bomb blast. A woman screamed from the opposite side of the square. She'd fallen, having tried to flee from another of the survivors who was inexplicably clutching a frag grenade.

Tsu'gan's combi-bolter was in his hands almost immediately and he shot the man through the chest. The grenade fell from the insurgent's grasp and went off.

The fleeing woman and several others were engulfed by the explosion. The screaming intensified.

Kadai bellowed for order, even as his sergeants went to join their battle-brothers in quelling the sudden panic.

Several cultists had infiltrated the survivor groups, intent on causing anarchy and massed destruction. They had succeeded. Respirator masks were the perfect disguise for their 'afflictions', bypassing the Stratosan soldiery and even the Adeptus Astartes.

Ko'tan Kadai knelt with the broken woman in his grasp, having gone to her when the smoke was still dissipating from the explosion. She looked frail and thin compared to his Adeptus Astartes bulk, as if the rest of her unbroken bones would shatter at his slightest touch. Yet, they did not. He held her delicately, as a father might cradle a child. She lasted only moments, eyes fearful, spitting blood from massive internal trauma.

'Brother-captain?' ventured N'keln, appearing at his side.

Kadai laid the dead woman down gently and rose to his full height. A thin line of crimson dotted his ebon face, the horror there having ebbed away, replaced by anger.

'Two combat squads,' he asserted, his iron-hard gaze finding Tsu'gan, who was close enough to hear him, but wisely displayed no discontent. 'Everyone is screened… *Everyone.*'

'Now we know why the survivors came out of hiding. The cultists wanted them to, so they could do this…' Ba'ken said softly to Dak'ir as the two Salamanders looked on.

Kadai touched the blood on his face then saw it on his fingers as if for the first time.

'We need only get a kill-team close enough to the Speaker to execute him and the cultists' resolve will fracture,' he promised. 'We move out now.'

Five kilometres filled with razor wire, pit falls and partially demolished streets. Cultist murder squads dredging the ruins for survivors to torture; human bombers hiding in alcoves, trembling fingers wrapped around grenade pins; eviscerator priests leading flocks with wire-sewn mouths. It was the most expedient route Techmarine Argos could find in order for his battle-brothers to reach Aura Hieron.

Only two kilometres down that hellish road, after fighting through ambushes and weathering continual booby traps, the Salamanders' assault had reached yet another impasse.

They stood before a long but narrow esplanade of churned plascrete. Labyrinthine track traps were dug in every three or four metres, crowned with spools of razor wire. The bulky black carapaces of partially sub-merged mines shone dully like the backs of tunnelling insects. Death pits were excavated throughout, well-hidden with guerrilla cunning.

A killing field; and they had to cross it in order to reach Aura Hieron. At the end of it was a thick grey line of rockcrete bunkers, fortified with armour plates. From slits in the sides constant tracer fire rattled, accompanied by the throbbing *thud-chank* of heavy cannon. The no-man's-land was blanketed by fire that lit up the darkness in gruesome monochrome.

The Salamanders were not the first to have come this way. The corpses of Stratosan soldiers littered the ground too, as ubiquitous and lifeless as sandbags.

'There is no way around.' Dak'ir's reconnaissance report was curt, hav-ing tried, but failed, to find a different angle of attack to exploit. In such a narrow cordon, barely wide enough for ten Space Marines to operate in, the Salamanders' combat effectiveness was severely hampered.

Captain Kadai stared grimly into the maelstrom. The Inferno Guard and Sergeant Omkar's Devastators were at his side, awaiting their rota-tion at the front.

No more than fifty metres ahead of them Tsu'gan and his squad were hunkered down behind a cluster of tank traps returning fire, Sergeant Lok and his Devastators providing support with heavy bolters. Each painful metre had been paid for with blood, and three of Tsu'gan's troopers were already wounded, but he was determined to gain more ground and get close enough to launch an offensive with krak grenades.

The battle line was stretched. They had gone as far as they could go, short of risking massive casualties by charging the cultists' guns head on. The insurgents were so well protected they were only visible as shadows until their twisted faces were lit by muzzle flashes.

Kadai was scouring the battle line, searching for weaknesses.

'What did you find, sergeant?' he asked.

'Only impassable blockades and un-crossable chasms, stretching for kilometres east and west,' Dak'ir replied. 'We could turn back, captain, get Argos to find another route?'

'I've seen fortifications erected by the Imperial Fists that put up less resistance,' Kadai muttered to himself, then turned to Dak'ir. 'No. We break them here or not at all.'

Dak'ir was about to respond when Tsu'gan's voice came through the comm-feed.

'Captain, we can make five more metres. Requesting the order to advance.'

'Denied. Get back here, sergeant, and tell Lok to hold the line. We need a new plan.'

A momentary pause in communication made Tsu'gan's discontent obvious, but his respect for Kadai was absolute.

'At once, my lord.'

'We need to get close enough to attack the wall with krak grenades and breach it,' said Tsu'gan, having returned to the Salamanders' second line to join up with Dak'ir and Kadai, leaving Lok to hold the front. 'A determined frontal assault is the only way to do it.'

'A charge across the killing ground is insane, Tsu'gan,' countered Dak'ir.

'We are wasting our ammunition pinned here,' Tsu'gan argued. 'What else would you suggest?'

'There must be another way,' Dak'ir insisted.

'Withdraw,' Tsu'gan answered simply, allowing a moment for it to sink in. 'Loath as I am to do it. If we cannot break through, then Cirrion is lost. Withdraw and summon the *Fire-wyvern*,' he said to Kadai. 'Use its missile payload to destroy the gravitic engines and send this hellish place to the ocean.'

The captain was reticent to agree.

'I would be condemning thousands of innocents to death.'

'And saving millions,' urged Tsu'gan. 'If a world is tainted beyond redemption or lost to invasion we annihilate it, excising its stain from the galaxy like a cancer. It should be no different for a city. Stratos *can* be saved. Cirrion cannot.'

'You speak of wholesale slaughter as if it is a casual thing, Tsu'gan,' Kadai replied.

'Ours is a warrior's lot, my lord. We were made to fight and to kill, to bring order in the Emperor's name.'

Kadai's voice grew hard.

'I know our purpose, sergeant. Do not presume to tell me of it.'

Tsu'gan bowed humbly.

'I meant no offence, my lord.'

Kadai was angry because he knew that Tsu'gan was right. Cirrion *was* lost. Sighing deeply, he opened the comm-feed, extending the link beyond the city.

'We will need Brother Argos to engage the Stratosan failsafe and blow the sky-bridges connecting Cirrion first, or it will take an entire chunk of the adjacent cities with it,' he said out loud to himself, before reverting to the comm-feed.

'Brother Hek'en.'

The pilot of the *Fire-wyvern* responded. The Thunderhawk was at rest on the landing platform just outside Nimbaros.

'My lord.'

'Prepare for imminent take off, and prime hellstrike missiles. We're abandoning the city. You'll have my orders within—'

The comm-feed crackling to life again in Kadai's battle-helm interrupted him. The crippling interference made it difficult to discern a voice at first, but when Kadai recognised it he felt his hot Salamanders blood grow cold.

It was Fugis. The Apothecary was alive.

'I blacked out after the fall. When I awoke I was in the sub-levels of the city. They stretch down for about two kilometres, deep enough for the massive lifter-engines. It's like a damn labyrinth,' Fugis explained with his usual choler.

'Are you injured, brother?' asked Kadai.

Silence persisted, laced with static, and for a moment he thought they'd lost the Apothecary again.

'I took some damage, my battle-helm too. It's taken me this long to repair the comm-feed,' Fugis returned at last. In the short pauses it was possible to hear his breathing. It was irregular and ragged. The Apothecary was trying to mask his pain.

'What is your exact location, Fugis?'

Static interference marred the connection again.

'It's a tunnel complex below the surface. But it could be anywhere.'

Kadai turned to Dak'ir. 'Contact Brother Argos. Have him lock on to Fugis's signal and send us the coordinates.'

Dak'ir nodded and set about his task. All the while heavy cannon were chugging overhead.

'Listen,' said Fugis, the crackling static worsening, 'I am not alone. There are civilians. They fled down here when the attacks began, and stayed hidden until now.'

There was another short silence as the Apothecary considered his next statement.

'The city is still not ours.'

Kadai explained the situation with the hydrogen gas amalgam on the surface, how they could not use their flamers or meltas, and that it only compounded the fact that the cultists were well-prepared and dug in. 'It is almost as if they know our tactics,' he concluded.

'The gas has not penetrated this deep,' Fugis told him. 'But I may have a way to stop it.'

'How, brother?' asked Kadai, fresh hope filling his voice.

'A human engineer. Some of the refugees were fleeing from the gas as well as the insurgents. His name is Banen. If we get him out of the city and to the Techmarine, Cirrion can be purged.' A pregnant pause suggested an imminent sting. 'But there is a price,' Fugis explained through bursts of interference.

Kadai's jaw clenched beneath his battle-helm.

*There always is…*

The Apothecary went on.

'In order to cleanse Cirrion of the gas, the entire air supply must be vented. Its atmospheric integrity will be utterly compromised. With the air so thin, many will suffocate before it can be restored. Humans hiding in the outer reaches of the city, away from the hot core of the lifter-engines, will also likely freeze to death.'

Kadai's brief optimism was quickly crushed.

'To save Cirrion, I must doom its people.'

'Some may survive,' offered Fugis, though his words lacked conviction.

'A few at best,' Kadai concluded. 'It is no choice.'

Destroying the city's gravitic engines had been bad enough. This seemed worse. The Salamanders, a Chapter who prided themselves on their humanitarianism, their pledge to protect the weak and the innocent, were merely exchanging one holocaust for another.

Kadai gripped the haft of his thunder hammer. It was black, and its head was thick and heavy like the ready tool of a forgesmith. He had fashioned it this way in the depths of Nocturne, the lava flows from the mountain casting his onyx flesh in an orange glow. Kadai longed to return there, to the anvil and the heat of the forge. The hammer was a symbol. It was like the weapon Vulkan had first taken up in defence of his adopted homeworld. In it Kadai found resolve and, in turn, the strength he needed to do what he must.

'We are coming for you, brother,' he said with steely determination. 'Protect the engineer. Have him ready to be extracted upon our arrival.'

'I will hold on as long as I can.'

White noise resumed.

Kadai felt the weight of resignation around his shoulders like a heavy mantle.

'Brother Argos has locked the signal and fed it to our auspex,' Dak'ir told him, wresting the Salamanders captain from his dark reverie.

Kadai nodded grimly.

'Sergeants, break into combat squads. The rest stay here,' he said, summoning his second in command.

'N'keln,' Kadai addressed the veteran sergeant. 'You will lead the expedition to rescue Fugis.'

Tsu'gan interjected.

'My lord?'

'Once we make a move the insurgents will almost certainly redirect their forces away from here. We cannot hold them by merely standing our ground,' Kadai explained. 'We need their attention fixed where we want it. I intend to achieve that by charging the wall.'

'Captain, that is suicide,' Dak'ir told him plainly.

'Perhaps. But I cannot risk bringing the enemy to Fugis, to the human engineer. His survival is of the utmost importance. Self-sacrifice is the Promethean way, sergeant, you know that.'

'With respect, captain,' said N'keln. 'Brother Malicant and I wish to stay behind and fight with the others.'

Malicant, the company banner bearer, nodded solemnly behind the veteran sergeant.

Both Salamanders had been wounded in the ill-fated campaign to liberate Cirrion. Malicant leaned heavily on the company banner from a leg wound he had sustained during the bomb blast in Aereon Square, whereas N'keln grimaced with the pain of his crushed ribs.

Kadai was incensed.

'You disobey my orders, sergeant?'

N'keln stood his ground despite his captain's ire.

'Yes, my lord.'

Kadai glared at him, but his anger bled away as he realised the sense in the veteran sergeant's words and clasped N'keln by the shoulder.

'Hold off as long as you can. Advance only when you must, and strike swiftly. You may yet get past the guns unscathed,' Kadai told him. 'You honour the Chapter with your sacrifice.'

N'keln rapped his fist against his plastron in salute and then he and Malicant went to join the others already at the battle line.

'Make it an act of honour,' he said to the others as they watched the two Salamanders go. They were singular warriors. All his battle-brothers were. Kadai was intensely proud of each and every one. 'Fugis is waiting. Into the fires of battle, brothers...'

'Unto the anvil of war,' they declared solemnly as one.

The Salamanders turned away without looking back, leaving their brothers to their fate.

The tunnels were deserted.

Ba'ken tracked his heavy bolter across the darkness, his battle-senses ultra-heightened with tension.

'Too quiet…'

'You would prefer a fight?' Dak'ir returned over the comm-feed.

'Yes,' Ba'ken answered honestly.

The sergeant was a few metres in front of him, the Salamanders having broken into two long files on either side of the tunnel. Each Space Marine maintained a distance of a few metres from the battle-brother ahead, watching his back and flanks in case of ambush. Helmet luminators strafed the darkened corridors, creating imagined hazards in the gathered shadows.

The Salamanders had followed the Apothecary's signal like a beacon. It had led them south at first, back the way they had come, to a hidden entrance into the Cirrion sub-levels. The tunnels were myriad and did not appear on any city schematic, so Argos had no knowledge of them. The private complex of passageways and bunkers was reserved for the Stratosan aristocracy. Portals set in the tunnel walls slid open with a ghosting of released pressure and fed off into opulent rooms, their furnishings undisturbed and layered with dust. Reinforced vaults lay unsecured and unguarded, their treasures still untouched within. Several chambers were jammed with machinery hooked up to cryogenic flotation tanks. Purple bacteria contaminated the stagnant gel-solutions within. Decomposed bodies, bloated with putrefaction, were slumped against the glass, their suspended existence ended when the power in Cirrion had failed.

Kadai raised his hand from up ahead and the Salamanders stopped.

Nearby, one step in the chain from Tsu'gan, Iagon consulted his auspex.

'Bio-readings fifty metres ahead,' he hissed through the comm-feed.

The *thud-chank* of bolters being primed filled the narrow space.

Kadai lowered his hand and the Salamanders slowly began to proceed, closing up as they went. They had yet to meet any cultist resistance, but that didn't mean it wasn't there.

Dak'ir heard something move up ahead, like metal scraping metal.

'*Hammer!*' a voice cried out of the dark, accompanied by the sound of a bolt-round filling its weapon's breech.

'*Anvil!*' Kadai replied with the other half of the code, and lowered his pistol.

Twenty metres farther on, a wounded Salamander was slumped against a bulkhead, his outstretched bolt pistol falling slowly.

The relief in Kadai's voice was palpable.

'Stand down. It's Fugis. We've got him.'

Banen stepped from the shadows with the small band of survivors. Short and unassuming, he wore a leather apron and dirty overalls that bulged with his portly figure. A pair of goggles framed his grease-smeared pate.

He didn't look like a man with the power to wipe out a city.

The gravitas of the decision facing Kadai was not lost on him as he regarded the human engineer.

'You can vent the atmosphere in Cirrion, cleanse the city of the gas?'

'Y-yes, milord.' The stammer only made the human seem more innocuous.

The Salamanders formed a protective cordon around the bulkhead where Fugis and the survivors were holed up, bolters trained outwards. The Apothecary's leg was broken, but he was at least still conscious, though in no condition to fight. With the discovery of the Apothecary an eerie silence had descended on the tunnel complex, as if the air was holding its breath.

Salamanders encircling them, Kadai stared down at Banen.

*I will be signing the death warrant of thousands...*

'Escort them back to Aereon Square,' he said to Brother Ba'ken. 'Commence the cleansing of the city as soon as possible.'

Ba'ken saluted. The Salamanders were breaking up their defensive formation when the held breath rushed back.

A few metres farther down the tunnel, a lone insurgent dropped down from a ceiling hatch, a grenade clutched in her thin fingers.

Bolters roared, loud and throaty down the corridor, shredding the cultist. The grenade went up in the fusillade, the explosion sweeping out in a firestorm. The Salamanders met it without hesitation, shielding the terrified humans with their armoured bodies.

Hundreds of footsteps clattered down to them from the darkness up ahead.

'Battle positions!' shouted Kadai.

A ravening mob of insurgents rounded the corner. Further hatchways in the walls and ceilings suddenly broke open as cultists piled out like fat lice crawling from the cracks.

Kadai levelled his pistol.

'Salamanders! Unleash death!'

A team of cultists brought up an autocannon. Dak'ir raked them with bolter fire before they could set it.

'Iagon...' shouted Tsu'gan over the raucous battle din.

'Atmosphere normal, sir,' the other Salamander replied, knowing precisely what was on his sergeant's mind.

Tsu'gan bared his teeth in a feral smile.

'Cleanse and burn,' he growled, and the flamer attached to his combi-bolter roared.

Liquid promethium ignited on contact with the air as a superheated wave of fire spewed hungrily down the corridor.

Shen'kar intensified the conflagration with his own flamer. The cultists were obliterated in the blaze, their bodies becoming slowly collapsing shadows behind the shimmering heat haze.

It lasted merely seconds. Smoke and charred remains were all that was left when the flames finally died down. Dozens of insurgents had been destroyed; some were little more than ash and bone.

'The fury of fire will win this war for the Salamanders,' said Fugis, as the Astartes were readying to split their forces once again. Ba'ken supported the Apothecary and was standing with the others that would be returning to Aereon Square.

Kadai was adamant that Fugis and the human survivors be given all the protection he could afford them. If that meant stretching his Salamanders thinly, then so be it. The captain would press on with only Tsu'gan, Dak'ir, Company Champion Vek'shen and Honoured Brother Shen'kar as retinue. The rest were going back.

'I am certain of it,' Kadai replied, facing him. 'But at the cost of thousands. I only hope the price is worth it, old friend.'

'Is any price ever worth it?' Fugis asked.

The Apothecary was no longer talking about Cirrion. A bitter remembrance flared in Kadai's mind and he crushed it.

'Send word when you've reached Aereon Square and the gas has been purged. We'll be waiting here until then.'

Fugis nodded, though it gave the Apothecary some pain to do so.

'In the name of Vulkan,' he said, saluting.

Kadai echoed him, rapping his plastron. The Apothecary gave him a final consolatory look before he had Ba'ken help him away. It gave Kadai little comfort as he thought of the thousands of innocents still in the city and their ignorance of what was soon to befall them, a fate made by his own hand.

'Emperor, forgive me...' he whispered softly, watching the Salamanders go.

Aura Hieron hung open like a carcass. It had been austerely beautiful once, much like the rest of Cirrion, stark silver alloyed with cold marble. Now it was an abattoir-temple. Blood slicked its walls, seeping down into the cracks of the intricate mosaic floor. Broken columns punctuated a high outer wall that ran around the temple's vast ambit. Statues set in shadowy alcoves had been beheaded or smeared in filth, their pale immortality defaced.

Crude sigils, exulting in the dark glory of the Cult of Truth, were daubed upon the stonework. A black altar, re-fashioned with jagged knives and stained with blood, dominated a cracked dais at the back of the chamber. Metal spars ripped from the structure of Cirrion's underbelly had been dragged bodily into the temple, tearing ragged grooves in the tarnished marble. Blackened corpses, the remains of loyal Stratosans, were hung upon them as offerings to the Chaos gods. A shrine to the Emperor of Mankind no longer, Aura Hieron was a haven for the corrupt now, where only the damned came to worship.

Nihilan revelled in the temple's debasement as he regarded the instrument of his malicious will from afar.

'We should not be here, sorcerer. We have what we came for,' rasped a voice from the shadows, redolent of smoke and ash.

'Our purpose here is two-fold, Ramlek,' Nihilan replied, his cadence grating. 'We have only achieved the first half.' The renegade Dragon Warrior overlooked the bloodied plaza of Aura Hieron from a blackened anteroom above its only altar. He was watching the Speaker keenly, beguiling and persuading the cultist masses basking in his unnatural aura with his dark-tongued rhetoric.

The brand Nihilan had seared into the hierophant's flesh over three months ago, when the Dragon Warriors had first come to Stratos, had spread well. It infected almost his entire face. The seed the sorcerer had embedded there would be reaching maturation.

'A life for a life, Ramlek. You know that. Is Ghor'gan prepared?'

'He is,' rasped the horned warrior.

Nihilan smiled thinly. The scar tissue on his face pulled tight with the rare muscular use. 'Our enemies will be arriving soon,' he hissed, psychic power crackling over his clenched fist, 'then we will have vengeance.'

Eyes like mirrored glass stared out from beneath a mausoleum archway, no longer seeing, unblinking in mortality. Tiny ice crystals flecked the dead man's lips and encumbered his eyelids so they drooped in mock lethargy. The poor wretch was arched awkwardly across a stone tomb, his head slack and lifeless as it hung backwards over the edge.

He was not alone. Throughout the temple district, citizens and insurgents alike lay dead, their breath and their life stolen away when the atmospheric processors had vented. Some held one another in a final desperate embrace, accepting of their fate; others fought, fingers clutched around their throats as they tried in vain to fill their lungs.

The ruins of the temple district were disturbingly silent. It was oddly appropriate. The quietude fell like a shroud over broken monoliths and solemn chapels, acres of cemeteries punctuated with mausoleums, sepulchres and hooded statues bent in sombre remembrance.

'So much death…' uttered Dak'ir, reminded of another place decades ago, and glanced to his captain. Kadai seemed to bear it all stoically, but Dak'ir could tell it was affecting him.

The Salamanders had passed through the city unchallenged, plying along the subterranean roads of the private tunnel complex. Though he had no map of the underground labyrinth, Techmarine Argos had extrapolated a route based on the position of the hidden entrance and his battle-brothers' visual reports, relayed to him as they progressed through its dingy confines. After an hour of trawling through the narrow dark, the Salamanders had emerged from a shadowy egress to be confronted with the solemnity of the temple district.

Kadai had told his retinue to expect resistance. Truthfully, he would have welcomed it. Anything to distract him from the terrible act he had been forced to commit against the citizens of Cirrion. But it was not to be – the Salamanders had passed through the white gates of the temple district without incident, yet the reminders of Kadai's act lurked in every alcove, in each darkened bolthole of the city.

Mercifully, Fugis and the others had arrived at Aereon Square without hindrance. Kadai was emotionally ambivalent when the Apothecary's communication had reached him over the comm-feed. It was a double-edged sword, salvation with a heavy tariff – annihilation for Cirrion's people.

'Aura Hieron lies half a kilometre to the north,' the metallic voice of Argos grated over the comm-feed, dispelling further introspection.

'I see it,' Kadai returned flatly.

He cut the link with the Techmarine, instead addressing his retinue.

'The people of Cirrion paid for a chance to end this war with their lives. Let us not leave them wanting. It ends this day, one way or the other. On my lead, brothers. In the name of Vulkan.'

Ahead, the temple of Aura Hieron loomed like a skeletal hand grasping at a pitch black sky.

Dak'ir crept through the darkened alcoves of the temple's west wall. Opposite him, across the tenebrous gulf of the temple's nave, Tsu'gan stalked along the other flanking wall.

Edging down the centre, obscured by shattered columns and the debris from Aura Hieron's collapsed roof, was Kadai and the rest of his retinue. They kept low and quiet, despite their power armour, and closed swiftly on their target.

Ahead of them cultists thronged in hundreds, respirators fixed over their sewn mouths, prostrate before their vile hierophant. The Speaker was perched on a marble dais and clad in dirty blue robes like his congregation of the depraved. Unlike the wire-mouthed acolytes abasing themselves before him, the Speaker was not mute. Far from it. A writhing purple tongue extruded from his distended maw, the teeth within just blackened nubs. The wretched appendage twisted and lashed as if sentient. Inscrutable dogma spewed from the Speaker's mouth, its form and language inflected by the daemonic tongue. Even the sound of his words gnawed at Dak'ir's senses and he shut them out, recognising the mutation for what it was – Chaos taint. It explained at once how this disaffected Stratosan native, who, up until a few months ago, had been little more than a petty firebrand, had managed to cajole such unswerving loyalty, and in such masses.

Surrounding the hierophant was the elite of those fanatical troops, a ring of eight eviscerator priests, kneeling with their chainblades laid out in front of them in ceremony.

* * *

It left a bitter tang in Tsu'gan's mouth to witness such corruption. Whatever foul rite these degenerate scum were planning, the Salamanders would end with flame and blade. He felt the zeal burn in his breast, and wished dearly that he was with his captain advancing down the very throat of the enemy and not here guarding shadows.

Let the Ignean skulk at the periphery, he thought. I am destined for more glorious deeds.

A garbled cry arrested Tsu'gan's arrogant brooding. Spewing an unintelligible diatribe, the Speaker gestured frantically towards Kadai and the other two Salamanders emerging from their cover to destroy him. His craven followers reacted with eerie synchronicity to their master's warning, and surged towards the trio of interlopers murderously.

Shen'kar opened up his flamer and burned down a swathe of maddened cultists with a war cry on his lips. Vek'shen charged into the wake of the blaze, the conflagration having barely ebbed, fire-glaive swinging. The master-crafted blade reaped a terrible harvest of sheared limbs and heads, spurts of incendiary immolating bodies with every flame-wreathed strike.

Kadai was like a relentless storm, and Tsu'gan's warrior heart sang to witness such prowess and fury. Channelling his fiery rage, the captain tore a ragged hole through one of the eviscerator priests with his inferno pistol, before crushing the skull of another with his thunder hammer.

As the wretched deacon went down, his head pulped, Kadai gave the signal and enfilading bolter fire barked from the alcoves as Tsu'gan and Dak'ir let rip.

As cultists fell, shot apart by his furious salvos, Tsu'gan could contain his battle lust no longer. He would not be left here like some sentry. He wanted to be at his captain's side, and look into his enemy's eyes as he slew them. Dak'ir could hold the perimeter well enough without his aid. In any case, the enemy was here amassed for slaughter.

Roaring an oath to Vulkan, Tsu'gan left his post and waded into the battle proper.

Dak'ir caught sight of Tsu'gan's muzzle flare and cursed loudly when he realised he had abandoned his orders and left the wall deserted. Debating whether to press the attack himself, his attention was arrested when he noticed Kadai, having bludgeoned his way through the mob, standing scant metres from the Speaker and levelling his inferno pistol.

'In the name of Vulkan!' he bellowed, about to end the threat of the Cult of Truth forever, when a single shot thundered above the carnage and the Speaker fell, his head half-destroyed by an explosive round.

Kadai felt the meat and blood of the executed Speaker spatter his armour, and started to lower his pistol out of shock. A strange lull fell over the fighting, enemies poised in mid-attack, that didn't feel entirely natural as the Salamanders captain traced the source of the shot.

Above him there was a parapet overlooking the temple's nave. Kadai's gaze was fixed upon it as a figure in blood-red power armour emerged from the gathered shadows, a smoking bolt pistol in his grasp.

Scales bedecked this warrior's battle-plate, like those of some primordial lizard from an archaic age. His gauntlets were fashioned like claws, with long vermillion talons, and eldritch lightning rippled across them in crackling ruby arcs. In one he clutched a staff, a roaring dragon's head at its tip rendered in silver; in the other his bolt pistol, which he returned to its holster. Broad pauldrons sat like hardened scale shells on the warrior's shoulders, a horn curving from each. He wore no battle-helm, and bore horrific facial scars openly. Fire had blighted this warrior's once noble countenance, twisting it, devouring it and remaking his visage into one of puckered tissue, angry wheals and exposed bone. It was the face of death, hideous and accusing.

A chill entered Kadai's spine as if he was suddenly drowning in ice. The spectre before him was a ghost, an apparition that died long ago in terrible agony. Yet, here it was in flesh and blood, called back from the grave like some vengeful revenant.

'Nihilan...'

'Captain,' the apparition replied, his voice cracked like dry earth baked beneath a remorseless sun, burning red eyes aglow.

Kadai's posture stiffened as the shock quickly passed, subjugated by righteous anger.

'Renegade,' he snarled.

Wracking pain gripped Dak'ir's chest as he beheld the warrior and was wrenched back into the otherworld of his dream...

*The temple faded as the grey sky of Moribar engulfed all. Bone-monoliths surged into that endless steel firmament, ossuary paths stretched into endless tracts of cemeteries, mausoleum fields and sepulchral vales. Through legions of tombs, across phalanxes of crypts, along battalions of reliquaries sunk in earthen catacombs, Dak'ir followed the grave-road until he reached its terminus.*

*And there beneath the cold damp earth, boiling, burning, its lambent glow neither warm nor inviting, was the vast churning furnace of the crematoria.*

*Pain lanced Dak'ir's body as the vision changed. He gripped his chest, but no longer felt his black carapace. He was a Scout once more, observing from the edge of the crematoria, the massive pit of fire large enough to swallow a Titan, burning, ever burning, down into the molten heart of Moribar.*

*Dak'ir saw two Astartes clambering at the edge of that portal to fiery death. Nihilan clung desperately to Captain Ushorak, his black power armour pitted and cracked with the intense heat emanating from below.*

*The terrible conflagration was in turmoil. It bubbled explosively, plumes of lava spearing the air in fiery cascades, when a huge pillar of flame tore from the crematoria. Dak'ir shielded his eyes as a massive fire wall obliterated the warriors from view.*

*Strong hands grasped Dak'ir's shoulder and wrenched him away from the blaze as the renegades they had come to bring to justice, not to kill, were immolated. Barely visible through the solid curtain of flame, Nihilan was screaming as his face burned...*

Dak'ir lurched back to the present, a sickening vertigo threatening to overwhelm him, and he reached out to steady himself. He tasted blood in his mouth and black spots marred his vision. Tearing off his battle-helm, he struggled to breathe.

Somewhere in the temple, someone was speaking...

'You died,' Kadai accused, looking up at the warrior on the parapet. He fought the invisible pressure stopping him from striking the renegade down, but his arms were leaden.

'I survived,' returned Nihilan, the effort to maintain the psychic dampening that held the battle in stasis against the Salamander's will creasing his scarred face.

'You should have faced justice, not death,' Kadai told him, then smiled vindictively. 'Overloading the crematoria, stirring up the volatile core of Moribar, you provoked it in order to escape and kill me and my brothers into the bargain. Ushorak's destruction was your doing, yours *and* his.'

'Don't you speak of him!' cried Nihilan, red lightning coursing through his eyes and clenched fists, writhing around his force staff and spitting off in jagged arcs. Exhaling fury, the Dragon Warrior recovered his composure. '*You* are the murderer here, Kadai – a petty marshal who'd do anything to catch his quarry. But perhaps you're right... I did die, and was *reborn.*'

Kadai raised his inferno pistol a fraction. Nihilan's grip was loosening. He was readying for it to slip completely, and slay the traitor where he stood, when the Speaker's body started to convulse.

'It doesn't matter any more,' the Dragon Warrior added, stepping back into the shadows of the parapet. 'Not for you...'

Kadai fired off his inferno pistol, melting away a chunk of parapet as Nihilan released his psychic hold. The Salamander was about to chase after him when a terrible aura enveloped the Speaker, lifting his prone corpse inexplicably so that it dangled just above the ground like meat on an invisible hook.

Slowly, agonisingly slowly, he raised his chin to reveal a ruined face destroyed by the bolt pistol's explosive round. Slick red flesh, wrapped partially around a bloody skull, shimmered in the ambient light. What remained of the Speaker's cranium was split open like an egg. Luminous cobalt skin was revealed beneath. Cracking bone gave way to a leering visage called forth from a dark unreality as something... *unnatural...* pulled itself forth into the material plane.

A lidless eye of fulgent black glared with otherworldly malevolence. The eight-pointed star, once burned into the Speaker's forehead, was now glowing upon this new horror. It was raw and vital, pulsing like a wretched heart as the warp-thing grew hideously. Bulbous protrusions tore from mortal flesh, spilling out with thickets of spines. Fingers splayed as if pulled taut by unseen threads, talons rupturing from them, long, sharp and black. The thing's distended maw, in mimicry of the Speaker's original mutation, stretched further and wider until it was a terrible lipless chasm, the lashing tongue within three-pronged and spiked with bloodied bone.

Cultists shrieked in fear and adoration as the Speaker's corpse was possessed. Eviscerator priests pledged their mute allegiance, turning their chainblades towards the Salamanders once again.

The creature was primal, wrenched from ethereal slumber and only partially sentient, a deep soul-hunger driving it. Roaring in fury and anguish, it surged forwards, devouring a pair of eviscerator priests closing on Kadai. Like some terrible basilisk, it consumed them whole, bones crunching audibly as it dragged the prey down its bulging gullet.

'Abomination...' Kadai breathed, gripping the haft of his thunder hammer as he prepared to smite the daemon. Nihilan had given his soul over to the dark powers now, and this was but a taste of his malfeasance.

'Die, hell-beast!' cried Vek'shen, stepping between his captain and the unbound daemon. Whirling his fire-glaive in a blazing arc, the Company Champion crafted an overhand blow that would've felled an ork warlord. The daemon met it with its talons and the glaive was held fast. Its tongue slid like lightning from its abyssal mouth, oozing swiftly around Vek'shen's power-armoured form. The Salamander gaped in a silent scream, breath pressed violently from his body, as he was crushed to death.

Kadai roared, launching himself at the beast, even as his battle-brother's flaccid corpse, dented where the daemon's tongue had clutched him, crashed to the ground.

Dak'ir was recovering his senses. Though he hadn't seen how, the Speaker was dead, shot in the back of the head, his body lying at Kadai's feet. It wasn't all that he'd missed while he was under the influence of his memory-dream. In the time it had taken for his Adeptus Astartes constitution and training to override the lingering nausea the remembrance had caused, Nihilan was already retreating into the shadows. Leaving his flank position, Dak'ir ran towards the nave determined to pursue, when a swathe of cultists impeded him.

'Tsu'gan!' he cried, gutting an insurgent with his chainsword and firing his bolter one-handed to explode the face of another, 'Stop the renegade!'

The other Salamander nodded in a rare moment of empathy and sped off after Nihilan.

Dak'ir was battling through the frenzied mob when he saw the Speaker's corpse rising and felt the touch of the warp prickle his skin…

Tsu'gan bolted across the nave, pummelling cultists with his fists, chewing up packed groups with explosive bursts of fire. Shen'kar was just visible in his peripheral vision, immolating swathes of the heretical vermin with bright streaks of flame.

Smashing through a wooden door at the back of the temple, Tsu'gan found a flight of stone steps leading up to the parapet. He took them three at a time with servo-assisted bounds of his power-armoured legs, until he emerged into a darkened anteroom.

Something was happening below. He heard Vek'shen bellow a call to arms and then nothing, as if all sound had fled in a sudden vacuum.

Burning red eyes regarded him coldly in the blackness.

'Tsu'gan…' said Nihilan, emerging from the dark.

'Traitorous scum!' the Salamander raged.

But Tsu'gan didn't raise his bolter to fire, didn't vanquish the renegade where he stood. He merely remained transfixed, muscles clenched as if held fast in amber.

'Wha–' he began, but found his tongue was leaden too.

'Sorcery,' Nihilan told him, the surface of his force staff alive with incandescent energy. It threw ephemeral flashes of light into the gloom, illuminating the sorcerer's dread visage as he closed on the stricken Astartes.

'I could kill you right now,' he said levelly. 'Snuff out the light in your eyes, and kill you, just like Kadai killed Ushorak.'

'You were offered redemption.' Tsu'gan struggled to fashion the retort, forcing his tongue into compliance through sheer willpower.

The sinister cast to Nihilan's face bled away and was replaced by indignation.

'Redemption was it? Spiritual castigation at the hands of Elysius, a few hours with his chirurgeon-interrogators, is that what was offered?' He laughed mirthlessly. 'That sadistic bastard would only have passed a guilty judgement.'

Stepping closer, Nihilan took on a sincere tone.

'Ushorak offered life. Power,' he breathed. 'Freedom from the shackles forcing us to serve the cattle of men, when we should be ruling them.'

The Dragon Warrior clenched his fist as he said it, so close now that Tsu'gan could smell his copper breath.

'You see, *brother*. We are not so dissimilar.'

'We are nothing alike, traitor,' snapped the Salamander, grimacing with the simple effort of speaking.

Nihilan stepped back, spreading his arms plaintively.

'A bolter shot to the head to end my heresy then?' His upturned lip showed his displeasure. 'Or stripped of rank, a penitent brand in place of my service studs?'

He shook his head.

'No... I think not. Perhaps I will brand you, though, *brother*.' Nihilan showed the Salamander his palm and spread his fingers wide. 'Would your resistance to corruption be stauncher than the human puppet, I wonder?'

Tsu'gan flinched before Nihilan's approach, expecting at any moment for all the turpitude of Chaos to spew forth from his hand.

'Cull your fear,' Nihilan rasped, making a fist as he sneered.

'I fear nothing,' barked Tsu'gan.

Nihilan sniffed contemptuously. 'You fear everything, Salamander.'

Tsu'gan felt his boots scraping against the floor as he was psychically impelled towards the edge of the parapet against his will.

'Enough talk,' he spat. 'Cast me down. Break my body, if you must. The Chapter will hunt you, renegade, and there will be no chance of redemption for you this time.'

Nihilan regarded him as an adult would a simple child.

'You still don't understand, do you?'

Slowly, Tsu'gan's body rotated so that he could see out onto the battle below.

Cultists fell in their droves, burned down by Shen'kar's flamer, or eviscerated by Dak'ir's chain-sword. His brothers fought tooth and nail, fending off the horde whilst his beloved captain fought for his life.

Kadai's artificer armour was rent in over a dozen places, a daemon-thing that wore the flesh of the Speaker assailing him. Talons like long slashes of night came down in a rain of blows against the Salamanders captain's defence, but he weathered it all, carving great arcs in riposte with his thunder hammer. Vulkan's name was on his lips as the lightning cracked from the head of his master-forged weapon, searing the daemon's borrowed flesh.

'I was devoted to Ushorak, just as you are to your captain...' Nihilan uttered in Tsu'gan's ear as he watched the battle with the hell-spawn unfold.

Kadai smashed the daemon's shoulder, shattering bone, and its arm fell limp.

'Kadai killed him,' Nihilan continued. 'He forced us to seek solace in the Eye. There we fled and there we stayed for decades...'

Ichor hissed from the tears in the daemon's earthly form, its hold on reality slipping as Kadai punished it relentlessly with fist and hammer.

'Time moves differently in that realm. For us it felt like centuries had passed before we found a way out.'

A chorus of screams ripped from the distended throat of the daemon-thing, as Kadai crushed its skull finally and banished it back into the warp, the souls it had consumed begging for succour.

'It *changed* me. Opened my eyes. I see much now. A great destiny awaits you, Tsu'gan, but another overshadows it.' Nihilan gave the faintest inclination of his head towards Dak'ir.

The Ignean was fighting valiantly, cutting down the last of the cultists and heading for Kadai.

'Even now he rushes to your captain's side...' Nihilan said, insidiously, 'Hoping to gain his favour.'

Tsu'gan knew he could not trust the foul tongue of a traitor, but the words spoken echoed his own long-held suspicions.

And so, unbeknownst to the Salamander, Nihilan *did* plant a seed. Not one born of daemonic essence. No, this came about through petty jealousy and ambition, through the very thing Tsu'gan had no aegis against – himself.

'This cult,' the Dragon Warrior pressed. 'It is *nothing*. Stratos is nothing. Even this city is meaningless. It was always about *him*.'

Kadai was leaning heavily on his thunder hammer, weakened after vanquishing the daemon.

Nihilan smiled, scarred flesh creaking.

'A captain for a captain...'

Realisation slid like a cold blade into Tsu'gan's gut.

Too late he saw the armoured shadow closing in. The Dragon Warriors springing their trap at last. By leaving his post, he had let them infiltrate the Salamanders' guard. The cultists were only ever a distraction; the true enemy was only now revealing itself.

He had been a fool.

'No!'

Sheer force of will broke Nihilan's psychic hold. Roaring the captain's name, Tsu'gan leapt off the parapet.

Hoarse laughter followed him all the way down.

Dak'ir had almost reached Kadai when he saw the renegade hefting the multi-melta. Shouting a warning, he raced to his captain's side. Kadai faced him, hearing the cry of Tsu'gan from above at the same time, and then followed Dak'ir's agonised gaze...

An incandescent beam tore out of the darkness.

Kadai was struck, and his body immolated in an actinic flare.

An intense rush of heat smashed Dak'ir off his feet, backwash from the terrible melta blast. He smelled scorched flesh. A hot spike of agony tortured his senses. His face was burning, just like in the dream...

Dak'ir realised he was blacking out, his body shutting down as his sus-an membrane registered the gross trauma he had suffered. Dimly, as if buried alive and listening through layered earth, he heard the voice of Sergeant N'keln and his battle-brothers. Dak'ir managed to turn his head. The last thing he saw before unconsciousness claimed him was

Tsu'gan slumped to his knees in front of the charred remains of their captain.

When Dak'ir awoke he was laid out in the Apothecarion of the *Vulkan's Wrath*. It was cold as a tomb inside the austere chamber, the gloom alleviated by the lit icons of the medical apparatus around him.

With waking came remembrance, and with remembrance, grief and despair.

Kadai was dead.

'Welcome back, brother,' a soft voice said. Fugis was thin-faced and gaunter than ever, as he loomed over Dak'ir.

Emotional agony was compounded by physical pain and Dak'ir reached for his face as it started to burn anew.

Fugis seized his wrist before he could touch it.

'I wouldn't do that,' he warned the sergeant. 'Your skin was badly burned. You're healing, but the flesh is still very tender.'

Dak'ir lowered his arm as Fugis released him. The Apothecary injected a solution of drugs through an intravenous drip-feed to ease the pain.

Dak'ir relaxed as the suppressants went to work, catalysing his body's natural regenerative processes.

'What happened?' His throat felt raw and abrasive, and he croaked the words. Fugis stepped away from Dak'ir's medi-slab to check on the instrumentation. He limped as he walked, a temporary augmetic frame fitted over his leg to shore up the break he had sustained in his fall. Stubborn to the point of bloody-mindedness, nothing would prevent the Apothecary from doing his work.

'Stratos is saved,' he said simply, his back to the other Salamander. 'With the Speaker dead and our flamers restored, the insurgents fell quickly. The storms lifted an hour after we returned to Aereon Square,' he explained. 'Librarian Pyriel arrived twenty minutes later with the rest of the company to reinforce N'keln, who had taken the wall and was already en route to Aura Hieron…'

'But too late to save Kadai,' Dak'ir finished for him.

Fugis stopped what he was doing and gripped the instrumentation panel he'd been consulting for support.

'Yes. Even his gene-seed was unsalvageable.'

A long grief-filled silence crept insidiously into the room before the Apothecary continued.

'A ship, Stormbird-class, left the planet but we were too late to give chase.'

The rancour in Dak'ir's voice could have scarred metal.

'Nihilan and the other renegades escaped.'

'To Vulkan knows where,' Fugis replied, facing the patient. 'Librarian Pyriel has command of Third Company, until Chapter Master Tu'Shan can appoint someone permanent.'

Dak'ir frowned.

'We're going home?'

'Our tour of the Hadron Belt is over. We are returning to Prometheus to reinforce and lick our wounds.'

'My face...' Dak'ir ventured after a long silence. 'I want to see it.'

'Of course,' said Fugis, and showed the Salamander a mirror.

Part of Dak'ir's facial tissue had been seared away. Almost half of his onyx-black skin had been bleached near-white by the voracious heat of the melta flare. Though raw and angry, it looked almost human.

'A reaction to the intense radiation,' Fugis explained. 'The damage has resulted in minor cellular regression, reverting to a form prior to the genetic ebonisation of your skin when you became an Astartes. I cannot say for certain yet, but it shows no sign of immediate regeneration.'

Dak'ir stared, lost in his own reflection and the semblance of human-ness there. Fugis arrested the Salamander's reverie.

'I'll leave you in peace, such as it is,' he said, taking away the mirror. 'You are stable and there's nothing more I can do at this point. I'll return in a few hours. Your body needs time to heal, before you can fight again. Rest,' the Apothecary told him. 'I expect you to be here upon my return.'

The Apothecary left, hobbling off to some other part of the ship. But as the metal door slid shut with a susurrus of escaping pressure, Dak'ir knew he was not alone.

'Tsu'gan?'

He could feel his battle-brother's presence even before he saw him emerge from the shadows.

'Brother,' Dak'ir croaked warmly, recalling the moment of empathy between them as they'd fought together in the temple.

The warmth seeped away, as a cold wind steals heat from a fire, when Dak'ir saw Tsu'gan's dark expression.

'You are unfit to be an Astartes,' he said levelly. 'Kadai's death is on your hands, Ignean. Had you not sent me after the renegade, had you been swift enough to react to the danger in our midst, we would not have lost our captain.' Tsu'gan's burning gaze was as chill as ice. 'I shall not forget it.'

Stunned, Dak'ir was unable to reply before Tsu'gan turned his back on him and left the Apothecarion.

Anguish filled his heart and soul as Dak'ir wrestled with the terrible accusations of his brother, before exhaustion took him and he fell into a deep and fitful sleep.

*For the first time in over forty years, the dream had changed...*

Sitting in the troop compartment of the Stormbird, Nihilan turned the device stolen from the vault in the depths of Cirrion over and over in his gauntlet. His fellow Dragon Warriors surrounded him: the giant Ramlek, breathing tiny gouts of ash and cinder from his mouth grille as he tried to calm his perpetual anger; Ghor'gan, his scaled skin shedding after he'd removed his battle-helm, cradling his multi-melta like a favoured pet; Nor'hak, fastidiously stripping and reassembling his weapons; and Erkine his pilot, the other renegade left behind to watch the Stormbird, forearm bone-blades carefully sheathed within the confines of his power armour as he steered the vessel to its final destination.

The Dragon Warriors had risked much to retrieve the device, even going as far as to establish the elaborate distraction of the uprising to cloak their movements. Kadai's death as part of that subterfuge had been a particularly satisfying, but unexpected, boon for Nihilan.

The Stormbird had been primed and ready before the trap in Aura Hieron was sprung. With eager swathes of suicidal cultists to ensure their escape, the renegades had fled swiftly, leaving the atmosphere of Stratos behind them as the engines of their extant craft roared.

'How little do they realise…' Nihilan rasped, examining every facet of the gilt object in his palm. Such an innocuous piece of arcana; within its twelve pentagonal faces, along the geodesic lines of esoteric script that wreathed its dodecahedral surface, there was the means to unlock secrets. It was the very purpose of the *decyphrex*, to reveal that which was hidden. For Nihilan that enigma existed in the scrolls of Kelock, ancient parchments he and Ushorak had taken over forty years ago from Kelock's tomb on Moribar. Kelock was a technocrat, and a misunderstood genius. He created something, a weapon, far beyond what was capable with the crippled science of the current decaying age. Nihilan meant to replicate his work.

Over a thousand years within the Eye of Terror, patiently plotting revenge, and now he finally was closing on the means to destroy his enemies.

'Approaching the *Hell-stalker*,' the sepulchral voice of Erkine returned over the vox.

Nihilan engaged the grav-harness. As it crept over his armoured shoulders, securing him for landing, he peered out of the Stormbird's vision slit. There across a becalmed and cobalt sea, a vessel of molten-red lay anchored. It was an old ship with old wounds, and older ghosts. The prow was a serrated blade, ripping a hole in the void. Cannons arrayed its flanks, gunmetal grey and powder-blackened. Dozens of towers and antennae reached up like crooked fingers.

*Hell-stalker* had entered the Eye a mere battle-barge and had come out something else entirely. It was Nihilan's ship and aboard it his warriors awaited him – renegades, mercenaries and defectors; pirates, raiders and reavers. There they gathered to heed of his victory and the slow realisation of their ambition – the total and utter destruction of Nocturne, and with it the death of the Salamanders.

# THE LABYRINTH

*Richard Ford*

Chainsword motors roared, bellowing at each other before their steel teeth clashed in a violent kiss, spitting sparks and black oil. They locked together, whining in fury, each relentless in its desire to rend and tear.

Invictus glared at his opponent across the biting blades, determined he would be triumphant, utterly convinced that he would be the victor this time.

It was not to be.

Genareas wrenched his weapon aside, pulling the whirring teeth apart and showering the battle deck with a metallic spray. Before Invictus could counter, the full weight of Genareas's shoulder guard smashed him in the face, sending him reeling. He lost his footing, arms flailing wildly in an attempt to keep his balance, but it was no good. He fell, the harsh clang of ceramite on corrugated steel filling the battle deck, and it was all Invictus could do to keep a hold on his buzzing chainsword. Before he could bring it to bear, Genareas had clamped his arm to the ground with a huge armoured foot, his own chainsword brandished threateningly, closing in towards his opponent's face. Invictus watched as the swirling teeth drew closer to his exposed flesh, and grimaced at their inevitable onslaught.

With a triumphant laugh, Genareas powered down the chainsword's motor, offering his arm to Invictus. 'Well fought, brother. But as we can see, you are still no match for me in the confines of the battle deck.'

Invictus took the proffered arm and was helped to his feet, once again feeling the sting of defeat pierce him more painfully than any physical wound ever could.

'One day, Brother Genareas,' he said. 'One day.'

Genareas only laughed the louder. 'Indeed, brother. And I look forward to that day. Now come. We are already late.'

Together they walked from the battle deck, Invictus several paces behind Genareas, as he always was. Though they were closer than any of their other battle-brothers among the Sons of Malice, having served together as Scouts and then Initiates, it seemed that Invictus was always in Genareas's shadow, always that one step behind. It was a failing that had plagued him for decades, despite the victories he had won in the service of his Chapter.

But tonight would be different – tonight Invictus would prove his worth.

They strode through the dimly illuminated passages of the Retaliator-class cruiser, until they arrived at the docking bay. As soon as the bay doors opened, the shrill hum of a thousand different voices assailed their ears. Servitors buzzed and whirred, piloting their automatons, driving the rows of prisoners of both familiar and extrinsic species onto the docking craft. Snouts mewled peevishly, jaws barked curses in alien tongues, and amidst them the all too familiar cries of weeping innocents pealed out to fill the bay with a cacophonous racket. They had brought offerings captured in every system they had travelled through, xenos from almost a hundred different species. Malice would undoubtedly be pleased with the largesse; the sacrificial pyre would burn brighter than ever before.

Such an extensive gathering of vile beings sickened Invictus to his core, but he knew it was necessary if the hunger of Malice was to be sated and his desires appeased. This pitiful host could not be silenced soon enough, and Invictus could only hope the slaughter would be underway soon.

With Genareas at his side, Invictus made his way across the packed hangar to where his brothers of the Sons of Malice waited. They were already filing into the belly of a growling Thunderhawk gunship, and the two tardy Space Marines were quick to join their fellows. As they boarded, Invictus could hear some of his brothers offering benediction through the vox-relay of his helmet. For himself he made no prayer as he strapped on his harness and prepared for take off – his trust in the skills of the pilot was absolute.

The ship's engines fired into life and it left the artificial gravity of the Retaliator's hangar. Through the gunship's narrow viewport, Invictus could see the colossal outline of a long-dead Imperial ship drawing closer, expanding in his field of vision like a vast beast inflating itself to ward off a curious predator. Every dent and surface burn was visible, and it was a wonder the gargantuan relic survived at all after spending millennia exposed in the vastness of space, with no defence against the empyreal elements.

It hung like a gargantuan, rotted hand – vast steel appendages spiralling out from the centre, some displaying their bulwarks to the cold vacuum of space like an eviscerated corpse. Here and there the ship vented a gaseous blast into the void as though snorting its last toxic breath. Twisted detritus meandered by, caught in the behemoth's gravitational field and forced to perform a perpetual waltz around the vast edifice.

They called it the *Labyrinth*. It had taken them a month of trawling the warp to return here, as they did once each century to honour the blood rites of their Chapter. It was consecrated ground for the Sons of Malice, the only place they could rally to since their home world of Scelus had been so wickedly defiled by the Astartes. No matter their commitments elsewhere, no matter the blood that had to be shed on other worlds, the Sons of Malice would always come back here at the appointed time, ready to make their sacrifices. Their rites had to be strictly observed to the abandonment of all other things.

It was the way of the Sons, and always had been.

The Thunderhawk weaved through the spinning flotsam surrounding the vast ship, and finally reached the *Labyrinth*'s docking hangar. There was a deafening roar as reverse thrusters were engaged, and the Thunderhawk glided in to gently greet the surface of the landing pad.

Once the doors opened, Invictus was quick to disembark, barely registering the flashing relay of information as it pattered across the inside of his visor, shining a blinking green light onto his face. It had been a hundred years since last he trod this sacred ground, and it never failed to fill him with awe.

The resplendence of the ship's bowels was in stark contrast to the desolate appearance of its outer shell. Rockcrete pillars soared a thousand feet into the air, linked by flying buttresses. These towering structures flanked ogival arches that led down shadowed passageways in every direction. Gargoyles of every conceivable shape and size leered from the darkness; antiquated depictions of whatever deities were worshipped here in aeons passed.

Now, only one deity was offered reverence in this cold empty vessel: the exalted Malice, the Renegade God, the Outcast, Malice the Lost, Hierarch of Anarchy and Terror. And He would soon receive nourishment aplenty when the feeding began.

They had discarded their armour and steam was rising from their bare flesh in the firelight. Every one of his brothers was covered in the ichor of their victims, each warrior now gore-strewn and glutted in the great hall.

Invictus had sated himself better than most. The blood was still fresh on his lips and chin where he had gorged on the stone-hard body of a trussed Astartes. To his credit, the servant of the Carrion Lord had not cried out as Invictus sank his teeth into him again and again, rending the flesh and muscle from his bones and feasting for the glory of Malice. Now, little was left of the dead Space Marine but a bloody stump, hanging like a carved joint of meat from a rusted chain.

The other sacrifices had not been as silent as that of Invictus, and the lofty heights of the massive hall still echoed with the ring of their unheeded screams for mercy. All around, the pyres burned, hot coals glowing bright with the charred remains of the night's hecatomb.

Faintly echoing from the distant, unexplored confines of the dead ship, Invictus was sure he could hear a noise, like something bellowing from the depths of its inhuman lungs. It repeated a phrase again and again, the strength of its voice carrying the words over what may have been miles, but try as he might Invictus could not hear them clearly. In the end he chose to ignore the sound, allowing it to blend in with the background hum of the creaking ship and the aftermath of the night's sacrifice.

He turned his attention to a raised mezzanine at one end of the great hall, where stood Lord Kathal, the greatest of them all, Chapter Master of the Sons of Malice, bedecked in his armour of office. Invictus could see his ancient face leering down, satisfied with the oblation his warriors had made. Every one of the Sons was now watching him, waiting for him to honour them with his words.

Kathal simply stared with those eyes of ice, seeming to savour the moment before he broke the silence.

'Brothers.' Kathal's voice was deep and resonant, filling the hall all the way to its high, dark ceiling. 'Malice is truly honoured this night. We have raised to Him a thousand souls in agony and terror. It is fitting that we offer Him such a bounteous sacrifice in preparation for our coming crusade.'

Invictus clenched his fists in anticipation. It was common knowledge that the Sons of Malice would soon march to war, embarking on a crusade the likes of which their Chapter had never seen before.

'For such a struggle we will need unparalleled warriors, men who have proven themselves in the Challenge of the Labyrinth. Only by succeeding at this trial can any of you prove your worth, and your suitability to stride amongst the ranks of the Doomed Ones.'

He felt a bite of quick excitement, and he knew his brethren felt it too. Each century, when the Sons of Malice returned to the carcass of the huge and ancient vessel, a select few would volunteer to face the Challenge of the Labyrinth. None were ever seen again, but it was said that those strong and cunning enough to overcome the trials of the Labyrinth were elevated to the Doomed Ones, Malice's sept of holy warriors. Every member of this elite coterie was granted Malice's divine gifts of untold power and sent off to walk the dark paths of the galaxy, slaying their enemies with cold efficiency. It was a position Invictus had long coveted, and this year he finally felt ready to pursue it.

'Which of you is strong enough, resourceful enough, and courageous enough to face the Labyrinth?' asked Kathal.

His head held high, his body still dripping with the gore of his recent sacrifice, Invictus strode forward to present himself before Kathal. He did not bow or show fealty, but thrust out his chin in defiance, keen to show his lack of trepidation and his worthiness for the ordeal ahead.

Lord Kathal smiled down in satisfaction, his wide leer cracking that ancient face almost in two. And after Invictus, others began to move forward, spurred on by his example and eager to show themselves equally as worthy. In the end, twenty warriors stood shoulder to shoulder with Invictus, presenting themselves to face the perils of the Labyrinth.

Glancing to his side, Invictus saw that his brother, Genareas, had also chosen this year to join the trial. It was inevitable that they would take this challenge together, but this time Invictus was determined to step out of his brother's shadow.

When he was sure that no more would take up the challenge, Lord Kathal beckoned his twenty warriors away from the great hall. The grim procession marched further into the dark heart of the rotting ship until finally they reached their goal. Before them stood a simple steel hatchway, which barred the way to the unseen terrors of the Labyrinth.

'Beyond this door lies your destiny,' said Kathal. 'You will all enter here unarmed and unarmoured. There is no rank beyond this entrance; you are all equal within the Labyrinth. Use what resources you can scavenge, and have faith in one another. At the far side of the ship awaits a portal to freedom. Any who can find it and step within its hallowed confines will receive the benediction of Malice. The rest will find only oblivion. To those of you I will not see again – die well, my brothers.'

With that, Kathal turned the great wheel that secured the hatch and it swung open on rusted hinges. Within was only darkness, but Invictus did not pause – stepping inside and leading the way for his brothers to follow.

Once they were all within, he heard the great door close behind him.

Flickering strobes filled the corridor with a dim red light, and the warriors were forced to wait for their keen eyes to adjust to the gloom before proceeding. While they lingered, Invictus was sure he could hear that bellowing voice once more, though its origin was still too distant for him to ascertain any meaning. The noise filled Invictus with a chill, but he would not allow it to stop him. They would never find victory skulking in the dark corridor of some dead ship and, steeling himself against the fear, he led his battle-brothers forward.

At first the going was easy, with the wide corridor funnelling them along an obvious route. As they moved, the warriors of the Sons scavenged what they could – steel bars, the sharp edges of torn bulwarks – anything that could be used as a weapon. Here and there they would discover an object of greater value gripped in the skeletal fingers of a long dead aspirant – a discarded bolter or a salvageable flamer. Invictus found a bolt pistol, its clip half full, and said silent thanks to Malice for his beneficence.

After an hour of tramping through the dimly lit passageways without incident, the twenty warriors came to a wide chamber. Six doors were set in the far wall, each one yawning wide, beckoning them forward into the blackness beyond.

'Which way?' asked Genareas.

The other warriors looked to one another uncertainly.

'Perhaps we should split our numbers here,' Invictus replied. 'If only death awaits us beyond one of these doors, then at least some of us might make it to the Labyrinth's end.'

Genareas nodded, as did the others. If the Labyrinth was as huge and dangerous as they feared, then splitting into smaller groups would serve them better than staying as a single unit and falling foul of the same deadly ensnarement.

The warriors quickly split into two squads, with Genareas and Invictus on opposing sides. Before they headed off through different passage-ways, Genareas offered his brother a nod – what might be a final salute. Whether he was wishing him luck or merely offering a silent challenge, Invictus did not know, but he returned the gesture in kind, and followed his own group into the dark.

Invictus led the way, his battle-brothers close behind. As they moved they could hear a tapping within the walls that grew more intense the further they delved into the shell of the dead ship. It was as though the noise were following their route along the arterial passageways. Several times they stopped, sensing unseen forms watching them, waiting to pounce at any moment, but each time their caution proved unfounded.

Again, something shuffled in the dark nearby, and the warriors quickly halted, brandishing their arms threateningly. They looked to one another uncertainly, until bold Brother Cainin stepped forward. He had fashioned a crude axe from the detritus of the tunnels and he held it forward, as though challenging the shadows themselves. With a quick swipe left and right Cainin cut the blackness from where the sound had emanated, as though attacking the shadows themselves.

Nothing.

He turned, shrugging with a smile as though they were all foolish – spooked by innocent sounds like a bunch of untested neophytes, not the cold, hard veterans they were.

It roared from the dark, huge arms clamping around Cainin, slaver-ing jaws biting deep into his neck. He had no time to scream as he was pulled into the shadows, blood spurting from his wounds as a savage, twisted beast tore clumps of his flesh away.

The remaining warriors opened fire with what weapons they had and Invictus pumped bolter shells at the place where seconds before his battle-brother had stood. Brother Vallius, crude autogun in hand, stepped forward to unleash an angry tirade of fire and was answered with a bloodcurdling cry of pain.

The echo of gunfire subsided and the corridor fell silent. None of the warriors moved, each one staring at the dark, waiting for something to come screaming forward, ready to grasp them with powerful arms and rend their flesh asunder.

Blood suddenly began to pool across the decking, and Invictus took a step forward. Before he could get any closer a thick, foetid arm flopped raggedly from the dark, its clawed hand twitching in the winking light. Brother Angustine reached up and diverted one of the dull spotlights that hung limply from its housing to shed some illumination on the creature. It was large, and like no xenos Invictus had ever seen. The body bore obvious marks of mutation, as though the creature had been exposed to the warp. Its fangs were bared from a lipless maw and its dead eyes stared blankly, bereft of pupils. The skin was hard like leather and its body was covered with open sores, exuding a weird, musky scent.

As his brothers checked the lifeless body of Cainin, Invictus knelt beside the creature, keen to get a closer look at the kind of beast they would be facing during the trial. Instantly his eyes were drawn to the mutant's upper arm. It bore some kind of mark, faded by the years and the mutation of its flesh, but it was still barely discernible in the guttering light – the black and white skull symbol of Malice.

He thought it strange that the creature should bear such a mark, but before he could speak of it Brother Mortigan beckoned them on down the corridor.

'We must keep moving,' he said. 'We do not know how many more of these creatures are stalking us in the dark. Our shots may attract more of them to our position.'

With that, they began to move on, leaving the dead creature and the body of battle-brother Cainin in the shadows behind them.

Invictus gave no further thought to the mark. He had more pressing matters to attend to – such as not falling foul of any more of these twisted beasts in the stygian tunnels.

Over the next few hours they made good progress through the rotting bulwarks and rusted corridors of the dead ship, but the tricks and traps of the Labyrinth began to take their toll.

Brother Kado, who single-handedly repelled an ork ambush at the Battle of Uderverengin, was beheaded by hidden las-wire as they traversed a narrow bridge. Brother Vallius, who took the head of Lord Bacchus at the Ansolom Gate, was crushed by a blast door that had at first seemed inoperable. Brother Mortigan, who stood beside Invictus as they watched the exterminatus of Corodon IV, was doused in corrosive waste as they navigated a scoriation duct.

With each death Invictus felt the pall of dread close in further, but he forced himself on. If anyone was to survive this trial and take their place among the Doomed Ones it would be him, and he would let nothing stand in his way.

Eventually, the six remaining warriors found themselves at the entrance to a wide chamber. Its floor was peppered with huge holes, as though something massive had punched through the solid decking with spiked fists of steel.

Invictus tentatively led the way, stepping over the threshold of the room as though the floor beyond might burn his bare feet. There did not appear to be any cunning traps awaiting them inside, and Invictus signalled his brothers to follow him as he skirted the edge of one of the great holes. Looking down, he could see that the huge punctured deck disappeared into the darkness below, and a sudden sense of foreboding began to fill him.

'Move quickly,' he ordered, stepping gingerly between the twisted metal. 'There is something not right here.'

It took Invictus scant seconds to realise what had put him on edge – the entire room stank of the same musk as the creature they had slain earlier – but by then it was too late.

Brother Angustine cried out in alarm, firing wildly with his autogun as a ferocious mutant beast rushed from the dark. The blaring report of automatic fire suddenly filled the room as more of the creatures began to pour in from all around. Invictus raised his bolt pistol, ready to add his own stream of fire to the deluge, when another of the creatures burst from the shadows ahead. He immediately altered his sightline, squeezing hard on the trigger three times. Each shot hit its target, bursting against the mutant's face, explosive rounds mashing flesh and pulping bone with each deafening impact. But even as one assailant fell, Invictus was attacked by a second that leapt at him from above. He swung his pistol around, letting off a sweeping volley of fire, but it was not enough to stop the mutant's wild lunge. It smashed into him, gripping him tightly with razor claws and snapping its fangs at his throat. Invictus fell back, his hands barely grasping at the beast's jaws in time to stop it tearing out his throat, but as he did so he lost his footing, falling back into the void as he and the mutant were pitched into one of the huge holes.

All he could hear as the shadows enveloped him was the desperate sound of his remaining battle-brothers fighting valiantly for their lives…

His eyes flicked open, suddenly assailed by the intermittent blinking of another defective spotlight. Lifting a hand to his head, Invictus could feel blood caking the side of his face. He had fallen Malice-knew how far, and struck his head on something solid. There was no telling how long he had been unconscious.

Panic suddenly gripped him as he realised he had lost his weapon. His mutant attacker could be anywhere, even now stalking him, readying itself to pounce. He leapt to his feet, eyes scanning desperately for something he could use as a weapon, and instantly he saw there was little need for alarm.

The room he had fallen into was packed with detritus – sharp edged machinery and torn bulwark panels lay scattered all around. It was only by the grace of Malice that he had not been cut to ribbons by the forest of junk. The mutant he had fallen with, however, had not been so lucky. Its body was impaled by a steel girder, poking up from the pile of scrap metal like a slanted flagpole. The end of the torn steel protruded from its mouth, and its black eyes stared vacantly. It looked almost pitiful.

There was silence above – Invictus's battle-brothers had either perished, or moved on, thinking him lost. From here he would have to proceed alone.

Making a quick search of the surrounding junk, Invictus managed to retrieve the bolt pistol, and then set about trying to locate an exit from the stifling chamber.

As he scrabbled around in the dark something reached out, grasping his wrist and holding the bolt pistol firmly. Invictus stretched out with his free hand, keen to halt the mutant's jaws before they could clamp themselves around his throat, but he suddenly stopped as he saw that it was not the baleful eyes of a mutant beast that regarded him from the shadows, but one of his battle-brothers. Though it was no one he recognised, the mark of Malice was plain to see on his upper arm. But that was not all – his skin was marred by sores, and his face had taken on a feral cast. It was plain he was in the early stages of mutation.

'Mercy, brother,' he said. 'I mean you no harm.'

With that he released Invictus's wrist, but remained in the dark confines of the shadows, seeming to find solace within them.

Invictus took a wary step backwards, readying himself to raise the bolt pistol at the slightest provocation. 'What has happened to you?' he asked.

'The Labyrinth, brother. Prolonged exposure condemns us to this.' He raised his arm, showing the weeping pustules and fledgling talons. 'I too volunteered for the Challenge a century ago, heeding the words of our Chapter Master. There were six of us that made it to the portal and what we thought was our victory. But it seems Kathal did not tell us all there is to know about his test. Once the first of us passed through the portal, it ceased to operate for the rest. We were trapped down here, forced to fight for our lives. I am the last of those survivors, but as you can see, survival means nothing. This place is warp-touched. It will not be long before I am one of them.' He gestured towards the mutant, impaled on the vast spike.

'Then there can be only one victor in this Challenge?' said Invictus.
'Indeed.'

'Then I must hurry. Is there a way out of this place?'

His tainted battle-brother beckoned towards the shadows. 'An exit
lies that way. But beware – their hive nestles along that path. It will be
impossible to pass.'

'I will find a way.' Invictus took a step towards the door.

'Before you leave,' the mutant's voice sounded almost desperate. 'Perhaps there is something you could do for me in return...'

Invictus raised the bolt pistol and fired a single round, exploding his
twisted battle-brother's face. Without a second look, he walked from the
metallic bone yard and further into the Labyrinth.

The sound of boltgun reports and the stench of promethium emanated
from up ahead. Invictus quickened his step, eager to join in the fray,
feeling the red mist of his battle haze descending. As he moved along the
tunnel the sounds and smells of combat intensified and his heart began
to pound with anticipation.

He could see the desperate skirmish now. Five of his battle-brothers
were fighting in a tight corridor, with mutants assailing them from
further ahead. Genareas was among them, unleashing a hellish conflagration from the tip of his salvaged flamer. Any beasts that were not
instantly immolated were riddled with bolter and autogun fire.

As Invictus joined his battle-brothers, Genareas looked across and
smiled. 'Where is your squad? Have you lost them so soon?'

Invictus smiled back. 'They did not fare as well as I,' he replied. 'But I
see that you are not without troubles of your own.'

More ravenous faces appeared at the end of the corridor, rushing
towards their doom, and Invictus added the sound of his own bolt pistol
to the staccato melody of gunfire.

'There is some kind of lair up ahead,' Genareas bellowed above the
din. 'It is packed with these creatures. We cannot make it through.'

'Then we will have to go around,' shouted Invictus, pointing to a sign
written in ancient and crumbling script above their heads. Genareas looked
up, nodding his agreement as he read the word 'Airlock' on the sign.

'Withdraw,' ordered Genareas, flooding the corridor with another torrent of liquid flame.

One by one, the remaining warriors moved back along the passage
in short sprints before turning and supporting their battle-brothers'
withdrawal with bursts of fire. Within seconds they were at the airlock,
leaving a trail of corrupted bodies in their wake.

Once all his battle-brothers were inside, Invictus pulled the ancient
lever, sealing the outer lock. At once, more of the mutant brood
appeared, flinging themselves at the reinforced hatch in their voracious
attempts to get at the escaping warriors.

Genareas was already at the airlock controls, reducing the pressure within the room so that they were not blown out into the immaterium once the outer door's seals were broken. Invictus and his brothers could only watch and wait as the creatures smashed their fists and heads against the toughened plasglass, unyielding in their desire to destroy the warriors inside.

'These beasts are insane,' said Brother Crassus, staring intently at the mad creatures. 'They would destroy themselves just to get to us.'

Invictus laughed. 'Take a good look. These creatures are what we are destined to become. All but one of us.'

'What do you mean?' asked Agon, as Invictus's words sparked a murmur of doubt from the rest.

'These things were once our brothers, the product of Challenges past. One of them spoke to me – it revealed that only the first of us to the transportation portal will be relayed to safety. The rest will be left behind, left to the vagaries of the warp.'

The warriors began to eye one another warily, unsure of how to take the news.

'We should discuss this later,' said Genareas. 'For now, I would suggest a deep breath and a tight grip.'

With that there came a sharp hiss, as the outer seal of the airlock began to lift, revealing the stark oblivion of the immaterium beyond.

Genareas was the first to brave the cold vacuum, shouldering his flamer and gripping the corrugated hull of the great ship for dear life. He was closely followed by Agon, then Crassus and Septimon. Invictus looked to Moloch, offering him the next place in line but his battle-brother shook his head, eyeing him suspiciously. With a shrug, Invictus made his way into the void, his fingers gripping hard to the strip of weathered metal that was his only lifeline. Just as Moloch joined him on the outer hull there came an almighty blast of air as the plasglass finally gave way under its vicious assault, depressurising the corridor within and blowing flailing mutants into the immaterium.

Invictus and his brothers quickly made their way across the hull, with the mutated bodies of what were once proud warriors floating away into the black behind them like so much flotsam.

Though their mucranoid glands would offer protection against the vacuum it would not last indefinitely, and Invictus felt relief wash over him as he saw Genareas opening another airlock up ahead.

Genareas and Agon made their way into the ship, and the other warriors quickened their pace along the handrail of the hull. Crassus was next into the airlock and Septimon was about to climb inside when Invictus felt the railing suddenly yield under his weight. The iron bolts securing the rail to the hull began to give way, and separate from the ship's corrugated surface. Invictus glanced back at Moloch, a wicked plan quickly formulating in his mind. One less rival would take him one step closer to victory, and besides, Moloch had always been his inferior.

Panic suddenly crossed Moloch's face as he saw Invictus's look of loathing.

Both Space Marines moved faster, desperate to reach the airlock before the railing came free altogether. Invictus managed to grip the inside of the door, feeling a strong hand grasp his wrist. With a last look back at Moloch, he pulled hard on the railing, wrenching the remaining rusted bolts from their housing and sending his battle-brother reeling into the immaterium. Moloch's mouth opened wide in a silent scream as he floated off, and Invictus was pulled inside to safety.

The warriors began to breathe easily once more as the outer seal was brought down with a hiss. Invictus looked to his brothers and saw that more than one of them was regarding him accusatorially.

'What happened to Moloch?' said Agon, bringing his autogun to bear.

'Do you accuse me, brother?' Invictus replied, reaching for the bolt pistol in his belt.

Before anyone could move, both battle-brothers had aimed their weapons. There was a sudden flurry of movement, as Genareas raised his flamer to point at Agon, and in turn Septimon and Crassus pointed their own weapons at Invictus.

'We have enough enemies without turning on each another,' said Genareas. 'If we cull our own numbers there is less chance we will even reach the portal to freedom. Once we find it, then we should allow our strength of arms to decide which of us survives. Until then, we are still brothers, we are still the Sons of Malice.'

Invictus slowly lowered his bolt pistol, and Agon did the same.

'Well met,' said Genareas. 'Let's get moving. It may not take these creatures long to work out our strategy.' With that he led the way from the airlock and along yet another seemingly endless tunnel.

The rest of the warriors followed in his stead, but they all regarded each other with a warier eye than they had previously – especially Invictus.

The tunnel dipped, drawing them ever downward as though into the abyss itself. Invictus knew that to be a ridiculous notion – they were on the foundering carcass of an ancient spaceship, and despite its artificial suspensors giving the illusion of gravity, there was no 'up' or 'down'.

Nevertheless, they seemed to be drawn deeper into the Labyrinth, and moisture began pooling at their feet. The further they penetrated, the deeper the waters got until they were soon wading waist deep through foetid green sludge.

Once again, that bellowing voice emanated from some hidden part of the ship, but this time it was much closer. Invictus strained to hear what was being said but he could still not discern the meaning. The phrase consisted of three words, each of a single syllable, howled over and over again. What foul litany, and whatever ancient alien tongue it was in, was impossible to tell, but one thing was for sure – the speaker was no ordinary mortal.

A sudden scream pierced the tunnel, rising louder than the distant roar, and every man turned as one. It was Crassus, who had been bringing up their rear. The warriors aimed their weapons as their brother was lifted into the air by some unseen hand, his body clearing the water that oozed all around them. Blood spurted from his mouth as he tried to scream once more, his body pierced from behind by a huge, spiked tentacle that burst through his chest and flailed around as though probing for another victim.

As the lifeless body of Crassus was discarded to sink below the surface of the mire, the squad opened fire, shredding the putrid thing that had impaled their brother. More appendages began to rise from the water all around, blindly searching for prey.

'Retreat,' yelled Agon. 'There are too many!'

Invictus began to wade through the morass as tentacles rose all around. Bolter fire streaked past him as he moved down the tunnel and up ahead he could see the passage rising out of the water to safety. Agon and Septimon fired over his head, pulverising the foul smelling feelers as they reached out towards him, and as Invictus moved past him, Genareas blasted a cloud of molten fire into the corridor.

The water level around them dropped as they climbed the passageway, but the probing tentacles still relentlessly pursued them. If they could make it through the open doorway ahead they would be free, but as they neared it, a blast hatch began to slowly descend, threatening to trap them in the corridor with the deadly spiked limbs.

Septimon was the first to the doorway, dropping his weapon and grasping the hatch as it lowered. Invictus could hear the grinding of gears as Septimon's great strength fought against the ancient mechanism that sought to entomb them.

Agon was the first through the gap braced open by his brother Septimon, and he was quickly followed by Genareas. As Invictus passed through he gave one last glance to Septimon, his face grimly set as he held open the heavy steel door. Then he was gone, the metal portal slamming down and sealing his brother in with the horde of disembodied tentacles.

Invictus sat in the dark corridor, panting for air. Genareas offered him his arm, and Invictus gratefully accepted it, rising to his feet, his every fibre seeming to ache.

'Where is Agon?' said Genareas, glancing down the corridor.

'He must think us near to our goal.'

'And he wishes to claim his place amongst the Doomed Ones and leave us to our fate in this place.'

'Then we must hurry,' Invictus replied, moving off down the passageway.

With their last reserves of energy, the two warriors pursued their errant brother, and this time it was Invictus who led the way, for once a step in front of Genareas.

The passageway gradually turned and widened into a dark hall, deep shadows cloistering it on either side. Great statues rose upwards from the dark, ancient sentinels that lined the hall, but Invictus paid them no heed, for up ahead was a much more majestic sight.

A great portal stood at the far end of the massive chamber, fulgurating blue disks dancing up and down its length, tempting Invictus – beckoning him ever closer. But between he and it was the sprinting form of Agon, way ahead, ready to claim the prize that was rightfully his.

'Agon!' Genareas cried.

As he neared the portal, Agon stopped, slowly turning with a smile.

'I am truly sorry, my brothers. But it seems I must leave you. I wish you–'

Something streaked from the dark, cutting Agon off mid sentence. A huge chitin claw, ancient and battered, gripped him around the waist, lifting him five metres into the air. Agon screamed, blood gurgling from his mouth as the claw squeezed tight. The two halves of his body fell to the ground, innards spilling onto the hard steel decking.

Then it walked from the shadows.

Four massive limbs carried its great bulk forward. It was a mass of flesh and steel, metal plates cauterised to a body of seething blubber. Two great claws reached out to the fore and clacked together menacingly. But it was the head that was the most hideous – a twisted, bloated replica of a face that might once have been human, but was now so savage and malign as to be almost unrecognisable.

As Invictus watched in horror, its great jaws opened and it bellowed forth its incessant call.

'*LET. ME. OUT!*' it screamed, filling the hall with its ear splitting roar.

It was now all too clear. This was no ancient war cry Invictus had been hearing – it was simply the maddened ranting of an insane mutant, caged for centuries and left to the mercy of the warp's corrupting influence.

And now it was the only thing standing in the way of victory.

Genareas was the first to move, stepping forward and unleashing a gout of flame that consumed the monster's head. When the inferno subsided, Invictus could see that the flames had not even left a mark on the beast's hardened carapace. He raised his bolt pistol, firing at the creature's eye, but the explosive rounds did nothing but cause it annoyance.

It roared once more, repeating its interminable request for release, before stomping forward on those thick and hideous limbs.

'I have only one shot left,' said Invictus. 'We must make this last round count.'

'I understand, brother,' Genareas replied, grasping his flamer by the stock.

The beast opened its maw, ready to bellow at them again, and Genareas took his chance, flinging the flamer into its gaping jaws.

Invictus raised the bolt pistol, waiting for his moment. He had only a split second window in which to fire, but he was a veteran of the Sons of Malice, a warrior unmatched on the field. A split second was more than he would ever need.

An explosive round pierced the promethium canister just as the flamer entered the behemoth's mouth, igniting the liquid flame within. It exploded, blowing the top of the mutant's head clean off, and silencing it forever. For a few seconds the body of the twisted juggernaut staggered on its four limbs, uncertain of whether or not it was dead. Then, like a tower suddenly robbed of its foundations, it collapsed to the ground.

Genareas smiled at his brother. 'And so it is just us two remaining,' he said. 'It is fitting that we should face one another this last time. We will fight, with nothing but our bare hands and our stone resolve, and the victor will claim the spoils.' He gestured towards the portal, which still flashed and quivered seductively. 'How I have waited for this day, Invictus. Ours is a kinship forged in a hundred battles, and tempered in the blood of a thousand vanquished enemies. This will be a battle to end all battles. I am only sorry that we cannot both march from here triumphant, but as you know, there can be only one champion.'

Invictus nodded his agreement. 'I too am sorry, brother,' he said, raising the bolt pistol. 'For when I said I had only a single round remaining, I lied.'

Genareas had little time to protest before Invictus squeezed the trigger, sending his brother's brains exploding from the back of his head.

Discarding the now empty pistol, Invictus strode towards the coruscating portal and stepped within the threshold of its glorious light.

He stood at the centre of a wide, carved circle. Ancient sigils intersected one another across its face, eliciting the notion of daemonic faces in his mind, but as soon as he tried to focus on them the faces were gone.

Surrounding him on all sides was the faint sparking light of a containment shield. Invictus found it hard to imagine what awaited him that would require such a safeguard; there was no way he would flinch in the face of his destiny. Nevertheless, he was not about to question the dictates of Lord Kathal.

Lining the periphery of the great hall were his brothers of the Sons of Malice, fully regaled in their armour, bearing the standards and livery of the Chapter. The sides of the hall rose in tiers, allowing each and every man to view the proceedings. Each would be able to watch as the ceremony took place, each would see as Invictus was elevated to the ranks of the Doomed Ones. This had never happened before, and Kathal must have deemed his victory in the Labyrinth a historic one to break with tradition in such a way.

From one end of the great hall, Invictus saw Lord Kathal approaching, flanked by his Librarians and their priestly attendants, bedecked in their cerulean robes. Servitors carried the Chapter's ancient tomes, and liturgies droned from the automated vox-units that hovered alongside the procession. But there was more: huge caskets pulled along by the grasping mechadendrites of the Chapter's Techmarines. What was in these caskets Invictus had no idea, but something about their unexpected appearance began to fill him with a sense of unease.

As the huge room filled with the scent of burning incense, a macabre silence seemed to descend upon the proceedings. It was an unnerving quiet, and Invictus's unease began to intensify into a stolid feeling of dread. This was not the exultant ritual he had been anticipating – it was more like a funeral march.

As the feeling intensified, Kathal approached him, his stone face grim in the hazy darkness.

'You have proven yourself the best among us, Invictus. You have proven you are without peer for your strength and cunning. You are the most potent, the latest to prove himself worthy to join the Doomed Ones.'

The Librarians had surrounded him now, a monotonous chant emanating from within their hooded robes. The ancient, dark language that was spewed forth by the vox-units grew louder with every passing second, and Invictus could feel something metallic on the air, as though a storm were brewing within the confines of the hall. The Techmarines had positioned the caskets, ten in all, in a circle around Invictus. They ceremoniously released the holy seals that bound their locks and revealed what was inside. Ten blank faces stared out at Invictus – ten silent warriors, their bodies still robust but their minds vacuous.

His unease suddenly turned to cold panic. He told himself this was all part of the ritual, that there was nothing to fear, but his base instincts were crying out for him to flee this place. With the containment field binding him in place though, flight was impossible.

'You are the eleventh hero, Invictus, the eleventh and final warrior. Look to your battle-brothers,' he gestured to the blank faces that glared with vacant expressions. 'Your predecessors, each one succeeding in the Challenge of the Labyrinth for the honour of joining the ranks of the Doomed Ones. For a thousand years have we searched for champions worthy of Him. And tonight, finally you are all assembled.

'Our crusade can now begin. Now we will be strong enough to take back that which was stolen from us – Scelus, our home world. None will stand in our way – not the forces of the foul Ruinous Powers nor the servants of the Carrion Lord. Not with Him by our side.'

Terror gripped Invictus as he looked down at the circle beneath his feet. Eldritch light was beginning to emanate from the carved runes, dancing and gambolling, flashing green and blue and red.

'Now you will learn what it is to be among the Doomed Ones,' continued Lord Kathal, taking a step backwards. 'Now Malice will show you what your victory has wrought.'

Invictus tried to speak, to demand to know what was happening to him, but he found his jaw would not move. The words simply would not come. The whisper of the Librarians rose, as did the vox-units, and they soon reached a crescendo. The light at Invictus's feet grew brighter, lashing upwards to sting his legs and bathe him in its iniquitous light.

'You are truly worthy, Invictus of the Sons,' Kathal screamed, raising his arms to the shadows of the rooftop. 'Can you hear Him calling? He has come to accept your tribute. He has come for the Labyrinth's eleven. He has come to walk among us.'

Invictus followed Kathal's gaze, lifting his head to the ceiling. Through the shadows he could see the outline of something huge, something that stared down with baleful eyes. Something wicked in the dark.

He screamed. Screamed for the pain that engulfed his body. Screamed for the terror in the depths of his soul. But no amount of screaming could halt the ritual now.

It began to descend, pulling with it the dark and the pain. Invictus raised his voice in a last tumultuous cry as his flesh began to flay from his bones.

As his body was consumed, he realised that not even the kindly release of oblivion could save him now…

In the great hall all was silent.

The Sons had watched as the light consumed the body of their brother Invictus, along with the ten other heroes of the Labyrinth, their limbs immolated, their torsos eviscerated, their heads contorting and twisting, writhing within a pool of black light.

And now what stood before them was no longer their brothers. Invictus and the rest were gone – gone to join the ranks of the legendary Doomed Ones.

What stood before them was the revenant they had worshipped for millennia. The eidolon that would stand at their vanguard as they retook what was rightfully theirs.

He could only be summoned by sacrifice – only by giving unto Him their best and most praiseworthy warriors could He walk among them.

And here He stood, gazing with eyes of fire – the Renegade God, the Outcast, the Lost, Hierarch of Anarchy and Terror…

…Malice.

# HEADHUNTED

*Steve Parker*

Something vast, dark and brutish moved across the pinpricked curtain of space, blotting out the diamond lights of the constellations behind it as if swallowing them whole. It was the size of a city block, and its bulbous eyes, like those of a great blind fish, glowed with a green and baleful light.

It was a terrible thing to behold, this leviathan – a harbinger of doom – and its passage had brought agony and destruction to countless victims in the centuries it had swum among the stars. It travelled, now, through the Charybdis Subsector on trails of angry red plasma, cutting across the inky darkness with a purpose.

That purpose was close at hand, and a change began to take place on its bestial features. New lights flickered to life on its muzzle, shining far brighter and sharper than its eyes, illuminating myriad shapes, large and small, that danced and spun in high orbit above the glowing orange sphere of Arronax II. With a slow, deliberate motion, the leviathan unhinged its massive lower jaw, and opened its mouth to feed.

At first, the glimmering pieces of debris it swallowed were mere fragments, nothing much larger than a man. But soon, heavier, bulkier pieces drifted into that gaping maw, passing between its bladelike teeth and down into its black throat.

For hours, the monster gorged itself on space-borne scrap, devouring everything it could fit into its mouth. The pickings were good. There had been heavy fighting here in ages past. Scoured worlds and lifeless wrecks were all that remained now, locked in a slow elliptical dance around the local star. But the wrecks, at least, had a future. Once salvaged, they would be forged anew, recast in forms that would bring death and suffering down upon countless others. For, of course, this beast, this hungry monster of the void, was no beast at all.

It was an ork ship. And the massive glyphs daubed sloppily on its hull marked it as a vessel of the Deathskull clan.

Re-pressurisation began the moment the ship's vast metal jaws clanged shut. The process took around twenty minutes, pumps flooding the salvage bay with breathable, if foul-smelling, air. The orks crowding the corridor beyond the bay's airlock doors roared their impatience and hammered their fists against the thick metal bulkheads. They shoved and jostled for position. Then, just when it seemed murderous violence was sure to erupt, sirens sounded and the heavy doors split apart. The orks surged forward, pushing and scrambling, racing towards the mountains of scrap, each utterly focused on claiming the choicest pieces for himself.

Fights broke out between the biggest and darkest-skinned. They roared and wrestled with each other, and snapped at each other with tusk-filled jaws. They lashed out with the tools and weapons that bristled on their augmented limbs. They might have killed each other but for the massive suits of cybernetic armour they wore. These were no mere greenskin foot soldiers. They were orks of a unique genus, the engineers of their race, each born with an inherent understanding of machines. It was hardcoded into their marrow in the same way as violence and torture.

As was true of every caste, however, some among them were cleverer than others. While the mightiest bellowed and beat their metal-plated chests, one ork, marginally shorter and leaner than the rest, slid around them and into the shadows, intent on getting first pickings.

This ork was called Gorgrot in the rough speech of his race, and, despite the sheer density of salvage the ship had swallowed, it didn't take him long to find something truly valuable. At the very back of the junk-filled bay, closes to the ship's great metal teeth, he found the ruined, severed prow of a mid-sized human craft. As he studied it, he noticed weapon barrels protruding from the front end. His alien heart quickened. Functional or not, he could do great things with salvaged weapon systems. He would make himself more dangerous, an ork to be reckoned with.

After a furtive look over his shoulder to make sure none of the bigger orks had noticed him, he moved straight across to the wrecked prow, reached out a gnarled hand and touched the hull. Its armour-plating was in bad shape, pocked and cratered by plasma fire and torpedo impacts. To the rear, the metal was twisted and black where it had sheared away from the rest of the craft. It looked like an explosion had torn the ship apart. To Gorgrot, however, the nature of the ship's destruction mattered not at all. What mattered was its potential. Already, visions of murderous creativity were flashing through his tiny mind in rapid succession, so many at once, in fact, that he forgot to breathe until his lungs sent him a painful reminder. These visions were a gift from Gork and Mork, the bloodthirsty greenskin gods, and he had received their like many times before. All greenskin engineers received them, and nothing, save the rending of an enemy's flesh, felt so utterly right.

Even so, it was something small and insignificant that pulled him out of his rapture.

A light had begun to flash on the lower left side of the ruined prow, winking at him from beneath a tangle of beams and cables and dented armour plates, igniting his simple-minded curiosity, drawing him towards it. It was small and green, and it looked like it might be a button of some kind. Gorgrot began clearing debris from the area around it. Soon, he was grunting and growling with the effort, sweating despite the assistance of his armour's strength-boosting hydraulics.

Within minutes, he had removed all obstructions between himself and the blinking light, and discovered that it was indeed a kind of button.

Gorgrot was extending his finger out to press it when something suddenly wrenched him backwards with irresistible force. He was hurled to the ground and landed hard on his back with a snarl. Immediately, he tried to scramble up again, but a huge metal boot stamped down on him, denting his belly-armour and pushing him deep into the carpet of sharp scrap.

Gorgrot looked up into the blazing red eyes of the biggest, heaviest ork in the salvage bay.

This was Zazog, personal engineer to the mighty Warboss Balthazog Bludwrekk, and few orks on the ship were foolish enough to challenge any of his salvage claims. It was the reason he always arrived in the salvage bay last of all; his tardiness was the supreme symbol of his dominance among the scavengers.

Zazog staked his claim now, turning from Gorgrot and stomping over to the wrecked prow. There, he hunkered down to examine the winking button. He knew well enough what it meant. There had to be a working power source onboard, something far more valuable than most scrap. He flicked out a blowtorch attachment from the middle knuckle of his mechanised left claw and burned a rough likeness of his personal glyph into the side of the wrecked prow. Then he rose and bellowed a challenge to those around him.

Scores of gretchin, the puniest members of the orkoid race, skittered away in panic, disappearing into the protection of the shadows. The other orks stepped back, growling at Zazog, snarling in anger. But none dared challenge him.

Zazog glared at each in turn, forcing them, one by one, to drop their gazes or die by his hand. Then, satisfied at their deference, he turned and pressed a thick finger to the winking green button.

For a brief moment, nothing happened. Zazog growled and pressed it again. Still nothing. He was about to begin pounding it with his mighty fist when he heard a noise.

It was the sound of atmospheric seals unlocking.

The door shuddered, and began sliding up into the hull.

Zazog's craggy, scar-covered face twisted into a hideous grin. Yes, there *was* a power source on board. The door's motion proved it. He, like Gorgrot, began to experience flashes of divine inspiration, visions of weaponry so grand and deadly that his limited brain could hardly cope. No matter; the gods would work through him once he got started. His hands would automatically fashion what his brain could barely comprehend. It was always the way.

The sliding door retracted fully now, revealing an entrance just large enough for Zazog's armoured bulk to squeeze through. He shifted forward with that very intention, but the moment never came.

From the shadows inside the doorway, there was a soft coughing sound.

Zazog's skull disintegrated in a haze of blood and bone chips. His headless corpse crashed backwards onto the carpet of junk.

The other orks gaped in slack-jawed wonder. They looked down at Zazog's body, trying to make sense of the dim warnings that rolled through their minds. Ignoring the obvious threat, the biggest orks quickly began roaring fresh claims and shoving the others aside, little realising that their own deaths were imminent.

But imminent they were.

A great black shadow appeared, bursting from the door Zazog had opened. It was humanoid, not quite as large as the orks surrounding it, but bulky nonetheless, though it moved with a speed and confidence no ork could ever have matched. Its long adamantium talons sparked and crackled with deadly energy as it slashed and stabbed in all directions, a whirlwind of lethal motion. Great fountains of thick red blood arced through the air as it killed again and again. Greenskins fell like sacks of meat.

More shadows emerged from the wreck now. Four of them. Like the first, all were dressed in heavy black ceramite armour. All bore an intricate skull and 'I' design on their massive left pauldrons. The icons on their right pauldrons, however, were each unique.

'Clear the room,' barked one over his comm-link as he gunned down a greenskin in front of him, spitting death from the barrel of his silenced bolter. 'Quick and quiet. Kill the rest before they raise the alarm.' Switching comm channels, he said, 'Sigma, this is Talon Alpha. Phase one complete. Kill-team is aboard. Securing entry point now.'

'Understood, Alpha,' replied the toneless voice at the other end of the link. 'Proceed on mission. Extract within the hour, as instructed. Captain Redthorne has orders to pull out if you miss your pick-up, so keep your team on a tight leash. This is *not* a purge operation. Is that clear?'

'I'm well aware of that, Sigma,' the kill-team leader replied brusquely.

'You had better be,' replied the voice. 'Sigma, out.'

It took Talon squad less than sixty seconds to clear the salvage bay. Brother Rauth of the Exorcists Chapter gunned down the last of the fleeing gretchin as it dashed for the exit. The creature stumbled as a single silenced bolt punched into its back. Half a second later, a flesh-muffled detonation ripped it apart.

It was the last of twenty-six bodies to fall among the litter of salvaged scrap.

'Target down, Karras,' reported Rauth. 'Area clear.'

'Confirmed,' replied Karras. He turned to face a Space Marine with a heavy flamer. 'Omni, you know what to do. The rest of you, cover the entrance.'

With the exception of Omni, the team immediately moved to positions covering the mouth of the corridor through which the orks had come. Omni, otherwise known as Maximmion Voss of the Imperial Fists, moved to the side walls, first the left, then the right, working quickly at a number of thick hydraulic pistons and power cables there.

'That was messy, Karras,' said Brother Solarion, 'letting them see us as we came out. I told you we should have used smoke. If one had escaped and raised the alarm...'

Karras ignored the comment. It was just Solarion being Solarion.

'Give it a rest, Prophet,' said Brother Zeed, opting to use Solarion's nickname. Zeed had coined it himself, and knew precisely how much it irritated the proud Ultramarine. 'The room is clear. No runners. No alarms. Scholar knows what he's doing.'

Scholar. That was what they called Karras, or at least Brothers Voss and Zeed did. Rauth and Solarion insisted on calling him by his second name. Sigma always called him Alpha. And his battle-brothers back on Occludus, homeworld of the Death Spectres Chapter, simply called him by his first name, Lyandro, or sometimes simply Codicier – his rank in the Librarius.

Karras didn't much care what anyone called him so long as they all did their jobs. The honour of serving in the Deathwatch had been offered to him, and he had taken it, knowing the great glory it would bring both himself and his Chapter. But he wouldn't be sorry when his obligation to the Emperor's Holy Inquisition was over. Astartes life seemed far less complicated among one's own Chapter-brothers.

When would he return to the fold? He didn't know. There was no fixed term for Deathwatch service. The Inquisition made high demands of all it called upon. Karras might not see the darkly beautiful crypt-cities of his home world again for decades... if he lived that long.

'Done, Scholar,' reported Voss as he rejoined the rest of the team.

Karras nodded and pointed towards a shattered pict screen and rune-board that protruded from the wall, close to the bay's only exit. 'Think you can get anything from that?' he asked.

'Nothing from the screen,' said Voss, 'but I could try wiring the data-feed directly into my visor.'

'Do it,' said Karras, 'but be quick.' To the others, he said, 'Proceed with phase two. Solarion, take point.'

The Ultramarine nodded curtly, rose from his position among the scrap and stalked forward into the shadowy corridor, bolter raised and ready. He moved with smooth, near-silent steps despite the massive weight of his armour. Torias Telion, famed Ultramarine Scout Master and Solarion's former mentor, would have been proud of his prize student.

One by one, with the exception of Voss, the rest of the kill-team followed in his wake.

The filthy, rusting corridors of the ork ship were lit, but the electric lamps the greenskins had strung up along pipes and ducts were old and in poor repair. Barely half of them seemed to be working at all. Even these buzzed and flickered in a constant battle to throw out their weak illumination. Still, the little light they did give was enough to bother the kill-team leader. The inquisitor, known to the members of Talon only by his call-sign, Sigma, had estimated the ork population of the ship at somewhere over twenty thousand. Against odds like these, Karras knew only too well that darkness and stealth were among his best weapons.

'I want the lights taken out,' he growled. 'The longer we stay hidden, the better our chances of making it off this damned heap.'

'We could shoot them out as we go,' offered Solarion, 'but I'd rather not waste my ammunition on something that doesn't bleed.'

Just then, Karras heard Voss on the comm-link. 'I've finished with the terminal, Scholar. I managed to pull some old cargo manifests from the ship's memory core. Not much else, though. Apparently, this ship used to be a civilian heavy-transport, Magellann class, built on Stygies. It was called *The Pegasus*.'

'No schematics?'

'Most of the memory core is heavily corrupted. It's thousands of years old. We were lucky to get that much.'

'Sigma, this is Alpha,' said Karras. 'The ork ship is built around an Imperial transport called *The Pegasus*. Requesting schematics, priority one.'

'I heard,' said Sigma. 'You'll have them as soon as I do.'

'Voss, where are you now?' Karras asked.

'Close to your position,' said the Imperial Fist.

'Do you have any idea which cable provides power to the lights?'

'Look up,' said Voss. 'See those cables running along the ceiling? The thick one, third from the left. I'd wager my knife on it.'

Karras didn't have to issue the order. The moment Zeed heard Voss's words, his right arm flashed upwards. There was a crackle of blue energy as the Raven Guard's claws sliced through the cable, and the corridor went utterly dark.

To the Space Marines, however, everything remained clear as day. Their Mark VII helmets, like everything else in their arsenal, had been heavily modified by the Inquisition's finest artificers. They boasted a composite low-light/thermal vision mode that was superior to anything else Karras had ever used. In the three years he had been leading Talon, it had tipped the balance in his favour more times than he cared to count. He hoped it would do so many more times in the years to come, but that would all depend on their survival here, and he knew all too well that the odds were against them from the start. It wasn't just the numbers they were up against, or the tight deadline. There was something here the likes of which few Deathwatch kill-teams had ever faced before.

Karras could already feel its presence somewhere on the upper levels of the ship.

'Keep moving,' he told the others.

Three minutes after Zeed had killed the lights, Solarion hissed for them all to stop. 'Karras,' he rasped, 'I have multiple xenos up ahead. Suggest you move up and take a look.'

Karras ordered the others to hold and went forward, careful not to bang or scrape his broad pauldrons against the clutter of twisting pipes that lined both walls. Crouching beside Solarion, he realised he needn't have worried about a little noise. In front of him, over a hundred orks had crowded into a high-ceilinged, octagonal chamber. They were hooting and laughing and wrestling with each other to get nearer the centre of the room.

Neither Karras nor Solarion could see beyond the wall of broad green backs, but there was clearly something in the middle that was holding their attention.

'What are they doing?' whispered Solarion.

Karras decided there was only one way to find out. He centred his awareness down in the pit of his stomach, and began reciting the Litany of the Sight Beyond Sight that his former master, Chief Librarian Athio Cordatus, had taught him during his earliest years in the Librarius. Beneath his helmet, hidden from Solarion's view, Karras's eyes, normally deep red in colour, began to glow with an ethereal white flame. On his forehead, a wound appeared. A single drop of blood rolled over his brow and down to the bridge of his narrow, angular nose. Slowly, as he opened his soul fractionally more to the dangerous power within him, the wound widened, revealing the physical manifestation of his psychic inner eye.

Karras felt his awareness lift out of his body now. He willed it deeper into the chamber, rising above the backs of the orks, looking down on them from above.

He saw a great pit sunk into the centre of the metal floor. It was filled with hideous ovoid creatures of every possible colour, their tiny red eyes set above oversized mouths crammed with razor-edged teeth.

'It's a mess hall,' Karras told his team over the link. 'There's a squig pit in the centre.'

As his projected consciousness watched, the greenskins at the rim of the pit stabbed downwards with cruelly barbed poles, hooking their prey through soft flesh. Then they lifted the squigs, bleeding and screaming, into the air before reaching for them, tearing them from the hooks, and feasting on them.

'They're busy,' said Karras, 'but we'll need to find another way through.'

'Send me in, Scholar,' said Voss from the rear. 'I'll turn them all into cooked meat before they even realise they're under attack. Ghost can back me up.'

'On your order, Scholar,' said Zeed eagerly.

Ghost. That was Siefer Zeed. With his helmet off, it was easy to see how he'd come by the name. Like Karras, and like all brothers of their respective Chapters, Zeed was the victim of a failed melanochromic implant, a slight mutation in his ancient and otherwise worthy gene-seed. The skin of both he and the kill-team leader was as white as porcelain. But, whereas Karras bore the blood-red eyes and chalk-white hair of the true albino, Zeed's eyes were black as coals, and his hair no less dark.

'Negative,' said Karras. 'We'll find another way through.'

He pushed his astral-self further into the chamber, desperate to find a means that didn't involve alerting the foe, but there seemed little choice. Only when he turned his awareness upwards did he see what he was looking for.

'There's a walkway near the ceiling,' he reported. 'It looks frail, rusting badly, but if we cross it one at a time, it should hold.'

A sharp, icy voice on the comm-link interrupted him. 'Talon Alpha, get ready to receive those schematics. Transmitting now.'

Karras willed his consciousness back into his body, and his glowing third eye sealed itself, leaving only the barest trace of a scar. Using conventional sight, he consulted his helmet's heads-up display and watched the last few per cent of the schematics file being downloaded. When it was finished, he called it up with a thought, and the helmet projected it as a shimmering green image cast directly onto his left retina.

The others, he knew, were seeing the same thing.

'According to these plans,' he told them, 'there's an access ladder set into the wall near the second junction we passed. We'll backtrack to it. The corridor above this one will give us access to the walkway.'

'If it's still there,' said Solarion. 'The orks may have removed it.'

'And backtracking will cost us time,' grumbled Voss.

'Less time than a firefight would cost us,' countered Rauth. His hard, gravelly tones were made even harder by the slight distortion on the comm-link. 'There's a time and place for that kind of killing, but it isn't now.'

'Watcher's right,' said Zeed reluctantly. It was rare for he and Rauth to agree.

'I've told you before,' warned Rauth. 'Don't call me that.'

'Right or wrong,' said Karras, 'I'm not taking votes. I've made my call. Let's move.'

Karras was the last to cross the gantry above the ork feeding pit. The shadows up here were dense and, so far, the orks had noticed nothing, though there had been a few moments when it looked as if the aging iron were about to collapse, particularly beneath the tremendous weight of Voss with his heavy flamer, high explosives, and back-mounted pro-methium supply.

Such was the weight of the Imperial Fist and his kit that Karras had decided to send him over first. Voss had made it across, but it was noth-ing short of a miracle that the orks below hadn't noticed the rain of red flakes showering down on them.

Lucky we didn't bring old Chyron after all, thought Karras.

The sixth member of Talon wouldn't have made it out of the salvage bay. The corridors on this ship were too narrow for such a mighty Space Marine. Instead, Sigma had ordered the redoubtable Dreadnought, formerly of the Lamenters Chapter but now permanently attached to Talon, to remain behind on Redthorne's ship, the *Saint Nevarre*. That had caused a few tense moments. Chyron had a vile temper.

Karras made his way, centimetre by centimetre, along the creaking metal grille, his silenced bolter fixed securely to the magnetic couplings on his right thigh plate, his force sword sheathed on his left hip. Over one massive shoulder was slung the cryo-case that Sigma had insisted he carry. Karras cursed it, but there was no way he could leave it behind. It added twenty kilogrammes to his already significant weight, but the case was absolutely critical to the mission. He had no choice.

Up ahead, he could see Rauth watching him, as ever, from the end of the gangway. What was the Exorcist thinking? Karras had no clue. He had never been able to read the mysterious Astartes. Rauth seemed to have no warp signature whatsoever. He simply didn't register at all. Even his armour, even his bolter for Throne's sake, resonated more than he did. And it was an anomaly that Rauth was singularly unwilling to discuss.

There was no love lost between them, Karras knew, and, for his part, he regretted that. He had made gestures, occasional overtures, but for whatever reason, they had been rebuffed every time. The Exorcist was unreachable, distant, remote, and it seemed he planned to stay that way.

As Karras took his next step, the cryo-case suddenly swung forward on its strap, shifting his centre of gravity and threatening to unbalance him. He compensated swiftly, but the effort caused the gangway to creak and a piece of rusted metal snapped off, spinning away under him.

He froze, praying that the orks wouldn't notice.

But one did.

It was at the edge of the pit, poking a fat squig with its barbed pole, when the metal fragment struck its head. The ork immediately stopped what it was doing and scanned the shadows above it, squinting suspiciously up towards the unlit recesses of the high ceiling.

Karras stared back, willing it to turn away. Reading minds and controlling minds, however, were two very different things. The latter was a power beyond his gifts. Ultimately, it wasn't Karras's will that turned the ork from its scrutiny. It was the nature of the greenskin species.

The other orks around it, impatient to feed, began grabbing at the barbed pole. One managed to snatch it, and the gazing ork suddenly found himself robbed of his chance to feed. He launched himself into a violent frenzy, lashing out at the pole-thief and those nearby. That was when the orks behind him surged forward, and pushed him into the squig pit.

Karras saw the squigs swarm on the hapless ork, sinking their long teeth into its flesh and tearing away great, bloody mouthfuls. The food chain had been turned on its head. The orks around the pit laughed and capered and struck at their dying fellow with their poles.

Karras didn't stop to watch. He moved on carefully, cursing the black case that was now pressed tight to his side with one arm. He rejoined his team in the mouth of a tunnel on the far side of the gantry and they moved off, pressing deeper into the ship. Solarion moved up front with Zeed. Voss stayed in the middle. Rauth and Karras brought up the rear.

'They need to do some damned maintenance around here,' Karras told Rauth in a wry tone.

The Exorcist said nothing.

By comparing Sigma's schematics of *The Pegasus* with the features he saw as he moved through it, it soon became clear to Karras that the orks had done very little to alter the interior of the ship beyond covering its walls in badly rendered glyphs, defecating wherever they pleased, leaving dead bodies to rot where they fell, and generally making the place unfit for habitation by anything save their own wretched kind. Masses of quivering fungi had sprouted from broken water pipes. Frayed electrical cables sparked and hissed at anyone who walked by. And there were so many bones strewn about that some sections almost looked like mass graves.

The Deathwatch members made a number of kills, or rather Solarion did, as they proceeded deeper into the ship's belly. Most of these were gretchin sent out on some errand or other by their slavemasters. The Ultramarine silently executed them wherever he found them and stuffed the small corpses under pipes or in dark alcoves. Only twice did the kill-team encounter parties of ork warriors, and both times, the green-skins announced themselves well in advance with their loud grunting and jabbering. Karras could tell that Voss and Zeed were both itching to engage, but stealth was still paramount. Instead, he, Rauth and Solarion eliminated the foe, loading powerful hellfire rounds into their silenced bolters to ensure quick, quiet one-shot kills.

'I've reached Waypoint Adrius,' Solarion soon reported from up ahead. 'No xenos contacts.'

'Okay, move in and secure,' Karras ordered. 'Check your corners and exits.'

The kill-team hurried forward, emerging from the blackness of the corridor into a towering square shaft. It was hundreds of metres high, its metal walls stained with age and rust and all kinds of spillage. Thick pipes ran across the walls at all angles, many of them venting steam or dripping icy coolant. There were broken staircases and rusting gantries at regular intervals, each of which led to gaping doorways. And, in the middle of the left-side wall, an open elevator shaft ran almost to the top.

It was here that Talon would be forced to split up. From this chamber, they could access any level in the ship. Voss and Zeed would go down via a metal stairway, the others would go up.

'Good luck using that,' said Voss, nodding towards the elevator cage. It was clearly of ork construction, a mishmash of metal bits bolted together. It had a bloodstained steel floor, a folding, lattice-work gate and a large lever which could be pushed forward for up, or pulled backwards for down.

There was no sign of what had happened to the original elevator.

Karras scowled under his helmet as he looked at it and cross-referenced what he saw against his schematics. 'We'll have to take it as high as it will go,' he told Rauth and Solarion. He pointed up towards the far ceiling. 'That landing at the top; that is where we are going. From there we can access the corridor to the bridge. Ghost, Omni, you have your own objectives.' He checked the mission chrono in the corner of his visor. 'Forty-three minutes,' he told them. 'Avoid confrontation if you can. And stay in contact.'

'Understood, Scholar,' said Voss.

Karras frowned. He could sense the Imperial Fist's hunger for battle. It had been there since the moment they'd set foot on this mechanical abomination. Like most Imperial Fists, once Voss was in a fight, he tended to stay there until the foe was dead. He could be stubborn to the point of idiocy, but there was no denying his versatility. Weapons, vehicles, demolitions… Voss could do it all.

'Ghost,' said Karras. 'Make sure he gets back here on schedule.'

'If I have to knock him out and drag him back myself,' said Zeed.

'You can try,' Voss snorted, grinning under his helmet. He and the

Raven Guard had enjoyed a good rapport since the moment they had met. Karras occasionally envied them that.

'Go,' he told them, and they moved off, disappearing down a stairwell on the right, their footsteps vibrating the grille under Karras's feet.

'Then there were three,' said Solarion.

'With the Emperor's blessing,' said Karras, 'that's all we'll need.' He strode over to the elevator, pulled the latticework gate aside, and got in. As the others joined him, he added, 'If either of you know a Mechanicus prayer, now would be a good time. Rauth, take us up.'

The Exorcist pushed the control lever forward, and it gave a harsh, metallic screech. A winch high above them began turning. Slowly at first, then with increasing speed, the lower levels dropped away beneath them. Pipes and landings flashed by, then the counterweight whistled past. The floor of the cage creaked and groaned under their feet as it carried them higher and higher. Disconcerting sounds issued from the cable and the assembly at the top, but the ride was short, lasting barely a minute, for which Karras thanked the Emperor.

When they were almost at the top of the shaft, Rauth eased the control lever backwards and the elevator slowed, issuing the same high-pitched complaint with which it had started.

Karras heard Solarion cursing.

'Problem, brother?' he asked.

'We'll be lucky if the whole damned ship doesn't know we're here by now,' spat the Ultramarine. 'Accursed piece of ork junk.'

The elevator ground to a halt at the level of the topmost landing, and Solarion almost tore the latticework gate from its fixings as he wrenched it aside. Stepping out, he took point again automatically.

The rickety steel landing led off in two directions. To the left, it led to a trio of dimly lit corridor entrances. To the right, it led towards a steep metal staircase in a severe state of disrepair.

Karras consulted his schematics.

'Now for the bad news,' he said.

The others eyed the stair grimly.

'It won't hold us,' said Rauth. 'Not together.'

Some of the metal steps had rusted away completely leaving gaps of up to a metre. Others were bent and twisted, torn halfway free of their bolts as if something heavy had landed hard on them.

'So we spread out,' said Karras. 'Stay close to the wall. Put as little pressure on each step as we can. We don't have time to debate it.'

They moved off, Solarion in front, Karras in the middle, Rauth at the rear. Karras watched his point-man carefully, noting exactly where he placed each foot. The Ultramarine moved with a certainty and fluidity that few could match. Had he registered more of a warp signature than he did, Karras might even have suspected some kind of extrasensory perception, but, in fact, it was simply the superior training of the Master Scout, Telion.

Halfway up the stair, however, Solarion suddenly held up his hand and hissed, 'Hold!'

Rauth and Karras froze at once. The stairway creaked gently under them.

'Xenos, direct front. Twenty metres. Three big ones.'

Neither Karras nor Rauth could see them. The steep angle of the stair prevented it.

'Can you deal with them?' asked Karras.

'Not alone,' said Solarion. 'One is standing in a doorway. I don't have clear line of fire on him. It could go either way. If he charges, fine. But he may raise the alarm as soon as I drop the others. Better the three of us take them out at once, if you think you can move up quietly.'

The challenge in Solarion's words, not to mention his tone, could hardly be missed. Karras lifted a foot and placed it gently on the next step up. Slowly, he put his weight on it. There was a harsh grating sound.

'I said *quietly*,' hissed Solarion.

'I heard you, damn it,' Karras snapped back. Silently, he cursed the cryo-case strapped over his shoulder. Its extra weight and shifting centre of gravity was hampering him, as it had on the gantry above the squig pit, but what could he do?

'Rauth,' he said. 'Move past me. Don't touch this step. Place yourself on Solarion's left. Try to get an angle on the ork in the doorway. Solarion, open fire on Rauth's mark. You'll have to handle the other two yourself.'

'Confirmed,' rumbled Rauth. Slowly, carefully, the Exorcist moved out from behind Karras and continued climbing as quietly as he could. Flakes of rust fell from the underside of the stair like red snow.

Rauth was just ahead of Karras, barely a metre out in front, when, as he put the weight down on his right foot, the step under it gave way with a sharp snap. Rauth plunged into open space, nothing below him but two hundred metres of freefall and a lethally hard landing.

Karras moved on instinct with a speed that bordered on supernatural. His gauntleted fist shot out, catching Rauth just in time, closing around the Exorcist's left wrist with almost crushing force.

The orks turned their heads towards the sudden noise and stomped towards the top of the stairs, massive stubbers raised in front of them.

'By Guilliman's blood!' raged Solarion.

He opened fire.

The first of the orks collapsed with its brainpan blown out.

Karras was struggling to haul Rauth back onto the stairway, but the metal under his own feet, forced to support the weight of both Astartes, began to scrape clear of its fixings.

'Quickly, psyker,' gasped Rauth, 'or we'll both die.'

'Not a damned chance,' Karras growled. With a monumental effort of strength, he heaved Rauth high enough that the Exorcist could grab the staircase and scramble back onto it.

As Rauth got to his feet, he breathed, 'Thank you, Karras... but you may live to regret saving me.'

Karras was scowling furiously under his helmet. 'You may not think of me as your brother, but, at the very least, you are a member of my team. However, the next time you call me psyker with such disdain, you will be the one to regret it. Is that understood?'

Rauth glared at him for a second, then nodded once. 'Fair words.'

Karras moved past him, stepping over the broad gap then stopping at Solarion's side. On the landing ahead, he saw two ork bodies leaking copious amounts of fluid from severe head wounds.

As he looked at them, wailing alarms began to sound throughout the ship.

Solarion turned to face him. 'I told Sigma he should have put me in charge,' he hissed. 'Damn it, Karras.'

'Save it,' Karras barked. His eyes flicked to the countdown on his heads-up display. 'Thirty-three minutes left. They know we're here. The killing starts in earnest now, but we can't let them hold us up. Both of you follow me. Let's move!'

Without another word, the three Astartes pounded across the upper landing and into the mouth of the corridor down which the third ork had vanished, desperate to reach their primary objective before the whole damned horde descended on them.

'So much for keeping a low profile, eh, brother?' said Zeed as he guarded Voss's back.

A deafening, ululating wail had filled the air. Red lights began to rotate in their wall fixtures.

Voss grunted by way of response. He was concentrating hard on the task at hand. He crouched by the coolant valves of the ship's massive plasma reactor, power source for the vessel's gigantic main thrusters.

The noise in the reactor room was deafening even without the ork alarms, and none of the busy gretchin work crews had noticed the two Deathwatch members until it was too late. Zeed had hacked them limb from limb before they'd had a chance to scatter. Now that the alarm had been sounded, though, orks would be arming themselves and filling the corridors outside, each filthy alien desperate to claim a kill.

'We're done here,' said Voss, rising from his crouch. He hefted his heavy flamer from the floor and turned. 'The rest is up to Scholar and the others.'

Voss couldn't check in with them. Not from here. Such close proximity to a reactor, particularly one with so much leakage, filled the kill-team's primary comm-channels with nothing but static.

Zeed moved to the thick steel door of the reactor room, opened it a crack, and peered outside.

'It's getting busy out there,' he reported. 'Lots of mean-looking bastards, but they can hardly see with all the lights knocked out. What do you say, brother? Are you ready to paint the walls with the blood of the foe?'

Under his helmet, Voss grinned. He thumbed his heavy flamer's igniter switch and a hot blue flame burst to life just in front of the weapon's promethium nozzle. 'Always,' he said, coming abreast of the Raven Guard.

Together, the two comrades charged into the corridor, howling the names of their primarchs as battle-cries.

'We're pinned,' hissed Rauth as ork stubber and pistol fire smacked into the metal wall beside him. Pipes shattered. Iron flakes showered the ground. Karras, Rauth and Solarion had pushed as far and as fast as they could once the alarms had been tripped. But now they found themselves penned-in at a junction, a confluence of three broad corridors, and mobs of howling, jabbering orks were pouring towards them from all sides.

With his knife, Solarion had already severed the cable that powered the lights, along with a score of others that did Throne knew what. A number of the orks, however, were equipped with goggles, not to mention weapons and armour far above typical greenskin standards. Karras had fought such fiends before. They were the greenskin equivalent of commando squads, far more cunning and deadly than the usual muscle-minded oafs. Their red night-vision lenses glowed like daemons' eyes as they pressed closer and closer, keeping to cover as much as possible.

Karras and his Deathwatch Marines were outnumbered at least twenty to one, and that ratio would quickly change for the worse if they didn't break through soon.

'Orders, Karras,' growled Solarion as his right pauldron absorbed a direct hit. The ork shell left an ugly scrape on the blue and white Chapter insignia there. 'We're taking too much fire. The cover here is pitiful.'

Karras thought fast. A smokescreen would be useless. If the ork goggles were operating on thermal signatures, they would see right through it. Incendiaries or frags would kill a good score of them and dissuade the others from closing, but that wouldn't solve the problem of being pinned.

'Novas,' he told them. 'On my signal, one down each corridor. Short throws. Remember to cover your visors. The moment they detonate, we make a push. I'm taking point. Clear?'

'On your mark, Karras,' said Solarion with a nod.

'Give the word,' said Rauth.

Karras tugged a nova grenade from the webbing around his armoured waist. The others did the same. He pulled the pin, swung his arm back and called out, 'Now!'

Three small black cylinders flew through the darkness to clatter against the metal floor. Swept up in the excitement of the firefight, the orks didn't notice them.

'Eyes!' shouted Karras and threw an arm up over his visor.

Three deafening bangs sounded in quick succession, louder even than the bark of the orks' guns. Howls of agony immediately followed, filling the close, damp air of the corridors. Karras looked up to see the orks reeling around in the dark with their great, thick-fingered hands pressed to their faces. They were crashing into the walls, weapons forgotten, thrown to the floor in their agony and confusion.

Nova grenades were typically employed for room clearance, but they worked well in any dark, enclosed space. They were far from standard-issue Astartes hardware, but the Deathwatch were the elite, the best of the best, and they had access to the kind of resources that few others could boast. The intense, phosphor-bright flash that the grenades produced overloaded optical receptors, both mechanical and biological. The blindness was temporary in most cases, but Karras was betting that the orks' goggles would magnify the glare.

Their retinas would be permanently burned out.

'With me,' he barked, and charged out from his corner. He moved in a blur, fixing his silenced bolter to the mag-locks on his thigh plate and drawing his faithful force sword, Arquemann, from its scabbard as he raced towards the foe.

Rauth and Solarion came behind, but not so close as to gamble with their lives. The bite of Arquemann was certain death whenever it glowed with otherworldly energy, and it had begun to glow now, throwing out a chill, unnatural light.

Karras threw himself in among the greenskin commandos, turning great powerful arcs with his blade, despatching more xenos filth with every limb-severing stroke. Steaming corpses soon littered the floor. The orks in the corridors behind continued to flail blindly, attacking each other now, in their sightless desperation.

'The way is clear,' Karras gasped. 'We run.' He sheathed Arquemann and led the way, feet pounding on the metal deck. The cryo-case swung wildly behind him as he moved, but he paid it no mind. Beneath his helmet, his third eye was closing again. The dangerous energies that gave him his powers were retreating at his command, suppressed by the mantras that kept him strong, kept him safe.

The inquisitor's voice intruded on the comm-link. 'Alpha, this is Sigma. Respond.'

'I hear you, Sigma,' said Karras as he ran.

'Where are you now?'

'Closing on Waypoint Barrius. We're about one minute out.'

'You're falling behind, Alpha. Perhaps I should begin preparing death certificates to your respective Chapters.'

'Damn you, inquisitor. We'll make it. Now if that's all you wanted…'

'Solarion is to leave you at Barrius. I have another task for him.'

'No,' said Karras flatly. 'We're already facing heavy resistance here. I need him with me.'

'I don't make requests, Deathwatch. According to naval intelligence reports, there is a large fighter bay on the ship's starboard side. Significant fuel dumps. Give Solarion your explosives. I want him to knock out that fighter bay while you and Rauth proceed to the bridge. If all goes well, the diversion may help clear your escape route. If not, you had better start praying for a miracle.'

'Rauth will blow the fuel dumps,' said Karras, opting to test a hunch.

'No,' said Sigma. 'Solarion is better acquainted with operating alone.'

Karras wondered about Sigma's insistence that Solarion go. Rauth hardly ever let Karras out of his sight. It had been that way ever since they'd met. Little wonder, then, that Zeed had settled on the nickname '*Watcher*'. Was Sigma behind it all? Karras couldn't be sure. The inquisitor had a point about Solarion's solo skills, and he knew it.

'Fine, I'll give Solarion the new orders.'

'No,' said Sigma. 'I'll do it directly. You and Rauth must hurry to the command bridge. Expect to lose comms once you get closer to the target. I'm sure you've sensed the creature's incredible power already. I want that thing eliminated, Alpha. Do not fail me.'

'When have I ever?' Karras retorted, but Sigma had already cut the link. Judging by Solarion's body language as he ran, the inquisitor was already giving him his new orders.

At the next junction, Waypoint Barrius, the trio encountered another ork mob. But the speed at which Karras and his men were moving caught the orks by surprise. Karras didn't even have time to charge his blade with psychic energy before he was in among them, hacking and thrusting. Arquemann was lethally sharp even without the power of the immaterium running through it, and orks fell in a great tide of blood. Silenced bolters coughed on either side of him, Solarion and Rauth giving fire support, and soon the junction was heaped with twitching green meat.

Karras turned to Rauth. 'Give Solarion your frags and incendiaries,' he said, pulling his own from his webbing. 'But keep two breaching charges. We'll need them.'

Solarion accepted the grenades, quickly fixing them to his belt, then he said, 'Good hunting, brothers.'

Karras nodded. 'We'll rendezvous back at the elevator shaft. Whoever gets there first holds it until the others arrive. Keep the comm-link open. If it goes dead for more than ten minutes at our end, don't waste any time. Rendezvous with Voss and Zeed and get to the salvage bay.'

Solarion banged a fist on his breastplate in salute and turned.

Karras nodded to Rauth. 'Let's go,' he said, and together, they ran on towards the fore section of the ship while Solarion merged with the shadows in the other direction.

'Die!' spat Zeed as another massive greenskin slid to the floor, its body opened from gullet to groin. Then he was moving again. Instincts every bit as sharp as his lightning claws told him to sidestep just in time to avoid the stroke of a giant chainaxe that would have cleaved him in two. The ork wielding the axe roared in frustration as its whirring blade bit into the metal floor, sending up a shower of orange sparks. It made a grab for Zeed with its empty hand, but Zeed parried, slipped inside at the same instant, and thrust his right set of claws straight up under the creature's jutting jaw. The tips of the long slender blades punched through the top of its skull, and it stood there quivering, literally dead on its feet.

Zeed stepped back, wrenching his claws from the creature's throat, and watched its body drop beside the others.

He looked around hungrily, eager for another opponent to step forward, but there were none to be had. Voss and he stood surrounded by dead xenos. The Imperial Fist had already lowered his heavy flamer. He stood admiring his handiwork, a small hill of smoking black corpses. The two comrades had fought their way back to Waypoint Adrius. The air in the towering chamber was now thick with the stink of spilled blood and burnt flesh.

Zeed looked up at the landings overhead and said, 'No sign of the others.'

Voss moved up beside him. 'There's much less static on the comm-link here. Scholar, this is Omni. If you can hear me, respond.'

At first there was no answer. Voss was about to try again when the Death Spectre Librarian finally acknowledged. 'I hear you, Omni. This isn't the best time.'

Karras sounded strained, as if fighting for his life.

'We are finished with the reactor,' Voss reported. 'Back at Waypoint Adrius, now. Do you need assistance?'

As he asked this, Voss automatically checked the mission countdown. Not good.

Twenty-seven minutes left.

'Hold that position,' Karras grunted. 'We need to keep that area secure for our escape. Rauth and I are–'

His words were cut off in mid-sentence. For a brief instant, Voss and Zeed thought the kill-team leader had been hit, possibly even killed. But their fears were allayed when Karras heaved a sigh of relief and said, 'Damn, those bastards were strong. Ghost, you would have enjoyed that. Listen, brothers, Rauth and I are outside the ship's command bridge. Time is running out. If we don't make it back to Waypoint Adrius within the next twelve minutes, I want the rest of you to pull out. Do *not* miss the pick-up. Is that understood?'

Voss scowled. The words *pull out* made him want to smash something. As far as his Chapter was concerned, they were curse words. But he knew Karras was right. There was little to be gained by dying here. 'Emperor's speed, Scholar,' he said.

'For Terra and the Throne,' Karras replied then signed off.

Zeed was scraping his claws together restlessly, a bad habit that manifested itself when he had excess adrenaline and no further outlet for it. 'Damn,' he said. 'I'm not standing around here while the others are fighting for their lives.' He pointed to the metal landing high above him where Karras and the others had gotten off the elevator. 'There has to be a way to call that piece of junk back down to this level. We can ride it up there and–'

He was interrupted by the clatter of heavy, iron-shod boots closing from multiple directions. The sounds echoed into the chamber from a dozen corridor mouths.

'I think we're about to be too busy for that, brother,' said Voss darkly.

Rauth stepped over the body of the massive ork guard he had just slain, flicked the beast's blood from the groove on his shortsword, and sheathed it at his side. There was a shallow crater in the ceramite of his right pauldron. Part of his Chapter icon was missing, cleaved off in the fight. The daemon-skull design now boasted only a single horn. The other pauldron, intricately detailed with the skull, bones and inquisitorial 'I' of the Deathwatch, was chipped and scraped, but had suffered no serious damage.

'That's the biggest I've slain hand-to-hand,' the Exorcist muttered, mostly to himself.

The one Karras had just slain was no smaller, but the Death Spectre was focused on something else. He was standing with one hand pressed to a massive steel blast door covered in orkish glyphs. Tiny lambent arcs of unnatural energy flickered around him.

'There's a tremendous amount of psychic interference,' he said, 'but I sense at least thirty of them on this level. Our target is on the upper deck. And he knows we're here.'

Rauth nodded, but said nothing. *We?* No. Karras was wrong in that. Rauth knew well enough that the target couldn't have sensed him. Nothing psychic could. It was a side effect of the unspeakable horrors he had endured during his Chapter's selection and training programmes— programmes that had taught him to hate all psykers and the terrible daemons their powers sometimes loosed into the galaxy.

The frequency with which Lyandro Karras tapped the power of the immaterium disgusted Rauth. Did the Librarian not realise the great peril in which he placed his soul? Or was he simply a fool, spilling over with an arrogance that invited the ultimate calamity. Daemons of the warp rejoiced in the folly of such men.

Of course, that was why Rauth had been sequestered to Deathwatch in the first place. The inquisitor had never said so explicitly, but it simply had to be the case. As enigmatic as Sigma was, he was clearly no fool. Who better than an Exorcist to watch over one such as Karras? Even the mighty Grey Knights, from whose seed Rauth's Chapter had been born, could hardly have been more suited to the task.

'Smoke,' said Karras. 'The moment we breach, I want smoke grenades in there. Don't spare them for later. Use what we have. We go in with bolters blazing. Remove your suppressor. There's no need for it now. Let them hear the bark of our guns. The minute the lower floor is cleared, we each take a side stair to the command deck. You go left. I'll take the right. We'll find the target at the top.'

'Bodyguards?' asked Rauth. Like Karras, he began unscrewing the sound suppressor from the barrel of his bolter.

'I can't tell. If there are, the psychic resonance is blotting them out. It's… incredible.'

The two Astartes stored their suppressors in pouches on their webbing, then Rauth fixed a rectangular breaching charge to the seam between the double doors. The Exorcist was about to step back when Karras said, 'No, brother. We'll need two. These doors are stronger than you think.'

Rauth fixed another charge just below the first, then he and Karras moved to either side of the doorway and pressed their backs to the wall.

Simultaneously, they checked the magazines in their bolters. Rauth slid in a fresh clip. Karras tugged a smoke grenade from his webbing, and nodded.

'Now!'

Rauth pressed the tiny detonator in his hand, and the whole corridor shook with a deafening blast to rival the boom of any artillery piece. The heavy doors blew straight into the room, causing immediate casualties among the orks closest to the explosion.

'Smoke!' ordered Karras as he threw his first grenade. Rauth discarded the detonator and did the same. Two, three, four small canisters bounced onto the ship's bridge, spread just enough to avoid redundancy. Within two seconds, the whole deck was covered in a dense grey cloud. The ork crew went into an uproar, barely able to see their hands in front of their faces. But to the Astartes, all was perfectly clear. They entered the room with bolters firing, each shot a vicious bark, and the greenskins fell where they stood.

Not a single bolt was wasted. Every last one found its target, every shot a headshot, an instant kill. In the time it took to draw three breaths, the lower floor of the bridge was cleared of threats.

'Move!' said Karras, making for the stair that jutted from the right-hand wall.

The smoke had begun to billow upwards now, thinning as it did.

Rauth stormed the left-side stair.

Neither Space Marine, however, was entirely prepared for what he found at the top.

* * *

Solarion burst from the mouth of the corridor and sprinted along the metal landing in the direction of the elevator cage. He was breathing hard, and rivulets of red blood ran from grape-sized holes in the armour of his torso and left upper arm. If he could only stop, the wounds would quickly seal themselves, but there was no time for that. His normally dormant second heart was pumping in tandem with the first, flushing lactic acid from his muscles, helping him to keep going. Following barely a second behind him, a great mob of armoured orks with heavy pistols and blades surged out of the same corridor in hot pursuit. The platform trembled under their tremendous weight.

Solarion didn't stop to look behind. Just ahead of him, the upper section of the landing ended. Beyond it was the rusted stairway that had almost claimed Rauth's life. There was no time now to navigate those stairs.

He put on an extra burst of speed and leapt straight out over them.

It was an impressive jump. For a moment, he almost seemed to fly. Then he passed the apex of his jump and the ship's artificial gravity started to pull him downwards. He landed on the lower section of the landing with a loud clang. Sharp spears of pain shot up the nerves in his legs, but he ignored them and turned, bolter held ready at his shoulder.

The orks were following his example, leaping from the upper platform, hoping to land right beside him and cut him to pieces. Their lack of agility, however, betrayed them. The first row crashed down onto the rickety stairs about two thirds of the way down. The old iron steps couldn't take that kind of punishment. They crumbled and snapped, dropping the luckless orks into lethal freefall. The air filled with howls, but the others didn't catch on until it was too late. They, too, leapt from the platform's edge in their eagerness to make a kill. Step after step gave way with each heavy body that crashed down on it, and soon the stairway was reduced almost to nothing.

A broad chasm, some thirty metres across, now separated the metal platforms that had been joined by the stairs. The surviving orks saw that they couldn't follow the Space Marine across. Instead, they paced the edge of the upper platform, bellowing at Solarion in outrage and frustration and taking wild potshots at him with their clunky pistols.

'It's raining greenskins,' said a gruff voice on the link. 'What in Dorn's name is going on up there?'

With one eye still on the pacing orks, Solarion moved to the edge of the platform. As he reached the twisted railing, he looked out over the edge and down towards the steel floor two hundred metres below. Gouts of bright promethium flame illuminated a conflict there. Voss and Zeed were standing back to back, about five metres apart, fighting off an ork assault from all sides. The floor around them was heaped with dead aliens.

'This is Solarion,' the Ultramarine told them. 'Do you need aid, brothers?'

'Prophet?' said Zeed between lethal sweeps of his claws. 'Where are Scholar and Watcher?'

'You've had no word?' asked Solarion.

'They've been out of contact since they entered the command bridge. Sigma warned of that. But time is running out. Can you go to them?'

'Impossible,' replied Solarion. 'The stairs are gone. I can't get back up there now.'

'Then pray for them,' said Voss.

Solarion checked his mission chrono. He remembered Karras's orders. Four more minutes. After that, he would have to assume they were dead. He would take the elevator down and, with the others, strike out for the salvage bay and their only hope of escape.

A shell from an ork pistol ricocheted from the platform and smacked against his breastplate. The shot wasn't powerful enough to penetrate ceramite, not like the heavy-stubber shells he had taken at close range, but it got his attention. He was about to return fire, to start clearing the upper platform in anticipation of Karras and Rauth's return, when a great boom shook the air and sent deep vibrations through the metal under his feet.

'That's not one of mine,' said Voss.

'It's mine,' said Solarion. 'I rigged the fuel dump in their fighter bay. If we're lucky, most of the greenskins will be drawn there, thinking that's where the conflict is. It might buy our brothers a little time.'

The mission chrono now read eighteen minutes and forty seconds. He watched it drop. Thirty-nine seconds. Thirty-eight. Thirty-seven.

Come on, Karras, he thought. What in Terra's name are you doing?

Karras barely had time to register the sheer size of Balthazog Bludwrekk's twin bodyguards before their blistering assault began. They were easily the largest orks he had ever seen, even larger than the door guards he and Rauth had slain, and they wielded their massive two-handed war-hammers as if they weighed nothing at all. Under normal circumstances, orks of this size and strength would have become mighty warbosses, but these two were nothing of the kind. They were slaves to a far greater power than mere muscle or aggression. They were mindless puppets held in servitude by a much deadlier force, and the puppeteer himself sat some ten metres behind them, perched on a bizarre mechanical throne in the centre of the ship's command deck.

*Bludwrekk!*

Karras only needed an instant, a fraction of a second, to take in the details of the fiend's appearance.

Even for an ork, the psychic warboss was hideous. Portions of his head were vastly swollen, with great vein-marbled bumps extending out in all directions from his crown. His brow was ringed with large, blood-stained metal plugs sunk deep into the bone of his skull. The beast's leering, lopsided face was twisted, like something seen in a curved mirror, the features pathetically small on one side, grotesquely overlarge on the other, and saliva dripped from his slack jaw, great strands of it hanging from the spaces between his tusks.

He wore a patchwork robe of cured human skins stitched together with gut, and a trio of decaying heads hung between his knees, fixed to his belt by long, braided hair. Karras had the immediate impression that the heads had been taken from murdered women, perhaps the wives of some human lord or tribal leader that the beast had slain during a raid. Orks had a known fondness for such grisly trophies.

The beast's throne was just as strange; a mass of coils, cogs and moving pistons without any apparent purpose whatsoever. Thick bundles of wire linked it to an inexplicable clutter of vast, arcane machines that crackled and hummed with sickly green light. In the instant Karras took all this in, he felt his anger and hate break over him like a thunderstorm.

It was as if this creature, this blasted aberration, sat in sickening, blasphemous parody of the immortal Emperor Himself.

The two Space Marines opened fire at the same time, eager to drop the bodyguards and engage the real target quickly. Their bolters chattered, spitting their deadly hail, but somehow each round detonated harmlessly in the air.

'He's shielding them!' Karras called out. 'Draw your blade!'

He dropped the cryo-case from his shoulder, pulled Arquemann from its scabbard and let the power of the immaterium flow through him, focusing it into the ancient crystalline matrix that lay embedded in the blade.

'To me, xenos scum!' he roared at the hulking beast in front of him.

The bodyguard's massive hammer whistled up into the air, then changed direction with a speed that seemed impossible. Karras barely managed to step aside. Sparks flew as the weapon clipped his left pauldron, sending a painful shock along his arm. The thick steel floor fared worse. The hammer left a hole in it the size of a human head.

On his right, Karras heard Rauth loose a great battle-cry as he clashed with his own opponent, barely ducking a lateral blow that would have taken his head clean off. The Exorcist's short-sword looked awfully small compared to his enemy's hammer.

Bludwrekk was laughing, revelling in the life and death struggle that was playing out before him, as if it were some kind of grand entertainment laid on just for him. The more he cackled, the more the green light seemed to shimmer and churn around him. Karras felt the resonance of that power disorienting him. The air was supercharged with it. He felt his own power surging up inside him, rising to meet it. Only so much could be channelled into his force sword. Already, the blade sang with deadly energy as it slashed through the air.

This surge is dangerous, he warned himself. I mustn't let it get out of control.

Automatically, he began reciting the mantras Master Cordatus had taught him, but the effort of wrestling to maintain his equilibrium cost him an opening in which he could have killed his foe with a stroke. The ork bodyguard, on the other hand, did not miss its chance. It caught Karras squarely on the right pauldron with the head of its hammer, shattering the Deathwatch insignia there, and knocking him sideways, straight off his feet.

The impact hurled Karras directly into Rauth's opponent, and the two tumbled to the metal floor. Karras's helmet was torn from his head, and rolled away. In the sudden tangle of thrashing Space Marine and ork bodies, Rauth saw an opening. He stepped straight in, plunging his shortsword up under the beast's sternum, shoving it deep, cleaving the ork's heart in two. Without hesitation, he then turned to face the remaining bodyguard while Karras kicked himself clear of the dead behemoth and got to his feet.

The last bodyguard was fast, and Rauth did well to stay clear of the whistling hammerhead, but the stabbing and slashing strokes of his shortsword were having little effect. It was only when Karras joined him, and the ork was faced with attacks from two directions at once, that the tables truly turned. Balthazog Bludwrekk had stopped laughing now. He gave a deafening roar of anger as Rauth and Karras thrust from opposite angles and, between them, pierced the greenskin's heart and lungs.

Blood bubbled from its wounds as it sank to the floor, dropping its mighty hammer with a crash.

Bludwrekk surged upwards from his throne. Arcs of green lightning lanced outwards from his fingers. Karras felt Waaagh! energy lick his armour, looking for chinks through which it might burn his flesh and corrode his soul. Together, blades raised, he and Rauth rounded on their foe.

The moment they stepped forward to engage, however, a great torrent of kinetic energy burst from the ork's outstretched hands and launched Rauth into the air. Karras ducked and rolled sideways, narrowly avoiding death, but he heard Rauth land with a heavy crash on the lower floor of the bridge.

'Rauth!' he shouted over the link. 'Answer!'

No answer was forthcoming. The comm-link was useless here. And perhaps Rauth was already dead.

Karras felt the ork's magnified power pressing in on him from all sides, and now he saw its source. Behind Bludwrekk's mechanical throne, beyond a filthy, blood-spattered window of thick glass, there were hundreds – no, thousands – of orks strapped to vertical slabs that looked like operating tables. The tops of their skulls had been removed, and cables and tubes ran from their exposed brains to the core of a vast power-siphoning system.

'By the Golden Throne,' gasped Karras. 'No wonder Sigma wants your ugly head.'

How much time remained before the ship's reactors detonated? Without his helmet, he couldn't tell. Long enough to kill this monstrosity? Maybe. But, one on one, was he even a match for the thing?

Not without exploiting more of the dangerous power at his disposal. He had to trust in his master's teachings. The mantras would keep him safe. They had to. He opened himself up to the warp a little more, channelling it, focusing it with his mind.

Bludwrekk stepped forward to meet him, and the two powers clashed with apocalyptic fury.

Darrion Rauth was not dead. The searing impact of the ork warlord's psychic blast would have killed a lesser man on contact, ripping his soul from his body and leaving it a lifeless hunk of meat. But Rauth was no lesser man. The secret rites of his Chapter, and the suffering he had endured to earn his place in it, had proofed him against such a fate. Also, though a number of his bones were broken, his superhuman physiology was already about the business of reknitting them, making them whole and strong again. The internal bleeding would stop soon, too.

But there wasn't time to heal completely. Not if he wanted to make a difference.

With a grunt of pain, he rolled, pushed himself to one knee, and looked for his shortsword. He couldn't see it. His bolter, however, was still attached to his thigh plate. He tugged it free, slammed in a fresh magazine, cocked it, and struggled to his feet. He coughed wetly, tasting blood in his mouth. Looking up towards the place from which he had been thrown, he saw unnatural light blazing and strobing. There was a great deal of noise, too, almost like thunder, but not quite the same. It made the air tremble around him.

Karras must still be alive, he thought. He's still fighting.

Pushing aside the agony in his limbs, he ran to the stairs on his right and, with an ancient litany of strength on his lips, charged up them to rejoin the battle.

Karras was failing. He could feel it. Balthazog Bludwrekk was drawing on an incredible reserve of power. The psychic Waaagh! energy he was tapping seemed boundless, pouring into the warlord from the brains of the tormented orks wired into his insane contraption.

Karras cursed as he struggled to turn aside another wave of roiling green fire. It buckled the deck plates all around him. Only those beneath his feet, those that fell inside the shimmering bubble he fought to maintain, remained undamaged.

His shield was holding, but only just, and the effort required to maintain it precluded him from launching attacks of his own. Worse yet, as the ork warlord pressed his advantage, Karras was forced to let the power of the warp flow through him more and more. A cacophony of voices had risen in his head, chittering and whispering in tongues he knew were blasphemous. This was the moment all Librarians feared, when the power they wielded threatened to consume them, when user became used, master became slave. The voices started to drown out his own. Much more of this and his soul would be lost for eternity, ripped from him and thrown into the maelstrom. Daemons would wrestle for command of his mortal flesh.

Was it right to slay this ork at the cost of his immortal soul? Should he not simply drop his shield and die so that something far worse than Bludwrekk would be denied entry into the material universe?

Karras could barely hear these questions in his head. So many other voices crowded them out.

Balthazog Bludwrekk seemed to sense the moment was his. He stepped nearer, still trailing thick cables from the metal plugs in his distorted skull.

Karras sank to one knee under the onslaught to both body and mind. His protective bubble was dissipating. Only seconds remained. One way or another, he realised, he was doomed.

Bludwrekk was almost on him now, still throwing green lightning from one hand, drawing a long, curved blade with the other. Glistening strands of drool shone in the fierce green light. His eyes were ablaze.

Karras sagged, barely able to hold himself upright, leaning heavily on the sword his mentor had given him.

I am Lyandro Karras, he tried to think. Librarian. Death Spectre. Space Marine. The Emperor will not let me fall.

But his inner voice was faint. Bludwrekk was barely two metres away. His psychic assault pierced Karras's shield. The Codicer felt the skin on his arms blazing and crisping. His nerves began to scream.

In his mind, one voice began to dominate the others. Was this the voice of the daemon that would claim him? It was so loud and clear that it seemed to issue from the very air around him. 'Get up, Karras!' it snarled. 'Fight!'

He realised it was speaking in High Gothic. He hadn't expected that.

His vision was darkening, despite the green fire that blazed all around, but, distantly, he caught a flicker of movement to his right. A hulking black figure appeared as if from nowhere, weapon raised before it. There was something familiar about it, an icon on the left shoulder; a skull with a single gleaming red eye.

*Rauth!*

The Exorcist's bolter spat a torrent of shells, forcing Balthazog Bludwrekk to spin and defend himself, concentrating all his psychic power on stopping the stream of deadly bolts.

Karras acted without pause for conscious thought. He moved on reflex, conditioned by decades of harsh daily training rituals. With Bludwrekk's merciless assault momentarily halted, he surged upwards, putting all his strength into a single horizontal swing of his force sword. The warp energy he had been trying to marshal crashed over him, flooding into the crystalline matrix of his blade as the razor-edged metal bit deep into the ork's thick green neck.

The monster didn't even have time to scream. Body and head fell in separate directions, the green light vanished, and the upper bridge was suddenly awash with steaming ork blood.

Karras fell to his knees, and screamed, dropping Arquemann at his side. His fight wasn't over. Not yet.

Now, he turned his attention to the battle for his soul.

Rauth saw all too clearly that his moment had come, as he had known it must, sooner or later, but he couldn't relish it. There was no joy to be had here. Psyker or not, Lyandro Karras was a Space Marine, a son of the Emperor just as he was himself, and he had saved Rauth's life.

But you must do it for him, Rauth told himself. You must do it to save his soul.

Out of respect, Rauth took off his helmet so that he might bear witness to the Death Spectre's final moments with his own naked eyes. Grimacing, he raised the barrel of his bolter to Karras's temple and began reciting the words of the *Mortis Morgatii Praetovo*. It was an ancient rite from long before the Great Crusade, forgotten by all save the Exorcists and the Grey Knights. If it worked, it would send Karras's spiritual essence beyond the reach of the warp's ravenous fiends, but it could not save his life.

It was not a long rite, and Rauth recited it perfectly.

As he came to the end of it, he prepared to squeeze the trigger.

War raged inside Lyandro Karras. Sickening entities filled with hate and hunger strove to overwhelm him. They were brutal and relentless, bombarding him with unholy visions that threatened to drown him in horror and disgust. He saw Imperial saints defiled and mutilated on altars of burning black rock. He saw the Golden Throne smashed and ruined, and the body of the Emperor trampled under the feet of vile capering beasts. He saw his Chapter house sundered, its walls covered in weeping sores as if the stones themselves had contracted a vile disease.

He cried out, railing against the visions, denying them. But still they came. He scrambled for something Cordatus had told him.

*Cordatus!*

The thought of that name alone gave him the strength to keep up the fight, if only for a moment. To avoid becoming lost in the empyrean, the old warrior had said, one must anchor oneself to the physical.

Karras reached for the physical now, for something real, a bastion against the visions.

He found it in a strange place, in a sensation he couldn't quite explain. Something hot and metallic was pressing hard against the skin of his temple.

The metal was scalding him, causing him physical pain. Other pains joined it, accumulating so that the song of agony his nerves were singing became louder and louder. He felt again the pain of his burned hands, even while his gene-boosted body worked fast to heal them. He clutched at the pain, letting the sensation pull his mind back to the moment, to the here and now. He grasped it like a rock in a storm-tossed sea.

The voices of the vile multitude began to weaken. He heard his own inner voice again, and immediately resumed his mantras. Soon enough, the energy of the immaterium slowed to a trickle, then ceased completely. He felt the physical manifestation of his third eye closing. He felt the skin knitting on his brow once again.

What was it, he wondered, this hot metal pressed to his head, this thing that had saved him?

He opened his eyes and saw the craggy, battle-scarred features of Darrion Rauth. The Exorcist was standing very close, helmet at his side, muttering something that sounded like a prayer.

His bolter was pressed to Karras's head, and he was about to blow his brains out.

'What are you doing?' Karras asked quietly.

Rauth looked surprised to hear his voice.

'I'm saving your soul, Death Spectre. Be at peace. Your honour will be spared. The daemons of the warp will not have you.'

'That is good to know,' said Karras. 'Now lower your weapon. My soul is exactly where it should be, and there it stays until my service to the Emperor is done.'

For a moment, neither Rauth nor Karras moved. The Exorcist did not seem convinced.

'Darrion Rauth,' said Karras. 'Are you so eager to spill my blood? Is this why you have shadowed my every movement for the last three years? Perhaps Solarion would thank you for killing me, but I don't think Sigma would.'

'That would depend,' Rauth replied. Hesitantly, however, he lowered his gun. 'You will submit to proper testing when we return to the *Saint Nevarre*. Sigma will insist on it, and so shall I.'

'As is your right, brother, but be assured that you will find no taint. Of course it won't matter either way unless we get off this ship alive. Quickly now, grab the monster's head. I will open the cryo-case.'

Rauth did as ordered, though he kept a wary eye on the kill-team leader. Lifting Bludwrekk's lifeless head, he offered it to Karras, saying, 'The machinery that boosted Bludwrekk's power should be analysed. If other ork psykers begin to employ such things...'

Karras took the ork's head from him, placed it inside the black case, and pressed a four-digit code into the keypad on the side. The lid fused itself shut with a hiss. Karras rose, slung it over his right shoulder, sheathed Arquemann, located his helmet, and fixed it back on his head. Rauth donned his own helmet, too.

'If Sigma wanted the machine,' said Karras as he led his comrade off the command bridge, 'he would have said so.'

Glancing at the mission chrono, he saw that barely seventeen minutes remained until the exfiltration deadline. He doubted it would be enough to escape the ship, but he wasn't about to give up without trying. Not after all they had been through here.

'Can you run?' he asked Rauth.

'Time is up,' said Solarion grimly. He stood in front of the open elevator cage. 'They're not going to make it. I'm coming down.'

'No,' said Voss. 'Give them another minute, Prophet.'

Voss and Zeed had finished slaughtering their attackers on the lower floor. It was just as well, too. Voss had used up the last of his promethium fuel in the fight. With great regret, he had slung the fuel pack off his back and relinquished the powerful weapon. He drew his support weapon, a bolt pistol, from a holster on his webbing.

It felt pathetically small and light in his hand.

'Would you have us all die here, brother?' asked the Ultramarine. 'For no gain? Because that will be our lot if we don't get moving right now.'

'If only we had heard *something* on the link...' said Zeed. 'Omni, as much as I hate to say it, Prophet has a point.'

'Believe me,' said Solarion, 'I wish it were otherwise. As of this moment, however, it seems only prudent that I assume operational command. Sigma, if you are listening–'

A familiar voice cut him off.

'Wait until my boots have cooled before you step into them, Solarion!'

'Scholar!' exclaimed Zeed. 'And is Watcher with you?'

'How many times must I warn you, Raven Guard,' said the Exorcist. 'Don't call me that.'

'At least another hundred,' replied Zeed.

'Karras,' said Voss, 'where in Dorn's name are you?'

'Almost at the platform now,' said Karras. 'We've got company. Ork commandos closing the distance from the rear.'

'Keep your speed up,' said Solarion. 'The stairs are out. You'll have to jump. The gap is about thirty metres.'

'Understood,' said Karras. 'Coming out of the corridor now.'

Solarion could hear the thunder of heavy feet pounding the upper metal platform from which he had so recently leaped. He watched from beside the elevator, and saw two bulky black figures soar out into the air.

Karras landed first, coming down hard. The cryo-case came free of his shoulder and skidded across the metal floor towards the edge. Solarion saw it and moved automatically, stopping it with one booted foot before it slid over the side.

Rauth landed a second later, slamming onto the platform in a heap. He gave a grunt of pain, pushed himself up and limped past Solarion into the elevator cage.

'Are you wounded, brother?' asked the Ultramarine.

'It is nothing,' growled Rauth.

Karras and Solarion joined him in the cage. The kill-team leader pulled the lever, starting them on their downward journey.

The cage started slowly at first, but soon gathered speed. Halfway down, the heavy counterweight again whooshed past them.

'Ghost, Omni,' said Karras over the link. 'Start clearing the route towards the salvage bay. We'll catch up with you as soon as we're at the bottom.'

'Loud and clear, Scholar,' said Zeed. He and Voss disappeared off into the darkness of the corridor through which the kill-team had originally come.

Suddenly, Rauth pointed upwards. 'Trouble,' he said.

Karras and Solarion looked up.

Some of the ork commandos, those more resourceful than their kin, had used grapnels to cross the gap in the platforms. Now they were hacking at the elevator cables with their broad blades.

'Solarion,' said Karras.

He didn't need to say anything else. The Ultramarine raised his bolter, sighted along the barrel, and began firing up at the orks. Shots sparked from the metal around the greenskins' heads, but it was hard to fire accurately with the elevator shaking and shuddering throughout its descent.

Rauth stepped forward and ripped the latticework gate from its hinges. 'We should jump the last twenty metres,' he said.

Solarion stopped firing. 'Agreed.'

Karras looked down from the edge of the cage floor. 'Forty metres,' he said. 'Thirty-five. Thirty. Twenty-five. Go!'

Together, the three Astartes leapt clear of the elevator and landed on the metal floor below. Again, Rauth gave a pained grunt, but he was up just as fast as the others.

Behind them, the elevator cage slammed into the floor with a mighty clang. Karras turned just in time to see the heavy counterweight smash down on top of it. The orks had cut the cables after all. Had the three Space Marines stayed in the cage until it reached the bottom, they would have been crushed to a fleshy pulp.

'Ten minutes left,' said Karras, adjusting the cryo-case on his shoulder. 'In the Emperor's name, run!'

* * *

Karras, Rauth and Solarion soon caught up with Voss and Zeed. There wasn't time to move carefully now, but Karras dreaded getting caught up in another firefight. That would surely doom them. Perhaps the saints were smiling on him, though, because it seemed that most of the orks in the sections between the central shaft and the prow had responded to the earlier alarms and had already been slain by Zeed and Voss.

The corridors were comparatively empty, but the large mess room with its central squig pit was not.

The Space Marines charged straight in, this time on ground level, and opened fire with their bolters, cutting down the orks that were directly in their way. With his beloved blade, Karras hacked down all who stood before him, always maintaining his forward momentum, never stopping for a moment. In a matter of seconds, the kill-team crossed the mess hall and plunged into the shadowy corridor on the far side.

A great noise erupted behind them. Those orks that had not been killed or injured were taking up weapons and following close by. Their heavy, booted feet shook the grillework floors of the corridor as they swarmed along it.

'Omni,' said Karras, feet hammering the metal floor, 'the moment we reach the bay, I want you to ready the shuttle. Do not stop to engage, is that clear?'

If Karras had been expecting some argument from the Imperial Fist, he was surprised. Voss acknowledged the order without dispute. The whole team had made it this far by the skin of their teeth, but he knew it would count for absolutely nothing if their shuttle didn't get clear of the ork ship in time.

Up ahead, just over Solarion's shoulder, Karras saw the light of the salvage bay. Then, in another few seconds, they were out of the corridor and charging through the mountains of scrap towards the large piece of starship wreckage in which they had stolen aboard.

There was a crew of gretchin around it, working feverishly with wrenches and hammers that looked far too big for their sinewy little bodies. Some even had blowtorches and were cutting through sections of the outer plate.

*Damn them,* cursed Karras. *If they've damaged any of our critical systems…*

Bolters spat, and the gretchin dropped in a red mist.

'Omni, get those systems running,' Karras ordered. 'We'll hold them off.'

Voss tossed Karras his bolt pistol as he ran past, then disappeared into the doorway in the side of the ruined prow.

Karras saw Rauth and Solarion open fire as the first of the pursuing orks charged in. At first, they came in twos and threes. Then they came in a great flood. Empty magazines fell to the scrap-covered floor, to be replaced by others that were quickly spent.

Karras drew his own bolt pistol from its holster and joined the fire-fight, wielding one in each hand. Orks fell before him with gaping exit wounds in their heads.

'I'm out!' yelled Solarion, drawing his shortsword.

'Dry,' called Rauth seconds later and did the same.

Frenzied orks continued to pour in, firing their guns and waving their oversized blades, despite the steadily growing number of their dead that they had to trample over.

'Blast it!' cursed Karras. 'Talk to me, Omni.'

'Forty seconds,' answered the Imperial Fist. 'Coils at sixty per cent.'

Karras's bolt pistols clicked empty within two rounds of each other. He holstered his own, fixed Voss's to a loop on his webbing, drew Arque-mann and called to the others, 'Into the shuttle, now. We'll have to take our chances.'

And hope they don't cut through to our fuel lines, he thought sourly.

One member of the kill-team, however, didn't seem to like those odds much.

'They're mine!' Zeed roared, and he threw himself in among the orks, cutting and stabbing in a battle-fury, dropping the giant alien savages like flies. Karras felt a flash of anger, but he marvelled at the way the Raven Guard moved, as if every single flex of muscle and claw was part of a dance that sent xenos filth howling to their deaths.

Zeed's armour was soon drenched in blood, and still he fought, swip-ing this way and that, always moving in perpetual slaughter, as if he were a tireless engine of death.

'Plasma coils at eighty per cent,' Voss announced. 'What are we waiting on, Scholar?'

Solarion and Rauth had already broken from the orks they were fight-ing and had raced inside, but Karras hovered by the door.

Zeed was still fighting.

'Ghost,' shouted Karras. 'Fall back, damn you.'

Zeed didn't seem to hear him, and the seconds kept ticking away. Any moment now, Karras knew, the ork ship's reactor would explode. Voss had seen to that. Death would take all of them if they didn't leave right now.

'Raven Guard!' Karras roared.

That did it.

Zeed plunged his lightning claws deep into the belly of one last ork, gutted him, then turned and raced towards Karras.

When they were through the door, Karras thumped the locking mecha-nism with the heel of his fist. 'You're worse than Omni,' he growled at the Raven Guard. Then, over the comm-link, he said, 'Blow the piston charges and get us out of here fast.'

He heard the sound of ork blades and hammers battering the hull as the orks tried to hack their way inside. The shuttle door would hold but, if Voss didn't get them out of the salvage bay soon, they would go up with the rest of the ship.

'Detonating charges now,' said the Imperial Fist.

In the salvage bay, the packages he had fixed to the big pistons and cables on either side of the bay at the start of the mission exploded, shearing straight through the metal.

There was a great metallic screeching sound and the whole floor of the salvage bay began to shudder. Slowly, the ork ship's gigantic mouth fell open, and the cold void of space rushed in, stealing away the breathable atmosphere. Everything inside the salvage bay, both animate and inanimate, was blown out of the gigantic mouth, as if snatched up by a mighty hurricane. Anything that hit the great triangular teeth on the way out went into a wild spin. Karras's team was lucky. Their craft missed clipping the upper front teeth by less than a metre.

'Shedding the shell,' said Voss, 'in three… two… one…'

He hit a button on the pilot's console that fired a series of explosive bolts, and the wrecked prow façade fragmented and fell away, the pieces drifting off into space like metal blossoms on a breeze. The shuttle beneath was now revealed – a sleek, black wedge-shaped craft bearing the icons of both the Ordo Xenos and the Inquisition proper. All around it, metal debris and rapidly freezing ork bodies spun in zero gravity.

Inside the craft, Karras, Rauth, Solarion and Zeed fixed their weapons on storage racks, sat in their respective places, and locked themselves into impact frames.

'Hold on to something,' said Voss from the cockpit as he fired the ship's plasma thrusters.

The shuttle leapt forward, accelerating violently just as the stern of the massive ork ship exploded. There was a blinding flash of yellow light that outshone even the local star. Then a series of secondary explosions erupted, blowing each section of the vast metal monstrosity apart, from aft to fore, in a great chain of utter destruction. Twenty thousand ork lives were snuffed out in a matter of seconds, reduced to their component atoms in the plasma-charged blasts.

Aboard the shuttle, Zeed removed his helmet and shook out his long black hair. With a broad grin, he said, 'Damn, but I fought well today.'

Karras might have grinned at the Raven Guard's exaggerated arrogance, but not this time. His mood was dark, despite their survival. Sigma had asked a lot this time. He looked down at the black surface of the cryocase between his booted feet.

Zeed followed his gaze. 'We got what we came for, right, Scholar?' he asked.

Karras nodded.

'Going to let me see it?'

Zeed hated the ordo's need-to-know policies, hated not knowing exactly why Talon squad was put on the line, time after time. Karras could identify with that. Maybe they all could. But curiosity brought its own dangers.

In one sense, it didn't really matter *why* Sigma wanted Bludwrekk's head, or anything else, so long as each of the Space Marines honoured the obligations of their Chapters and lived to return to them.

One day, it would all be over.

One day, Karras would set foot on Occludus again, and return to the Librarius as a veteran of the Deathwatch.

He felt Rauth's eyes on him, watching as always, perhaps closer than ever now. There would be trouble later. Difficult questions. Tests. Karras didn't lie to himself. He knew how close he had come to losing his soul. He had never allowed so much of the power to flow through him before, and the results made him anxious never to do so again.

How readily would Rauth pull the trigger next time?

Focusing his attention back on Zeed, he shook his head and muttered, 'There's nothing to see, Ghost. Just an ugly green head with metal plugs in it.' He tapped the case. 'Besides, the moment I locked this thing, it fused itself shut. You could ask Sigma to let you see it, but we both know what he'll say.'

The mention of his name seemed to invoke the inquisitor. His voice sounded on the comm-link. 'That could have gone better, Alpha. I confess I'm disappointed.'

'Don't be,' Karras replied coldly. 'We have what you wanted. How fine we cut it is beside the point.'

Sigma said nothing for a moment, then, 'Fly the shuttle to the extraction coordinates and prepare for pick-up. Redthorne is on her way. And rest while you can. Something else has come up, and I want Talon on it.'

'What is it this time?' asked Karras.

'You'll know,' said the inquisitor, 'when you need to know. Sigma out.'

Magos Altando, former member of both biologis and technicus arms of the glorious Adeptus Mechanicus, stared through the wide plex window at his current project. Beyond the transparent barrier, a hundred captured orks lay strapped down to cold metal tables. Their skulls were trepanned, soft grey brains open to the air. Servo-arms dangling from the ceiling prodded each of them with short electrically-charged spikes, eliciting thunderous roars and howls of rage. The strange machine in the centre, wired directly to the greenskins' brains, siphoned off the psychic energy their collective anger and aggression was generating.

Altando's many eye-lenses watched his servitors scuttle among the tables, taking the measurements he had demanded.

I must comprehend the manner of its function, he told himself. Who could have projected that the orks were capable of fabricating such a thing?

Frustratingly, much of the data surrounding the recovery of the ork machine was classified above Altando's clearance level. He knew that a Deathwatch kill-team, designation *Scimitar*, had uncovered it during a purge of mining tunnels on Delta IV Genova. The inquisitor had brought it to him, knowing Altando followed a school of thought which other tech-magi considered disconcertingly radical.

Of course, the machine would tell Altando very little without the last missing part of the puzzle.

A door slid open behind him, and he turned from his observations to greet a cloaked and hooded figure accompanied by a large, shambling servitor which carried a black case.

'Progress?' said the figure.

'Limited,' said Altando, 'and so it will remain, inquisitor, without the resources we need. Ah, but it appears you have solved that problem. Correct?'

The inquisitor muttered something and the blank-eyed servitor trudged forward. It stopped just in front of Altando and wordlessly passed him the black metal case.

Altando accepted it without thanks, his own heavily augmented body having no trouble with the weight. 'Let us go next door, inquisitor,' he said, 'to the primary laboratory.'

The hooded figure followed the magos into a chamber on the left, leaving the servitor where it stood, staring lifelessly into empty space.

The laboratory was large, but so packed with devices of every conceivable scientific purpose that there was little room to move. Servo-skulls hovered in the air overhead, awaiting commands, their metallic components gleaming in the lamplight. Altando placed the black case on a table in the middle of the room, and unfurled a long mechanical arm from his back. It was tipped with a las-cutter.

'May I?' asked the magos.

'Proceed.'

The cutter sent bright red sparks out as it traced the circumference of the case. When it was done, the mechanical arm folded again behind the magos's back, and another unfurled over the opposite shoulder. This was tipped with a powerful metal manipulator, like an angular crab's claw but with three tapering digits instead of two. With it, the magos clutched the top of the case, lifted it, and set it aside. Then he dipped the manipulator into the box and lifted out the head of Balthazog Bludwrekk.

'Yes,' he grated through his vocaliser. 'This will be perfect.'

'It had better be,' said the inquisitor. 'These new orkoid machines represent a significant threat, and the Inquisition must have answers.'

The magos craned forward to examine the severed head. It was frozen solid, glittering with frost. The cut at its neck was incredibly clean, even at the highest magnification his eye-lenses would allow.

It must have been a fine weapon indeed that did this, Altando thought. No typical blade.

'Look at the distortion of the skull,' he said. 'Look at the features. Fascinating. A mutation, perhaps? Or a side effect of the channelling process? Give me time, inquisitor, and the august Ordo Xenos will have the answers it seeks.'

'Do not take *too* long, magos,' said the inquisitor as he turned to leave. 'And do not disappoint me. It took my best assets to acquire that abomination.'

The magos barely registered these words. Nor did he look up to watch the inquisitor and his servitor depart. He was already far too engrossed in his study of the monstrous head.

Now, at long last, he could begin to unravel the secrets of the strange ork machine.

# AND THEY SHALL KNOW NO FEAR...

*Darren Cox*

009.009.832.M41
04.52

'Three minutes until blackout.'

The vox crackle from the Land Raider's driver pulled Castellan Marius Reinhart from his silent liturgies. Bathed in the interior's red light, he released himself from his assault harness and stood. His armour's gyro-stabilisers steadied him against the buck of the transport's passage as he peered over the driver's shoulder.

Through the forward viewport he watched as flashes of lightning fractured the night and revealed a landscape of icy rock and jagged peaks. Above, strange auroras moved across a sea of churning storm clouds. Even over the rumble of the Land Raider's tracks he could hear the slow roll of thunder.

'How far are we from our target?'

The Land Raider's co-driver adjusted a series of brass dials on the forward console. 'At our current speed, auspex readings mark us thirty minutes out.'

'Do we have any readings from the keep, any residual power spikes?'

'Negative, castellan, the storm is jamming the majority of our forward sensors. There is no way to say for certain.'

Reinhart growled a curse under his breath. They were going in blind. Atmosphereologists aboard the Black Templar flagship, the *Revenant*, had warned him and his Sword Brethren about the dangers of the

215

electromagnetic storm raging over Stygia XII's upper polar region – and over their waiting target. The forge world's storms could affect the machine-spirit of even the most basic device – a fact necessitating their insertion by Thunderhawk transports just beyond the storm's perimeter. Though a direct flight through the storm would have saved the most time, there was no way to tell if the Thunderhawk's systems could withstand the fury of the electromagnetic pulses. The risk was too great and their cargo too precious. The Land Raiders would have to get them as close as possible.

Reinhart keyed his vox, triggering the command channel connecting him to the rest of his battle-brothers in the convoy. 'Escalade Two, Escalade Three, we're approaching the storm's blackout perimeter. Be prepared for vox interference.'

Two of the twelve amber runes displayed on his visor flashed briefly. Chaplain Mathias, commanding the second Land Raider, and Brother-Sergeant Janus, commanding the third, had received and understood.

Through the viewport Reinhart could see the track ahead narrowing into a rocky defile.

'Understood, Escalade Three.' The driver turned in his seat, addressing Reinhart. 'We're moving into a single ingress line. Escalade Three will take point.'

Reinhart nodded and turned back to the Land Raider's hold, grasping an overhead stabiliser. In preparation, the interior of the hold had been stripped bare, leaving room only for its cargo and three occupants.

'Brother Cerebus, Brother Fernus, prepare the Ark's shield.'

On either side of the hold, two Techmarines, their helmets heavy with neural cables, turned towards him and nodded. They bowed over a great armoured casket – what they called the Ark. Its surface was incised with the baroque runes of the Adeptus Mechanicus, and grav-engines kept it suspended just above the floor.

Chanting the rites of activation, the Techmarines coupled their grafted servo-arms with the Ark's forward actuators. Moments later a heavy thrum vibrated through the hold. A pale shimmer began to enshroud the Ark. Reinhart could not help but watch in awe as the machine-spirit was drawn from its slumber by the warrior-priests.

He found himself joining them in a prayer of his own.

*'Emperor, protect us in this hour of need, may You see the truth of our actions. Allow us to be the instruments of Your will and steer our hands on this blessed duty.'*

With the Techmarines' rite complete Reinhart could barely see the Ark through the coalescing motes of energy that surrounded it. Lexmechanics aboard the *Revenant* had built the shield to specifically retard the effects of Stygia XII's storms and protect the Ark's internal functions. If it failed, millions would pay the price.

'Castellan, we have contact. Escalade Three is taking fire.'

Reinhart whirled back to the viewport just as the heavy staccato thump of rounds stitched across the exterior of their own Land Raider. 'Where? Where is it coming from?' He braced himself as a violent shudder ripped through the hull of the transport. Alarms sounded in time with the strobing of combat lamps.

'They've taken out our starboard sponson!' The co-driver shouted over the hail of gunfire. 'It's an ambush, right and left, above us, from the cliffs–'

In front of them, Escalade Three blossomed into a searing ball of flame. Shrapnel from its shredded hide clanged against their forward armour. At once five runes disappeared from Reinhart's visor.

'Holy Throne!' The driver, panic evident in his eyes, glanced over his shoulder at Reinhart. 'They must have ruptured a fuel cell. Whoever they are, they have some heavy ordinance.'

Reinhart ignored him. Unwilling to admit their fate, he keyed his vox and tried to reach Escalade Three. Only static answered. Brother-Sergeant Janus plus Brothers Gorgon, Sangrill, Charsild and Eklain were five of the Templars' most experienced and bravest Sword Brethren, each of them champions and legends in their own right. Together, they had all survived countless battles on countless worlds, and now they were gone. The loss was staggering.

'Castellan, your orders? Do we search for survivors?'

Reinhart blinked. 'They're all dead. Drive – get us out of here.'

With the heavy growl of turbine engines, the driver punched the throttle forward. Reinhart looked back to Cerebus and Fernus, both of whom stood protectively to either side of the Ark. Their Mechanicus power axes were held ready, shoulder-mounted bolters on-line. 'Be ready! This is going to get rough!' he yelled over the cacophony.

Another violent lurch nearly sent him sprawling to the hold's decking. A second series of alarms began to wail.

'We can't take much more, Castellan! We have armour breaches in three locations! If we continue to sustain this–' A terrific blast of flame and smoke engulfed the cabin in front of Reinhart. Hot shrapnel flew in all directions, pinging off the ablative plates of his artificer-forged power armour. Beneath him, the Land Raider shuddered to a stop.

Oily smoke began to fill the hold. Cerebus inserted a diagnostic cable from his chest plate into the Land Raider's secondary codifier. The machine's screenplate flickered as lines of scripture scrolled across its surface. The Techmarine's augmented voice came over Reinhart's vox reflecting nothing of the anarchy that boiled around them. 'The Land Raider is crippled, Castellan. Evacuation is the only option before the engine's plasma coils go critical.'

Reinhart nodded. 'Escalade Two, this is Escalade One. Acknowledge.'

Amid the crackle of static, Mathias's vox keyed up. Reinhart heard the thunderous boom of bolter fire in the background. 'I acknowledge,

Castellan. Your Land Raider is blocking the track. We can't get around.
We are dismounting and moving to your position to secure the Ark.'

Good, Reinhart thought. The Ark comes first; all of them would willingly sacrifice their lives to protect it. He drew his filigreed bolt pistol, its
balanced weight a perfect extension of his armoured gauntlet. Whispering his *Litany of Devotion*, he clasped the weapon's binding chain around
his wrist, each link graven with the litany's sacred words.

'Brother Cerebus, Brother Fernus, exit forward.' He gestured towards the
hatch beneath the smoking crew cabin where the remains of the driver
and co-driver crisped in the dying flames. 'Chaplain Mathias and our
battle-brothers in Escalade Two are moving to cover you. Get through to
the target as quickly as possible. May the Emperor be with you.'

Without waiting for their response, Reinhart turned, flipped open
an access panel, and punched the quick release of the port side hatch.
Explosive bolts blew the armoured door outwards. With a roar, Reinhart
leapt into the frozen night of Stygia XII.

Through swirling snow he was met by streaks of tracer fire lancing
down from darkened figures in the crags. Las-pulses and solid shot tore
up the ground around him in explosions of rock and ice.

Within moments the crunch of footfalls and the bellow of war chants
alerted him to Brother Apollos's approach from the direction of Escalade
Two. The giant Sword Brother marched through the gunfire as if striding
through a heavy gale. Shells whined and spat off his ornate Terminator
armour. He bore his giant thunder hammer chained to his wrist; in his
other, a heavy storm bolter tracked and fired. The newest of Castellan's
squad – and the youngest – Apollos had been awarded his tabard just
a year prior. In that time, Reinhart had met few who could match his
fervour in battle.

Next to the hulking Terminator, a giant himself but dwarfed in Apollos's shadow, was Brother Ackolon. The prime helix of the Apothecarion
was emblazoned on his shoulder pad, his narthecium strapped securely
to his back. Together, the Space Marines laid down a withering fusillade
of fire, their blazing muzzle flashes lending a daemonic cast to their
already terrifying countenances.

Apollos reached the shadow of the burning Land Raider and crashed
against its buckled armour, shielded against the fire from the opposite
cliffside. He pulverised the rock face looming over them in a shower of
bolter shells, sending shadowy foes diving for cover. Ackolon followed
close behind and crouched next to Reinhart, slamming a fresh magazine
into his bolter. 'Castellan, Chaplain Mathias with Brothers Dorner, Gerard, and Julius are moving up the right; your orders?'

'Keep moving,' Reinhart voxed over the hammer of his bolter, even as
a smoking slug blew a chunk from his ceramite leg guard. 'They'll cut
us to pieces if we remain exposed in this Throne-forsaken defile much
longer!'

Ackolon nodded. 'The Emperor protects!' He motioned to Apollos and the two Space Marines burst from the cover of the crippled Land Raider, charging through the smoke and haze of gunfire. Reinhart fired a final volley, blowing two of the enemy from the cliff, then followed.

Ahead, he could see the towering forms of Cerebus and Fernus fighting their way through the defile – the Ark between them – its shield sparking each time a round found its surface. Paralleling him across the narrow track, Chaplain Mathias, his golden skull helm gleaming, led the three remaining Sword Brethren at a full run, their bolters streaking angry gouts of automatic fire.

Reaching the two Techmarines, Reinhart and his squad flowed seamlessly into a wide formation around the Ark. From their left, a rocket, spitting a fiery contrail, hissed through the air and detonated at Brother Julius's feet.

The blast vaporised his legs, blowing away his helmet and a good portion of his breastplate. The Templar fell, screaming hate around mouthfuls of bloody froth. Still, Julius's bolter roared. Ackolon dashed to him, and began dragging him along, firing from the hip. Brother Gerard moved to help. Before he could reach them, a stray round blew through the knee joint of his armour. Blood sprayed, steaming on the frozen ground.

Reinhart knew the situation was slipping from his grasp. Enemies they had yet to identify held the high ground, the rough terrain rendering them next to impossible to acquire. Worse yet, the storm of gunfire lacing the air around them only seemed to be intensifying.

With two battle-brothers down, the squad moved into a tight circle, doing their best to cover all angles of fire. A sudden, earth-shaking detonation washed the defile in blinding firelight – the crippled Land Raider had finally succumbed to its wounds. Then, as abruptly as it had started, the gunfire ceased.

From somewhere forward of their position, where the defile opened into a deep valley, came the echoing booms of multiple engines. Reinhart risked a glance upwards.

Dorner heard the booms as well, mistaking them for enemy fire. 'Incoming!' he yelled.

Reinhart held up a fist. 'Hold your fire; those are jump packs.' With the words barely uttered, the sound of thumping bolters filled the night once more. Tracer rounds streaked down from the sky into the enemy positions high in the rocks.

'Stay alert! Everyone hold their position.'

In the momentary respite, Reinhart removed his helmet, its vox and visor readings going dead from the interference of the storm. The others followed suit. None of them could risk being blind and unable to communicate if the fighting broke out again.

Reinhart moved to Brother Gerard. The injured Space Marine, blood colouring the lower leg of his power armour, stood over Ackolon and the stricken Brother Julius. The Castellan laid a hand on his shoulder. 'How is your knee, brother?'

Gerard continued to scan the defile, his bolter sweeping left and right. 'A minor wound. I can still fight,' he said.

Reinhart looked down at Ackolon. 'Brother Julius?'

Ackolon shook his head. 'Massive trauma. I've already removed his gene-seed.'

Reinhart scanned the rocks. He felt the stares of his men. He looked back at Ackolon. 'Then he will serve the Chapter in death,' he said loud enough for all of them to hear. 'So will we all, if that is what the Emperor's will demands of us.'

Overhead, the sound of bolter fire ceased, but Reinhart's heightened senses could pick out the faint echo of a more intense exchange from somewhere deeper in the valley. Subtle flashes flickered in the darkness. An ochre cast stained the sky, a great conflagration raging just out of sight. He knew it could only be coming from one place. What he did not know was what waited for them there.

Chaplain Mathias, the black cross of their Chapter tattooed on his forehead, moved to Reinhart's side. 'Castellan, our... *rescuers*... approach.'

Reinhart turned. He glanced at Mathias, disgust at their situation evident on the Chaplain's grim face. From the direction of the valley a squad of women – armoured in crimson and sable – advanced. Catechisms of the Ecclesiarchy adorned their tabards, stitched in High Gothic around the blood-red petals of a single rose. Each carried a finely worked, Godwyn-Deaz pattern bolter of gold and silver. It was the signature weapon of those female orphans raised in the schola progenium and inducted as Adepta Sororitas battle-sisters of the Orders Militant.

The lead sister broke from her flanking guard. Reinhart moved to meet her, Mathias a step behind.

Beneath short-cropped midnight-black hair, old scars lined what would have been an attractive face. Her marred beauty was accentuated by an augmetic targeting reticule that replaced her left eye; the jewelled lens glowed a baleful red. 'Brother Astartes,' she said, her voice as cold as the biting wind. 'I am Sister Superior Helena Britaine of the Third Celestian Squad of the Order of the Bloody Rose.'

'Castellan Marius Reinhart of the Sword Brethren of the Black Templars,' Reinhart gestured to Mathias. The Chaplain stepped forward, his skull helm held in the crook of his arm, his crozius arcanum – topped with a glittering Imperial eagle – cradled in the other. 'This is Chaplain Mathias Vlain.'

The Sister Superior nodded. 'Well met, brothers of the Emperor.' Her single blue eye drifted past the two Astartes to the others who still waited, bolters at the ready. 'My Seraphim have driven the enemy from the cliffs. It should be safe for the moment. I can offer medical assistance to any of your battle-brothers who require it.'

'We have our own Apothecary,' Reinhart said, then stepped closer, his voice low. 'What I do need are answers. How have you and your sisters come to be here?'

Sister Helena's eye narrowed. 'I would ask the same of you, Castellan. We were given no word of your coming.'

'We did not offer any word, Sister Superior, and if you are not willing to give me the answers I need, I suggest you take me to someone who will.'

Helena studied the towering Space Marine for a moment. 'Very well, Castellan,' she said finally. 'I will take you. But be warned: Chaos has assuredly tainted this place.'

Interrogator Edwin Savaul of the Ordo Hereticus took a ragged breath of the mountain air as he surveyed the siege's progress. He stood at a shattered casement high in an ancient tower, a tower his men dubbed 'the Spike.' With walls forged from the ironite stone indigenous to Stygia XII, the Spike was one of two towers guarding the entrance to the valley from the winding defile beyond. All that remained of the second was a finger of crumbling stone, a place avoided by the simple Guardsmen, who claimed the unquiet dead haunted its collapsed halls.

From his perch, Savaul could easily see the gothic fortress stretching into the night sky, commanding the far side of the valley like a dark cathedral cut from the stone of the mountain. From its decaying battlements glowing streaks of criss-crossing las-fire and tracer rounds webbed the valley floor. Explosions rocked the broken landscape just beneath the walls, an area that had also received a name: 'the cemetery.' Everywhere, flashing light illuminated the forms of struggling soldiers.

Savaul turned to face the chamber's dank interior. A ring of flickering lumoglobes circled the room, their snaking power cables stretching across the floor's cracked flagstones. The harsh light stung his eyes. 'Are we any closer?' he asked.

Veteran Captain Dremin Vlorn of the Fourth Inquisitorial storm trooper regiment emerged from where he waited in the chamber's entry portal. He limped into the room, his grizzled face streaked with soot and dried blood. A stylized 'I' – the mark of Inquisitorial conditioning – stood out on either ridge of his sunken cheeks. He placed his helmet on the only piece of furniture: a large, smoke-blackened quarter panel of a blasted Vindicator tank turned into a makeshift table. The captain's exhaustion was palpable. 'The gates hold, interrogator. Our troops still can't get close enough to plant the breaching charges.'

Savaul stepped from the ruined window, one hand in the pocket of his ankle-length storm coat, its high black collar framing a face devoid of pigment. 'Where is Sister Superior Helena? I expected her report along with yours.'

'She should be just behind me,' the captain replied, tugging his gloves free. 'She took her Celestian and Seraphim squads to investigate a disturbance in the defile about an hour ago. I saw them descending the switchbacks as I entered the Spike.'

'A disturbance?'

Vlorn shrugged. 'There were reports of gunfire.'

Savaul's disturbingly blue eyes searched the captain's face. He had become adept at detecting a man turned by the warp. It appeared Veteran Captain Vlorn's conditioning remained uncorrupted. Savaul engaged the safety of the laspistol in his pocket and placed the weapon on the table. Vlorn looked up in alarm.

'None of us are safe from the warp's taint, veteran captain. Especially here. I would expect you to deal with me in the same manner, were I no longer… pure.'

Vlorn inclined his head. 'Understood, interrogator.'

A sound brought both men around. Footsteps echoed from the shadows beyond the chamber's portal – slow and measured, like the tread of a Titan. As they grew nearer, dust began to sift from the ceiling stones. A moment later Sister Superior Helena entered the room, stepping aside to make way for the mammoth figure in her wake. Savaul sucked in a sharp breath at the sheer scale of the newcomer.

*Astartes.* He had seen one once from a distance, but nothing could match the awe or the terror of seeing one up close. They truly were monsters.

Helena stepped forward. 'Interrogator Savaul, I present Castellan Marius Reinhart of the Black Templars.'

Reinhart stared down at them, flint eyes sparkling, one half of his tanned face covered in tattooed lines of High Gothic script. At close to three metres tall, encased in ornate black power armour, the Space Marine dominated the room. His tabard was the colour of aged parchment. Scorched and ripped, it bore the ebony cross of the Templars' heraldry. An ancient blade hung at his side.

Silent, the giant nodded in greeting and stepped around the table, his gaze drawn to the maps spread upon its scarred surface. Armoured fingers lifted the vellum schematics of the besieged fortress's walls and gridded layouts of troop dispersements. All of them watched, drawn into a hushed silence, entranced.

He let the maps fall back to the table. His gaze swept them all, and then his unwavering eyes locked with Savaul's. 'What troubles this place, interrogator?'

Savaul swallowed, feeling as though he had emerged from a dream. All the power and authority due an Inquisitorial agent flooded back in an instant. He straightened. 'Castellan, I welcome you,' he said, ignoring the question. 'Your arrival is most propitious. I will require your forces to join the assault on the gates of the fortress. I'm sure you saw the situation on your descent from the defile.'

A strange, reverberating growl came from the Space Marine. It took a moment for Savaul to realize it was laughter.

'Interrogator,' he said, any hint of mirth now gone from his voice, 'If you think I have come here to relieve you, you are mistaken.'

'I... I'm afraid I don't understand. Surely you have come at our request for aid. My envoys left with the call three days ago.'

Reinhart glanced down, again studying the map of the fortress. 'Do you know, interrogator, what this place is that you lay siege to?'

Savaul looked from Helena to Vlorn, but neither noticed his glance. They simply stared at Reinhart, puzzlement evident on both of their faces. Savaul was beginning to feel as though he lacked some vital piece of information – a feeling he was not accustomed to. 'Planetary records on file with Stygia XII's Administratum centre in Capitalis Acheron report that this fortress was in existence upon the planet's settlement. Its builders are unknown, possibly xenos, a rumour causing it to be shunned by the local populace. They call it Stormhelm. Further records indicate–'

'Your records are lacking, interrogator,' Reinhart interrupted. Savaul, unused to such disrespect, stood open-mouthed. Reinhart moved to the room's gaping window, the glow of the siege-flames lighting his face. 'The bastion's true name is Montgisard; a chapter keep of my order founded by Marshal Gervhart during his execution of the Athelor Crusade. That was close to three thousand years prior to Stygia XII's official settlement date. After millennia of faithful service it was declared *Vox in Excelso* – dissolved – and thus abandoned. However, the memory of our Chapter is long, and none of our keeps are ever truly forgotten. We have returned at the behest of High Marshal Ludoldus to reclaim Montgisard.' Reinhart turned back to the table. 'So, I ask you again: who has defiled this place?'

Savaul said nothing for a moment, unable to comprehend how his ordo could have been ignorant of these facts. Still, it changed nothing. The needs of the Templars would have to come second, if at all. A world's fate hinged upon the Inquisition's success. Savaul chose his next words carefully.

'Castellan, I thank you for enlightening us on the history of this site. This fortress, whether you call it Montgisard or Stormhelm, has become an infested hive of taint and corruption – and, as near as we can tell, is the Archenemy's base of operations on Stygia XII. We are here on orders from my master, Inquisitor Abraham Vinculus of the Ordo Hereticus, to cleanse this taint.' Savaul motioned to Helena.

The Battle Sister moved to the table and gestured to the map outlining troop placements. 'We arrived on-site a week ago,' she said. 'Shortly thereafter, the storm manifested, cutting our communication lines. Nothing in, nothing out.' She looked up at Reinhart. 'Our situation could not be more dire. The cult of the Archenemy has turned out to be much larger than anticipated. A sizeable portion of the Stygian Planetary Defence Force has turned traitor, enslaved by the warp's corruption.' She motioned to Vlorn. 'Veteran Captain Vlorn and his storm-troopers have executed the brunt of the assault, with my sisters acting as the tip of the spear.'

Vlorn's gruff voice cut in. 'The bastards have dug in and they have a taste for blood. Though we lay siege, it is actually we who are encircled. They've taken the high ground around us, and the gates of Stormhelm refuse to fall.' A touch of grudging admiration laced the veteran captain's words. 'You Astartes know how to build a door.'

'Why not simply pull out, fight your way back through the defile, and return with additional forces?'

Helena and Vlorn looked to Savaul, a sudden uneasiness to their features.

Savaul looked down, composed himself, and then raised his eyes to meet the full force of Reinhart's gaze. 'Retreat is not an option, Castellan. We–' Savaul hesitated.

The hulking Space Marine's voice cracked with impatience. 'Speak, man! My time is short!'

'As is ours, Castellan!' Savaul reached to the inner-pocket of his storm coat and withdrew a rolled parchment. 'Have you heard of a Necrolectifier?'

'No, interrogator, I have not.'

Savaul unrolled the scroll and placed it on the table. A coruscating mass of arcanographs and warp glyphs crawled across the blood-stained parchment. Reinhart snarled, stepping back from the table. 'What abomination is this?'

The interrogator laid a splayed hand across the parchment, never taking his eyes from Reinhart. 'This scroll holds the design of a warp gate, a physical portal between our universe and the realm of Chaos. It requires four artefacts, four Necrolectifiers, vile items capable of focusing enough daemonic energy to rip a hole through the fabric of our reality into the maelstrom of the warp. Castellan, they are planning to open this gate.'

'But you have captured this scroll,' Reinhart said. 'You have foiled their plan, correct?'

'No, Castellan, this scroll is not the key; it was drawn by a captured heretic during interrogation – a physical representation of the knowledge my excruciators drew from him. It tells us the cultists within Montgisard already hold the Necrolectifiers, the knowledge of their proper arrangement, and the rituals required to activate them. It tells us that on any given year, at the ninth hour of the ninth day of the ninth month, a portal may be opened, a portal through which the legions of the warp may pass.'

Savaul's voice lowered to a whisper. 'Castellan, this is the ninth day, of the ninth month of 832.M41 and very soon it will be the ninth hour. Unless this fortress is destroyed first, you can be assured this gate will open, then this world will burn – and the thousands of souls living here will burn with it.'

The meeting with the interrogator had taken longer than Reinhart expected. The time he had spent with Savaul made it plain to him the man's resolve was unbendable, and that the situation at Stormhelm posed a very real threat to the success of the Templars' mission. Now, more than ever, time was of the essence.

He found his battle-brothers waiting for him in one of the tower's undercrofts. Its western wall had collapsed, the rubble cleared to give easy access to the tower's exterior. Beyond the wall a marshalling yard had been levelled. A hive of activity swarmed across its packed surface. Ordnance officers bellowed while loading crews thronged around a handful of damaged Vindicator tanks awaiting the ministrations of overworked enginseers.

Dorner and Apollos stood watchful at the undercroft's crude exit, observing the tumult outside, their bolters at low guard. Gerard sat on a battered munitions crate, his leg elevated while Ackolon applied a battlefield dressing. Chaplain Mathias talked in hushed tones with the Techmarines, not far from the floating Ark. They all turned at Reinhart's approach.

Mathias stepped to the forefront. 'Castellan?'

Reinhart looked at each of them in turn. 'I will tell you simply, brothers: Chaos has gained a foothold here. The Archenemy occupies Montgisard. At minimum two regiments of traitor guard and militia lie within. In three hours they will attempt to open a warp gate within the fortress's grand chapel, and this world will die in the apocalypse that follows.'

Mathias's face darkened. 'Then we dare not lose another moment. The power cells of the shield will last another two hours at most.'

'I am well aware of the cells' capacity, Chaplain,' he replied. He brushed past Mathias and strode to the Ark, running his hands across the shield's crackling surface. So much hope hinged on what lay within. 'The Inquisition's forces are desperate. They have been engaged here over a week and are no closer to breaking the fortress's gates.'

Mathias followed Reinhart to the Ark. 'Castellan, I am afraid I don't see how their situation has any bearing on our mission here.'

'It bears on our mission, Chaplain Mathias, because I have told them we would help–'

'By Terra,' Mathias snapped. 'You told them what? I must protest this!' he growled, the muscles in his jaw knotting. 'Were this any other circumstance I would agree.' He looked to the Marines around him. 'We all would, but aiding the Inquisition is not an option. We have an oath and only one directive here. The fate of this world, our lives if need be, are secondary.'

Reinhart felt Ackolon move up beside him. 'Castellan, you know we would follow you anywhere, but Chaplain Mathias is right. Stygia XII has not yet fallen. We can return once our task is done.'

Reinhart faced the Apothecary. 'Are the two of you finished?'

Startled by the iron in the Castellan's tone, Ackolon stepped back. Dorner and Apollos exchanged concerned looks.

'I have pledged to help them, yes,' he repeated. 'But for the first time in my life I must betray my word. We must feign compliance with them because I suspect that our comrades in the Inquisition will not help us, and I fear that whatever lies in wait within those halls will be more than we can handle alone. You and Mathias are right, Ackolon. Our task is more important and I will see it done at any cost, even if we must turn our backs on them.'

Reinhart looked back to the Ark. 'And when that time comes, may the Emperor forgive us all.'

The wind howled across the escarpment, snow and ice scouring the rock. It had taken the small battlegroup of Reinhart's men and the Sister Superior's Celestian squad just under an hour to climb the steep crags leading up to Montgisard's flank. It was an hour they could ill afford. The black ramparts of the fortress at last loomed above them.

Carved from the very rock and sheathed in armoured layers of rusting iron, the impregnable walls had bore witness to the week-long slaughter in the valley before them. Now, however, a haunting stillness cloaked the valley. Following the Castellan's orders, Veteran Captain Vlorn and his men had pulled back – every hand needed to prepare for the massed artillery barrage that was to come. In response, the enemy's guns had gone silent.

Reinhart squinted through the gale, double-checking the codifier readout in his vambrace. Lines of interference spiked across the display. With the storm raging he was surprised it worked at all. The glowing schematic of Montgisard – something all of the Templars had been given prior to making planetfall – showed the entrance to an auxiliary passage at this location. The hidden tunnel would give them access to the fortress's lower levels and hopefully allow them to approach their target with minimal contact. It had perturbed Interrogator Savaul, Vlorn and the Sister Superior that this piece of information was lacking from their own maps. To Reinhart, this boded well. If the Inquisition did not know about the passage, it was possible the enemy was equally ignorant.

To either side, the armoured forms of his battle-brothers, along with the twelve members of Sister Superior Helena's Celestian squad, hugged the steep walls of the mountain trail. Interrogator Savaul stood behind him, wrapped in the leather of his storm coat, breath frosting on the wind. Reinhart scowled. The man's albino skin was a beacon against the darkness. Luckily, the rocky outcroppings kept them shielded from the watchful eyes of the Archenemy's sentries patrolling the heights above.

Reinhart looked down at Cerebus where he knelt next to Fernus, the Techmarine's servo arms manipulating the tunnel door's locking mechanism hidden in the rock. 'How long?'

'Thirty seconds, Castellan.'

Reinhart nodded; he motioned for the battlegroup to prepare for entry. The silent gesture travelled down the line. Next to him, Savaul drew his silver-plated laspistol, its barrel stamped with the crimson sigil of the Inquisition.

The Castellan heard a loud hiss, a sound not unlike the sudden decompression of a Thunderhawk's airlock, and the rock face in front of the Techmarines split to reveal a shadowed portal. From the opposite side of the door Apollos tossed a pair of glowing phosphorus rods into the tunnel beyond. The rods' fizzling light slowly grew steady. Motioning for the others to follow, Reinhart slid forward, his bolt pistol raised.

Silence greeted them, the low passage dark and empty. As they had hoped, the enemy had not discovered this part of the tunnel. After the last of them had filed through, Cerebus activated the door's inner mechanism and sealed the portal behind them. Reinhart moved to Gerard's side. 'Try your auspex,' he said.

Slinging his bolter, Gerard pulled his auspex from his belt and thumbed its activator switch. The scanner's display sputtered then blinked to life. Gerard looked over at Reinhart, relief evident on his face. 'The Emperor is watching over us.'

Reinhart nodded. They had expected the ironite walls of Montgisard to block the effects of the storm but couldn't know for certain until they had reached this point. None of them had relished the idea of descending into the fortress blind.

Keeping his voice low Reinhart addressed the rest of the group. 'Let's move. The generator room is straight ahead.'

They descended quickly through the tunnel and minutes later emptied into their first objective. The chamber they entered stretched away into the gloom: a long gallery of dormant generators lined its stone walls and disappeared into the upper shadows of the room. Weapons braced, Helena and her battle-sisters fanned out. Cerebus and Fernus moved to an archaic panel of codifiers, and began working to restore the fortress's power. Chaplain Mathias entered last with the remaining Templars flanking the floating Ark. Reinhart noticed Savaul watching it, the hunger in his eyes warring with nervous anticipation.

Reinhart had told the interrogator the Ark was a high-yield reactor core capable of powering the fortress's system of defence turrets, part of the protocol required to reclaim the stronghold. However, it could be used in another capacity. Placed in the heart of Stormhelm, it could be rigged to detonate – the resultant explosion strong enough to destroy the fortress. For the interrogator it was an answer to his prayers: a weapon capable of foiling the Archenemy's plans in one fell strike. Reinhart only wished he could have told the man the truth.

They waited in the near darkness until, finally, a series of thumps travelled down the gallery as generators awoke one by one, causing banks of suspended lumoglobes to flicker to life. Reinhart looked over to the Techmarines. 'Only quadrant sigma up to the grav lifts. We don't want the entire fortress to know we're here.'

'These grav lifts, they will take us to where we can plant the reactor?' Savaul asked, perspiration beading on his brow.

Reinhart hesitated; he could not look him in the eye. 'The grav lifts are as far as we go.' He turned and motioned Gerard to him. With a slight limp the Space Marine advanced to the Castellan's side. 'Take point with Apollos and keep me advised of any contact.'

Reinhart turned to address them all. 'I want noise discipline from this point forward. Sister Superior Helena, you and your squad have the rear. The Ark stays between your squad and mine.'

Helena nodded, her features lost beneath her Sabbat pattern helm.

From a great distance, the percussive boom of massed ordinance vibrated down through the halls. Captain Vlorn and his men had begun their bombardment as planned. With any luck, it would pull the enemy from the lower levels.

With drilled precision, the small force moved into the halls of ancient Montgisard.

For what seemed like miles, they stalked through the fortress's lower chambers. Thankfully, they were empty of enemy troops. Vlorn's bombardment appeared to have done its job in pulling them to the surface levels. Each step took the battlegroup deeper into the nightmare that had once been the Templar stronghold. Everywhere, the walls were awash in horrific glyphs and grotesque scenes depicted in rotting blood and viscera. Even to the Space Marines the stench was nearly unbearable.

'Contact, twenty metres.' Gerard knelt in the vaulted corridor, the green glow of his auspex tinting his face. Reinhart's raised fist halted the formation behind him. He moved to Gerard's shoulder.

'How many?'

'It looks like a patrol; I count fifteen, just around the next junction.'

Apollos looked over at Reinhart, a hard grin splitting his face. 'I guess they want to know who turned the lights on.'

Reinhart motioned to Dorner. 'Spread the word, contact in two minutes,' he said. 'We will take them. The sisters and Savaul will protect the Ark with Cerebus and Fernus.'

Dorner glanced over his shoulder at the waiting Sororitas. 'They might not like that.'

Reinhart drew his ancient battle blade, a massive bastard sword blessed and inscribed with the sacred oaths of his Chapter. 'Once this begins,' he said, 'there will be plenty for them to do.'

To Apollos and Mathias, he said: 'We will lead the strike. Gerard, Dorner and Ackolon, you will support us with bolter fire. No one gets through our line, understood?'

They all nodded. Reinhart stepped to the forefront, flanked by Apollos and Mathias as Dorner rushed off to warn the rest of the battlegroup. The sound of disruptive energy crackled through the air as Mathias triggered his crozius arcanum. Apollos activated his thunder hammer, waves of gleaming power rolling across its surface.

Moments later, Dorner returned. He nodded to Reinhart. 'We're ready.'

Gerard took a final reading from his auspex. 'Twenty metres and still approaching'

Reinhart glanced to the rear and saw the battle-sisters spreading out in a formation around the Ark.

Mathias's voice brought him around. 'Here they come.'

The patrol rounded the corner; a dozen lost souls of the militia clad in armour streaked with gore and marked with foul symbols of Chaos. The cultists stumbled to a halt, shocked at what lay before them.

With a thunderous roar, Reinhart charged followed closely by Apollos and Mathias. Superheated bolter rounds screamed past them to shred the enemy's forward rank, exploding flesh, blood and bone. In seconds, the Astartes were among them. The deafening crack of Apollos's thunder hammer splintered the armour of a former guardsman. To Reinhart's left, Mathias waded into the fray, his crozius trailing bloody arcs through the air. Snarling, the Castellan ducked a thrusting rifle butt; with a savage two-handed downward cut, he opened the cultist from shoulder to hip. Blood washed the floor. Twirling the blade, he pivoted and swept the weapon in a tight arc, decapitating a charging foe.

It was over in a heartbeat, the floor littered with the enemy's crushed and eviscerated bodies. Reinhart whirled to check their rear. He could see Savaul, his white face paler still at the brutal effectiveness of the Sword Brethren.

Gerard activated his auspex again, his smoking bolter still ready in the opposite hand. 'I've got more, converging from the last junction to our rear.' He looked closer. 'And ahead. Throne! They're crawling all over the main plasma coil chamber.'

Reinhart knew they couldn't afford to get bogged down in a protracted fight. Pumping his arm, he yelled back to the others through the haze that filled the corridor. 'The game is up! Expect contact forward and to our rear! We've got to punch through to the grav lifts! Move! Move!'

They broke into a run, Cerebus and Fernus increasing the output of the Ark's propulsion engines to keep pace. The reverberating thump of the battle-sisters' bolters exploded from behind them. Reinhart heard a sucking *whoosh* followed by an eruption of gurgling screams. The air grew hot, the stench of promethium masking that of decay as a Sororitas flamer did its holy work.

The embattled force stormed down the last few metres of the corridor and plunged through a yawning doorway. Close on Apollos's heels, Reinhart burst into the seemingly infinite space of the plasma coil chamber. Floor after floor of open gantries ringed the room and stretched upwards into the cavernous void above. Rising from a deep pit, the plasma coil dominated the chamber's centre: a monstrous pillar of brass machinery that arced and crackled with pent-up energies. Stabilising beams sprouted from its skin like the disjointed spokes of an endless wheel, each strut hung with scarlet rags, banners scrawled with the blasphemous litanies of Chaos.

Former guardsman swarmed the gantries above, their Imperial uniforms now a mockery of filth and gore. Gunfire spewed down from the heretics' positions as Reinhart's force dashed across the room. Firing upwards, the Castellan waved his men past. One Sister stumbled as multiple rounds tore through her armour. Her body twisted under the impacts; unable to stop her momentum, she fell screaming over the edge of the coil's pit.

Apollos reached the exit at the far side of the chamber and turned; his bolter blazing, he provided covering fire for the rest of the squad who rushed through. Dorner hurried into position at his side. Together, they answered the cultists with a hellish barrage of their own. Bolters roared, and a gruesome rain of torn and mangled bodies fell from the upper floors.

Bringing up the rear, Savaul and Helena raced towards Reinhart. The Sister Superior's helmet was gone, a bloody gash down her face. Both fired blindly behind them.

'Move, Castellan! They're right behind us!' Helena yelled.

Reinhart fell in step behind them, back-pedalling and firing a furious volley into the horde of screaming cultists that burst from the corridor they had just vacated. He grunted in annoyance as a lucky shell punched through his shoulder joint, lodging near his collarbone. Already off-balance, a blast of autogun fire stitched across his breastplate and sent him sprawling.

Seeing him fall, Helena and Savaul turned back. Helena slung her bolter and, together with Savaul, dragged the Astartes to his feet. As she did so, she tore a krak grenade from her belt, pulled the pin with her teeth, and pitched it into the oncoming mass. A horrific blast ripped through the horde, pulverising the thronged bodies into a cloud of blood vapour and shredded flesh.

Together, the three stumbled through the exit hatch between Apollos and Dorner. The Space Marines swung in behind them, letting loose a final round of fire before punching the hatch activator that sent the door booming closed behind them, the hollow thump of rounds continuing to bang against its armoured shell.

They stood now in another wide corridor, once again, thankfully devoid of the enemy.

Flexing his shoulder, Reinhart could feel the wound closing with the shell still lodged painfully against his collarbone. He had fought with worse injuries. He looked at Helena and Savaul. The Sister Superior was organising the eight remaining members of her squad. Savaul, attended by Ackolon, was bent against the wall catching his breath and holding his side where a grazing round had cut through. They made no mention of what they had done for him and neither did he.

Fernus, his red tabard in rags, moved past Dorner and Apollos to the hatch activator. He looked over his shoulder at Reinhart. 'This door has no locking mechanism; it won't hold them long.'

The sudden thunder of a bolter round startled them all. The hatch activator exploded in a shower of sparks. They all turned to see Mathias lowering his bolt pistol. 'It should hold them now,' he said. Holstering the weapon, Mathias stepped forward, raising his crozius arcanum. 'All of you steel yourselves. In this fateful hour, the Emperor's eyes are upon us. May we all go to Him knowing that we have done our duty and stayed true to His will.'

Reinhart could not help but think these last words were directed at him.

By the time they reached the grav lift chamber the Ark's shield had died and Reinhart's time had run out. He could no longer hide the true nature of his squad's mission. He could see this fact on all his men's faces as they set up a perimeter around the lifts. They and the Sisters had bled together, a bond formed of shared hardship. Savaul and Helena had saved his life. Only Mathias seemed resolute in what they had to do. Reinhart knew he had to follow the Chaplain's example.

The Ark waited on the first of three grav lifts: circular pads set into the floor adorned with the Templar cross. The battle-sisters had split. Two stood guard at each of the stairwells that emptied into the room's four corners. The Techmarines worked at a bank of codifiers that controlled the lifts.

'How far up do we have to plant the reactor?' Savaul asked, watching the Techmarines work. His face was sunken and splattered with dried blood; one hand still clutched his wounded side.

Reinhart looked behind him. Mathias stood at the foot of the Ark, his manner cold and aloof. Apollos and Ackolon locked eyes on the floor, unable to meet his gaze. Never had he felt the weight of duty as acutely as he did at that moment. He looked back to Savaul. Helena had come to stand beside the injured interrogator.

'We are not going up, interrogator.'

Savaul's head snapped around. 'What? I thought you said the reactor needed to be set near the ground floor.'

Reinhart hardened his voice. 'I mean we are not destroying the fortress, Savaul.' He motioned to the Ark. 'That is not a reactor and it cannot be rigged to detonate.'

Savaul turned to face him fully, his voice quivering with rage. 'What, by the Throne, are you talking about?'

'What I told you was a reactor core for Montgisard's defences is in fact a sarcophagus housing the remains of one of our Chapter's most decorated Sword Brethren. His name is Ezekial Yesod, and he clings to life by a thread.'

Helena stepped forward, her face a mask of fury. 'Then what has all this been about, Castellan? Why have you brought us here, if not to exterminate this threat?'

'My battle-brothers and I have not come here to reclaim Montgisard, Sister Superior. We are here because this grav lift will take us down to the keep's lowest sepulchre, where one of our Chapter's most venerated Dreadnoughts sleeps. There, we will inter Brother Yesod so that he may continue to fight in the Emperor's name.'

Savaul pushed past Helena, to stand toe to toe with Reinhart. 'Is fighting in the Emperor's name not what we're already doing here? Throne, man! Don't you realise that by doing this you will condemn hundreds of thousands of His servants to death?'

Reinhart stared down at the trembling interrogator. 'This world is not yet lost.' He motioned to the waiting sarcophagus. 'But thousands of light years away, a battle is being fought. An entire system stands on the brink of destruction, and what lies in Brother Yesod's mind could mean the difference between victory and defeat. Interment within the Dreadnought is his only chance. The loss of Stygia XII would be a mere ripple in an ocean of lost souls if I were to let him die.'

He looked past Savaul to Helena. 'Come with us, all of you. Once our task is done we will return to our battle-barge and explain the conditions here. High Marshal Ludoldus will send aid, and we can return and save this planet before it is too late.'

Helena shook her head, a look of sorrow filling her eyes. 'It will be too late, Castellan. The Archenemy will already have opened the warp gate. We must do everything we can now to stop it.'

Gerard's voice cut the air. 'Castellan, contact again, approaching from the stairwells. Ten minutes, maximum.'

Reinhart stepped back, called to the Techmarines. 'Prepare the lift.' He looked again at Savaul and Helena. 'I will only offer this once more: come with us.'

Savaul's head sank, his shoulders wilting in defeat. 'Then we are on our own.'

'Unless you come with us, yes.'

Helena stepped forward. 'This man Ezekial, you claim that by saving him you will save millions of others?'

Reinhart nodded. 'That is correct, Sister Superior.'

Helena fixed him with a cold stare. 'You know you used us, you lied to us.'

'If there had been another way…' Reinhart let the words trail off.

Helena only smiled. She looked at Savaul. 'You have command, it's your choice.'

Savaul drew in a deep breath. 'I cannot let this atrocity go unanswered. We must try.' He looked at the empty lift next to him, then to Reinhart. 'Send us up and we will destroy the gate or die trying.'

Reinhart stared at him for a moment. He truly did wish there was another way. 'Send them up, Fernus,' he said finally.

Savaul turned without another word.

Helena looked up at Reinhart. 'Goodbye, Castellan. I ask you to remember one thing: Duty and honour do not always go hand in hand.'

Reinhart watched them gather on the lift, and then they were gone, shooting upwards into the heart of the keep and into the midst of the waiting enemy.

He turned. 'Everyone to the lift, prepare for descent.'

All of them moved, circling around the Ark. All of them except Apollos.

'Brother Apollos,' Reinhart said. 'I believe I gave an order.'

The young Terminator stared back at him. 'Castellan… I request permission to follow them, to lend the support of my bolter.'

Reinhart glanced to the others.

Gerard looked up from his auspex. 'Five minutes, Castellan.'

Apollos stepped to the lift. 'Castellan, Chaplain Mathias said the eyes of the Emperor are upon us. I believe he speaks the truth. I believe you can complete this task without me. Let me help them, Castellan.'

'Brother Apollos,' Mathias said, his voice edged with venom. 'Your Castellan has given you an order.'

Reinhart stepped from the lift. 'No, Mathias, Brother Apollos speaks true. The rest of you go and we will do what we can to help them. Take the Ark, inter Ezekial, and then get out. If we are unsuccessful in closing the gate advise the High Marshal of what you've seen here and return to save this world. It is our duty. This is my final order. May the Emperor go with you.'

* * *

The crypt waited for them at the heart of Montgisard's deepest catacombs. Their approach from the grav lift had been a quiet one, Gerard's
auspex showing no sign of the enemy, but they knew that wouldn't last
for long. Following the schematics downloaded to their armour, the
crypt's brass doors emerged from the darkness, glinting beneath the
stark beams of their armour's search lamps. The formidable doors were
an imposing sight, each at five metres tall and nearly as wide, their brass
surface worked with the image of Dorn smiting the forces of Chaos at
the gates of the Imperial Palace.

With Ackolon and Dorner flanking the portal, the Techmarines started
to examine the doors but Mathias waved them back. He pulled an
adamantium necklace from beneath his armour, an amulet of polished
obsidian hanging from its beaded length.

'High Marshal Ludoldus bestowed this rosarius upon me before our
departure,' he said in an awe-hushed voice. 'It belonged to Reclusiarch
Gideon Amesaris. He served beneath High Marshal Gervhart.' The Chaplain knelt before the doors. 'It was he who designed these doors almost
four thousand years ago.' With reverence Mathias fitted the sacred rosarius into an ornate depression within the door. He turned the amulet. A
series of clicks answered and with a hiss the doors rumbled open.

Beyond, statues carved in the grim shapes of ancient Templars holding aloft iron lanterns circled the perimeter of the room. As the doors
boomed open the lanterns guttered to life. Their amber glow filled the
chamber; its sectioned walls covered in dusty, bas-relief carvings of forgotten battles.

In the chamber's centre stood the cyclopean hull of a venerable
Dreadnought draped in cobwebs. Its chest plate was open, revealing a
darkened cavity within.

Mathias stood. 'We must work quickly.'

Together, the Space Marines brought the Ark forward, resting it just
above a low altar at the foot of the colossal war machine. The smell of
holy oils and sacred unguents permeated the air. Stepping back, Gerard
and Dorner took up posts at the crypt's threshold while Cerebus and
Fernus flanked the Ark.

The Techmarines began to chant, manipulating a succession of rune-
marked dials along the Ark's side. Piece by piece its armoured shell
folded back to reveal a golden sarcophagus, its surface glinting in the
amber light.

Gerard's voice once again brought the warning. 'They're coming,' he
said. 'More than I can count.'

'Hold them back,' Mathias replied. 'At any cost. We only need
minutes.'

Gerard and Dorner drew their chainswords and kicked them into
life even as the sound of the screaming cultists began to echo through
the darkness of the hall beyond. Ackolon put himself between the

sarcophagus and the door's threshold, his bolter levelled. 'Hurry, Chaplain.'

Reinhart and Apollos found the battle-sisters and Savaul in a long gallery leading to Montgisard's chapel. They had formed a ragged line across the width of the hall. Step-by-step, they struggled through a seething mass of carnage, the space before them boiling with the streak of las-rounds, bolter shells and intermittent gouts of roaring flame. The stink of blood and promethium choked the air.

'Throne,' Apollos whispered.

Reinhart hefted his blade. 'Come, Apollos. For the sword of Dorn.'

The Terminator looked over at him. 'For the sword of Dorn, Castellan.'

Together, they charged into the centre of the battle-sisters line. Helena spotted them first. A grim smile crossed her features.

'The Templars are with us!' she shouted.

A cheer from the sisters rolled over the din.

With Reinhart and Apollos leading, they formed a wedge and drove into the screaming cultists. The writhing mass was frenzied to the point of suicide, hell-bent on keeping the Emperor's faithful from reaching the chapel. Within moments, the blood of the enemy dripped from Reinhart's armour, his blade a whirling blur of slaughter, his bolt pistol screaming its song of death. Through the carnage he could see Apollos. With every swing the Terminator's thunder hammer cleaved away huge swaths of cultists. Savaul fought in his shadow, a surgical grace to his movements, each shot of his laspistol toppling a crazed heretic.

Ahead of them lay their goal: the towering bronze doors of the chapel.

Reinhart ducked the swing of a whining chainaxe and blew the wielder's head away in a shower of gore. He vaulted the fallen heretic, watching as a Sister stumbled beneath the blow of a crackling power maul. Successive rounds tore her arm off and then her left leg below the knee. Her death grip discharged her flamer in a wide arc, the white flame incinerating all those standing before her. A cultist fell before Apollos, his ribcage crushed beneath the Terminator's armoured boot.

Reinhart breathed hard, his armour wrenched and scorched, the skin of his face blistered. Only four of Helena's sisters remained, but the doors were within reach. They had to keep moving.

'The doors, Apollos, the doors!'

Apollos nodded. With a thunderous bellow the Terminator dropped his shoulder and plunged through the heretics, striking the doors with the full force of his weight and shattering them in an explosion of fragmenting wood and twisted bronze.

Reinhart and the others followed close on his heels... into hell.

Brother Dorner died in the first moments of the cultists' charge. It was an errant shot, catching him in the throat and blowing out the back of his neck in a shower of blood. He fell to his knees, chainsword still raised in a blow that would never come, then pitched forward on his face. Gerard roared in fury and waded into the corridor. Hacking like a man possessed, the Sword Brother tore a bloody swathe through the maddened heretics. The floor became slick with blood and for a moment the foe recoiled from his savage onslaught.

At the threshold of the crypt, Ackolon pumped round after round into the melee; behind him, Mathias and the Techmarines continued their work. He risked a hurried glance.

The Chaplain stood before the altar and chanted the sacred rite of interment as the Techmarines' servo-arms lifted the sarcophagus up and into the yawning cavity of the Dreadnought. For a moment, through the fogged glass set into the sarcophagus's lid, the Apothecary caught a glimpse of an emaciated face. Brass tubes and wires inlaid with lexmechanical runes glistened from its eyes, ears, nose and mouth.

A scream of warning from Gerard brought him about just as a traitor militia officer lunged at him with his sword. Ackolon caught the weapon in his gauntlet. Snarling he snapped the blade in half and put a bolter round through the officer's chest. With a startled look in his eyes, the heretic fell to the floor.

Ahead of him, Gerard continued to scream: not in warning but in pain. The Space Marine had dropped his bolt pistol and was pressing his hand against his temple as he fought. Blood ran from his eyes. Ackolon noticed the rime of frost that crackled its way up the crypt doors and then he spotted the robed psyker at the back of the corridor.

Gerard's agonised voice shrieked over the tumult. 'Get out, Ackolon! I can't hold it! Pull back! Close the do–' With a loud crack Gerard's head split.

Ackolon grunted as a las-round scorched across his check and burned away his ear. He dove for the door. Wrenching Mathias's rosarius from the lock, he rolled into the crypt firing on full auto to keep the heretics at bay.

The doors boomed shut and Ackolon swung to his feet. 'Chaplain Mathi–' He stared in horror at the scene before him. Cerebus and Fernus were sprawled across the altar, a single bolt shot through each of their heads. Mathias stood over them, his pistol drawn, his armour caked in psychic frost.

Mathias glared at him, blood haemorrhaging from his eyes and nose. The Chaplain staggered forward and fell to his knees. 'Ackolon... ki... kill me! The psyker, I... have expunged him, but I can't hold... at bay for... for long!' Even as he spoke, Mathias began to raise his pistol, his arm trembling. Behind them, the crypt doors started to buckle.

Ackolon placed his bolter to Mathias's head, closed his eyes, and fired. Then, dropping his weapon, he sank to his knees and waited for his own death.

The violent squeal of heavy pneumatics brought him around. Ackolon looked up in awe. Somehow, Cerebus and Fernus had completed the rite of interment before Mathias killed them.

Like a vengeful god of death, the Dreadnought rose above him. The hollow pitch of Ezekiel's voice trumpeted from the war machine's loudspeaker.

'Take me to the enemy, Apothecary.'

Reinhart choked on the smell of corruption as he stormed through the shattered doors behind Apollos. The interior was a charnel house. Flayed bodies and blood-soaked banners hung from the flying buttresses ribbing the chapel's nave. Heaps of stone pews were piled like children's building blocks near the chapel doors to make room for an undulating mass of Chaos worshipers. Two massive fires, a nebulous green tint to their flames, burned at either side of the sacristy's altar. Within the flames, blackened human forms chained to iron stakes cried out in torment. At the Templars' appearance the heretics spun. Screaming their fury, they poured down the nave.

With Helena and Savaul beside him, the Castellan slammed against a toppled marble pew, his eyes burning in the acrid air. Apollos hunkered against the heap across from them while Helena's sisters turned and defended the splintered doors. They were surrounded.

Helena rose from the cover of the pew, her bolter kicking. 'By the Emperor, the altar!' she yelled, oblivious to the gunfire tearing up the marble around her.

Reinhart punched home a fresh magazine and stood to add his own firepower.

Where the sacristy's rear wall once stood a tenebrous ripple of sickening warp energies now spiralled, twisting the laws of reality between the four anchor points of the Necrolectifiers. At the altar's base nine robed warp priests chanted, their shaven skulls branded with ruinous curses.

'Is it open?' Apollos roared.

Helena shook her head. 'No, but almost. We only have minutes.'

'The priests! Aim for the priests!' Savaul screamed.

As one, they poured fire over the heads of the cultists only to see their shells detonate just short of their target.

Reinhart spat a curse. 'What is this heresy?'

'Psykers!' Savaul yelled.

Behind them one of the sisters fell, her body hacked apart as she was pulled through the doors.

'We're going to have to get close!' Apollos shouted.

Helena let loose another barrage and fell back behind cover. 'We'll never make it. We have no defence against the warp. Their energies will tear us apart even if that mob doesn't.'

Apollos raked down another wave of cultists. They were almost on them. 'We're running out of time!'

The warp gate began to darken.

Reinhart looked at his companions, each in turn. He knew there was only one option. The Emperor's eyes were upon him. 'Give me all of your grenades!' he yelled to Helena.

She looked at him, a question on her lips, even as understanding blazed in her eyes. Unclipping her last two, she handed them over.

Reinhart ripped away a portion of his tabard, binding up her grenades with two of his own. He kept one in his hand.

From across the streaking avenue of fire Apollos watched, realising Reinhart's intent. 'No!' he screamed. 'Let me go, I have the best chance!'

A sudden, deafening eruption blew apart what remained of the chapel doors. A shattered piece of lintel struck Apollos in the temple, knocking the young Terminator unconscious. Helena's remaining sisters simply ceased to exist, their bodies vaporised.

Reinhart shook himself from his dazed concussion, a heavy ringing in his ears. He felt warmth streaming down his chest. A bloody crater smoked just below his shoulder. Next to him, Helena coughed in the swirling dust, her face covered in blood from a deep gash across her forehead. Her left leg was gone. Savaul lay unconscious next to them. Through the roiling haze they could see a thronging horde of cultists climbing over the rubble of the devastated doorway.

'Can you hold them?' Reinhart asked.

Helena braced her bolter and nodded. She smiled at Reinhart. 'You do know what true honour is, Marius Reinhart.'

'The Emperor protects, Helena,' he said and briefly grasped her hand.

The Battle Sister smiled again. 'The Emperor protects, Castellan.'

Reinhart vaulted from cover. Hugging the grenades close to his body, he charged through the haze. It took a moment for the Chaos worshippers to realise what dashed between them. But, before they could react, the trembling discharge of an assault cannon shook the chapel's foundations and ripped them to bloody pulps. A grenade arced over the Castellan's head and detonated in a cloud of heavy smoke – masking his approach. Reinhart glanced over his shoulder as he covered the last few metres and saw the silhouette of an ancient Dreadnought in the shadow of the ruined threshold.

He whispered a word of thanks, then turned and emerged from the smoke in the midst of the unsuspecting psykers. Thumbing away the pin of his grenade, he barrelled onto the altar's landing. He felt the first stabs of pain within his mind but they were too late.

'The Emperor does protect,' he said, and the gate was shut amidst lightning and flame.

They found him in the smoking rubble outside the chapel's entrance; his body and armour shattered, his features burnt. He awoke as a young

Templar Neophyte knelt next to him. His crusted eyes cracked open, miraculously intact.

Ackolon blinked.

The shadowed forms of Templars picked their way past them, bolters aimed. He tried to focus on the man leaning over him.

'Brother,' the Neophyte said. 'Hold on. The Apothecaries will be here soon.'

Ackolon coughed, attempted to raise his head. He knew his wounds were mortal 'How... Where?'

'The *Revenant*, brother, your flagship. High Marshal Ludoldus himself sent us after we received a call for aid from an inquisitor named Vinculus. It appears we're working with the Ordo Hereticus now.' he said. 'A crusade has been called against the remainder of the cult you and Castellan Reinhart stopped here.'

'The others...'

'Brother Apollos and the interrogator live, sir, we are pulling them out now. Brother Yesod has already been extracted.'

Ackolon nodded. He began to go cold. What little feeling he had left was slowly fading. He struggled to rise again.

'What is your name, Neophyte?' he rasped.

'Helbrecht, sir.'

Ackolon fell back, his vision blurring. He thought he could hear Reinhart and the others calling his name. 'Tell them, Helbrecht,' he whispered, 'tell them we knew no fear...'

And then he too joined his battle-brothers.

# NIGHTFALL

*Peter Fehervari*

*'Terrible things wait amongst the stars and only a terror greater still
may ward against them. So the Lords have taught us and thus have
They shaped and shielded us through the hungry night. But strength
demands sacrifice and Sarastus must pay its dues. Know then, that
every thirteenth year, upon the dawn of the Black Star, our Lords
shall descend and terrible will be their wrath should our tribute
prove unworthy.'*

'The Blind and the Bound'
The Revelations of True Night

Sarastus was just another forgotten world left to rot in the backwaters of
the Imperium. The life of a hive-world was measured by its productiv-
ity and when the seams of its industry ran dry, the planet had quietly
slipped off the Imperial charts. Soon after that the darkness had come.

True Night had touched Sarastus three times, each visitation miring
the planet deeper in damnation. Four of the great hive cities now lay
silent, their will to live smothered beneath decades of fear. Carceri,
once the greatest, was now merely the last. Blighting the plains like a
vast scab, it was a black ziggurat of heaped tiers, its spires clutching
hopelessly at the sky. The manufactorums were still, the hab-warrens
shadow-haunted mausoleums. Of its massed millions perhaps some
hundred thousand remained, huddling in the lowest tiers, far from the
touch of the stars. The prophets of True Night ruled them with an iron

hand, but they were as fearful as their thralls, for in the balance of Sarastus the only ones who truly mattered were the sacrifices.

To the prophets who chose them, they were the blessed; to the thralls who surrendered and mourned them, they were just the ghouls. All were ragged, skeletal shadows with gaunt faces and hungry eyes. Most would kill on a whim and many wouldn't hesitate to make a meal of the dead. Cast into the uppermost tier of the hive they scavenged and murdered beneath an open sky, striving to prove themselves worthy of the darkness. When True Night fell none were older than thirteen.

Judgement began with a song, a drone so deep it stirred the entire hive. Throughout the day it rose in pitch and complexity, blossoming as the sun waned, charging the air with potential. As night drew near, the planet itself seemed to hold its breath, as if playing dead for the stars. But while the thralls trembled and the priests mumbled prayers, the ghouls thrilled to it. This was *their* night!

Tantalising and threatening by turns, the call drew them to the walled plaza nestling at the peak of the hive. Long ago the square had hosted the elite of Carceri, but now only these feral youths remained to pass through the crumbling majesty of the gates. They came in a trickle and then a tide, none sparing a glance for the imperious faces glowering down from the lintels; they knew nothing of the past, and cared even less. They were here for the Needle, because tonight the Needle sang.

Gazing up at the gently vibrating monolith that dominated the centre of the plaza, Zeth felt the old awe welling up again. No matter how many times he saw it, the Needle was a shocking, impossible thing. About twenty feet across, it was a vast splinter woven from twisted iron spars, every inch encrusted with black barbs. One end was embedded deep in the rockcrete of the plaza, the other ascended in angular coils to disappear amongst the clouds. It was the brand of the star gods on Sarastus and it was Zeth's only friend.

Most of the ghouls feared the monolith, but Zeth had always been drawn to it. During the first terrifying days of his ordeal he'd hidden in its shadow, finding strength in its agonised contours. Soon afterwards the visions had begun. They were just teasing flashes – *a rich darkness glittering midnight blue* – *a black-feathered king dying from within and without* – *the howl of a hunter high above*... There were never enough pieces to complete the picture, but Zeth knew the Needle had given him an *edge*. He'd glimpsed enough of the future to get ahead of the game.

Losing himself in the Needlesong, Zeth remembered the words of the scarred prophet, 'Listen for the Needle. It's their mark and your measure. Time will come when you'll hear it sing and then you'd best be ready, for the Lords will be close. Win their favour and you'll taste the stars, fail them and you'll be worse than dead...'

The weak would be culled and the strong would be taken. It was a simple promise that had become the vicious core of Zeth's soul. He was ready for the test. He was *hungry* for it. Impatiently he watched the sun bleed into the horizon.

As was their way, the masters of Sarastus returned on the eve of Nightfall. Their vessel was a jagged predator, slicing between the stars like a serrated knife. Its hull, a blue so deep it was almost black, bore no ornamentation or marks of allegiance. It was a creature of shadows, much like its crew.

From the shrouded recesses of his command throne, Vassaago observed the world he had enslaved. Flickering holo-reports veiled his bleakly handsome features in a web of light and shadow, but his eyes were changeless black orbs. Impassively he assessed the prospects for this harvest. Another hive had died and the last was teetering on the brink of extinction.

'Lord, I must prepare for the harrowing.' The words were spoken in a discordant electrical hiss and Vassaago frowned, turning to the thing hovering beside him.

The sorcerer had entered his service a mere century ago and he still considered it an outsider. It claimed an Astartes heritage, but its demeanour had more in common with the extremes of the Mechanicum. The tattered swathes of its robes completely hid its physique and Vassaago had never seen so much as a hand emerge from that formless mass. Stranger still was the absence of anything recognisable as a face. Perhaps the coarse iron sheet it wore was just a mask, but if so it made no concessions to anything remotely human. *Such as eyes...* It was an uncanny creature to be sure, but Vassaago had entertained stranger allies over the millennia.

'Do not dissemble with me, Yehzod. I know it is your precious Black Sun that draws you,' Vassaago challenged.

'Our interests are concordant. The anomaly will facilitate a prime yield.'

'Indeed? I believe this world has grown stale. Previously we took only six newbloods...'

'Six that proved exceptional,' Yehzod insisted, but Vassaago's attention had already returned to the holo-screens and after a moment the sorcerer took the opportunity to drift away. Watching the creature from the corner of his eye, Vassaago knew it was correct. The six *had* been exceptional. Perhaps there was still meat on this carcass after all...

Stealthily the ship stalked the hive, following it into the planet's night side. As the sun was occluded the vessel's hull rippled with scintillating flashes of energy and its primal spirit stirred into troubled awareness. Neither wholly machine nor yet daemon, the ancient predator recognised this place and shuddered uneasily.

Crouched in the assault bay amongst his armoured brethren, Zhara'shan could sense the ship's disquiet, reading its mood in every nuance of the flight: the erratic pulse of the thrusters, the lethargy of the stabilisers, even the flicker of the lights... The old devil was skittish, as it always was when they hunted here. It was a wary beast and Zhara'shan sometimes grew tired of its reticence, but he had faith in it. Certainly he trusted it over his watchful, murderous brethren.

His eyes hidden beneath his helmet, he glanced warily at Haz'thur. Inevitably, the massive warrior had positioned himself just to Zhara'shan's right, not quite challenging his authority, but visibly staking a claim. The talonmaster regarded his unwelcome shadow with distaste. Haz'thur's armour was a fibrous mass of tumours and spines that pulsed with a life of its own, its monstrosity completed by the huge bone cleavers jutting from his wrists. Typically he disdained a helmet, revelling in the horror his serpentine features evoked in his prey. Although a youth beside Zhara'shan, the giant had embraced the ravages of the warp with zeal. Some amongst the talon even whispered of daemonic possession...

Zhara'shan grimaced. Like all his kind he had tasted the glory of the warp, but his own changes were refined, precise... *controlled*. The rampant perversions sported by Haz'thur could only end in madness and dissolution. If such abominations were the future then the Long War was already lost.

Abruptly the fierce jet streams of Sarastus caught them, buffeting and rattling the craft. They were entering the atmosphere and tradition demanded the vigil. Zhara'shan's bellow drew the eyes of the talon.

'Brothers, we ride the storm and the storm rides within our hearts!' He ignored the low, mocking chuckle from Haz'thur. 'We are masters of the tempest, never slaves. Seek the eye and chain the storm!' With a snarl Zhara'shan twisted his body into a stylised stance and became rigid. Swiftly the talon followed his lead, each warrior freezing into his own unique posture. Even Haz'thur obeyed, dropping into a bestial crouch.

Striving for perfect stillness they compensated for the turbulence with minute motions. Each knew that to slip or scuffle, even to make the slightest sound, would invite the scorn of his brothers. Their discipline filled Zhara'shan with fierce pride. Balance was the lynchpin of their craft, enabling them to skim the warp without being consumed.

Like a menagerie of nightmare statues, the silent raptors waited for Nightfall.

Nightfall. Zeth shivered at the thought of it. Not just any night, but *True Night*. Soon all the pain and the horror was going to pay off...

'This is gonna be a bloodfest. We gotta evac this zone, chief.' Vivo's reedy voice broke Zeth's reverie and he scowled.

'You planning to run out on us, Vivo?' Zeth's tone dripped poison and the gangly youth blanched. He was the weakest link in Zeth's pack, but all of them were wired. He sighed theatrically. 'Listen up, it's Nightfall! Needle's where we gotta be. Just stick with the plan and I'll get you all to the stars.'

Shaking his head, Zeth scanned the plaza. Things *were* pretty wild. There were hundreds clustered around the Needle now: razers and flesheaters and darkscars all standing shoulder to shoulder, their gang rivalries on hold for Nightfall. But Zeth could already taste the violence in the air. High above, the sky rumbled.

A violent judder shook the craft and Haz'thur felt himself slipping. Only an act of brutal concentration saved him and he snarled inwardly. Covertly he eyed Zhara'shan, certain that the ancient had caught his error. Doubtless the talonmaster would seek to humiliate him after the harvest, but the fool would never get the chance. The mood of the warband was changing and relics like Zhara'shan were losing favour. Already the talon was drawn to Haz'thur and when the time came none would defy him. Bristling beneath Zhara'shan's contempt, Haz'thur had long hungered to lash out, but the sorcerer had urged patience.

Thinking of the mystic, Haz'thur recalled the truths that had been revealed to him. He had seen the future! A future of slaughter unfettered by any justification save its own raw beauty, where his body would shape itself to the whims of the moment and the Long War would become the Eternal War! Seething with tension, Haz'thur endured the vigil.

Lurking amongst the roiling clouds, the ship sensed the obscenity approaching. There was nothing its sensors could detect, nothing its tainted logic core could quantify, just an absolute certainty of *wrongness*. Bitterly it turned its attention to the stone-clad chamber that ached like a void in its guts.

Ensconced within his sanctum, levitating within a circle of arcane wards, Yehzod quietly decided the fate of the talonmaster and dismissed the ship's hatred. Like Zhara'shan, the ship was another vexing element of this warband that needed addressing, but for now the impending anomaly consumed his attention. The Black Sun was returning to Sarastus and every detail had to be recorded, every nuance evaluated. Despite decades dedicated to the enigma, he had made little progress in fathoming its nature, but its *promise* captivated him. Satisfied that his wards were intact, the sorcerer reached into the void to bear witness to impossibility.

It arrived with a silent scream, the insane potential sound of space being defiled by *otherness*. Reality itself recoiled, waves of causality twisted into chaos by the intruder's presence. Fighting back at some fundamental level, the materium coagulated around the rift, struggling to quarantine the infected space. Reality held and the invader was contained.

Contained, but not quite isolated. Trapped in a bubble of order it manifested as a vast black star radiating poisonous light.

True Night fell on Sarastus.

The darkness was sudden and complete, yet Zeth could see right across the plaza. Every pale face and glinting blade and grey charm, all raked the eyes with unnatural sharpness. It was all stark high-contrast detail, bleached of colour and every hint of warmth. *Ghost light...*

A voice whimpered, another answered, superstitious dread spreading through the crowd like wildfire. They wanted to flee, but the Needle's song held them. The monolith burned a bright white, like a negative image of its former self. It was alive with coruscating energy, arcs of black lightning crackling between its thorns. Suddenly its song flared into an awful, soul-scraping whine.

Something began to fracture inside the ghouls. With a lost wail someone raced forward, arms outstretched to embrace the metal siren. Immediately the boy was caught up in the crackling eddies swirling around the monolith and drawn up into the maelstrom. Spiralling up through the forest of thorns he was shredded and charred, rendered down into a ragged ruin before coming to rest impaled on the spines high above.

A second youth leapt into the whirlwind, then a third, a fourth. Soon dozens of supplicants had joined the lethal dance, gyrating about the Needle and screaming joyfully as it mangled them, body and soul.

On Zeth and his pack the tug was gentle, almost playful. He knew the Needle wanted him to win through, wanted him to make it to the stars. He didn't really know why, and his instincts told him there would be a price to pay, but Zeth figured he'd deal with that later. After all, he was already in hell, so what did he have to lose?

Abandoning the cage of his flesh, the sorcerer cast his spirit into the plaza and hovered invisibly above the chaos. Observing the shrieking monolith, Yehzod was filled with pride, remembering the tiny daemon-seed he had planted there so long ago. Nurtured by the noxious light of the Black Sun and feeding on the decay of the hive, it had germinated into a titan! Unfortunately, while it was a useful tool for the harvest, it had revealed little about the sun. He had deduced that the anomaly violated space at a metaphysical level, literally corroding the soul of a planet, but the *mechanism* completely eluded him.

He turned his attention to the test animals and assessed the carnage. Once again the pitiful creatures displayed remarkable fortitude. For every one that succumbed to the lure, three more resisted. Many had fallen to their knees, hands clasped over their ears to block out the song. Others stood rigid, eyes screwed shut, their lips mouthing prayers or obscenities, focusing on anything but the call. They confirmed his hypothesis that brutality bred resistance to the anomaly. Even so, too many were dying and Lord Vassaago would expect a live yield from this harvest. It would be imprudent to disappoint him quite yet…

Reluctantly Yehzod commanded the monolith to desist. As always, it resisted and he lashed it with his will, brutally driving it into submission. Its strength had grown exponentially since the last harvest. It was more hostile, more enigmatic, *more a creature of the Black Sun…*

Gradually the cacophony died down and the Needle subsided into a dull, lifeless grey. The ghouls gawked at the slumbering monster, their faces bright with ghost light. At some point during the slaughter it had begun to rain and now the first rumbles of thunder rolled across the plaza. Still the monolith remained silent. Slowly, uncertainly, a murmur washed through the crowd, beginning as relief and daring for jubilation.

Zeth almost pitied them. They thought the test was over when it had only just begun. Ignoring the whoops and cheers he watched the seething sky.

A sonorous bell reverberated through the assault bay and the hatch swung open. Instantly the chamber was transformed into a riot of wind and rain. It would have scattered ordinary men, but for the raptors it was bliss. Exploding from the rigour of the vigil they scuttled towards the hatch. Hunched beneath their baroque jump packs, clawed feet skittering along the decking, they moved in ragged, avian bursts, hungry for freedom.

Thrusting aside an insolent brother Zhara'shan claimed the spearhead. As talonmaster the first jump was his by right! Instinctively he rounded on Haz'thur, the flensing claws springing free from his gauntlets, but the abomination was hanging back in the shadows. Surprised, Zhara'shan growled low in his throat. His instincts had been honed through the pitiless millennia and he knew something was wrong here…

Abruptly he realised his brothers were watching him expectantly. *Did they think he feared the jump?* The thought seared him with horror, swiftly followed by an overpowering need to kill. Already he could see the bay transformed into a blood-drenched charnel house. Savagely fighting down the fury, he swung around and plunged into the tempest.

Haz'thur stalked forward, noting with satisfaction that the others were giving him precedence. Already they understood the new shape the talon was taking. Contemptuously he appraised the stunted, almost uniform extent of their mutations. Yes, a new shape was undeniably called for. *Several in fact!* With a guttural chuckle he leapt after the talonmaster.

Freefalling through the maelstrom, Zhara'shan urged the wind to flay him of doubt. He thrust his arms wide, recklessly obstructing his streamlined form and inviting the full wrath of the wind. It answered with a vengeance, raking the gnarled flesh of his armour and making him howl with release. At one with the storm, he tasted the only peace he recognised.

As he fell, Haz'thur fixed his eyes on the dark speck of the talon-master far below and grinned savagely. He had received the command during the vigil, the sorcerer's words a silken whisper in his mind: *the talonmaster was not to return from the harrowing.*

Spying the tip of the monolith jabbing through the clouds, Zhara'shan reluctantly ignited his jetpack to veer away. The thing was a spawn of the Black Sun and not to be trusted. *Much like the faceless bastard who had led them on this trail…* With a clarity born of the storm, Zhara'shan suddenly knew he would kill the sorcerer. Lord Vassaago's schemes be damned, once this harvest was done he would tear out the cancer devouring his warband. With a satisfied snarl the talonmaster flipped into a knifing dive, streaking towards the distant spires.

Cautiously Zeth approached the silent monolith. The pack kept their distance, but Zeth told himself he had nothing to fear. Tentatively he reached out towards a long, dagger-like thorn, hesitating at the thought of the remnants sizzling in the branches above.

'You want me for something…' *Something other than charred meat.* 'And I want…' *To break them all and unmake them all and bring them all down screaming and drowning in their own lies.* The words erupted unbidden from somewhere dark and hungry deep within Zeth's soul. They were shockingly alien, yet achingly familiar. *True words.*

Stunned, Zeth staggered back, the thorn snapping free in his grasp. He stared at it in confusion. When had he actually touched the thing? He'd reached out, but then he'd hesitated…

The thought was sliced apart by an ululating cry. Rippling down from the clouds, it was a bestial sound that froze the ghouls as surely as the Needle's lure. Zeth recognised it in a heartbeat.

A tall darkscar, his face a patchwork of ritual wounds, seized the moment, 'Hear the Midnight Fathers and open your hearts to True Night!' His voice was deep and rich, belying his youth. 'We have endured the Sacrament of Divine Shredding and now the Lords are come amongst us!'

Zeth could see he had them. In a crazy way he was even right. That cry from above had sealed the deal. All his visions had been real. The Lords were here!

'The things you've seen up here in the Spires, they're nothing! Up there…' The darkscar jabbed at the sky. 'Up there it's all pain and death! The only thing you've got to ask is this: am I a hunter… or am I just meat?'

And then something streaked out of the sky and the preacher was gone.

\* \* \*

Soaring back into the clouds, his prey hooked delicately between the shoulder blades, Haz'thur whooped with delight. He lived for these moments of elegant slaughter, his perfect offerings to the chaos swirling at the heart of everything. But this time the true joy lay in cheating the talonmaster of the first kill!

Twisting into the wind he saw Zhara'shan watching him. They regarded each other from a hovering standstill as the others circled them. This affront had crossed the line between insolence and open challenge. A reckoning was inevitable. All that remained was a question of when. Haz'thur waited, ropes of drool dripping from his maw in anticipation of the clash. His claws flashing free, Zhara'shan ignited his thrusters… and dived towards the plaza.

Haz'thur laughed, knowing it wasn't fear that had driven away his rival. Despite his long millennia in the darkness, the talonmaster was still driven by *duty*. In his heart, the ancient monster was still a Space Marine.

Zeth caught the momentary blur of shadows as a second ghoul was snatched from the bewildered crowd. It happened in an eye-blink, the work of a master. The third was slower and Zeth spied something man-like and impossibly huge.

*Night Lord.* The name slipped into his mind, redolent with promise. He didn't know if it was another gift from the Needle or a revelation from something deeper, but his heart sang to it. Recognising their game, recognising *them*, Zeth sank into a crouch beside the monolith and watched. The strikes weren't random. They were only taking the real crazies: berserk razers, fanatical darkscars, gibbering flesheaters… and anyone that ran for the gate. *Culling the weak.*

Glancing at his pack, Zeth winced. They were bunched together, just staring at the clouds! He needed to get them into cover, but he wasn't going to risk shouting for the sky-struck fools. This wasn't the time to get noticed, or distracted. Unwillingly, his eyes were drawn back to the Night Lords' game. *It was beautiful…*

As he hooked another kill onto his shoulder spikes, Zhara'shan considered Haz'thur's challenge. It had been inevitable, yet it had surprised him. Had his talon forgotten that the mission always came first? *Had they fallen so far?* The Night Lords had entered the Long War bound by an oath to tear down the lie that was the Imperium, but watching his rapacious, shrieking brethren he wondered what bound them now.

Troubled, Zhara'shan's preternatural gaze wandered back to the youth he had spied hiding beside the monolith. It was a scrawny thing, its face bone white against lank black hair, but its stillness had caught his eye. Twice already he had spared it, convinced it wasn't hiding out of cowardice. No, there was no fear there, yet it was free of the rage or faith that so often blinded the fearless…

A brother whipped past him, hissing reproachfully. The talon was growing weary of the shadow play and their insolence incensed him. If Haz'thur took the lead now would they follow him? Surely their loyalty, no, their *fear* of the talonmaster hadn't waned so far? Bitterly he added Haz'thur's name to the personal harvest he would reap after this mission. Howling a command, he dropped from the cloud cover.

The crowd fell silent as they spied the jagged black shapes emerging from the clouds. Spiralling above the plaza in swift arcs, their paths interweaving with arrogant precision, the flyers were inscribing something across the sky. Zeth watched it form and fade, over and again. It was just a phantom incarnated in the contrails of their jets, but the eightfold star was still potent. Zeth recoiled, torn between loathing and longing, struggling to ground himself. Time was running out and his pack was frozen in the killing ground...

Suddenly Zeth was running out into the open, shouting, 'Plan is on!' That got their attention, along with all the crazies and probably the Night Lords too. 'You want to live, go for the Needle!'

Unquestioning, Brox and Kert dashed towards him, but then Vivo sneered, 'You're crazy chief, Needle's a trap! We're going to the stars with the angels!' He was a rat but he had easy answers and the pack was frayed enough to listen. The hackles on the back of Zeth's neck were tingling in anticipation of rending claws. *He didn't have time for this...*

On impulse Zeth glared into Vivo's eyes, opening the shutters to the terrible dark country so recently revealed by the Needle. Vivo only caught a glimpse of the truth, but it shredded his mind in an instant. By the time he hit the ground he'd already died a thousand times.

Floating above the plaza, Yehzod reeled as a spike of blacklight energy ricocheted through him. It was just an echo, but its lingering malice almost shattered his astral projection. Coldly subsuming confusion to curiosity, the sorcerer scanned the plaza. He had glimpsed a mind behind the attack, but the scene below was an impenetrable quagmire of psychic torment. Gauging the screaming, scrabbling animals, Yehzod felt the first stirrings of unease. Could there truly be such a mind amongst these wretches? *A mind that could focus the Black Star?*

Zeth stared at Vivo's corpse, confusion vying with horror vying with... joy? How had he done that? And why did he care when it had felt so good? *And why could he taste blood?*

Hearing the sudden murmur in the crowd, Zeth realised they were all tasting it. *The blood was in the rain.* Looking up, he saw the black rivulets pouring down from high above. Urgently he pulled Brox and Kert down into the shadow of the Needle, already knowing it was too late for the others.

Without warning the downpour exploded into a storm from hell. Glistening viscera, ragged limbs and unrecognisable raw fragments hailed down on the frantic mob as the hunters butchered their catch. With a chorus of hoots and harsh chirps they swept back and forth, showering the mob with gore as they spiralled ever lower. The ghouls were in turmoil, desperately ducking and diving to avoid the flyers, many slipping in the blood and tripping their neighbours.

Zeth saw a Night Lord glide low over the crowd, his clawed feet just skimming their heads. His helmet was carved into the visage of a snarling wolf, its lupine ears flaring into stylised bat wings, the eyes lambent with cold fire. As he swept over them he whispered, his harsh rasp somehow cutting through the chaos, *'We are the darkness between the stars… Die for us… We are the promise of murder in your hearts… Kill for us… We are the truth behind the lies… Kill or die…'*

It was like a trigger to some deep-rooted switch in their souls. First the razers went berserk, lashing out with crude clubs and cleavers, then the darkscars fell on unbelievers with their bone knives and the sane creeds fought back, shados and nailz and statiks all turning on each other in the name of True Night. And all the while the Night Lords circled above, taunting and tormenting, but only killing those who fled.

Watching his pack die, Zeth felt nothing.

Arms outstretched, Haz'thur streaked between a pair of fleeing ghouls, neatly bisecting both at the waist, turning two into four. He spun, wondering how far their legs would run unburdened, but they just flopped over. This was poor sport and his blood sang to the tune of the rabid mob. Hearing the talonmaster finish his vainglorious speech Haz'thur knew it was time. Slavering with anticipation he jetted back into the clouds.

Watching his rival soar skyward, Zhara'shan felt his instincts prickle uneasily, but the newbloods demanded his attention. They fought with impressive ferocity but few promised any true depth to their darkness. Once again his thoughts turned to that strange, quiet ghoul. There had been something of the raptor vigil in its stillness and he wondered if it still lived. Intrigued, he flew towards the monolith.

Zeth saw the malevolent eight-pointed star reappear in the sky, blazing with fulfilment, glutted on the blood sacrifice of the ghouls. Recognising the moment, he chewed his lip, suddenly uncertain.

'We going to be okay, chief?' Brox asked, his eyes wide. The big ghoul had never been the sharpest player in the pack, but he'd always been loyal.

'Just stick with the plan,' Zeth said. 'Go. Both of you.' Nervously Brox and Kert ducked into the recesses of the Needle… and disappeared. Zeth knew this was the turning point. He could just slip away now and the

Night Lords would never know. Come dawn he'd be King of the Spires.

But then the moment passed. It would never have been enough anyway. Zeth looked up and the wolf-helmed Nightlord was there.

The ghoul was looking straight at him. As Zhara'shan had soared towards the Needle its eyes had met his unerringly. *As if it had been waiting for him.* The strangeness had brought him to a standstill and now they took each other's measure, the mayhem around them forgotten. Warily, Zhara'shan wondered what its connection was with the monolith. *Was it another spawn of the Black Sun?*

Suddenly the ghoul's eyes flicked upwards, its warning coming a heartbeat before Zhara'shan heard the thrusters. He spun with a snarl and Haz'thur's clawed feet struck him squarely in the chest. The abomination's blistering dive tore the talonmaster from the sky, pounding him into the plaza with savage force. Three ghouls burst into bloody ruins beneath him and the rockcrete surface cracked wide open. Instinctively Zhara'shan rolled aside as Haz'thur's talons ripped towards him and the abomination crashed down onto the rockcrete.

His balance perfect, Haz'thur landed on his feet and spun after his rival, swinging down with those monstrous bone cleavers. Unable to recover, Zhara'shan could only roll and roll again, the shattered bones of his composite ribs tearing his chest like broken glass. A fraction too slow, he took a glancing blow to one of his shoulder pauldrons. The armour held, but it was enough to break the rhythm of his escape and Haz'thur was on him in an instant, a foot stamping down onto his chest and pinning him to the ground.

'Your Long War is a lie…' The abomination's voice was hoarse with pleasure, his drool spattering over the talonmaster's armour. 'And you were always blind to True Night!'

As the bone cleavers slashed down Zhara'shan ignited his jump pack. The explosive force tore him away from his rival, blasting him through the legs of the screaming throng. He gritted his teeth against the agony as he flashed along the rockcrete in a shower of sparks, the abused jump pack bucking and roaring under him like a living thing. Suddenly the exhaust jets spewed fire, scorching his armoured legs and leaving a wake of flame in his passing. Desperately he tried to cut the power, but the tortured machine-spirit was beyond tethering. Even as he fumbled for the locking clamps he knew it was too late.

Zhara'shan's bold manoeuvre had sent Haz'thur crashing to the ground, his legs swept from under him. As he leapt to his feet a crunching boom echoed across the plaza, followed a moment later by the vivid bloom of flames against the sky. His eyes glittering, Haz'thur threw back his head and bellowed his victory to the stars.

His joy was lanced by a stabbing agony in his thigh and he whirled around, but his attacker was already springing away, its black dagger glistening with Haz'thur's blood. Unbelievably it was just another ghoul, thinner than most and sickly pale. Glancing back, it flashed him a cold grin before ducking into the seething crowd.

With a bestial roar Haz'thur launched himself after his attacker, tearing into the throng like a primal tide of destruction, slicing and biting and crushing his way through the ghouls. Some tried to flee, others turned on him with their pitiful weapons, but all were reduced to shreds of meat and bone in his wake. And then he was through and his quarry was waiting for him.

It was less than twenty paces away, lurking beside the monolith, its eyes cold and calculating. Briefly a fading, rational part of Haz'thur's mind surged up through the rage, cautious and questioning. What was this creature? How could its feeble blade even scratch his armour, let alone pierce it? He was a god beside this worm, so how had it drawn blood?

As if sensing Haz'thur's doubt, the ghoul pointed at him, then slowly, deliberately ran a finger across its throat. And then it ducked into the shadow of the monolith and vanished. Gone in an eye blink.

*Not a ghoul, but a ghost...*

Hissing, Haz'thur leapt to the spot the creature had occupied only moments before, furiously sniffing for a scent, searching the dark whorls of the Needle for a huddled shape. *What trickery was this?*

And then he saw them, those cold grey eyes, peering at him through the iron web. *Inside the Needle!* Lightning fast, Haz'thur punched through the crevice, but the ghost was already gone, ducking away into the darkness. A gleam of admiration flashed through the rage as Haz'thur scanned the weave of the monolith. Yes, there were ragged gaps aplenty for a worm to crawl through, but what kind of fool would hide inside that killing machine? The answer surged back on the crest of his rage: *the kind that would taunt a raptor!*

Suddenly he was savaging the Needle. The iron was hard but brittle and it buckled rapidly beneath his bone cleavers.

The core of the Needle was a hollow vertical shaft. Zeth guessed it ran the whole length of the hive and maybe even beyond, but he'd only ever gone a few tiers deep. Scrambling down its gnarled guts, he heard the hunter ripping its way inside. Iron fragments tumbled past, rapidly lost in the abyss below and he shuddered, wondering whether a fall into that darkness would ever end.

*But he wasn't going to fall.*

He'd made this climb countless times over the years, finding gaps in the weave that led to other tiers of the hive. Of course they were all abandoned, but there'd been plenty to scavenge and he'd prepared well for this night.

With a final screech of tortured metal the Night Lord broke through and Zeth abandoned caution, speeding down the shaft. He glimpsed the others waiting below, crouched in a chamber on the other side of the web. He was almost there...

Suddenly something vast and dark plummeted past, the ferocity of its wake almost dislodging him. It struck the side of the shaft below with a violent clang and ricocheted away into the darkness. Glancing down, he saw a flare of light bloom in the depths. A heartbeat later the shaft reverberated with the roar of an engine and the light came streaking up.

Leaping recklessly into the Needle, Haz'thur had dropped like a stone into the abyss beyond. *That warp-cursed ghost had tricked him!* Rocketing furiously back up the shaft he swiped at his quarry, missing by a hair's breadth as it slipped through another crawl hole. Furious, he jetted backwards and coiled into a huddled ball of spikes. Thrusters burning, he launched himself at the iron barrier.

The crash of the raptor's entry shook the rockcrete corridor, but the sprinting ghouls didn't look back. The shimmering glow-globes weren't the only things they'd planted along this stretch of tunnels. Over the years they'd turned the place into a death trap and one misstep would kill them as surely as their hunter's claws.

Leaping an almost invisible wire Zeth felt the panic rising in him. He'd planned for a better lead, but the raptor's sheer physical power had surprised him. Suddenly all the years of scheming and scavenging seemed pitiful, but he held onto the Needle's promise. *He would taste the stars...*

Haz'thur's wild cannonball dive ripped through the web and carried him careening into the wall only thirty paces beyond. The impact pulverized the rockcrete and shook the whole chamber. Bellowing, he exploded from the ragged crater in a shower of debris, crashing down into a feral crouch. His head flicked about in rapid, avian jerks as he assessed the territory. Low ceiling, drab rockcrete walls threaded with pipes, passages branching off on all sides... Not a true tier then, just a service layer for the clockwork of the hive. It would be a maze of tight tunnels and cluttered chambers that would favour his prey and fight his bulk. *Clever little ghost.*

But he had their scent. There were three and they were close. Unable to jump, let alone fly in the confined warren, he skittered towards the exit... and the ground collapsed beneath his feet. Inhuman reflexes kicking in, he snagged the lip of the pit and leapt out, impelled by a jab of thrust. Peering back down he snarled at the nest of spikes jutting from the gloom. *A trap?* His ceramite armour would have crushed the pitiful spines like matchsticks, but the sheer arrogance of it affronted him. *Did the prey presume to hunt him?*

The traps came thick and fast after that, Haz'thur's furious pursuit triggering a new attack at every twist and turn of the tunnels. Mostly they were variants on the same themes; crude pitfalls, collapsing ceilings and tripwires that released spring-loaded spikes or swinging girders. Occasionally there was something unique, a shower of acid or a rigged laspistol, but all were the clumsy toys of a child playing at war. At first Haz'thur's instincts had compelled him to avoid the traps, but soon he was tripping them with scornful abandon, laughing as spikes shattered against his armour and dodging whirling debris with bravado.

By the time the prey came in sight his mood had grown almost sanguine and he was tempted to prolong the hunt. At thirty paces he teased them with a keening wail, enticing one of the three to glance back. Moments later the fool had impaled itself on a bed of nails. As he whipped past, Haz'thur beheaded the screaming wretch with a flick of the wrist. Predictably it hadn't been the ghost. No, the ghost was sly, but even so its life hung by a thread only twenty paces long...

Drenched in sweat, his heart hammering wildly, Zeth knew they couldn't last much longer. Even Kert's slip-up hadn't slowed the hunter. When the fool had got himself spiked the dark thing inside Zeth had cheered, desperate for anything to delay those claws, but it hadn't made a damned bit of difference. Even so, that shadow was now eyeing Brox hungrily, looking for an angle to make him count...

The placid ghoul's breathing was steady beside Zeth's ragged gasps. Dim but strong, that was Brox. And so very loyal. The idiot could have pulled ahead long ago, but there he was, sticking shoulder to shoulder with Zeth despite the devil breathing down their backs.

*Sacrifice the fool! Freeze him!*

The thoughts lashed across Zeth's mind with a brutal logic that shocked him. The worst thing was he knew he could do it. All he had to do was reach out with his mind and *twist*. It would be so easy and it made such sense! But Brox was the last of his pack...

They swept round a corner and Zeth saw their destination looming just ahead. This was the endgame! They were so close, but so was the hunter...

*Do it now!*

And then they were bursting into the old generatorium storeroom, weaving through the heaped metal barrels, straining for the open hatchway on the far side. But then Zeth's heart sank in despair. They'd never get the blast door closed in time! From outside the storeroom they'd have to turn and *pull* it shut. It would take precious seconds they'd never have... but if someone just *pushed* it from the inside...

Zeth glanced at Brox and the cold thing inside him reared up.

*Do it!*

* * *

Exploding into the storeroom Haz'thur saw the bigger animal suddenly turn on the ghost, thrusting it into the tunnel beyond. Excited by their conflict he stormed forward, the reek of promethium assaulting his finely tuned sense of smell. *Promethium?* He felt the tripwire break.

Staggering from the storeroom Zeth glanced back and caught a glimpse of Brox's face. The big ghoul's expression was tranquil, empty. And then the hatch slammed shut and the concussion followed an instant later. It buckled the solid metal hatch and tore the ground from under Zeth's feet. Huddled in a ragged heap, he lay in the darkness long after the tremor had passed. Two thoughts hounded each other through his mind, vying for his soul: *I didn't... I did...*

Haz'thur awoke to a world of raw pain. Every breath tore through his chest like a gust of broken glass and his nostrils twitched to the stench of his own charred flesh. His remaining eye had fixed on the maze of fissures in the ceiling above. There was significance to be found in that twisting conjunction of empty spaces. Besides, he couldn't move his neck, or anything else for that matter. Only the claws of his left foot still offered the ghost of a twitch. *The ghost...* The ghost had killed him. The same ghost that was looking down at him now with those cold, grey eyes. As it knelt over him something dark slithered behind the grey and suddenly he was gazing up into twin black suns. For the briefest instant he knew fear, and then the black thorn came down.

When Zeth emerged from the Needle the sky was streaked with red and the plaza swam with it. The bodies were everywhere, razers and flesheaters and darkscars all alike in the unravelled simplicity of death. The survivors were gathered in a bewildered huddle, almost as ragged and bloody as the dead, their faces slack with the shock of just being alive.

The raptors were there too, but now they were still and silent. It was as if the sun's rays had petrified them where they stood, transforming them into dark statues. Their wolf-helmed leader crouched amongst them. His armour was a scorched wreck and his hunched posture spoke of barely contained agony, but he was alive. That was good, Zeth thought. He would need allies amongst them.

His eyes found the ones who would decide his fate. A faceless creature was skimming silently over the dead, the seething swathe of its robes never quite touching the ground. It was like a spectral carrion bird, seeking some arcane logic in the weave of the carnage. An armoured giant stalked silently by its side, the tapers of his sable cloak wet with the blood of trampled corpses.

*Sorcerer and lord.* Once again the words just slipped into Zeth's mind, along with an understanding that these ancient nightmares were not to be approached boldly. They would come to him in their own time. So

Zeth waited, eyes fixed on the gore-spattered ground. And finally they came.

'Have we bled this world so dry?' The lord's voice was a desiccated whisper. 'So dry... that such a stunted creature can endure the harrowing?'

The sorcerer made no reply, but Zeth suddenly felt the barbed tendrils of its mind reaching out...

*Digging into his soul... Tearing through the walls like paper... Seeing through to his edge...*

Desperately Zeth brandished his sacrifice. 'A kill... a kill for True Night!' Hanging from his hand was the bloody rag of Haz'thur's flayed face.

With a smooth gesture the lord silenced the psychic assault and leant forward. His handsome, bloodless features might have been carved from white marble, but they were pooled with shadows and his eyes were a lustreless black.

'You claim to have killed a raptor?' No anger in that voice, just an ancient bitterness that was somehow worse. To answer with anything less than excellence would be fatal.

'He was... weak, lord.' Zeth breathed, waiting for death. The moments stretched into a dark eternity beneath that withering gaze. And then the ancient nodded.

'Yes, he was. And weakness is the only sin this galaxy truly despises.' The lord turned to the sorcerer. 'We will take this one.'

'It is dangerous.' The words were a hissing, electrical buzz.

'I would hope so, sorcerer.' There was the faintest trace of amusement in that bleak voice.

'Lord Vassaago, its essence has been tainted by... an element I am unable to quantify.'

Zeth fought down a wave of hatred for the faceless bastard. It had tasted the touch of the Needle on him and it was afraid, afraid of the power he would become...

'We are all tainted, Yehzod.' Zeth almost flinched at the acid in Vassaago's voice. 'It is the reason we must endure.'

'Lord, it is unpredictable.' Yehzod urged.

'We shall see...' Vassaago answered, turning his back on them.

*Yes, you will*, the Needle promised.

# ONE HATE

### Aaron Dembski-Bowden

*I am the future of my Chapter.*

*My masters and mentors often tell me this. They say I, and those like me, hold the Chapter's soul in our hands. We wear the black, and we are the beating heart of a reborn brotherhood.*

*It is our duty to remember. We are charged to recall the traditions that came before the moment when our Chapter stood on the edge of extinction.*

*My name is Argo. In a Chapter with few remaining relics, I am blessed above my brothers in the tools of war in my possession.*

*My armour was born when the Imperium was born – repaired, amended and maintained in the centuries since by generations of warriors, slaves, servitors and serfs. My bolter roared on the battlefields of the Horus Heresy, and has been carried in the red-marked hands of thirty-seven Astartes since the day of its forging. Each of their names is etched into the dark iron of the weapon, along with the name of the world that claimed their lives. The eyes of my helm have stared out onto ten thousand wars, and seen a million of mankind's foes die.*

*Around my neck is a gift from the Ecclesiarchy of Holy Terra: an aquila symbol of priceless worth and imbued with the warding secrets of a technology almost lost to time. My armour is black, for I am death itself. My helm is the skull of every battle-brother that died in every battle fought by my Chapter in the ten millennia since our founding.*

*More than that, my face is the victorious leer of the dying Emperor.*

*And why am I charged with this responsibility? Why do I wear the black?*

*Because I hate. I hate more than my brothers, and my hatred runs blacker, deeper, purer than theirs.*

*One hate stands above all others. One hate that burns in our blood and barks from the mouths of five hundred bolters when we stand together in war. It is a hatred with many names: the greenskin, the ork, the kine.*

*To us, they are simply the Enemy.*

*We are the Crimson Fists, the shield-hand of Dorn, and we have survived extinction when all others would have fallen into worthless memory. Our hatred takes us across the stars in service to the Throne.*

*And now it brings us to Syral.*

Syral. A lone orb around a diminutive sun, on the edge of Segmentum Tempestus.

The single celestial child of a red star that was taking thousands of years to die. The sun's waning would take thousands of years before its eventual expiration, and the planet it warmed was still of great use to the Imperium.

Syral was an agri-world, with the globe's landmasses given over to expansive and fertile continents of foodstuffs and livestock. Syral's great oceans were similarly plundered by Imperial need. Beneath their dark surface, the tides concealed hydroponics facilities the size of cities, harvesting the edible wealth of the depths. As a planet, Syral had but one colossal purpose: to export a system's worth of food ready for purchase by the worlds nearby that lacked such natural bounty. Syral fed three hive-worlds, from the spires of the rich to the slums of the destitute, as well as several Imperial Navy fleets and regiments of the Imperial Guard warring in nearby crusades.

From space, Syral was the blue-green of mankind's ancestral memory, as if drawn from an artist's imaginings of the impious ages of Old Terra. However, the face of a world can change a great deal in a year.

'The Fists are back.'

Lord General Ulviran looked at Major Dace, who had spoken those words. With his thin face, ice-blue eyes and aquiline nose, the lord general was a natural when it came to bestowing withering looks on those among his staff that disappointed him. He gave one of those glances to Dace now. The major looked away, suitably chastised.

The gunship sat idle, as it had for several minutes now, its landing stanchions and velocity thrusters still hissing with occasional jets of steam as they released flight pressure and settled into repose. Across the side of this midnight-blue vulture of a vessel, an engraved symbol stared back at the horde of Guardsmen that waited. A clenched fist, as red and dark as good wine.

The gunship's forward ramp lowered like a mouth opening. Ulviran was put in mind – as he always was when seeing an Astartes Thunder-hawk – of a great steel bird of prey. When its forward ramp lowered, just beneath the cockpit window, the bird seemed to roar with the sound of whining hydraulics.

'I count four,' Major Dace said, making this his second most obvious observation that day. Four armoured forms, each more than a head taller than a normal man, tramped down the clanking ramp.

'Just four...' the major added a moment later. Ulviran would gladly have shot him, had he been able to think of a reason to do so. Not even a good reason, just a legal one. Dace was an asset on the battlefield, but at staff meetings his dullard observations were a tedium his fellow officers could easily do without.

The Astartes made no move to approach the crowd of Guardsmen. They stood as still as statues, monstrous bolters held to their eagle-emblazoned chests. Ulviran took stock of the situation. The Astartes were back, and it was not the time to stand around gawping. Control. The scene warranted control. Maybe there could be some dignity salvaged from this whole tawdry development. Having the Astartes arrive would be a cause for celebration right enough, but Ulviran recalled every single word in the missive he'd composed to Chapter Master Kantor of the Crimson Fists. Begging was the only word for it, really. He'd begged for aid, and here it was: deliverance once more. He was not a man who enjoyed resorting to begging. It had galled him even as he'd dictated the distress call.

Ulviran strode forward to meet the giants as they stood stone-still in the shadow of their avian gunship. He noted with unnoticeable displeasure that the heavy bolter turrets on the Thunderhawk's wing tips panned across the camp, as if seeking threats even amongst Imperial forces. Did the Fists not even consider the Guard capable of holding their own base camp secure against the enemy? In that moment, deliverance or not, the lord general hated their damned arrogance.

'Welcome back,' he said to the first of the Astartes, who was undoubtedly the commander of this small team.

The warrior looked at the lord general, his snarling visored helm turning down to regard the human. This close, no more than an arm's length from the towering warriors, Ulviran felt his gums ache from the pressuring hum of the squad's power armour. The whine of energy was more tactile than audible, making his eyes water and prickling the skin on the back of his neck. He swallowed as the Astartes made the sign of the aquila, the warrior's gauntleted hands forming the salute and banging against his armoured chest. Even the smallest of movements made their armour joints purr in a low mechanical snarl.

Ulviran returned the salute. His neck hurt a little, looking up like this, and he unwillingly flinched when the Astartes spoke.

'With all due respect,' the voice was a crackling, vox-distorted growl, far deeper than a normal man's, 'why are you addressing me?'

Ulviran hadn't expected this level of disrespect, nor this degree of informality. He was a lord general, after all. Planets lived and died by his tactical expertise.

262        Space Marines

The general took in the details of the warrior's armour. The suit was the blue of a starless midnight sky, trimmed in places with a bold red, nowhere more noticeable than the clenched fist on the warrior's shoulder pad. A scroll detailing oaths and matters of unknowable honour was draped from the warrior's other shoulder pad, moving slightly in the gentle wind. Hanging from a thick chain that had been made into a bandolier, oversized, misshapen skulls knocked quietly together as the Astartes moved. From the pronounced lower jaws and brutish bone structure, Ulviran knew they were the skulls of orks. In life, they'd been big orks, most likely leaders among their bestial kind. In death, they were impressive trophies.

This Astartes was clearly the leader of the squad. None of the others wore trophies to match.

'I am addressing you because I assumed you were in command.' He adopted the tone of one speaking to a small child, which his men would have found both laughable and insane had they heard. The thrill of authority over these giants rushed through the lord general's blood. He would, after all, brook no disrespect.

'Do I look like a brother-captain to you?' the Astartes asked, and Ulviran wondered if the warrior's vox-speakers made his voice into a growl, or if it was naturally that low.

Ulviran nodded in response to the question. He was determined not to be intimidated.

'To my eyes, yes, you do.'

'Well, I'm not.' Here the Astartes looked to his fellows. 'Not yet, anyway.' Ulviran heard something at the edge of his hearing – a series of quiet clicks coming from the helms of the armoured men. He assumed, quite correctly, that they were laughing with each other over a private vox-channel.

The Astartes draped in skulls, chains and scrolls detailing his many victories inclined his head at one of the others.

'He's the sergeant.'

Ulviran turned to face this next one, making the sign of the aquila once more.

Before the lord general could speak, this next Astartes – who was clad in a blood-coloured toga draped around his armour – shook his helmed head.

'No, lord general,' the Astartes intoned, his voice as much a mechanical rumble as the first one's had been. 'You do not address me, either.'

Ulviran's patience was reaching its end.

'Then who am I to address?'

The robed warrior nodded in the direction of the Thunderhawk, at the newest arrival striding down the ramp. This Astartes was clad in plate of charcoal-black, and even without much knowledge of Astartes technology it was clear to Ulviran that the dark suit of power armour was an antique, dating back centuries – probably even millennia. The black warrior's helmed face was a grinning skull, the red eye lenses lending it a daemonic cast as he looked left and right, surveying the landing site.

Ulviran swallowed, unaware of how his Adam's apple bobbed and betrayed his nervousness. *Throne,* he thought. *A Chaplain.*

The Astartes in the red toga offered the lord general a slight bow.

'You address him.'

In private, they discussed Syral. The Chaplain stalked around the large table with its map-covered surface. Here in the lord general's command room, aboard his personal Baneblade, *The Indomitable Will,* the human and the Astartes shared words away from the ears of others.

'We handed you this world four months ago.'

Those words chilled the lord general's blood. They were an insult, certainly, but they were also an unarguable truth.

'Circumstances change, Brother-Chaplain.' And they had. Ork reinforcements had come in flooding waves, washing the western hemisphere in a tide of greenskin invaders. The Imperium's easy victory, largely bought by the surgical strikes of the Crimson Fists four months before, was nothing more than a pleasant memory and a tale of what might have been. The Imperial Guard had been falling back ever since.

The Chaplain's vox-voice was edged by growls, as if the man spoke at an octave almost too low for words.

'You are losing Syral,' the Astartes said. His skullish face stared at the human across the room.

'I know better than to argue that assessment,' came the lord general's reply. 'I'd wager that I see it clearer than you, for I've been watching it happen for months.'

Ulviran watched as the Chaplain reached up to his helm and pulled the release catches on his armoured collar. With a serpentine hiss of venting pressure, the locks disengaged and the Astartes removed his skulled helmet, reverently lifting it then laying it on the table before him. Its red eyes were dimmed now the helm was detached from the armour's power supply, but they still glared at the lord general in dull accusation.

'I am not here to chastise you, lord general.'

Ulviran smiled to hear the warrior's true voice. It was deep and reso-nant, but with a gentility shaping the words. The Chaplain was, by the lord general's best guess, close to thirty years of age, but with the Astartes it was almost impossible to tell. He didn't even know for certain if they *did* age; he'd always taken the trope for granted that one determined a Space Marine's age by the scars on their flesh and the inscriptions etched into their armour.

Had this Astartes been allowed to grow as a normal man, he might have been considered handsome. Even as the product of intensive genetic enhancement since puberty, the Chaplain was a fair example of his kind. The Astartes was almost two heads taller than a normal man, with features and body mass to match, but Ulviran saw something undeniably human within the warrior's dark-blue eyes and the half-smile he wore.

The lord general liked him immediately. For Ulviran, who prided himself on being a fine reader of men, this was a rare development.

'Brother-Chaplain–'

'Argo,' he interrupted. 'My name is Argo.'

'As you wish. I must ask you, Argo, how did you respond so quickly to our...' he didn't want to say *to our plea*, '...to our request for reinforcement?'

Argo met his gaze. The half-smile left his face, and the warrior's eyes narrowed. The silence that followed the general's question bordered on becoming awkward.

'Just good fortune,' the Chaplain said at last, the smile returning. 'We were close to the system.'

'I see. And are you alone?'

The Chaplain spread his hands in benefice. One gauntlet was the same coal black as the warrior's armour. The other, his left, was painted blood red in keeping with the traditions of his Chapter.

'I bring with me the brothers of Squad Demetrian, of the Fifth Battle Company.'

'Yourself and four others. Nothing more?'

'The Chapter serfs and servitors responsible for the flight and maintenance of our Thunderhawk.'

'No more Astartes.' It was a statement of resignation, not a question.

'As you say,' the Chaplain offered a shallow but sincere bow, 'no more Astartes.'

Ulviran was noticeably ill at ease. 'As much as I thank the Throne and your Chapter Master for any assistance the Fists offer, especially so quickly, I had hoped for a... bolder show of support.'

'Hope is the first step on the road to disappointment. Four months ago, we broke the Enemy's back here. I assume you recall the date.'

'I do. The men still speak of it. They call it Vengeance Night.'

'Very apt. We left the enemy reeling, lord general. We left them bloody, their armies shattered from our assaults across the globe. I was at the Siege of the Cantorial Palace. I was part of the strike force that destroyed the palace itself, and I was there when Brother Imrich of the Fifth took the head of Warlord Golgorrad in the battle amongst the smoking rubble. We are back, lord general, and I humbly suggest you be grateful for even the small blessing that one squad of our Chapter represents.'

'I am grateful, to you and your Chapter Master.'

'Good. I apologise for any harshness in my tone. Now, let us talk of strategy.' The Chaplain pointed with his red hand at the largest map spread across the table. 'Southspire, the capital city, unless I am mistaken.'

'You are not.'

'And, according to the sensor sweeps made by my Thunderhawk as we broke orbit, the city – and the site of the Cantorial Palace at the city's heart – is once more in the hands of the enemy.'

'It is.'

Argo's blue eyes met Ulviran's, drilling into the officer with an unblinking lack of mercy.

'So when do we take it back?'

The interior bay of the Thunderhawk echoed with Argo's footfalls, his clanking tread ringing from the iron skin of the inert machinery stored there. Chapter serfs in robes of deep blue stepped aside, making the sign of the aquila as he passed. Argo nodded to each one in kind, whispering benedictions for them all. They thanked him and moved about the business of attending to the gunship's innards and readying the stored machinery. Argo's eyes raked along the heavy digging equipment stored in the hold, and his mood turned black.

Squad Demetrian was training. He heard them long before he saw them. Climbing a ladder to the next deck, Argo thumped the door release to the communal 'quarters', a room where Astartes remained strapped in flight seats when the gunship took to the skies. In the small usable space between the twin rows of seats, two of Squad Demetrian duelled in full armour.

The two warriors could not have been less alike. His armour draped in scrolls of his deeds, bone tokens of fallen foes, and the skulls of seven orks hanging from his chain bandolier, Imrich was a whirlwind of movement. Kicks, punches, elbow thrusts, headbutts – all thrown into a duel with shortswords, added between the moves of the clashing blades.

Opposing him was Toma, embodying pure economy of motion. Where Imrich's fury twinned with his skill, Toma's movements were calculated to the finest degree by a lightning mind that drove his vicious combat reflexes. His blade snapped into position to block and thrust in a silver blur, stopping precisely at each twist, never overbalancing, never overreaching, with Toma never giving ground.

'I'll wear you down, Deathwatch,' Imrich teased. Their gladius blades locked again, and the two helms glared at each other only half a metre apart.

Toma said nothing. Displayed on the polished iron of his unique shoulder pad was the stylised symbol of the Holy Inquisition. He always fought in silence. His recent return from three years in the specialist Ordo Xenos Deathwatch Chapter hadn't changed that.

The fight came to an end when Argo cleared his throat. Disengaging from one another, Imrich and Toma resheathed their blades.

'I had you, Deathwatch.' Imrich saluted his opponent with his clenched left fist against his heart.

'Sure you did, hero.' Toma's voice was toneless as he returned the gesture.

'I had you.'

'The day you have me is the day the Emperor rises from the Throne and dances all night long.'

Brother-Sergeant Demetrian silenced them both with a fist pounded against the metal wall.

'News, Brother-Chaplain?' the sergeant asked.

Argo removed his helm and gave them his half-smile. 'They think we're here in answer of a distress call.'

The squad looked at the Chaplain, awaiting further explanation. Now this had their interest up.

'You didn't tell them the truth,' said Demetrian. The veteran's scarred face was a map of battles fought across a hundred systems. Both his gauntlets were crimson; he'd served time in the Crusade Company among the best of the best, and on the knee of his armour, a Black Templar cross was proudly displayed. The Declates Crusade, when the Templars and the Fists broke ranks to fight in mixed units, was a point of great honour for both Chapters. Demetrian had been there. A roll of his honours was recorded in acid-etched lettering on a gold tablet in the Chapter's fortress-monastery back home on Rynn's World.

Argo nodded. 'I thought it best to retain the illusion of our compliance. The truth would breed animosity.'

'No surprise,' Demetrian's words were as clipped and to the point as ever. 'The plan remains the same?'

'We fight until the Cantorial Palace. Then we do the duty entrusted to us. I saw the maps of Southspire and the enemy's forces spread across the sector. A new warlord leads the enemy on the far side of the city, and the Guard ready for their last attempt at a big push. The city itself is flooded with roaming bands of foes.'

'Numbers?'

'Thousands within the city. Tens of thousands at the edge, where the warlord waits.'

'I like those odds,' Imrich said. They all heard the smile in his words, even from behind his helm.

Argo shook his head. 'This is not a war we can win without the Guard.'

Now Toma spoke up. He sat in one of the restraining seats, meticulously dismantling and cleaning the sacred bolter given to him by the Ordo Xenos during his tenure in the Inquisitorial kill-teams.

'Will the Guard win this war without us?'

Argo shrugged. 'We have our orders.'

Toma pressed on. 'And once we leave?'

'The Emperor protects,' the Chaplain replied.

Imrich's skulls rattled as he turned. 'So we flee a war that the Imperium is losing? I don't like the thought of running from the kine.'

'Duly noted, but Chapter Master Kantor was clear in his priorities,' Argo said. 'And you will do penance for your disrespect of the Enemy, Brother Imrich.'

It was a matter of small shame among some of the Crimson Fists that they referred to the greenskins as *kine*. On Rynn's World, another agriworld, it was slang for 'cattle'.

'Yes, Brother-Chaplain,' Imrich growled.

'Hate the inhuman, slaughter the impure, and praise the Emperor above all. But always respect the foe.'

'Yes, Brother-Chaplain.' Imrich wanted to insist Argo stopped quoting the litanies at him. Instead he bowed his head. He knew better than to apologise.

'When do we move out?' Demetrian cut in.

'Tomorrow night, the Guard will advance,' Argo said, as he held his golden aquila medallion in his red-fingered gauntlet. 'And we advance with them.'

Dawn found Argo in the cockpit of the Thunderhawk, still in his armour. He sat in one of the command thrones, his elbows on his knees, staring out of the window. He had not slept. He was Astartes. He barely needed sleep.

Toma came to him as he mused on the coming battle. The quiet warrior was a powerful credit to the squad, and Argo – who was over a century younger than the Deathwatch specialist – always welcomed his presence. He suspected it would not be long before the captain of the Fifth selected Toma for promotion into the Crusade Company, or to lead his own squad into the field of war.

'Another dawn, Brother-Chaplain.' Toma took the command throne next to Argo, sitting and holding his helm in his hands. The Deathwatch had aged him, Argo saw. New scars, faded from fast treatment but still noticeable, pitted the warrior's cheek and temple.

'Acid burns,' Argo said, gesturing with a gloved hand, his black one. 'The Deathwatch kept you busy.'

'I can't say,' Toma replied. His face was as expressive as stone.

'Can't or won't?' Argo asked, already knowing the answer.

'Both.'

'The Ordo Xenos keeps its secrets close.'

'It does.' Toma's expression was edged with thought as he replayed hazy recollections, little more than echoes, through his mind. Oaths had been sworn. Promises were made. Memories were torn from the mind by psyk-enhanced meditation and the ungentle scouring of arcane machinery.

It was the first time Argo had seen his fellow Fist's neutral mask slip, and he found it fascinating.

'We go to war today,' the Chaplain said. 'We are a poor portion of the Fifth's strength, but we are the Fifth nevertheless. In the fires of war, we are forged. And yet I sense a burden on your soul, brother.'

Toma nodded. This was why he had come.

'It's Vayne.'

Brother-Apothecary Vayne was in the Thunderhawk's confined apothecarion, little more than an operating table and racks of monitoring equipment fastened to the small room's walls. Already prepared for the battle tonight, he was in full armour with one exception: his head was bare. The white-faced helm that marked him as an Apothecary rested on the surgery table, and this was the first thing Argo saw as he entered. The second thing was Vayne himself, adjusting data readouts on his arm-mounted narthecium. As Argo watched, several surgical spikes and knives snapped back into the bulky medical unit housed on Vayne's forearm.

Vayne eventually turned to the sound of thrumming power armour, though his enhanced senses would have detected the Chaplain's approach long before he came into the room.

'Argo,' he said in subdued greeting.

'Vayne,' the Chaplain nodded back.

The atmosphere between the two men was nothing short of ugly. Seven years before, they'd served together as novices in Nochlitan's Scout squad. Seven years since the final trials to become Astartes, when Argo had been chosen to wear the black, and Vayne the white.

A Chaplain and an Apothecary drawn from the same Scout unit. Sergeant Nochlitan, who like Demetrian had served admirably in the Crusade Company among the Chapter's elite, had been honoured by Chapter Master Kantor himself for honing such excellence in a novice squad.

With the Chapter still in its perilous rebuilding stage, the finest warriors of the Crimson Fists were often charged with the duty of training novice squads. It was no shame to step away from the First Company to the role of Scout-sergeant, and Nochlitan was one of the most respected.

Beyond a few scars, Argo looked no different. The same could not be said for the Apothecary. Half of Vayne's face was gone, replaced by cold, smooth steel shaped to resemble his features. Despite its artistry, the exquisite workmanship was clear evidence of a terrible wound that had almost been Vayne's death. Vayne's left eye, an augmetic lens of synthetic scarlet crystal, whirred in its circular socket as the Apothecary focused his gaze on the Chaplain.

'You're looking well,' he remarked. Argo didn't reply. He watched as Vayne limped around the surgical table, and considered the rest of the Apothecary's newly-restored body.

Daemon-fire had done this to Vayne, during the Cleansing of Chiaro two months before. Fresh from the victory on Syral and the destruction of the Cantorial Palace, the Crimson Fists had entered the warp for several weeks to reach Chiaro, answering a call for aid by the planetary governor. Mutant cults were spreading in the rotting industrial sectors of his world. A true purge was needed to stamp the problem out, after the local defence forces had failed to quell the matter.

The Fists had not failed. It took a month and was not without casualties, but their duty was done. The rest of the strike force returned to Rynn's World at the behest of Chapter Master Kantor. Argo and Squad Demetrian had returned to Syral aboard the support cruiser *Vigil*.

It had been a cold, quiet journey back to Syral. They were the only Astartes on board, except for a single Apothecary from the Fifth Company that remained to preside over Vayne's injuries – and act in his stead if the younger man died.

Vayne had suffered as the servitors and his potential replacement rebuilt his body. He was almost certain to die, given the massive burns sustained and their initial refusal to heal. The Chapter would lose a gifted healer in a time when the Fists most desperately needed to reclaim and preserve their fighting strength. Had Vayne died, it would have been a true loss.

From shoulder to fingertips, his left arm was augmetic. It connected internally to the bionic sections of his spine and collarbone, purring in a smooth hiss of expensive augmentation that Argo's keen hearing could detect even underneath the background hum of their power armour. As with his left arm, so too was his left leg bionic – from hip to toes. The augmentations were still new, still untested in battle, and although Argo doubted a normal human could discern the minute inconsistencies in Vayne's gait and posture, to Astartes senses it registered as a subtle but noticeable hitch in his stride. A limp.

It was temporary, until the augmetics aligned with Vayne's body patterns and wholly fused with his biorhythms. The leg ended in a splayed claw of a foot for enhanced stability: a cross of blackened metal that connected to the well-armoured ankle joint and the heavy musculature of the bionic shin and calf above.

'Your attitude is beginning to create strain within your squad,' Argo began. 'I am told you are melancholic.'

Vayne scowled. His false eye hummed in its socket as it tried to conform to his facial expression.

'Brother-Sergeant Demetrian has said nothing.'

'You were saved because you have value to the Chapter. You stand in high regard for your skills. Why are you unbalanced by wounds which heal even as we speak?'

Vayne watched his own crimson left gauntlet close and open, repeating the motion several times. It was his bionic arm, and feeling was slow in returning.

'I trained a lifetime in my own body. Now I fight in someone else's.'

'It is still your body.'

'Not yet. There is acclimatisation to come.'

'Then you will acclimatise. There is no more to say.'

'You don't see? This is not false pathos, Argo. I was perfect before, made in the Emperor's image in accordance with his ancient and most sacred designs.'

'You still are.'

'No. I am a simulacrum.' He clenched his augmetic hand into a numb fist. 'I am the best imitation we are capable of creating. I am no longer perfect.'

'Our brothers in the Iron Hands would dispute that diagnosis.'

Vayne scoffed. 'Those uninspired slaves of the Mechanicum? They make war at the pace of toothless old men.'

'If you resort to insults against our brother Chapters, I will lose my temper as well as my patience.'

'My point is that I am no Iron Hand. And I have no wish to be some half-flesh imitation Astartes.'

'You will acclimatise,' Argo stepped forward, taking Vayne's helm from the table and looking down at the white faceplate.

'Even so, until then I am a liability to my brothers.'

Argo handed his friend the helmet and shook his head. 'You are petulant beyond my comprehension. Only in death does duty end. We are the Fists. We are the shield-hand of Dorn. We do not weep and cower from battle because of pain or fear or worries of what might yet be. We fight and die because we were made to fight and die.'

Vayne took the helm and smiled without humour. Half of his face didn't follow the expression.

'What amuses you?'

'You are blind, Argo. You may preserve the soul of our Chapter, but I preserve its body. I harvest the gene-seed of the fallen, and I ensure the wounded will fight again. So listen to me, *brother*. I fear nothing but allowing my failures to harm my brethren. I am not at peak performance, and I am unused to the wounds I still wear under this armour. That is the source of my unbalance.'

'You lose your own argument. You fear to let down your brothers because your battle skills are hindered for a short while. Vayne, you are harming your brothers far more with your withdrawn attitude and the bitterness leaking from your every word. You are eroding their trust in you, and destroying their confidence.'

Argo's battle-collar pulsed a single blip. He tensed his neck, activating the pearl-like vox-bead attached to his throat, which picked up the vibrations of his vocal chords.

'Brother-Chaplain Argo. Speak.'

'Brother-Chaplain,' it was Lord General Ulviran. 'I have a request to ask of you and your warriors.'

'I will be with you shortly,' Argo said, and killed the link. The silence between Argo and Vayne returned.

'Your point is taken,' Vayne conceded. 'I will not allow my melancholy to taint my squad any longer.'

'That is all I demand.' Argo was already turning to leave.

'I remember a time when you could not make such demands of me, Argo.'

'I remember a time when I did not need to make them.'

The Fists shed blood before the Guard's night-time advance. Under Ulviran's request, Argo and Demetrian led the squad into the shattered remains of the city's western sector.

In the minutes leading up to deployment, Argo had gathered the warriors together in the shadow of their Thunderhawk. Dozens of Guardsmen around the camp looked on, dallying about their business while they watched the Astartes soldiers perform their rite. The Fists ignored them all.

With his gladius, Argo sliced the palms of each warrior's left hand. They, in turn, pressed their bleeding hands against the chest piece of the Fist next to them.

Imrich rested his hand on the embossed silver eagle decorating Toma's breastplate. The Larraman cells in his blood scabbed and sealed the gash quickly, but not before his palm left a dark smear on Toma's Imperial symbol.

'My life for you,' Imrich said, then removed his hand and fastened his helm. Toma was next, pressing his bleeding hand against Vayne's breastplate.

'My life for you,' the Deathwatch veteran said, before donning his own helm. Vayne forced a smile. He had to perform the rite with his remaining flesh hand, his right instead of his left, and did so without complaint.

When it came to the Chaplain's turn, Argo rested his hand on Demetrian's armour, as tradition necessitated the officiating Chaplain to honour the ranking officer.

'My life for you,' Argo said. A moment later, his senses were submerged in the audiovisual chaos of his battle helm. On the eye lens displays, he saw the flickering readouts of the squad's vital signs, communication runes, lists of vox-channels, sight-altering lens options, thermo-conditional and local atmospheric readouts, and a cluster of information pertaining to the myriad functions of his armour.

All of the information added up to one thing.

'Ready,' he voxed to the others, blink-clicking most of the lens displays into transparency.

'Ready,' they voxed back. They'd started walking then, loping strides that emitted a chorus of mechanical growls from their armour joints.

The Guardsmen parted like a split sea as the Astartes neared them.

With blood on their Imperial eagles, the Crimson Fists went to war.

That had been three hours ago. The Fists took a Guard Chimera troop transport to the city limits, and were advancing through the western edge of Southspire. It was a scouting run, and progress was predicted – by Lord General Ulviran – to be fast. Intelligence had pinned enemy resistance in this section of the city to be minimal. Only at the city's centre was resistance expected to pick up.

Intelligence had been wrong about that.

Argo crouched in the ruins of what had once been an Administratum building, where hundreds of barely-educated civilians typed their lives away into the cogitators that amassed Syral's exportation data. Pressed against a wall half tumbled down months ago from Imperial Basilisk shelling, the Chaplain waited unmoving, listening to the thrum of his power armour and the sounds of several foes breathing nearby.

Roaming bands of greenskins claimed this part of the city. Squad Demetrian had abandoned the Chimera long before, in favour of stalking through the ruins and clearing a path for the Guard's advance tonight.

Argo heard the xenos trampling closer, around the corner. They muttered to each other in their guttural, swinish tongue. The Chaplain tasted bile in his mouth. Their inhumanity repelled him.

He heard the bestial things pause in their lazy search, heard them snuffing at the air and grunting. They had his scent, he was sure of it, and his blood ran hot as he clenched his short combat sword in one hand, his bolter in the other.

At his hip hung his deactivated crozius arcanum, the symbolic weapon of his role in the Chapter. Capped by an eagle-shaped maul fashioned from blackened adamantium, it was a fearsome bludgeon when sheathed in its crackling power field. Argo's crozius had belonged to Ancient Amentus, one of the first Crimson Fists Chaplains; a founder of the Chapter from when the primarch divided the Imperial Fists Legion ten millennia before. Upon an arm-length haft of dark metal, the inscription *Traitor's Bane* was written in High Gothic.

He treasured the relic weapon, which still felt unfamiliar in his fists even after seven years. Against detritus such as these greenskins, his gladius was more than enough to suffice. He would not let the filthy blood of weakling xenos mar an honourable weapon dating back to the Great Crusade.

The first of the creatures, alert now, came around the corner. In its fists was a collection of scrap that evidently served the greenskin as a firearm. Argo surged to his feet, superhuman reflexes enhanced even further by his armour, and before the ork could utter a sound, it was falling backwards with the hilt of the Chaplain's gladius protruding from its eye socket.

Argo rounded the corner to meet the others head-on and his bolter barked, spitting detonating shells into green flesh. Eleven of them. Each hulking figure was momentarily outlined by a flicker of light in his helm's vision, cycling through target locks. But eleven was too many, even for an Astartes. In a flashing moment of anger, Argo cursed himself for not listening carefully to their breathing and trying to discern their numbers. It was his failing, he knew. He'd acted in rage, and now it was going to kill him.

The brutish creatures ran at him even as they took fire, massive fists gripping jagged axes that were pieced together from vehicle parts and industrial machinery. Argo's bolter cut down three orks as his targeting reticule flitted between weak points in the greenskins' piecemeal armour.

'You dare exist in mankind's galaxy!' Argo's bolter spat its last shell which destroyed an ork from the jaw up. He clamped the weapon to his thigh with its magnetic seal and threw his fist forward, shattering the forehead of the first greenskin to come in range. 'Die! Die knowing the Crimson Fists will cleanse the stars of your taint!'

Axes slashed towards him, which Argo weaved to avoid. A step back took him within reach of the first ork he'd felled, and he snatched up his gladius from the wretch's skull. Rivulets of dark blood slid along the silver blade, and the Astartes grinned behind his death's head mask.

'Come, alien filth. I am Argo, son of Rogal Dorn, and I am your death.' The mob of orks ran in and Argo met them, the primarch's name on his lips.

*'Break left.'*

The voice crackled over the vox and Argo obeyed instantly, throwing himself into a roll that scattered a dust cloud in the ruins of the building. He came up, blade in hand, just as the speaker joined him in the fight.

The midday sun flashed from Toma's iron shoulder guard as he hammered the greenskins from behind. His bolter disgorged a stream of shells that exploded on impact in bursts of clear, hissing liquid. As he fired one-handed, he plunged his gladius into the throat of the closest greenskin, giving it a savage twist to half-sever the creature's head. Four of the orks fell back, the horrendously potent acid from Toma's prized bolt rounds overriding even the orkish resilience to pain as it ate through their flesh like holy fire.

All of this happened before Argo's two hearts had time to beat twice.

The last two orks leapt at the Fists to die in futility. Toma impaled the first through the chest, shattered its face with a brutal headbutt, and fired a single bolt at point-blank range into the alien's temple. The skull gave way in a shower of gore as the explosive shell performed its sacred function. Gobbets of flesh and bone hissed as they spun away, eaten by the mutagenic acid in Toma's Inquisition-sanctioned ammunition.

Argo grappled with the second ork, his gauntlets wrapped around the thing's throat as it broke its thick nails scrabbling at his armour. He bore the howling greenskin to the ground, his weighty armour crushing the life from its chest as he strangled it in trembling fists.

'Die…'

The ork's answer was to roar voicelessly, its red eyes burning with rage. The Astartes grinned in mimicry of his helm and leaned close to the thing's face. His voice was a whisper through his vox-speakers.

'I *hate* you.'

Toma stood to the side, reloading his bolter and scanning the ruins for more foes. Argo's skulled face pressed against the choking ork's forehead. Orkish sweat left dark smears against his bone-cream faceplate.

'This is the Emperor's galaxy.' With a final surge of effort, he squeezed with all his strength. Vertebrae popped and cracked under the pressure. 'Mankind's galaxy. *Our* galaxy. Know that, as your worthless life ends.'

'Brother-Chaplain…' Toma said.

Argo barely heard. He let the creature fall dead and rose to his feet, savouring the taste of copper, bitter and hot, on his tongue. His rage had not killed him, after all. The enemy lay dead in great numbers.

'Brother-Chaplain,' Toma repeated.

'What?' Argo unclasped his bolter, reloading it now with the proper litany to the machine-spirit within.

There was a moment when Argo was sure Toma would say something; chide him for letting his fury get the better of him and lead him into reckless combat. Despite the break with tradition and authority, Argo would have accepted the criticism from a warrior like Toma.

Toma said nothing, but the silence passing between the two Astartes was laden with meaning.

'Report,' Argo said to break the quiet.

'Imrich and Vayne report their section is clear now. Brother-Sergeant Demetrian reports the same.'

'Resistance?'

'Vayne and Demetrian described it as savage.'

'And Imrich?'

'He described it as thrilling.'

Argo nodded. He was running low on ammunition, and knew the others must be as well.

'Prepare for withdrawal.'

As Toma voxed Argo's orders to the others, the young Chaplain looked out across the ruined city. Small by Imperial standards – large settlements were rare on an agri-world – yet the focus of so much destruction.

On the other side of Southspire, the new warlord waited with the bulk of his horde. And in the heart of the city, the broken remains of the Cantorial Palace: the Fists' true goal, surrounded by foes.

Argo's blood boiled as he spat a curse behind his mask. He wanted to press on. The palace was no more than a handful of hours away, but resistance from the roaming warbands was intense. With another squad of Astartes, just five more men, he'd have taken the chance. But alone, it was suicide.

'What's that noise?' Toma said.

Argo levelled his bolter. He'd heard it, too. Drums. The music of primitives, echoing across the city like the pounding heartbeat of an angry god.

'It's a warning.'

The Imperial Guard advanced that night, and the weather turned bitter as if the heavens recognised the humans' intent.

Basilisks softened up the way ahead with relentless bombardments each hour. Ulviran was content to endure this halting advance, frequently cutting forward progress to establish another artillery barrage that took an age to set up. He pored over maps and holo-displays in his Baneblade's command room as Imperial guns pounded their own city into dust.

The big push consisted of the surviving elements of the Radimir Third Rifles, Seventh Irregulars and Ninth Armoured. These were the so-called 'Revenants', named for the many times Radimir had replaced entire regiments due to losses against the greenskins in Segmentum Tempestus. Rebirth at the precipice of extinction was a blessing familiar to the Crimson Fists, and the Chapter had fought well with the soldiers of Radimir countless times across the centuries.

Hundreds of Guardsmen clad in the gunmetal grey of the Radimir Revenants marched alongside rattling Sentinels in the vanguard of the assault, flanked by Leman Russ battle tanks in half a dozen variants. Radimir was close to being a forge world in terms of its armoured exports. No Revenant regiment ever went to war short of armour support.

The bulk of Ulviran's forces followed the vanguard: six thousand men including a detachment of storm troopers serving as his ceremonial guard, riding alongside his Baneblade in eight black-painted Chimeras.

At the rear of this main force came the artillery: Griffons and Basilisks, their punishing guns stowed and locked until the next time Ulviran brought the column to a halt and ordered them to set up a shelling storm kilometres ahead.

Last of all came the rearguard, made of the lord general's veteran Guard squads interspersed with auxiliary units, medical transports and supply trucks.

The Fists' Thunderhawk gunship remained back at the abandoned base camp at the city's edge, ready to be summoned. For a short while, until Argo scattered them, Squad Demetrian marched in the vanguard of the force, forming the vicious tip of the Imperium's conquering blade. In

scything rain and howling winds, as the elements battered down upon
the miserable Imperial advance, the war to retake Southspire began. The
Fists soon bled away into the night, leaving Argo alone.

Major Dace, who had been present in the Baneblade's command
room when Argo reported the Fists' scouting run, couldn't resist voxing
the Chaplain now. Argo's suit insulated him from the noise of the rain
slashing against his ceramite armour, and he tensed his throat to activate
his vox-bead as it chimed.

'Brother-Chaplain Argo. Speak.'

'This is Major Dace of the Revenants.' Argo smiled as he heard the
voice. The ritual processes that had moulded his body like clay, forming him into an Astartes, had given him a memory close to eidetic. It
was known by most imperial commanders who worked with Astartes
that Space Marines possessed preternatural capacities for instant
recollection.

'Have we met?' Argo asked with his half-smile in place. He didn't let
his amusement leak into his voice. It had the desired effect; Dace's feathers were ruffled.

'I don't see your foretold resistance, Brother-Chaplain. All is quiet on
the advance, is it not?'

'I can still hear the drums,' Argo noted. And he could, setting a distant
rhythmic percussion to the thunder grinding across the sky.

'I can't,' Dace said.

'You are comfortably hidden in a tank, major.' Argo closed the link
and added, 'And you are only human.'

The Fists had been killing greenskins their entire unnaturally long
lives. Ulviran, no stranger to the orkish hordes himself, trusted Argo's
belief that the drums pounded as a challenge to the Imperials. The new
warlord, a curse upon his black heart, knew they were coming, and the
drums of war beat to show he welcomed the coming bloodshed. The
storm swallowed their noise now. Only the Astartes could make it out,
and it was dimmed even to their senses.

'Ulviran to all units,' crackled the lord general's hourly message. 'Dig
in for bombardment. Shelling to commence in thirty minutes.'

Argo bit back a curse. Too slow, much too slow. His thoughts were
plagued by the Thunderhawk full of digging equipment back at the base.

'Brother-Chaplain?'

The communication rune that flashed on his reddish lens display was,
thankfully, not Dace. Imrich's vital signs registered as almost a kilometre
ahead.

'How goes the scouting, Brother Imrich?'

'Lord,' Imrich responded, speaking quietly and clearly. 'I've found the
kine.'

'So have I, sir.' This was Vayne, a kilometre to the west.

'Contact,' voxed Demetrian. His readouts pinned him in the south.

Argo looked over his shoulder, at the procession of ocean-grey tanks with rain sluicing off their hulls.

'Numbers?' he asked them all over the squad's shared channel. The weather was banishing vox integrity, masking all the words in a haze of crackles and hisses.

'I count over a thousand, easily,' Vayne said. 'Perhaps two.'

'Same,' added Demetrian.

'I've got more. I've got lots more.' Imrich sounded overjoyed. But then, knowing Imrich, he probably was. 'Twice that number, I'm sure of it. If we hear from Toma,' Imrich added, 'we're in a world of trouble.'

The Deathwatch specialist had been sent to the south, stalking a good distance behind the rearguard.

The vox clicked live again. 'Brother-Chaplain, come in.' said Toma. The rest of his message was cut off by Imrich's delighted laughter.

With a cold feeling of metallic-tasting finality in his throat, Argo voxed the lord general.

Ulviran listened without hesitation. He ignored Dace's complaints and pulled the column into a still-advancing defensive spread that, admirably, took less than half an hour to form. No small feat for that many soldiers and vehicles. The organisational aspects of war were where Ulviran most prided himself. An orderly army was a victorious one. The faster orders were obeyed, the more men survived. It was a simple mathematic he liked, and had a talent for putting it into practice.

'The shelling,' Argo voxed to him, 'is doing nothing. The warlord has put significant force into the city against us, and the horde ahead is falling back to draw us in.'

Ulviran glared down at the hololithic display of the city projected onto the large table. His Baneblade rumbled as it rolled on.

'We're surrounded.'

'If we stop now, lord general, we will be. The pincers will close around us the moment we halt. If we push on at speed, we can make it to the Cantorial Palace and engage the forward elements before the rest of the noose can close around our throats.'

Ulviran liked that. Turn the ambush into an attack.

'Strike first, strike hard, and prepare to repel the rest of the attackers once the main force is crushed.' It sounded good. It sounded right. But…

'I am going purely on your word for this, Brother-Chaplain.'

'Good,' the Astartes replied, and ended the link.

'The Cantorial Palace?' voxed Demetrian.

'Yes. Squad, form up. We're taking the prize.'

The Cantorial Palace had been the seat of the planetary governor, and a masterpiece of gothic design; as skeletally, broodingly Imperial as would be expected.

All that remained was a series of shattered walls and a small mountain of rubble, where once battlements and ridged towers had risen around a central bastion. The previous greenskin warlord had claimed it as his lair, until the Crimson Fists had dissuaded him of the notion four months ago. Refuting his claim of ownership involved razing the building to the ground with infiltrating sappers, and even then, the gigantic xenos clad in its primitive power armour had survived to claw itself free from the smoking rubble.

Imrich had battled the warlord in the stone wreckage, finally taking its head after a long and bloody duel. He wore Warlord Golgorrad's skull on his bandolier, giving it pride of place on his chest.

The ork forces of this nameless new warlord evidently favoured the former site of battle. It was to be the anvil upon which the Imperial forces would be crushed by the flanking hordes.

Ulviran's army did not march sedately to a doom surrounded by foes. Time was of the essence, and the Revenants powered on to meet the larger force ahead. Men held to the side of speeding tanks and rode atop vehicle roofs. Within the hour, the Guard spilled with overwhelming force into the great plaza district where the Cantorial Palace's bones jutted from the ground.

The armoured fist of the Revenant advance crashed into the scattered greenskin lines. Rubble rained down as tanks unleashed the fury of their cannons, and a staccato chorus of heavy bolter fire filled the air between the thunder of main guns. Lacking entrenchments, the orks counter-charged the armoured column, finding walls of Imperial Guard coming to meet them. Las-fire sliced across the night, illuminating the battlefield like some hellish pre-dawn in scarlet sunlight.

The rain lashed down on troopers in cold-weather gear as they fired in disciplined ranks, and the orks still came on in a roaring wave that drowned out the sound of thunder above.

Imperial records came to know this battle as the Night of the Axe, when the Radimir regiments on Syral were decimated by the hordes of xenos creatures they faced. Losses stood at forty-six per cent, utterly damning Lord General Ulviran's planned big push to face the new warlord that still lay in wait on the other side of the city. The Guard was bloody and beaten, and although thousands survived the assault, it was nowhere near enough to storm the warlord's position with any hope of success. The Radimir's one slim hope of survival on the kine-infested world – to strike the warlord down and cast the hordes into disarray – was gone. In turning the ambush into an attack of their own, the Guard had delayed their destruction but not avoided it.

However, for the purposes of the Crimson Fists, the Night of the Axe was neither the most critical juncture in the war for Syral, nor was it even recorded in their rolls of honour despite the harvest of lives reaped by Squad Demetrian of the Fifth Company.

The Fists, in true Astartes autonomy, had a sacred duty of their own to perform. This came to light the following morning, as the broken Guard made to move on from the scene of slaughter.

The sector was a mess of bloodshed and battle fallout. The corpses of thousands of orks and humans lay scattered over a square kilometre of annihilated urban terrain. The air thrummed with the growl of engines, frequently split by the cries of wounded men ringing out as they were tended by medics or died in agony, unfound among the charnel chaos that littered the ground.

Argo walked among the dead, gladius plunging down to end the lives of any greenskins that still drew breath. He listened to the general vox-channel as he performed his bloody work, making a mental note of casualties suffered by the Guard. He knew they were sure to be destroyed if they pressed on to face the warlord, just as surely as they'd be destroyed when the warlord's armies came hunting for them. He felt a moment of pity for the Guard. The Revenants were brave souls who'd always stood their ground in the face of the enemy. It was a shame to see them expire like this, in utter futility.

But the Fists would be long gone by then.

As he approached the edge of the colossal vista of rubble that made up the bones of the Cantorial Palace, he activated his vox and sent the signal he'd ached to send since his arrival. A single acknowledgement blip was the only answer he received, and the only answer he required.

Squad Demetrian stood a short distance from the lord general's Baneblade, honouring their wargear through daily prayer and muttered rituals. There they remained, ignoring the Guard all around, until thrusters shrieked in the sky above.

'What in the name of hell is that doing here?' Lord General Ulviran asked Major Dace as they looked up at the dark shape coming in to land with a howl of engines. The two officers left the cooling shadows of the command tank and approached the Astartes. Behind the warriors, throwing up a blizzard of dust, their Thunderhawk kissed the rubble-strewn ground and settled on its clawed stanchion feet.

'Are you leaving?' Ulviran demanded of Argo, aghast as he shouted above the cycling-down engines.

'No.'

'Then what–'

'Move aside, lord general,' the Chaplain said. 'We need room for our equipment. And if you would be so kind as to move your Baneblade, it would be appreciated.'

Dace, a short and rotund example of Radimir manhood, drew himself up to his unimpressive full height. 'We move out within the hour! You can't do… whatever it is you're doing.'

'Yes,' Argo said, 'I can.' His skullish helm glared down at the fat man. 'And if you try to stop me, I will kill you.'

To his credit, Dace did a fine job at appearing unmoved by the vox-growled threat.

'We have orders from Segmentum Command, and the Crimson Fists must abide by them.'

'That's an amusing fiction,' Argo smiled, knowing the humans couldn't see his expression. 'Feel free to entertain that fantasy as you get out of our way.'

Ulviran looked stricken, like he'd just taken a gut wound. He watched in mute sickness as servitors and robed serfs unloaded portable industrial equipment down the Thunderhawk's ramp.

'If you do not move aside,' Argo said with false patience in his voice, 'the Thunderhawk lander coming from orbit with more equipment will be forced to destroy your Baneblade to make room to land.'

'Equipment?' Dace was indignant. 'For what?'

It was Ulviran who answered. He'd seen the drills and clawed scoops on the machinery being unloaded.

'Digging…' The lord general's face was wrinkled in thought.

Argo favoured the officers with a bow. 'Yes. Digging. Now move aside, if you please.'

Defeated and confused, the two men backed away. Dace was red-faced and scowling, Ulviran subdued and voxing orders to make room for further Astartes landings.

When the Guard left just under an hour later, three Thunderhawks were nested in the ruins of the Cantorial Palace, each one freed of its cargo of servitors, serfs and machinery.

'They're heading west,' Imrich nodded towards the rolling Guard column.

'Then they'll die well,' the Chaplain snapped, and his hand cut through the air in a gesture to the work crews.

Drills ground into stone, scoops clawed piles of rubble aside, and the serfs of the Crimson Fists Chapter began to dig.

It took three days to make the first discovery.

By this time, the Guard were nearing the edge of Southspire, mere hours from their final encounter with the greenskin warlord. The Fists remained at the Cantorial Palace, silently admiring the Revenants' decision to die on the offensive, rather than retreat and die in their makeshift fort-camp.

Three days had passed since the Guard rolled out.

Three days of random sieges and petty assaults punctuating the sunlit hours and the long nights. Although the orks had been crushed in the area, wandering bands of savages still attacked the Crimson Fists' position. Each of the attempts made by the snorting, roaring mobs were met with torrents of heavy bolter fire from the grounded Thunderhawks and the seasoned killing prowess of Squad Demetrian as they maintained a perimeter vigil day and night, never resting, never sleeping.

On the evening of the third day, as the dull sun fell below the horizon, one of the serfs cried out. He'd found something, and the Astartes came running.

The first boy was dead.

His Scout's armour was largely intact, as was his body. Vayne was the one to lift the corpse from its rubble grave, treating it with all due honour as he laid it out on the ground by the first Thunderhawk. Argo came over once the examinations were complete to intone the Rite of Blessed Release. He knelt by the body, pressing his slit palm to the slain boy's forehead and leaving a smear of blood that mixed with the dirt on the child's dusty face.

'Novice Frael,' Vayne consulted his narthecium, tapping at the keypad as he examined the readout. 'Age thirteen, initial stages of implantation.'

'There's very little decay,' Argo observed in a soft voice.

'No. Blood and tissue samples indicate he died three or four days ago. My guess would be the day before we arrived.'

'Four months,' Argo whispered, looking back over the rubble. 'He was under there for *four months*, and we were three days too late. That…'

'What?' Vayne closed his narthecium and reset the data display. Surgical cutting tools snicked back into his bracer.

'That isn't… fair,' Argo finished. He knew how foolish the words sounded.

'If he'd been fully human,' Vayne said, 'he'd have died in the first two weeks. Thirst. Starvation. Trauma. It was a miracle his initial implantations even allowed him to survive this long. Almost sixteen weeks, Argo. That's worthy of the rolls of honour itself.'

They'd avoided discussing the odds up until now. It was a mission none of the squad expected to fulfil with anything approaching glory.

'Sixteen weeks.' Argo closed his eyes, though his helm stared at Vayne, its gaze unbroken.

'Even without the sus-an membrane,' Vayne was tapping keys on his narthecium bracer, 'our physiology will allow the slowing of the metabolism and the near-cessation of many bio-functions. It is still within the edge of prospective boundaries that an Astartes from the gene-seed of Rogal Dorn could survive the duration.'

Argo nodded. Full Astartes could survive, could *potentially* survive. That, however, wasn't the true issue. The Chaplain looked over his shoulder, where the corpse of the young novice lay.

'Kine,' snapped the vox. 'Kine at the south perimeter.'

Argo and Vayne were already running. 'That's penance for you, Imrich.'

'Yes, Brother-Chaplain. I'll do it right after we kill these whoreson aliens who've taken such umbrage at my trophies.'

* * *

The second body was discovered fifty metres away, two hours later. It was a dry husk, deep in waterless decay, and it took Vayne several minutes to identify the corpse as Novice Amadon, age fifteen, at the secondary stage of Astartes implantation.

'He's been dead for months,' Vayne said, without needing to point out the crushed ribcage and severed right leg. Scraps of Scout armour still clung to the dry fleshy remnants. 'He was killed when the palace fell.'

The Chaplain was conducting the funerary rite on Novice Amadon when the first survivor was found.

'Argo,' the vox crackled live with Vayne's excited voice. 'Blood of the primarch, Argo, come over here now.'

Argo clenched his teeth. 'A moment, please.' He pressed his cut palm to the ruined corpse's skull.

'Argo, *now*.'

The Chaplain forced his twin hearts to slow in their beat as he suppressed his eagerness and finished the rite. Such things were a matter of tradition. Such things mattered, and the dead must be respected for their sacrifice. After what seemed an age, he rose to his feet and moved over to where Vayne and Demetrian were helping the survivor from the rubble.

His targeting reticule outlined the figure in a flash, indicating a failed lock-on. A runic symbol flashed onto his retinas. Gene-seed failsafe. Target denied.

The figure was bone-thin, on shaking legs. Argo's lens display conceded to a passive lock on the emaciated wraith, and at first all he saw was the digital displays of low-pulsing life signs under the figure's name. He couldn't believe anyone, even an Astartes, could be that weak and still live.

The name registered at last, a moment before Vayne and Demetrian brought the figure close enough to recognise. Hollow-cheeked, sunken-eyed and looking more dead than alive, the older Astartes grinned when he saw Argo. The Chaplain didn't miss the resemblance between the survivor's wasted face and his own skull helm.

'Who have you found?' Imrich voxed, sounding annoyed to be missing the discovery.

Argo tried to speak but couldn't form the words. It was Vayne who answered.

'Nochlitan. We found Scout-sergeant Nochlitan.'

The skeletal figure, the sergeant responsible for training both Argo and Vayne in the same squad, kept grinning as he took in the hulking form of Argo's black battle armour.

'Hello, my boy,' Nochlitan said, and his voice was strong despite a scratchy edge and the veteran's shivering limbs. 'You took your damn time.'

'We… We didn't know…'

'I can see why they made you a Chaplain with oratory like that.' The sergeant paused to cough, a dry rasp of a sound that brought blood to his lips. 'Now stop standing around slack-jawed and save the rest of my boys.'

Three of them had survived. Three of the ten.

It was enough to justify the mission – far more than enough. A single Fist novice would have justified the risk. For four months they had survived in the rubble, and they each emerged as wasted husks, life-signs barely flickering on Vayne's narthecium. Nochlitan was the only one with the power of speech remaining to him. The two novices, in their ruined armour, were little more than tangles of withered limbs, barely breathing, drifting in and out of silent delirium.

The squad had been entombed since the Cantorial Palace had fallen. Nochlitan's Scout squad were embattled in the undercroft as the explosives ticked towards detonation, and had been unable to escape the blast area.

Seven dead. Three alive. A small but blessed victory, torn from the jaws of catastrophe.

As the servitors stored the digging equipment and the serfs readied the Thunderhawks for orbital flight, Argo sat with Nochlitan in the modest apothecarion. Vayne tended to the two novices, neither one older than sixteen.

'Dorn's holy hand,' Nochlitan said, fixing the Chaplain with his grey eyes. 'What happened to Vayne?'

'A daemon.'

'Is it dead?'

'Of course it's dead.'

'Yes, of course. You see that one there?' Nochlitan waved a weak hand in the direction of the stretcher next to him. 'That's Novice Zefaray.'

Zefaray wheezed into a rebreather mask that covered half of his face. Lines of angry tissue marked his temples and neck, where veins stood out like lightning streaks.

Argo watched the boy's laboured breathing. Zefaray was the Scout squad's Epistolary candidate, marked by the Chapter Librarium for the power of his psychic gift.

'He will be greatly honoured by Chapter Master Kantor for this,' the Chaplain said.

'Damn right he will. Almost killed him, you know. Day and night, screaming into the warp and hoping one of the Librarium would hear. We were trapped close to one another. He would whisper and mutter, speaking of how he was riding a hundred minds to reach one we could trust so many systems away.'

Argo didn't know what to say. It was a psychic feat of incredible strength. When one of the Chapter's Epistolaries had reported the weak yet crazed contact, it had been all the incentive the Chapter's highest echelons had needed. A recovery operation was mounted immediately.

'Great things ahead for him,' Nochlitan grinned. 'Did you find my bolter, boy?'

They hadn't. It showed on Argo's face.

'Ah, well.' Nochlitan lay back on the stretcher, plugged into an array of tubes and wires. 'I'll miss that weapon, without a doubt. It was a fine gun. A fine gun. I killed a genestealer patriarch genus with that bolter. Tore its head clean off.'

'We'll be taking off in a few minutes. The *Vigil* waits in orbit. Once aboard, we make haste to Rynn's World as soon as we break away from Syral.'

Nochlitan sat up again, trembling and overtaxing his remaining strength as his glare speared Argo's eyes.

'You told me the Radimir were still here. Still advancing on this new warlord.'

'They are. They'll engage the enemy's main force this afternoon, if initial projections were correct.'

'You'd abandon the Revenants? Boy, what's wrong with you?'

'Please don't call me "boy", sir. Chapter Master Kantor–'

'Pedro Kantor, blessings upon my old friend, isn't here, my boy. You are. And by Dorn's holy hand, you want to face the Emperor one day knowing you ran from this fight?'

'The odds are… beyond overwhelming. Everything we came to achieve would be void if we die in this battle.'

Nochlitan grasped at Argo's bracer, clenching the smooth black ceramite in a thin-fingered claw that shook as if palsied.

'You are the future of this Chapter.' His grey eyes were the colour of summer storms. 'You shape the path these novices will one day walk.'

Argo rose to his feet, letting his mentor's hand slip from his arm, and left the room without a word.

The Thunderhawk screamed across the night sky, its downward thrusters kicking in as it hovered four hundred metres high. Its wing-mounted bolters aimed at the ground, barking in an unremitting stream. The servitors slaved to the weapons didn't even need to aim. They couldn't miss the horde below: a sea of green skin and chattering weapons, ringing a diminished cluster of grey.

The Revenants' last stand.

The guns cut out after a minute, autoloaders cycling but not opening fire again. On the ground, the armoured divisions of the Radimir kept up their onslaught against the ork host in the city's ruins, and Ulviran watched the Crimson Fists gunship as it stayed aloft, out of enemy fire range.

'It's the Fists,' Dace said, and Ulviran smiled to himself at the man's painfully obvious statement. *Good old Dace. No better man to die with.*

'We did well, Dace. Almost reached that bastard warlord, eh?'

'We did fine, sir.' The major was still looking up at the sky, ignoring the war hammering around him.

'So what are the Fists doing, exactly?' the lord general asked. 'My eyes aren't what they once were.'

'They're...'

Argo's lens displays registered the altitude as he fell. The ground soared up fast in his red-tinted vision, and he clutched his sword and bolter tightly, blink-clicking the propulsion icon at the edge of his sight. The weighty jump pack on his back fired in a roaring kick, slowing his descent, but he still landed with jarring force ahead of the others.

He hit the ground running and his weapons sang. Left and right, he slashed his gladius into flesh and fired a relentless stream from his bolter, clearing a space around him in the thick of the churning orkish tide.

Toma was next, thudding to the ground and repeating Argo's lethal sprint. Then Demetrian, then Vayne. Imrich was last, much to his gall. The others, whirling and killing, heard his curses as they started without him.

Twenty metres ahead of them through the ocean of writhing orkish flesh, unmistakeable in salvaged armour that swelled his form to the size of an Astartes Dreadnought, was the greenskin warlord.

Imrich landed and opened up his bolter, running for the brute.

'He's mine!' he voxed to the others. 'That skull is mine!'

In two gauntleted fists, one red, one black, the ancient weapon *Traitor's Bane* was wreathed in coruscating waves of sparking force. The relic mace smashed aside three orks in a single swing, sending their broken forms to the ground still twitching with energy.

'No.' Argo stopped screaming the Litanies of Hate, drawing breath to reply to Imrich and the squad behind him.

'The kine lord is *mine.*'

# LEGENDS OF THE
# SPACE MARINES

# HELL NIGHT

*Nick Kyme*

*It can't rain all the time…*

The trooper's mood was sullen as he helped drag the unlimbered lascannon through the mire.

The Earthshakers had begun their bombardment. A slow and steady *crump-crump* – stop – *crump-crump* far behind him at the outskirts of bastion headquarters made the trooper flinch instinctively every time a shell whined overhead.

It was ridiculous: the deadly cargo fired by the siege guns was at least thirty metres at the apex of its trajectory, yet still he ducked.

Survival was high on the trooper's list of priorities, that and service to the Emperor of course.

*Ave Imperator.*

A cry to the trooper's right, though muffled by the droning rain, got his attention. He turned, rivulets teeming off his nose like at the precipice of a waterfall, and saw the lascannon had foundered. One of its carriage's rear wheels was sunk in mud, sucked into an invisible bog.

'Bostok, gimme a hand.'

Another trooper, Genk, an old guy – a *lifer* – grimaced to Bostok as he tried to wedge the butt of his lasgun under the trapped wheel and use it like a lever.

Tracer fire was whipping overhead, slits of magnesium carving up the darkness. It sizzled and spat when it pierced the sheeting rain.

Bostok grumbled. Staying low, he tramped over heavily to help his fellow gunner. Adding his own weapon to the hopeful excavation, he

289

pushed down and tried to work his way under the wheel.

'Get it deeper,' urged Genk, the lines in his weathered face becoming dark crevices with every distant flash-flare of siege shells striking the void shield.

Though each hit brought a fresh blossom of energy rippling across the shield, the city's defences were holding. If the 135th Phalanx was to breach it – for the Emperor's glory and righteous will – they'd need to bring more firepower to bear.

'*Overload the generators,*' Sergeant Harver had said.

'*Bring our guns close,*' he'd said. '*Orders from Colonel Tench.*'

Not particularly subtle, but then they were the Guard, the Hammer of the Emperor: blunt was what the common soldiery did best.

Genk was starting to panic: they were falling behind.

Across a killing field dug with abandoned trenches, tufts of razor wire protruding like wild gorse in some untamed prairie, teams of Phalanx troopers dragged heavy weapons or marched hastily in squad formation.

It took a lot of men to break a siege; more still, and with artillery support, to bring down a fully functioning void shield. Men the Phalanx had: some ten thousand souls willing to sacrifice their lives for the glory of the Throne; the big guns – leastways the shells for the big guns – they did not. A Departmento Munitorum clerical error had left the battle group short some fifty thousand anti-tank, arrowhead shells. Fewer shells meant more boots and bodies. A more aggressive strategy was taken immediately: all lascannons and heavy weapons to advance to five hundred metres and lay void shield-sapping support fire.

Bad luck for Phalanx: wars were easier to fight from behind distant crosshairs. And safer. Bad luck for Bostok, too.

Though he was working hard at freeing the gun with Genk, he noticed some of their comrades falling to the defensive return fire of the secessionist rebels, holed up and cosy behind their shield and their armour and their fraggin' gun emplacements.

Bastards.

Bet they're dry too, Bostok thought ruefully. His slicker came undone when he snagged it on the elevation winch of the lascannon and he swore loudly as the downpour soaked his red-brown standard-issue uniform beneath.

There was a muted cry ahead as he fastened up the slicker and pulled his wide-brimmed helmet down further to keep out the worst of the rain – a heavy bolter team and half an infantry squad disappeared from view, seemingly swallowed by the earth. Some of the old firing pits and trenches had been left unfilled, except now they contained muddy water and sucking earth. As deadly as quicksand they were.

Bostok muttered a prayer, making the sign of the aquila. Least it wasn't him and Genk.

'Eye be damned, what is holding you up, troopers?'

It was Sergeant Harver. The tumult was deafening, that and the artillery exchange. He had to bellow just to be heard. Not that Harver ever did anything but bellow when addressing his squad.

'Get this fraggin' rig moving you sump rats,' he barracked. 'You're lagging troopers, lagging.'

Harver munched a fat, vine-leaf cigar below the black wire of his twirled moustache. He didn't seem to mind or notice that it had long been doused and hung like a fat, soggy finger from the corner of his mouth.

A static crackle from the vox-operator's comms unit interrupted the sergeant's tirade.

'More volume: louder Rhoper, louder.'

Rhoper, the vox-operator, nodded, before setting the unit down and fiddling with a bunch of controls. The receiver was amplified in a few seconds and returned with the voice of Sergeant Rampe.

'...*Enemy sighted! They're here in no-man's land! Bastards are out beyond the shield! I see, oh sh*–'

'Rampe, Rampe,' Harver bellowed into the receiver cup. 'Respond, man!' His attention switched to Rhoper.

'Another channel, trooper – at the double, if you please.'

Rhoper was already working on it. The comms channels linking the infantry squads to artillery command and one another flicked by in a mixture of static, shouting and oddly muted gunfire.

At last, they got a response.

'...*aggin' out here with us! Throne of Earth, that's not poss*–'

The voice stopped but the link continued unbroken. There was more distant weapons fire, and something else.

'Did I hear–' Harver began.

'Bells, sir,' offered Rhoper, in a rare spurt of dialogue. 'It was bells ringing.'

Static killed the link and this time Harver turned to Trooper Bostok, who had all but given up trying to free the lascannon.

The bells hadn't stopped. They were on this part of the battlefield too.

'Could be the sounds carrying on the wind, sir?' suggested Genk, caked in mud from his efforts.

Too loud, too close to be just the wind, thought Bostok. He took up his lasgun as he turned to face the dark.

Silhouettes lived there, jerking in stop-motion with every void impact flare – they were his comrades, those who had made it to the five hundred metre line.

Bostok's eyes narrowed.

There was something else out there too. Not guns or Phalanx, not even rebels.

It was white, rippling and flowing on an unseen breeze. The rain was so dense it just flattened; the air didn't zephyr, there were no eddies skirling across the killing ground.

'Sarge, do we 'ave Ecclesiarchy in our ranks?'

'Negative, trooper, just the Emperor's own: boots, bayonets and blood.'

Bostok pointed towards the flicker of white.

'Then who the frag is that?'

But the flicker had already gone. Though the bells tolled on. Louder and louder.

Fifty metres away, men were screaming. And running.

Bostok saw their faces through his gun sight, saw the horror written there. Then they were gone. He scanned the area, using his scope like a magnocular, but couldn't find them. At first Bostok thought they'd fallen foul of an earth ditch, like the heavy bolter and infantry he'd seen earlier, but he could see no ditches, no trench or fire pit that could've swallowed them. But they'd been claimed all right, claimed by whatever moved amongst them.

More screaming; merging with the bells into a disturbing clamour.

It put the wind up Sergeant Harver – Phalanx soldiers were disappearing in all directions.

'Bostok, Genk, get that cannon turned about,' he ordered, slipping out his service pistol.

The lascannon was well and truly stuck, but worked on a pintle mount, so could be swivelled into position. Genk darted around the carriage, not sure what was happening but falling back on orders to anchor himself and stave off rising terror. He yanked out the holding pin with more force than was necessary and swung the gun around towards the white flickers and the screaming, just as his sergeant requested.

'Covering fire, Mr Rhoper,' added Harver, and the vox-operator slung the boxy comms unit on his back and drew his lasgun, crouching in a shooting position just behind the lascannon.

Bostok took up his post by the firing shield, slamming a fresh power cell into the heavy weapon's breech.

'Lit and clear!'

'At your discretion, trooper,' said Harver.

Genk didn't need a written invitation. He sighted down the barrel and the targeting nub, seeing a flicker, and hauled back the triggers.

Red beams, hot and angry, ripped up the night. Genk laid suppressing fire in a forward arc that smacked of fear and desperation. He was sweating by the end of his salvo, and not from the heat discharge.

The bells were tolling still, though it was impossible to place their origin. The void-shrouded city was too far away, a black smudge on an already dark canvas, and the resonant din sounded close and all around them.

Cordite wafted on the breeze; cordite and screaming.

Bostok tried to squint past the driving rain, more effective than any camo-paint for concealment.

The flickers were still out there, ephemeral and indistinct... and they were closing.

'Again, if you please,' ordered Harver, an odd tremor affecting his voice.

It took Bostok a few seconds to recognise it as fear.

'Lit and clear!' he announced, slamming in a second power cell.

'Not stopping, sir,' said Rhoper and sighted down his lasgun before firing.

Sergeant Harver responded by loosing his own weapon, pistol cracks adding to the fusillade.

Casting about, Bostok found they were alone; an island of Phalanx in a sea of mud, but the advanced line was coming to meet them. They were fleeing, driven wild by sheer terror. Men were disappearing as they ran, sucked under the earth, abruptly silenced.

'Sarge…' Bostok began.

Onwards the line came, something moving within it, preying on it like piranhas stalking a shoal of frightened fish.

Harver was nearly gone, just firing on impulse now. Some of his shots and that of Genk's lascannon were tearing up their own troops.

Rhoper still had his wits, and came forwards as the heavy weapon ran dry.

'F-f…' Harver was saying when Bostok got to his feet and ran like hell.

Rhoper disappeared a moment later. No cries for help, no nothing; just a cessation of his lasgun fire and then silence to show for the end of the doughty vox-officer.

Heart hammering in his chest, his slicker having now parted and exposing him to the elements, Bostok ran, promising never to bemoan his lot again, if the Emperor would just spare him this time, spare him from being pulled into the earth and buried alive. He didn't want to die like that.

Bostok must have been dragging his feet, because troopers from the advanced line were passing him. A trooper disappeared to his left, a white flicker and the waft of something old and dank presaging his demise. Another, just ahead, was pulled asunder, and Bostok jinked away from a course that would lead him into that path. He risked a glance over his shoulder. Harver and Genk were gone – the lascannon was still mired but now abandoned – fled or taken, he didn't know.

Some of the Phalanx were staging a fighting withdrawal. Gallant, but what did they have to hold off? It was no enemy Bostok had ever seen or known.

Running was all that concerned him now, running for his life.

Just reach the artillery batteries and I'll be fine.

But then a hollow cry echoed ahead, and Bostok saw a white flicker around the siege guns. A tanker disappeared under the earth, his cap left on the grille of the firing platform.

The fat lump of numbing panic in his chest rose into Bostok's throat and threatened to choke him.

Can't go back, can't go forwards…

He peeled off to the left. Maybe he could take a circuitous route to bastion headquarters.

No, too long. They'd be on him before then.

In the dark and the rain, he couldn't even see the mighty structure. No beacon-lamps to guide him, no searchlights to cling to. Death, like the darkness, was closing.

The bells were tolling.

Men screamed.

Bostok ran, his vision fragmenting in sheer terror, the pieces collapsing in on one another like a kaleidoscope.

Got to get away… Please Throne, oh pl–

Earth became swamp beneath his feet, and Bostok sank. He panicked, thinking he was about to be taken, when he realised he'd fallen into an earth ditch, right up to his chin. Fighting the urge to wade across, he dipped lower until the muddy water reached his nose, filling his nostrils with a rank and stagnant odour. Clinging to the edge with trembling, bone-cold fingers, he prayed to the Emperor for the end of the night, for the end of the rain and the cessation of the bells.

But the bells didn't stop. They just kept on tolling.

*Three weeks later…*

'Fifty metres to landfall,' announced Hak'en. The pilot's voice sounded tinny through the vox-speaker in the Chamber Sanctuarine of *Fire-wyvern*.

Looking through the occuliport in the gunship's flank, Dak'ir saw a grey day, sheeting with rain.

Hak'en was bringing the vessel around, flying a course that would take them within a few metres of Mercy Rock, the headquarters of the 135th Phalanx and the Imperial forces they were joining on Vaporis. As the gunship banked, angling Dak'ir's slit-view downward, a sodden earth field riddled with dirty pools and sludge-like emplacements was revealed. The view came in frustrating slashes.

Dak'ir was curious to see more.

'Brother,' he addressed the vox-speaker, 'open up the embarkation ramp.'

'As you wish, brother-sergeant. Landfall in twenty metres.'

Hak'en disengaged the locking protocols that kept the Thunderhawk's hatches sealed during transit. As the operational rune went green, Dak'ir punched it and the ramp started to open and lower.

Light and air rushed into the gunship's troop compartment where Dak'ir's battle-brothers were sat in meditative silence. Even in the grey dawn, their bright green battle-plate flashed, the snarling firedrake icon on their left pauldrons – orange on a black field – revealing them to be Salamanders of the 3rd Company.

As well as illuminating their power armour, the feeble light also managed to banish the glare from their eyes. Blazing red with captured fire, it echoed the heat of the Salamanders' volcanic home world, Nocturne.

'A far cry from the forge-pits under Mount Deathfire,' groaned Ba'ken.

Though he couldn't see his face beneath the battle-helm he was wearing, Dak'ir knew his brother also wore a scowl at the inclement weather.

'Wetter too,' added Emek, coming to stand beside the hulking form of Ba'ken and peering over Dak'ir's broad shoulders. 'But then what else are we to expect from a monsoon world?'

The ground was coming to meet them and as Hak'en straightened up *Fire-wyvern* the full glory of Mercy Rock was laid before them.

It might once have been beautiful, but now the bastion squatted like an ugly gargoyle in a brown mud-plain. Angular gun towers, bristling with autocannon and heavy stubber, crushed the angelic spires that had once soared into the turbulent Vaporis sky; ablative armour concealed murals and baroque columns; the old triumphal gate, with its frescos and ornate filigree, had been replaced with something grey, dark and practical. These specific details were unknown to Dak'ir, but he could see in the structure's curves an echo of its architectural bearing, hints of something artful and not merely functional.

'I see we are not the only recent arrivals,' said Ba'ken. The other Salamanders at the open hatch followed his gaze to where a black Valkyrie gunship had touched down in the mud, its landing stanchions slowly sinking.

'Imperial Commissariat,' replied Emek, recognising the official seal on the side of the transport.

Dak'ir kept his silence. His eyes strayed across the horizon to the distant city of Aphium and the void dome surrounding it. Even above the droning gunship engines, he could hear the hum of generatoria powering the field. It was like those which protected the Sanctuary Cities of his home world from the earthquakes and volcanic eruptions that were a way of life for the hardy folk of Nocturne. The air was thick with the stench of ozone; another by-product of the void fields. Even the constant rain couldn't wash it away.

As *Fire-wyvern* came in to land with a scream of stabiliser-jets, Dak'ir closed his eyes. Rain was coming in through the hatch and he let it patter against his armour. The dulcet ring of it was calming. Rain – at least the cool, wet, non-acidic kind – was rare on Nocturne, and even against his armour he enjoyed the sensation. There was an undercurrent of something else that came with it, though. It was unease, disquiet, a sense of watchfulness.

*I feel it too*, a voice echoed inside Dak'ir's head, and his eyes snapped open again. He turned to find Brother Pyriel watching him intently. Pyriel was a Librarian, a wielder of the psychic arts, and he could read people's thoughts as they might read an open book. The psyker's eyes flashed cerulean-blue before returning to burning red. Dak'ir didn't like the idea of him poking around in his subconscious, but he sensed that Pyriel had merely browsed the surface of his mind. Even still, Dak'ir looked away and was glad when the earth met them at last and *Fire-wyvern* touched down.

The cold snap of las-fire carried on the breeze as the Salamanders debarked.

Across the muddied field, just fifty metres from the approach road to Mercy Rock, a commissarial firing squad was executing a traitor.

An Imperial Guard colonel, wearing the red-brown uniform of the Phalanx, jerked spastically as the hot rounds struck him, and was still. Tied to a thick, wooden pole, he slumped and sagged against his bonds. First his knees folded and he sank, then his head lolled forward, his eyes open and glassy.

A commissar, lord-level given his rank pins and trappings, was looking on as his bodyguards brought their lasguns to port arms and marched away from the execution site. His gaze met with Dak'ir's as he turned to go after them. Rain teemed off the brim of his cap, a silver skull stud sat in the centre above the peak. The commissar's eyes were hidden by the shadow the brim cast, but felt cold and rigid all the same. The Imperial officer didn't linger. He was already walking away, back to the bastion, as the last of the Salamanders mustered out and the exit ramps closed.

Dak'ir wondered at what events had delivered the colonel to such a bleak end, and was sorry to see *Fire-wyvern* lifting off again, leaving them alone in this place.

'Such is the fate of all traitors,' remarked Tsu'gan with a bitter tang.

Even behind his helmet lens, Tsu'gan's stare was hard. Dak'ir returned his glare.

There was no brotherly love between the two Salamanders sergeants. Before they became Space Marines, they had hailed from opposite ends of the Nocturnean hierarchy: Dak'ir, an Ignean cave-dweller and an orphan, the likes of which had never before joined the ranks of the Astartes; and Tsu'gan, a nobleman's son from the Sanctuary City of Hesiod, as close to aristocracy and affluence as it was possible to get on a volcanic death world. Though as sergeants they were both equals in the eyes of their captain and Chapter Master, Tsu'gan did not regard their relationship as such. Dak'ir was unlike many other Salamanders, there was a strain of humanity left within him that was greater and more empathic than that of his brothers. It occasionally left him isolated, almost disconnected. Tsu'gan had seen it often enough and decided it was not merely unusual, it was an aberration. Since their first mission as Scouts on the sepulchre world of Moribar, acrimony had divided them. In the years that followed, it had not lessened.

'It leaves a grim feeling to see men wasted like that,' said Dak'ir. 'Slain in cold blood without chance for reparation.'

Many Space Marine Chapters, the Salamanders among them, believed in order and punishment, but they also practised penitence and the opportunity for atonement. Only when a brother was truly lost, given in to the Ruinous Powers or guilty of such a heinous deed as could not be forgiven or forgotten, was death the only alternative.

'Then you'd best develop a stronger stomach, *Ignean*,' sneered Tsu'gan, fashioning the word into a slight, 'for your compassion is misplaced on the executioners' field.'

'It's no weakness, brother,' Dak'ir replied fiercely.

Pyriel deliberately walked between them to prevent any further hostility.

'Gather your squads, brother-sergeants,' the Librarian said firmly, 'and follow me.'

Both did as ordered, Ba'ken and Emek plus seven others falling in behind Dak'ir whilst Tsu'gan led another same-sized squad from the dropsite. One in Tsu'gan's group gave Dak'ir a vaguely contemptuous look, before turning his attention to an auspex unit. This was Iagon, Tsu'gan's second and chief minion. Where Tsu'gan was all thinly-veiled threat and belligerence, Iagon was an insidious snake, much more poisonous and deadly.

Dak'ir shrugged off the battle-brother's glare and motioned his squad forwards.

'I could see his attitude corrected, brother,' hissed Ba'ken over a closed comm-link channel feeding to Dak'ir's battle-helm. 'It would be a pleasure.'

'I don't doubt that, Ba'ken,' Dak'ir replied, 'but let's just try and stay friendly for now, shall we?'

'As you wish, sergeant.'

Behind his battle-helm, Dak'ir smiled. Ba'ken was his closest ally in the Chapter and he was eternally grateful that the hulking heavy weapons trooper was watching his back.

As they marched the final few metres to the bastion gates, Ba'ken's attention strayed to the void shield on the Salamanders' right. The commissar lord, along with his entourage, had already gone inside the Imperial command centre. Overhead, the skies were darkening and the rain intensified. Day was giving way to night.

'Your tactical assessment, Brother Ba'ken?' asked Pyriel, noting his fellow Salamander's interest in the shield.

'Constant bombardment – it's the only way to bring a void shield down.' He paused, thinking. 'That, or get close enough to slip through during a momentary break in the field and knock out the generatoria.'

Tsu'gan sniffed derisively.

'Then let us hope the humans can do just that, and get us to within striking distance, so we can leave this sodden planet.'

Dak'ir bristled at the other sergeant's contempt, but kept his feelings in check. He suspected it was half-meant as a goad, anyway.

'Tell me this, then, brothers,' added Pyriel, the gates of the bastion looming, 'why are they falling back with their artillery?'

At a low ridge, just below the outskirts of the bastion, Basilisk tanks were retreating. Their long cannons shrank away from the battlefield as the tanks found parking positions within the protective outer boundaries of the bastion.

'Why indeed?' Dak'ir asked himself as they passed through the slowly opening gates and entered Mercy Rock.


'Victory at Aphium will be won with strong backs, courage and the guns of our Immortal Emperor!'

The commissar lord was sermonising as the Salamanders appeared in the great bastion hall.

Dak'ir noticed the remnants of ornamental fountains, columns and mosaics – all reduced to rubble for the Imperial war machine.

The hall was a vast expanse and enabled the Imperial officer to address almost ten thousand men, mustered in varying states of battle-dress. Sergeants, corporals, line troopers, even the wounded and support staff had been summoned to the commissar's presence as he announced his glorious vision for the coming war.

To his credit, he barely flinched when the Astartes strode into the massive chamber, continuing on with his rallying cry to the men of the Phalanx who showed much greater reverence for the Emperor's Angels of Death amongst them.

The Fire-born had removed battle-helms as they'd entered, revealing onyx-black skin and red eyes that glowed dully in the half-dark. As well as reverence, several of the Guardsmen betrayed their fear and awe of the Salamanders. Dak'ir noticed Tsu'gan smiling thinly, enjoying intimidating the humans before them.

'*As potent as bolt or blade,*' old Master Zen'de had told them when they were neophytes. Except that Tsu'gan deployed such tactics all too readily; even against allies.

'Colonel Tench is dead,' the commissar announced flatly. 'He lacked the will and the purpose the Emperor demands of us. His legacy of largesse and cowardice is over.'

Like black-clad sentinels, the commissar's storm troopers eyed the men nearest their master at this last remark, daring them to take umbrage at the defamation of their former colonel.

The commissar's voice was amplified by a loudhailer and echoed around the courtyard, carrying to every trooper present. A small cadre of Phalanx officers, what was left of the command section, were standing to one side of the commissar, giving off stern and unyielding looks to the rest of their troops.

This was the Emperor's will – they didn't have to like it; they just had to do it.

'And any man who thinks otherwise had best look to the bloody fields beyond Mercy Rock, for that is the fate which awaits he without the courage to do what is necessary.' The commissar glared, baiting dissension. When none was forthcoming, he went on. 'I am taking command in the late colonel's stead. All artillery will return to the battlefront immediately. Infantry is to be mustered in platoon and ready for deployment as soon as possible. Section commanders are to report to me in the strategium. The Phalanx will mobilise tonight!' He emphasised this last point with a clenched fist.

Silence reigned for a few moments, before a lone voice rang out of the crowd.

'But tonight is Hell Night.'

Like a predator with its senses piqued, the commissar turned to find the voice.

'Who said that?' he demanded, stalking to the front of the rostrum where he was preaching. 'Make yourself known.'

'There are things in the darkness, things not of this world. I've seen 'em!' A gap formed around a frantic-looking trooper as he gesticulated to the others, his growing hysteria spreading. 'They took Sergeant Harver, took 'im! The spectres! Just sucked men under the earth… They'll ta–'

The loud report of the commissar's bolt pistol stopped the trooper in mid-flow. Blood and brain matter spattered the infantrymen nearest the now headless corpse as silence returned.

Dak'ir stiffened at such wanton destruction of life, and was about to step forward and speak his mind, before a warning hand from Pyriel stopped him.

Reluctantly, the Salamander backed down.

'This idle talk about spectres and shadows haunting the night will not be tolerated,' the commissar decreed, holstering his still-smoking pistol. 'Our enemies are flesh and blood. They occupy Aphium and when this city falls, we will open up the rest of the continent to conquest. The lord-governor of this world lies dead, assassinated by men he trusted. Seceding from the Imperium is tantamount to an act of war. This rebellion will be crushed and Vaporis will be brought back to the light of Imperial unity. Now, prepare for battle…'

The commissar looked down his nose at the headless remains of the dead trooper, now lying prone.

'…and somebody clear up that filth.'

'He'll demoralise these men,' hissed Dak'ir, anger hardening his tone.

Two infantrymen were dragging the corpse of the dead trooper away. His bloodied jacket bore the name: Bostok.

'It's not our affair,' muttered Pyriel, his keen gaze fixed on the commissar as he headed towards them.

'The mood is grim enough, though, Brother-Librarian,' said Ba'ken, surveying the weary lines of troopers as they fell in, marshalled by platoon sergeants.

'Something has them spooked,' snarled Tsu'gan, though more out of contempt for the Guardsmen's apparent weakness, than concern.

Pyriel stepped forward to greet the commissar, who'd reached the Salamanders from the end of the rostrum.

'My lord Astartes,' he said with deference, bowing before Pyriel. 'I am Commissar Loth, and if you would accompany me with your officers to the strategium, I will apprise you of the tactical situation here on Vaporis.'

Loth was about to move away, determined to send the message that he, and not the Emperor's Angels, was in charge at Mercy Rock, when Pyriel's voice, resonant with psy-power, stopped him.

'That won't be necessary, commissar.'

Loth didn't looked impressed at he stared at the Librarian. His expression demanded an explanation, which Pyriel was only too pleased to provide.

'We know our orders and the tactical disposition of this battle. Weaken the shield, get us close enough to deploy an insertion team in the vicinity of the generatoria and we will do the rest.'

'I– that is, I mean to say, very well. But do you not need–'

Pyriel cut him off.

'I do have questions, though. That man, the trooper you executed: what did he mean by "spectres", and what is Hell Night?'

Loth gave a dismissive snort.

'Superstition and scaremongering – these men have been lacking discipline for too long.' He was about to end it there when Pyriel's body language suggested the commissar should go on. Reluctantly, he did. 'Rumours, reports from the last night-attack against the secessionists, of men disappearing without trace under the earth and unnatural denizens prowling the battlefield. Hell Night is the longest nocturnal period in the Vaporan calendar – its longest night.'

'Tonight?'

'Yes.' Loth's face formed a scowl. 'It's sheer idiocy. Fearing the dark? Well, it's just damaging to the morale of the men in this regiment.'

'The former colonel, did he supply you with these… *reports*?'

Loth made a mirthless grin.

'He did.'

'And you had him shot for that?'

'As my duty binds me, yes, I did.' Loth had a pugilist's face, slab-flat with a wide, crushed nose and a scar that ran from top lip to hairline that pulled up the corner of his mouth in a snarl. His small ears, poking out from either side of his commissar's cap, were ragged. He was stolid when he spoke next. 'There is nothing lurking in the darkness except the false nightmares that dwell in the minds of infants.'

'I've seen nightmares made real before, commissar,' Pyriel took on a warning tone.

'Then we are fortunate to have angels watching over us.' Loth adjusted his cap and straightened his leather frockcoat. 'I'll weaken the shield, be assured of that, nightmares or no.'

'Then we'll see you on the field, commissar,' Pyriel told him, before showing his back and leaving Loth to wallow in impotent rage.

'You really took exception to him, didn't you brother?' said Emek a few minutes later, too curious to realise his impropriety. They were back out in the muddy quagmire. In the distance, the sound of battle tanks moving into position ground on the air.

'He had a callous disregard for human life,' Pyriel replied. 'And besides… his aura was bad.' He allowed a rare smirk at the remark, before clamping on his battle-helm.

Overhead, the sky was wracked with jagged red lightning and the clouds billowed crimson. Far above, in the outer atmosphere of Vaporis, a warp storm was boiling. It threw a visceral cast over the rain-slicked darkness of the battlefield.

'Hell Night, in more than just name it seems,' said Ba'ken, looking up to the bloody heavens.

'An inauspicious omen, perhaps?' offered Iagon, the first time he'd spoken since landfall.

'Ever the doomsayer,' remarked Ba'ken under his breath to his sergeant.

But Dak'ir wasn't listening. He was looking at Pyriel.

'Form combat squads,' said the Librarian, when he realised he was under scrutiny. 'Tsu'gan, find positions.'

Tsu'gan slammed a fist against his plastron, and cast a last snide glance at Dak'ir before he divided up his squad and moved out at a steady run.

Dak'ir ignored him, still intent on Pyriel.

'Do you sense something, Brother-Librarian?'

Pyriel eyed the darkness in the middle distance, the no-man's land between the bastion and the shimmering edge of the far off void shield. It was as if he was trying to catch a glimpse of something just beyond his reach, at the edge of natural sight.

'It's nothing.'

Dak'ir nodded slowly and mustered out. But he'd detected the lie in the Librarian's words and wondered what it meant.

False thunder wracked the sky from the report of heavy cannons at the rear of the Imperial battle line. Smoke hung over the muddied field like a shroud, occluding the bodies of the Phalanx troopers moving through it, but was quickly weighed down by the incessant rain.

They marched in platoons, captains and sergeants hollering orders over the defensive fire of rebel guns and the dense *thuds* of explosions.

Heavy weapons teams, two men dragging unlimbered cannons whilst standard infantry ran alongside, forged towards emplacements dug five hundred metres from the shield wall.

Incandescent flashes rippled across the void shield with the dense shell impacts of the distant Earthshaker cannons and from lascannon and missile salvoes, unleashed when their crews had closed to the assault line.

In the midst of it all were the Salamanders, crouched down in cover, at the edges of the line in five-man combat squads.

Librarian Pyriel had joined Dak'ir's unit, making it six. With the flare of explosions and the red sky overhead, his blue armour was turned a lurid purple. It denoted his rank as Librarian, as did the arcane paraphernalia about his person.

'Our objective is close, brothers. There...' Pyriel indicated the bulk of a generatorium structure some thousand metres distant. Only Space Marines, with their occulobe implants, had the enhanced visual faculty to see and identify it. Rebel forces, hunkered down in pillboxes, behind trenches and fortified emplacements, guarded it. In the darkness and the rain, even with the superhuman senses of the Astartes, they were just shadows and muzzle flashes.

'We should take an oblique route, around the east and west hemispheres of the shield,' Dak'ir began. 'Resistance will be weakest there. We'll be better able to exploit it.'

After Tsu'gan had secured the route, the Salamanders had arrived at the five hundred metre assault line, having stealthed their way to it undetected before the full Imperial bombardment had begun. But they were positioned at the extreme edges of the line – two groups east, two groups west – in the hope of launching a shock assault into the heart of the rebel defenders and destroying the generatoria powering the void shield before serious opposition could be raised.

'Brother Pyriel?' Dak'ir pressed when a response wasn't forthcoming.

The Librarian was staring at the distant void shield, energy blossoms appearing on its surface only to dissipate seconds later.

'Something about the shield... An anomaly in its energy signature...' he breathed. His eyes were glowing cerulean-blue.

For once, Dak'ir felt nothing, just the urge to act.

'What is it?'

'I don't know...' The psychic fire dimmed in the Librarian's eyes behind his battle-helm. 'Oblique assault – one primary, one secondary. East and west,' he asserted.

Dak'ir nodded, but had a nagging feeling that Pyriel wasn't telling them everything. He opened a comm-channel to the other combat squads.

'We move in, brothers. Assault plan *serpentine*. Brother Apion, you are support. We will take primary. Brother Tsu'gan–'

'We are ready, Ignean,' came the harsh reply before Dak'ir had finished.

'Assault vector locked, I am the primary at the western hemisphere. Tsu'gan out.'

The link was cut abruptly. Dak'ir cursed under his breath.

Taking out his plasma pistol and unsheathing his chainsword, running a gauntleted finger down the flat of the blade and muttering a litany to Vulkan, Dak'ir rose to his feet.

'Fire-born, advance on my lead.'

Emek's raised fist brought them to a halt before they could move out. He had his finger pressed to the side of his battle-helm.

'I'm getting some frantic chatter from the Phalanx units.' He paused, listening intently. 'Contact has been lost with several secondary command units.' Then he looked up. During the pregnant pause, Dak'ir could sense what was coming next.

'They say they're under attack... from *spectres*,' said Emek.

'Patch it to all comms, brother. Every combat squad.'

Emek did as asked, and Dak'ir's battle-helm, together with his brothers', was filled with the broken reports from the Phalanx command units.

'*...ergeant is dead. Falling back to secondary positions...*'

'*...all around us! Throne of Earth, I can't see a target, I can't se–*'

'*...ead, everyone. They're out here among us! Oh hell, oh Emperor sa–*'

Scattered gunfire and hollow screams punctuated these reports. Some units were attempting to restore order. The barking commands of sergeants and corporals sounded desperate as they tried to reorganise in the face of sudden attack.

Commissar Loth's voice broke in sporadically, his replies curt and scathing. They must hold and then advance. The Imperium would brook no cowardice in the face of the enemy. Staggered bursts from his bolt pistol concluded each order, suggesting further executions.

Above and omnipresent, the sound of tolling bells filled the air.

'I saw no chapel or basilica in the Phalanx bastion,' said Ba'ken. He swept his gaze around slowly, panning with his heavy flamer as he did so.

'The rebels?' offered Brother Romulus.

'How do you explain it being everywhere?' asked Pyriel, his eyes aglow once more. He regarded the blood-red clouds that hinted at the churning warp storm above. 'This is an unnatural phenomenon. We are dealing with more than secessionists.'

Dak'ir swore under his breath; he'd made his decision.

'Spectres or not, we can't leave the Phalanx to be butchered.' He switched the comm-feed in his battle-helm to transmit.

'All squads regroup, and converge on Phalanx command positions.'

Brother Apion responded with a rapid affirmative, as did a second combat squad led by Brother Lazarus. Tsu'gan took a little longer to capitulate, evidently unimpressed, but seeing the need to rescue the Guardsmen from whatever was attacking them. Without the support fire offered by their heavy guns, the Salamanders were horribly exposed to the secessionist artillery and with the shield intact they had no feasible mission to prosecute.

'Understood.' Tsu'gan then cut the link.

Silhouettes moved through the downpour. Lasgun snap-shot fizzed out from Imperial positions, revealing Phalanx troopers that were shooting at unseen foes.

Most were running. Even the Basilisks were starting to withdraw. Commissar Loth, despite all of his fervour and promised retribution, couldn't prevent it.

The Phalanx were fleeing.

'Enemy contacts?'

Dak'ir was tracking through the mire, pistol held low, chainsword still but ready. He was the fulcrum of a dispersed battle-formation, Pyriel to his immediate left and two battle-brothers either side of them.

Ahead, he saw another combat squad led by Apion, the secondary insertion group. He too had dispersed his warriors, and they were plying every metre of the field for enemies.

'Negative,' was the curt response from Lazarus, approaching from the west.

Artillery bombardment from the entrenched rebel positions was falling with the intense rain. A great plume of sodden earth and broken bodies surged into the air a few metres away from where Dak'ir's squad advanced.

'Pyriel, anything?'

The Librarian shook his head, intent on his otherworldly instincts but finding no sense in what he felt or saw.

The broken chatter in Dak'ir's ear continued, the tolling of the bells providing an ominous chorus to gunfire and screaming. The Phalanx were close to a rout, having been pushed too far by a commissar who didn't understand or care about the nature of the enemy they were facing. Loth's only answer was threat of death to galvanise the men under his command. The bark of the Imperial officer's bolt pistol was close. Dak'ir could make out the telltale muzzle flash of the weapon in his peripheral vision.

Loth was firing at shadows and hitting his own men in the process; those fleeing and those who were standing their ground.

'I'll deal with him,' promised Pyriel, snapping out of his psychic trance without warning and peeling off to intercept the commissar.

Another artillery blast detonated nearby, showering the Salamanders with debris. Without the Earthshaker bombardment, the rebels were using their shell-hunting cannons to punish the Imperials. Tracer fire from high-calibre gunnery positions added to the carnage. That and whatever was stalking them through the mud and rain.

'It's infiltrators.' Tsu'gan's harsh voice was made harder still as it came through the comm-feed. 'Maybe fifty men, strung out in small groups, operating under camouflage. The humans are easily spooked. We will find them, Fire-born, and eliminate the threat.'

'How can you be–'

Dak'ir stopped when he caught a glimpse of something, away to his right.

'Did you see that?' he asked Ba'ken.

The hulking trooper followed him, swinging his heavy flamer around.

'No target,' Ba'ken replied. 'What was it, brother?'

'Not sure…' It had looked like just a flicker of… *white robes*, fluttering lightly but against the wind. The air suddenly became redolent with dank and age.

'Ignean!' Tsu'gan demanded.

'It's not infiltrators,' Dak'ir replied flatly.

Static flared in the feed before the other sergeant's voice returned.

'You can't be sure of that.'

'I know it, brother.' This time, Dak'ir cut the link. It had eluded him at first, but now he felt it, a… *presence*, out in the darkness of the killing field. It was angry.

'Eyes open,' he warned his squad, the half-seen image at the forefront of his mind and the stench all too real as the bells rang on.

Ahead, Dak'ir made out the form of a Phalanx officer, a captain according to his rank pins and attire. The Salamanders headed towards him, hoping to link up their forces and stage some kind of counter-attack. That was assuming there were enough troopers left to make any difference.

Commissar Loth was consumed by frenzy.

'Hold your ground!' he screeched. 'The Emperor demands your courage!' The bolt pistol rang out and another trooper fell, his torso gaping and red.

'Forward, damn you! Advance for His greater glory and the glory of the Imperium!'

Another Phalanx died, this time a sergeant who'd been rallying his men.

Pyriel was hurrying to get close, his force sword drawn, whilst his other hand was free. In the darkness and the driving rain he saw… *spectres*. They were white-grey and indistinct. Their movements were jagged, as if partially out of synch with reality, the non-corporeal breaching the fabric of the corporeal realm.

Loth saw them too, and the fear of it, whatever this phenomenon was, was etched over his pugilist's face.

'*Ave Imperator*. By the light of the Emperor, I shall fear no evil,' he intoned, falling back on the catechisms of warding and preservation he had learned in the schola progenium. '*Ave Imperator*. My soul is free of taint. Chaos will never claim it whilst He is my shield.'

The spectres were closing, flitting in and out of reality like a bad pict recording. Turning left and right, Loth loosed off shots at his aggressors, the brass rounds passing through them or missing completely, driving on to hit fleeing Phalanx infantrymen instead.

With each manifestation, the spectres got nearer.

Pyriel was only a few metres away when one appeared ahead of him. Loth's shot struck the Salamander in the pauldron as it went through and through, and a damage rune flared into life on the Librarian's tactical display inside his battle-helm.

'*Ave Imp–*' Too late. The spectre was upon Commissar Loth. He barely rasped the words–

'*Oh God-Emperor…*'

–when a blazing wall of psychic fire spilled from Pyriel's outstretched palm, smothering the apparition and banishing it from sight.

Loth was raising his pistol to his lips, jamming the still hot barrel into his mouth as his mind was unmanned by what he had seen.

Pyriel reached him just in time, smacking the pistol away before the commissar could summarily execute himself. The irony of it wasn't lost on the Librarian as the bolt-round flew harmlessly into the air. Still trailing tendrils of fire, Pyriel placed two fingers from his outstretched hand onto Loth's brow, who promptly crumpled to the ground and was still.

'He'll be out for several hours. Get him out of here, back to the bastion,' he ordered one of the commissar's attendants.

The attendant nodded, still shaken, calling for help, and together the storm troopers dragged Loth away.

'And he'll remember nothing of this or Vaporis,' Pyriel added beneath his breath.

Sensing his power, the spectres Pyriel had seen had retreated. Something else prickled at his senses now, something far off into the wilderness, away from the main battle site. There was neither time nor opportunity to investigate. Pyriel knew the nature of the foe they were facing now. He also knew there was no defence against it his brothers could muster. Space Marines were the ultimate warriors, but they needed enemies of flesh and blood. They couldn't fight mist and shadow.

Huge chunks of the Phalanx army were fleeing. But there was nothing Pyriel could do about that. Nor could he save those claimed by the earth, though this was the malice of the spectres at work again.

Instead, he raised a channel to Dak'ir through his battle-helm.

All the while, the bells tolled on.


'The entire force is broken,' the captain explained. He was a little hoarse from shouting commands, but had rallied what platoons were around him into some sort of order.

'Captain…'

'Mannheim,' the officer supplied.

'Captain Mannheim, what happened here? What is preying on your men?' asked Dak'ir. The rain was pounding heavily now, and *tinked* rapidly off his battle-plate. Explosions boomed all around them.

'I never saw it, my lord,' Mannheim admitted, wincing as a flare of incendiary came close, 'only Phalanx troopers disappearing from sight. At first, I thought enemy commandos, but our bio-scanners were blank. The only heat signatures came from our own men.'

Malfunctioning equipment was a possibility, but it still cast doubt on Tsu'gan's infiltrators theory.

Dak'ir turned to Emek, who carried the squad's auspex. The Salamander shook his head. Nothing had come from the rebel positions behind the shield, either.

'Could they have already been out here? Masked their heat traces?' asked Ba'ken on a closed channel.

Mannheim was distracted by his vox-officer. Making a rapid apology, he turned his back and pressed the receiver cup to his ear, straining to hear against the rain and thunder.

'Not possible,' replied Dak'ir. 'We would have seen them.'

'Then what?'

Dak'ir shook his head, as the rain came on in swathes.

'My lord...' It was Mannheim again. 'I've lost contact with Lieutenant Bahnhoff. We were coordinating a tactical consolidation of troops to launch a fresh assault. Strength in numbers.'

It was a rarefied concept on Nocturne, where self-reliance and isolationism were the main tenets.

'Where?' asked Dak'ir.

Mannheim pointed ahead. 'The lieutenant was part of our vanguard, occupying a more advanced position. His men had already reached the assault line when we were attacked.'

Explosions rippled in the distance where the captain gestured with a quavering finger. These were brave men, but their resolve was nearing its limit. Loth, and his bloody-minded draconianism, had almost pushed them over the edge.

It was hard to imagine much surviving in that barrage, and with whatever was abroad in the killing field to contend with too...

'If Lieutenant Bahnhoff lives, we will extract him and his men,' Dak'ir promised. He abandoned thoughts of a counter-attack almost immediately. The Phalanx were in disarray. Retreat was the only sensible option that preserved a later opportunity to attack. Though it went against his Promethean code, the very ideals of endurance and tenacity the Salamanders prided themselves on, Dak'ir had no choice but to admit it.

'Fall back with your men, captain. Get as many as you can to the bastion. Inform any other officers you can raise that the Imperial forces are in full retreat.'

Captain Mannheim motioned to protest.

'Full retreat, captain,' Dak'ir asserted. 'No victory was ever won with foolish sacrifice,' he added, quoting one of Zen'de's Tenets of Pragmatism.

The Phalanx officer saluted, and started pulling his men back. Orders were already being barked down the vox to any other coherent platoons in the army.

'We don't know what is out there, Dak'ir,' Ba'ken warned as they started running in Bahnhoff's direction. Though distant, silhouettes of the lieutenant's forces were visible. Worryingly, their las-fire spat in frantic bursts.

'Then we prepare for anything,' the sergeant replied grimly and forged on into the churned earth.

Bahnhoff's men had formed a defensive perimeter, their backs facing one another with the lieutenant himself at the centre, shouting orders. He positively sagged with relief upon sighting the Emperor's Angels coming to their aid.

The Salamanders were only a few metres away when something flickered into being nearby the circle of lasguns and one of the men simply vanished. One moment he was there, and the next... gone.

Panic flared and the order Bahnhoff had gallantly established threatened to break down. Troopers had their eyes on flight and not battle against apparitions they could barely see, let alone shoot or kill.

A second trooper followed the first, another white flicker signalling his death. This time Dak'ir saw the human's fate. It was as if the earth had opened up and swallowed him whole. Except the trooper hadn't fallen or been sucked into a bog, he'd been *dragged*. Pearlescent hands, with thin fingers like talons, had seized the poor bastard by the ankles and pulled him under.

Despite Bahnhoff's efforts his platoon's resolve shattered and they fled. Several more perished as they ran, sharing the same grisly fate as the others, dragged down in an eye-blink. The lieutenant ran with them, trying to turn the rout into an ordered retreat, but failing.

Emboldened by the troopers' fear, the things that were preying on the Phalanx manifested and the Salamanders saw them clearly for the first time.

'Are they daemons?' spat Emek, levelling his bolter.

They looked more like ragged corpses, swathed in rotting surplices and robes, the tattered fabric flapping like the tendrils of some incorporeal squid. Their eyes were hollow and black, and they were bone-thin with the essence of clergy about them. Priests they may once have been; now they were devils.

'Let us see if they can burn,' snarled Ba'ken, unleashing a gout of promethium from his heavy flamer. The spectres dissipated against the glare of liquid fire coursing over them as Ba'ken set the killing fields ablaze, but returned almost as soon as the fires had died down, utterly unscathed.

He was about to douse them again when they evaporated like mist before his eyes.

An uncertain second or two passed, before the hulking Fire-born turned to his sergeant and shrugged.

'I've fought tougher foes–' he began, before crying out as his booted feet sank beneath the earth.

'Name of Vulkan!' Emek swore, scarcely believing his eyes.

'Hold him!' bellowed Dak'ir, seeing white talons snaring Ba'ken's feet and ankles. Brothers Romulus and G'heb sprang to their fellow Salamander's aid, each hooking their arms under Ba'ken's. In moments, they were straining against the strength of the spectres.

'Let me go, you'll tear me in half,' roared Ba'ken, part anger, part pain.

'Hang on, brother,' Dak'ir told him. He was about to call for reinforcements, noting Pyriel's contact rune on his tac-display, when an apparition mat-erialised in front of him. It was an old preacher, his grey face lined with age and malice, a belligerent light illuminating the sockets of his eyes. His mouth formed words Dak'ir could not discern and he raised an accusing finger.

'Release him, hell-spawn!' Dak'ir lashed out with his chainsword, but the preacher blinked out of existence and the blade passed on harmlessly to embed itself in the soft earth behind him. Dak'ir raised his plasma pistol to shoot when a terrible, numbing cold filled his body. Icy fire surged through him as his blood was chilled by something old and vengeful. It stole away the breath from his lungs and made them burn, as if he had plunged naked beneath the surface of an arctic river. It took Dak'ir a few moments to realise the crooked fingers of the preacher were penetrating his battle-plate. Worming beyond the aegis of ceramite, making a mockery of his power armour's normally staunch defences, the grey preacher's talons sought vital organs in their quest for vengeance.

Trying to cry out, Dak'ir found his larynx frozen, his tongue made leaden by the spectral assault. In his mind his intoned words of Promethean lore kept him from slipping into utter darkness.

*Vulkan's fire beats in my breast. With it I shall smite the foes of the Emperor.*

A heavy pressure hammered at his thunderous hearts, pressing, pressing…

Dak'ir's senses were ablaze and the smell of old, dank wood permeated through his battle-helm.

Then a bright flame engulfed him and the pressure eased. Cold withered, melted away by soothing heat, and as his darkening vision faded Dak'ir saw Pyriel standing amidst a pillar of fire. At the periphery, Ba'ken was being dragged free of the earth that had claimed him. Someone else was lifting Dak'ir. He felt strong hands hooking under his arms and pulling him. It was only then as his body became weightless and light that he realised he must've fallen. Semi-conscious, Dak'ir was aware of a fading voice addressing him.

'Dragging your carcass out of the fire again, Ignean…'

Then the darkness claimed him.

The strategium was actually an old refectory inside the bastion compound that smelled strongly of tabac and stale sweat. A sturdy-looking cantina table had been commandeered to act as a tacticarium, and was strewn with oiled maps, geographical charts and data-slates. The vaulted ceiling leaked, and drips of water were constantly being wiped from the various scrolls and picts layering the table by aides and officers alike. Buzzing around the moderately sized room's edges were Departmento Munitorum clerks and logisticians, counting up men and materiel with their styluses and exchanging dark glances with one another when they thought the Guard weren't looking.

It was no secret that they'd lost a lot of troops in the last sortie to bring down the void shield. To compound matters, ammunition for the larger guns was running dangerously low, to 'campaign-unviable' levels. Almost an hour had passed since the disastrous assault, and the Imperial forces were no closer to forging a battle-plan.

Librarian Pyriel surveyed the tactical data before him and saw nothing new, no insightful strategy to alleviate the graveness of their situation. At least the spectres had given up pursuit when they'd entered the grounds of Mercy Rock, though it had taken a great deal of the Epistolary's psychic prowess to fend them off and make retreat possible.

'What were they, brother?' said Tsu'gan in a low voice, trying not to alert the Guard officers and quartermaster who had joined them. Some things – Tsu'gan knew – it was best that humans stayed ignorant of. They could be weak-minded, all too susceptible to fear. Protecting humanity meant more than bolter and blade; it meant shielding them from the horrifying truths of the galaxy too, lest they be broken by them.

'I am uncertain.' Pyriel cast his gaze upwards, where his witch-sight turned timber and rockcrete as thin as gossamer, penetrating the material to soar into the shadow night where the firmament was drenched blood-red. 'But I believe the warp storm and the spectres are connected.'

'Slaves of Chaos?' The word left a bitter taste, and Tsu'gan spat it out.

'Lost and damned, perhaps,' the Librarian mused. 'Not vassals of the Ruinous Powers, though. I think they are… *warp echoes*, souls trapped between the empyrean and the mortal world. The red storm has thinned the veil of reality. I can *feel* the echoes pushing through. Only, I don't know why. But as long as the storm persists, as long as Hell Night continues, they will be out there.'

Only a few metres away, oblivious to the Salamanders, the Guard officers were having a war council of their own.

'The simple matter is, we cannot afford a protracted siege,' stated Captain Mannheim. Since Tench's execution and the commissar's incapacitation, Mann-heim was the highest ranking officer in the Phalanx. His sleeves were rolled up and he'd left his cap on the tacticarium table, summing the charts.

'We have perhaps enough munitions for one more sustained assault on the void shield.' The quartermaster was surveying his materiel logs, a Departmento Munitorum aide feeding him data-slates with fresh information that he mentally recorded and handed back as he spoke. 'After that, there is nothing we possess here that can crack it.'

Another officer, a second lieutenant, spoke up. His jacket front was unbuttoned and an ugly dark sweat stain created a dagger-shaped patch down his shirt.

'Even if we did, what hope is there while those things haunt the darkness?'

A patched-up corporal, his left eye bandaged, blotched crimson under the medical gauze, stepped forward.

'I am not leading my platoon out there to be butchered again. The secessionists consort with daemons. We have no defence against it.'

Fear, Tsu'gan sneered. Yes, humans were too weak for some truths.

The second lieutenant turned, scowling, to regard the Salamanders who dwelt in the shadows at the back of the room.

'And what of the Emperor's Angels? Were you not sent to deliver us and help end the siege? Are these foes, the spectres in the darkness, not allied to our faceless enemies at Aphium? We cannot break the city, if you cannot rid us of the daemons in our midst.'

Hot anger flared in Tsu'gan's eyes, and the officer balked. The Salamander snarled with it, clenching a fist at the human's impudence.

Pyriel's warning glance made his brother stand down.

'They are not daemons,' Pyriel asserted, 'but warp echoes. A resonance of the past that clings to our present.'

'Daemons, echoes, what difference does it make?' asked Mannheim. 'We are being slaughtered all the same, and with no way to retaliate. Even if we could banish these... *echoes*,' he corrected, 'we cannot take on them *and* the void shield. It's simple numbers, my lord. We are fighting a war of attrition which our depleted force cannot win.'

Tsu'gan stepped forward, unable to abstain from comment any longer.

'You are servants of the Emperor!' he reminded Mannheim fiercely. 'And you will do your part, hopeless or not, for the glory of Him on Earth.'

A few of the officers made the sign of the aquila, but Mannheim was not to be cowed.

'I'll step onto the sacrificial altar of war if that is what it takes, but I won't do it blindly. Would you lead your men to certain death, knowing it would achieve nothing?'

Tsu'gan scowled. Grunting an unintelligible diatribe, he turned on his heel and stalked from the strategium.

Pyriel raised his eyebrows.

'Forgive my brother,' he said to the council. 'Tsu'gan burns with a Nocturnean's fire. He becomes agitated if he cannot slay anything.'

'And that is the problem, isn't it?' returned Captain Mannheim. 'The reason why your brother-sergeant was so frustrated. Save for you, Librarian, your Astartes have no weapons against these echoes. For all their strength of arms, their skill and courage, they are powerless against them.'

The statement lingered, like a blade dangling precariously over the thread of all their hopes.

'Yes,' Pyriel admitted in little more than a whisper.

Silent disbelief filled the room for a time as the officers fought to comprehend the direness of their plight on Vaporis.

'There are no sanctioned psykers in the Phalanx,' said the second lieutenant at last. 'Can one individual, even an Astartes, turn the tide of this war?'

'He cannot!' chimed the corporal. 'We need to signal for landers immediately. Request reinforcements,' he suggested.

'There will be none forthcoming,' chided Mann-heim. 'Nor will the landers enter Vaporis space whilst Aphium is contested. We are alone in this.'

'My brother was right in one thing,' uttered Pyriel, his voice cutting through the rising clamour. 'Your duty is to the Emperor. Trust in us, and we will deliver victory,' he promised.

'But how, my lord?' asked Mannheim.

Pyriel's gaze was penetrating.

'Psychics are anathema to the warp echoes. With my power, I can protect your men by erecting a psy-shield. The spectres, as you call them, will not be able to pass through. If we can get close enough to the void shield, much closer than the original assault line, and apply sufficient pressure to breach it, my brothers will break through and shatter your enemies. Taking out the generatoria first, the shield will fail and with it the Aphium resistance once your long guns have pounded them.'

The second lieutenant scoffed, a little incredulous.

'My lord, I don't doubt the talents of the Astartes, nor your own skill, but can you really sustain a shield of sufficient magnitude and duration to make this plan work?'

The Librarian smiled thinly.

'I am well schooled by my Master Vel'cona. As an Epistolary-level Librarian, my abilities are prodigious, lieutenant,' he said without pride. 'I can do what must be done.'

Mannheim nodded, though a hint of fatalism tainted his resolve.

'Then you have my full support and the support of the Phalanx 135th,' he said. 'Tell me what you need, my lord, and it shall be yours.'

'Stout hearts and steely resolve is all I ask, captain. It is all the Emperor will ever ask of you.'

Tsu'gan checked the load of his combi-bolter, re-securing the promethium canister on the flamer element of the weapon.

'Seems pointless, when we cannot even kill our foes,' he growled.

The bellicose sergeant was joined by the rest of his brothers at the threshold to Mercy Rock, in the inner courtyard before the bastion's great gate.

Behind them, the Phalanx platoons were readying. In the vehicle yards, the Basilisks were churning into position on their tracks. Anticipation filled the air like an electric charge.

Only two Salamanders were missing, and one of those was hurrying to join them through the thronging Guardsmen from the makeshift medibay located in the bastion catacombs.

'How is he, brother?' Emek asked, racking the slide to his bolter.

'Unconscious still,' said Ba'ken. He'd ditched his heavy flamer and carried a bolter like most of his battle-brothers. Dak'ir had not recovered from the attack by the spectre and so, despite his protests, Ba'ken had been made de facto sergeant by Pyriel.

'I wish he were with us,' he muttered.

'We all do, brother,' said Pyriel. Detecting a mote of unease, he asked, 'Something on your mind, Ba'ken?'

The question hung in the air like an unfired bolt-round, before the hulking trooper answered.

'I heard Brother-Sergeant Tsu'gan over the comm-feed. Can these things even be fought, brother? Or are we merely drawing them off for the Guard?'

'I saw the Ignean's blade pass straight through one,' Tsu'gan muttered. 'And yet others seized upon Ba'ken as solid and intractable as a docking claw.'

Emek looked up from his auspex.

'Before they attack, they corporealise; become flesh,' he said, 'Although it is flesh of iron with a grip as strong as a power fist.'

'I had noticed it too,' Pyriel replied. 'Very observant, brother.'

Emek nodded humbly, before the Librarian outlined his strategy.

'Our forces will be strung out across the killing field, four combat squads as before. I can stretch my psychic influence to encompass the entire Phalanx battle line but it will be a comparatively narrow cordon, and some of the spectres may get through. Adopt defensive tactics and wait for them to attack, then strike. But know the best we can hope for is to repel them. Only I possess the craft to banish the creatures into the warp and that won't be possible whilst I'm maintaining the psychic shield.'

'Nor then will you be able to fight, Brother-Librarian,' said Ba'ken.

Pyriel faced him, and there was an unspoken compact in his low voice. 'No, I'll be temporarily vulnerable.'

*So you, brothers, will need to be my shield.*

The severity of the mission weighed as heavy as the weather. Captain Mannheim had been correct when he'd spoken in the strategium: for all their strength of arms, their skill and courage, they *were* powerless against the spectres. Almost.

Pyriel addressed the group. 'Fire-born: check helm-displays for updated mission parameters and objectives.'

A series of 'affirmatives' greeted the order.

'Switching to tac-sight,' added Tsu'gan. A data stream of time-codes, distances and troop dispositions filled his left occulobe lens. He turned to Pyriel just as the great gates to Mercy Rock were opening. 'I hope you can do what you promised, Librarian, or we are all dead.'

Pyriel's gaze was fixed ahead as he donned his battle-helm.

'The warp storm is unpredictable, but it also augments my own powers,' he said. 'I can hold the shield for long enough.'

On a closed channel, he contacted Tsu'gan alone.

'My psychic dampener will be low,' he warned. 'If at any moment I am compromised, you know what must be done.'

*If I am daemonically possessed by the warp*, Tsu'gan read between the Librarian's words easily enough.

A sub-vocal 'compliance' flashed up as an icon on Pyriel's display.

'Brothers Emek, Iagon?' the Librarian asked with the gates now yawning wide. The gap in the wall brought lashing rain and the stench of death.

Emek and Iagon were interrogating overlapping scan patterns on their auspexes in search of warp activity in the shadows of the killing field.

'Negative, brother,' Emek replied. Iagon nodded in agreement.

The way, for now at least, was clear.

Despite the rain, a curious stillness persisted in the darkness of Hell Night. It was red and angry. And it was waiting for them. Pyriel was drawn again to the patch of wilderness, far off in the distance.

*Just beyond my reach…*

'Into the fires of battle…' he intoned, and led the Salamanders out.

Dak'ir awoke, startled and awash with cold sweat. He was acutely aware of his beating hearts and a dense throbbing in his skull. Disorientating visions were fading from his subconscious mind… An ashen world, of tombs and mausoleums lining a long, bone-grey road… The redolence of burning flesh and grave dust… Half-remembered screams of a brother in pain…

…*Becoming one with the screams of many, across a dark and muddied field… The touch of rain, cold against his skin… and a bell tolling… 'We are here…' 'We are here…'*

The first was an old dream. He had seen it many times. But now new impressions had joined it, and Dak'ir knew they came from Vaporis. He tried to hold onto them, the visions and the sense memories, but it was like clutching smoke.

With the thinning of the unreal, the real became solid and Dak'ir realised he was flat on his back. A wire mattress with coarse sheets supported him. The cot groaned as he tried to move – so did Dak'ir when the daggers of pain pierced his body. He grimaced and sank back down, piecing together the immediate past. The attack by the spectral preacher came back to him. A remembered chill made him shiver.

'You're pretty well banged up,' said a voice from the shadows. The sudden sound revealed just how quiet it was – the dull reply of heavy artillery was but a faint thudding in the walls. 'I wouldn't move so quickly,' the voice advised.

'Who are you?' rasped Dak'ir, the dryness in his throat a surprise at first.

A high-pitched squeal grated against the Salamander's skull as a Phalanx officer sitting in a wheelchair rolled into view.

'Bahnhoff, my lord,' he said. 'You and your Astartes tried to save my men in the killing field, and I'm grateful to you for that.'

'It's my duty,' Dak'ir replied, still groggy. He managed to sit up, despite the horrendous pain of his injuries and the numbness that lingered well after the preacher had relinquished his deathly grip. Dak'ir was gasping for breath for a time.

'*Lieutenant* Bahnhoff?' he said, remembering; a look of incredulity on his face when he saw the wheelchair.

'Artillery blast got me,' the officer supplied. 'Platoon dragged me the rest of the way. Took *me* off the frontline too, though.'

Dak'ir felt a pang of sorrow for the lieutenant when he saw the shattered pride in his eyes.

'Am I alone? Have my brothers gone to battle without me?' Dak'ir asked.

'They said you were too badly injured. Told us to watch over you until they returned.'

'My armour…' Dak'ir was naked from the waist up. Even his torso bodyglove had been removed. As he made to swing himself over the edge of the cot, enduring still further agonies, he saw that his battle-plate's cuirass was lying reverently in one corner of the room. His bodyglove was with it, cut up where his brothers had needed to part it to treat his wounds. Dak'ir ran his finger over them. In the glow of a single lume-lamp they looked like dark bruises in the shape of fingerprint impressions.

'Here… I found these in a storage room nearby.' Bahnhoff tossed Dak'ir a bundle of something he'd been carrying on his lap.

The Salamander caught it, movement still painful but getting easier, and saw they were robes.

'They're loose, so should fit your frame,' Bahnhoff explained.

Dak'ir eyed the lieutenant, but shrugged on the robes nonetheless.

'Help me off this cot,' he said.

Together, they got Dak'ir off the bed and onto his feet. He wobbled at first, but quickly found his balance, before surveying his surroundings.

They were in a small room, like a cell. The walls were bare stone. Dust collected in the corners and hung in the air, giving it an eerie quality.

'What is this place?'

Bahnhoff wheeled backwards as Dak'ir staggered a few steps from the cot.

'Mercy Rock's catacombs. We use it as a medi-bay,' the lieutenant's face darkened, 'and morgue.'

'Apt,' Dak'ir replied with grim humour.

A strange atmosphere permeated this place. Dak'ir felt it as he brushed the walls with his finger-tips, as he drank in the cloudy air.

*We are here…*

The words came back to him like a keening. They were beckoning him. He turned to Bahnhoff, eyes narrowed.

'What is that?'

'What is *what*, my lord?'

A faint scratching was audible in the sepulchral silence, as a quill makes upon parchment. Bahnhoff's eyes widened as he heard it too.

'All the Munitorum clerks are up in the strategium…'

'It's coming from beneath us,' said Dak'ir. He was already making for the door. Wincing with every step, he betrayed his discomfort, but gritted his teeth as he went to follow the scratching sound.

'Are there lower levels?' he asked Bahnhoff, as they moved through a shadowy corridor.

'Doesn't get any deeper than the catacombs, my lord.'

Dak'ir was moving more quickly now, and Bahnhoff was wheeling hard to keep up.

The scratching was getting louder, and when they reached the end of the corridor the way ahead was blocked by a timber barricade.

'Structurally unsafe, according to the engineers,' said Bahnhoff.

'It's old…' Dak'ir replied, noting the rotten wood and the gossamer webs wreathing it like a veil. He gripped one of the planks and tore it off easily. Compelled by some unknown force, Dak'ir ripped the barricade apart until they were faced by a stone stairway. It led into a darkened void. The reek of decay and stagnation was strong.

'Are we going down there?' asked Bahnhoff, a slight tremor in his voice.

'Wait for me here,' Dak'ir told him and started down the steps.

'Stay within the cordon!' bellowed Tsu'gan, as another one of Captain Mannheim's men was lost to the earth.

An invisible barrier stretched the length of the killing ground that only flared incandescently into existence when one of the spectres struck it and recoiled. Like a lightning spark, the flash was born and died quickly, casting the scene starkly in its ephemeral life. Gunnery teams slogged hard to keep pace and infantry tramped hurriedly alongside them in long thin files, adopting firing lines once they'd reached the two hundred metre marker. Las-bursts erupted from the Phalanx ranks in a storm. Barking solid shot from heavy bolters and auto-cannon added to the sustained salvo. So close to the void shield, the energy impact returns were incandescently bright and despite the darkness, made several troopers don photoflash goggles. For some, it was just as well that their vision was impeded for shadows lurked beyond Librarian Pyriel's psychic aegis and not everyone was immune to them.

The barrier was narrow, just as Pyriel had warned, and as the Phalanx had tried to keep pace with the Salamanders on the way to the advanced assault line some stepped out of it. A muted cry and then they were no longer seen or heard from again. By the time the firing line was erected, some several dozen troopers were missing. The Salamanders, as yet, had not succumbed.

Tsu'gan saw the flickering white forms of the warp echoes through the Librarian's psychic shield. They lingered, angry and frustrated, ever probing to test the limits of Pyriel's strength. Though he couldn't see his face through his battle-helm, Tsu'gan knew by the Epistolary's juddering movements that he was feeling the strain. He was a vessel now for the near-unfettered power of the warp. Like a sluice gate let free, the energy coursed through him as Pyriel fought hard to channel it into the shield. One slip and he would be lost. Then Tsu'gan would need to act quickly, slaying him before Pyriel's flesh was obtained by another, heralding the death of them all, Salamanders or no.

One of the creatures breached the barrier wall, corporealising to do it, and Tsu'gan lashed out with his fist.

It was like striking adamantium, and he felt the shock of the blow all the way up his arm and into his shoulder, but did enough to force the creature back. It flashed briefly out of existence, but returned quickly, a snarl upon its eldritch features.

'Hard as iron you said,' Tsu'gan roared into the comm-feed as the weapons fire intensified.

Overhead the Earthshaker shells were finding their marks and the void shield rippled near its summit.

Emek battered another of the spectres back beyond the psychic cordon, the exertion needed to do it evident in his body language.

'Perhaps too conservative,' he admitted.

'A tad, brother,' came Tsu'gan's bitter rejoinder. 'Iagon,' he relayed through his battle-helm, 'what are the readings for the shield?'

'Weakening, my lord,' was Iagon's sibilant reply, 'but still insufficient for a break.'

Tsu'gan scowled.

'Ba'ken…'

'We must advance,' the acting sergeant answered. 'Fifty metres, and apply greater pressure to the shield.'

At a hundred and fifty metres away, the danger from energy flares cast by void impacts and friendly fire casualties from the Earthshakers was greatly increased, but then the Salamanders had little choice. Soon the bombardment from the Basilisks would end when they ran out of shells. The void shield had to be down before then.

'Brother-Librarian,' Tsu'gan began, 'another fifty metres?'

After a few moments, Pyriel nodded weakly and started to move forwards.

Tsu'gan turned his attention to the Phalanx.

'Captain Mannheim, we are advancing. Another fifty metres.'

The Phalanx officer gave a clipped affirmative before continuing to galvanise his men and reminding them of their duty to the Emperor.

Despite himself, the Salamander found he admired the captain for that. The bells tolled on as the Imperial forces resumed their march.

The stairs were shallow and several times Dak'ir almost lost his footing, only narrowly avoiding a plunge into uncertain darkness by bracing himself against the flanking walls.

Near the bottom of the stairwell, he was guided by a faint smudge of flickering light. Its warm, orange glow suggested candles or a fire. There was another room down here and this was where the scratching sound emanated from.

Cursing himself for leaving his weapons in the cell above, Dak'ir stepped cautiously through a narrow portal that forced him to duck to get through and into a small, dusty chamber.

Beyond the room's threshold he saw bookcases stuffed with numerous scrolls, tomes and other arcana. Religious relics were packed in half-open crates, stamped with the Imperial seal. Others, deific statues, Ecclesiarchal sigils and shrines were cluttered around the chamber's periphery. And there, in the centre, scribing with ink and quill at a low table, was an old, robed clerk.

The scrivener looked up from his labours, blinking with eye strain as he regarded the giant, onyx-skinned warrior in his midst.

'Greetings, soldier,' he offered politely.

Dak'ir nodded, uncertain of what to make of his surroundings. A prickling sensation ran through his body but then faded as he stepped into the corona of light cast by the scrivener's solitary candle.

'Are you Munitorum?' asked Dak'ir. 'What are you doing so far from the strategium?' Dak'ir continued to survey the room as he stepped closer. It was caked in dust and the grime of ages, more a forgotten storeroom than an office for a Departmento clerk.

The scrivener laughed; a thin, rasping sort of a sound that put Dak'ir a little on edge.

'Here,' said the old man as he backed away from his works. 'See what keeps me in this room.'

Dak'ir came to the table at the scrivener's beckoning, strangely compelled by the old man's manner, and looked down at his work.

*Hallowed Heath – a testament of its final days*, he read.

'Mercy Rock was not always a fortress,' explained the scrivener behind him. 'Nor was it always alone.'

The hand that had authored the parchment scroll in front of Dak'ir was scratchy and loose but he was able to read it.

'It says here that Mercy Rock was once a basilica, a temple devoted to the worship of the Imperial Creed.'

'Read on, my lord...' the scrivener goaded.

Dak'ir did as asked.

'"...and Hallowed Heath was its twin. Two bastions of light, shining like beacons against the old faiths, bringing enlightenment and understanding to Vaporis,"' he related directly from the text. '"In the shadow of Aphium, but a nascent township with lofty ambitions, did these pinnacles of faith reside. Equal were they in their fervour and dedication, but not in fortification–"' Dak'ir looked around at the old scrivener who glared at the Salamander intently.

'I thought you said they were not fortresses?'

The scrivener nodded, urging Dak'ir to continue his studies.

'"–One was built upon a solid promontory of rock, hence its given appellation; the other upon clay. It was during the Unending Deluge of 966.M40 when the rains of Vaporis continued for sixty-six days, the heaviest they had ever been in longest memory, that Hallowed Heath sank down beneath a quagmire of earth, taking its five hundred and forty-six patrons and priests with it. For three harrowing days and nights the basilica sank, stone by stone, beneath the earth, its inhabitants stranded within its walls that had become as their tomb. And for three nights, they tolled the bells in the highest towers of Hallowed Heath, saying, "We are here!", "We are here!" but none came to their aid."'*

Dak'ir paused as a horrible understanding started to crawl up his spine. Needing to know more, oblivious now to the scrivener, he continued.

'"Aphium was the worst. The township and all its peoples did not venture into the growing mire for fear of their own lives, did not even try to save the stricken people. They shut their ears to the bells and shut their doors, waiting for a cessation to the rains. And all the while, the basilica sank, metre by metre, hour by hour, until the highest towers were consumed beneath the earth, all of its inhabitants buried alive with them, and the bells finally silenced."'*

Dak'ir turned to regard the old scrivener.

'The spectres in the killing field,' he said, 'they are the warp echoes of the preachers and their patrons.'

'They are driven by hate, hate for the Aphiums who closed their ears and let them die, just as I am driven by guilt.'

*Guilt?*

Dak'ir was about to question it when the scrivener interrupted.

'You're near the end, Hazon, read on.'

Dak'ir was compelled to turn back, as if entranced.

'"*This testament is the sole evidence of this terrible deed – nay; it is my confession of complicity in it. Safe was I in Mercy Rock, sat idle whilst others suffered and died. It cannot stand. This I leave as small recompense, so that others might know of what transpired. My life shall be forfeit just as theirs were, too.*"'

There it ended, and only then did Dak'ir acknowledge that the old man had used his first name. He whirled around, about to demand answers… but he was too late.

The scrivener was gone.

The Earthshaker barrage stopped abruptly like a thumping heart in sudden cardiac arrest. Its absence was a silent death knell to the Phalanx and their Adeptus Astartes allies.

'It's done,' snarled Tsu'gan, when the Imperial shelling ended. 'We break through now or face the end. Iagon?'

'Still holding, my lord.'

They were but a hundred metres from the void shield now, having pressed up in one final effort to overload it. Without the heavy artillery backing them up, it seemed an impossible task. All the time, more and more Phalanx troopers were lost to breaches in the psychic shield, dragged into dank oblivion by ethereal hands.

'I feel… *something*…' said Pyriel, struggling to speak, 'Something in the void shield… Just beyond my reach…'

Despite his colossal efforts, the Librarian was weakening. The psychic barrier was losing its integrity and with it any protection against the warp echoes baying at its borders.

'Stand fast!' yelled Mannheim. 'Hold the line and press for glory, men of the Phalanx!'

Through sheer grit and determination, the Guardsmen held. Even though their fellow troopers were being swallowed by the earth, they held.

Tsu'gan could not help but feel admiration again for their courage. Like a crazed dervish, he raced down the line raining blows upon the intruding spectres, his shoulders burning with the effort.

'Salamanders! We are about to be breached,' he cried. 'Protect the Phalanx. Protect your brothers in arms with your lives!'

'Hail Vulkan and the glory of Prometheus!' Ba'ken chimed. 'Let Him on Earth witness your courage, men of the Phalanx.'

The effect of the sergeants' words was galvanising. Coupled with Mannheim's own stirring rally, the men became intractable in the face of almost certain death.

Tsu'gan heard a deep cry of pain to his left and saw Lazarus fall, impaled as Dak'ir had been by eldritch fingers.

'Brother!'

S'tang and Nor'gan went to his aid as Honorious covered their retreat with his flamer.

'Hold, Fire-born, hold!' Tsu'gan bellowed. 'Give them nothing!'

Tenacious to the end, the Salamanders would fight until their final breaths, and none so fiercely as Tsu'gan.

The battle-hardened sergeant was ready to make his final pledges to his primarch and his Emperor when the comm-feed crackled to life in his ear.

'You may have cheated death, Ignean,' snapped Tsu'gan when he realised who it was. 'But then survival over glory was always your–'

'Shut up, Zek, and raise Pyriel right now,' Dak'ir demanded, using the other Salamander's first name and mustering as much animus as he could.

'Our brother needs to marshal all of his concentration, Ignean,' Tsu'gan snapped again. 'He can ill afford distractions from you.'

'Do it, or it will not matter how distracted he becomes!'

Tsu'gan snarled audibly but obeyed, something in Dak'ir's tone making him realise it was important.

'Brother-Librarian,' he barked down the comm-feed. 'Our absent brother demands to speak with you.'

Pyriel nodded labouredly, his hands aloft as he struggled to maintain the barrier.

'Speak…' the Librarian could scarcely rasp.

'Do you remember what you felt before the first assault?' Dak'ir asked quickly. 'You said there was something about the shield, an anomaly in its energy signature. It is psychically enhanced, brother, to keep the warp echoes *out*.'

Through the furious barrage a slim crack was forming in the void shield's integrity, invisible to mortal eyes but plain as frozen lightning to the Librarian's witch-sight. And through it, Pyriel discerned a psychic undercurrent straining to maintain a barrier of its own. With Dak'ir's revelation came understanding and then purpose.

'They want vengeance against Aphium,' said Pyriel, beginning to refocus his psychic energy and remould it into a sharp blade of his own anger.

'For the complicity in their deaths over a thousand years ago,' Dak'ir concluded.

'I know what to do, brother,' Pyriel uttered simply, his voice drenched with psychic resonance as he let slip the last of the tethers from his psychic hood, the crystal matrix dampener that protected him psychically, and laid himself open to the warp.

'In Vulkan's name,' Dak'ir intoned before the link was overwhelmed with psychic static and died.

'Brother Tsu'gan…' Pyriel's voice was deep and impossibly loud against the battle din. A tsunami of raw psychic power was coursing through him, encasing the Librarian in a vibrant, fiery aura. '…I am about to relinquish the barrier…'

Tsu'gan had no time to answer. The psychic barrier fell and the warp echoes swept in. Thunder split the heavens and red lightning tore across boiling clouds as the warp storm reached its zenith.

Already, the breach Pyriel had psychically perceived was closing.

'Maintain positions!' roared Mannheim, as his men were being taken. 'Keep firing!'

Secessionist fire, freed up from mitigating the Imperial artillery barrage, was levelled at the Phalanx. Mannheim took a lucky las-round in the throat and was silenced.

Tsu'gan watched the officer fall just as Pyriel burst into violent conflagration. Running over to Mannheim, he scooped the fallen captain up into his arms, and watched as a bolt of flame lashed out from Pyriel's refulgent form. It surged through the void shield, past the unseen breach, reaching out for the minds of the Librarian's enemies…

Deep in Aphium rebel territory, in an armoured bunker sunk partially beneath the earth, a cadre of psykers sat in a circle, their consciousnesses locked, their will combined to throw a veil across the void shield that kept out the deeds of their ancestors. It was only around Hell Night when the blood storm wracked the heavens and brought about an awakening for vengeance, a desire for retribution, that their skills were needed.

One by one they screamed, an orange fire unseen by mortal eyes ravaging them with its scorching tendrils. Flesh melted, eyes ran like wax under a hot lamp, and one by one the psyker cadre burned. The heat inside the bunker was intense, though the temperature gauge suggested a cool night, and within seconds the psykers were reduced to ash and the defence of Aphium with it.

Upon the killing field, Tsu'gan detected a change in the air. The oppressive weight that had dogged them since mustering out for a second time on Hell Night had lifted, like leaden chains being dragged away by unseen hands.

Like mist before the rays of a hot sun, the warp echoes receded into nothing. Silence drifted over the killing field, as all of the guns stopped. The void shield flickered and died a moment later, the absence of its droning hum replaced by screaming from within the city of Aphium.

'In Vulkan's name…' Tsu'gan breathed, unable to believe what was unfolding before his eyes. He didn't need to see it to know the spectres had turned on the rebels of Aphium and were systematically slaying each and every one.

It wasn't over. Not yet. Pyriel blazed like an incendiary about to explode. The Librarian's body was spasming uncontrollably as he fought to marshal the forces he'd unleashed. Raging psychic flame coursed through him. As if taking hold of an accelerant, it burned mercilessly. Several troopers were consumed by it, the mind-fire becoming real. Men collapsed in the heat, their bodies rendered to ash.

'Pyriel!' cried Tsu'gan. Cradling Captain Mann-heim in his arms, he raised his bolter one-handed.

*…you know what you must do.*

He fired into Pyriel's back, an expert shot that punctured the Librarian's lung but wasn't fatal. Pyriel bucked against the blow, the flames around him dwindling, and sagged to his knees. Then he fell onto his side, unconscious, and the conflagration was over.

'Tsu'gan. Tsu'gan!'

It took Tsu'gan a few seconds to realise he was being hailed. A curious stillness had settled over the killing field. Above them the red sky was fading as the warp storm passed, and the rain had lessened. On the horizon, another grey day was dawning.

'Dak'ir…'

Stunned, he forgot to use his derogatory sobriquet for the other sergeant.

'What happened, Zek? Is it over?'

Mannheim was dead. Tsu'gan realised it as the officer went limp in his arms. He had not faltered, even at the end, and had delivered his men to victory and glory. Tsu'gan's bolter was still hot from shooting Pyriel. He used it carefully to burn an honour marking in Captain Mannheim's flesh. It was shaped like the head of a firedrake.

'It's over,' he replied and cut the link.

A faded sun had broken through the gathering cloud. Errant rays lanced downwards, casting their glow upon a patch of distant earth far off in the wilderness. Tsu'gan didn't know what it meant, only that when he looked upon it his old anger lessened and a strange feeling, that was not to last in the days to come, spilled over him.

Rain fell. Day dawned anew. Hell Night was ended, but the feeling remained.

It was peace.

# COVER OF DARKNESS

### Mitchel Scanlon

It was a night made for war by stealth. The night sky was moonless, with an opaque covering of clouds hiding the light of the stars. Cresting a ridge on his bike, Sergeant Kergis of the White Scars paused for a moment and scanned the arid landscape spread out before him. Ahead, the twisting maze of gullies and snaking furrows of the region known as Volcan's Cradle were bathed in Stygian blackness. To Kergis's mind, it seemed a favourable omen. Success in their mission was dependent on catching the enemy unawares. Tonight, the darkness would be their ally.

Turning his bike to follow the sinuous curve of the ridge slope as it descended toward the next gully, Kergis spared a glance at the rest of the eight-man squad behind him. His men travelled in single file, the lights of their bikes turned off, their armour covered in a thick layer of dust courtesy of the terrain around them. Occasionally, there was the ominous clatter of falling stones as they dislodged a few small rocks in crossing the slope, but the White Scars negotiated these hazards with the smooth assurance born of a lifetime spent in the saddle.

Reaching the foot of the slope in safety, they pushed on with their journey, following the trail of the gully as it headed northward. Much of Volcan's Cradle was open plain: a vast dusty expanse of dried lava created by millions of years of volcanic activity. But the need for stealth had forced Kergis and his men to take a circuitous route to their target, hugging the zigzag contours of a series of ravines and gullies in the western part of the region, cut by the effect of rain erosion on the yielding surface of the lava plain. It had made their path through the Cradle longer and more difficult, but given the nature of their mission it was vital they stayed clear of enemy patrols.

'I am reading movement,' Kergis heard the voice of Arik, a fellow White Scar, on his helmet-vox as they sped through the gully. 'Several vehicles from the size of the contact. The auspex puts them at six kilometres away, moving towards us on a bearing twelve degrees north-north-west.'

'An interception force?' Kergis voxed back.

'No,' Arik's voice was confident. 'Based on their bearing, I'd say it's a routine patrol. If we stay to our plotted course and maintain our speed, we will be long gone by the time they get here.'

'Good. We can't be more than a kilometre away from the geyser field by now. Take the lead, Arik. You will be our pathfinder. The rest of us will follow behind you.'

Throttling back his bike, Kergis allowed the other man to overtake him. Briefly pressing his right fist across his breast in a salute as he passed, Arik took up the sergeant's position at the head of the line of White Scars and veered eastward as he came to a fork in the gully. Kergis and the others followed suit.

The darkness would have been impenetrable to any normal man, but thanks to their enhanced eyesight and the autosenses of their armour the White Scars could navigate the desolate terrain of the Cradle with equal facility by day or night. The same sharpness of the senses alerted Kergis to the stink of sulphur long before the geyser fields became visible.

During the briefing that preceded the mission, a Techmarine named Goju had attempted to outline the unusual conditions which underpinned the geography of the Cradle. The planetary crust was thin here, he had explained, likening it to a frail wafer laid across a huge broiling sea of lava. In some places, the crust had cracked due to the enormous stresses upon it, creating a path to the surface for red-hot magma.

In the area the White Scars were headed for, the magma had heated the water stored underground in naturally formed aquifers, causing geysers and thermal springs to emerge in place of lava. Such phenomena were relatively common in the unstable volcanic landscape of the Cradle, but Kergis and his men would be travelling through the largest geyser field in the region, riding tens of kilometres through dangerous territory in the hope of keeping their presence hidden from the enemy.

Following Arik's lead, the squad of bikers emerged from the gully and sped on through the short distance of open plain separating them from the geyser field. Ahead, a strange and deadly landscape lay ready to greet them.

'Keep your helmets sealed and respiratus systems engaged,' Arik warned as they entered the geyser field. 'Leave at least five metres between you and the man in front. And stay on my track. The ground is fragile here. If it gives way beneath the weight of your bike, you'll be swimming in boiling water.'

According to the Imperial survey maps Kergis had inspected before making planetfall, it was known simply as Geyser Field Septimus. The prosaic title hid a sinister reality. The entire area was dotted with steaming vents and smoking craters. The colours were mostly concealed by the night, but Kergis knew the ground was covered in a thick multi-hued residue in startling shades of red, green and yellow, alongside vast white carpets of glittering salt crystals. The residue and the crystals were accumulated from the minerals leached from the rocks by the underground heat and brought to the surface as tiny particles over thousands of years every time one of the geysers erupted.

Kergis did not doubt the geyser field would be beautiful by daylight, but it was also treacherous. The vapours rising from the vents included deadly gases as well as scalding superheated steam, while the sluggish liquid bubbling in some of the craters was concentrated acid created by the same leached minerals responsible for the coloured residue. Enemy patrols tended to avoid the geyser field with good reason. By any standard, it was a lethal environment.

Carefully staying to the line of Arik's trail as it twisted between the smouldering vents, Kergis checked his auspex for any sign of the enemy patrol detected earlier. Seeing no trace of them, Kergis was pleased. The range of the auspex on his bike was limited, but even if the enemy were nearby there was little chance of his squad being detected while they were in the geyser field.

The throaty roar of the White Scars' engines was drowned out by the noises of the vents around them. Listening to the hiss of steam and the cackle of bubbling acid, Kergis was reminded of the sounds of breathing. It was as though they had intruded into the domain of a massive, slumbering beast, an illusion underlined by the occasional *whoosh* as one of the geysers erupted. The sound brought to mind the sea-leviathans that inhabited the oceans of Chogoris: gargantuan creatures that emerged periodically from the waves to breathe out through their blowholes, emitting great clouds of spray before returning once more to the deep.

Having never seen a body of open water until he was thirteen years of age and already on the path to becoming a White Scar, Kergis had always regarded the sea and its denizens with awe. He was Astartes, so he did not fear them. Still, they impressed him.

Inside Kergis's helmet, a warning sensor flashed an angry red to draw his attention to the rising levels of poisonous gases in the air outside, already far beyond human tolerance. He ignored it. The geyser field was a labyrinth of death, but the sergeant trusted Arik to guide them through it. Arik had always shown an unerring ability to find the correct trail through any terrain, no matter how difficult.

It was not an uncommon talent on their home world. Countless generations spent navigating the shifting pathways of the endless plains of Chogoris meant that some were born with a special aptitude for finding their way, whatever the circumstance. They were not psykers. It was simply that they took more notice of the subtle clues around them, whether in the landscape, the weather or the stars, relying on the patterns of past experience to guide them onto the best path to their destination.

In Arik's case he was aided by the fact his bike was equipped with a more powerful auspex unit than the others in the squad, but Kergis had no doubt he could have guided them through the geyser field without it. Even if Arik had never left Chogoris, never become Astartes, he would have been a pathfinder to his people, responsible for guiding his tribe to the watering holes for their herds and the best winter pastures.

As the White Scars moved deeper into the geyser field, the clouds of steam and poison grew thicker. Soon, visibility was reduced to a few metres. Still, they pushed onward, each warrior trusting to the man in front to lead him safely through the miasma.

It was no more than Kergis would have expected. The habit of mutual trust was deeply ingrained between his men. Their bonds of brotherhood were strong; bonds forged and tempered across a hundred battlefields. With it came a sense of debt, of obligation. Kergis did not doubt that any man in the squad would be willing to die for his brothers.

Certainly, it was part of the reason he had come to Volcan's Cradle.

'Tephra VII,' Jurga Khan had said to him, two days earlier. 'It has been an Imperial world for ten thousand years. Our great Primarch Jaghatai Khan, may his memory always be honoured, played a part in its liberation. But a year ago it was all undone. Chaos has seized this place, Kergis. Now, it falls to us to follow in the footsteps of our primarch. This planet will be liberated again. And the White Scars will be the spearhead, the first among the liberators.'

They were standing on the strategium deck of the strike cruiser *Warrior of the Plains*. A few minutes earlier Jurga Khan had concluded a briefing for the squad leaders under his command, indicating the roles they would be expected to play in the coming invasion. When the briefing was done, the Khan had dismissed everyone except Kergis. Even the Chapter serfs had been sent to perform duties elsewhere on the ship, ensuring the two men's privacy.

Courtesy of the strategium's display units, a shimmering translucent globe hovered in the air showing a hololithic representation of Tephra VII. Kergis noticed part of the planet's power grid had been highlighted, creating a network of fine golden lines that crisscrossed the northern hemisphere.

'We will make our first strike here,' Jurga Khan said, lifting an armoured finger to indicate a city. 'The planetary capital, Chaldis, is the main centre of the enemy's power. If we can defeat them here, in one assault, we will break the backbone of their resistance. But the city is protected by void shields. It will not be easy. We may face heavy losses.'

Kergis nodded. The invasion and re-conquest of Tephra VII was a major undertaking. The *Warrior of the Plains* was one of nearly thirty Imperial ships massing at the edge of the system. As the only Astartes taking part in the invasion, the White Scars could expect to bear the brunt of the fighting in the crucial opening stages when the enemy's defences were first breached.

'But there is a way we can lessen some of the price in blood,' his commander continued.

The Khan moved his finger to point to an area several thousand kilometres to the east of the capital. Responding to the movement, the hololithic globe turned to reveal a low-lying plain, surrounded by mountains to form a massive basin. Significantly, the golden lines of the power network all seemed to lead to the same region.

'The locals call this place Volcan's Cradle,' the Khan said. 'Goju will give you an in-depth briefing on the region and its conditions later, but you can take it for granted it is hard country. It's a desolate, volcanic wasteland. No one would ever go there, except for this…'

The Khan pressed his finger into the surface of the globe. The hololith shimmered and changed as the floating image zoomed in to a three-dimensional representation of a large manufactory complex, evidently based on the data from reconnaissance picts. Studying the image, Kergis realised the facility was situated on the slopes of a smouldering volcano.

'It is some kind of power generating facility?' he said, comparing the design to similar buildings he had seen on other worlds, even fought over, in his time as a White Scar.

'Geothermal,' Jurga Khan told him. 'You are looking at a power plant situated on the Ignis Mons, the largest active volcano in the Cradle region. Goju will explain the particulars to you, but it is my understanding they generate power by harnessing the heat of underground magma. Tephra VII is deficient in promethium and other fuels, so a number of such facilities were built in ancient times to provide for the planet's needs. The Ignis Mons complex supplies power to almost the entire western section of the northern hemisphere, including the void shields protecting the capital.'

'So, if this facility is destroyed, the shields go down?'

'Exactly. There are supposed to be backup power sources to supply the void shields in the event of an emergency. But the systems are old and it is believed the enemy have been lax in their maintenance. To add to its value as a target, the Mons complex also supplies power to the planet's sensor array network. If we destroy it, the enemy will be blind as well as shield-less.'

'But the enemy must also be aware of its value. The target will be well-defended?'

'It is,' Jurga Khan nodded. 'Including the forces manning a series of sentry points surrounding the area, the enemy can call upon at least two

thousand warriors to defend the complex. Added to which, the main
access ways into the facility are protected by multiple bunkers and other
secure emplacements armed with autocannons and anti-tank weapons. The heart of the facility is situated deep underground, so orbital
bombardment won't work. It would take a major assault to capture the
Mons. And not only would that warn the enemy of our intentions, it
would divert manpower away from the main assault on Chaldis.'

'But there is another way?' Kergis asked him. The Khan's briefing
seemed to be headed in one direction and he could see its logical conclusion. 'A stealth assault by a small team, ideally to be inserted into
the area under cover of darkness. It would be their task to destroy the
complex, or at least sabotage it to deny its use to the enemy. Given the
importance of the mission, and its risks, it is a task for Astartes rather
than Imperial Guardsmen.'

'Very good,' Jurga Khan smiled, the expression highlighting the honour scars crosshatching his features. 'Perhaps you missed your calling
with the Stormseers, Kergis. You seem to have read my mind.'

'It was simply that I could see your intention, my Khan. When you
assigned tasks to the other sergeants during the briefing earlier, I was
surprised when myself and my squad were left without duties. Then,
you called me aside to this briefing out of earshot of the others. I have
never known you do something without reason. It suggested you had a
particular mission in mind for me and my men.'

'Not a psyker, then,' the Khan's smile deepened. 'Simply a man with
the mind of a regicide master, always able to think several moves ahead
of his commander. I said you missed your calling as a Stormseer. Perhaps I was in error, and your true calling was as a savant.'

He raised a hand good-naturedly to stifle Kergis's protests.

'There is no shame in having a sharp mind, Kergis. The histories record
that Jaghatai Khan, may he always be honoured, possessed one of the
great military minds of his era. Too often we forget our primarch's example in this. We honour our warriors for feats of arms, but we forget it is
a man's mind and the character of his heart which wins battles as much
as the strength of his sinews. In this case, I chose you for this mission
because you are well served in all three of those qualities.'

'My Khan's words honour me.' Kergis bowed in obeisance.

'No more than your character merits it.' The Khan's face became serious. 'Besides, there were other considerations. Before you joined this
company, you served with Kor'sarro Khan during the Hunt for Voldorius. I know you fought side by side with the Raven Guard, and learned
some of their tricks of stealth. I know you have passed some of these
lessons on to the men in your squad. I hear you emphasise to them that
the lightning attack is negated in value if the enemy knows which direction it will come from. Such skills may be important on Tephra.'

Raising his hand again, Jurga Khan banished the hololith with a gesture. As the shimmering image of the geothermal complex faded away, the Khan's expression grew darker. He lowered his hand to hover over the manual control of the hololithic generator.

'But there is something else, Kergis. Another reason I chose you for this mission. The same reason I decided to banish the others and hold this briefing in private. You will soon see I had good cause for secrecy.'

Jurga Khan's hand moved over the control system's keypad, inputting a coded sequence of numbers. In response to the code, the hololithic generators hummed to life once more and a new image began to form.

'The attack on Chaldis is scheduled to begin in a little over two days. It will be a dawn assault, meaning you and your men will be expected to infiltrate the complex the night before. But there are other considerations at work here beyond the re-conquest of this world. What I am going to show you is for your eyes alone. It is not to be shared with your squad. In time, when the matter is resolved, the need for such secrecy may pass. But for the present, it is better we keep this between ourselves.'

The new hololith coalesced, revealing a pict-image taken at a distance of an armoured figure standing on top of a plascrete bunker.

'A Naval Lightning adapted for long-range reconnaissance took a series of picts two days ago during a high-speed sweep over the Ignis Mons,' the Khan said. 'The images are grainy, but you can clearly see the commander of the enemy garrison as he oversees the disposition of his troops.'

At a gesture from the Khan's hand, a second pict appeared. It was taken from a slightly different angle, but it showed the same figure. Helpfully, the enemy commander had craned his head up to look skyward, presenting a clearer image of his face. Seeing it, Kergis felt a sick feeling in the pit of his stomach. He barely heard his Khan's next words.

'It is almost as though he knows the spy-ship is there and is looking at it. Impossible, of course. The Lightning was moving at too high an altitude for anyone on the ground to spot it. But you see the reason for secrecy? This is an event of dark moment, Kergis. The honour of our Chapter is at stake.'

Kergis nodded, his mind still reeling at the revelation of the identity of the garrison commander. Standing on top of the bunker was a figure in battered white power armour emblazoned with a lightning insignia. Kergis could hardly believe it, but he saw the face of an old comrade, a man he had believed dead.

He saw the face of a battle-brother, a White Scar.

A friend.

The rendezvous point was situated seven kilometres from the target. Having successfully navigated though the geyser field courtesy of Arik's pathfinding skills, Kergis and his men reached the meeting place with fifteen minutes to spare. Seeking to stay out of sight, they hid their bikes in a low-lying gully that had once formed the riverbed of a long dead stream. While the rest of the squad stayed with their bikes, Kergis and his second-in-command, Gurban, climbed the gully's eastern wall on foot to check their surroundings.

'It seems quiet,' Gurban whispered, once he had scanned the area with a handheld auspex. 'I'm not reading any enemy patrols. But there's no sign of Balat and his men, either.'

Balat was a sergeant in the White Scars' 10th Company. When Kergis was told he would rendezvous with a squad of Scouts under Balat's command before making his approach on the target, he had been pleased. He and the Scout-sergeant were old comrades. Before Balat had transferred across to 10th Company, they had served together for several decades. Balat had been the sergeant of the squad Kergis had served in during his early days as a battle-brother. Kergis had always regarded the older man as something of a mentor.

'I would be more surprised if we did see them,' Kergis replied. He raised his hand in a thumb-sideways gesture to signal to the men in the gully that the area was clear but they should remain wary. Then, he turned back to Gurban.

'Keep your eyes sharp,' he told him. 'A broken undulating landscape like this one can play havoc with the auspex. It creates dead spots the sensors can't reach. A platoon could be hiding within fifty metres of us and we wouldn't know it.'

As though in proof of his words, the sound of a birdcall abruptly broke the silence. Kergis recognised it as the cawing of a razorhook, a sharp-beaked carrion eater native to the plains of Chogoris. Having been expecting the signal, Kergis had already removed his helmet. Decades ago, on a world called Quintus, a Raven Guard Space Marine named Melierax had taught him the vox-amplifiers in an Astartes helmet gave an unnatural timbre to attempts to imitate the sound of birds. An unknowing listener hearing the noise would be less likely to assume it was a genuine birdcall and ignore it.

Kergis responded to the razorhook's cawing by whistling three times in imitation of another native Chogorian bird. In reply, the cawing stopped. After a second, he became aware of dim shapes moving through the darkness towards them. Kergis kept his hand on his bolt pistol, ready in case it was a trick, but as the figures came closer he recognised the face of his old sergeant, Balat.

'It is good to see you again,' he said, clasping Balat's hand once the Scouts had joined them in the gully. 'What is our situation?'

Before answering, Balat made a signal to his men. Silently, they deployed to take up sentry posts around the lip of the gully.

'The immediate area is clear,' Balat said, once the Scouts had moved into position. 'Enemy patrols don't like to come this close to the geyser field in case the wind blows the poison clouds towards them. Still, it is better to be careful.'

Satisfied his men had covered every approach to their location, Balat walked a little distance along the bottom of the gully with Kergis beside him until they were out of earshot of the others.

'I made planetfall with my squad forty-eight hours ago,' the Scout-sergeant said. 'In that time, the enemy have tripled their patrols. This entire region has become a hotbed of activity.'

'Do you think they detected your arrival?'

'Perhaps,' Balat shrugged. 'We were inserted by Thunderhawk, as you were. The pilots did their best to fly us in under the enemy's sensor network, but it is possible we were detected. But, if that is the case, the enemy don't appear to be actively searching for us. We have seen no fly-ers, nor any sign of auspex sweeps. Rather than being a direct response to our arrival, it seems more likely they have stepped up their patrols because they are expecting trouble.'

'It would make sense,' Kergis agreed. 'They must know an invasion is coming. They may even have detected our reconnaissance flights. And they would realise the power complex is a target. They have probably increased their patrols as a precaution.'

'Even so, it is strange they have not brought in flyers or auspex,' Balat said. 'Why take half-measures if they think the invasion is coming? They must know the landscape of the Cradle makes an attack by stealth a real possibility. You would think they would take every step they could to prevent it.'

Balat shook his head in frustration. He was old, even by Astartes standards. He had nearly four centuries behind him, the years etched as lines on his face as surely as the many honour scars he wore as mark of his deeds. Kergis had heard rumours that Balat had once respectfully declined a promotion to become Master of the Watch back on Chogoris. In its place, he had asked to remain a simple sergeant and transferred to the 10th Company so he could pass on his skills to new generations of White Scars. Having experienced Balat's tutorship himself, Kergis had no doubt the Chapter's Scouts would be better warriors for it.

'Still, we should not be surprised if we find it difficult to divine the enemy's plans,' Balat said. 'It was always the same in the battle with Chaos. Do you remember Cernis? We thought to catch Voldorius una-wares there, but he was ready for us.'

'I remember,' Kergis nodded. Briefly, he thought of the battle in the polar wastes. He remembered the race across the ice fields and the mon-strous enemy they had fought under the northern lights. His memories brought to mind other battles: he thought of Kavell and icy Zoran, of the underhives of Modanna and the guntowers of Quintus. He thought of his encounter with the Bloodtide. He had come far and survived much. With Balat as his mentor, he had learned lessons in every battle.

'It was always so,' the Scout-sergeant continued. 'Of all the enemies we face, Chaos is the most treacherous, its champions the most cunning.'

Abruptly, Balat fell quiet. Staring intently at Kergis, he grimaced.

'You are smiling. I have said something amusing?'

'Forgive me, arban,' Kergis said, using a traditional Chogorian word for sergeant. Strictly speaking its meaning translated simply as 'leader of ten men', but among the White Scars it had grown to mean much more. The word held no official standing, but it was used commonly when referring to a sergeant whose courage and wisdom were highly regarded. It was meant as a mark of honour, a term of great respect.

'I was reminded of the old days when I served in your squad as a newly promoted battle-brother,' Kergis continued. 'To become a White Scar, I had passed through trials that not one in ten thousand men could have survived. On my first day, you told me not to get too cocky.'

'I was right,' Balat scowled. 'Arrogance is a dangerous vice in a warrior. It blinds him to his own weaknesses and the enemy's strengths.'

'Yes,' Kergis agreed. 'You taught me what it truly means to be Astartes. You moulded me to be a better warrior, a better servant of the Chapter and our Khan. I was smiling because the lessons continue. Despite the passing of a century, I am still the student and you the master. And, to be truthful, I was also smiling because your motive is transparent. In discussing Chaos and reminding me of Voldorius, you were not talking idly. You had a specific aim in mind.'

'Subtlety was never one of my own vices,' Balat admitted grudgingly. 'I have been fully briefed on the details of your mission. Including the identity of the enemy commander.'

'And you were wary I might need reminding of my duty?'

'No, not that. Never that.' All through their conversation, Balat had continued to stare at Kergis's face. Now, his gaze became more searching, more insightful. 'I simply hoped to remind you that Borchu is gone. Don't let your hand be slowed by the memory of past friendship. Strike fast, and strike to kill. If you hesitate, the enemy will make use of it.'

'Sound advice,' Kergis nodded again. 'I will follow it, I promise you.'

He glanced briefly above their heads. The sky was dark and overcast. Night still held its grip over the Cradle.

'But now, my men and I need to make ready. The darkness will not last forever. And we need to be at the Ignis Mons before dawn.'

It soon became apparent Balat and his Scouts had made able use of their time on Tephra VII. In their forty-eight hours in the Cradle, while being careful to stay out of sight, they had observed every aspect of the defences surrounding the Ignis Mons.

By the time he and Kergis met at the rendezvous, Balat possessed the kind of in-depth intelligence that might well prove vital to the successful outcome of their mission. While Kergis and his men watched and listened, he sketched out the positions of the ring of sentry points, minefields and hidden bunkers protecting the Mons. He provided an analysis of the enemy's patrol schedules, indicating the route each patrol took through the Cradle. He had even prepared a map outlining a suggested approach to their objective. Checking the approach and finding no flaw in it, Kergis ordered his men to memorise it.

Once Balat had passed on all the intelligence, the two groups took their leave of each other.

The pre-arranged mission plan called for the Scouts to remain behind and cover the line of retreat of Kergis's squad. At the same time, they would guard the mission team's bikes. They were close enough to the target that Kergis and his men could no longer use their vehicles for fear the sound of their engines would give them away. As much as it pained them as White Scars to leave their bikes behind, they had no choice. Henceforth, they would continue their mission on foot.

It was not the only change which had been forced upon them by the needs of the mission. Ordinarily, at least two of the men in his squad would have been equipped with meltas or other heavy weapons. Instead, the nature of their mission in the Cradle meant they had left behind their heavy weapons in order to carry more explosives. Each man in the squad carried a grey, polyleather satchel filled with demolition charges and detonators: necessary equipment to sabotage the power plant. To save on weight, their only other arms were bolt pistols, knives and their normal close combat weapons.

'May the spirits of your ancestors go with you,' Balat said, once preparations had been made and Kergis was ready to leave. The rest of Kergis's squad stood nearby, watching as the two sergeants clasped hands once more in parting.

'May they be your guide and guardians. May they strike the stones from your path and leave your enemies grieving in your wake.'

'And may your ancestors ride with you also,' Kergis responded, completing the form of a traditional Chogorian farewell. 'May they always be beside you.'

To Kergis's surprise, Balat refused at first to release his grip once the goodbyes were done. While their hands were still joined he leaned forward, whispering a few words out of hearing of the others.

'Good luck,' he said. 'I know the choice you have made. It honours you. But do not assume this will be our last meeting. I will see you again, Kergis. I count on it.'

'I hope you are right, arban,' Kergis answered quietly. 'Things will fall where they may. Whatever the outcome, you should know I have always valued your guidance.'

The contact was broken. With nothing more to be said, Kergis turned and took his place at the head of his squad. With a gesture, he set them moving. With half the night gone already, they could not afford to waste an instant. Seven kilometres of hard terrain lay ahead before they reached their target.

Despite that, as he and his men followed a path through the gully, he spared a glance behind him. Balat was consulting with one of his Scouts, his head nodding sagely as he corrected some of his men's positioning. A moment later the line of the gully turned, blocking Kergis's last sight of his old mentor.

Despite Balat's good wishes, he did not expect that the two of them would meet again.

In the end it was easier to infiltrate his men into the immediate vicinity of the Ignis Mons than Kergis would have expected. Although Balat's warnings of increased activity proved accurate, the sentries and patrols guarding the approaches to the enemy stronghold were surprisingly badly organised and half-hearted in the performance of their duty. Kergis did not doubt that the enemy's troops would fight fanatically to the last man to repel an Imperial invasion. But when it came to the more drudging tasks of soldiery, the night patrols and the long boring hours on watch, the enemy's lack of discipline told against them.

Even as Kergis and his men moved to within sight of the lower slopes of the Mons, the same defects of organisation among the enemy's defences were readily apparent. Any halfway competent commander would have ordered the ground of the lower slopes bulldozed and cleared so as to provide open fields of fire for the defenders' guns. As it was, the entire area was littered with rocky outcrops and dense patches of wiry scrub, as well as the occasional low ridge of dried lava.

The landscape provided Kergis and his men with ample cover as they made their way closer to their target. Similarly, the laxity of the enemy sentries meant they were able to reach the very edge of the slopes without having to once unsheathe their knives.

Suddenly, as Kergis crept onto the foot of the Mons, he heard voices approaching. Careful not to make any noise, he signalled to his men to stay in cover and sought refuge in the shadow of a weathered boulder. As the voices came closer he crouched in the darkness, waiting. His knife was in his hand, the blade smudged with volcanic ash to dull its reflection.

There were two of them. As the enemy sentries drew nearer, he was able to distinguish their voices and footsteps. They were arguing quietly amongst themselves, making no attempt to hide their presence. Listening as he waited, Kergis learned they had been assigned to sentry duty as punishment for failing to recite the litany properly during a rite of offering on a recent day of worship; a collective failure that each one blamed on the other.

As the footsteps came closer, Kergis was struck by the banality of their evil. From their conversation it was clear the rite they were referring to involved the blood sacrifice of innocent victims to the gods of Chaos. Yet, the sentries were more concerned with a petty grievance against their immediate superior in the cult hierarchy.

'It ain't right that Sinner Grell punished us,' the one on the left said. 'The litany's long and the Hierarch speaks so fast it's hard to keep up. I bet Sinner Grell don't know it no better than we do. He had the easy part, holding the salver for catching the blood. He ain't careful, somebody will tell the Hierarch what he does with the sacrifices before we kills 'em.'

They were his last words. Waiting until the sentries had walked past him, Kergis was on him in an instant. Clamping a hand over the man's mouth, he dragged the knife across his throat.

Hearing the sound of movement, the second sentry turned towards his partner. His eyes widening as he saw Kergis, he tried to raise his autogun. He was dead long before he could fire the weapon. Gurban emerged from the darkness behind him to press a hand over the second man's mouth and cut his throat just as Kergis had done to the first.

'We will take the bodies with us,' Kergis whispered to Gurban once he was sure the killing of the sentries had not raised any alarms. 'They are less likely to be discovered if we dump them in the tunnels.'

Gurban nodded. Kergis had made no gesture of thanks to the other man for killing the second sentry, nor would Gurban have expected one. Aware that his squad were nearby, Kergis had assumed that one of them would back him up when he launched his attack. If the position had been reversed and it was one of his men who had been left exposed by the sudden arrival of the sentries, Kergis would have behaved exactly as Gurban had done in supporting him. Such behaviour was taken for granted among the White Scars. As brother Astartes, they relied on each other implicitly.

Nearby, the rest of the squad emerged from cover. Motioning them to him, Kergis waited until they were huddled around him before he issued his orders.

'The entrance to the tunnels is that way,' he whispered, pointing to an area of the slope that was close at hand. Looking at the helmeted faces the men around him, he gave orders to several of the squad members in turn. 'I will take the lead. Osol, you will help Gurban carry the bodies. Doshin, shift some of the dust to cover the blood splatter from the sentries, then take a piece of scrub bush and use it to obscure our tracks. Arik, you're with me. The rest of you, follow behind us.'

The huddle dissolved as the squad followed his commands. Climbing the slope with Arik by the side of him, Kergis kept his senses sharp for any sign of the enemy. The lower reaches of the Ignis Mons were little more than a gentle incline, but the slopes of the volcano soon began to grow steeper.

Ahead, two kilometres above them, Kergis could see the smoking peak of the Mons. It was lit by a dull red glow from the lake of lava hidden inside it. They were on the northern slope, out of sight of the geothermal complex which was situated on the southern one, but they maintained the same habits of stealth that, so far, had taken them within striking distance of their objective. The most dangerous leg of the journey still lay ahead of them.

'I can see the hatchway,' Arik whispered over a secure channel on their vox. 'It is in the low depression thirty metres away, at three degrees south-south-west.'

'I see it, too,' Kergis replied. 'Signal to the others to stay back in case the enemy have left any unpleasant surprises waiting for us.'

While Arik communicated his orders to the rest of the squad by gesture, Kergis made his way cautiously across the slope.

The cone of the volcano and the ground beneath it were riddled with man-made tunnels designed to bleed off the hot magma and prevent the Ignis Mons from erupting. The same tunnels channelled the excess magma to heat steam which was then re-directed to drive turbines to create an energy supply for the planet's cities. Based on the information gathered from debriefing some of the Imperial refugees who had escaped the fall of Tephra VII, the invasion forces had learned some of the tunnels beneath the Ignis Mons had not been used for centuries. Assuming the intelligence was right, Kergis and his men could use the tunnels to sneak into the power complex right under the noses of the enemy.

The access hatchway into the tunnels was set in a shallow well of plascrete to help protect it from the elements. Despite such precautions, its surface was pitted and scarred with rust. It was clear it had not been opened for some time.

Checking the surface of the hatchway for heat, Kergis took hold of the wheel-like opening mechanism and experimentally tried to turn it. The hatchway held fast, its inner workings rusted in place by centuries of disuse. Kergis increased the pressure incrementally, wary in case his gene-wrought strength caused the wheel to shear off in his hands. With a protesting squeal of rusted metal, the wheel started to move. Slowly, he managed to turn it half a revolution.

The shriek as the hatch finally came free seemed as loud as a gunshot in the silence of the night. Expecting to see sentries hurrying towards their position, Kergis waited with Arik beside him, carefully scanning their surroundings. To his surprise, there was no sign of activity. Evidently, the remaining sentries had been too far away to hear it.

'Quickly,' Kergis said, easing himself into the tunnel. 'The moment I give the all clear, tell the men to follow me. I don't want to test our luck out here any longer than necessary.'

Inside, the tunnel was dark and quiet. There was a vaguely sulphurous smell in the air; a side-effect, Kergis assumed, of the proximity of a live volcano. It was clear, however, that the intelligence from the refugees had been correct. The air was warm and damp, but it was obvious the tunnel had not been put to work in recent times.

The inner surface of the tunnel was rough with a residue of dried lava, but overlaying it was a thick layer of undisturbed dust. The tunnel itself was over four metres tall. Standing with ease once he had dropped through the hatchway, Kergis signalled to Arik above him that everything was all right.

Soon, the rest of the squad had joined him in the tunnel. As the last man dropped through, Doshin shut the hatchway behind him. Meanwhile, Gurban and Osol dumped the bodies of the dead sentries to one side of the tunnel.

'We will move forward in single file,' Kergis told his men once they were ready to proceed. 'If we meet the enemy, we will fight with swords and knives. We will only use our bolt pistols as weapons of last resort. Remember, the sound of a shot might echo across the whole length of these tunnels, alerting the enemy.'

The squad nodded their understanding. Turning, Kergis faced into darkness. The tunnels were even blacker than the night had been outside.

He and his men carried compact luminators attached to the sides of their helmets. He gave a signal to switch them on. The dull glow of the luminators revealed the shape of the tunnel in their immediate vicinity. Beyond it, there lay yet more darkness.

They had been furnished with a layout of the tunnel network courtesy of an ancient survey blueprint from the planetary archives; one of thousands of such documents the planetary governor and his retinue had taken with them when they fled the fall of their world to Chaos. Ordinarily, Kergis would have expected a governor to spend more time defending his planet and less saving some mouldering parchments, but on this occasion he supposed the man's weak backbone had played in his favour. Always assuming, of course, that the tunnels had not been substantially altered in the millennia since the survey had been completed.

'Move out,' he voxed his men.

As one, they marched forward into the darkness.

An hour later, they had made steady progress. The tunnel layout recorded in the survey blueprints had proven to be accurate, allowing the squad to move faster than Kergis had expected. The luminators supplied only limited radiance, but this was not an insurmountable obstacle. Within minutes, the White Scars' eyes had begun to grow accustomed to the gloom. Soon, they could see as well in the tunnels as they had in the moonless night on the approach to the Ignis Mons.

By Kergis's reckoning, they were another three quarters of an hour from their destination.

'We need to pick up speed,' he told his men. 'The assault will be easier if we time our attack to the middle of the workers' shift, when they are likely to be at their most tired and dull-witted. From now on, double-time.'

Uncomplaining, the squad followed his example and broke into a jog.

Their objective was the control room which oversaw the operation of the lava tunnels. It was the most critical part of the facility. The White Scars were carrying a number of demolition charges with them; more than enough, he hoped, to destroy the control systems responsible for directing the movement of lava. Back on the strike cruiser, Goju, the Techmarine attached to their company, had given the squad an in-depth briefing, highlighting what each piece of the control apparatus looked like and where to place the charges to achieve the greatest effect. If the White Scars were successful in their plan of sabotage, the geothermal complex would be destroyed.

It would be harsh medicine for the people of Tephra VII. Assuming the invasion was a success, the newly liberated population in the western regions would be left without power. But the needs of victory outweighed any other consideration. First, Tephra VII would have to be liberated from the yoke of Chaos.

Compared to that noble aim, anything else was of secondary importance.

The White Scars had travelled another half a kilometre before they discovered the tunnels had guardians. Hunters by nature, these guardians did not practise the lax habits of the sentries protecting the slopes of the Mons. They did not announce their presence with loud footsteps or idle conversation. They were not even human.

Kergis and his men had reached a place where the tunnel they were following suddenly opened out into a broad, empty space at least a hundred metres long and an equal distance wide. The ceiling high above was partially hidden in the gloom, but Kergis could see it was gently rounded, while the floor of the chamber was rough and uneven due to a coating of dried lava.

Entering cautiously into the hemispherical expanse, Kergis noted that the walls were dotted with the entrances of dozens of other tunnels, some of them set high above the floor of the chamber.

'What is it, do you think?' Gurban asked as he followed Kergis into the open. In keeping with Chapter tactics, the rest of the squad had stayed back at the mouth of the tunnel, ready to cover them in the event of an ambush.

'Some kind of overflow chamber, perhaps?' Kergis shrugged. 'If Goju was here, we could ask him.'

Summoning up the tunnel blueprints on his helmet display, he checked for the chamber in the layout. There was no sign of it.

'Whatever it is, it was built after the survey blueprints were made. Still, it doesn't look as though it was created recently. The stonework appears ancient. What does the auspex say?'

'The area reads clear,' Gurban said, grimacing as he checked the handheld unit he was carrying. 'But the reading may be unreliable. The tunnel walls are warm, hot even in places. I think some of these disused tunnels run parallel to pockets of lava. The temperature fluxions are confusing the auspex.'

'Understood,' Kergis said. He contacted the rest of the squad by vox. 'The auspex readings are unclear. Gurban and I will remain on point. Osol, you'll cover the others as last man. The rest of you, spread out. We move with caution.'

Blades at the ready, the White Scars fanned out across the chamber. Taking the lead with Gurban at his side, Kergis followed the lessons he had first learned as a Scout, then later as a battle-brother under the tutelage of Balat.

Given the proliferation of tunnels entering into the chamber, there were dozens of places an ambusher could hide. Rather than allowing his attention to become fixated on any particular point, Kergis broadened his perception and tried to take in the totality of his surroundings, relying on his armour's autosenses to supply him with a continuous feed of details. Above all else, he attuned himself to respond to any sign of movement – be it sight or sound – from the various tunnel mouths around him. At the same time, he listened for a warning shout from any of his fellow White Scars, each of whom acted as an extra set of eyes and ears for their brothers.

In the end, it was the smell that warned him of the enemy's presence. He picked up on a rank odour. It was only the merest trace. An animal stench, familiar yet elusive.

'Contact!' Gurban yelled a warning as the proximity alert on the auspex in his hand burst suddenly into noisy life. 'I make a dozen at least. They are all around us...'

The rest of his words were lost as the first of the attackers emerged from their hiding places to ambush the White Scars.

Kergis caught a blurred glimpse of slavering jaws as their owner leapt towards him. He responded with a sweep of his sword, the blade of the power weapon sizzling eagerly through the air as it hurried to meet its target. The blow caught the creature in the flanks in mid-leap. Kergis heard the attacker scream as his armour was splashed with hot alien gore.

Amid the stench of blood he smelled the same rank odour he had sensed before, stronger this time. It was a charnel smell of malice and corruption, one he recognised from bloody encounters on a dozen different worlds.

A second creature emerged from a nearby tunnel and bounded towards him. This time, given more opportunity to ready his defence, Kergis was able to take in the full nature of the creature as it charged. To any man who was not Astartes, it would have seemed a source of terrifying horror; a thing of nightmare given swift and shrieking life.

The beast was perhaps two metres long. Its body was lean and hungry, with powerful rippling muscles and a head that seemed too large for its torso. Its legs ended in sharp claws that gouged scratches into the surface of the ground as it ran. The oversized head ended in a long snout set with a row of massive, interlocking fangs. The first beast had been covered in matted fur, but this one was disturbingly hairless. Its skin was a leprous ashen shade of grey.

As the creature began its death-leap towards him, Kergis saw a pair of bony hooks emerge from concealed sheaths on its shoulders, ready to strike in unison with its jaws. Holding to the last moment with the confident assurance of a skilled swordsman, Kergis waited until the creature was almost upon him before he lashed out with his sword.

The blow caught the beast in the centre line of its skull. The head and brain were split down the middle, killing it.

Propelled by momentum, the dead creature's body continued moving. Sidestepping it with ease, Kergis heard it flop to the ground behind him.

In the brief breathing space accorded by the death of the second attacker, he snapped a quick glance towards his men. Behind him, the rest of the squad were each busy with their own battles, fighting with knives and whirring chainswords against the teeth and claws of a horde of similar monsters.

Kergis turned, intent on offering aid to his brothers. Suddenly, he felt a blow hit his side. Caught unawares, it knocked him from his feet.

Too late, he realised the creatures attacked in *threes*.

Falling to the ground, Kergis found himself looking up at a pair of red, rage-filled eyes. The third beast was bigger than either of its two fellow hunters. It had Kergis on his back, its weight pressing down on his chest. His sword arm was held gripped in its jaws. Kergis tried to pull the arm free, but the creature's hold was too strong.

As he struggled, it bit down harder into his arm. Incredibly, Kergis saw the teeth had made an impression on the ceramite skin of his armour. A minute series of cracks had begun to appear in the armour's surface. Kergis would have hardly thought it possible, but the creature gave every impression of being able to bite through his armour if he gave it long enough. Unable to bring his sword to bear as long as his right arm was in its grip, Kergis's left hand scrabbled to free his knife, then stabbed the creature with all his strength.

He felt a brief moment of resistance as the blade cut through the beast's tough outer skin before sliding deep into its body. The monster seemed indifferent to the blow; if anything, its grip on his arm tightened.

Kergis pulled out the knife and stabbed it again. And again. The blade of the knife arced back and forth in a rapid succession of blows, making a bloody ruin of the creature's side as Kergis fought desperately to kill it.

Abruptly, his efforts were rewarded. Still gripping tightly on his sword arm, the beast closed its eyes and died.

Kergis's view of his fellow White Scars was obscured by the body of the creature on top of him, but as he recovered his breath he became dimly aware the struggle around him had been brought to a close. The noises of war, the battle cries of his men and roars of the creatures had faded. In their place he heard a strange, mournful howl echo in the distance.

Unsure of the sound's origin, Kergis pushed the creature's bulk to one side. Unable to break its death-grip on his arm, he managed to work his power sword free and took it in his left hand. Then, activating the blade, he sliced through the upper and lower jaws of the dead animal's snout just below the point where they gripped his arm.

With nothing left to maintain their hold, the two parts of the severed snout came away. Looking down at the indentations that the beast's fangs had left in his armour, Kergis could not help but wonder how much longer it would have taken the monster to crack through his defences.

Now that the beast was dead, Kergis could see it was different from its fellows. Gazing at the dozen or so creatures lying dead around the chamber, he observed that each individual bore only the vaguest signs of kinship to the others. He saw fur and armoured scales, retractable claws and envenomed fangs, poison-weeping musk glands and iridescent insect eyes; sometimes all combined in the body of a single creature. For all that, however, there was a resemblance between each and every one of them, no matter how slight. It was as though each of the monsters had been badly drawn from memory to the same basic design.

'Ugly beasts, aren't they?'

It was Arik. Looking up, Kergis saw the rest of the squad had gathered around him. He was relieved to see there were no casualties among them. Despite the deadly nature of their opponents, his men had passed through the fight unscathed.

'What were they?' Osol asked. He was the youngest man in the squad, with barely half a decade as a battle-brother behind him.

'A hunting pack,' Kergis replied. 'A Chaos warband may raid on dozens, even hundreds of worlds. Sometimes, they capture particularly fearsome examples of the local animals, predators especially. Some they use for sport, but others they breed together, creating hybrid monstrosities that they train as hunting packs. Making use of the powers of Chaos, they can combine even completely different animals, creating chimera creatures like these. We have fought them before, maybe a dozen times. Each time the creatures look different. But the smell is always the same.'

'They must have left them down here because they knew the tunnels would be a target for infiltrators,' Arik said. 'You realise the noise of the fight may have warned the enemy of our presence?'

'No,' Kergis shook his head. 'It doesn't necessarily follow. We are deep underground, and none of us fired our bolt pistols. The enemy may not have heard the battle at all. Or, if they did, they may rely on the hunting pack to have killed us. What concerns me more right now is the howling.'

The sound had continued, growing louder as the creature making it moved closer to their position. In his long service as an Astartes, Kergis had never heard anything to match it. It was a keening sound, long and ululating, rising and falling in pitch in a harsh, continuous wail. The noise of it was grating, even disturbing.

Kergis would have preferred to believe no human voice was capable of making such a sound, but the howling seemed to speak wordlessly of all too human emotions. Kergis recognised a sound born of rage and insanity. There was a squall of white noise underlying it, which seemed to indicate the howl was issuing from a vox unit, but there was no mistaking the raw seething emotion behind it. Kergis heard tones of outrage, grief and betrayal. Above all else, he heard the sound of madness.

'It started in the middle of the fight,' Arik said. 'When the hunting pack heard it, they fled.'

'Spread out,' Kergis ordered his men. 'It's getting closer. Given that sound, we can assume it's hostile. And if it scared the hunting pack away, it must be dangerous.'

The howling grew louder. Although the sound echoed around the chamber, it was clear which tunnel it was coming from. Taking a step forward, Gurban raised his auspex and tried to gain a reading.

'It's big,' he said. 'From the size of the contact, it must be barely able to fit in the tunnel.'

'All of you, check your bolt pistols and melta charges,' Kergis said as Gurban stepped back to join the line of White Scars standing in the centre of the chamber. 'But only use them if you hear my order. If possible, we will try to use our blades.'

Privately, he doubted the White Scars' swords were up to the task of killing the thing lumbering its way towards them, but he was willing to try so long as there was any chance of maintaining the element of surprise in their mission.

The volume of the howling had risen to an ear-splitting roar. Kergis pressed the activation rune on his power sword as a dark shape emerged from the mouth of the tunnel.

As the creature stepped forward, Kergis saw it clearly for the first time. He realised he and his men were in deep trouble.

His name was long forgotten. If his current captors referred to him by any name at all they called him Shulok-ahk-alim-neg, a phrase meaning 'he howls without end' in the corrupt argot favoured by the warband's leaders. Or else, they simply called him Shulok.

He did not care. His true name had been lost on the day his brothers betrayed him.

Once, he had been handsome and well featured. He was strong of limb and purpose. He was Astartes. When his brothers rebelled against the Emperor, he had followed their example. Ultimately, they had been defeated in their struggle, but they consoled themselves with the thought they had helped deliver a deathblow to the Emperor and all His works.

The years would prove them wrong. The Emperor's followers refused to accept His demise. They placed Him on a golden throne, a corpse-god effigy to rule over a conquered galaxy. Incredibly, the Imperium He had founded prospered and grew stronger.

Angered by this inexplicable development, Shulok and his brothers had begun to raid the Imperium's territory. Bitter and vengeful after their defeat, they sought to destroy the Emperor's dominions in piece-meal fashion.

In truth, there was no longer any grand strategy or noble aim. Once, they had made war in the name of ideas. But defeat had changed everything. Now, they simply killed for killing's sake. They fought to bring destruction to their enemies, with no thought of high ideals or consequence.

To the mind of the creature who would one day become Shulok, they had been wonderful times. His memories had been blurred and darkened by the years, but he remembered the heady sense of freedom, of licence. He had fought across the stars with his brothers beside him. He had known glory and victory.

Then, one day he died.

He remembered it vividly. They had fought beneath a giant red sun. A warrior with a crimson fist had raised a bolt pistol as the two of them struggled in hand-to-hand combat. Point blank, the barrel opening of the bolt weapon seemed huge, a yawning chasm. He had tried to grab the pistol, to deflect the shot, but it was too late. There was a bright flash from the muzzle and his world passed to darkness.

After that, there came the betrayal. He awoke to find his body felt strangely numb. Puzzled by unfamiliar sensations, he tried to lift his arms to inspect them. What he saw once he did so made him cry out in anguish.

He had been encased in a metal shell. His body, too badly injured to be healed, had been entombed inside a cold sarcophagus, henceforth to serve as the central cortex piloting a hulking war machine.

Raging at his imprisonment, he had screamed for release. Alternating between fury and bouts of pleading, he had called for someone, anyone, to have mercy. Even death would be better than an eternity trapped inside a machine. He had begged to be killed.

His only answer had come with cruel laughter. Focusing on the sound, he had realised several of his brothers stood nearby. Standing at their head was their leader, the warsmith. He smiled, his expression insufferably smug and mocking.

'Kill you? I think not. You are a resource to us now, a valuable one.

And, really, you can't complain. We simply took you at your promise all those times you uttered our battle cry. "Iron within, iron without." Now, my friend, you truly are an iron warrior.'

It was then that the creature who would one day be known as Shulok began to earn his name. He started to howl, giving vent to pain and frustration as he strained against the chains his brothers had used to bind him.

From that day on, the howling had never ended. The men who betrayed him were dead and gone, killed in a long ago battle he could barely remember. But even with their deaths his captivity and his torment had not ended. Over the course of thousands of years he had been passed from warband to warband, traded as a chattel or captured as part of the spoils of war.

Through it all, the howling continued.

It had become a reflex. A man of flesh and blood cannot scream forever; he needs rest and sleep. But a machine knows no such limitations. After thousands of years, the vox unit in his war machine body still gave voice to the same keening, strident shriek.

His reason had long since left him, his wits broken in the centuries since his betrayal. If there was one saving grace left to him, it was that he could still take pleasure in killing his enemies.

In particular, he cherished the killing of Astartes, especially the heirs of the loyalist Legions who had taken the Emperor's side in the rebellion. He hated them most of all. They reminded him of all he had lost. Killing them gave him respite, creating a brief moment of joy that drowned out his pain and anguish, even if only for a second.

In recent days he had been accorded little opportunity for killing of any kind. Weary of his howling, his current captors had imprisoned him in the disused tunnels beneath the Ignis Mons. Left to wander alone, he had soon discovered the only creatures other than himself in the tunnels were the warband's hunting animals. He had tried to stalk them, to sate his need for killing, but they proved to be difficult quarry, too quick and wily to be easily caught.

The lack of killing had made his existence even harder to endure. Until, one day, the sounds echoing through his underground domain had brought news of the presence of fresh prey in the tunnels.

Soon, the roar of the hunting animals and the smell of blood had seemed to confirm his hopes, bringing him hurrying to investigate. Stepping forward from the confined space of the tunnels into open territory, he saw nine figures clad in white power armour emblazoned with a lightning insignia.

*White Scars.*

A thrill of anticipation ran through him.

The pistons of his leg hydraulics hissing like a pit of angry vipers, he strode forward into the chamber and made ready to kill them.

* * *

'Dreadnought!'

Forewarned by his auspex a split second before the metal giant emerged from the tunnel, Gurban shouted out a desperate warning.

The war machine was huge. Dust fell where its massive hulking shoulders had scraped against the tunnel walls. Still howling as it moved into the chamber, it advanced with thudding, foreboding footsteps. Its exterior was a dull gunmetal grey in colour, overlaid with riveted Chaos symbols in brass and copper. On one shoulder, Kergis could see an ancient skull insignia indicating the Dreadnought had once belonged to the Iron Warriors. The skull had been crudely scratched out and defaced, but the outline of the insignia was still visible.

Unlike the majority of Astartes Chapters, the White Scars had never made great use of Dreadnoughts. To warriors accustomed to the freedom of the plains of their home world Chogoris, the idea of being entombed in a walking sarcophagus seemed like a fate worse than death.

Despite this, as the Chaos Dreadnought advanced on his position Kergis was forced to grant that the machine was impressive. He did not doubt that a group of lesser warriors might have decided to flee rather than face the monster. But he and his men were White Scars. They were made of sterner stuff.

The Dreadnought came closer, eager to begin the fight.

'Switch to bolt pistols!' Kergis called out to his men. 'Rapid fire! Aim for the legs!'

Fanning out to create more room between themselves and their opponent, the men of the squad drew their pistols and began firing. Following their sergeant's order they aimed at the Dreadnought's legs, hoping to knock out the motive hydraulics enabling its movement.

It was an old lesson of the plains that an immobilised enemy was nearly as good as dead. When facing a more powerful opponent, the White Scars would often attempt to hamstring him in order to take the greatest advantage of their manoeuvrability on their bikes. Kergis realised that the tactic was less likely to be successful in the relatively confined space of the overflow chamber, especially as the White Scars were on foot. The most he could hope for was that if they destroyed the Dreadnought's movement capability it would allow them to outflank and overwhelm it.

Despite the hail of gunfire, the Dreadnought was unaffected. Almost contemptuous of the White Scars' efforts, it brandished the plasma cannon fitted to its left arm.

Kergis dived to the ground just in time as a stream of plasma scythed through the air over his head. Going into a roll, he came up and fired his bolt pistol at the war machine again. He aimed for the shadowed recess where its head met his body, hoping to find a weak point in the heavy armour protecting it from the front.

Meanwhile, his men had spread out in a wide circle around their

enemy. Adapting their more normal tactics to the situation, they fired
on the move, each individual Space Marine alternating between phases
of advance, retreat and sideways movement in an attempt to confuse
the Dreadnought.

Greeted with multiple, moving targets the Dreadnought seemed
briefly stymied. Until, seeking to make use of the opportunity presented
by the enemy's uncertainty, Osol moved behind the machine and made
a sudden dash for its back. In his hand, he held the round shape of a
melta bomb.

Guessing his intent Kergis almost called out a warning, but kept his
silence for fear of alerting the Dreadnought. His worst fears were quickly
realised. As Osol came within a few paces, the Dreadnought suddenly
turned, its legs remaining motionless as it pivoted its upper body
around one hundred and eighty degrees on its central axis. Catching
Osol by surprise, it smashed him to the ground with a blow from the
power claw on its right arm.

Using the heavy gauntlet as a club, it hammered repeatedly on Osol's
inert form. Attempting to rescue his battle-brother, Doshin swept into
the fray firing his bolt pistol. Turning once more on its axis, the Dreadnought moved with surprising swiftness. It raised its plasma cannon to
meet Doshin's attack, leaving the charging White Scar staring down the
muzzle of the weapon at nearly point-blank range.

'No!'

Activating his power sword, Kergis charged forward to intervene.

It was too late. The plasma weapon fired with a blinding light.
Doshin's head was atomised in an instant, leaving his body still standing, the seared flesh smouldering from the heat of the energy discharge.

Caught in the backwash of the blast as he leapt forward, Kergis's sword
strike was deflected. Instead of biting deep into the Dreadnought's arm,
he caught it a glancing blow on the shoulder. Shuddering as the crackling energy field surrounding the blade sliced off a layer of its metal skin,
the Dreadnought bellowed in rage and hit the White Scar sergeant with
a heavy, backhanded blow.

The force of it sent Kergis hurtling bodily across the chamber. He
landed with a jarring impact, skidding to a halt beside the cadaver of
one of the dead hunting animals. Pulling himself up, he saw his men
had increased their attacks against the Dreadnought to distract it from
going after their sergeant.

Kergis was about to charge back into the battle when he realised he
was no longer holding his power sword. Evidently, it had slipped from
his grip when the Dreadnought hit him.

Looking about desperately, he saw it lying on the floor of the chamber near the Dreadnought's feet. Spotting it, he almost cried out in
frustration. The sword was the most potent weapon he possessed. In
the absence of the heavy weapons his squad had given up to carry

explosives, it was the best weapon they had against the Dreadnought. Without it, there was precious little chance that he and his men could even hurt the machine, much less kill it.

For a moment, it appeared to Kergis that he and his men were doomed. He would fight to the last, they all would, but there seemed no prospect of their survival. Worse, their mission would be a failure. At dawn, when their brothers assaulted the city of Chaldis they would find the enemy shields were still in place. The likely result would be a bloodbath. The success of the invasion would be at risk.

Then, abruptly, he spotted something in the chamber floor that changed everything.

There was a spider web of cracks in the surface of the floor around the Dreadnought. With each crunching footstep more cracks appeared, adding to the pattern as the great weight of the war machine pressed down on the stone. More tellingly, Kergis could see tiny wisps of steam and smoke rising from among some of the cracks, almost lost in the thin clouds of dust that hugged the chamber floor. At the same time, he noticed the ground beneath his feet was hot to the touch. Looking down, he saw the floor was not composed of the same stonework as the walls of the chamber. Instead, it appeared almost identical to the rocks he had seen while travelling through the Cradle.

With a sudden burst of inspiration, Kergis realised the chamber he was standing in was a sphere, not a hemisphere. He and his men had mistaken a bed of dried lava for the chamber floor. It seemed likely there was yet more lava beneath it, red-hot and still liquid.

A dangerous plan forming in his mind, Kergis's hands scrabbled in the satchel he carried with him. Then, lifting his bolt pistol to fire a rapid series of shots, he charged across the chamber towards the Dreadnought.

'Pull back!' he yelled to his men as he drew closer to the machine. 'Keep firing, but pull back, all of you! That is an order! Leave this monster to me.'

With no time to explain his plan, he could only hope the habit of obedience was so deeply engrained that his men would follow his orders without question.

Ahead, it was almost as if the Dreadnought was waiting for him. Instead of firing its weapons, it spread its arms wide in a taunting gesture and encouraged Kergis to continue his charge. Sprinting closer as the bolt pistol in his hand ran out of ammunition and fell silent, Kergis let out an emphatic battle cry.

'For the Khan and the Emperor! For victory!'

The Dreadnought leaned its great bulk forward, ready to meet his charge. But instead of facing the monster head-on, Kergis changed tack. At the very last instant before he moved into range of its grasp he threw himself to the ground, relying on the momentum of the charge to carry him forward as his body skidded across the filmy, dusty surface of the lava floor. Catching the Dreadnought by surprise, Kergis slid between its articulated legs and emerged behind the machine. His momentum exhausted, he slowed to a gentle stop a few metres behind the Dreadnought.

The sound of its howling briefly changing timbre to a cry of rage at the trick, the Dreadnought turned on its axis and angrily moved its arm into a firing position. Levelling the plasma weapon at Kergis as he lay on the ground, it prepared to blast him to oblivion. In response, Kergis lifted a small, handheld remote detonator, making sure the Dreadnought could see it before he pressed the ignition stud.

Too late, the machine realised the White Scar had left something beneath it in his skidding journey underneath its body. Looking down, it saw the dark compact shape of a polyleather satchel lying on the ground at a point almost equidistant between its feet.

The contents of the satchel detonated with a roar that drowned out the Dreadnought's howl of anguish.

The explosion did not penetrate its armour, but it was enough to fatally weaken the ground beneath the monster's feet. With its arms flailing madly, the Dreadnought began to fall screaming as the floor immediately underneath it shattered and gave way, pitching it headlong into a suddenly revealed abyss of burning lava situated below the level of the chamber floor. For the first time in thousands of years the Dreadnought's howls of pain and anguish were replaced by the sounds of fear as it tumbled into a lake of fire. It made a splash as it landed, sending droplets of hissing magma flying into the air as it sank into the red heat of a flowing sea of lava.

Nearby, luck had been on Kergis's side. Although the floor had collapsed to within a few centimetres of his position, the ground had held firm underneath him. Rising to his feet, he saw that his sword lay on the floor barely a metre away. He reached over to pick it up. Behind him, the mouth of the newly created pit was obscured by a pall of steam and rising smoke, as hot air from the lava well met the colder air of the overflow chamber.

Casting a quick glance around him, Kergis could see that his men had followed his orders to pull back. He was the closest man to the edge of the pit. The remaining members of the squad were congregated twenty metres away, on the other side. As he leaned forward to grip the hilt of his sword, he raised his other hand to signal to his men that he was all right.

His presence of mind in immediately seeking out the sword saved his life as one of the Dreadnought's arms suddenly emerged from inside the pit and lashed through the air beside him. Caught by a glancing blow, Kergis was knocked to the ground as the monster's blindly groping claw latched on to his leg and began to pull him into the hole. From the other side of the pit he heard his men call out in horror as they rushed to help him. But they were too far away. With a remorseless strength born of a desire for vengeance, the Dreadnought began to drag him towards the edge of the abyss.

His free hand scrabbling at the floor as he tried to arrest his journey, Kergis turned on his side and attempted to bring the sword to bear. At last, his hand found purchase as the Dreadnought's arm tugged him onto the crumbling lip of the pit. Digging his hand into the relatively soft surface of the floor, Kergis managed to create enough of a handhold to resist the monster's strength.

He held on with all his might, his muscles aching with the strain as the Dreadnought fought mercilessly to pull him into the abyss. Suspended on the edge of the pit, he glanced down and saw the Dreadnought glaring up at him, its body half-submerged in burning lava. Flames and steam billowed from its body as the lava found a way past its defences through the crevices in its armour. The monster was being burned alive inside its own skin. Yet, still, it clung on to Kergis's leg, intent on dragging him to hell with it.

At last, Kergis was able to twist around and bring his sword to bear. He slashed downward, the descending arc of his power sword trailing bright flashes of sparks as the energy field of the blade ignited tiny micro-pockets of flammable gas rising from the lava. Unlike the last time he had struck the Dreadnought, this time the blade hit its mark squarely. It cut through the lava-weakened armour of the Dreadnought's arm, severing it at the elbow.

Its hold on his leg lost, the Dreadnought sank into the boiling lava like a tired swimmer. Its last sound was a final, despairing howl. Then, it was gone.

'Sergeant!' Kergis felt hands at his shoulder. 'Quickly, take my hand! We won't let you fall!'

It was Arik. Together with Gurban, the pathfinder had leapt across the pit to help rescue him. Soon, they had pulled Kergis away from the mouth of the hole. The three of them stood watching the smoke rising from the pit as the other men of the squad rushed to join them.

'That was a close one,' Arik said to Kergis, once he could see the sergeant had regained his breath. 'For a moment, I thought we'd lost you.'

'For a moment I thought the same myself,' Kergis admitted.

He paused for a second to listen. From further ahead he heard the sound of a distant klaxon, echoing shrilly around the tunnels. Evidently, the fight with the Dreadnought had alerted the enemy to their presence.

It seemed they no longer had the element of surprise on their side.

Osol was dead. In the aftermath of the fight, it became clear the White Scars had lost two of their number in return for the Dreadnought's death. Kergis had known Doshin had been killed, his head blasted to atoms by the thing's plasma cannon, but the death of Osol came as an unpleasant surprise. He had seen the younger Space Marine fall, but he had still harboured hopes that Osol might have survived the attack.

As it was, those hopes had been swiftly dashed. The Dreadnought's hammering blows had smashed through Osol's helmet and crushed his skull like an eggshell.

The death of both men was a bitter loss to the squad, but Kergis found the death of Osol to be an especial cause for sorrow. The young White Scar had been rough around the edges, but he had showed great promise. Kergis knew he was not alone in expecting that Osol would one day rise high in the Chapter.

Sadly, that promise would never be fulfilled.

'We have lost our brothers,' he said to his men afterwards, once they had taken the weapons and ammunition from the dead men's bodies, along with the explosives and their few personal effects. 'But we know all that was good in them is not lost. They will be remembered in the tales we tell around the campfire, and in the annals maintained by the Chaplains. And their gene-seed has survived their deaths. Through it, they will serve as the forebears of future White Scars.'

His hands were slick with blood as he spoke. As the ranking warrior among his men, it had fallen to Kergis to remove the progenoid glands from Osol and Doshin. He had placed the harvested glands into a cryo-flask and given it to Gurban for safekeeping. In time, the progenoids would be returned to Chogoris where the Chapter Apothecaries would use them in the creation of more new White Scars. Osol and Doshin were dead, but their gene-seed would live on.

While Kergis had performed the bloody work of removing the progenoids, the other members of the squad had removed their helmets as a mark of respect. Now, Kergis looked around at their faces, one by one.

'Remember the teachings of the Stormseers,' he said to his men. 'Even in death, our brothers are still with us. They sit at our shoulder. Their spirits guide us and watch us.'

'In death, their spirits are still with us,' the squad intoned quietly, echoing his words with their heads bowed and their voices as one.

It was a phrase and a sentiment taken from the ancient funerary rites still practised on the plains of Chogoris. The pressure of time meant that Kergis could do little except say a few words over the bodies of his dead brothers. If they had been on Chogoris, things would have been different. As warriors fallen in battle, Osol and Doshin would have been accorded the highest of honours. Instead, the current situation meant the best Kergis and his men had been able to do was to set booby traps to kill any enemy or scavenger who might try to defile their dead brothers' remains.

'We should be on our way,' Gurban said, once their preparations were done. 'The enemy will be looking for us, but they'll have a hard time searching all these tunnels. We'll have the best chance of reaching our objective if we push on now, before they can get the search properly organised.'

'Agreed,' Kergis nodded. 'But there has been a change of plan. I won't be going with you.'

If he had claimed the Emperor had appeared to him in a vision, he doubted it would have had more of an effect on his men. Their faces looked thunderstruck.

'I cannot explain the whole of it,' Kergis said, lifting a hand to stifle the squad's protests. 'I can only say that there is more to our mission here than you were told. I was given a second secret task, to be accomplished alongside the main objective of our mission. I had hoped to complete the main objective first, but events have become our master in this. Now the enemy knows we are here, the only way to achieve both tasks is to split our forces. Gurban, you will lead the squad to the main objective and complete the sabotage as planned. As for the second task, I will continue alone and complete it by myself.'

'But sergeant...' Arik's expression was aghast. 'You can't leave us now. At least let us know what is going on. If you have to leave, let us know that it serves some purpose.'

'I'm sorry,' Kergis turned to Gurban. 'The mission falls to you now. Remember the importance of what we were sent to do here. If the power supply to the void shield isn't interrupted the assault on Chaldis may fail. Our brothers are counting on you, Gurban. I have every faith you will not let them down.'

'I will not allow us to fail,' Gurban nodded, solemnly. 'But what of you, sergeant? When we are attacking the main objective, where will you be?'

'I will be hunting for the master of this place,' Kergis said. 'He has business with the White Scars that cannot be allowed to go unfinished.'

The overflow chamber was a juncture point in the tunnels, so it was there that Kergis took his leave of the squad. Using the survey blueprint to guide him he chose a tunnel that brought him closer to the main body of the power complex while his comrades followed a path deeper into the bowels of the facility. Their objective was the control room overseeing the operation of the lava tunnels, while his lay in the higher reaches of the complex.

All through the journey the sound of the klaxon reverberated through the tunnels. Evidently, the sounds of the battle against the Dreadnought and the explosion that tipped it into the lava pit had stirred up a hornets' nest of enemy activity. All too aware that this might make things harder for Gurban and the others, Kergis decided he would do what he could to ease his brothers on their path through the complex.

It was not difficult. The fact an alarm had been raised meant there were sentries and search parties moving throughout the area. Some of them would be in Kergis's way. By killing them as swiftly and noisily as possible he could achieve two aims at once: clearing the pathway to his own objective while simultaneously drawing the enemy away from the rest of the squad. If luck was on his side every enemy in the complex would soon be chasing him, leaving Gurban and the others with a relatively clear path to the control room.

Given the sheer number of enemy troops now swarming throughout the facility, it was not long before he was able to put his plan into practice.

'We have found the intruder!' the search party leader screamed into his vox. 'He is Astartes… wearing white armour like the blessed one… he…'

Kergis ended the man's words with a shot from his bolt pistol, the round hitting him in the middle of his forehead and detonating inside his skull.

There were five other men in the group, one of dozens of such search parties currently scouring the Mons. They were armed with autoguns and wore robes indicating their membership in one of the many foul cults which had flourished on Tephra VII since it had fallen to Chaos.

Even by the standard of the scum that frequently attached itself to Chaos warbands, they were poor warriors. They were actively searching for an intruder, supposedly on their guard, but Kergis had been able to get behind them with ease. He had encountered them a little while after he emerged from the lava tunnels into the complex proper. By then, they were the sixth or seventh group of guards he had encountered. He had killed so many he had begun to lose count.

The rest of the search party quickly followed their leader into death. Armed with his power sword, he made short work of them.

'Search Group Nine, are you still there? Nine, can you hear me?'

The leader's vox had fallen to the ground and continued to squawk long after its owner and his comrades were dead. Treading on it, Kergis crushed it.

Turning away from the carnage he had just wrought with barely a thought, Kergis hurried his steps and pushed on through the complex. Still guided by the survey blueprints he had been given as part of the mission, he travelled a twisting trail through the Mons, frequently punctuated by bloody encounters with small parties of the enemy garrison.

Wary of the danger he might be overwhelmed by sheer weight of numbers, he was careful to stay away from the main areas of the complex that were likely to feature the greatest concentrations of the enemy's strength. Instead, he stayed to the byways, relying on a network of maintenance tubes and access hatchways to take him through the complex. In this, the facility's very nature worked in his favour.

Inside, the power complex was a vast and uncoordinated maze of rooms and corridors, open spaces and storage areas. It had quickly become clear the enemy lacked the same blueprints that he possessed.

Without them, they could only trail in confusion in Kergis's wake while he journeyed unerringly to his target.

His objective was situated in the higher levels of the complex, in the area the warband's leaders had set aside as their quarters. As Kergis followed a twisting path through the tubes and hatchways, he noticed the sentries and guard posts appeared to thin in numbers as he rose higher through the facility.

To his mind it seemed curious that the enemy had chosen to leave their leaders' quarters relatively unprotected. A small, quiet voice in his mind wondered whether he was missing something. It was almost as if the enemy had left the path to their leaders' quarters clear, though any motive they might have had to do so eluded him.

Dismissing his thoughts as idle fancies, he continued on his journey.

Before long he found himself within sight of his objective. Moving quietly down a long corridor on one of the upper floors of the complex, he peered around a corner and saw two sentries standing outside a closed doorway. Based on the survey blueprints, and the intelligence gathered from Imperial refugees who had escaped Tephra after its fall, Kergis knew the doorway was the entrance to the private quarters of the leader of the warband responsible for garrisoning the Mons. Through those doors, he would find his target.

Watching the sentries from cover, he waited until their heads were turned away from him. Then, he struck. He ran towards them, all too aware of the sound of his footsteps as they boomed off the metal surface of the floor. It could not be helped. The time for stealth had passed, replaced by the need for quick, decisive action.

Hearing the footsteps running towards them, the sentries turned and raised their autoguns. Their response came too late. Having crossed the distance to their position in barely the time it took them to lift their guns, Kergis lashed out twice with his power sword. In those two movements, the sentries were dead.

Cautiously, Kergis tried to open the doors into the warband leader's quarters and found them unlocked. Pushing them ajar as quietly as possible, he advanced silently into the chamber beyond. He saw a room decorated in a strangely spartan manner. There were almost no furnishings, beyond a metal cot at one end of the room and a chair situated in the centre. Kergis noticed they were sized for Astartes rather than ordinary humans. The rest of the room was bare. There was evidence the walls had once been decorated with friezes and mosaics, probably Imperial in nature, but they had been roughly gouged and chopped from the surface, leaving a detritus of dust and plaster sitting on the floor.

His sword and bolt pistol at the ready, Kergis moved further into the room.

'Hello, arban,' a familiar voice said behind him.

\* \* \*

'Borchu?' Kergis had said two days earlier as he stood with Jurga Khan in the strategium, staring at the reconnaissance pict of the armoured figure.

'Yes, it is him,' Jurga Khan agreed, nodding. 'You see now why I thought it best to give you this mission? Borchu was in your squad.'

'But he is dead,' Kergis said, his voice disbelieving. 'He was killed in the caverns of Nephis-Ra. I saw him die myself.'

'His body was never recovered,' the Khan reminded him. 'I have read your battle report. His body was lost in a cave-in after he had been felled by enemy fire. That section of the caverns was destroyed three days later when the enemy unleashed a captured Deathstrike armed with a plasma warhead. It was assumed Borchu's body was annihilated in the blast with everything else.'

The Khan's expression darkened.

'It now seems that assumption was in error.'

'But he was dead,' Kergis said. 'I saw him fall myself. He was hit in the chest by a lascannon. It was at close range and the beam went straight through him, emerging from his back. There is no way anyone could have survived it – otherwise, I would have tried to rescue him. But it was pointless. The heat of the beam would have cooked his internal organs instantly.'

At first, Jurga Khan did not answer. Instead, he made a gesture with his hand and caused another pict to appear. It was taken at the same angle as the previous one, but it showed a close-up of the armoured figure's chest. Despite the grainy nature of the image it was clear the chest plate of the armour had been repaired by an unknown hand. The workmanship was poor and it was readily apparent to Kergis's trained eye that the damage which had occasioned the repair work had been caused by something which had drilled a fist-sized hole through the armour's ceramite surface. Even if he had not seen the wound inflicted himself, his decades spent on the battlefield would have told him precisely which weapon had created the hole.

A lascannon.

'It is impossible,' Kergis said quietly. 'I don't want to believe it, but I must accept the evidence of my own eyes. It is Borchu. Still, I cannot believe he would turn against us. It was his nature to be loyal.'

'He may not have turned on us,' the Khan replied. 'Despite appearances, Borchu may well have died on Nephis-Ra. We have fought enemies who have been possessed by daemons in the past. Normally, the daemons can only possess a living body, but all things are possible for the creatures of the warp. Perhaps Borchu's body was recovered by the enemy after he died and a daemon now uses it. Or perhaps Borchu's body really was destroyed and a daemon or some xenos creature has shifted its appearance to resemble him. Whatever the truth, it is an abomination. Our Chapter is dishonoured as long as a creature of the enemy wears the face of one of our fallen brothers.'

'Then, the dishonour must be avenged,' Kergis said, lifting a hand to indicate the figure in the pict. 'I will seek him out. Whether it truly is Borchu, or a daemon using his appearance, I will kill him. The Chapter's honour will be restored.'

'You understand the full ramifications of what you are saying?' Jurga Khan asked him. 'I have already agreed, on behalf of our Chapter, that we will lead the assault on Chaldis. I have also agreed to send a mission to sabotage the power complex on the Ignis Mons. I agreed to both these tasks before I saw these picts and spotted Borchu, but that hardly matters. As Khan my words must be iron. If not, if we fail in either mission, our company will be dishonoured. Similarly, whatever his true nature may be, we will also be dishonoured if we fail to act against this "Borchu".'

'I understand,' Kergis said, his voice hard and unyielding. 'And I know there may be a price to be paid. But no matter the price or what it costs me, I promise you I will kill Borchu – whoever or whatever he may be.'

'Hello, arban,' the thing wearing Borchu's face said. 'What, no smile of greeting? No warm words of welcome for a comrade you had thought lost? I am disappointed.'

Somehow, it had gotten behind him. Kergis had been sure he had checked every corner of the room before advancing, but the creature that was not Borchu had managed to find a hiding place all the same.

Cautiously, Kergis turned to face it. The room was gloomy, with few sources of illumination, but even as he stared at the armoured figure half-hidden in the shadows he knew at once it was not his former comrade. The face and the armour were the same, but the skin held a blue-white pallor Kergis associated with the recently deceased. At the same time, the creature's eyes rippled with seething and unearthly energies as though its physical form was barely able to contain the maelstrom inside it.

Even without these signs, Kergis would never have mistaken it for Borchu. In life his friend had been a good-natured, hearty fellow, always laughing. The creature before him now might wear Borchu's likeness but it was unable to copy his bearing.

'What is the matter, arban?' the thing said, taking a step forward. 'Don't you know me? Don't you recognise your old friend?'

'You are not Borchu,' Kergis replied, his expression severe. 'You may wear his face, but I know your real nature. You are a daemon, some carrion thing that stole his body. Nothing more.'

'Yes,' the creature smiled. For the moment it stayed where it was, not moving closer, but Kergis saw it carried a power axe in its hands. 'To be honest, I didn't think I'd fool you by pretending to be Borchu. But I had to try. Really, you'd be surprised how often even the clumsiest pretence will work. There is something weak in the heart of man. Show them the face of a friend, even one thought long dead, and they will believe almost anything. But you are stronger than that. Aren't you, *Kergis*?'

In response, Kergis was silent. He knew better than to be lulled by the daemon's words. His senses were alert, carefully reading the thing's stance for any sign it was about to attack. The magazine of his bolt pistol was full, but he was aware it would take almost a miracle to kill the thing with that weapon. His best chance would be to take the head from its shoulders with his power sword, but to do that he would need to move within range of the axe. He watched for an opening, waiting for the moment to strike.

'Aren't you curious as to how I knew your name?' the daemon's mocking smile grew broader. 'You must have wondered? Ordinarily, I'd tell you I learned it from Borchu himself. I'd explain I captured his soul as it was leaving his body, a split second before I entered his physical remains and made them my new home. It would be a lie, of course. But, again, you'd be surprised how often such simple untruths are effective.'

Under cover of its words, the daemon had moved one of its feet fractionally forward of its partner. Recognising the change as evidence it was preparing to attack him, Kergis waited for the daemon to shift its weight from one foot to the other. Once it did so, he knew the attack would not be long in coming.

'It is all a matter of how you play it,' the daemon continued. 'Typically, I'd say something like "Borchu always hated you, you know". And you'd wonder whether I was telling the truth or not. It is the nature of human beings to always wonder whether their fellows secretly despise them. If I told you Borchu really did hate you, it would only confirm your worst suspicions. I would not even have to sell the lie too hard. You would convince yourself I was telling the truth. Humans are such easy marks.'

For all Kergis's watchfulness the daemon nearly killed him then. Even as the White Scar waited, it attacked suddenly without having to shift its weight first.

Too late, Kergis realised his error. He had let the fact the daemon was wearing Borchu's body gull him into thinking it would act like a mortal opponent, not a daemonic one.

Leaping effortlessly across the room towards him, the daemon brought its axe down in a deadly arc. Kergis barely managed to dodge the blow in time. Unbalanced, he struck out with a sideways slash of his blade. The daemon parried it easily, before delivering a counter-blow with the butt of his axe-shaft that sent Kergis staggering backward.

The daemon charged forward to press home its advantage, but Kergis was ready. He lashed out once more with his sword. The daemon blocked it, but by doing so it had left the repaired section on the chest plate of its armour exposed. Even as the sword and axe locked together, Kergis lifted his bolt pistol and fired a salvo of shots into the daemon's chest at point-blank range.

The daemon screamed in rage and pain. Striking again with the butt of its axe it hit the bolt pistol and knocked it from Kergis's hand. It tried to follow the strike with another attack from the blade of the axe, but Kergis saw it coming. He leapt backward, landing with catlike agility as he put several metres between himself and his enemy.

'You know, that actually almost hurt me,' the daemon said, lifting a hand to inspect the damage.

The salvo of bolts had blown away the patchwork repair to the armoured plate, revealing a dark wound in the chest of the daemon's host body. Instead of blood oozing out, Kergis saw sparks of eldritch fire leak from the hole. For an instant, the sparks played around the daemon's probing fingers. Then, they were gone.

'Still, there's no real damage done,' the daemon grinned insidiously. 'Not like the last time we met. You think of it often no doubt, Kergis. The good old days, eh?'

Kergis found he was beginning to hate the creature's smile, not to mention its habit of making insinuating, viperous asides every time it spoke. At the same time, he realised he might be able to play the daemon at its own game; using words to distract it in the same way as it was evidently trying to distract him.

'We have met before?' he asked.

'Surely you're not trying to claim you don't remember?' The daemon's grin deepened as his Astartes opponent took the bait. 'Granted, it was decades ago. But really, I thought you'd remember. Of course, my name was different then. I called myself *Nullus*.'

'Nullus?' Despite his awareness that the daemon would say anything to trick him, Kergis felt a shock run through him. 'I encountered a possessed Traitor Marine on Quintus who called himself by that name. He served as a lieutenant to the daemon prince Voldorius.'

'Indeed, I did,' the daemon said. 'Of course, I did look different in those days, so I can understand that you were slow to recognise me. You remember, Kergis? You killed my host body on Quintus. Sometimes, it feels like it took an eternity for me to find another one. It can be a difficult business finding a suitable body. Which is why I was so happy when I came upon your dear, departed former comrade.'

'And that's why you stole Borchu's body? Revenge?'

'It was part of the motive, I'll grant you.' The daemon's voice was like a satisfied oily purr. 'I had already attached myself to the invasion of this world, close to Chogoris. It occurred to me if I made myself visible enough it was bound to bring the White Scars to me. Naturally, I had no way of knowing it was you they'd send. That was an unexpected bonus.'

'And you did this because I cut you down on Quintus?'

'Hardly.' The daemon rolled its eyes in a curiously human gesture. 'Oh, I'd hoped I would get to settle accounts with you one day. But my aim here goes far beyond any such petty annoyances. I have been an enemy of the White Scars for thousands of years. Does that surprise you,

Kergis? I have stalked your Chapter from its earliest days. I was there in the very beginning, on the plains of Chogoris, even before the Emperor came. I know your planet of old, and I knew your primarch.'

'Now I know you are lying,' Kergis told the daemon. 'If you really were such a formidable enemy, I would have heard of you. You forget, the White Scars have their own way of dealing with their foes. If you truly ranked as an ancient enemy of the Chapter, you would have been targeted long ago by the Masters of the Hunt for destruction. You would have been killed and your skull would be sitting on a pike along the road to Khum Karta. Your name would be known from the roster of the hunt.'

'My name? You don't know my name. Not my true name, at any rate. I didn't always call myself Nullus. I'll admit you won't find me mentioned in the annals of your Chapter or in the tales the Chaplains tell, but everything I have told you is true. I am an old enemy of the White Scars, perhaps the *oldest*. I fought against Jaghatai Khan on Chogoris, just as I had fought against many other petty chieftains on your home world. In the old days, the days before the Imperium, your people knew me, Kergis. They called me *Kagayaga*. You know *that* name, I'm sure.'

Again, Kergis felt a shock run through him. The daemon was right. The name was familiar to him, although he had not heard it for over a century.

Kagayaga. It was a word from the old Chogorian dialect. Literally, it meant 'the whisper in the darkness'. It was a name to conjure nightmares. In the ancient folklore of Kergis's home world, Kagayaga had been the title given to a mythical monster. According to the tales he was an invisible, bodiless horror; a malicious spirit who haunted the plains and sometimes stole into the hearts of men while they were sleeping in order to compel them to perform evil acts.

Even today, it was still common for mothers on Chogoris to warn their offspring that Kagayaga would come for them if they did not behave themselves. Kergis had heard the same tales himself in his own childhood at his mother's knee.

Kagayaga. It was impossible. Kergis did not know how the daemon had come to know the name, but he did not believe the creature's claim for an instant. Kagayaga did not exist. He was a fictional figure used to frighten children. A figment of his people's ancient imaginings.

It was clear the daemon was trying to trick him, to frighten him by evoking the terrors of his childhood. It would not work. Kergis was a White Scar. He was Astartes. He was beyond such fears.

'I see you know the name,' the daemon said. 'I thought you would.'

'You are lying,' Kergis replied coldly. 'Kagayaga is a name to frighten children, nothing more. He does not exist.'

'By all means tell yourself that if you find it gives you comfort.' The daemon's smile had grown even more smug and insufferable. 'But, really we both know the truth, don't we? I am Kagayaga. But then, I have used so many names it hardly makes a difference. I am Borchu. I am Nullus. I am no one. I am the voice inside your mind. The whisper in the darkness.'

The daemon moved a step closer to him, shifting the great weight of the axe lightly from hand to hand as though making a game of it.

'For reasons of my own I have a need for the body of a White Scar,' the daemon said. 'Poor Borchu's body is so badly damaged I won't be able to use it for much longer. If only you knew the effort I have to expend just to hold it together and stop his damaged organs from spilling all over the floor like rotten fruit. No, I need something *fresher*. Not too fresh, naturally. It's true I can possess a living host, but it is difficult. One has to find the moral flaw, a chink in the victim's soul, in order to gain entrance. No, what I really need is the body of a recently killed victim. Your body, for example.'

Without warning, the daemon suddenly leapt forward to attack him again.

Kergis was ready for it. He dodged the first blow, counter-attacking with a low strike towards his opponent's legs. The daemon sidestepped it easily, responding with an axe-head strike aimed at Kergis's chest. The fight continued, the blows raining back and forth only to be blocked or eluded as they struggled without either being able to best the other.

They were evenly matched in terms of skill, but Kergis realised the odds were stacked against him. The daemon held all the advantages. As yet none of its blows had connected, but Kergis did not need to feel the force of them to know the warp-abomination was physically stronger than he was. At the same time, it was tireless and seemingly immune to pain.

Kergis was Astartes, with all the benefits it entailed. At the root, though, he was only a mortal man, while the daemon was something darker, ancient and more powerful. Given enough time, he knew it would wear him down.

The monster had shown him its weakness, though. While it baited and mocked him, Kergis had seen the daemon's arrogance. Experience told him it was a flaw he could use to create an opening.

'I believe you are getting slower, Kergis,' the daemon said as the duel between them continued. 'That last parry was hardly of the standard I'd expect from an Astartes. You're getting tired, aren't you?'

'I am feeling a little extended, it is true,' Kergis replied, trying to keep the strain from his voice as he blocked another strike from the axe. 'But it is only to be expected. I had a bike beneath me last time I killed you. The extra running involved in this battle has taken its toll.'

'The bike was the only reason you won last time,' the daemon commented acidly. He might be immune to physical pain, but evidently Kergis's words had struck a nerve. 'This time, it will be different.'

'I agree,' Kergis came back at him. 'This time, I am not part of a larger White Scars army. I am not accompanied by the best part of a company of warriors, most of them on bikes. I am on my own, on foot, at a disadvantage. Yet still, I am holding my own against you. I see now my Khan was right in sending me here alone. It would have been a waste of resources to have sent a bigger force after you, when one sergeant on his own is equal to the task.'

Kergis let his barbed words hang in the air for a moment before twisting the knife.

'Perhaps you are Kagayaga, after all. A bogeyman whose name is invoked to frighten children. Scaring children would seem to be all you are good for.'

His words provoked an immediate response. Its face a mask of rage, the daemon swung its axe in a powerful two-handed strike intending to cut Kergis in half. Expecting the reaction, the White Scar dodged the clumsy blow and responded with a low, rising cut while the daemon was still off-balance.

His blow caught the daemon's host body in the midriff, slicing through armour and exiting just below the shoulder. Showing the first real sign of pain, the daemon briefly lost its balance and fell to its knees. Trying to regain its feet, it lifted its axe to defend itself. But, as it looked up, it saw the bright flash of Kergis's sword arcing towards it as the White Scar prepared to deliver the coup de grace.

'For Borchu,' Kergis said, as he brought the sword down and took the daemon's head from its shoulders.

It felt like a benediction.

Afterwards, Kergis would never know how long he stood over the headless corpse. With the destruction of its host body, the fell light of the daemon's eyes had been immediately extinguished. Nullus, or Kagayaga, had been banished back to wherever it was daemons went when their physical forms were destroyed. Kergis was left alone with the body of a friend.

Ordinarily, Kergis would have felt pride or exultation in the aftermath of victory. This time, he felt only sorrow. He had defeated the daemon, but though he had driven the thing from Borchu's body he was acutely aware of a loss to his Chapter.

Unlike Osol or Doshin, Borchu's gene-seed would never be used to create new White Scars. For all Kergis knew, the progenoid glands inside Borchu's corpse were still intact. But that same body had been possessed by a daemon, a thing of Chaos. It did not matter that the daemon was gone. Borchu's body was irredeemably tainted.

Similarly, Kergis suspected the record of Borchu's deeds would be quietly purged from the tales the Chaplains told to remind the White Scars of their fallen brethren. No one would want to be reminded of Borchu now. Whatever his achievements in life, his body had suffered ignominy and dishonour after his death. It did not matter that Borchu himself had been innocent of that dishonour. The tales the Chaplains told were as much lessons as anything else. There seemed no good lesson to be learned from Borchu's post-mortem disgrace.

It could not be helped, but to Kergis it felt like he had lost his old comrade a second time.

Abruptly, he felt a tremor run through the floor beneath his feet, bringing him back to the present. It was followed by another tremor, and another, each one more insistent than the last.

Kergis knew at once what it meant. Gurban and the others had succeeded in their mission of sabotage. They had destroyed the control systems responsible for holding the eruptions of the Ignis Mons in check. Once the damage had been done it was only a matter of time before the magma pressure built up to a critical level, resulting in an eruption that would engulf the power complex in a rising wave of red-hot lava. After being kept under artificial control for so long, it was likely the eruption would progress quickly. At most, Kergis supposed he might have ten minutes to escape the complex before it was destroyed.

Ten minutes. It was barely enough time for him to find his way out from the complex, never mind the fact it was teeming with enemy troops, none of whom would take it well that he had just killed their leader.

In all likelihood, Kergis expected to die on the Ignis Mons. He had suspected as much from the very beginning. He had known it was the most probable outcome once he had volunteered for his part of the mission. Jurga Khan and Balat had both said as much to him, at different times and in their own individual ways.

Yet, Kergis had accepted the potential sacrifice ahead of him gladly. The fact that the daemon-possessed Borchu was the leader of the garrison guarding the Mons had left the White Scars facing a conflict between duty and honour.

On one hand, the honour of the Chapter dictated the creature had to be destroyed. On the other, they were already committed to destroying the power plant – a mission vital to the success of the coming invasion. Unable to see any other way to achieve this dual purpose, and unwilling to let more of his brothers be put at risk, Kergis had accepted the mission knowing it would probably be his last. It was a suicide run from the very beginning.

Still, if he was to die on this strange world far from home, he would die fighting. Retrieving his bolt pistol and igniting the blade of his power sword once more, Kergis took a last glance at Borchu's body and turned for the door leading from the chamber.

Expecting to find dozens of enemy warriors waiting for him on the other side, he prepared for the onslaught, opened the door and stepped out into the corridor.

Unexpectedly, it was quiet.

It was empty except for the bodies of the two sentries he had killed earlier. Surprised at his good fortune, Kergis hurried on down the corridor. No matter how far he went there was no sign of the massed ranks of enemy fighters he had expected. The upper levels of the complex seemed almost eerily deserted.

Then, Kergis turned a corner and saw dozens of bodies lying strewn across a broad, open hallway. They were cultists, like the ones he had met earlier, and they had died with great violence. From the amount of autogun casings littering the floor it was clear they had fought savagely, but their killer had cut through them like a scythe through wheat.

'Hello, sergeant.' A smiling figure stood waiting for him in the centre of the hallway. 'I had hoped to catch up with you earlier. But it took longer to kill this scum than I expected.'

It was Arik. Staring at him in disbelief, Kergis realised he was the reason there had been no enemies waiting when he left the daemon's quarters.

'I discussed the matter with Gurban after we planted the charges in the control room,' Arik said. 'We decided it really didn't need all five of us to fight our way out of the complex once the job was done. And Gurban thought you might need a pathfinder. I realise, strictly speaking, we violated your orders. But I hoped you might forgive us if I helped you escape before the volcano erupts.'

'Perhaps I will forgive you,' Kergis smiled back. 'Always assuming you actually have a plan to escape and you aren't just hoping for a miracle.'

'A miracle couldn't hurt,' Arik shrugged. 'But I notice on the blueprints there's a landing pad at the top of complex. If we can reach it before the whole place is destroyed, we might be able to seize a shuttle.'

As though underlining his words, another tremor shook through the walls around them.

'All right,' Kergis said. 'You're the pathfinder. Find us a path out of this hellhole.'

Together, they ran down the hallway.

The sun was rising by the time they reached the landing pad, the first glimmerings of dawn painting the sky a vibrant red.

Having taken advantage of the confusion caused by the worsening tremors rumbling through the complex, Kergis and Arik fought their way to an ancient shuttle sitting on the landing pad. It was a light cargo lifter of the kind designed to ferry supplies and the occasional passenger to distant outposts.

Boarding the shuttle before the crew could lift off, the two White Scars killed them without breaking stride. Kergis took the controls, while Arik searched through the channels on the shuttle's vox for the telltale comms-chatter that would indicate the invasion of Tephra VII was underway.

Kergis had seen a fuel tanker parked beside the shuttle when they came on board. As he triggered the engines, he found himself hoping the tanker had finished its work rather than not yet started it.

In the event, the engines purred into life smoothly. Except for a few desultory bursts of autogun fire plinking against their hull, they took off without incident. Hurtling through the vast smoke cloud now billowing from the summit of the Mons, Kergis sped westward as the tremors shaking through the complex reached a final crescendo.

Sparing a glance behind him, he saw the eruption of the Ignis Mons. Lava issued from the summit and poured down the slopes, an inexorable and slow moving blanket of death.

There was no question their primary mission had been successful. The power complex, along with the body of Borchu, would be engulfed and destroyed. The void shields protecting Chaldis would come down.

After much adjustment of the unfamiliar controls of the shuttle's vox, Arik found a great welter of encrypted chatter across a dozen channels on Imperial wavelengths. Hearing it, they smiled in satisfaction.

The invasion had begun.

Somewhere, out in the desolate Cradle, Gurban and the other men from the squad would be on their way to rendezvous with Balat and his Scouts, before heading for a pre-arranged extraction point where a Thunderhawk would be waiting to take them back to the *Warrior of the Plains*. With any luck, Kergis and Arik would be there before them.

Kergis's smile grew broader when he thought of the surprised looks his comrades would be sure to wear when they arrived and saw him and Arik already waiting for them.

Today, at this time and place, it was a good day to be alive. The mission had achieved its aims. Hopefully, soon, Tephra VII would be free. A daemon had been slain. An old comrade laid to rest.

Kergis did not fool himself his current mood of contentment would last for long. Experience told him to enjoy it while he could, for he knew such times were fleeting. Soon, there would be new conflicts, new dangers, new battles. The galaxy was not made for times of peace.

In the grim darkness of the forty-first millennium there was only war.

# THE RELIC

*Jonathan Green*

The horde spread across the unsullied blue-white wilderness of the ice fields like an oily black stain. Filthy clouds of greasy smoke rose from the exhausts of fossil fuel-guzzling machines, sending sooty trails into the frozen air to mark their passing. Every warbike and cobbled-together trukk left a petrochemical smear across both land and sky behind it, marking the horde's progress across the polar wilderness as another region of the planet fell to the furious predations of the alien invaders.

An unstoppable tide of savage, growling machinery poured out across the riven glacier. Before it, still a league or more away, the stalwart line of armour that the Emperor's chosen had decreed would not be breached approached. Today – at this time and in this place, amidst the desolate ice fields of the Dead Lands of Armageddon – the Astartes would make their stand against the green tide.

Warbike outriders gunned their throttles excitedly, while those boyz clinging to the sides of guntrukks, wartraks and battlewagons cannibalised from captured vehicles of Imperial design fired off round after round from their heavy calibre shootas in their overeagerness to engage with the enemy.

The drop-pod fell from heaven like the wrath of the Emperor Himself. The force of its landing sent shuddering tremors through the iron-hard ice sheet, a network of treacherous crevasses fracturing outwards from the point of impact.

The echoing gunshot retort of the pod's landing still rumbling across the fractured face of the glacier, the armoured landing craft opened and from it emerged the instrument of the Emperor's holy vengeance.

Autoloaders clattered into operation as the barrels of an assault cannon noisily cycled up to speed. The four blunt digits of a huge robotic fist, easily large enough to crush an ork's skull, flexed and whirred, servo-motors in each finger giving it a crushing force equal to that exerted by a crawling glacier.

With heavy, pistoning steps, the revered Dreadnought emerged from the cocoon of its drop-pod, some monstrous metal beetle birthing from its adamantium shell, roused and ready for war.

Bio-linked sensors scanned the rapidly-advancing line of greenskin vehicles, the Dreadnought's machine-spirit-merged sentience processing the constant stream of information – everything from average velocities to weapon capabilities to wind shear – and waited. Experience won on a thousand battlefields across a hundred worlds – including this Emperor-forsaken rock in particular – came into play, recalled from the depths of mind-linked implants. The orks weren't going anywhere. He could afford to be patient. Revenge was a dish served best cold, after all.

Heavy weapons fire chewed the frozen ground in front of him. The foul xenos had seen him fall from the heavens on wings of fire like some avenging angel and now that he was in their sights they were directing everything in their crude arsenal directly at him.

Shells threw chips of ice the size of Predator shells from the bullet-pitted surface of the glacier, many raining back down to strike against the Dreadnought's ancient adamantium armour. It had stood up to much worse over the centuries. The ice shards shattered harmlessly against its hull, some exploding into powder.

As the orks drew closer still and their haphazard targeting devices found their range at last, the greenskins let fly with rockets, high calibre shells and even smoky flamethrowers in their eagerness to engage with the ancient.

The Dreadnought disappeared amidst clouds of sooty smoke and roiling flames, the glacier reverberating now to the explosions and impacts of the orks' weapons which were, in general, noisy and heavy on the pyrotechnics, but not all that accurate or effective.

And all the time the ork line surged forwards, steadily closing on the Dreadnought's position.

Preceded by a torrent of cannon and bolter fire, the Dreadnought stepped from the smoke of its supposed destruction, swivelling about its waist axis, raking the hurtling ork vehicles with its arm-mounted weapons. The standard that hung from its banner-pole was scorched black and still smouldering at the edges, the halo of iron spikes surmounting its armoured body glowing orange in the oily flames lapping at its pockmarked hull.

Three times the height of a man, larger than many of the ork machines and as heavy as a warbuggy, armoured with adamantium plates and carrying an arsenal that rivalled the firepower of a battlewagon, it would take more than that to halt this juggernaut's advance.

It took the Dreadnought's symbiotic machine-spirit mere nanoseconds to divine the ancient's position relative to the speeding ork vehicles and select a succession of suitable targets. The Dreadnought opened up with its assault cannon and storm bolter again, a hail of hard shells reaping their own whirlwind of death and destruction.

'Death to the invaders!' Brother Jarold of the Black Templars Solemnus Crusade bellowed, his augmented voice booming from vox-casters built into his Dreadnought body-shell. What little of him that was still flesh and blood spasmed in fury, thrashing and sloshing within the amniotic fluids of his sarcophagus-tank. 'Cleanse this place of the xenos taint, in the name of the primarch and the Emperor. Death to the defilers of Armageddon!'

The squadron of warbikes leading the Kult of Speed in its attack was the first to taste his wrath. Burning rubber shredded under the attention of the Dreadnought's assault cannon, sending several bikes and their riders cart-wheeling over the ice, as sheared axles and wheel-less spokes stabbed into the ice, flipping the screaming machines through the air to land in broken piles upon the iron-hard glacier.

Those orks unfortunate enough to land at Jarold's feet had limbs and skulls crushed beneath his relentless, pounding footfalls.

A burst of storm bolter fire found a promethium barrel lashed to the side of a wartrak. The fuel inside touched off, blowing the vehicle apart, spreading pieces of wartrak up to twenty-five metres away across the ice field.

With a series of hollow pops, the launchers arrayed across the Dreadnought's broad shoulders sent a fusillade of shells arcing into the pack of vehicles behind the disintegrating line of warbikes.

Unable to stop in time, some of the ork bikes skidded past the Dreadnought, and having already missed one target chose instead to rev their engines and plough on towards the advancing line of Astartes armour.

Three bikes crashed and burned as Brother Jarold's weapons-fire took them down, and just as many again collided with the wrecked vehicles.

Many of the ork drivers were horrified to discover that the Dreadnought still stood after their concerted bombardment of it, and swerved at the last moment to avoid the immovable hulk. But one wasn't quick enough and cleared the choking exhaust trail of another bike to find itself directly on top of the Dreadnought.

The warbike hit Brother Jarold with the force of a missile. Even as the bike hit him, Jarold grabbed hold of it with his huge power fist, the vehicle swinging up into the air in his grasp as its momentum spun them both around. The ork rider was still clinging to the wide handlebars when a direct hit from Brother Jarold's storm bolter ignited the contents of the bike's fuel tank, as he released the vehicle at the height of its rising arc. The bike spun through the air above him and became a fiery comet, annihilating another ork rider that was rounding on the Dreadnought as the bike crashed back down to earth.

The Dreadnought's deep strike insertion and deadly combination of

cannon and bolter fire had decimated the front line of the ork Speed
Freeks. And all the while, unheard over the roar of bike and trukk,
assault cannon and bolter, as well as the concussive booms of fuel-tank
explosions, Brother Jarold called down the wrath of the Emperor and
His primarchs on the heads of the xenos filth.

The promethium roar of crude ork engines was joined by the well-
tuned growl of the superior Astartes armour as the bikes of the Black
Templars' rapid deployment force and its supporting land speeder
squadron closed on the drop-pod's homing beacon.

If the orks had been surprised by the fury of the Dreadnought's initial
attack, it proved to be only a foretaste of what was to come as Ansgar's
Avengers – the strike force mustered in memory of the fallen Emperor's
Champion – engaged the enemy.

*Clouds of bittersweet incense swirled and ascended into the vault of the battle-
chapel, filling the cathedral space with a sparkling aromatic mist. Shapes
swam in and out of the constantly shifting vapours, giving glimpses of fluted
columns a hundred metres tall, skull and cross adorned buttresses and statues
commemorating the fallen of the Chapter.*

*The skull-set glow-globes had been dimmed and the forests of candles were
in the process of being snuffed out by a trundling cenobyte servitor while its
partner, following on behind, proceeded to trim their wicks and clear away
the crusted wax that coated the black iron candelabra, like a series of frozen
cataracts.*

*The sound of the pitted oak doors opening – the doors so old now the wood
was black – resounded throughout the battle-chapel like the boom of distant
gunfire. Chaplain Wolfram opened his eyes, finishing the prayer that was
on his lips. He rose to standing from where he had been kneeling before the
Solemnus Shrine, his eyes falling once again upon the empty indentations
where the Black Sword, the Champion's laurel-wreathed helm and the lovingly
ornamented Armour of Faith should have lain.*

*Wolfram turned, one armoured hand – every knuckle of the gauntlet
embossed with the Templars' black cross and white skull insignia, a permanent
memento mori to the one charged with watching over the souls of the crusaders
– closing around the haft of his crozius arcanum. The ancient artefact was both
a Chaplain's badge of office and a potent weapon in its own right. A disruptor
field generator was concealed within the wooden shaft of the relic, that one
simple addition turning the flared blades of the Templar cross that surmounted
it into a lethal power axe.*

*The sound of echoing footfalls on the stone-flagged floor of the cathedral
space carried to the Chaplain through the muffling clouds rising from the
glowing nuggets of flame-flecked incense smouldering within their braziers.
Chaplain Wolfram relaxed his grip on his crozius.*

*The booming footsteps came closer, the incense smoke parting as a colossal
shape, that was neither man nor machine but something of both, something*

*greater than either, stepped into the light of the candles that guttered in the breeze of its advance.*

Wolfram noted the battle-damaged banner pole and the deeply etched Gothic lettering upon the Dreadnought's hull and bowed.

'In the name of Him Enthroned on Holy Terra, well met, Brother Jarold,' he said. 'And what brings you to this place of sanctuary, still an hour from matins?'

'May the Emperor's blessings be upon you, Brother-Chaplain,' the machine-tempered voice of the ancient responded.

'You are not slumbering with your brother Dreadnoughts aboard Forgeship Goliath?'

'Now is not the time for rest.'

'But our recent endeavours on Armageddon have cost us dear,' the Chaplain warned. 'Rest is what is needed now.'

'I cannot sleep, brother, not when there is still so much of His holy work left undone. And besides, I have slept for long enough already.'

'Then what can I do for you, brother?' the Chaplain asked.

'I would seek your counsel,' the Dreadnought said in a voice like the slamming of sepulchre doors.

'From me, brother?' Wolfram asked, caught off guard for a moment by Brother Jarold's honesty. Ancients were usually the ones who shared their hard-won wisdom with the rest of the Chapter; they were not the ones who came seeking it from others. 'You are troubled?'

'Yes, I am troubled, Brother-Chaplain.' The Dreadnought broke off.

'Speak, brother. You have nothing to feel ashamed of.'

'But I do.'

'I see. You speak of the loss of Brother Ansgar.'

'I do, brother. When the Emperor's chosen one needed me most, I was found wanting.'

'You have prayed about this?'

'I have sat in penitent vigil ever since my return to the fleet. I have thought on Brother Ansgar's fate and nothing else.'

'I too have spent time in prayer and contemplation on the same matter,' Wolfram admitted.

'You have, brother?'

'I have. You cannot blame yourself for what happened. Blame the beast, the heretic xenos that blight the world below still. Purge yourself of your guilt in the crucible of war. Smite the xenos with bolter and fist and cannon, all in the name of vengeance. Use the rage that the Emperor has placed within your soul to bring down His wrath upon the greenskin. Show no remorse. Show the alien no pity and you will have nothing to fear.'

Silence descended between Chaplain and Dreadnought as the latter considered the former's words.

'So you believe that this is all part of some greater plan? His divine plan for Armageddon? For our crusade? For me?'

'I do not know, Brother Jarold,' Wolfram admitted with a shake of his head,

Space Marines

'but what I do know is that no one has come forward since to take on the mantle of champion, having received His divine inspiration, and there are plenty who would be ready for such a role.'

'So you believe Brother Ansgar is still alive.' The Dreadnought's augmented voice suddenly sounded strangely like that of a young petitioner, yet to be admitted to the brotherhood, desperate for reassurance.

'That is what I know. Somewhere, and perhaps only barely, but the Emperor would not leave us without a source of inspiration to lead us at a time such as this, with the conflict to decide the fate of this world still raging around us. And Brother Ansgar does not have to fight alongside us to inspire we of the Solemnus Crusade to great deeds.'

Incense-smoke coiled about the motionless form of the monolithic Dreadnought. When Brother Jarold spoke again, the vibrations of his vox-casters sent ripples through the curling smoke, creating new eddying patterns within it.

'Then my course is plain,' he said.

Chaplain Wolfram looked up at the scrollwork decorations of Jarold's Dreadnought-locked sarcophagus.

'This day I vow that I shall not rest until Brother Ansgar has been found and we bear him back in triumph, or that we might lay his body to rest and reclaim the relics of our Chapter – the sanctified weapons that are the most potent symbols of his office.

'I shall petition Marshal Brant to muster an army that we might avenge Brother Ansgar and our Chapter against the orks of the Blood Scar Tribe,' the Dreadnought said. 'And then we shall return to Armageddon.'

Brother Jarold surveyed the wreckage that was all that remained of the Speed Freeks expeditionary force. The kult's predilection for speed had proved their undoing. Stronger armour and better armament would have perhaps given them a better fighting chance against the inviolable armour of the Black Templars battleforce.

Sensors that saw in wavelengths ranging from infra-red to ultraviolet scanned the devastation searching for life-signs. If any greenskin had survived the Black Templars' wrath they would not remain alive for long.

The once pristine white wilderness was now befouled with the gouged ruts of tyre tracks, blackened mounds of snow and ice thrown up by the artillery shells of both sides, promethium spills and fossil-fuel slicks turning the ice desert black. Some puddles still burned, the oily smoke rising from them adding their own acrid pollution to the devastated wilderness. Impact craters pockmarked the glacier where some heavy shells had missed their targets; where others had hit, debris from large ork vehicles lay strewn across the snow.

The kult's battlewagon had met its end when the machine-spirit of Techmarine Isendur's personal Razorback transport targeted the battlewagon's primary weapon power cell. A single, directed pulse from the Razorback's twin-linked lascannon and the resulting detonation had not only taken out the gun-bristling battlewagon itself, but also a guntrukk, a warbuggy and three assorted warbikes.

This had also been the turning point in the battle, a devastating blow from which the orks never recovered. All that was left of them now were piles of burning debris, blackened craters in the ice and piles of crushed and eviscerated carcasses.

Brother Jarold stood at the centre of the devastation, amidst the splintered axle-shafts, buckled wheel-housings and twisted chassis of the orks' ramshackle vehicles.

Behind the imposing presence of the watchful Dreadnought massed the Black Templars of the Solemnus Crusade. That same crusade had set out twelve years before to avenge the atrocity perpetrated against the Templars' Chapter Keep on the world of Solemnus by the greenskins that fought under the banner of the Scarred Ork.

There were injuries among the crusaders, the most severe being the loss of a limb sustained by Brother Baldulf under the wheels of an ork warbike, although it wouldn't stop him from marching to battle alongside his brethren, his chainsword held high. But there were no brothers to mourn that day, to be marked on the roll of the fallen, maintained within the battle-chapel at the heart of the Solemnus fleet's flagship battle barge, the *Divine Fury*.

The Emperor was truly smiling upon their endeavours that day; for sixty-three verified enemy kills not one Black Templar had fallen to the aliens. It was all the proof Brother Jarold needed to feel vindicated that their search for their lost champion was the will of Him Enthroned on Holy Terra.

Brother Jarold gave thanks to the Emperor, the Primarch Dorn and Lord Sigismund, their Chapter-founder, that their sanctified boltguns had functioned fully during their battle with the greenskins and that not one of their war machines had been damaged beyond repair during the conflict.

The Black Templars land speeder squadron had decimated the ork bikes and trukks, the Rhinos and Razorbacks finishing off what Typhoon and Tornado had started, while the Space Marines bike squadron and two-manned attack bikes had harried those orks that attempted to flee the battlefield.

The bark of a storm bolter firing echoed across the ice field like the retort of a heavy artillery piece. It had a number of the Black Templars raking the mounds of debris and bodies with boltgun and flamer, seeking the source of the sound, ready to bring the fight to the enemy once again. Instead they found Brother Jarold, blue smoke coiling from the muzzles of his storm bolter – a weapon so large it would not look out of place mounted on one of the fleet's precious Predators or Vindicators. The body of a greenskin Jarold had targeted spasmed as it was blown in two by the mass-reactive rounds.

Techmarine Isendur approached Jarold. The Dreadnought dwarfed even the crimson-armoured Techmarine, whose twitching servo-arm

– which seemed to move with a life all of its own – made him appear even taller than the average superhuman Space Marine. Behind him, Isendur's servitor team were making repairs to superficial damage sustained by the Razorback in the battle, or keeping an unstinting watch over those working on the machine, depending on their designation and degree of sentient programming.

Sensing the Techmarine's presence before he had a chance to speak Jarold asked, 'Are our brothers ready to move on the objective again?'

'Affirmative, brother,' the other replied in that familiar emotionless way of his, that was so out of character when compared with the passion and zeal exhibited by the rest of the crusade's fanatical warriors. 'At your command.'

'How far do you judge us to be from our target?

'Twelve point zero-seven-six kilometres,' the Techmarine intoned. It had been remarked upon on more than one occasion that Isendur was more akin to the machines to which he ministered than his brother Space Marines.

'And the nature of the signal,' Jarold said. 'Is it still as it appeared from orbit?'

'More so,' Isendur said. 'As hypothesised, the anomalous readings detected from orbit are indicative of some form of primitive teleportation technology.'

Grim satisfaction warred with Jarold's overriding sense of guilt and barely-supressed rage. The memory of the moment Jarold witnessed the mech-enhanced greenskin warboss teleport out of the devastated mekboy's lab blazed within his mind as hot and red as the moment when he had been cut down by a rusting cybernetic claw. That had earned him the privilege of being encased within the Dreadnought shell that had formerly been the living tomb of Ancient Brother Dedric.

The moment Emperor's Champion Ansgar had been taken from right in front of him re-played itself through his mind for what seemed like the thousandth time…

*He saw himself closing on the alien tyrant again, a sphere of crackling emerald light surrounding the ork and his unconscious prisoner. He watched again as the green glare of the crackling shield intensified.*

*And then, just as his crashing steps brought him within reach of the xenos brute, with a sub-sonic boom the sphere of light imploded, plunging the ruins of the laboratory into sudden darkness. Only a retina-searing after-image remained, trapped within the sensor-linked optic nerves of Jarold's physical body, but of Emperor's Champion Ansgar and the alien warboss Morkrull Grimskar there was no sign…*

'Then the command is given,' Jarold said simply.

Wherever the orks were using their wildly unpredictable teleportation technology, there was the possibility that the re-constructed Grimskar, nemesis of the Solemnus Crusade, would be there too. And if the greenskin warboss *was* there, there was also the possibility that they would find Ansgar too.

Isendur made an adjustment to the signum he held out before him in one crimson gauntlet. Servo-motors whined as the Dreadnought turned to observe the Techmarine with its faceless sarcophagus front. 'Brother Isendur? Is there something else?'

'I am picking up another signal,' the Techmarine said.

'Another teleport signal?' Jarold asked.

'No. It is weak, like a resting pulse.'

'What is its source?'

'Bearing zero six-seven point three.'

'And what would you hazard is the nature of this signal?'

'There is a fifty-two per cent probability that it is electromagnetic interference caused by isotopes buried in the bedrock beneath the glacier,' the Techmarine explained. 'But there is also a twenty-three per cent probability that it is interference caused by the disruption of the planet's magnetic field by the teleportation matrix. One way or the other, probability tells us that it is likely not worth pursuing.'

'But what of the other twenty-five per cent?' Jarold enquired.

'There is a possibility that it is a signal from a dormant power source. But it is unlikely.'

'What sort of power source?' Jarold pressed.

'Like that of a dying power cell.'

'As might be found inside a Deathstorm automated weapons system. Or a Dreadnought.'

'It is increasingly unlikely but still a slim possibility,' Isendur persisted, not prepared to have his logic refuted. 'If our mission is to find the source of the teleport signal I would recommend that we move on that target forthwith and ignore this weaker signum reading.'

The knowledge that there was a possibility – no matter how slim – that the signal was the last sign of a lost brother Dreadnought, whether Templar or otherwise, played on Jarold's mind. Dreadnoughts were potent weapons of the Astartes Chapters and revered relics. An entire battleforce would willingly fight to reclaim a fallen Dreadnought brother. Only in the direst circumstances would a Space Marine commander abandon such a sacred relic to the field of battle.

To recover such a potent treasure, whatever Chapter it might belong to, would be of incalculable value to the war effort. Just one Dreadnought could help bolster the Astartes forces on one of Armageddon's numerous war-fronts, and who knew what impact that could have in the long term on the struggle for the contested planet.

'I respect your opinion, Brother-Techmarine, you know that. You and your brethren of the Forge have tended to me on numerous occasions, but you see only the logic of variables and algorithms. I have the benefit of experience and the wisdom of years and I disagree. We shall investigate the source of this other signal and then, when we have resolved what it is, we will press on towards our primary objective.'

'Very well, brother,' Isendur conceded. 'As you wish.'

The Dreadnought turned to survey the re-ordered ranks of the Black Templars' strike force.

'Brothers,' he declaimed, his voice booming over the burning battlefield, flurries of snow hissing as they melted in the licking flames of the promethium fires. 'The word is given. In the name of the Emperor, Primarch Dorn and Lord Sigismund.'

'Is this the place?' Jarold asked, scanning the blizzard-scoured ice valley. The ice sheet rose up before them to meet the frozen slopes of a ridge of razor-edged peaks beyond which curious green corposant flickered and danced across the sky.

'Affirmative,' Techmarine Isendur replied, consulting the signum in his hand once more.

The hulking black Dreadnought and the crimson-armoured Techmarine stood before a wall of blue ice as solid and as impenetrable as rockcrete.

'So where, precisely, is the source of the signal?'

'Six point eight-nine metres downwards. If we are to discover the source of the signal we are going to have to dig.'

'Then we dig,' Jarold stated bluntly.

'Leave it to me, brother,' Isendur said. The Techmarine signalled the waiting column. 'Brothers Larce and Nyle,' he said, summoning those two crusaders. Jarold understood what it was he had in mind.

Larce, flamer in hand, and Nyle, bearing his thrice-blessed meltagun, joined them before the wall of blue ice.

'Brothers,' Jarold said. 'Let the Emperor's holy fire cleanse these xenos-blighted lands.'

Techmarine Isendur directing their fire, Larce and Nyle hit the glacier with everything their weapons could muster.

Initiate Tobrecan brought his bike up to join them and directed a series of searing blasts from the plasma gun mounted on the front of his machine at the glacier. When the steam and mist cleared, Brothers Larce and Nyle stepped up again, while Initiate Isen drove his attack bike forwards, Gunner Leax turning his multi-melta on the metres thick ice.

The Space Marines' flamers and plasma weapons swiftly melted a shaft through the ice to the source of the signal Isendur had located via his signum. Steaming geysers of cloud rose from the hole in the glacier as the boiling water bubbling at the bottom of the pit re-condensed as it came into contact with the cold air.

'Now then, Brother-Techmarine,' Jarold said, standing at the edge of the cone-shaped shaft, 'let us see what lies buried here.'

Using his servo-arm to assist him in his descent, Techmarine Isendur clambered into the steaming shadows of the ice pit. The rest of the strike force waited in tense anticipation to see which would be proved right; the Techmarine or the Dreadnought.

Bracing himself within the shaft Isendur looked down at the shadow still locked beneath one last remaining layer of ice.

'You were right,' his voice rose from the bottom of the pit. There was no hint of annoyance or praise in its tone.

'I was right,' the Dreadnought rumbled with righteous satisfaction.

'Do we wake him?' the Techmarine asked, something like awe tingeing his words, as he stared down at the statuesque creation of frost-rimed adamantium beneath him. A faint red glow pulsed weakly behind the ice, and yet as regular as a heartbeat.

'He is a brother Space Marine.'

'He is a Crimson Fist,' the Techmarine testified.

'But our brother nonetheless. So we wake him.'

He remembered...

*Thunder rumbled over the ice fields and frozen, broken peaks of the Dead Lands. It was the crack and boom of heavy artillery fire. The iron-hard ground shook with the force of an earthquake, more so than it did at his own wrathful steps.*

He remembered...

*Rank upon rank of Space Marines, squad after squad of his fellow battle-brothers, marching against the enemy, their Chapter banners flying proudly above them. Magnificent in their regal blue power armour, their left hands blood-red – recalling the ceremony conducted at the initiation of new Chapter Masters in the former Imperial Fists Legion – their battle-consecrated boltguns cinched tight to their chest plates ready to deliver the Emperor's ultimate justice to the enemy.*

And he remembered...

*The war machine. A stompa, the rank and file troops of the Armageddon militia had called it. A mobile war-altar dedicated to the hated greenskins' brutal heathen gods. An icon to thoughtless bloodshed and mindless destruction.*

He remembered...

*Marching to war across the bitter wastes, shoulder to shoulder with his battle-brothers, the ork host charging to meet them, the glacier's surface fracturing beneath the greenskins' advance, the freezing wind as sharp and as cold as a blade of ice slicing the air between them.*

He remembered...

*Faced with insurmountable odds, a new strategy had to be formed, shaped within the heat of battle.*

He remembered volunteering, proud that he should be the one to bring an end to this conflict. He remembered sound and heat and light. He remembered dying a second time.

And then, amidst the clamour of battle and the cataclysmic roar of destruction, he heard a voice.

'Brother,' it said. 'Awake.'

\* \* \*

The dull red glow behind the visor of the Dreadnought's sarcophagus helm pulsed more brightly with every word the Dreadnought spoke. Its voice was phlegmy and cracked from age and lack of use.

'I am sorry, brother, but what did you say?'

A sound like vox-distorted coughing crackled from the ancient. Then the Dreadnought tried again.

'You are on Armageddon, brother,' Jarold replied. 'You are here, within the Dead Lands.'

The coughing resumed, rose to a crescendo and then subsided at last.

'No. When is it?' the ancient asked. 'My internal chronograph appears to be malfunctioning.'

Techmarine Isendur answered in terms precise to three decimal places.

The Crimson Fist was silent for several long moments.

'How long have you been here, brother?' Jarold dared to ask at last. 'Since the conflict began?'

'You mean to tell me that Armageddon has been a contested world all this time?' the Crimson Fist said with something like disbelieving incomprehension.

'Yes, since the abomination Ghazghkull Mag Uruk Thraka fell upon this world for a second time.'

'A second time?'

Jarold regarded the ancient suspiciously.

'Tell me, brother, how long have you been trapped here, entombed within the ice?'

Several moments more passed before the venerable Dreadnoughtwas able to speak again. 'Fifty years, brother Templar. I have been trapped here, lost, for fifty years.'

The vehicles had been parked up and the massed force of Brother Jarold's avenging angels had formed a circle of unbreakable armour. All were included, from the newest neophyte to the oldest initiate. The formation of the praying Space Marines served as a barricade against the biting winds that swept across the Dead Lands, stabbing at any exposed flesh with knives of ice. It affected the neophytes – Gervais, Feran, Eadig and Galan – worst, for they were yet to earn the right to wear the full power armour as worn by their brethren and their heads were exposed. But if the freezing wind caused them any discomfort they didn't show it. Weakness of the flesh was not permitted of a Space Marine.

Brother Jarold stood on one side of the circle and opposite him loomed the Venerable Rhodomanus of the Crimson Fists.

The latter's crimson and regal blue paintwork was in stark contrast to the predominantly black and white power armour of the Templars – although some of the older, more ornamented suits worn by those veterans among the battleforce were traced with gold and red as well.

The moaning wind whirled flurries of snow around them but over the voice of the blizzard, Brother Jarold's booming prayers could be heard quite plainly.

'We shall bring down His almighty wrath and fury upon the xenos and drive the greenskin from the face of this planet!' Jarold bellowed. 'For the Emperor and the primarch!'

'For the Emperor and the primarch!' his battle-brothers responded with fervent zeal.

'For the Emperor and the primarch,' Venerable Rhodomanus echoed.

Brother Jarold had not needed to ask the ancient whether he would deign to join the Templars on the continuation of their mission. To awaken to a world fifty years into his future and so unchanged despite the passage of time, and yet finding his brother Crimson Fists with whom he had fought shoulder to shoulder against the greenskins gone, the prospect of fighting alongside the Templars had given him a noble purpose. Here was a chance to finish what he and his brothers had started.

For what purpose could there be for a Space Marine, other than eternal service? If he were denied the right to serve Him Enthroned on Holy Terra, a Space Marine's long life, and all the battles he had fought, everything he had achieved in His holy name would count as naught.

The Black Templars and Crimson Fists – two Chapters formed in the aftermath of the Heresy ten thousand years before – were both successor Chapters of the original Imperial Fists Legion, created from the very genetic material of the Primarch Rogal Dorn. Templar and Fist owed their very existence to the lauded Rogal Dorn, so there had never been any question as to whether Rhodomanus would join the Black Templars of the Solemnus Crusade. They were brothers-in-arms; that was all that mattered.

Brother Jarold surveyed the assembled Templars, the ancient Fist and the ice-clad vista beyond.

'It is time,' he said, scanning the ridge of sickle-shaped peaks on the horizon. 'Whatever the source of the anomalous signals detected by the fleet, it lies beyond that ridge.

'Today we show the greenskins why they should fear us. We let them see why we are fear incarnate. Today we take the fight to the enemy. Today we purge the Dead Lands of the xenos plague that blights this world.

'Move out!'

Their act of worship concluded, with renewed steel in their hearts, shielded by the armour of their faith as much as by the ceramite of their power armour, the circle broke up as the Space Marines returned to their vehicles. With a roar of mighty engines, like the wrathful prayers of Brother Jarold himself, Ansgar's Avengers moved out.

The force progressed slowly, in order to never leave the Dreadnoughts far behind. Brother Jarold had deployed into the heart of the Dead Lands by drop-pod and the Templars had not anticipated having another ancient join them in their quest to find the source of the anomalous readings. There was no means of transporting them, other than for them to continue under their own propulsion.

But it still did not take them long to climb the icy slopes of a pass between the jagged obsidian-black peaks. Initiate-pilot Egeslic took his land speeder on ahead, to scout out what lay in wait for them on the other side of the ridge. He returned presently, guiding his speeder deftly over the ice, compensating for wind shear as he descended from the crest of the pass, and brought the vehicle to a hovering halt beside the clumping Dreadnought.

'Brother Jarold,' Egeslic said, 'you should see this for yourself.'

'That,' said Techmarine Isendur, pointing into the heart of the crater that had been dug into the ice, 'is the source of the anomalous readings.'

From the Space Marines' position at the mouth of the pass, sheltered by the shadows of the looming wind-scoured ice sculptures that surmounted the ridge in impossible overhangs, Brother Jarold surveyed the rift in the ice below them.

The ork-dug crevasse was a hive of seemingly disorganised industry. Everywhere he looked he saw orks. The foul xenos covered the glacier in a thick, dense green carpet as they swarmed over the dig site, the clamour of their mining machines ringing from the ice walls around them. There were customised digging machines, and other ork vehicles had been pressed into strange service here too. Some of these machines bore banner poles, bearing the iconography that demonstrated the ork tribe's loyalty. The sight of the Scarred Ork again – the ugly steel-cut tribal glyph bearing a rust red lightning bolt scar that bisected its crude simulacra features – filled Brother Jarold with both righteous satisfaction and indignation in equal measure.

They had found the one tribe that Jarold had hoped they would. The orks labouring within the ice pit were of the Blood Scar tribe. Truly the Emperor was smiling upon their endeavours that day.

But focusing again upon the coarse alien totem Jarold felt rage burn within him like he had not known since the moment the re-constructed warboss Morkrull Grimskar had made his cowardly escape, taking the body of the Emperor's Champion Ansgar with him as he teleported out of the mekboy's crumbling lab smothered within the foetid green depths of the equatorial jungle.

'Is there a teleportation device somewhere here?' Jarold demanded of the Techmarine, watching the waves of green corposant rolling across the underside of the thick clouds that covered the arctic valley. He had to be certain.

'I have recalibrated the signum and fine-tuned the signal, brother,' the Techmarine said. 'And there is.'

Excitement pulsed through the husk of Jarold's mortal remains locked within the life-preserving amniotic tank of the Dreadnought's sarcophagus.

Had they really tracked down their long-sought-for quarry at last? Was the warboss here? And if he was, was Brother Ansgar with him?

Jarold gazed down into the crater again and treacherous doubt began to creep between his thoughts of righteousness revenge. But it was not the size of the ork horde that filled Brother Jarold's mind with appalled awe and wonder but the effigy that they had virtually finished digging out of the solid ice of the glacier that had spilled between the frost-chiselled peaks into this valley like some great frozen and fractured river.

Venerable Rhodomanus saw it too. And remembered.

*The war machine. An appalling amalgamation of scavenged weapons and armour, the product of unholy alien engineering and genetically pre-programmed habit, the living embodiment of ork savagery and the relentless desire for war.*

*The monster – for it was a monster – crashed across the glacier, decimating the Crimson Fists' frontline. The Space Marines brought their armour and heavy weapons to bear but it was too little compared to the might of the monstrous god-machine that now marched to war before them.*

*Desperate times called for desperate measures and Rhodomanus had never known them more desperate. Something had to be done to bring about the destruction of this angry god.*

*And so, supported by his noble brethren Fists, he had strode forth to conquer the beast in one final act of self-sacrifice. His battle-brothers falling one by one at his side, giving their lives – all of them – that he might complete his final mission, weathering shoota, kannon, gatler and a storm of rokkits, the ancient was able to breach the stompa's shields and place the thermal charges at its very feet.*

*'The Emperor protects,' he intoned, quietly resigned to his fate.*

*Then all was white noise, heat and light.*

*For one brief moment the ice of millennia became a torrent of liquid water again and the blazing stompa sank beneath the sudden waves. The force of the blast hurled Rhodomanus across the sky like a blazing comet and he thought he heard the Emperor calling him to serve at his side in the next world...*

'The idol lives,' Rhodomanus breathed.

It was clear to all – and not just Techmarine Isendur's practised eye – that the orks had finished carving the remains of the war machine from the body of the glacier and were now busy attempting to re-activate it; re-fuelling it, testing its growling motive systems and firing off bursts of random weapons-fire from its many and varied weapon emplacements.

There was a hungry roar of pistons firing and thick billows of greasy black smoke gouted from the proliferation of smoke-stacks and exhaust flues that rose from the back of the alien war idol.

'That, I take it, is not the source of the signal we have been tracking, is it?' Jarold quizzed the Techmarine standing beside him.

'No, brother. That is.' Isendur pointed with his power axe.

'I see it,' Rhodomanus said.

Jarold looked again, refocusing his optical sensors, and then he saw it too.

It was a vast assemblage of iron beams and girders, crackling brass orbs and endless spools of cabling. It was supported by an immense scaffold and yet the whole massive structure had been hidden by the blizzard and the bulk of the ork effigy standing before it.

The device culminated in a huge gun-barrelled probe that Jarold imagined to be a beam transmitter, supported on strong gantry arms.

'By Sigismund's sword!' Jarold gasped.

'Its designation in this warzone is an ork teleporter, I believe,' Isendur said.

'We should warn the fleet,' Jarold said. 'We cannot allow the xenos filth continued access to such weaponry or technology,' he added as he pondered the matter in hand. It was clear to Jarold now that the orks intended to teleport their scavenged stompa out of the ice-locked Dead Lands to be used on another war front and bolster their forces there. Such a reinforcement could turn the tide of battle in the orks' favour. Such a thing could not be allowed to happen.

'Yes, brother,' Isendur replied.

Tense moments later, with Jarold watching the heavens as if he expected the *Divine Fury* to deliver a thunderbolt directly from heaven against the stompa, the Techmarine made his report. 'The interference being generated by the teleporter that we detected from orbit is now preventing my signal from getting through to the crusade fleet,' he said, delivering his bad tidings without any obvious emotion.

They were alone down there.

'We are going to have to deal with the stompa and the teleporter ourselves,' Rhodomanus declared. 'We cannot allow the greenskins to make it away from here with their idol intact. It is against the will of the Emperor.'

'Then we shall face the enemy in battle once again; fight them hand to hand if that is what it takes,' Jarold said, his assault cannon whining as it began to run up to speed. 'Just the way we like it.'

With the roar of bike engines and heavy armour running at maximum speed, the Black Templars poured through the ridge pass and into the carved crevasse in the ice before the orks had any warning as to what was happening.

'No pity! No remorse! No fear!' Brother Jarold boomed as he tramped down the glacial slopes towards the great ork-gouged hole, the toe-hooks of his Dreadnought feet locking him securely in place on the treacherous ice.

'There is only the Emperor!' Rhodomanus joined, urging the crusading Space Marines on. 'He is our shield and our protector!'

First came the bikes and attack bikes, pouring over the lip of the ridge, past the clumping Dreadnought. Then came the Razorbacks and the Rhinos, the heavy armour grinding over the ice of the glacier, pounding it to shards beneath their tracks, heavy bolter fire riddling both the ice sheet and those orks that had mustered enough awareness to try to do something about the approaching Space Marines.

The land speeder squadron hurtled over the ridge after the rest of the Templar armour past the advancing battleforce, the *whub-whub-whub* of their engines thrumming through the ice, the Tornado's assault cannon rattling off hard rounds into the milling orks as they hurried to respond to this new threat.

With a whooshing roar, the Typhoon fired off a barrage of missiles. The rockets corkscrewed through the air and impacted in a series of scathing detonations amidst the moving ork armour. Bodies, armour plating and wheels were thrown into the air to land in broken burning piles.

With a searing scream, the lascannon mounted on Techmarine Isendur's Razorback fired, a blinding spear of light burning through the constant snow flurries and illuminating the crevasse like an incendiary shell-burst. A moment later the crater was illuminated again as an ork halftrakk exploded in a sheet of flame, the las-blast having hit both its fuel tank and the rokkits loaded into the back of it.

There was the *crack* and *crump* of frag grenades detonating amidst the greenskin horde, and orks fell in their dozens.

Some of the orks had climbed aboard their trukks and bikes again. They revved their engines as they turned their vehicles to face the oncoming Black Templars armour.

The orks were rallying. Jarold's crusaders had made the most of the advantage that stealth and the blessings of the Emperor had brought them but now the enemy were starting to organise a cohesive defence.

As war trukks and heavy orkish bikes began to converge on the advancing Templar armour, those battle-brothers piloting the fleet's venerated vehicles urged them forwards, Techmarine Isendur making supplication to the Omnissiah in the same unmodulated tone, over and over.

At the bottom of the crater, in the shadow of the dug-out idol, the two sides met with a roar of over-revving engines and the scream of shearing metal. Sparks flew, armour plating buckled, axles sheared and fuel tanks ruptured. Orks were thrown over the hulls of Rhinos and land speeders. Milling grots were crushed under the tracks of Rhinos and ork bikes alike. Others among the horde were gunned down by the blazing, blessed bolters of the Templars, the ork guns unable to match the reliability or accuracy of the Space Marines' arsenal.

But despite their primitive design there was one thing that the ork guns had over the Templars' weapons; there were more of them. Far more. It was becoming painfully apparent that the Templars were drastically outnumbered, at least twenty to one. Although the Emperor's chosen were renowned for their fighting prowess, those were odds that tested even a Space Marine. There was a very real danger that sheer weight of numbers would see them overwhelmed, if the orks were able to unify their attack.

But Brother Jarold – now part of the rearguard, finishing off those greenskins that had evaded the Templars' guns – had realised this would be the case before he had committed his fighting force to this action.

It was clear that the Blood Scar orks were planning on teleporting the stompa from this location, to deploy elsewhere on Armageddon. Jarold's plan had always been to infiltrate the dig site and bring down the war-effigy or, failing that, seize and hold the colossal ork teleporter until Isendur found a way to destroy it.

With a scream of failing engines, Initiate-Pilot Egeslic's land speeder ploughed into the surface of the glacier: an ork shokk attack gun had made a lucky hit. A gaggle of snarling boyz piled onto the downed speeder, burying Egeslic and Initiate-gunner Fraomar beneath a flurry of thumping axes and stabbing serrated knives.

The two Rhinos slewed to a halt in the middle of the crater, dropped their hatches and the troops they were carrying poured out in a tide of funereal black and gleaming white. Boltguns barking and chainswords screaming, they met the milling rabble head on. They might be outnumbered, but they were in the thick of battle, which was the only place where a Templar might hope to win his honour-badges.

Venerable Rhodomanus' multi-melta pulsed, and a swarm of orks died as their blood boiled and their own bodily fluids broiled their internal organs.

The ice field was lit up again, this time as a sphere of actinic light exploded into life like a miniature sun at the periphery of the Templar lines. The explosion pushed a great wave of concussive force before it as the land speeder Typhoon and its remaining payload of missiles were obliterated by a direct hit from the stompa's now active deth kannon.

Brother Jarold stood firm, as ork bikes tumbled end over end past him, carried before the bow-wave of explosive force. He then turned his assault cannon on the surviving greenskins now running from the epi-centre of destruction, holy wrath pounding through what little remained of him that was still flesh and blood.

'Brother Jarold,' Techmarine Isendur's voice crackled over the comm-net, the interference caused by the orks' unstable teleporter technology affecting even close range communications.

'What is it, brother? Report.'

'We have our objective.' Isendur declared with something dangerously like emotion tingeing his words. 'The teleporter is ours.'

* * *

'Your objective is the teleporter; reconvene there,' Jarold commanded, his battle-brothers hearing him through the comm in their helmets, his words also carrying to them over the bestial roars and bolter fire of the battlefield. 'Repeat, rally at the teleporter.'

The device was huge, on a monumental scale that even an ancient such as Venerable Rhodomanus had never witnessed before. It was too big a target to miss. The Templars had teleport technology themselves, of course, hidden within the bowels of the Forge-ship *Goliath* where it was carefully tended and operated by the Techmarine Masters of the Forge and their servitors, but they had nothing approaching the size of this brutal piece of esoteric machinery.

Techmarine Isendur felt something approaching heretical awe on seeing the monstrous device arrayed before him in all its terrible, alien glory.

The Templars were brutally outnumbered by the thuggish orks, but by launching a surprise attack, the vengeful Space Marines had been able to penetrate far into the dig site; the either arrogant or idiotic orks having failed to post anything like enough sentries to create an effective defensive perimeter. They had probably not thought to be interrupted out here in the trackless frozen wastes of the Dead Lands for little could survive in these bitter wastes other than the alien orks. But then, from what Jarold had witnessed first-hand, it seemed that orks could survive pretty much anywhere.

The Templars' fast-moving, heavy armour had been able to penetrate the ork crater that held the ice-locked stompa with ease, the Razorbacks and Rhinos ploughing into the aliens and their scratch-built vehicles as if blessed Sigismund himself were smiting the foul xenos from beyond the stars, where he now stood at Primarch Dorn's right hand.

But now the initially bewildered orks had rallied and were mounting an effective counter-attack against the Black Templars' lightning assault.

Despite the crusading Chapter's prowess in hand-to-hand combat, even hardened fighters such as Brother Jarold's avenging warriors would be hard-pressed to overcome when facing such impossibly overwhelming odds.

The best they could hope for was to sell themselves dear. They might not have found their lost Brother Ansgar or their nemesis, the warlord Morkrull Grimskar, but they could end their crusade here, denying the ork host the war machine that the greenskins had fought so hard to win again.

Bikes – in both the black and white livery of the Templars and the scruffy red kustom paint jobs of the orks – roared past Brother Jarold as he stomped across the battlefield. He took aim and fired. The front wheel of a warbike that was pursuing a Space Marine attack bike – its gunner whooping wildly as it took pot-shots at the noble Templars – disintegrated in a hail of cannon fire. The wheel struts dug into the ice, halting the bike's forward motion. The vehicle flipped over, hurling the ork gunner into the path of a hurtling land speeder – the surprised-looking greenskin bouncing off the hull with the unmistakable sound of breaking bone – while the bike's driver was crushed beneath the great weight of the bike landing on top of it and crushing its spine.

Jarold turned his bolter on a gaggle of greenskins that charged him, large-calibre shootas and clumsy chain-bladed weapons in their meaty paws. A burst of flesh-shredding gunfire and then he was through. Nothing now stood between him and the ork teleporter.

And he wasn't the only one to have made it to the objective. Sergeant Bellangere had led the men under his command by example – bolt pistol in one hand, chainsword in the other dripping with alien gore – and hadn't lost a single member of his squad in the process. He and his troops were even now finishing off the last of the resistance being put up by the orks that crawled all over the vast gantries of the teleporter, an augmented mekboy falling to Bellangere's gutting chainblade.

Jarold turned to survey the smoking craters and tight knots of fighting that characterised the battlefield dig-site. The crumpled wreckage of a devastated Rhino lay nearby, as did the smouldering remains of a bike. Most of the Templar armour had made it through to the objective, but not all. Jarold caught glimpses of scratched black and blistered white amidst the bodies of the slain between billows of smoke from burning wrecks strewn across the combat zone.

On seeing his fallen battle-brothers Jarold felt his blood boil. The machine-spirit that resided with him inside his Dreadnought body informed him of the names of each and every one of the fallen – Initiate Garr and Gunner Heolstor, Brother Derian, Brother Eghan and Brother Clust of Squad Garrond, Clust's heavy bolter lying useless on the ice under his eviscerated body.

Brother Jarold was shaken from his enraged reverie by what felt like an earthquake.

The ground shook, splinters of ice twenty metres tall breaking free of the glacier as the stompa began to move. The orks had finally coaxed their idol into unnatural life once more.

Like Brother Rhodomanus it had lain locked in the ice for the last fifty years. Like Brother Rhodomanus it now had a second chance to finish what Ghazghkull Mag Uruk Thraka's hordes had started half a century ago.

At the growl of the effigy's engines, filthy smoke poured from its chimney-exhausts, filling the cerulean blue sky with stinking black clouds.

The stompa's wrecking ball attachment – the krusher itself looking like a huge rusted boulder – came whirling around over the top of its pintle arm mount, crashing down on top of a Rhino with all the force of a meteorite impact. The tank's adamantium plates buckled under the force of the wrecking ball blow, sending the troop transport bouncing off the uneven ice-gouged bedrock that had lain buried beneath the glacier until the orks had dug it up.

As Jarold watched, what was left of Neophyte Feran rocketed skyward as an ork skorcha engulfed his body in flame, detonating the krak grenades he carried at his waist.

Raging to the heavens at the death of another battle-brother, and one who had not yet had the chance to prove himself in glorious battle to his brethren's satisfaction, the Dreadnought turned his blazing weapons on the ork responsible.

The barrels of his assault cannon glowing red hot, his mind-linked machine-spirit informed him that his auto-loaders would soon be out of ammunition. But if today was his day to die a second death then he would make it his vow to take as many of the Blood Scar orks with him as possible.

Jarold surveyed the scorched glacier around him. The remaining Black Templar armour had formed a cordon around the teleporter, every vehicle's guns pointing outwards towards the enemy now pouring over the ground towards their position. The aliens' fury at the audacity of the Templars in taking the teleporter spurred them on, the savage brutes giving voice to harsh barks and hoots of wild abandon.

'Brothers!' Jarold declared, his voice echoing strangely from the derricks and hoists of the corposant-sheathed structure. 'This day we show the xenos filth that Armageddon is not theirs for the taking. This day we show the orks that we will leave no wrong unavenged, no slight unchallenged. This day we will deliver the Emperor's divine retribution upon the heads of the greenskin defilers of this world in the name of Primarch Dorn and his servant Lord Sigismund.'

Jarold turned his storm bolter on another charging ork and took its head off with one mass-reactive round.

'Brothers! Today we sell ourselves dear in the name of the Emperor that we might deny the orks another victory upon the shores of Armageddon. We have a new mission. We will not depart this world until we have ensured that they may never make use of their teleporter or their war-idol again. Today is a good day to die!'

With a scream of rending metal, lightning-drenched claws tore through the chugging engine of an ork wartrak as its armour plating melted under the intense heat-blast of a multi-melta.

As the smoke and flames died back again, the Black Templars Dreadnought watched with grim satisfaction as the still more imposing and ornamented form of Venerable Rhodomanus strode through the devastation to reach the protection of the cordon of crusader armour, crushing a flailing ork beneath one colossal foot whilst snatching the mangled body of another from the wrecked wartrak and quartering its head between the crimson talons of his colossal power fist.

'No, brother,' the ancient boomed. 'I am sorry to contradict you, but today is not your day to die.'

As he reached the Templars line, Rhodomanus turned his multi-melta on an ork bike, igniting its fuel tank; the vehicle and its rider disappeared in a sheet of incandescent flame.

'It is not your destiny to give your lives in sacrifice to stop this blasphemy,' the ancient went on, as if making his decree. 'Your mission is not yet done. You must live to fight another day.'

Jarold did not interrupt, but listened, considering Rhodomanus's words as he targeted the ork manning the flamethrower mounted on the back of a rumbling halftrakk.

'This is my battle, brother,' Rhodomanus continued. 'It is up to me to accomplish what I and my brother Fists tried to do fifty years ago.'

The ancient was right. This was not the Templars' battle. The destruction of the ork war machine had never been their objective. Brother Ansgar still awaited them, somewhere. And it was up to Jarold and the others to find him. It was as they had sworn it.

But none of that changed the fact that they were severely outnumbered and completely surrounded, with little hope of being able to turn the tide of battle in their favour now, unable to even call for extraction by the fleet.

The superstructure of the incomparable ork device in whose shadow they now sheltered hummed and twanged as orkish hard rounds and crackling energy beams spanged off its pylons and girders.

'Do you think you can fathom the workings of this teleporter?' Jarold asked his Techmarine.

'All ork machines are primitive and alien,' Isendur replied, 'but I would predict a seventy per cent chance of success.'

'Then set to work,' Jarold instructed. 'By the Emperor, I want this thing operational and locked onto the fleet in orbit as soon as is humanly possible.'

With a dull crump the speeding guntrukk exploded, obliterated by the massed barrage of heavy weapons that pounded it.

Standing side by side against the horde, the Dreadnoughts Jarold and Rhodomanus locked onto a new target and a warbike disintegrated into shrapnel.

Only a matter of metres away, Brother Huarwar died as he was decapitated at close quarters by a heavily mekanised ork. Roaring in grief-stricken pain, Jarold broke from the circle, advancing on the creature responsible, litanies of hate spouting from his vox-casters like bile as he shredded the alien's augmented body with raking bolter and cannon fire.

'Brother Isendur!' he bellowed over the howls of the orks and the savage chatter of their guns, ignoring the succession of hard rounds that rattled off his own adamantium body-shell as if they were no more than the stings of rad-midges. 'Give me some good news!'

'I have subjugated what passes for the device's machine-spirit, patching a link via one of my servitors and dominating it with a liturgical sub-routine, and, through its transmitter array, have located the fleet in orbit and Forge-ship *Goliath*–'

'Brother!' Jarold boomed, bisecting an ork from midriff to neck with a barrage of bolter fire. 'Is it ready?'

'Aye, brother,' Isendur replied. 'It is ready.'

'Then begin the evacuation.'

As the two Dreadnoughts held back the press of the ork horde with bolter and fist, cannon and melta, at Jarold's command the strike force moved back beneath the beam emitter of the huge gantry, never once turning their backs on the enemy, claiming a dozen ork lives for every step they took in retreat.

It was not the Templars' way to retreat in the face of greater numbers of the enemy. But for the brethren of the Solemnus Crusade, this was their last action. They could not afford to sacrifice their lives so freely, not when their holy work remained undone. They were yet to recover Brother Ansgar's body and repay the warboss Morkrull Grimskar for all the monster had taken from them when the orks of the Blood Scar tribe razed the Chapter Keep on Solemnus.

They had all sworn it – every crusading battle-brother, from neophyte to initiate, Techmarine to Apothecary, Dreadnought to Marshal, Chaplain to Champion – and they could not relinquish the fight until their vow had been fulfilled, not when a way out of this impossible situation had presented itself.

So large was the ork teleporter – it having been intended to beam something as gargantuan as the stompa to another arena of battle – that the entirety of the survivors of Jarold's battleforce could fit within the circumference of the projection plate beneath the enormous beam emitter.

They would go together. That was how Brother Jarold wanted it. Whether their plan worked, and the teleporter returned them to the Forge-ship *Goliath*, or scattered their component atoms to the stars, they would go together. The only ones they would leave behind were one tech-servitor to initiate the firing sequence of the teleporter's beam-gun, and Venerable Brother Rhodomanus of the Crimson Fists.

'Brother Jarold,' came Techmarine Isendur's voice with something almost like urgency in his usually unexcitable tone. 'Our departure now waits only on your presence upon the plate.'

Jarold turned to Rhodomanus, swivelling about the pivot of his waist bearing, as if he were about to address the venerable, blasting a leaping axe-wielding ork out of the air with a single, well-placed shot.

'Go, brother,' Rhodomanus said, before the other could speak. 'Go to meet your destiny and leave me to face mine.'

'It has been an honour,' Jarold stated stoically.

'Aye, it has been that,' the ancient agreed.

'Die well, brother. For the primarch.'

'For Dorn. Now go.'

Rhodomanus directed another shot from his multi-melta into the press of the ork pack, the heat blast clearing ten metres around him in every direction.

Taking his leave, Brother Jarold defiantly turned his back on the orks and marched to join his battle-brothers at the heart of the humming teleporter, the venerable laying down covering fire behind him, like some colossal avatar of the Emperor's retribution.

And as he did so, he began to intone Dorn's litany of service.

'What is your life?' he began. 'My honour is my life.'

An ork fell to scything fire from his storm bolter.

'What is your fate? My duty is my fate.'

Another was impaled on the crackling blades of his lightning fist.

'What is your fear? My fear is to fail.'

As he retreated behind Rhodomanus, Brother Jarold gave voice to the defiant battle cry in one last act of defiance directed at the alien orks.

'No pity!' Brother Jarold boomed.

'No remorse!' his battle-brothers responded, taking up his battle cry.

'No fear!' they bellowed in unison, clashing their weapons against their holy armour in a clattering cacophony of defiance.

Corposant crawled over and around the superstructure of the ork teleporter in writhing serpents of sick green light. With an apocalyptic scream like the sundering of the heavens, the beam-emitter fired.

Rhodomanus did not look back. He knew the Templars were gone.

'And what is your reward?' he asked, his voice rising like a challenge against the ravening greenskins. 'My salvation is my reward!'

Three orks fell to a withering hail of bolter fire.

'What is your craft? My craft is death!'

The multi-melta put an end to another ork bike.

'What is your pledge?'

The venerable Dreadnought hesitated. He could see the stompa advancing on him now, and him alone, belching smoke into the air from its exhaust-stacks, its colossal mass shaking the ground with its every step.

'My pledge is eternal service!'

As the stompa closed on the teleporter at last, with heavy, purposeful steps that sent tremors skittering through the bedrock that lay beneath the glacier, an inescapable fact wormed its way into the spirit-linked mind of the ancient. This was to be his last stand, but even the glorious sacrifice of a venerable Dreadnought might not be enough to stop the stompa.

Rhodomanus and his brother Fists had been unable to destroy it fifty years before, during the Second War for Armageddon, only managing to delay the inevitable by trapping it within the glacier. And now, fifty years on, what hope was there for him as he stood before the devastatingly powerful war machine?

But still he kept firing, directing blast after blast of his multi-melta at the gun emplacements that bristled from the effigy's carapace, at the stompa's armour itself, and its crew, when his spirit-linked targeter could lock onto them.

The stompa loomed before him, blocking his view of the crater and the rest of the horde, the macabre god-machine filling his world. Nothing else mattered now. There was only the ancient and the idol, two relics from another battle for Armageddon, ready to make the final moves of a power play begun five decades before.

Sparkling emerald flame consumed the ork teleporter once more, power relays humming as the device came online again. Rhodomanus's optical sensors homed in on the roasted remains of the tech-servitor fused to the esoteric device by its last firing. The servitor was dead, so how was it that the teleporter was powering up to fire at all?

It was only then that Rhodomanus realised that in his face-off with the stompa he had backed himself onto the empty platform and now stood directly beneath the beam emitter.

A nimbus of actinic light formed at the centre of the teleporter, also directly beneath the focusing beam of the vast construction, surrounding him with its suffused essence. Something was being beamed back to the teleporter.

He felt the tingle of it at his very core, in every fibre of his body that was still flesh and blood. And the machine-spirit of his Dreadnought body felt the exhilarating rush of a trillion calculations as the impossible machine read and recorded the position of every atom within his body, the connection of every synapse, the binary pattern of every recollection-code stored within his memory implants. He was beaming out.

Framed by the skeletal structure of the alien device, the stompa seemed to peer down at him with the telescoping sights of its cannon-barrel eyes.

Through his one remaining mortal eye Rhodomanus saw adamantium, steel, ceramite and flesh become first translucent and then transparent. At the same time he saw something else taking shape within the sphere of light with him, becomingly steadily more opaque as it solidified around his departing form.

For the briefest nano-second he and the object shared the same space – his machine-spirit merging with its primitive programmed consciousness. Fifty metres long and weighing a hundred tonnes – the energy build-up already taking place within its plasma reactor perilously close to the point of critical mass and detonation – the torpedo was capable of blowing a hole in the side of an ork kill kroozer with armour plating several metres thick. The venerable's own machine-spirit continued the countdown to destruction.

*Five.*

*Four.*

*Three.*

*Two.*

Suffer not the alien to live, he thought.

And then actinic light blinded his optical sensors and the bleak white wastes of the Dead Lands, the collapsing structure of the teleporter and the impotently raging stompa. Everything vanished, melting into black oblivion, and Brother Rhodomanus was gone.

The battle-barge *Pride of Polux* hung in high orbit above Armageddon's second largest landmass.

All was still within the reclusiam. Captain Obiareus, Commander of the Crimson Fists 3rd Company, was alone with his thoughts and his strategium. There were not many minutes in the day when he could say that, and he savoured those times when it was the case. But such precious moments made all the difference to his command. They were those times when he could step back, reflect, consider and plan.

He sat, the elbows of his power armour resting on the cuisses of his armoured legs, gauntlets locked together before his face. His lips touched the reliquary that hung from his neck on its golden chain and which he held within his hands as reverentially as a father might cradle a newborn. He stared out of the roof-high windows of the reclusiam at the silent void beyond, pondering again his Chapter's gains and losses on the planet below, alone with his thoughts and the stars.

Footsteps disturbed the captain's contemplations, the sound of ceramite ringing from the stone-flagged floor shattering the silence of the reclusiam. Obiareus looked up in annoyance.

Brother Julio approached the strategium, head bowed respectfully.

'What is it?'

'My lord,' Julio began. 'We have received a hail from Marshal Brant of the Black Templars Solemnus Crusade. He wishes to speak with you, my lord.'

'The Templars wish to speak with us?'

'Yes, my lord.'

'Regarding what matter?' Obiareus probed further.

'They have news, my lord.' Brother Julio faltered, as if hardly able to believe what he himself was saying.

'Yes? What news?'

'News of Venerable Rhodomanus,' Brother Julio said hesitantly.

'Brother Rhodomanus?' Now it was Obiareus's turn to express his disbelief. 'Brother Rhodomanus lost to us these fifty years past since the first war fought against the xenos for this world?'

'Yes, my lord,' Julio confirmed, 'but lost no longer. Venerable Rhodomanus has returned.'

# TWELVE WOLVES

### Ben Counter

The sons of Fenris look not only to the future, but also to their noble past and so my task is a most arduous one. Think not that the saga I speak comes to this tongue easily, or that to bend the ear of a mead-soaked Blood Claw is a task any less worthy than bringing the bolter and chainsword to the Emperor's foes! No, indeed, to tell these tales of the past, and to have them listened to by the Brothers of the Wolf, is a task whose difficulty is matched only by the weight of the duty I bear in telling them.

I hear you now, throaty and raucous, demanding to hear a saga of some great battle or feat of arms that will fill your hearts with fire. Lord Russ fighting the One-Eyed traitor, you cry! The many crimes of the Dark Angels, you demand, so that we might feast and drink and remember our grudges! But my purpose here is not to serve this feasting throng with whatever bloody tale they desire. No, I have gathered you by this roaring fire, in the grand hall of the Fang where generations of Space Wolves have celebrated their victories and toasted their dead, because there is a lesson I have to impart.

I do not need an Astartes' augmented senses to hear your sighs. What use, you whisper to yourselves, is a saga not dripping with the blood of foes and thundering with the sound of chainblade on heretic flesh? Fear not! There will be blood. Could an old thrall like me, a broken, haggard thing kept in pity by the Chapter whose standards I failed to reach in my youth, hope to survive if he spoke of anything but battles and glory to a roomful of Astartes? It is from the Wolf Priests themselves, the guardians of your spirits, that I learned this tale, and they know better than to impart lessons that will not be heeded.

It is in a great battle of the past, then, that our tale takes place. Those attentive young wolves will know of the Age of Apostasy, one of the direst lessons that mankind has ever had to learn, during which the corrupt clergy of the Imperial Creed sought to seize power for themselves. It is a long and grim story in its own right that I will not tell here. Suffice it to say that it was a time of blindness, fear and chaos, when the Imperium of Man sought to crumble in a way not threatened since the dark times of Horus. Among the many tales of sorrow in this time, our story concerns that of the Plague of Unbelief, when a wicked man named Cardinal Bucharis carved out an empire of his own, throwing off Imperial authority to rule as a king!

Bucharis, while a cunning and fearless man, was a fool. For as his empire grew, conquered by renegades of the Imperial Guard and armies of mercenary cutthroats, he came to the threshold of Fenris. Arrogant in the extreme, Bucharis did not halt there and turn back, afeared of the Space Wolves who called it their home then as you do now. No, he sent his armies to Fenris, to conquer its savage peoples and force the Space Wolves to cede their world to him!

Ah, yes, you laugh. Who could have thought that an Apostate Cardinal and a host of mere men could defeat the Space Wolves on their home world? But it happened that at this time very few Space Wolves were at the Fang, with most of them having joined the Wolf Lord Kyrl Grimblood on a crusade elsewhere in the galaxy. The Space Wolves left there to face Bucharis's villains numbered little more than a single Great Company, along with the newly-blooded novices and the thralls who dwell within the Fang. Bucharis, meanwhile, bled the garrisons of his empire white to flood Fenris with soldiers and lay siege to the Fang. Do not think that the Fang was impregnable to them! Any fortress, even this ancient and formidable mountain hold, can fall.

In the third month of this siege two Space Wolves were abroad in the valleys and foothills around the Fang. They were patrolling to disrupt and observe the enemy forces, as the sons of Fenris were wont to do at that time in the battle. One of them, and his name was Daegalan, was a Long Fang such as those battered, leather-coloured Astartes who watch us even now from the back of the hall. They have heard this tale many times, but take note, young Blood Claws and novices, that they still listen, for they understand its lesson well. The other was much like you. His name was Hrothgar, and he was a Blood Claw. Daegalan was wise and stern, and had taken Hrothgar as a student to teach him the ways of war that, with the Fang and the Chapter in great peril, he had to learn very quickly.

Imagine a mountain ridge at night, bare flint as sharp as knives clad in ice that glinted under the many stars and moons of mother Fenris. It overlooked a wide, rocky valley, cleared of snow by tanks and shored up by engineers, like a black serpent winding between the flinty blades of the Fang's foothills. Now you are there, the story can begin.

Two Astartes made their way up to the lip of this ridge. One of them wore a wolf skin cloak about his shoulders, and across his back was slung a missile launcher. This was Daegalan. His face was like a mask of tanned leather, so deeply lined it might have been carved with a knife, his grey-streaked hair whipping around his head in the night's chill wind. He wore on his shoulder pad the symbol of Wolf Lord Hef Icenheart, who at that time was directing the defence of the Fang from its granite halls. The other, with the red slash marks painted on his shoulder pad, was Hrothgar. The scars, where the organs of an Astartes were implanted, were still red on his shaven scalp. His chainsword was in his hand, for it rarely left, and his armour was unadorned with markings of past campaigns.

'See, young cub,' said Daegalan. 'This is the place where our enemy creeps, like vermin, thinking he is hidden from our eyes. Look down, and tell me what you see.'

Hrothgar looked over the edge of the ridge into the valley. The night's darkness was no hindrance to the eyes of an Astartes. He saw a track laid along the bottom of the valley, along which could be wheeled the huge siege guns and war machines which Bucharis's armies hoped would shake the sides of the Fang and bring its defences down. Slave labour on the worlds the Cardinal had captured had created countless such machines and they filled the bellies of spacecraft supplying his war on Fenris. Indeed, it was the mission of the two Astartes to locate and disrupt the bringing of these war machines to a location where they could fire on the Fang.

Many Guardsmen, from the renegade Rigellian regiments who had thrown their lot in with Bucharis, guarded the tracks, knowing that soon the precious war machines would come trundling along it.

'I count twenty of the enemy,' said Hrothgar. 'Imperial Guard all, they are reasonably trained – not the equal of a Space Wolf, of course, but dangerous if they can fire upon us in great numbers. See, Long Fang, they have assembled defences of flak-weave and ammunition crates, and they seem ready for an attack by such as us. They know the importance of their mission.'

'Good,' said Daegalan, 'for a first glance. But our task here is to destroy these enemies. What can you see that will ensure they fall?'

'This one, 'said Hrothgar, 'is the officer that leads them. See the medals and badges of rank on his uniform? That silver skull on his chest is granted by the heretic Cardinal to followers who show great ruthlessness in leading the troops. Upon one sleeve are the marks of his rank. In his hand is a map case, surely marking out the route of these tracks. This man must die first, for with their leader dead, the others will fall into disarray.'

Daegalan smiled at this, and showed the grand canine teeth that are the mark of a true Long Fang. May you who listen to this one day sport such fangs as these, sharp and white, to tell the tale of your years spent fighting with the Sons of Russ! 'Young Blood Claw,' said Daegalan, 'can it be that even with the eyes of an Astartes you are so blind? You must learn the lessons of the Twelve Wolves of Fenris, those great beasts who even now hunt through the mountains and snowy plains of our world. Each wolf is taken as the totem of one of our Great Companies, and for good reason.' Daegalan here tapped the symbol of his Great Company on his shoulder pad. 'I wear the symbol of Wolf Lord Icenheart. He took as his totem Torvald the Far-Sighted, the wolf whose eyes miss nothing. This wolf of Fenris teaches us to observe our enemy, much as we would love to get our claws around his throat first, for it is in looking ahead that the victory can sometimes be won before a blow is struck.

'Look again. The man you see is indeed an officer, and no doubt a ruthless one at that. But there is another. There, seated on an ammunition crate, his lasgun propped up by his side. See him? He is reading from a book. Even these old eyes can read its title. It is the *Collected Visions*, a book written by the Apostate Cardinal himself, serving as a collection of his madness and heresies. Only the most devout of his followers, when the night is this cold and the mission is this crucial, would read it so earnestly. This man may not be the officer who leads these soldiers on paper, but he leads them in reality. He is their spiritual heart, the one to whom they turn for true leadership. This man must die first, for when it is shown that the most devout of them is no more than meat and bone beneath our claws, then all their hope shall flee them.'

Hrothgar thought upon this, and he saw the truth in the Long Fang's words.

'Then let us fight,' said the Blood Claw. 'The reader of books shall die first, beneath these very hands!'

'Alas, I have but two missiles left,' said Daegalan, 'otherwise I would sow fire and death among them from up here. I shall fight alongside you, then. When you tear the heart from them, I shall slay the rest, including that officer to whom you paid so much attention.'

With this Hrothgar vaulted down from the ridge and crashed with a snarl into the heart of the enemy. He charged for the spiritual leader, and was upon him before the other Guardsmen had even raised their lasguns! At that time the Space Wolves were sorely lacking of ammunition for their guns and power packs for their chainswords, and so it was with his hands that Hrothgar hauled the reader of books into the air and dashed his brains out against the rocks.

'He is dead!' came the cry from the Guardsmen. 'He who assured us that the divine Cardinal would deliver us, he whose survival proved to us the sureness of our victory! He is dead!' And they wailed in much terror.

Daegalan was among them now. He was not as fast as the Blood Claw, but he surpassed him in strength and cunning. He fought with his knife, and plunged it up to the hilt in the skull of the first Guardsman who faced him. Another died, head cracked open by the swinging of his fist, and then another, speared through the midriff. The officer, who was shouting and trying to steel the hearts of his men, fell next, knocked to the ground and crushed beneath Daegalan's armour-shod feet.

It was, but the space of a few heartbeats, as a non-Astartes might reckon it, that the enemy were torn asunder and scattered. Those that were not dead cursed their fates and fled into the snowy wilderness, eager to face the teeth and claws of Mother Fenris rather than spend another moment in that blood-spattered valley.

The hot breath of the two Astartes was white in the cold as they panted like predators sated from the hunt. But this hunt was not finished. For from down the tracks came the sound of steel feet on the rocks, and the roaring voice of an engine. And before the Astartes could ready themselves, from the frozen darkness lumbered a Sentinel walker.

Many of you have seen such a thing, and perhaps even fought alongside them, for they are commonly used by the armies of the Imperial Guard. This, however, was different. Its two legs were reinforced with sturdy armour plates and its cab, in which its traitor driver cowered, was as heavily plated as a tank. It had been made with techniques forgotten to the masters of the forge worlds today, and it bore as its weapon a pair of autocannon. This was no mere spindly scouting machine! This was an engine of destruction.

'Despair not!' shouted the headstrong Hrothgar as this monster came into view. 'You shall not have to face this machine, old man, wizened and decrepit as you are! I shall ensure this traitor's eyes are on me alone. All you need do, venerable one, is fire that missile launcher of yours!'

Daegalan had it in mind to scold the Blood Claw for his insolence, but it was not the time for such things.

Hrothgar ran into view of the Sentinel. He fired off shots from his bolt pistol, and the Sentinel turned to hunt him through the valley's shadows. But Hrothgar was fast and valiant, and even as the Sentinel's mighty guns opened fire he sprinted from rock to rock, from flinty fissure to deep shadow, and every shell spat by the Sentinel's guns was wasted against unyielding stone. At that time it happened a flurry of snow was blown up by Mother Fenris's icy breath and Hrothgar ventured closer still, diving between the metal feet of the Sentinel, knowing that he was too fast and his movements too unpredictable for the machine's pilot to fire upon him with accuracy.

So infuriated was the pilot of the Sentinel that he forgot, as lesser soldiers than Astartes are wont to do, the true threat he was facing. For

Daegalan the Long Fang had indeed taken aim with his missile launcher, the only weapon the Astartes had between them that might pierce the machine's armour. With a roar the missile fired, and with a vicious bark it exploded. The rear of the Sentinel was torn clear away, and the pilot mortally wounded. Exposed to the cold night, the blood from his many wounds froze. But he did not have long to suffer this fate, for Hrothgar the Blood Claw climbed up the legs of the Sentinel and tore out the traitor's spine with his bare hands.

'You may think,' said Daegalan, 'to have angered this old Long Fang with your insolence, but in truth you have expounded the lesson of another of Fenris's wolves – or rather, two of them, for they are Freki and Geri, the Twin Wolves who were companions of Leman Russ himself. See how this enemy, a match for both of us, was destroyed by the fruits of our brotherhood! When wolves fight as a pack, as one, they slay foes that would confound them if they merely attacked as individuals. You have learned well, though you did not know it, the lesson of the Twin Wolves!'

With that, the two Astartes set about destroying the tracks, and for many days as a result the walls of the Fang were spared the bombardment of Bucharis's war machines, and the lives of many Space Wolves were surely spared.

Now, it was about this time that the Apostate Cardinal, accursed Bucharis himself, was upon Fenris directing the siege of the Fang. You already know that he was a man possessed of great arrogance and blindness to the rage he inflamed in those who suffered under his conquest. He was also a wrathful man, much given to extravagant punishments and feats of cruelty when angered. Having heard from a subordinate that his war machines (which he expected to shatter the Fang and slay all those within) would be delayed by the actions of the Astartes, he flew into a rage. He supposed that a great host of Space Wolves had done this deed, and that with their destruction the defenders of the Fang would be greatly weakened in number. A foolish man, I hear you cry. Indeed he was, but he was also a very dangerous man, whose foolishness lay not in an inability to achieve his goals but in ignorance of the consequences his cruelty would have. You know, of course, that Bucharis was eventually to meet an end as befits a man like him, but that is a story for another time.

Many units of the Imperial Guard were sent to punish the host of Astartes that Bucharis believed to be abroad in the foothills of the Fang. They were men picked by Bucharis's warmaster, the renegade Colonel Gasto, from the regiments of Rigellians he commanded. They had been well versed in the beliefs of Bucharis, which were heretical in the extreme and shall not be spoken of by this humble tongue. They believed Bucharis's lies that the Imperium had fallen and that only by obeying Bucharis could they hope to survive its collapse. Gasto gave them tanks and heavy weapons, and the kind of murderous cutthroat mercenaries that Bucharis had swayed to his cause to lead them.

These men and machines left the great siege encampment of the Rigellian Guard and headed for the Fang, ordered on pain of death to destroy the Astartes.

Meanwhile, Daegalan the Long Fang and Hrothgar the Blood Claw were making their way back to the Fang, for their mission was completed. Though it was now daylight a storm had fallen over the area and Mother Fenris was breathing ice across the flinty hills. Terrible gales blew and showers of ice fell like daggers.

'Remember,' said Daegalan as he led Hrothgar up the slippery slope of a barren hill, 'that it is cruel weather such as this that makes every blasted and inhospitable place the domain of Haegr, the Mountain Wolf. For he endures all, indeed, he thrives in such inhospitable climes. It is to him that we must look, for is it not so that the physical endurance of an Astartes is a weapon in itself, and that by taking this hazardous path we make better time towards the Fang and further confound our enemies?'

Hrothgar did not answer this, for while he was young and vigorous, the Long Fang was so much inured to hardships and gnarled by Fenris's icy winds that the old Astartes did not feel the cold as much as the Blood Claw. But he did indeed recall the Mountain Wolf and, knowing that the sons of Fenris are made of stern stuff, he shrugged off his discomfort and the two made good speed over the hills.

It was at the pinnacle of the next hill that a break in the storm gave them a glimpse of the Fang. It was the first time they had seen it in many days. Daegalan bade his companion to stop, and look for a moment upon the Fang itself.

'This tooth of ice and stone, this spear piercing the white sky, does this not fill your heart with gladness, young Blood Claw?'

'Indeed,' said Hrothgar, 'I am now struck by the majesty of it. It gladdens me to think of the despair our foes must suffer when they see it, for those are the slopes they must climb! Those are the walls they must breach!' And all of you have seen the Fang and, I do not doubt, imagined how any foe might hope to silence the guns that stud its sides or climb the sheer slopes that guard its doors more surely than any army.

'Then you feel,' said Daegalan, 'the howl of Thengir in your veins! For he is the King Wolf, the monarch of Fenris, and everything under his domain is alight with glory and majesty. So you see, ignorant and insolent young cub, that another of Fenris's wolves has a lesson to teach us today.'

Hrothgar did indeed hear Thengir, like a distant howl, speaking of the kingly aspect of the Fang as it rules over all the mountains of Fenris.

'And mark also the Wolf Who Stalks Between Stars,' continued Dae-galan, 'as you look above the Fang to the moons that hang in the sky. The Stalker Between Stars was the totem of Leman Russ himself, and even now his symbol adorns the Great Wolf's own pack. Our pawprints may be found even on distant worlds and the farthest-flung corners of the Imperium. So long as we, like that wolf, hunt abroad among the stars, then Fenris is not merely the ground beneath our feet but also any place where the Sons of Fenris have trod, where the Space Wolves have brought fang and fire to their enemies!'

Hrothgar's hearts swelled with pride as he thought of the mark the Space Wolves had left upon the galaxy beyond Fenris. But the Astartes could not tarry for long, and quickly made their way on.

Soon Daegalan saw the white tongues of engine exhausts nearby, and knew that the traitor Guard were close. He led Hrothgar into a winding valley, deep and dark even when the sun broke through the blizzards. Many such valleys lead through the foothills of the Fang, chill and black, and within their depths lurk many of the most deadly things with which Mother Fenris has populated her world.

'I can tell,' said Daegalan after some time, 'your frustration, young Blood Claw. You wish to get to grips with the foe and cover your armour with their blood! But remember, if you will, that another wolf stalks beside us. Ranek, the Hidden Wolf, goes everywhere unseen, silent and cunning. In just such a way do we stalk unseen. Do not scorn the Hid-den Wolf, young one! For his claws are as sharp as any other, and when he strikes from the shadows the wound is doubly deep!'

Hrothgar was a little consoled by this as he listened to the engines of the enemy's tanks and the voices of the soldiers raised as they called to one another. They could not traverse the foothills of the Fang as surely as a Space Wolf, and many of them were lost as they stumbled into gorges or fell through thin ice. Driven by their fear of Bucharis they made good time but paid for it in lives, and with every step the force became more and more ragged. Hrothgar imagined slaying them as he emerged from hiding, and he smiled.

'Now you think of killing them by the dozen,' continued Daegalan, for he never passed by the opportunity to instruct a younger Astartes. 'But ask yourself, in this butchery you imagine, is there any place for me, your battle-brother? You need not reply, for of course there is not. I do not admonish you this, Blood Claw. Quite the opposite, I commend you to the spirit of Lokyar, the Lone Wolf. While the Twin Wolves teach us of brotherhood, Lokyar reminds us that some-times we must fight alone. He is the totem of our Wolf Scouts, those solitary killers, and now he may be your totem, too, for it is Lokyar whose path you tread as you imagine yourself diving into our enemy alone.'

\* \* \*

Now our two Astartes came to the head of the valley, where it reached the surface. They espied before them fearsome barricades set up by the traitor Guard, the bayonets of the heretics glinting in the sun that now broke through the storm clouds. Dozens of them were waiting for the Astartes, and they were trembling for they believed that a host of Astartes would stream from the black valley.

'Ah, may we give thanks to Mother Fenris,' said Hrothgar the Blood Claw, 'for she has guided our friends to meet us! What a grand reunion this shall be! I shall embrace our friends with these bloody hands and I shall give them all gifts of a happy death!'

'Now I see the battle favours the youthful and the heedless of danger,' said Daegalan in reply, 'and is content to leave the old and cunning behind. Go, Brother Hrothgar! Bestow upon them the welcome your young wolf's heart lusts for! And remember the Iron Wolf, too, for he watches over the artificers of our Chapter forge wherein your armour was smelted. Trust in him that your battlegear will turn aside their laser fire and their bullets, and run with him into battle!'

Hrothgar recalled, indeed, the Iron Wolf, whose pelt can turn aside even the teeth of the kraken who haunt the oceans of Fenris. And he ran from the darkness of the valley. The soldiers opened fire as one and bolts of red laser fell around the Blood Claw like a rain of burning blood. But his armour held firm, the Iron Wolf's teachings having guided well the artificers of the Fang.

Ah, how I wish I had the words to describe Hrothgar in that bloody hour! His armour was red to the elbow and the screams of his enemies were like a blizzard gale howling through the mountains. He leapt the barriers the traitors had set up and even as he landed, men were dying around him. He drew his chainsword and its teeth chewed through muscle and bone. One heretic he spitted through the throat, throwing him off with a flick of a wrist, and a heartbeat later a skull was staved in by a strike from his gauntleted fist. He cut them apart and crushed them underfoot. He threw them aside and hurled them against the rocks. He took the lasgun from one and stabbed him through the stomach with his own bayonet. Some traitors even fell to their own laser fire as the men around them fired blindly, seeing in their terror Astartes charging from every shadow.

Daegalan followed Hrothgar into the fray. Some leader amongst the traitors called out for a counterattack and bullied a few men into charging at Hrothgar with their bayonets lowered. Daegalan fell amongst them, his combat knife reaping a terrible toll. He cut arms and heads from bodies, and when he was faced by the officer alone he grabbed the heretic fool with both arms. He crushed the life out of the man, holding him fast in a terrible embrace.

The Guardsmen fled, but Hrothgar was not done. Some he followed behind outcrops of rock where they sought to hide. He hauled them out, as a hunter's hounds might drag an unwilling prey from a burrow, and killed them there on the ground. When they tried to snipe at him from some high vantage point he trusted in his armour to scorn their fire and clambered to meet them, holding them above his head and throwing them down to be dashed to pieces against the rocks below.

When the traitors bled, their blood froze around their wounds, for Mother Fenris had granted the Astartes a day bright yet as cold as any that had ever passed around the Fang. Blood fell like a harvest of frozen rubies. Now Daegalan and Hrothgar rested in the centre of this field of bloody jewels, as bright and plentiful as if Mother Fenris herself was bleeding. They were exhausted by their killing and they panted like wolves after the kill, their breath white in the cold. They were covered in blood, their faces spattered with it, their pack emblems and Great Company totems almost hidden. Silently, each gave thanks to Fenris herself for the hunt, and even to Cardinal Bucharis for his foolishness and arrogance, for it was he who had sent them such prey.

Above them loomed the Fang, wherein their battle-brothers waited to receive the news of their success. Prey lay dead all around them, and the majesty of Fenris was all about. What more could a Space Wolf ask for? It was indeed a good day, and may you young pups have many such hunts ahead of you.

'Well fought, my brother,' said Daegalan. 'It is well that the Apostate Cardinal stumbled upon Fenris, for without his ill fortune we would not have such hunts upon our very doorstep!'

'He should have a statue in the Hall of Echoes,' agreed Hrothgar. 'Was there ever a man who did more for the glory of the Space Wolves? I think I shall toast him with a barrel of mead when we celebrate this hunt.'

They laughed at that, and it was to this sound that the rumble of engines grew closer and a shadow fell over them. For the mercenaries who led the Guardsmen were hard-bitten and foul-minded men, well versed in the low cunning of war, and they had prepared a trap for the Astartes.

The force the Space Wolves had slaughtered were just the vanguard of the army sent to punish them. Bucharis had sent in his fear ten times that number, sorely stretching the forces that besieged the Fang elsewhere. They had with them tanks: Reaper-class war machines such as can no longer be made by the forge worlds of the Mechanicus. Six of these machines had survived the journey, and they all rumbled into view now, their guns aiming at the place where the two Astartes stood.

The Guardsmen, though sorely pressed by the harsh journey through the foothills, numbered hundreds, and they had brought many heavy weapons with which to destroy the Astartes from afar – for they feared to face the claws and teeth of the Space Wolves up close, and rightly so. Their leaders, Bucharis's chosen mercenaries, were strong and brutal men who wore pieces of uniform and armour from a dozen places they had plundered, and all wore the scars of war like banners proclaiming their savagery. They, too, were afraid of the Astartes, but they turned their fear into brutality and so the men under them obeyed them out of terror.

One such man addressed the Astartes through the vox-caster of his tank. By the standards of such men, it was a bold thing to do indeed!

'Astartes!' he called to them. 'Noble sons of Fenris! The honoured Lord Bucharis, monarch of his galactic empire, has no quarrel with the Space Wolves. He seeks only to grant protection to those within the fold of his generosity. For the Imperium has fallen, and Terra lies aflame and ruined. Lord Bucharis promises safety and sanity for those who kneel to him!

'But we do not ask you to kneel. How could we, mere men, demand such of Astartes? No, we ask only that Lord Bucharis count Fenris among the worlds of his empire. What do you care for this grim and frozen place, its savage peoples and its bitter oceans? To the Space Wolves, of course, we shall leave the Fang, and the right to rule yourselves, excepting a few minor and quite necessary obeisances to Lord Bucharis's undoubted majesty. So you see, there is no need for you to fight any more. There is nothing left for you to prove. Stand down and place yourselves within our custody, and we shall deliver you safely unto the Fang where you can pass on word of Lord Bucharis's matchless generosity.'

The Astartes, of course, saw through these lies. They knew the Imperium was eternal, and had not fallen, and moreover they believed no more than you do that Bucharis meant to destroy the Space Wolves and take the Fang for himself. No doubt he wished to install himself in our great fortress, and to use as his throne room the hall wherein Leman Russ himself once held court! The only answer to such a speech lies at the tip of a wolf's claws, or in the gnashing of his fangs!

'Now, young wolf,' said Daegalan, 'we face our death. How blessed are we that we can look it in the face as it comes for us. And moreover, we die on Fenris, on the ground upon which we were born, and first ran with our packs in the snow. This is the world that forged us into the Astartes we are, that gave us the strength and ferocity to be accepted into the ranks of the Space Wolves. Now we shall repay that honour by choosing this very ground for our deaths! How blessed are we, Blood Claw, and how blessed am I that it is beside my brother that I die.

'And do not think that we shall die alone. For I hear the snarling of Lakkan, the Runed Wolf, upon the wind. Once Lakkan walked across Fenris, and wise men read the symbols he left in his footprints. These men were the first Rune Priests and those who still follow the path of Lakkan even now watch us from the Fang. They scry out our deeds, and they shall record them, and give thanks as we do that we die a death so fine.'

Daegalan now drew his bolt pistol. He had but a single magazine of bolt shells, for at that time the Astartes were sorely pressed for ammunition with their fortress besieged. Hrothgar, in turn, drew once more his chainsword. Its teeth were clotted with the frozen blood of traitors, but soon, he knew, he would plunge it into a warm body and thaw out that blood so its teeth could gnash again.

'I do not seek death,' said the Blood Claw, 'as easily as you do, old man.'

'Your saga shall be a fine one,' replied Daegalan, 'though it is short.'

'Perhaps you are right,' said Hrothgar, and in that moment the guns of the tanks were levelled at the place where they stood in the field of blood rubies. 'You are a Long Fang, after all, and wise. But I fear that in all you have taught me you have made a single error.'

'And what might that be, Blood Claw?' said Daegalan. 'What omission have I made that is so grave I must hear of it now, in the moment of my death?'

Now a strange countenance came upon Hrothgar the Blood Claw. His teeth flashed like fangs and his eyes turned into the flinty black orbs of the hunting wolf. 'You have spoken of the wolves of Fenris that follow us and impart to us their lessons. Twelve of them you have described to me, each one mirroring an aspect of Fenris or of the teachings the Wolf Priests have passed down to us. These lessons were well earned, and I thank you for them, Brother Daegalan. But I am wiser than you in but one aspect.'

'Speak of it, you cur!' demanded Daegalan with much impatience, for the guns of the traitor tanks were now aimed at them, awaiting the order to fire, as were the heavy weapons of the Guardsmen.

'I have counted twelve Fenrisian wolves in your teachings, each one taken as the totem of a Great Company of the Space Wolves. But here you are mistaken. For I know that in truth, there are not twelve wolves. There are thirteen.'

It is time, I fear, for this old tongue to lie still and for a draught of mead to warm this thrall's bones. You wish the story to continue? I have no doubt you foresee great bloodshed of the kind you love to hear. And there was bloodshed after that moment, it is true. Terrible it was, perhaps worse than any that fell upon the face of Mother Fenris during the besieging of the Fang. But it is not for me to speak of it. I hear you groan, and a few even flash your fangs in anger! But look to the Long Fangs who sit at the back of the hall. Do they growl their displeasure? No, for they know the truth. A thrall such as I has no place speaking of such things. Even the most ancient among the children of Russ, the mighty Dreadnoughts who have marched to war for a thousand years or more, would not speak of it.

There is, however, a legend told among the people of Gathalamor, the world where the Apostate Bucharis first came to prominence. They are a fearful and religious people, for upon them has fallen the burden of redeeming their world from the stain the Apostate left upon it. But sometimes they speak of legends forbidden by the cardinals of their world, and among them is this one, brought back, it is said, by the few survivors of the armies who fought on Fenris.

Once an army was sent by Bucharis to destroy the Astartes who had been sowing much death and confusion among the besieging forces. The army cornered the Astartes but found, much to their delight, that they faced not a Battle Company or even a single pack, but a single Space Wolf.

In some versions of the tale there was not one Space Wolf, but two. The difference matters not.

Now the soldiers drove their tanks into range and took aim at the Astartes. And they awaited only the order to open fire, which would surely have been given but a moment later. But then they were struck by a great and monstrous fear, such as rarely enters the hearts even of the most cowardly of men.

The Space Wolf was an Astartes no more. In fact, he appeared as nothing that could once have been a man. A bestial countenance overcame him, and the winds howled as if Fenris herself was recoiling in disgust. Talons grew from his fingers. His armour warped and split as his body deformed, shoulders broadening and spine hunching over in the aspect of a beast. The soldiers cried that a daemon had come into their midst, and men fled the sight of it. Even the gunners in their tanks did not think themselves safe from the horror unfolding in front of them.

And then there came the slaughter. The beast charged and butchered men with every stroke of its gory claws. It tore open the hulls of their tanks and ripped out the men inside. In its frenzy it feasted on them, and strips of bloody skin and meat hung from its inhuman fangs. Men went mad with the force of its onslaught. The leaders of that army fired on their own men to keep them from fleeing but the beast fell on them next and the last moments of their life were filled with terror and the agony of claws through their flesh.

The soldiers were thrown to the winds of Fenris and scattered. Some say that none survived, either torn down by the beast or frozen to death as they cowered from it. Others insist that a single man survived to tell the tale, but that he was driven hopelessly mad and the legend of the Beast of Fenris was all that ever escaped his quivering lips.

But this is a tale told by other men, far from the Fang and the proud sons of Fenris who dwell therein, and I shall dwell upon it no more.

Now it came that many days later, when the battle had waxed and waned as battles do, a pack of Grey Hunters ventured forth from the Fang to drive off the traitor Guardsmen who were thought to be encamped in the foothills. There they came across a place like a field of rubies, where frozen blood lay scattered across the snowy rocks with such great abandon that it seemed a great battle had been fought there, though the pack-mates knew of no such battle.

'Look!' cried one Space Wolf. 'Someone yet lives! He is clad in the armour of a Space Wolf and yet he is not one, for see, his bearing is that of an animal and his face bears no trace of the human we all were before becoming Astartes.'

The pack leader bade his battle-brothers to cover him with their bolt-guns as he went to see what they had found. As he approached he saw countless bodies torn asunder, many with the marks of teeth in their frozen flesh, and still others dead in the ruins of their tanks.

The figure in the centre of the battlefield indeed wore the power armour of an Astartes, but split apart and ruined as if rent from within. He crouched panting in the cold, as if fresh from a hunt. His form was not that of a human, but of a beast.

'He is touched by the Wulfen,' said the pack leader. 'The Thirteenth Wolf of Fenris has walked here, and its inhumanity has found a place to dwell inside this Blood Claw. Some flaw in his gene-seed went unnoticed during his novicehood, and now it has come to the fore in this place of bloodshed.'

Another Space Wolf cried out. 'There lies another of our battle-brothers, dead beside him! What appalling wounds he has suffered! What monstrous force must have torn his armour so, and what claws must have ripped at his flesh!'

'Indeed,' said the pack leader, 'this noble brother was a Long Fang, one of that wise and hardy breed, and he shall be borne by us to a proper place of resting within the Fang. Alas, I knew him – he is Brother Daegalan, I recognise him by his pack markings. But see, the claws of the survivor made these wounds! His teeth have gnashed at the fallen Astartes's armour, and even upon his bones.'

The pack was much dismayed at this. 'What Space Wolf could turn on his brother?' they asked.

'Mark well the path of the Wulfen,' said the pack leader sternly. 'His is the way of deviant and frenzied bloodshed. He cares not from whom the blood flows as long as the hunting is good. This ill-fated Long Fang is testament to that – when this Blood Claw ran out of foes to slay, under the Wulfen's influence he turned upon his brother.'

The pack spoke prayers to mighty Russ and to the ancestors of the Chapter, and all those interred in the Fang, to watch over them and protect them from such a fate as suffered by the two Astartes.

You might think that a beast such as they found should have been put down, but imagine for a moment you were confronted by such a sight. It would surely be impossible for you to kill one such as Hrothgar, for though a warped and pitiable thing he was still a Son of Fenris and to slay him was still to slay a brother. So the pack brought Daegalan's body and Hrothgar, still living, to the Fang. I have heard it said they led him by a chain like an animal, or that they called upon a Wolf Priest to administer a powerful concoction that sedated him long enough to be carried to the Fang.

And so it came to be that Daegalan the Long Fang was given his rightful place among the packmates who had fallen over the decades, and there he lies still. As for Hrothgar, well, he was interred in a similar way, this time in a cell hollowed out from the rock of the Fang's very heart where from the lightless cold none can hope to escape.

Hush! Cease the sound of clinking tankards. Ignore the crackling of the fire. Can you hear it? That scratching at the walls? That is Brother Hrothgar, scrabbling at the boundaries of his cell, for he is now but an animal and yearns to run in the snows of Fenris, hunting beast and brother alike. But sometimes he remembers who he once was, and the Long Fang who fought alongside him, and then he lets out a terrible mournful howl. You can hear it in the longest of Fenris's nights, echoing around the heart of the Fang.

Now, my tale has come to an end. Perhaps now you understand why it was to a lowly thrall that this saga has been given to tell, and not one of the venerable Wolf Priests or well-scarred Long Fangs who uttered its grim words. What true Space Wolf could bear to have such things pass his lips?

And perhaps a few of you have even understood the lesson that lies at its heart. The rest will have to listen for Hrothgar's claws, for Hrothgar's howl, and perhaps the truth will come to you.

Remember always, whether you hunt in the wilds that Mother Fenris tends, or you stalk between the stars, the thirteen wolves hunt beside you.

# THE RETURNED

*James Swallow*

The skies above the Razorpeak range wept oil. Low cowls of cloud, grey as ancient stone, ranged from horizon to horizon, grudging to allow only a faint glow of sunlight to pierce them from the great white star of Gathis. The clouds moved upon the constant winds, the same gales that howled mournfully through the jagged towers of the mountains, the same heavy gusts that reached up to beat at the figure of Brother Zurus.

The slick rain, dark with the metallic scent of oceans and the tang of rotting biomass, fell constantly upon the landing platform where he stood. Zurus watched it move in wave fronts across the granite and steel. The storms hammered, as they always did, against the constructions men had built high up here in the tallest crags. The platform was only one of many extensions, cupolas and balconies emerging from the sheer sides of the tallest fell among the Razorpeaks. The earliest, most primitive tribes of Gathis II had christened it the Ghostmountain, a name not in honour of its white-grey stone, but in recognition of the many dead that haunted it, so lethal were its slopes. Thousands of years later and the name was, if anything, more fitting.

Once, before men had come from Terra to colonise this world, there had been a true peak atop the Ghostmountain, a series of serrated spires that rose high enough that they could pierce the cloud mantle. Now a great walled citadel stood in their place, the living rock of the peak carved and formed by artisans into halls, donjons and battlements of stark, grim aspect. At each point of the compass, a hulking tower rose, opening into the sculpted shape of a vast raptor screaming defiance at elements and enemies. These warbirds put truth to the name of the great fortress-monastery atop the Ghostmountain: the Eyrie.

One of the great eagles stood at his back, and like the raptor, Zurus was watchful. He peered out from under the hood of his heavy, rain-slick over-robe, waiting for the roiling, churning sky to release to him his responsibility. In the far distance, down towards the settlements of Table City and the lowhill coasts where the tribals lived, great jags of bright lightning flashed, and on the wind the grind of thunder reached his ears a few moments later, cutting through the steady hiss of the falling rains.

Zurus was soothed by the sound. He found it peaceful, and often when he was far from Gathis, perhaps upon the eve of battle at some distant alien battleground, he would meditate upon the sounds of the rainfall and find his focus in it. And so, when he had awoken at dawn this day, he had at once sensed something amiss. Zurus exited his sleeping cell and found only rays of weak sunlight reaching down the passages of the dormitoria; and outside, a break in the clouds, and a silence in the air.

A rare thing. By the ways of the Gathian tribes, an omen of ill fortune when the eternal tears of Him Upon The Throne ceased to fall, and with them the protection the God-Emperor of Mankind provided. After a time, the rain began again, as constant as it ever was, but Zurus had witnessed the moment of silence, and was on some level unsettled by it.

As he had crossed through the gate to venture out to the landing platform, a figure in red-trimmed robes was waiting for him in the lee of the entranceway.

Thryn, the Librarian Secundus. The old warrior's sallow, bleak features always measured Zurus whenever he turned to face him. The look in his eyes was no different from the expression he had shown when the battle brother had first seen the psyker, on the fateful day the Chapter had recruited Zurus into their fold. Many decades ago now.

Thryn nodded towards the open gate and the sky beyond. 'The rain returns,' he noted.

'It never leaves,' Zurus replied. The exchange of words had a ritual quality to them.

The Librarian's lip curled in something that a generous observer might have considered a smile. 'If only that were so. The light of naked sun upon the peaks... It does not bode well.'

Zurus gathered in his robes, unfurling the hood. 'I have no time for omens.'

Thryn's mouth twisted; the old warrior could sense a bald untruth even without the use of his witch-sight. 'You are ready for this, brother?' he asked, turning to stare out at the empty landing pad. 'You did not need to take on this duty alone. Other men–'

'It is right that I do it,' Zurus spoke over the Librarian. 'It is right,' he repeated.

Thryn turned back to study him for a long moment, then stepped away, out of his path. 'As you wish.' The Librarian banged his fist against the inner door of the gateway and halted. Metal gears began to grind as the saw-toothed hatchway drew open. When Thryn spoke again, he did not face him. 'But remember this, Zurus. What comes today, what you go to meet... You have not faced the like before.'

Something in the other warrior's tone chafed on him. 'If you think I will falter when... *if* the time comes, you are mistaken. I do not shrink from death.'

Thryn gave a low chuckle. 'That much is certain. We are Doom Eagles, brother. Death is part of us.'

'I know the difference between friend and foe,' Zurus insisted. 'I know what the Archenemy looks like. I can tell a traitor when I see one.'

The inner gate clanged open. 'I have no doubt you believe that. But Chaos has faces it has never shown to you, kinsman. Do not forget that.' Thryn walked away, back into the fortress.

The thunder was closer now, sullen and deep enough to echo in his bones. His companion rains drew hard across the metal decking as if they were scouring it, preparing it for the arrival; and then it came to him that the tone of the storm-sound had changed, a new note growing loud, fast approaching.

Zurus looked up, following his hearing. The oily rain touched his face, streaking over an aspect that was a maze of scars. He saw a shape up there, only the suggestion of it really, a shadowed thing with broad wings and a hooked profile. A vast eagle, falling towards him, talons extending.

The sound was strident, and it opened the cowl of cloud cover for a brief instant. On pillars of orange fire and hard jet-noise, a gunmetal-silver drop-ship suddenly emerged from the haze, dropping fast. Rain sluiced from the steel wings and across the blocky, rigid angles of the Thunderhawk's blunt nose. Zurus's robes snapped and billowed as the thruster backwash buffeted him, but he did not move from his sentinel stance.

The drop-ship landed firmly, the slow impact resonating through the landing platform. Engines keening as they powered down, the craft settled on hydraulic skids, lowering itself to the deck as if it were thankful to have completed its journey. Zurus saw motion behind the windows of the cockpit, but nothing distinct. He found he was holding his breath, and chided himself, releasing it. The Astartes warrior resisted the urge to throw a glance over his shoulder, back towards the Eyrie. He had no doubt Thryn was at some gallery window far above him, watching.

With a crunch of cogs, the Thunderhawk's drop ramp unfolded, a mouth opening to show the dark interior of the transport craft. A servitor was the first to shamble out, head bobbing as it chewed on the punchcard containing its command strings. The machine-slave dragged a wheeled trolley behind it, half-covered by the tattered remains of a war cloak.

Zurus's gaze was momentarily drawn to the trolley as it was pulled past him; he saw the distinct and unmistakable shape of ceramite armour heaped within the wheeled container. The silver wargear, the trim of red and ebon, as familiar to him as the scar-patterns on his own face. Doom Eagle armour, but corroded and damaged in a fashion no son of Aquila would ever willingly countenance.

When he looked back there was a hooded man at the top of the ramp. He was looking down at his hands, and the streams of rainwater spattering off his upturned palms. He resembled a pilgrim accepting a benediction.

The Thunderhawk's sole passenger spoke, after a moment. 'The rains,' he began, in a low, crack-throated voice. 'I thought I might never see them again.' He took in a deep, long breath through his nostrils. 'On the wind. I smell Chamack.' There was a smile in the words.

Zurus nodded. Down in Table City, leagues away from the Eyrie, the great bio-matter refineries that fabricated lubricant oil from the fibres of the sinuous Chamack sea-plant worked night and day, and the heavy, resinous odour was always present in the air. Zurus only ever noticed it by its absence.

The moment passed and the new arrival bowed his head. He began to walk down the ramp, but in two quick steps Zurus had crossed to the bottom of the gangway and stood blocking his path. The other man faltered, then halted.

'Who are you?' said Zurus. 'Let the ghosts of the mountain hear your name.'

From beneath the other man's hood, eyes narrowed and became cold. 'The ghosts know who I am, brother. I am a Gathis-born son, as you are.'

'You must say the words,' insisted Zurus. 'For protocol's sake.'

Hands tightened into fists, before vanishing into folds of the dripping robes. 'The protocols of which you speak are for outsiders. *Strangers.*'

Zurus searched the face concealed beneath the hood for any sign of subterfuge or malice. 'Say the words,' he repeated.

The other man said nothing, and the moment stretched too long. Then finally, with a fall of his shoulders, the new arrival relented. 'My name is Tarikus. Warrior of the Adeptus Astartes. Brother-Sergeant of the esteemed Third Company of the Doom Eagles Chapter. And I have returned home.'

*Tarikus.* Zurus had been there on the day that name had been added to the Walls of Memory in the great Relical Keep. He had watched with due reverence as a helot carved the name into the polished black marble, etched there for eternity among the hundredfold dead of the Chapter. Zurus had been there to hear the Chaplains announce Tarikus's loss, and cement it in the annals of Doom Eagle history. Two whole Gathian cycles now, since he had been declared *Astartes Mortus*. Many seasons come and gone, his life become a revered memory among all the honoured fallen.

The other man drew back his hood for the first time and walked on, down towards the end of the drop ramp.

Zurus took a wary step backwards and met the gaze of a dead man.

'Is it him?'

Thryn did not turn away from the rain-slicked windowpane, watching the two men far below on the landing platform. He saw Brother Zurus step aside and allow the passenger from the Thunderhawk to stride back towards the gate. The Librarian clearly saw the tawny, battle-scarred aspect of the man, lit by a momentary pulse of high lightning. 'That remains to be seen, lord,' said Thryn, at length.

In the shadowed gloom of the observation gallery, Commander Hearon folded his arms across his barrel chest and his ever-present frown deepened. The answer was unsatisfactory to the Chapter Master of the Doom Eagles. 'I allowed him to be brought here on your advice, old friend,' Hearon rumbled. 'I did so because I thought you could give me the answer I wanted.'

'I will,' Thryn replied. 'In time.'

'Not too much time,' said the Chapter Master. 'Voices call for a swift end to the matter of this... return. Chief among them the Chaplains and your senior, Brother Tolkca.'

Thryn nodded. 'Yes, I imagine the Librarian Primus is ill-tempered at the thought of such a thing being placed in my hands.'

Hearon gestured at the air. 'He is at battle a sector distant. You are here. If he's irked by my decision, he may take it up with me on his return.' The commander leaned in. 'There is no precedent for this, Thryn. Death is the closure of all things, the last page in the passage of a life. For that book to be re-opened once we have written the final entry...' Hearon trailed off. 'This man... if that is what he is... must be put to the question. The truth of him must out.'

The Librarian nodded again, musing. Thryn had pored over the battle records and honours listed under the name of Tarikus. A veteran of bloody conflicts and engagements on worlds such as Thaxted and Zanasar, he had risen to the rank of Brother-Sergeant with command of a tactical squad under Consultus, the current captain of the Third Company. The Third had a history of ill fate; two commanders in succession had been lost to them during the last Black Crusade of the Archtraitor Abaddon, at Yayor and then again at Cadia, but Tarikus had survived them all – even the great massacre at Krypt, where the Doom Eagles had lost many men on the surface of that brutal, frigid planetoid.

It was only after the destruction of the planet Serek, on a voyage back to the Segmentum Tempestus, that the luck of Brother Tarikus had run dry. The medicae frigate he had been aboard was ambushed by the hated Red Corsairs, and torn apart. Tarikus had not been among the Astartes who made it to the saviour pods before the wrecked ship had plunged into a star. He was given the honour of a worthy end, and declared dead, with all the ritual and rite such a tribute entailed.

But now… Now a ghost walked the halls of the Eyrie.

Thryn was well aware that some brother Chapters of the Doom Eagles regarded their association with matters of death as unusual. *Morbid*, even *macabre*; he had heard these slights from warriors of the Space Wolves and the White Scars, even brothers of the Ultramarines, the very Legion his Chapter had been drawn from. Some viewed the character of the Doom Eagles and saw an *obsession* with fatality; but this was a short-sighted, narrow view.

The Doom Eagles were gifted with an understanding of the universe. They knew the truth, that all life is born dying, moment by moment. What others saw as fatalism, they saw as pragmatism, a manner born out of knowledge that life and joy were transient things, that the only constants in existence were despair, loss – and ultimately the embrace of death. *We are already dead*, so said the first words of the oath of the Chapter. The Doom Eagles understood that death was always close; and so they fought harder, strove longer, to perform their duties before the cloak of Final Sleep came upon them. They had no illusions.

Death was the end of all things. Nothing could come back from the void beyond it. This knowledge was the pillar upon which stood every-thing the Chapter believed in.

Tarikus, by his presence, his mere existence, challenged that.

Hearon spoke again. 'You have my authority to do as much as required in order to cut to the core of this circumstance.' The Chapter Master turned away. 'I ask you only be certain.'

Thryn felt a tightening in his gut as the full scope of Hearon's com-mand became clear to him. 'And if I cannot be certain, my lord? What would you have me do then?'

'There is no scope for doubts, brother.' Hearon paused at the edge of the chamber's shadows and nodded towards the window. 'End him if you must. Our ghosts remain dead.'

Tarikus awoke, and his first reaction was one of shock. It faded quickly, to be replaced by a twinge of annoyance; ever since his escape from the prison on Dynikas V, each new slumber ended with the same tremor of fear and uncertainty, and it angered him.

Each time, he expected to find himself back in the searing metal cell, his ash-smeared skin slick with sweat against the hard surface of his sleeping pallet, the humid air about him resonating with heat. It was as if his subconscious mind could not willingly accept that he had found his freedom. He had experienced so many strange tortures during his imprisonment in that light-forsaken hell that even now, weeks after breaking out of the cursed place, some seed of doubt remained lodged in his thoughts, some tiny part of him too afraid to accept the reality presented to it for fear it would be torn away a moment later.

The stone and steel of the prison on Dynikas V was no more, his tormentors consumed by tyranid swarms, the prison itself scoured to the bedrock by Astartes lance fire; but the walls still stood in Tarikus's mind, and he wondered if they would ever fall.

With a sigh, he pushed such thoughts away, rose and moved to the simple fresher unit in the corner of his room. Perhaps there was an irony in the fact that this small chamber was also called a 'cell', but its function was dedicated to providing silence and peace, not confinement. He ran cold, brackish water over his face, glancing at the small circular window high in the wall. A simple pattern of acid-etching covered the glassaic; the shape of a spread-winged eagle and upon that the lines of a human skull. The sigil of his Chapter. Seeing it made Tarikus's chest tighten; the symbol meant so much to him. It had been his life for so long, and in the darkest moments of his incarceration, he had thought never to lay eyes upon it again.

Men of the steady and dour nature that characterised most of the Astartes of the Doom Eagles Chapter were not often given to moments of open excitement or joy, and yet Tarikus could not deny that he felt something close to those emotions deep within him, a strange elation at being home once more, but tempered with apprehension at what was to come next.

A day now since he arrived on the Thunderhawk. A day, after a sullen greeting from this Brother Zurus; none of his questions answered, mind, only the offer of a spartan meal and the room and rest. *A place where you can reflect,* Zurus had said. It was not lost on Tarikus that, although the door to his chamber had not been locked, a discreet gun-servitor had been stationed nearby. And he knew without needing to search for them that audial and visi-spectrum aura sensors were concealed in the covings above him.

They were watching him closely. He expected as much.

Should he have been affronted by such surveillance? On some level he was. On another, he understood the motivation behind it. Trust was a precious commodity in the Imperium of Mankind, and it was only in places where bonds of brotherhood and fealty ran strong that it could be spent. The ranks of the Adeptus Astartes were one such place, but when outsiders ventured into that circle – *outsiders and strangers*, Tarikus reminded himself – the wellspring quickly ran dry.

His own kinsmen did not trust him, and for reasons that a cursed fate had forced upon him.

Tarikus grimly considered the unfairness of it, the hard reality of callous outcome that was the way of his bleak universe. After Serek, where he and his squad had engaged a force of Necrontyr and ultimately been compelled to flee a planet in its death throes, he had healed aboard a hospitaller ship. In a narthecia-induced slumber, his enhanced physiology working to repair the damage of a poor teleport reversion, he had slept the voyage away – at least until the Traitor-kin had ambushed them. Too weak to fight them all, Tarikus had been captured even as his brothers escaped, thinking him dead. From there, the whoreson Red Corsairs sold him like chained cattle to the master of the Dynikas prison – and he had remained in that place for month after month, year after year, confined with other Astartes stolen from battlefields or presumed dead. Forgotten men turned into laboratory animals, test subjects for the amusement of the self-styled primogenitor who called himself Fabius Bile.

Tarikus had expected to die there – but then he was a Doom Eagle, and Doom Eagles always expected death. Still, when the chance for freedom came, he embraced it with all his might, aware that his service to the Golden Throne was not yet over. In his soul, Tarikus knew that he was not ready to perish, not on Dynikas, not at the hands of Bile and his freak-army of modificate mutants. He had not been granted permission to die.

He heard footsteps out in the corridor, then a voice. 'Tarikus,' called Zurus, 'will you join me?'

The Doom Eagle gathered in his duty tunic and over-robe, then opened the cell door. 'Are we going somewhere?'

Zurus nodded once. 'I have something I wish you to see.'

They walked, and Zurus did his best to observe his charge without making his scrutiny an open challenge. Tarikus seemed no different from the man shown in his file picts, or captured by the imagers of servo-skulls in battle footage. He carried himself like an Astartes should, and with no prompting the warrior showed all the correct fealty and honour towards the sacrosanct statuary ringing the gates of the great circlet corridor, which ran the circumference of the Eyrie. If anything, Tarikus seemed almost moved to see the great carving of Aquila, first of the Doom Eagles and chosen of the Second Founding. Zurus looked up from his own deep bow a moment quicker than usual, examining the curve of the other man's shoulders.

Finally, Tarikus stood and straightened. 'Perhaps you wish to set an hourglass at my side, brother. That might be method enough to gauge my piety.'

'I am not an inquisitor,' replied Zurus, a little too swiftly. In truth, he wondered what the representatives of the Ordo Hereticus might have done if they knew of Tarikus and his circumstances – or indeed that of the other handful of Astartes, who had been liberated from Dynikas by brothers of the Blood Angels Chapter. To spend months, years even, in a gaol ruled by one of the most notorious traitors of the Heresy... Could anyone, even a chosen warrior of the Emperor's Astartes, emerge untouched by the experience? Could a Space Marine survive such a thing and not be tainted in some fashion? Zurus held the question in his thoughts as he spoke again. 'You are among kinsmen here.'

'And who better to judge me?' Tarikus looked around, his hard gaze sweeping the ranges of the curving corridor, the galleries overhead and the gloomy alcoves where lume-light did not fall. 'Where are my other watchers? Nearby, I'd imagine.'

Zurus resisted the urge to look where Tarikus did. He knew full well that the Librarian Thryn was somewhere close at hand, studying them both. He wondered what Thryn thought of them; outwardly, the two Doom Eagles were similar in aspect, although Zurus's hairless scalp was paler – the legacy of his origin in the sea-nomad tribes, unlike Tarikus, who was a son of the high-mountain kindred. They were both as good an example of the aspect of a son of Aquila as one could hope to find on the Ghostmountain; but it was what lay beneath that aspect that could not be quantified.

That which could not be valued in the weight of coin; this was what Zurus had to quantify. If Tarikus was found wanting, it would mean ignoble death – the worst of fates for a Doom Eagle to suffer.

A party of Scouts passed close, and Zurus guessed by their garb and weapons they had returned from a training sortie out in the equatorial island chains. He gave the youths a terse nod that was returned, but none of them acknowledged the presence of Tarikus, passing him by without making eye contact. Zurus saw him stiffen at the slight, but he said nothing. After a moment, he nodded to himself, as if accepting something.

'Where are my men?' said the other warrior, without meeting his gaze. 'It has been two years since I last saw them, and this question I have asked more than once. Do they live still?'

Zurus had been ordered not to speak of Tarikus's former comrades-in-arms, but the command sat poorly with him. He could not in good conscience remain silent on the matter. At length, he gave a nod. 'They live,' Zurus admitted. At Serek, Tarikus had led a number of good, steadfast Space Marines – Brothers Korica, Petius and Mykilus – each of whom had survived the Red Corsair attack on the medicae frigate.

'I wish to see them.'

Zurus shook his head. 'Perhaps later.'

Tarikus shot him a glare. 'Do not lie to me, brother. Grant me that, at least.'

He sighed. 'What do you expect me to say, Tarikus? What did you think would happen when you returned here?' Zurus gestured around. 'Did you think we would welcome you with open arms? Take you in as if nothing had happened? You said it yourself. Two years, brother. A long time in the heart of darkness.'

The other man's gaze dropped to the ornate stone floor, and despite himself, Zurus felt a pang of sympathy for him. 'I'm a fool, then,' said Tarikus. 'Naïve to think that I could return and pick up where I left off.' He shook his head. 'I only want to return. That is all.'

Zurus frowned and walked on. 'Come,' he told Tarikus, 'you must see this. You'll understand better when you do.'

The Eyrie's central feature was a great octagonal tower, tallest of the citadels that reached for the sky, deepest of those that plunged levels down into the heart-rock of the Ghostmountain. The Reclusiam was a million memorials to countless deaths across the galactic disc. Entire floors were given over to relics recovered from the sites of terrible battles and brutal wars across the entire span of the Imperium. Many were from conflicts in which the Doom Eagles had taken a direct part, but others were from atrocities so soaked in despair and fatality that warriors of the Chapter had been drawn to visit them.

The Doom Eagles were born from the Legion of the Ultramarines in the wake of the Horus Heresy, in the shadow of great Aquila. He had been a warrior of Guilliman during the Siege of Terra, and along with the rest of the Ultramarines, battles fought during the race to reinforce humanity's home world waylaid them at a most crucial moment. As Chapter history told it, Aquila had been so wracked with guilt and despair at arriving too late to protect the Emperor from his mortal wounds at the hands of Horus, that he had sworn an oath never again to delay in defence of the Imperium. When the time of the Second Founding came, Aquila willingly broke away to forge the Doom Eagles and make his belief manifest in them. The first Master made it a tenet of his new Chapter that every son of Gathis would understand the cost of hesitation, of failure – and with it, the great guilt that came in step.

He would have them see these things, know them first-hand. And so, the relics; gathered by brothers on pilgrimages to places of battle and failed wars, each item a piece of despair and calamity made solid and real.

Many levels of the Reclusiam were such grim museums, halls reverent with shards of stone and bone, glass and steel. Armageddon, Rocene, Malvolion, Telemachus, Brodra-kul, and countless other war-sites, all represented here. And in the hallowed core, brought to this place by Aquila himself, the silver-walled chamber where pieces of shattered masonry from the Imperial Palace lay alongside a feather from the wing of Sanguinius and a shard of the Emperor's own battle armour.

It was said that those with the witch-sight could hear the ghost-screams in the tower. If that were so, if these relics could indeed contain a fraction of the pain and anguish that had enveloped them, then Zurus was glad the great chorus of sorrow thundering silent in the air was hidden from him.

This was not their destination, however. With Tarikus quiet at his side, the Space Marine rode the grav-car that ran the brass rails following the length of the tower. They rode up and up, beyond the ranges of the death-relics of strangers and into the Hall of the Fallen.

The largest open space inside the Eyrie, the vast walls, floor and ceiling were sheathed in great tiles of polished obsidian, each the size of a Land Raider. Hanging at right angles from complex armatures, some from floor to ceiling, others suspended at differing heights, were free-floating panels of the same dark stone. At a distance, the glassy black panes seemed clouded somehow, but as one drew closer, definition unfolded.

Each panel was perfectly laser-etched into thin strips; each strip sported a half-globe of glass, behind which lay a random item. Upon the strip, the name of a Doom Eagle claimed by death. Next to each name, inside the glass, a relic: a fragment of armour, an eye-lens, a bolt shell, an honour-chain. Every artefact, something touched by the dead. A piece of them, to be held in trust for as long as the Chapter existed.

The grav-car changed tracks, joining a conveyor that took them across the span of the hall, down and across in zigzag motions toward one of the tallest of the panels.

Zurus looked down towards the floor far below. Somewhere down there was the memorial of Aquila, and beside it a cracked helmet under glass. It had no dressing, no great and ostentatious detail to set it aside from every other marker. The First Master had ordered it so, knowing that in death, all men were in unity.

He glanced up and saw that Tarikus was also looking downward. *Mimicking me,* he wondered? *Or is he feeling the reverence that I feel?*

At last, the grav-car rattled to a halt some distance up the face of a suspended wall and Zurus gestured towards the pane that hung before them. Behind a glass bubble, an Astartes combat blade was visible, the fractal edge still bright and sharp even though the length of the knife was dirty and pitted with use.

Tarikus saw the weapon and took a half step towards it, then stopped dead. 'It's mine,' he said. The tone of his voice was peculiar; there was something like fear in it.

Zurus nodded and indicated the memorial panel. 'Look here, brother.' There in Gothic script, etched by the hand of some machine-slave stoneworker, letters lined in heavy silver. As if he had no control over the action, Tarikus reached out and ran his fingers over the shape of his name. 'No...' began the other Astartes, shaking his head.

Zurus nodded again. 'You were lost, brother. You know our laws and diktats. Your name was cast from the rolls. The ceremony of loss completed and sanctified. Your name, carved here, in memoriam. By the lights of the Chapter and all of Gathis–'

The other Doom Eagle turned abruptly to face him, a curious shade of emotion in his dark eyes. 'I am dead,' he said, finishing Zurus's sentence for him. 'I no longer exist.'

Tarikus strode from the gates of the Reclusiam across the processional bridge with such pace and intent that it was a long moment before he realised he had nowhere to go. He slowed and the grief he had tried to outrun caught up with him, as if it were only his swift tread that had kept it at bay.

In his darkest moments, trapped in that hated prison cell, Tarikus had encountered a great dread within himself that had shocked him with its potency. He had feared that he was *forgotten*; that after he was lost in deep space, the many sorties and battles he had fought, the honours he had earned, all would count for nothing among his brethren. He feared that all he had done would be meaningless.

But now he saw that the greater horror was this – that he had been *remembered*, in so final and damning a way as to make each breath he drew now a phantom. In the eyes of Great Aquila and his Chapter, Brother-Sergeant Tarikus had perished aboard that lost medicae frigate, years past. His kinsmen had counted him gone and made their peace with that fact.

Was it any wonder the Scouts had looked away from him, unsettled by his presence? For a Chapter so intimate with the manners of death, to see a warrior return from it must have shaken them to their core. Our ghosts remain dead, Tarikus thought, recalling the words written in the *Prayer Mortalis*.

Zurus called his name and he turned as the other Doom Eagle approached him, his pale face set like ice.

'This must be undone,' Tarikus began, but Zurus waved him into silence.

'Do you understand, brother?' Zurus demanded of him. 'You see now why your reappearance is… problematic?'

Tarikus felt a swell of anger inside him, and let it rise. 'Don't speak to me as if I am some whining neophyte. I am a battle-brother of this Chapter with honour and glory to my name!'

'Are you?' The question slipped from Zurus's lips.

He glared at the other warrior. 'Ah. I see. At first I thought you were concerned that my wits might have been dulled by my confinement, that perhaps you suspected my spirit damaged by my experiences… But it's more than that, isn't it?' Tarikus made a spitting sound and advanced on the other Doom Eagle. 'Can it be that you doubt the evidence of your own eyes, *brother*?' He put savage emphasis on the last word.

'The truth–'

Tarikus's anger was strong now, and he refused to let Zurus speak. 'What do you presume?' He spread his hands. 'Are you waiting for me to shed my skin, to transform into some hell-spawned Chaos daemon? Is that what you think I am?'

Zurus's gaze did not waver. 'That question has been asked.'

He took a quick step forward and prodded Zurus in the chest with his finger. 'I know what I am, kinsman,' snarled Tarikus. 'A warrior loyal to Holy Terra!'

'Perhaps,' said Zurus, 'or perhaps you are only a thing which believes that to be true. Something that only resembles Brother-Sergeant Tarikus.'

Muscles bunched in his arm, and for a long second Tarikus wavered on the verge of striking the other Space Marine across the face. That another Doom Eagle would dare to impugn the honour of a kinsman lit his fury still higher, reasons be damned.

And in that moment, through the lens of his cold anger, Tarikus discerned something else: a greasy, electric tingle across his skin and the sense of a hundred eyes staring at him. He relaxed his stance and turned away, glaring about across the length of the high marble bridge. The only sound was the clatter of heat exchangers working far below in the depths of the Ghostmountain.

To the air he spoke a demand. 'Show yourself, witch-kin.' Tarikus shot a look at Zurus, and the other warrior's expression confirmed his suspicions. He turned away again, ranging around. 'Come, brother. If you wish to damn my name, at least do me the courtesy of looking me in the eye when you do so,'

'As you wish.' The voice came from behind him, close and low. Tarikus found a figure in the lee of a carved support, swamped by red-trimmed robes. The Doom Eagle had looked in that direction only moments earlier, and there had been nothing there. Only shadows.

The psyker walked closer, dropping his hood. Cold, hard eyes bit into Tarikus, searching for any sign of weakness. He betrayed none.

'I am Thryn,' said the Librarian. 'My name is known.'

Tarikus nodded once. 'I have heard of you. A chooser of the faithful.'

'But not you,' Thryn replied. 'It was not my duty on the day you were picked from the aspirants to join this Chapter, all those decades ago. Perhaps, if it had been, this question would already be answered.'

'There is no question,' Tarikus retorted. 'What you see before you is all that I am. Doom Eagle. Adeptus Astartes. Son of Gathis.'

Thryn cocked his head. 'The enemy hides in plain sight. A tactic the followers of the Ruinous Powers are quite fond of. They have warped many a mind in the past. It is only sensible that we must be certain that has not happened here.'

Tarikus met Thryn's burning gaze and refused to look away. 'Do you know what kept me centred for all those months inside that hellhole, witch-kin? It was my faith in my brothers, my Chapter and my Emperor. Was I wrong to believe that? Have I been forsaken?'

'That is the question we must ask of you, Tarikus,' said Thryn.

'You dare ask me to prove myself?' The fury boiled inside him. 'After all that I have done in Aquila's name, you question *me*?' He advanced on the psyker until they were face to face. He could feel the prickling aura of the Librarian's controlled mind-force pressing on his flesh. 'This is your greeting for a lost brother, who by the grace of He That Is Most Mighty, has had the temerity to survive. Nothing but disdain and isolation. Accusations and disrespect.'

'This is the universe we live in,' offered Zurus.

Tarikus paused, holding Thryn's gaze. 'Perhaps you would have preferred it if I allowed myself to die in confinement.'

Thryn cocked his head. 'That would have brought a definite end to this matter, to be sure.'

'Then I apologise for daring to live,' Tarikus shot back. 'It must be very inconvenient for you.'

'There is still time,' said the psyker. 'But not much time.'

Tarikus was silent for a long moment, and with an effort, he calmed himself and shuttered away his annoyance. That there was some logic in the challenge posed by Zurus and Thryn only made matters worse; but rather than resist it, Tarikus drew in a breath and looked to his heart, to the soul and spirit that made him a Doom Eagle.

'So be it,' he said grimly. 'If I must be questioned, then I must be questioned. This is the way of things. I will face it and not flinch. Tell me what must be done to put this challenge to its end.'

'You're certain?' asked Zurus. 'It will be difficult. Some have been broken by less.'

'Tell me,' repeated Tarikus, glaring at the psyker.

Thryn looked back at him with a level, even gaze. 'There are rituals of purity. Rites of passage. You will be tested.' The psyker turned to leave. 'Tomorrow, at dawn–'

Tarikus's hand shot out and grabbed the Librarian's forearm, halting him instantly. 'No,' said the Doom Eagle. 'We will begin this now.'

Thryn studied him. 'You understand what you will face?'

'*Now*,' repeated Tarikus.

They began with the Talons.

A mechanism made of bright, polished steel, and as cold as polar ice, it wrapped around Tarikus and held the Doom Eagle in its grip. It resembled an artificer's vice, scaled up to the size of a giant. A great oiled screw turned, bringing knurled blocks of metal towards one another in an inexorable approach. From each block grew a fan of wicked barbs, claws modelled on the talons of the great raptors that rode the thermals of the Razorpeak range.

Tarikus stood between them, clad only in thin exercise robes. The muscles of his arms and legs bunched and became iron-solid as he settled in against the blocks. Only his strength and fortitude held back a crushing death. He breathed evenly, pacing himself, marshalling his strength rather than spending it all in a single effort.

The Talons pressed in. They never tired. The slow-turning gears pushed against the Space Marine's resistance, daring him to falter for just a moment; and there was the insidious thing about the trial. If the warrior relaxed, even for an instant, the blocks would lurch forward by a full hand's span, reducing the space between by a good measure – but in doing so, giving him a moment's respite from the struggle. Thus, the Talons preyed on fatigue and inattention. After hours, days between the blocks, a warrior might consider letting them close the distance a little, just to take a precious second of rest before they reached their stops and started to press in once again; but that was the route to failure. So it was said, Hearon himself once managed a lunar month in the Talons and never gave any quarter.

Tarikus was there for days. With no windows in sight, he could only make the most basic reckoning of the passing hours. And unlike Hearon's trial, Tarikus was not left alone with his struggle. From the shadows about the Talons, figures moved and called out to him, bombarding him constantly with questions and demands. They asked him to recite lines of catechism and Chapter rote, or they hectored him over every last point of the story he told of his confinement in Bile's prison. The interrogation went on and on, without end, circling his thoughts until he felt his mind going numb.

Thryn was among his questioners; perhaps he was only one of them, perhaps he was all of them, but as sweat dripped from Tarikus's limbs and acid slowly filled his veins, the warrior did not give the answers the Librarian wanted. He told the same story over and over, he recited his hymnals and prayers as he should have, all the while resisting the constant, blinding pressure. Denied food, denied water, denied release, he stood his ground.

Then without warning, a week into the trial, it ended. The Talons retracted, and Tarikus fell to the deck, his muscles twitching and cramping. It took him a moment to get back to his feet. Dimly, he was aware of figures in the cowled robes of Chapter serfs crowding towards him.

He frowned. This could not be the end of it. He had not suffered enough.

He was correct.

Tarikus was stripped naked and put into the hold of a rotorflyer. The aircraft left the Ghostmountain with a sudden upward lurch, and almost as quickly it began a steep downward arc. The Doom Eagle had barely enough time to register the howl of winds over the hull of the craft before the deck beneath him parted and he fell.

Tarikus landed hard on a shelf of icy rock, a harsh bombardment of sleet angling across it towards a sudden, sheer drop into the mist. He glanced up to see the flyer power away on flickering blades and caught sight of the Eyrie beyond it. They had deposited him on one of the nearby peak sides, little more than half a kilometre distant from the Ghostmountain as the eagle flew, but uncrossable without a jet pack or a wing-glider.

He cast around, searching for something to shield himself from the punishing weather, and found only a canted slab of rock. Aching from the strain of the Talons, Tarikus made it into the poor cover and found mud and lichen in the lee. The fungus he ate, the mud he smeared over his flesh to hold in his body heat.

He wondered if this was some kind of punishment. Had he failed the first test in some way that had not registered in his mind? Or had Thryn and those who sat in judgement of him tired of the game and made their choice, left him out here to die of exposure? Both seemed unlikely; a bolt shell to the back of his head would have ended him far faster than starvation or hypothermia, and the Doom Eagles were not given to cause suffering where it need not occur – there was enough of that to go around in the universe, without adding to the volume of it.

As he half-dozed behind his rough shelter, Tarikus imagined the scrutiny of distant eyes, watching him from the windows of the fortress-monastery he thought of as his home. He felt darkness crowd in on him, a numbness spreading through his body. Still they questioned him, only now it was without words, now it was with the force of ruthless nature. Now it was Gathis itself, the voice of the Ghostmountain and the Razor-peaks, that challenged him.

And still, the answer that was sought was not given. By the following dawn, Tarikus had died.

Thryn sensed his master's displeasure before he entered the observation gallery. It filled the space around him like a cold fog, present in everything and ready to become an ice-storm at a moment's notice.

Within he found Hearon at the heavy window, and off to one side the figure of Brother-Captain Consultus. The warrior was clad in his wargear, and he stood at stiff attention, eyes focused on a distant point beyond the far wall. Consultus looked like carved stone, immobile and rigid; but Thryn saw past that, reading the steady churn of emotions inside the captain of the Third.

The Luckless Third, so the other company commanders called them, but never to their faces. Thryn considered this and saw truth in it; the return of Tarikus was just one more piece of ill fortune laid at the boots of Consultus and his men.

Hearon threw a glance at the Librarian. 'You have an answer for me?'

'I do not, lord,' he replied.

'Where is he now?'

The psyker gestured with a nod. 'In the Apothecarion. He was recovered before brain death could occur. He will live.'

'For what that is worth.' Thryn's master made a negative noise. 'Does your witch-sight fail you? Look into his soul, tell me what you see.'

'I have,' admitted the psyker, 'and I can draw no conclusion. Resilient as he is, his psyche was tormented by imprisonment and suffering, but that is to be expected. But this is not a case of black and white. There are many shades of grey.'

'I disagree,' Hearon replied. 'The question is a direct one. Is Tarikus to be trusted? Yes or no?'

'He has endured the trials,' ventured the captain. 'Survived, once again.'

'I know your opinion already,' Hearon snapped. 'Repeating it serves no purpose.' He looked back at Thryn.

'The captain is quite correct,' said the Librarian. 'His flesh withstands great punishment. He does not waver beneath chastisement that would kill a warrior of lesser courage.'

Hearon grimaced. 'That is a thing of meat and blood,' he said, with a terse gesture. 'And we know those can be controlled.' The Chapter Master shook his head. 'No, it is the question of Tarikus's spirit that tasks me. His soul is where the question lies.'

'His faith in the Emperor is strong.' Thryn paused, framing his words. 'His faith in his Chapter also.'

'*Even after we have done this to him,*' Hearon was looking at Consultus as he said the words. 'I don't need Thryn's powers to pluck that thought from your mind, brother-captain.'

'It is so, lord,' Consultus replied.

'Let no man here labour under the mistaken belief that I take pleasure in this,' Hearon grated. 'But Tarikus is one man. My responsibilities are to a Chapter one thousand strong, to a heritage of ten millennia. The Doom Eagles are my charge, and if I must shoulder the guilt of persecuting a single kinsman in order to protect them, I will do so without hesitation. It is only a grain of sand against the weight of Aquila's holy remorse.'

Thryn was silent for a moment. He knew full well why he had been called to this meeting, and why too Consultus, as Tarikus's former commanding officer, had been brought in as a witness. 'There is word from the Council of Eagles?'

Hearon nodded. Modelled after the High Council of Terra, the Doom Eagles encompassed a commission of men of highest rank who would draw together on matters of import facing the Chapter. The group would offer advice to the Chapter Master, and while ultimately Hearon held the sanction over all commands, he drew upon the knowledge and advice of all his company captains, his senior Chaplain, Apothecary, Forge Master and Librarian. 'The greater body of my warriors question the need to prolong this matter. The risk outweighs the gain. The damage that might be wrought by a single turncoat among our number is huge when compared against the value of one veteran sergeant.'

'Is it?' Consultus said quietly. 'Do we not damage the Chapter ourselves if we reject a warrior whose only crime was a failure to die?'

'The others believe he is tainted?' asked Thryn.

'The others suggest that Tarikus be put down,' said the captain, with no little venom.

Hearon ignored Consultus's interruption. 'I… am not convinced.'

'My lord?'

The Chapter Master returned to the window. 'The Doom Eagles have always been the most pragmatic of the Adeptus Astartes. We have no time for vacillation. That we may never again delay… Those words are etched on our hearts.' He paused. 'Some of our battle-brothers say we should excise this man and move beyond. End him, and confirm what has already been laid to stone; that Tarikus of the 3rd is dead and gone.'

Thryn cocked his head. 'And yet?'

'And yet…' repeated Hearon, glancing toward Consultus, 'I cannot in all good conscience end this in so cursory a manner. When death comes to claim me, I find myself asking how I could go to the Emperor's side and answer for this. That I would allow a Son of Gathis to meet the sword's edge all because of an unanswered question?' He shook his head. 'That will not stand.'

Thryn's eyes narrowed. 'There is another way, lord. A method I have yet hesitated to employ. A weirding, if you will. '

'Do what you must.' The Chapter Master looked over his shoulder at Thryn. 'You *will* bring me an answer, Librarian.'

'Even if Tarikus is destroyed by it?' said Consultus.

'Even if,' Hearon replied.

Zurus exited the south range after morning firing rites, and found the three of them waiting for him. He hesitated, for a moment uncertain how to respond, then beckoned the Space Marines to follow him. They moved to a worktable in the far corner of the arming hall, and he took the only stool and sat upon it. With careful, spare motions, Zurus dismantled his bolt pistol and set about the work of cleaning the weapon.

As he expected, it was Korica who spoke first. 'Lord,' he began, tension thick in his tone, 'we have talked amongst ourselves of… of this matter, and we have questions.'

'Indeed?' said Zurus, taking apart the trigger assembly. 'Questions seem to be the matter of the day.' From the corner of his eye, he saw the other two Doom Eagles exchange glances; one of them, his face dark and intense with old fire scarring, the other sallow of features with a single silver ring in his ear and the helix electoo of an Apothecary upon his neck. He read conflict in their aspects. It came as no surprise; he felt the same thing they did, to some degree.

'There is much talk in the galleries,' Korica went on, gesturing with his carbon-and-steel augmetic arm. 'Rumour and hearsay. We would know the truth.'

Zurus stopped and studied the pieces of his gun. 'Would you?' he said, a warning in his manner. 'Tell me, brother, would you also have me go against the express orders of the Chapter Master?'

'We would never disobey a legal command, brother-sergeant,' said the Apothecary. 'You know that.'

He nodded. 'Aye, Petius, I do.' Zurus glanced at the scarred warrior. 'Mykilus? As your kinsmen have spoken, I trust you must have something to venture as well?'

The other Doom Eagle gave a slow nod. 'Sir,' he began, 'you have commanded our squad for two cycles and we have been bound in blood and fire together. No disrespect to you is intended... but Tarikus was our sergeant for a long time. He saved each of our lives on one battleground or another. We thought him dead, and now we learn that he still lives...' Mykilus trailed off, unable to find the right words.

'Aquila's remorse runs strong in us,' said Korica. 'We believed Tarikus had been killed at the hands of the Red Corsairs. We brought back his knife. We share the guilt at giving up on him.' He shook his head. 'We let him down. We should have done more. Searched longer.'

Zurus looked up for the first time. 'No,' he said flatly. 'Do not torment yourselves. You could not have known.'

'We want to see him, sir,' said Petius.

'Impossible.' Zurus shot a glance at the Apothecary. 'It is forbidden. He is to remain in isolation until he has been judged.'

Korica's face twisted in anger. 'Tarikus is no traitor. We know the man better than any other battle-brother on the Ghostmountain! He is steadfast!'

Zurus studied the faces of the three men. 'Is that what you all think?' He got a chorus of nods in return – and yet, the warrior could sense some tiny inklings of doubt lurking behind the hard eyes of his men. The very same hesitation he himself experienced. 'I took on the mantle of Tarikus's stewardship for one reason,' Zurus went on. 'Because of what I knew of the man whom I had succeeded. I did it because of what you told me of him.' He didn't add that in truth, Brother Zurus had always felt as if he could not measure up to the shadow of the squad's former commander.

'Then tell us what you think, sir,' said Mykilus. 'If we cannot speak to him ourselves, tell us your thoughts.'

'Aye,' added Petius. 'You have looked him in the eye. What did you see?'

Zurus sighed. 'One of us.' His gaze dropped to the disassembled bolter. 'Or so it seemed.'

'Chaos does not lurk within the heart of Brother Tarikus,' grated Korica. 'I would stake my life on that.'

'Are you sure?' Zurus returned to his work. 'Trapped in the heart of madness, tormented every moment of every day by the foulest traitor-genius hell ever spawned? Could a man not be twisted under such pressure?'

'A man, perhaps,' said Petius. 'But not a Doom Eagle.'

'Not Tarikus,' insisted Korica.

Zurus was silent for a long time, carefully rebuilding the weapon. 'It is no wonder you wish Tarikus to be found pure,' he said, at length. 'Each of you carry the guilt of speaking his death when in fact he had only been lost. But that remorse will pale into nothing if he is proven to be tainted.'

'If that is so,' Mykilus began, his voice leaden, 'then we three will be the ones to send him into oblivion.'

'But it is *not*,' Korica insisted. 'And we three will be there to welcome him back once this mistrust is swept away!'

The gun went back together smoothly, and Zurus tested the action before returning it to his holster. Finally, he rose and walked away.

At the threshold of the chamber door he paused and glanced back at his men. *But not really my men*, he told himself. *Tarikus's men*.

'Are you coming?' he asked.


He was at peace.

Sleep, pure and real. Tarikus struggled to remember the last time he had rested so well, free from nightmares and horrific recollections. Sluggish amniotic fluid swathed him, and he drifted in a tiny, warm ocean of his own. His fingers brushed the inside of a glassy orb. No sound reached him here.

*Peace*. And all he had needed to do to find it was to die.

He knew that what he experienced now was not true death; he had known that even as the cold had crept into his flesh, tightening about his bio-implant organs, pushing him towards nothingness. No, this was the little-death of the healing trance, the strange state between where the engines of his Astartes physiology were left to work their chemical magicks. He had been here before. After the battle for Krypt. After the narrow escape from Serek–

*Serek*. Tarikus suppressed a shudder. Memory of that incident returned to him with harsh clarity. After Serek, he had been in a trance like this, repairing damage wrought by a forced teleport transition. And it had been inside a medicae tank such as this one that he had watched the Red Corsairs come to take him. It came back in hard punches of sense-memory – bolt shells cracking the glassaic, his body sluicing out with the liquid on to the deck, still broken, still unready. The renegades coming in to attack him. Blood mixed with the yellowish amnio-fluid. Fighting and killing; but ultimately, failing.

A shiver ran the length of him. Suddenly the warm liquid was as cold as the mountainside.

Tarikus took a breath of the oxygenated medium and felt the chill bore deeper. Out beyond the walls of the medicae tank shapes moved to and fro. They might have been other Astartes, perhaps come to observe this curiosity, this warrior back from the dead, this soul in limbo – or perhaps they were just servitors, going about their tasks, making sure Tarikus did not perish. Not yet.

He did not have permission to die. Aquila had not granted it.

The Doom Eagle looked inside himself and dared to wonder what a real death might feel like. He had been close to that abyss so many times, but never fallen to it; and now, in this moment of great darkness he dared to wonder if death would be the better end for him. If he had perished aboard the hospitaller ship, or perhaps in the cells of the Dynikas prison, then all that happened now would not have come to pass. Tarikus's Chapter would continue on, untroubled by the aberration of his chance survival. The pestilent questions would not have been asked. Constancy would not be challenged.

He felt hollow inside. In his prison cell, whenever he could snatch a moment away from the eyes of the mutant guards and the modificate freaks, he had prayed to the Golden Throne that he might live to see home once more. And in all that time, he had never once thought that he would not be trusted by his own kinsmen.

Conflict raged inside him. At once he hated Thryn and the others for daring to doubt him, but at the same moment he understood why they did so. If matters had been different, if it had been Zurus returning to Gathis and not Tarikus, then what choices would *he* have made in the same place? What questions would Tarikus have demanded answers for?

It came to him that the only way he would be able to prove himself would be to give up the last breath in his body. In death, truth could not be hidden.

The door to the psyker's sanctum opened on oiled pistons and a grave voice issued out from the darkness inside. 'Enter, Zurus. If you must.'

Zurus did as he was bid. Thryn's meditation chamber was little bigger than the accommodation cell where the sergeant laid his head, but it had the illusion of depth thanks to the strange jumble of shadows cast by electro-candles atop a series of iron stands, each at the corner of a mathematical shape carved into the floor.

Thryn rose from a kneeling cushion and pushed aside a fan of imager plates. Zurus glanced at them and saw only unreadable texts and oddly blurred images. He swallowed and failed to hide a grimace. The air in here was strange, almost oily, but with an acid tingle on the bare flesh of his face and hands.

Thryn glared at him. The psyker was in his wargear, and about his head in a blue-white halo, the crystalline matrix of a psionic hood glowed softly. 'You're interrupting my preparations, brother. And you have no good reason.'

Zurus met his hard look with one of his own. 'I have every reason–' he began.

'I'll save you the trouble of explaining yourself to me, shall I?' snapped the Librarian. 'You've been swayed by Tarikus. You've listened to his men, and felt their anxiety for their former commander's fate.' He turned away. 'And as you have never truly felt content as the leader of Tarikus's former squad, you wish to have him return to our fold so you can be free of your conflicts. Is that close to the truth?'

Zurus bristled at the other warrior's tone. 'You make us sound like mewling, weak children! You mock men who dare to show compassion and loyalty to their brothers!'

'Pragmatism is the watchword of the Doom Eagles,' Thryn continued. 'We do not let matters of sentimentality cloud our vision.'

'You think fidelity is something to be dismissed, witch-kin?' Zurus advanced on him. 'Is your warp-touched heart so empty that you forget your bonds of brotherhood?'

'I have forgotten nothing,' Thryn replied. 'But some must bear the burden to voice the questions that no others can utter. Some must dare to speak the hard words that no brother wishes to hear!' He turned to face him, the psy-crystals flickering. 'This obligation is mine. I will see it to its end.'

Zurus's shoulders sagged. 'How much further must this go? You have looked into his mind – tell me, have you sensed the taint of Chaos in his thoughts?'

Thryn shook his head. 'I have not.'

'And the testing of his flesh, first the Talons and then the wind and ice. Did his body belie the touch of the Archenemy at any time?'

'It did not,' intoned the Librarian.

'Then how can you let this go on? Tarikus is not corrupted!'

Thryn nodded. 'I agree.' It was not the answer Zurus was expecting. Before he could speak again, the psyker continued. 'I agree that his mind and his body are sound. But it is not those that I seek to test, brother. It is his soul. That which is the most ephemeral, yet the most powerful element of a life.' Thryn sighed, and something of the bleak aspect of his face softened. 'We know the insidious ways of Chaos, the Emperor blight them. Tarikus may carry a seed of darkness within him and never know it. It has happened before. He may live out a long life, and then one day, at an appointed time, or at some word of command, be transformed into something horrific. All that, if the smallest sliver of warp-stigma lies buried in his aura.'

Zurus frowned. 'The only way to be sure is to kill him, is that what you mean? If you end him and he erupts into some hell beast, you are proven right. If he dies, then he was innocent and just, and goes to the Emperor's side.' He snorted. 'A poor choice for Tarikus on either account.'

'This matter cannot be brought to a close while doubt still exists,' insisted Thryn.

'Then you'll do it?' Zurus snapped. 'And not just the little-death this time, but a cold-blooded murder?'

'Lord Hearon has granted me latitude to do whatever I must to end this uncertainty. And I will end it, this day.' Thryn returned to the centre of the room and knelt once more.

Zurus felt the tingle on his skin of psy-power in the air, the near-storm sense of it growing by the second. 'What will you do?'

Thryn bowed his head. 'Go now, brother. You will know soon enough.'

He lingered at the threshold for a long moment, then stepped through and allowed the hatch to close behind him. Cogs worked and seals fell into place, and Zurus stood outside, staring at the strange hexagram-matric wards etched into the metal, wondering what final trial Tarikus was about to face.

A sound came to him, echoing down the stone corridor. It sounded like thunder, but it could just as easily have been the report of distant shellfire.

Tarikus awoke, and he was in hell.

He fell hard, the rough metal plating of the floor rising up to slam into his knees and arms. He groaned and coughed up a river of sting-ing bile and thick amnio-fluid. Black streaks of blood threaded the ejecta from his lips. The warrior felt strange; his body seemed wrong, the impulses from his fingertips somehow out of synchrony with the rest of his nerves. He tried to shake himself free of the sensation but it would not leave him. Tarikus's flesh hung on him like an ill-fitting suit of clothes.

He looked up and blinked, his eyes refusing to focus properly. Lights and shadows jumped around him, blurring into shapes that he could not define. Something hove close and he perceived a hand reaching out to him, offering assistance.

'Here,' said a thick, resinous voice. 'To your feet. Come. There is much work to do.'

He took the grip, and felt peculiar talons where fingers should have been; but he was already rising, legs working, muscles tightening.

Light flashed, too slow to be storm-glow, the thunder-pulse with it too quick, too near. *Gunfire?* The sluggish thought trickled down through the layers of his awareness.

Tarikus jerked his hand away. 'Who are you? What is happening?'

Harsh laughter answered him. 'So many questions. Be still, warrior. All will be made clear.' One of the shadows came closer, looming large.

'Don't fight it, Tarikus. Let it happen.' He heard another low, callous chuckle. 'It will be less painful.'

There was heat at his back, burning and steady like the beating of a pitiless sun; and in the air about him, he perceived motes of dust falling in a slow torrent. He saw steel walls. Chains and broken glass. 'What is happening?' he shouted, but his words were lost in the blazing roar of a weapon. He knew that sound: a heavy bolter cannon on full automatic fire, impacts cutting into flesh and ceramite.

'You have done well,' he was told. 'Better than we could have expected. You opened the way for us.' The shadow-man came closer. 'Our perfect weapon.'

'What?' Tarikus raised his hands in self-defence. 'I do not understand–'

'Then look at me,' said the voice. 'And know the truth.'

The light chose that moment to come again, and in its hard-edged, unflinching glare Tarikus saw a thing that resembled an Astartes, but one made of flayed meat, broken bone and corroded iron. A face of gallows-pale flesh leered at him and twisted in amusement. Beneath it, on the figure's chest, was the design of a star with eight razor-tipped points.

'Traitor!' Tarikus shouted the word.

The corrupted warrior nodded. 'Yes, you are.'

He stumbled backwards, shaking his head. His skull felt heavy and leaden. 'No…'

'Your hands. Look at your hands.'

Tarikus could not help but glance downward. The meat of his hard, calloused fingers was gone, and in its place were arcs of bone that glistened like black oil.

'The change is already upon you. It's coming now. Let it happen.'

Ice filled his gut and Tarikus thrashed at the air, smashing aside a support frame, crashing back into the opened medicae tank where he had been healing. He tried to give a wordless shout of denial, but the sound would not form in his constricting throat. His muscles bunched and he shuddered, losing balance. Tarikus could feel a wave of something terrible billowing up inside him, reordering the meat and blood of his body as it moved. He spat and acid flew from his lips, spattering the walls with tiny smoking pits where the droplets fell. He tried to reject it, and failed.

He could hear battle beyond the doors of the chamber now, fast and lethal. Thunder rumbled all around, echoing through the stone at his feet. The Eyrie was under attack.

The Traitor Marine took a step towards him. When it spoke again, there was almost concern in its words. 'The Primogenitor told me it would not be an easy transformation. But hold on, kinsman. You will be renewed in all but a moment. And then you will join us fully.'

'I am not your kinsman!' Tarikus roared, and the words were ragged animal sounds torn from the throat of some monster, not from his lips, not from the mouth of a Doom Eagle. 'What have you done to me?'

Another chuckle. 'You did this to yourself, Tarikus. Don't you recall?' The room seemed to contract, the walls closing in on them both. 'On Dynikas. When you cast off your master. When you finally understood?'

'Understood… what?' All around him the stone of the medicae chamber flowed like wax into different shapes, and through the haze across his twitching vision the walls momentarily turned into planes of steel, vibrating with heat. The cell. The chains and the walls and the cell. *Did I never really leave? Have I always been there?*

The Traitor cocked its head. 'You understood that you had been discarded. Forgotten. That your corpse-god is ashes and lies. That you mean nothing to the men who tried to make you their slave.'

Tarikus stumbled away, shaking his head, denying every word. 'No!' He tried to launch himself towards the other warrior, but the sudden heat robbed him of every ounce of energy. In place of sweat, oily fluids seeped from his skin, draining his vitality with them.

'Don't you remember?' The Traitor gestured around, and Tarikus saw a distorted liquid mirror shimmer in the air. Upon it he saw himself in rags, kneeling before a towering figure in a coat made of human skin, a giant brass spider emerging from its back.

*Fabius Bile.*

'No…' he insisted. 'This is a trick! That did not happen! I would never break my oath!' Tarikus lurched back to his feet. 'I would not turn!'

'But you did,' said the voice. 'Because they hated you, forgot you.' The Traitor gestured and Tarikus saw a line of figures in tarnished silver armour standing high behind him. Their proportions were monstrous; they towered like Dreadnoughts, each one jeering and mocking him. They had faces he knew: Zurus and Thryn. At their shoulders: Korica, Mykilus and Petius. And above them all, as tall as a Titan, Aquila himself.

Tarikus reached out his mutating talon-hand and they shrank away; and then the worst of it. As one, all the Doom Eagles turned their backs on him, casting him aside.

Suddenly the room was tight and small about him, the space at the bottom of a pit that stretched up and away, walls too sheer to climb, light too far to reach.

'Poor Tarikus,' said the voice, soothing and unctuous. 'Is it any wonder you accepted the gift?'

Terror filled him at the words, but he could not stay silent. 'What gift?'

The Traitor opened its claw-hand and in it lay a feather, a small curl of plume alike to those that an eagle might leave behind in passing. It was ink-black, a colour so deep and strong that Tarikus immediately knew that to touch it would be poison to him.

No sooner had he laid eyes on the barb than his chest began to burn. Tarikus gasped and clawed at the wet strips of torn tunic shrouding his torso and ripped them away. His transformed talon hands caught the surface of his skin and great rents appeared in the meat of him. From the wounds he had made, no blood flowed; instead cascades of tiny black feathers issued out, spilling from his body. He roared and felt his throat filling with a swarming mass. Tarikus retched and spat a plug of wet, matted quills from his lips.

'Do you see now?' said the Traitor. 'A Chapter that rejected you, left you to perish in the cold, pitiless void. A cadre of false brothers who fled when their lives were in jeopardy. The lies you were told about fealty and honour, but all of it sand. Is it any wonder you were broken?' The other warrior leaned in. 'Is it any wonder you let us remake you in the Primogenitor's name?' He nodded. 'And now the last shroud is released from you, kinsman. Now you are free to be one of us… and our first act will be to grind this Ghostmountain to dust.'

Tarikus could not stop himself from trembling. The worst of it was not the visions, or the perhaps-memories, or the sense of his own body slipping away from him. No, the worst of it was that he could not be sure. The Traitor's words had the edge of truth to them.

How often in those long months in that cell had he lain in torment, one single question desperate on his lips. *Why have I been forgotten?* His every waking moment as an Adeptus Astartes had been in service of something greater than himself, and in return, in exchange for the surety of fate and death the Doom Eagles gave, Tarikus had the priceless gift of brotherhood. The certain knowledge of comradeship among his kindred, the knowing that he would never be lost, not so long as a single son of Gathis still drew breath. *So why did they never come for me? Why did they count me dead and be done, never to speak my name again?*

'Because it is a lie,' said the Traitor. 'And has ever been one.' He gestured around. '*We* will never lie to you, Tarikus. You will always know the truth with us.' The hand extended out to him once more. 'Take it.'

The thunder outside and the flashes of blue-white light coursed all around him. Tarikus looked up and saw the outstretched hand, the turncoat Astartes – and beyond, the shadows of the Doom Eagles.

They were judging him.

Time halted for Tarikus, and the questions that had bombarded him since he had returned to the Eyrie were echoing through his mind. The accusations welled up from within.

He could imagine a shade of himself – a weaker, broken Tarikus – who might have had the flaw of character to yield to the strain of his confinement on Dynikas. This ghost-Tarikus, this pale copy of him, made bitter by his abandonment, clawing in desperation for the one thing every Space Marine wanted… The bond of brotherhood. Without their comradeship, the Astartes were nothing. Everything they were was built upon that foundation. What horror it would be to lose that, to be cast adrift and counted as unkindred. A weakened soul, captured at the lowest moment, might be persuaded to bend the knee to a former foe for just a taste of that blessed bond once again. A fragile spirit, yes, who would willingly hide their new loyalty beneath the cloak of the old, and carry poison back to those who had deserted them. Poison and murder, all in the name of revenge.

Suddenly, events were moving again, and he was aware of the Traitor nodding. 'Yes. You see now, don't you?'

But that shade, that weakling who appeared in his thoughts... Whatever it was, it was not Tarikus, son of Gathis, scion of Aquila. He drew himself up and with a vicious shove, pushed the turncoat aside.

Tarikus glared up at the silent, condemning gazes of his Doom Eagle brethren, peering at the phantoms of their faces. 'I am not a heretic.' He spoke, and with each word that left his mouth, Tarikus felt his vitality returning to him. A sense of righteous power enveloped him, and with it the wrongness of his changed body bled away. Moment by moment, he began to feel *correct*. With every breath, he moved closer to the warrior he had always been – and with a surge of strength, Tarikus realised that he had not felt so certain of anything in years. Not since before he had been taken prisoner. 'Judge me if you will,' he shouted, 'I do not fear it! You will look inside my heart and see only fealty! I am Tarikus!'

The hazed faces of his former squad mates danced there in the wraith-light. Korica: impulsive and brave. Mykilus: steadfast and strong. Petius: taciturn and measured. They did not turn from him. They had not forgotten him.

Behind him, the Traitor was getting to its feet, coming towards him with murder in its eyes. 'Fool–'

He silenced the enemy by grabbing his throat and tightening his grip until the Traitor could only make broken gurgles. Gunfire-thunder rumbled louder and louder in his ears and Tarikus bellowed to make himself heard. 'I am a Doom Eagle! My fidelity will never falter!' He threw his enemy to the ground. 'I did not break! *I will never break!*'

A great pressure, silent but deafening, pushed out from inside his thoughts, and all at once the warped walls around him exploded like glass beneath a hammer.

Tarikus swept around; he was intact, unchanged. Everything that had happened in the phantom room was gone, vanished like shafts of sunlight consumed by clouds. He stood before the open healing tank, then turned and found the Librarian Thryn coming back to his feet. The psyker was nursing an ugly bruise forming at his throat. He spat and eyed the other Astartes.

'You?' said Tarikus. He sniffed the air, scenting the greasy tang of spent mind-power. 'You cast a veil over me... All of it illusions and game-play.'

'Aye,' Thryn replied, rough-voiced. 'And you almost tore the breath from me in the process.'

Tarikus advanced towards the psyker, his hands contracting into fists. Anger burned in his eyes, and the question of Thryn being clad in armour and himself not didn't cross his thoughts. 'I should beat an apology from you, witch-kin.'

'You should be thanking me,' Thryn retorted. 'At last, I finally saw into you. Saw what you hid from us.'

'I hid nothing,' Tarikus spat.

Thryn shook his head. 'Don't lie to me, not now. You hid your fear, Tarikus. The black and terrible fear that came upon you in the darkest moments of your confinement, when just for a moment, you wondered what would happen if you weakened.' The Librarian gave a crooked, unlovely smile. 'How very human of you.'

Gradually, Tarikus's fists relaxed. 'I looked into the darkness, across the edge of the abyss,' he said slowly. 'And I turned away.'

Thryn nodded. 'Indeed you did. And now I have the answer I wanted.' He offered his hand to the other Doom Eagle. 'Your integrity is assured. You are returned to us, brother. In body, mind… and in soul.'

Tarikus shook his hand in the old fashion, palm to wrist. 'I never left,' he said.

'When will there be an end to this?' grated Korica. He glared at Zurus, and the other warrior nodded slightly.

'I have no answer for you,' admitted the sergeant. He looked away, his gaze crossing the towering black marble fascias of the memorial towers, each reaching up and away towards the ornate ceiling far overhead. He saw something moving; a travel platform, dropping towards them.

Mykilus saw it too, and he pointed. 'Look there.'

Petius took a tentative step towards the edge of the gantryway, then halted. Like all of them, he was unsure of what meaning lay behind the urgent summons that had brought them to the relical.

In the next moment, the platform had arrived and a figure in duty robes stepped off, pushing past them.

'Tarikus?' Zurus could not keep the amazement from his voice. He had truly believed that he would never see the errant Astartes again. Thryn was not known for his lenience in matters of judgement. Then his thoughts caught up with him and Zurus allowed himself a small smile. He had been right about his lost brother; suddenly, all the doubts he had harboured about this duty and his part in Tarikus's ordeal were swept away, and it was as if a great weight fell from his shoulders.

Korica extended his augmetic arm towards Tarikus, but the veteran pushed past him, not slowing. The other Doom Eagles followed Tarikus down the length of the gantryway until he halted before a particular memorial slab.

Zurus knew what would come next the instant before it happened. The veteran's fist shot out and punched through the bubble of glassaic at the end of the panel and then folded around the death-remnant inside.

He watched the other warrior draw out a blood-streaked hand, and in it, a battle-worn combat blade. Tarikus looked down at the knife, and then up at them for the first time. His steady, clear-eyed gaze crossed each one of them in turn, ending with Zurus. The veteran opened his mouth to speak – and then thought better of it. Instead, Tarikus acted.

With a slow, steady draw of blade point over stone, he etched a heavy line through his own name, erasing the record of his death. He reclaimed his life. Mykilus was the first to speak. 'Welcome back, sir.' He bowed his head. 'If we had only known that the Red Corsairs had not killed you–'

'No.' Tarikus held up his hand. 'You will not speak of that again. And by my order, you will not carry any guilt over what happened.' He stepped forward and moved from brother to brother, tapping each on the shoulder in turn. 'I hold no malice. You did no wrong that day.'

Then he was looking at Zurus. The Doom Eagle sighed, and made a decision of his own. He reached beneath his robes and his hand returned with a fetter of black and silver links pooled in the palm; it was the honour-chain that signified his command of the battle squad. He offered it. 'This also belongs to you, I believe.'

Tarikus showed quiet surprise. 'The squad is yours, brother. You have made it so. These men are your men.'

Zurus shook his head. 'No. It has been my honour to lead them into battle in the name of the Emperor and Aquila, but I have never been their commander, not in the manner you were. I have only been... the caretaker of that post. You have seniority over me, the laurel and the honours. It is your right to reclaim your prior status.'

The veteran came closer, his brow furrowing. 'You are sure you wish to step down, Zurus? I know my brothers would not have followed you if you had not been worthy of it.' He nodded at the chain.

Zurus pressed the links into Tarikus's hand. 'I will not take that which by right is yours.' He stepped away. 'I will find another place in the Chapter.'

'You already have a place, sir,' said Korica. He glanced at Tarikus, and the veteran sergeant nodded.

'Aye,' said the other Doom Eagle. 'I have need of good men, who see clearly and fight well.' Tarikus held up the honour chain. 'I will accept this on condition that you remain in the squad as my second.'

Zurus thought on the offer, then nodded. 'That seems a fair bargain.'

Tarikus was silent for a long moment; then he wrapped the chain about the hilt of the knife and put it into his belt. 'Come, then, kinsmen. The enemy tasks me.' He gestured up towards the distant roof, where glimmers of constant storm-light flickered. 'I have been dead long enough.'

Zurus followed his commander's gaze upward to where the rain fell, steady and ceaseless as the Emperor's wrath.

# ʊ
# CONSEQUENCES

*Graham McNeill*

Author's note
*This story is set between the events of* Warriors
of Ultramar *and* Dead Sky, Black Sun.

The cold water pooled in a depression in the centre of the stone floor
of the cell, before spilling through the cracked stonework to unknown
destinations. This deep beneath the rock of the Fortress of Hera, water
dripped from the rugged ceiling, leached through thousands of metres
of hard granite from the river that thundered along the length of the
Valley of Laponis high above.

Only the thinnest sliver of light from below the thick, iron door illuminated the cell, but it was enough for its occupant, due to enhanced
vision that allowed him to see almost as well at night as in daylight. Not
that there was anything to see within the cell's dank confines, merely an
iron ring set into the wall where a prisoner could be kept chained until
such time as he was removed for sentencing or punishment.

The cell's solitary occupant was not chained to the wall or restrained
in any way. There would be little point in chaining one whose strength
could easily break any such fetters, tear the iron ring from the wall or
who secreted an acidic saliva that, given time, would eat away at even
the strongest of metals.

The prisoner had already sworn an oath that he would not attempt
to escape or hamper his gaolers in any way and his word was accepted
as truth.

He sat cross-legged, supporting his weight on his hands, holding his
body a centimetre from the cold floor of the cell. An aquila tattoo flexed
on his right shoulder as he tensed and released his muscles. Inscribed

upon the flesh of his left was a number in the curling script of High Gothic.

The prisoner heard the clip of approaching footsteps over the steady *drip-drip* of the water from the ceiling and lowered himself to the floor, uncrossing his legs and standing in one smooth motion. His hair was dark and short, though longer than he kept it normally, and his thundercloud eyes smouldered with promised threat. Two golden studs glittered on his forehead and, though he was powerfully muscled, taller and broader than the mightiest of humans, he knew he was much weaker and leaner than he should be.

A knotted mass of scar tissue writhed across his flat stomach, paler than the rest of his skin, but it was merely the largest of an impressive collection of scars and battle wounds that criss-crossed his skin in a macabre web.

He heard the rattle of keys and the heavy door groaned open, spilling warm light into the cell. He squinted briefly, before his eyes quickly adjusted to the increased illumination and saw a blue-robed helot dressed in the garb of a gaoler with a dark hood covering his face.

Behind him, two giants in brightly polished Terminator armour stood with golden-bladed polearms carried across their chests. Their bulk filled the wide corridor, braziered torchlight flickering across the blue ceramite surfaces like fiery snakes. The prisoner bowed to his gaoler and said, 'Is it time?'

The helot nodded – it was forbidden for one such as he to address the prisoner – and indicated that he should leave the cell.

The prisoner bowed his head below the level of the stone lintel and stood in front of the Terminators, before marching through the fire-lit tunnels towards whatever fate the Master of the Ultramarines had decreed for him.

As he made his way up the rough-hewn steps of the detention level, Uriel Ventris wondered again at the path that had led him to this place.

Six days earlier, the battered and war-weary form of the Ultramarine strike cruiser *Vae Victus* limped towards the blue jewel of Macragge. Her armoured hide seemed to hang loose on her frame, like a beast starved of food and entering its dying days. The journey through the warp from Tarsis Ultra had taken the better part of six months, though upon re-entering real space and calibrating the ship's chronometers against local celestial bodies, it was noted that a time dilation of a year and a half had passed. Such anomalies in the apparent flow of time while travelling through the fluid medium of warpspace were not uncommon; rather, they were an accepted price to be paid for a method of travel that allowed a ship to cross the galaxy without spending generations in the journey.

Indeed, such a relatively minor time dilation was remarkable given the vast distance travelled by the *Vae Victus*. Tarsis Ultra lay to the north of Segmentum Tempestus, while Macragge orbited her star in the eastern reaches of Ultima Segmentum, half the galaxy away.

In the forward hangars of the ship, three Thunderhawk gunships were securely tethered to the deck – one in dire need of the ministrations of a Techmarine and a team of mono-tasked servitors before it would fly again, so stripped of its armaments and armour was it. Here, a lone Space Marine knelt in prayer between two parallel rows of corpses covered in sky-blue sheets. Another Space Marine, armoured in black, with a skull-faced helm, stood at the end of the rows of bodies, chanting a soft mantra to the fallen and calling upon the Emperor to guide each warriors to His side.

The bodies lined up on either side of him were the dead of the Fourth Company, the cost to the Ultramarines for honouring an ancient debt sworn by their primarch to aid the people of Tarsis Ultra in times of need. Such a price was high, terribly high, but it was a price the Ultramarines willingly paid for the sake of honour.

The Space Marine kneeling between the corpses raised his head and smoothly rose to his feet. Captain Uriel Ventris hammered his fist twice into his breastplate in the warrior's Honour to the Fallen. These were his men, his warriors. They had followed him into battle on Pavonis against traitors and a monstrous alien star god and thence to Tarsis Ultra where they had fought with courage and honour against the terrifying threat of the extra-galactic predators known as the tyranids. They had saved Tarsis Ultra, but had paid a heavy blood price for the victory.

There, Uriel had fought shoulder to shoulder with brother Space Marines, the Mortifactors, an honourable Chapter whose lineage could be traced back to Blessed Guilliman, but whose doctrines and belief structure had changed so radically as to make them unrecognisable from their parent Chapter.

To the Mortifactors, death was venerated above all things, and the wisdom of the dead was sought through the visions of their Chaplains. Blood rites and the worship of those who had passed through this life in ages past was the norm for the Mortifactors and, though initially horrified by such deviation from the pages of the Codex Astartes, Uriel had found that he had more in common with the warriors of the Mortifactors than he cared to admit.

It was not a pleasing revelation.

Astador, the Chaplain of the Mortifactors, had said it best: 'You and I are both Angels of Death, Uriel.'

But it had taken him many months of hard fighting and harder choices to realise the truth of this. Despite the protests and outrage of Sergeant Learchus, Uriel had followed Astador's vision quests and emerged triumphant, where a strict adherence to the Codex would have seen them defeated in the earliest stages of the war. Pulled between two opposing philosophies, Uriel had made his choice and had found the balance between following the spirit and the letter of the Codex. He knew such behaviour marked him out amongst his brethren, but his former captain, Idaeus, had taught him the value of such insights and he knew in his heart that he had done the right thing.

Uriel looked along the line of corpses and felt a great weight settle upon him.

He had almost died in the belly of the tyranid hive ship, an insidious alien poison causing his blood to clot throughout his body. Only the devotion of his oldest friend and comrade, Pasanius, had saved his life, the veteran sergeant almost bleeding himself dry to save his captain's life. The wounds he had suffered in the conflict had mostly healed, though the mass of plasflesh that sealed the gaping wound in his torso was a constant dull, throbbing ache. Techmarine Harkus and Apothecary Selenus had reconstructed his left shoulder and clavicular pectoralis major with augmetic sinews and muscle grafts following a battle with a tyranid guardian organism, and his blood still underwent regular transfusions to ensure its purity.

But he had not died, he had triumphed and through his and countless others' sacrifice, Tarsis Ultra had been saved, though it would never be the same again. Uriel had seen enough on Ichar IV to know that once a planet was infected with the taint of these vile xeno creatures, it would forever be impossible to remove.

The bodies had been prepared for transport to the crypts beneath the Fortress of Hera; Chaplain Clausel was performing the *Finis Rerum* and Selenus had reverently removed the progenoid glands from the fallen. Upon their return to Macragge, each battle-brother would be interred in his own sepulchre and Uriel himself would go to the Shrine of the Primarch in the Temple of Correction and carve the names of the dead onto the bronze-edged slabs of smooth black marble that ran along the curved inner wall of the sanctum.

Clausel's chanting came to an abrupt end and Uriel turned to face the skull-visaged Chaplain, reflecting that perhaps the Mortifactors were not so different after all. For wasn't a Chaplain nothing more than a vision of Death incarnate? Frequently the last face a warrior saw before passing from this mortal coil was that of a Chaplain, the warrior who prepared his body before its journey to the halls of the dead.

He nodded to Clausel, feeling a tonal shift in the vibrations running through the hull as the ship's main engines powered down. The *Vae Victus* had achieved orbit and they were ready to descend to Macragge.

Awe. Humility. A sense of history that stretched back ten thousand years. All these feelings and more flooded Uriel's body as he entered the Temple of Correction once more. He remembered the last time he had set foot in this mighty marble edifice before he had set off for the world of Tarsis Ultra. Then he had been but a newly tested captain, with the weight of his next command heavy on his shoulders and a life of service before him. Everything had seemed simpler back then, before the burden of choice had entered his life.

As always, the Temple was thronged with pilgrims and the faithful, many of whom had journeyed further than he to be here. Many women carried babes in swaddling clothes and Uriel knew that a great many would have been both conceived and born during the pilgrimage to Macragge. Heads bowed as he passed and shouted blessings followed him. There were whispered prayers of thanks that one of the Emperor's chosen had come to this place to worship with them.

Uriel marched through the marble corridors, the dazzling white of the walls veined with thin traceries of gold and sepia and the floor paved with stone from the rocks at the base of Hera's Falls.

Finally, he entered the inner sanctum, beams of multicoloured light spearing from the gargantuan dome above. Refracted by cunning artifice through the crystals that made up its structure, each beam interwove with the others to create a dazzling internal rainbow. Hundreds of people knelt before the gently glowing Sepulchre of the Primarch, their voices raised in songs of praise to his memory. The sense of wonderment and rapture in the chamber was palpable and Uriel dropped to one knee, feeling unworthy of gazing too long on the face of his Chapter's founding father.

Being in the presence of such a magnificent hero of the Imperium, even though his heart had ceased to beat nearly ten thousand years ago, was a humbling experience, made all the more so for his own sense of unworthiness after the battles on Tarsis Ultra. Had he not cast aside this legendary warrior's teachings in favour of his own initiative and the primitive rites of a death-worshipper? Such arrogance, such hubris. Who was he to second-guess the wisdom of this hero, who was the flesh and blood progeny of the Emperor himself?

'Forgive me, my lord,' whispered Uriel, 'for I am unworthy of your love. I come before you to honour the names and deeds of your sons who fell in battle. They fought with courage and honour, and are deserving of a place at your side. Grant them surcease of their sorrows until they are ready to be reborn in your image through the holy mysteries of their gene-seed.'

He stood and made his way to the marble slabs set into the inner circumference of the wall, finding the section designated for the members of Fourth Company. So many slabs, so many names of those who had given their lives for the Chapter. He moved to the last slab with names upon it and, though he had seventy-eight names to carve, he needed neither list nor record to remember each warrior. Each face and name was indelibly etched on his memory and even if he lived to see out his days as one of the Chapter's Masters, he would never forget those who had died under his command.

He fished out a small chisel and hammer from his belt and began delicately chipping the marble to fashion the first name. He smoothed the inner edges of each letter with a hard-edged sanding stone, ready for those more skilled than he to apply the gold leaf to each name.

Name followed name, and Uriel lost track of time as he relived each warrior's character and personality through the simple act of carving their name. Daylight dimmed: the dome's rainbow fading and vanishing before rising anew the following morning. Days passed, though Uriel stopped for neither food nor water. Helots tasked with the care and maintenance of the temple enquired at regular intervals if he wished for anything, but were dismissed with a curt shake of the head. After three days they stopped asking.

As the rainbow crept down through the air to the stone floor of the temple on the fifth day of Uriel's vigil, he smoothed the last edge of the final name. His arms ached from the precise and painstaking movements of carving, but he was pleased with the results. All seventy-eight warriors would now remain part of the Chapter's heritage forever more and he felt their silent acceptance of his vigil as light and warmth filled the temple.

He pushed himself to his feet, pocketing his craftsman's tools, and made his way back to the centre of the temple. Though he had not eaten, drunk or slept these last days, he felt more refreshed than ever, as though a cool spring flowed through his veins, washing away the old Uriel and leaving only a dedicated warrior of the Emperor in his stead. The songs of the many pilgrims echoed in his skull and Uriel felt a great welcoming embrace.

Uriel closed his eyes and prayed, giving thanks for being afforded the chance to serve his Chapter and the Emperor. He joined in song with the pilgrims and many were the rapturous faces that beamed radiantly from the assembled congregation as his voice joined theirs.

They sang of duty, of courage and of sacrifice. They sang until they were hoarse and could raise their voices no more. They sang until tears spilled from their eyes and a swelling sense of brotherhood filled the temple. A choking tide of emotions welled within Uriel's chest as more and more voices joined the choir of praise.

As the latest hymn came to a rousing climax, ending in an exhilarated round of exultation, Uriel saw a trio of Space Marines in burnished blue armour enter the temple. That in itself was nothing unusual, but then Uriel realised the leader of the group was none other than Captain Sicarius of the Second Company, Commander of the Watch and Master of the Household. Uriel also saw that the Terminators who followed him were armed, something normally unheard of within the sanctum of the primarch.

Sicarius stopped before Uriel and said, 'Ventris.'

Though both were captains, Sicarius was still senior to him, and thus Uriel bowed his head, saying, 'Captain Sicarius, it is good to see you again.'

Sicarius's granite features were harder and colder than Uriel had ever known.

'Uriel Ventris of Calth,' said Sicarius formally. 'By the power invested in me by Lord Calgar and by the Emperor of Mankind, you are to surrender yourself into my keeping, that I might render you into the custody of your peers and effect their judgement upon you.'

Uriel suspected he knew the answer already, but asked, 'On what charge?'

'Heresy,' spat Sicarius, as though the word itself were repugnant to him. 'Do not offer any resistance, Ventris, there are more warriors without and it will do no good to create discord before these people.'

Uriel nodded and said, 'Thank you for letting me finish my work here. I know you could have come sooner.'

'That was for the dead, not for you,' snapped Sicarius.

'Thank you anyway.'

Sicarius nodded to the Terminators.

'Take him to the dungeons.'

The halls of Marneus Calgar, Master of the Ultramarines, were set atop the highest peak of the mountains, amidst the golden domes and marble-pillared temples of the Fortress of Hera. Though the day was hot, the air here was temperate, a fine mist of water from Hera's Falls sapping the worst of the heat. A perfectly symmetrical structure, the Chapter Master's chambers enclosed a central, sunken courtyard that was open to the azure sky above, its cloisters wrapped in cool shadows, its balconies draped in ancient, gold-stitched battle honours.

At its centre, a foaming fountain splashed. Carved in the likeness of Konor, the first Battle King of Macragge, it was surrounded by statuary depicting long-dead heroes of Macragge, artfully arranged so that they gave homage to their ancient king.

The last time Uriel had set foot here, it had been to receive his orders to depart for Pavonis and it had been a momentous occasion for him. Now, after a night in the dungeons and stripped of his armour, it was the scene of his disgrace.

And worse, it was the scene of his oldest friend's disgrace.

Pasanius stood beside him, similarly manacled and dressed in a blue chiton.

His own fall from grace he would accept, but to see Pasanius dragged down with him was almost too much for him to bear.

Surrounding Lord Calgar were the various Masters of the Chapter present on Macragge, in whose hands his ultimate fate lay. Captain Sicarius, Master of the Watch, sat to his left, next to Captain Galenus,

Master of the Marches, who in turn flanked Fennias Maxim, the Master of the Forge. Opposite them sat Captain Ixion, Chief Victualler, Captain Antilochus, Chief of Recruits and the heroic Captain Agemman of the First Company. The great and good of the Ultramarines sat in judgement of him and at their head sat Lord Calgar, his liege lord and Chapter Master.

Calgar looked older than Uriel remembered him, his piercing gaze sadder and his stern, patrician features more careworn than he remembered. The disappointment in his lord's eyes was too much and Uriel dropped his gaze, shame burning hot in his breast.

And last of all, seated beside Calgar, was Learchus.

Veteran sergeant of Fourth Company, Learchus had fought beside Uriel and, though it broke his heart, he knew now the source of the accusations against Pasanius and himself.

He should have seen it coming. In the final hours of the war on Tarsis Ultra, Learchus had as good as told him that he would seek redress for Uriel's flagrant disregard of the Codex Astartes. Much as he wanted to feel anger towards Learchus for this, Uriel could not bring himself to feel anything but pride in his sergeant. He was an Ultramarine through and through and had done nothing wrong. Indeed, had the circumstances been reversed, Uriel might well have found himself where Learchus was now.

At some unseen signal, Captain Sicarius rose from his seat, his long red cloak billowing around him as he stepped down into the sunken courtyard. He stared at Uriel and Pasanius with a look of loathing, pulling a wax-sealed vellum scroll from beneath his cloak.

He looked towards Calgar, who nodded solemnly.

'Uriel Ventris. Pasanius Lysane. On this, the nine hundredth and ninety-ninth year of the tenth millennium of his Imperial Majesty's rule, you are hereby charged with seventeen counts of the crime of heresy. Do you understand the gravity of these charges?'

'I do,' said Uriel.

'Aye,' said Pasanius, in a tone that made no secret of his contempt for this hearing. 'Though to drag us here after the great victory we won at Tarsis Ultra does nothing but shame the memories of those who died there. We fought the Great Devourer with courage, honour and faith. No man here can ask more than that!'

'Be silent!' thundered Sicarius. 'You will answer only those questions I ask of you and you are to volunteer no more information than that. Do you understand me?'

Pasanius's lip curled, but he said nothing and merely nodded.

Apparently satisfied, Sicarius circled the fountain and stood before Uriel, his gaze boring into him, as though he were attempting to force him to admit his guilt by sheer force of personality.

'You are a protégé of Captain Idaeus, are you not?'

'You know I am, Captain Sicarius,' answered Uriel evenly.

'Answer the question, Ventris,' retorted Sicarius.

'My rank is captain, you have not found me guilty yet and will address me by my title until such time as I may be convicted by this body.'

Sicarius pursed his lips, but knew it would do him no good to press the point and reluctantly conceded.

'Very well, captain. If we may proceed?'

'Yes, I served in Fourth Company under Captain Idaeus for ninety years, before rising to its captaincy following his death on Thracia.'

'Could you describe the circumstances of his death for us?'

Uriel took a deep breath to calm his rising temper. The tale of Idaeus's final battle was well known to every man here and he could see no purpose in reiterating it.

'Captain Ventris?'

'Very well,' began Uriel. 'The world of Thracia was one of a number that had rebelled against the lawful rule of the Emperor's representatives in the Ulenta sector and it was rumoured that the uprising had been instigated by followers of the Dark Powers. We were attached to the crusade forces of Inquisitor Appolyon and had been tasked with several surgical strikes against key enemy positions to facilitate the advance of Imperial Guard units closing on the capital city of Mercia.'

'And what was your final mission in this crusade?' asked Sicarius.

'Guard units were advancing along a narrow frontage, with one flank open to assault across a number of bridges. Squads of Fourth Company were tasked with their destruction.'

'An easy task surely?'

'In theory, yes. Intelligence indicated that the bridges were lightly held by poor quality opposition.'

'But that proved not to be the case, did it not?' asked Sicarius.

'No, bridge two-four was held by inferior troops, and we easily dealt with them without loss. Once the bridge was ours, we began rigging it for destruction, under the direction of Techmarine Tomasin.'

'May he always be remembered,' intoned Fennias Maxim from the edge of the courtyard.

'And then what happened?'

'As we prepared the bridge for destruction, the weather deteriorated markedly and we received fragmentary reports of the enemy moving in our direction. Within minutes we were under attack from a battalion-sized force of enemy units intent on seizing the bridge.'

'A fearsome prospect,' observed Sicarius.

'Not in this case,' said Uriel. 'Though this opposition was of a higher calibre than that tasked with holding the bridge, we were able to keep them at bay, though in the course of the fighting, our Thunderhawk gunship was shot down by enemy flak tanks.'

'So you were trapped,' stated Sicarius. 'Truly a desperate situation. At what point did the enemy attack again?'

'Just before dawn we were attacked by warriors of the Night Lords Legion.'

A collective gasp went around the courtyard. Though every warrior knew of the fallen Legions, to hear their name spoken so brazenly was still a shock. To mention such things was as unseemly as it was unbelievable.

'We were able to hold them off, but as the battle dragged on, it soon became clear that we would not be able to hold our position.'

'So what did you do?'

'The explosives were rigged, but Techmarine Tomasin had died in the initial attack. Without his detonator mechanism, we had no way of triggering the charges to destroy the bridge. During the night, Captain Idaeus had sent our assault squads to attempt to detonate the explosives manually using krak grenades. They were unsuccessful, but the principle was sound.'

'I'm sorry, Captain Ventris, I don't understand,' said Sicarius, cocking his head to one side.

'Don't understand what?'

'This plan of Idaeus's, it is obviously one that does not refer to the tactica of the Codex Astartes. Are you sure it was his plan?'

Uriel was about to answer that of course it was, when he was seized by a sudden memory of the frantic battle on bridge two-four. Sicarius smiled and Uriel saw how deftly he had been manoeuvred into this admission of guilt. Slowly he shook his head.

'No, it was not Captain Idaeus's plan,' he said. 'It was mine.'

Sicarius stepped back, arms raised at his sides.

'It was your plan,' he said triumphantly.

'But it worked, damn it,' roared Pasanius. 'Don't you see that? The bridge was destroyed and the campaign won!'

'Irrelevant,' responded Sicarius. 'A victory is not a victory unless it is won with the principles of the primarch. We have all read of the Mortifactors in Captain Ventris's after-action reports from Tarsis Ultra. We all see where the path of deviance from the Codex leads. Tell me, sergeant, would you have us become the Mortifactors?'

Pasanius shook his head. 'No, of course not.'

'But you would have us follow their methods?'

'No, that's not what I said,' growled Pasanius. 'I just meant that whatever breaches of the Codex we made, they were only small.'

'Sergeant,' said Sicarius, as though speaking to a small child, 'our faith in the Codex is a fortress, and no crack in a fortress can be accounted small. If we take small steps down their path, each tiny indiscretion becomes that little bit easier, doesn't it? After a hundred such breaches of the Codex's teachings, what matters another ten, or a hundred? That is why you must be punished, Captain Ventris, for where you tread, others follow. You are a captain of the Ultramarines and must comport yourself appropriately.'

Uriel glared as Sicarius climbed the steps back to his seat and the Master of the Forges, Fennias Maxim, descended to the courtyard. His leather-tough skin was the colour of aged oak and completely hairless. Dark, hooded eyes, one replaced with a blinking red metriculator augmetic, transfixed Uriel as Fennias circled them, his hands laced behind his back. A hissing servo-arm, folded into a recumbent position on his back, wheezed as it flexed in time with his breath and his heavy, metal legs thumped on the stonework of the courtyard.

'I have spoken to Techmarine Harkus,' he barked suddenly.

Uriel knew where Maxim was heading and said, 'I ordered him to strip the Thunderhawk down to its bare bones. He was only obeying my orders and no blame should be attached to him for his actions on Tarsis Ultra.'

Maxim stepped close and lowered his thunderous face into Uriel's.

'I know,' he hissed. 'Did you think I would not know that?'

'No,' replied Uriel, 'I merely wished to be clear on the subject.'

'Tell me why you desecrated such a holy machine, one that had seen honourable service for almost a millennium and had carried you into battle on occasions too numerous to count. How could you turn your back on such a noble spirit and treat it so cruelly?'

'I had no choice,' said Uriel simply.

'No choice?' scoffed Maxim. 'I find that hard to believe.'

'I do not lie, Master,' said Uriel darkly. 'To destroy one of the tyranid's hive ships we had to get the planet's defence lasers firing again, and the only way we could do it was to transport fresh energy capacitors to a site that had the best chance of killing it. The only craft available that stood any chance of reaching this site and making it back was the Thunderhawk. Even then I was forced to order the gunship stripped down to its minimum weight to ensure we would have enough fuel to get us there and back.'

'You angered its war-spirit. I have since ministered to it and great is its wrath. Were I you, I would not trust my life to it again until you have begged its forgiveness and performed the necessary rites of obeisance.'

Maxim turned his back on Uriel and returned to his seat as, one by one, each of the Chapter's Masters came forward to highlight an example of Uriel's disregard for the teachings of the Codex Astartes.

They knew everything from both the Pavonis and Tarsis Ultra campaigns, the events on the space hulk, *Death of Virtue*, and the battle with the dark eldar on the return leg of the journey.

His frustration grew as example after example of his recklessness was paraded before him. While he could not deny the veracity of these claims, he could refute with reason and proof of their merit, but as the day wore on, he saw that the Chapter Masters were not interested in his truth. He had deviated from the Codex Astartes, the most heinous crime imaginable, and nothing could atone for such a breach of trust and faith.

As the sun dipped below the tiled roof of Lord Calgar's chambers, Uriel's temper was fraying and he knew he was in danger of losing it completely. These men did not want truth; they wanted a scapegoat for the dead of Tarsis Ultra and to set an example to the rest of the Chapter that there was no other way than the Codex.

He wanted to scream in frustration, but pursed his lips and bit down on his anger.

Purple shadows lengthened on the floor of the courtyard. Evening moths gathered around the torches that were hung from the balconies.

Marneus Calgar stood and swept his gaze around the assembled Masters before striding into the centre of the courtyard to face Uriel and Pasanius. He stared into Uriel's eyes and Uriel met his gaze unflinchingly. Whatever his fate, he would face it on his feet like the warrior he knew himself to be, and damn the consequences.

At last, Lord Calgar said, 'It saddens me to see what has become of you both. I saw greatness within you and hoped that one day you might have taken your place amongst this Chapter's mightiest heroes. But nothing in this life is set in stone and you stand before me accused of the darkest of crimes. Tomorrow you shall have your chance to refute your accusers and present your defence. Think well on what you wish to say. I urge you to spend this night in prayer. Look to the Emperor for guidance and remember your oaths of allegiance to this Chapter and all that once meant to you when next you stand before me.'

The first slivers of moonlight crested the roof as Uriel and Pasanius were led back to their cells.

The cell was dark and filled with a musty odour of damp and helplessness. A chain dangled from a ring set in the wall and water dripped from the ceiling to disappear down a crack in the stone floor.

'Do I need to chain you?' enquired one of the Terminators, his voice hissing through his helmet-vox.

'No,' said Uriel. 'You have my word I will give you no trouble.'

The Terminator nodded as though he had expected as much and closed the cell's door, bolting and locking it with thick chains and mechanical wards.

Uriel bunched his fists and paced the cell like a caged animal. He would not try to escape, but tomorrow, he would hurl every one of the accusations levelled at him back at those who stood in judgement over him. They had not witnessed the circumstances that had driven him to this point.

Where were they on the walls of Tarsis Ultra? Where were they when he had stood defiant before the might of an ancient star god and allowed its vile xeno taint into his mind? Where were they when he had almost died in their name? He knew he was reacting with his heart and not his head, but couldn't help himself. The injustice of it all made him sick and he slumped on the floor of the cell, listening to the dripping water and framing what he would say.

Some hours later, as he lay sprawled on the cold, damp floor, Uriel heard the soft pad of footsteps approach. Furtive steps, like those of a man afraid of being discovered, drew near, and even through the thickness of the stone walls and iron door, Uriel's enhanced hearing could tell that whoever was approaching his cell was a Space Marine.

He swivelled upright and sat with his back to the wall opposite the door. Keys rattled and the door swung inwards, a hooded figure blocking the light. The figure stepped into the cell and pulled back his hood.

'It is good to see you, Captain Ventris,' said a deep voice, rich with age and experience.

'Captain Agemman?' said Uriel, recognising the voice. Agemman was the Captain of the First Company: the veterans, the best and bravest of the Chapter. Amongst his titles was Regent of Ultramar, the man to whom the Master of the Ultramarines entrusted the safety of Macragge in his absence. After the death of Captain Invictus, hero of the First Company who had died fighting the tyranids of Hive Fleet Behemoth, Agemman had taken on the role of rebuilding the destroyed company. Only now, two hundred and fifty years after its complete destruction, was it returned to full strength and the Banner of Macragge unfurled once more.

Agemman had been an inspiration to them all while training at Agiselus and all through their elevation to the ranks of the Adeptus Astartes at the Fortress of Hera. His noble bearing and courage of spirit were shining lights amid the darkness. What could he want with Uriel?

'Aye,' replied Agemman, holding out his hand. 'Courage and honour.'

'Courage and honour,' said Uriel, accepting Agemman's hand.

Agemman folded his arms within his robe and glanced around him in distaste at the bleakness of the cell.

'It is galling to see a warrior of such courage treated so,' he said.

'You pick a strange time to come and see me, captain. What are you doing here?'

'I come on behalf of Lord Calgar, Captain Ventris.'

'Lord Calgar? I do not understand—'

'I know all about you, Uriel,' interrupted Agemman. 'I followed your progress all the way through Agiselus. I recognised your potential and I rejoiced when you were selected to come to the Fortress of Hera and become an Ultramarine. I gave thanks for the victory on Vorhn's World and mourned with you after Black Bone Road. I know all of what you did while serving with the Deathwatch and I know why you will never speak of it.'

'Why are you telling me this?' asked Uriel, suddenly wary.

'So that you will know that I speak true, Uriel Ventris,' explained Agemman. 'You stand accused of the gravest crime an Ultramarine can commit and your life hangs by the most slender of threads. You would do well to heed my words.'

Agemman closed the cell door.

'Much depends on it...'

Dawn broke clear and bright over the mountains, casting long shadows over the pale rocks and highland forests. A cool breeze blew down the length of the Valley of Laponis, and Uriel felt a curious light-headedness as he marched up the smooth-worn steps carved into the rock that led to the chambers of Marneus Calgar. Despite the armed guards escorting them, his step was lighter and his heart unclouded by anger or resentment. He knew now what he had to do and, with the choice so clear before him, there was no more doubt or uncertainty.

He was saddened that Pasanius would be tarred with the same brush, but there was little he could do to prevent that now.

Captain Agemman had spoken simply and clearly for an hour and Uriel had been struck by his simple honesty and the force of his words. When he had finished, they had shaken hands in the warrior's grip, wrist to wrist, and said their farewells. Agemman had wished him well and departed, no doubt to take the same message to Pasanius. As they climbed the stairs to their fate, one glance at Pasanius's face told Uriel that he had accepted Agemman's words and chosen the same path. Uriel was humbled by his comrade's loyalty and managed a wan smile as they reached the esplanade at the top of the steps and approached the many-pillared portico that led to the chambers of Marneus Calgar.

They passed between the Terminator guards into the shadowed vestibule before emerging once more into the sunlit courtyard. Though they had been taken from their cells at first light, the Masters of the Chapter were already gathered, their ceremonial cloaks of office draped around their shoulders and laurels of judgement wreathing their skulls.

They took their place before the statue of Konor, facing Lord Calgar and standing at parade rest, with their arms ramrod straight at their sides. The armed warriors retreated from the courtyard and not a soul moved until the echoing clang of the bronze doors rang out.

Marneus Calgar stepped down into the courtyard to stand before Uriel and Pasanius. His augmetic eye burned a steady red, his features unreadable. Uriel knew that Calgar had sent Agemman to their cells last night and, though he knew it meant his undoing, could find no anger in his heart for this act, just a simple understanding of what it meant to be a true Ultramarine.

The Lord of the Ultramarines strode around the fountain, addressing the assembled Masters.

'Brother Ultramarines, today is a day of judgement. We have heard much that condemns these warriors in the eyes of our brethren, but we are men of honour and would not think of deciding their fate without first giving them a chance to refute these charges and answer the accusations against them.'

Calgar completed his circuit of the gurgling fountain and stood before Uriel, locking his gaze with him.

'Captain Ventris, you have the right to speak and defend yourself.'

Uriel took a deep breath and said, 'I waive that right and accept the judgement of my lords upon me.'

A ripple of surprise rose from the masters and hurried glances were exchanged as Lord Calgar gave an imperceptible nod of his head to Uriel. Calgar then asked Pasanius the same question and received the same answer. Uriel saw Learchus's face harden and knew it pained the sergeant to have brought this upon him, but Uriel now knew that Learchus had no choice but to do so. He nodded to Learchus in a gesture of peace and respect between them.

Uriel faced the Master of the Ultramarines as he spoke again to him. 'You do not wish to give an account of yourself and enter a plea to your peers?'

'No,' said Uriel. 'I willingly submit myself to your judgement.'

Lord Calgar turned from Uriel and ascended to his throne, arranging his cloak about him before addressing the assembled masters.

'These men have broken faith with the Codex Astartes, and, by their own admission, abandoned its teachings,' began Calgar. 'Their fate is now in my hands and on the morrow I shall render my verdict. We shall convene again at dawn tomorrow at Gallan's Rock where judgement will be passed.'

Though he had known they were to be punished, Uriel felt his heart sink as Calgar spoke.

Gallan's Rock was a place of execution.

The noise of Hera's Falls was deafening. Torrents of water fell hundreds of metres to the jagged rocks below, cascading into a spume-covered pool of glacially cold water. The sharp white rocks glistened and sparkled with quartz, and emerald green highland fir grew right up to the edge of the cliffs. Sunlight crept over the mountaintops and bathed everything in the glow of molten gold. It was, thought Uriel, one of the most beautiful vistas he had been privileged to lay his eyes upon, as though nature, realising that this might well be the last thing he saw, had striven to produce the most wondrous vision for him to take into the next life.

He and Pasanius marched in silence after the Chapter's Masters, their chains removed and armour stored in the Fourth Company's armorium. Both wore unadorned black chitons, their bare feet warmed by the sun-kissed earth.

No guards accompanied the sombre column. Though guilty, they were still Ultramarines and would meet their fate with courage and honour. The climb from the Fortress of Hera had taken two hours and they stood now before Gallan's Rock, an angular slab of black marble that speared out from the valley side.

In ancient times, convicted criminals had been hurled to their deaths on the rocks below and it had been on this very spot that the sword of Roboute Guilliman had cut the head from the traitor king, Gallan, who had murdered his adopted father with an envenomed blade and attempted to take control of Macragge.

The Masters gathered at the edge of the cliff, a thin veil of water soaking their armour, and as he approached them, Uriel felt the fabric of his chiton cling to his skin as it became saturated.

Without any words being spoken, Uriel and Pasanius marched onto the rock and slowly inched their way towards the end. Uriel experienced a moment's vertigo as he lost sight of the cliff edge in his peripheral vision. The black rock was slippery underfoot, but he supposed it didn't much matter whether he fell now or not.

They reached the end of the rock and knelt, the stone hard and cold against their skin. Uriel looked over the edge, the drop dizzyingly high and the rocks below indelibly stained with the blood of the condemned. His own would soon join it and, strangely, the thought did not trouble him overmuch. Agemman had made it clear what was at stake and Uriel was Ultramarine enough to grasp the truth of his words and make the right decision.

He felt a hand grip his shoulder and glanced over at Pasanius. His friend and comrade in arms was stoic and stared across the valley, savouring the beauty of their surroundings.

'I regret nothing of what we have achieved,' said Pasanius. 'We acted with courage and honour and no man can ask more of us than that.'

Uriel felt his chest tighten and nodded, too overcome with admiration for his friend to speak. He nodded as he heard footsteps behind him, bowing his head and closing his eyes as he awaited the push that would send him plummeting to his death.

He felt armoured gauntlets take hold of his chiton and heard the voice of Lord Calgar.

'A true judgement has been returned against you and the Codex Astartes has but one punishment for your crimes. Though you are warriors of courage and it pains me to lose such valiant fighters, I have no choice in my verdict.

'Just as we all are, I too am bound by the Codex and must obey its teachings in sentencing you to death.'

The grip on Uriel's chiton tightened.

'There are many ways one can achieve death, many ways to meet your fate. To waste a life that may yet bring retribution to the enemies of the

Emperor is a sin in and of itself. It is therefore my judgement that you be bound by a Death Oath, and take the light of the Emperor into that abominable region of space where many a true warrior has met his end – the Eye of Terror. I bind you to take your fire and steel into the dark places until such time as you meet your destiny.'

Uriel stood motionless in the torch-lit gatehouse as the Masters of the Chapter circled him. Fully clad in his armour, his golden-hilted sword sheathed at his side, he felt a lightness in his heart he had not felt in many months. Though to journey into the Eye of Terror, that region of space where the madness and corruption of the warp spilled into real space, was as certain a death sentence as if had they been pushed from Gallan's Rock, Uriel knew that this was somehow right.

Pasanius stood beside him, also fully armoured, his customary flamer held tightly in his silver bionic arm. Chaplain Clausel read from an ancient leather-bound tome with gold edged pages and the musty aroma of a book that had sat unopened for many centuries.

Verses from the *Book of Dishonour*, words that had not been spoken in over six thousand years, were uttered in time with the Masters' footsteps as they removed everything that marked them as Ultramarines from their armour and weapons.

His company tattoo had been burned from the skin of his left shoulder and the Chapter symbols of the Ultramarines had been painted over, leaving his shoulder guards an unblemished blue. The golden eagles were removed from his breastplate and waist and the purity seals and honour badges were unclipped and placed in a sandarac reliquary box.

Learchus would lead the Fourth Company in his absence and Uriel could think of no one he would rather have commanding his surviving warriors and rebuilding the company.

Marneus Calgar watched them having their insignia removed from their armour impassively. Uriel knew Lord Calgar did not want to have to do this, but the Chapter Master had no choice but to place the Death Oath upon them. It had been that or an ignominious end on the rocks at the foot of Hera's Falls.

He remembered Agemman's words, spoken in a calm and even voice in his cell as though they were being whispered in his ear even now. Agemman had spoken of the great and good name of the Ultramarines, a name that stood for truth, courage and faith in the Emperor. No truer Chapter of Space Marines existed, and to plant any seeds of doubt of that in the minds of its own warriors was to damn it as surely as if it were to embrace the Ruinous Powers. A Chapter's strength came from its belief in itself, a power that devolved from the force of its Chapter Master and was embodied within those he appointed beneath him.

The Chapter was held together by such valour and to allow any one man to undermine that was to erode the very foundations of the

Ultramarines. Each warrior looked up to his superiors as embodiments of the Codex and to see a captain flaunt its teachings was to invite disaster.

The rot of dissention had to be cut out before it infected the entire Chapter and brought about the ruin of the Ultramarines. There could be no other way. The strength in Agemman's voice had cut through the bitterness and frustration consuming Uriel, and he had seen the ramifications should his methods and actions become widespread. The Ultramarines would become little more than roving bands of warriors, visiting such vengeance as they deemed appropriate upon whomever they chose. Before long, there would be little to distinguish them from the renegades who gave praise to the Dark Gods and Uriel was gripped by a horrifying vision of a future where blood-soaked Ultramarines were as feared and reviled as those who trod the path of Chaos.

Agemman had not ordered either of them in what they must do, but had left them to choose the right path.

Uriel had known what that choice must be: accept the judgement of Lord Calgar and show the Chapter that the way chosen by the Ultramarines was true. They must accept the Death Oath so that the Chapter might live on as it always had.

At last, Clausel closed the book and bowed his head as Uriel and Pasanius marched past him towards the doors of the gatehouse.

'Uriel, Pasanius,' said Lord Calgar.

The two Space Marines stopped and bowed to their former master.

'The Emperor go with you. Die well.'

Uriel nodded as the doors swung open. He and Pasanius stepped into the purple twilight of evening. Birds sang and torchlight flickered from the high towers of the outermost wall of the Fortress of Hera.

Before the door closed, Calgar spoke again, his voice hesitant, as though unsure as to whether he should speak at all.

'Varro Tigurius spoke with me last night,' he began. 'He told me that he had been granted a vision of you and Pasanius upon a world taken by the Dark Powers. A world that tasted of dark iron, with great wombs of daemonic flesh rippling with monstrous, unnatural life. As he watched, fell surgeons – like monsters themselves – hacked at them with blades and saws and pulled bloodstained figures from within. Though appearing more dead than alive, these figures lived and breathed, tall and strong, a dark mirror of our own glory. I know not what this means, Uriel, but its evil is plain. Seek this place out. Destroy it.'

'As you command,' said Uriel and walked into the night.

Ahead was a wide, cobbled esplanade, two parallel lines of Ultramarines lining the route they would take towards the main gate of the Fortress. The entirety of the Chapter's strength on Macragge awaited them, over five hundred Space Marines, their weapons clasped across their chests and heads held high.

Uriel and Pasanius marched between the lines of fellow Space Marines, each warrior snapping to attention and smoothly turning his back on them as they passed. The outer wall of the Fortress towered above them and Uriel could not help but look over his shoulder at the glittering marvel of the Fortress of Hera as he strode from its majesty.

The hundred-metre-high golden gate swung smoothly open, and Uriel felt a tremendous sense of stepping into the unknown seize him. Once they passed through that gate, they would no longer be Ultramarines, they would be stepping into the vastness of the galaxy to fulfil their Death Oath on their own, and the thought sent a realisation of what they had lost through him.

As the gateway drew closer, he saw Learchus in the line of Space Marines ahead of him. He reached his former sergeant and saw that Learchus was not turning his back as every other Ultramarine had.

Uriel stopped and said, 'Sergeant, you must turn your back.'

'No, captain, I will not, I will see you on your way.'

Uriel smiled and held out his hand to Learchus, who shook it proudly.

'I will look after the men of the company until you return,' promised Learchus.

'I know you will, Learchus. I bid you farewell, but now you must turn from us.'

Learchus nodded slowly and saluted before turning his back on his former captain.

Uriel and Pasanius continued on their long walk, finally passing into the shadow of the massive wall and leaving the Fortress of Hera behind.

And the gates slammed shut.

# THE LAST DETAIL

*Paul Kearney*

The monsoon rains came early that year, as if the planet itself were tugging down a veil to hide its broken face. Even cowering in the bunker, the boy and his father could hear them, thunderous, massive, a roar of noise. But the rainstorm was nothing to that which had gone before – in fact even the bellowing of the monsoon seemed almost like a kind of silence.

'It stopped,' the boy said. 'All the noise. Perhaps they went away.'

The man squeezed his son's shoulder but said nothing. He had the wiry, etched face of a farmer, old before his time, but as hard as steel wire. Both he and his son had the sunken, hollow look of folk who have not eaten or drunk in days. He passed a dry tongue over his cracked lips at the sound of the rain, then looked at the flickering digits of the comms bench.

'It'll be dawn soon. When it comes, I'm going to look outside.'

The boy clenched him tighter. 'Pa!'

'It'll be all right. We need water, or we won't make it. I think they've gone, son.' He ruffled his boy's hair. 'I think it's over, whatever it was.'

'They might be waiting.'

'We need the water. It'll be all right, you'll see.'

'I'm coming with you.'

The man hesitated a second, and then nodded. 'All right then – whatever we find out there, we'll meet it together.'

A summer dawn came early in the planet's northern hemisphere. When the man set his shoulder to the bunker door only a few hours had passed. The heavy steel and plascrete door usually swung light and noiseless on its hinges, but now he had to throw himself at it to grind it open centimetre by centimetre. When the opening was wide enough for a man's bicep, he stopped, and sniffed the air.

'Get the respirators,' he snapped to his son. 'Now!'

They tugged on the cumbersome masks, and immediately their already enclosed world became tinier and darker still. They breathed heavily. The man coughed, took deep breaths.

'Some kind of gas out there, a chemical agent – but it's heavy. It's seeped down the stairs and pooled there. We've got to go up.' He looked round himself at the interior of the bunker with its discarded blankets, the dying battery-fed lights and useless comms unit. A pale mist was pouring in through the opened door almost like a kind of liquid, and with it, the gurgling rainwater of the passing monsoon.

'This place is compromised,' he said. 'We have to get out now, or we'll die here.'

They pushed together at the door. It squealed open angrily, until at last there was a kind of light filtering down on them from above. The man looked up. 'Well, the house is gone,' he said calmly.

They clambered over wet piles of debris which choked the stone stairs, until at last they stood at the top.

Inside a ruin. Two walls still stood, constructed out of the sturdy local stone, but that was all. The rest was blasted rubble. The clay tiles of the roof lay everywhere, and the boy saw his favourite toy, a wooden rifle his father had carved for him, lying splintered by what had been their front door. The rain was easing now, but he still had to rub the eyepieces of his respirator clear every few seconds.

'Stay here,' the man said. He walked forward, out of the shadows of their ruined home, his boots crunching and clinking on broken glass and plastic, splashing through puddles. Around them, the pale mist was receding. A wind was blowing, and on it the rain came down, washing everything clean. The man hesitated, then pulled off his respirator. He raised his face to the sky and opened his mouth, feeling the rain on his tongue.

'It's all right,' he said to his son. 'The air is clean now. Take it off, boy, but don't touch anything. We don't know what's contaminated.'

All around them for as far as the eye could see, the countryside which had once been their farm, a green and pleasant place, was now a stinking marsh of shell-holes. The trunks of trees stood up like black sword-blades, their branches stripped away, the bark burnt from their boles. Here and there, one of their cattle, or a piece of one, lay bloated and green and putrid. Smoke rose in black pillars along the horizon.

Such was their thirst that they had nothing to say, but stood with their tongues out trying to soak up the rain. It streamed into the boy's mouth, reinvigorating him. Nothing in his life had ever felt so good as that cold water sinking into his parched mouth. He opened his eyes at last, and frowned, then pointed skywards, at the broken wrack of clouds which the wind was lashing across the sky.

'Pa, look,' he said, eyes wide with wonder. 'Look at that– it's like a cathedral up-ended in the clouds.'

His father looked skywards, narrowed his eyes, and curled a protective arm about the boy's shoulders. Many kilometres away, but still dominating the heavens, a vast angular shape hung shining above the earth, all jagged with steeples and adornments and improbable spikes. It broke out in a white flash as the sun caught it turning, and then began to recede, in a bright flare of afterburners. After a few seconds they caught the distant roar of its massive engines. As the sun rose higher, so they lost sight of it in the gathering brightness of the morning.

'It's moving out of orbit,' the man said.

'What is it – is the God-Emperor inside it, Pa?'

'No, son.' The father's arm curled tighter about his son's shoulders. 'It is the vessel of those who know His face. It is the Emperor's Angels, here in our sky.'

The man looked around him. At the reeking desolation, the craters, the puddled steaming meres of chemicals.

'We were their battleground,' he said.

They ranged over what was left of the farm during the next few days, setting out containers to catch rainwater, gathering up what remained of their canned goods, and throwing away anything which the man's rad-counter began creaking at. At night they made camp in the ruins of the farmhouse and coaxed fire out of the soaked timbers which had once upheld its roof.

'Is the whole world like this?' the boy asked, gazing into the firelight one night, huddled under an old canvas tarp that the rain beat upon.

'Could be,' his father said. 'Perreken is a small place, not much more than a moon. Wouldn't take much to trash the whole thing.'

'Why would the Emperor's Angels do this to us?' the boy asked.

'They do things for reasons we can't fathom,' his father told him. 'They are the Wrath of the Emperor made real, and when their anger sweeps a world, no-one escapes it, not even those they are sworn to save. They are our protectors, boy, but also, they are the Angels of Death.'

'What are they like – have you ever seen one, Pa?'

The man shook his head. 'Not I. I did my spell in the militia same as most, and that's as far as my knowledge of things warlike goes. I don't think they ever even came close to this system before. But that was a big Imperial ship in the sky the other morning, I'm sure of it – I seen pictures when I was your age. Only they ride in ships like that – the *Astartes* – the Angels of the God-Emperor.'

* * *

Three days later the boy and his father were trudging through the black shattered crag north of their farm which had once been a wooded hillside, looking to see if any of their stock had by some chance survived the holocaust. Here, there had been a rocky knoll some two hundred metres in height, which gave a good view down the valley beyond to the city and its spaceport. It seemed the hill had been bombed heavily, its conical head now flattened. Smoke still hissed out of cracks in the hillside, as molten rocks cooled underground. Out towards the horizon, the city smoked and flickered with pinpoints of flame.

'Pa! Pa!' the boy shouted, running and tumbling among the rocks – 'Look here!'

'Don't touch it!'

'It's – it's – I don't know what it is.'

Looming over them was a hulk of massive, shattered metal, a box of steel and ceramite broken open and still sparking and glowing in places. It had legs like those of a crab, great pincers, and the barrels of autocannon on its shoulders. Atop it was what might once have been a man's head, grotesquely attached, snarling in death. It was a machine which was almost an animal, or an animal which had become a machine. Carved onto the bullet-pocked carcass of the thing were unspeakable scenes of slaughter and perversity, and it was hung with rotting skulls, festooned with spikes and chains.

'Come away,' the man told his son hoarsely. 'Get away from it.'

They backed away, and were suddenly aware that all down the slope below them were other remnants of battle. Bodies, everywhere, most of them shaven-headed, snarling, mutilated men, many with a pointed star cut into their foreheads. Here and there a bulkier figure in heavy armour, horned helmets, dismembered limbs, entrails underfoot about which the flies buzzed in black clouds.

'They fought here,' the man said. 'They fought here for the high ground.'

The boy, with the curiosity of youth, seemed less afraid than his father. He had found a large firearm, almost as long as himself, and was trying to lift it out of its glutinous glue of mud and blood.

'Leave that alone!'

'But Pa!'

'That's an Astartes weapon.' The man knelt and peered at it, wiping the metal gingerly with one gloved hand. 'Look – see the double-headed eagle on the barrel – that's the badge of the Imperium. The Space Marines fought here, on this hill. These are the dead of the great enemy lying around us, heretics cursed by the Emperor. The Astartes saved us from them.'

'Saved us,' the boy repeated grumpily. He pointed at the burning city down in the valley. 'Look at Dendrekken. It's all burnt and blown up.'

'Better that than under the fist of the Dark Powers, believe me,' the man said, straightening. 'It's getting dark. We've come far enough for one day. Tomorrow we'll try and get down to the city, and see who else is left.'

That night, shivering beside their campfire amid the bodies of the dead, the boy lay awake staring at the night sky. The clouds had cleared, and he was able to see the familiar constellations overhead. Now and again he saw a shooting star, and now and again he was sure he saw other things gliding in the dark between the stars. New constellations glittered, moving in formation. He found himself wondering about those who lived out there in that blackness, travelling in their city-sized ships from system to system, bearing the eagle of the Imperium, carrying weapons like the massive bolter he had found upon the battlefield. What must it be like, to live like that?

He got up in the middle hours of the night, too restless and hungry for sleep. Stepping away from the fire, he clicked on his little battered torch, an old wind-up contraption he had had since he was a toddler. He walked out upon the rocky, blasted slope upon which the bodies of the dead lay contorted and rotting, and felt no fear, only a sense of wonder, and a profound restlessness. He picked his way down the slope and apart from his yellow band of torchlight there was no other radiance in the world save for the stars.

And one other thing. Off to his left he caught sight of something which came and went, an infinitesimal red glow. Intrigued, he made his way towards it, sliding his knife out of the sheath at his waist. He crouched and padded forwards, as quiet as when hunting in these same hills with his father's old lasgun. Several times the light died altogether, but he was patient, and waited until he could see it again. It was at the foot of a looming, broken crag which stood up black against the stars.

Something half-buried in rubble, but still with a shine to it that reflected back the torchlight. It was a helmet, huge, fit for a giant. It looked almost like a massive skull. In the eye-sockets were two lenses, one cracked and broken, and the other with that flickering scarlet light oozing out of it. The boy knelt down and gently tapped the helmet with the butt of his knife. There was a hiss as of static, and the thing moved slightly, making him spring backwards in fright. He saw then that it was not just a helmet. Buried in the fallen stone there was a body attached to the helm. Off to one side lay a massive hemispherical shape – the boy could have sat in it – and painted upon it in white was the symbol of a double-headed axe. A shoulder-guard made for a giant.

The boy scraped and scratched frantically at the stones, levering away the looser ones, uncovering more and more of the buried figure. There was a gleam of silver below the helm, and he saw that he had unearthed shining wings engraved upon a mighty breastplate, and in the centre of the wings, a skull emblem. He stared, open-mouthed. This was no

Chaos fiend, no armoured heretic. He had found one of *them*, one of the Astartes his father talked about.

A fallen angel, he thought.

'Pa!' he shouted. 'Pa, come here quick and see this!'

It took them most of the remainder of the night to uncover the buried giant. As dawn broke, and the relentless rain began again, so the water washed the mud and caked filth and blood from its armour, making it gleam in the sunrise. Dark blue metal, as dark as an evening sky, save for the white silver wings on the chest. The boy and his father knelt, panting before it. The armour was dented and broken in places, and loose wiring sprang out of gashes in the metal. There were bullet-holes in the thigh, and here and there plates had been buckled out of shape by some inconceivable force, bent out of place; the heavy dark paint scraped off them so they could see the bare alloy underneath.

The boy's father wiped his brow, streaking it with mud. 'Help me with the helmet, boy – let's see if we can get a look at him.'

They felt around the helmet seal with their fingertips, that savage visage staring up at them, immobile. The boy's quicker fingers found the two pressure points first. There were two clicks, and a hiss, then a loud crack. Between the two of them they levered up the mass of metal, and eased it off. It rolled to one side, clinking on the stones, and they found themselves staring at the face of an Astartes.

The skin was pale, as though it seldom saw the sun, stretched tight across a huge-boned skull, long and somehow horse-like. It was recognisably human, but out of scale, like the face of a great statue. A metal stud was embedded above one colourless eyebrow. The head was shaved, criss-crossed with old scars, though a bristle of dark hair had begun to regrow on it. The right eye was gone – he had been shot through the lens of his helmet – but the hole was already healed, a ragged whorl of red tissue.

Then the left eye opened.

The boy and his father tumbled backwards, away from the glare of the eye. The giant stirred, his arm coming up and then falling back again. A rasping growl came up from somewhere deep in the barrel-wide chest, and the legs quivered. Then the giant groaned, and was still again, but now his teeth were bared and clenched – white, strong teeth which looked as though they could snap off a hand. He spoke, a slur of pain-filled words.

The boy's father approached the giant on hands and knees. 'You're among friends here. We're trying to help you, lord. The fighting is over. The enemy is gone. Can you hear me?'

The eye, bloodshot and as blue as midwinter ice, came to rest on the boy's father. 'My brothers,' the giant said. 'Where are they?' His voice was deep, the accent so strange that the boy could barely understand him.

'They've gone. I saw the great ship leave orbit myself, six days ago.'

A deep snarl, a cross between rage and grief. Again, the helpless movement of the massive limbs.

'Help me. I must stand.'

They tried, tugging at the cold metal armour. They managed to get him sitting upright. His gauntleted hand scrabbled at the rubble.

'My bolter.'

'It's not here – it must be buried, as you were. We had to dig you out.'

He could not raise himself. The single eye blinked. The Astartes spat, and his spittle spattered against the rocks, bright with blood.

'My armour is dead. We must get it off. Help me. I will show you what to do.'

The rain came lashing down. They struggled in the muck and gravel around the giant, clicking off one piece after another of the armour which enclosed him. The boy could not lift any of them, strong though he was. His father grunted and sweated, corded muscles standing out along his arms and chest, as he set each piece of the dark blue carapace to one side. The massive breastplate almost defeated them all, and when it came free the giant snarled with pain. As it fell away, slick, mucus-covered cables slid out of his torso along with it, and when they sucked free, the boy saw that his chest was pocked with metal sockets embedded in his very flesh. The armour had been part of him.

He had been shot through the thigh, but the wound was almost closed. It was a raised, angry lump, in the midst of which was a suppurating hole. The Astartes looked at it, frowning. 'Something's in there. My system should have fixed it by now.' He probed the hole with one finger, teeth bared against the pain, and raised his bloody pus-covered digit to his face and sniffed at it. 'Something bad.' He put a knuckle to his empty eye-socket. 'It feels hot. I have infection in me.' His voice held a note of incredulity. 'This should not be.' He thought for a moment. 'They used chemical agents in the fighting. Maybe biological too. It would seem my system has been compromised.'

The Astartes looked at the man who knelt by him. 'I must rejoin my brethren. I need a deep space comms link. Do you know where there would be such a thing?'

The boy's father tugged at his lower lip. 'In the city, at the spaceport I suppose. But the city is pretty much destroyed. There may be nothing left.'

The Astartes nodded again. Something like humanity came into his surviving eye. 'I remember. Our Deep Strike teams made planetfall not far from the landing fields. The Thunderhawks took out positions all up and down the pads. They had drop-ships there, three of them. We got them all.'

'Who were they, lord, if I might ask?'

The Astartes smiled, though the effect was less humorous than ferocious on that massive, brutal face. 'Those who brought us here were the enemies of Man – a Chaos faction my Chapter has been charged with eradicating for decades now. They call themselves the *Punishers*. They meant to take over your world and use it as a bridgehead to conquer the rest of the system. My brothers and I saved you from that fate.'

'You destroyed my world,' the boy said, high and shrill with anger. 'You didn't save anything – you burnt us to ash!'

The giant regarded him gravely. 'Yes, we did. But I promise you that the Punishers would have done worse, had they been allowed. Your people would have been cattle to them, mere sport for the vilest appetites imaginable. Those who died quickly would have been the lucky ones. You will rebuild your world – it may take twenty years, but you can do it. Had it been tainted by Chaos, there would have been nothing for it but to scald it down to the very guts of the planet, and leave it an airless cinder.'

The man grasped his son's arm. 'He's young – he knows nothing.'

'Well, consider this part of his education,' the Astartes snapped. 'Now find me something we can use to splint my leg – and something to lean on that will take my weight. I must get mobile – and I need a weapon.'

Their search took much of the day, until finally they hit upon dismantling one of the discarded weapons lying on the battlefield and using the recoil rod within the firing mechanism to splint the Astartes's thigh. As he tied it tight about his lacerated flesh with lengths of wire, the giant ground his teeth, and pus popped out of the hot, red wound in his leg. The boy's father retrieved the weapon his son had found the day before. The Astartes's eyes lit up as he saw it, then narrowed again as he popped the magazine and checked the seat of the rounds within. 'Maybe thirty, if we're lucky. Well, a working bolter is worth something. Now hand me that pole.'

The pole was part of the innards of one of the great biomechanical carcasses which littered the field. The Astartes regarded it with disgust, wiping it clean with wet soil and sand. He used it as a staff, and was finally able to lever himself upright. In his free fist he held the bolter. He found its weight hard to manage in his weakened state however, and so fashioned a sling from more gleaned wire so that he might let it swing at his side. The wire of the sling cut into his shoulder, slicing the skin, but he seemed not to feel the pain.

'It'll be dark soon,' the boy's father said. 'We should perhaps stay here another night and then set off at dawn.'

'No time,' the Astartes said. Now that he was upright he seemed even huger, half as tall again as the man in front of him, his hands as big as shovels, his chest as wide as a dining table. 'I see in the dark. You can follow me.' With that, he set off, hobbling down the slopes of the shattered hillside to the valley below, where the sun was setting in a maelstrom of black cloud and toiling pillars of even blacker smoke, still rising from the stricken city that was their destination.

* * *

They walked half the night. The ground they traversed was broken by great bombardments and littered with the wreckage of war machines, some tracked, some wheeled, and some it seemed fashioned with arms and legs. They stopped once beside a great burnt-out carcass which squatted as tall as a building. So shot to pieces was it that its original shape could hardly be made out, but the Astartes limped up to it and carefully, reverently clicked off a metal seal with a tattered remnant of parchment still clinging to it. He bowed his head over this relic. 'Ah, brother,' he whispered.

'What is it?' the boy asked, even as his father tried to hush him.

'One of my battle-brothers; a spirit so bold, so fine, he chose to be encased in this mighty Dreadnought after his own body was destroyed, to carry on the fight, to stay with us, his brethren. His friends. His name was Geherran. He was with my company, and saved us from these–' Here the Astartes gestured at the other wrecks which stood round about, evil, crab-like structures adorned with all manner of ordnance, emblazoned with sickening symbols, '–these defilers. Abominations of Chaos. He broke them, took their heaviest fire upon himself so we might bring them down one by one.'

The Astartes blinked his one eye, then straightened, and limped on without another word.

The boy and his father followed him through a graveyard of the great machines, awed by their size, and the way in which they had been blasted to pieces where they stood. As the planet's two moons began to rise, it seemed they were in the midst of some ancient arena, where the dead had been left forgotten in mounds about them. But the dead were all twisted, snarling, white-faced and putrid. In the moons' light, it did not do to look at them too closely.

They entered the suburbs of the city and began to encounter signs of life. Rats flickered and squealed amid avalanches of rubble, and here and there a dog growled at them from the deepest shadows, eyes alight with madness, luminous foam dripping from its jaws. Once, a stream of cockroaches, each as big as a man's fist, went chittering across their path, dragging some unidentifiable chunk of carrion with them as they went. The Astartes watched them go thoughtfully, hefting the bolter.

'Such creatures are not native to this world, am I right?'

The boy's father was wide-eyed. 'Not that I have heard.'

'Something has been happening here. My brothers would not have left this world again so quickly unless there was a good reason. My guess is something called them out of orbit. A secondary threat of some kind.'

'You think they destroyed all the enemy down here on the surface?'

'We do not leave jobs half done.'

'How do you know?' the boy piped up. 'You were buried under a ton of stone, dead to the world. They left you behind.'

The Astartes turned, and in his eye they could see a light not unlike that in the dog's caught by lamplight. But he said nothing. The boy was cuffed across the back of his head by his father.

They moved on, more slowly now, for the Astartes was straining to keep his massive firearm at the ready. An ordinary man would struggle to lift, let alone fire it. His metal staff clicked against the plascrete underfoot, and stones skittered aside as his feet found their way. Watching him, the boy realised that the giant was near the end of his strength, and now he noticed also that the Astartes was leaving a thickly stippled trail of dark liquid in his wake. He was bleeding to death. He pointed this out to his father, who grasped up at the giant's arm.

'Your leg – you must let me look at it.'

'My systems should have taken care of it. I am infected. Some kind of bio-agent. I can feel it in my skull, like red-hot worms writhing behind my eyes. I need an Apothecary.' The Astartes was panting heavily. 'How far to the spaceport?'

'Another four or five kilometres.'

'Then I will rest, for now. We must find somewhere to lay up until daylight. I don't like this place, these ruins. There is something here.'

'No bodies,' the boy said, making his companions stare at him. He shrugged. 'Where are all the dead people? There's nothing but vermin left.'

'Lean on me,' the boy's father said to the ailing giant. 'There are houses on our right, up ahead, and they look more intact. We'll find one with a roof.'

By they time they bedded down for what remained of the darkness the Astartes was shivering uncontrollably, though his skin was almost too hot to touch. They gathered rainwater out of puddles and broken crockery and sipped enough of the black, disgusting liquid to moisten their mouths. The air was full of smoke and soot which left a gritty taste on the tongue and there were sparks flying in the midst of the reek.

'The fires are up north, towards the spaceport,' the boy's father said, rubbing his aching shoulder.

The Astartes nodded. He stroked the bolter in his lap as though it comforted him. 'It may be best if I go on alone,' he said.

'My other shoulder is still good enough to lean on.'

The giant smiled. 'What are you, a farmer?'

'I was. I had cattle. Now I have rocks and ash.'

'And a son, who still lives.'

'For now,' the man said, and he looked at the filthy, pinched face of his son, who lay sleeping like an abandoned orphan, wrapped in the charred rags of a blanket on the floor.

'Think of him, then – you have accompanied me far enough.'

'Yes,' the boy's father said dryly. 'And you are in such tremendous shape. You want rid of us because you think something bad is up ahead, at the spaceport, and you want to spare us.'

The giant inclined his head. 'Fighting is my life, not yours.'

'Something tells me this thing is not over. Your brothers overlooked something when they left. This is my world we are on – I will help you fight for it. There is nothing behind me but burnt earth, anyway.'

'So be it,' the Astartes said. 'At daybreak we will walk out together.'

Daybreak did not come. Instead there was only a slight lightening of the darkness, and in the sky ahead, a glow which had nothing to do with the colour of flame. The two moons were setting amid oceans of smoke, and the smoke itself was tinted on its underside, a colour like the underbelly of a maggot.

The Astartes rose unaided. His remaining eye seemed to have sunk into his skull, so that it was but a single gimlet gleam in his soot-blackened face. He cast aside his iron staff and stood upright as the pus ran yellow and pink from his swollen leg. The agony of it brought the sweat running down his forehead, but his face was impassive, at peace.

'The Emperor watch over us,' he said quietly as the boy and his father rose in turn, rubbing their smarting eyes. 'We must be quick and quiet now, like hunters.'

The three set off.

The scream burst ahead of them like a fire in the night, a tearing shriek which rose to the limits of human capacity, and then was cut off. There was a murmur, as of a distant engine, heavy machinery moving. And when it stopped they heard another sound, murmuring through the heavy smoke and the preternatural darkness. Voices, many voices chanting in unison.

The three of them went to ground in a burning house as the gledes and coals of the rafters spat and showered them. Some hissed as they landed on the sweat of the Astartes's back, but he did not so much as twitch.

'Cultists,' he said, listening. 'They're at the work of the warp, some ceremony or sorcery.'

His two companions stared at him, uncomprehending.

'Followers of the Dark Powers,' he explained, 'gulled or tortured into subservience. They are fodder for our guns.' Carefully, he unloaded the magazine from his bolter, eyed the rounds, and then kissed the cold metal before reloading. He eased back the cocking handle with a double click, like the lock of a door going back and forth.

'How far to the spaceport now?'

'We're almost on it,' the man told him. He was gripping his son's shoulder until his knuckles showed white. 'Up ahead the road turns to the right, and there's a gate, and walls – the spaceport is within.'

'I doubt the walls still stand,' the Astartes said with grim humour.

'There's a guardpost and a small barracks for the militia just within the gate – and an armoury out back, by the control tower. Ammunition, lasguns.'

'Lasguns,' the Astartes said with a kind of contempt. 'I am used to heavier metal, my friend. But it may be worth checking out. We need something to up our killing power. From here in, you stay close to me, both of you.'

He sprang up, and was off with barely a limp. With astonishing speed he sprinted to the end of the street and disappeared into the shell of the last house on the right. After a moment's hesitation, the man and his son got up and followed him.

He was right – the walls had been blasted away. In fact most of the buildings on this side of the spaceport lay in ruins, and the landing pads themselves were cratered with massive shell-holes and littered with the debris of all sorts of orbital craft. At the western end, three tall towers of twisted wreckage stood out, the smoke wreathing them, fires still burning deep in their tangled hulls.

'Punisher drop-pods' the Astartes said. 'We got all three.'

'There's another one,' the boy spoke up, pointing.

They peered together, squinting in the smoke. The boy was right. A fourth, undamaged drop-pod was squatting to the east, where the damage to the landing pads was less severe. Infantry was marching down its ramps.

The Astartes's face creased with hatred. 'It would seem my brothers and I were not as thorough as we thought. We must get word to my company, or your planet will fall to the enemy after all. We must have comms!'

'It'll be in the control tower, out yonder – if it's still intact,' the man said, jerking his head to the north. Dimly through the smoke they could make out a pale white pillar with a cluster of grey plascrete buildings around its foot. There seemed to be no enemy activity out in that direction, but with the smoke and gathering darkness it was hard to be sure.

'Then that is where we go,' the Astartes said simply. 'My brothers must be brought back to this world to cleanse it – or else they will have to extinguish it from space – get down!' This last was in a hiss. A troop of enemy infantry marched past. Strange, angular bald-headed men with heavily tattooed faces. They wore long leather coats adorned with studs and chains and what seemed to be human body parts. They bore lasguns, and chattered and snarled incessantly as they passed by.

'Their talk hurts my ears,' the boy said, rubbing his head.

'The warp infects them,' the Astartes told him. 'If we cannot cleanse this place, then it will begin to infect the remainder of your people.' He lifted a hand to the wound where his eye had been, then dropped it again. 'To the tower, then.'

\* \* \*

They ran, right into the heart of the foul-smelling smoke. The boy became dizzy, and found it hard to breathe, and the distant chanting of the cultists seemed to cloud over his thinking. He faltered, and found himself standing still, staring vacantly, aware that he was missing something.

Then he found himself lifted into the air and crushed against an enormous, fever-hot body. The Astartes had picked him up and tucked him under his free arm, still running.

Out of nowhere a cluster of pale faces appeared in the smoke. Before they could even raise their weapons the Astartes was upon them. A kick broke the ribcage of one and sent him hurtling off into the darkness. The heavy bolter was swung like a club and smashed the heads of two more into red ruin, almost decapitating them. The fourth got off a red burst of lasgun fire that spiked out harmlessly into the air, before the Astartes, dropping the boy, had him by the throat. He crushed the man's windpipe with one quick clench of his fist, and tossed him aside.

'Get the weapons,' he said to the man and the boy, panting. 'Grenades, anything.' He bent over and coughed, and a gout of dark liquid sprayed out of his mouth to splatter all over the plascrete landing strip. He swayed for a second, then straightened. When his companions had retrieved two lasguns and a sling of grenades from the bodies he nodded. 'Someone may have seen that las-fire. If we run into more of them, do not stop – keep running.'

They set off again. The giant was hobbling now, and left a trail of blood behind him, but he still set a fearsome pace, and it was all the man and his son could do to keep up with him, as they fought for air in the reeking hell that surrounded them.

At last the white pillar of the control tower appeared out of the smoke – and a band of cultists at its foot. They saw the shapes come running out of the darkness at them and set up a kind of shriek and began firing wildly. Las-fire came arcing through the air.

In return the Astartes halted, set the bolter in his shoulder, and began firing.

Short bursts, no more, two or three rounds at a time. But when the heavy ordnance hit the cultists it blew them apart. He took down eight of them before the first las-burst hit him, in the stomach. He staggered, and the bolter-muzzle dropped, but a second later he had raised it again and blew to pieces the cultist who had shot him.

The boy and his father lay on the ground and started firing also, but the heavy Chaos lasguns were unwieldy and hard to handle – their shots went wild. The boy fumbled with the sling of grenades and popped out one thumb-sized bomb. There was a tiny red button at the top of the little cylinder. He pressed it, and then tossed the thing at the cultists. It clinked on the base of the tower and lay at their feet. One looked at it with dawning horror on his face, and then the grenade exploded, and splattered him in scarlet fragments across the white painted wall of the control tower, along with three of his comrades.

The rest broke and ran, quickly disappearing into the toiling darkness. The Astartes sank to one knee, leaning on his bolter. His other hand was bunched in a fist where the lasgun had burnt a black hole through his torso from front to back.

'You need my shoulder again, I think,' the man said, helping up the maimed giant. 'Not far to go now. Lean on me, my friend. I will get you there.'

The Astartes managed a strangled laugh, but said no more.

They found the door ajar, a tall steel affair whose command-box had been blown out. The man made as if to enter but the Astartes held him back. 'Grenade first,' he rasped.

The boy tossed another of the little explosives inside. He was smiling as he did so, and when the thing went off, he laughed.

'I am glad everyone finds this so amusing,' his father said, as he stepped inside.

Two dead bodies, blown to pieces in the confined chamber at the base of the tower. There was an elevator, but the boy punched its buttons in vain.

'No power, Pa,' he said. 'The whole place is dead.'

'Stairs,' the Astartes gasped.

'Listen,' the man said. 'Outside – can you hear it?'

A confused babel, a roaring, bellowing sound of voices, some shrill, some deep. Even as they listened, it grew louder.

'Get the door closed,' the Astartes snapped. 'Block it, jam it – use anything you can.'

They slammed the heavy steel door shut, and piled up whatever they could find in the way of wreckage and furniture against it. The Astartes, with an agonised cry, wrenched a stretch of iron piping free of the wall and wedged it against the steel. Seconds later, the cacophony of voices was right outside, and they were hammering on the door. Gunfire sounded, and shells rang loudly against the metal.

'That won't hold them,' the man said. He and his son were white-faced, and sweat was cutting stripes down the grime on their faces.

'Up,' the Astartes said impatiently. 'We must go up. You first, then your boy. I will hold the rear. Any sounds ahead of you, start firing and keep firing.'

'We're trapped here,' the man said unsteadily.

'Move!' the giant barked.

The stairs wound round the inside of the tower like the thread of a screw. They laboured up them in almost pitch darkness, the sound of their own harsh breathing magnified by the plascrete to left and right, their feet sounding hollow on the metal steps. Several times the Astartes paused to listen as they ascended, and once he ordered them to halt.

'Anyone got a light?' he asked.

'I have,' the boy said. There was a whirring sound, and then a feeble glow began, yellow and flickering. It strengthened as the boy kept winding up his torch.

'Good for you,' the Astartes said. 'Give me those grenades.' He popped one out of the sling and peered at it.

'They copy us in everything – these are just like Imperial charges. They have three settings: instant, delay and proximity. The most obvious one is delay, the red button on top – give thanks to the Emperor you picked that one back outside. You twist the top of the cylinder for the other settings.' He did so. 'Move up the stairs.' He set down the little cylinder upright, pressed the red button on its top, and then followed them. Behind him there were three tiny clicks, and then silence.

'The next thing to approach that is going to have a surprise. I just hope there are no rats in here. Move out.'

Round the tower they went by the flickering glow of the boy's clockwork torch. Finally they came to another steel door. It was very slightly ajar, and there were voices on the far side. The boy reached for the grenades, but the Astartes stopped him. 'We need this place intact. Get behind me.'

He kicked open the door and there was a roar of bolter fire, a stuttering series of flashes, and then a click as the bolter's magazine came up empty. The Astartes roared and lunged forward.

Behind him, the boy and his father burst through the doorway, coughing on the cordite stink that filled the space beyond. They were in a large circular room filled with consoles and monitors, with huge windows that overlooked the entire spaceport. A trio of cultists lay dead, their innards scattered like red streamers across the electronic wall-consoles of the tower. On the far side of the room, a titanic battle was raging, smashing back and forth, sending chairs flying, filling the air with broken glass. The Astartes was struggling with a dark, armoured figure almost as massive as himself, and the two were grappling with each other, bellowing like two bulls intent on mayhem. The boy and his father stood staring, lasguns almost forgotten in their hands.

The Astartes was knocked clear across the room. He crashed into the heavy blast-proof glass of the tower and the impact spidered it out in a web of cracks. His adversary straightened, and there was the sound of horrible, unhinged laughter.

'Brother Marine!' the voice gargled, 'You have not come dressed for the occasion! Where is your blue livery now, Dark Hunter? Can't you see you are on the wrong world? This place is ours now!'

The speaker was clad in power armour similar to that they had found the Astartes wearing, but it was bone-white in colour, and a black skeleton had been picked out upon it with ebony inlays. Its bearer wore a helm adorned with two great horns, and the light from his eye sockets glowed sickening green. The many-arrowed star of Chaos had been engraved on his breastplate, and in his hand he held a cruel monomolecular blade which shone with blood.

'How many of you are left now, heretic?' the Astartes spat. 'My brothers will wipe you from this system as a man wipes shit from the sole of his boot.'

'Big words, from the mouth of a cripple,' the Chaos warrior snarled. He drew a bolt pistol from its holster and aimed it at the Astartes's head.

The boy and his father both raised their lasguns and fired in the same moment. The man missed, but his son's burst caught the enemy warrior just under the armpit. The fearsome figure cried out in pain and anger, and dropped the knife. The pistol swung round.

'What are these, brother– pets of yours? They need chastising.'

He opened fire. The pistol bucked in his hand and the impact of the heavy rounds sent the boy's father smashing back against the wall behind, ripping open his chest and filling the air with gore. The Chaos warrior stepped forward, still firing, and the bolter shells blew open the wall in a line of explosions as he followed the flight of the boy, who had dropped his lasgun and was scrabbling on hands and knees for the shelter of the consoles. The magazine clicked dry, and the warrior flicked it free, reaching in his belt for another one. 'Such vermin on this world – they must be exterminated to the last squealing morsel.'

'I agree,' the Astartes said.

The Chaos warrior spun round, and was staggered backwards by the force of the blow. He fell full length on his back. Dropping his pistol, his hands came up to his chest to find the hilt of his knife buried in his own breastplate. There was a thin, almost inaudible whine as the filament blade continued to vibrate deep in his body cavity.

The Astartes, his face a swollen mask of blood, dropped to his knees beside his prone enemy.

'We have two hearts each, you and I,' he said. 'That is how we are made. We were created for the betterment of Man, to make this galaxy a place of order and peace.' He gripped the knife blade, slapping his struggling adversary's hands aside, and pulled the weapon free. A thin jet of blood sprang out, and the Chaos warrior grunted in agony.

'Let me see if I can find that second heart,' the Astartes said, and he plunged the knife downwards again.

The boy crept out of his hiding place and crouched by the mangled remains of his father. His face was blank, wide eyes in a filthy blood-spattered mask. He closed his father's staring eyes and clenched his own teeth on a sob. The he stood up and retrieved his lasgun.

The Astartes was lying by the wall in a pool of his own blood, his dead enemy sprawled beside him. His body was white as ivory, and the blood leaking from his wounds had slowed to a trickle. He looked up at the boy with his remaining eye. They stared at one another for a moment.

'Help me up,' the Astartes said at last, and the boy somehow climbed behind him and pushed his immense torso upright.

'Your father–' the Astartes began, and then there was a dull boom from below them.

'The grenade,' the boy said dully. 'They're on the stairs.'

'Toss another one down there and then lock the door,' the Astartes said. 'Bring me over that bolt pistol when you're done.'

'What's the point?' the boy asked, sullen. His eyes were red and bloodshot. He looked like a little old man, shrunken and defeated.

'Do as I say,' the Astartes cracked out, glaring. 'It's not over while we live, not for us, not for your world. Now toss the grenade!'

The boy looked round the door.

'There's movement on the stairs,' he said, calm now. He pressed the red button on the explosive and threw it down the stairs. It bounced and clinked and clicked as it went down the steps. He shut the heavy metal door and slid the bar-lock in place. Another boom, closer than the first. There were screams below them, and the floor quivered. The boy handed the Astartes the bolt pistol, and the giant ripped the ammo belt off the fallen Chaos Marine, clicking in a fresh magazine and cocking the weapon.

'I've found the comms,' the boy said, across the room. He flicked several switches up and down. 'At least I think so – it looks like a comms unit anyway. But it's dead. There's no power.'

The Astartes laboured over to the boy on his hands and knees. Blood dripped out of his mouth and nose and ears. He sounded as though he were breathing through water.

'Yes, that's it. Old-fashioned. But it still needs power.' He sighed deeply. 'Well, that's that then.'

The boy stared at the dead lights on the console. He was frowning. He did not even start when the first battering began on the door to the control room, and a slavering and snarling on the other side of it, as though a herd of beasts milled there.

'Power,' he said. 'I have power – I have power here.' His face quickened. 'My torch!'

He drew it out of the bag of oddments at his waist. 'I can attach it – I can plug it in and get it running!'

The Astartes drew himself up and sat on the creaking chair before the console. 'A fine idea, but you'll never crank up enough power with that little hand-held dynamo.'

'There must be something!'

They stared at the dead array of lights and switches before them. The comms unit was a relic, a patched up antique for use on a far-flung border world. The Astartes's good eye narrowed.

'Plug in your torch and start winding,' he said.

'But–'

'Just do it!' He scrabbled open the wooden drawer below the console, while behind them both, blow after heavy blow was rained down on the door to the chamber. The lock-bar bent inwards. A chorus of cackles and growls sounded on the other side, like the memory of a fevered nightmare.

'Sometimes they hang on to the most obsolete of technologies on worlds like yours,' the Astartes said. He smiled. 'Because they still work.' From a tangle of junk in the drawer, he produced a contraption of wires and a small knobbed device. He stared at it, considering a moment, and then set it up on the bench, plugging it into the adaptor socket. Immediately, a small green light came on within it.

'Built to last,' he muttered. He closed his eye, and then began tapping down on the device. A high series of clicks and tones was audible. He adjusted the frequency with an ancient circular dial, and there was a faint crackle.

The two of them were so intent, the boy turning the handle on his creaking torch, the giant tapping away on the strange device, that they were almost oblivious to the grinding and banging at the room's door.

'Is it working?' the boy asked.

'The signal is going out. The code is ancient; a relic of old Earth, but we still use it in my Chapter, for its simplicity. It is elegant, older even than the Imperium itself. But like many simple, elegant things in this universe, it has endured.'

The Space Marine stopped his tapping. 'Enough. We must see if we can get you out of here.'

'There's no way out,' the boy said.

'There's always a way out,' the Astartes told him. He turned and fired at the plexi-glass of the control tower. It shattered and cascaded in an avalanche of jagged shards. Then he reached into the console drawer with a fist and produced a long coil of dull coppery wire.

'It will slice your hands as you go down,' he said to the boy, 'but you must hold on. When you get to the bottom, start running.'

'What about you?'

The Space Marine smiled. 'I will be on the other end. Now do it.'

The door burst open, and was flung back against the wall with a clang. A huge figure loomed out of the darkness, and more were behind it.

The Astartes was slumped by the huge broken maw of the plexiglass window, a glint of wire wrapped round one arm, disappearing into the smoky vacancy beyond. He bared his teeth in a rictus.

'What kept you?' he asked the hulking shapes as they advanced on him. Then he raised his free arm and fired a full magazine from the bolt pistol into the intruders. Screams and yowls rent the air, and the foremost two shapes were blasted off their feet.

But more were behind them. The howling mob in the doorway poured into the room, firing bolters as they came, the heavy rounds blasting everything to pieces.

Away from the tortured little world, the vastness of hanging space was utterly silent, peaceful, but in the midst of that peace tiny flowers of light bloomed, white and yellow, lasting only an instant before lack of oxygen snuffed them out. From a distance – a great distance – they seemed minute and beautiful, brief jewels in the blackness. Closer to, the story was different.

There were craft floating in the blackness, immense structures of steel and ceramite and titanium and a thousand other alloys, constructed with an eye to utility, to endurance. Made for destruction. They looked like vast airborne temples created for the worship of a deranged god, kilometres long, their flanks bristling with turrets and batteries. About them, smaller craft wheeled and dove like flycatchers on the hide of a rhino.

Within the largest of these craft an assemblage of giants stood clad in shining dark blue armour, unhelmed, their pale faces reflecting back the distant infernos that were on the viewscreens to their front. All around them, travesties of man and machine worked silently, murmuring into their stations, hands of flesh working in harmony with limbs of steel and muti-hued wiring. Incense hung in the air, mixed with the unmistakable fragrance of gun-oil.

'You're sure of this, brother?' one of the giant figures said, not turning his head from the scenes of kinetic mayhem on the screens about him.

'Yes, captain. The signal lasted only some forty-five seconds, but there was no doubting its content. Several of my comms-techs know the old code, as do the Adeptus Mechanicus. It is a survival from ancient days.'

'And the content of the message?'

'One phrase, repeated again and again. Captain, the phrase was *Umbra Sumus*.'

At this, all the standing figures started and turned towards the speaker. They were all two and a half metres high, clad in midnight-blue armour. All had the white symbol of the double-headed axe on one of their shoulderguards. They carried their helms in the crook of their arms, and bolt-pistols were holstered on their thighs.

'Mardius, are you sure – that is what it said?'

'Yes, captain. I have triple checked. The signal was logged and recorded.'

The captain drew in a sharp breath. 'The motto of our order.'

'*We are shadows.* Yes, captain. No Punisher would ever utter those words – the hatred they feel for the Dark Hunters is too great. It is my belief one or more of our brethren sent it from the surface of the planet; he was contacting us in the only way he could. Or warning us.'

'The signal cut off, you say?'

'It was very faint. It may have been cut off or it may merely have passed out of our range-width. We are too far away to scan the planet. The signal itself took the better part of ten days to reach us.'

'Brother Avriel,' the captain snapped. 'Who was unaccounted for after we left the surface?'

Another of the giants stepped forward. 'Brother Pieter. No trace was found of him. We would have searched longer, but–'

'But the Punishers had to be pursued. Quite right, Avriel. No blame is attached to my query. It was the priority at the time.' The captain stared up at one of the giant screens again. Within the massive nave of the starship, there was almost silence, except for the clicks and muttering of the adepts at their posts.

'No other communications from planetside?'

'None whatsoever, captain. Their infrastructure was comprehensively destroyed during our assault, and it was a backwater to begin with. One spaceport, and nothing but suborbital craft across the whole planet.'

'Yes, yes, I am aware of the facts of the campaign, Avriel.' The captain frowned, the studs on his brow almost disappearing in the folds of scarred flesh there. At last he looked up.

'This engagement here is almost concluded. The Punisher flotilla has been crippled and well nigh destroyed. As soon as we have finished off the last of their strike craft we will turn about, and set a course for Perreken.'

'Go back?' one of the Astartes said. 'But it's been weeks. If it was Pieter–'

'Avriel,' the captain snapped, 'What is our estimated journey time to the planet?'

'At best speed, some thirty-six days, captain.'

'Emperor guide us, that's a long time to leave a Brother-Marine alone,' one of the others said.

'We do this not just for our brother,' the captain told them. 'If any taint of Chaos has remained on the planet then it must be burnt out, or our mission in this system will have utterly failed. We return to Perreken, brothers – in force.'

The ceremony was almost complete. For weeks the cultists and their champions had danced and prayed and chanted and wept. Now their mission was close to its fruition. Across the plascrete of the landing pads, a dark stain had grown. This was no burn mark, no sear of energy weapon or bombardment crater. Within its shadow the ground bubbled like soup left too long on a stove. It steamed and groaned, cracking upwards, segments of plascrete floating on the unquiet surface. The screaming chant of the cultists reached a new level, one that human ears could barely comprehend. Hundreds of them were gathered around the unquiet, desecrated stain of earth.

\* \* \*

'Hold your fire until I give the word,' the boy said, and up and down the line the order was passed along. In a series of impact craters to the east of the spaceport scores of men and women lay hidden by the broken rubble. They were a tatterdemalion band of ragged figures weighed down by bandoliers of ammunition and a bewildering assortment of weaponry, some modern and well-kept, some ancient and worn-out. Once, a long time ago it seemed now, they had been civilians, non-combatants. But now that distinction had ceased to exist on Perreken.

A black-bearded man who lay beside the boy was chewing on his thumbnail nervously. 'If we've got this wrong, then all of us will die here today,' he said.

'That is why I didn't get it wrong,' the boy said. He turned to stare at his companion and the black-bearded man looked away, unable to meet those eyes.

Almost three months had passed since the boy had slid down a piece of wire held by a dead Space Marine. In that time he had broadened, grown taller, and yet more gaunt. The flesh of his face had been stripped back to the bone by hunger and exhaustion, and his eyes were blank with the look of a man who has seen too much. Despite his youth, no one questioned his leadership. It was as if his fellow fighters recognised something unique in him, something none of the rest of them possessed.

The boy held an Astartes bolt pistol in his hands, and as he lay there in the crater with the rank sweat of fear filling the air around him, he bent his head and kissed the double-headed eagle on the barrel. Then he fumbled in the canvas satchel at his side and produced a mess of wires and a little control panel. A green light burned on the heavy battery still in the satchel.

'Send it,' he said to the black-bearded man. 'It's time.'

His companion began tapping clicks out on the elderly wired contraption. 'May the Emperor smile on us today,' he muttered. 'And may His Angels arrive on time.'

'When the Astartes say they will do something, they do it,' the boy said. 'They gave their word. They will be here.'

Across the landing fields, the cultists were dancing and stamping and screaming their way into a frenzy. Some of the madly cavorting figures had once been smallholders and blacksmiths and businessmen, friends and neighbours of the ragged guerrillas who lay in wait among the craters to the east. Now they had been turned into chattels of the Dark Gods, worshippers of that which drew its strength from the warp. And now the warp had stirred them into a kind of ecstasy, and it fed off their worship, their blood-sacrifices. The patch of ground which they circled darkened further, popping and undulating as though cooked on some great invisible flame.

And inside that roiling cauldron, something stirred. There was a momentary glimpse of something breaking the surface, like the fin of a great whale at sea. The earth spat upwards, as though trying to escape whatever writhed beneath it. The cultists went into paroxysms, prostrating themselves, shrieking until the blood vessels in their throats burst and sprayed the air with their life fluids. Farther back from the edge, the armour-clad champions of their kind stood and stamped and clashed power swords against their breastplates. The darkness thickened over them all like a shroud.

The boy lay and watched them with his face disfigured by hatred and fear. Up and down the line there was a murmur as his fellow fighters brought their weapons into their shoulders. Some were priming home-made bombs, others were checking magazines. They were an underfed, rancid, ill-equipped band, but they held their position with real discipline, waiting for their young leader's word.

I did that, the boy thought. I made them like this. I am good at it.

He could barely remember a time now when he had been a mere farm boy, living on a green planet where the skies were blue and there was fresh food to be had, clean water to drink. He could barely even remember his father. That boy who had known a father was someone else, from another time. All he could remember now was the endless smoke-shrouded landscape, the constant fear, the explosions of bloody violence, the carnage. And the face of the Astartes who had died while helping him to live. That, he could not forget.

Nor could he forget the moment of sheer bubbling joy and relief when the ancient comms device he had found in the city had proved to work as well as that which they had found in the control tower. One of the older men knew the ancient code by heart and taught it to him. When the first message had come clicking back at them from a far-flung starship on the other side of the system it had seemed like a benediction from the God-Emperor Himself. It was enough to engender hope, to help him recruit fighters from the shattered survivors of the population. They had lived like rats, scavenging, scurrying for weeks and then months in the ruins of their world. Until today. Today they would stand up and take it back.

That was the plan.

The boy clambered to his feet just as the battery-fed contraption in the satchel clicked by itself in a sharp staccato final message.

An incoming message.

The boy smiled. 'Open fire!' he shouted.

And all around him hell erupted.

The chanting of the cultists faltered. They looked up, distracted, angry, shocked. The first volley cut down almost a hundred. Then the ragged guerrillas followed the boy's lead and charged forward across the broken plascrete of the landing field, firing as they came and yelling at the top of their voices.

The ring of cultists opened up, fraying under the shock of the assault. But there were many hundreds more of them further west by their drop-pods. These now set up a cacophony of fury, and began running eastwards to meet the attack.

The boy went to one knee, picking his targets calmly, firing two or three rounds into each. The enemy formation had splintered – they were confused, scattered, but in their midst their champions were restoring discipline quickly, shooting the more panicked of their underlings, roaring at the rest to stand fast.

*Now*, the boy thought. *It must be now.*

In the sky above the spaceport, eye-blinding lights appeared, lancing even through the heavy smoke and the preternatural night. With them came a sullen, earth-trembling roar.

In an explosion of concrete and soil, a behemoth thundered to earth. It was dozens of metres tall, painted midnight blue, and on its multi-faceted sides was painted the sigil of the double-headed axe. It scattered the cultists through the air with the force of its impact, and in its wake came another, and another, and then two more. It was as if a series of great metal castles had suddenly been hurled to earth.

With a scream of straining metal, long hatches fell down from the sides of these monstrous apparitions, as though they were the petals opening on a flower. These hatches hit the ground and buried themselves in earth and shattered stone and the bodies of the screaming cultists, becoming ramps. And down the ramps came an army, a host of armour-clad warriors blazing a bloody path with the automatic fire of bolters, melta guns, plasma rifles and rocket launchers. In their midst hulking Dreadnoughts strode, picking up the cultist champions in their clawed fists and tossing them away like discarded rags. They belched flame as they came, incinerating the cultists, boiling their flesh within their armour, making of them black desiccated statues.

And overhead the engines of destruction swooped down to unloose cargoes of bombs on the unholy stain which the Chaos minions had inflicted upon the tortured planet. As they went off, so in their brilliant light something bestial and immense could be seen twisting and thrashing in its last agonies. It sank down below the level of the plascrete launch pad as though below the surface of a lake, bellowing, and as the missiles rained down on it, so the blackened earth became solid again, and the stain became that of normal charred earth and stone, the desecration lifted before it could be consummated.

The boy stood with his bolt pistol forgotten in his hands, staring at that great storm of fire, a scene like the ending of a world. He felt the concussion of the shells beat at the air in his very lungs, and the heat of them crackled the hair on his head, but he stood oblivious. Tears shone in his eyes as he watched the obliteration of those who had destroyed his home, and in that moment there was only a single thought in his mind.

He stared at the massive, fearsome ranks of the advancing Space Marines, and thought: this is me – this is what I want to be.

Thus did the Dark Hunters Chapter of the Adeptus Astartes return to the planet of Perreken, to save a world, and to retrieve the remains of one of their own.

# THE TRIAL OF THE MANTIS WARRIORS

## C S Goto

A faint mist of light hung in the darkness, casting the vaulted chamber into a grimy and spectral half-life. Specks of dust danced suspended in the twilight, hazing the shadows with interference. From the apex of the central dome a single cone of light cut clarity into the heart of the gold-edged Imperial aquila that was etched into the deck. The hall seemed to fade away from this shining pillar of truth, retreating into the heavy shadows of its circular perimeter, where hints of grave faces haunted the darkness. Standing between the wings of the double-headed eagle, as though entrapped by the single column of light, Acting Chapter Master Neotera's eyes shone with fierce resolve and disbelief. How had it come to this?

His bearing proud despite the humiliation, Neotera held his gaze directly ahead, showing no signs of listening to the whispers of accusation and allegation that hissed around the dark recesses of the Council of Judgement. Held in the beam of light, his armour glittering like a polished emerald, he could not see the faces of the ghostly, shadow-veiled judges. But he knew who they were. They could not disguise their voices from him, and they did not try. This was a court of honour, and the purpose of the darkness was not to hide their identity from him, but rather to hide them from his shame. It did not matter who they were; it mattered who he was, and what he had done.

The new master of the Mantis Warriors wore no shackles; nobody feared that he would attempt to escape his fate. Under one arm he held his helmet, so that his long, black hair cascaded freely down his back.

The tendrils of his elaborate tattoos could be seen reaching around his neck, and his pale blue eyes glimmered aquamarine in the spotlight. Hanging at his other side was *Metasomata*, his revered and elaborately curved blade, celebrated throughout the Religiosa Realms as the *Venom of Tamulus*; it seemed to shimmer with control and restraint just fractions from the hand of its master. Amongst the legends of the Mantis Warriors, only the account of the Maetrus's *Foundation of the Mantidae* rivalled in glory that of the *Purgation of Traanquility*, in which Neotera was reputed to have purified the overrun jungles of the home world in the discipline of the Old Way, with no armour and only his blade strung across his back and devotion in his heart.

The members of the Council of Judgement knew him well, and they acknowledged him as a Space Marine of peerless honour. None feared his lethal weapon or his celebrated skill at bladed combat. Many had fought at his side in previous campaigns, and more than one owed him their life. The autocannons embedded into the walls as precautions against the criminal, the violent, or the deranged lay dormant and inactivated. Yet Neotera stood before them now as their prisoner. They could see how he held his gaze directly ahead, firm and unwavering, not insulting them by looking at them as he awaited their judgement on the charges of treachery and rebellion. He waited, already resolved to die at their word, to take his shame before the Emperor himself, and to purge the sins of his battle-brothers in the fires of a pyre. No others would suffer for his crimes.

'Do you have nothing to say, Master Neotera?'

*Will you say nothing?*

The impersonal voices from the shadows were firm and unyielding, yet Neotera could feel the compassion in them. He knew that many in the council wanted to understand what he had done. They wanted him to *explain*, as though explanations were possible or helpful. There were those in the council who would have once called him brother, who would have followed him into the depths of the Maelstrom itself, taking the righteous fury of the Emperor into the heart of Chaos. They had seen *Metasomata* carve venom-tinged light into the darkness of the worlds lost in the fringe of the Maelstrom. They wanted to believe that his fall had a reason, that he had lost himself to some kind of irresistible sorcery, that he was no longer the Space Marine he once was. They wanted to find something of him in his explanation, a part of him or his story that could be salvaged for the archives or even for their own personal reassurance. Yet their compassion was underscored by fear, fear that there might be no such explanation, that others might be tempted to make the same choices that he had made. Fear that there was actually nothing wrong with Neotera at all, and that he could be any one of them.

Fear provoked denial. And denial brought anger into the words of others.

'Do you ridicule this council, Mantis Warrior?'

*Do you find us unworthy even of your words?*

'Do you hold us in contempt even now?'

The voices and thoughts swirled around him, challenging his pride, daring him to break his silence and to attempt to argue. The psychic interrogations probed at his mind, making him dizzy and nauseous. His soul cried out in anger and horror, demanding that he turn the indignance back at his accusers but simultaneously pleading for them to stop asking for words and to simply condemn him. He had nothing to say to them. There was nothing that words could undo.

The silent Chapter Master meant no further offence to this revered and ghostly council, and he refused to be drawn into a contest of words. His crimes were clear for all to see; he had denied nothing. He would not make things worse for his battle-brothers or for the honour of the Mantis Warriors by engaging in the cheap competition of excuses and explanations. He was of the Adeptus Astartes, one of the Emperor's chosen servants, and he would not play the grubby word-games of servitors, Arbites or inquisitors. History would judge him harshly for his silence, but nobody could judge him more severely than he judged himself. For history, he cared not one iota. For himself, he had given up all hope of salvation – he had taken steps from which there was no returning, and he would not shame his name further by scrambling hopelessly for the last pathetic phantasms of deliverance. He accepted his damnation, and so the condemnation of this revered council held no greater horror for him. Once the fall begins, there is only flame and sword.

*Your crimes are heinous beyond our understanding.*

'You must help us to understand, Mantis Warrior.'

*Will you say nothing, Neotera? Will you not help us?*

'If you say nothing, we can offer no mercy.'

There was a long, resigned silence as the judges waited without hope of hearing a response. The hearing had been in session for three days already, and the Mantis Warrior had not yet spoken, other than to acknowledge his name and rank when he had first been brought before the council. He had not even taken advantage of his right to know whom he faced; which great Chapters the Masters and senior Librarians had been drawn from to compose this Council of Judgement. For three entire days, he had not moved, not a finger or a flicker of an eyelid, and a fine sprinkling of dust had settled out of the air onto the broad, emerald shoulders of his ceremonial armour. He was a statue, the very icon of the immaculate and devoted warrior. And yet he stood before a punitive court that had not been convened for countless centuries; he stood with no defence against the charges and no hope of emancipation.

He was guilty.

For the last three days, his mind had gradually turned in on itself. A question spiralled and spun through his thoughts, but it was not one of those thrown at him by his judges.

*How had it come to this?*

The question obsessed him, as though it had woven itself into the very fabric of his being. He had been sure. He had been right. And yet, how had it come to this? Not for the first time in his long and brutal life, Neotera recognised the potential of his soul to embrace the kind of fanatical focus and devotion of the Mantis Religiosa. He could feel how easy it would be to release the last vestiges of his sense of self, undeserving as it was, and to lose his will in the vast and blinding brilliance of the Emperor's terrible magnificence. The Religiosa lived as the lost and the saved, having no sense of their own needs and only a pure devotion to the Imperial Will.

The intrepid and pious Captain Maetrus of the Second Company had only recently discovered a possible source of this tendency in some Mantis Warriors; he hypothesised that it was connected to a uniquely altered neuro-toxic function of the preomnor implant in the Chapter's gene-seed. However, rather than seeing it as a curse that condemned its victims to the life of fanatical devotion of the Mantis Religiosa, Maetrus argued that such dark mysticism was a reward. The heightened sense of focus and the contracted perception of space and time that accompanied it sharpened a Space Marine's reflexes to an unprecedented degree, sometimes even giving the impression of mild precognition. During the last years of the war, Maetrus had sought Neotera's permission to develop a specialist cadre of Space Marines able to harness this blessed curse, claiming that they might tip the balance in the seemingly interminable battles with the Fire Angels and Carcharadons. He had wanted to call them the Praying Mantidae, but the demands of the war had stretched resources to breaking point – before they had finally broken in such spectacular fashion – and Neotera had not been able to spare the Space Marines that Maetrus requested.

Neotera wanted to close his eyes and swim in his regrets and laments.

*How had it come to this?*

The temptation to surrender himself to the light was almost overwhelming. He had felt it before, and it had helped him in situations even more lethal than the one he was in now. For the tiniest and most horrifying moment, Neotera wondered whether this descending battle-haze would be enough for him to unleash the *Venom of Tamulus* on those who sat in false judgement over him. There were only twelve of them – he had beaten worse odds before. Perhaps it was they who sinned against the Emperor? Perhaps the Mantis Warriors had been right after all – it was their righteous duty to cut down these heretics and hypocrites who dared to stand in judgement over him.

But the moment passed in a heartbeat, and then the appalling shame of his thoughts crashed even more weight into his overburdened soul.

He knew they had been wrong, that their war against the agents of the Imperium had been mistaken, that his own judgement had failed him, and that in his failure resided the damnation of all his battle-brothers. It was he, and he alone, who should bear the fury and the agony and the shame. Clinging to even the faintest hope that he had been right and that the edifice of the Imperium of Man itself was mistaken just compounded his crimes with egregious arrogance. He could not even stand to let the idea enter his head; it violated the very foundations of his being.

Even hidden within the confines of his own thoughts, Neotera felt his crimes worsening and his soul screaming in anguish. Yet, to the judges around him, he was a statue of control and composure. His eyes unblinking and his breath all but indiscernible. The certainty of his guilt hardened in his resolve, and his jaw clenched imperceptibly.

*How had it come to this?*

While his eyes kept Neotera crisply and painfully in the spotlight on the aquila, his thoughts searched desperately for answers. He didn't want explanations for the Council, but part of him needed to know when it had all gone wrong. Why hadn't he *seen* it?

He realised that Maetrus had seen the truth first. The brilliant captain had sent a communiqué to Neotera just before the Star Phantoms had finally broken the defensive barricade around Badab itself. Even as the Phantom drop pods thundered down into the Palace of Thorns, Maetrus had known that Huron's heart was black and filled with the taint of Chaos. At the same time, Neotera was fighting desperately to hold position in his battle-barge, engaged in the endgame of the war against the Loyalist coalition that had warred with Commander Huron's Astral Claws. Neotera had watched Maetrus break formation and turn the guns of his cruiser, *Tortured Soul*, against the ships in the collapsing defences of the Astral Claws. Maetrus had turned his fire against his own allies, breaking the Mantis Warrior formation in two by joining his guns with those of the Star Phantoms and breaking open a corridor for their drop-pods. And Neotera had only been able to bellow his disbelief at this insubordination and treachery – he had not seen the truth even then. In the heat of the battle, Maetrus had offered no explanation but had simply said that he 'trusted that Master Neotera would do the same.' Finally, when Lord Huron's own cruiser punched out of the atmosphere and cut through the Exorcists' blockade, Neotera had watched with slowly dawning understanding as Maetrus threw the *Tortured Soul* into pursuit and charged into the Maelstrom with guns blazing in the tyrant's wake. It was then, and only then, that Neotera understood what he had done. The horror had been beyond his capacity to comprehend, as though the galaxy had suddenly collapsed around him, leaving him standing alone and desolate in the ruins. He had fallen to his knees and gazed up into the heavens to see the constant, brilliant light of the Emperor, but he had seen only darkness.

The exit-ramp crashed down to the ground, kicking up a great cloud of dust from the moon's surface. As the mist of dirt billowed around him, Shaidan stood on the ramp and scanned the scene, his double-bladed Mantis Staff held vertically in one hand by his side. He had not been back to this place since the forging of his weapon in the hidden and half-forgotten furnaces of the moon's core. But this was not the return he had expected.

Beyond the rim of the crater that provided cover for his Thunderhawk, Shaidan could see flashes and streaks of bolter fire and energy discharges. Explosions shuddered through the shifting dust, making the ground ripple like a grey, liquid desert. Giant plumes of powder erupted into the thin atmosphere, obscuring the stars, marking impacts over the tightly arcing horizon. Banks of Space Marines were dug into cover in improvised bunkers to the right, forming a steadfast siege of the obscured Astartes facility in the cave at the foot of the mountain to the left. Above the trenches in the plain, standards of quartered blue and bone shook erratically in the airless atmosphere as the ground trembled beneath them. The Novamarines' starburst was clear to see, proudly and defiantly planted on this husk of a moon orbiting Badab Prime.

As his gunship had descended towards the moon, Shaidan had quickly identified the heavily camouflaged entrance to the cave, which had long ago been blown into one of the volcanoes that peppered the surface of the perpetually dark side of the moon. Despite the efforts of the Astral Claws to keep the location of their base hidden, Shaidan's keen eyes could detect the dull red light and the constant wisps of heat that seeped out of the cave mouth. The tunnels ran straight through to a lattice of magma chambers, from which the base and the mine beneath it had drawn its power for centuries, and then down into the bowels of the moon and the now-abandoned mines. The Librarian could remember the labyrinth of red-shadowed passageways from all those years before. And now a barrage of fire hailed in and out of the cave mouth, transforming it into a vision of a flame-breathing dragon emerging from the ancient and fiery depths, lighting the entrance to the secret base like a beacon.

Three squads of Mantis Warriors charged out of the Thunderhawk, filing past Shaidan on either side and fanning out to make a line along the lip of the crater. As Shaidan himself stepped off the ramp into the wake of the Space Marines, the engines of the gunship roared and the gunship pivoted as it rose out of the crater, bringing its main guns around to cover the Mantis Warriors. Great gouts of fire erupted from the Thunderhawk's lascannons and heavy bolters, spraying the ground around the dug-in formations of the siege forces of the Novamarines, forcing them into cover for just long enough for the Mantis Warriors to crest the crater and begin their charge.

As Shaidan clambered over the lip of the crater, with threads of bolter fire searing over his head, he saw the Mantis Warriors already braced into formation. They had come to this little moon for a rendezvous with a detachment of Astral Claws, who had assured them that Badab Prime was being virtually ignored by the coalition arrayed against them. Back on the *Tortured Soul*, Captain Maetrus had been characteristically suspicious and had dispatched Shaidan with three heavily armed squads; they would not be caught unaware because of the naïveté or over-confidence of their allies.

For a moment, Shaidan watched the Devastator squad brace themselves in the low gravity for heavy fire from their missile launchers and plasma cannons, throwing force into the mix of shells and las-fire from the Thunderhawk and rending the makeshift barricades of the Novamarines into banks of flame and raw energy. As the torrent of fury pounded the enemy line, the two Mantis assault squads blasted off the ground, spilling flame from their jump packs as they screeched over the lunar surface, spluttering staccatos of bolter fire and hurling grenades over the barricades into the trenches beyond. In the thin atmosphere, the assault squads seemed to flash with unnatural speed, and they were over the battered siege line in an instant.

But something was wrong. The attack of the Mantis Warriors had been smooth and by the book: they had hit the formation of Novamarines with sudden and overwhelming force, and they might have expected to be mopping up the fringes of the skirmish by now. Instead, there was an eerie quiet in the theatre as the assault squads hovered over the barricades, their bolt pistols silent and their chainswords still holstered.

From his position on the edge of the landing crater, Shaidan could see Sergeant Treomar of the first assault squad drop out of the sky into the unseen trench. A few seconds later, the sergeant reappeared above the barricade, hovering easily, and turned to face Shaidan. The vox-unit in his ear hissed.

'Librarian Shaidan. The trench is deserted. The treacherous Novamarines have fled.'

Shaidan turned on his heel, immediately realising what had happened. 'The mines! This moon is riddled with tunnels just under the surface; they've dropped into the mines!'

Even as he spoke, he saw a great plume of moon dust erupt into the sky from the crater behind him, directly beneath the low-hovering Thunderhawk. A hole opened suddenly in the ground and a squad of Novamarines stormed out, their bolt pistols coughing and their chainswords brandished. As Shaidan spun his force staff and vaulted down into the crater to check their advance, he saw a team of Novamarines, carrying missile launchers, emerging behind the vanguard.

Behind them, labouring through the dust, came the trundling weight of a Thunderfire cannon and the elaborate profile of a Techmarine in its wake. Despite himself, Shaidan found himself admiring the execution of the Novamarines' plan.

With just a few strides and one low-grav leap, Shaidan was down amongst the Novamarines. Immediately his Mantis Staff ignited with coruscating force as the Librarian spun it in a smooth arc around him, slicing one of its twin blades through the abdomen of one Space Marine while punching a burst of lightning from his other hand into the helmet of another. The two Novamarines recoiled under the assault, their bodies suddenly sagging as they tumbled backwards in the faint gravity, crashing into their battle-brothers, who brushed them aside and took their place between the Librarian and the emerging Devastator squad.

Meanwhile, the Mantis Warriors assault squads roared into view over the edge of the crater, charging back from the abandoned barricades in the plain. They opened fire with their bolt pistols but were unwilling to throw grenades while Shaidan remained engaged. But the Novamarines had moved with great efficiency. The Thunderfire cannon was firmly planted on its tracks and its quad-barrels were already fully adjusted, angled down into the curving walls of the crater. There was a sudden and abortive blaze from the barrels and then silence; for a moment it seemed that the cannon had misfired. But then the ground convulsed and shuddered, as though the moon were suddenly wracked with agony, and a huge subterranean detonation shattered the side of the crater and the landscape beyond. The lip of the crater crumpled and collapsed beneath the hovering figures of the assault squads. Great cracks ripped into the lunar surface around the devastator squad in the plain, swallowing three Space Marines whole, as clouds of dust were ejected into the atmosphere and jets of lava pulsed up from the ruptured magma chambers beneath the volcanic region.

Under cover of the tremor shells, lines of missiles streamed out of the Novamarine launchers and punched into the underbelly of the Mantis Thunderhawk as it banked and pitched in an attempt to get clear of the crater. The missiles punched relentlessly into the gunship's armour, one after another slamming into the same spot beneath the engine block. The armour was not designed for such extreme, close-range punishment and Shaidan could actually see the crack open in the adamantium just before the next flurry of rockets split the armoured panel away and crashed into the engine.

For a long, agonising second, the Thunderhawk shook and started to pitch. Tendrils of smoke escaped from the stern and intensifying flickers of flame started to lick out from between the cracking armoured panels. Then the gunship pitched abruptly and rolled sharply to the side; it lost its altitude in less than a second and crunched into the lunar surface just beyond the crater, smashing down next to the devastators. The impact shook the already unstable ground, and the landscape convulsed. After a fraction of a second, the downed Thunderhawk shifted and seemed to settle, but then the ground beneath it collapsed and it fell a hundred metres down into roiling lava streams below, bringing half of the remaining Devastators with it. As it sunk into the pyroclastic flow, the heat finally detonated the engine core, and the Thunderhawk shattered into an explosive ball of fire.

From the bridge of the *Tortured Soul* the atmosphere of Badab Primaris seemed to be on fire. The planet blazed like a small star as the oxygen in the ozone layer raged with flame. Captain Maetrus watched the ships that vied for superiority in different levels of orbit. His own cruiser was caught in between two banks of blockades: the defences of the Astral Claws in low orbit, barely above the thermosphere and supported by volleys from ground-based artillery on the planet below, and the siege line of the loyalists that sought to cut Badab off from the rest of the Maelstrom Zone. The two massive bulks of tonnage unleashed constant broadsides across the intervening space, lacing the fire-tainted darkness with searing lines of lance-fire and torpedo trails. Rapid strike vessels and destroyers darted through the theatre, manoeuvring around each other and attempting to approach enemy cruisers closely enough to launch boarding actions.

The First Company led the reserve companies in the defence of the Endymion cluster, where battle with the loyalists had been joined. Meanwhile, about half of the dwindling Mantis Warriors fleet had been pulled into the last-ditch defence of Badab, the final stronghold of the rebellion and the seat of Lord Lugft Huron, Master of the Astral Claws and most loyal servant of the Emperor. The Second Company, as usual, was in the vanguard, engaged where the fighting was most fierce. The *Tortured Soul* had been in almost constant battle for the last eight years – Maetrus had been on the bridge when they had captured the *Red Harbinger* from the Fire Hawks and plunged the Mantis Warriors into war all those years before. But not even this ancient and venerable vessel could withstand the kind of hammering that it was receiving now. The ship's great spirit remained unbroken and determined, but its systems were gradually collapsing under the relentless strain. The decks shuddered with impacts and the halls echoed with bootfalls as servitors and Space Marines strove to control damage and effect repairs. Whole sections of some decks were constantly and irrevocably ablaze, while others had been torn open to the absolute cold of space.

Over the years of battle, most of the ship's components had been cycled through a system of redundancy to ensure that it was always fully functional and able to withstand even the most formidable assault, but now there was nothing left in reserve. A serious hit on the control systems, life support, or even the engine block would leave the glorious ship all but dead.

A new warning light pulsed on the control deck and a siren sounded, unheard amidst the other alerts and noise. Maetrus flicked his eyes away from the fiery planet on the viewscreen and noted the warning. They were being boarded. With the number of gaping holes in the hull, it had only been a matter of time before one of the Exorcists or Star Phantoms ships had found a breach through which to deploy a boarding party.

'Sergeant,' muttered Maetrus almost inaudibly, as though the words didn't really need to be spoken, 'take two squads down to the breach and repel boarders. When Librarian Shaidan returns from Badab Primaris I'll send him to support you. Now go.'

Sergeant Audin's helmet tilted slightly, indicating his comprehension; then he turned swiftly and marched out of the bridge. As the door slid open a thin gust of smoke and the smell of charred metal wisped onto the deck.

Maetrus turned his attention back to the viewscreen. A formation of frigates was manoeuvring into an intricate assault pattern around the *Piercing Nova*, one of the Astral Claws' strike cruisers. The *Nova* was ill-equipped as part of a defensive blockade and its crew could hardly be accustomed to repelling this kind of battering – Astartes strike cruisers were designed to seize planets, not to hold them. But the Astral Claws had no choice as Badab's planetary defences were gradually being hammered into the ground by the bombardment canons of the besieging loyalist coalition.

The battle for Badab was all but over; it was just a matter of time now. There were no supplies or reinforcements coming through the Exorcists' blockade: the Executioners and the Lamenters had been crushed in an ambush by the Minotaurs nearly four years earlier – they had done the unthinkable, and surrendered. The secessionists were shattered; the Mantis Warriors were now Huron's only hope of survival, and Maetrus knew that this faint hope depended on his Second Company.

It was the kind of sight that an Adeptus Astartes might dream about. The heavens were full of war, with massive and terrible forces aligned against each other, and nothing but heroism and devotion lay between death and glory. An entire planet lay in ruins, its atmosphere a blazing inferno enwrapped in flaming clouds. In the mire was a desperate last stand, and spiralling around it was an overwhelming and malignant force bent on the destruction of a people, of a Chapter. Maetrus could see little hope of victory in the theatre before him, and he had no intention of seeking a retreat, even if he could somehow escape the immovable line of Exorcists that held the system in isolation. But his mind was no longer engaged in thoughts of victory or defeat. He had not entered this war believing that it could be won, but only believing that it should be fought. Sometimes honour was not about winning, but merely about dying the right way. For him, realised Maetrus, this war had always been about dying. It had been a long and blood-drenched pathway towards his death.

A great, stuttering explosion broke Maetrus's reflection. One of the capital ships of the Star Phantoms deployment convulsed and then blew apart, scattering debris and spinning shards of metal through the Astral Claws' faltering line and into the atmosphere of Badab. It was the *Spectre of Fear*, the cruiser to which Maetrus had despatched his last squad of Mantis Religiosa. He had known that they would not return, but had also been certain that they would not die without glory. The death of a strike cruiser was no less of a testament than those devoted Space Marines deserved. The Religiosa had somehow managed to board the embattled vessel and presumably fought their way to the engine core, where they had probably triggered a critical overload, staying to defend their sabotage until the engine finally blew. It would make no difference to the outcome of the battle.

'Give me a dozen squads of those Space Marines, and I will give you victory in any battle,' he muttered to himself, his eyes glittering with resigned admiration.

'If we gave you a dozen squads of Religiosa, captain, the Mantis Warriors would quickly be vanquished.' The response from Shaidan was unexpected.

'Then we must find a way of harnessing that power without losing the minds of our Space Marines to such unquestioning devotion, my friend. Imagine a Religiosa who *returned*. Shaidan, when did *you* return?' asked Maetrus, finally turning on his heel at the unexpected sound of the Librarian's voice.

'This moment, captain. I bring news from Badab Primaris.' Shaidan had removed his psychic hood and his long black hair hung loosely over his shoulders. His face was lined with grime and blood, but his piercing green eyes seemed to look into Maetrus's weary soul as he inclined his head to show his respects. He had never seen the captain's spirit so morose.

'I would prefer bad news,' replied Maetrus. 'The battle is on the brink of a spectacular finale, Shaidan. Good news may simply delay something glorious. Unless you have a miracle, give me bad news.'

'My news may have no bearing on the outcome of the battle, captain. But I think you might call it bad news nonetheless.'

Maetrus considered the face of the Librarian before him, old beyond its years and aching with the wisdom of power. 'You will tell me that Huron has surrendered?' He laughed without humour. 'And that he requests his allies to stand down?'

'I bring no such message, captain. Rather, I bring a report.' Shaidan's friendly tone stiffened. 'I rendezvoused with the Astral Claws on a moon of Badab Primaris, as you requested, captain. They were right that the loyalists are now so focused on breaking the defences of Huron's home world that reaching the minor planet should have been relatively simple.'

'Should have been?'

'Yes, captain. You were also right to note that other forces are at work in this theatre. We met with some inconvenience due to a small contingent of Novamarines. They were... persistent.'

'I think we should skip to the point, Shaidan,' mocked Maetrus gently, inclining his head back towards the viewscreen and the raging battle it showed. He liked this Librarian, and saw in his careful manner the promise of high command one day. But not today. 'There are some other things that require my attention today. And you are needed by Audin, who is repelling a boarding party even as we speak.'

Shaidan nodded, seeing the sad mixture of respect and resigned urgency in Maetrus's face. 'Lugft Huron's will is unbroken. He will fight until his Chapter is no more.' Despite the need for rapidity, Shaidan paused to collect the correct words. 'Yet the Astral Claws are no longer themselves, captain.'

'No riddles, Librarian. This is not the time.'

'Maetrus, I almost failed to recognise the squad that I had been sent to meet. In place of the proud colours of the Astral Claws, each Space Marine had painted over his armour in random ways, obscuring their Chapter insignia and even covering the Imperial aquila.'

'These were renegades? Deserters?'

'No captain, this was one of the elite squads employed by Huron as his palace guard. This was the squad that he entrusted to rendezvous with me.'

Maetrus stared. 'What are you saying, Shaidan?' There was anger in his voice; his lack of comprehension fuelled his frustration. 'Has all discipline in the ranks collapsed? I cannot believe it.'

'I cannot be sure, captain, but I believe that this is a new discipline. It seems that Huron has instructed his battle-brothers that the Siege of Badab is evidence that the Emperor has forsaken them at last. He claims that the Emperor's gaze has been corrupted by the bureaucrats of the Imperium and that it can no longer differentiate between loyalty and tyranny. Rumours spread that Lord Huron had gouged the aquila from his shoulder, and vowed to continue his fight for truth *for the Emperor*, even if no longer in the Emperor's name. The Space Marines related a rumour that Huron had insisted that since the Emperor could no longer recognise friend from foe, he would demonstrate his loyalty by ending his service to a muddled mind and by showing it the clarity that it has lost. This, he is supposed to have said, would be the ultimate and most selfless kind of service – risking his own damnation to bring the Emperor Himself back into the light. Hearing this, it seems that units in the Astral Claws have desecrated their armour in similar – or not so similar – ways.'

Maetrus stared as his mind raced to process the information. Hearsay and stories were always rife during war, and this war had dragged on for a decade, pitting the Astral Claws against the corrupt and hypocritical Imperium of Man itself. He could understand that tensions would be incredibly high within that Chapter, but he had never heard of the will of a Chapter being broken so completely by battle fatigue or stress. For the sake of the Emperor, Space Marines were not mere Guardsmen! The Adeptus Astartes were built for perpetual war; this was their very reason for being. He could not believe that Huron or his Claws had broken. It was simply not possible. They should be relishing the prospect of their glorious and righteous deaths, not bleating about being forsaken.

*Unless...* hesitated Maetrus, *unless Huron knows that he's wrong.*

As soon as the thought hit him, he felt the power of its truth. Huron *was* wrong. And he *knew* that he was wrong. He had deliberately misled them for his own self-serving ends. He had... Maetrus could hardly finish the thought. He had turned them against the Emperor! And they had *believed* him... They were too credulous to see the truth – they wanted to help this Chapter, in whom they thought they saw something of themselves, striving for perfection in a galaxy that misunderstood and feared them. They mistook the Astral Claws for themselves, and so lost themselves forever. And Huron knew what he was taking from them. He knew, and he took their souls without even the decency to reveal his claws. Even the agents of Chaos had more honour than that kind of power-mongering and politicking; at least they had the decency to tempt the unwary with the promise of supernatural power.

Suddenly it was all very clear and unambiguous, and Maetrus realised that the rebellion had never felt right to him. He had assumed that the sinking terror in his heart had simply been because of the way that the war was tearing the segmentum apart, but now he realised that the horror was more simple and direct: the rebellion was wrong.

'Captain?' asked Shaidan, watching Maetrus's face gradually set into fury.

'Librarian, you will assist with the repulsion of the boarding party. You should know, however, that if either you or Sergeant Audin wish to avert a mutiny, you will need to be back on the control deck in less than ten minutes to commit your own.'

'You will inform Master Neotera before you act, captain?' Shaidan's question was formal and procedural, as though he were simply going through the motions. The observance of protocol calmed his spirit, which roared for action. His soul felt the perfect righteousness of Maetrus's decision, in a way that it had not felt for nearly a decade.

'Of course.' Maetrus's gaze was level. His fury had settled into a fierce resolve.

'Then we will return to receive further orders once the boarding party has been destroyed, captain.' With that, Librarian Shaidan nodded curtly and turned to leave. Spinning his ornate, double-bladed force-staff in his hand he marched from the bridge without a backward glance.

'Ruinus!'

An attentive Space Marine stepped forward from his position guarding the doors to the control deck.

'Captain?'

'You heard Librarian Shaidan's report, sergeant?'

'Yes, captain.'

'You will understand that I need to get a message to the Chapter Master. I do not require a response, and there is no time to wait for one. I trust that you will transmit my communication in due time?' Maetrus eyed him carefully.

'Yes, captain. Of course.' There was no flicker of doubt. Maetrus even thought he saw a flash of relief and pride, as though a painful and debilitating wound had suddenly been healed.

'Inform Master Neotera that the *Tortured Soul* will be turning its guns against the Astral Claws imminently. Request no permission and ask no pardon, but please explain that I trust he would do the same in our position. Indeed, I trust he will do the same.'

Neotera turned away from Ruinus. 'Sergeant Soron! Train the starboard weapons batteries onto the *Piercing Nova* and prepare the bombardment cannon to hit the planetary defences. We are going to make this into the right death if it is the last thing we do.'

As the Thunderhawk exploded, the ground in the crater began to crumble away. Shaidan strode forward over the faltering dust, pushing into the squad of Novamarines that clustered around their heavy weapons in the heart of the crater, trying to defend their retreat back down into the subterranean tunnels and mineshafts of the ageless moon. His Mantis Staff blazed with green, phosphorescent venom, reminiscent of the megafauna of Tranquility itself. He lashed and stabbed with the glorious weapon, pushing it through plates of blue and bone power armour in a fury of indignation, righteousness and vengeance. As he advanced through bolter fire and lashing chainswords, he muttered an ancient machine curse, spitting his thoughts towards the Thunderfire cannon just as it teetered clumsily back into the tunnel. It seemed to pause and twitch, as though it had been slighted by the insult. The Techmarine behind it snapped his head around as though struck. And then the cannon simply stopped, whining to a halt in the mouth of the Novamarines' escape route.

As his assault squads dropped down into a semicircle around the far side of the crater, forming an enveloping firing line on the more stable ground of that bank, Shaidan took aim and launched his staff like an ethereal javelin, sending it searing through the remnants of the Novamarine squad and piercing the great barrel of the Thunderfire cannon.

There was a flash and the inaudible crackle of an unspeakable energy discharging, and then the cannon exploded, radiating superheated shrapnel and high-explosive shells like a giant scattergun. The remaining Novamarines took the full force of the detonation, and the Techmarine who had been tending to the cannon was all but incinerated in the blast. The escape tunnel, the Novamarines' only path out of the crater, collapsed completely.

As the Novamarines finally fell under the disciplined volleys of bolter fire from the assault squads, Shaidan focused his thoughts for a moment of quickening and seemed to flash across the disintegrating crater in a blur of emerald light. A moment later, he was lifting his unblemished Mantis Staff out of the ruin of the cannon, and the next he was back across the crater before the last standing Novamarine.

The Mantis Warriors assault squads ceased fire and all eyes turned to Shaidan as he stood imperiously before the defeated foe. The Novamarine before him wore the insignia of a veteran sergeant, and his armour was scored with the evidence of countless battles. He stood with proud defiance before the Librarian, meeting his eerie, emerald gaze through the implacable shield of his helmet's visor.

Shaidan inspected him, a faint psychic light flickering around the nodes in the hood that covered the back of his head. The Badab Secession, the Liberation Wars as they were known to the righteous, had cost the Astartes so many lives. He had killed countless loyalists himself, and he had seen so many of his sacred brethren fall. Yet he found it hard to believe that any of the Adeptus Astartes could take this lightly or find any joy in their victories. Every victory meant the loss of valuable gene-seed and each death was a cut in the flesh of the Emperor himself.

Yet, it was a consequence of the nature of the Astartes that battles rarely resulted in prisoners. It was not that Space Marines lacked mercy or compassion – indeed, the Mantis Warriors prided themselves on their compassionate natures – but rather they lacked the will to surrender. No matter what the odds or the chances of survival, a Space Marine found his very being in fighting. Without the fight, how could he demonstrate his devotion to duty, and without duty a Space Marine was nothing, perhaps worse. Compassion was for others; for the self there was nothing.

So, Shaidan inspected the last of the Novamarines on Badab Primaris—with interest, quite willing to accept his surrender, but fully prepared for the likelihood that this sergeant would still believe he could win some kind of victory, despite the dozen or so guns trained on him and the magnificent Librarian standing before him.

The Librarian gazed into the Space Marine's eyes, seeing straight through the opaque visor of his helmet as though it weren't even there. He saw no fear and no desperation. There was no frantic scheming for an escape. The gaze was level and calm, and the eyes shone with deepest sincerity. But there was also something else: this sergeant hated him.

He was repulsed by the Mantis Warriors, as though they represented something horribly corrupt and disgusting. For a fraction of a second, Shaidan recoiled from the force of the hatred, shocked to see it in the eyes of one of the Astartes. Composing himself, the Librarian probed a little further, reaching into the sergeant's thoughts, where he found unending stories of the horrors and perversions perpetrated by the Astral Claws and their allies in this war. The sergeant felt that the Emperor was on his side.

Shaidan nodded to the sergeant, understanding his reasons, misguided by the lies of war as they may have been, and he turned his back on the Space Marine. In that instant, the Novamarine snatched his bolt pistol from its holster and squeezed a shell into the Librarian's back.

But Shaidan was gone before the shell could impact. With the lightning speed of the quickening, the Librarian flashed out of sight. The first the sergeant knew of where Shaidan had gone was when he felt the burning cold of the twin-bladed Mantis Staff slice effortlessly through the back of his neck. Instinctively, the Novamarine tried to turn to face his foe. Even as the twin blades severed his spinal column he managed to twist the grip of his bolt pistol around and fire one last shot. As his head fell to the ground, the shell punched through his own armour and abdomen and cracked into Shaidan's chest plate, where it stuck, lacking the power to break through another layer.

As the sergeant's crimson life spilled into the grey lunar dust at his feet, Shaidan could feel his surprise and gratitude. The Novamarine had not expected such honour, and his death was sullied by his own sudden but deep-seated doubt. For his part, Shaidan mourned the fact that one of the Astartes could expect so little from the Mantis Warriors.

*How has it come to this?*

The vox-bead in his ear hissed suddenly. 'Mantis Warrior. We have been expecting you.'

Shaidan looked up to the rim of the crater and saw a contingent of Space Marines assembling, silhouetted against the starry sky. He looked over to Sergeant Treomar on the wall of the crater, who nodded an acknowledgement and signalled that these were the Astral Claws they had been sent to meet. But his signal seemed hesitant, as though he were not immediately sure who the newcomers were.

'It is good of you to join us, Astral Claw,' replied Shaidan as he climbed towards his hosts. He wondered why the Claws had neither warned nor helped them, but it was not the way of the Mantis Warriors to complain or reprimand, and certainly not to suggest that they would have benefited from assistance in a battle that they had already won without it. 'Your timing is impeccable, friend,' the Librarian said sarcastically.

'We have much to discuss, Librarian,' came the voice again. 'And time is short.'

As Shaidan climbed out of the crater he got his first clear look at the Space Marines of the Astral Claws. Despite himself, he stared at them with disbelief. They were arrayed before him in the great splendour of the ancient armour of the Adeptus Astartes, which glinted like multi-coloured jewels in the starlight. And yet there were too many colours. The splendid gold and blue of the Astral Claws, about which Maetrus had told him so much after his visit to the Palace of Thorns, were obscured and hidden, peeking furtively out from beneath gaudy daubs of colour, black and crude, bloody patterns of red. They were like the perverted progeny of Astartes and eldar, if it were not heretical even to imagine such things. And even stranger, Shaidan could see that the Imperial aquila had been prised off the armour of some and obscured or desecrated on others.

He stood on the very brink of the collapsing crater, looking between the detachment of bizarre Astral Claws and the honourable corpses of the Novamarines that littered the dissipating lunar dust. He could feel Sergeant Treomar and the assault squads shifting uneasily, as though unsure about the next move. They were tense and ready for anything.

'Yes, time is short, friend,' said Shaidan at last, 'and I can see that you must have a great deal to report to us. First, you will permit us to reclaim the gene-seed of our fallen brethren, then we will talk.' He nodded over towards the mouth of the cave that held the base they had been trying to reach, and he winced when he saw that the double-headed eagle carved into the rock above the cave had been defaced. 'We will also thank you if you can spare a Thunderhawk or other transport for our voyage back to the fleet. I'm sure Captain Maetrus and the Chapter Master will be eager to hear my report.'

'Master Neotera, this council need hide nothing from you, and we should tell you that we are fully aware of the events of the war that you unleashed on this sector. You need not trouble yourself to tell us the details of how you finally surrendered before the gathered might of the Novamarines, Carcharadons and Sons of Medusa after the Lamenters had broken at Optera, how you routed the Marines Errant on Bellero-phon's Fall, how you miraculously escaped Tranquility II, or even how you managed to capture the *Red Harbinger* from the Fire Hawks back in 904. We do not need this information from you – it is already a matter of record. The gaps, such as they are, can be filled in by any number of observers. We do not ask for a confession of these acts, for they are undeniable. The blood has been spilled, the Space Marines have been slaughtered, and whole planets have been ravaged. All at your command. We do not seek denials or descriptions.

'What we cannot judge is *why*. What we require of you is *explanation*. What did you seek to achieve? Why would you desert the light of the Emperor and forge an alliance with the Tyrant of Badab? And what could have driven you to launch those first attacks against the Fire Hawks, knowing that such acts would drag the Imperium into the kind of war unknown since the Great Heresy itself? Even Huron himself dared not strike at his fellow Space Marines – it was only with you that the petty insurgency became a war. How were you convinced to turn away from the honour and devotion of the Astartes? What kind of promises could buy the soul of the Chapter Master of the Mantis Warriors and guardian of the Endymion Cluster?'

*What did the cowardly shape-changer offer you, Mantis? Did he promise you a seat at the right hand of a tyrant or liberty from the discipline of the Adeptus? Did he taunt you with the artefacts of his xenos allies, or tempt you with the forbidden knowledge of his corrupted brethren? How did he turn your will against the father of us all, and twist your spirit into treachery? Or would you have us believe that he did nothing… that you were already lost, and that you found a kindred spirit in this traitor? Is the great legacy of the Mantis Warriors nothing but an illusion, a cover to hide your own tainted gene-seed? Have you been hiding like cowards for a thousand years, living in pretence and hypocrisy and treating us all like fools? Are you to be damned as well as condemned, Mantis Lord?*

'You must *explain*, Neotera. We are not beyond mercy here.' The shadow-veiled words were not without kindness.

Do you not know me at all? The thoughts stayed inside his head. Of course you do not know me. I cannot even recognise myself. I have no answers to your questions, and I would offer none even if they burned like firebrands in my mind. We are beyond these words and reasons now. Deeds are done; we must be measured by them just as we must be held to account for them. How can you taunt me with the *threat* of mercy? Do you think I want your mercy or your forgiveness? Do you think I can go on knowing what I have done, what I have allowed myself to do? Your mercy mocks me and offends yourselves; do not belittle us all with this kind of talk. I am undeserving of your kindness, and you should know even the Emperor in His infinite wisdom would offer me nothing less than condemnation. In the fall, there is only flame and sword. Speak your judgement and rid yourselves of me.

'I seek no mercy.' Barely more than a breath, he wasn't sure if he had spoken the words out loud, yet they wisped around the hall like the scent of poison.

*Ah, the silent Mantis speaks after all.* Venom was laced through the disembodied thoughts; they ridiculed him, as if certain that he would be broken. *We just offer you a little selfish hope and your resolve shatters. Mercy and treachery are such an exquisite pair. Did Huron offer you mercy? Did you hear the whispered echoes of Horus himself, offering to bring you back into his fold? Was this all it took, feeble-minded insect? Can your soul be bought for a little mercy?*

*I seek no mercy*, he repeated in his mind, clenching his jaw in the agony of self-betrayal. He had not meant to speak, but his resolve was so powerful and consuming that it had vocalised almost by itself. *I seek no mercy* – the thoughts spiralled around inside his head like a mantra, and just once in three days had they leaked out into the air. It was as though he were becoming the words; he was giving them physical meaning through the remains of his life.

Yet see how easily even those four brief words could be twisted and contorted. Their purity was sullied and despoiled as soon as they left his mouth. Before they had even reached the ears of his judges, their psychic resonance had already been distorted by the noxious mind of the nameless Librarian who wanted nothing more than for the Mantis Warriors to fall into the abyss, to leave them dishonoured and desecrated by the judgement of history. There was genuine hatred in that mind, and it oozed toxically into Neotera's head. The Chapter Master could feel a hunger for profit and spoils in those psychic intrusions, and he realised that not all of his judges were here for vengeance, justice, or knowledge; some were in pursuit of ships and worlds.

'So you are unrepentant, Neotera?'

Even the voices of reason misunderstood him. How could they find him unrepentant when his very being screamed in torment at his deeds? If only he could take back those four simple words and let his devoted silence remain unbroken. But the words could not be revoked, no more than the actions that had brought him to this place. Words could not explain what he had done, and any words that he uttered would only pervert even further the faith that remained in his heart; they would be twisted and tortured until they no longer resembled themselves and he could not see truth from lies. He knew when his choices had been made, and it was becoming clear to him that he had been wrong for many years. But he knew – deep in his soul he knew – that his intentions had been pure.

Intentions are nothing. A servant is judged by his deeds. I seek no mercy. I offer no words and no excuses. I stand ready to bear the unendurable.

The Palace of Thorns was everything that they had been led to expect. It was the ostentatious seat of power on the home world of a proud Space Marine Chapter, full of the pomp and regalia of military exploits and glory. Great statues towered over the gates and reached their arms into arches over vaulted ceilings. Ornate frescoes filled the walls, depicting the most awesome and legendary victories of the Astral Claws: the Purification of the Badab system itself, the Scouring of Tesline, and the Reclamation of Mundus IV. The Chapter Master's honour guard stood sentinel in the corridors and halls, resplendent in their gunmetal and gold armour, like majestic kings surveying their realms. And the Imperial aquila, the universal sign of devotion and loyalty to the Emperor, held pride of place on each of the grand spires that pushed up towards the heavens.

The contingent of Mantis Warriors was unfazed by the grandeur as they swept through the corridors on their way to the throne room. Their own fortress monastery on Tranquility III was no less glorious, and even the jungle surrounding it could inspire awe. However, their delegation to Badab was understated. Four squads of Space Marines acted as honour guards for a command squad of unusual austerity and gravity: the Chapter Master himself strode through the hallways of the Palace of Thorns. His guards shone in emerald battle armour, polished to the point of ceremonial splendour, yet they moved with the kind of focused caution that spoke of veiled distrust. As a special token of good faith, Lord Huron had permitted them to enter his palace fully armed; and not quite willing to return the confidence, the Mantis Warriors had taken full advantage of his offer. On the landing field beyond the gates, a group of deep green Thunderhawks held heavy reinforcements.

On their approach to the Badab system, the Mantis Warriors had seen for themselves the evidence of Huron's recent activities. They had heard the rumours and reports, but seeing the evidence gave the official accounts of insurgency and revolt more power and resonance. The adjoining space-lanes were littered with debris and the ruined masses of raided freighters, damaged beyond salvage or repair. Before they had agreed to the rendezvous on Badab, Huron had warned them what they might see and how it might appear to them. He had not sought to deny anything, but had invited the Mantis Warriors to bear witness to the facts.

He had explained that many of the apparently civilian ships had been unmarked, covert Imperial gunships, sent to spy on the Badab system. He claimed that he had discovered that such ships were normal parts of all mercantile convoys to Adeptus Astartes controlled systems, and he had challenged them to forcefully inspect the sparse shipping lanes around their own domain if they doubted him. He argued calmly that there were powerful factions in the Imperium that hated and distrusted the Astartes, jealous of their intimacy with the spirit of the Emperor and their resemblance of his body. These factions were now in the ascendant at the Terra-bound end of Segmentum Ultima, where fear of the Maelstrom mixed with distrust of the glory of the Astartes to produce officiousness and insidious suspicion. Huron had told Master Sartag that the Mantis Warriors were also being watched.

As the *Venomous Blade* had cut its way into the outskirts of the Badab system, Neotera had seen the torn prow of an Imperial light cruiser tumbling through the wreckage of a group of freighters. In amongst the debris, he could see the twisted remains of weapons batteries and the charred icon of the aquila. It seemed that Huron was telling the truth about the presence of the Imperium's eyes in this sector.

On the edge of the star-system, the *Blade* had registered a wide spread of signals on its long-range scanners. A fleet of battleships was assembling in the interstellar space between Badab and Rigant. Most of the signatures were too indistinct to be accurately discerned, but those at the vanguard had the solid and menacing echo of Space Marine strike cruisers and frigates. The unusual shape of the *Rapturous Rex*, the legendary Fire Hawks star fortress, was at the heart, as the formation slowly shifted and manoeuvred. They were less than a warp-jump away, but probably several days under normal power. They were waiting for something, and their presence suggested that their attention was fixed on Badab. Perhaps Huron's paranoia was not without substance? Would the Imperium really send Space Marines against their own again? What kind of Chapter would heed such a call?

In one of his first communiqués, before the trouble had exploded into bloodshed in the Golgothan Wastes, Huron had asked Sartag about the frequency with which the Mechanicus demanded a sample of Mantis Warrior gene-seed. At first, the Chapter Master had not understood why another Chapter would request such information; it had seemed disrespectful to the point of being insulting. He had been suspicious of Huron's motives, and then fearful that rumours about the Mantis Warriors were spreading to neighbouring systems. Captain Maetrus of the Second Company, the Prophet Captain as he was known, had cautioned many times about the suspicions that could be raised about the Chapter if the mental state of the Mantis Religiosa were to be misunderstood as some kind of genetic anomaly. Maetrus was especially concerned that the condition, which sometimes enhanced a Space Marine's reflexes to such an extent that they seemed to develop mild precognitive abilities, might appear to represent the spontaneous onset of psychic tendencies. Given the proximity of the Mantis Warriors' realm to the Maelstrom and the conditions of constant internecine war on some of its core systems, it was not beyond imagination that the Mechanicus would seek to police their gene-seed even more vigorously than that of other Chapters. Yet Maetrus was adamant that the condition was a normal state of mind, and was determined to develop a training programme that would enable all Mantis Warriors to harness this natural ability.

In any case, Sartag had not been willing to share information about the frequency of contact from the Mechanicus until Huron had openly admitted that he had made a decision not to submit the gene-seed of the Astral Claws for inspection any more. He had spoken passionately about the ways in which the Mechanicus had lost their legitimacy when they had reinterpreted themselves as a form of genetic police, monitoring the Astartes and holding over them the threat of disestablishment should they fail to meet some arbitrary criteria. Huron had called this oppression. He had labelled it as an evil against the spirit of the Emperor – nobody had ever monitored the Emperor's genetic make-up to try and restrain his development. The Imperium needed the free development of the Astartes, just as it had once needed the free development of the Emperor to give it form, whether it was willing to admit this or not.

Even worse, Huron had attempted to convince the Mantis Warriors that there were corrupt Space Marine Chapters that knew of this agenda, and which sought to exploit it for their own selfish advancement. He worried that the Imperium was not above turning these lackey Space Marines against their fellow Adeptus Astartes, turning one Chapter against another in a horrible civil war in order to prevent the truth being realised. With barely disguised disgust, Huron had named the Ultramarines and the Imperial Fists, with their intimate ties to the Administratum, as the most likely to turn against the most free-thinking Chapters – those that held the true legacy of the Emperor in their genes.

They had listened to Huron with a mixture of horror and empathy. His words were not without truth – the Mantis Warriors knew the angst and insecurity of dark secrets, like many other Chapters – but they did not dare to trust them. However, the presence of the Fire Hawks in the Maelstrom Zone seemed to confirm Huron's suspicions.

And now, as the heavy, illuminated doors to the throne room pushed slowly open, Neotera stood before Lugft Huron himself for the first time. The Chapter Master sat on the far side of the hall, raised on a dais and seated in the most elaborate throne Neotera had ever seen. Fanned out behind him were the twelve Space Marines that comprised his personal guard, each holding their bolters formally across their chest-plates. Along each side of the long room, arrayed as though for inspection, were twin lines of Space Marines in full battle armour. The chamber was brilliant with gold and black.

Neotera paused in the doorway, genuinely admiring the awesome scene. His pause slowly lengthened into a hesitation as he calculated the mass of firepower that was assembled before him and weighed it against the reports of Huron's insurrection. Despite the evidence en route to the planet, Neotera was not quite convinced that his master could trust this Huron, the alleged Tyrant of Badab. But behind him were assembled the finest thirty Mantis Warriors from the First and Second Companies, veterans and heroes all, and Neotera knew that they would not be cowed by this attempt at intimidation. However, he also realised that this display of power effectively nullified any 'trust' that Huron had claimed to show by permitting them to enter his palace armed for battle.

'Chapter Master Yarvan Sartag, Master of the Mantis Warriors and guardian of the Endymion Cluster, I bid you welcome to my hall.' Huron rose as he spoke, his formal words echoing slightly in the high room, and started down the steps of the podium, as though to meet Sartag on the level floor. 'I am grateful that you made the journey. Communications are insecure, and it is no longer easy for me to travel far out of this system, as you will appreciate.'

'Master Huron,' acknowledged Sartag with less exaltation, 'your reception honours us.' He strode across the marbled floor while Neotera and the rest of the Mantis Warriors fell into line behind him.

'We have much to discuss, Yarvan,' began Huron as they faced each other and bowed slightly, his eyes burning with a deep and hidden light. 'Grave matters of concern for the whole Imperium. The salvation of our brother Astartes rests in our hands – we are the Emperor's last hope. Can I count on you, brother?'

Neotera was no longer sure how much time had passed. He was beginning to feel the effects of sleep deprivation; his head felt heavier than usual, as though he were concussed, and his thoughts moved like wraiths through smoke. He was not tired, but over the years he had learned to recognise the slight hazing of his mind as the activity of his catalepsean node as it shifted his fatigued consciousness around his brain to keep him functioning without sleep. Judging by the mist that had settled over his thoughts, like the dust that was gathering on the shoulders of his armour, he had been standing on the aquila for nearly seven days. He had not moved in that time, and he could only recall speaking four ill-judged words. His mind was full of the questions and accusations of the council of judges – their persistent and powerful siege of his psyche had gradually permeated his staunch resolve, and he could feel a dizziness caused by the internalisation of his interrogators' combination of malice and mercy. But he knew that he could not break, not again.

The questions had thrown his thoughts back into reflection, and he had lost himself in the past for a while. But for how long? And how many of his thoughts could the judges see? Were they simply prodding his mind into recollection and then watching his thoughts betray him? There were certainly a number of powerful Librarians in the shadows amongst the faceless judges, but Neotera was not attuned enough to know exactly what might be the dimensions of their powers. Perhaps his resolve not to speak was serving no purpose after all. Perhaps the council could recover the answers it sought without the crassness of language. But then why ask the questions? Why go through the motions of a trial if they could simply empty his brain and sift through his memories themselves?

Unless it was a test. They wanted to see what he would say, whether he would crack, how he would attempt to justify himself, and then measure his words against the inner voice of his soul. Did he believe his own words? Was there deceit in his heart? Did he seek to excuse himself or to blame others? Was there any honour left in him, even after all the horrors he had perpetrated on the galaxy, even after he had violated his most sacrosanct oaths of loyalty?

But he had said nothing. Just those four words: I seek no mercy. He had not tried to *explain*. Although, he knew, his mind had been racing constantly, questing for answers to the questions they posed, for the questions were his own as well: how had it come to this? Did they have the answers? Had they managed to discern the truth from his fevered reflections? Could they *explain* it to him? He needed to know as much as they did. More. For it was his soul that was falling into the inferno, not theirs.

If they could see into his mind, he should be told. He needed to know. He deserved to know. His soul screamed for the knowledge.

How did it come to this? I deserve to know. The thoughts hissed out, like gas from a cracked tank.

*You deserve nothing, Mantis Lord.*

The bitter thoughts mocked his indignation and seeped with disgust. But he knew that they were right: he deserved nothing. His protests, although intended only for his own thoughts and not for the minds of the council, were unworthy of him and the Librarian's derision was fully justified.

Once again, the pain of self-betrayal wracked his soul, vying with the bottomless horror of his treachery against all that he held to be true and just. It was unbearable, yet he endured. He wasn't even sure that he recognised himself anymore. How had it come to this? How had *he* come to this?

A heavy grinding sound told him that the main doors to the hall were sliding open. Keeping his eyes directly ahead, he traced the movement of footfalls as they fanned out into the shadows of the vaulted ceiling around the edge of the chamber. As far as he was aware, this was the first time that the door had opened and anyone had entered or left since the hearing began. But, he realised, he could not even be sure of this petty little fact – he had lost faith in the integrity of his mind. Was he actually being driven mad? Had he been mad from the start? Had he ever truly been loyal to the Emperor?

'Khoisan Neotera, Chapter Master of the Mantis Warriors and guardian of the Endymion Cluster, this council finds you guilty of the most terrible crimes imaginable to the Imperium of Man.' The voice, deep and raw and unused to diplomacy, washed over Neotera like a dark tide. The horror of its words soothed him like a balm: he was guilty; he would not be forgiven. The relief was real and almost physical.

'You have plotted against the light of the Emperor Himself. You have spilt the blood of His most loyal servants, and you have brought Chaos into the very heart of the Emperor's realm. You have offered no defence of your actions, no explanations of your deeds, and you have asked for no leniency. It was the intention of this council that you should be executed for your crimes, and that your gene-seed should be cast into the void. In addition, we intended to dismantle the Mantis Warriors, to strip your Space Marines of their armour and weapons, to quarantine your home world, and to condemn the remaining Mantis Warriors to live as penitants, rebuilding the worlds that they have destroyed.'

The voice paused, and Neotera could feel a dozen pairs of eyes studying him. He did not flinch or even blink. He bit down on his jaw and focused his mind on the words: he needed to be clear-headed to hear the verdict and he realised that there was more to come. There was a sudden and sinking panic that the judge would revoke his condemnation, and then a shock that he was feeling panic for the first time in his life, since the Trials on Tranquility when he was first inducted into the Mantis Warriors. What had become of him? Had his treachery really pushed him into madness?

*We will take Tranquility, insect lord. Your kind will never pollute its forests again. Now it is mine.* The unidentified thoughts were faint and torn, as though shredded by malice. Even in his fevered state, Neotera could sense the presence of a self-serving spite once again.

'And yet, Khoisan, there are those on this council who do not believe that your silence shows a lack of repentance. Some who do not find your bearing arrogant. Some, indeed, who believe that your egregious deeds were not motivated by hatred or self-interest, but rather that you were misled by the cunning of others.'

The words seemed like flames. What were they saying? Were they trying to find a way to save him after all? Did they really retain the faith in him that he had even lost in himself? They had used his personal name – nobody had called him Khoisan for over a hundred years. Did they seek to show *affection* to him?

*I am a Mantis Warrior. I need no love from you. I seek no mercy.* The thoughts whispered desperately through his mind.

'Nonetheless, Chapter Master,' came another voice, 'your actions speak eloquently and terribly for themselves. In the end, your intentions do not concern us, except in so far as they help us to understand how one such as you might be turned so completely from the light. And you have offered us no help in that regard.'

I seek no mercy.

'Mantis Master,' came yet another voice, the female voice of an inquisitor or Sister Sororitas. 'It is the opinion of this council that the Mantis Warriors are not beyond salvation – that they followed dutifully and loyally the commands of their Master, and that their Master was himself convinced that his commands were in accord with the will of the Emperor. The Chapter shall be excommunicated for one hundred years, during which time we expect that they will demonstrate penitence and loyalty enough to be brought back into the sight of the Emperor. As for your world, Mantis Lord, it will never again give birth to your kind – it is yours no longer. The rights of the Mantis Warriors to that place are forfeit forever; should they survive their penitence, they must begin again elsewhere. They must seek rebirth as well as redemption.'

*It is mine.*

Neotera's gaze did not waver and he said nothing. An image of the great fortress monastery flickered through his mind, engulfed in an inferno of flames as the emerald banners of the Mantis Warriors turned to cinders and blew away in the wind. The loss of his home world tortured his soul, piercing to the very foundation of his almost-forgotten humanity. Yet it was not a terminal end; he could see through the conflagration of horror to the tiniest glimmer of hope that survived the flames. Despite himself, the redemption of his loyal battle-brothers brought him profound relief and happiness. Barely perceptibly, a single tear trickled slowly over the scar on his cheek.

I seek no mercy. For myself, nothing. I seek no mercy. Already this is too much.

*But then there is you, Mantis. Even if you were deluded and confused, like a civilian fool being tempted into Chaos with promises of riches, of power, or of fame, then you are little more than a despicable excuse for an Astartes, with a pathetic will and a clouded mind. Your credulity offends the Emperor. His light is not ambiguous or unclear – it is brilliant, pristine and untarnished by doubts or interpretations. Even if you are not evil by intent, your naïveté provides a space for it to grow. This is worse: you make others do evil unknowingly. Your fallen master's leadership is what dragged your brothers into this war and turned them against themselves. In the end, even the devoted Captain Maetrus mutinied against you.*

*Consider this, Mantis Lord, your judgement tore your entire Chapter from the fold. You mutinied against the Emperor Himself – this is more than mutiny, it is heresy. And then your most celebrated captain mutinied against you. Civil wars within civil wars. How should we interpret these actions? Should we see Maetrus as evidence that there is yet integrity in your Chapter, despite his disappearance? Or should we conclude that credulity is a flaw in the gene-seed of the Mantis Warriors as a whole? Are you genetically untrustworthy, Mantis? Do you have any place in the Imperium of Man? Can the Emperor gaze on you with anything other than pity, derision, or disgust?*

'You will not be executed, Master Neotera.' The voice seemed somehow familiar, but Neotera's mind was reeling with such nausea after the psychic charges that he could not call a name to mind. And now the vocalised words struck horror into his heart. A terrible despair sank upon him, as though a world had fallen onto his shoulders. Were they going to offer him mercy?

'You will be stripped of your armour and imprisoned in the Penitentiacon. There you will live out your life in darkness and isolation. You will have no distractions from your own conscience, and you will find the truth of your treachery or you will die without ever understanding it.'

Neotera's mind staggered. The world fell onto his shoulders and crushed him through the aquila at his feet. His constant and resolute gaze began to swim, before he pulled his will together though sheer self-discipline and screaming anguish. He gritted his teeth against the horror of disbelief: he would not be executed for his deeds, but how could he go on living like this?

*You asked for no mercy. We offer you none.*

# ⚒ ORPHANS OF THE KRAKEN

*Richard Williams*

I am not yet dead.

I am only on the brink. I cannot tell anymore how long I have been here. My first heart begins its beat. I count the minutes until it finishes and begins again. I clutch at the sound as long as I can. It is my only reminder that I am still alive.

It is not fear that holds me from the edge. I see what is ahead and it welcomes me. But I have made an oath. Until I have held to my word, I cannot allow myself to fall.

The tyranid hive ship drifted silently in space. I watched it through my window. It was vast and it was an abomination, ugly beyond description, organic but no creation of any natural god. It was also, as best as we could determine, very, very dead.

My name is Brother Sergeant Tiresias of the Astartes Chapter Scythes of the Emperor, and I came here searching for legends.

I command the 21st Salvation Team, and if that sounds like a grand title then let me correct you now. It is not. There were eight of us at the beginning, myself and seven neophytes. Battle-brothers in training, youths, juveniles, children. I am told that they are our future. I know better; we do not have a future.

By that day I had been in their company, and they in mine, for over two years. Our time together had not been easy, nor without loss. The three empty seats beside me were testimony to that. But the three we had left behind had not disappointed me nearly as greatly as the four who remained. They had slunk to the far end of the assault boat, gathered around one of their number who was making some small adjustment to the squad's heavy bolter. They spoke softly, thinking they would not be heard.

'There... I think it'll work better that way.'

'Are you sure, Brother Narro? It is not Codex.'

'Of course he's sure, Hwygir. Who're you going to trust? Your brother here who's been slicing up these vermin as long as you have, or a book written by some hoary old creaker? These bugs weren't even around back then so the codex is as much use as a–'

'Show some respect, Vitellios,' the fourth of them interrupted. 'The sergeant can hear you.'

'Pasan. I tell you, after all he's put us through, I don't give a scrag if he does.'

It had not always been like this. At the start, in our first few insertions, their voices had been full of hope and they had spoken of what we might find. They had repeated the stories they had heard during their training: rumours of Space Marines wearing the insignia of the Scythes still alive inside the tyranid bio-ships; stories of Navy boarding parties surrounded, nearly destroyed, before being saved by such warriors who then disappeared back into the depths; stories of bio-ships convulsing and crumpling in the midst of battle, though untouched by any external force. Stories. Legends. Myths.

They believed, though. They fantasised that, in every dead bio-ship we sought, whole companies of Astartes waited. That they had not been annihilated in the onslaught of Hive Fleet Kraken at all. That Hive Fleet Kraken, that almighty judgement upon us which had destroyed fleets and consumed worlds, might have simply overlooked them. And so they had survived, forgotten, until these seven brave neophytes arrived to rescue them and become heroes to the Chapter, and become legends themselves.

Myths. Fantasies. Lies. As I already knew and they, once they stepped aboard a bio-ship for the first time, quickly discovered.

'Ten seconds!' the pilot's voice crackled over the intravox. 'Brace! Brace! Brace!'

I braced. Here we went again. Another legend to chase, another myth to find, another lie to unmask. How many more before we finally accept it? How many more until we finally decide to end it all?

My wards advanced cautiously from our insertion point into the ship. They fell into their formation positions with the ease of long experience. The hivers, the up-spire Narro and the trash Vitellios, took turns on point and edge. The trog savage Hwygir carried the heavy bolter on his shoulder further back as snath. Pasan, one of the few of the neophytes to have been born, as I, on noble Sotha, walked in the tang position to allow him to command.

If our auspexes and scanners had not already told us that the hive ship was dead, we would have known the instant we stepped aboard. The corridors were dark; the only light our own torches. As they illuminated our path ahead we could see the skin of the walls sagging limply from its ribs, its surface discoloured and shrivelling. The door-valves gaped open, the muscles that controlled them wasted.

We waded through a putrid sludge. Though it moved like a sewer it was no waste product, it was alive. It was billions of microscopic tyranid organisms, released by the bio-ship at the moment of its death and designed solely to consume the flesh of their dead parent, consume and multiply. More creatures, gigantic to the microbes, tiny to us, floated amongst them, eating their fill, then were speared and devoured by larger cousins who hunted them.

The hive ship was dead, and in death it became filled with new life. Each creature, from the sludge-microbe up, was created to feed and to be fed upon in turn, concentrating the bio-matter of the ship into apex predators that would bound gleefully aboard the next bio-ship they encountered to be re-absorbed and recycled. In this way, the tyranid xenoforms transformed the useless carcass of their parent into another legion of monsters to take to the void. The carcass of their parent, and any other bio-matter foolish enough to have stepped onboard.

'Biters! To the right!' Vitellios called. The lights on the gun barrels swung around in response. I heard the double shot as Vitellios and Pasan fired and then the screech of their target.

'Step back! Step back!' Pasan ordered automatically. 'Narro!'

Scout Narro had his bolter ready and triggered a burst of fire at the creatures. The shells exploded in their midst, bursting their fat little bodies and tossing them to the side.

The shots would alert every active tyranid nearby. Pasan swivelled his shotgun with its torch across the leathery walls of the chamber, searching for more. Vitellios simply blasted every dark corner. There was another screech for his trouble. The Scouts swung their weapons towards the noise, illuminating the target with blazing light.

There was nothing there. The corner was empty. The sludge rippled slightly around the base of the armoured buttress supporting the wall, but that was all.

I waited for Pasan to order Vitellios to investigate. I saw the acolyte's helmet turn to the hiver, his face shining gold from his suit lights. I waited for him to give the order, but he did not. He turned his head back and started to move out of position himself.

'Scout Pasan, hold!' I ordered angrily. 'Scout Vitellios, assess that area.'

Vitellios, expecting the order, stepped forward with a confidence no one in his situation should have. He enjoyed it, though, defying the others' expectations, claiming that places like this reminded him of home.

Though having seen myself the lower hive levels on the planet where he was born, I would not disagree.

Vitellios prodded the floor beneath the sludge to ensure it was solid and then stepped right into the corner. He shone his torch up to where the armoured buttress ended just short of the roof.

'Vitellios!' Narro whispered urgently. 'It's moving!'

Vitellios had an underhiver's instincts. He did not question. He did not waste even a split-second to look at the buttress that had suddenly started shifting towards him; he simply ran.

'Hwygir!' he called as he sprinted clear, kicking up a spray of sludge behind him.

Hwygir pulled the trigger on the big gun. The hellfire shell sped across the chamber and smashed into the buttress even as it launched itself at the Scout fleeing away. The sharp needles within the shell plunged into the creature's body, pumping acid, and it spasmed. It tore itself from the wall, revealing the tendrils and sucker-tubes on its underside and collapsed into the sludge, there to be recycled once more.

What it revealed, what it had slowly been consuming, was even more horrific. Three metres high, even collapsed against the wall, was a tyranid monster the size of a Dreadnought. Its skin was armoured like a carapace, its limbs ended in claws like tusks, its face was all the more dreadful for having been half-eaten away.

'Fire!' Vitellios shouted, and he, Pasan and Narro poured a half dozen rounds into the juddering, foetid corpse.

'It is dead already, neophytes. Do not waste your ammunition.' Shaking my head, I rechecked the auspex for the beacon's signal. 'This way.'

I had begun with seven neophytes under my command. On the hive ship identified as #34732 *Halisa*, we stumbled across a colony of dormant genestealers and Neophyte Metellian was killed. On #10998 *Archelon*, Neophyte Quintos lost an arm and part of his face to a tyranid warrior corpse that had more life in it than he had assumed. It almost bested me before I caught it with my falx and finally put an end to it. On #51191 *Notho*, Neophyte Varos slipped through an orifice in the floor. When we finally located him in the depths of the ship, he had been crushed to death.

We have inserted into over a dozen dead hive ships now. We Salvation Teams have probably stepped aboard more bio-ships than any other human warrior. Perhaps more than any alien as well. When I speak, it is with that experience. For all the vaunted diversity of the tyranid fleet, for all that Imperial adepts struggle to catalogue them into thousands of ship classes; the truth is that once you are in their guts they are all the same: the same walls of flesh, the same valve portals; the same cell-chambers leading to the major arteries leading to the vital organs at the ship's heart.

But for all the now routine horrors I have witnessed within these ships, on occasion they can still surprise me.

'God-Emperor...' Narro whispered as he looked out across the expanse.

The beacon had taken us up, but the tubule we followed did not lead into another cell-chamber, nor even into an artery. Instead it dropped away into a cavity so vast that our torches could not reach the opposite wall. At our feet, the sludge slovenly poured over the ledge in an oozing waterfall into the darkness on the floor. To our left, one side of the cavity was filled with a row of giant ovoids; each one as big as, bigger even, than our mighty Thunderhawks. They glistened with a sickly purple sheen as we shone a light upon them. Several of them were split open. One was cracked. Inside, emerging from it, still clenched tight upon itself in a rigor of death, I saw the creature these birthing sacs contained.

Bio-titans.

Bio-titans. Massive war-engines that, even hunched like spiders, towered over our heaviest tanks on the battlefield. Screaming, hideous, living machines bristling with limbs, each one a weapon, which had carved apart so many Imperial lines of defence.

'There... there's another one,' Pasan said and I shone my torch after his. It wasn't just one. The cavity was filled with these monsters, every one collapsed, knocked aside, dead. Their bloated bodies and scything limbs were barely distinguishable from the flesh of the hive ship beneath them.

It was Narro who finally broke the silence.

'Hierophants,' he concluded as he peered at them. 'Immature, judging from their size.'

'You mean these are runts?' Vitellios exclaimed, his usual cocksure manner jolted from him.

'Oh, indeed,' Narro replied. 'Certain reports from defence troopers quite clearly–'

'Of course they are, Scout Vitellios,' I interrupted. 'Do not underestimate our foe in the future. Acolyte Pasan, the beacon leads us forwards, organise our descent.'

Pasan stepped along the cliff-face, examining the floor far beneath. The other neophytes watched the path or checked their weapons.

'Honoured sergeant... could you... could you look at this?' Pasan asked me quietly.

Throne! Could this boy not even command as simple a task as this by himself?

'What is it, acolyte?' I said, biting down on my irritation as I went over to him.

'The floor...' He lay down flat and angled his torch to the base of the cavity directly beneath us. 'They look... they're biters, aren't they? It's covered with them.'

I looked; he was right. What appeared to be solid ground was indeed the segmented backs of a thousand biters packed together as though they were crammed in a rations can.

'And what will you do about it, acolyte?'

Pasan hesitated. Vitellios did not.

'We should head back, we can find a way around–'

I cut him off. 'An Astartes does not retreat in the face of common insects, neophyte. He finds a way through.'

I turned back to Pasan and watched the youth think. He finally produced an answer and looked at me for approval. His plan was sound, but still I was unimpressed by his need for my validation.

'What are you waiting for, acolyte? That is your plan, issue your orders.'

'Yes, sergeant. Culmonios, load a hellfire shell and deploy here.'

Hwygir nodded with all the eagerness of one who knows his inferiority and only wishes to be accepted. He had been birthed Hwygir, most certainly on some dirt rock floor on Miral. He had chosen the name Culmonios when he became an Astartes, I found it distasteful to address a stunted savage such as he with such a noble appellation. I used it in speech at first, but I could never bring myself to think it. Only Pasan still used it now.

The trog hefted the bulky heavy bolter to the lip of the ledge.

'He'll need bracing,' Vitellios muttered.

'I was just coming to that,' Pasan replied. 'Vitellios, dig in and brace him. Narro too. Have the next shell ready as soon as he fires.'

Finally I saw something of command coming to Pasan. He organised the squad into a firing team slowly and methodically. He even carved into the tubule wall itself to provide a steadier base to shoot directly down at the floor and strapped the heavy weapon to Hwygir tightly to ensure the recoil at such an awkward angle did not tear it from his hand.

'Fire!' Pasan ordered finally. The squad braced and Hwygir pulled the trigger. 'Reload. Adjust aim. Fire. Reload. Adjust aim. Fire. Reload.' Pasan continued, the squad following along. 'Halt!'

He and I looked over the edge. The flesh scouring acid of the hellfire had eaten into the biters and, without a foe close by, they had scattered away from the wall and started to feed instead on the corpses of the bio-titans, leaving a path clear across the cavity. It was as I had expected.

What I had not expected was what had now been revealed, the food on which the biters had been feasting. I looked down, my throat tight in horror, at the field of damaged and pockmarked power armour now on display, black and yellow like my own. The feast had been my brothers.

I had only ever seen such a sight before in my dreams, my nightmares of Sotha's destruction. I was there at the fall, but I did not witness the worst of it. By the time our last lines were being overrun, I was already aboard a Thunderhawk, unconscious, my chest and legs a mess of cuts and bio-plasma burns. A sergeant had pulled me from the barricade as I fell, thrown me upon an exhausted ammo-cart returning for fresh supplies and then stepped back into the battle. None who survived knew my rescuer's name.

I do not know how I made it from the ammo-cart onto one of the escaping Thunderhawks. I do remember how the Thunderhawk spiralled and dropped as it desperately sought to dodge through the rain of landing spores still pouring down, now unopposed, upon my home. I was awake in time to feel the last tug of Sotha's gravity upon me as we left it to be consumed by our foe, and to know that we had failed our holy duty.

We cleared the bio-titan birthing cavity of the biters and lesser xenoforms. It took nearly a full day, with the mysterious beacon still a steady pulse upon our auspex, but it had to be done. This place was no longer a simple obstacle to be surmounted in our larger search; it was sacred ground. We called back to the boat and ordered our retainer workers despatched to join us. When they arrived they added their firepower to our own in the final clearance of the cavity. My wards stayed on watch while our retainers began their work to recover our fallen brothers. We counted, as best we could, the armour of thirty-seven battle-brothers. Over a third of a company had died in this place, battling the fledgling bio-titans as they burst from their sacs. What a fight it must have been.

The armour bore the markings of the Fifth Company. They had not been on Sotha when Kraken came. They had fought and died months before. Chapter Master Thorcyra had despatched them to the very edges of the sectors the Scythes protected, responding to reports of rebellion and xenos incursion, while he himself led a force to counter an uprising to the galactic north. He did not know then that those incursions were the mere tip of the emerging Hive Fleet Kraken. We received a few routine reports back from the Fifth, garbled by psychic interference, and then they were swallowed by the shadow in the warp.

By the time another company was free to go after them the truth of the Kraken had emerged, as had the threat it posed to Sotha itself. A general recall was ordered, every battle-brother was called back in defence of our home. And so the Fifth became just another mystery, a hundred warriors amongst the millions who had already died at the talons of the Kraken and the billions more who were to follow.

'So it's true,' Senior Retainer Gricole said as he approached me in the birthing cavity. 'Another mystery solved.'

'Get your men working with all speed, Gricole. Secure the area so I can lead my wards on. We are here for the living more than the dead.'

Gricole ordered his men to their tasks, as I did my wards. But then he returned to my side and regarded me sceptically.

'You have something you wish to say?' I asked.

A Chapter retainer, a servant, would never consider questioning a full battle-brother. But not Gricole. I had found him on Graia, a hydropon-sprayer turned militia captain in the face of the hive fleet. His woman was long dead, spared the sight of the tyranid assault, his children died fighting under his command. He had seen the worst that the galaxy held; he was not going to be intimidated by me. He spoke his mind when it pleased him. I respected him for that.

'You can't think there's any chance they're still kicking,' Gricole said in his broad Graian accent. 'That they've been living, battling, inside one of these monsters all this time?'

I looked down at him. 'You are human, Gricole. I know it is hard for you to understand. The human soldier needs regular supply: food, ammunition, shelter, sleep, even fresh orders from those of a higher rank to reassure him that he has not been forgotten. Without any one of those the human soldier cannot function. He weakens and breaks. We are Astartes; we are not the same as you. We can eat what you cannot, sleep yet still be on our guard, and to give an Astartes a mission is to give him a purpose which he will seek to fulfil until ordered to stop or until the Emperor claims him.'

Gricole listened to me closely, nodding in thought, then he spoke again. 'So d'ya think there is a chance?' he repeated.

Gricole was being wilful. 'Consider for whom we are searching here.' I assented. 'This is the Fifth Company: Captain Theodosios, Commander Cassios, Lieutenant Enero, Ancient Valtioch. If anyone could survive it would be warriors such as these.'

'I understand.' Gricole nodded. 'And so... do you think there is a chance?' he asked a third time. He smiled, bearing his stained brown teeth. Such stubborn impertinence, if it had been from a neophyte I would not have stood it for a moment, but unlike them Gricole had earned such familiarity with blood.

'The truth then?' I drew breath and looked away. 'Of course not. Death is all we will find in this ship. It is all we will ever find on these missions. You have seen the same as I. Even dead, these ships consume all within them. How can there be survivors? Master Thracian's Salvation Teams are a fool's errand.'

I had let my bitterness against the new Chapter Master show again. It did not matter in front of Gricole, however; I trusted his discretion.

'He told me he called us Salvation Teams for we will be the salvation of the Chapter,' I continued, still angry at the far distant commander. 'Do you know what the brothers of the Battle Company call us?'

Gricole shook his head gently.

'Salvage squads,' I said.

'Hmph,' he muttered. 'Catchy.'

Salvage squads. It was meant as an insult, but I found the name more fitting with each new insertion. Despite our efforts, we had found none of our missing. None living, at least. What we did find was salvage. The tyranid xeno-species can plunder every last atom of use, but their booty of choice is biological material. Our flesh. This they choose over any other.

The fruit of our own labours then were those items a hive ship, especially if crippled by an assault party's attack, might overlook. Weapons, armour; our tools of destruction. It did not come only from fellow Scythes; the Astartes equipment we found came in an array of colours: yellow and red, blue, silver, black and green. Irrespective of whether those Chapters might consider it sacrilegious, we took it. Our orders were precise: salvage it all.

Gricole's men worked quickly and with determination. Like Gricole himself, they were born on worlds that had fallen to Kraken: Miral, Graia, and others, worlds that we had tried to defend in our long retreat from Sotha. The Chapter's original retainers all died defending Sotha; no matter how young, how old, how injured or frail, they had picked up a weapon and given their lives to buy a few more seconds for their masters, for we Astartes, to escape.

We did escape, but at that time our flight appeared only to delay our destruction. The survivors of Sotha stumbled back to the Miral system, there to report the loss of our home to our returning Chapter Master. Thorcyra was stunned, near-shattered by the news. Some advised further retreat against such overwhelming odds, but he rejected the notion and led us all in oaths of defiance. The Kraken was approaching and we would stand and die in the jungles of Miral.

The Kraken came, and we made our stand on the rocky crags of a place named the Giant's Coffin. We fought hard, and we died once again. I do not know if Thorcyra believed some miracle would save us, that perhaps his faith alone might bring the blessing of the Emperor upon us and grant us some astounding victory. It was not to be. Thorcyra fell, torn apart by his foes, and Captain Thracian ordered the retreat. And, once more, I survived.

If you think I was grateful for my life, you would be mistaken. To leave behind so many brothers once was a tragedy that cut deep into my soul. To have to do so again was more than any man could endure. My body survived Miral, but my spirit did not. As I watched Captain Thracian swear the oaths of a Chapter Master on the bridge of the *Heart of Cronus*, I was certain that my next battle would be my last.

But after Miral, I am ashamed to say, we grew more cautious. Thracian did not believe any other world worth the extinction of our Chapter, short of Holy Terra itself. We were told no longer to contemplate the possibility of victory, only of what damage we could cause before we would retreat again. Thracian planned our withdrawals to the last detail and demanded their precise execution. Brothers died, but none without reason. But I felt the dishonour burn inside me each time the order was given to abandon another world to the Kraken, to retreat while others fought on. I obeyed, but I rejected Thracian's orders to leave all other defenders to their fate and I brought back with me those I could who had proven themselves worth saving. I was not alone in such actions and those brothers and I shamed Thracian into allowing such noble men as Gricole to remain with us.

The signal from the beacon led us deeper into the ship. We located one of the major arterial tubes, but we found it packed with biters. They were not feeding, rather they had fed themselves to bursting and were dragging their distended bodies along the ground, all heading into the ship. A few hellfire shells here would not have made a dent in their number, and so reluctantly I ordered the Scouts to find another route. The hard muscle wall of the artery cut across all the chambers on our level, barring any further progress, until Pasan noticed the sludge draining in a corner. There was a valve in the floor, kept from closing by the thick sludge's flow. It was too small for us, but we wedged it open wider. I should have sent one of the Scouts first, but I did not wish to be trapped above a panicking neophyte who had lost his nerve. I stowed my pistol, drew my falx, and plunged headfirst straight down into the tight shaft.

At once, I felt that the sludge might suffocate me as I forced myself down. I had only my helmet light to shine ahead of me, but there was nothing to see except the sludge seeping ahead. I moved slowly, leading with my falx and levering the shaft open, then deliberately pressing the wall back and widening the area as I went. My only comfort was the thought that any tyranid xenoform who might have lurked in such a place would have been dissolved by the sludge long before.

The line about my waist pulled tight and then went slack as my wards climbed down after me.

World after world fell to the Kraken, but under Thracian we small remnant of the once proud, once brave, once honourable Scythes of the Emperor survived. But then, against such odds, I told myself still that it was solely a matter of time. The absolution of a violent death would still be mine. Then came Ichar IV.

The tendrils of the Kraken had concentrated against that world and there, ranged against them, amidst a great gathering of Imperial forces stood the Ultramarines. Together, they smashed the body of the Kraken. The planet was nearly destroyed, its defenders were decimated, but the tyranids were scattered.

It was the victory for which we Scythes had prayed so fervently, the victory that Thracian had told us we could no longer achieve.

And we were not there.

Word of the victory at Ichar IV filtered through to the latest planet on which we had taken refuge. Bosphor, I think its name was. Still, even then we did not know the extent to which the Kraken had been cast back. We continued to prepare the planet's defences, trained their wide-eyed troops in the combat doctrines we had learned at bitter cost. We waited for the Kraken to come and turn the skies red with their spores. But the bio-ships never came.

It was only then that I realised that I had survived. That I would survive, not just a few more days, a few more weeks, until the next battle, but decades more. It was only then that we counted the cost and the truth of our plight struck home. Of all my battle-brothers, only one in ten survived. One in ten.

Our officers, who had stood and fought even as they ordered others to retreat, were wiped out nearly to a man. Our vehicles, our machines of war, had been abandoned; our own blessed ancestors in their Dreadnought tombs had been torn to pieces by the Kraken's claws. Their voices and memories, our connection to our legacy and that of the Chapter before us, were lost to us forever.

Thracian told us that it was not the end. That the dead would be honoured, but that their ranks would be filled, that we would rise once more and be as we once were.

I knew, even as I stood listening to his words, how wrong he was. More youths might be recruited, more Astartes might wear the colours, more mouths might shout our battle cries and recite our oaths. But it would not be us. Everything that had made us a Chapter of Space Marines, everything beyond the ceramite of our armour, the metal of our weapons, the cloth of our banners, was gone.

The termagants scuttled across the slope. The tendrils that covered the area, the curved floor, the walls, even hanging from the roof, would normally have reached out at any movement and grasped at it, but instead they lay flaccid. One of the termagants paused and lowered its head, sniffing; it turned quickly to the rest of its brood and they changed direction. They moved with purpose, they sensed an intruder. They saw a light ahead of them and closed in around it. The leader reached down with one of its mid-claws to pick up the torch, while the others sniffed closer, discerning that the scent-trails had divided. It was then that the trap was sprung.

The half-dozen tendrils closest to the torch suddenly burst as the frag grenades tied to them detonated. The termagants howled as the shrapnel tore into their bodies. Narro, Pasan and Vitellios rose up from their hiding places on to one knee and targeted those few creatures still standing. When the last of them fell, hissing and jerking, I ordered ceasefire and had the Scouts cover me as I approached the carnage. The termagants appeared dead: their weapon-symbiotes hung limply from their claws, limbs were severed and all were covered in their own tainted ichor. I took no chances and raised my falx and cut the head off each one. It was little victory. I felt no more revenged for having done so. I never did. Soon the biters would move in and begin to eat, and through them the dead flesh of these 'gaunts would be reformed into the next generation.

'These freaks wouldn't last a minute in the underhive,' Vitellios said as he lit his helmet light and swaggered over to admire his handiwork. 'Even a yowler would scope a dome before picking up a piece of trash. These 'gaunts are not too smart.'

I looked down at the torch. In the midst of the violence it was still shining. I picked it up and switched it off.

'Extinguish your helm-light, neophyte,' I ordered. 'Pasan, form a watch. Don't assume that these were alone. Narro, come here.'

The Scouts followed my orders instantly, even Vitellios. He was an arrogant upstart, but not when his own neck was on the line. He had been picked out from amongst the scum pressed into service as militia in the defence of the hive-world Radnar. Barely into his teens, he was already the leader of several gangs of juves who had run rampage through a few underhive sectors. The Scythe Apothecaries had removed his gang markings, tattoos and the kill-tags of the dozen men he claimed to have bested, but they could not extract the smug superiority he carried with him. His training record identified him as a natural leader. I disagreed. To lead, one must first learn how to follow, a task he continually failed. He may have been born to lead a gang of hive-trash, but never command Astartes.

'What do you think, Narro?' I asked, indicating the tyranid bodies. Unlike Pasan, Scout Narro always grasped instantly whatever task I had for him. He had been recruited from Radnar as well and he, at least, had come from one of the noble families. He had already been marked for additional training that would lead him to become a Techmarine when he became a full battle-brother. He picked up one of the severed heads and peered fascinated at its sharp and vicious features.

"Gaunt genus, obviously. Termagant species.'

'Correct,' I replied. 'Go on.'

'Strange, though, to see them here...'

'Within a hive ship? Yes, truly bizarre, neophyte,' I directed him back. 'Are they fresh? Have they just been birthed?'

We had learned the hard way that newborn xenoforms were one of the danger signs. Even within a dead ship, certain vestigial reflexes might induce fresh tyranid fiends from their sacs if an interloper triggered them. Yet another defence against grave robbers such as us. If these termagants were freshly hatched then more of them might descend upon us at any moment.

'It is...' Narro murmured. 'It is not easy to say conclusively.'

'Then give me your best guess,' I replied curtly. 'Show me that Forge Master Sebastion's efforts with you were not wasted.'

Narro put the head down and ran a gloved hand down the flank of the slug-body, examining the texture of the flesh. I grimaced in disgust at such contact.

'No. They are not,' he said finally, and I let a fraction of the breath I had held escape. 'You see this scarring, and the skin, and this one here has lost part of its...' he began to explain.

'Thank you, neophyte,' I dismissed him before he could digress.

'But what Sebastion said was...' he began with fervour, then faltered when he saw my expression. But then I relented and nodded for him to continue.

'Master Sebastion, in his teachings, speaks of how in the assault upon Sotha and Miral and the rest, the ships of the Kraken released millions of such creatures and expended them as... as a company of Marines would the shells of their boltguns. Yet we Salvation Teams have rarely encountered them. He believed that, because they must be so simple to produce and had so little purpose once their ship was dead, that they were the first to be reabsorbed...'

Beneath my gaze, his voice trailed away.

'Thank you, neophyte,' I told him clearly. 'That is all.'

I looked towards our path ahead. If the auspex could be trusted then the beacon was close. Once it was recovered I could quit this insertion and leave the ship to rot. I did not want to delay any further, but then, out of the corner of my eye, I saw Narro reach down and grasp something. He had picked up the 'gaunt head again and was about to stow it in his pack.

'Drop it,' I told him.

He fumbled to explain: 'But if it is rare I only thought it might provide insight, if I could study–'

'Drop it, neophyte,' I ordered again. It had been Narro's affinity with the holy ways of the machine that had first brought him to Sebastion's attention, but his curiosity had bled from the proper realm of the Imperial enginseer into the living xenotech of the tyranid. I had overheard him speak to his brothers of his fanciful ideas of where such study could lead; to a weapon, some ultimate means to destroy the Kraken and its ilk and drive them back into the void. He did not understand the danger. The young never did.

'And consider in future to what infection or taint such trophies may expose you and your brothers. Save your thoughts of study until you are assigned to Mars. Until then, do not forget that you are here to fight.'

Shamed, Narro released it and the snarling, glassy-eyed trophy rolled a metre down the slope until it was lost in a knot of tendrils.

'There is an explanation for why these 'gaunts may have survived,' he said.

'And that is?'
'This ship... It is not dead.'

It was a ridiculous idea, but even so I felt the briefest chill at the thought. Every scan we had done of the hive ship before insertion told us that it was exactly as it appeared to be: a lifeless husk. But what if...? Could it still...?

No, I told myself as we continued on. I was no whelp neophyte. I would not fall prey to such paranoia. Every instinct I had, instincts honed from two long years of such expeditions, told me that this ship was dead. If it had been alive, we would never have made it this far. We would have been surrounded and destroyed within the first hundred steps. We certainly would not have been able to ambush those 'gaunts; some creature, some tiny insect would have been watching us and through it, the ship would have seen through our design.

We went deeper, the atmosphere thickening as we went. We climbed ridges of flesh and traversed the crevices between, squeezed our way through tiny capillaries and valves, and down passages ribbed with chitinous plates or covered with polyps crusted with mucus. We passed over caverns crammed with bulbs on stalks so that they resembled fields of flowers, and under roofs criss-crossed with lattices of tiny threads like spiders' webs. And everywhere we saw the same decay, the slow deconstruction of this grotesque, complex organism back into raw bio-matter by the biters and the smaller creatures they fed upon.

'There it is!' the cry finally went up. Vitellios shone his torch into a wall-cavity and there it was indeed, driven into the flesh-wall like a service stud. A piece of human technology, bound in brass and steel, as alien in this place as any tyranid xenoform would be aboard a human craft.

Excited, my wards crowded in to see. I batted them back, telling them to set watch. I did not wish to be taken unawares now of all times. Narro scraped away the translucent skin that had grown over the metal. I saw him instinctively reach to deactivate the signal and I grabbed his hand away. He looked at me askance and I slowly shook my head. He nodded in understanding and levered open the beacon's cover, exposing its innards. He groaned in dismay.

'What is it?' Pasan backed towards us, shotgun up, and glanced at the beacon.

'The data-slate,' Narro explained. 'Acid. It's been burned through.'

There was something more though. I looked closer. There were markings on the interior of the casing, distorted by the acid-damage, but still recognisable. They had been scratched by human hand and not tyranid claw.

'But it doesn't make sense...' Narro thought out loud.

'What doesn't make sense?' Pasan replied, the concern clear in his voice.

VIDE SUB, it read. Vide Sub. It was not code. It was High Gothic. An order. A command.

'Why would they destroy the message and leave the beacon transmitting?'

Look down.

The floor burst into a mass of scythes and talons as the monster exploded from its hiding place. The force of its eruption launched me into the air and threw me to the side. I smashed headfirst into a flesh-wall and slumped down to my knees.

'God-Emperor! Get back!' I heard someone cry as I slipped to the ground.

I forced myself onto my back. The gun-torches danced across the chamber as the Scouts moved. Pasan's was stationary, skewed at an angle, far to the other side. Vitellios's jumped as he sprinted away. One still remained in the centre; Hwygir was turning, bringing his heavy weapon to bear. His light caught the monster for an instant; it reared, jaws and mandibles gaping wide, as it swept two scything claws above its head to cut down the diminutive figure standing in its way. The Scout pulled the trigger and the monster's black eyes sparked orange with the ignition of the shells.

The first bolt clipped the bone of the claw even as it cut down towards him and ricocheted away. The second passed straight through the fleshy arm before detonating on the other side. But the third struck hard between two ribs of its exoskeleton. The explosion jolted the monster from its attack even as its blowback blinded Hwygir for a critical moment. The injured claw retracted early, the other was forced off its line and carved a bloody streak down the side of the Scout's leg instead of chopping his head in two.

Both Hwygir and the monster stumbled back for a moment. The savage dropped the sights of the heavy bolter, trying to blink his eyes clear, and his torch swivelled away from the monster just as it sprang and flipped over, digging back underground. Its thick snake-tail shot from the darkness, puncturing the casing of the heavy weapon on Hwygir's shoulder with such force as to knock it into the side of his head and leave him stunned.

'Burrower! Get clear!' It was Vitellios, shouting from cover.

Vitellios on one side and Pasan on the other desperately flashed their torches in every direction, hoping to catch a glimpse of the creature before it struck again.

'There!' Vitellios shouted.

'There!' Pasan cried.

They were facing in different directions. Vitellios had already fired; the hollow bark of a shotgun blast hitting nothing but the empty air echoed back to us. I pulled the torch from my pistol and twisted it in my hand. It blossomed with light in every direction.

'Quiet, you fools!' I hissed at them, drawing my falx as well. 'It's a ravener. It goes after the vibrations!'

They both stopped talking at that. I looked about the cavern in the dim, grey light. There was nothing on the surface to suggest any movement beneath. Hwygir was moving slightly beside the hole from which the ravener had burst. I saw Narro as well; he was lying beneath the beacon, smashed between it and the ravener's first attack. Hwygir saw him too and started slowly to crawl over to him, leaving the heavy bolter where it had fallen.

'No, you...' I cursed, but the trog did not hear me. Pasan did though. He suddenly stepped forwards, then picked up his feet and started to run. Great, booming, heavy steps. Not towards the heavy weapon, but away from it. I sensed, rather than saw, the ravener below us twist within the ship's flesh to go after him.

'Pasan! I order you–' I called after him, but I knew he was not going to stop.

I jerked my head around to Vitellios. 'Get the bolter. I'll get him.' I snapped, and powered after the running Scout.

Pasan knew both I and the ravener were after him now and quickened his pace over the leathery surface. In a shower of flesh and fluid, the ravener burst not from the floor, but from the wall. Pasan leapt and rolled, but the tyranid beast caught his leg in one of its grasping hands, flicked him around and hammered him against a chitinous strut. The shotgun flew from Pasan's hands as his body went limp, and it drew a claw back to slice him in two.

I bellowed at the beast as I ran and fired my pistol as fast as it allowed. My snap-shots blew the flesh from the walls and the beast indiscriminately and it twisted in pain. It coiled, ready to burrow again, and I dropped my pistol and raised my falx with both hands. The ravener leapt. I swung. The falx's tip pierced its carapace and hooked inside. I was yanked off my feet as the ravener dug down at an extraordinary rate. It dragged me on and I braced as I sped towards the hole it had created. My body hit the ground splayed across the hole and went no further. The ravener threatened to pull my weapon from my hands, but my grip was like steel. It thrashed beneath me, churning up the ship-flesh around it. Its tail, still in the air, whipped back and forth, battering at my side. I held on. It strained even harder against the hook of the falx and I felt it begin to tear itself clear. The next time the tail struck, I seized it with one arm, then released the falx and grasped it with my other.

'Vitellios!' I called. He was already running towards me, the heavy bolter cradled in his arms.

Beneath me, the ravener spiralled in my grip to try and escape; its scythes lashed up and punctured my armour, but I was too close for it to cut deep. Vitellios, only a few steps away, brought the bolter up, ready to fire. With a heave, I wrenched it out of the ground to give Vitellios a clear shot and, as I did so, it coiled into the air. Part of its thorax came free and I saw it grow an ugly pyramid-like cyst. It was a weapon, and it was pointed straight at me.

Vitellios and the ravener fired at exactly the same instant. The hive-trash pumped the beast full of bolt-shells that burrowed down along the length of its body and exploded. The bio-weapon shot a burst of slugs into me that burrowed up into my body and did nothing more.

I collapsed over the tyranid's remains. I did not know then what had hit me, only that my armour had been pierced. There was pain, but it was not incapacitating. I had seen brothers hit by tyranid weapons go mad or be burnt from the inside out, but as my hearts beat all the harder to race my blood around my veins I felt neither come upon me.

'How do, sergeant? You okay?' Vitellios had fallen to his knees beside me, his tone even more self-satisfied in victory. 'Caught ourselves a big one today.'

'Coward,' I replied coldly.

'What?' He looked shocked. 'Coward? I just saved your–'

'After you ran. After you fled.'

'I... That wasn't...' He was incensed. Almost ready to reload that bolter and use it on me. I did not care. 'That was doctrine! You're ambushed, you break free! Then you look to strike back!'

'Leaving your brothers to fend for themselves? Do not use doctrine to try to excuse that.'

Pasan had come round and was struggling upright. I heaved myself to my feet; my blessed body was raging, fighting to repair the damage done to it, but I would not show these neophytes even a hint of my weakness.

'You're pathetic. Both of you,' I told them. 'Pasan, get yourself up. Vitellios, go back. Check on the others.'

Vitellios stomped away and called after his brothers.

'Narro! Hwygir! If you're dead, raise your hands...' After a moment's pause, he turned back to me: 'They're good.'

Then he made a gesture in my direction that I am certain would have meant something to me had I been born amongst hive-trash like him, and continued away. Pasan was on his feet now, his helmet facing shattered, his face cut, bruised and crumpled.

'Honoured sergeant–' he began.

'Later,' I said. 'You will explain your actions later. Let us just get ourselves off this piece of thrice-damned filth.'

We hobbled back to where Narro and Hwygir had fallen. In spite of Vitellios's ignoble sense of humour, both still lived. I caught sight of the beacon again and the order scrawled there: VIDESUB. Look down. Another joke.

But it wasn't. For Vitellios spoke up again, and this time his voice was neither smug nor bitter. It was in awe.

'Sergeant Tiresias.' He shone his torch down into the hole below the beacon where the ravener had hibernated. In the violence of its awakening, however, it had scratched open a cavity even further beneath. Down there, glinting back in the light, shone the shoulder armour of a Space Marine. And upon that armour was inscribed the legend:

## CASSIOS

The Space Marine's vital signs barely registered on our auspex. His metabolism was as slow as a glacier. He might easily have been mistaken for dead, but we knew better. Even in suspended animation, he was an impressive figure. His chest was the size of a barrel, his armour was crafted and worked with a pattern of lamellar, festooned with images of victories and great feats through the owner's life. The neophytes stood, slack-jawed, gaping at him. For once, I shared their sense of wonder.

We dug him from his cradle and commenced the ritual to rouse him there. It was not worthy of a survivor, a hero such as he, to be borne back to his home as though he were an infant. I would not have the retainers see him in such a state. I would give him the chance to stand alone, if he willed it, and return as a hero should.

We waited on guard, expectant, for an hour or more. Tending our own wounds, but staying silent aside from checking the auspex readings. Then, finally, his chest heaved. His eyes opened.

Commander Cassios stepped from the darkness of the tunnel and into the beams of the powerful floodlights set up by the retainer crews working within the cavern of the bio-titans.

Gricole saw him at once and called his workers to order. They stood, hushed, as Commander Cassios walked amongst them. He, in turn, acknowledged them, and appeared about to speak, and then he saw what their work was. He dropped to his knees, resting his hands upon the armour of his men. His head was bowed, he was praying. Gricole ordered his men away and I did the same with my wards. A warrior such as Cassios deserved to be allowed to keep such a moment private.

After they had cleared away from the cavity, he stood and moved through the rest of the armour and possessions that Gricole's men had been carefully storing.

'Valens. Nikos. Leo. Abas. Tiberios. Messinus. Herakleios.' Names; he could name each one just from what little remained.

'Theodosios. He was my captain.' I realised that Cassios was addressing me. 'It was so hard for him to ask me to lead the diversionary attack. I volunteered. I insisted! I knew that our company only stood a chance of escape if he was leading the way…' his voice trailed off.

I brought Cassios out with me and took him back to the boat. Only Gricole was waiting for us there. He looked at me, concerned. He tried to see to my wounds, but I waved him away. My Astartes physiology had started healing me from the moment I was wounded; whatever poison the ravener had pumped into me, my body would defeat that just as I had overcome the beast. In any case, I had a more pressing task to address, though it was one I would have given my life not to have to fulfil.

The 5th Company had fought and died against the Kraken before the rest of us had even known it had emerged from the void. Cassios had been here ever since. He believed he had lost his men. He did not know he had lost so much more.

The days and weeks after Ichar IV were ones of celebration for the militia defenders of Bosphor, who had never fought the Kraken and now never would. My brother Astartes and I were in no mood to join them and we retreated to our ships.

Some of us immersed ourselves in prayer, others in rage. A few, gripped by madness at what they had seen and what they had lost, rampaged around the ship until they were forcibly restrained. There were accidents. At least, we called them accidents. We Astartes have no word for the act where a brother chooses to end his service in such a manner. It is not spoken of, but his gene-seed is sequestered, marked as potentially deviant, as though it was a disease of the body and not of the soul.

I thought I had seen every reaction there was to the tragedy of our Chapter. I was wrong. When I told Cassios of the battles, of the losses, of what we had been reduced to, he showed me something different. He showed me the response of a hero.

Cassios had had his eyes closed, standing perfectly still, for nearly a minute. Then his face screwed up in rage, but he did not shout, he breathed. He took great heaving breaths as though he could blow the emotion out from his body and into the air. Then his eyes opened.

'And what is being done?' he asked.

'About what?'

'What is being done to revenge ourselves against this abomination? What is being done to strike back? What is being done to rid our space of this bastard xenos curse for good?'

I placed my hand upon his shoulder.

'As soon as we return to the *Heart of Cronus* they will tell you all. We will leave at once. Your brothers will be most eager to see you again.'

I smiled at him, but he did not return it.

'We cannot leave before we are finished here.'

'Before we are finished?' I asked. 'You are here with us. What more is there?'

Cassios tilted his head a fraction, indicating out the window. 'This ship, nearly half my company, it killed them, feasted on them.'

'And it is dead now,' I reassured him.

'We did not kill it.'

'No, but perhaps our brother-Chapters did on Ichar IV or perhaps it was the servants of the Navy. I understand you want satisfaction, commander. Believe me, I want that for every brother we lost. But our service is done. You cannot kill it again.'

'You misunderstand me, brother-sergeant. It was never killed. The ship still lives.'

Thracian disappeared from our midst then; for several days we were told he had secluded himself to meditate upon the Emperor's will for our Chapter, but then we discovered he had left us entirely on some secret task. He had told us before that we would take the time to rebuild, restore ourselves, and there were many who disagreed with that intention.

I do not expect you to understand. We are Astartes. We are not like you. We do not wake in the morning and muse upon what our purpose may be that day. We know. From the day we are chosen to the day that we die we know what our purpose is. We fight in the name of the Emperor. If we are ordered, then we go. If we are struck, we strike back. If we fall, then we do so knowing that others will take our place. We do not pause, we do not hold back, we do not relent.

We fight. That is our service to the Emperor. That is what we are. If we do not fight, then we do not serve Him. If we do not serve Him, we are lost. One might as soon as tell a mechanicus not to build, a missionary not to preach, a telepath not to think, a ship not to sail. How can they? What use are they without it? And yet that was what Thracian was asking us to do because if we were to suffer the casualties of even the most minor of campaigns, it would be enough to finish us for good. If we wanted to survive, we could not lose anymore. We could not lose anymore, so we could no longer fight. And for how long?

Our armoury, our training grounds, a whole world of our recruits that had been lost with Sotha, perhaps those could be restored. But what of the gene-seed? Both in our living brothers and in our stores lost with Sotha, both now devoured by the Kraken. Without gene-seed there could be no more Astartes, and gene-seed can only be grown within an Astartes, from the progenoid glands implanted in us as youths. There were barely more than a hundred of us left. Most had already had their glands taken when they had matured, to be kept safe in the gene-banks of Sotha. Those few of us in whom they had still not matured... how many new generations would it take to recover our numbers? How many years would the Chapter be leashed, unable to put more than a bare company into the field? Fifty? A hundred? Could we ever recover or would we just fade into ghosts of what we had been? A cautionary tale: the Chapter that feared its own end so greatly they placed themselves above their oaths, their service to Him.

No, better to end it all with a final crusade. That is what my commander, Brother-Sergeant Angeloi, said to me, and I agreed as many others did in the corridors of the *Heart of Cronus*. When Thracian returned to us we would tell him what his men had decided and we would require his acceptance. This was not for glory, this was for our souls. We had been great once, let our story end well in a great crusade that would end only when the last of us fell. Other Chapters would then stand forward to take up our duty and our spirits would join His light as His proud warriors and our names would be spoken with glory as long as mankind endured.

'Trust me, commander–' I raised my voice higher, trying to make him see sense.

'You may trust me, sergeant. I have been aboard that monster for nearly three years. Do not doubt what I say.'

'The auspex–'

'The auspex is wrong. Our technology, blessed be His works, has been wrong as often as it has been right. We are not some dependent xenos like the tau, we rely on human flesh and blood, and there is a spark of life there, I know it.'

'Even so,' I declared, 'it does not matter.'

Cassios blinked. That had surprised him.

'It does not matter?' Cassios raised his eyebrow. 'Explain yourself, sergeant.'

'So it lives, despite the auspex, despite what we saw aboard, the ship lives. It does not matter. We will still leave. We will send a despatch to the battlefleet, they will send a warship and destroy it for good.'

'You said yourself, sergeant, the battlefleet is fully engaged with the hive fleets splintered from Ichar IV. There will be no warship, and this abomination will heal and be the death of further worlds. It is not befitting an Astartes to pass his duty on to lesser men.'

'Then we will return with all our brothers. With *our* warships. We shall destroy this beast ourselves.'

'We are here now. We shall finish it now. Make your preparations for reinsertion. That is my last word on the matter.'

'But it is not mine…' I told him.

'Are you challenging my authority, sergeant?'

'No,' I replied calmly. 'You are challenging mine, commander. This team is mine. This mission is mine. And you… are not permitted to command.'

'What?'

'You have been aboard that ship three years, brother,' I spoke softly. 'Surrounded by the xenos, one of them just centimetres from you. We do not know what has happened to you. *You* do not even know. Doctrine is clear. Until you return with us, until you are examined by the Apothecary and purified, you have no authority to hold.'

To that, Cassios had no answer.

* * *

I left Cassios to himself and started walking back along the narrow corridors of the assault boat. I headed for the Apothecarion. I was sick. I
did not know if it was the other injuries or the infection of the ship, but
whatever war was being waged inside me against the ravener's venom,
I was losing. My guts burned, my head felt as though it was floating
above my body. I stumbled on a step and, at that noise, the neophytes
appeared from the next cabin. Concerned, they rushed to my side, but I
waved them away. No weakness. No weakness in front of them.

'Get away... get away...' I tried to push them off, and stagger on. I saw
them back away as my vision dimmed. I did not feel the deck hit me.

Even in my poison-fever, I could not escape my wards. They plagued
my mind as the toxin did my body. In my dreams I saw them clearly. I
saw how each would add to the slow disintegration of my Chapter; to
its reduction to a shadow of its former self. Hwygir was unable to step
beyond the feral thinking of the savage world on which he had been
born. Was that the purpose for which the Astartes were created? To be
unthinking barbarians? No.

Narro was the reverse, his mind too open. His young fascination
with the xenos was a danger he did not comprehend. He thought to
save humanity by studying the technology of its enemies, using such
xenotech against them, integrating it within our own forces, within
ourselves. His path would lead us to create our own monsters, corrupt
our blessed forms and thereby our spirits. We Astartes may have bodies
enhanced to be greater than any normal human, but our souls remain
those of men. The only knowledge an Astartes needs of a xenos is how
it may be destroyed. Anything more is heresy.

Vitellios, I could see however, was destined for a different kind of heresy. Years of training, hypno-conditioning in the ways of the Chapter,
and still he clung to his old identity. His arrogant presumption of self-
importance. That he might be right and the Chapter might be wrong.
Our history lists those Astartes who doubted the Emperor, and each of
their names is blackened: Huron, Malai, Horus, and the rest.

Pasan, though, was my greatest disappointment. Every advantage that
could be offered, a destiny nigh pre-ordained, and this lacklustre boy
was the result. Insipid, full of self-doubt, unable to grasp the mantle of
leadership even when presented to him. If half-men like him were to
be the future of the Scythes then, Emperor help me, I would rather the
Chapter had stood and died at Sotha.

'Gricole,' I croaked when next I awoke. 'How am I?'

Gricole raised the dim light a fraction and bent to study the readings
from the medicae tablet.

'Your temperature is down. Your hearts are beating slower. And your
urine... is no longer purple. I would guess you are through the worst.'

I coughed. It cleared my throat. 'Good,' I said, my voice stronger. 'Too much time has been wasted already.'

I levered myself up and off the tablet. I felt a touch of weakness in my legs.

'The time has not been completely wasted,' Gricole began. 'We have been making some progress–'

'We have set out for home?' They should have waited until I was conscious again, but in this instance I would forgive them. 'How far have we gone?'

I looked into Gricole's stout, troubled face. I pushed past him, out of the Apothecarion, and to a porthole. The hive ship filled my view.

I turned back to my retainer, my thoughts gripped with suspicion. 'They have not gone onto the ship without me?' I strode across the room, my weakness vanishing before my anger. 'I expressly forbade it!'

I stalked out into the antechamber. My four wards were there. Startled, they stumbled to attention.

'Who was it?' I demanded. 'One of you? All of you? Who here did not understand my orders?'

I looked pointedly at Vitellios, but he stared straight ahead, not moving a muscle.

'You will find your tongues or I will find them for you,' I said sternly.

'Honoured sergeant.' It was Pasan. 'Your orders were understood and followed. We have not left this craft.'

His words were bold, but the slightest quiver in his voice betrayed his nervousness. I stepped close to him and studied him carefully.

'Then explain to me, Neophyte Pasan, what is this progress that you have made?'

I saw his eyes flick for an instant behind me, to Gricole, and then away. He blinked with a moment's indecision.

'We found a–' Narro started.

'Quiet,' I overruled. 'Neophyte Pasan can speak for himself.'

'We have… we have been mapping the surface,' he spoke, gaining confidence with each word. 'We found an aperture that we believe will lead us straight to our target.'

'Is this impertinence, Pasan? We recovered the beacon. What target is this?'

'My men,' Cassios said from the entrance hatch. He stepped into the antechamber. 'My apologies, brother-sergeant, we could not make you aware during your indisposition. These Scouts were fulfilling my instructions.'

'It is a second beacon, honoured sergeant.'

I looked from Cassios to Pasan. 'Another beacon? Our auspex read only the one.'

Vitellios chipped in. 'It signalled only once, at the exact time we discovered the commander's beacon.'

'It makes sense, sergeant,' now Narro spoke again. 'If some of the xenoforms can detect the beacon's signal you would not wish to lead them to all your hiding places. You would wait until a rescue party might be close, close enough to reach a primary beacon. Then once we accessed that, it must have sent a signal to all the secondary beacons to begin transmitting.'

'And one replied. Once.' I looked back at Cassios, but he was concentrated upon the neophytes' explanation. 'Our auspex did not detect a second signal at that time.'

'Not our squad auspex, no,' Narro continued, 'but the one on the boat did. It is noted within the data-log. It is at the far end of the ship, so deep inside we would not have detected it.'

'Very well. Commander?' I fixed my gaze upon Cassios. 'Do you know what we may find?'

'Our boarding parties struck all across the ship. There are several for whom I have not accounted.' He shook his head sadly. 'I only pray they were as lucky as I and that we may reach them in time.'

My wards appeared convinced, but I was not. Yet if more of our brothers were still sent aboard that abomination, I could not leave them behind.

'So, Scout Pasan, tell me. What is this aperture that you have discovered?'

'Arse!' Vitellios swore as he took another grudging step along the dim tunnel. 'I can't believe I have to climb up this bio-ship's arse.'

His overblown irritation elicited a smattering of laughter from the other neophytes.

'Keep the chatter off the vox!' I snapped at them all, my patience worn thin. There was no atmosphere in this part of the ship so we were fully encased within our armour with only the squad-vox to keep in contact. I was still not recovered, I felt weak, uncomfortable, and my discomfort frustrated me even further. Such petty inconveniences should be nothing to an Astartes. My body should be healed fully, not still ailing. I pushed on, the temperature rising and my temper shortening with each step.

How had I come to this? Reduced to a haemorrhoid on a hive ship's backside! Was this what heroes of the Astartes did? Would, one day, a new generation of battle-brothers listen in hushed tones to the tale of this adventure?

'Brother-sergeant?' Cassios's voice came through to me. He had set it to a private channel. Cassios, though, would be my salvation. When we returned home after this insertion, we would not be met by a Techmarine adept to catalogue our salvage. No, we would have an honour guard fitting for the hero we would restore.

'Commander?'

'I asked the neophytes, during the days you were inconvenienced, of the circumstances of my rescue.'

'With what purpose?' I had intended my query to be polite, but as I heard it back through the vox it had the tinge of accusation.

'No more than to further my understanding of them. It struck me that Scout Pasan in particular showed considerable courage in leading the ravener away, allowing the heavy bolter to be retrieved.'

'It would have shown considerable courage had I ordered him to do it,' I said, my voice sounding testy, 'but in the midst of battle, you must act as one. You cannot have a single person deciding to act alone, expecting everyone else to understand his meaning.'

'And yet at other times you have remarked on his failure to use initiative. That he has waited for orders.'

'He must learn to judge between the two. That is also part of leadership; when to act and when to listen to others.'

'You truly believe he is the right one to groom as acolyte?'

I knew to whom Cassios was referring, but I held firm in my opinion. 'Pasan is Sothan. Like you and I. One of the last. He has it within him. He merely needs to discover it.'

The conversation ended shortly after that. Cassios did not understand; he had spent two days with the neophytes. I had fought alongside them for over two years. My mind dwelt on Cassios's behaviour. It had been the neophytes who had pushed for this second insertion yet I knew it was exactly what he wished. There are reasons why any Space Marine discovered still living aboard a hive ship must be examined by the Apothecarion before returning to duty. It is not the constant danger and warfare, our minds are enhanced so that we may fight without rest, but it is the unknown influence of the greater tyranid consciousness that bears down on each and every living thing within its grasp. No one yet knows what effect that may have.

There is another reason as well. Not all tyranid xenoforms are created simply to destroy their enemies. Many are designed to infiltrate their minds, turn them against their friends and lead them into traps to be devoured. Cassios's behaviour seemed normal, but then perhaps that was a sign. How normal should a man be after such an experience?

I led them on in silence. The torches on our suits illuminated only a fraction of the gloom ahead of us. In truth, we did not know what function this part of the hive ship performed. Pasan had found the entrance at the stern of the vessel; it had been small, shrivelled, but the tunnel had widened out considerably after we had penetrated the initial portal. The bio-titan birthing cavity was nothing to the size of this cavern. Walking along the middle, the lowest point, we could see neither wall nor ceiling. We might as well have been walking upon the surface of a planet, the only difference being that the ground sloped upwards rather than down as it disappeared into the darkness on either side. It was desolate; there

were no remains here of any of the lesser tyranid creatures that we had
waded through in our earlier expeditions. The floor was bare, a series of
shallow crests as though we were on the inside of a giant spring, and the
footing was firm. It appeared as though we had found the one part of
the vessel where nothing had ever lived.

Or I may have spoken too soon. I noticed to my right Cassios stop
suddenly, he kneeled and held his gauntleted hand on the ground.

'Something's coming. Take cover,' his commanding voice coming
through the vox crackled around the inside of my helmet. What cover? I
asked myself, but Cassios was already breaking to one side.

'To the right,' I ordered my wards after him. They responded instantly,
ready to follow him. We ran for a minute until the rising wall hove up
into view, soaring above our heads into the shadow. Cassios climbed the
slope until it was as steep as we could manage and then stopped there,
looking further ahead.

'What is it?' I asked him. The auspex showed nothing.

'Do you not see them?'

I peered into the gloom. 'No,' I said.

He bade us wait, however, and within a few moments I saw what he
had seen. A ridge emerged ahead of us, stretching across the horizon, as
though a mighty hand had gripped the ship from the outside and was
squeezing it up towards us. I heard my wards gasp as they saw it too.

'Holy Throne...'

'God-Emperor...'

'Sotha preserve us...'

'What in the name of a hive-toad's spawn-baubles are those?'

The ridge was no muscle contraction: it was a phalanx of huge tyranid
creatures of a sort I had never seen before. Each as big as a tank, as big
as a Baneblade, packed tightly together so there was not a centimetre
between them, and moving as a line slowly towards us. Their armoured
eyeless heads were down, so low as to be ploughing over the surface in
front of them, dragging their bulbous bodies behind. Their limbs had
atrophied so they oozed their way forward like snails. I did not know
what their slime would do, but their weight alone would crush us. I
looked to the left, to the right, there was no way around; they ringed
the circumference of the cavern, somehow sticking to the walls even as
they arched round and became the ceiling. I doubted whether all the
weaponry we had to hand would be enough to stop one of these brutes
in its tracks.

I looked down the line, searching for a tank-beast that appeared
smaller or weaker. If we targeted one with concentrated fire there might
be a chance, but my attention was dragged away when my wards suddenly let out a great cheer. Cassios was advancing, climbing the curving
slope as he went. He had gone mad, I realised, the sight of his foe had
driven his wits from him.

'After him!' I ordered the Scouts. I would be damned if I would let him die now, after all he had survived, before he could be welcomed back home. We chased him as quickly as we could, struggling at the steep angle this close to the wall. He charged ahead of us, not even drawing his weapon. Scrabbling higher, he leapt from the cavern wall onto the top of the nearest tank-beast's head. Then, balanced precariously as the beast chomped forward, his power sword appeared in his hand and he stabbed down.

The tank-beast did not seem to notice.

'Back!' I shouted, appalled, to the others. 'Back! Firing positions!'

The beasts' pace had appeared slow from a distance, but up close they ground forwards with surprising speed. On such a slope, it was as if a Land Raider was barrelling towards us, teetering on a single tread.

'Stay on the curve! Stay high!' Cassios's voice blasted into our helmets as we fell back and he stabbed down again. I glanced behind, this time the beast acknowledged the strike with a flicker of its head that nearly threw Cassios off, but then it returned to its path and he regained his grip.

The Scouts stood ready to fire, but I hesitated, fearing the volley would hit the commander.

'Fire above me!' Cassios ordered, and we fired a battery of shells and shot over Cassios's head as he ducked and swung again. He cut to the right side of the beast's head, on the underside of where he was crouching. This time the beast shied slightly away from the barrage, but again returned to its course.

'Again!' He cut. We fired, the beast looming before us as though we were insects.

'Again!' he cried one last time before the beast steamrollered over us. We fired and he jammed the sword in as deep as it would go. The beast reacted. It squirmed away from our shot and lazily snapped towards the pinprick causing it pain. Its weight shifted and the upper edge of its body detached from the wall. For the first time we glimpsed the immense pores and suckers that had held it fast. As those came away from the surface, its weight shifted even further and more suckers came loose. With the inertia of a battleship ramming another, it slowly toppled down upon the tank-beast to its side and both monstrous creatures halted for a moment in confusion. Above them, their collision had left a gap. None of us needed to be told what to do.

We raced forwards to pass through before the tank-beast recovered. As we crossed into the valley we had created in the advancing ridge, it regained its grip and lumbered back. The valley's wall closed in upon us and I willed every last jolt of energy to my legs. The walls slammed shut as we shot from them and skidded upon the deep coating of mucus the tank-beasts left behind. I gained purchase for an instant before Hwygir, out of control, knocked me flying. We slid down the curved wall of the cavern right back into the centre until we finally stuck where the mucus was pooling.

I cut through the groans on the vox, demanding my squad to report. Haltingly, they did so. Slowly, trying not to fall again, I picked myself up from the laden ground and then checked the others. Cassios was rising as well. Hwygir was holding the heavy bolter high in the air, keeping it dry. Narro and Pasan were scraping the fluid off themselves as Vitellios just stood there, a look of horror on his face as he stared down at the mucus dripping off from every part of him.

'I've been slimed,' he said.

I forwent commenting that such dross reminded me of the grime-swamp where he'd been birthed; I had more pressing concerns.

'Neophytes, get yourselves up. Check your weapons, check your weapons!' I chivvied Vitellios. 'Straighten yourselves and get ready to move.'

I stepped away a little to check my own pistol and could not help but reflect once more on the new depths to which my command had sunk. I saw Cassios stepping around the neophytes, congratulating them individually. It did not matter, as soon as I returned him to the *Heart of Cronus* I would request transfer to the Battle Company and no one would be able to deny me.

'What is this place anyway?' I overheard Vitellios ask the rest.

'A no good place,' Hwygir concluded.

Narro was already working on hypotheses. 'Maybe some kind of alimentary canal, maybe a funnel or blow-hole.'

'Maybe the barrel of a bio-cannon?' Pasan queried.

'One big cannon,' Vitellios said.

'Either way, I just hope there's nothing bigger coming up out the pipe.'

I allowed them their inane chatter this once. I had checked my pistol and by His grace it still functioned. Our weapons last hundreds of years for a reason. I holstered it and then punched the auspex back to life to check the path ahead. I looked at its readings and then punched it again. The readings did not change. My body still moved, taking a few steps forward, but my brain, for this moment, had frozen. There *was* something bigger coming up the pipe. It wasn't a tank-beast or a carnifex or even a bio-titan. It was the spark of life that Cassios had claimed to sense. Ahead of us, growing, feeding, ready to be born, was a creature far larger than any we had encountered. It was the Kraken's offspring. It was another hive ship.


'Brother Tiresias?' The lieutenant stopped me as I walked the corridors of the *Heart of Cronus*.

'Brother Hadrios,' I responded, surprised. 'I thought you were away with Master Thracian?'

'We have just returned,' the lieutenant said flatly, his eyes heavy. 'He wishes to see you. You will come with me.'

He turned away, expecting me to follow. After a moment's hesitation, I did. The lieutenant offered no further conversation and so we walked in silence. He led me to the Master's chambers and left me there. The chambers were still dark, the mosaics along its walls unlit, unprepared for their master's return, much as the rest of us. This was not how I expected matters to unfold. We imagined we would have forewarning when Thracian reappeared, to gather our strength so that we might confront him together and demonstrate our collective will. Instead, he had stolen back like a thief in the night and taken us off-guard.

A line split down the panelling on one side and the chamber filled with light. Hidden in the light, Master Thracian stood. I imagine that I have already created in your mind's eye a character for Master Thracian. A careful man, a smaller man; lesser than those who came before him. Desperate, perhaps. Petty. Failing. Let me dispel that character from your mind now. No man can become an Astartes without the potential for greatness, and no Astartes can become the master of a Chapter without a part of that greatness realised. Thracian was no exception and he was to achieve even more over those next few years. He was big, big even for one of our kind, but his face had stayed thin. His long hair was still black where Chapter Master Thorcyra's had turned grey, and he wore his beard shorter. He was wearing a simple robe in the Chapter's colours and beneath it a vest of ceremonial scale armour, fastened loosely across his chest. I knew him to be a fierce warrior, a master tactician, and brave without question, but at that moment I saw him only as the obstacle to our Chapter finding the destiny it deserved.

I bowed; he bid me stand.

'Brother Tiresias, welcome. I regret that my absence had to be of such great duration,' he spoke. 'I understand that Brother-Captain Romonos has kept the Battle Company busy.'

Busy, yes, with small raids, petty battles and hasty withdrawals.

'I am told that you brought honour upon the Chapter by your actions during the campaign upon Tan.'

'My thanks, Master.' I nodded without emotion, but I relaxed a little. So this was merely to be a little perfunctory commendation. I would humour him and then find Sergeant Angeloi and tell him that our opportunity had come.

'What did you think of that campaign?' he asked.

'It was a great success. A significant victory,' I spouted what I knew I should say and bit my tongue on the rest.

The Chapter Master regarded me. 'I have read the reports, Tiresias, I asked what you thought.'

'Master, I have said already what I think. I do not know what you require from me.'

'That is an order,' he said calmly.

Well, if that was what he wished, that is what he would have. 'The campaign on Tan…' I snorted. 'The campaign on Tan was a joke. No, worse, it was a travesty. A few skirmishes, and standing guard throughout an evacuation. Providing support to others instead of leading from the front, where an Astartes should be. It does not even deserve to be called a campaign, let alone a victory.'

I stopped then. I had said too much, far too much. I had breached protocol, discipline, even simple good judgement. I looked at the Master, but his face was without expression.

'Did we lose any of our brothers?' he asked quietly.

I knew he knew already, but he wanted me to say it. 'No, no brothers lost. A few injured. Most minor. One more serious.'

'Brother Domitios, yes, but he will recover. I know also, Tiresias, that when he fell it was you who went to his defence. It was you who skewered the xenos beast that threatened him. It was you who saved his life.'

I nodded again. It was true, but I did not think it remarkable. Astartes are trained to do nothing less.

'You acquitted yourself well, brother. Very well,' the Master continued. 'You have always done so, even when you have had misgivings about the orders you have been given. That is why I wished you to speak your mind. Why I am talking to you now.'

'Do not mistake my words, Master.' I countered. 'I understand the value of restraint, of retreat when circumstances dictate. We defended the orbital stations, but we did not even try to save that planet. We did not even step foot upon the surface. Before we even entered the system we were defeated in our hearts.'

I paused. Thracian let the silence hang in the air between us for a long moment. 'You wish for it to be as it was.' he said.

'Yes!' I gasped. 'Kraken is broken, its fleets are scattered. We do not need to sell our lives merely to delay their advance. If we commit ourselves in force we can win a victory, a true victory. As Calgar did on Ichar IV, as we did at Dal'yth Tertius, and Translock. Yes, I wish to fight as we did, with every weapon, every muscle, every sinew at our command. Come victory or death, to fight as an Astartes should.'

I had not expected to burst out with such sentiments now, to anticipate the statement that Sergeant Angeloi was readying to give him. I expected Thracian to roar back at me, but his reply was very quick.

'One day, Tiresias, we shall fight like that again. But for now it cannot be. For now, any action where no brother is lost must be victory enough,' he said simply. 'I know that it is far easier to say than it is to accept in one's heart. That is my challenge, one of them at least, to help us understand what has happened to us. How we must change. So many brothers dead; Sotha gone, mere rubble in space. The noble Scythes of the Emperor, loyal reapers of mankind's foes, cut down ourselves by the Great Devourer. It is not a fate we deserved.'

He stepped away from me, his robe brushing lightly over the polished floor.

'I understand your frustration, but you must have hope in our future. And that is what I left you to acquire. Here.'

He keyed a sequence into a control and the mosaics along the walls rose smoothly, revealing pict-screens behind. They all displayed images of one of the ship's hangar bays. It had changed greatly. The fighters had gone; the machinery had all been stripped away. In their place, a bizarre maze had been constructed. Plasteel walls covered and painted to resemble the corridors of a tyranid bio-ship. Inside the maze I could see Space Marines advancing in their squads; not Space Marines, no, they were too small. They were neophytes.

As I watched, one of them trod upon a pressure-switch. A trapdoor in the floor opened and he vanished before even catching his breath to shout.

'Traps, creatures, combat servitors programmed with tyranid attack patterns. It is as real as we can make it. We have paid close attention to the data we gathered fighting these monstrosities, after all, it came to us dear.'

'How many?' I asked, my voice a whisper.

'Three hundred in total, and more to come. Young, untested, but keen. All orphans of the Kraken like ourselves. All ready to be baptised with tyranid blood.' Thracian placed his hand upon my shoulder then. 'They only need leadership, guidance, from brothers like you. Sergeant Angeloi recommended you specifically, Tiresias. Promotion and this, your first command.'

I opened my mouth, but found for once no words were waiting there. Thracian continued:

'You see, Tiresias, one day it shall be as it was. And it shall not take a hundred years, or even fifty. When the next hive fleet comes to plague these sectors we will be ready to answer the Emperor's call.'

I stepped back a little, and Thracian's hand fell from me.

'I will... thank you, Master. I will be sure to thank my sergeant when I–'

And then I saw a look in Thracian's golden eyes.

'I will ensure you will have the chance to send a message after him,' he interrupted. 'Brother-Sergeant Angeloi has already departed to join the xenos hunters of the Inquisition, the fabled Deathwatch. Given our experiences, they requested as many brothers as we could spare to help spread the knowledge of the forms of the tyranid blight and how each may best be destroyed. I granted him, and a few others, the honour of carrying our name and our teachings to the galaxy.'

A few others, Thracian said, but in truth over forty brothers had gone already, reassigned to the Deathwatch. They were nearly a third of our strength and each one of them was one of Angeloi's crusaders. And the chance to compel Thracian to order one last, glorious campaign had gone with them.

'Now rest a moment, brother,' Thracian directed me to sit, 'and allow me to share with you how your new command will aid our Chapter's salvation.'

I never discovered the truth behind the creation of the neophyte companies. The recruits themselves I knew were, just like Gricole and our retainers, from the worlds of the long retreat. Even before the hive fleet arrived in the Sotha system, even while my squad-brothers prepared the planet's defences, plans were being made so that the Scythes might rise again.

The best of the youngsters of Sotha had already been secretly evacuated. Each place we turned to make our stand, Miral, Graia, and the rest; while my brothers fought and died, the most promising youths were recruited and rescued. Harvested by us, I suppose, while those left behind were harvested by the xenos.

But the gene-seed, that was the question. Three whole companies of neophytes and more to come, Thracian had promised. How was it possible? There were many theories. A few were sensible; that Thorcyra had been forewarned of the attack on Sotha and ordered the gene-seed to be removed in secret, or that the old Chapter Master had struck an agreement with the Inquisition to return our gene-tithe and whether the Deathwatch Marines were the only price he had had to pay. Other theories were darker, that Thracian had found or purchased arcane or alien tech that allowed progenoids to develop artificially far faster than in a Space Marine, or that most of the neophytes did not receive true gene-seed, they were merely bio-engineered and would never mature into true Astartes. I even heard a whisper that the gene-seed was not ours; that before the Salvation Teams there were squads designated Reaper Teams. I do not credit such thoughts, however; no Astartes would stoop to such measures even if the future of the Chapter depended upon it.

But then, I have had cause to wonder, can you ever be sure what lengths a creature will go in order to ensure the survival of its children?

'A kilometre and a half long, millions of tonnes, and a face only a hormagaunt could love...' Vitellios murmured, watching the muscles of the hive ship's offspring ripple beneath its hull-skin.

'And it's trying to get out,' Pasan said.

This was it then, the source of the 'gaunts we had encountered, the spark of life that Cassios had sworn existed. The bloated biters we had seen were not venturing inwards to wait; they were coming here to feed this offspring on the bio-matter of the corpse of its parent.

'Very well,' I decided. 'As soon as we return to the boat, we will send a despatch to the closest battlegroup, Ultima priority. They will respond to that.'

'No,' Cassios said.

I scoffed. 'I assure you, commander, they will!' But then, through the visor of his faceplate, I saw the expression in his eyes.

'They will still be too late. We are the only ones who are close enough and we are here to kill that creature.'

I had had enough of him. He had challenged my command once already and I was not going to waste my breath diverting him from such vainglorious stupidity.

'As you wish, commander,' I told him and gave the signal for the Scouts to gather and follow. 'I will ensure your final action is recorded with the proper honour.' I had walked several steps before I realised my wards were not with me.

'Ensure it is recorded for all of us,' Vitellios spoke up.

I should have seen it. I should have seen it as soon as I saw them standing with Cassios as he convinced me there were others within the ship that may be saved. They were not looking at me to lead them; they were looking at me to see whether I believed their lie.

'A second beacon?' I did not look at Cassios, but rather at Narro. He knew I would have trusted him to double-check the auspex readings.

'It was not his idea,' Pasan said. 'Nor was it the commander's. It was mine.'

'Yours?' I shot back at my acolyte.

It was Cassios who replied. 'I would have left you back there. It is clear to me that you have failed as their teacher and you have failed even as their leader. But Brother Pasan wanted you here.'

I looked away from him; there was nothing he could say to me. Two days it had taken him, two days to take the loyalties of the wards I had cared for for two years. I looked back at Pasan. 'Why did you want me here? So that you may see my face as you disgrace me?'

'No,' Pasan said. 'So that you may have the chance to join us.'

'Join you?' I exclaimed. 'For what purpose would I do that? What do you offer but the futile waste of your lives?'

Pasan replied, but the four of them may as well have spoken as one.

'To know what it is to fight as an Astartes.'

I could not credit this from such youths. 'You do not know,' I told them. 'You have never seen the full Chapter deployed in battle. Squad after squad standing proud in their armour, bolters raised. Reciting your battle-oaths with one voice and then marching forwards, knowing your brothers are there for you as you are there for them. You draw such strength from them, being not one warrior fighting alone, but one of a thousand fighting together. Ten hundred bodies forming a single weapon. Until you have experienced that... you do not really know what it is to fight as an Astartes.'

The neophytes were silent. I felt my words had reached them at last.

'You are right, honoured sergeant,' Pasan said. 'We do not know. We have never experienced that. But then, when will we?'

'When you are full battle-brothers,' I said.

'Will we? Even if we do as you say. We leave here now, with you; we survive to take a place in the Battle Company,' Pasan glanced at his brother-Scouts for support. 'When will we ever march into battle a full Chapter strong? How long will it take us to recover before we do anything more than nip and pinch at our enemies? A hundred years, two hundred? How much more will be lost to the devourer by then?'

Pasan stood forwards and Vitellios stepped with him.

'I know you think little of me,' the hive-trash said. 'That I don't take being a high and mighty Astartes seriously. But there's one thing I am serious about. My life. I joined to scour our galaxy of the alien bastards that slaughtered my world. I didn't raise myself up from hive-trash, put myself through all the trials to be chosen as a Scythe so I could dig through the dead and grow old training the next generation. I didn't do all I've done just to become an antiquated relic…'

'As I am, you mean?' I snapped back. I was beyond anger, I was furious. I raised my hand and Vitellios braced himself for the blow, but Pasan stepped in front of him.

'Why are you against us?' he cried. 'We all know that this is what you truly want. We've heard you rail to Gricole often enough.'

'Now you are spying upon me as well?' I said, incredulous.

Hwygir grunted in the corner, 'A small craft, our transport.'

'You are not the only one with an Astartes' senses,' Vitellios chipped in, but Pasan cut him off.

'No excuses, honoured sergeant. You wanted us to hear. You wanted us to know how much you resented this mission, resented us for what we took you from. Now here is your chance. There is the enemy. We can reach it. We can kill it. Yes, some of us, all of us may die. But is this not the chance for glory you want?'

All four of them were standing now, united against me, yet united in favour of everything I believed. The anger that had flared inside me vanished.

'Yes, it is,' I agreed with them. 'More than you know. Every sinew and muscle in my body craves to carry the fight to the xenos without caution, without restraint. To serve as an Astartes should serve.'

'Then you are with us!' Pasan shouted.

'But then…' I continued. 'I look deeper than my muscle, I look into my bones. And there, inscribed a thousand times, is the oath I took to the master of this Chapter to obey his orders and the Emperor's word therein. It is an oath that I have never broken, and never will. As for the rest… I give it up.'

I swept my arm up and pointed at them. 'You are my witness! You hear me now! I give up my glory, I give up my revenge, I give up my hope of what I could have been,' I shouted even though they were close, but I knew I was not addressing them. 'I accept it cannot be as it was! A battle where no brother falls is glory enough!'

I saw their faces, they thought me mad, but in truth I was healed. The weight of the loss of my brothers, the weight of my rage that I had survived when they had not was lifted. I took a breath and breathed free for the first time since Sotha.

'No glory,' I finished quietly, 'is greater than the future of our Chapter. We are not greater than it, none of us. Any Astartes who thinks they are... there is a word for those...'

'Renegades,' Cassios said from behind me. 'But which of us is the renegade, brother? You, who defend our Chapter's crippled body or I, who defend its soul?'

'It's starting to move...' Narro reported.

'Then we shall as well,' Cassios gestured to the Scouts, once my wards, now his men, then turned back to me. 'I offer you the chance to fight as a Scythe should, with his hand, his oath on his lips and his brothers by his side. If you do not come, let it be upon you.'

'It shall be upon me,' I stated, 'but I shall come. I take this oath now: you may take these children to their deaths but I shall bring them back again.'

It was to be the final insertion of the 21st Salvation Team. The ship, the offspring, was grinding itself forward down the lifeless channel. We blew a hole through the young, unhardened skin as close to our target as we could manage. If the offspring noticed our pinprick at all its reaction was lost amidst the wild throes of its agonising birth. The chambers inside could not be more different than the dead, dark halls of its parent. Luminescent algae lit our path, the ground was springy beneath our boots, the wall-skin taut, the door valves firm, and the noise... each chamber and tunnel vibrated with the screeching noise as the offspring pulsed and squirmed out into space, but below that you could hear the hum, the pulse, the beat of its life all around you. The life the Scythes were here to take.

We moved quickly. Cassios led the way, allowing his warrior instincts to draw him towards the creature's heart. The Scouts followed a step behind; their excitement did not dull their skill, and nor did their fear. They moved easily, not in a single formation, but always shifting from one to another, running, covering. First Vitellios would run, as Pasan protected him, then Narro as Vitellios did the same, then Hwygir would charge up, bursting as ever with pride at being entrusted with the vital heavy weapon. They protected one another. For two years I had tried to find one amongst them suited to be their leader; at that moment I realised that they did not need one. They fought as one: as Hwygir reloaded, Narro shot into the tyranids to keep them from recovering; as Narro was caught by a tendril, Pasan forced his gun down into its maw and blew its brain out; as Pasan forced open a door-valve, Vitellios destroyed the creature lurking above it; as Vitellios ran quickly back from a new rush of 'gaunts, I lent my fire to his to halt them where they stood.

Our foes were not the fearsome monsters of Macragge and Ichar IV. The ship had grown only its most basic defenders: termagants, other 'gaunts and the like; and it itself was focused on its struggle towards freedom. However, its plight, its vulnerable state, triggered a response from the creatures barring our path that was all the more visceral. Cassios did not care, he simply battered them aside. These tyranids, who had overwhelmed countless star systems with force of numbers, now found themselves overwhelmed in turn by Cassios's simple force. Every chamber we encountered he stormed, every 'gaunt in his way fell to the shells of his pistol or the curved edge of his power sword. He gave them no chance to gather, but charged into the thick of them, relying on his speed to spoil their aim and his thick armour to protect his flesh. That it did for him, but it did not for the rest of us and we suffered our first loss.

'Brother!' Hwygir shouted after Narro as he stumbled. One of the shots of bio-acid aimed too quickly at Cassios had flown past the commander and struck Narro. Across the vox, I heard him clamp down on his scream. Hwygir had already raised the heavy bolter and was struggling across to check on him.

'Keep us covered!' I yelled at him and shoved his weapon around to face the closing enemy. I heard his frustrated roar as he fired, but my focus was on the stricken Narro. He was still breathing. I rolled him and saw his arm clutching his side. Without ceremony I pulled the arm away to see the wound and discovered that the arm ended at the wrist. His hand had been eaten away.

His eyes snapped open, he looked down in shock at his stump and breathed in to holler in pain. I punched him sharply in the chest and he gasped instead, winded.

'Overcome it!' I shouted into his ear. 'You shall build yourself a new one.'

He struggled to nod as his Astartes metabolism kicked in and dampened the shock and the pain. I took his weapon and handed him my pistol.

'Sergeant!' Hwygir called back as he released the trigger for a moment. 'How is–'

I looked up as Hwygir turned his head to ask after his brother. I saw the shot hit the back of his helmet and the blood splatter on the inside of his face-plate as the tiny beetles of the bio-weapon bored through his skull and ate the flesh of his face from the inside. The savage fell and, in that instant, I felt the loss of a brother.

I dived towards his body firing wildly to force his killers to scuttle back. I cannot claim any sentimentality – I had fought too long to allow such feelings cloud my reactions – it was solely his weapon I was after.

I rose and aimed the heavy bolter. I had not fired one in battle since the long retreat from Sotha. I pulled the trigger, felt the reassuring recoil and watched as its shells blew a line of bloody death across the 'gaunts' first ranks.

The offspring lurched suddenly to one side and all of us, tyranid and Space Marine alike, were knocked from our feet. Hwygir and the 'gaunt bodies rolled away. I hefted the cumbersome gun and scrambled back where Cassios and the rest of the squad had regrouped.

'It's accelerating,' Cassios said without a glance back towards where Hwygir had fallen. 'We have to move faster.'

'Does it matter?' Vitellios asked. 'We're inside it now, it's not getting away!'

'Every second we delay gives it time to call in more beasts.'

'Then what are we waiting for?' he jumped up, ever the fearless one, and smashed the butt of his shotgun against the next door-valve. The valve shrank back and he led us through. He made it a single step before a set of jaws within the valve snapped shut, razor-sharp teeth puncturing the length of Vitellios's body from his ankle to his head. I grabbed his arm, wedged the barrel under his shoulder and fired into the darkness, into whatever monster lay beyond. The door-mouth rippled in pain and slid back into the walls. It was too late, though, for Vitellios. His face was fixed in an expression of surprise, no last witticism to give. The hive-trash fell and I felt the loss of a brother.

It was then that we truly understood that it was not just these 'gaunts: every single piece of flesh around us wished us dead. The wall algae blazed brightly as we came near to draw the beasts, bulbed stalks burst and covered us in spores that sought to burrow into our armour, cysts showered us with bio-acid, even the muscles of the floor rippled as we fired, to disrupt our aim. It would have been enough to stop any human warriors, but we are Astartes. The Angels of Death. And all the offspring's efforts could not keep us from our quest's end.

'We are close,' Cassios declared, as another 'gaunt lay in pieces at his feet.

'How close?' I shouted as I delivered another volley of fire against the creatures pursuing us.

'Can't you hear it?'

I could hear nothing over the explosions of the bolt shells and the roar of the offspring's progress. It must be close to birthing now, but I did not care. Gricole would see it as soon as it emerged, he would know to carry a message back to the fleet. Others would know, they just would not know what had happened to us.

'I hear it!' Pasan cried, and then I heard it too: a deep throbbing sound.

'Brothers!' Cassios announced. 'I give you the heart of the beast!'

The single organ, if it was just one, filled the chamber beyond. It was a giant column, surrounded by red bloated chambers. From the top of each chamber split massive leeches that surmounted the top of the pillar and descended into the centre. It looked as though eight great Sothan phantine beasts were drinking from a pool. The entire structure constantly pulsed and shifted as gallons of fluid pumped through it each second. It was the energy cortex, and it was covered by tyranids. Smaller 'gaunts with bio-weapons, larger ones with great scything claws, a few at the top even had wings.

'It's a trap,' Pasan gasped. 'It let us get this far...'

'It's not a trap if we know it's coming,' Cassios told him.

No, it's insanity. I glanced at Cassios again; his eyes were at peace. Perhaps he really had been tainted, perhaps all he had done was in service of some xenos impulse inserted into his brain. Perhaps all the while we had been inside the offspring, the offspring had been inside him.

'Why don't they attack?' Pasan whispered.

'Maybe... maybe...' Narro's mind raced, he was feeling the disorientation worst of all. 'Maybe they did not wish to risk fighting here, risk damaging the cortex.'

But then the great thundering of the offspring as it climbed out the channel of its parent reached a crescendo and went silent. It was out. It was into space. My faith was with Gricole. He would do what needed to be done. It just remained for me to do the same, call this assault off, to save the lives I could. But Cassios was already advancing, a brace of mining charges in his hand. I stopped him and held one of the charges up.

'It's set to instant detonation,' I told him.

'Of course,' he replied and we locked gazes for the last time.

'Then we stay here. They deserve the chance, Cassios. Give them that.'

He shrugged, uncaring. This was to be the epic of his death; whether others were with him did not matter. I looked at my last two wards – Narro quickly nodded agreement with me, and so too, slowly, did Pasan.

'Cover him,' I told them, as Cassios raised his power sword high and cried:

'For Sotha! For the Emperor! Death! Death! Death!'

My wards and I fired in unison: heavy bolter, boltgun and pistol together, blowing holes in the ranks of the tyranid. The tyranids responded in kind, releasing a volley of borer-beetles, bio-acid and toxin-spines against Cassios as he charged.

Cassios slammed to a halt and flinched, drawing his cloak around him. I saw his mighty frame collapse under the onslaught.

'No!' Pasan shouted and sprinted after him, spraying fire wildly as he went. The hormagaunts had already leapt from the energy cortex and were surging towards the downed commander. I did not call to bring Pasan back, I saved my breath, he would not come. I had lost him long before. Instead I trained the heavy bolter to clear his path. The first of the hormagaunt wave exploded as my shell hit home, the one behind stumbled and was knocked down by those behind it, pushing forwards, the third leapt and my next shell caught its leg and its body cart-wheeled away in pieces. The fourth reached Cassios and took the brunt of Pasan's fire. The next rank sprang, arcing high to clear the bodies before them. Two fell to my shells, one to Narro's, but three fell upon the son of Sotha. One sliced through his gun and then his arm, the second caught his knee and cut deep into his side and the third split his head straight down the middle. The son of Sotha fell and I felt the loss of a part of myself.

Then, in a crackling arc of light, the three 'gaunts were carved apart themselves. Cassios rose, his cloak dissolved, his armour cracked and scarred. Blood streamed from the split in his armour at the neck. He spun to face the approaching horde and threw himself into their midst.

He was beyond our help now. I might have only seconds to fulfil my oath and save who I could. I turned to Narro, the last of my wards, and told him:

'I never thought it would be you. But it is best that it is.'

He looked at me, confused. I shook my head and pointed to our escape. This one at least I would save, I thought, the most brilliant of them. Perhaps, I thought, that would be enough. But I was not to be allowed even that. Above us, I heard a familiar bestial scream, first one, then a second. Without thinking, I brought the heavy bolter up straight into the ravener's face.

The brutal claw carved through the heavy bolter even as I pulled the trigger. The round rocketing down the barrel suddenly struck bone and exploded. Shrapnel burst through the barrel-cover and flew at me. I stumbled back, dropping the useless heavy weapon and clutching my face. I pulled the ruined helmet off, blinking to catch the ravener's next attack. I looked and saw it collapsed on the ground, its claw blown off, its face a mass of blood and bone. The second still held Narro's body impaled upon its scythe-claws as it twisted towards me. I drew my falx. This was to be the end.

The second ravener leapt, its two scythe-claws high. I dove forwards. The scythes came down but I was inside their reach and they glanced off my shoulders. My falx was already embedded through its chestbone. Its mid-limbs plunged through my armour and unloaded its venom as I twisted and pushed it off my blade. I staggered back, holding my guts inside my body, I was still not dead. Neither was it. It flew at me in one last attack, my falx came up and caught its scythes as they came down and pushed them to one side. As its blades went down mine cut back across its gaping mouth and sliced its head open.

I felt its ichor splatter my face, I tasted it as my mouth opened to roar my defiance. At that moment, somewhere behind me, a dying hand released its grip upon the mining charges and the chamber was filled with the Emperor's wrath.

\* \* \*

I woke aboard a dead ship, a ravener my bedside companion. I rolled the corpse away. I dragged myself to my feet and began to search about the dark and lifeless chamber. Whether the tyranids had fled or died on the spot from the psychic shock I did not know. I was searching for something else. I found it. I thought it impossible for any one, any Astartes, to live through that. I was right. The body of Commander Cassios was a shell. But I was not there for sentiment, I did not do that. I was there in the hope that something inside him survived. I grimaced in pain as I felt the bite of the ravener poison. A stronger dose this time, from a young beast, rather than a stale relic. I took the reductor from my pack and placed it first against Cassios's throat and then against his chest, and took from him the Chapter's due.

My second heart finishes its beat. My recollection concludes, as it always does, with the memory of dragging myself into this hole and, even as the bio-poison burned its way around my body, focusing on my training, slowing my mind, suspending my system and halting the poison's spread. It was too late for me; I know that. I will die when I wake. Pasan, Vitellios, Narro, Hwygir; Cassios had taken them in, but I will carry them out again. I know they are dead, their bodies lost, perhaps more bio-matter for the devourer, but their spirits live on. Two of them in the reductor in my hand, in the progenoid glands of Commander Cassios from which new gene-seed and two new Astartes would arise. And two of them my own shell. The glands in my throat and in my chest that would bear two more. Cassios and I are lost, as we should have been long ago. These four are the future of the Scythes now, and I will live and bear the pain of poison until I deliver them back home.

'Sergeant! Over here!' the neophyte called.

Sergeant Quintos, commanding the 121st Salvation Team, strode over to his ward. The neophyte gestured down with his torch into a crevice in the floor of the dead bio-ship. Sergeant Quintos activated the light built into his bionic arm. He had lost the original years before when he himself had been a scout in a Salvation Team. Down there, glinting back in the light, shone the shoulder armour of a Space Marine. And upon that armour was inscribed the legend:

## TIRESIAS

# AT GAIUS POINT

*Aaron Dembski-Bowden*

## I

The memory of fire. Fire and falling, incineration and annihilation.
   Then darkness.
   Absolute silence. Absolute nothing.

## II

I open my eyes.
   There before me, outlined by scrolling white text across my targeting display, is a shattered metal wall. Its architecture is gothic in nature – a skeletal wall, with black steel girders like ribs helping form the wall's curvature. It is mangled and bent. Crushed, even.
   I do not know where I am, but my senses are awash with perception. I hear the crackle of fire eating metal, and the angry hum of live battle armour. The sound is distorted, a hitch or a burr in the usually steady thrum. Damage has been sustained. My armour is compromised. A glance at the bio-feed displays shows minor damage to the armour plating of my wrist and shin. Nothing serious.
   I smell the flames nearby, and the bitter rancidity of melting steel. I smell my own body; the sweat, the chemicals injecting into my flesh by my armour, and the intoxicatingly rich scent of my own blood.
   A god's blood.
   Refined and thinned for use in mortal veins, but a god's blood nevertheless.
   A dead god. A slain angel.
   The thought brings my teeth together in a grunted curse, my fangs scraping the teeth below. Enough of this weakness.

I rise, muscles of aching flesh bunching in unison with the fibre-bundle false muscles of my armour. It is a sensation I am familiar with, yet it feels somehow flawed. I should be stronger. I should exult in my strength, the ultimate fusion of biological potency and machine power.

I do not feel strong. I feel nothing but pain and a momentary disorientation. The pain is centralised in my spinal column and shoulder blades, turning my back into a pillar of dull, aching heat. Nothing is broken – bio-feeds have already confirmed that. The soreness of muscle and nerve would have killed a human, but we are gene-forged into greater beings.

Already, the weakness fades. My blood stings with the flood of adrenal stimulants and kinetic enhancement narcotics rushing through my veins.

My movement is unimpeded. I rise to my feet, slow not from weakness now, but from caution.

With my vision stained a cooling emerald shade by my helm's eye lenses, I take in the wreckage around me.

This chamber is ruined, half-crushed with its walls distorted. Restraint thrones lie broken, torn from the floor. The two bulkheads leading from the chamber are both wrenched from their hinges, hanging at warped angles.

The impact must have been savage.

The… impact?

The crash. Our Thunderhawk crashed. The clarity of recollection is sickening… the sense of falling from the sky, my senses drenched in the thunder of descent, the shaking of the ship in its entirety. Temperature gauges on my retinal display rose slowly when the engines died in exploding flares that scorched the hull, and my armour systems registered the gunship's fiery journey groundward.

There was a final booming refrain, a roar like the carnosaurs of home – as loud and primal as their predator-king challenges – and the world shuddered beyond all sanity. The gunship ploughed into the ground.

And then… Darkness.

My eyes flicker to my retinal display's chronometer. I was unconscious for almost three minutes. I will do penance for such weakness, but that can come later.

Now I breathe in deep, tasting the ashy smoke in the air but unaffected by it. The air filtration in my helm's grille renders me immune to such trivial concerns.

'Zavien,' a voice crackles in my ears. A momentary confusion takes hold at the sound of the word. The vox-signal is either weak, or the sender's armour is badly damaged. With the ship in pieces, both could be true.

'Zavien,' the voice says again.

This time I turn at the name, realising it is my own.

Zavien strode into the cockpit, keeping his balance on the tilted floor through an effortless combination of natural grace and his armour's joint-stabilisers.

The cockpit had suffered even more than the adjacent chamber. The view window, despite the thickness of the reinforced plastek, was shattered beyond simple repair. Diamond shards of the sundered armourglass twinkled on the twisted floor. The pilot thrones were wrenched from their support columns, cast aside like detritus in a storm.

Through the windowless viewport there was nothing but mud and gnarled black roots, much of which had spilled over the lifeless control consoles. They'd come down hard enough to drive the gunship's nose into the earth.

The pilot, Varlon, was a mangled wreck sprawled face-down over the control console. Zavien's targeting reticule locked onto his brother's battered armour, secondary cursors detailing the rents and wounds in the deactivated war plate. Blood, thick and dark, ran from rips in Varlon's throat and waist joints. It ran in slow trickles across the smashed console, dripping between buttons and levers.

His power pack was inactive. Life signs were unreadable, but the evidence was clear enough. Zavien heard no heartbeat from the body, and had Varlon been alive, his gene-enhanced physiology would have clotted and sealed all but the most grievous wounds. He wouldn't still be bleeding slowly all over the controls of the downed gunship.

'Zavien,' said a voice to the right, no longer over the vox.

Zavien turned from Varlon, his armour snarling in a growl of joint-servos. There, pinned under wreckage from the collapsed wall, was Drayus. Zavien moved to the fallen warrior's side, seeing the truth. No, Drayus was not just pinned in place. He was impaled there.

The sergeant's black helm was lowered, chin down on his collar, green eyes regarding the broken Imperial eagle on his chest. Jagged wreckage knifed into his dark armour, the ravaged steel spearing him through the shoulder guard, the arm, the thigh and the stomach. Blood leaked through his helm's speaker grille. The biometric displays that flashed up on Zavien's visor told an ugly story, and one with an end soon to come.

'Report,' Sergeant Drayus said – the way he always said it – as if the scene around them were the most mundane situation imaginable.

Zavien kneeled by the pinned warrior, fighting back the aching need in his throat and gums to taste the blood of the fallen. Irregular and weak, a single heartbeat rattled in Drayus's chest. One of his hearts had shut down, likely flooded by internal haemorrhaging or burst by the wreckage piercing his body. The other pounded gamely, utterly without rhythm.

'Varlon is dead,' Zavien said.

'I can see that, fool.' The sergeant reached up one hand, the one not half-severed at the forearm, and clawed with unmoving fingers at the collar joint beneath his helm. Zavien reached to help, unlocking the helmet's pressurised seals. With a reptilian hiss, the helmet came free in Zavien's hands.

Drayus's craggy face, ruined by the pits and scars earned in two centuries of battle, was awash in spatters of blood. He grinned, showing blood-pinked teeth and split gums. 'My helm display is damaged. Tell me who is still alive.'

Zavien could see why it was damaged – both eye lenses were cracked. He discarded the sergeant's helm, and blink-clicked the runic icon that brought up the rest of the squad's life signs on his own retinal display.

Varlon was dead, his suit powered down. The evidence of that was right before Zavien's eyes.

Garax was also gone, his suit transmitting a screed of flat-line charts. The rangefinder listed him as no more than twenty metres away, likely thrown clear in the crash and killed on impact.

Drayus was dying, right here.

Jarl was…

'Where's Jarl?' Zavien asked, his voice harsh and guttural through his helm's vox speakers.

'He's loose.' Drayus sucked in a breath through clenched teeth. His armour's failing systems were feeding anaesthetic narcotics into his blood, but the wounds were savage and fatal.

'My rangefinder lists him as a kilometre distant.' Even with its unreliability compared to a tracking auspex, it was a decent enough figure to trust.

The sergeant's good hand clenched Zavien's wrist, and he glared into his brother's eye lenses with a fierce, bloodshot stare. 'Find him. Whatever it takes, Zavien. Bring him in, even if you have to kill him.'

'It will be done.'

'After. You must come back, after.' Drayus spat onto his own chest, marking the broken Imperial eagle with his lifeblood. 'Come back for our gene-seed.'

Zavien nodded, rising to his feet. Feeling his fingers curl in the need to draw weapons, he stalked from the cockpit without a backward glance at the sergeant he would never see alive again.

*Jarl had awoken first.*

*In fact, it was truer to say that Jarl had simply not lost his grip on consciousness in the impact, for his restraints bound him with greater security than the standard troop-thrones. In the shaking thunder of the crash, he had seen Garax hurled through the torn space where a wall had been a moment before. He had heard the vicious, wet snap of destroyed vertebrae and ruined bone as Garax had crashed into the edge of the hole on the way out. And he had seen Zavien thrown from his restraint throne to smash sidelong into the cockpit bulkhead, sliding to the floor unconscious.*

*Enveloped in a force cage around his own restraint throne, Jarl had seen these things occurring through the milky shimmer-screen of electrical force, yet had been protected against the worst of the crash.*

*Ah, but that protection had not lasted for long. With the gunship motion-less, with his brothers silent, with the Thunderhawk around him creaking and burning in the chasm it had carved in the ground, Jarl tore off the last buckles and scrambled over the wreckage of what had been his power-fielded throne. The machine itself, its generator smoking, reeked of captivity. Jarl wanted to be far from it.*

*He glanced at Zavien, stole the closest weapons he could find in the chaos of the crash site, and ran out into the jungle.*

*He had a duty to fulfil. A duty to the Emperor.*

*His father.*

Zavien's blade and bolter were gone.

Without compunction, he took Drayus's weapons from the small arming chamber behind the transport room, handling the relics with none of the care he would otherwise have used. Time was of the essence.

The necessary theft complete, he climbed from the wreck of the gun-ship, vaulting down to the ground and leaving the broken hull behind. In one hand was an idling chainaxe, the motors within the haft chuck-ling darkly in readiness to be triggered into roaring life. In the other, a bolt pistol, its blackened surface detailed with the crude scratchings of a hundred and more kill-runes.

Zavien didn't look at the smoking corpse of his gunship in some poignant reverie. He knew he would be back to gather the gene-seed of the fallen if he survived this hunt.

There was no time for sentiment. Jarl was loose.

Zavien broke into a run, his armour's joints growling at the rapid movement as he sprinted after his wayward brother, deep into the jungles of Armageddon.

### III

They call it Armageddon.

Maybe so. There is nothing to love about this planet.

Whatever savage beauty it once displayed is long dead now, choked under the relentless outflow of the sky-choking factories that vomit black smog into the heavens. The skies themselves are ugly enough – a greyish-yellow shroud of weak poison embracing the strangled world below. It does not rain water here. It rains acid, as thin, weak and strangely pungent as a reptile's piss.

Who could dwell here? In such impurity? The air tastes of sulphur and machine oil. The sky is the colour of infection. The humans – the very souls we are fighting to save – are dead-eyed creatures without passion or life.

I do not understand them. They embrace their enslavement. They accept their confinement within towering manufactories filled with howling machines. Perhaps it is because they have never known freedom, but that is no true excuse to act as brain-killed as a servitor.

We fight for these souls because we are told it is our duty. We are dying, selling our lives in the greatest war this world has ever known, to save them from their own weakness and allow them to return to their lightless lives.

The jungle here... We have jungles on my home world, yet not like this.

The jungles of home are saturated with life. Parasites thrive in every pool of dark water. Insects hollow out the great trees to build their chittering, poisonous hives. The air, already swarming with stinging flies, is sour with the reptilian stench of danger, and the ground will shake with the stalking hunts of the lizard predator-kings.

Survival is the greatest triumph one can earn on Cretacia.

The jungle here barely deserves the name. The ground is clinging mud, leaving you knee-deep in sulphuric sludge. What ragged life breathes the unclean air is weak, irritating, and nothing compared to the threats of home.

Of course, the jungles here possess a danger not even remotely native to the planet itself. They swarm with the worst kind of vermin.

With the planet locked in the throes of invasion, I am all too aware of what brought down our Thunderhawk.

*A pack of them hunted up ahead.*

*As soon as he heard their piggish snarls and barking laughter, Jarl's tongue ached with a raw, coppery urgency. His teeth itched in their sockets, and he felt his heartbeat in the soft tissue around his incisors.*

*His splashing sprint through the jungle became a hunched and feral stride, while the chainblade in his grip growled each time he gunned the trigger. Small arms fire rattled in his direction even before he cleared the line of trees. They knew he was coming, he made sure of that.*

*Jarl ignored the metallic rainfall of solid rounds clanging from his war plate. The trees parted and revealed his prey – six of them – hunkered around a tank made of scavenged, rusted scrap.*

*Greenskins. Their fat-mouthed pistols crashing loud and discordant, their brutish features illuminated by the flickering of muzzle flashes.*

*Jarl saw none of this. His vision, filtered through targeting reticules, saw only what his dying mind projected. A far greater enemy, the ancient slaves of the Ruinous Powers, feasting on the bodies of the loyal fallen. Where Jarl ran, the skies were not the milky-yellow of pus, but the deep blue of nightfall on ancestral Terra. He did not splash through black-watered marshland. He strode across battlements of gold while the world ended around him in a storm of heretical fire.*

*Jarl charged, his scream rendered harsh and deafening by his helm's vocalisers. The chainsword's throaty roar reached an apex in the moment before it was brought down onto the shoulder of the first ork.*

*The killing fury brought darkness again, but the blackness now was awash with blessed, sacred red.*

Zavien heard the slaughter. His pace, already at a breakneck sprint through the vegetation, intensified tenfold.

If he could catch Jarl, catch him before his brother made it to Imperial lines, he would avert a catastrophe of innocent blood and the blackest shame.

His red and black war plate – the dark red of arterial blood, the black of the void between worlds – was a ruined mess of burn markings, silver gougings where damage in the crash had scored away the paint from the ceramite's surface, and mud-spattered filth as he raced through the swamp.

Yet when one carries the pride of a Chapter on one's shoulders, necessity lends strength to aching limbs and the false muscles of broken armour.

Zavien burst into the clearing where his brother was embattled. His trigger fingers clenched at once – one unleashing a torrent of bolter shells at his brother's back, the other gunning the chainaxe into whirring, lethal life.

'Jarl!'

*Treachery.*

*What madness was this? To be struck down by one's own sons? Sanguinius, the Angel of Blood, turns from the twisted daemons he has slain and dismembered. One of his own sons screams his name, charging across the golden battlements while the heavens above them burn.*

*The primarch cries out as his son's weapon speaks in anger. Bolt shells crack against his magnificent armour. His own son, one of his beloved Blood Angels, is trying to kill him.*

*This cannot be happening.*

*And, in that moment, Sanguinius decides it is not. There is heresy at work here, not disloyalty. Blasphemy, not naked betrayal.*

*'What foulness grips you!' the Angel cries at his false son. 'What perversion blackens the soul of a Blood Angel and warps him to serve the Archenemy?'*

*'Sanguinius!' the traitor son screams. 'Father!'*

Zavien roared Jarl's name again, not knowing what his brother truly heard. The cries that returned from his brother's vox-amplifiers chilled his blood – a bellowed, clashing litany of archaic High Gothic and the tongue of Baal that Jarl had never learned.

Surrounded by the ravaged bodies of dead greenskins, the two brothers came together. Zavien's first blow was blocked, the flat of Jarl's chainblade clashing against the haft of his axe. Jarl's armour was pitted and cracked with smoking holes from the impact of bolt shells, yet his strength was unbelievable. Laughing in a voice barely his own, he hurled Zavien backwards.

Unbalanced by his brother's insane vigour, Zavien fell back, rolling into a fighting crouch, shin-deep in marshwater.

Again, Jarl shouted in his unnerving, ancient diction – words Zavien recognised but did not understand. As with Jarl, he had never learned Baalian, and never studied the form of High Gothic spoken ten thousand years before.

*'Let this not be your end, my son. Join me! We will take the fight to Horus and drown his evil ambitions in the blood of his tainted warriors!'*

*Sanguinius removes his helm – a sign of honour and trust despite the war raging around them – and smiles beneficently at his wayward son. His benevolence is legendary. His honour without question.*

*'It need not be this way,' the Angel of Blood says through his princely smile. 'Join me! To my father's side! For the Emperor!'*

Zavien stared at his brother, barely recognising Jarl's face in the drooling, slack-jawed grin that met his gaze. His brother's features were red; a shining wetness from eyes that cried blood.

A meaningless screed of syllables hammered from Jarl's bleeding mouth. It sounded like he was choking on his own demented laughter.

'Brother,' Zavien spoke softly. 'You are gone from us all.'

He rose to his feet, casting aside the empty bolt pistol. In his red gauntlets, he clutched the chainaxe two-handed, and stared at the brother he no longer knew.

'I am not your son, Jarl, and I am no longer your brother. I am Zavien of the Flesh Tearers, born of Cretacia, and I will be your death if you will not let me be your salvation.'

Jarl heaved a burbling laugh, bringing bloody froth to his lips as he wheezed in a language he shouldn't know.

*'You disgrace my bloodline,' the Angel said with infinite sorrow, his godlike heart breaking at the blasphemy before his eyes. 'The Ultimate Gate calls to me. A thousand of your masters will fall by my blade before they gain entrance to the Emperor's throne room. I have no more patience for your puling heresy. Come, traitor. Time to die.'*

*Sanguinius unfurled his great white wings, pearlescent and sunlight-bright in the firestorm wreathing the battlements. With tears in his eyes, tears of misery at the betrayal of one of his own sons, he launched forward to end this blasphemy once and for all.*

And I realise I cannot beat him.

When we are shaped into what we are, when we are denied our humanity to become weapons of war, it is said that fear is purged from our physical forms, and triumph is bred into our bones. This is an expression, an attempt at the kind of crude verse forever attributed to the warrior-preachers of the Adeptus Astartes.

It is true that defeat is anathema to us.

But I cannot beat him. He is not the warrior I trained with for decades, not the brother whose every move I can anticipate.

His chainblade, still wet with green gore, arcs down. I block, barely, and am already skidding back in the sulphuric mud. His strength is immense. I know why this is. I am aware of the… the genetic truths at play. His mind cannot contain his delusional fury. He is using everything he has, *everything*, powering his muscles with more force and expending more energy than a functioning mind can allow. I can smell the alkaline reek of his blood through the damage in his armour – combat narcotics are flooding his system in lethal quantities. In his madness, he cannot stem the flood of battle narcotics fusing with his bloodstream.

His strength, this godly power, will kill him.

But not quickly enough.

A second deflected slice, a third, and a fourth that crashes against my helm; a blocked headbutt that crunches into my bracer and dulls my arm; a kick that hammers into my chestplate even as I lean aside to dodge.

A thunderclap. My vision spins. Fire in my spine.

I think my back is broken. I try to say his name, but it comes out as a scream.

Rage, black and wholesome, its tendrils bearing the purest intent, creeps in at the edge of my vision.

I hear him laughing and damning me in a language he shouldn't know.

Then I hear nothing except the wind.

*Sanguinius lifts the traitor with contemptuous ease.*

*Held above his head, the blasphemer thrashes and writhes. The Angel of Blood stalks to the edge of the golden battlements, laughing and weeping all at once at the carnage below. It is a tragedy, but it is also beautiful. Mankind using its greatest might and achievements as it attempts to engineer its own demise. Titans duel in their hundreds, with millions of men dying around their iron feet. The sky is on fire. The entire world smells of blood.*

*'Die,' the Angel curses his treacherous son with a beauteous whisper, and hurls him from the battlements of the Imperial Palace into the maelstrom of war hundreds of metres below.*

*Freed of his burden and his bloodline's honour restored, the Angel in gold makes haste away.*

*His duty is not yet done.*

\* \* \*

## IV

Consciousness returned with the first impact.

A jarring crunch of armour against rock jolted Zavien from his lapse into the murky haze of near-unconsciousness. Feeling himself crashing down the cliff side, he rammed his hand down hard into the rock – a claw of ceramite clutching at the stone. The Astartes grunted as his arms snapped straight, taking his weight, arresting his tumbling fall.

Damage runes flicked up on his retinal display, a language of harsh white urgency. Zavien ignored them, though it was harder to ignore the pain throughout his body. Even the injected chemical anaesthetic compounds from his armour and the nerve-dulling surgery done to him couldn't entirely wash it away. That was a bad sign.

He clawed his way back up the cliff, teeth clenched, gauntlets tearing handholds into the stone where nature hadn't provided any.

Once at the top, the Flesh Tearer retrieved the chainaxe that had flown from his grip, and broke into a staggering run.

He almost killed me.

That is a hard truth to swallow, for we were evenly matched for all of our lives. My armour is damaged, operating at half capacity, but it still lends me strength as I run. Behind me, the wrecked greenskin tank remains alone, its crew slain, the rest of its missiles aiming into the sky with no one to fire them.

Curse those piggish wretches for bringing down our gunship.

I run on, gathering speed, slowing only to hack hanging vegetation from my path.

I recall the topography of this region from the hololithic maps at the last war council. The mining town of Dryfield is to the east. Jarl's rage-addled mind will drive him to seek out life. I know where he is going. I also know that unless something slows him down…

He will get there first.

Sister Amalay D'Vorien kissed the bronze likeness of Saint Silvana, and let the necklace icon fall back on its leather cord. The weak midday sun, what brightness penetrated the gauzy, polluted cloud cover, was a dull presence in the heavens, only occasionally reflecting glare off the edges of *Promethia*, the squad's Immolator tank.

Her own armour was once silver, now stained a faint, dull grey from exposure to the filthy air of this world. She licked her cracked lips, resisting the desire to drink from the water canteen inside the tank. Second Prayer was only an hour before, and she'd slaked her thirst with a mouthful of the brackish water, warmed as it was by the tank's idling engine.

'Sister…' called down Brialla from the Immolator's turret. 'Did you see that?'

Amalay and Brialla were alone while the rest of their squad patrolled the edges of the jungle. Their tank idled on the dirt road, with Amalay circling the hull, bolter in hand, and Brialla panning her heavy flamers along the tree lines.

Amalay whispered a litany of abasement before duty, chastising herself for letting her mind wander to thoughts of sustenance. Her bolter up and ready, she moved around to the front of the Immolator.

'I saw nothing,' she said, eyes narrowed and focused. 'What was it?'

'Movement. Something dark. Remain vigilant.'

There was a tone colouring Brialla's voice, on the final words. A suggestion of disapproval. Amalay's laxity had been noticed.

'I see nothing,' Amalay spoke again. 'There's… No, wait. *There.*'

The 'something' broke from its crouch in the vegetation at the tree line. A blur of crimson and black, with a chainblade revving. Amalay recognised an Astartes instantly, and the threat a moment later. Her bolter barked once, twice, and dropped from her hands to clatter to the dirt. The gun crashed once more from its vantage point on the ground, a loud boom that hammered a shell into the tank's sloped armour plating.

Even as this last shot was fired, Amalay's head flew clear of her shoulders, white hair catching the wind before the bleeding wreckage rolled into the undergrowth.

Brialla blasphemed as she brought the flamer turret around on protesting mechanics, and wrenched the handles to aim the cannons low.

The Astartes was cradling Amalay's headless body, speaking to it in a low snarl. Her sister was already dead. Brialla squeezed both triggers.

Twin gouts of stinking chemical flame roared from the cannons, bathing Amalay and the Astartes in clinging, corrosive fire. She was already whispering a lament for her fallen sister, even as she blistered the armour and skin from Amalay's bones.

It was impossible to see through the reeking orange miasma. Brialla killed the jets of flame after seven heartbeats, knowing whatever had been washed in the fire would be annihilated, purged in the burning storm.

Amalay. Her armour blackened, its joints melted, her hands reduced to blackened bone. She lay on the ground, incinerated.

A loud thud clanged on the tank's roof behind Brialla. She turned in her restraint throne, the slower turret cycling round to follow her gaze. Already, she was trying to scramble free of her seat.

The Astartes was burning. Holy fire licked at the edges of his war plate, and his joints steamed. He eclipsed the sun, casting a flickering shadow over her. His armour was black, charred, but not immolated. As she hauled herself out of her restraints, he levelled a dripping chainsword at her face.

'The Flesh Tearers!' she screamed into the vox-mic built into her armour's collar. 'Echoes of Gaius Point!'

In anciently-accented Gothic, her killer said six whispered words.
*'You will pay for your heresy.'*

I watch from the shadows of the trees.

The Sororitas are tense. While one of them performs funerary rites over the destroyed bodies of their sisters, three others stalk around the hull of their grey tank, bolters aimed while they stare into the jungle through gunsights.

I can smell the corpses beneath the white shrouds. One is burned, cooked by promethium chemical fire. The other had bled a great deal before she died, torn to pieces. I do not need to see the remains to know this is true.

For now, I hide, crouched and hidden. The jungle masks the ever-present charged hum of my armour from their weak, mortal ears, while I listen to fragments of their speech.

Jarl's trail has grown cold, even the smell of his potent blood lost in the billion scents of this sulphuric jungle. I need focus. I need direction.

But as soon as I draw near enough to see the sisters' steel-grey armour and the insignias of loyalty they each wear, I curse my fortune.

The Order of the Argent Shroud.

They were with us at Gaius Point.

Echoes of that battle will haunt us all until the Chapter's final nights.

'My auspex senses something,' I hear one of them say to her sisters. I make ready to move again, to taste shame and flee. I cannot confront them like this. They must not know of our presence. 'Something alive,' she says. 'And with a power signature.'

'Flesh Tearer!' one of the sisters calls out, and my blood freezes in my veins. It is not fear I feel, but true, sickening dread as she uses our Chapter's sacred name. *How can they know?*

'Flesh Tearer! Show yourself! Face the Emperor's judgement for the barbarity of your tainted Chapter!'

My teeth clench. My fingers quiver, then grip the chainaxe tighter. *They know.* They know a Flesh Tearer did this. Their wretched slain sisters must have warned them.

Another female voice, the one carrying the auspex scanner, adds to the first one's cries. 'We were at Gaius Point, decadent filth! Face us, and face retribution for your heresy!'

They know what happened at Gaius Point. They saw our shame, our curse, and the blood that ran that day.

They believe I butchered two of their sisters here, and now lay the sins of my brother Jarl upon my shoulders.

Gunfire rings out. A bolter shell slices past my pauldron, shredding vegetation.

'I see him,' a female voice declares, 'There!'

My trigger finger strokes the Engage rune on the chainaxe's haft. After a heartbeat's hesitation, I squeeze. Jagged, whirring teeth cycle into furious life. The weapon cuts air in anticipation of the moment it will eat flesh.

They *dare* to blame me for this…

They open fire.

I am not a heretic.

But this must end.

## V

Zavien reached Dryfield just as the sun was setting.

He had left the jungle behind three hours before. The lone warrior's run came to an end at the fortified walls – outside the mining settlement, he heard no sound from within, only the desperate howl of the wind across the wasteland.

Hailing the walls, calling for sentries, earned him no response.

The settlement's gates were sealed: a jury-rigged amalgamation of steel bars, flakboard and even furniture piled high behind the double doors in the wall ringing the village. These pitiful defences were the colony's attempts to reinforce their walls against the ork hordes sweeping across the planet.

With neither the time nor the inclination to hammer the gates open through force, Zavien mag-locked his axe to his back and punched handholds in the metal wall itself, dragging himself to the ramparts fifteen metres above.

The village was a collection of one-storey buildings, perhaps enough to house fifteen families. A dirt track cut through the village's centre like an old scar; evidence of the supply convoys that made it this far out from the main hives, and the passage of ore haulers who came to profit from the local copper mine. Low-quality metal would be in great demand by the planet's impoverished citizens, who could afford no better.

The largest building – indeed, the only one that was more than a hut made from scrap – was a spired church bedecked in crudely-carved gargoyles.

Zavien acknowledged all of this in a heartbeat's span. The Astartes scanned the ramshackle battlements around the village, then turned to stare at the settlement itself.

No sign of movement.

He walked from the platform, falling the fifteen metres to the ground and landing in a balanced crouch.

He came across the first body less than a minute later.

A woman. Unarmed. Slumped against the wall of a hovel, a bloodsmear decorating the wall behind her. She was carved in half, and not cleanly.

The wide streets between the ramshackle huts and homes were decorated with trails of blood and the tracks of weight dragged through the dirt. All of these led to the same place. Whomever had come here and slain the colonists had dragged the bodies to the modest church with its shattered windows and corroded walls of flakboard and red iron.

Zavien's retinal locator display was finally picking up faint returns from Jarl's war plate. His brother was inside, no longer running. And from the silence, no longer killing.

The Flesh Tearer stalked past the weaponless corpse, limp in its lifeless repose, slain by his own sword in his brother's hands. Zavien had seen such things before – they were images he would never forget while he still drew breath.

He felt cold, clinging shame run through his blood like a toxin. Just like at Gaius Point.

It wasn't supposed to happen.

At Gaius Point.

It was never supposed to happen.

That night, they had damned themselves forever.

It should have been a triumph worthy of being etched onto the armour of every warrior that fought there.

The Imperial front line was held by the Point's militia and the Order of the Argent Shroud, who had rallied the people of the wasteland town into an armed fighting force and raised morale to fever pitch through their sermons and blessings in the name of the God-Emperor.

The greenskins descended in a swarm of thousands, hurling themselves at the town's barricades, their mass forming a sea of bellowing challenges, leathery flesh and hacking blades.

At the battle's apex, the Sisters and the militia were on the edge of being overwhelmed. At last, and when it mattered most, Gaius Point's frantic distress calls were answered.

They came in Thunderhawks, boosters howling as they soared over the embattled horde. The gunships kissed the scorched earth only long enough to deploy their forces: almost two hundred Astartes in armour of arterial red and charcoal black. The rattling roar of so many chainblades came together in a ragged, ear splitting chorus, sounding like the war-cry of a mechanical god.

Zavien was in the first wave. Alongside Jarl and his brothers, he hewed left and right, his blade's grinding teeth chewing through armour and bloody, fungal flesh as the sons of Sanguinius reaped the aliens' lives.

The orks were butchered in droves, caught between a hammer and anvil, being annihilated from behind and gunned down from the front.

Zavien saw nothing but blood. Xenos blood, stinking and thick, splashing across his helm. The smell of triumph, the reek of exultant victory.

He was also one of the first to the barricades.

By then, he couldn't see. He couldn't think. His senses were flooded by stimuli, all of it aching, enticing and maddening. He tried to speak, but it tore from his lips as a cry aimed at the polluted skies. Even breathing did nothing but draw the rich scent of alien blood deeper into his body, disseminating it through his system. To be so saturated by xenos taint ignited a fire in his mind, tapping into the gene-deep fury that forever threatened to overwhelm him.

Driven on by the ceaseless urge to drown his senses in the purity of enemy blood, Zavien disembowelled the last ork before him, and vaulted the barricade. He had to kill. *He had to kill.* He was born for nothing else.

He and his brothers had been fighting in ferocious hand-to-hand battle for two hours. The enemy was destroyed. The joyous cheers of the militia died in thousands of throats as, in a wave of vox-screams and howling chainswords, half of the Flesh Tearers broke the barricades and ran into the town.

With no foes left to slay, the Astartes turned their rage upon whatever still lived.

*The Angel mourned the slain.*

*Their deaths were a dark necessity on the path to redemption. The prayers he chanted to the ceiling of the Emperor's throne room inspired tears in his eyes, and tears in the eyes of the thousands of loyal soldiers staring on.*

*'We must burn the slain,' he whispered through the silver tears. 'We must forever remember those who died this day, and remember the foulness that turned their hearts against us.'*

*'Sanguinius!' a voice cried from behind. It echoed throughout the chamber, where a million banners hung in the breezeless air, marking every regiment ever sworn to fight and die for the young Imperium of Man.*

*The Angel tilted his head, the very image of patient purity.*

*'I thought I killed you, heretic.'*

'Jarl!'

Wheezing, mumbling, with bloody saliva running in strings from his damaged mouth grille, Jarl staggered around to face his brother.

What burbled from his mouth was a mixture of languages, wet with the blood in his throat. The chemical reek of Jarl's body assaulted Zavien's senses even over the smell of his brother's burned armour and the reek of the slain. The combat narcotics flooding Jarl's body were eating him alive.

Zavien did nothing but stare for several moments after he called his brother's name. The dead were everywhere, piled all across the floor of the church, a slumbering congregation of the slaughtered. Perhaps a hundred of them, all dragged here after the carnage. Perhaps many of them had been found here in worshipful service, and only half the village had needed to be dragged. Trails of streaked, smeared blood marked the floor.

'Burn the bodies,' Jarl said in grunted Cretacian, the tongue of their shared home world, amongst a screed of words Zavien couldn't make out. 'Purge the sin, burn the bodies, cleanse the palace.'

Zavien raised his chainaxe. In sickening mirror image, his blood-maddened brother raised his dripping chainsword.

'This ends now, Jarl.'

There was a bark of syllables, a drooling mess of annihilated words.

*The Angel raised his golden blade.*

*He had been so foolish. This was no mere heretic. Had he been blinded all along? Yes… the machinations of the tainted traitors had shrouded his golden eyes from the truth. But now… Now he saw everything.*

*'Yes, Horus,' he said with a smile that spoke of infinite regret. 'It ends now.'*

## VI

The brothers met in the defiled church, their boots struggling to grip the mosaic-laid floor, awash as it was with innocent blood. The whining roar of chainblades was punctuated by crashes as the weapons met. Jagged teeth shattered with every block and parry, clattering against nearby wooden pews as they were torn from their sockets.

Zavien's blood hammered through his body, tingling with the electric edge of combat stimulants. Jarl was a shadow of the warrior he had been – frothing at the mouth, raving at allies that didn't exist, and half-crippled by the lethal battle-drug overdose that was burning out his organs.

Zavien blocked his brother's frantic, shaking cuts. Every time his axe fell, he'd carve another chasm into Jarl's armour. Ultimately, only one warrior was aware enough to know this would never be settled by chainblades.

With a last block and a savage return, Zavien smashed Jarl's blade aside and kicked it from his grip. Its engine stuttered to a halt, resting on the tiled ground. Jarl watched it fly from his grip with delayed, bleeding vision.

Before he could recover, Zavien's hands were at his throat. The Flesh Tearer squeezed, his hands crunching into Jarl's neck, collapsing the softer joint-armour there and vicing into the flesh beneath.

Jarl fell to his knees as his brother strangled him. His genhanced physiology was poisoned by both the curse and the narcotics, and his sight began to darken as his body could take no more punishment.

Darken, yet clear.

Deprived of air, unable to even draw a shred of breath, he mouthed a voiceless word that never left the confines of his charred helm.

*'Zavien.'*

Zavien wrenched his grip to the side, snapping the bones of his brother's spine, and still strangling.

He stood like this for some time. Night had fallen before the warrior's gauntlets released their burden and Jarl's body finally slumped to the ground.

There the madman rested, asleep among those he had slain.

'It is done,' Zavien spoke into his squad's vox channel, his eyes closed as only silence replied.

'Jarl is dead, brothers. It is done.'

He chose to finish what his brother had begun. Even in madness, there sometimes hides a little sense.

The bodies had to be burned. Not to purify any imagined heresy, but to hide the evidence of what had happened here.

It was never supposed to happen. Here, or at Gaius Point. They had damned themselves, and all that remained was to fight as loyally as they could before righteous vengeance caught up with them all.

As the church burned, pouring thick black smoke into the polluted sky, the sound of engines grumbled from the horizon.

Orks. The enemy was finally here.

Zavien stood among the flames, immune to them, his axe in his hand. The fire would draw the aliens closer. There was no way he could defend the whole village against them, but the thought of shedding and tasting their blood before he finally fell ignited his killing urge.

His fangs ached as the vehicles pulled in to a halt outside.

No.

Those engine sounds were too clean, too well-maintained. It was the enemy. But it was not the greenskins.

I walk from the church, the broken axe in my hand.

There are twenty of them. In human unison, impressive enough even if it lacks the perfection of Astartes unity, they raise their bolters. The Sisters of the Order of the Argent Shroud. The silver hulls of their tanks and their own armour are turned a flickering orange-red in the light of the fire that should have hidden our sins.

Twenty guns aim at me.

The thirst fades. My hunger to taste blood trickles back into my throat, suddenly ignorable.

'We were at Gaius Point,' the lead sister calls out. Their eyes are narrowed at the brightness of the flame behind me.

I do not move. I tell them, simply:

'I know.'

'We have petitioned the Inquisition for your Chapter's destruction, Flesh Tearer.'

'I know.'

'That is all you have to say for yourself, heretic? After Gaius Point? After killing the squad of our sister Amalay D'Vorien? *After massacring an entire village?*'

'You came to pass judgement,' I tell her. 'So do it.'

'We came to defend this colony against your wretched blasphemy!'

They still fear me. Even outnumbered and armed only with a shattered axe, they still fear me. I can smell it in their sweat, hear it in their voices, and see it in their wide eyes that reflect the flames.

I look over my shoulder, where Jarl's legacy burns. Motes of amber fire sail up from the blaze. My brother's funeral pyre, and a testament to what we have all become. A monument to how far we have fallen.

We burn our dead on Cretacia. Because so many are killed by poisons and beasts and the predator-king reptiles, it is a mark of honour to die and be burned, rather than be taken by the forest.

It was never meant to be like this. Not here, and not at Gaius Point.

Twenty bolters open fire before I can look back.

I don't hear them. I don't feel the wet, knifing pain of destruction.

All I hear is the roar of a Cretacian predator-king, the fury rising from its reptilian jaws as it stalks the jungles of my home world. A carnosaur, black-scaled and huge, roaring up to the clear, clean skies.

It hunts me. It hunts me now, as it hunted me so long ago, at the start of this second life.

I reach for my spear, and…

*Zavien clutches the weapon against his chest.*

*'It is death itself,' he grunts to his tribal brothers as they crouch in the undergrowth. The tongue of Cretacia is simple and plain, little more than the rudiments of true language. 'The king-lizard is death itself. It comes for us.'*

*The carnosaur shakes the ground with another slow step closer. It breathes in short sniffs, mouth open, jaws slack, tasting the air for scents. A grey tongue the size of a man quivers in its maw.*

*The spear in his steady grip is the one he made himself. A long shaft of dark wood with a fire-blackened point. He has used it for three years now, since his tenth winter, to hunt for his tribe.*

*He does not hunt for his tribe today. Today, as the sun burns down and bakes their backs, he hunts because the gods are in the jungle, and they are watching. The tribes have seen the gods in their armour of red metal and black stone, always in the shadows, watching the hunting parties as they stalk their prey.*

*If a hunter wishes to dwell in paradise among the stars, he must hunt well when the gods walk the jungles.*

*Zavien stares at the towering lizard-beast, unable to look away from its watery, slitted red eye.*

*He shifts his grip on the spear he crafted.*

*With a prayer that the gods are bearing witness to his courage, he throws the weapon with a heartfelt scream.*

The Flesh Tearer crashed to the bloodstained ground, face down in the dust.

'Cease fire,' Sister Superior Mercy Astaran said softly. Her sisters obeyed immediately.

'But he still lives,' one of them replied.

This was true. The warrior was dragging himself with gut-wrenching slowness, one-armed and with a trembling hand, through the dirt. A dark trail of broken armour and leaking lifeblood pooled around him.

He raised his shaking hand once more, dug the spasming fingers into the ground, and dragged himself another half-metre closer to the burning church's front door.

'Is he seeking to escape?' one of the youngest sisters asked, unwilling to admit her admiration for the heretic's endurance. One arm lost at the elbow, both legs destroyed from the knees down, and his armour a cracked mess that leaked coolant fluids and rich, red Astartes blood.

'It is hardly escape to crawl into a burning building,' another laughed.

'He wishes to die among the blasphemy he caused,' Astaran said, her scowl even harsher in the firelight. 'End him.'

A single gunshot rang out from the battle-line.

Zavien's fingers stopped trembling. His reaching hand fell into the dust. His eyes, which had first opened to see the clear skies of a distant world, closed at last.

'What should we do with the body?' Sister Mercy Astaran asked her commander.

'Let the echoes of this heresy remain as an example, at least until the greenskins take control of the surrounding wastelands. Come sisters, we do not have much time. Leave this wretch for the vultures.'

# VICTORIES OF THE
# SPACE MARINES

# RUNES

*by Chris Wraight*

Baldr Svelok slammed hard into the acid-laced rock. His plate crunched against the stone, sending warning runes flashing across his helm-feed. Instinct told him another blow was coming in fast, and the Wolf Guard ducked. A massive tight-balled fist tore into the rock where his head had been, showering him with shards where the impact had obliterated the cliff.

Svelok dodged the next crashing fist, his augmented limbs moving with preternatural speed. He almost made it, but the monster's talons raked down across his right shoulder-guard, sending him sprawling to the ground and skidding across pools of acid. He landed with a heavy crack, and something snapped across his barrel chest boneplate. He felt blood in his mouth, and his head jerked back from the impact.

Throne, he was being taken apart. That did *not* happen.

He spun onto his back, ignoring the heavy crunch as the creature's clawed foot stamped down just millimetres from his arm. It towered into the storm-wracked sky, a living wall of obsidian, five metres high and crowned with dark, curving spikes. Lightning reflected from the facets of its organic armour, glinting off the slick ebony. Somewhere in the whirl of jagged, serrated limbs was a monotasking mind, a basic alien intelligence filled with an urge to protect its territory and drive the infiltrating humans back into space.

Svelok had never seen a xenos like it. The closest he could get was a creature of demi-myth on Fenris, the Grendel, but these bastards were encased in plates of rock and had talons like lightning claws.

'You all die the same way,' he growled. His voice was a jagged-edged rasp, scraped into savagery by old throat wounds. He sounded as terrifying as he looked.

The storm bolter screamed out a juddering stream of mass-reactive bolts, sending ice-white impact flares across the creature's armoured hide. It staggered, rocking back on its heels, clutching at the hail of rounds as if trying to pluck them from the air. The torrent was relentless, perfectly aimed and deadly.

The magazine clicked empty. Boosted by his armour-servos, Svelok leapt to his feet, mag-locked the bolter and grabbed a krak grenade.

Amazingly, the leviathan still stood. It was reeling now, its hide cracked and driven in by the barrage of bolter fire, but some spark of defiance within it hadn't died. A jagged maw, black as Morkai's pelt, cracked open, revealing teeth like a row of stalactites. It lurched back into the attack, talons outstretched.

Whip-fast, Svelok hurled the grenade through the open mouth. The massive jaws snapped shut in reflex and the Space Wolf crouched down against the oncoming blast. There was a muffled boom and the xenos was blown apart, its iron-hard shell smashed open and spread out like a splayed ribcage. The behemoth crumbled in a storm of shards, toppled, and was gone.

'Feel the wrath of Russ, filth!' roared Svelok, leaping back to his feet, fangs bared inside his helmet. He seized a fresh magazine, spun round and slammed the rounds into the storm bolter's chamber. There'd been three of them, massive stalking beasts carved from the stone around them, horrors of black, tortured rock bigger than a Dreadnought.

Now there were none. Rune Priest Ravenblade loomed over the smoking remains of the largest, his runestaff thrumming with angry, spitting witchfire. Lokjr and Varek had taken out the third, though the Grey Hunters' armour was scarred and dented from the assault. The xenos monsters were tough as leviathan-hide.

'What in *Hel* are these things?' Lokjr spat over the comm, releasing the angry churn of his frostblade power axe.

'Scions of this world, brother,' replied Ravenblade coolly.

'Just find me more to kill,' growled Varek, reloading his bolter and sweeping the muzzle over the barren landscape.

Svelok snarled. His blood was up, pumping round his massive frame and filling his bunched muscles with the need for movement. The wolf-spirit was roused, and he could feel its feral power coiled round his hearts. He suppressed the kill-urge with difficulty. His irritation with Ravenblade was finding other outlets, and that was dangerous.

'How far, and how long?' he spat, flexing his gauntlet impatiently.

'Three kilometres south,' said Ravenblade, consulting the auspex. 'One hour left.'

'Then we go now,' ordered Svelok, combat-readiness flooding his body again. 'There'll be more xenos, and I still haven't seen one bleed.'

Kolja Ravenblade loped alongside the others, feeling his armoured boots thud against the unyielding rock. Gath Rimmon, the planetoid they'd been on for less than an hour, was a hellish maelstrom of acid-flecked storms. The sky was near-black, lit only by boiling electrical torment that scored the heavens with a tracery of silver fire. In every direction the landscape was dark and glossy, cut from unyielding rock and glinting dully in the flickering light. Acid pooled across the jagged edges, hissing and spitting as it splashed against the Astartes' armour. The four Space Wolves ran south through narrow defiles of jet, each worn down by millennia of erosion, each as pitiless and terrible as the ice-fields of Fenris in the heart of the Long Winter.

This world was angry. Angry with them, angry with itself. Somewhere, close by, Ravenblade could feel it. It was like the beat of a heart, sullen and deep. That was the sound that had drawn him here, echoing across the void, lodged in the psychic flesh of the universe. Something was hidden on Gath Rimmon, something that screamed of perversion.

And it was being guarded.

'Incoming!' bellowed Varek, halting suddenly and sending a volley of bolter fire into the air.

Ravenblade pulled out of his run and swept his staff from its mag-lock. His helm-display ran red with signals – they were coming from the sky. He spoke a single word and the shaft blazed with fluorescent power, flooding the land around.

Above them, dozens of creatures were flinging themselves from the high rock, talons of stone outstretched. They were carved from the same material as the planet, each of them crudely animated creatures of inorganic, immutable armour. Eight spindly legs curved down from angular abdomens, crowned with extended rigid plates for controlled gliding. At the end of the metre-long body, wide jaws gaped, lined with teeth of rending daggers. They plummeted towards the Space Marines soundlessly, like ghosts carved out of solid adamantium.

'Fell them!' ordered Svelok, his storm bolter spitting controlled bursts at the swooping xenos. The rounds all hit, sparking and exploding in showers of shattered rock. The Wolf Guard made killing look simple. A shame, thought Ravenblade, that he had no time for anything else.

Varek's bolter joined in the chorus of destruction, but some xenos still got through, wheeling down and twisting through the corridors of fire.

For those that made it, Lokjr waited. The massive warrior, his armour draped in the pelt of a white bear and hung with the skulls of a dozen kills, spun arcs of death with the whirring blade of his frost axe.

'For the honour of Fenris!' he roared, slamming the monomolecular edge in wide loops, slicing through the glistening rock-hide and tearing the flyers apart as they reached him.

Watching the carnage unfold, Ravenblade grasped his staff in both hands, feeling the power of his calling well up within him. The wind spun faster around his body, coursing over the rune-wound armour. Acid flecks spat against his ancient vambraces, fizzing into vapour as raw aether rippled across steel-grey ceramite.

'In the name of the Allfather,' he whispered, feeling the dark wolf within him snarl into life. The runes on his plate blazed with witchlight, blood-red like the heart of a dying star. He raised the staff above his head, and the wind accelerated into a frenzied whine. A vortex opened, swirling and cascading above the four Space Marines, billowing into the tortured air above them.

'Unleash!'

A column of lightning blazed down from the skies. As it reached Ravenblade's outstretched staff it exploded into a corona of writhing, white-hot fire, lashing out from the Rune Priest in whip-fronds of dazzling brilliance.

The surviving flyers were blasted open, ripped into slivers by the leaping blades of lightning, crushed and flayed by the atomising power of the storm. The Rune Priest had spoken, and the creatures of Gath Rimmon had no answer to his elemental wrath.

As the last of them crunched to the ground, Ravenblade released the power from the staff. The skirling corona rippled out of existence and a shudder seemed to bloom through the air.

By contrast with the fury of the storm, the Rune Priest stood as still and calm as ever. Unlike his brothers, his pack-manner was stealthy. If he hadn't been picked out by Stormcaller, perhaps the path of the Lone Wolf would have called for him.

Kilometres above them, the natural storm growled unabated. The planet had been cowed, but remained angry.

'Russ damn you, priest,' rasped Svelok, crushing a fallen flyer beneath his boot and crunching the stone to rubble. His helm was carved in the shape of a black wolf's head, locked in a perpetual curling grimace. In the flickering light its fangs glistened like tears. 'You'll bring more to us.'

'Let them come!' shouted Varek, laughing harshly over the comm.

Svelok turned on him. The Wolf Guard was a hand's breadth taller and broader than the Grey Hunter, though the aura of his ever-present battle-lust made him twice as terrifying. His armour was pitted and studded with old scars, and they laced the surface like badges of honour. Rage was forever present with him, frothing under the surface. Ravenblade could sense it through the layers of battle-plate, pulsing like an exposed vein.

'Don't be a fool!' Svelok growled. 'There's no time for this.'

Ravenblade regarded the Wolf Guard coldly. Svelok was as angry as the planet, his hackles raised by a mission he saw no use or glory in, but he was right. Time was running out. They all knew the acid tide was racing towards them. In less than an hour the ravines would be filling up, and ceramite was no protection against those torrents.

'I'll be the judge of that, brother,' warned the Rune Priest. 'We're close.'

Svelok turned to face him, his bolter still poised for assault. For a moment, the two Space Wolves faced one another, saying nothing. Svelok had no patience with the scrying arts, and no faith in anything but his bolter. He had almost a century more experience on the battlefront than Ravenblade, and took orders from no one but his Wolf Lord and Grimnar. Handling him would be a test.

'We'd better be,' he snarled at last, his voice thick with disdain. 'Move out.'

Six kilometres to the north, Gath Rimmon's dark plains were deserted. The tearing wind scoured the stone, whipping up the acid that remained on it and sending curls of vapour twisting into the air.

In the centre of a vast, tumbled plateau of rock was a circular platform. Exposed to the atmosphere, it looked raw and out of place. Lightning flashed across the heavens, picking out the smooth edge of the aberration.

Suddenly, without any signal or warning, a crystalline pinprick began to spiral over the platform. It spun rapidly, picking up speed and flashing with increasing intensity. It moulded itself, forming into a tall oval twice the height of a man. At its edge, psychic energy coursed and crackled. The rain whipped through it, vaporising and bouncing from the perimeter.

Then there was a rip. The surface of the ellipse sheered away. One by one, figures emerged from the portal. Eight of them. As the last stepped lightly from the oval, the perimeter collapsed into nothingness, howling back into a single point of nullity.

The arrivals were man-shaped, though far slighter than humans, let alone Space Marines. Six were clad in dark green segmented armour. They carried a chainsword in one hand and a shuriken pistol in the other. Their closed-faced helmets were sleek and tapered, and all had twin blasters set into the jowls. They fell into position around the platform, their movements silent and efficient.

Their leader remained in the centre. He was arrayed in the same armour, though his right hand was enclosed in a powerclaw and the mark of his shrine had been emblazoned across his chest. He moved with a smooth, palpable menace.

Beside him stood a figure in a white mask carrying a two-handed force sword. The blade swam with pale fire, sending tendrils of glistening energy snaking towards the ground. He wore black armour lined with bone-coloured sigils and warding runes. Ruby spirit stones studded the surface, glowing angrily from the passage through the webway. He wore no robes of rank over his interlocking armour plates, but his calling was unmistakable. He was a psyker and a warrior. Humans, in their ignorance, called such figures warlocks, knowing little of what they spoke.

'You sense it, Valiel?' asked the claw-fisted warrior.

'South,' nodded the warlock. 'Be quick, exarch; the tides already approach.'

The exarch made a quick gesture with his chainsword, and the bodyguard clustered around him.

'Go fast,' he hissed. 'Go silent.'

As one, the eldar broke into a run, negotiating the treacherous terrain with cool agility. Like a train of ghosts, they slipped across the broken rocks, heading south.

Svelok felt battle-fury burning in his blood, filling his muscles and flooding his senses. He was a Space Wolf, a warrior of Fenris, and his one purpose was to kill. This chase, this *running*, was horrifying to him. Only the sanctity of his mission orders restrained him from turning and taking the wrath of Russ to every Grendel-clone on the planet. He knew the acid ocean was coming. He knew that the entire globe would soon be engulfed in boiling death. Even so, turning aside from the path of the hunt for the sake of a Rune Priest's dreams sickened him.

They were coming to the end of a long, narrow defile. The stone walls, serrated and near-vertical, blocked any route but south. A few metres ahead, hidden by a jutting buttress of rock, the route turned sharply right.

Svelok's helm-display flickered, and he blink-clicked to augment the feed. There were proximity signals on the far side of the buttress. Plenty of them.

Varek whooped with pleasure. 'Prey!' he bellowed, picking up the pace. By his side, the bear-like Lokjr kicked his frost axe into shimmering life and returned a throaty cry of aggression. 'Fodder for my blade, brother!'

Only Ravenblade remained silent, and his wolf-spirit remained dark. Svelok ignored him. Energy coursed through his own superhuman limbs, energy that needed to be dissipated. He was a Wolf Guard, a demigod of combat, the mightiest and purest of the Allfather's instruments of death, and this is what he'd been bred for.

'Kill them all!' he roared, his hearts pounding as he tore round the final corner and into the ravine beyond. His muscles tensed for impact, suffused with the expectation of righteous murder. A kind of elation bled into the fanged smile under his helm.

Past the buttress, tall cliffs of stone soared away on either side, cradling a narrow stretch of open ground. The massive Grendel-creatures were there, stalking like Titans across the stone, silent and dark. Flyers swooped among them. There were smaller creatures too, all encased in the acid-washed rock-hide of their kind, multi-faceted and covered in diamond-hard spikes and growths. Their vast mouths opened, each ringed with armour-shredding incisors.

Something was in their midst, hunted and cowering. The xenos had come to slay.

'Humans!' called out Lokjr, barrelling into the nearest walker. His frost axe slammed against its trailing leg, throwing up shards and sparks.

'Preserve them,' ordered Ravenblade, dropping to one knee and spraying bolter fire up at the circling flyers.

Svelok charged into the nearest spiked xenos, ducking under a clumsy swipe and punching up with his power fist. The stone chest shattered as the crackling disruption field tore through it. He threw an upper-cut at the monster's head, ripping away spikes, before cracking it apart with a savage back-handed lunge. What was left of the xenos fell away and he ploughed on, heading to the heart of the melee.

A dozen weapon-servitors, grey-skinned and fizzing from the acid in the air, were being torn apart by two of the Grendels. Even as Svelok raced to intercept, a big one was ripped limb from limb by a talon-thrust, its pallid flesh impaled on the tips of massive claws, implanted machinery snapping and crunching. Las-blasts spat out in all directions, bouncing harmlessly from the rock-hide of the xenos.

'What are they doing here?' growled Varek, taking down his target with a volley of superbly positioned bolter rounds and whirling to confront the first of the slower-moving walkers.

Svelok sent a column of bolter shells into another spiked creature and charged into assault range. Above him, a Grendel was turning, its massive fists clenching with intent.

'Russ only knows,' he snapped. 'Just finish them!'

There was a crack of thunder above them and forks of lightning plunged from the sky. As coolly as ever, Ravenblade had got to work. Bolts of searing witchfire slammed down, punching through rock-hide and breaking limbs apart. The rain of whining destruction was withering, and the smaller flyers were cut down from the air.

Svelok engaged the nearest Grendel, glorying in the crackling aura of his power fist. The wolf-spirit howled within him, and he crunched his fist into the creature's leading knee-joint. The stone shell shattered, bringing the massive xenos down. It plunged its own fist at Svelok's head, but the Space Wolf was already moving, darting to the left and releasing a barrage of rounds at the Grendel's open mouth. The bolts exploded, dousing the monster in a cataclysm of sparks.

'Death to the alien!' roared Svelok, his ragged voice ringing out of his helm's vox-unit and echoing across the ravine. His fist clenched around the trigger, and the twin barrels spat more streams of rock-tearing bolts.

Thrown back by the fury of the assault, the Grendel toppled, broken limbs grasping for purchase. Svelok leapt after it. His armour powered him into the air and on top of the creature's chest. He plunged down, pinning the monster, his power fist thrumming. Twice, three, four times he punched, his arm moving like a piston, his disruptor-shrouded gauntlet tearing up stone and delving into the heart of the xenos. It cracked, stove, crunched, shattered.

Then he leapt free, whirling to face his next target, clenching the power fist for another assault.

The Space Marines had sliced through the xenos as they'd been made to do. Only one of the big walkers remained. Ravenblade had it enclosed in an aura of blazing light, raised from the ground, coils of lightning crackling between it and the Rune Priest's staff. Helpless, it writhed within the nimbus of psychic power, trapped inside like an insect in amber. Ravenblade uttered a single word. The cracks in the creature's armour blazed white-hot, frozen for a second in a lattice of blazing tracery, then it blew itself apart in an orgy of bursting aether-fuelled immolation. Massive chunks of broken hide tore through the air, smoking and fizzing from the Rune Priest's warp-born energies.

Varek and Lokjr let their heads fall back and howled their victory, swinging their weapons around them like the barbarous warriors of Fenris they'd once been.

'For the Allfather!' Svelok bellowed, giving vent to his battle-fury. As Lokjr raised his massive arms in a gesture of defiance and triumph, the skulls at his belt clattered and swirled around him.

Only the Rune Priest remained unmoved. He let the vast power at his command bleed away and strode silently forwards. The bodies of servitors lay before him, ripped to shreds by the acid, or the xenos, or both. In the middle of them all hunched a human shape, clad in some kind of suit and unsteadily regaining its feet.

Svelok cursed under his breath. What was *wrong* with the priest? Were his fangs so blunted by meddling in runes that he couldn't revel in the joy of victory like a Son of Russ should? He reined in his own exuberance grudgingly, and made his way to the cowering form on the ground. Varek and Lokjr took up guard around them, no doubt eager for more combat.

The survivor was clad in bulky armour of an ancient template, blood-red in colour and fully covering his body. It looked obsolete, scored with the patina of years and covered in esoteric devices Svelok didn't recognise. Brass-coloured implants studded the surface, humming sclerotically and issuing hisses of steam. As the human rose, servos whined in protest and a thicket of mechadendrites scuttled out from hidden panels at his shoulders to begin repairing surface damage. Across his chest was the skull of the Adeptus Mechanicus, pitted and worn from age.

The man's face was hidden beneath a translucent dome of plexiglass filled with a thin blue mist. His head was little more than a dark shadow within that clouded interior, though the spidery shapes of augmetic rebreathers and sensor couplings could be made out.

'Speak, mortal,' ordered Svelok in Low Gothic, determined to interrogate him before Ravenblade could.

A series of clicks emerged from the dome. Eventually, hidden behind a wall of distortion, speech emerged from a vox-unit mounted on his sternum. There was no emotion in it, barely any humanity. It had been filtered through some proxy mechanism, cleansed of its imperfections and rendered blank and sterile. Svelok felt nothing but disgust.

'Adeptus Astartes,' came the voice. Then a train of jumbled clicks. 'Low Gothic, dialect Fenris Vulgaris. Recalling.'

Ravenblade stayed silent. Even through the barrier of the runic armour, Svelok could feel his keen interest in the pheromones his packbrother emitted. Something had got the prophet worked up. Another vision? Or something else? He suppressed a low throat-rattle of irritation. There was no time for this.

'Identify as Logis Alsmo 3/66 Charis. Departmento Archeotech IV Gamma.'

Another pause.

'I should add,' he said. 'Thank you.'

They came to a standstill. As they'd headed south, the plains had given way to twisting, steep-sided gorges. Pools of fluid could be seen glistening at the base of the defiles, harbingers of the deluge to come. They were closing on their quarry, but time was running out. The acid was coming.

'What do you sense?' asked the exarch.

The warlock remained silent, his head inclined to one side. Above him, the sides of the gorge soared upwards.

'Mon-keigh,' he said at last. 'And something else.'

Even as Valiel finished speaking, there was a crack in the rock face closest to him. The warriors snapped into a defensive cordon around the warlock.

A pillar of rock seemed to detach from the cliff nearest them. As it did so, jagged arms broke free from the torso, showering corrosive fluid. Silent as death, an eyeless creature, obsidian-clad and uncurling talons of stone, began to move towards them. Further down the gully, spiked variants detached, unfurling glossy limbs and exposing gem-like teeth.

'This world dislikes intruders,' said Valiel.

The exarch hissed an order, and the troops fanned out into a line in front of the warlock. The creatures lumbered nearer.

'Was *this* in your visions?' asked the exarch over his shoulder.

Valiel let the psychic surface of his witchblade fill with energy. These creatures hadn't been, but then glimpses of the future were always imperfect. That was what made the universe so interesting.

'You don't need to know. Just kill them.'

* * *

Ravenblade glanced at his auspex. Thirty-nine minutes.

'Your purpose here, tech-priest,' he said, towering over the logis. 'Speak quickly – I can kill you as well as those xenos.'

He could still feel the dark wolf within him panting, circling impatiently, thirsting for more release. It would have to wait. There was also a shard of fear from the logis, generated by the vestigial part of whatever humanity he'd once had. The Space Wolves towered over him, their massive war-plate draped in gruesome trophies and adorned with runes of destruction.

'Rune Priest,' said the logis. 'Artificer armour, Fenris-pattern.'

Svelok growled his displeasure. 'Stop babbling, mortal, or I'll rip your arms off. Answer him.'

The logis shrank back, cogitators whirring. Communication in anything other than binaric seemed difficult.

'Gath Rimmon,' Charis said. 'Third world Iopheas Secundus system. Acid surface, total coverage, impenetrable, sensor-resistant, hyper-corrosive. No settlement possible, no surveys archived.'

Svelok took a half-step forwards, his gauntlet curling into a fist. 'We know this!' he rasped over the mission channel to Ravenblade. 'He's wasting our time.'

'Let him speak,' replied Ravenblade. His voice was calm, but firm.

'Single satellite, class Tertius, designation Riapax. Orbit highly irregular. Period 5,467 solar years. Proximity induces tidal withdrawal across polar massif for three local days, total exposure thirty-four standard hours. Opportunity for exploration. Sensors detect artefact. Mission dispatched. Xenos infiltration unanticipated.'

'What kind of artefact?'

'Unknown. Benefit analysis determined by age. Assessed Majoris Beta in priority rank system Philexus. Resources deployed accordingly.'

'You have a location?'

'Signal intermittent, 2.34 kilometres, bearing 5/66/774.'

'Then we need him,' said Ravenblade to Svelok on the closed channel.

'Forget it,' said Svelok. 'Too weak.'

'He has a lock. We don't have time to waste looking.'

'Morkai take you, prophet!' cried Svelok, spitting with vehemence. 'What *is* this thing? We diverted a *strike cruiser* for your visions.'

Ravenblade remained impassive. Svelok was the deadliest killer he'd ever seen, a single-minded inferno of perfectly controlled rage and zeal. Despite all of that, the Wolf Guard had no idea of the power of the Wyrd and the knowledge it gave Ravenblade. How could he? How could anyone but a Rune Priest understand?

'He comes with us. We have less than an hour to find it and return to the pick-up coordinates. The acid is returning, brother. When it comes, the chance will have gone for another five millennia.'

'Then let it lie. This worm can scurry after it.'

Ravenblade felt the dark wolf issue a low psychic growl, hidden to all but his aether-attuned instinct. Svelok was a stubborn bastard, as stubborn as the Great Wolf himself, but there were other ways of deciding this.

'Enough.'

He twisted open a casket hanging from his neck to reveal a dozen pieces of bone, each inscribed with a single rune on both sides. He spilled the pieces into his gauntlet's palm, marking how each fell. As he worked, he saw Svelok turn away in exasperation. The Wolf Guard had no time for the runes. That was his problem.

Ravenblade studied the sigils. Rune patterns were complex and subtle things. He opened his mind to the patterns in the abstract shapes. Across time and space, the angular outlines locked into their sacred formation. The sequence fell into place. He had his sign.

'The runes never lie, brother,' he said. 'We are meant to be here, and we are on the right course. The strands of fate demand it. And there's something else.'

He looked at Svelok, and this time spoke over the standard vox. Another element had emerged, one he'd not foreseen.

'I sense xenos,' he announced. 'They are here.'

The exarch called his warriors back. None of the creatures remained alive. Two had died in the assault, their fragile armour rent by the talons of the world's guardians. Once the shell was broken, the acid rain did the rest.

'Safeguard the spirit stones,' ordered Valiel, sheathing his witchblade and bringing his breathing under control. The survivors did his bidding silently.

'Are we near?' The exarch's voice, muffled by a damaged speech matrix, was tainted with accusation. Valiel regarded him carefully. The exarch was the deadliest killer he'd ever seen, a relentless master of close-ranged combat. Despite all of that, the warrior had little idea of the full power of the warp and the knowledge it gave Valiel. How could he? How could anyone but a warlock understand?

'See for yourself.'

Before them, the series of winding gullies opened out into a wide valley which ran towards the southern horizon. At the far end of the valley was a cliff of cloud, flecked with pale lightning at its base. A distant roar came from it, just like the sea coming in.

'The tides approach,' said the exarch, resentment still in his voice. He feared nothing but that which he couldn't fight. So it was with all those lost on the warrior path.

'What we seek lies on the precipice of danger,' said Valiel. 'Remember your vows, killer.'

The warriors returned and waited. Valiel could sense their doubt, just like their master's.

'Follow me,' said the warlock. He didn't wait for the exarch's assent. Now, above all else, he trusted in the vindication of his vision. The artefact was at hand. Ignoring the acid rain as it streaked across his armour, the warlock strode down the floor of the gorge and into the valley beyond.

Svelok's pack broke from the cover of the gorges and into a wide, bowl-shaped valley. At its far end, a few kilometres distant, the storm raged unabated. A low roar echoed from the mountain walls on either side. The tide-line was almost visible. Even now the rocks underfoot were sodden with puddles of gently hissing fluid. The planet's inhabitants had been driven off for now, but the pack was still being shadowed by flyers, circling out of bolter range like vultures.

They kept running, kept the pace tight. Twenty-five minutes. Raven-blade could taste the acrid stench of the distant acid ocean. Readings scrolled down his helm-display detailing atmospheric toxicity. Nothing his armour couldn't handle. For now.

'Bearing,' he ordered over the mission channel.

'Imminent, Space Marine,' responded the logis, struggling to match the pace in his archaic armour. 'Recommend halt.'

The Space Wolves came to a standstill and waited for Charis to catch up. The rain streaked and steamed from their battle-plate. Lokjr's bear pelt was being eaten away, and the runes of Ravenblade's pauldrons were still glowing an angry red, like wounds washed in iodine.

'Located,' said Charis. A laser-sight extended from his right shoulder and pointed out a piece of flat rock a few metres distant.

'Russ, that's nothing!' mocked Varek.

'Silence!' ordered Svelok, his mood clearly still dark. 'We'll examine it.'

As Ravenblade approached the site he had a sudden lurch of remembrance. He'd seen it before. Like a déjà vu, the blank gap in the stone loomed up towards him. He had no doubts. This was where he'd been drawn to.

No more than five metres square, a shaft had been bored directly down into the valley floor. It plunged vertically, sides smooth and open to the elements. It was perfectly black, as if it went all the way down to Hel. There were no steps, and few hand-holds. Far above them, the thunder growled, echoing from the valley sides.

'That's it?' demanded Svelok.

Ravenblade nodded, mag-locking his staff. 'Where we're meant to be, brother.'

'You *sense* it?'

The psychic signal filled Ravenblade's mind, drowning out the pheromone-signatures of his battle-brothers. All that he could sense was the thing that had drawn him, and the stench of the xenos. Both were close.

'Trust me.'

Svelok turned away. 'Lokjr, you'll hold. Drop anything that gets close. Varek, take point. We're going down.'

Panels on Charis's gauntlets and vambraces opened up, revealing clawed extensions capable of gripping the rock face. The Space Marines, with their occulobe-enhanced vision and superhuman poise, needed no such aids.

Varek swung himself over the edge, his boots finding instant purchases against the rock, and started to descend.

Ravenblade turned away, reaching for the runes again. Surreptitiously, keeping them shielded from Svelok, he spilled the bone fragments into his palm once more.

'What do you see?' The rumbling voice was Lokjr's. Unlike his superior, the Grey Hunter had a pious respect for the readings.

Ravenblade stared at the figures resting on his gauntlet. The fragments glistened pale in the darkness. Shapes swam before his eyes, resisting interpretation. Elk, Fire, Axe, Death, Ice. None of them stood in their proper relations. There was no pattern. Ravenblade felt a rare pang of unease. For the first time in his life, over a hundred years of service, the runes were blank. There was nothing.

'All is as it should be,' he said, snatching up the bones and putting them away. 'Time to go.'

Svelok went carefully but quickly, testing each hold before placing his weight on it. He knew as well as the others that when the tide came up the valley floor it would cascade down the shaft on top of them. Whatever happened, they had to be back up on the surface before then. Damn that priest. This mission was pointlessly dangerous. They didn't even know what they were hunting down. His pack-brothers respected the Wyrd, but he'd never trusted it. There was a thin line between augmentation and corruption, and Rune Priests walked it perilously.

He blink-clicked a feed from Ravenblade's auspex to his helm display. Twenty minutes.

'Report,' he snapped.

There was a low thud from below him as Varek leapt to the bottom of the shaft.

'At the base,' he responded. 'No targets.'

Svelok checked his proximity readings.

'Teeth of Russ,' he spat. 'Where are those xenos?'

He crunched to the ground beside Varek. On three sides, the stone walls continued to the level of the floor. The fourth opened out into a small underground chamber carved roughly from the rock. As Ravenblade and Charis completed the descent, the lumen-beams of the Space Marines' helms ran across the enclosed space.

A circular access hatch had been carved into the floor of the chamber.

Svelok's helm detected the force field across it – one strong enough to withstand five thousand years of acid erosion.

'The mechanism may prove–' started Charis.

A blast rang out across the chamber, and the embedded control panel exploded with a gout of oily smoke. The field shimmered and gave out.

'Varek, with me,' barked Svelok, his bolter barrel glowing from the discharge. 'Priest, keep an eye on the mortal.'

Then he leapt through the hatch, landing heavily several metres down and throwing up a cloud of fragile debris. He sprang away, whirling his bolter round.

Still no targets. His lumen-beam ran over banks of equipment. Cogitators, they looked like, ancient and dark. He heard a crash behind him as Varek joined him. Together they swept the space with their weapon muzzles.

Nothing. The room was empty. It had been empty for millennia. A chamber no more than ten metres square, packed with defunct machinery, heavy with decay. Coils of translucent piping lay breached and desiccated in the dust. Bundles of machine-spirit conduits led from cogitator banks to an elaborate brass altar, black with age, studded with skulls and obscure control runes. There was a faint hum from somewhere, as if the force field had a counterpart hidden in the chamber. Cracked crystal viewports were as dark and lifeless as the shaft above them, and the floor was thick with ancient dust.

Ravenblade and Charis clambered down from the hatch via footholds in the wall. Svelok lowered his bolter and widened his lumen-beam.

The altar was the centrepiece. Though tarnished and old, the pipes and embellishments were massively complex. The hum came from its base, and a faint power reading registered on his helm display. Sitting on the altar was a box. A small, black box. Fascinated, Charis edged towards it.

Svelok turned to Ravenblade.

'You sensed xenos,' he said. 'Where are they?'

The Rune Priest didn't reply. He was looking at the space where Svelok had landed. There was a shattered ribcage on the floor, brittle with age. Other bones littered the floor. Ravenblade snapped his gaze towards the altar.

'They're here, Space Wolf.'

Charis's voice had taken on a fresh clarity, and he suddenly seemed to have no trouble with rendering Gothic. Svelok and Varek spun round to face him. The logis withdrew his gauntlet and exposed a grey-fleshed claw of a hand, riddled with mechanical components. He took the box.

'They've always been here.'

Valiel dropped through the hatch, landing lightly on the pristine metal floor. He sprang clear, making room for the warriors to follow. The dark green figures leapt into the room, rolling away and uncoiling into attack poses, the exarch close behind.

The chamber was harshly lit and lined with gleaming machinery. Coils of translucent pipes pumped coolant from cogitator banks to an elaborate brass altar, studded with skull-and-cog devices and surmounted by a humming containment field. Runes flickered across crystal viewports as the arcane clusters of machinery clicked through their protocols. A low humming gave away the power stored in the room, enough to supply a protective field of prodigious strength.

The chamber's lone occupant whirled round to face them. A human, wearing bright red armour. The close-fitting plates were covered in gleaming mechadendrites, all clicking animatedly, sparkling under the bright strip lighting. His domed helmet had been retracted, revealing a thin, young face. Only a few augmetics marred the taut skin, though there were already fresh incisions on his cheeks where more would be added.

He looked terrified.

Valiel let a ripple of sapphire pass down his blade.

*Kill*, he ordered psychically.

The warriors sprang towards the human. Two kept low, sending a stream of metal from their mandiblasters. Two more leapt into the air, chainswords whirling. The exarch took the direct route, firing from his shuriken pistol as he swung his claw into position.

It all happened in a single heartbeat, and yet the human reacted. That should have been impossible.

Mandiblaster darts homed in and folded out of existence. Shuriken bolts disappeared, winking into nothingness. The man raised his hand and the warriors crumpled into agony. Valiel felt their psychic screams as their souls were ripped from their bodies and sucked, howling, into the box. Dark tongues of matter like strings of ink shot out from the box. They clamped on to the exarch, tearing his spirit from his body. His broken husk fell to the floor, his faceplate distorted into a many-dimensioned mess.

So quick. Valiel remained calm, feeding his blade energy. Tendrils of aether-born plasma curled round his armour like the tails of cats.

'So you've learned some of its tricks,' he said in heavily-accented Gothic. 'That won't help you. If you keep using it, they'll find you.'

Logis Alsmo Charis walked forwards. As he did so the box folded up and switched aspect in his hand. At times it resembled a cube, at others a pyramid, others a rhomboid. Every heartbeat, a new shape. Valiel knew, as the human could not, that it was folding across many dimensions as well. It was an abomination, the product of a mind beyond the imagination of a mon-keigh, and its power had been proscribed on the craftworlds for millennia. Despite his long training, Valiel felt his gaze drawn to it.

So terrible. So beautiful.

'You think I came here to use it?' the logis said, his voice growing in confidence. His fear was fading. 'I came here to hide it. The trail will die.'

'Then so will you.'

Charis flexed his fingers, already laced with steel slivers of augmetic technology.

'I'll find a way.'

He launched a lashing column of black fire from the box.

Valiel sprang clear, kindling the witchblade as he rose. He somer-saulted clear of the box's blast, landing lightly on a cogitator bank. His blade shot out, spitting a flurry of brilliant silver stars towards the human. The man evaded the strikes and leapt back towards the warlock.

His outline shimmered like a Warp Spider's. The box was shifting him.

Charis twisted the box. A black mirror flew into being, rotating across the chamber, reflecting thousands of possible states on its shimmering surface. Valiel knew what it was instantly. He twisted away, but the glass enveloped him. As it passed through him, bulging like water across his body, he felt his soul dragged from his body, folded into miniscule shards of pain-filled insignificance. He was pulled from the bank and crashed to the floor.

The surface of the warped glass shattered. Valiel came to a halt, prone, locked down. His sword clattered away. He felt his essence dissipated. There was no physical pain, but the psychic agony was unbearable. He stifled his screams as the human loomed over him. The box was still in his hand, and was changing shape quickly now.

'Unwise, to try and prevent me.'

Valiel let his eyes flicker to the roof.

*Too powerful. Why was I led here?*

He opened his tormented mind, bent all his fading power towards the multiple paths stretching away from this moment. The structure of the universe always gave you options.

*I am only a part of this.*

Valiel felt the humming malevolence of the box grow. With all the strength that remained in him, he locked away everything he knew about the device, its origins, his mission. History, time itself, condensed into a single form. A glyph. A key. One with the right power would know how to use it.

With a cry of agonised effort, a final blast of witchfire streaked from his clenched fingers, tugging at those strands of his soul still gathered together, tearing the psychic sinews of his inner self.

Charis moved quickly, trying to deflect it with the box, but the bolt flew clear, striking the metal rim of the hatch above, cracking it and careering across the roof. As the flame burned out it left a trail behind it on the stone. An intricate trail.

Charis ignored it. The last traces of terror had left his eyes, and flickers of a confident hatred distorted his features.

'A waste,' he spat, spinning the box-forms on his palm idly. 'You're no different from the rest. Think carefully on that, alien filth. *Your* people started this. *I* will finish it.'

Valiel tried to speak, but his mouth no longer obeyed him. The mon-keigh was mistaken about that, like so much else. He knew nothing of the varied allegiances of Valiel's ancient kind. The mon-keigh were so crude, so *simple*.

The box opened. Defenceless, Valiel felt his soul dragged into isolation, his remaining essence torn from his material form and sucked within the shifting walls of the device. For an instant, while his eyes still worked, he caught a glimpse of what was inside. Part of him understood what was in there, knew it from myths and scraps of legend. He could see movement, layers, shifting upon shifting, the dark heart revolving before a...

He tried to scream, but his vocal chords were no longer his own.

The box clicked shut.

Charis looked down at the burnt-out corpse of the warlock. Not as powerful as he'd been led to fear. The dark ones had been worse.

He hurried over to the altar and placed the box in the receptacle he'd made for it. Leaving it was hard, but he had to master the secrets of it, and *they* were coming. He withdrew his hand and his armoured gauntlet extended over the exposed flesh, sealing him in against the acid. He depressed a rune on the nearby panel and the cogitators clicked into life, feeding the containment field, keeping it safe. A whiff of ozone burst across the chamber, and the air began to crackle with bounded energies.

The tides were returning. The xenos had delayed but not defeated him. With a final glance across the chamber, Charis let the dome close over his head. He had to leave – they'd be tearing space apart to find him. Once he was safely away, there was work to be done. Lore to be studied. Secrets to be uncovered. And then the long years of stasis while he waited for Riapax to uncover the shaft again.

So much to do before he'd be back. But then there was so much to learn.

Ravenblade's staff burst into flame, kindling on the angular incisions inscribed along the shaft, and the dark wolf's hackles raised. The box held by Charis was shedding psychic energy. *Incredible* amounts. It was opening and closing in on itself with dizzying speed.

Svelok and Varek moved instantly.

'Lokjr!' Svelok barked into the comm-link. 'Down here. Now!'

The sergeant barrelled across the chamber, power fist crackling. Varek let fly a stream of rounds, each aimed with exact precision: head, neck, armour joints. As they hit, they folded out of existence. Nothing left as much as a mark.

Then Svelok was in range. He hurled a heavy blow with the power fist, aiming for the gap between shoulder and helmet. Charis fell back astonishingly quickly, but the fist still caught him, sinking into the armour. It disappeared. The ceramite crumpled and distorted, and the disruption field flew wildly out of frequency.

Svelok fell back with a snarl and snapped up his storm bolter. Before he could get a round away Charis's gauntlet punched him heavily in the face. As the fist impacted, black flames exploded from the blow, spiralling out like seeker flares. Svelok was hurled backwards, feet flung from the ground before crashing into a bank of cogitators. The muzzle of his wolf-helm had been folded in on itself.

'Death, traitor!' roared Varek, tearing straight at Charis, discarding his bolter for his fists. He smashed into the logis, closing his gauntlet over the box, aiming to tear it away.

'No!' cried Ravenblade, swinging his staff into position.

Varek bellowed in agony as his arm was sucked from real space, dragging him after it. The limb was ripped into a vortex of distortion, blood flying in concentric spirals, armour cracking and flesh tearing.

Ravenblade let fly with a searing ball of lightning, engulfing Charis's breastplate and ramming him against the altar. What was left of Varek slumped against the floor, gurgling in a froth of blood, half of his body ripped away. Ravenblade swung round for a second strike, and his staff crackled with storm-pulled fury.

He didn't even see the blast from the box. All he felt was the pain as it hit him. The rending, mind-unlocking pain. That was what the device was for, its only purpose. It had been made by a master of technology so advanced that it looked like sorcery. In that moment, exposed to its searching mind, Ravenblade knew its name. In the ancient xenos language now only spoken in one city in the galaxy, it was the *Ayex Commorragh*. The Heart of Agony.

Black fire shattered his defences, tore through his psychic wards. He felt himself being lifted backwards, armour aflame. He hit the wall with a crack, crashing into the rock. The fire kept coming. Blood trickled down the inside of his helmet. He felt his breastplate rip away, exposing the flesh beneath. The black carapace bubbled and split, shredding the skin, tearing up the muscle.

'For the Allfather!'

Ravenblade half-heard Lokjr's charge into the chamber, his frost axe pulsating with energy. Charis whirled to deal with him, but Svelok was back on his feet too, his bolter spitting. Ravenblade felt consciousness slipping away, and fought to hold on to it. He was collapsing into shock. He needed to fix on something. Anything.

He let his head fall back. His eyes flicked to the roof. That was when he saw it. Blasted into the ceiling of the chamber, scored in witchfire, was the thing that had drawn him. The rune. It had been in his dreams for months, deep in the void, out on the strike cruiser. It was the key.

It was enough. His mind unlocked.

Deep within him, crippled and bloody, the dark wolf opened its yellow eyes. A succession of images raced through his consciousness, overlapping with each other as they crowded into his mind. He sensed the souls thronging around him, impossibly old, long-dead. There was a warlock in a white mask and black armour. He'd been here, five thousand years ago.

More images rushed into his mind. Another planet, covered in Adeptus Mechanicus complexes, hells of industry. Dark shapes streaked across the burning skies, jagged-winged flyers, crewed by nightmares. There were men and women running, faces contorted with terror. Among them strode thin-limbed corsairs. Eldar they were too, but of a different kind. In the midst was the architect of the Heart, the haemonculus, hunched over his machinery of terror, watching the slaves being herded through the webway portal. His skin was grey, riddled with black veins. The eyes were pitiless wells of ennui, windows on to a heart driven cold by centuries of horror. There was a terrible intelligence there, a mastery of forbidden arts. He'd used the box to create pain from outside the bounds of the universe. That, and that alone, was why it had been made.

The vision shifted. There was fighting, ranks of human troops moving through the shattered cityscape. The corsairs were driven back. The haemonculus had lingered too long, and soldiers in carapace armour, skitarii, ordinatus, all piled into the vision. There were crippling explosions, massed volleys of las-fire, a retreat. The webway portal closed. The nightmares were gone.

It shifted again. In the midst of the ruination, surrounded by weeping survivors and smouldering rubble, a young logis came. He looked handsome, his flesh as yet unmarked by the touch of the Machine-God. He bent down, drawn by a strange black box. It had a certain pleasing construction. He took it, covering it in his robes. He'd keep it secret, learn how to use it.

But the nightmares knew how to find the box. They came back, pursuing him across the stars. While he had it, they could find him. He could never rest long enough to master it. It had to be hidden. Somewhere far away. Safe while he learned what it was. Safe until the trail died and he could come back to collect it.

Ravenblade snapped back into consciousness. The visions shuddered into nothing. He hadn't been summoned here by the box. He'd been summoned here by the witchfire rune, left by the xenos whose presence he still sensed. The real world rushed into focus around him. All that remained of the mind-transfer were five words.

*I have weakened the portal.*

Ravenblade tried to pull himself up. Even his superhuman constitution was near collapse. Blood, half-coagulated, pumped from his exposed chest. Lokjr and Svelok fought on. They were being ripped apart. None of their weapons bit. They ducked around the vicious blasts of black fire with all their skill, but the end was only a matter of time. Even as he watched, Ravenblade saw Lokjr's frost axe suddenly pulled across dimensions and smashed into scraps of metal by the Heart.

He dragged himself into a half-seated position, lungs burning. Charis had closed the hatch above them, sealing them in. He had control over every device in the room and had ensured that none of them would escape.

But Ravenblade was a son of Fenris, and escape was the last thing on his mind. Just like Svelok, he was a dealer in death, a predator, a hunting beast of the endless war. Only the manner of the kill differed.

Ravenblade closed his charred eyes and opened his mind to the immaterium. The dark wolf growled with pleasure. The runes on his armour went black as Ravenblade pulled all his remaining power to himself. He went back to the essence of his Rune Priest training, the primal tools of his art.

The elements. And this was a world of storms.

'Unleash.'

Ravenblade screamed as the pain coursed through his body and mind. Far above, he could sense the torrent answer his call. Clouds boiled and raced, hurtling to the source of the summons. Acid oceans, already close, surged across the blasted land, swollen unnaturally by the power at Ravenblade's command.

The rain increased. It became a deluge, hammering against the rocks. Even shielded by twenty metres of stone, Ravenblade could feel the breaking fury. Corrosive fluid rushed across the valley floor and down the shaft above the chamber, bubbling and churning. He piled on more energy, ignoring the warnings of terminal stress from his body. He felt his primary heart give out, but still the maelstrom responded to the call. He could sense the weight of the acid as it pressed against the hatch. The metal began to steam.

He opened his eyes. Lokjr had been cast aside, his face half-dissolved by the Heart. Even as he watched, Svelok was thrown backwards, a two-metre tall giant in full power armour hurled like a doll across the chamber, shattering machines as he skidded along the floor. Then Charis came for him.

'Russ guide me,' whispered Ravenblade, seizing his bolt pistol from its holster, swinging it upwards and firing at the hatch.

The metal exploded instantly, blowing shards across the chamber, unleashing the torrent. Acid sheeted down. The cogitators fizzed and exploded, sending blooms of sparks skittering across the floor. Ravenblade went into spasms of fresh agony as the searing liquid ran across his open wounds. His back arched as he cried out, doused in gouts of boiling liquid pain.

Too slow, Charis's naked hand was snatched back into its gauntlet. The acid tore through the exposed flesh, eating through skin, bone and metal. The logis shrieked in his turn, his fear unfiltered by the vox-distorter. He tried to clutch the box, but his fingers were gone, washed into the slew of ankle-deep acid bubbling at his feet. It tumbled from his grip, dropping into the seething, corroding mass.

As it hit the liquid, it flipped into a dizzying array of shapes. For a moment it spun desperately, its walls folding impossibly fast. Then, feeling even its infinite malignance threatened, the spinning stopped. There was a shudder, and the air around it burned away in a sudden blaze of ozone. The acid bath surged into a boiling sphere, furious and infused with black fire. The box emitted a deafening scream, as if a million tortured voices had been sucked back into the mortal plane for an instant.

Then the acid ball exploded in a blinding, whirling inferno. At its core, the box folded itself out of existence and the psychic backwash from its departure tore out from the epicentre.

Ravenblade cried aloud as the warp echo scored his exposed soul. Eyes bleeding, lungs burning, he hauled himself to his knees, trying to shelter his open chest cavity from the tumbling rain. Every move was a symphony of agony, physical and psychic.

'You... *killed* it!'

Charis stumbled towards him, his remaining gauntlet clutching impotently. Freed from the protection of the box, his armour was corroding fast. Mechadendrites extended, blades whirring. The Rune Priest, chest ripped open, psychic senses seared away, had no defences left. He snatched the bolt pistol into position, but it slipped through his broken fingers.

'For Russ!'

His voice ringing with rage, Svelok burst from the acid like a leviathan rising from the ocean, armour streaming with fluid. He staggered into range and smashed his fist straight through Charis's visor. The glass shattered, cracking the logis back against the altar and snapping his spine. For a moment, Ravenblade caught a glimpse of a hideously ruined face within, riddled with augmetics. Then it was gone, consumed by the foaming deluge.

Ravenblade's vision wavered. He was close to passing out. The acid burned against his chest, eating its way into his core. The liquid was now knee-deep around him.

'We have to go, priest,' Svelok rasped, his battle-plate pitted and steaming. The combat-fury was gone from his voice, replaced by grim resolve. He dragged Ravenblade to his feet, sending fresh needles of pain shooting through his body.

'The staff,' gasped the Rune Priest.

'No time.'

Svelok hauled Ravenblade to the footholds, shouldering the Rune Priest's massive armoured weight. Fluid showered down from the portal,

sluicing over Ravenblade's breastplate, snaking under the ruined carapace, worming into his wounds. His organs were failing.

He gritted his teeth. Not yet.

Svelok went first up the ladder, pulling Ravenblade after him. His
strength was incredible. It was all Ravenblade could do to hang on, keep
his feet on the holds, stay conscious.

The ascent up the rock was a nightmare. Falling acid burned through
the armour plate with horrifying speed. Every agonising step saw their
protection thinned a little more. Ravenblade watched the runes on his
vambrace blaze red as the liquid sank into the impressions. The runes
he'd carved himself, now smoking into oblivion.

They reached the top of the shaft. Shouldering his bulk against the torrent, Svelok pulled himself back onto the valley floor. With an almighty
heave, he dragged Ravenblade up behind him.

The fury of the heavens had been unleashed. Lightning streaked across
the angry sky. Rain fell in swathes. Acid swilled across the full width of
the valley floor, bubbling and foaming. To the south, there were white-
topped waves. Riapax was heading back into the void, and the ocean was
reclaiming its own. They were out of time.

Ravenblade's helm lenses flickered and went dark. Acid must have got
into the mechanism.

'Nearly as... bad as... Fenris,' he gasped, feeling the tightness in his
throat grow.

Svelok dragged Ravenblade to his feet, pulling the Rune Priest's arm
over his shoulder. Despite his wounds, he was still a furnace of energy
and determination. For the first time, Ravenblade began to see his true
value to the pack. He was everything a Son of Russ should be.

'Nearly as,' Svelok agreed grimly, dragging them both to higher
ground. They reached a flat-topped outcrop, jutting from the rising acid
around them. It wouldn't last long. Even now the liquid at its foot was
knee-deep. It would soon be waist-deep.

The two of them clambered onto the rock shelf. Ravenblade collapsed
against the stone, his breath ragged. Far above them, thunder rolled
across the valley. The torrent surged by, washing against the edges of
their little island.

Svelok bent over Ravenblade, trying to shield the stricken Rune Priest
from the downpour.

'Hold on, prophet,' he said, then corrected himself. '*Brother*. We're not
dead yet.'

The Wolf Guard hid his emotions poorly. Ravenblade could sense the
full range of frustration and regret. They were far from the pick-up location. Better to prepare for the end, to meet the Allfather with honour.
Battle-rage had its place, but not now.

As for himself, he could no longer feel anything in his limbs. His torso
was lost in a dull ache, the nerve-endings burned away. A task had been

achieved on Gath Rimmon, even if it wasn't the one he'd expected.

'They were blank,' coughed Ravenblade, tasting the blood in his mouth.

'What were?' Svelok's voice was no longer coloured with suspicion. Two battle-brothers had gone. Two pack-members. The bond between them was severed. Now a third strand would be cut.

The roar above them got louder. It wasn't just thunder. There were lights in the clouds, and the whine of engines.

'The runes,' said Ravenblade. He saw the huge shadow of a Thunder-hawk descend from above, searchlights whirling. That was good. Svelok would live to tell the saga.

'Don't speak, brother.'

The pain went. The Allfather had granted him that, at least.

'I will speak,' Ravenblade croaked, letting the last of the air in his lungs bleed away. 'You must learn from this, Wolf Guard. We were part of a greater pattern here. There is always a pattern.'

His vision faded to black.

'Your fury gives you strength, but it is fate that guides you. Remember it.'

The dark wolf gave him a final, mournful look, then loped into the shadows. Ravenblade was truly alone then, just as he had been before taking the Canis Helix.

'Even across so much time and space,' he rasped, feeling Morkai steal upon him. 'The runes never lie.'

# THE REWARDS OF TOLERANCE

*by Gav Thorpe*

Encased in a flickering Geller field, the *Vengeful* slid through the psychic tides of the warp. The field flared intermittently as it crossed the path of itinerant warp denizens, becoming a shell of writhing, fanged faces and swirling colours. In the turmoil of its wake, dark shapes gathered in a flitting shoal; occasionally a creature would speed forwards and hurl itself at the strike cruiser, seeking the life force of those within. Each time the unreal predators were hurled back by a flash of psychic force.

Sitting in the Navigator's cockpit Zacherys, former Librarian of the Avenging Sons, gazed out into the warp through eyes ablaze with blue energy. Sparks crackled from the pinpricks of his pupils and thick beads of sweat rolled down his cheeks. With a trembling hand, he reached out to the comm-unit and switched to the command frequency.

'I can hear them whispering,' he growled.

There was a hiss of static before the reply came through the speakers.

'Hold them as long as you can,' said Gessart, the ship's captain. Once master of an Avenging Sons company, he now led a small renegade band only two dozen strong. 'We'll reach safe exit distance in less than an hour.'

The comm buzzed for a few seconds more and fell silent. Left alone in the quiet, Zacherys could not help but listen to the voices pawing at the edge of his hearing. Most were gibberish, some snarled threats, others begged Zacherys to let down his guard. A mellifluous voice cut through, silencing them with its authority.

*I can take you to safety*, it said. *Listen to me, Zacherys. I can protect you.*

*All I ask is a small favour. Just let me help you. Open your thoughts to me. Let me see your mind and I will grant your desires.*

The sensation of claws prising at the sides of Zacherys's thoughts suddenly disappeared, like a great pressure released by an opening airlock. The chittering stopped and the Geller field stabilised, becoming a placid oily-sheened bubble once more.

Zacherys relaxed his fingers, loosening his fist on the arm of the Navigator's chair, indentations left in the metal from his fierce grip. He took a deep breath and closed his eyes. When he opened them, they had returned to normal, the burst of psychic energy drawn back into his mind.

Thank you, he thought.

*You are welcome*, replied the voice.

What do I call you? Zacherys asked.

*Call me Messenger*, it said.

What are you? A daemon?

*I am Messenger. I am the one that will open your mind to your true power. I will show you the full scope of your abilities. Together we will grow stronger. We will both be pupil and teacher.*

We need to break out of warp space, thought Zacherys. I cannot resist another attack.

*Allow me*, said Messenger. *Call to me when you return. I will be waiting.*

The streaming rivers of psychic energy surrounding the *Vengeful* bucked and spiralled, turning upon themselves until they split into an immaterial whirlpool. Through the widening hole, Zacherys could see the blue glow of a star.

Fingers moving gently across the steering panel, he guided the *Vengeful* towards the opening. The strike cruiser burst out of the immaterium with a flash of multi-coloured light. The rift behind fluttered for a moment and disappeared. Silence followed; the emptiness of space. Zacherys looked around and saw a dense swathe of stars: the northern arm of the galactic spiral spread out before him. He smiled with relief and prodded the automatic telemetry systems into action. It was time to find out where they were.

The renegade Space Marines gathered in the briefing hall. The twenty-four warriors barely filled a quarter of the large chamber, which was designed to house a whole Space Marine company. Gessart looked down from the briefing podium and marvelled at how quickly his followers had asserted their individuality. After decades of loyal service to their Chapter – centuries in the case of some – the Space Marines were rediscovering their true selves, throwing off millennia of tradition and dogma.

All of them wore armour blackened with thick paint, their old livery and symbols obliterated. Some had gone further, taking their gear down to the armoury to chisel off Imperial insignia and weld plates over aquilas and other icons of the Imperium. A few had painted new mottos across the black to replace the devotional texts that had been removed. In a neat script, Willusch had written 'The Peace of Death' along the rim of his left shoulder pad. Lehenhart, with his customary humour, had daubed a white skull across the face of his helm, a ragged bullet hole painted in the centre of its forehead. Nicz, Gessart's self-appointed second-in-command, sat with a chainsword across his lap, a thin brush in his left hand, putting the finishing touches to his own design: 'The Truth Hurts', written in red paint to resemble smeared blood.

Zacherys was the last to attend. The psyker nodded to Gessart as he sat down, confirming the location estimate he had passed on earlier. Gessart smiled.

'It seems that though the Emperor looks over us no more, we have not yet been abandoned by the galaxy,' he announced. 'Helmabad is more than a dozen light years behind us. That's the only good news. We are dangerously low on supplies, despite what we salvaged from Helmabad. We are six thousand light years away from safety; a considerable distance. If we are to complete our journey to sanctuary in the Eye of Terror, we will need more weapons and equipment, as well as food.'

Gessart rasped a hand across the thick stubble on his chin. The Space Marines all looked at him attentively, faces impassive as they received this news. Some habits were harder to break than others and they waited in silence for their leader to continue.

'Whether by luck, fate or some other power, our half-blind flight through the warp has brought us within a hundred light years of the Geddan system. The system is virtually lifeless, but it's a chartist captains' convoy meeting point; merchant ships from across the sector converge there to make the run down past the ork territories towards Rhodus. We'll take what we need from the merchantmen.'

'Those convoys have Imperial Navy escorts,' said Heynke.

'Usually nothing more than a few frigates and destroyers,' said Nicz before Gessart could answer. 'Not too much for a strike cruiser to overcome.'

'If this were a fully-manned ship, I'd agree,' said Gessart. 'But it isn't. If there's a light escort we'll try to cut out a cargo ship or two and avoid confrontation. If there's a more sizeable Imperial Navy presence we cannot risk an open battle. The task is to gather more supplies, not expend what little we have.'

Nicz conceded the point with a shrug.

'You're in charge,' the Space Marine muttered.

Gessart ignored the slight and turned his attention to Zacherys.

'Can you guide us to Geddan in a single jump?'

The psyker looked away for a moment, obviously unsure.

'I think I can manage that,' he said eventually.

'Can you, or can't you?' snapped Gessart. 'I don't want to drop into the middle of something we aren't expecting.'

Zacherys nodded, uncertainly at first and then with greater conviction.

'Yes, I have a way to do it,' the psyker said. 'I can take us to Geddan.'

'Good. There is another issue that needs to be resolved before we leave,' said Gessart. He looked directly at Nicz, who glanced to either side, surprised by his commander's attention.

'Something I've done?' said Nicz.

'Not yet,' replied Gessart. 'The menial crew are still loyal to us, but they do not know the full facts of what happened on Helmabad. If we have to fight at Geddan, there can be no hesitation. I want you to ensure that they will open fire on command, even against an Imperial vessel. I want every weapon system overseen by one of us, and dispose of any crew that may prove problematic.'

'Dispose?' said Nicz. 'You mean kill?'

'Don't get carried away, we cannot run the ship without them. But leave them with no doubt that we are still their masters and they will follow our instructions without question.'

'I'll see that it is done,' said Nicz, patting his chainsword.

'Are there any questions?' Gessart asked the rest of the Space Marines. They exchanged glances and shook their heads until Lehenhart stood up.

'What happens when we reach the Eye of Terror?' he asked.

Gessart considered his reply carefully.

'I don't know. We'll have to go there and find out. At the moment, nobody knows what we have done. I'd rather keep it that way.'

'What if Rykhel somehow survived on Helmabad?' asked Heynke. 'What if he contacts the rest of the Avenging Sons?'

'Between the rebels and the daemons, Rykhel is dead,' said Nicz.

'But what if he isn't?' insisted Heynke.

'Then our former battle-brothers will attempt to live up to their name,' said Gessart. 'That's why we're going to the Eye of Terror. Nobody would dare follow us into that nightmare. Once we attack the convoy word will spread about what we have done. We have one chance to do this right. If we fail, the Emperor's servants will be looking for us, and getting to the Cadian Gate will be all the harder for it.'

'So let's not mess it up,' said Lehenhart.

Zacherys's hand hesitated over the warp engine activation rune on the console beside his Navigator's chair. He glanced at the panel above it, looking at the fluctuating lines of green fading into orange and then surging with power into green again. Although the warp engine was not fully active, the psyker could feel the boundaries of reality thinning around the *Vengeful*. Through the canopy around him, he saw the stars wavering, the darkness between them glowing occasionally with rainbows of psychic energy.

He had promised Gessart that he would get the ship to Geddan, thinking he would use the daemon Messenger to do so. He was having second thoughts, but could not back down. Not only would Zacherys face the scorn of the others, the ship was stranded in wilderness space. At some point they would have to re-enter the warp or simply stay here and eventually die from starvation – a prospect even more harrowing for a Space Marine than a normal man. Doubtless they would kill each other before that fate overtook them.

Taking a deep breath, Zacherys touched the rune. From the *Vengeful*'s innards a deep rumbling reverberated through the ship, increasing to a rapid vibration that whined in Zacherys's ears.

The starfield around the *Vengeful* wavered and spun, engulfing the starship with a whirl of colours: the eye of a kaleidoscopic storm of the material and immaterial. Zacherys engaged the drive and the strike cruiser lurched into the warp; not a physical strain of inertia but a stretching of the mind, filled with momentary flashes of memory and dizziness. For the psyker, the transition welled up at the base of his skull, suffusing his thoughts with pressure as synapses flared randomly for a heartbeat.

It was over in a moment. The *Vengeful* was sliding along the psychic current, Geller field sparkling around it. Zacherys opened his mind up to the power of the warp and felt the shifting energies around him. He could sense the ebb and flow of the immaterium, but he was no Navigator; he lacked true warp-sight. Though he could feel the titanic psychic power surging around the ship, he could see only a little along their route, enough to avoid the swirls and plunging currents that would hurl them off-course, but little more.

Messenger? he thought. There was no reply and Zacherys became fearful that the creature had tricked him back into warp space, to drift on the tides until the Geller field finally failed and they were set upon by the daemons and other denizens that hungered after their souls.

'Foolish,' Zacherys muttered to himself.

The ship was buffeted by a wave of energy and Zacherys's focus turned to the steering controls as he attempted to ride the surge. As with the warp jump itself, he felt this not in the pit of his stomach like a man upon an ordinary sea, but as crests and troughs of sensation behind his eyes, along every nerve.

He regained some control, moving the *Vengeful* into a calmer stream of power. He was making a huge mistake.

Zacherys's hand hovered over the emergency disengage rune, which would rip open the fabric of real/warp space and dump the *Vengeful* back into the material galaxy. There was no telling what damage would be done to the warp engines, or those on board, and Zacherys would have to confess all to Gessart.

It seemed such an ignominious end. So soon after taking the first steps on the road to freedom. It made a mockery of Zacherys's aspirations; his hopes to understand the nature of his abilities and his place between the real and unreal. The bright path leading from Helmabad he had seen in his visions was guttering and dying, swallowed by the formless energy of the void.

*I am here.*

Zacherys let out an explosive breath of relief.

I need your help, he thought.

*Of course you do*, replied Messenger. *Look how perilous your situation has become, flinging yourselves into our domain without heed to the dangers.*

I need a guide, thought Zacherys. Can you show me the way ahead?

*As I told you before, you must lower your defences and allow me to enter your mind. I must see with your eyes to guide you. Do not worry; I will protect you from the others.*

Zacherys's hand was shaking as he leaned over towards the Geller field controls. It would be a rash act, dooming not just the psyker but every soul on board the *Vengeful*. What option did he have?

*Indeed*, said Messenger. *You have cast yourselves upon the whims of cruel fate. Yet, there is no need to succumb to despair. You can still control your destiny, with me beside you.*

What do you get as your part of the bargain? asked Zacherys. Why should I trust you?

*I get your mind, my friend. And your loyalty. We need each other, you and I. In this world you are at my mercy; but I have no reach into your world other than with your hands. We shall help each other, and both shall benefit.*

You could destroy the ship, thought Zacherys.

*What would I gain? A momentary gratification, a brief peak of power and nothing more. Do not mistake me for the mindless soul-eaters that flock after your ship. I too have my ambitions and desires, and a mind and body such as yours can take me closer to them.*

You will possess me, drive me from my own flesh!

*You know that I cannot. Your armour against me is your will, strengthened over your whole life. We would wage war against each other constantly, neither victorious. You are no normal mortal; you are a Space Marine still, with all the power that entails.*

Klaxons screeched across the *Vengeful* as Zacherys punched in the first cipher to unlock the Geller field controls. Within moments, Gessart was on the comm.

'What is it? Warp breach?' the warband leader demanded.

'There is nothing to fear,' said Zacherys, convincing himself as much as the commander. The blaring was joined by a host of flashing red lights on the display board as Zacherys keyed in the next sequence. 'Everything is under control.'

He tapped out the last digits and pressed the deactivation rune. With a screech that could only be heard inside his head, Zacherys cut the Geller field. The bubble of psychic energy around the starship imploded, the full pressure of the warp rushing into and through the *Vengeful*.

Zacherys felt cold, a freezing chill of the void that encrusted every cell of his being. With gritted teeth, he put his head back against the chair.

'The moment of truth,' he whispered. 'I am at your mercy, Messenger. Prove me right or wrong.'

The bitter cold vanished, replaced by warmth that glowed through Zacherys's limbs. He felt the heat expanding outwards, engulfing the rest of the ship. The energy of the warp remained, not pushed back like it was with the Geller field, but the *Vengeful* settled in an oasis of calm, resting gently upon the stilled psychic tide.

Zacherys opened his eyes. Other than the tingling in his nerves, the psyker felt no different. He flexed his fingers and looked around until he was confident that he was in full control of his faculties. He laughed, buoyed up by a sudden feeling of ecstasy that suffused his body.

And then he felt it.

It was indistinct, like the tendrils of a light fog, spreading through his mind, dribbling along the course of his thoughts. It was a dark web, an alien cancer latching on to all of his emotions, every hope and fear, dream and disappointment, suckling upon his centuries of experience. Zacherys sensed satisfaction seeping through him, leeched from his new companion.

*Such delights we have to offer one another. But for another time. Tell me, my friend: where do you wish to go?*

Gessart paced the command bridge as he waited for the results of the initial sensor sweep. Zacherys had done an admirable job, dropping the ship out of warp space just outside the orbit of Geddan's fourth world. Gessart wondered how the psyker had overcome the graviometric problems that normally prevented ships from emerging so close to a celestial body, but decided against asking for details; the former Librarian's strangely contented expression and the incident with the collapsing Geller field warned Gessart that there was something odd happening, but he could not afford the distraction for the moment.

'Seven signatures on response, captain,' announced Kholich Beyne, the head of the *Vengeful*'s non-Space Marine crew. The young man checked something on the data-slab in his hands. 'No military channels in use.'

'Confirm that,' said Gessart. 'Are there any Imperial Navy vessels?'

Kholich headed over to the sensor technicians and conferred briefly with each. He turned back to Gessart with a solemn expression.

'Confirm that there are no Imperial Navy vessels in the system, captain. The convoy is assembling around the fifth planet. From their comms chatter, they are expecting to receive their escort in the next day or two.'

'Defences in that grid?' Gessart stopped his pacing and knotted his hands behind his back, trying to stay calm.

'We're not picking up any orbital defences, captain. It seems unlikely that the convoy would gather without some form of protection.'

'Surface-to-orbit weapons, most likely,' said Gessart. 'Nothing that can attack us if we get amongst the convoy before they start opening fire.'

He rounded on the comms team.

'Transmit our identifier to the convoy ships. Tell them we will be approaching.'

'If they require an explanation, captain?' asked Kholich. 'What do we tell them?'

'Nothing,' replied Gessart, heading towards the bridge doors. 'Find out who the civilian convoy captain is and inform him that I'll be boarding his vessel and speaking to him in person.'

'Very well, captain,' said Kholich as the armoured doors slid open with a rumble. 'I'll inform you of any developments.'

Though not considered a large vessel by Imperial standards, the *Vengeful* dwarfed the merchantman carrying Sebanius Loil, the man who had identified himself as the merchant commander of the convoy. Following a terse conversation, during which Gessart had done most of the talking, the trader had acquiesced to the Space Marine's demand to be allowed on board. Now Gessart and his warriors were fully armoured and crossing the few hundred kilometres between the strike cruiser and the *Lady Bountiful* aboard their last surviving Thunderhawk gunship.

Gessart looked at the merchantman through the cockpit canopy, noticing the three defence turrets clustered around her midsection: short-ranged weapons that might fend off a lone pirate but which would be hard-pressed to overload even one of the *Vengeful*'s void shields. Beyond the *Lady Bountiful* was the rest of the convoy, visible only as returns on the Thunderhawk's scanners, separated from each other by several thousand kilometres of vacuum. Four were of similar size, but two of the ships were immense transports, three times the size of the *Vengeful*. Fortunately they were empty, destined to pick up their cargo of an Imperial Guard regiment en route to the warzone in Rhodus.

Bright light streamed from an opening that stretched a quarter of the length of the *Lady Bountiful* as the ship slid back its loading bay doors to allow the Thunderhawk to land. Nicz eased the gunship into a course and speed parallel with the merchantship and then fired the landing thrusters to guide them into the bay.

A lone man waited for Gessart as the Thunderhawk's ramp lowered to the deck, smoke and steam billowing across the bare rockcrete floor. He was stocky, clad in a heavy fur-lined coat with puffed shoulders slashed with red. Sebanius Loil warily watched the Space Marines with one good eye and an augmetic device riveted into his face in place of the other. Lenses clacked as the merchant focussed on Gessart. A servo whined as

Loil lifted his right hand in welcome, the sleeve of the coat falling back to reveal a three-clawed metal hand.

'Welcome aboard the *Lady Bountiful*, captain,' said Loil. His voice was a hoarse whisper and through the ruff of the coat Gessart could see more bionics; an artificial larynx bobbed up and down at Loil's throat.

Gessart did not return the greeting. He looked at his warriors over his shoulder and signalled them to spread out around the docking bay.

'I'm taking your cargo,' he said.

Loil did not seem surprised by this pronouncement. He lowered his cybernetic arm with a whirr and held out his good hand towards Gessart.

'You know that I cannot allow that, captain,' said the merchant. 'My cargo is destined for Imperial forces fighting at Rhodus. I have an agreement with the Departmento Munitorum.'

The bionic hand delved into a deep pocket and produced a data-crystal. Loil offered it towards Gessart as proof of his contract.

'You have no choice in the matter,' said Gessart as he thrust Loil aside. 'Your compliance will be for your own good.'

'You cannot seriously threaten us with force,' said Loil, following Gessart as the Space Marine stalked across the bay towards the main doors. Gessart darted the man a look that confirmed he could very well make such a threat. Loil paled and his artificial eye buzzed erratically. 'This is intolerable! I will…'

The trader's words petered away as Zacherys thudded down the ramp. The psyker's eyes were orbs of golden energy. Zacherys turned that infernal gaze upon Loil, who recoiled in horror, holding up his hands in front of his ravaged face. The merchant whimpered and fell to his knees, tears coursing down his scarred cheeks. Zacherys stood over the man for a moment, looking down, lips pursed in contemplation.

'Where is the main cargo hold?' asked Gessart.

Zacherys looked up, broken from his thoughts by Gessart's questions.

'Aft,' said the former Librarian. 'Four bays, all filled with crates. Too much for the Thunderhawk, we will have to bring the *Vengeful* alongside and dock directly.'

Zacherys held out a hand above Loil's head. He twitched his armoured fingers and the merchant looked up, meeting the psyker's gaze. The gold of Zacherys's eyes spread down his right arm and engulfed the head of the merchant before disappearing. Zacherys smiled and lifted his hand further. The ship's captain rose jerkily to his feet, swaying slightly.

'Lead me to the bridge,' said Zacherys.

Loil's first steps were faltering as he resisted the control of the psyker, scraping his feet across the floor. Zacherys twisted his wrist a fraction and Loil mewled like a wounded animal, knees buckling. The merchant righted himself and stumbled on, Zacherys following with long, slow strides.

The double doors hissed open, revealing a cluster of crew members holding an assortment of weapons: shotguns, autoguns, lasrifles. They stared in disbelief as their captain shuffled through the open doors, Zacherys and Gessart close behind. On their heels, the rest of the Space Marines hefted their bolters meaningfully.

'What do we do, Captain Loil?' asked one of the men, lasgun trembling in his grip.

'Wh-whatever they say,' hissed the merchant. 'Do whatever they say.'

The men looked uncertain. Gessart towered over them, fists clenched.

'Make ready to unload your cargo to our vessel,' he said slowly. 'Comply and no harm will come to you. Disobey and you will be killed. Put down your weapons.'

Most of them did as they were told, their guns clattering on the deck. One, face twisted with indignation, raised his shotgun. He didn't have time to pull the trigger. Gessart's fist slammed into his face, snapping the crewman's neck and hurling him across the corridor.

'Pass the word to your crewmates,' said Gessart. 'Unloading will begin in ten minutes.'

Zacherys made Loil cut the comm-link and then released his psychic grip on the merchant. The man swooned to the floor, head banging loudly against the deck. Blood oozed from a gash in the captain's scalp. It didn't matter; he had served his purpose. The rest of the convoy would be gathering on the *Lady Bountiful* to await boarding and 'inspection' by the Space Marines.

I think I pushed him too far, thought Zacherys as he noticed blood leaking from Loil's ears and nose.

*It does not matter*, replied Messenger. *There are more of his kind, weak and pathetic, than there are stars in your galaxy. Did you feel how easy it was to control his feeble mind?*

I did, replied Zacherys. The thrill of using the man as a puppet ebbed away, leaving Zacherys strangely empty. What else can I do?

*Whatever you desire. You power will no longer be chained by the dogma of weaklings. The full force of y– Wait! Did you feel that?*

I felt nothing, thought Zacherys. What is it?

*Let me show you.*

Zacherys felt the daemon shifting inside him, pulling back its tendrils from his limbs, coalescing its power in his brain. His witchsight flared into life – the psychic sense that allowed Zacherys to feel the thoughts of others, sense their emotions and locate the spark of their minds in the warp. Zacherys's golden eyes did not see the cramped bridge of the merchantman or the bloodied bodies of the three officers lying crumpled by the door. His thoughts expanded through the ship and beyond, touching on the moon below, sensing the minds of the crew aboard the *Vengeful* alongside. Out and out his mind stretched, reaching through the veil that separated reality from the warp.

And then he felt them.

They were indistinct, faint reflections of presence like shadows in darkness. They were not in the warp; even before his pact with Messenger, Zacherys could tell the approach of a ship by its wake in the immaterium. They were somewhere else.

What are they, he asked? Where are they?

*Between here and there, in their little tunnels burrowed through dimensions. The children of the Dark Prince; you call them eldar.*

Zacherys strained to focus on their location, but could not fix upon them. They were close, within the system. He broke off the search and forced himself back to his mortal senses.

'Gessart, we might have a problem,' he barked over the comm.

Out of glimmering stars of silver, the eldar ships emerged into real space, a little over twenty thousand kilometres away on the starboard bow. Gessart cursed the rudimentary scanner arrays of the *Lady Bountiful*, which were painfully short-ranged and slow. He opened up a channel to the *Vengeful*.

'Kholich, I'm transmitting coordinates. Give me a full augur sweep of that area. Three eldar ships detected. I want to know course, speed and type in two minutes.'

Gessart's fingers danced over the transmitter controls as he sent the information to the strike cruiser.

'We have to assume they are hostile,' he said as he stabbed the transmit rune. Zacherys, Nicz, Lehenhart and Ustrekh were with him in the bridge while the others oversaw the transfer of the cargo containers from the hold to the bays of the *Vengeful*. 'How much longer until we have what we need?'

'Not long enough,' replied Nicz. 'Assuming they come for us as quick as they can.'

'They will,' said Zacherys. 'They are predators and they are hunting. I feel their desire for the kill.'

Gessart flexed his gauntleted fingers with agitation.

'If we cut and run now, we might get away,' he muttered, more to himself than his companions. 'But then we will have to find more supplies before we reach the Eye. Yet, we have no idea of their strength or intent. A stiff warning may force them to break off. They cannot know our numbers either.'

'I say we fight,' said Ustrekh. 'They've come here looking for easy pickings. They'll have little stomach for a real battle.'

Gessart turned to Lehenhart, knowing the veteran would have his own thoughts on the matter.

'It won't take them long to get here,' said Lehenhart. 'Whatever we're going to do, we have to decide quickly. If we leave it too late to run, their ships can easily overhaul a strike cruiser. If we're going to fight, we had best start preparing our defences.'

Gessart sighed. That observation didn't make the choice any easier. The comm chimed in his ear before he could say anything else.

'This is *Vengeful*,' came Kholich's tinny voice. 'Confirm three vessels on a closing course. Warships, cruiser-class. We're beating to orders, arming weapon batteries and setting plasma reactors to battle readiness. Do you wish us to break from docking?'

Gessart glared at the main screen, searching for a sign of the attackers but they were still too far away to be seen against the darkness of space. On the scanner, he could see the merchant ships closest to the eldar turning away, scattering in all directions like sheep before wolves.

'Remain docked,' said Gessart.

'Captain, we will not have battle manoeuvrability whilst attached to the *Lady Bountiful*.'

'Do not question my orders! Continue loading until the enemy are ten thousand kilometres away and then break docking. Take up escort position on the *Lady Bountiful*. We will remain aboard the trader. Signal the civilian fleet to maintain formation and make best speed to our location.'

'Understood, captain.'

The link crackled and fell silent. With a sub-vocal order, he switched the comm to his command channel, addressing the Space Marines of his force.

'Arm the crew,' he said. 'Let them fight for their vessel alongside us. If nothing else, they will be a distraction to the enemy. Remember that we do not fight for the Emperor, nor to protect these people and their ships. This is a battle we must win because our survival depends upon it. Fail here and we are doomed. Better to die in battle now than to eke out a worthless existence drifting the stars. Our destiny is in our hands and though we are no longer slaves to the Imperium, we are still Space Marines!'

The eldar were not dissuaded from their attack by the presence of the *Vengeful*. The three warships swooped in for the kill, sleek, fast and deadly. On the *Lady Bountiful's* flickering scanner, Gessart watched the pirates circling around one of the other merchantmen.

'Detect laser weaponry fire,' Kholich reported from the strike cruiser. 'They are targeting the engines of the *Valdiatius Five*. Shall we move to intercept, captain?'

Gessart quickly assessed the situation on the scanner. As well as the *Lady Bountiful*, three other ships were already within range of the *Vengeful's* batteries. The rest of the convoy were making slow progress and the eldar would fall upon each in turn without having to risk a confrontation with the strike cruiser if it maintained its current position.

'Put yourself between the raiders and the rest of the convoy,' he told Kholich. 'Force them towards our position.'

'Affirmative, captain, moving to intercept,' replied Kholich.

'Engage at long range only,' Gessart added. It was unlikely the eldar would risk boarding a Space Marine vessel, but he didn't want to risk losing the strike cruiser. He turned to Nicz, who was at the helm and engine controls. 'Can you manoeuvre this piece of scrap?'

'Engines and control systems responding well,' replied Nicz without looking up. 'The ship's a mess on the outside, but Loil kept the important functions well maintained.'

'Can you simulate thruster difficulties?'

Nicz glanced at Gessart, guessing his intent.

'I can set them up with intermittent firing,' he said. 'We'll fall behind the rest of the ships and make ourselves an easy target.'

'Do it,' said Gessart, returning his attention to the scanner screen.

As he had hoped, the eldar were unwilling to tackle the strike cruiser directly, despite having more ships. As the *Vengeful* cut through the scattered ships of the convoy, the pirates broke away from their attack and retreated, putting several thousand kilometres between themselves and the escort.

The *Lady Bountiful* trembled violently as Nicz misfired the engines. His armour was bathed with an orange glow as warning lights flickered across the panel in front of him.

'Venting plasma,' he announced.

The ship shook again and rocked to starboard as a plume of super-heated gas exploded from emergency exhausts along the portside stern. Nicz was deliberately clumsy in his attempts to correct their course, causing the ship to list sideways for several minutes while the main engines stuttered with flaring blasts of fire. Another glance at the scanner confirmed to Gessart that the three other merchant ships close to the *Lady Bountiful* were pulling away, heading directly from the eldar attack.

'Come on, take the bait,' Gessart muttered. 'Look at us, we're crippled. Come and get us!'

His attention was fixed on the scanner display, but the vague blobs of green that represented the eldar ships were too inaccurate to track any heading changes. He growled with frustration and fought the urge to slam his fist through the useless piece of equipment.

'Kholich, report!' he snapped. 'What are the enemy doing?'

'They've altered course towards you, captain,' Kholich reported. 'Not at full speed. They seem cautious.'

'They're waiting to see what you are going to do,' Nicz cut in across the comm. 'Move further away from our position.'

'Captain?' Kholich was uncertain, surprised by the break in protocol.

'Move out of weapons range of the *Lady Bountiful*,' Gessart said. 'But stand ready to come about and make full speed to our position if needed. Keep me informed of the eldar's movement, these scanners are worthless.'

'Affirmative, captain.'

Gessart broke the link and rounded on Nicz, stalking across the bridge to slam an open hand into the Space Marine's armoured chest.

'Stay off the command channel!' Gessart growled. 'I am still in charge.'

Nicz knocked away his leader's hand and stepped forwards, the grille of his helm a few centimetres from Gessart's.

'You're just guessing,' Nicz replied calmly. 'You haven't any more idea what to do than the rest of us. We should be aboard the *Vengeful*, chasing down these scum.'

'They would run rings around us, and you know it,' snapped Gessart. 'If they split up, we'll have no chance of catching any of them. We need to draw them in, convince them to board. That's when we'll have the advantage.'

Nicz stepped back and his shock was clear in his voice.

'You intend to counter-board one of their ships?'

'If possible. We will have to see how badly they want to fight.'

Nicz said nothing but a shake of the head made it clear what he thought of Gessart's plan. Gessart turned away and returned to his place at the command controls. His fingers drummed the side of the scanner display as he waited to find out what the eldar would do next.

'They're using cutters on the starboard bow!' Lehenhart reported. 'Decks six and seven.'

'Meet me at Lehenhart's position,' Gessart told his warriors. One of the eldar warships had snared the *Lady Bountiful* in a gravity net and had pulled her alongside to board. The other two raiders had taken up a position a few thousand kilometres away to block the path of the *Vengeful* if it tried to intervene.

Gessart swung around to face Nicz. 'Can I trust you to keep an eye on the other two ships?'

'I'll tell you if either of them tries to board,' the Space Marine replied.

Gessart nodded and ran out of the bridge. He pounded along the uppermost deck until he came to a stairwell. Ducking sideways to fit his bulk through the low door, he hurled himself down the metal steps three at a time, the mesh buckling slightly under the impact of his boots. Three decks down, he squeezed into a narrow passageway flanked by rows of small cabins. Turning to his left he headed towards the bow of the ship. After a few hundred metres the corridor split to the left and right. Bolter fire ran along the bare metal walls from starboard.

Unslinging his storm bolter, Gessart slowed to a jog, eyes scanning the open doorways ahead. He saw nothing until Lehenhart advanced into view along the gallery at the end of the passage, his bionic right hand holding his bolter in a firing position, serrated combat knife in the left. Bright blue lances of laser light erupted from ahead of the Space Marine, zipping past him as he shifted to his left and returned fire, his bolter blazing three times, the roar of each round echoing along the corridor around Gessart.

Glancing over his shoulder at the thump of booted feet, Gessart saw Willusch, Gerhart and Johun a few dozen strides behind him. Over the comm, he heard the reports of others closing in from aft.

Lehenhart had moved out of sight; as Gessart turned into the starboard gallery he saw the Space Marine holding a landing ahead, firing down the stairwell. Five eldar bodies lay sprawled on the decking. Gessart paused for a moment to examine the dead aliens.

Each was as tall as a Space Marine, though far slighter of build. They had thin, angular faces, their almond-shaped eyes wide with the gaze of the dead, ears slightly pointed, brows high and arched. They appeared to have no uniform, though all five wore close-fitting tunics of iridescent scales. One was swathed in the ragged remains of a long red cloak, half his chest missing from a bolt detonation; another was sprawled across the corridor face-down, two holes in the back of his high-collared, dark blue coat. Two of the others were female, their hair wound in elaborate blonde braids spattered with bright red blood, skin-tight suits of black and white beneath their mesh armour; the last half-sat against the wall, narrow chin on chest, head shaven but for a blue scalplock, wearing a broad-shouldered black jacket studded with glistening gems, his legs naked but for knee-high boots.

Long-barrelled lasrifles lay on the floor next to each body, of similar design but each decorated with different coloured gemstones and swirling golden filigrees. Gessart picked up one of the weapons and examined it. It was elegant, powered by some form of crystal cell in the thin stock of the weapon. It crumpled easily as he tightened his grip, no sturdier than the creature that had wielded it.

Reaching Lehenhart, Gessart leaned over the balustrade and saw lithe figures darting from cover to cover on the landing below. He snatched two fragmentation grenades from his belt, thumbed the activation studs and dropped them over the edge. The stairwell rang with twin detonations; shrapnel and smoke filled the enclosed space, a lingering scream signalling that he had found at least one target.

'Do we wait, or go to them?' asked Lehenhart.

Gessart dragged up his memory of the ship's layout; he had to assume the eldar had scanned the vessel and knew something of its configuration as well. The upper four decks only extended for a third of the ship and did not connect to the hold directly. If the eldar were after the cargo – which was no longer aboard – they would have to go down to the lower six decks. With only twenty-five Space Marines to cover the hold, loading bays, docking areas and crew quarters, it would be hard to concentrate any resistance.

'Counter-attack!' Gessart told his warriors. 'Make them pay in blood for ever setting foot on this ship!'

A fusillade of bright blasts and blurring discs filled the stairwell. Gessart recognised shuriken catapult fire amongst the laser shots. He leaned over the railing and unleashed a hail of fire from his storm bolter, the explosive ammunition ripping a trail of splintering metal across the landing below. Slender shapes darted from the shadows and he was engulfed by a hail of razor-sharp projectiles. Pushing himself back, he glanced down at his armour and saw a row of barbed discs embedded across his chest plastron.

'With me,' he growled, pounding down the steps. He heard Lehenhart and the others close behind.

The railing buckled as Gessart grabbed a hold to swing around a turn in the steps. Enemy fire stormed up to meet him; las-bolts seared the paint from his armour while more shurikens sliced through his left arm and leg.

With a leap, he crashed to the landing. There were more than a dozen eldar taking cover in the two doorways; they were dressed in the same strange mix of coats, cloaks and armour he had seen on the bodies above. Quicker than a heartbeat, some of the alien warriors leapt to attack, wielding chainswords with glittering teeth and long blades that gleamed with energy.

Gessart let loose with another burst of fire, shredding an eldar directly in front of him. Before he could adjust his aim, two more were upon him, the teeth of their chainswords shrieking as they skittered across his right shoulder pad and backpack. He swung the storm bolter like a club, aiming for the head of one of his attackers. The eldar dropped cat-like to all fours and then leapt past, dragging her chainsword across the side of Gessart's helm. He took a step back, trying to keep both assailants in view.

Lehenhart arrived at a run, smashing his fist into the back of one of the eldar. The alien bent awkwardly and flopped to the ground, limbs twitching. Gessart had no time to spare a further glance for his warriors coming in behind him as more eldar appeared at the doorway ahead, pistols and swords gripped by slender fingers.

Gessart turned his right shoulder towards them and charged with a roar. Most of the eldar scattered quickly from his path but one was caught with nowhere to go; he was smashed bloodily into the wall by the headlong rush. A warning siren sounded in Gessart's ears as blades bit deep into his backpack and legs, the eldar like a swarm of wasps, darting in to strike before swiftly retreating out of reach.

The Space Marine swung a booted foot at the closest, looking to sweep away the pirate's legs. The eldar nimbly somersaulted over Gessart's attack and landed with sure-footed grace to fire his pistol directly into Gessart's face.

Gessart's finger tightened instinctively on the trigger as he reeled back. Through the cracked lenses of his helm he saw the alien bisected by bolts, sheared through by detonations across his scale-armoured stomach.

Detecting the patter of feet behind him, Gessart swung around to confront a new attacker, but found only empty air. The eldar were falling back, disappearing quickly along both passageways. Willusch and Lehenhart set off after them but Gessart called them back.

'They'll pick each of us off if we split up,' he said. 'Let's not run into an ambush.'

He quickly took stock of the scene. Two of his warriors lay still on the steps, their armour and flesh cut through to the bone in dozens of places. Another three were bleeding heavily from wounds to their arms and legs.

'Report in!' he barked over the comm.

The replies painted a complicated picture. Some of his Space Marines had fended off an eldar advance along the portside, causing significant casualties for no losses. Another group had been caught out on their way to support Gessart and two of their number had fallen in moments before the eldar had swiftly withdrawn. Those who had been stationed by the aft holds were still making their way towards the bow and had yet to encounter any foes.

Unfortunately the *Lady Bountiful* had no internal scanners to keep track of the pirates. Gessart looked for Heynke, who had the force's only functional auspex. The Space Marine was at the top of the flight of steps, bolter in his hands, guarding the approach from above. His armour appeared undamaged, in stark contrast to the others, who all showed signs of the brief but fierce fight.

'Heynke, use the auspex,' Gessart said, checking the ammunition counter on his storm bolter. Seventeen rounds left. He had two more magazines at his belt. More than enough for the moment.

Heynke hooked his bolter to his belt and unslung the scanning device. His armoured fingers coaxed the machine into life, his helm reflecting the pale yellow of the display. Heynke moved the auspex around, trying to get a fix on the lifesigns of the eldar.

'Most have reached the upper decks,' he reported. 'Too much interference from the superstructure for an accura... Hold on, something strange.'

'What is it?' demanded Gessart leaping up the steps to stand beside Heynke.

'Look for yourself,' the Space Marine said, holding the auspex towards Gessart.

The semi-circular screen was filled with bright lines – the power conduits running through the walls of the ship. The eldar showed as fainter traces, little more than pale yellow smudges. The largest concentration was two decks above in the crew mess hall. They were not moving.

'What do you think they are up to?' asked Heynke.

Gessart did not know and any speculation he might offer was abruptly stopped by a buzzing over the comm. The static lasted for a few moments, scaling higher in pitch, and then stopped. There was a pause before he heard a voice, the words slightly stilted with a mechanical edge to them.

'Commander of the Space Marines,' it said. 'I have found the air upon which you speak. Heed the wisdom of my words. This loss of life is senseless and is not of benefit to myself or to you. I have become aware that we should not be adversaries. I detect the eyes that see far and know that you are aware of where I am. I have knowledge that you would wish I share with you. Meet me where we can hold conference and we will discuss this matter like civilised creatures.'

The link crackled again and fell silent.

'Was that…?' said Lehenhart. 'Did that bastard override our comm-frequency?'

'How?' said Heynke.

'Forget how, did you hear what he said?' This was from Freichz. 'He wants a truce!'

Gessart's comm chimed again, signalling a switch to the private channel. He bit back a snarl of frustration at this fresh interruption.

'Yes?' he snapped.

'Gessart, we have a serious problem,' replied Zacherys. 'Ships have broken through the warp boundary. I believe it is the Imperial Navy escort for the convoy.'

'Did you hear the pirate commander?'

'I did. I believe this is the information he wished to pass to us. Somehow he knows that we are protecting the fleet for ourselves. I would recommend that you hear what he has to say.'

'Agreed. Meet me at the aft entrance to the mess hall.' Gessart switched to general transmission. 'Take up guard positions around the mess hall but do not enter. This may be some kind of trick, so stay alert.'

He snapped off more precise orders and instructed Tylo, the Apothecary, to set up an aid station in one of the holds so that the wounded could be tended. With these preparations made, Gessart headed up the stairwell, uncertain what to expect.

Zacherys met Gessart outside the mess hall. There was bright eldar blood splashed across the psyker's armour, some of it still steaming and bubbling. Gessart decided it would be better not to ask. The main doors of the mess hall slid open in front of them and they stepped inside, weapons in hand.

The mess hall was a wide open space, divided by long tables and benches riveted to the floor. At the centre several dozen eldar waited, some of them with weapons ready, most of them lounging across the tables and seats. Gessart's eye was immediately drawn to the one at the centre of the group, who leaned against the end of a table with his legs casually crossed, arms folded. He was dressed in a long coat of green and red diamond patches, which reached to his booted ankles. A ruff of white and blue feathers jutted from the high collar, acting as a wispy halo for his narrow, sharp-cheeked face. His skin was almost white, his hair black and pulled back in a single braid plaited with shining thread. Dark eyes fixed on Gessart as the Space Marine stomped across the metal floor and stopped about ten metres away.

The eldar straightened and his lips moved faintly. The words that echoed across the hall came not from his mouth, but from a brooch upon his lapel, shaped like a thin, stylised skull.

'What is the name of he who has the honour of addressing Aradryan, Admiral of the Winter Gulf?'

'Gessart. Is that a translator?'

'I understand your crude language, but will not sully my lips with its barbaric grunts,' came the metallic reply.

Zacherys moved up next to Gessart and Aradryan's eyes widened with shock and fear. He looked at Gessart with a furrowed brow.

'That you consort with this sort of creature is ample evidence that you are no longer in service to the Emperor of Mankind. We have encountered other renegades like yourselves in the past. My assumptions are proven correct.'

'Zacherys is one of us,' said Gessart with a glance towards the psyker. 'What do you mean?'

'Can you not see that which dwells within him?' The machine spoke in a flat tone but Aradryan's incredulity was clear.

'What do you want?' demanded Gessart.

'To save needless loss for both of us,' Aradryan replied, opening his hands in a placating gesture. 'You will soon be aware that those whose duty it is to protect these vessels are close at hand. If we engage in this pointless fighting they will come upon us both. This does not serve my purpose or yours. I propose that we settle our differences in a peaceful way. I am certain that we can come to an agreement that accommodates the desires of both parties.'

'A truce? We divide the spoils of the convoy?'

'It brings happiness to my spirit to find that you understand my intent. I feared greatly that you would respond to my entreaty with the blind ignorance that blights so many of your species.'

'I have become a recent acquaintance of compromise,' said Gessart. 'I find it makes better company than the alternatives. What agreement do you propose?'

'There is time enough for us both to take what we wish before these new arrivals can intervene in our affairs. We have no interest in the clumsy weapons and goods these vessels carry. You may take as much as you wish.'

'If you don't want the cargo, what is your half of the deal?'

'Everything else,' said Aradryan with a sly smile.

'He means the crews,' whispered Zacherys.

'That is correct, tainted one,' said Aradryan. The eldar pirate fixed his large eyes on Gessart, the hint of a smile twisting his thin lips. 'Do you accede to these demands, or do you wish that we expend more energy killing one another in a pointless display of pride? You must know that I am aware of how few warriors you have should you choose to fight.'

'How long before the escort arrives?' Gessart asked Zacherys.

'Two days at the most.'

'You have enough time to unload whatever you wish and will not be hampered by my ships or my warriors. You have my assurance that you will be unmolested if you offer me the same.'

Gessart stared at Aradryan for some time, but it was impossible to discern the alien's thoughts from his expression. He knew that he could no more trust an eldar than he could take his eye off Nicz, but there seemed little choice. He suppressed a sigh, wondering what it was that he had done to deserve a succession of impossible decisions lately: between protecting innocents and killing the enemy on Archimedon, between millions of rebels and a host of daemons at Helmabad, and now he had to make a bargain with an alien or risk being destroyed by those he had once fought alongside.

'The terms are agreed,' said Gessart. 'I will order my warriors to suspend fighting. I have no control over the crews of the convoy.'

'We are capable of dealing with such problems in our own way,' said Aradryan. 'Be thankful that this day you have found me in a generous mood.'

Gessart hefted his storm bolter and fixed the eldar pirate with a cold stare.

'Don't give me an excuse to change my mind.'

All available space aboard the *Vengeful* was packed with pillaged supplies. Crates filled the hangars that had berthed lost Thunderhawks; ammunition boxes were piled high in the chapel and Reclusiam; crew quarters that would never again house battle-brothers were used as storage for medical wares and maintenance parts. Gessart was exceptionally pleased with the haul; they had enough to survive for several years if necessary.

He stood on the bridge of the strike cruiser as it broke dock from the civilian transport. It had taken more than a day to ferry everything across, and two of the convoy's ships had been left untouched: there simply wasn't room to take on board anything else. As the *Vengeful* powered away one of the eldar cruisers slipped past, the swirl of its gravity nets hooking onto the cargo hauler. The alien ship glided serenely on, its yellow hull fluctuating with black tiger stripes, its solar sails shimmering gold.

'Are we ready to jump?' Gessart asked Zacherys.

'At your command,' came the reply.

Gessart caught Nicz staring at him.

'Don't tell me that you disapprove,' said Gessart.

'Not at all, quite the opposite,' replied Nicz. 'I wondered if Helmabad was a unique moment, but I see that I might be wrong.'

'Let me convince you,' said Gessart, striding to the gunnery control panel.

The systems had been at full power since their first arrival so he knew the eldar would not detect a spike in power. The lock-on was another matter. His fingers danced over the controls as gun ports slid open along the starboard side of the strike cruiser. The eldar ship was only a few hundred kilometres away and the targeting metriculators found their range within seconds.

'What are you doing?' said Nicz

'Leaving the Imperial Navy something to play with,' Gessart replied with a smile.

Gessart tapped in the command for a single salvo and pressed the firing rune. The *Vengeful* shook as the ship unleashed a full broadside at the eldar cruiser. On the main screen explosions blossomed around the alien ship, snapping the main sail mast and rippling along the hull. Flames billowed from exploding gases, the pressure of their release causing the cruiser to yaw violently.

'Zacherys, take us into the warp.'

# BLACK DAWN

### by C L Werner

Labourers bustled about the busy star port of Izo Primaris, capital city of Vulscus. Soldiers of the Merchant Guild observed the workers with a wary eye and a ready grip on the lasguns they carried. Hungry men from across Vulscus were drawn to the walled city of Izo Primaris seeking a better life. What they discovered was a cadre of guilds and cartels who maintained an iron fist upon all commerce in the city. There was work to be had, but only at the wages set by the cadre. The Merchant Guild went to draconian extremes to ensure none of their workers tried to augment their miserable earnings by prying into the crates offloaded from off-world ships.

As a heavy loading servitor trundled away from the steel crates it had unloaded, a different sort of violation of the star port's custom was unfolding. Only minutes before the steel boxes had rested inside the hold of a sleek galiot. The sinister-looking black-hulled freighter had landed upon Vulscus hours before, its master, the rogue trader Zweig Barcelo, having quickly departed the star port to seek an audience with the planetary governor.

Behind him, Zweig had left his cargo, admonishing the Conservator of the port to take special care unloading the crates and keeping people away from them. He had made it clear that the Guilders would be most unhappy if they were denied the chance to bid upon the goods he had brought into the Vulscus system.

Most of the crates the servitors offloaded from the galiot indeed held an exotic menagerie of off-world goods. One, however, held an entirely different cargo.

A small flash of light, a thin wisp of smoke and a round section of the steel crate fell from the side of the metal box. Only a few centimetres in size, the piece of steel struck the tarmac with little more noise than a coin falling from the pocket of a careless labourer. The little hole in the side of the crate was not empty for long. A slender stick-like length of bronze emerged from the opening, bending in half upon a tiny pivot as it cleared the edges of the hole. From the tip of the instrument, an iris slid open, exposing a multifaceted crystalline optic sensor. Held upright against the side of the box, the stick-like instrument slowly pivoted, searching the area for any observers.

Its inspection completed, the compact view scope was withdrawn back into the hole as quickly as it had materialised. Soon the opposite side of the steel crate began to spit sparks and thin streams of smoke. Molten lines of superheated metal disfigured the face of the box as the cargo within cut through the heavy steel. Each precise cut converged upon the others, forming a door-like pattern. Unlike the small round spy hole, the square carved from the opposite side of the crate was not allowed to crash to the ground. Instead, powerful hands gripped the cut section at each corner, fingers encased in ceramite immune to the glowing heat of the burned metal. The section was withdrawn into the crate, vanishing without trace into the shadowy interior.

Almost as soon as the opening was finished, a burly figure stalked away from the crate, his outline obscured by the shifting hues of the camo-cloak draped about his body. The man moved with unsettling grace and military precision despite the heavy carapace armour he wore beneath his cloak. In his hands, he held a thin, narrow-muzzled rifle devoid of either stock or magazine. He kept one finger coiled about the trigger of his rifle as he swept across the tarmac, shifting between the shadows.

Brother-Sergeant Carius paused as a team of labourers and their Guild wardens passed near the stack of crates he had concealed himself behind. The single organic eye remaining in his scarred face locked upon the leader of the wardens, watching him carefully. If any of the workers or their guards spotted him, they would get their orders from this man. Therefore the warden would be the first to die if it came to a fight.

A soft hiss rose from Carius's rifle, long wires projecting outwards from the back of the gun's scope. The Scout-sergeant shifted his head slightly so that the wires could connect with the mechanical optic that had replaced his missing eye. As the wires inserted themselves into his head, Carius found his mind racing with the feed from his rifle's scope, a constantly updating sequence indicating potential targets, distance, obstructions and estimated velocity.

Carius ignored the feed from his rifle and concentrated upon his own senses instead. The rifle could tell him how to shoot, but it couldn't calculate when. The Scout-sergeant would need to watch for that moment when stealth would give way to violence. There were ten targets in all. He estimated he could put them down in three seconds. He didn't want it to come to that. There was just a chance one of them might be able to scream before death silenced him.

The work crew rounded a corner and Carius shook his head to one side, ending the feed from his rifle and inducing the wires to retract back into the scope. He rose from the crouch he had assumed and gestured with his fingers to the shadows around him. Other Scouts rushed from the darkness, following the unspoken commands their sergeant had given them. Three of them formed a defensive perimeter, watching for any other workers who might stray into this quadrant of the star port. The other six assaulted the ferrocrete wall of the storage facility, employing the lowest setting of the melta-axes they had used to silently cut through the side of the cargo crate.

Carius watched his men work. The ferrocrete would take longer to cut through than the steel crate, but the knife-like melta-blades would eventually open the wall as easily as the box. The Scout Marines would then be loosed upon Izo Primaris proper.

Then their real work would begin.

Mattias held a gloved hand to his chin and watched through lidded eyes as the flamboyant off-worlder was led into the conference hall. The governor of Vulscus and the satellite settlements scattered throughout the Boras system adopted a manner of aloof disdain mixed with amused tolerance. He felt it was the proper display of emotion for a man entrusted with the stewardship of seven billion souls and the industry of an entire world.

Governor Mattias didn't feel either aloof or amused, however. The off-worlder wasn't some simple tramp merchant looking to establish trade on Vulscus or a wealthy pilgrim come to pay homage to the relic enshrined within the chapel of the governor's palace.

Zweig, the man called himself, a rogue trader with a charter going back almost to the days of the Heresy itself. The man's charter put him above all authority short of the Inquisition and the High Lords of Terra themselves. For most of his adult life, Mattias had been absolute ruler of Vulscus and her outlying satellites. It upset him greatly to know a man whose execution he couldn't order was at large upon his world.

The rogue trader made a garish sight in the dark, gothic atmosphere of the conference hall. Zweig's tunic was fashioned from a bolt of cloth so vibrant it seemed to glow with an inner light of its own, like the radioactive grin of a mutant sump-ghoul. His vest was a gaudy swirl of crimson velvet, vented by crosswise slashes in a seemingly random pattern. The hologlobes levitating beneath the hall's vaulted ceiling reflected wildly from the synthetic diamonds that marched along the breast of the trader's vest. Zweig's breeches were of chuff-silk, of nearly transparent thinness and clinging to his body more tightly than the gloves Mattias wore. Rough, grox-hide boots completed the gauche exhibition, looking like something that might have been confiscated from an ork pirate. The governor winced every time the ugly boots stepped upon the rich ihl-rugs which covered the marble floors of his hall. He could almost see the psycho-reactive cloth sickening from the crude footwear grinding into its fibres.

Zweig strode boldly between the polished obsidian columns and the hanging nests of niktiro birds that flanked the conference hall, ignoring the crimson-clad Vulscun excubitors who glowered at him as he passed. Mattias was tempted to have one of his soldiers put a shaft of las-light through the pompous off-worlder's knee, but the very air of arrogance the rogue trader displayed made him reconsider the wisdom of such action. It would be best to learn the reason for Zweig's bravado. A rogue trader didn't live long trusting that his charter would shield him from harm on every backwater world he visited. The Imperium was a big place and it might take a long time for news of his demise to reach anyone with the authority to do anything about it.

The rogue trader bowed deeply before Mattias's table, the blue mohawk into which his hair had been waxed nearly brushing across the ihl-rugs. When he rose from his bow, the vacuous grin was back on his face, pearly teeth gleaming behind his dusky lips.

'The Emperor's holy blessing upon the House of Mattias and all his fortune, may his herds be fruitful and his children prodigious. May his enterprise flourish and his fields never fall before the waning star,' Zweig said, continuing the stilted, antiquated form of address that was still practised in only the most remote and forgotten corners of the segmentum. The governor bristled under the formal salutation, unable to decide if Zweig was using the archaic greeting because he thought Vulscus was such an isolated backwater as to still employ it or because he wanted to subtly insult Mattias.

'You may dispense with the formality,' Mattias cut off Zweig's address with an annoyed flick of his hand. 'I know who you are, and you know who I am. More importantly, we each know what the other is.' Mattias's sharp, mask-like face pulled back in a thin smile. 'I am a busy man, with little time for idle chatter. Your charter ensures you an audience with the governor of any world upon which your custom takes you.' He spat the words from his tongue as though each had the taste of sour-glass upon them. 'I, however, will decide how long that audience will be.'

Zweig bowed again, a bit more shallowly than his first obeisance before the governor. 'I shall ensure that I do not waste his lordship's time,' he said. He glanced about the conference hall, his eyes lingering on the twin ranks of excubitors. He stared more closely at the fat-faced ministers seated around Mattias at the table. 'However, I do wonder if what I have to say should be shared with other ears.'

Mattias's face turned a little pale when he heard Zweig speak. Of course the rogue trader had been scanned for weapons before being allowed into the governor's palace, but there was always the chance of something too exotic for the scanners to recognise. He had heard stories about jokaero digi-weapons that were small enough to be concealed in a synthetic finger and deadly enough to burn through armaplas in the blink of an eye.

'I run an impeccable administration,' Mattias said, trying to keep any hint of suspicion out of his tone. 'I have no secrets from my ministers, or my people.'

Zweig shrugged as he heard the outrageous claim, but didn't challenge Mattias's claim of transparency. 'News of the recent... fortunes... of Vulscus has travelled far. Perhaps farther than even you intended, your lordship.'

An excited murmur spread among the ministers, but a gesture from Mattias silenced his functionaries.

'Both the Adeptus Mechanicus and the Ecclesiarchy have examined the relic,' Mattias told Zweig. 'They are convinced of its authenticity. Not that their word was needed. You only have to be in the relic's presence to feel the aura of power that surrounds it.'

'The bolt pistol of Roboute Guilliman himself,' Zweig said, a trace of awe slipping past his pompous demeanour. 'A weapon wielded by one of the holy primarchs, son of the God-Emperor Himself!'

'Vulscus is blessed to have such a relic entrusted to her care,' Mattias said. 'The relic was unearthed by labourers laying the foundation for a new promethium refinery in the Hizzak quarter of Izo Secundus, our oldest city. All Vulscuns proudly remember that it was there the primarch led his Adeptus Astartes in the final battle against the heretical Baron Unfirth during the Great Crusade, ending generations of tyranny and bringing our world into the light of the Imperium.'

Zweig nodded his head in sombre acknowledgement of Mattias's statement. 'My... benefactors... are aware of the relic and the prosperity it will surely bestow upon Vulscus. It is for that reason they... contracted me... to serve as their agent.'

The rogue trader reached to his vest, hesitating as some of the excubitors raised their weapons. A nod of the governor's head gave Zweig permission to continue. Carefully he removed a flat disc of adamantium from a pocket inside his vest. Wax seals affixed a riotous array of orisons, declarations and endowments to the disc, but it was the sigil embossed upon the metal itself that instantly arrested the attention of Mattias and his ministers. It was the heraldic symbol of House Heraclius, one of the most powerful of the Navis Nobilite families in the segmentum.

'I am here on behalf of Novator Priskos,' Zweig announced. 'House Heraclius is anxious to strengthen its dominance over the other Great Families sanctioned to transport custom in this sector. The novator has empowered me to treat with the governor of Vulscus to secure exclusive rights to the transportation of pilgrims to view your sacred relic. The agreement would preclude allowing any vessel without a Navigator from House Heraclius to land on your world.'

There was no need for Mattias to silence his ministers this time. The very magnitude of Zweig's announcement had already done that. Every man in the conference hall knew the traffic of pilgrims to their world would be tremendous. Other worlds had built entire cathedral cities to house lesser relics from the Great Crusade and to accommodate the vast numbers of pilgrims who journeyed across the stars to pay homage to such trifles as a cast-off boot worn by the first ecclesiarch and a dented copper flagon once used by the primarch Leman Russ. The multitudes that would descend upon Vulscus to see a relic of such import as the actual weapon of Roboute Guilliman himself would be staggering. To give a single Navigator House a monopoly on that traffic went beyond a simple concession. The phrase 'kingmaker' flashed through the governor's mind.

'I will need to confer with the full Vulscun planetary council,' Mattias said when he was able to find his voice. House Heraclius would be a dangerous enemy to make, but conceding to its request would not sit well with the other Navigators. The governor knew there was no good choice to make, so he would prefer to allow the planetary council to consider the matter – and take blame for the consequences when they came.

Zweig reached into his pocket again, removing an ancient chronometer. He made a show of sliding its cover away and studying the phased crystal display. Slowly, he nodded his head. 'Assemble the leaders of your world, governor. I can allow you time to discuss your decision. Novator Priskos is a patient... man. He would, however, expect me to be present for your deliberations to ensure that a strong case is made for House Heraclius being granted this concession.'

Mattias scowled as Zweig fixed him with that ingratiating smile of his. The governor didn't appreciate people who could make him squirm.

'That which serves the glory of the God-Emperor is just and will endure. That which harms the Imperium built by His children is false and shall be purged by flame and sword. With burning hearts and cool heads, we shall overcome that which has offended the Emperor's will. Our victory is ordained. Our victory is ensured by our faith in the Emperor.'

The words rang out through the ancient, ornate chapel, broadcast from the vox-casters built into the skull-like helm of Chaplain Valac, repeated by the speakers built into the stone cherubs and gargoyles that leaned down from the immense basalt columns that supported the stained plexiglass ceiling far overhead. Stars shone through the vibrant roof, casting celestial shadows across the throng gathered within the massive temple.

Each of the men who listened to Valac's words was a giant, even the smallest of their number over two metres in height. Every one of the giants was encased in a heavy suit of ceramite armour. The bulky armour was painted a dull green, dappled with blacks and browns to form a camouflaged pattern. Only the right pauldron was not covered in the patchwork series of splotches or concealed by fabric strips of scrim. The thick plate of armour above the right shoulder of each giant bore a simple field of olive green broken by a pair of crossed swords in black. It was a symbol that had announced doom upon a thousand worlds. It was the mark of the Adeptus Astartes, the heraldry of the Chapter of Space Marines called the Emperor's Warbringers.

'This day I remind the Fifth Company of its duty,' Valac continued, his armoured bulk pacing before the golden aquila looming above the chapel's altar. Unlike the rest of the Warbringers, who had removed their helms when they entered the holy shrine, the Chaplain kept his visage locked behind his skull-like mask of ceramite. He alone had not covered his armour in camouflage, his power armour retaining its grim black colouration.

'The Emperor expects us to do that which will bring honour upon His name. All we have accomplished in the past is dust and shadow. It is the moment before us that is of consequence. We do not want to fail Him. Through our victory, we shall show that we are proud to serve Him and to know that He has chosen us to be His mighty servants.

'The Fifth Company is ready for anything and we shall not be found lacking. Let no doubt enter your mind. We have no right to decide innocence or guilt. We are only the sword. The Emperor will know His own. The Emperor has commanded and we will follow His holy words before all others. In this hour of reflection and contemplation, we see victory before us. We need only deny the temptations of doubt and seize it. That is the duty of this hour!'

At the rear of the chapel, Inquisitor Korm listened to Chaplain Valac preach to his fellow Warbringers. A guest upon the Warbringers' battle-barge, the inquisitor had decided to keep himself as inconspicuous as possible. Even Korm felt a trickle of fear in his heart as he heard Valac's fiery words, as he watched the Chaplain instil upon the armoured giants kneeling before him a cold, vicious determination to descend upon their enemies without mercy or quarter. Korm knew he was hearing the death of an entire city echoing through the vaulted hall of the chapel. A twinge of guilt flickered through his mind as he considered how many innocent people were going to die in a few hours.

Korm quickly suppressed the annoying emotion. He'd done too many things over his life to listen to his conscience now. Ten thousand, even a million hapless citizens of the Imperium were a small price to pay for the knowledge he sought. Knowledge he alone would possess because only he knew the secret of the relic that Governor Mattias had unearthed.

626 *Space Marines*

Unleashing the Warbringers upon Vulscus was a brutal solution to Korm's problem, but the inquisitor had learned long ago that the surest way to victory was through excessive force.

If there was one thing the Warbringers did better than anyone, it was excessive force. Korm smiled grimly as he listened to the Chaplain's closing words.

'Now, brothers, rise up and let the Emperor's enemies discover the price of heresy! Let the storm of judgement be set loose!'

The factory worker crumpled into a lifeless heap as the vibro-knife punctured his neck and slashed the carotid artery. Carius lowered the grimy corpse to the peeling linoleum tiles that covered the floor. The Scout-sergeant pressed his armoured body against the filthy wall of the hallway and brought the tip of his boot against the clapboard door the worker had unlocked only a few seconds before. Slowly, Carius nudged the door open. Like a shadow, he slid into the opening, closing the portal behind him.

Scout-Sergeant Carius had been lurking in the dusty archway that marked a long-forgotten garbage chute, biding his time as he waited for the factories of Izo Primaris to disgorge their human inmates. He had watched as workers trudged down the hall, shuffling down the corridor half-dead with fatigue. He had let them all pass, maintaining his vigil until he saw the man he wanted. Carius's victim was just another nameless cog in the economy of the Imperium, a man of no importance or consequence. The only thing that made him remarkable was the room he called home. That minor detail had caused fifteen centimetres of gyrating steel to sink into the back of the man's neck.

Carius paused when he crossed the threshold, his ears trained upon the sounds of the dingy apartment he had invaded. He could hear the mineral-tainted water rumbling through the pipes, could fix the lairs of sump-rats in the plaster walls, could discern the pebbly groan of air rattling through vents. The Scout-sergeant ignored these sounds. It was the slight noise of footsteps that had his attention.

The apartment was a miserable hovel, ramshackle factory-pressed furnishings slowly decaying into their constituent components. A threadbare rug was thrown across the peeling floor in some vain effort to lend a touch of dignity to the place. A narrow bed was crushed against one wall, a scarred wardrobe lodged in a corner. Table, chairs, a mouldering couch, a lopsided shelf supporting a sorry collection of crystal miniatures, these were the contents of the apartment. These, and a wide window looking out upon the boulevard.

Carius followed the sound of footsteps. The main room of the apartment had two lesser ancillary chambers – a pail closet and a galley. It was from the galley that the sounds arose.

The Scout-sergeant edged along the wall until he stood just at the edge of the archway leading into the galley. The pungent smell of boiling veg-etables struck his heightened olfactory senses, along with a suggestion of sweat and feminine odour. Carius dug his armoured thumb into the wall, effortlessly ripping a clump of crumbly grey plaster free. Without turning from the archway, he threw the clump of plaster against the apartment door. The impact sounded remarkably like a door slamming shut; the fragments of plaster tumbling across the floor as they exploded away from the impact resembled the sound of footsteps.

'Andreas!' a woman's voice called. 'Dinner is–'

The worker's wife didn't have time to do more than blink as Carius's armoured bulk swung out from the wall and filled the archway as she emerged from the galley to welcome her husband. The vibro-knife stabbed into her throat, stifling any cry she might have made.

Carius depressed the vibro-knife's activation stud, ending the shivering motion of the blade and slid the weapon back into its sheath. Walking away from the body, he shoved furniture out of his way, advancing to the window. The sergeant stared through the glazed glass and admired the view of the boulevard outside. From the instant he had inspected the building from the street below, he had expected this room to offer such a vantage point.

The apartment door opened behind him, but Carius did not look away from the window. He knew the men moving into the room were his own.

'Report,' Carius ordered.

'Melta bombs placed at power plant,' one of the Scouts stated, his voice carrying no inflection, only the precise acknowledgement of a job completed.

'Melta bombs in position at defence turrets nine and seven,' the other Scout said.

Carius nodded his head. The two Scouts had been charged with tar-gets closest to their current position. It would take time for the others to reach their targets and filter back. The sergeant studied the chronometer fixed to the underside of his gauntlet. The attack would not begin for some hours yet. His squad was still ahead of schedule. By the time they were finished, all of Izo Primaris's defence turrets would be sabotaged, leaving the city unable to strike any aerial attackers until it could scram-ble its own aircraft. Carius shook his head as he considered what value the antiquated militia fighters would have against a Thunderhawk. The defence turrets had been the only real menace the Space Marines could expect as they made their descent from the orbiting battle-barge, the *Deathmonger*.

Other melta bombs would destroy the city's central communications hub and disable the energy grid. Izo Primaris would be plunged into confusion and despair even before the first Warbringers descended upon the city.

The local planetary defence force was of little concern to the Warbringers. Unable to contact their central command, they would be forced to operate in a disjointed, fragmented fashion, a type of combat for which they were unprepared. There was only one factor within Izo Primaris that might prove resilient enough to react to the havoc preceding the Warbringers' assault.

Carius motioned with his hand, gesturing for the two Scout Marines to occupy rooms to either side of the apartment he had secured. The Scouts slipped back into the hall with the same silence with which they had entered. Carius unslung the needle rifle looped over his shoulder. The back of the scope opened, sending wires slithering into his artificial eye.

Through the prism of the rifle's scope, Carius studied the massive, fortress-like structure of plasteel and ferrocrete that rose from the squalor of the district like an iron castle. A gigantic Imperial aquila was etched in bronze upon each side of the imposing structure, the precinct courthouse of the city's contingent of the Adeptus Arbites.

Brutal enforcers of the *Lex Imperialis*, the Imperial Law that bound every world within the Imperium, the Arbites had the training, the weapons and the skill to prove a troublesome obstacle if allowed the chance. Carius and his Scouts would ensure the arbitrators did not get that chance. Their mission of sabotage completed, the Scouts would fan out across the perimeter of the courthouse. Sniper fire would keep the arbitrators pinned down inside their fortress. In time, the arbitrators would find a way around the lethal fire of Carius and his men. By then, however, the Warbringers should have accomplished their purpose in Izo Primaris.

Carius watched as armoured arbitrators paced about the perimeter fence separating the courthouse from the slums around it. His finger rested lightly against the trigger of his rifle, the weapon shifting ever so slightly as he maintained contact with the target he had chosen.

When the signal came, Carius and his Scouts would be ready.

It wasn't really surprising that the planetary council of Vulscus met in a section of the governor's palace. Mattias was a ruler who believed in allowing his subjects the illusion of representation, but wasn't foolish enough to allow the council to actually conduct its business outside his own supervision. Even so, there were times when the representatives of the various merchant guilds and industrial combines could be exceedingly opinionated. Occasionally, Mattias had found it necessary to summon his excubitors to maintain order in the council chamber.

The debate over the proposal Zweig had brought to Vulscus was proving to be just such a divisive subject. Lavishly appointed guilders roared at fat promethium barons, the semi-mechanical tech-priests lashing out against the zealous oratory of the robed ecclesiarchs. Even the handful of wiry rogues representing the trade unions felt they had to bare their teeth and demand a few concessions to compensate the unwashed masses of workers they supposedly championed. As soon as one of the industrialists or guilders tossed a bribe their way, the union men would shut up. The others would be more difficult to silence.

Arguments arose over the wisdom of defying the other Great Families by honouring the request of House Heraclius. Some felt that the pilgrims should be able to reach Vulscus by whatever means they could, others claimed that by having a single family of Navigators controlling the traffic there would be less confusion and more order. Those guilders and industrialists who already had exclusive contracts with House Heraclius to ship goods through the warp sparred with those who had dealings with other Navigators and worried about how the current situation would impact their own shipping agreements.

Throughout it all, Mattias watched the planetary council shout itself hoarse and wondered if perhaps he should have bypassed them and just made the decision himself. If anyone had been too upset with his decision, he could have always sent the militia to re-educate them.

He glanced across the tiers of the council chamber to the ornate visitors' gallery. No expense had been spared to make the gallery as opulent and impressive as possible. Visiting dignitaries were surrounded by vivid holo-picts of assorted scenes of Vulscun history and culture, the walls behind them covered in rich tapestries depicting the wonders of Vulscun industry and the extensive resources of the planet and her satellites. If the vicious debates of the planetary council failed to interest a visiting ambassador, the exotic sculptures of Vulscun beauties would usually suffice to keep him entertained.

Zweig, however, didn't even glance at the expensive art all around him in the gallery. He stubbornly kept watching the debate raging below him, despite the tedium of such a vigil. Mattias could tell the rogue trader was bored by the whole affair. He kept looking at his antique chronometer.

The governor chuckled at Zweig's discomfort. The man had asked for this, after all. He'd kept pestering Mattias about when the council could be gathered and if all the leaders of Vulscus would be present to hear him make his case for Novator Priskos. Despite repeated assurances from the governor, Zweig had been most insistent that all of the men who controlled Vulscus should be in attendance when he introduced the Navigator's proposal.

Well, the rogue trader had gotten his wish. He had presented his proposal to the planetary council. Now he could just sit back and wait a few weeks for their answer.

Mattias chuckled again when he saw Zweig fussing about with his chronometer again. The governor wondered if the rogue trader might consider selling the thing. Mattias had never seen a chronometer quite like it. He was sure it would make an interesting addition to his private collection of off-world jewellery and bric-a-brac.

The governor's amusement ended when there was a bright flash from Zweig's chronometer. At first Mattias thought perhaps Zweig's incessant toying with the device had caused some internal relay to explode. It was on his lips to order attendants to see if the rogue trader had been injured, but the words never left his mouth.

Shapes were appearing on the gallery beside Zweig, blurry outlines that somehow seemed far more real than the holo-picts playing around them. With each second, the shapes became more distinct, more solid. They were huge, monstrous figures, twice the height of a man and incredibly broad. Though their outlines were humanoid, they looked more machine than man, great bulky brutes of tempered plasteel and adamantium.

Mattias stared in shock as the strange manifestations began to move, lumbering across the gallery. The giants were painted in a dull olive drab, mottled with splashes of black and brown to help break up their outlines. If not for the confusing blur of colour, the governor might have recognised them for what they were sooner. It was only when one of the giants shifted its arm, raising a hideous rotary autocannon over the railing of the gallery, that the governor saw the ancient stone cruciform bolted to the armoured shoulder. It was then that he knew the armoured giants surrounding Zweig were Space Marines.

The chronometer Zweig had been toying with was actually a homing beacon. The Space Marines had fixed the beacon's location and teleported down into the council chamber. There could be no doubt as to why. For some reason, the rogue trader had brought death to the leaders of Vulscus.

A hush fell upon the chamber as the councillors took notice of the five giants looming above them from the gallery. Arguments and feuds were forgotten in that moment as each man stared up into the waiting jaws of destruction. Some cried out in terror; some fell to their knees and pleaded innocence; others made the sign of the aquila and called upon the Emperor of Mankind.

Whatever their reaction, their end was already decided. In unison, the Warbringers in their heavy Terminator armour opened fire upon the cowering councillors. Five storm bolters tore into the screaming men, bursting their bodies as though they were rotten fruit.

In a matter of seconds, the ornate council chamber became a charnel house.

Sirens blared throughout Izo Primaris. Smoke curled skywards from every quarter, turning the purplish twilight black with soot. Crisis control tractors trundled into the streets, smashing their way through the evening traffic, oblivious to any concern save that of reaching the stricken sections of the city. No industrial accident, no casual arson in a block of filthy tenements, not even the tragic conflagration of the opulent residence of a guilder could have provoked such frantic, brutal reaction. The explosions had engulfed the defence batteries, all five of the massive forts crippled in the blink of an eye by melta bombs.

Even as the crisis tractors smashed a path through the crowded streets, tossing freight trucks and commuter sedans like chaff before a plough, more explosions ripped through the city. Lights winked out, a malignant darkness spreading through the capital. A pillar of fire rising from the heart of the metropolitan sprawl was the only monument to the site of Izo Primaris's central power plant. It would be hours before tech-priests at the substations would be able to redirect the city's energy needs through the battery of back-up plants. They wouldn't even try. To do that, the tech-priests required absolution from their superiors.

The destruction of the communications hub made the earlier explosions seem tame by comparison. Plasteel windows cracked a kilometre and a half away from the cloud of noxious smoke that heralded the silencing of a planet. A skyscraper of ferrocrete and reinforced armaplas, the communications tower had bristled with satellite relays and frequency transmitters, its highest chambers, five hundred metres above the ground, devoted to the psychic exertions of the planet's astropaths. Governor Mattias, always mindful of his own security and power, had caused all communications on Vulscus to be routed through the tower, where his private police could check every message for hints of sedition and discontent.

Now the giant tower had fallen, brought to ruin by the timed blast of seven melta bombs planted in its sub-cellars. With the death of the hub, every vox-caster on Vulscus went silent.

All except those trained upon a different frequency. A frequency being relayed from a sinister vessel in orbit around the world.

Izo Primaris maintained three militia garrisons within its walled confines. Two infantry barracks and a brigade of armour. Despite the silence of the vox-casters and their inability to raise anyone in central command, the soldiers of the Vulscun planetary defence forces were not idle. Lasguns and flak armour were brought from stores, companies and regiments were quickly mustered into formation.

There was nothing to disturb the hasty muster of soldiers at the two infantry barracks. The tank brigade was not so fortunate. The Scout Marine who had visited them had not placed melta bombs about their headquarters or tried to sabotage the fifty Leman Russ-pattern tanks housed in the base's motor pool. What he had done instead was even more deadly.

A bright flash burst into life at the centre of the courtyard where the tankmen were scrambling to their vehicles. A survivor of the massacre in the council chamber would have recognised that flash, would have shouted a warning as hulking armoured shapes suddenly appeared.

From the orbiting battle-barge, five more Terminators had followed a homing beacon and been teleported with unerring precision to their target.

The olive-drab giants opened fire upon the tankmen, tearing their bodies to pieces with concentrated fire from their storm bolters. One of the Space Marines, his bulky armour further broadened by the box-like weapon system fastened to his shoulders, targeted the tanks themselves. Shrieking as they shot upwards from the cyclone missile launcher, a dozen armour-busting krak missiles streamed towards the militia tanks. The effect upon the armoured vehicles was much like that of the storm bolters upon the stunned tankmen. Reinforced armour plate crumpled like tinfoil as the missiles slammed home, their shaped warheads punching deep into the tanks' hulls before detonating. The effect was like igniting a plasma grenade inside a steel can. The tanks burst apart from within as the explosives gutted their innards.

In a few minutes, the surviving tankmen retreated back into their barracks, seeking shelter behind the thick ferrocrete walls. The Terminators ignored the sporadic lasgun fire directed on them, knowing there was no chance such small arms fire could penetrate their armoured shells. They turned away from the barracks, maintaining a vigil on the gated entryway to the motor pool.

Despite the carnage they had wrought, the mission the Terminators had been given was not one of slaughter. It was to keep the tanks from mobilising and spreading out into the city where they might interfere with the Warbringers' other operations.

Carius followed the read from his scope and opened fire. He aimed thirteen centimetres above the arbitrator he had chosen for his victim, allowing for the pull of gravity upon his shot. The slender sliver-like needle struck home, slicing through the arbitrator's jaw just beneath the brim of his visor. The Enforcer didn't even have time to register pain before the deadly poison upon the needle dropped him. His body twitched and spasmed upon the cobblestones outside the courthouse, drawing in other arbitrators, rushing to investigate their comrade's plight. Three more of the Enforcers were dropped as the other snipers staged around the courthouse opened fire.

The arbitrators fell back into their fortress, employing riot shields to protect themselves as they withdrew. Carius kept his rifle aimed upon the entrance of the courthouse. Experience and the mem-training he had undergone when a neophyte told Carius what to expect next. These arbitrators were especially well trained, the sergeant conceded. They beat his estimate by a full minute when they emerged from the courthouse in a phalanx, employing their riot shields to form a bulwark against the sniper fire.

Emotionlessly, Carius scanned the crude defensive line. He nodded his head slightly when he saw the man he wanted. The Judge wore a stormcloak over his carapace armour and a golden eagle adorned his helmet. Carius aimed at that bit of ostentation, sending a poisoned needle sizzling through one of the riot shields to embed itself in the beak of the eagle. The Judge felt the impact of the shot, ducking his head and reaching to his helmet. The Scout-sergeant wasn't disappointed when he saw the Judge's face go white when his fingers felt the slivers of Carius's bullet embedded in his helmet.

The Judge rose and shouted at the arbitrators. It was again to the credit of the Enforcers that they did not allow the Judge's panic to infect them and their second retreat into the courthouse was made in perfect order, the phalanx never disintegrating into a panicked mob.

Carius leaned back, resting his elbows against the sill of the window. The next thing the arbitrators would try would be to use one of their Rhino armoured transports to affect a breakout. Brother Domitian would be in position with his heavy bolter to thwart that attempt. After that, the Enforcers would have to think about their next move.

Carius was content to let them think. While the arbitrators were thinking they would be safely contained inside the courthouse where they couldn't interfere with the Warbringers.

With the defence batteries destroyed and communications down, there was no warning for the people of Izo Primaris when five gun-laden assault craft descended upon the city. Two of the powerful Thunderhawk gunships hurtled into the ferrocrete canyons of the city, guided through the black maze of the darkened metropolis by holo-maps taken by the battle-barge from orbit. As the Thunderhawks progressed only a dozen metres above the streets, their speed gradually slowed. Intermittent bursts of lascannon fire slammed into the sides of buildings or gouged craters from the tarmac. Screams of terror rose from civilians as they streamed from their wounded homes, filling the streets with a mass of frightened humanity.

Coldly, with a callous precision, the Warbringers employed the heavy bolters mounted upon their Thunderhawks to herd the frantic mob through the streets. The objective of this brutal tactic soon showed itself. The infantry regiments were finally marching from their garrisons, trying to restore order to the stricken city. The desperate mob rushed into the face of their marching columns.

The militia commanders hesitated to give the order to open fire on their own people. The delay could not be recovered. Even as the belated command was given, the civilians were crashing into the soldiers, confusing their ranks, breaking the cohesion of their units.

The Thunderhawks dropped still lower, the ramps set into the rear of their hulls opening. Green-armoured giants jumped from the moving gunships, rolling across the tarmac as they landed. Each of the

Warbringers was soon on his feet again, the lethal bulk of a boltgun clenched in his steel gauntlets. While the militia still fought to free themselves of the civilian herd, the Space Marines moved into position, establishing a strongpoint at the intersection nearest their enemies.

Both Thunderhawks surged forwards with a burst of speed, sweeping over the embattled troops. One soldier managed to send a rocket screaming up at one of the gunships, the warhead impacting against the hull and blackening the armour plate. Any jubilation over the attack was quickly extinguished as the Thunderhawks reached the rear of the militia columns. Spinning full around, the gunships came back, their lascannons blazing. The withering fire slammed into the militia regiments, forcing them forwards. It was their turn to be herded through the streets, herded straight into the waiting guns of the Warbringers on the ground.

Of the remaining Thunderhawks, one sped across Izo Primaris to disgorge its cargo of power-armoured giants at the armour base so that they might support the action entrusted to the Terminators. The other two made straight for the governor's palace.

The compound was in a state of siege, frightened citizens hammering at its gates, demanding answers from their leaders. The red-uniformed excubitors held the mob back, employing shock mauls to break the arms of anyone trying to climb over the walls, using laspistols on those few who actually made it over the barrier.

The gunships unleashed the fury of their heavy bolters into both mob and guards, the explosive rounds shearing through the crimson armour of the excubitors as though it were paper. Citizens fled back into the darkened streets, wailing like damned souls as terror pounded through their hearts. The excubitors attempted to fall back to defensive positions, but the punishment being visited on them by the heavy bolters soon caused the guards to abandon that plan and retreat back into the palace itself.

In short order, a landing zone had been cleared. The Thunderhawks descended into the lush gardens fronting Governor Mattias's palace, the backwash of their powerful engines crushing priceless blooms imported from Terra into a mess of mangled vegetation. Armoured ramps dropped open at the rear of each gunship, ceramite-encased giants rushing to assume a perimeter around the garden. Two machines, lumbering monstrosities twice as tall as even the gigantic Space Marines, emerged from the Thunderhawks behind the Warbringers. Vaguely cast in a humanoid form, the torso of each machine encased the armoured sarcophagus of a crippled Warbringer, his mind fused to the adamantium body which now housed it. The Dreadnoughts were revered battle-brothers of the Warbringers, ancient warriors who fought on through the millennia in their ageless metal tombs.

The two Dreadnoughts fanned out across the gardens, one training its deadly weapons on the wall at the front of the compound, the other facing towards the palace itself. Almost immediately the huge machine was spurred into action as solid shot from a heavy stubber mounted in an ornate cupola began firing upon it. The bullets glanced off the Dreadnought's thick hull, barely scratching the olive drab paint that coated it. Power hissed through the over-sized energy coils of the immense weapon that was fitted to the machine's left arm. When the coils began to glow with the intensity of a supernova, the Dreadnought pivoted at its waist and raised the arm towards the cupola.

A blinding burst of light erupted from the nozzle that fronted the Dreadnought's cumbersome weapon. The blazing ball of gas sizzled across the gardens, striking the cupola at its centre. Instantly the structure vanished in a great cloud of boiling nuclear malignance as the charged plasma reacted with the solid composition of the cupola. The sun gun immolated the excubitors who had fired upon the Dreadnought, reduced their heavy stubber to a molten smear and fused the cupola into something resembling a charred brick.

After that, an eerie silence fell across the compound. The governor's guards were not about to provoke the wrath of the Dreadnoughts a second time.

With the Dreadnoughts in command of the exterior, the twenty Warbringers left the defence of the perimeter to their ancient brethren and rushed the palace itself. Gilded doors designed to withstand the impact of a freight tractor were quickly shattered by the chainswords of the Space Marines, the diamond-edged blades tearing through the heavy oorl-wood panels and the plasteel supports.

As the first Warbringers breached the doors and entered the palace itself, Inquisitor Korm emerged from one of the Thunderhawks, his imposing figure dwarfed by the huge armoured warriors who flanked him. Captain Phazas held his helmet in the crook of his arm, exposing a leathery face and a forehead bristling with steel service studs. Chaplain Valac, as ever, kept his countenance locked behind the death's head mask of his helm.

Phazas pressed a finger against his ear, closing one eye as he digested the vox-cast being relayed to him. 'Squad Boethius has secured the council building,' he told Korm. The captain's grim face twisted in a scowl. 'Zweig reports that Governor Mattias escaped before the operation was complete. Some kind of personal force field.'

'We will track down the heretic,' Korm assured the fearsome Phazas. 'There is no escape for him. With his regime broken, he will try to flee Vulscus.' The inquisitor's eyes burned with a fanatical light, his lip curling in disgust. 'First he will try to secure his most precious treasure.'

'The obscene shall be cast low in the midst of their obscenity,' Chaplain Valac's stern voice intoned. 'For them, death is but the doorway to damnation.'

Korm turned away from Valac and directed his attention back to Phazas. 'Have your men search the palace, sweep through it room by room. Mattias must not leave the compound with the relic.'

'The Warbringers know their duty,' Phazas answered, annoyance in his tone. 'The heretic will be found. The relic will be recovered.' He spoke as though both tasks had already been accomplished, statement rather than speculation. Korm knew better than to question the captain's belief in his men.

A man didn't live long enough to become an inquisitor if he were a fool.

Governor Mattias had retreated to a fortified bunker deep beneath his palace. The Warbringers had intercepted the governor before he could reach his escape route: a private tunnel connecting the complex to the underrail network beneath Izo Primaris. Twenty excubitors had been killed in the ensuing firefight. Mattias and his ten surviving guards had fallen back to the bunker.

Designed to be proof against rebellion and civil unrest, the governor's bunker proved no obstacle to the Warbringers, warriors used to breaching the bulkheads of renegade starships and assaulting the citadels of xenos armies. The huge plasteel doors that blocked the entrance to the bunker were quickly reduced to slag by a concentrated blast from a plasma cannon. The Warbringers rushed through the opening while molten metal still dripped from the frame.

One of the power-armoured giants vanished in a burst of light, flesh and ceramite liquefied by the searing energy that smashed into him. Instantly the other Warbringers flattened against the walls, voxing warnings to their comrades. Mattias only had a few guards left to him, but these last excubitors had something the others didn't. They had a multi-melta.

The crimson-armoured excubitors swung the heavy weapon around on its tripod. Nestled behind a ferrocrete pillbox, the guards tried to bring their deadly weapon to bear on the Warbringers already in the corridor. The armoured giants could see the barrels of the multi-melta pivoting within the narrow loophole. One of the Warbringers racked his boltgun and emptied a clip into the pillbox, the explosive rounds digging little craters in the thick surface, drawing the attention of the gun crew.

As the multi-melta swung around to fire on the shooter, he threw himself flat to the floor. The superheated beam of light flashed through the air above him, melting the stabiliser jets and air purification intakes on the Warbringer's backpack, but doing no harm to the Space Marine himself.

Instantly, the other Warbringers in the corridor charged the pillbox. It would take three seconds for the multi-melta to cool down enough to be fired again. The Space Marines intended to have the strongpoint disabled before then. The foremost of the armoured giants reached to his belt, removing a narrow disc of metal. He flung this against the face of the pillbox, black smoke filling the corridor as the blind grenade exploded. The optical sensors built into the Warbringers' helmets allowed them to pierce the dense cloud of inky smoke. The excubitors inside the pillbox were not so fortunate. Frantically they tried to fire the multi-melta into the darkness, the blazing beam of light striking only the ferrocrete wall of the bunker.

Pressed against the face of the pillbox, two of the Warbringers pushed tiny discs through the loophole, then turned away as the frag grenades detonated inside the strongpoint. The menace of the multi-melta was over.

The Warbringers swept around the now silent pillbox, pressing on down the corridor. Las-bolts cracked against their power armour as they converged upon an armaplas barricade thrown across the middle of the hallway, the governor and the last of his guards mounting a hopeless last-ditch effort to defy the oncoming Space Marines.

'This is an unjust act!' Mattias shrieked. 'I have paid the Imperial tithe, I have exceeded the conscription levels for the Imperial Guard! You have no right here! Vulscus is loyal!'

The governor's desperate plea went unanswered by the Space Marines sweeping down the hall. Precise shots from the huge boltguns the Warbringers bore brought death to two of the remaining excubitors. A third threw down his weapon, climbing over the barricade in an effort to surrender. A bolt-round tore through his chest, splattering his organs across the armaplas fortification. The orders the Warbringers were under had been explicit: no prisoners.

'Surrender the relic,' the sepulchral voice of Chaplain Valac boomed through the bunker, magnified by the vox-amplifiers built into his skull-faced helm. The black-armoured Warbringer marched down the corridor, the winged crozius clenched in his fist glowing with power as he approached the barricade. 'Atone for your faithlessness and be returned to the Emperor's grace in death.'

The governor cringed as he heard Valac's words, but quickly recovered. His face pulled back in a sneer of contempt. 'The relic? That is why you have destroyed my city?' Bitter laughter choked Mattias's voice. 'The noble Adeptus Astartes, sons of the Emperor! Common thieves!'

Perhaps the governor might have said more, but his tirade had focused every bolter in the corridor upon him. Mattias was thrown back as the concentrated fusillade struck him, tossing his body back from the edge of the barricade. The last two excubitors, their reason broken by the hopelessness of their situation, broke from cover and charged straight towards the Warbringers, their lasguns firing harmlessly at the power-armoured giants.

Chaplain Valac pressed forwards, climbing over the barricade and walking towards the crumpled body of Governor Mattias. The governor's reductor field had prevented the fusillade from ripping apart his body, but hadn't been equal to the momentum of the shots. The impact had hurled him across the corridor to crash against the unyielding ferrocrete wall.

There was no sympathy as Valac stared down at the broken governor. Even with half his bones shattered, Mattias tried to defend the object cradled against his chest. Wrapped tightly in a prayer rug soaked in sacred unguents and adorned with waxen purity seals and parchment benedictions, even now the governor could feel the supernatural power of the relic giving him strength.

'You have no right,' Mattias snarled at Valac. 'Roboute Guilliman left it here, left it for Vulscus!'

'No,' Valac's pitiless voice growled. He raised the heavy crozius he carried, energy bristling about the club-like baton. 'He didn't leave it.' The Chaplain brought his staff smashing down, its power field easily bypassing the reductor field that protected the governor. Mattias's head was reduced to pulp beneath Valac's blow.

Grimly, Valac removed the relic from the bloodied corpse. Turning away from Mattias's body, the Chaplain began stripping away the pious adornments that surrounded the relic, flinging them aside as though they were unclean filth. Soon he exposed a bolt pistol of ancient pattern, its surface encrusted by millennia of decay and corrosion.

'You have secured the relic,' Inquisitor Korm beamed as he marched down the corridor, Captain Phazas beside him. A triumphant smile was on Korm's lean face. 'We must get it to the fortress on Titan so that the Ordo Malleus may study it.'

Valac shook his head. 'No,' he intoned. His fist clenched tighter about the bolt pistol, the pressure causing some of the corrosion to flake away, exposing the symbol of an eye engraved into the grip of the gun. 'It is an abomination and must be purged. You have brought us here to do the Emperor's work, and it shall be done.'

Korm stared in disbelief at the grim Warbringer Chaplain. The inquisitor had been the one who had uncovered the truth about the relic so recently discovered on Vulscus, a truth locked away in the archives on Titan. Roboute Guilliman had indeed been on Vulscus, but it had not been the Ultramarines or their primarch who had brought the planet into the Imperium, though such was the official version preached by the Ecclesiarchy and taught in sanctioned histories of the world. The real liberators had been the Luna Wolves. If a primarch had left a relic upon a Vulscun battlefield, it had been left by that of the Luna Wolves. It had been left by the arch-traitor, Warmaster Horus.

The fearsome Chaplain marched across the bunker to the shambles that had been left of the pillbox. Clenching the relic in one hand, Valac ripped the damaged multi-melta from the emplacement. Korm gasped in alarm as he understood the Chaplain's purpose. The relic was tainted, a thing of heresy and evil to be sure, corrupting even the innocent by pretending to be something holy. But it was more important that it be studied, not destroyed!

Phazas laid a restraining hand upon Korm's shoulder before the inquisitor could interfere. 'Two fates present themselves,' the captain told him. 'You can return to Titan a hero who has brought about the destruction of an unholy thing. Or you can be denounced as a Horusian radical and perish with the relic. Make your choice, inquisitor.'

Sweat beaded Korm's brow as he watched Chaplain Valac throw the relic onto the ground and aim the heavy multi-melta at it. At such range, the bolt pistol would be reduced to vapour, annihilated more completely than if it had been cast into the centre of a sun.

Korm knew he would share the same annihilation if he broke faith with the Warbringers. The Adeptus Astartes had a very narrow definition of duty and honour. Anything tainted by contact with heresy was a thing to be destroyed.

As he watched Valac obliterate the relic, Korm decided to keep quiet. He'd been an inquisitor for a long time. A man didn't last that long if he were a fool.

# THE LONG GAMES AT CARCHARIAS

*By Rob Sanders*

The end began with the *Revenant Rex*.

An interstellar beast. Bad omen of omens. A wanderer: she was a regular visitor to this part of the segmentum. The hulk was a drifting gravity well of twisted rock and metal. Vessels from disparate and distant races nestled, broken-backed amongst mineral deposits from beyond the galaxy's borders and ice frozen from before the beginning of time. A demented logic engine at the heart of the hulk – like a tormented dreamer – guided the nightmare path of the beast through the dark void of Imperial sectors, alien empires of the Eastern Fringe and the riftspace of erupting maelstroms. Then, as if suddenly awoken from a fevered sleep, the daemon cogitator would initiate the countdown sequence of an ancient and weary warp drive. The planetkiller would disappear with the expediency of an answered prayer, destined to drift up upon the shores of some other bedevilled sector, hundreds of light years away.

The *Revenant Rex* beat the Aurora Chapter at Schindelgheist, the Angels Eradicant over at Theta Reticuli and the White Scars at the Martyrpeake. Unfortunately the hulk was too colossal and the timeframes too erratic for the cleanse-and-burn efforts of the Adeptus Astartes to succeed: but Chapter pride and zealotry ensured their superhuman efforts regardless. The behemoth was infested with greenskins of the Iron Klaw Clan – that had spent the past millennia visiting hit-and-run mayhem on systems across the segmentum, with abandoned warbands colonising planetary badlands like a green, galactic plague. The Battlefleet Ultima, where it could gather craft in sufficient time and numbers, had twice attempted

641

to destroy the gargantuan hulk. The combined firepower of hundreds of Navy vessels had also failed to destroy the beast, simply serving to enhance its hideous melange further.

All these things and more had preyed upon Elias Artegall's conscience when the *Revenant Rex* tumbled into the Gilead Sector. Arch-Deacon Urbanto. Rear Admiral Darracq. Overlord Gordius. Zimner, the High Magos Retroenginericus. Grand Master Karmyne of the Angels Eradicant. Artegall had either received them or received astrotelepathic messages from them all.

'Chapter Master, the xenos threat cannot be tolerated...'

'The Mercantile Gilead have reported the loss of thirty bulk freighters...'

'Master Artegall, the greenskins are already out of control in the Despot Stars...'

'That vessel could harbour ancient technological secrets that could benefit the future of mankind...'

'You must avenge us, brother...'

The spirehalls of the Slaughterhorn had echoed with their demands and insistence. But to war was a Space Marine's prerogative. Did not Lord Guilliman state on the steps of the Plaza Ptolemy: 'There is but one of the Emperor's Angels for every world in the Imperium; but one drop of Adeptus Astartes blood for every Imperial citizen. Judge the necessity to spill such a precious commodity with care and if it must be spilt, spill it wisely, my battle-brothers.'

Unlike the Scars or the Auroras, Artegall's Crimson Consuls were not given to competitive rivalry. Artegall did not desire success because others had failed. Serving at the pleasure of the primarch was not a tournament spectacle and the *Revenant Rex* was not an opportunistic arena. In the end, Artegall let his battered copy of the Codex Astartes decide. In those much-thumbed pages lay the wisdom of greater men than he: as ever, Artegall put his trust in their skill and experience. He chose a passage that reflected his final judgement and included it in both his correspondence to his far-flung petitioners and his address to the Crimson Consuls, First Company on board the battle-barge *Incarnadine Ecliptic*.

'From *Codicil CC-LXXX-IV.ii: The Coda of Balthus Dardanus, 17th Lord of Macragge* – entitled *Staunch Supremacies*. "For our enemies will bring us to battle on the caprice of chance. The alien and the renegade are the vagaries of the galaxy incarnate. What can we truly know or would want to of their ways or motivations? They are to us as the rabid wolf at the closed door that knows not even its own mind. Be that door. Be the simplicity of the steadfast and unchanging: the barrier between what is known and the unknowable. Let the Imperium of Man realise its manifold destiny within while without its mindless foes dash themselves against the constancy of our adamantium. In such uniformity of practice and purpose lies the perpetuity of mankind." May Guilliman be with you.'

'And with you,' Captain Bolinvar and his crimson-clad First Company Terminator Marines had returned. But the primarch had not been with them and Bolinvar and one hundred veteran sons of Carcharias had been forsaken.

Artegall sat alone in his private Tactical Chancelorium, among the cold ivory of his throne. The Chancelorium formed the very pinnacle of the Slaughterhorn – the Crimson Consuls fortress-monastery – which in turn formed the spirepeak of Hive Niveous, the Carcharian capital city. The throne was constructed from the colossal bones of shaggy, shovel-tusk Stegodonts, hunted by Carcharian ancestors, out on the Dry-blind. Without his armour the Chapter Master felt small and vulnerable in the huge throne – a sensation usually alien to an Adeptus Astartes' very being. The chamber was comfortably gelid and Artegall sat in his woollen robes, elbow to knee and fist to chin, like some crumbling statue from Terran antiquity.

The Chancelorium began to rumble and this startled the troubled Chapter Master. The crimson-darkness swirl of the marble floor began to part in front of him and the trapdoor admitted a rising platform upon which juddered two Chapter serfs in their own zoster robes. They flanked a huge brass pict-caster that squatted dormant between them. The serfs were purebred Carcharians with their fat, projecting noses, wide nostrils and thick brows. These on top of stocky, muscular frames, barrel torsos and thick arms decorated with crude tattoos and scar-markings. Perfectly adapted for life in the frozen underhive.

'Where is your master, the Chamber Castellan?' Artegall demanded of the bondsmen. The first hailed his Chapter Master with a fist to the aquila represented on the Crimson Consuls crest of his robes.

'Returned presently from the underhive, my lord – at your request – with the Lord Apothecary,' the serf answered solemnly. The second activated the pict-caster, bringing forth the crystal screen's grainy picture.

'We have word from the Master of the Fleet, Master Artegall,' the serf informed him.

Standing before Artegall was an image of Hecton Lambert, Master of the Crimson Consuls fleet. The Space Marine commander was on the bridge of the strike cruiser *Anno Tenebris*, high above the gleaming, glacial world of Carcharias.

'Hecton, what news?' Artegall put to him without the usual formality of a greeting.

'My master: nothing but the gravest news,' the Crimson Consul told him. 'As you know, we have been out of contact with Captain Bolinvar and the *Incarnadine Ecliptic* for days. A brief flash on one of our scopes prompted me to despatch the frigate *Herald Angel* with orders to locate the *Ecliptic* and report back. Twelve hours into their search they intercepted the following pict-cast, which they transmitted to the *Anno Tenebris*, and which I now dutifully transmit to you. My lord, with this every man on board sends his deepest sympathies. May Guilliman be with you.'

'And with you,' Artegall mouthed absently, rising out of the throne. He took a disbelieving step towards the broad screen of the pict-caster. Brother Lambert disappeared and was replaced by a static-laced image, harsh light and excruciating noise. The vague outline of a Crimson Consuls Space Marine could be made out. There were sparks and fires in the background, as well as the silhouettes of injured Space Marines and Chapter serfs stumbling blind and injured through the smoke and bedlam. The Astartes identified himself but his name and rank were garbled in the intruding static of the transmission.

'...this is the battle-barge *Incarnadine Ecliptic*, two days out of Morriga. I am now ranking battle-brother. We have sustained critical damage...' The screen erupted with light and interference.

Then: 'Captain Bolinvar went in with the first wave. Xenos resistance was heavy. Primitive booby traps. Explosives. Wall-to-wall green flesh and small arms. By the primarch, losses were minimal; my injuries, though, necessitated my return to the *Ecliptic*. The captain was brave and through the use of squad rotations, heavy flamers and teleporters our Consul Terminators managed to punch through to an enginarium with a power signature. We could all hear the countdown, even over the vox. Fearing that the *Revenant Rex* was about to make a warp jump I begged the captain to return. I begged him, but he transmitted that the only way to end the hulk and stop the madness was to sabotage the warp drive.'

Once again the lone Space Marine became enveloped in an ominous, growing brightness. 'His final transmission identified the warp engine as active but already sabotaged. He said the logic engine wasn't counting down to a jump... Then, the *Revenant Rex*, it – it just exploded. The sentry ships were caught in the blast wave and the *Ecliptic* wrecked.'

A serf clutching a heinous wound on his face staggered into the reporting Space Marine. 'Go! To the pods,' he roared at him. Then he returned his attention to the transmission. 'We saw it all. Detonation of the warp engines must have caused some kind of immaterium anomaly. Moments after the hulk blew apart, fragments and debris from the explosion – including our sentry ships – were sucked back through a collapsing empyrean vortex before disappearing altogether. We managed to haul off but are losing power and have been caught in the gravitational pull of a nearby star. Techmarine Hereward has declared the battle-barge unsalvageable. With our orbit decaying I have ordered all surviving Adeptus Astartes and Chapter serfs to the saviour pods. Perhaps some may break free. I fear our chances are slim... May Guilliman be with us...'

As the screen glared with light from the damning star and clouded over with static, Artegall felt like he'd been speared through the gut. He could taste blood in his mouth: the copper tang of lives lost. One hundred Crimson Consuls. The Emperor's Angels under his command. The

Chapter's best, gone with the irreplaceable seed of their genetic heritage. Thousands of years of combined battle experience lost to the Imperium. The Chapter's entire inheritance of Tactical Dreadnought Armour: every suit a priceless relic in its own right. The venerable *Ecliptic*. A veteran battle-barge of countless engagements and a piece of Carcharias among the stars. All gone. All claimed by the oblivion of the warp or cremated across the blazing surface of a nearby sun.

'You must avenge us, brother–'

Artegall reached back for his throne but missed and staggered. Someone caught him, slipping their shoulders underneath one of his huge arms. It was Baldwin. He'd been standing behind Artegall, soaking up the tragedy like his Chapter Master. The Space Marine's weight alone should have crushed the Chamber Castellan, but Baldwin was little more than a mind and a grafted, grizzled face on a robe-swathed brass chassis. The serf's hydraulics sighed as he took his master's bulk.

'My lord,' Baldwin began in his metallic burr.

'Baldwin, I lost them…' Artegall managed, his face a mask of stricken denial. With a clockwork clunk of gears and pistons the Chamber Castellan turned on the two serfs flanking the pict-caster.

'Begone!' he told them, his savage command echoing around the bronze walls of the Chancelorium. As the bondsmen thumped their fists into their aquilas and left, Baldwin helped his master to the cool bone of his throne. Artegall stared at the serf with unseeing eyes. They had been recruited together as savage underhivers and netted, kicking and pounding, from the fighting pits and tribal stomping grounds of the abhuman-haunted catacombs of Hive Niveous. But whereas Artegall had passed tissue compatibility and become a Neophyte, Baldwin had fallen at the first hurdle. Deemed unsuitable for surgical enhancement, the young hiver was inducted as a Chapter serf and had served the Crimson Consuls ever since. As personal servant, Baldwin had travelled the galaxy with his superhuman master.

As the decades passed, Artegall's engineered immortality and fighting prowess brought him promotion, while Baldwin's all-too-human body brought him the pain and limitation of old age. When Elias Artegall became the Crimson Consuls' Chapter Master, Baldwin wanted to serve on as his Chamber Castellan. As one century became the next, the underhiver exchanged his wasted frame for an engineered immortality of his own: the brass bulk of cylinders, hydraulics and exo-skeletal appendages that whirred and droned before the throne. Only the serf's kindly face and sharp mind remained.

Baldwin stood by as Artegall's body sagged against the cathedra arm and his face contorted with silent rage. It fell with futility before screwing up again with the bottomless fury only an Adeptus Astartes could feel for his foes and himself. Before him the Crimson Consul could see the faces of men with whom he'd served. Battle-brothers who had been

his parrying arm when his own had been employed in death-dealing;
Space Marines who had shared with him the small eternities of deep
space patrol and deathworld ambush; friends and loyal brethren.

'I sent them,' he hissed through the perfection of his gritted teeth.

'It is as you said to them, my lord. As the Codex commanded.'

'Condemned them…'

'They were the door that kept the rabid wolf at bay. The adamantium
upon which our enemies must be dashed.'

Artegall didn't seem to hear him: 'I walked them into a trap.'

'What is a space hulk if it not be such a thing? The sector is safe. The
Imperium lives on. Such an honour is not without cost. Even Guilliman
recognises that. Let me bring you the comfort of his words, my master.
Let the primarch show us his way.'

Artegall nodded and Baldwin hydraulically stomped across the chamber to where a lectern waited on a gravitic base. The top of the lectern
formed a crystal case that the Castellan opened, allowing the preserva-
tive poison of argon gas to escape. Inside, Artegall's tattered copy of the
Codex Astartes lay open as it had done since the Chapter Master had
selected his reading for the First Company's departure. Baldwin drifted
the lectern across the crimson marble of the Chancelorium floor to the
throne's side. Artegall was on his feet. Recovered. A Space Marine again.
A Chapter Master with the weight of history and the burden of future
expectation on his mighty Astartes' shoulders.

'Baldwin,' he rumbled with a steely-eyed determination. 'Were your
recruitment forays into the underhive with the Lord Apothecary fruitful?'

'I believe so, my lord.'

'Good. The Chapter will need Carcharias to offer up its finest sons, on
this dark day. You will need to organise further recruitment sweeps. Go
deep. We need the finest savages the hive can offer. Inform Lord Fabian
that I have authorised cultivation of our remaining seed. Tell him I need
one hundred Crimson Consuls. Demigods all, to honour the sacrifice of
their fallen brethren.'

'Yes, Chapter Master.'

'And Baldwin.'

'My master?'

'Send for the Reclusiarch.'

'High Chaplain Enobarbus is attached to the Tenth Company,' Baldwin informed Artegall with gentle, metallic inflection. 'On training
manoeuvres in the Dry-blind.'

'I don't care if he's visiting Holy Terra. Get him here. Now. There are
services to organise. Commemorations. Obsequies. The like this Chapter has never known. See to it.'

'Yes, my master,' Baldwin answered and left his lord to his feverish
guilt and the cold words of Guilliman.

* * *

'By now your lids are probably frozen to your eyeballs,' growled High Chaplain Enobarbus over the vox-link. 'Your body no longer feels like your own.'

The Crimson Consuls Chaplain leant against the crumbling architecture of the Archaphrael Hive and drank in the spectacular bleakness of his home world. The Dry-blind extended forever in all directions: the white swirl, like a smazeous blanket of white, moulded from the ice pack. By day, with the planet's equally bleak stars turning their attentions on Carcharias, the dry ice that caked everything in a rime of frozen carbon dioxide bled a ghostly vapour. The Dry-blind, as it was called, hid the true lethality of the Carcharian surface, however. A maze of bottomless crevasses, fissures and fractures that riddled the ice beneath and could only be witnessed during the short, temperature-plummeting nights, when the nebulous thunderhead of dry ice sank and re-froze.

'Your fingers are back in your cells, because they sure as Balthus Dardanus aren't part of your hands any more. Hopes of pulling the trigger on your weapon are a distant memory,' the High Chaplain voxed across the open channel.

The Chaplain ran a gauntlet across the top of his head, clearing the settled frost from his tight dreadlocks and flicking the slush at the floor. With a ceramite knuckle, he rubbed at the socket of the eye he'd lost on New Davalos. Now stapled shut, a livid scar ran down one side of his brutal face, from the eyelid to his jaw, where tears constantly trickled in the cold air and froze to his face.

'Skin is raw: like radiation burns – agony both inside and out.'

From his position in the twisted, frost-shattered shell that had been the Archaphrael Hive, Enobarbus could hear fang-face shredders. He fancied he could even spot the tell-tale vapour wakes of the shredders' dorsal fins cutting through the Dry-blind. Archaphrael Hive made up a triumvirate of cities called the Pale Maidens that stood like ancient monuments to the fickle nature of Carcharian meteorology. A thousand years before the three cities had been devastated by a freak polar cyclone colloquially referred to as 'The Big One' by the hivers. Now the ghost hives were used by the Crimson Consuls as an impromptu training ground.

'And those are the benefits,' Enobarbus continued, the High Chaplain's oratory sailing out across the vox waves. 'It's the bits you can't feel that you should worry about. Limbs that died hours ago. Dead meat that you're dragging around. Organs choking on the slush you're barely beating around your numb bodies.'

He had brought the tenth Company's Second and Seventh Scout sniper squads out to the Pale Maidens for stealth training and spiritual instruction. As a test of their worth and spirit, Enobarbus had had the Space Marine Scouts establish and hold ambush positions with their sniper rifles in the deep Carcharian freeze for three days. He had bombarded them endlessly with remembered readings from the Codex

Astartes, faith instruction and training rhetoric across the open channels of the vox.

Behind him Scout-Sergeant Caradoc was adjusting his snow cloak over the giveaway crimson of his carapace armour plating and priming his shotgun. Enobarbus nodded and the Scout-sergeant melted into the misty, frost-shattered archways of the Archaphrael Hive.

While the Scouts held their agonising positions, caked and swathed in dry ice, Enobarbus and the Scout-sergeants had amused themselves by trapping fang-face shredders. Packs of the beasts roamed the Dry-blind, making the environment an ever more perilous prospect for travellers. The shredders had flat, shovel-shaped maws spilling over with needle-like fangs. They carried their bodies close to the ground and were flat but for the razored dorsal fin protruding from their knobbly spines. They used their long tails for balance and changing direction on the ice. Like their dorsals, the tails were the razor-edged whiplash that gave them their name. Their sharp bones were wrapped in an elastic skin-sheen that felt almost amphibious and gave the beasts the ability to slide downhill and toboggan their prey. Then they would turn their crystal-tipped talons on their unfortunate victims: shredding grapnels that the creatures used to climb up and along the labyrinthine crevasses that fractured the ice shelf.

'This is nothing. Lips are sealed with rime. Thought is slow. It's painful. It's agony. Even listening to this feels like more than you can bear.'

Enobarbus pulled his own cape tight about his power armour. Like many of his calling the High Chaplain's plate was ancient and distinct, befitting an Adeptus Astartes of his status, experience and wisdom. Beyond the heraldry and honorifica decorating his midnight adamantium shell and the skullface helmet hanging from his belt, Enobarbus sported the trappings of his home world. The shredder-skin cape hung over his pack, with its razor dorsal and flaps that extended down his arms and terminated in the skinned creature's bestial claws: one decorating each of the High Chaplain's gauntlets.

'But bear it you must, you worthless souls. This is the moment your Emperor will need you. When you feel you have the least to give: that's when your primarch demands the most from you. When your battle-brother is under the knife or in another's sights – this is when you must be able to act,' the High Chaplain grizzled down the vox with gravity. Switching to a secure channel Enobarbus added, 'Sergeant Notus: now, if you will.'

Storeys and storeys below, down in the Dry-blind where Enobarbus and the Scout-sergeants had penned their captured prey, Notus would be waiting for the signal. A signal the Chaplain knew he'd received because of the high-pitched screeches of the released pack of shredders echoing up the shattered chambers and frost-bored ruins of the hive interior. The Codex Astartes taught of the nobility of aeon-honoured combat tactics and battle manoeuvres perfectly realised. It was Guilliman's way. The Rules of Engagement. The way in which Enobarbus was instructing his Scouts. But in their war games about the Pale Maidens, Enobarbus wasn't playing the role of the noble Space Marine. He was everything else the galaxy might throw at them: and the enemies of the Astartes did not play by the rules.

With the Scouts undoubtedly making excellent use of the hive's elevation and dilapidated exterior – as scores of previous Neophytes had – Enobarbus decided to engage them on multiple fronts at once. While the starving shredders clawed their way up through the ruined hive, intent on ripping the frozen Scouts to pieces, Scout-Sergeant Caradoc was working his way silently down through the derelict stairwells and halls of the hive interior with his shotgun. The High Chaplain decided to come at his Scouts from an entirely different angle.

Slipping his crozius arcanum – the High Chaplain's sacred staff of office – from his belt and extending the shredder talons on the backs of his gauntlets, Enobarbus swung out onto the crumbling hive wall exterior and began a perilous climb skywards. The shell of the hive wall had long been undermined by the daily freeze-thaw action of Carcharian night and day. Using the sharpened point of the aquila's wings at the end of his crozius like an ice pick and the crystal-tipped claws of the shredder, the High Chaplain made swift work of the frozen cliff-face of the dilapidated hive.

'There is nothing convenient about your enemy's desires. He will come for you precisely in the moment you have set aside for some corporal indulgence,' Enobarbus told the Scouts, trying hard not to let his exertions betray him over the vox. 'Exhaustion, fear, pain, sickness, injury, necessities of the body and as an extension of your bodies, the necessities of your weapons. Keep your blade keen and your sidearm clean. Guilliman protect you on the reload: the most necessary of indulgences – a mechanical funeral rite.'

Heaving himself up through the shattered floor of a gargoyle-encrusted overhang, the High Chaplain drew his bolt pistol and crept through to a balcony. The tier-terrace was barely stable but commanded an excellent view: too much temptation for a sniper Scout. But as Enobarbus stalked out across the fragile space he found it deserted. The first time in years of such training exercises he'd discovered it as such.

The High Chaplain nodded to himself. Perhaps this cohort of Neophytes was better. Perhaps they were learning faster: soaking up the wisdom of Guilliman and growing into their role. Perhaps they were ready for their Black Carapace and hallowed suits of power armour. Emperor knows they were needed. Chapter Master Artegall had insisted that Enobarbus concentrate his efforts on the 10th Company. The Crimson Consuls had had their share of past tragedies.

The Chapter had inherited the terrible misfortune of a garrison rotation on the industrial world of Phaethon IV when the Celebrant Chapter could not meet their commitments. Word was sent that the Celebrants were required to remain on Nedicta Secundus and protect the priceless holy relics of the cardinal world from the ravages of Hive Fleet Kraken and its splintered tyranid forces. Phaethon IV, on the other hand, bordered the Despot Stars and had long been coveted by Dregz Wuzghal, Arch-Mogul of Gunza Major. The Crimson Consuls fought bravely on Phaethon IV, and would have halted the beginnings of Waaagh! Wuzghal in its tracks: something stirred under the factories and power plants of the planet, however. Something awoken by the nightly bombing raids of the Arch-Mogul's 'Green Wing'. Something twice as alien as the degenerate greenskins: unfeeling, unbound and unstoppable. An ancient enemy, long forgotten by the galaxy and entombed below the assembly lines and Imperial manufacturing works of Phaethon, skeletal nightmares of living silver: the necrons. Between greenskin death from above and tomb warriors crawling out of their stasis chambers below, the industrial worlders and their Crimson Consuls guardians hadn't stood a chance and the Chapter lost two highly-decorated companies. As far as Enobarbus knew, the necron and the Arch-Mogul fought for Phaethon still.

The High Chaplain held his position. The still air seared the architecture around him with its caustic frigidity. Enobarbus closed his eyes and allowed his ears to do the work. He filtered out the freeze-thaw expansion of the masonry under his boots, the spiritual hum of the sacred armour about his body and the creak of his own aged bones. There it was. The tell-tale scrape of movement, the tiniest displacement of weight on the balcony expanse above. Back-tracking, the High Chaplain found a craterous hole in the ceiling. Hooking his crozius into the ruined stone and corroded metal, the Crimson Consul heaved himself noiselessly up through the floor of the level above.

Patient, like a rogue shredder on ambush in the Dry-blind – masked by the mist and hidden in some ice floor fissure – Enobarbus advanced with agonising care across the dilapidated balcony. There he was. One of the 10th Company Scouts. Flat to the steaming floor, form buried in his snow cloak, helmet down at the scope of his sniper rifle: a position the Neophyte had undoubtedly held for days. The balcony was an excellent spot. Despite some obstructive masonry, it commanded a view of the Dry-blind with almost the same breathtaking grandeur of the platform below. Without a sound, Enobarbus was above the sniper Scout, the aquila-wing blade-edge of his crozius resting on the back of the Scout's neck, between the helmet and the snow cloak.

'The cold is not the enemy,' the High Chaplain voxed across the open channel. 'The enemy is not even the enemy. You are the enemy. Ultimately you will betray yourself.'

When the Scout didn't move, the Chaplain's lip curled with annoyance.

He locked his suit vox-channels and hooked the Scout's shoulder with the wing-tip of the crozius.

'It's over, Consul,' Enobarbus told the prone form. 'The enemy has you.'

Flipping the Scout over, Enobarbus stood there in silent shock. Cloak, helmet and rifle were there but the Scout was not. Instead, the butchered body of a Shredder lay beneath, with the hilt of a gladius buried in its fang-faced maw. Enobarbus shook his head. Anger turned to admiration. These Scouts would truly test him.

Enobarbus switched to the private channel he shared with Scout-Sergeant Notus to offer him brief congratulations on his Scouts and to direct him up into the ruined hive.

'What in Guilliman's name are–' Enobarbus heard upon the transferring frequency. Then the unmistakable crack of las-fire. The High Chaplain heard the Scout-sergeant roar defiance over the vox and looking out over the Dry-blind, Enobarbus saw the light show, diffused in the swirling miasma, like sheet lightning across a stormy sky. Something cold took hold of the High Chaplain's heart. Enobarbus had heard thousands of men die. Notus was dead.

Transferring channels, Enobarbus hissed, 'Override Obsidian: we are under attack. This is not a drill. Second and Seventh, you are cleared to fire. Sergeant Caradoc, meet me at the–'

Shotgun blasts. Rapid and rushed. Caradoc pressed by multiple targets. The crash of the weapon bounced around the maze of masonry and worm-holed architecture.

'Somebody get me a visual,' the High Chaplain growled over the vox before slipping the crozius into his belt. Leading with his bolt pistol, Enobarbus raced for the fading echo of the sergeant's weapon. Short sprints punctuated with skips and drops through holes and stairwells.

'Caradoc, where are you?' Enobarbus voxed as he threaded his way through the crumbling hive. The shotgun fire had died away but the Scout-sergeant wasn't replying. 'Second squad, Seventh squad, I want a visual on Sergeant Caradoc, now!'

But there was nothing: only an eerie static across the channel. Rotating through the frequencies, Enobarbus vaulted cracks and chasms and thundered across frost-hazed chambers.

'Ritter, Lennox, Beade...' the High Chaplain cycled but the channels were dead. Sliding down into a skid, the shredder-skin cape and the greave plates of his armour carrying him across the chamber floor, Enobarbus dropped down through a hole and landed in a crouch. His pistol was everywhere, pivoting around and taking in the chamber below. An Astartes shotgun lay spent and smoking nearby and a large body swung from a creaking strut in the exposed ceiling. Caradoc.

The Scout-sergeant was hanging from his own snow cloak, framed in a gaping hole in the exterior hive wall, swinging amongst the brilliance of the Dry-blind beyond. The cloak, wrapped around his neck as it was, had been tied off around the strut like a noose. This wouldn't have been enough to kill the Space Marine. The dozen gladius blades stabbed through his butchered body up to their hilts had done that. The sickening curiosity of such a vision would have been enough to stun most battle-brothers but Enobarbus took immediate comfort and instruction from his memorised Codex. There was protocol to follow. Counsel to heed.

Snatching his skull-face helmet from his belt, Enobarbus slapped it on and secured the seals. With pistol still outstretched in one gauntlet, the High Chaplain felt for the rosarius hanging around his neck. He would have activated the powerful force field generator but an enemy was already upon him. The haze of the chamber was suddenly whipped up in a rush of movement. Shredders. Lots of them. They came out of the floor. Out of the roof. Up the exterior wall, as the High Chaplain had. Snapping at him with crystal claws and maws of needle-tip teeth. Enobarbus felt their razored tails slash against his adamantium shell and the vice-like grip of their crushing, shovel-head jaws on his knees, his shoulder, at his elbows and on his helmet.

Bellowing shock and frustration, Enobarbus threw his arm around, dislodging two of the monsters. As they scrambled about on the floor, ready to pounce straight back at him, the High Chaplain ended them with his bolt pistol. Another death-dealer tore at him from behind and swallowed his pistol and gauntlet whole. Again, Enobarbus fired, his bolt-rounds riddling the creature from within. The thing died with ease but its dagger-fang jaws locked around his hand and weapon, refusing to release. The darkness of holes and fractured doorways continued to give birth to the Carcharian predators. They bounded at him with their merciless, ice-hook talons, vaulting off the walls, floor and ceiling, even off Caradoc's dangling corpse.

Snatching the crozius arcanum from his belt the High Chaplain thumbed the power weapon to life. Swinging it about him in cold fury, Enobarbus cleaved shredders in two, slicing the monsters through the head and chopping limbs and tails from the beasts.

The floor erupted in front of the Space Marine and a hideously emaciated shredder – big, even for its kind – came up through the frost-shattered masonry. It leapt at Enobarbus, jaws snapping shut around his neck and wicked talons hooking themselves around the edges of his chest plate. The force of the impact sent the High Chaplain flailing backwards, off balance and with shredders hanging from every appendage.

Enobarbus roared as his armoured form smashed through part of a ruined wall and out through the gap in the hive exterior. The Crimson Consul felt himself falling. Survival instinct causing his fist to open, allowing the crozius to be torn from him by a savage little shredder. Snatching at the rapidly disappearing masonry, Enobarbus elongated his own shredder claw and buried the crystal-tipped talon in the ancient rockcrete. The High Chaplain hung from two monstrous digits, shredders in turn hanging from his armour. With the dead-weight and locked jaw of the pistol-swallowing shredder on the other arm and the huge beast now hanging down his back from a jaw-hold on his neck, Enobarbus had little hope of improving his prospects. Below lay thousands of metres of open drop, a ragged cliff-face of hive masonry to bounce off and shredder-infested, bottomless chasms of ice waiting below the white blanket of the Dry-blind. Even the superhuman frame of the High Chaplain could not hope to survive such a fall.

Above the shrieking and gnawing of the beasts and his own exertions, Enobarbus heard the hammer of disciplined sniper fire. Shredder bodies cascaded over the edge past the High Chaplain, either blasted apart by the accurate las-fire or leaping wildly out of its path. Enobarbus looked up. The two talons from which he hung scraped through the rockcrete with every purchase-snapping swing of the monsters hanging from the Crimson Consul. There were figures looking down at him from the edge. Figures in helmets and crimson carapace, swathed in snow cloaks and clutching sniper rifles. On the level above was a further collection looking down at him and the same on the storey after that.

Enobarbus recognised the Scout standing above him.

'Beade…' the High Chaplain managed, but there was nothing in the blank stare or soulless eyes of the Neophyte to lead Enobarbus to believe that he was going to live. As the barrel of Beade's rifle came down in unison with his Space Marine Scout compatriots, the High Chaplain's thoughts raced through a lifetime of combat experience and the primarch's teaching. But Roboute Guilliman and his Codex had nothing for him and, with synchronous trigger-pulls that would have been worthy of a firing squad, High Chaplain Enobarbus's las-slashed corpse tumbled into the whiteness below.

The Oratorium was crowded with hulking forms, their shadows cutting through the hololithic graphics of the chamber. Each Crimson Consul was a sculpture in muscle, wrapped in zoster robes and the colour of their calling. Only the two Astartes on the Oratorium door stood in full cream and crimson ceremonial armour, Sergeants Ravenscar and Bohemond watching silently over their brothers at the circular runeslab that dominated the chamber. The doors parted and Baldwin stomped in with the hiss of hydraulic urgency, accompanied by a serf attendant of his own. The supermen turned.

'The Reclusiarch has not returned as ordered, master,' Baldwin reported. 'Neither have two full Scout squads of the 10th Company and their sergeants.'

'It's the time of year I tell you,' the Master of the Forge maintained through his conical faceplate. Without his armour and colossal servo-claw, Maximagne Ferro cut a very different figure. Ferro wheezed a further intake of breath through his grilles before insisting: 'Our relay stations on De Vere and Thusa Minor experience communication disruption from starquakes every year around the Antilochal Feast day.'

The Slaughterhorn's Master of Ordnance, Talbot Faulks, gave Artegall the intensity of his magnobionic eyes, their telescrew mountings whirring to projection. 'Elias. It's highly irregular: and you know it.'

'Perhaps the High Chaplain and his men have been beset by difficulties of a very natural kind,' Lord Apothecary Fabian suggested. 'Reports suggest carbonic cyclones sweeping in on the Pale Maidens from the east. They could just be waiting out the poor conditions.'

'Enjoying them, more like,' Chaplain Mercimund told the Apothecary. 'The Reclusiarch would loathe missing an opportunity to test his pupils to their limits. I remember once, out on the–'

'Forgive me, Brother-Chaplain. After the Chapter Master's recall?' the Master of Ordnance put to him. 'Not exactly in keeping with the Codex.'

'Brothers, please,' Artegall said, leaning thoughtfully against the runeslab on his fingertips. Hololithics danced across his grim face, glinting off the neat rows of service studs running above each eyebrow. He looked at Baldwin. 'Send the 10th's Thunderhawks for them with two further squads for a search, if one is required.'

Baldwin nodded and despatched his attendant. 'Chaplain,' Artegall added, turning on Mercimund. 'If you would be so good as to start organising the commemorations, in the High Chaplain's absence.'

'It would be an honour, Chapter Master,' Mercimund acknowledged, thumping his fist into the Chapter signature on his robes earnestly before following the Chamber Castellan's serf out of the Oratorium. Baldwin remained.

'Yes?' Artegall asked.

Baldwin looked uncomfortably at Lord Fabian, prompting him to clear his throat. Artegall changed his focus to the Apothecary. 'Speak.'

'The recruitment party is long returned from the underhive. Your Chamber Castellan and I returned together – at your request – with the other party members and the potential aspirants. Since they were not requested, Navarre and his novice remained on some matter of significance: the Chief Librarian did not share it with me. I had the Chamber Castellan check with the Librarium…'

'They are as yet to return, Master Artegall,' Baldwin inserted.

'Communications?'

'We're having some difficulty reaching them,' Baldwin admitted.

Faulks's telescopic eyes retracted. 'Enobarbus, the *Crimson Tithe*, the Chief Librarian…'

'Communication difficulties, all caused by seasonal starquakes, I tell you,' Maximagne Ferro maintained, his conical faceplate swinging around to each of them with exasperation. 'The entire hive is probably experiencing the same.'

'And yet we can reach Lambert,' Faulks argued.

Artegall pursed his lips: 'I want confirmation of the nature of the communication difficulties,' he put to the Master of the Forge, prompting the Techmarine to nod slowly. 'How long have Captain Baptista and the *Crimson Tithe* been out of contact?'

'Six hours,' Faulks reported.

Artegall looked down at the runeslab. With the loss of the Chapter's only other battle-barge, Artegall wasn't comfortable with static from the *Crimson Tithe*.

'Where is she? Precisely.'

'Over the moon of Rubessa: quadrant four-gamma, equatorial west.'

Artegall fixed his Chamber Castellan with cold, certain eyes.

'Baldwin, arrange a pict-link with Master Lambert. I wish to speak with him again.'

'You're going to send Lambert over to investigate?' Faulks enquired.

'Calm yourself, brother,' Artegall instructed the Master of Ordnance. 'I'm sure it is as Ferro indicates. I'll have the Master of the Fleet take the *Anno Tenebris* to rendezvous with the battle-barge over Rubessa. There Lambert and Baptista can have their enginseers and the Sixth Reserve Company's Techmarines work on the problem from their end.'

Baldwin bowed his head. The sigh of hydraulics announced his intention to leave. 'Baldwin,' Artegall called, his eyes still on Faulks. 'On your way, return to the Librarium. Have our astropaths and Navarre's senior Epistolary attempt to reach the Chief Librarian and the *Crimson Tithe* by psychic means.'

'My lord,' Baldwin confirmed and left the Oratorium with the Master of the Forge.

'Elias,' Faulks insisted as he had done earlier. 'You must let me take the *Slaughterhorn* to Status Vermillion.'

'That seems unnecessary,' the Lord Apothecary shook his head.

'We have two of our most senior leaders unaccounted for and a Chapter battle-barge in a communications black-out,' Faulks listed with emphasis. 'All following the loss of one hundred of our most experienced and decorated battle-brothers? I believe that we must face the possibility that we are under some kind of attack.'

'Attack?' Fabian carped incredulously. 'From whom? Sector greenskins? Elias, you're not entertaining this?'

Artegall remained silent, his eyes following the path of hololithic representations tracking their way across the still air of the chamber.

'You have started preparing the Chapter's remaining gene-seed?' Artegall put to the Lord Apothecary.

'As you ordered, my master,' Fabian replied coolly. 'Further recruiting sweeps will need to be made. I know the loss of the First Company was a shock and this on top of the tragedies of Phaethon IV. But, this is our Chapter's entire stored genetic heritage we are talking about here. You have heard my entreaties for caution with this course of action.'

'Caution,' Artegall nodded.

'Elias,' Faulks pressed.

'As in all things,' Artegall put to his Master of Ordnance and the Apothecary, 'we shall be guided by Guilliman. The Codex advises caution in the face of the unknown – *Codicil MX-VII-IX.i: The Wisdoms of Hera*, "Gather your wits, as the traveller gauges the depth of the river crossing with the fallen branch, before wading into waters wary." Master Faulks, what would you advise?'

'I would order all Crimson Consuls to arms and armour,' the Master of Ordnance reeled off. 'Thunderhawks fuelled and prepped in the hangers. Penitorium secured. Vox-checks doubled and the defence lasers charged for ground to orbit assault. I would also recall Roderick and the Seventh Company from urban pacification and double the fortress-monastery garrison.'

'Anything else?'

'I would advise Master Lambert to move all Crimson Consuls vessels to a similarly high alert status.'

'That is a matter for the Master of the Fleet. I will apprise him of your recommendations.'

'So?'

Artegall gave his grim consent, 'Slaughterhorn so ordered to Status Vermillion.'

'I can't raise the Slaughterhorn,' Lexicanum Raughan Stellan complained to his Librarian Master.

'We are far below the hive, my novice,' the Chief Librarian replied, his power armour boots crunching through the darkness. 'There are a billion tonnes of plasteel and rockcrete between us and the spire monastery. You would expect even our equipment to have some problems negotiating that. Besides, it's the season for starquakes.'

'Still...' the Lexicanum mused.

The psykers had entered the catacombs: the lightless labyrinth of tunnels, cave systems and caverns that threaded their torturous way through the pulverised rock and rust of the original hive. Thousands of storeys had since been erected on top of the ancient structures, crushing them into the bottomless network of grottos from which the Crimson Consuls procured their most savage potential recruits. The sub-zero stillness was routinely shattered by murderous screams of tribal barbarism.

Far below the aristocratic indifference of the spire and the slavish poverty of the habs and industrial districts lay the gang savagery of the underhive. Collections of killers and their Carcharian kin, gathered for security or mass slaughter, blasting across the subterranean badlands for scraps and criminal honour. Below this kingdom of desperados and petty despots extended the catacombs, where tribes of barbaric brutes ruled almost as they had at the planet's feral dawn. Here, young Carcharian bodies were crafted by necessity: shaped by circumstance into small mountains of muscle and sinew. Minds were sharpened to keenness by animal instinct and souls remained empty and pure. Perfect for cult indoctrination and the teachings of Guilliman.

Navarre held up his force sword, *Chrysaor*, the unnatural blade bleeding immaterial illumination into the darkness. It was short, like the traditional gladius of his Chapter and its twin, *Chrysaen*, sat in the inverse criss-cross of scabbards that decorated the Chief Librarian's blue and gold chest plate. The denizens of the catacombs retreated into the alcoves and shadows at the abnormal glare of the blade and the towering presence of the armoured Adeptus Astartes.

'Stellan, keep up,' Navarre instructed. They had both been recruited from this tribal underworld – although hundreds of years apart. This familiarity should have filled the Carcharians with ease and acquaintance. Their Astartes instruction and training had realised in both supermen, however, an understanding of the untamed dangers of the place.

Not only would their kith and kin dash out their brains for the rich marrow in their bones, their degenerate brothers shared their dark kingdom with abhumans, mutants and wyrds, driven from the upper levels of the hive for the unsightly danger they posed. Navarre and Stellan had already despatched a shaggy, cyclopean monstrosity that had come at them on its knuckles with brute fury and bloodhunger.

Navarre and Stellan, however, were Adeptus Astartes: the Emperor's Angels of Death and demigods among men. They came with dangers of their own. This alone would be enough to ensure their survival in such a lethal place. The Crimson Consuls were also powerful psykers: wielders of powers unnatural and warp-tapped. Without the techno-spectacle of their arms, the magnificence of their blue and gold plating, their superhuman forms and murderous training, Navarre and Stellan would still be the deadliest presence in the catacombs for kilometres in any direction.

The tight tunnels opened out into a cavernous space. Lifting *Chrysaor* higher, the Chief Librarian allowed more of his potential to flood the unnatural blade of the weapon, throwing light up at the cave ceiling. Something colossal and twisted through with corrosion and stalactitular icicles formed the top of the cavern: some huge structure that had descended through the hive interior during some forgotten, cataclysmic collapse. Irregular columns of resistant-gauge rockcrete and strata structural supports held up the roof at precarious angles. This accidental architecture had allowed the abnormality of the open space to exist below and during the daily thaw had created, drop by drop, the frozen chemical lake that steamed beneath it.

A primitive walkway of scavenged plasteel, rock-ice and girders crossed the vast space and, as the Space Marines made their tentative crossing, Navarre's warplight spooked a flock of gliding netherworms. Uncoiling themselves from their icicle bases they flattened their bodies and slithered through the air, angling the drag of their serpentine descent down past the Space Marines and at the crags and ledges of the cavern where they would make a fresh ascent. As the flock of black worms spiralled by, one crossed Stellan's path. The novice struck out with his gauntlet in disgust but the thing latched onto him with its unparalleled prehensility. It weaved its way up through his armoured digits and corkscrewed up his thrashing arm at his helmetless face.

Light flashed before the Lexicanum's eyes. Just as the netherworm retracted its fleshy collar and prepared to sink its venomous beak hooks into the Astartes' young face, Navarre clipped the horror in half with the blazing tip of *Chrysaor*. As the worm fell down the side of the walkway in two writhing pieces, Stellan mumbled his thanks.

'Why didn't you use your powers?' the Chief Librarian boomed around the cavern.

'It surprised me,' was all the Lexicanum could manage.

'You've been out of the depths mere moments and you've already forgotten its dangers,' Navarre remonstrated gently. 'What of the galaxy's dangers? There's a myriad of lethality waiting for you out there. Be mindful, my novice.'

'Yes, master.'

'Did it come to you again?' Navarre asked pointedly.

'Why do you ask, master?'

'You seem, distracted: not yourself. Was your sleep disturbed?'

'Yes, master.'

'Your dreams?'

'Yes, master.'

'The empyreal realm seems a dark and distant place,' Navarre told his apprentice sagely. 'But it is everywhere. How do you think we can draw on it so? Its rawness feeds our power: the blessings our God-Emperor gave us and through which we give back in His name. We are not the only ones to draw from this wellspring of power and we need our faith and constant vigilance to shield us from the predations of these immaterial others.'

'Yes, master.'

'Behind a wall of mirrored-plas the warp hides, reflecting back to us our realities. In some places it's thick; in others a mere wafer of truth separates us from its unnatural influence. Your dreams are one such window: a place where one may submerge one's head in the Sea of Souls.'

'Yes, master.'

'Tell me, then.'

Stellan seemed uncomfortable, but as the two Space Marines continued their careful trudge across the cavern walkway, the novice unburdened himself.

'It called itself Ghidorquiel.'

'You conversed with this thing of confusion and darkness?'

'No, my master. It spoke only to me: in my cell.'

'You said you were dreaming,' Navarre reminded the novice.

'Of being awake,' Stellan informed him, 'in my cell. It spoke. What I took to be lips moved but the voice was in my head.'

'And what lies did this living lie tell you?'

'A host of obscenities, my lord,' Stellan confirmed. 'It spoke in languages unknown to me. Hissed and spat its impatience. It claimed my soul as its own. It said my weakness was the light in its darkness.'

'This disturbed you.'

'Of course,' the Lexicanum admitted. 'Its attentions disgust me. But this creature called out to me across the expanse of time and space. Am I marked? Am I afflicted?'

'No more than you ever were,' Navarre reassured the novice. 'Stellan, all those who bear the burden of powers manifest – the Emperor's sacred gift – of which he was gifted himself – dream themselves face to face with the daemonscape from time to time. Entities trawl the warp for souls to torment for their wretched entertainment. Our years of training and the mental fortitude that comes of being the Emperor's chosen protects us from their direct influence. The unbound, the warp-rampant and the witch are all easy prey for such beasts and through them the daemon worms its way into our world. Thank the primarch we need face such things for real with blessed infrequency.'

'Yes, my lord,' Stellan agreed.

'The warp sometimes calls to us: demands our attention. It's why we did not return to the Slaughterhorn with the others. Such a demand led me beyond the scope of the Lord Apothecary's recruitment party and down into the frozen bowels of Carcharias. Here.'

Reaching the other side of the cavern, Navarre and Stellan stood on the far end of the walkway, where it led back into the rock face of pulverised masonry. Over the top of the tunnel opening was a single phrase in slap-dash white paint. It was all glyph symbols and runic consonants of ancient Carcharian.

'It's recent,' Navarre said half to himself. Stellan simply stared at the oddness of the lettering. 'Yet its meaning is very old. A phrase that predates the hives, at least. It means, "From the single flake of snow – the avalanche".'

Venturing into the tunnel with force sword held high, Navarre was struck by the patterns on the walls. Graffiti was endemic to the underhive: it was not mere defacement or criminal damage. In the ganglands above it advertised the presence of dangerous individuals and marked the jealously guarded territories of House-sponsored outfits, organisations and posses. It covered every empty space: the walls, the floor and ceiling, and was simply part of the underworld's texture. Below that, the graffiti was no less pervasive or lacking in purpose. Tribal totems and primitive paintings performed much the same purpose for the barbarians of the catacombs. Handprints in blood; primordial representations of subterranean mega-vermin in campfire charcoal; symbolic warnings splashed across walls in the phosphorescent, radioactive chemicals that leaked down from the industrial sectors above. The Carcharian savages that haunted the catacombs had little use for words, yet this was all Navarre could see.

The Chief Librarian had been drawn to this place, deep under Hive Niveous, by the stink of psychic intrusion. Emanations. Something large and invasive: something that had wormed its way through the very core of the Carcharian capital. The ghostly glow of *Chrysaor* revealed it to Navarre in all its mesmerising glory. Graffiti upon graffiti, primitive paintings upon symbols upon markings upon blood splatter. Words. The same words, over and over again, in all orientations, spelt out in letters created in the layered spaces of the hive cacography. Repetitions that ran for kilometres through the arterial maze of tunnels. Like a chant or incantation in ancient Carcharian: they blazed with psychic significance to the Chief Librarian, where to the eyes of the ordinary and untouched, among the background scrawl of the hive underworld, they would not appear to be there at all.

'Stellan! You must see this,' Navarre murmured as he advanced down the winding passage. The Librarian continued: 'Psycho-sensitive words, spelt out on the walls, a conditioned instruction of some kind, imprinting itself on the minds of the underhivers. Stellan: we must get word back to the Slaughterhorn – to Fabian – to the Chapter Master. The recruits could be compromised…'

The Chief Librarian turned to find that his novice wasn't there. Marching back up the passage in the halo of his shimmering force weapon, Navarre found the Lexicanum still standing on the cavern walkway, staring up at the wall above the tunnel entrance with a terrible blankness. 'Stellan? Stellan, talk to me.'

At first Navarre thought that one of the deadly gliding worms had got him, infecting the young Space Marine with its toxin. The reality was much worse. Following the novice's line of sight, Navarre settled on the white painted scrawl above the tunnel. The ancient insistence, 'From the single flake of snow – the avalanche' in fresh paint. Looking back at the Lexicanum, Navarre came to realise that his own novice had succumbed to the psycho-sensitive indoctrination of his recruiting grounds. All the wordsmith had needed was to introduce his subjects to the trigger. A phrase they were unlikely to come across anywhere else. The timing intentional; the brainwashing complete.

Stellan dribbled. He tried to mumble the words on the wall. Then he tried to get his palsied mouth around his master's name. He failed. The young Space Marine's mind was no longer his own. He belonged to someone else: to the will of the wordsmith – whoever they were. And not only the novice: countless other recruits over the years, for whom indoctrination hid in the very fabric of their worlds and now in the backs of their afflicted minds. All ready to be activated at a single phrase.

Navarre readied himself. Opened his being to the warp's dark promise. Allowed its fire to burn within. Slipping *Chrysaen* from its chest scabbard, the Chief Librarian held both force blades out in front of him. Each master-crafted gladius smoked with immaterial vengeance.

For Stellan, the dangers were much more immediate than brainwashing. Stripped of his years of training and the mental fortitude that shielded an Astartes Librarian from the dangers of the warp, Stellan succumbed to the monster stalking his soul.

Something like shock took the Crimson Consul's face hostage. The novice looked like he had been seized from below. Somehow, horribly, he had. The Librarian's head suddenly disappeared down into the trunk of his blue and gold power armour. An oily, green ichor erupted from the neck of the suit.

'Ghidorquiel…' Navarre spat. The Chief Librarian thrust himself at the quivering suit of armour, spearing his Lexicanum through the chest with *Chrysaor*. The stink of warp-corruption poured from the adamantium shell and stung the psyker's nostrils. Spinning and kicking the body back along the treacherous walkway, Navarre's blades trailed ethereal afterglow as they arced and cleaved through the sacred suit.

Howling fury at the materialising beast within the armour, the Chief Librarian unleashed a blast wave of raw warp energy from his chest that lit up the cavern interior and hit the suit like the God-Emperor's own fist.

The suit tumbled backwards, wrenching and cracking along the walkway until it came to rest, a broken-backed heap. Even then, the armour continued to quiver and snap, rearranging the splintered ceramite plating and moulding itself into something new. On the walkway, Navarre came to behold an adamantium shell, like that of a mollusc, from which slithered an explosion of tentacles. Navarre ran full speed at the daemon while appendages shot for him like guided missiles. Twisting this way and that, but without sacrificing any of his rage-fuelled speed, the Chief Librarian slashed at the beast, his blinding blades shearing off tentacular length and the warp-dribbling tips of the monster feelers.

As the psyker closed with the daemon nautiloid, the warp beast shot its appendages into the fragile walkway's architecture. Hugging the snapping struts and supports to it, the creature demolished the structure beneath the Crimson Consul's feet.

Navarre plummeted through the cavern space before smashing down through the frozen surface of the chemical lake below. The industrial

waste plunge immediately went to work on the blue and gold of the
Librarian's armour and blistered the psyker's exposed and freezing flesh.
Navarre's force blades glowed spectroscopic eeriness under the surface
and it took precious moments for the Space Marine to orientate himself
and kick for the surface. As his steaming head broke from the frozen acid
depths of the lake, Navarre's burn-blurry eyes saw the rest of the walkway collapsing towards him. Ghidorquiel had reached for the cavern
wall and, pulling with its unnatural might, had toppled the remainder
of the structure.

Again Navarre was hammered to the darkness of the lake bottom,
sinking wreckage raining all about the dazed psyker. Somewhere in the
chaos *Chrysaen* slipped from Navarre's grip. Vaulting upwards, the Space
Marine hit the thick ice of the lake surface further across. Clawing uselessly with his gauntlet, skin aflame and armour freezing up, Navarre
stared through the ice and saw something slither overhead. Roaring pain
and frustration into the chemical darkness, the Chief Librarian thrust
*Chrysaor* through the frozen effluence. Warpflame bled from the blade
and across the ice, rapidly melting the crust of the acid bath and allowing the Crimson Consul a moment to suck in a foetid breath and drag
himself up the shoreline of shattered masonry.

Ghidorquiel was there, launching tentacles at the psyker. Hairless
and with flesh melting from his skull the Librarian mindlessly slashed
the appendages to pieces. All the Space Marine wanted was the daemon.
The thing dragged its obscene adamantium shell sluggishly away from
the lake and the enraged Astartes. Navarre bounded up and off a heap
of walkway wreckage, dodging the creature's remaining tentacles and
landing on ceramite. Drawing on everything he had, the Chief Librarian
became a conduit of the warp. The raw, scalding essence of immaterial
energy poured from his being and down through the descending tip of
his force sword. *Chrysaor* slammed through the twisted shell of Stellan's
armour and buried itself in the daemon's core. Like a lightning rod, the
gladius roasted the beast from the inside out.

Armour steamed. Tentacles dropped and trembled to stillness. The
daemon caught light. Leaving the force blade in the monstrous body,
Navarre stumbled down from the creature and crashed to the cavern
floor himself. The psyker was spent: in every way conceivable. He could
do little more than lie there in his own palsy, staring at the daemon
corpse lit by *Chrysaor's* still gleaming blade. The slack, horrible face of
the creature had slipped down out of the malformed armour shell: the
same horrific face that the novice Stellan had confronted in his dreams.

Looking up into the inky, cavern blackness, Navarre wrangled with the
reality that somehow he had to get out of the catacombs and warn the
Slaughterhorn of impending disaster. A *slurp* drew his face back to the
creature; sickeningly it began to rumble with daemonic life and throttled laughter. Fresh tentacles erupted from its flaming sides and wrapped

themselves around two of the crooked pillars of rockcrete and metal that were supporting the chamber ceiling and the underhive levels above.

All Navarre could do was watch the monster pull the columns towards its warp-scorched body and roar his frustration as the cavern ceiling quaked and thundered down towards him, with the weight of Hive Niveous behind it.

The Oratorium swarmed with armoured command staff and their attendants. Clarifications and communications shot back and forth across the chamber amongst a hololithic representation of the Slaughterhorn fortress-monastery that crackled disturbance every time an officer or Crimson Consuls serf walked through it.

'They discovered nothing, my lord,' Baldwin informed Artegall in mid-report. 'No High Chaplain; no Scout squads; nothing. They've scoured the Dry-blind around the Pale Maidens. They're requesting permission to bring the Thunderhawks back to base.'

'What about Chief Librarian Navarre?' Artegall called across the Oratorium.

'Nothing, sir,' Lord Apothecary Fabian confirmed. 'On the vox or from the Librarium.'

'Planetary Defence Force channels and on-scene Enforcers report seismic shift and hive tremors in the capital lower levels,' the Master of the Forge reported, his huge servo-claw swinging about over the heads of the gathering.

'What about the *Crimson Tithe*?'

'Patching you through to Master Lambert now,' Maximagne Ferro added, giving directions to a communications servitor. The hololithic representation of the Slaughterhorn disappeared and was replaced with the phantasmal static of a dead pict-feed that danced around the assembled Crimson Consuls.

'What the hell is happening up there, Maximagne?' Artegall demanded, but the Master of the Forge was working furiously on the servitor and the brass control station of the runeslab. The static disappeared before briefly being replaced by the Slaughterhorn and then a three-dimensional hololith of the Carcharian system. Artegall immediately picked out their system star and their icebound home world: numerous defence monitors and small frigates were stationed in high orbit. Circling Carcharias were the moons of De Vere, Thusa Major and Thusa Minor between which two strike cruisers sat at anchor. Most distant was Rubessa; the Oratorium could see the battle-barge *Crimson Tithe* beneath it. Approaching was Hecton Lambert's strike cruiser, *Anno Tenebris*. The hololithic image of the Adeptus Astartes strike cruiser suddenly crackled and then disappeared.

The Oratorium fell to a deathly silence.

'Maximagne...' Artegall began. The Master of the Forge had a vox-headset to one ear.

'Confirmed, my lord. The *Anno Tenebris* has been destroyed with all on board.' The silence prevailed. 'Sir, the *Crimson Tithe* fired upon her.'

The gathered Adeptus Astartes looked to their Chapter Master, who, like his compatriots, could not believe what he was hearing.

'Master Faulks,' Artegall began. 'It seems you were correct. We are under attack. Status report: fortress-monastery.'

'In lockdown as ordered, sir,' the Master of Ordnance reported with grim pride. 'All Crimson Consuls are prepped for combat. All sentry guns manned. Thunderhawks ready for launch on your order. Defence lasers powered to full.'

Captain Roderick presented himself to his Chapter Master: 'My lord, the Seventh Company has fortified the Slaughterhorn at the Master of Ordnance's instruction. Nothing will get through – you can be sure of that.'

'Sir,' Master Maximagne alerted the chamber: '*Crimson Tithe* is on the move, Carcharias bound, my lord.'

Artegall's lip curled into a snarl. 'Who the hell are they?' he muttered to himself. 'What about our remaining cruisers?'

Faulks stepped forwards indicating the cruisers at anchor between the hololithic moons of Thusa Major and Thusa Minor. 'At full alert as I advised. The *Caliburn* and *Honour of Hera* could plot an intercept course and attempt an ambush…'

'Out of the question,' Artegall stopped Faulks. 'Bring the strike cruisers in above the Slaughterhorn at low orbit. I want our defence lasers to have their backs.'

'Yes, my master,' Faulks obeyed.

'Baldwin…'

'Lord?'

'Ready my weapons and armour.'

The Chamber Castellan nodded slowly, 'It would be my honour, master.' The Crimson Consuls watched the serf exit, knowing what this meant. Artegall was already standing at the head of the runeslab in a functional suit of crimson and cream power armour and his mantle. He was asking for the hallowed suit of artificer armour and master-crafted bolter that resided in the Chapter Master's private armoury. The gleaming suit of crimson and gold upon which the honourable history of the Crimson Consuls Chapter was inscribed and inlaid in gemstone ripped from the frozen earth of Carcharias itself. The armour that past Masters had worn when leading the Chapter to war in its entirety: Aldebaran; the Fall of Volsungard; the Termagant Wars.

'Narke.'

'Master Artegall,' the Slaughterhorn's chief astropath replied from near the Oratorium doors.

'Have you been successful in contacting the Third, Fifth or Eighth Companies?'

'Captain Neath has not responded, lord,' the blind Narke reported, clutching his staff.

Artegall and Talbot Faulks exchanged grim glances. Neath and the 8th Company were only two systems away hunting Black Legion Traitor Marine degenerates in the Sarcus Reaches.

'And Captain Borachio?'

Artegall had received monthly astrotelepathic reports from Captain Albrecht Borachio stationed in the Damocles Gulf. Borachio had overseen the Crimson Consuls contribution to the Damocles Crusade in the form of the 3rd and 5th Companies and had present responsibility for bringing the Tau commander, O'Shovah, to battle in the Farsight Enclaves. Artegall and Borachio had served together in the same squad as battle-brothers and Borachio, beyond Baldwin, was what the Chapter Master might have counted as the closest thing he had to a friend.

'Three days ago, my lord,' Narke returned. 'You returned in kind, Master Artegall.'

'Read back the message.'

The astropath's knuckles whitened around his staff as he recalled the message: '... encountered a convoy of heavy cruisers out of Fi'Rios – a lesser sept, the Xenobiologis assure me, attempting to contact Commander Farsight. We took a trailing vessel with little difficulty but at the loss of one Carcharian son: Crimson Consul Battle-Brother Theodoric of the First Squad: Fifth Company. I commend Brother Theodoric's service to you and recommend his name be added to the Shrine of Hera in the Company Chapel as a posthumous recipient of the Iron Laurel...'

'And the end?' Artegall pushed.

'An algebraic notation in three dimensions, my lord: Kn $\Omega$ iii – $\pi$ iX (Z-) – ⊠ v.R (!?) 0-1.'

'Coordinates? Battle manoeuvres?' Talbot Faulks hypothesised.

'Regicide notations,' Artegall informed him, his mind elsewhere. For years, the Chapter Master and Albrecht Borachio had maintained a game of regicide across the stars, moves detailed back and forth with their astropathic communiqués. Each had a board and pieces upon which the same game had been played out; Artegall's was an ancient set carved from lacquered megafelis sabres on a burnished bronze board. Artegall moved the pieces in his mind, recalling the board as it was set up on a rostra by his throne in the Chancelorium. Borachio had beaten him. 'Blind Man's Mate...' the Chapter Master mouthed.

'Excuse me, my lord?' Narke asked.

'No disrespect intended,' Artegall told the astropath. 'It's a form of victory in regicide, so called because you do not see it coming.'

The corridor outside the Oratorium suddenly echoed with the sharp crack of bolter fire. Shocked glances between Artegall and his Astartes officers were swiftly replaced by the assumption of cover positions. The armoured forms took advantage of the runeslab and the walls either side of the Oratorium door.

'That's inside the perimeter,' Faulks called in disbelief, slapping on his helmet.

'Well inside,' Artegall agreed grimly. Many of the Space Marines had drawn either their bolt pistols or their gladius swords. Only Captain Roderick and the Oratorium sentry sergeants, Bohemond and Ravenscar, were equipped for full combat with bolters, spare ammunition and grenades.

With the muzzle of his squat Fornax-pattern bolt pistol resting on the slab, the Master of Ordnance brought up the hololithic representation of the Slaughterhorn once more. The fortress-monastery was a tessellation of flashing wings, towers, hangars and sections.

'Impossible…' Faulks mumbled.

'The fortress-monastery is completely compromised,' Master Maximagne informed the chamber, cycling through the vox-channels.

Bolt shells pounded the thick doors of the Oratorium. The Seventh Company captain held a gauntleted finger to the vox-bead in his ear.

'Roderick,' Artegall called. 'What's happening?'

'My men are being fired upon from the inside of the Slaughterhorn, my lord,' the captain reported bleakly. 'By fellow Astartes – by Crimson Consuls, Master Artegall!'

'What has happened to us?' the Chapter Master bawled in dire amazement.

'Later, sir. We have to get you out of here,' Faulks insisted.

'What sections do we hold?' Artegall demanded.

'Elias, we have to go, now!'

'Master Faulks, what do we hold?'

'Sir, small groups of my men hold the Apothecarion and the north-east hangar,' Roderick reported. 'The Barbican, some Foundry sections and Cell Block Sigma.'

'The Apothecarion?' Fabian clarified.

'The gene-seed,' Artegall heard himself mutter.

'The Command Tower is clear,' Faulks announced, reading details off the hololith schematic of the monastery. Bolt-rounds tore through the metal of the Oratorium door and drummed into the runeslab column. The hololith promptly died. Ravenscar pushed Narke, the blind astropath, out of his way and poked the muzzle of his weapon through the rent in the door. He started plugging the corridor with ammunition-conserving boltfire.

'We must get the Chapter Master to the Tactical Chancelorium,' Faulks put to Roderick, Maximagne and the sentry sergeants.

'No,' Artegall barked back. 'We must take back the Slaughterhorn.'

'Which we can do best from your Tactical Chancelorium, my lord,' Faulks insisted with strategic logic. 'From there we have our own vox-relays, tactical feeds and your private armoury: it's elevated for a Thunderhawk evacuation – it's simply the most secure location in the fortress-monastery,' Faulks told his master. 'The best place from which to coordinate and rally our forces.'

'When we determine who they are,' Fabian added miserably. Artegall and the Master of Ordnance stared at one another.

'Sir!' Ravenscar called from the door. 'Coming up on a reload.'

'Agreed,' Artegall told Faulks. 'Captain Roderick shall accompany Master Maximagne and Lord Fabian to secure the Apothecarion; the gene-seed must be saved. Serfs with your masters. Sergeants Ravenscar and Bohemond, escort the Master of Ordnance and myself to the Tactical Chancelorium. Narke, you will accompany us. All understood?'

'Yes, Chapter Master,' the chorus came back.

'Sergeant, on three,' Artegall instructed. 'One.' Bohemond nodded and primed a pair of grenades from his belt. 'Two.' Faulks took position by the door stud. 'Three'. Roderick nestled his bolter snug into his shoulder as Faulks activated the door mechanism.

As the door rolled open, Ravenscar pulled away and went about reloading his boltgun. Bohemond's grenades were then followed by replacement suppression fire from Captain Roderick's bolter.

The brief impression of crimson and cream armour working up the corridor was suddenly replaced with the thunder and flash of grenades. Roderick was swiftly joined by Bohemond and then Ravenscar, the three Space Marines maintaining a withering arc of fire. The command group filed out of the Oratorium with their Chapter serf attendants, the singular crash of their Fornax-pattern pistols joining in the cacophony.

With Roderick's precision fire leading the Lord Apothecary and the Master of the Forge down a side passage, Bohemond slammed his shoulder through a stairwell door to lead the other group up onto the next level. The Crimson Consuls soon fell into the surgical-style battle rotation so beloved of Guilliman: battle-brother covering battle-brother; arc-pivoting and rapid advance suppression fire. Ravenscar and Bohemond orchestrated the tactical dance from the front, with Artegall's pistol crashing support from behind and the Master of Ordnance covering the rear with his own, while half dragging the blind Narke behind him.

Advancing up through the stairwell, spiralling up through the storeys, the Astartes walked up into a storm of iron: armoured, renegade Crimson Consuls funnelled their firepower down at them from a gauntlet above. Unclipping a grenade, Ravenscar tossed it to his brother-sergeant. Bohemond then held the explosive, counting away the precious seconds before launching the thing directly up through the space between the spiral stair rails. The grenade detonated above, silencing the gunfire. A cream and crimson body fell down past the group in a shower of grit. The sergeants didn't wait, however, bounding up the stairs and into the maelstrom above.

Dead Crimson Consuls lay mangled amongst the rail and rockcrete. One young Space Marine lay without his legs, his helmet half blasted from his face. As blood frothed between the Adeptus Astartes' gritted teeth the Space Marine stared at the passing group. For Artegall it was too much. Crimson Consuls spilling each other's sacred blood. Guilliman's dream in tatters. He seized the grievously wounded Space Marine by his shattered breastplate and shook him violently.

'What the hell are you doing, boy?' Artegall roared, but there was no time. Scouts in light carapace armour were spilling from a doorway above, bouncing down one storey to the next on their boot tips, bathing the landings with scattershot from their shotguns. Bolt-rounds sailed past Faulks from below, where renegade Crimson Consuls had followed in the footsteps of their escape. The shells thudded into the wall above the kneeling Artegall and punched through the stumbling astropath, causing the Master of Ordnance to abandon his handicap and force back their assailants with blasts from a recovered bolter.

'Through there!' Faulks bawled above the bolt chatter, indicating the nearest door on the stairwell. Again Bohemond led with his shoulder, blasting through the door into a dormitory hall. The space was plain and provided living quarters for some of the Slaughterhorn's Chapter serfs. Bright, white light was admitted from the icescape outside through towering arches of plain glass, each depicting a bleached scene from the Chapter's illustrious history, picked out in lead strips.

Ravenscar handed Artegall his bolter and took a blood-splattered replacement from the stairwell for himself.

'There's a bondsman's entrance to the Chancelorium through the dormitories,' Artegall pointed, priming the bolter. Their advance along the window-lined hall had already been ensured by the bolt-riddled door being blasted off its hinges behind them.

'Go!' Faulks roared. The four Space Marines stormed along the open space towards the far end of the hall. The searing light from the windows was suddenly eclipsed, causing the Astrartes to turn as they ran. Drifting up alongside the wall, directed in on their position by the renegade Astartes, was the sinister outline of a Crimson Consuls Thunderhawk. As the monstrous aircraft hovered immediately outside, the heavy bolters adorning its carrier compartment unleashed their fury.

All the Space Marines could do was run as the great accomplishments of the Chapter shattered behind them. One by one the windows imploded with anti-personnel fire and fragmentation shells, the Thunderhawk gently gliding along the wall. The rampage caught up with Ravenscar who, lost in the maelstrom of smashed glass and lead, soaked up the heavy bolter's punishment and in turn became a metal storm of pulped flesh and fragmented armour. At the next window, Artegall felt the whoosh of the heavy bolter rounds streak across his back. Detonating about him like tiny frag grenades, the rounds shredded through his pack and tore up the ceramite plating of his armoured suit. Falling through the shrapnel hurricane, Artegall tumbled to the floor before hitting the far wall.

Gauntlets were suddenly all over him, hauling the Chapter Master in through an open security bulkhead, before slamming the door on the chaos beyond.

By comparison the command tower was silent. Artegall squinted, dazed, through the darkness of the Chancelorium dungeon-antechamber, his power armour steaming and slick with blood, lubricant and hydraulic fluid.

As Artegall came back to his senses, he realised that he'd never seen this part of his fortress-monastery before; traditionally it only admitted Chapter serfs. Getting unsteadily to his feet he joined his battle-brothers in stepping up on the crimson swirl of the marble trapdoor platform. With Sergeant Bohemond and Master Faulks flanking him, the Chapter Master activated the rising floor section and the three Crimson Consuls ascended up through the floor of Artegall's own Tactical Chancelorium.

'Chapter Master, I'll begin–'

Light and sound, simultaneous.

Bohemond and Faulks dropped as the backs of their heads came level with the yawning barrels of waiting bolters and their skulls were blasted through the front of their faceplates. Artegall spun around but found that the bolters, all black paint and spiked barrels, were now pressed up against the crimson of his chest.

His assailants were Space Marines. Traitor Astartes. The galaxy's arch-traitors. The Warmaster's own – the Black Legion. Their cracked and filthy power armour was a dusty black, edged with gargoylesque details of dull bronze. Their helmets were barbed and leering and their torsos a tangle of chains and skulls. With the smoking muzzle of the first still resting against him, the second disarmed the grim Chapter Master, removing his bolter and slipping the bolt pistol and gladius from his belt. Weaponless, he was motioned round.

Before him stood two Black Legion officers. The senior was a wild-eyed captain with teeth filed to sharp points and a flea-infested wolf pelt hanging from his spiked armour. The other was an Apothecary whose once-white armour was now streaked with blood and rust and whose face was shrunken and soulless like a zombie.

'At least do me the honour of knowing who I am addressing, traitor filth,' the Chapter Master rumbled.

This, the Black Legion captain seemed to find amusing.

'This is Lord Vladivoss of the Black Legion and his Apothecary Szekle,' a voice bounced around the vaulted roof of the Chancelorium, but it came from neither Chaos Marine. The Black Legion Space Marines parted to reveal the voice's owner, sitting in Artegall's own bone command throne. His armour gleamed a sickening mazarine, embossed with the necks of green serpents that entwined his limbs and whose heads clustered on his chest plate in the fashion of a hydra. The unmistakable iconography of the Alpha Legion. The Space Marine sat thumbing casually through the pages of the Codex Astartes on the Chapter Master's lectern.

'I don't reason that there's any point in asking you that question, renegade,' Artegall snarled.

The copper-skinned giant pushed the anti-gravitic lectern to one side, stood and smiled: 'I am Alpharius.'

A grim chuckle surfaced in Artegall. He hawked and spat blood at the Alpha Legionnaire's feet.

'That's what I think of that, Alpha,' the Chapter Master told him. 'Come on, I want to congratulate you on your trademark planning and perfect execution. Alpharius is but a ghost. My Lord Guilliman ended the scourge – as I will end you, monster.'

The Legionnaire's smile never faltered, even in the face of Artegall's threats and insults. It grew as the Space Marine came to a private decision.

'I am Captain Quetzal Carthach, Crimson Consul,' the Alpha Legion Space Marine told him, 'and I have come to accept your unconditional surrender.'

'The only unconditional thing you'll get from me, Captain Carthach, is my unending revulsion and hatred.'

'You talk of ends, Chapter Master,' the Legionnaire said calmly. 'Has Guilliman blinded you so that you cannot see your own. The end of your Chapter. The end of your living custodianship, your shred of that sanctimonious bastard's seed. I wanted to come here and meet you. So you could go to your grave knowing that it was the Alpha Legion that had beaten you; the Alpha Legion who are eradicating Guilliman's legacy one thousand of his sons at a time; the Alpha Legion who are not only superior strategists but also superior Space Marines.'

Artegall's lips curled with cold fury.

'Never...'

'Perhaps, Chapter Master, you think there's a chance for your seed to survive: for future sons of Carcharias to avenge you?' The Alpha Legion giant sat back down in Artegall's throne. 'The Tenth was mine before you even recruited them – as was the Ninth Company before them: you must know that now. I lent you their minds but not their true allegiance: a simple phrase was all that was needed to bring them back to the Alpha Legion fold. The Second and Fourth were easy: that was a mere administrative error, holding the Celebrants over at Nedicta Secundus and drawing the Crimson Consuls to the waiting xenos deathtrap that was Phaethon IV.'

Artegall listened to the Alpha Legionnaire honour himself with the deaths of his Crimson Consul brothers. Listened, while the Black Legion

Space Marine looked down the spiked muzzle of his bolter at the back of the Chapter Master's head.

'The Seventh fell fittingly at the hands of their brothers, foolishly defending your colourfully-named fortress-monastery from a threat that was within rather than without. The Eighth, well, Captain Vladivoss took care of those in the Sarcus Reaches – and now the good captain has earned his prize. Szekle,' the Alpha Legion Space Marine addressed the zombified Chaos Space Marine. 'The Apothecarion is now in our hands. You may help yourself to the Crimson Consuls remaining stocks of gene-seed. Feel free to extract progenoids from loyalists who fought in our name. Fear not, they will not obstruct you. In fact, the completion of the procedure is their signal to turn their weapons on themselves. Captain Vladivoss, you may then return to Lord Abaddon with my respects and your prize – to help replenish the Black Legion's depleted numbers in the Eye of Terror.'

Vladivoss bowed, while Szekle fidgeted with dead-eyed anticipation.

'Oh, and captain,' Carthach instructed as Artegall was pushed forwards towards the throne, 'leave one alive, please.'

With Captain Vladivoss, his depraved Apothecary and their Chaos Space Marine sentry descending through the trapdoor on the marble platform with Bohemond and Faulk's bodies, Carthach came to regard the Chapter Master once again.

'The *Revenant Rex* was pure genius. That I even admit to myself. What I couldn't have hoped for was the deployment of all your First Company Terminator veterans. That made matters considerably easier down the line. You should receive some credit for that, Chapter Master Artegall,' Carthach grinned nastily.

A rumble like distant thunder rolled through the floor beneath Artegall's feet. Carthach seemed suddenly excited. 'Do you know what that is?' he asked. The monster didn't wait for an answer. Instead he activated the controls in the bone armrest of Artegall's throne. The vaulted ceiling of the Tactical Chancelorium – which formed the pinnacle of the Command Tower – began to turn and unscrew, revealing a circular aperture in the roof that grew with the corkscrew motion of the Tower top.

The Alpha Legionnaire shook his head in what could have been mock disappointment.

'Missed it: that was your Slaughterhorn's defence lasers destroying the strike cruisers you ordered back under their protection. Poetic. Or perhaps just tactically predictable. Ah, now look at this.'

Carthach pointed at the sky and with the Chaos Space Marine's bolter muzzle still buried in the back of his skull, Artegall felt compelled to look up also. To savour the reassuring bleakness of his home world's sky for what might be the last time.

'There they are, see?'

Artegall watched a meteorite shower in the sky above: a lightshow of tiny flashes. 'I brought the *Crimson Tithe* back to finish off any remaining frigates or destroyers. I don't want surviving Crimson Consuls running to the Aurora Chapter with my strategies and secrets; the Auroras and their share of Guilliman's seed may be my next target. Anyway, the beautiful spectacle you see before you is no ordinary celestial phenomenon. This is the Crimson Consuls Sixth Company coming home, expelled from the *Crimson Tithe*'s airlocks and falling to Carcharias. The battle-barge I need – another gift for the Warmaster. It has the facilities on board to safely transport your seed to the Eye of Terror, where it is sorely needed for future Black Crusades. Who knows, perhaps one of your line will have the honour of being the first to bring the Warmaster's justice to Terra itself? In Black Legion armour and under a traitor's banner, of course.'

Artegall quaked silent rage, the Chapter Master's eyes dropping and fixing on a spot on the wall behind the throne.

'I know what you're thinking,' Carthach informed him. 'As I have all along, Crimson Consul. You're pinning your hopes on Captain Borachio. Stationed in the Damocles Gulf with the Third and Fifth Companies... Did you find my reports convincing?'

Artegall's eyes widened.

'Captain Borachio and his men have been dead for two years, Elias.'

Artegall shook his head.

'The Crimson Consuls are ended. I am Borachio,' the Alpha revealed, soaking up the Chapter Master's doom, 'and Carthach ... and Alpharius.' The captain bent down to execute the final, astrotelepathically communicated move on Artegall's beautifully carved Regicide board. Blind Man's Mate.

Artegall's legs faltered. As the Crimson Consul fell to his knees before Quetzal Carthach and the throne, Artegall mouthed a disbelieving, 'Why?'

'Because we play the Long Game, Elias...' the Alpha Legionnaire told him.

Artegall hoped that the Black Legion's attention span didn't extend half as far as their Alpha Legion compatriots. The Space Marine threw his head back, cutting his scalp against the bolter's muzzle. The weapon smacked the Chaos Space Marine in the throat – the Black Legion savage still staring up into the sky, watching the Crimson Consuls burn in the upper atmosphere.

Artegall surged away from the stunned Chaos Space Marine and directly at Carthach. The Alpha Legion Marine snarled at the sudden, suicidal surprise of it all, snatching for his pistol.

Artegall awkwardly changed direction, throwing himself around the other side of the throne. The Black Legion Space Marine's bolter fire followed him, mauling the throne and driving the alarmed Carthach even further back. Artegall sprinted for the wall, stopping and feeling for the featureless trigger that activated the door of the Chapter Master's private armoury. As the Chaos Space Marine's bolter chewed up the Chance-lorium wall, Artegall activated the trigger and slid the hidden door to one side. He felt hot agony as the Chaos Space Marine's bolter found its mark and two rounds crashed through his ruined armour.

Returned to his knees, the Chapter Master fell in through the dark-ness of the private armoury and slid the reinforced door shut from the inside. In the disappearing crack of light between the door and wall, Artegall caught sight of Quetzal Carthach's face once more dissolve into a wolfish grin.

Throwing himself across the darkness of the armoury floor, the felled Crimson Consul heaved himself arm over agonising arm through the presentation racks of artificer armour: racks from which serfs would ordi-narily select the individual plates and adornments and dress the Chapter Master at his bequest. Artegall didn't have time for such extravagance. Crawling for the rear of the armoury, he searched for the only item that could bring him peace. The only item seemingly designed for the single purpose of ending Quetzal Carthach, the deadliest in the Chapter's long history of deadly enemies. Artegall's master-crafted boltgun.

Reaching for the exquisite weapon, its crimson-painted adamantium finished in gold and decorated with gemstones from Carcharias's rich depths, Artegall faltered. The bolt-rounds had done their worst and the Chapter Master's fingers failed to reach the boltgun in its cradle. Sud-denly there was sound and movement in the darkness. The hydraulic sigh of bionic appendages thumping into the cold marble with every step.

'Baldwin!' Artegall cried out. 'My weapon, Baldwin... the boltgun.'

The Chamber Castellan slipped the beautiful bolter from its cradle and stomped around to his master. 'Thank the primarch you're here,' Artegall blurted.

In the oily blackness of the private armoury, the Chapter Master heard the thunk of the priming mechanism. Artegall tensed and then fell limp. He wasn't being handed the weapon: it was being pointed at him through the gloom. Whatever had possessed the minds of his Neophyte recruits in the Carcharian underhive had also had time to worm its way into the Chamber Castellan, whose responsibility it was to accompany the recruitment parties on their expeditions. Without the training or spiritual fortitude of an Astartes, Baldwin's mind had been vulnerable. He had become a Regicide piece on a galactic board, making his small but significant move, guided by an unknown hand. Artegall was suddenly glad of the darkness. Glad that he couldn't see the mask of Baldwin's kindly face frozen in murderous blankness.

Closing his eyes, Elias Artegall, Chapter Master and last of the Crim-son Consuls, wished the game to end.

# HEART OF RAGE

## by James Swallow

In the blood-warm gloom, amid the shrouding, cloying thickness of the air, the heart beat on. A clock ticking towards death, a ceaseless rhythm echoing through his body. A cadence that inched him, pulse by throbbing pulse, towards the raging madness of the Thirst.

Engorged with vital fluid, the heart pressed against the inside of his ribcage, trip-hammer impacts growing faster and faster, reaching out, threatening to engulf him. His every sense rang with the force of it, the rushing in his ears, his arrow-sharp sight fogged and hazy, the scent of old rust thick in his nostrils... And the taste.

Oh yes, the taste... Congealing upon his tongue, the heavy meat-tang like burned copper, the wash across his fangs. The aching, delirious need to drink deep.

Clouds of ruby and darkness billowed about him, surrounded him, dragged him roaring into the void, damned and destined to surrender to it. These were the enemies that he and all his kindred could never defeat, the unslakable Red Thirst and its terrible twin, the berserker fury of the Black Rage. These were the legacy of The Flaw, the foes he would face for eternity, beyond all others, for they were trapped within him. Woven like threads of poison through the tapestry of his DNA, the bane-gift of his lord and master ten thousand years dead.

*Sanguinius.* Primarch and noblest among the Emperor's sons. The Great Angel, the Brightest One. The shockwave of the master's murder, millennia gone yet forever resonant, thundered in his veins. The power of the primarch's angelic splendour and matchless strength filled him...

And yet the other face of that golden coin was dark, dark as rage, dark as fury, darker than any hell-spawned curse upon creation.

Their boon and their blight. The malevolent mirror of the beast inside every brother of the Blood Angels Chapter.

Brother-Codicier Garas Nord knelt upon the chapel's flagstones, the only sound about him the whisper of servo-skulls high overhead, watching the lone Space Marine with indifferent attention.

Hunched forwards in prayer, his broad frame was alone before the simple iron altar. Wan light cast by biolumes cast hollow colour over his face. It glittered across the sullen indigo of his battle armour and the gold chasing of the metal skull upon his chest. The glow caught the deep, rich red of his right shoulder pauldron and the sigil of his Chapter, a winged drop of crimson blood. It glittered upon the matrix of fine crystal about his bowed head, where the frame of a psychic hood rose from his gorget – and it caught in accusing shadows the faint trembling of Nord's gauntleted hands, where they met and crossed in the shape of the Imperial aquila.

Nord's eyes were closed, but his senses were open. His hands tightened into fists. The ominous echoes of the dream still clung to him, defeating his every attempt to banish them.

He released a sigh. Visions were no stranger to him. They were as much a tool to his kind as the hood or the force axe sheathed upon his back. Nord had The Sight, the twisted blessing of psionic power, and with it he fought alongside his brothers in the Adeptus Astartes, to bolster them upon the field of conflict. In his time he had seen many things, great horrors spilling into the world from the mad realms of the warp, forms that pulled at reason with their sheer monstrosity. Darkness and hate... And once in a while, a glimpse of something. A possibility. A future.

It had saved his life on Ixion, when prescience turned his head, a split second before a las-bolt cut through the air. He still wore the burn scar from that near-hit across his cheek, livid against his face.

But this was different. No flash of reflex, just a dream, over and over. He could not help but wonder – was it also a warning?

His kind... They had many names – telekine, witchkin, warp-touched, *psyker* – but beyond it all he was something more. A son of Sanguinius. A Blood Angel. Whatever visions of fate his mind conjured for him, his duty came before them all.

If the spirit of Sanguinius were to beckon him towards a death, then he prayed that it would be a noble sacrifice; an ending not in the wild madness of the Black Rage, but one forged in honour. A death worthy of his primarch, worthy of one who had perished protecting Holy Terra and the Emperor himself from the blades of arch-traitors.

'Nord.' He sensed the new presence in the chapel, the edges of a hard, disciplined psyche, a thing forged like sword-blade steel.

The Codicier opened his eyes and looked up at the statue of the Emperor behind the altar. The Emperor looked down, impassive and silent. The eyes of the carving seemed to track Nord as he bowed before it. It offered only mute counsel, but that was just and right. For now, whatever troubled the Codicier was his burden to carry.

Nord rose to find Brother-Sergeant Kale approaching, his boots snapping against the stone floor. He sketched a salute and Kale nodded in return.

'Sir,' he began. 'Forgive me. I hoped to take a moment of reflection before we embarked upon the mission proper.'

Kale waved away his explanation. 'Your tone suggests you did not find it, Garas.'

Nord gave his battle-brother a humourless smile. 'Some days peace is more difficult to find than others.'

'I know exactly what you mean.' Kale's hand strayed to his chin and he rubbed the rasp of white-grey stubble there with red-armoured fingers. 'I doubt I have had a moment's quiet since we embarked.' He gestured towards the chapel doors and Nord walked with him.

The Codicier studied the other man. They were contrasts in colour and shade, the warrior and the psyker.

Sergeant Brenin Kale's wargear was crimson from head to toe, dressed with honour-chains of black steel and gold detailing, purity seals and engravings that listed his combat record. Under one arm he carried his helmet, upon it the white laurel of a veteran. He wore a chainsword in a scabbard along the line of his right arm, the tungsten fangs of the blade grey and sharp. His face was pale and pitted, the mark of radiation damage, and he sported a queue of wiry hair from a top-knot; and yet there was a patrician solidity to his aspect, a strength and nobility that time and war had not yet diminished.

Nord shared Kale's build and stature, as did every son of Sanguinius, the bequest of the gene-seed implantation process each Adeptus Astartes endured as an initiate. But there the similarity ended. Where Kale was sallow of face, Nord's skin was rust-red, like the rad-deserts of Baal Secundus, and the laser scar was mirrored on his other cheek by the electro-tattoo of a single blood droplet, caught as if falling from the corner of his eye. Nord's hairless scalp was bare except for the faint tracery of a molly-wire matrix just beneath the flesh, implanted to improve connectivity with his psychic hood. And his armour was a uniform blue everywhere except his shoulder, contrasting against the red of the rest of his battle-brothers. The colour set him apart, showed him for what he was beneath the plasteel and ceramite. Witchkin. Psyker. A man without his peace.

Within the chapel, one might have thought they stood inside a church upon any one of billions of hive-worlds across the Imperium. If not for the banners of the Adeptus Astartes and the Navy, the place would be no different from all those other basilicas: sacred places devoted to the worship of the God-Emperor of Humanity. But this church lay deep in the decks of the frigate *Emathia*, protected by vast iron ribs of hull-metal, nestled between the accelerator cores of the warship's primary and secondary lance cannons.

Nord left the sanctum behind, and – so he hoped – his misgivings, walking in easy lockstep with his sergeant. Half-human servitors and worried crew serfs scattered out of their way, clearing a path for the Space Marines.

'We left the warp a few hours ago,' offered Kale. 'The squad is preparing for deployment.'

'I'll join them,' Nord began, but Kale shook his head.

'I want you with me. I have been summoned to the bridge.' A sourness entered the veteran's tone. 'The tech-priest wishes to address me personally before we proceed.'

'Indeed? Does he think he needs to underline our mission to us once again? Perhaps he believes he has not repeated it enough.' Nord was silent for a moment. 'I may not be the best choice to accompany you. I believe our honoured colleague from the Adeptus Mechanicus finds my presence... discomforting.'

Kale's lip curled. 'That's one reason I want you there. Keep the bastard off balance.'

'And the other?'

'In case I feel the need to kill him.'

Nord allowed himself a smirk. 'If you expect me to dissuade you, brother-sergeant, you have picked the wrong man.'

'Dissuade me?' Kale snorted. 'I expect you to assist!'

The gallows humour of the moment faded; to casually discuss the murder of a High Priest of the Magos Biologis, even in rough jest, courted grave censure. But the eminent magos gathered dislike to him with such effortless ease, it was hard to imagine that the man wanted anything else than to be detested. Scant weeks they had been aboard the *Emathia* on its journey to this light-forsaken part of the galaxy, and in that time the Exalted Tech-Priest Epja Xeren had shown only aloof disrespect for both the Blood Angels and the frigate's hardy officers.

Nord wondered why Xeren had not simply used one of the Mechanicus's own starships for this operation, or employed his cadre's tech-guard. Like many factors surrounding this tasking, it sat uneasily with the Codicier; he sensed the same concern in Kale's emotional aura.

'This duty...' said Kale in a low voice, his thoughts clearly mirroring those of his battle-brother, 'it has the stink of subterfuge about it.'

Nord gave a nod. 'And yet, all the diktats from the Adeptus Terra were in order. Despite his manner, the priest is valued by the Imperial Council.'

'Civilians,' grunted the sergeant. 'Politicians! Sometimes I wonder if arrogance is the grease upon their wheels.'

'They might say the same of us. That we Adeptus Astartes consider ourselves to be *their* betters.'

'Just so,' Kale allowed. 'The difference is, where we are concerned, that fact is true.'

Emathia's ornate bridge was a vaulted oval cut from planes of brass and steel, dominated by great lenses of crystal ranging down towards the frigate's bow. Below the deck, in work-pits among the ship's cogitators, hunchbacked servitors hissed to one another, busying themselves with the running of the vessel. Officers in blue-black tunics walked back and forth, overseeing their work.

The ship's commander, resplendent in a red-trimmed duty jacket, turned from a gas-lens viewer and gave the Astartes a bow.

'Sergeant Kale, Brother Nord. We're very close now. Come.' Captain Hyban Gorolev beckoned them towards him.

Nord liked the man; Gorolev had impressed him early on with his grasp of Adeptus Astartes protocol and the careful generosity with which he commanded *Emathia*'s crew. Nord had encountered Navy men who ruled their ships through fear and intimidation. Gorolev was quite unlike that; he had a fatherly way to him, a mixture of sternness tempered by sincerity that bonded his crew through mutual loyalty. Nord saw in the captain the mirror of brotherhood with *his* kindred.

'The derelict is near,' he was saying. Gorolev's sandy-coloured face was fixed in a frown. 'Interference continues to defeat the scrying of our sensors, however. There is wreckage. Evidence of plasma fire…' He trailed off.

Nord sensed the man's apprehension but said nothing, catching sight of a readout thick with lines of text in Gothic script. He saw recitations that suggested organic matter out there in the void. Unbidden, the Codicier's gaze snapped up and he stared out through the viewports. The ghost of a cold, undefined emotion began to gather at the base of his thoughts.

'Adeptus Astartes.' The voice had all the tonality of a command, a summons, a demand to be given fealty.

Filtered and machine-altered, the word emitted from a speaker embedded in a face where a mouth had once been. Eyes of titanium clockwork measured the Blood Angels coldly. Flesh, what there was of it, was subsumed into carbide plates that disappeared beneath a hood. A great gale of black robes hung loose to pool upon the decking, concealing a form that was a collection of sharp angles; the silhouette of a body that bore little resemblance to anything natural-born. Antennae blossomed from tailored holes in the habit, and out of hidden pockets, manipulators and snake-like mechadendrites moved, apparently of independent thought and action.

This thing that stood before them at the edge of the frigate's tacti-carium, this not-quite-man seemingly built from human pieces and scrapyard leavings... This was Xeren.

'Your mission will commence momentarily,' said the tech-priest. He shifted slightly, and Nord heard the working of pistons. 'You are ready?'

'We are Adeptus Astartes,' Kale replied, with a grimace. The words were answer enough.

'Quite.' Xeren inclined his head towards the hololithic display, which showed flickers of hazy light. 'This zone is filthy with expended radia-tion. It may trouble even your iron constitution, Blood Angel.'

'Doubtful.' Kale's annoyance was building. 'Your concern is noted, magi. But now we are here, I am more interested in learning the identity of this hulk you have tasked us to secure for you. We cannot prosecute a mission to the best of our abilities without knowing what we will face.'

'But you are Adeptus Astartes,' said Xeren, making little effort to hide his mocking tone. Before Kale could respond, the tech-priest's head bobbed. 'You are quite right, brother-sergeant,' he demurred. 'I have been secretive with the specifics of this operation. But once you see your target, you will understand the need for such security.'

There was a clicking sound from Xeren's chest; Nord wondered if it might be the Mechanicum cyborg's equivalent of a gasp.

'Sensors are clearing,' noted Gorolev. 'We have a clean return.'

'Show me,' snapped Kale.

Earlier during the voyage, just to satisfy his mild interest, Nord had allowed his psychic senses to brush the surface of Xeren's mind. What he had sensed there was unreadable; not shrouded, but simply *inhuman*. Nothing that he could interpret as emotions, only a coldly logical chain of processes with all the nuance of a cogitator program. And yet, as the hololith stuttered and grew distinct, for the briefest of moments Nord was certain he felt the echo of a covetous thrill from the tech-priest.

'Here is your target,' said Xeren.

'Throne of Terra...' The curse slipped from Gorolev's lips as the image solidified. '*Xenos!*'

It resembled a whorled shell, a tight spiral of shimmering bone curved in on itself. Coils of fibrous matter that suggested sinew webbed it, and from one vast orifice along the ventral plane, a nest of pasty tenticular forms issued outwards, grasping at nothing.

It lay among a drift of broken chitin and flash-frozen fluids, listing. Great scars marked the flanks of the alien construct, and in places there were craters, huge pockmarks that had exploded outwards like city-sized pustules.

There seemed to be no life to it. It was a gargantuan, bilious corpse. A dead horror, there in the starless night.

'This is what you brought us to find?' Kale's voice was loaded with menace. 'A *tyranid* craft?'

'A hive ship,' Xeren corrected. The tech-priest ignored the silence that had descended on the *Emathia*'s bridge, the mute shock upon the faces of Gorolev's officers.

'A vessel of this tonnage is no match for a tyranid hive,' said Nord. 'Their craft have defeated entire fleets and pillaged the crews for raw bio-mass to feast upon!'

'It is dead,' said the priest. 'Have no fear.'

'I am not afraid,' Nord retorted, 'but neither am I a fool! The tyranids are not known as "the Great Devourer" without reason. They are a plague, organisms that exist solely to consume and replicate. To destroy all life unlike them.'

'You forget yourself.' Xeren's tone hardened. 'The authority here is mine. I have brought you to this place for good reason. Look to the hive. It is dead,' he repeated.

Nord studied the image. The xenos craft exhibited signs of heavy damage, and its motion and course suggested it was unguided.

'My orders come from the highest echelons of the Adeptus Mechanicus,' continued the tech-priest. 'I am here to oversee the capture of this derelict, in the name of the God-Emperor and Omnissiah!'

'Capture...' Kale echoed the word. Nord saw the veteran's sword-hand twitch as he weighed the command.

'Consider the bounty within that monstrosity,' Xeren addressed them, Adeptus Astartes and officers all. 'Nord is quite correct. The tyranids are a scourge upon the stars, a virus writ large. But like any virus, it must be studied if a cure is to be found.' A spindly machine-arm whirred, moving to point at the image. 'This represents an unparalleled opportunity. This hive ship is a treasure trove of biological data. If we take it, learn its secrets...' He gave a clicking rasp. 'We might turn the xenos against themselves. Perhaps even tame them...'

'How did you know this thing was here?' Nord tore his gaze from the display.

Xeren answered after a moment. 'The first attempt to take the hive was not a success. There were complications.'

'You will tell us what transpired,' said Kale. 'Or we will go no further.'

'Aye,' rasped Gorolev. The captain had turned pale and sweaty, his fingers kneading the grip of his holstered laspistol.

Xeren gave another clicking sigh, and inclined his head on whining motors. 'A scouting party of Archeo-Technologists boarded the craft under the command of an adept named Indus. We believe that a splinter force from a larger hive fleet left this ship behind after it suffered some malfunction. Evidence suggests–'

'This Adept Indus,' Kale broke in. 'Where is he?'

Xeren looked away. 'The scouting party did not return. Their fate is unknown to me.'

'Consumed!' grated Gorolev. 'Throne and Blood! Any man that ventures in there would be torn apart!'

'*Captain*,' warned the brother-sergeant.

The tech-priest paid no attention to the officer's outburst. 'It is my firm belief that the hive ship, although not without hazards, is dormant. For the moment, at least.' He came closer on iron-clawed feet. 'You understand now why the Adeptus Mechanicus wish to move with alacrity, Blood Angel?'

'I understand,' Kale replied, and Nord saw the tightening of his jaw. Without another word, the veteran turned on his heel and strode away. Nord moved with him, and they were into the corridor before the Space Marine felt a hand upon his forearm.

'Lords.' Gorolev shot a look back towards the bridge as the hatch slammed shut, his eyes narrowing. 'A word?' Suspicion flared black in the man's aura.

'Speak,' Kale replied.

'I've made no secret of my reservations about the esteemed tech-priest's motive and manner,' said the captain. 'I cannot let this pass without comment.' His face took on the cast of anger and old fear. 'By the Emperor's grace, I am a veteran of many conflicts with the xenos, those tyranid abominations among them.' Gorolev's words brimmed with venom. 'Those… *things*. I've seen them rape worlds and leave nothing but ashen husks in their wake.' He leaned closer. 'That hive ship should not be studied like some curiosity. It should be *atomised*!'

Kale held up a hand and Gorolev fell silent. 'There is nothing you have said I disagree with, ship-master. But we are servants of the God-Emperor, Nord and I, you and your crew, even Xeren. And we have our duty.'

For a moment, it seemed as if Gorolev was about to argue; but then he nodded grimly, resigned to fulfilling his orders. 'Duty, then. In the Emperor's name.'

'In the Emperor's name,' said Kale.

Nord opened his mouth to repeat the oath, but he found his voice silenced.

So fleeting, so mercurial and indistinct that it was gone even as he turned his senses towards it, Nord felt… *Something*.

A gloom, stygian-deep and ominous, passing over him as a storm cloud might obscure the sun. There, and gone. A presence. A mind?

The sense of black and red clouds pressed in on the edges of his thoughts and he pushed them away.

'Nord?' He found Kale studying him with a careful gaze.

He cleared his thoughts with a moment's effort. 'Brother-Sergeant,' he replied. 'The mission, then?'

Kale nodded. 'The mission, aye.'

* * *

The boarding torpedo penetrated the hull of the tyranid vessel high along the dorsal surface. Serrated iron razor-cogs bit into the bony structure and turned, ripping at shell-matter and bunches of necrotic muscle, dragging the pod through layers of decking, into the voids of the hive ship's interior.

Then, at rest, the seals released and the Space Marines deployed into the alien hulk, weapons rising to the ready.

Sergeant Kale led from the front, as he always did. He slipped down from the mouth of the boarding torpedo, playing his bolt pistol back and forth, sweeping the chamber for threats. Nord was next, then Brother Dane, Brother Serun and finally Corae, who moved with care as he cradled his flame-thrower. The weapon's pilot lamp hissed quietly to itself, dancing there in the wet, stinking murk.

The Codicier felt the floor beneath his boots give under his weight; the decking – if it could be called that – was made up of rough plates of bone atop something that could only be flesh, stretching away in an arching, curved passageway. By degrees, the chamber lightened as Nord's occulobe implant contracted, adjusting the perception range of his eyes.

Great arching walls that resembled flayed meat rose around the Blood Angels, along with fluted spires made of greasy black cartilage that drooled thin fluids. Puckered sphincters lay sagging and open, allowing a slaughterhouse stench to reach them. Here and there were the signs of internal damage, long festering wounds open and caked with xenos blood.

Nord picked out glowing boles upon the walls arranged at random intervals; it took a moment before he realised that they were actually fist-sized beetles, clinging to the skin-walls, antennae waving gently, bodies lit with dull bio-luminescence.

There were more insectile creatures in the shadows, little arachnid things that moved sluggishly, crawling in and out of the raw-edged cuts.

'Damage everywhere,' noted Serun, his gruff voice flattened by the thick air of the tyranid craft. 'But no signs of weapons fire.'

'It appears the tech-priest was right.' Kale examined one of the walls. 'Whatever fate befell this ruin, it was not caused by battle.' He beckoned his men on. 'Serun, do you have a reading?'

Brother Serun studied the sensor runes on the auspex device in his hand. 'A faint trace from the adept's personal locator.' He pointed in an aftward direction.

'That way.'

Kale's gaze drifted towards Nord. 'Is he alive, this man Indus?'

The psyker stiffened; warily extending his preternatural senses forwards. He could discern only the pale glitters of thought-energy from the spider-things and the lamp-beetles; nothing that might suggest a reasoning mind, let alone a human one. 'I have no answer for you, sir,' he said at length.

'With caution, then, brothers.' Kale walked on, and they followed him, silent and vigilant.

The corridor narrowed into a tube, and Nord imagined it a gullet down which the Adeptus Astartes were travelling. He had encountered tyranids before, but only upon the field of battle, and then down the sights of a missile launcher. He had never ventured aboard one of their craft, and it was exactly the horror he had expected it to be.

Tyranid vessels were not the product of forges and shipyards; they were spawned. Hive ships were spun out of knots of meat and bone, grown on the surface of captured worlds in teeming vats filled with a broth of liquefied biomass. They were living things, animals by some vague definition of the term. Electrochemical processes and nerve ganglions transmitted commands about its flesh; pheremonic discharges regulated its internal atmosphere; exothermic chemistry created light and heat. Its hull was skeletal matter, protecting the crew that swarmed like parasites inside the gut of the craft. Together, the hive was a contained, freakish ecosystem, drifting from world to world driven by the need to feed and feed.

Even in this half-dead state, Nord could taste the echo of that aching, bone-deep craving, as if it were leaking from the twitching walls. The fleshy wattles that dangled from the ceiling, the corpse-grey cilia and phlegmy deposits around his feet, all of it sickened him with its dead stench and the sheer, revolting affront of the tyranids' very existence. This xenos abortion was everything that the Imperium, in all its human glory, was not. A chaotic riot of mutant life, disordered and rapacious, without soul or intellect. The absolute antithesis of the civilisation the Adeptus Astartes had fought to preserve since the days of Old Night.

Nord's hand tightened around his pistol; the urge to kill this thing rose high, and he reined it in, denying the tingle of a building Rage before it had freedom to form.

The chamber broadened into an uneven space, dotted with deep pits of muddy liquid that festered and spat, gaseous discharges chugging into the foetid air. Mounds of fatty deposits lay in uneven heaps, the ejecta from the processes churning in the ponds.

Serun gestured. 'Rendering pools. Bio-mass is brought here to be denatured into a liquid slurry.'

Corae spoke for the first time since they had boarded. 'To what end?'

'To feed the hive,' Serun replied. 'This… gruel is the raw material of the tyranids. They consume it, shape it. It is where they are born from.'

Kale dropped to his haunches. 'And where they kill,' he added. The sergeant picked something metallic from the spoil heaps and turned it in his fingers. A rank sigil of iron and copper, a disc cut to resemble a cogwheel. Upon it, the design of a skull, the symbol of the Adeptus Mechanicus.

Corae turned his face and spat in disgust. 'Emperor protect me from such a fate.'

'More here,' said Brother Dane. With care, he drew to him a twisted shape afloat on one of the pools. It was a man's ribcage and part of a spine, but the bone was rubbery and distended where acidic fluids had eaten into it. It crumbled like wet sand in the Blood Angel's grip.

'Adept Indus, perhaps, and his scout team…' Kale suggested. He turned to face Nord and saw the psyker glaring into the dimness. 'Brother?'

The question had barely left his lips when the Codicier gave an explosive shout. '*Enemy*!'

The shapes came at them from out of the twisted, sinewy ropes about the walls. Three beasts, bursting from concealment as one, attacking from all sides.

Corae was quick, clutching the trigger bar of his flamer. A bright gout of blazing promethium jetted from the bell-mouth of the weapon and engulfed the closest tyranid in flames, but on it came, falling into the red wave of death.

The second skittered across the ground, low and fast, dragging itself in loping jerks by its taloned limbs and great curved claws. Dane, Serun and the sergeant turned their bolters on it in a hail of punishing steel.

The third found Nord and dove at him, falling from the ceiling, spinning about as it came. He flung himself backwards, his storm bolter crashing, his free hand reaching for the hilt of his force axe.

The tyranid landed hard and rocked off its hooves; Nord got his first good look at the thing and recognition unfolded in his forebrain, the legacy of a hundred hypnogogic combat indoctrination tapes. A lictor.

Humanoid in form, tall and festooned with barbs, they sported massive scything talons and a cobra-head tail. Where a man would have a mouth, the lictors grew a wriggling orchard of feeder tendrils. They were hunter-predator forms, deployed alone or in small packs, stealthy and favoured of ambush attacks. Unless Nord and his brothers killed them quickly, they would spill fresh pheromones into the air and summon more of their kind.

He reversed and met the alien with the flickering crystal edge of the axe, reaching into his heart and finding the reservoir of psychic might lurking within him. As the axe-head bit into the lictor's chest, Nord channelled a quickening from the warp along the weapon's psi-convector and into the xenos's new wound. Its agonised shriek battered at him, and he staggered as it tried to claw through his armour. Nord's bolter crashed again, hot rounds finding purchase in the pasty flesh of its thorax. He withdrew the axe again and struck again, over and over, riding on the battle-anger welling up inside him.

The Blood Angel was dimly aware of a death-wail off to his right, half-glimpsing another lictor fall as it was opened by shellfire and chain-blade; but his target still lived.

A talon swept down, barbs screeching as they scored Nord's chest plate; in turn he let the axe fall again, this time severing a monstrous limb at the joint. Gouts of black blood spurted, burning where it landed, and the Codicier threw a wall of psionic pressure outwards, battering at the wounded creature.

The lictor's hooves slipped on the lip of a bio-pool and it stumbled backwards into the lake of stringy muck; instantly the churning acids ate into the tyranid and it collapsed, drowning and melting.

Nord regained his balance and waved a hand in front of his visor as oily smoke wafted past; the third tyranid was also dying, finally succumbing to Corae's flamer and the impacts of krak grenades.

A mechanical voice grated through his vox-link. *'Kale. Respond. This is Xeren. We have detected weapons fire. Report status immediately.'*

Ignoring the buzzing of the tech-priest, the psyker approached the last dying lictor as Corae took aim with his flame-thrower, twisting the nozzle to adjust the dispersal pattern. The force axe still humming in his hand, his psychic power resonating through him, Nord caught the sense of the tyranid's animal mind, trapped in its death throes. He winced, the touch of it more abhorrent to him than anything he had yet witnessed aboard the hive ship.

Yet there, in the mass of its unknowable, alien thoughts, he glimpsed something. Great swirling clouds of red and black. And men, robed men with skeletal limbs of metal and copper cogs about their necks.

Corae pulled the trigger and laid a snake of fire over the beast, boiling its soft tissues beneath the hard chitin armour. Nord sheathed his axe and heard the voice again. Xeren seemed impatient.

*'Perhaps you should not engage every tyranid you see.'*

Kale was plucking spent flesh hooks from the crevices of his armour with quick, spare motions. 'The xenos did not offer us the choice, priest. And I remind you who it was that told us this ship was dead.'

*'Where the tyranids are concerned, there are degrees of death. The ship is dormant, and so the majority of the swarm aboard should be quiescent. But some may retain a wakeful state... I suggest you avoid further engagements.'*

'I will take that under advisement,' Kale retorted.

Xeren continued. *'You are proceeding too slowly, brother-sergeant, and without efficiency. Indus is the primary objective. Divide your forces to cover a greater area. Find him for me.'*

The sergeant holstered his gun, and any reply he might have made was rendered pointless as the tech-priest cut the vox signal.

Serun's hands closed into fists. 'He dares bray commands as if he were our Chapter Master? The scrawny cog has no right–'

'Decorum, kinsman,' said Kale. 'We are the sons of Sanguinius. A mere tech-priest is not worth our enmity. We'll find Xeren's lost lamb soon enough and be done.'

'If he still lives,' mused Corae, nudging the powdery bones with his boot.

* * *

Reluctantly, Brother-Sergeant Kale chose to do as the tech-priest had suggested; beyond the bio-pool chamber the throat-corridors branched and he ordered Dane to break off, taking Corae and Serun with him. Brother Dane's element would move anti-spinwards through the hive ship's interior spaces, while Nord and his commander ventured along the other path.

The psyker threw the veteran a questioning look when he voiced the orders; in turn Kale's expression remained unchanged. 'Xeren and I agree on one point,' he noted. 'We both wish this mission to be concluded as quickly as possible.'

Nord had to admit he too shared that desire. He thought of Gorolev's words aboard the *Emathia*. The ship-master was right; this monstrous hulk was an insult every second it was allowed to exist.

Dane's team vanished into the clammy darkness and Nord followed Kale onwards. They passed through more rendering chambers, then rooms seemingly constructed from waxy matter, laced with spherical pods, each one wet and dripping ichor. They encountered other strange spaces that defied any interpretation of form or function; hollows where tooth-like spires criss-crossed from floor and ceiling; a copse of bulbous, acid-rimed fronds that resembled coral polyps; and great bladders that throbbed, thick liquid emerging from them in desultory jerks.

And there were the creatures. The first time they came across the alien forms, Nord's axe had come to his hand before he was even aware of it; but the tyranids they encountered were in some state that mirrored death, a strange hibernative trance that rendered them inert.

They crossed a high catwalk formed from spinal bone, and Kale used the pin-lamp beneath the barrel of his boltgun to throw a disc of light into the pits below. The glow picked out the hulking shape of a massive carnifex, its bullet-shaped head tucked into its spiny chest in some mad parody of a sleeping child.

The rasping breaths of the huge assault organism fogged the air, bone armour and spines scraping across one another as its chest rose and fell. Awake, it could have killed the Blood Angels with a single blast of bio-poison from its slavering venom cannons.

Around the gnarled hooves of the slumbering carnifex, a clutch of deadly hormagaunts rested, shiny oil-black carapaces piled atop one another, clawed limbs folded back, talons sheathed. Nord gripped the force axe firmly, and it took a near physical effort for him to turn from the gallery of targets before him. Instead they moved on, ever on, picking their way in stealth through the very heart of the hive's dozing populace.

'Why do they ignore us?' Kale wondered, his question transmitted to the vox-bead in Nord's ear.

'They are conserving their strength, brother-sergeant,' he replied. 'Whatever incident caused this ship to fall away from the rest of its hive fleet, it must have drained them to survive it. I would not question our luck.'

'Aye,' Kale replied. 'Terra protects.'

'I–'

The force axe fell from Nord's fingers and the impact upon the bone deck seemed louder than cannon fire. Suddenly, without warning, *it* was there.

A black and cloying touch enveloping his thoughts – the same sense of something alien he had felt aboard the *Emathia*.

A presence. A mind. Clouds, billowing wreaths of black and red, surrounding him, engulfing him.

'There… is something else here,' he husked. 'A psychic phantom, just beyond my reach. Measuring itself against me.' Nord's heart hammered in his chest; he tasted metal in his mouth. 'Not just the xenos… More than that.'

He grimaced, and strengthened his mental bulwarks, shoring them up with raw determination. The dark dream uncoiled in his thoughts, the rumbling pulse of the Red Thirst in his gullet, the churn of the Black Rage stiffening his muscles. All about him, the shadows seemed to lengthen and loom, leaking from the walls, ranging across the sleeping monsters to reach for the warrior with ebon fingers.

Nord gasped. 'Something is awakening.'

Across the plane of the hive ship's hull, Brother Dane brought up his fist in a gesture of command, halting Corae and Serun. 'Do you hear that?' he asked.

Corae turned, the flamer in his grip. 'It's coming from the walls.' They were the last words he would utter.

Flesh-matter all around the squad ripped and tore into bleeding rags as claws shredded their way towards the Astartes. With brutal, murderous power, a tide of chattering freaks boiled in upon them, spines and bone and armoured heads moving in blurs. They were so fast that in the dimness they seemed like the talons of single giant animal, reaching out to take them.

Gunfire lit the corridor, the flat bang of bolter sounding shot after shot, the chugging belch of fire from the flamer issuing out to seek targets. In return came screaming – the blood-hungry shrieks of a warrior brood turned loose to find prey.

The horde of tyranid soldier organisms rolled over the Space Marines with no regard for their own safety; mindless things driven on by killer instinct and a desire to feed, they had no self to preserve. They were simply the blades of the hive, and the very presence of the intruders was enough to drive them mad.

Perhaps beings with intellect might have sensed the hand of something larger, something at the back of their thoughts, compelling them, driving them to destroy. But the termagants knew nothing but the lust to rip and rend.

Symbiotic phero-chemical links between the tyranids and the engineered bio-tools in their claws sent kill commands running before them. Like everything in their arsenal, the weapons used by the warriors were living things. Their fleshborers, great bell-mouthed flutes of chitin, spat clumps of fang-toothed beetles that chewed through armour and flesh in a destructive frenzy.

Numberless and unstoppable, the brood swallowed up Corae and Serun, opening them to the air in jets of red. Dane was the last to fall, his legs cut out from under him, his bolter running dry, becoming a club in his mailed fists. At the end of him, a storm of tusk blades pierced his torso, penetrating his lungs, his primary and secondary hearts.

Blood flooded his mouth and he perished in silence, his last act to deny the creatures the victory of his screams.

Brother Nord stumbled and fell to one knee, clutching at his chest in sympathetic agony. He felt Dane perish in his thoughts, heard the echo of the warrior's death, and that of Corae and Serun. Each man's ending struck him like a slow bullet, filling his gut with ice.

Nord's heart and its decentralised twin beat fast, faster, faster, his blood singing in his ears in a captured tempest. The same trembling he had felt back in the chapel returned, and it was all he could do to fight it off.

He became aware of Brother-Sergeant Kale helping him to his feet, dimly registering his squad commander guiding him away from the hibernaculum chamber and into the flesh-warm humidity of the corridor beyond.

'Nord! Speak to me!'

He tried to answer but the psychic undertow dragged on him, taking all his effort just to stay afloat and sensate. The shocking resonance was far worse than he had ever felt before. There had been many times upon the field of combat where Nord had tasted the mind-death of others, sometimes his foes, too often his battle-brothers... But this... This was of a very different stripe.

At once alien and human, unknowable and yet known to him, the psychic force that had compelled the termagant swarm reached in and raked frigid claws over the surface of his mind. A part of him screamed that he should withdraw, disengage and erect the strongest of his mental barriers. Every second he did not, he gave this force leave to plunge still deeper. And yet, another facet of Nord's iron will dared to face this power head-on, driven by the need to know it. To know it and *destroy* it.

Against the sickness he felt within, Nord tried to see the face of his enemy. The mental riposte was powerful; it hit him like a wall and he recoiled, his vision hazed crimson.

With a monumental psychic effort, Nord disengaged and slumped against a bony stanchion, his dark skin sallow and filmed with sweat.

He blinked away the fog in his vision and found his commander. Kale's pale face was grave in the dimness. 'The others?' he whispered.

'Dead,' Nord managed. 'All dead.'

The sergeant gave a grim nod. 'The Emperor knows their names.' He hesitated a moment. 'You felt it? With your witchsight, you saw... the enemy?'

'Aye.' The psyker got to his feet. 'It tried to kill me. Didn't take.'

Kale stood, drumming his fingers on the hilt of his chainsword. 'This... force that assaulted you?'

He shook his head. 'I've never sensed the like before, sir.'

'Do you know where it is?' The veteran gestured around at the walls with the chainsword.

Nord nodded. 'That, I do know.'

He heard the hunter's smile in the sergeant's voice. 'Show me.'

At the heart of every tyranid nest, one breed of creature was supreme. If the carnifexes and termagants, ripper swarms and biovores were the teeth and talons of the tyranid mass, then the commanding intellect was the hive tyrant. None had ever been captured alive, and few had been recovered by the Imperium intact enough for a full dissection. If the lictors and the hormagaunts and all the other creatures were common soldiery, the hive tyrants were the generals. The conduit for whatever passed as the diffuse mind of this repugnant xenos species.

Some even said that the tyrants were only a sub-genus of something even larger and more intelligent; a cadre of tyranid capable of reasoning and independent thought. But no such being had ever been seen by human eyes – or if it had, those who had gazed upon it did not live to tell.

It was the hive ship's tyrant that the Blood Angels sought as they entered the orb-like hibernacula, the tech-priest's objective now ranked of lesser importance. If a tyrant was awake aboard this vessel, then none of them were safe.

'It's not a tyranid,' husked Nord. 'The thought-pattern I sensed... It wasn't the same as the lictor's.' He paused. 'At least, not in whole.'

Kale eyed him. 'Explain, brother. Your gift is a mystery to me. I do not understand.'

'The mind that touched my thoughts, that rallied the creatures who attacked us. It is neither human nor xenos.'

The sergeant halted. 'A daemon?' He said the word like a curse.

Nord shook his head. 'I do not sense the taint of Chaos here, sir. This is different...' Even as the words fell from his lips, the psyker felt the change in the air around them. The wet, damp atmosphere grew sullen and greasy, setting a sickly churn deep in his belly.

Kale felt it too, even without the Codicier's preternatural senses. The sergeant drew his chainsword and brandished it before him, his thumb resting on the weapon's activation stud.

A robed figure, there in the dimness. Perhaps a man, it advanced slowly towards them, feet dragging as if wounded. And then a voice, brittle and cracked.

'Me,' rasped the newcomer. 'You sense me, Adeptus Astartes.' The figure moved at the very edge of the dull light from the lamp-beetles. Nord's eyes narrowed; threads of clothing, cables perhaps, seemed to trail behind the man, away into the dark.

Kale aimed his gun. 'In the Emperor's name, identify yourself or I will kill you where you stand.'

Hands opened in a gesture of concession. 'I do not doubt you already know who I am.' He bowed slightly, and Nord saw cords snaking along his back. 'My name is Heraklite Indus, adept and savant, former Magos Biologis Minoris of the Adeptus Mechanicus.'

'*Former?*' echoed Kale.

Indus's shadowed head bobbed. 'Oh, yes. I attend a new master now. Let me introduce you to him.'

The strange threads pulled taut and lifted Indus off his feet, to dangle as a marionette would hang from the hands of a puppeteer. A shape that dwarfed him lumbered out of the black, drawing into the pool of light.

White as bleached bone, crested with purple-black patches of armour shell, it bent to fit its bulk inside the close quarters of the hibernacula; a hive tyrant, in all its obscene glory.

Two of its four arms were withered and folded to its torso, the pearlescent surface of their claws cracked and fractured. The other arms ended in ropey whips of sinew that threaded across the floor and into the adept's flayed spine, glittering wetly where bone was revealed beneath his torn robes.

And yet... The towering tyranid's breathing was laboured and rough, and from its eye-spots, its great fanged jaws, its fleshy throat-sacs, thin yellow pus oozed over crusted scabs. For all the horror and scale, the tyrant seemed slack and drained, without the twitchy, insectile frenzy of its lessers. A stinking haze of necrotic decay issued from it; Nord had tasted the scent of death enough times to know that this alien beast was mortally wounded.

'What have you done, Indus?' demanded Kale, his face twisted in disgust. In all his years, the veteran sergeant had never seen the like.

'Neither human nor xenos.' Nord repeated his earlier statement, the words suddenly snapping into hard focus. With a whip-crack thought, he sent a savage mental probe towards the adept; Indus spun to face him with a glare and the telepathic feint was deflected easily.

The adept nodded slowly. 'Yes, Blood Angel. We are the same. Both blessed with witchsight. Both psykers.' Indus cocked his head. 'Xeren never told you. How like him.'

'No matter,' growled Kale. Without hesitation, the sergeant opened fire and Nord followed suit, both Space Marines turning their weapons on the ugly, abhorrent pairing.

The hive tyrant shifted, drawing Indus close in a gesture of protection, shielding the adept from the bolt-rounds that whined off its chitinous armour. Its head lolled back and a high screech issued from between its teeth; in reply there were hoots and howls from all around the Adeptus Astartes.

In moments, sphinctered rents in the hibernacula walls drew open, spilling dozens of mucus-slicked hormagaunts into the chamber. The chattering beasts rose up in a wave and the Blood Angels went to their blades. Kale's chainsword brayed as it chewed through bone; Nord's force axe cut lightning-flash arcs into meat, as barbed grasping claws dragged them down.

Nord caught a telepathic spark as blood from a cut gummed his right eye shut; he drew up his mental shields just as the hive tyrant released a scream of psychic energy upon them.

The wave of pain blasted across the chamber and the Codicier saw his battle-brother stumble, clutching his hands to his head in agony. Nord fared little better, the tyranid's telepathic onslaught sending him spinning. For long moments he waited for death to fall upon him, for the mass of hormagaunts to take the opportunity to rip him apart – but they did not.

Instead, the hissing monsters retreated, forming into a wall before the Space Marines, shielding Indus and the tyrant.

Nord went to Kale and helped him to his feet. The sergeant had lost his bolter in the melee, and he still shook from the after-effect of the psychic scream.

'We could have killed you,' said Indus. 'We chose not to.'

'You speak for the xenos now?' spat Nord.

Indus gave a crooked smile. 'A soldier's limited mindset. I had hoped for better from one with the sight.' He came forwards, the shuffling tyrant at his back. 'I found this creature near death, you understand? Too weak to fight me. I pushed in, touched its thoughts…' The adept gave a gasp of pleasure. 'And what I saw there. Such riches. The knowledge of flesh and bone, nerve and blood, an understanding! More than the scribes of the Magos Biologis could ever hope to learn. Race memory, Adeptus Astartes. Millions of years of it, to drink in…'

'Fool,' replied the Blood Angel. 'Can you not see what you have done? The creature is near death! It used what strength it had to lure you in, place you in its thrall! It uses you like it uses these mindless predators!'

He gestured at the hormagaunts. 'When it is healed, it will reawaken every horror that walks or crawls within this hive, and turn again to the killing of men!'

'You are wrong,' Indus retorted. 'I have control here! I spared your lives!'

'I?' snapped Kale. 'A moment ago you said "we". Which is it?'

'The hive answers to me!' he shouted, the warrior creatures howling in empathy. 'I gave myself to the merging, and now see what I have at my hands...' Indus drew in a rattling breath. 'That is why Xeren sent you here. He is like you. Afraid. Jealous of what we are.'

'The priest knew of this?' hissed Kale.

Indus chuckled. 'Xeren saw it happen. He fled! He sent you to find us, praying you would destroy us so his cadre could take this hive for itself.'

Nord nodded to himself. 'Aboard a ship filled with killing machines, a deed only an Astartes could do.'

'You've seen the power of these creatures,' said the adept. 'This is only a tiny measure of what the swarm is capable of.' He extended a skeletal cybernetic arm towards the psyker. 'There is such majesty here, red in tooth and claw, Blood Angel. Come see it. Join me.' New, fang-mouthed tentacles issued forth from the tyrant's stunted arms, questing towards the Codicier. 'Our union is vast and giving, for those with the gift...'

His eyes narrowed, and with one sweeping blow, Brother Nord sliced down with his axe, severing the probing limbs in a welter of acidic blood. The tyrant screamed and rocked backwards.

'A grave mistake,' snarled Indus. 'You have no idea what you have denied yourself.'

'I know full well,' came the reply. 'My blood stays pure, by the Emperor's grace and the might of Sanguinius! You have willingly defiled yourself, debased your humanity... For that there can be no forgiveness.'

'We are not monsters!' shouted Indus, amid his howling chorus. 'You are the destroyers, the disunited, the infection! You are the hate! The rage and the thirst!'

Too late, Nord's mind sensed the build of warp energy once more, resonating between the tyrant and the Mechanicum psyker. Too late, the cold understanding reached him. 'No...' he breathed, staggering backwards. 'No!'

'Nord?' The question on Brother Kale's lips was suddenly ripped away by a new, thunderous shockwave of dark power.

Perhaps it was the hive tyrant, with its hate for all things alien to it, perhaps it was Indus in his crazed fury. Whatever the origin, the burning blade of madness swept across the Blood Angels and ripped open their minds.

Nord held on to the ragged edge of the abyss, as once more the red and black clouds enveloped him. The dream! The vision in his roaring heart was upon him! His moment of foresight damning and terrifyingly real.

The strength of the psychic blast tore away any self-control, burning down to the basest, most *monstrous* instincts a man could conceal; and for an Adeptus Astartes of the Blood Angels Chapter, the fall to such madness was damning.

The gene-curse. The flaw. The Red Thirst's wild and insatiable desire for blood, the Black Rage's uncontrollable berserker insanity. These were the twin banes Nord fought to endure. Fought and held against. Fought... And finally... resisted.

But Brother-Sergeant Brenin Kale had none of the Codicier's psychic bulwarks. His naked mind absorbed the power of the tyrant's fury... and *fell*.

The man that Nord's comrade had been was gone; in his place was a beast clothed in his flesh.

Kale threw himself at the Codicier, his chainsword discarded and forgotten, hands in claws, his mouth wide to release a bellow of pure anger. The Blood Angel's fangs glittered in the light, and darkness filled his vision.

Nord collided with Kale with a concussion that sounded across the chamber, scattering dithering hormagaunts, crushing others with the impact. Kale's mailed fists rained blow after blow upon Nord's battle armour, the crimson tint of fury in the sergeant's aura stifling him.

He cried out the other man's name, desperately trying to reach through the fog of madness, but to no avail. Nord fought to block the impacts as they struggled against one another, locked in close combat; he could not bring himself to hit back.

His skull rang with each strike, his vision blurring. There was no doubt that Kale could kill him. He was no match for the old veteran's strength and prowess, even in such a state. Kale's frightening speed and instinctive combat skills would overwhelm him. He had little choice. If he could not end this madness quickly, Kale would tear open his throat and drink deep.

He glimpsed a rent in Kale's armour, a deep gouge that had penetrated the ceramite sheath. 'Brother,' he whispered. 'Forgive me.'

Nord's hand closed around the hilt of his combat blade, turning the fractal-edged knife about. Without pause, he buried it deep in his old friend's chest, down to the hilt. The blade penetrated plasteel, flesh and muscle; it punctured Kale's primary heart and the veteran's back arched in a spasm of agony.

Nord let him fall, and the other man dropped to the bony deck, pain wracking him, robbing him of his rage.

A different kind of fury burned in the psyker. One pure and controlled, as bright as the core of a star. Blue sparks gathering around the crystal matrix of his psychic hood, Nord turned and found his force axe, sweeping it up to aim at Indus.

'You will pay in kind for this, adept,' he snarled. 'Know that. In the name of Holy Terra, you will pay.'

Nord closed his eyes and let the power flow into him. Blazing actinic flares of warp energy sputtered and flew around the Blood Angel's head as the hormagaunts shook off their pause and came at him. Channelling the might of heroes though his bones, through his very soul itself, he unleashed his telepathic might through the force axe.

The blast turned the air into smoke and battered away the xenos beasts, sending them shrieking into the dark. Indus bellowed in pain as his flesh was wracked with agony, and the tyrant hooted in synchrony with him.

It took unbearable minutes for the psychic blast to dissipate, for the adept's crooked mind to shake off the aftershock.

Finally, through the myriad senses of the howling, confused tyranids, he saw only the scorched bone deck of the hibernacula.

The Adeptus Astartes were gone.

With Kale's body across his shoulder, Brother Nord ran as swiftly as the bulk of his battle armour would allow, always onwards, never looking back. His storm bolter ran hot in his hand as the Codicier placed shots into any tyranid that crossed his path. He did not stop to engage them, did not pause in his headlong flight.

Nord could feel Indus reaching out, probing the hive ship for him, drawing more and more of the sleeping xenos from their hibernation with each passing moment. He crossed the high bone bridge above the pits and saw the carnifex stirring, moaning as it rose towards wakefulness.

The psyker understood a measure of what had transpired here; Indus or the hive tyrant – or whatever unholy fusion of the two now existed – must have sensed him for the very first time as the *Emathia* made its approach. Hungry for another thrall, the hive mind allowed Nord and Kale to approach the core of the ship, while dispatching Dane and the other battle-brothers. He suppressed a shudder; it wanted *him*. It wanted to engulf him, subsume him into that same horrific unity.

Nord spat in loathing. Perhaps a weakling mind, a man like the bio-adept, perhaps he might have fallen to such a thing... But Nord was a Blood Angel, an Adeptus Astartes – the finest warrior humanity had ever created. Whatever dark fate awaited him, his duty came before them all.

His duty...

'Brother...' He heard the voice as they came to the chamber where the boarding torpedo had made its breach.

Nord lowered his comrade to the ground and he saw the light of recognition in the sergeant's eyes. The mental force Indus had turned on Kale was, at least for the moment, dispelled. 'What... did I do?' Kale's voice was a gasp, thick with blood and recrimination. 'The xenos...'

'They are close,' he replied. 'We have little time.'

\* \* \*

Kale saw Nord's dagger deep in his chest and gave a ragged chuckle. 'Should... I thank you for this?'

The psyker dragged the injured warrior into the boarding capsule, ignoring the question. 'You will heal. Your body's implants are already destroying infection, repairing your wounds.' He stood up and punched a series of commands into a control panel.

Kale's pale face darkened. 'Wait. What... are you doing?'

Nord didn't meet his gaze. 'Indus will find us again soon enough. He must be dealt with.' The psyker scowled at the vox-link and gave a low curse; the channel was laced with static, likely jammed by some freakish tyranid organism bred just for that task.

Kale tried to lift himself off the deck, ignoring the pain of his fresh, bloody scars, but the acid burn of tyranid venom in his flesh left him gasping, shaking with pain. 'You can't... go back. Not alone...'

The other warrior reached into a weapons locker, searching for something. 'I beg to differ. I am the *only* one who can go back. This enemy has already claimed the lives of three Blood Angels. There must be payment for that cost.' He glanced at the veteran. 'And Xeren's perfidy cannot stand unchallenged.'

Through his blurred vision, the sergeant saw the Codicier gather a gear pack to him, saw him slam a fresh clip of bolt shells into his weapon. 'Nord,' he growled. 'You will stand down!'

The psyker hesitated at the airlock, looking back into the gloom of the hive ship beyond. 'I regret I cannot obey you, brother. Forgive me.'

Without another word, Nord stepped through, letting the brass leaves of the hatch close behind him. Then the razor-cogs began to turn, the boarding torpedo drawing back into the void amid gushes of outgassing air.

Fuming, Kale dragged himself to the viewport, a trail of dark blood across the steel deck behind him, in time to see the hive ship's hull falling away.

The capsule turned away to find the *Emathia* hanging in the blackness, and with a pulse of thrusters, it set upon a return course towards the frigate.

Nord threw himself into the melee, storm bolter crashing, his force axe a spinning cascade of psychic fury. 'Indus!' he cried. 'I am here! Face me if you dare!'

In the confines of the corridors, he fought with termagants and warriors, stamped ripper swarms into paste beneath his boots, killed and tore and blazed a path of destruction back through the hive. Nord became a whirlwind of blade and shell, deep in the mad glory of combat.

His body sang with pain from lacerations, toxins and impacts, but still he fought on, bolstering himself with the power of his own psionic quickening. The shadows of the Rage and the Thirst were there at his back, reaching for him, ready to take him, and he raced to stay one step ahead. He could not be consumed: *not yet*. His heavy burden rattled against his chest plate.

*Soon*, he told himself, sensing the red and the black. *Very soon*.

Crossing the bone bridge once more, he shouted his defiance – and the tyranids replied in kind.

Winged fiends and fluttering, gas-filled spores fell around him, the gargoyle broods tearing through the air, daring him to attack. He unloaded the storm bolter, tracer shells cutting magnesium-bright flashes in the dark; but for each he killed there were five more, ten more, twenty. The spores detonated in foetid coughs of combustion and without warning the bridge was severed.

Nord fell, his weapons lost, down into the pit where the carnifex lurked. Impact came hard and suffocating, as the Blood Angel sank into a drift of soft, doughy matter collecting around the hive's egg sacs. Tearing the sticky strings of albumen from his armour, he tore free–

And faced his foe.

'You should have fled while you had the chance.' Indus's voice had taken on a fly-swarm buzz. 'We will take you now.'

Flanked by mammoth thorn-backed beasts, the hive tyrant bowed, as if mocking him, allowing Indus to dangle before Nord upon his tendrils. More tentacles snaked forwards, questing and probing.

The aliens waited to taste the stink of his fear, savouring the moment; Nord gave them nothing, instead bending to recover his axe where it had fallen.

'This will be your end, adept,' he said. 'If only you could see what you have become.'

'We are the superior!' came the roar in return. 'We will devour all! You are the prey! You are the beasts!'

Nord took a breath and let the dark clouds come. 'Yes,' he admitted, 'perhaps we are.'

The Black Rage and the Red Thirst, the curses that he had fought against for so long, the twin madness at the core of his being... The psyker let his defences fall before them. He gave himself fully to the heart of the rage, let it fill him.

Power, burning nova-bright, swept away every doubt, every question in his mind. Suddenly it was so very clear to him; there was only the weapon and the target. The killer and the killed.

The aliens charged, and Nord ripped open the gear pack at his belt, drawing the weapon within, running to meet them, racing towards the hive tyrant.

Indus saw the lethal burden in the Blood Angel's hand and felt a cold blade of fear lance through him; the tyrant shook in sympathetic panic. 'No–' he whispered.

'In the name of Sanguinius and the God-Emperor,' the Codicier snarled, baring his fangs, 'I will end you all!'

Captain Gorolev jerked up from the console, his expression set in fear. 'The cogitators register an energy increase aboard the hive ship!'

Xeren's head turned to face him atop his snake-like neck. 'I am aware.'

Gorolev took a step towards the Mechanicus magi. 'That ship is a threat!' he snapped. 'We have completed recovery of the boarding torpedo, and your scouts are lost! We should destroy the xenos! There is no reason to let them live a moment longer!'

'There is every reason!' Xeren's manner of cold, silky dismissal suddenly broke. He rounded on the frigate's commander, his mechadendrites and cyber-limbs rising up behind him in a fan, angry serpents hissing and snapping at the air. All trace of his false politeness faded. 'You test me and test me, ship-master, and I will hear no more! You *will* do as I say, or your life will be forfeit!'

'You have no right–' Gorolev was cut off as Xeren reached out a hand, showing brass micro-lasers where fingers should have been.

'I have the authority to do anything,' he grated. 'That hive is worth more than your life, captain. More than the lives of your worthless crew, more than the lives of Kale and his Space Marines! I will sacrifice every single one of you, if that is what it will cost!'

A silence fell across the bridge; Gorolev's eyes widened, but not in fear of Xeren. He and his officers stared beyond the tech-priest, to the open hatchway behind him.

There, filling the doorway, was a figure clad in blood-red. Xeren spun, his limbs, flesh and steel, coming up before him in a gesture of self-protection.

Brother-Sergeant Kale entered, carrying himself with a limp, his pale face stained with spilled vitae and smoke. His eyes were black with an anger as cold and vast as space.

Armour scarred from tyranid venom and claw, blemished with bitter fluids, he took heavy, purposeful steps towards the tech-priest. 'My brothers lie dead,' he intoned. 'The blame is yours.'

'I… I was not…' Xeren's cool reserve crumbled.

'Do not cheapen their sacrifice with lies, priest,' growled Kale, his ire building ever higher as he came closer. 'You sent us to our deaths, and you smiled as you did it.'

Xeren stiffened, drawing himself up. 'I only did what was needed! I did what was expected of me!'

'Yes,' Kale gave a slow nod, and reached up to his chest, where the hilt of a combat knife protruded from a scabbed wound. 'Now I do the same.'

With a shout of rage and pain, Kale tore the knife free and swept it around in a fluid arc. The blade's mirror-bright edge found the tech-priest's throat and cut deep, severing veins and wires, bone and metal. The Blood Angel leaned into the attack and took Xeren's head from his neck. The cyborg's body danced and fell, crashing to the deck in a puddle of oil.

'Energy surge at criticality...' Gorolev reported, as alert chimes sounded from the cogitator console.

Kale said nothing, only nodded. He stepped up to the viewport, over Xeren's headless corpse, and watched the hive ship. His hands drew up to his chest in salute, taking on the shape of the Imperial aquila.

'In His name, brother,' he whispered.


He was falling.

Somewhere, far beyond his thoughts in the world of meat and bone, he was dying. Claws tearing at him, serpentine tendrils cutting into him, cilia probing to find grey matter and absorb it.

Nord fell into the cascade of sensation. The blood roaring through him. The flawless, diamond-hard perfection of his anger driving him on, into the arms of the enemy.

He had never feared death; he had only feared that when the moment came, he would be found wanting.

That time was here, and he was more certain of his rightness than ever before.

The clouds of billowing crimson, the swelling mist of deep, deep night; they came and took him, and he embraced it.

Somewhere, far beyond his thoughts, a bloody, near-crippled hand curled about the grip of a weapon, tight upon a trigger. And with a breath, a slow and steady breath, that hand released. Let go. Gave freedom to the tiny star building and churning inside.

The fusion detonator Nord had recovered from the weapons locker, the secret burden he had carried back into the heart of the hive ship. Now revealed, now empowered and unleashed.

The new sun grew, flesh and bone crisping, becoming pale sketches and then vapour; and in that moment, as the light became all, in its heart Brother Nord saw an angel, golden and magnificent. Reaching for him. Offering his hand.

Beckoning him towards honour, and a death most worthy.

# BUT DUST IN THE WIND

### by Jonathan Green

The Thunderhawk gunship dropped through the planet's exosphere like a star falling from heaven, its scorched and scarred hull-plating glowing hot as molten gold. Beneath it lay a vast shroud of cloud cover and beneath that the frozen world of Ixya.

Clouds boiled and evaporated at the caress of the burning craft, and as the vessel continued its descent, those on board were afforded their first view of the snowball world at last.

Ixya might look no more than a vast planet-sized chunk of ice drifting silently through space at the far reaches of the freezing depths of the Chthonian Subsector, but according to the data the Chapter's archivists on board the *Phalanx* had been able to coax from the ancient Archivium's cogitators, it was the foremost provider of essential ores and precious metals to the forge worlds of the Chthonian Chain.

Platinum, iridium, plutonium and uranium were all found buried within the crust of the planet, even though it was compressed beneath ten kilometres of crushing ice in some places. Iron ore was found in vast quantities in great seams running practically the entire circumference of the planet's equator and it was the only attainable source of a number of rarer elements for twelve parsecs.

But all that was currently visible to the Thunderhawk's pilot was kilometre after kilometre of fractured ice sheet, crawling glaciers and frost-formed blades of frozen mountain ridges.

'Any lock on the source of the signal yet?' Sergeant Hesperus enquired of the battle-brother piloting the craft.

'Triangulating now, sir,' Brother-Pilot Teaz replied via the vessel's internal comm.

There was a pause, accompanied by an insistent pinging sound as the *Fortis*'s machine spirit gazed upon the blue-white world through its auspex arrays, seeking to pinpoint the source of the distress signal. Mere moments later, the servitor hard-wired into the gunship's systems in the co-pilot's position began to burble machine code, its eyes glassy and unblinking as it continued to stare perpetually out of the front glasteel shield of the Thunderhawk's cockpit.

'Scanners indicate that it is coming from a location three hundred kilometres from our current position. Signs are that it is uninhabited. But...' Teaz trailed off.

'What is it, brother? What else is the *Fortis* telling you?'

'Very little at that location. But there is a large settlement – a Mechanicus facility of some kind two hundred kilometres from here.'

'The miners,' Hesperus mused. 'And the distress signal isn't coming from there?'

'No, brother-sergeant.'

'And yet the facility is inhabited?'

'Reading multiple life-signs, sergeant. Cogitator estimates somewhere within the region of three thousand souls.'

'And are you reading any other settlements of comparable size anywhere else upon the planet's surface?'

'No, sir. This would appear to be the primary centre of human occupation.'

'Then I think we should pay our respects to the planetary authorities, don't you, Brother Teaz?'

'Shall I hail them, sergeant?' the pilot asked.

'No, brother, that won't be necessary. Besides, I am sure they already have us on their scopes and if they don't already know of our imminent arrival, then they soon will. I think it only right that we meet with those charged with the care of this world face to face. After all, first impressions matter.'

'You think they will brave this blizzard to meet us, brother?'

'If they have any sense, they would brave the warp itself rather than leave a detachment of Imperial Fists unattended.'

'Very good, sir. Landing site acquired. Planetfall in five minutes.'

Keying his micro-bead, Sergeant Hesperus addressed the other battle-brothers on board, strapped within the ruddy darkness of the Thunderhawk's belly hold.

'Brothers of Squad Eurus, the time has come,' Hesperus said, taking up the venerable thunder hammer that it was his honour to wield in battle along with the storm shield that bore his own personal battle honours. 'Lock helmets, bolters at the ready. We make planetfall in five.'

\* \* \*

Like a spear of burning gold, cast down from heaven by the immortal Emperor Himself, Thunderhawk *Fortis* made planetfall on the snow-bound world.

With a scream of turbofan afterburners and attitude thrusters – the jet-wash from the craft momentarily disrupting the blizzard sweeping across the barely-visible mass of chimneys, pylons and refinery barns – the *Fortis* touched down on the landing pad located within the facility's outer defensive bulwark.

Power to the engines was cut and the Doppler-crashing white noise of the fans descended to a deafening whine, the craft's landing struts flexing as they took the weight, as the great golden bird settled on the plasteel and adamantium-reinforced platform.

By the time the disembarkation ramp descended and Sergeant Hesperus led the battle-brothers of Squad Eurus out onto the hard standing of the firebase, the Space Marines' ceramite boots crunching on the ice-patched rockcrete, the welcoming committee was already trooping out onto deck to greet them. The blunt shapes of shuttle craft and grounded orbital tugs squatted on the platform, their hard profiles softened by drifts of snow.

Three men, diminutive by the standards of the Emperor's finest, made the long walk from the shelter of an irising bunker door to where Squad Eurus had formed themselves up in a perfectly straight line, ready to receive them.

Although he was at least half a head shorter than either of his two companions, from his bearing, along with the red sash and ceremonial badge of office, to his straining dress jacket, ursine fur cloak, and polished grox-hide jackboots, Hesperus knew at once that the Space Marines' arrival on Ixya had brought none other than the planetary governor – the Emperor's representative himself – to receive them. It was a good sign; Sergeant Hesperus liked to be appreciated.

The three men faced the nine mighty Adeptus Astartes of the Imperial Fists Chapter, resplendent in their black-iron trimmed golden yellow power armour, the jet packs they wore making them appear even more intimidating. Every member of the welcoming committee had to look up to meet Hesperus's visored gaze.

With a hiss of changing air pressures, Sergeant Hesperus removed his helmet and peered down at the shortest of the three. He had to admire the man; his steely expression of resolute determinedness did not falter once.

The governor had a face that looked like it had been carved from cold marble. His pate was balding but the white wings of hair that swept back from his temples and covered his chin gave him an appropriately aristocratic air.

The man held the Space Marine's gaze for several seconds and then bowed, his ursine-skin cloak sweeping the powdered snow from the landing deck.

'We are honoured, my lords.' He rose again and carefully considered the smart line of Space Marines. 'I am Governor Selig, Imperial administrator of this facility and by extension this world. I bid you welcome to Aes Metallum.' Hesperus considered that the man's chiselled expression did not offer the same welcome his words offered. Governor Selig was suspicious of them.

A wry smile formed at the corner of the sergeant's mouth. And so would I be, Hesperus thought, if I were governor and a fully-armed assault squad of Imperial Fists Space Marines arrived unannounced on my watch.

Governor Selig turned to the man at his right hand, a military man wearing a cold-weather camo-cloak over the uniform of a militia officer. 'May I introduce Captain Derrin of the Ixyan First Planetary Defence Force,' – the man saluted smartly and the governor turned to the towering, semi-mechanoid thing shrouded by a frayed crimson robe to his left – 'and Magos Winze of the Brotherhood of Mars who oversees our mining operation.'

Hesperus noted the huge ceramite and steel representation of the Cult Mechanicus's cybernetic skull heraldry on the towering facade of the structure before the landing pad, the details of the huge icon blurred by the snow that had settled upon it.

'Welcome to Aes Metallum,' the tech-priest hissed in a voice that was rusty with age and underlain by the wheezing of some augmetic respiratory function. A buzzing cyber-skull – looking like a miniature version of the Cult's crest – hovered at the adept's shoulder.

Hesperus acknowledged the tech-priest's greeting with a curt nod of his head.

'What can we do for you, sergeant?' Selig asked.

'Ask not what you can do for us,' Hesperus countered, 'but what we can do for you.'

'My lord?'

'The strike cruiser *Fury's Blade* picked up a faint automated distress call being broadcast from this world three standard days ago. Our glorious Fourth Company was en route from the *Phalanx,* our fortress-monastery, to the Roura Cluster, to bolster the defence of the Vendrin Line against the incursions of the alien eldar. However, it was deemed appropriate to send a single Thunderhawk and accompanying assault squad to assess the level of threat that had triggered this distress beacon accordingly. I presume you are aware of this distress signal yourselves, are you not?'

To his credit, Governor Selig's steely expression didn't change one iota. 'Yes we are, thank you, brother,' he stated unapologetically.

'An explorator team is currently carrying out a survey of that region,' Magos Winze explained, 'searching for new mineral reserves we suspect may be located in the area.'

'And have you sent rescue squads to investigate?' Hesperus challenged.

Governor Selig turned his gaze from the looming Astartes to the officer at his side. 'Captain Derrin?'

'No, sir.'

Hesperus looked at him askance.

'And might I ask why not?'

Captain Derrin indicated the blizzard howling about them with a gesture. The clinging flakes were steadily turning the Imperial Fists' armour from dazzling yellow to white gold.

'It's the ice storm, sir,' he said, pulling his cold-weather camo-cloak tighter about him as he shivered in the face of the freezing wind. 'We're only at the edge of it here but further north it's at its most intense – so cold it'll freeze the promethium inside the tanks of a Trojan. The flyers and armour we have at our disposal are not able to withstand its full force.'

Hesperus turned from the captain to the tech-priest, the altered adept's mechadendrites seeming to twitch with an epileptic life all of their own.

'You can confirm this, magos?'

'Captain Derrin is quite correct,' Winze wheezed. 'Aes Metallum's been locked down for three days. However, our meteorological auspex would seem to suggest that the storm is moving east across the Glacies Plateau. In two days it should be safe to send out a team to investigate.'

'Have you had any pict-feed or vox-communication with the explorator team since the storm began?' Hesperus pressed.

'No. Nothing but the signal put out by the automated beacon.'

The Imperial Fist on Hesperus's right, Battle-Brother Maestus, keyed his micro-bead. 'Do you think it could be the eldar, brother-sergeant?'

At mention of the enigmatic alien raiders, Governor Selig's expression faltered for the first time since he had welcomed the Astartes to Ixya.

'The distress beacon could be explained by any one of a dozen or more scenarios,' Magos Winze interjected. 'A snowplough could have fallen into an ice fissure, or the team saw the storm coming and triggered the distress beacon hoping for a quick extraction. We would not wish to keep you from your holy work, brother.'

'We may yet be needed here,' Hesperus countered. He turned to Maestus. 'Remaining here will not tell us whether the eldar are poised to attack this world as well. It is time we followed the signal to its source.'

He addressed each of the Ixyan welcoming committee in turn. 'Captain Derrin, ice storm or no, mobilise your men. Magos Winze, see that your servants run diagnostics of all this facility's defences; I want them primed and ready for action. Governor, good day to you.'

'But–' Selig began before Hesperus cut him off with a curt wave of an armoured hand.

'It is better that you prepare for the worst and ultimately face nothing than it is to do nothing and reap the bitter harvest that follows as a result of your inaction. Look to your defences. Secure the base. We shall return presently. Squad Eurus, move out.'

And with that the nine golden giants boarded the *Fortis* again. Only a minute later, as Governor Selig and the rest of the welcoming committee returned to the shelter of the bunker, the *Fortis* lifted off from the landing platform, the snow flurries returning as the Thunderhawk was swallowed up by the blizzard.

The Fortis shook as the freezing winds assailed it, the constant staccato of hailstones pounding its hull-plating like a remorseless barrage of autocannon fire. But the Thunderhawk, as capable of short range interplanetary travel as it was of atmospheric flight, resisted and held firm, Brother-Pilot Teaz steering a course through the hurricane winds and hail towards the spot indicated by the chiming distress signal.

'This is the place,' Teaz said as the Thunderhawk's forward motion suddenly slowed, holding it in a hover above the ice and the snow for a moment before bringing it down in the middle of a whiteout so intense that for all the visibility there was, they might as well have landed on the dark side of the planet; if that had been the case, at least then the Thunderhawk's lamps would have been able to make a difference.

Squad Eurus disembarked from the craft again, Teaz remaining on board as before, in case there was the need for a hasty extraction or the Space Marines found themselves involved in an encounter that required heavier firepower to resolve it than was carried by the members of Hesperus's team.

And yet continued sensor sweeps carried out by the *Fortis's* instruments during the short hop from the Aes Metallum facility, now one hundred kilometres to the south-west, had revealed nothing. No signs of life, no indication of an alien presence, nothing at all. It seemed that there was nothing out there beyond the howling ice storm, other than whatever anomalous geological feature it was that had led the explorers here in search of mineral deposits in the first place.

'Search pattern delta. Battle-Brother Ngaio, I want you up front,' Hesperus instructed his squad members via the helmet comm. He would have struggled to make himself heard by his battle-brothers otherwise, even with their Lyman's ear implants.

In response the nine Imperial Fists began to fan out from the landing site, sweeping the snow-shriven wilderness with their weapons, each alike – bolter in one hand, chainsword in the other, except in Battle-Brother Verwhere's case, who targeted the illusory shapes created by the flurries of gale-blown snow with his plasma pistol. Battle-Brother Ngaio advanced at the forefront, at the apex of the expanding semi-circle of warriors, his chainsword mag-locked to his hip, replaced in his gauntleted hand by the auspex he was carrying.

Hesperus moved forwards, between Ngaio and Battle-Brother Ahx. Then came Ors and Jarda. To Ngaio's left were arrayed, in the same formation, Battle-Brothers Maestus, Verwhere, Haldrich and Khafra.

Not one of them had been born on the same world – Jarda had not even set foot on one of the vassal worlds of the galaxy-spanning Imperium until after he had been inducted into the Imperial Fists Chapter, having been void-born, while Khafra was from the desert necropolis world of Tanis – but they were all brothers nonetheless. They might not have the same predominant eye colour, skin tones, hair or bone structure, but thanks to the gene-seed they all bore inside them now, they were all Imperial Fists and shared the common physiological traits of a Space Marine.

The Imperial Fists gathered their aspirants from a whole network of worlds, many of which they had visited before in the ten millennia since the *Phalanx* had set out upon its never-ending quest to bring the Emperor's mercy and justice to the galaxy. But although the brothers of Squad Eurus might not have come from a common culture or been born of a common ancestry before joining the ranks of the Imperial Fists, since their induction into the Chapter – second only, other agencies claimed, to Great Guilliman's Adeptus Astartes paragons, the Ultramarines – they were all Sons of Dorn now, the superhuman essence of the primarch having been passed down to them through his blessed gene-seed.

Hesperus peered through the whiteout, everything coloured now by the heat spectrum of his helmet's infrared arrays. But even the HUD struggled to reveal any more than he could already see with his own occulobe-enhanced sight.

Shapes came into relief out of the impenetrable whiteness, ice-obscured objects delineated by the subtle variations in light and shade that existed even within this white darkness. Huge things with tyred wheels and caterpillar track-sections, twice as tall as a Space Marine, and bucket scoops large enough to contain a land speeder emerged from the storm-wracked ice-desert.

Servos in his suit whirred as Hesperus scanned left and right, surveying the frozen wrecks of earth-moving machines and the explorators' abandoned equipment.

'Where are the bodies?' he heard Brother Jarda wonder aloud over the helmet comm.

Hesperus had been thinking the same thing. Here were the explorator team's machines, left to be claimed by the ice and snow, but there was no sign of the crews that had driven the hundred kilometres across the ice sheet to bring them to this place.

'Sergeant Hesperus,' Brother Ngaio voxed. 'I have something.'

'It's all right, brother, I see it too,' Hesperus replied.

'No, I mean there's a structure, sir.'

'A structure?'

'It should be right in front of us.'

A gust of biting wind suddenly swept the ice sheet all about them clear of snow and – beyond the frozen, broken shapes of the earthmovers and drilling rigs – Hesperus saw it. It was a great rift in the glacier, as if a great cube had been cut out of the ice where the explorators had dug down into the ice, exposing...

Hesperus tensed.

It was a pyramid. It was caked in ice, half-buried by the drifts of snow. What little of it that was visible appeared to be made from a seamless piece of some unrecognisable compound that looked like dark silver, but it was pyramidal in form and there was no mistaking its origin.

'The soulless ones,' Hesperus growled. Not the renegade eldar they had been expecting perhaps, but xenos nonetheless – something even more alien than the piratical raiders. Something utterly inimical to life.

'Brothers, with me,' Sergeant Hesperus instructed, leading the march down the rutted slope of ice that had been carved from the ice sheet by the explorators' machines. 'Brother Teaz, remain with the *Fortis*,' he commanded the Thunderhawk's pilot. 'We may be in need of the *Fortis*'s legendary firepower before too long.'

The rest of the Imperial Fists formed up behind him, trooping after him into the hole, which was ten metres deep and more than six times that across, that had been carved into the ice of Ixya.

Over the keening of the wind Sergeant Hesperus imagined he could hear another sound, like the echoes of the desperate cries and terrified screams of those who had met their end here. For there was no one left to find. They would not find anyone alive this day; of that fact Hesperus was certain.

The nine Space Marines gathered before the looming pyramidal spike of alien metal, their weapons trained on the xenos structure.

'You think they're in there?' Brother Maestus asked. He and Hesperus had a unique relationship within the squad, since they had been aspirants together almost sixty years before.

'I think that something unspeakable woke, walked from this tomb and took them.'

'Do we attempt a rescue?' Brother Verwhere asked, his plasma pistol ready in his hand, trained at the curious spherical and hemispherical hieroglyphs etched into the otherwise perfectly smooth surface of the pyramid.

'And rescue what, exactly?' Hesperus challenged his brother. 'We would find nothing alive in there, I can assure you.'

He took a step back from the towering structure.

'This is only the tip of the iceberg,' he said, smiling darkly. 'No, we pull back, return to the Aes Metallum facility. We send an astropathic message to our brethren aboard the *Phalanx* and the *Fury's Blade* and we prepare for a battle the like of which I'll wager this world has never seen.'

'Sir, I have something on the auspex,' Ngaio announced, the adrenaline rush detectable in his tone.

'Range?' Hesperus demanded, scanning the ice-locked structure in front of him, searching for any sign that the sepulchre was about to open and disgorge its unholy host.

'Sixty metres. Moving this way.'

'Vladimir's bones! Where did that come from?'

'Nowhere, sir. It came out of nowhere!'

'Direction!' Hesperus demanded.

'Heading two-seven-nine degrees!' Ngaio stated, turning to face the approaching menace, bolter in one hand, auspex still gripped tightly in the other.

'Squad Eurus!' Hesperus called to his companions over the sheet ice and howling gale. 'Ready yourselves. The enemy chooses to show itself.'

And then he saw it through the blizzard, a black beetle shape gliding towards the Imperial Fists through the whirling snow.

More than twice as large as a Space Marine, the construct hovered over the frozen ground towards them, its flight unaffected by the powerful wind shear.

Eight articulated metal limbs hung from the iron carapace of its body. The thing reached out with its forelimbs and with a ringing of blades the tips each ratcheted open to form three savage cutting claws. Multiple asymmetrical artificial eyes scanned the Space Marines, pulsing with the eerie green light of an unfathomable xenos intelligence.

'Fire at will!' Hesperus commanded and a cacophony of bolter fire immediately filled the ice hole like the barking of angry hate-dogs.

Mass-reactive shells exploded from the resilient carapace of the construct. The arachnoid-thing jerked and faltered, rotating wildly about its centre of gravity as the battle-brothers found their target.

The spyder-like construct surged forwards again, closing the distance between the Space Marines and it. And was it merely the strange acoustics set up by the flesh-scouring wind keening through the teeth of the weird ice formations that clung to the pyramid, or at that moment did the xenos-construct give voice to a disharmonic shriek of its own?

With a high-pitched scream, a pulse of rippling blue-white energy burned through the whipping winds of the ice storm and struck the soaring spyder. There was an explosion of sparks and one of the construct's fore-claws went whirling away into the storm. The limb landed in a wind-blown drift, still twitching with a macabre life of its own. As the spyder recovered and closed, Brother Verwhere stood his ground, his plasma pistol still trained on the construct as he waited for the weapon to recharge.

Sergeant Hesperus strode forwards, ready to bolster Verwhere's defence. If the spyder evaded the next shot from his plasma pistol, he would ensure that the thing did not escape the wrath of his thunder hammer.

As the spyder construct closed on them, Brother Verwhere fired again,

the shot making a molten mess of the thing's head and sending it
ploughing into the ice in a sparking, crackling mess, bolts of green lightning arcing from its metal carcass.

'We have multiple contacts,' Ngaio declared clearly over the comm,
one eye on the blizzard of returns now painting the scope of his auspex.

And then the snowstorm birthed a host of figures even more maca-
brely grotesque and yet, at the same time, hauntingly familiar. They
possessed the form of hunched humanoid creatures and advanced at
a gambolling gait, darting through the ice and snow, reaching for the
Space Marines with hands shaped into glinting razor-sharp talons, as
long as a man's arm, dripping blood and sticky with gore.

And as if the presence of such soulless, inhuman things was not bad
enough, then the grisly trophies with which they had adorned themselves made their very existence all the more mind-wrenching. Their
ghoulish garb – the shredded skins they had flayed from the bodies of
their victims – eradicated any lingering doubt within the minds of the
Space Marines as to the fate of the lost survey team.

As the sinister silver and crimson figures stalked towards them out of
the blizzard, Squad Eurus opened fire with their bolt pistols, the rattle
of gunfire warped by the wind into something that sounded not unlike
the drumming of iron bones on a taut skin of human hide.

Metal bodies jerked and spun, clipped by the mass-reactive shells, or
were thrown backwards into the snow when a direct hit was scored.

Hearing a thrumming, insistent buzzing noise, Sergeant Hesperus's
attention was drawn away from the approaching alien automatons and
onto the approach of another three of the hovering spyder-things.

'Defence pattern gamma,' Hesperus commanded and the eight battle-
brothers present reacted immediately, forming a tight circle of ceramite
and adamantium armour between the pyramid and the Thunderhawk.
With every angle covered, they lay down suppressing fire, dropping spyders and the flayed ones before they could even get close.

'Sergeant,' Teaz's voice came over the comm, 'look to the pyramid.'

Hesperus stepped forwards and dropped another of the skin-wrapped
metal skeletons with his crackling thunder hammer and stared at the
frozen structure even though he already knew what he would see there.

Under its cladding of ice and snow, part of the pyramid's solid surface
appeared to have liquefied and now rippled like quicksilver. Defying all
the laws of physics, the liquid surface remained at a slant, ripples gliding out from its centre as if a pebble had been dropped into a pool of
mercury.

All this happened in only a matter of seconds. His attention still half
on the approaching xenos constructs, Hesperus turned and spun, bringing his hammer down on another of the spyder-things even as it reached
for him with snapping pincer-claws.

Something was emerging from the pool of liquid metal that had formed in the side of the pyramid. At the periphery of his vision, Hesperus saw a skeletal metal thing step out from the fluid shimmering surface and begin to stalk towards the Space Marines' line. Its gleaming metal skull was hung low between its armoured shoulders, its crystal eyes glowing with a malign intelligence. In its gauntlet-like hands the inhuman warrior carried a bizarre-looking weapon of alien design, but nonetheless lethal for all that. Hesperus had read a treatise disseminated by the Cult Mechanicus that postulated how such weapons operated and recognised the glowing green rods that formed what could best be described as the barrel of the gun as a linear accelerator chamber. Beneath this, the firearm sported a cruel, scything blade – a lethal close quarters combat attachment.

'We're not prepared for this,' Hesperus muttered. It was not the way of an Imperial Fists commander to readily give the order to retreat. The Chapter was notorious even amongst the Adeptus Astartes for the stubborn determination of its warriors, who would stand and fight long after the brethren of other Chapters would have quit the field of battle. But nor was it the Imperial Fists way to waste such a precious commodity as experienced battle-brothers, by fighting a suicidal action which would not win them the day and which, in the case of Ixya and the Aes Metallum facility, would leave the Emperor's loyal subjects open to attack, with no hope of victory in the face of the xenos threat.

There was a steady stream of the skeletal warriors emerging from the quicksilver pool now, without there being any indication as to when the reinforcements might come to an end.

Beside him Brother Ors's chainsword bit through the spine of a warrior, sending chewed-up chunks of metal vertebrae flying and leaving shorn gold wiring exposed.

In the face of ever-increasing numbers, having no idea how many there might still be to come, Hesperus called the retreat.

'Squad Eurus! Ignite jump packs and fall back to the *Fortis*. We are leaving – now!'

He did not fall back lightly; it was not the Imperial Fists' way. But Hesperus knew from bitter experience, that where there was one necron, a multitude might follow.

'Brother Teaz,' he called into the comm, once again. 'Covering fire, now!'

One after another, in quick succession, the Space Marines' jump packs ignited with a roar and Squad Eurus rocketed skywards.

A split second later searing laser light streaked over their heads and down into the excavation site, exploding spyders and warriors where it struck as the grounded Thunderhawk's strafing fire found targets even through the obscuring blizzard.

Pulses of sickly green lightning burst from the weapons of the advancing warriors, chasing them from the depths of the whiteout, evaporating the falling snow and lending the snowstorm an eerie, otherworldly cast.

Almost as quickly as the Thunderhawk's laser barrage had begun it cut out again.

'Brother Teaz!' Hesperus called into the comm as he began to descend again towards the waiting Thunderhawk. 'We need covering fire, now!'

He could make out the silhouette of the great adamantium craft on the ice beneath them now. What he could not hear, however, was the roar of turbofan engines running up to take-off speed and he could not see pulses of laser-light spitting from the *Fortis's* guns.

As he and his brother Space Marines dropped lower he understood the reason for the Thunderhawk's unprepared condition. The hull of the craft appeared to ripple as if its adamantium plates had fractured and acquired some unnatural form of life.

As they came closer still, Hesperus could see that the undulating surface was in fact formed from myriad beetle-like constructs that were swarming all over the *Fortis*, jamming its flight controls, clogging its propulsion systems and interfering with its weapon arrays.

There were more of the beetling machines burrowing up through the ice to join the host already smothering the Thunderhawk. If the craft was to be of any use to the Imperial Fists in their flight from this xenos-cursed place, the silver scarabs had to be eliminated.

'Squad Eurus, deploy grenades.'

As well as being armed with bolt pistols and chainswords, each of the Space Marines also carried a number of grenades. Mag-locking their chainswords to their armoured suits, the battle-brothers of Squad Eurus slowed their rapid descent, dropped the primed frag charges where the swarm was thickest, training their pistols on the scarabs interfering with the weapons systems and the Thunderhawk's engines, removing them with precision shots to free the more delicate parts of the craft from the xenos swarm infestation.

The grenades detonated as they hit, sending fragments of alien artifice flying, turning the beetle-things into just so much more shrapnel, clearing a score of the creatures from the fuselage with every blast.

As the Space Marines dropped the last twenty metres to the landing site, they opened up with their bolters, their own strafing fire clearing yet more of the insidious scuttling things from the stricken *Fortis*.

Hesperus landed hard, the ice shuddering beneath his feet. He was up and at the swarm in the time it took him to rise from the crouch in which he braced himself as he landed, batting the scrabbling scarabs clear of the wings of the Thunderhawk, sending a dozen flying with every powerfully concussive blow of his hammer.

But the Space Marines' action against the Thunderhawk was making a difference now. Slowly, the flyer's turbofan engines began to whine as the cockpit controls came online again and Brother-Pilot Teaz coaxed the great craft into life.

Striding into the thick of the skittering beetle-things, Hesperus made his way to the *Fortis's* hold access and, with well-placed sweeps of his crackling hammer head, he beat the scarabs clear of the hatch.

'Brother Teaz, can you hear me now?'

'Re– *czzz*– ving you now, s– *czz*– geant.'

'Then open up and let us in.'

With a grinding whine the embarkation hatch opened and Squad Eurus boarded the Thunderhawk. Brother Khafra, the last on board punched the switch to activate the closing mechanism as the *Fortis* lifted off, shaking the snow from its landing struts and sending the last of the scarabs tumbling from its surface where they had persistently clung onto the outer hull.

As the Thunderhawk continued to gain altitude, Brother-Pilot Teaz swung its nose round, pointing it back in the direction of the mining facility. Sergeant Hesperus, his hearts still racing within the hardened shell of his ribs, peered through the closing crack of the outer hatch and uttered a heartfelt prayer to Dorn and the Emperor. A multitude filled the excavation site before the frozen pyramid, the legions woken by the explorators' innocent interference darkening the snow and ice with their innumerable host.

'Brothers,' he said, 'we return to the facility to prepare for a siege.'

'What news, sergeant?' Governor Selig asked as the great and the good of Aes Metallum met the Imperial Fists again upon the adamantium skirt of the shuttle pad.

Hesperus removed his helmet again before answering the governor.

'Nothing good I fear,' he said, his face hard.

'But did you find the missing explorators?'

'What was left of them.'

The governor stared at him aghast. Hesperus took a long, slow breath, carefully composing what he was about to say in his mind first.

Selig blanched as Sergeant Hesperus told him what had befallen the explorator team and what would soon befall the mining facility. For those who had once claimed this frozen hell as their own had woken from the slumber of aeons to take it back.

'Governor, were it not for our presence upon this world, I would say that the fate of this world was sealed, that Ixya was doomed. But you see here before you ten of the Emperor's finest warriors, each one worth a hundred of those who fight within the Emperor's inestimable armies, and as a result this world is not yet doomed. For as long as you have us to bolster your defence of this bastion, there is still hope.'

'Throne be praised,' Selig gasped, making the sign of the aquila across his chest.

'The Emperor protects.'

Magos Winze's circling mechadendrites formed the holy cog symbol in supplication to the Omnissiah of Mars, accompanied by a chirrup of machine code-prayer.

'Captain Derrin,' Hesperus said, turning to the commander of Ixya's planetary defence force. 'What armour have you? Aircraft? Gun emplacements? How many men do you have at your command? What other defensive measures? I need an inventory of everything you have got at your disposal. You too, Magos Winze. Tell me everything.'

When Captain Derrin had finished running through the militia's resources on Ixya – from the flight of Valkyries, through to Hades breaching drills, Sentinel power-lifters and Trojan support vehicles – aided by the tech-priest's indefatigable augmented memory, Sergeant Hesperus looked at each of the three men and said, 'Then we prepare for war!'

'Permission to speak honestly, brother-sergeant,' Brother Maestus said over a closed comm channel so that only Hesperus could hear him.

'For you, Maestus, always.'

'Sir, it is not enough,' the battle-brother said, gravely.

'I know that, brother,' Hesperus replied, 'but what would you have me tell Selig and the others? Take away their hope and we take away the best weapon these people have at their disposal. As it stands, this facility may well be doomed, but if we can hold the enemy at bay long enough, then it is still possible that reinforcements may arrive in time.'

He hesitated and then turned back, calling after the departing tech-priest. 'Magos Winze, a word if you would be so kind.'

Winze appeared to rotate at the waist and then glided back across the hard deck towards them. 'How may I assist you, sergeant?'

'How are the refined minerals you produce here transported to the forge worlds of this subsector?'

'Why,' the adapted adept croaked rustily, 'Mechanicus transport vessels arrive on a regular basis to transport the ores and isotopes we refine here to Croze, Incus and Ferramentum III.'

'And when is the next shipment due to leave?'

'Why, the *Glory of Gehenna* is coming in-system as we speak,' Magos Winze announced, augmetic nictitating eyelids clicking in quick succession. 'Would I be correct in the assumption that you are now cogitating what I predict you to be cogitating, sergeant?'

'Hail the *Glory of Gehenna*. We shall have need of the might of Mars as well as the might of the strength of Dorn's legacy this day.'

Like some leviathan void-spawn birthed in the cold, dark depths of space, the Mechanicus vessel *Glory of Gehenna* coasted in the exosphere of the frozen planet a thousand kilometres below, like some vast and ancient cetacean trawling the shallows of an arctic sea.

The servitor bound from the waist down into the ordnance post of the nave-like bridge rotated to face the command pulpit and a string of machine code emanated from the speaker grille that stood in place of a mouth.

The tech-priest at the pulpit-comm smiled in satisfaction, a hundred artificial muscle-bundles articulating the near-dead flesh of his mouth into something approximating the correct facial expression.

'Target confirmed,' Magos Kappel said.

While on the surface of the snowball world everyone and everything – from caterpillar-tracked servitors, as large as a full-grown grox and twenty times as strong, to huge earthmoving machines – was pressed into service in preparing the mining facility for the siege that was to come, the *Glory of Gehenna* prepared to deliver a dolorous blow against the enemy and pre-empt the xenos attack on Aes Metallum Hive.

Dropping into low orbit, the Mechanicus vessel locked onto the coordinates relayed from the surface by Thunderhawk *Fortis*'s machine spirit, the signal boosted by Magos Winze's Mechanicus-maintained communication arrays.

A seismic shudder passed along the length of the *Glory of Gehenna* as with a silent scream the vessel's port and starboard laser batteries fired on the surface of Ixya. They hit the ground with a deviation of only point zero six degrees, due to atmospheric distortion, and pounded the excavation site and the xenos ruins with everything the servants of the Machine-God on board could coax from the ancient weapons batteries, channelling as much energy as they could from the leviathan's ancient plasma core.

Atmospheric gases were split into their component elements as the beams of focused retina-searing light, as hot as the heart of a sun, speared down through the cloud-festooned atmosphere of the planet, setting the sky on fire, mere nanoseconds later reaching their target on the ground.

Ice melted and water boiled as the furious heat of the *Glory of Gehenna*'s attack burned away the layers of frozen glacier within which the doomed explorator team had found the alien pyramid waiting for them.

Hundreds of the inhuman constructs were wiped out in the initial phase of the bombardment. The skeletal warriors were reduced to their component parts, as units of tomb spyders and swarms of scarabs, too numerous to count, were eradicated alongside them.

In only a matter of seconds half the emerging necron force had been eradicated by one decisive, pre-emptive strike.

But as the clouds of steam drifted clear of the burn site and the whirling snow returned, it soon became apparent to those monitoring the results of the orbital barrage, from both the heavens and one hundred kilometres away within the rockcrete bunkers of the Aes Metallum base, that despite wiping out a significant portion of the burgeoning necron host, the blasphemous structure on the ground – the pyramid itself

– still stood. The only thing that had altered about its status was that much more of it had been uncovered by the scouring laser lances as their furious barrage cut through ice many metres deep, exposing not just the primary pyramid, but the peaks of two smaller structures that lay in its deathly shadow.

'Magos Winze,' the adept-master of the *Glory of Gehenna* said, speaking into the pulpit comm-link, addressing the senior adept on the surface. 'I regret to report that the target still stands.'

'Understood, Magos Kappel,' a static-distorted voice replied, echoing back across the gulf of space from the planet below, echoing like the voice of some disembodied machine spirit between the ornamented metal ribs of the bridge nave. 'Our initial sensor scans suggest that too.'

'We are charging batteries for a second attempt,' Magos Kappel continued, and then broke off abruptly. 'Wait, auspex arrays are detecting fresh activity in the vicinity of the structures.' He stared at the data-splurge scrolling across the pulpit monitor screen. 'Just a nanosecond...'

A series of live-feed data-inputs from the various servitor scanner stations ranged throughout the bridge spiked as a dramatic change in energy output was detected, centred upon the three xenos structures.

No more than four kilometres from the pyramidal hibernation sepulchres, the compacted snow covering the ice sheet fractured like the sun-baked clay bed of a receding summer watering hole. Three crescent-shaped pylon structures shuddered up out of the snow, seismic tremors rippling through the glacier, quantities of the white powder falling from them in fresh cascades as more and more of the pylons were revealed. Each supported a huge green crystal emitter, and all three were already pulsing with pent-up esoteric energies. Finally the alien devices shuddered to a halt, the last of the clinging snow dropping from them in blocks of melting slush.

With the whining thrum of ancient machinery grinding into operation again after countless millennia of inaction, the three pylons rotated slowly, like morning flowers turning to follow the sun. As one they turned and as one their energising crystals glowed into deadly life, as an aetheric light began to trickle like a shower of pulverised emerald dust from the tips of each crescent. With a crack, like the ignition of a thousand rocket launchers, the gauss annihilators fired.

Whips of coruscating energy lashed out from the crystals, focused by the vanes that projected from the pylons to either side of each emitter that harnessed their unimaginable power, streaming it into a lethal crackling discharge kilometres in length.

The annihilator beams merged a thousand metres up, cutting through the tortured atmosphere, their combined lethal lightning fingertips reaching into the exosphere, not stopping until they made contact with the *Glory of Gehenna* itself.

The annihilating beams stripped the shields from the Mechanicus vessel within seconds setting the port weapons batteries on fire and tearing through the hull plating. The carefully regulated artificial atmosphere on board the ship ignited as it bled out into the void in rippling waves of flame a hundred metres long.

As the beams continued to rip through the Mechanicus vessel, the *Glory of Gehenna* was clearly doomed. Listing badly to port, the ship commenced its descent, its blunt prow glowing magma-red as it plunged head-long through Ixya's upper atmosphere.

The blazing wreckage of the *Glory of Gehenna* fell on Ixya like the divine wrath of the God-Emperor of Mankind Himself. It struck the ice sheet two hundred kilometres east of Aes Metallum, the shockwave of its crash-landing rippling through the crust of ice and rock, hitting Aes Metallum only a minute later, followed by a dense white cloud, a tsunami of snow that was thrown up into the freezing air as the concussive energies raced outwards from the epicentre of the crash site.

The distant crump and boom of its reactor core was also the sound that signalled the beginning of the assault on Aes Metallum.

'Brother-sergeant, they are here,' Ngaio announced from his place on the northern bulwark of the defended facility.

Before its catastrophic death, perpetrated by the gauss annihilators, the *Glory of Gehenna* had eradicated much of the necron force as Magos Kappel tried to destroy the pyramidal structure. But out of the thousands that had already emerged from the tomb, hundreds had still survived the orbital bombardment. And that surviving vanguard force had now reached the walls of the mining facility.

Aes Metallum already had two semi-circular rings of defences, based on the Phaeton pattern – the rear of the facility being shielded by the towering cliff face against which it had been built – but the Imperial Fists had worked hard to bolster these by barricading the gates with earthmoving vehicles. Magos Winze's tech-priests had done what they could to hard-wire a number of the servitors available to them into the gun emplacements in redoubts and atop the bulwarks of the base. Atop the cliffs behind the refinery works and the ore-processing sheds stood yet more servitor-tasked Tarantula gun turrets, covering the reverse approach.

But the Imperial Fists had also used the mining equipment and facilities available to them to prepare a few other surprises with which to challenge the enemy's assault.

Skimming towards them now, over the wind-whipped ice, advanced the destroyers. To the untrained eye they looked like anti-gravitic speeders, only where a land speeder needed a separate pilot, in this example of heretical xenos machinery, the vehicle and its pilot were one and the same. Rising from the prow of each of the skimmer bodies was the torso, arms and head of a humanoid automaton. These mechanoids were more heavily armoured than the warriors Squad Eurus had encountered at the excavation site and were noticeably more heavily armed as well.

As Hesperus peered through a pair of magnoculars at the approaching skimmers he could see that each of the constructs had had its right arm melded into an energy cannon that pulsed with malevolent emerald energy.

'On my mark,' Hesperus announced into his helm comm, 'activate forward countermeasures.'

The Imperial Fists, the serried ranks of the militia and even the miners of Aes Metallum, who had exchanged hammer-drills for autoguns, waited. The sense of tense anticipation shared by the Space Marines, the half-human things of the Adeptus Mechanicus, and the mortal defenders of Aes Metallum, was a living breathing thing, and its breathing was shallow and its pulse panic-fast.

'Wait for it,' Hesperus muttered under his breath. 'Wait for it.'

They waited. The destroyers drew nearer.

And now scuttling swarms of scarabs, the trooping warriors of the necron host and other skulking or swiftly darting things appeared as the snowstorm abated at last.

Gauss weapons glowed with a foetid green light as the advancing host prepared to fire on the mining facility's defenders.

The destroyers were in range of the defenders' guns now and, more worryingly, the aliens' own weapons were in range too, ready to give the defenders a taste of their lethal lightning discharges.

'Mark!' Hesperus shouted into the comm.

A split second later, the bulwarks of the base were rocked by a series of detonations that threw up great clouds of white snow and black rock that enveloped the speeding necron destroyers. As the Imperial Fists and militia conscripts had worked to strengthen the base's forward defences, teams of miners, under the supervision of tech-priests, had cut trenches in the ice in which they had laid the explosives they normally used as part of the mining process to open new seams of precious ore. But they had been put to a more war-like use this day.

A moment later, the destroyers emerged from the smoke and fresh-falling snow, trailing smoke, their carapaces scorched and dented. Some were listing badly. One had almost lost its cannon-arm to the charge it had passed over. Another skewed sideways, collided with one of its fellows and the two of them then ploughed into the frozen ground, triggering another detonation that had failed to fire first time round.

Broadcasting on all channels, Sergeant Hesperus cried, 'For Ixya, for Aes Metallum, and for the *Glory of Gehenna*!' His cry was echoed by the miners and militia while their tech-priest overseers made the sign of the cog and offered up prayers of supplication to the Omnissiah for the thousand souls that had perished aboard the mighty Mechanicus vessel.

Then Hesperus spoke again, standing atop the battlements overlooking the main gate of the facility, behind which had been parked a host of heavy, earth-moving and drilling machinery to form an additional barricade behind the vulnerable entrance. Thrusting his thunder hammer into the sky, he shouted – so that all could hear – 'Primarch. Progenitor, to your glory!'

'And to the glory of Him on Earth!' his brothers bellowed in response.

The necron advance hit the outer bulwark like a hammer blow. Destroyers and tomb spyders sprouting particle projectors blasted battlements, gun emplacements and defenders alike with coruscating beams of molecule-shredding energy and searing bolts of hard-white light.

A turret-mounted autocannon magazine cooked off, not thirty metres from the main gate, the gun emplacement disappearing in an expanding ball of black smoke and oily orange flame.

Men caught in the coruscating emerald beams screamed briefly and then died as layer after layer of their bodies was stripped away by the gauss guns.

Necron warriors advanced by the score, rank after rank of the relentless warriors, each locating their targets on the battlements and then picking them off with mechanical precision. Other things, only partially humanoid in form – the elongated spines of their armoured skeleton bodies tapering to lethal shocking blades – moved with bewildering speed, blinking in and out of existence, vanishing in one position only to reappear at the foot of the base's defences. Then they would blink out of existence again and re-materialise atop the battlements, striking with whip-like arms and deadly scalpel-fingers.

More of the facility's guardians screamed and died, in horror as much as in agony as they were cut down by a grotesque vision of their own mortality made manifest.

The ground itself appeared to be moving. And then, through the drifting smoke and whirling snow, the panicked defenders of the curtain defences saw the seething mass of scarabs closing on them, crawling over everything in sight.

With a roar of turbofans, the Thunderhawk *Fortis* swept low over the icy no-man's-land before the walls of Aes Metallum, twin-linked heavy bolters raking the troops massed on the ground in front of the siege works. Where the massive-reactive shells hit, necrons were blown into their component parts, mechanoid body parts raining back down onto the sullied snow in a shower of twisted black metal and fused components.

A second later, Captain Derrin's Valkyries screamed overhead, great blooms of orange fire blossoming in their wake and more of the undying legion fell – destroyers, spyders and warriors alike.

A dreadful scream – like the rending of reality itself – ripped the heavens asunder. Green fire blazed across the firmament and tore the

*Space Marines*

snow-white skies apart as the trailing Valkyrie disintegrated in shredding flames.

The red harvest had begun.

Sergeant Hesperus batted aside another darting robotic wraith-form, the crackling head of his thunder hammer pulverising its living metal cranium. The thing slid back down the second curtain wall, throwing up a stream of sparks behind it as it scraped against the adamantium-reinforced bulwarks.

The defenders of Aes Metallum had had to abandon the outer defensive ring after a concerted pounding attack by a trio of heavy destroyers had breached the main gate. But losses had been heavy on both sides. As the Imperial Fists performed a rearguard action, the surviving militia troopers and others involved in the defence of the facility retreated behind the second curtain wall and the refinery barns and processing manufactorums beyond. Battle-Brother Verwhere triggered another trap, igniting the promethium store that had been positioned between the two gates with a well-placed shot from his plasma pistol.

Flames rose twenty metres into the freezing air, licking at the mechanoid forms pouring through the breach in the base's defences, but doing little in the way of any real harm.

A coruscating cord of dread lightning tore across the sundered ice-field, shredding the tyres from a massive spoil plough and sending the machine sliding sideways.

The particle whip reached out again, sending half a dozen of the curtain wall's defenders to their deaths.

Sergeant Hesperus's gaze immediately went to the source of this devastating attack.

Standing serenely at the centre of the necron strike force, clad in crumbling vestments, was a thing apart from the others of its kind now marching into the compromised mining facility. Its body was the colour of antique silver inlaid with hieroglyphs of gold, its skull tarnished with the fractal patterns of the patina of epochs past. It scanned the progress of the battle raging all around it with tactical interest as it directed its forces into the fray.

It was the calm at the centre of the storm, the eye of the hurricane, and in its hands it clasped its staff of power. With a silent gesture it guided its warriors forwards, towards the breach, glittering arcs of energy crackling between its skeletal digits, its entire being suffused with ancient power.

This was the focus of the necron force's esoteric energies. For this was their lord. As their mechanoid master passed by, those among their number that had had fallen to the Imperials rose to fight again, living metal re-knitting itself, repairing damaged limbs and forging their armoured shells anew.

'Brothers,' Hesperus spoke into the comm, directing his own troops into the fray, 'we have our target. The xenos lord cannot be allowed to stand any longer. It is a blasphemy in the sight of the Emperor. In the name of Dorn, ignite jump packs.'

To which the battle-brothers of Squad Eurus replied in unison, 'And Him on Earth!'

Hesperus's body smashed through the ranks of the milling necrons, sending a number of the xenos flying as his armour-hard body collided with them. His hurtling flight was brought to a sudden stop by the dozer blade of a heavy earth-mover. The bodywork of the huge digger buckled at the impact and Hesperus dropped to the ground, momentarily stunned by the blast from the necron's arcane weapon.

Recovering quickly, he got to his feet again, grey tendrils of smoke rising from the scorched ceramite plates of his power armour. If it hadn't been for the now dented storm shield that he still held fast in his left hand, he would have been lucky to survive the staff of light's unkind ministrations at all.

Raising his thunder hammer above his head once more, he began to pound towards the silver and gold ancient a second time, hammer held high, an unintelligible bellow of battle-rage on his lips. The pace of his pounding footfalls began to pick up as he covered the expanse of ice before his target.

As he ran, servos in his armoured greaves squealing, the necron prepared itself for another onslaught from the Imperial Fists. With his eyes locked on the necron lord, Hesperus could still see the broken and mangled metal carcasses of fallen xenos warriors knit themselves back together – as if he was watching a pict-feed of the destruction of the alien host running backwards – the undying automatons rising from the sullied snow to fight again at their master's side.

Hesperus readied himself both physically and mentally for the necron's retaliatory attack that was sure to come, but kept running.

Hearing the hot roar of a jump pack above him, he looked up and saw Battle-Brother Maestus, shorn of one arm already, descend upon the necron from the sky like the wrath of Dorn himself.

As Maestus dropped on the necron, Hesperus could tell that something was wrong with his battle-brother's jump pack immediately. The Space Marine was doing his damnedest to direct his wild plunge directly onto the target, rather than making a controlled leap across the ice-field. The trail of smoke trailing from the port gravitic thruster attested to the problem as well.

But Hesperus had no idea just how badly damaged Brother Maestus's jump pack was until, preceded by a cry of 'For Dorn!' from the plunging Space Marine, the pack's power core overloaded, resulting in a detonation as powerful as that of a cluster of thermal charges.

Time suddenly slowed for Hesperus as he watched the scene unfold before him as if he were watching a pict-feed playing at half-speed.

He saw the jump pack rip apart like burnt paper as the blast consumed it. He saw Brother Maestus reduced to his component atoms as the resulting fireball from the sub-atomic explosion consumed him. He saw the necron's tattered robes burn away to nothing on the nuclear wind. He watched as the skeletal lord warped, melted and disintegrated nano-seconds later. Then the hungry flames were washing over him and the shockwave hit, sending him somersaulting backwards once more across the vaporised ice-field.

Sergeant Hesperus picked himself up for a second time and gazed in stunned shock across the ice-field, knowing what he would see there. Nothing at all.

Brother Maestus was gone. Of the necron master, there was no sign either. All that remained was the solidifying bowl of a melted crater focused on the epicentre of the catastrophic blast. For thirty metres in every direction lay the fallen of the necron host: warriors and wraiths, scarabs and spyders, all obliterated by the blast, their cybernetic components fused into lumps of useless metal, the flicker of artificial automaton intelligence in their eyes fading to the black of oblivion.

The loss of Battle-Brother Maestus was a dolorous wound in the very heart of Squad Eurus, but his passing had dealt an even more dolorous blow against the enemy. Maestus's sacrifice had taken down the entity that had led the necrons into battle. With the ancient's passing the attacking force was as good as defeated.

'Squad Eurus,' Hesperus commanded. 'Sound off!'

As the seven surviving battle-brothers under his immediate command signalled their condition to their sergeant and the rest of the squad, Hesperus stared in wonder at the debris littering the battlefield all around them.

Even as the remaining necron warriors continued to stride towards the mining facility over the ice with lethal purpose blazing in their incandescent eye-sockets, they began to shimmer, their armoured bodies becoming blurred and hazy. And then suddenly Hesperus was staring right through them until they weren't actually there at all.

Even the battle debris of necron constructs besmirching the snow and the crater-gouged ice – up-ended spyders and sparking scarabs included – shimmered and phased out of existence. Soon even the spectral forms of the steel skeletons were no more.

If it had not been for the great smouldering wounds scarring the bulwarks of the base, the wrecked earth-movers, the devastated Trojans, the downed Valkyrie and the bodies of those who had died defending the facility, Hesperus could have believed that there hadn't been an attack launched on the base at all. Of the enemy there was now no sign.

The Imperial allies had won. Aes Metallum had been saved but at a price, a price that had been paid in the blood and the lives of militia troopers, tech-adepts and one battle-brother of the lauded Imperial Fists Chapter.

A leaden silence descended over the blizzard-blown wastes, falling across the battlefield like a funerary shroud, as autoguns, las weapons and the huge autocannon emplacements ceased firing.

Then, intermittently at first, Hesperus's acute hearing registered the utterances of disbelief of the Ixyans. Many men had died, but Aes Metallum still stood and the enemy had been vanquished.

Gathering pace and momentum, like a snowball rolling downhill, the gasps turned to emotional whoops of joy and of relief, mixed with wailing cries of intense emotion and heartfelt howls of grief.

But, as the sounds of jubilant celebration increased, overwhelming all other expressions of emotion, ringing from the cliffs behind the base, the Imperial Fists remained silent. Their sergeant's dour mood reflected how they all felt.

Hesperus's helm comm crackled into life.

'Sergeant? Are you receiving me?' It was Brother Teaz.

'Receiving,' Hesperus confirmed. 'Where are you, brother?'

'Sir, I'm eighty kilometres north of the facility.'

'What news?'

For a moment Hesperus could hear nothing but the hiss of static over the helm comm. He knew immediately that the news was going to be bad.

'Reinforcements are moving in on your position from the north-east.'

Hesperus took a deep breath, trying hard to dispel the chill that had now permeated even his ossmodula-hardened bones. 'Reinforcements, brother?'

'Well, no, sir, not really, I suppose. It would appear that the force that attacked Aes Metallum was only the vanguard of a much larger reaper force that has risen from inside the pyramid.'

'How much larger, Brother Teaz?'

'A thousand times, sir.'

'Their number is legion,' Hesperus breathed.

The remaining members of Squad Eurus met with Governor Selig, Captain Derrin and Magos Winze in the shell of a manufactorum temple. None of them had escaped the battle for the base unscathed. The governor had acquired a haunted, hollow-eyed expression. Captain Derrin's right arm was bound up in a sling that was now soaked with blood. Even the magos showed signs of having played his part in the battle for Aes Metallum: a half-shorn mechadendrite convulsed spastically and there was no sign of his attendant cyber-skull.

'But the battle is won, brother-sergeant,' Selig protested, a haunted look in his eyes. 'The necrontyr are defeated. I witnessed their destruction

with my own eyes. You and your men bested them and in their rout the
blasphemies quit not only the battlefield but reality itself!'

'The force we defeated was merely the vanguard,' Hesperus stated
bluntly, 'but a fraction of the legion of undying xenos constructs that is
even now marching on this base.'

'But our hard-won victory cost us dear,' Derrin said hollowly. 'We
shall not survive another battle like it, I fear.'

'Whatever else happens, we must not despair,' Sergeant Hesperus told
the Ixyans.

'You have been in touch with your brethren?' the magos queried, his
croaking words washed through with a static buzz.

'We have reported our status but they are too far away to be able to
relieve Ixya and are already on course for the Chthonian Chain. Even if
they broke off from that Chapter-sanctioned campaign, they would not
reach us in time. The only ones who stand between the necrontyr and
their re-conquest of this world is us.'

'But Captain Derrin has made an accurate assessment of the situation.
Those who remain cannot hope to win this day.'

'Perhaps not,' Hesperus admitted, 'but that does not mean that the
necrontyr shall either.'

'Please explain yourself, Astartes,' the tech-priest crackled.

'Magos, from where does Aes Metallum get its power?'

'We take our energy from the boiling heart of this world, deep, deep
below the ice.'

'As I suspected, geothermally.'

'Your point being, sergeant?'

'Captain Derrin, you are right; I fear none of us shall see another
dawn, but our deaths shall not be in vain.'

The governor's shoulders sagged, his head hung low.

'We must prepare to sell ourselves dear. We shall die this day, yes, but
we shall die as heroes all. For it is in our power to ensure that no more
Imperial lives are lost. Through our actions here, this day, we can keep
the rest of the Imperium safe from the menace being birthed here.

'Magos Winze – broadcast a repeating signal via your satellite network
that Ixya is *Terra Perdita*. Then do all that is necessary to ensure that you
overload the geothermal grid. We shall use Aes Metallum's very power
source, the beating heart of this Emperor-given world, to split it asunder.
This base, and everything in it, shall be destroyed in a volcanic eruption
the like of which Ixya has not seen in ten thousand years. We may die
this day, but so shall the undying legions of the necrontyr!'

Hesperus's tone was all vehement righteousness.

'In time our battle-brothers will visit this world and our deaths shall
be avenged. But for the time being we shall tear this planet apart and
blow this place sky high, in His name!'

Sergeant Hesperus stood atop the inner curtain wall of Aes Metallum, with the battle-brothers of Squad Eurus at his side.

Behind them were gathered the remnants of the militia, indentured miners and Mechanicus-mustered servitors, battle-weary but resolute the lot of them. The Imperial Fist's rhetoric had lent them the strength they needed to face the end with courage and resolve. Every man, tech-adept and servitor was ready to sell himself dear if it meant they might deny the necrontyr this world and, through their own deaths, bring about the destruction of their hated enemy.

Bowing his head, Hesperus led his battle-brothers in prayer. 'Oh Dorn, the dawn of our being. Lead us, your sons, to victory.'

Hesperus stared, his immovable gaze focused beyond the limits of the ice-field. As far as his occulobe-enhanced eyes could see, to both left and right, the far horizon glinted silver. The ice storm had blown itself out at last, revealing the necrontyr in all their morbid might as they advanced in a solid line of living metal.

Hesperus hefted his hammer in his hand, the blackened storm shield already in place on his left arm, and heard the hum of Brother Ver-where's energising plasma pistol, accompanied by the clatter of bolt pistols being primed and the growl of chainswords running up to speed.

'In the name of Dorn!' Hesperus bellowed, his eyes still locked on the seething tide of dark metal.

'And Him on Earth!' his fellow battle-brothers shouted, giving the antiphonal response, their battle-cry almost drowned out by the roar of turbofan engines as the *Fortis* roared overhead, to meet the enemy head-on and make the first strike against the xenos hordes.

Through the cockpit of the craft Brother-Pilot Teaz could see the advancing horde in all its terrible glory. Truly could the term innumerable be applied to the host. Where the Imperial Fists had faced hundreds of the mechanical warriors during the initial attack on Aes Metallum, here thousands advanced on the right flank, thousands on the left, thousands more forming the central block, an unstoppable mass of moving metal. From this height individual necrons looked not unlike the scarab swarms that now turned the sky black above them as millions of the beetle-form constructs took to the air.

Hesperus cast his eyes from the soaring Thunderhawk to the seething mass of silent metal warriors that stretched from the ancient sepulchre complex to the very gates of the devastated refinery, covering every centimetre of the ice wastes in between.

The planet's ancient masters had returned: the necrontyr. Their number was legion.

And they would show no mercy to the servants of the Emperor – not that the Imperial Fists would have sought it – for their name was death.

And today, Sergeant Hesperus decided, was a good day to die.

*That we, in our arrogance, believed that humankind was first among the races of this galaxy will be exposed as folly of the worst kind upon the awakening of these ancient beings. Any hopes, dreams or promises of salvation are naught but dust in the wind.*

Excerpted from the *Dogma Omniastra*

# EXHUMED

### by Steve Parker

The Thunderhawk gunship loomed out of the clouds like a monstrous bird of prey, wings spread, turbines growling, airbrakes flared to slow it for landing. It was black, its fuselage marked with three symbols: the Imperial aquila, noble and golden; the 'I' of the Emperor's Holy Inquisition, a symbol even the righteous knew better than to greet gladly; and another symbol, a skull cast in silver with a gleaming red, cybernetic eye. Derlon Saezar didn't know that one, had never seen it before, but it sent a chill up his spine all the same. Whichever august Imperial body the symbol represented was obviously linked to the Holy Inquisition. That couldn't be good news.

Eyes locked to his vid-monitor, Saezar watched tensely as the gunship banked hard towards the small landing facility he managed, its prow slicing through the veils of windblown dust like a knife through silk. There was a burst of static-riddled speech on his headset. In response, he tapped several codes into the console in front of him, keyed his microphone and said, 'Acknowledged, One-Seven-One. Clearance codes accepted. Proceed to Bay Four. This is an enclosed atmosphere facility. I'm uploading our safety and debarkation protocols to you now. Over.'

His fingers rippled over the console's runeboard, and the massive metal jaws of Bay Four began to grate open, ready to swallow the unwelcome black craft. Thick toxic air rushed in. Breathable air rushed out. The entire facility shuddered and groaned in complaint, as it always did when a spacecraft came or went. The Adeptus Mechanicus had built this station, Orga Station, quickly and with the minimum systems and

727

resources it would need to do its job. No more, no less.

It was a rusting, dust-scoured place, squat and ugly on the outside, dank and gloomy within. Craft arrived, craft departed. Those coming in brought slaves, servitors, heavy machinery and fuel. Saezar didn't know what those leaving carried. The magos who had hired him had left him in no doubt that curiosity would lead to the termination of more than his contract. Saezar was smart enough to believe it. He and his staff kept their heads down and did their jobs. In another few years, the tech-priests would be done here. They had told him as much. He would go back to Jacero then, maybe buy a farm with the money he'd have saved, enjoy air that didn't kill you on the first lungful.

That thought called up a memory Saezar would have given a lot to erase. Three weeks ago, a malfunction in one of the Bay Two extractors left an entire work crew breathing this planet's lethal air. The bay's vid-picters had caught it all in fine detail, the way the technicians and slaves staggered in agony towards the emergency airlocks, clawing at their throats while blood streamed from their mouths, noses and eyes. Twenty-three men dead. It had taken only seconds, but Saezar knew the sight would be with him for life. He shook himself, trying to cast the memory off.

The Thunderhawk had passed beyond the outer picters' field of view. Saezar switched to Bay Four's internal picters and saw the big black craft settle heavily on its landing stanchions. Thrusters cooled. Turbines whined down towards silence. The outer doors of the landing bay clanged shut. Saezar hit the winking red rune on the top right of his board and flooded the bay with the proper nitrogen and oxygen mix. When his screen showed everything was in the green, he addressed the pilot of the Thunderhawk again.

'Atmosphere restored, One-Seven-One. Bay Four secure. Free to debark.'

There was a brief grunt in answer. The Thunderhawk's front ramp lowered. Yellow light spilled out from inside, illuminating the black metal grille of the bay floor. Shadows appeared in that light – big shadows – and, after a moment, the figures that cast them began to descend the ramp. Saezar leaned forwards, face close to his screen.

'By the Throne,' he whispered to himself.

With his right hand, he manipulated one of the bay vid-picters by remote, zooming in on the figure striding in front. It was massive, armoured in black ceramite, its face hidden beneath a cold, expressionless helm. On one great pauldron, the left, Saezar saw the same skull icon that graced the ship's prow. On the right, he saw another skull on a field of white, two black scythes crossed behind it. Here was yet another icon Saezar had never seen before, but he knew well enough the nature of the being that bore it. He had seen such beings rendered in paintings and stained glass, cut from marble or cast in precious metal. It was a figure of legend, and it was not alone.

Behind it, four others, similarly armour-clad but each bearing different iconography on their right pauldrons, marched in formation. Saezar's heart was in his throat. He tried to swallow, but his mouth was dry. He had never expected to see such beings with his own eyes. No one did. They were heroes from the stories his father had read to him, stories told to all children of the Imperium to give them hope, to help them sleep at night. Here they were in flesh and bone and metal.

Space Marines! Here! At Orga Station!

And there was a further incredible sight yet to come. Just as the five figures stepped onto the grillework floor, something huge blotted out all the light from inside the craft. The Thunderhawk's ramp shook with thunderous steps. Something emerged on two stocky, piston-like legs. It was vast and angular and impossibly powerful-looking, like a walking tank with fists instead of cannon.

It was a Dreadnought, and, even among such legends as these, it was in a class of its own.

Saezar felt a flood of conflicting emotion, equal parts joy and dread.

The Space Marines had come to Menatar, and where they went, death followed.

'Menatar,' said the tiny hunched figure, more to himself than to any of the black-armoured giants he shared the pressurised mag-rail carriage with. 'Second planet of the Ozyma-138 system, Hatha Subsector, Ultima Segmentum. Solar orbital period, one-point-one-three Terran standard. Gravity, zero-point-eight-three Terran standard.' He looked up, his tiny black eyes meeting those of Siefer Zeed, the Raven Guard. 'The atmosphere is a thick nitrogen-sulphide and carbon dioxide mix. Did you know that? Utterly deadly to the non-augmented. I doubt even you Adeptus Astartes could breathe it for long. Even our servitors wear air tanks here.'

Zeed stared back indifferently at the little tech-priest. When he spoke, it was not in answer. His words were directed to his right, to his squad leader, Lyandro Karras, Codicier Librarian of the Death Spectres Chapter, known officially in Deathwatch circles as Talon Alpha. That wasn't what Zeed called him, though. 'Tell me again, Scholar, why we get all the worthless jobs.'

Karras didn't look up from the boltgun he was muttering litanies over. Times like these, the quiet times, were for meditation and proper observances, something the Raven Guard seemed wholly unable to grasp. Karras had spent six years as leader of this kill-team. Siefer Zeed, nicknamed Ghost for his alabaster skin, was as irreverent today as he had been when they'd first met. Perhaps he was even worse.

Karras finished murmuring his Litany of Flawless Operation and sighed. 'You know why, Ghost. If you didn't go out of your way to anger Sigma all the time, maybe those Scimitar bastards would be here instead of us.'

Talon Squad's handler, an inquisitor lord known only as Sigma, had come all too close to dismissing Zeed from active duty on several occasions, a terrible dishonour not just for the Deathwatch member in question, but for his entire Chapter. Zeed frequently tested the limits of Sigma's need-to-know policy, not to mention the inquisitor's patience. But the Raven Guard was a peerless killing machine at close range, and his skill with a pair of lightning claws, his signature weapon, had won the day so often that Karras and the others had stopped counting.

Another voice spoke up, a deep rumbling bass, its tones warm and rich. 'They're not all bad,' said Maximmion Voss of the Imperial Fists. 'Scimitar Squad, I mean.'

'Right,' said Zeed with good-natured sarcasm. 'It's not like you're biased, Omni. I mean, every Black Templar or Crimson Fist in the galaxy is a veritable saint.'

Voss grinned.

There was a hiss from the rear of the carriage where Ignatio Solarion and Darrion Rauth, Ultramarine and Exorcist respectively, sat in relative silence. The hiss had come from Solarion.

'Something you want to say, Prophet?' said Zeed with a challenging thrust of his chin.

Solarion scowled at him, displaying the full extent of his contempt for the Raven Guard. 'We are with company,' he said, indicating the little tech-priest who had fallen silent while the Deathwatch Space Marines talked. 'You would do well to remember that.'

Zeed threw Solarion a sneer, then turned his eyes back to the tech-priest. The man had met them on the mag-rail platform at Orga Station, introducing himself as Magos Iapetus Borgovda, the most senior adept on the planet and a xeno-heirographologist specialising in the writings and history of the Exodites, offshoot cultures of the eldar race. They had lived here once, these Exodites, and had left many secrets buried deep in the drifting red sands.

That went no way to explaining why a Deathwatch kill-team was needed, however, especially now. Menatar was a dead world. Its sun had become a red giant, a K3-type star well on its way to final collapse. Before it died, however, it would burn off the last of Menatar's atmosphere, leaving little more than a ball of molten rock. Shortly after that, Menatar would cool and there would be no trace of anyone ever having set foot here at all. Such an end was many tens of thousands of years away, of course. Had the Exodites abandoned this world early, knowing its eventual fate? Or had something else driven them off? Maybe the xeno-heirographologist would find the answers eventually, but that still didn't tell Zeed anything about why Sigma had sent some of his key assets here.

Magos Borgovda turned to his left and looked out the viewspex bubble at the front of the mag-rail carriage. A vast dead volcano dominated the skyline. The mag-rail car sped towards it so fast the red dunes and rocky spires on either side of the tracks went by in a blur. 'We are coming up on Typhonis Mons,' the magos wheezed. 'The noble Priesthood of Mars cut a tunnel straight through the side of the crater, you know. The journey will take another hour. No more than that. Without the tunnel–'

'Good,' interrupted Zeed, running the fingers of one gauntleted hand through his long black hair. His eyes flicked to the blades of the lightning claws fixed to the magnetic couplings on his thigh-plates. Soon it would be time to don the weapons properly, fix his helmet to its seals, and step out onto solid ground. Omni was tuning the suspensors on his heavy bolter. Solarion was checking the bolt mechanism of his sniper rifle. Karras and Rauth had both finished their final checks already.

If there was nothing here to fight, why were they sent so heavily armed, Zeed asked himself.

He thought of the ill-tempered Dreadnought riding alone in the other carriage.

And why did they bring Chyron?

The mag-rail carriage slowed to a smooth halt beside a platform cluttered with crates bearing the cog-and-skull mark of the Adeptus Mechanicus. On either side of the platform, spreading out in well-ordered concentric rows, were scores of stocky pre-fabricated huts and storage units, their low roofs piled with ash and dust. Thick insulated cables snaked everywhere, linking heavy machinery to generators supplying light, heat and atmospheric stability to the sleeping quarters and mess blocks. Here and there, cranes stood tall against the wind. Looming over everything were the sides of the crater, penning it all in, lending the place a strange quality, almost like being outdoors and yet indoors at the same time.

Borgovda was clearly expected. Dozens of acolytes, robed in the red of the Martian Priesthood and fitted with breathing apparatus, bowed low when he emerged from the carriage. Around them, straight-backed skitarii troopers stood to attention with lasguns and hellguns clutched diagonally across their chests.

Quietly, Voss mumbled to Zeed, 'It seems our new acquaintance didn't lie about his status here. Perhaps you should have been more polite to him, paper-face.'

'I don't recall you offering any pleasantries, tree-trunk,' Zeed replied. He and Voss had been friends since the moment they met. It was a rapport that none of the other kill-team members shared, a fact that only served to further deepen the bond. Had anyone else called Zeed *paper-face*, he might well have eviscerated them on the spot. Likewise, few would have dared to call the squat, powerful Voss *tree-trunk*. Even fewer would have survived to tell of it. But, between the two of them, such names were taken as a mark of trust and friendship that was truly rare among the Deathwatch.

Magos Borgovda broke from greeting the rows of fawning acolytes and turned to his black-armoured escorts. When he spoke, it was directly to Karras, who had identified himself as team leader during introductions.

'Shall we proceed to the dig-site, lord? Or do you wish to rest first?'

'Astartes need no rest,' answered Karras flatly.

It was a slight exaggeration, of course, and the twinkle in the xeno-heirographologist's eye suggested he knew as much, but he also knew that, by comparison to most humans, it was as good as true. Borgovda and his fellow servants of the Machine-God also required little rest.

'Very well,' said the magos. 'Let us go straight to the pit. My acolytes tell me we are ready to initiate the final stage of our operation. They await only my command.'

He dismissed all but a few of the acolytes, issuing commands to them in sharp bursts of machine code language, and turned east. Leaving the platform behind them, the Deathwatch followed. Karras walked beside the bent and robed figure, consciously slowing his steps to match the speed of the tech-priest. The others, including the massive, multi-tonne form of the Dreadnought, Chyron, fell into step behind them. Chyron's footfalls made the ground tremble as he brought up the rear.

Zeed cursed at having to walk so slowly. Why should one such as he, one who could move with inhuman speed, be forced to crawl at the little tech-priest's pace? He might reach the dig-site in a fraction of the time and never break sweat. How long would it take at the speed of this grinding, clicking, wheezing half-mechanical magos?

Eager for distraction, he turned his gaze to the inner slopes of the great crater in which the entire excavation site was located. This was Typhonis Mons, the largest volcano in the Ozyma-138 system. No wonder the Adeptus Mechanicus had tunnelled all those kilometres through the crater wall. To go up and over the towering ridgeline would have taken significantly more time and effort. Any road built to do so would have required more switchbacks than was reasonable. The caldera was close to two and a half kilometres across, its jagged rim rising well over a kilometre on every side.

Looking more closely at the steep slopes all around him, Zeed saw that many bore signs of artifice. The signs were subtle, yes, perhaps eroded by time and wind, or by the changes in atmosphere that the expanding red giant had wrought, but they were there all the same. The Raven Guard's enhanced visor-optics, working in accord with his superior gene-boosted vision, showed him crumbled doorways and pillared galleries.

Had he not known this world for an Exodite world, he might have passed these off as natural structures, for there was little angular about them. Angularity was something one saw everywhere in human construction, but far less so in the works of the hated, inexplicable eldar. Their structures, their craft, their weapons – each seemed almost grown rather than built, their forms fluid, gracefully organic. Like all righteous warriors of the Imperium, Zeed hated them. They denied man's destiny as ruler of the stars. They stood in the way of expansion, of progress.

He had fought them many times. He had been there when forces had contested human territory in the Adiccan Reach, launching blisteringly fast raids on worlds they had no right to claim. They were good foes to fight. He enjoyed the challenge of their speed, and they were not afraid to engage with him at close quarters, though they often retreated in the face of his might rather than die honourably.

Cowards.

Such a shame they had left this world so long ago. He would have enjoyed fighting them here.

In fact, he thought, flexing his claws in irritation, just about any fight would do.

Six massive cranes struggled in unison to raise their load from the circular black pit in the centre of the crater. They had buried this thing deep – deep enough that no one should ever have disturbed it here. But Iapetus Borgovda had transcribed the records of that burial, records found on a damaged craft that had been lost in the warp only to emerge centuries later on the fringe of the Imperium. He had been on his way to present his findings to the Genetor Biologis himself when a senior magos by the name of Serjus Altando had intercepted him and asked him to present his findings to the Ordo Xenos of the Holy Inquisition first.

After that, Borgovda had never gotten around to presenting his work to his superiors on Mars. The mysterious inquisitor lord that Magos Altando served had guaranteed Borgovda all the resources he would need to make the discovery entirely his own. The credit, Altando promised, need not be shared with anyone else. Borgovda would be revered for his work. Perhaps, one day, he would even be granted genetor rank himself.

And so it was that mankind had come to Menatar and had begun to dig where no one was supposed to.

The fruits of that labour were finally close at hand. Borgovda's black eyes glittered like coals beneath the clear bubble of his breathing apparatus as he watched each of the six cranes reel in their thick polysteel cables. With tantalising slowness, something huge and ancient began to peek above the lip of the pit. A hundred skitarii troopers and gun-servitors inched forwards, weapons raised. They had no idea what was emerging. Few did.

Borgovda knew. Magos Altando knew. Sigma knew. Of these three, however, only Borgovda was present in person. The others, he believed, were light-years away. This was *his* prize alone, just as the inquisitor had promised. This was *his* operation. As more of the object cleared the lip of the pit, he stepped forwards himself. Behind him, the Space Marines of Talon Squad gripped their weapons and watched.

The object was almost entirely revealed now, a vast sarcophagus, oval in shape, twenty-three metres long on its vertical axis, sixteen metres on the horizontal. Every centimetre of its surface, a surface like nothing so much as polished bone, was intricately carved with script. By force of habit, the xeno-heirographologist began translating the symbols with part of his mind while the rest of it continued to marvel at the beauty of what he saw. Just what secrets would this object reveal?

He, and other radicals like him, believed mankind's salvation, its very future, lay not with the technological stagnation in which the race of men was currently mired, but with the act of understanding and embracing the technology of its alien enemies. And yet, so many fools scorned this patently obvious truth. Borgovda had known good colleagues, fine inquisitive magi like himself, who had been executed for their beliefs. Why did the Fabricator General not see it? Why did the mighty Lords of Terra not understand? Well, he would make them see. Sigma had promised him all the resources he would need to make the most of this discovery. The Holy Inquisition was on his side. This time would be different.

The object, fully raised above the pit, hung there in all its ancient, inscrutable glory. Borgovda gave a muttered command into a vox-piece, and the cranes began a slow, synchronised turn.

Borgovda held his breath.

They moved the vast sarcophagus over solid ground and stopped.

'Yes,' said Borgovda over the link. 'That's it. Now lower it gently.'

The crane crews did as ordered. Millimetre by millimetre, the oval tomb descended.

Then it lurched.

One of the cranes gave a screech of metal. Its frame twisted sharply to the right, titanium struts crumpling like tin.

'What's going on?' demanded Borgovda.

From the corner of his vision, he noted the Deathwatch stepping forwards, cocking their weapons, and the Dreadnought eagerly flexing its great metal fists.

A panicked voice came back to him from the crane operator in the damaged machine. 'There's something moving inside that thing,' gasped the man. 'Something really heavy. Its centre of gravity is shifting all over the place!'

Borgovda's eyes narrowed as he scrutinised the hanging oval object. It was swinging on five taut cables now, while the sixth, that of the ruined crane, had gone slack. The object lurched again. The movement was clearly visible this time, obviously generated by massive internal force.

'Get it onto the ground,' Borgovda barked over the link, 'but carefully. Do not damage it.'

The cranes began spooling out more cable at his command, but the sarcophagus gave one final big lurch and crumpled two more of the sturdy machines. The other three cables tore free, and it fell to the ground with an impact that shook the closest slaves and acolytes from their feet.

Borgovda started towards the fallen sarcophagus, and knew that the Deathwatch were right behind him. Had the inquisitor known this might happen? Was that why he had sent his angels of death and destruction along?

Even at this distance, some one hundred and twenty metres away, even through all the dust and grit the impact had kicked up, Borgovda could see sigils begin to glow red on the surface of the massive object. They blinked on and off like warning lights, and he realised that was exactly what they were. Despite all the irreconcilable differences between the humans and the aliens, this message, at least, meant the same.

Danger!

There was a sound like cracking wood, but so loud it was deafening.

Suddenly, one of the Deathwatch Space Marines roared in agony and collapsed to his knees, gauntlets pressed tight to the side of his helmet. Another Adeptus Astartes, the Imperial Fist, raced forwards to his fallen leader's side.

'What's the matter, Scholar? What's going on?'

The one called Karras spoke through his pain, but there was no mistaking the sound of it, the raw, nerve-searing agony in his words. 'A psychic beacon!' he growled through clenched teeth. 'A psychic beacon just went off. The magnitude–'

He howled as another wave of pain hit him, and the sound spoke of a suffering that Borgovda could hardly imagine.

Another of the kill-team members, this one with a pauldron boasting a daemon's skull design, stepped forwards with boltgun raised and, incredibly, took aim at his leader's head.

The Raven Guard moved like lightning. Almost too fast to see, he was at this other's side, knocking the muzzle of the boltgun up and away with the back of his forearm. 'What the hell are you doing, Watcher?' Zeed snapped. 'Stand down!'

The Exorcist, Rauth, glared at Zeed through his helmet visor, but he turned his weapon away all the same. His finger, however, did not leave the trigger.

'Scholar,' said Voss. 'Can you fight it? Can you fight through it?'

The Death Spectre struggled to his feet, but his posture said he was hardly in any shape to fight if he had to. 'I've never felt anything like this!' he hissed. 'We have to knock it out. It's smothering my... gift.' He turned to Borgovda. 'What in the Emperor's name is going on here, magos?'

'Gift?' spat Rauth in an undertone.

Borgovda answered, turning his black eyes back to the object as he did. It was on its side about twenty metres from the edge of the pit, rocking violently as if something were alive inside it.

'The Exodites...' he said. 'They must have set up some kind of signal to alert them when someone... interfered. We've just set it off.'

'Interfered with what?' demanded Ignatio Solarion. The Ultramarine rounded on the tiny tech-priest. 'Answer me!'

There was another loud cracking sound. Borgovda looked beyond Solarion and saw the bone-like surface of the sarcophagus split violently. Pieces shattered and flew off. In the gaps they left, something huge and dark writhed and twisted, desperate to be free.

The magos was transfixed.

'I asked you a question!' Solarion barked, visibly fighting to restrain himself from striking the magos. 'What does the beacon alert them to?'

'To that,' said Borgovda, terrified and exhilarated all at once. 'To the release of... of whatever they buried here.'

'They left it alive?' said Voss, drawing abreast of Solarion and Borgovda, his heavy bolter raised and ready.

Suddenly, everything slotted into place. Borgovda had the full context of the writing he had deciphered on the sarcophagus's surface, and, with that context, came a new understanding.

'They buried it,' he told Talon Squad, 'because they couldn't kill it!'

There was a shower of bony pieces as the creature finally broke free of the last of its tomb and stretched its massive serpentine body for all to see. It was as tall as a Warhound Titan, and, from the look of it, almost as well armoured. Complex mouthparts split open like the bony, razor-lined petals of some strange, lethal flower. Its bizarre jaws dripped with corrosive fluids. This beast, this nightmare leviathan pulled from the belly of the earth, shivered and threw back its gargantuan head.

A piercing shriek filled the poisonous air, so loud that some of the skitarii troopers closest to it fell down, choking on the deadly atmosphere. The creature's screech had shattered their visors.

'Well maybe *they* couldn't kill it,' growled Lyandro Karras, marching stoically forwards through waves of psychic pain, 'But *we* will! To battle, brothers, in the Emperor's name!'

Searing lances of las-fire erupted from all directions at once, centring on the massive worm-like creature that was, after so many long millennia, finally free. Normal men would have quailed in the face of such an overwhelming foe. What could such tiny things as humans do against something like this? But the skitarii troopers of the Adeptus Mechanicus had been rendered all but fearless, their survival instincts overridden by neural programming, augmentation and brain surgery. They did not flee as other men would have. They surrounded the beast, working as one to put as much firepower on it as possible.

A brave effort, but ultimately a wasted one. The creature's thick plates of alien chitin shrugged off their assault. All that concentrated firepower really achieved was to turn the beast's attention on its attackers. Though sightless in the conventional sense, it sensed everything. Rows of tiny cyst-like nodules running the length of its body detected changes in heat, air pressure and vibration to the most minute degree. It knew exactly where each of its attackers stood. Not only could it hear their beating hearts, it could feel them vibrating through the ground and the air. Nothing escaped its notice.

With incredible speed for a creature so vast, it whipped its heavy black tail forwards in an arc. The air around it whistled. Skitarii troopers were cut down like stalks of wheat, crushed by the dozen, their ribcages pulverised. Some were launched into the air, their bodies falling like mortar shells a second later, slamming down with fatal force onto the corrugated metal roofs of the nearby storage and accommodation huts.

Talon Squad was already racing forwards to join the fight. Chyron's awkward run caused crates to fall from their stacks. Adrenaline flooded the wretched remains of his organic body, a tiny remnant of the Astartes he had once been, little more now than brain, organs and scraps of flesh held together, kept alive, by the systems of his massive armoured chassis.

'Death to all xenos!' he roared, following close behind the others.

At the head of the team, Karras ran with his bolter in hand. The creature was three hundred metres away, but he and his squadmates would close that gap all too quickly. What would they do then? How did one fight a monster like this?

There was a voice on the link. It was Voss.

'A trygon, Scholar? A mawloc?'

'No, Omni,' replied Karras. 'Same genus, I think, but something we haven't seen before.'

'Sigma knew,' said Zeed, breaking in on the link.

'Aye,' said Karras. 'Knew or suspected.'

'Karras,' said Solarion. 'I'm moving to high ground.'

'Go.'

Solarion's boltgun, a superbly-crafted weapon, its like unseen in the armouries of any Adeptus Astartes Chapter but the Deathwatch, was best employed from a distance. The Ultramarine broke away from the charge of the others. He sought out the tallest structure in the crater that he could reach quickly. His eyes found it almost immediately. It was behind him – the loading crane that served the mag-rail line. It was slightly shorter than the cranes that had been used to lift the entombed creature out of the pit, but each of those were far too close to the beast to be useful. This one would do well. He ran to the foot of the crane, to the stanchions that were steam-bolted to the ground, slung his rifle over his right pauldron, and began to climb.

The massive tyranid worm was scything its tail through more of the skitarii, and their numbers dropped by half. Bloody smears marked the open concrete. For all their fearlessness and tenacity, the Mechanicus troops hadn't even scratched the blasted thing. All they had managed was to put the beast in a killing frenzy at the cost of their own lives. Still they fought, still they poured blinding spears of fire on it, but to no avail. The beast flexed again, tail slashing forwards, and another dozen died, their bodies smashed to a red pulp.

'I hope you've got a plan, Scholar,' said Zeed as he ran beside his leader. 'Other than *kill the bastard*, I mean.'

'I can't channel psychic energy into *Arquemann*,' said Karras, thinking for a moment that his ancient force sword might be the only thing able to crack the brute's armoured hide. 'Not with that infernal beacon drowning me out. But if we can stop the beacon… If I can get close enough–'

He was cut off by a calm, cold and all-too-familiar voice on the link.

'Specimen Six is not to be killed under any circumstances, Talon Alpha. I want the creature alive!'

'Sigma!' spat Karras. 'You can't seriously think… No! We're taking it down. We have to!'

Sigma broadcast his voice to the entire team.

'Listen to me, Talon Squad. That creature is to be taken alive at all costs. Restrain it and prepare it for transport. Brother Solarion has been equipped for the task already. Your job is to facilitate the success of his shot, then escort the tranquilised creature back to the *Saint Nevarre*. Remember your oaths. Do as you are bid.'

It was Chyron, breaking his characteristic brooding silence, who spoke up first.

'This is an outrage, Sigma. It is a tyranid abomination and Chyron will kill it. We are Deathwatch. Killing things is what we do.'

'You will do as ordered, Lamenter. All of you will. Remember your oaths. Honour the treaties, or return to your brothers in disgrace.'

'I have no brothers left,' Chyron snarled, as if this freed him from the need to obey.

'Then you will return to nothing. The Inquisition has no need of those who cannot follow mission parameters. The Deathwatch even less so.'

Karras, getting close to the skitarii and the foe, felt his lip curl in anger. This was madness.

'Solarion,' he barked. 'How much did you know?'

'Some,' said the Ultramarine, a trace of something unpleasant in his voice. 'Not much.'

'And you didn't warn us, brother?' Karras demanded.

'Orders, Karras. Unlike some, I follow mine to the letter.'

Solarion had never been happy operating under the Death Spectre Librarian's command. Karras was from a Chapter of the Thirteenth

Founding. To Solarion, that made him inferior. Only the Chapters of the First Founding were worthy of unconditional respect, and even some of those...

'Magos Altando issued me with special rounds,' Solarion went on. 'Neuro-toxins. I need a clear shot on a soft, fleshy area. Get me that opening, Karras, and Sigma will have what he wants.'

Karras swore under his helm. He had known all along that something was up. His psychic gift did not extend to prescience, but he had sensed something dark and ominous hanging over them from the start.

The tyranid worm was barely fifty metres away now, and it turned its plated head straight towards the charging Deathwatch Space Marines. It could hardly have missed the thundering footfalls of Chyron, who was another thirty metres behind Karras, unable to match the swift pace of his smaller, lighter squadmates.

'The plan, Karras!' said Zeed, voice high and anxious.

Karras had to think fast. The beast lowered its fore-sections and began slithering towards them, sensing these newcomers were a far greater threat than the remaining skitarii.

Karras skidded to an abrupt halt next to a skitarii sergeant and shouted at him, 'You! Get your forces out. Fall back towards the mag-rail station.'

'We fight,' insisted the skitarii. 'Magos Borgovda has not issued the command to retreat.'

Karras grabbed the man by the upper right arm and almost lifted him off his feet. 'This isn't fighting. This is dying. You will do as I say. The Deathwatch will take care of this. Do not get in our way.'

The sergeant's eyes were blank, lifeless things, like those of a doll. Had the Adeptus Mechanicus surgically removed so much of the man's humanity? There was no fear there, certainly, but Karras sensed little else, either. Whether that was because of the surgeries or because the beacon was still drowning him in wave after invisible wave of pounding psychic pressure, he could not say.

After a second, the skitarii sergeant gave a reluctant nod and sent a message over his vox-link. The skitarii began falling back, but they kept their futile fire up as they moved.

The rasping of the worm's armour plates against the rockcrete grew louder as it neared, and Karras turned again to face it. 'Get ready!' he told the others.

'What is your decision, Death Spectre?' Chyron rumbled. 'It is a xenos abomination. It must be killed, regardless of the inquisitor's command.'

Damn it, thought Karras. I know he's right, but I must honour the treaties, for the sake of the Chapter. We must give Solarion his window.

'Keep the beast occupied. Do as Sigma commands. If Solarion's shot fails...'

'It won't,' said Solarion over the link.

It had better not, thought Karras. Because, if it does, I'm not sure we *can* kill this thing.

Solarion had reached the end of the crane's armature. The entire crater floor was spread out below him. He saw his fellow Talon members fan out to face the alien abomination. It reared up on its hind-sections again and screeched at them, thrashing the air with rows of tiny vestigial limbs. Voss opened up on it first, showering it with a hail of fire from his heavy bolter. Rauth and Karras followed suit while Zeed and Chyron tried to flank it and approach from the sides.

Solarion snorted.

It was obvious, to him at least, that the fiend didn't have any blind spots. It didn't have eyes!

So far as Solarion could tell from up here, the furious fusillade of bolter rounds rattling off the beast's hide was doing nothing at all, unable to penetrate the thick chitin plates.

I need exposed flesh, he told himself. I won't fire until I get it. One shot, one kill. Or, in this case, one paralysed xenos worm.

He locked himself into a stable position by pushing his boots into the corners created by the crane's metal frame. All around him, the winds of Menatar howled and tugged, trying to pull him into a deadly eighty metre drop. The dust on those winds cut visibility by twenty per cent, but Solarion had hit targets the size of an Imperial ducat at three kilometres. He knew he could pull off a perfect shot in far worse conditions than these.

Sniping from the top of the crane meant that he was forced to lie belly-down at a forty-five degree angle, his boltgun's stock braced against his shoulder, right visor-slit pressed close to the lens of his scope. After some adjustments, the writhing monstrosity came into sharp focus. Bursts of Astartes gunfire continued to ripple over its carapace. Its tail came down hard in a hammering vertical stroke that Rauth only managed to sidestep at the last possible second. The concrete where the Exorcist had been standing shattered and flew off in all directions.

Solarion pulled back the cocking lever of his weapon and slid one of Altando's neuro-toxin rounds into the chamber. Then he spoke over the comm-link.

'I'm in position, Karras. Ready to take the shot. Hurry up and get me that opening.'

'We're trying, Prophet!' Karras snapped back, using the nickname Zeed had coined for the Ultramarine.

Try harder, thought Solarion, but he didn't say it. There was a limit, he knew, to how far he could push Talon Alpha.

Three grenades detonated, one after another, with ground-splintering cracks. The wind pulled the dust and debris aside. The creature reared up again, towering over the Space Marines, and they saw that it remained utterly undamaged, not even a scratch on it.

'Nothing!' cursed Rauth.

Karras swore. This was getting desperate. The monster was tireless, its speed undiminished, and nothing they did seemed to have the least effect. By contrast, its own blows were all too potent. It had already struck Voss aside. Luck had been with the Imperial Fist, however. The blow had been lateral, sending him twenty metres along the ground before slamming him into the side of a fuel silo. The strength of his ceramite armour had saved his life. Had the blow been vertical, it would have killed him on the spot.

Talon Squad hadn't survived the last six years of special operations to die here on Menatar. Karras wouldn't allow it. But the only weapon they had which might do anything to the monster was his force blade, *Arquemann*, and, with that accursed beacon drowning out his gift, Karras couldn't charge it with the devastating psychic power it needed to do the job.

'Warp blast it!' he cursed over the link. 'Someone find the source of that psychic signal and knock it out!'

He couldn't pinpoint it himself. The psychic bursts were overwhelming, drowning out all but his own thoughts. He could no longer sense Zeed's spiritual essence, nor that of Voss, Chyron, or Solarion. As for Rauth, he had never been able to sense the Exorcist's soul. Even after serving together this long, he was no closer to discovering the reason for that. For all Karras knew, maybe the quiet, brooding Astartes had no soul.

Zeed was doing his best to keep the tyranid's attention on himself. He was the fastest of all of them. If Karras hadn't known better, he might even have said Zeed was enjoying the deadly game. Again and again, that barbed black tail flashed at the Raven Guard, and, every time, found only empty air. Zeed kept himself a split second ahead. Whenever he was close enough, he lashed out with his lightning claws and raked the creature's sides. But, despite the blue sparks that flashed with every contact, he couldn't penetrate that incredible armour.

Karras locked his bolter to his thigh plate and drew *Arquemann* from its scabbard.

This is it, he thought. We have to close with it. Maybe Chyron can do something if he can get inside its guard. He's the only one who might just be strong enough.

'Engage at close quarters,' he told the others. 'We can't do anything from back here.'

It was all the direction Chyron needed. The Dreadnought loosed a battle-cry and stormed forwards to attack with his two great power fists, the ground juddering under him as he charged.

By the Emperor's grace, thought Karras, following in the Dreadnought's thunderous wake, don't let this be the day we lose someone.

Talon Squad was *his* squad. Despite the infighting, the secrets, the mistrust and everything else, that still meant something.

Solarion saw the rest of the kill-team race forwards to engage the beast at close quarters and did not envy them, but he had to admit a grudging pride in their bravery and honour. Such a charge looked like sure suicide. For any other squad, it might well have been. But for Talon Squad...

Concentrate, he told himself. The moment is at hand. Breathe slowly. He did.

His helmet filtered the air, removing the elements that might have killed him, elements that even the Adeptus Astartes implant known as the Imbiber, or the multi-lung, would not have been able to handle. Still, the air tasted foul and burned in his nostrils and throat. A gust of wind buffeted him, throwing his aim off a few millimetres, forcing him to adjust again.

A voice shouted triumphantly on the link.

'I've found it, Scholar. I have the beacon!'

'Voss?' said Karras.

There was a muffled crump, the sound of a krak grenade. Solarion's eyes flicked from his scope to a cloud of smoke about fifty metres to the creature's right. He saw Voss emerge from the smoke. Around him lay the rubble of the monster's smashed sarcophagus.

Karras gave a roar of triumph.

'It's... it's gone,' he said. 'It's lifted. I can feel it!'

So Karras would be able to wield his psychic abilities again. Would it make any difference, Solarion wondered.

It did, and that difference was immediate. Something began to glow down on the battlefield. Solarion turned his eyes towards it and saw Karras raise *Arquemann* in a two-handed grip. The monster must have sensed the sudden build-up of psychic charge, too. It thrashed its way towards the Librarian, eager to crush him under its powerful coils. Karras dashed in to meet the creature's huge body and plunged his blade into a crease where two sections of chitin plate met.

An ear-splitting alien scream tore through the air, echoing off the crater walls.

Karras twisted the blade hard and pulled it free, and its glowing length was followed by a thick gush of black ichor.

The creature writhed in pain, reared straight up and screeched again, its complex jaws open wide.

Just the opening Solarion was waiting for.

He squeezed the trigger of his rifle and felt it kick powerfully against his armoured shoulder.

A single white-hot round lanced out towards the tyranid worm.

There was a wet impact as the round struck home, embedding itself deep in the fleshy tissue of the beast's mouth.

'Direct hit!' Solarion reported.

'Good work,' said Karras on the link. 'Now what?'

It was Sigma's voice that answered. 'Fall back and wait. The toxin is fast acting. Ten to fifteen seconds. Specimen Six will be completely paralysed.'

'You heard him, Talon Squad,' said Karras. 'Fall back. Let's go!'

Solarion placed one hand on the top of his rifle, muttered a prayer of thanks to the weapon's machine-spirit, and prepared to descend. As he looked out over the crater floor, however, he saw that one member of the kill-team wasn't retreating.

Karras had seen it, too.

'Chyron,' barked the team leader. 'What in Terra's name are you doing?

The Dreadnought was standing right in front of the beast, fending off blows from its tail and its jaws with his oversized fists.

'Stand down, Lamenter,' Sigma commanded.

If Chyron heard, he deigned not to answer. While there was still a fight to be had here, he wasn't going anywhere. It was the tyranids that had obliterated his Chapter. Hive Fleet Kraken had decimated them, leaving him with no brothers, no home to return to. But if Sigma and the others thought the Deathwatch was all Chyron had left, they were wrong. He had his rage, his fury, his unquenchable lust for dire and bloody vengeance.

The others should have known that. Sigma should have known.

Karras started back towards the Dreadnought, intent on finding some way to reach him. He would use his psyker gifts if he had to. Chyron could not hope to beat the thing alone.

But, as the seconds ticked off and the Dreadnought continued to fight, it became clear that something was wrong.

From his high vantage point, it was Solarion who voiced it first.

'It's not stopping,' he said over the link. 'Sigma, the damned thing isn't even slowing down. The neuro-toxin didn't work.'

'Impossible,' replied the voice of the inquisitor. 'Magos Altando had the serum tested on–'

'Twenty-five… no, thirty seconds. I tell you, it's not working.'

Sigma was silent for a brief moment. Then he said, 'We need it alive.'

'Why?' demanded Zeed. The Raven Guard was crossing the concrete again, back towards the fight, following close behind Karras.

'You do not need to know,' said Sigma.

'The neuro-toxin doesn't work, Sigma,' Solarion repeated. 'If you have some other suggestion…'

Sigma clicked off.

I guess he doesn't, thought Solarion sourly.

'Solarion,' said Karras. 'Can you put another round in it?'

'Get it to open wide and you know I can. But it might not be a dosage issue.'

'I know,' said Karras, his anger and frustration telling in his voice. 'But it's all we've got. Be ready.'

Chyron's chassis was scraped and dented. His foe's strength seemed boundless. Every time the barbed tail whipped forwards, Chyron swung his fists at it, but the beast was truly powerful and, when one blow connected squarely with the Dreadnought's thick glacis plate, he found himself staggering backwards despite his best efforts.

Karras was suddenly at his side.

'When I tell you to fall back, Dreadnought, you will do it,' growled the Librarian. 'I'm still Talon Alpha. Or does that mean nothing to you?'

Chyron steadied himself and started forwards again, saying, 'I honour your station, Death Spectre, and your command. But vengeance for my Chapter supersedes all. Sigma be damned, I *will* kill this thing!'

Karras hefted *Arquemann* and prepared to join Chyron's charge. 'Would you dishonour all of us with you?'

The beast swivelled its head towards them and readied to strike again.

'For the vengeance of my Chapter, no price is too high. I am sorry, Alpha, but that is how it must be.'

'Then the rest of Talon Squad stands with you,' said Karras. 'Let us hope we all live to regret it.'

Solarion managed to put two further toxic rounds into the creature's mouth in rapid succession, but it was futile. This hopeless battle was telling badly on the others now. Each slash of that deadly tail was avoided by a rapidly narrowing margin. Against a smaller and more numerous foe, the strength of the Adeptus Astartes would have seemed almost infinite, but this towering tyranid leviathan was far too powerful to engage with the weapons they had. They were losing this fight, and yet Chyron would not abandon it, and the others would not abandon him, despite the good sense that might be served in doing so.

Voss tried his best to keep the creature occupied at range, firing great torrents from his heavy bolter, even knowing that he could do little, if any, real damage. His fire, however, gave the others just enough openings to keep fighting. Still, even the heavy ammunition store on the Imperial Fist's back had its limits. Soon, the weapon's thick belt feed began whining as it tried to cycle non-existent rounds into the chamber.

'I'm out,' Voss told them. He started disconnecting the heavy weapon so that he might draw his combat blade and join the close-quarters melee.

It was at that precise moment, however, that Zeed, who had again been taunting the creature with his lightning claws, had his feet struck out from under him. He went down hard on his back, and the tyranid monstrosity launched itself straight towards him, massive mandibles spread wide.

For an instant, Zeed saw that huge red maw descending towards him. It looked like a tunnel of dark, wet flesh. Then a black shape blocked his view and he heard a mechanical grunt of strain.

'I'm more of a meal, beast,' growled Chyron.

The Dreadnought had put himself directly in front of Zeed at the last minute, gripping the tyranid's sharp mandibles in his unbreakable titanium grip. But the creature was impossibly heavy, and it pressed down on the Lamenter with all its weight.

The force pressing down on Chyron was impossible to fight, but he put everything he had into the effort. His squat, powerful legs began to buckle. A piston in his right leg snapped. His engine began to sputter and cough with the strain.

'Get out from under me, Raven Guard,' he barked. 'I can't hold it much longer!'

Zeed scrabbled backwards about two metres, then stopped.

No, he told himself. Not today. Not to a mindless beast like this.

'Corax protect me,' he muttered, then sprang to his feet and raced forwards, shouting, '*Victoris aut mortis!*'

Victory or death!

He slipped beneath the Dreadnought's right arm, bunched his legs beneath him and, with lightning claws extended out in front, dived directly into the beast's gaping throat.

'Ghost!' shouted Voss and Karras at the same time, but he was already gone from sight and there was no reply over the link.

Chyron wrestled on for another second. Then two. Then, suddenly, the monster began thrashing in great paroxysms of agony. It wrenched its mandibles from Chyron's grip and flew backwards, pounding its ringed segments against the concrete so hard that great fractures appeared in the ground.

The others moved quickly back to a safe distance and watched in stunned silence.

It took a long time to die.

When the beast was finally still, Voss sank to his knees.

'No,' he said, but he was so quiet that the others almost missed it.

Footsteps sounded on the stone behind them. It was Solarion. He stopped alongside Karras and Rauth.

'So much for taking it alive,' he said.

No one answered.

Karras couldn't believe it had finally happened. He had lost one. After all they had been through together, he had started to believe they might all return to their Chapters alive one day, to be welcomed as honoured heroes, with the sad exception of Chyron, of course.

Suddenly, however, that belief seemed embarrassingly naïve. If Zeed could die, all of them could. Even the very best of the best would meet his match in the end. Statistically, most Deathwatch members never made it back to the fortress-monasteries of their originating Chapters. Today, Zeed had joined those fallen ranks.

It was Sigma, breaking in on the command channel, who shattered the grim silence.

'You have failed me, Talon Squad. It seems I greatly overestimated you.'

Karras hissed in quiet anger. 'Siefer Zeed is dead, inquisitor.'

'Then you, Alpha, have failed on two counts. The Chapter Master of the Raven Guard will be notified of Zeed's failure. Those of you who live will at least have a future chance to redeem yourselves. The Imperium has lost a great opportunity here. I have no more to say to you. Stand by for Magos Altando.'

'Altando?' said Karras. 'Why would–'

Sigma signed off before Karras could finish, his voice soon replaced by the buzzing mechanical tones of the old magos who served on his retinue.

'I am told that Specimen Six is dead,' he grated over the link. 'Most regrettable, but your chances of success were extremely slim from the beginning. I predicted failure at close to ninety-six point eight five per cent probability.'

'But Sigma deployed us anyway,' Karras seethed. 'Why am I not surprised?'

'All is not lost,' Altando continued, ignoring the Death Spectre's ire. 'There is much still to be learned from the carcass. Escort it back to Orga Station. I will arrive there to collect it shortly.'

'Wait,' snapped Karras. 'You wish this piece of tyranid filth loaded up and shipped back for extraction? Are you aware of its size?'

'Of course, I am,' answered Altando. 'It is what the mag-rail line was built for. In fact, everything we did on Menatar from the very beginning – the construction, the excavation, the influx of Mechanicus personnel – all of it was to secure the specimen alive, still trapped inside its sarcophagus. Under the circumstances, we will make do with a dead one. You have given us no choice.'

The sound of approaching footsteps caught Karras's attention. He turned from the beast's slumped form and saw the xeno-heirographologist, Magos Borgovda, walking towards him with a phalanx of surviving skitarii troopers and robed Mechanicus acolytes.

Beneath the plex bubble of his helm, the little tech-priest's eyes were wide.

'You… you bested it. I would not have believed it possible. You have achieved what the Exodites could not.'

'Ghost bested it,' said Voss. 'This is his kill. His and Chyron's.'

If Chyron registered these words, he didn't show it. The ancient warrior stared fixedly at his fallen foe.

'Magos Borgovda,' said Karras heavily, 'are there men among your survivors who can work the cranes? This carcass is to be loaded onto a mag-rail car and taken to Orga Station.'

'Yes, indeed,' said Borgovda, his eyes taking in the sheer size of the creature. 'That part of our plans has not changed, at least.'

Karras turned in the direction of the mag-rail station and started walking. He knew he sounded tired and miserable when he said, 'Talon Squad, fall in.'

'Wait,' said Chyron. He limped forwards with a clashing and grinding of the gears in his right leg. 'I swear it, Alpha. The creature just moved. Perhaps it is not dead, after all.'

He clenched his fists as if in anticipation of crushing the last vestiges of life from it. But, as he stepped closer to the creature's slack mouth, there was a sudden outpouring of thick black gore, a great torrent of it. It splashed over his feet and washed across the dry rocky ground.

In that flood of gore was a bulky form, a form with great rounded pauldrons, sharp claws, and a distinctive, back-mounted generator. It lay unmoving in the tide of ichor.

'Ghost,' said Karras quietly. He had hoped never to see this, one under his command lying dead.

Then the figure stirred and groaned.

'If we ever fight a giant alien worm again,' said the croaking figure over the comm-link, 'some other bastard can jump down its throat. I've had my turn.'

Solarion gave a sharp laugh. Voss's reaction was immediate. He strode forwards and hauled his friend up, clapping him hard on the shoulders. 'Why would any of us bother when you're so good at it, paper-face?'

Karras could hear the relief in Voss's voice. He grinned under his helm. Maybe Talon Squad was blessed after all. Maybe they would live to return to their Chapters.

'I said fall in, Deathwatch,' he barked at them; then he turned and led them away.

Altando's lifter had already docked at Orga Station by the time the mag-rail cars brought Talon Squad, the dead beast and the Mechanicus survivors to the facility. Sigma himself was, as always, nowhere to be seen. That was standard practice for the inquisitor. Six years, and Karras had still never met his enigmatic handler. He doubted he ever would.

Derlon Saezar and the station staff had been warned to stay well away from the mag-rail platforms and loading bays and to turn off all internal vid-picters. Saezar was smarter than most people gave him credit for. He did exactly as he was told. No knowledge was worth the price of his life.

Magos Altando surveyed the tyranid's long body with an appraising lens before ordering it loaded onto the lifter, a task with which even his veritable army of servitor slaves had some trouble. Magos Borgovda was most eager to speak with him, but, for some reason, Altando acted as if the xeno-heirographologist barely existed. In the end, Borgovda became irate and insisted that the other magos answer his questions at once. Why was he being told nothing? This was *his* discovery. Great promises had been made. He demanded the respect he was due.

It was at this point, with everyone gathered in Bay One, the only bay in the station large enough to offer a berth to Altando's lifter, that Sigma addressed Talon Squad over the comm-link command channel once again.

'No witnesses,' he said simply.

Karras was hardly surprised. Again, this was standard operating procedure, but that didn't mean the Death Spectre had to like it. It went against every bone in his body. Wasn't the whole point of the Death-watch to protect mankind? They were alien-hunters. His weapons hadn't been crafted to take the lives of loyal Imperial citizens, no matter who gave the command.

'Clarify,' said Karras, feigning momentary confusion.

There was a crack of thunder, a single bolter-shot. Magos Borgovda's head exploded in a red haze.

Darrion Rauth stood over the body, dark grey smoke rising from the muzzle of his bolter

'Clear enough for you, Karras?' said the Exorcist.

Karras felt anger surging up inside him. He might even have lashed out at Rauth, might have grabbed him by the gorget, but the reaction of the surviving skitarii troopers put a stop to that. Responding to the cold-blooded slaughter of their leader, they raised their weapons and aimed straight at the Exorcist.

What followed was a one-sided massacre that made Karras sick to his stomach.

When it was over, Sigma had his wish.

There were no witnesses left to testify that anything at all had been dug up from the crater on Menatar. All that remained was the little spaceport station and its staff, waiting to be told that the excavation was over and that their time on this inhospitable world was finally at an end.

Saezar watched the big lifter take off first, and marvelled at it. Even on his slightly fuzzy vid-monitor screen, the craft was an awe-inspiring sight. It emerged from the doors of Bay One with so much thrust that he thought it might rip the whole station apart, but the facility's integrity held. There were no pressure leaks, no accidents.

The way that great ship hauled its heavy form up into the sky and off beyond the clouds thrilled him. Such power! It was a joy and an honour to see it. He wondered what it must be like to pilot such a ship.

Soon, the black Thunderhawk was also ready to leave. He granted the smaller, sleeker craft clearance and opened the doors of Bay Four once again. Good air out, bad air in. The Thunderhawk's thrusters powered up. It soon emerged into the light of the Menatarian day, angled its nose upwards, and began to pull away.

Watching it go, Saezar felt a sense of relief that surprised him. The Adeptus Astartes were leaving. He had expected to feel some kind of sadness, perhaps even regret at not getting to meet them in person. But he felt neither of those things. There was something terrible about them. He knew that now. It was something none of the bedtime stories had ever conveyed.

As he watched the Thunderhawk climb, Saezar reflected on it, and discovered that he knew what it was. The Astartes, the Space Marines... they didn't radiate goodness or kindness like the stories pretended. They were not so much righteous and shining champions as they were dark avatars of destruction. Aye, he was glad to see the back of them. They were the living embodiment of death. He hoped he would never set eyes on such beings again. Was there any greater reminder that the galaxy was a terrible and deadly place?

'That's right,' he said quietly to the vid-image of the departing Thunderhawk. 'Fly away. We don't need angels of death here. Better you remain a legend only if the truth is so grim.'

And then he saw something that made him start forwards, eyes wide.

It was as if the great black bird of prey had heard his words. It veered sharply left, turning back towards the station.

Saezar stared at it, wordless, confused.

There was a burst of bright light from the battle-cannon on the craft's back. A cluster of dark, slim shapes burst forwards from the under-wing pylons, each trailing a bright ribbon of smoke.

*Missiles!*

'No!'

Saezar would have said more, would have cried out to the Emperor for salvation, but the roof of the operations centre was ripped apart in the blast. Even if the razor-sharp debris hadn't cut his body into a dozen wet red pieces, the rush of choking Menatarian air would have eaten him from the inside out.

'No witnesses,' Sigma had said.

Within minutes, Orga Station was obliterated, and there were none.

Days passed.

The only thing stirring within the crater was the skirts of dust kicked up by gusting winds. Ozyma-138 loomed vast and red in the sky above, continuing its work of slowly blasting away the planet's atmosphere. With the last of the humans gone, this truly was a dead place once again, and that was how the visitors, or rather returnees, found it.

There were three of them, and they had been called here by a powerful beacon that only psychically gifted individuals might detect. It was a beacon that had gone strangely silent just shortly after it had been activated. The visitors had come to find out why.

They were far taller than the men of the Imperium, and their limbs were long and straight. The human race might have thought them elegant once, but all the killings these slender beings had perpetrated against mankind had put a permanent end to that. To the modern Imperium, they were simply xenos, to be hated and feared and destroyed like any other.

They descended the rocky sides of the crater in graceful silence, their booted feet causing only the slightest of rockslides. When they reached the bottom, they stepped onto the crater floor and marched together towards the centre where the mouth of the great pit gaped.

There was nothing hurried about their movements, and yet they covered the distance at an impressive speed.

The one who walked at the front of the trio was taller than the others, and not just by virtue of the high, jewel-encrusted crest on his helmet. He wore a rich cloak of strange shimmering material and carried a golden staff that shone with its own light.

The others were dressed in dark armour sculpted to emphasise the sweep of their long, lean muscles. They were armed with projectile weapons as white as bone. When the tall, cloaked figure stopped by the edge of the great pit, they stopped, too, and turned to either side, watchful, alert to any danger that might remain here.

The cloaked leader looked down into the pit for a moment, then moved off through the ruins of the excavation site, glancing at the crumpled metal huts and the rusting cranes as he passed them.

He stopped by a body on the ground, one of many. It was a pathetic, filthy mess of a thing, little more than rotting meat and broken bone wrapped in dust-caked cloth. It looked like it had been crushed by something. Pulverised. On the cloth was an icon – a skull set within a cog, equal parts black and white. For a moment, the tall figure looked down at it in silence, then he turned to the others and spoke, his voice filled with a boundless contempt that made even the swollen red sun seem to draw away.

'Mon-keigh,' he said, and the word was like a bitter poison on his tongue.

*Mon-keigh.*

# PRIMARY INSTINCT

### S P Cawkwell

*Victory does not always rest with the big guns.*
*But if we rest in front of them, we shall be lost.*

– Lord Commander Argentius,
Chapter Master, Silver Skulls

The soaring forests of Ancerios III steamed gently in the relentless heat of the tropical sun. Condensation beaded and rose, shimmering in a constant haze from the emerald-green and deep mauve of the leaves. This was a cruel, merciless place where the sultry twin suns raised the surface temperature to inhospitable levels. The atmosphere was stifling and barely tolerable for human physiology.

However, the party making their way through the jungle were not fully human.

The dark Anceriosan jungle had more than just shape, it had oppressive, heavy form. There was an eerie silence, which might once have been broken by the chattering of primate-like creatures or the call of exotic birds. In this remote part of the jungle, there was no sign of the supposed native fauna. What plant life that did exist had long since evolved at a tangent, adapting necessarily to the living conditions. Everything that grew reached desperately upwards, yearning towards the suns. Perhaps there was a dearth of animal life, but these immense plants thrived and provided a home for a countless variety of insects.

There was a faint stirring of wind, a shift in the muggy air, and a cloud of insects lifted on the breeze. They twisted lazily, their varicoloured forms catching and reflecting what little smattering of dappled sunlight managed to penetrate this far down. They twirled with joyful abandon on the zephyr that held them in its gentle grasp, riding the updraught through to a clearing.

The cloud abruptly dissipated as a hand clad in a steel-grey gauntlet scythed neatly through it. Startled, the insects scattered as though someone had thrown a frag grenade amongst them. The moment of confusion passed swiftly, and they gradually drifted back together in an almost palpably indignant clump. They lingered briefly, caught another thermal and were gone.

Sergeant Gileas Ur'ten, squad commander of the Silver Skulls Eighth Company Assault squad 'The Reckoners', swatted with a vague sense of irritation at the insects. They flew constantly into the breathing grille of his helmet and whilst the armour was advanced enough and sensibly designed in order not to allow them to get inside, the near-constant *pit-pit-pit* of the bugs flying against him was starting to become a nuisance.

He swore colourfully and hefted the weight of the combat knife in his hand. It had taken a great deal more work than anticipated to carve a path through to the clearing, and the blade was noticeably dulled by the experience.

Behind him, the other members of his squad were similarly surveying the damage to their weapons caused by the apparently innocent plant life. Gileas stretched out his shoulders, stiff from being hunched in the same position for so long, and spun on his heel to face his battle-brothers.

'As far as I can make out, the worst threats are these accursed insects,' he said in a sonorous rumble. His voice was deep and thickly accented. 'Not to mention these prevailing plant stalks and the weather.'

The Assault squad had discovered very quickly that the moisture in the air, coupled with spores from the vegetation that they had hacked down, was causing a variety of malfunctions within their jump packs. Like so much of the rediscovered technology that the Adeptus Astartes employed, the jump packs had once been things of beauty, things that offered great majesty and advantage to the Emperor's warriors. Now, however, they were starting to show signs of their age. Fortunately, the expert and occasionally lengthy ministrations of the Chapter's Techmarines kept the machine-spirits satisfied and ensured that even if the devices were not always perfect, they were always functional.

Gileas sheathed his combat knife and reached up to snap open the catch that released his helmet. There was an audible *hiss* of escaping air as the seals unlocked. Removing the helmet, an untidy tumble of dark hair fell to his shoulders, framing a weather-tanned, handsome face that was devoid of the tattoos that covered the rest of his body beneath the armour. Like all of the Silver Skulls, Gileas took great pride in his honour markings. He had not yet earned the right to mark his face. It would not be long, it was strongly hinted, for the ambitious Gileas was reputedly earmarked for promotion to captain. It was a rumour which had stemmed from his own squad and had been met with mixed reactions from others within the Chapter. Gileas repeatedly dismissed such talk as hearsay.

He cast dark, intelligent eyes cautiously around the clearing, clipping his helmet to his belt and loosening his chainsword in the scabbard worn down the line of his armoured thigh. The twisted, broken wreckage of what had once been a space-going vessel lay swaddled amidst fractured trees and branches. Whatever it was, it was mostly destroyed and it most certainly didn't look native to the surroundings. This was the first thing they had encountered in the jungle which was clearly not indigenous.

Reuben, his second-in-command, came up to Gileas's side and disengaged his own helmet. Unlike his wild-haired commanding officer, he wore his hair neat and closely cropped to his head. He considered the destroyed vessel, sifting through the catalogue of data in his mind. It was unlike anything he had ever seen before. Any markings on its surface were long gone with the ravages of time, and it was nearly impossible to filter out any sort of shape. Any form it may have once taken had been eradicated by the force of impact.

'It doesn't look like a wraithship, brother,' he said.

'No,' grunted Gileas in agreement. 'It certainly bears no resemblance to that thing we were pursuing.' He growled softly and ran a hand through his thick mane of hair. 'I suspect, brother, that our quarry got away from us in the webway. Unfortunate that they escaped the Emperor's justice. For now, at least.' His hand clenched briefly into a fist and he swore again. He considered the vessel for a few silent moments. Finally, he shook his head.

'This has been guesswork from the start,' he acknowledged with reluctance. 'We all knew that there was a risk we would end up chasing phantoms. Still…' He indicated the wreck. 'At least we have something to investigate. Perhaps this is what the eldar were seeking. There's no sign of them in the atmosphere. We may as well press our advantage.'

'You think we're ahead of them?'

'I would suggest that there's a good chance.' Gileas shrugged lightly. 'Or maybe we're behind them. They could already have been and gone. Who knows, with the vagaries of the warp? The *Silver Arrow*'s Navigator hadn't unscrambled her head enough to get a fix on chronological data when we left. Either way, it's worth checking for any sign of passage. Any lead is a good lead. Even when it leads nowhere.'

'Is that you or Captain Kulle speaking?' Reuben smiled as he mentioned Gileas's long-dead mentor.

The sergeant did not reply. Instead, he grinned, exposing ritualistically sharpened canines that were a remnant of his childhood amongst the tribes of the southern steppes. 'It matters little. Whatever this thing is, it's been here for a long time. This surely can't be the ship we followed into the warp. It isn't one of ours and that's all we need to know. You are all fully aware of your orders, brothers. Assess, evaluate, exterminate. In that order.'

He squinted at the ship carefully. Like Reuben, he was unable to match it to anything in his memory. 'I feel that the last instruction might well be something of a formality though. I doubt that anything could have survived an impact like that.'

The ship was practically embedded in the planet's surface, much of its prow no longer visible, buried beneath a churned pile of dirt and tree roots. Hardy vegetation, some kind of lichen or moss, clung to the side of the vessel with grim determination.

The sergeant glanced sideways at the only member of the squad not clad head-to-foot in steel-grey armour and made a gesture with his hand, inviting him forwards.

Resplendent in the blue armour of a psychic battle-brother, Prognosticator Bhehan inclined his head in affirmation before reaching his hand into a pouch worn on his belt. He stepped forwards until he was beside the sergeant, hunkered down into a crouch and cast a handful of silver-carved rune stones to the ground. As Prognosticator, it was important for him to read the auguries, to commune with the will of the Emperor before the squad committed themselves. To a man, the Silver Skulls were deeply superstitious. It had been known for entire companies to refuse to go into battle if the auguries were poor. Even the Chapter Master, Lord Commander Argentius, had once refused to enter the fray on the advice of the *Vashiro*, the Chief Prognosticator.

This was more, so much more than ancient superstition. The Silver Skulls believed without question that the Emperor projected His will and His desire through His psychic children. These readings were no simple divinations of chance and happenstance. They were messages from the God-Emperor of Mankind, sent through the fathomless depths of space to His distant loyal servants.

The Silver Skulls, loyal to the core, never denied His will.

Prognosticators served a dual purpose in the Chapter. Where other ranks of Adeptus Astartes had Librarians and Chaplains, the Silver Skulls saw the universe in a different way. Those battle-brothers who underwent training at the hands of the Chief Prognosticator offered both psychic and spiritual guidance to their brethren. Their numbers were not great: Varsavia did not seem to produce many psykers. As a consequence, those who did ascend to the ranks of the Adeptus Astartes were both highly prized and revered amongst the Chapter.

Gileas knew that the squad were deeply honoured to have Bhehan assigned to them. He was young, certainly; but his powers, particularly those of foresight, were widely acknowledged as being amongst the most veracious and trustworthy in the entire Chapter.

'I'm feeling nothing from the wreck,' said Bhehan in his soft, whispering voice. The young Prognosticator hesitated and frowned at the runes, passing his hand across them once again. He considered for a moment or two, his posture stiff and unyielding. Finally, he relaxed. 'If it were a wraithship, if it were the one we were pursuing, its psychic field would still be active. This one is assuredly dead. Stone-cold dead.' He frowned, pausing just long enough for Gileas to quirk an eyebrow.

'Is that doubt I'm detecting there?' The Prognosticator looked up at Gileas, his unseen face, hidden as it was behind his helmet, giving nothing away. He glanced back down at the runes thoughtfully. The scratched designs on their surfaces were a great mystery to Gileas. However, the Prognosticators understood them, and that was all that mattered. An eminently pragmatic warrior, Gileas never let things he didn't understand worry him. He would never have vocalised the thought, but it was an approach he privately felt many others in the Chapter should adopt.

Bhehan shifted some of the runes with a practiced hand, turning some around, lining others up, making apparently random patterns on the ground with them. A pulsing red glow briefly animated the Space Marine's psychic hood as he brought his concentration to bear on the matter at hand.

Finally, after some consideration, he shook his head.

'An echo, perhaps,' he mused, 'nothing more, nothing less.' He nodded firmly, assertiveness colouring his tone. 'No, Brother-Sergeant Ur'ten,' he said, 'no doubt. The Fates suggest to me that there was perhaps something alive on board this ship when it crashed. Any sentience within its shell has long since passed on. Subsumed, perhaps, into the jungle. Eaten by predators, or simply died in the crash.'

He gathered up the runes, dropping them with quiet confidence back into his pouch, and stood up. 'The Fates,' he said, 'and the evidence lying around us.' He nodded once more and removed his helmet. The face beneath was surprisingly youthful, almost cherubic in appearance, and reflected Bhehan's relative inexperience. For all that, he was a field-proven warrior of considerable ferocity. Combined with the powers of a Prognosticator, he was a formidable opponent, something the sergeant had already tested in the training cages.

Gileas nodded, satisfied with the outcome. 'Very well. Reuben, take Wulfric and Jalonis with you and search the perimeter for any sign of passage. All of this...' He swept his hand around the clearing to indicate the crash site. 'All of this may simply be an eldar ruse. I have no idea of the extent of their capabilities, but they are xenos and are not to be trusted. Not even in death. Tikaye, you and Bhehan are with me. Seeing as we're here anyway, let's get this ship and the surrounding area checked out. The sooner it's done, the sooner we can move on to the next location.' He grinned his wicked grin again and rattled his chainsword slightly.

The entire group moved onwards, aware of a shift in the weather. A storm front was rolling in. It told in the increased ozone in the air, the faint tingle of electricity that heralded thunder. Following his unit commander, Bhehan absently dipped a hand into the pouch at his side and randomly selected a rune. The tides of Fate were lapping against his psyche strongly, and the closer they got to the craft, the more intense that sensation became.

He briefly surfaced from his light trance to stare with greater intensity at the rune he had withdrawn and he stiffened, his eyes wide. He considered the stone in his hand again and tried to wind the rapidly unravelling thoughts in his mind back together. As though a physical action could somehow help him achieve this, he raised a hand and grabbed at his fair hair.

Noticing the sudden movement, Gileas moved to the Prognosticator's side immediately. 'Talk to me, brother. What do you see?'

A faint hint of wildness came into the psyker's eyes as he turned to look up at the sergeant. 'I see death,' he said, his voice notably more high-pitched than normal. 'I see death, I smell corruption, I taste blood, I feel the touch of damnation. Above all, above all, above all, I *hear* it. Don't you hear it? I hear it. The screams, brothers. The screaming. They will be devoured!'

He pulled wretchedly at his hair, releasing the rune which fell to the floor. A thin trail of drool appeared at the side of the psyker's mouth and he repeatedly drummed his fist against his temple. Gileas, despite the respect he had for the Prognosticator, reached out and caught his battle-brother's arm in his hand.

'Keep your focus, Brother-Prognosticator Bhehan,' he rebuked, his tone mild but his manner stern. 'We need you.' He'd seen this before; seen psykers lose themselves to the Sight in this way. Disconcertingly, where Bhehan was concerned, the Sight had never been wrong.

It did not bode well.

'We are not welcome here,' the psyker said, his voice still edged with that same slightly unearthly, eerie, high-pitched tone. 'We are not welcome here and if we set one foot outside of the ship, it will spell our doom.'

'We *are* outside the ship…' Tikaye began. Gileas cast a brief, silencing glance in his direction. The young psyker was making little sense, but such were the ways of the Emperor and it was not for those not chosen to receive His grace to question. The sergeant patted Bhehan's shoulder gruffly and gave a grim nod. 'The faster this task is completed, the better. Double-time, brothers.'

He leaned down and picked up the rune that Bhehan had dropped, offering it back to the psyker without comment.

* * *

The other party, led by Reuben, had skirted the perimeter of the clearing. At first there had been nothing to suggest anything untoward had occurred. Closer investigations by Wulfric, a fine tracker even by the Chapter's high standards, had eventually revealed recently trampled undergrowth.

Reuben took stock of what little intelligence they had gathered on this planet, far out on the Eastern Fringe of the galaxy. There had been suggestions of some native creatures, but as of yet, they had encountered none. Worthless and of little value, the planet had been passed over as unimportant and uninhabited with no obviously valuable resources or human life.

Just because there were no previous sightings of any of the indigenous life forms, of course, did not mean that there were none to actually *be* seen.

Reuben waved his bolter to indicate that Wulfric should lead on and the three Space Marines plunged back into the jungle, following what was a fairly obvious trail. They did not have to travel far before they located their quarry, a few feet ahead of them, in a natural glade formed by a break in the trees.

The creature seemed totally ignorant of their presence, affording them a brief opportunity to assess it. An overall shade of dark, almost midnight-blue, the alien was completely unfamiliar. Without any frame of visual reference, the thing could easily be one of the presumably indigenous life forms. Muted conversations amongst the group drew agreement.

A slight adjustment to his optical sensors allowed Reuben a closer inspection. The thing had neither fur, nor scales or even insectoid chitin covering its body. It was smooth and unblemished with the same pearlescent sheen to its form that the insects seemed to have. Its limbs were long and sinewy; the musculature of the legs suggesting to Reuben's understanding of xenobiology that it could very probably run and jump exceptionally well. The arms ended in oddly human-like five-fingered hands. Frankly, Reuben didn't care about its lineage or whether it had ever displayed any intelligence. In accordance with every belief he held, with every hypno-doctrination he had undergone, he found it utterly repulsive.

He reacted in accordance with those beliefs and teachings at the exact moment the alien turned its head in their direction, emitting a bone-chilling screech that tore through the jungle. It was so piercing as to be almost unbearable. Reuben's enhanced auditory senses protected him from the worst of it, but it was the sort of noise that he genuinely suspected could shatter crystal. Unearthly. Inhuman.

*Alien.*

Acting with the intrinsic response of a thousand or more engagements, Reuben flicked his bolter to semi-automatic and squeezed the trigger. Staccato fire roared as every projectile found its target. It was joined, seconds later, by the mimicking echo of the weapons in his fellow Space Marines' hands.

At full stretch, the xenos was easily the size of any of the Space Marines shooting at it. It showed no reaction to the wounds that were being ripped open in its body by the hail of bolter fire. It was locked in a berserk rage, uncaring and indifferent to the relentless attack. As the explosive bolts lacerated its body, dark fluid sprayed onto the leaves, onto the ground, onto the Silver Skulls.

Still it kept coming.

Reuben switched to full-automatic and unloaded the remainder of the weapon's magazine. Wulfric and Jalonis followed his example. Eventually, mortally wounded and repelled by the continuous gunfire, the abomination emitted a strangled scream of outrage. It crumpled to the ground just short of their position, spasms wracking its hideous form, and then all movement ceased.

Smoke curled from the ends of three bolters and the moment was broken only by the crackle of the vox-bead in Reuben's ear.

'Report, Reuben.'

'Sergeant, we found something. Xenos life form. Dead now.'

Reuben could hear the scowl in his sergeant's voice. 'Remove its head to be sure it *is* dead, brother.' Reuben smiled. 'We're coming to your position. Hold there.'

'Yes, brother-sergeant.'

Not wishing to take any chances, Reuben swiftly reloaded his weapon and stepped forwards to examine the xenos. It had just taken delivery of a payload of several rounds of bolter fire and had resisted death for a preternaturally long time. As such, he was not prepared to trust to it being completely deceased. His misgivings proved unfounded.

Moving towards the alien, any doubt of its state was dismissed: thick, purple-hued blood oozed stickily from multiple wounds in its body, pooling in the dust of the forest floor, settling on the surface and refusing to soak into the ground. It was as though the planet itself, despite being parched, rejected the fluid. The pungent, acrid scent of its essential vitae was almost sweet, sickly and cloying in the thick, humid air around them. Wrinkling his nose slightly against its stench, Reuben moved closer.

Lying on the ground, the thing had attempted to curl into an animalistic, defensive position, but was now rapidly stiffening as rigor mortis took hold. Reuben could see its eyes, amethyst-purple, staring glassily up at him. Even in death, sheer hatred shone through. The Adeptus Astartes felt sickened to the stomach at its effrontery to all that was right.

Just to be on the safe side, he placed the still-hot muzzle of his bolter against its head and fired a solitary shot at point-blank range into it. Grey matter and still more of the purplish blood burst forth like the contents of an over-ripe fruit.

Reuben crouched down and considered the xenos more carefully. The head was curiously elongated, with no visible ears. The purple eyes were over-large in a comparatively small face. A closer look, despite the odour that roiled up from it, suggested that they may well have been multi-faceted. The head was triangular, coming to a small point at the end of which were two slits that Reuben could only presume were nostrils.

Anatomically, even by xenos standards it seemed *wrong*. In a harsh environment like the jungle, any animal would need to adapt just in order to survive. This thing, however, seemed as though it was a vague idea of what was right rather than a practical evolution of the species. It was a complex chain of thought, and the more Reuben considered it, the more the explanation eluded him. It was as though the answer was there, but kept just out of his mental grasp.

For countless centuries, the Silver Skulls had claimed the heads of their victims as trophies of battle, carefully extracting the skulls and coating them in silver. Thus preserved, the heads of their enemies decorated the ships and vaults of the Chapter proudly. However, the longer Reuben stared at the dead alien, any urge he may have had to make a prize of it ebbed away. Forcing himself not to think on the matter any further, he turned back to the others.

Wulfric had resumed his search of the surrounding area and even now was gesturing. 'It wasn't alone. Look.' He indicated a series of tracks leading off in scattered directions, mostly deeper into the jungle.

Reuben gave a sudden, involuntary growl. It had taken three of them with bolters on full-automatic to bring just one of these things to a halt, and even then he had half-suspected that if he hadn't blasted its brains out, it would have got back up again.

'Can you make out how many?'

'Difficult, brother.' Wulfric crouched down and examined the ground. 'There's a lot of scuffing, plus with our passage through, it's obscured the more obvious prints. Immediate thoughts are perhaps half a dozen, maybe more.' He looked up at Reuben expectantly, awaiting orders from the squad's second-in-command. 'Of course, that's just in the local area. Who knows how many more of those things are out there?'

'They probably hunt in packs.' Reuben fingered the hilt of his combat knife.

Unspoken, the thoughts passed between them. If one was that hard to put down, imagine what half a dozen of them or more would be like to keep at bay. Reuben made a decision and nodded firmly.

'Good work, Wulfric. See if you can determine any sort of theoretical routes that these things may have taken. Do a short-range perimeter check. Try to remain in visual range if you can. Report anything unusual.'

'Consider it done,' replied Wulfric, getting to his feet and reloading his bolter. Without a backwards glance, the Space Marine began to trace the footprints.

The snapping of undergrowth announced the impending arrival of the other three Adeptus Astartes. Straightening, Reuben turned to face his commanding officer. He punched his left fist to his right shoulder in the Chapter's salute and Gileas returned the gesture.

All eyes were immediately drawn to the dead creature on the floor.

'Now that,' said Gileas after a few moments of assessing the look and, particularly, the stench of the alien, 'is unlike anything I have ever seen before. And to be blunt, I would be perfectly happy if I never see one again.'

Reuben dutifully reported the incident to his sergeant. 'Sorry to disappoint you, but Wulfric believes there could be anything up to a half-dozen other creatures similar to this one in the vicinity. I sent him to track them.'

Gileas frowned as he listened, his expression darkening thunderously. 'Any obvious weaknesses or vulnerable spots?'

'None that were obvious, no.'

Gileas glanced at Reuben. They had been brothers-in-arms for over one hundred years and were as close as brothers born. He had never once heard uncertainty in Reuben's tone and he didn't like what he heard now. He raised a hand to scratch at his jaw thoughtfully.

'These things are technically incidental to our mission,' he said coolly, 'but we should complete what we have started. It may retain some memory, some thought or knowledge about those we seek.' He turned to the Prognosticator, who was standing slightly apart from the others. 'Brother-Prognosticator, much as it pains me to ask you, would you divine what you can from this thing?'

'As you command.' Bhehan lowered his head in acquiescence and moved to kneel beside the dead alien. The sight of its bloodied and mangled body turned his stomach – not because of the gore, but because of its very inhuman nature. He took a few deep, steadying breaths and laid a hand on what remained of the creature's head.

'I sense nothing easily recognisable,' he said, after a time. He glanced up at Reuben. 'The damage to its cerebral cortex is too great. Virtually all of its residual psychic energies are gone.' His voice held the slightest hint of reproach.

Gileas glanced sideways at Reuben, who smiled a little ruefully. 'It was you who suggested I remove its head to be sure it was dead, Gil,' he said, the use of the diminutive form of his sergeant's name reflecting the close friendship the two shared. 'I merely used my initiative and modified your suggestion.'

The sergeant's lips twitched slightly, but he said nothing. Bhehan moved his hand to the other side of the being's head without much optimism.

*A flash of something. Distant memories of hunting…*

As swiftly as it had been there, the sensation dwindled and died.

Instinctively, and with the training that had granted him the ability to understand such things, Bhehan knew all that was needed to be known.

'An animal,' said Bhehan. 'Nothing more. Separated from the pack. Old, perhaps.' He shook his head and looked up at Gileas. 'I'm sorry, brother-sergeant. I cannot give you any more than that.'

'No matter, Prognosticator,' said Gileas, grimly. 'It was worth a try.' He surveyed the surrounding area a little more, looking vaguely disappointed. 'This is a waste of time and resources,' he said eventually. 'I propose that we regroup, head back the way we came, destroy the ship in case it is, or contains, what the eldar were seeking, and get back to the landing site. We'll have time to kill, but I'm sure I can think of something to keep us occupied.'

'Not another one of your impromptu training sessions, Gileas,' objected Reuben with good-natured humour. 'Don't you ever get tired of coming up with new and interesting ways to get us to fight each other?'

'No,' came the deadpan reply. 'Never.'

Bhehan allowed the Reckoners to discuss their next course of action amongst themselves, waiting for the inevitable request to see what the runes said. He kept his attention half on their conversation, but the other half was caught by something in the dirt beside the dead alien's head. From his kneeling position, he reached over and scooped it up in one blue-gauntleted hand.

Barely five centimetres across, the deep wine-red stone was attached to a sturdy length of vine: a crudely made necklace. Bhehan's brow furrowed slightly as he glanced again at the corpse. It had felt feral and not even remotely intelligent, but then most of its synapses had been shredded by Reuben's bolter. Putting a hand back against its head yielded nothing. He was feeling more psychic emanations from the trees themselves than from this once-living being. Of course, the charm may not have belonged to the animal; perhaps it had stolen it. It was impossible to know for sure without employing full regression techniques. For that option, however, the thing needed to be alive.

The young Prognosticator brought the stone closer to his face to study it more intently, and another flash of memory seared through his mind. This one, though, was not the primal force of nature that he had felt from the dead xenos. This was something else entirely. Sudden flashes emblazoned themselves across his mind. Shadowy images wavered in his mind's eye, images that were intangible and hard to make out.

A shape. Male? Maybe. Human? Definitely not. Eldar. It was eldar. Wearing the garments of those known as warlocks. It was screaming, cowering.

It was dying. It was being attacked. A huge shape loomed over it, blocking out the sunlight…

'Prognosticator!'

Gileas's sudden bark brought the psyker out of the trance that he had not even realised he'd fallen into. He stared at the sergeant, the brief look of displacement on his face swiftly replaced by customary attentiveness.

'My apologies, brother-sergeant,' he said, shaking his mind clear of the visions. He got to his feet and stood straight-backed and alert, the images in his mind already faded. 'Here, I found this. It might give us some clue to what happened here.' He proffered the stone and Gileas stared at it with obvious distrust before taking it. He held it up at arm's length and studied it as it spun, winking in the sunlight.

'I've seen something like this before,' he said thoughtfully. 'The eldar wear them. Something to do with their religion, isn't it?'

'In honesty, I'm not completely sure,' replied Bhehan. 'I haven't had an opportunity to study one this closely. We, I mean the company Prognosticators, have many theories...' Seeing that the sergeant wasn't even remotely interested in theories, the psyker tailed off and accepted the object back from Gileas, who seemed more than pleased to be rid of it.

'If this is an eldar item,' said Gileas, grimly, 'then it's not too much of a leap of faith to believe that they've been present, or *are* present, on this planet. Increases the odds of that wreck being eldar and also that this planet may well have been their ultimate destination.'

The others concurred. The sergeant nodded abruptly. 'Then we definitely return to the ship and we destroy the whole thing. We make damn sure that they find nothing when they get here. Are we in accord?'

He glanced around and all nodded agreement. They clasped their hands together, one atop the other. Gileas looked sideways at Bhehan who, surprised by this unspoken invitation into the brotherhood of the squad, laid his hand on the others.

'Brothers all,' said Gileas, and the squad responded in kind.

'Fetch Wulfric back,' commanded Gileas. Tikaye nodded and voxed through to his battle-brother.

There was no reply.

'Wulfric, report,' Tikaye said into the vox, even as they began heading in the direction he had taken, weapons at the ready.

They moved deeper still into the jungle.

It was rapidly becoming far more densely packed, the vibrant green of the trees and plants creating an arboreal tunnel through which the five giants marched. Despite the overriding concern at their companion's whereabouts, the Adeptus Astartes welcomed the moment's relief from the constant squinting brought about by standing in the direct sunlight. As they made their way with expediency through the trees, light filtered through to mottle the dirt and scrub of the forest floor. Parched dust marked their passage, rising up in clouds around their feet.

'Brother Wulfric, report.' Tikaye continually tried the vox, but there was still nothing. Bhehan extended the range of his psychic powers, reaching for Wulfric's awareness, and instead received something far worse. His nostrils flared as a familiar coppery scent assailed him, and he turned slightly to the west.

'It's this way,' he said, with confidence.

'You are sure, brother?'

'Aye, brother-sergeant.'

'Jalonis, lead the way. I will bring up the rear.' Gileas, with the practical and seemingly effortless ease that he did everything, organised the squad. They had travelled a little further into the trees when a crack as loud as a whip caused them all to whirl on the spot, weapons readied and primed. The first fall of raindrops announced that it was nothing more than the arrival of the tropical storm. The thunder that had barely been audible in the distance was now directly above them.

The vox in Gileas's ear crackled with static and he tapped at it irritably. These atmospherics caused such frustrating communication problems. It had never failed to amaze Gileas, a man raised as a savage in a tribe for whom the pinnacle of technological advancement was the longbow, that a race who could genetically engineer super-warriors still couldn't successfully produce robust communications.

More static flared, then Jalonis's voice broke through. It was a scattered message, breaking up as the Space Marine spoke, but Gileas had no trouble extrapolating its meaning.

'...Jal... found Wulfric... t's left... him anyway. Dead ah... maybe... dred metres or so.'

Gileas acknowledged tersely and accelerated his pace.

Another crack of thunder reverberated so loudly that Gileas swore he could feel his teeth rattle in his jaw. The light drizzle gave way rapidly to huge, fat drops of rain. The canopy of the trees did its best to repel them, but ultimately the persisting rain triumphed. The bare heads of the Silver Skulls were soaked swiftly. Gileas's hair, wild and untamed at the best of times, soon turned to unruly curls that clung tightly around his face and eyes. He put his helmet back on, not so much to keep his head dry, but more to reduce the risk of his vision being impaired by his own damp hair getting in the way.

The moment he put his helmet back on, he knew what he would find when he reached Jalonis. The information feed scrolling in front of his eyes told him everything that he needed to know. A sense of foreboding stole over him, and he murmured a prayer to the Emperor under his breath.

The precipitation did nothing to dispel the steaming heat of the forest, but merely landed on the dusty floor where it was immediately swallowed into the ground as though it had never been.

'Sergeant Ur'ten.'

Jalonis stood several metres ahead, a look of grim resignation on his face. 'You should come and see this. I'm afraid it's not pretty.'

Jalonis, a practical man by nature, had ever been the master of understatement. What Gileas witnessed as he looked down caused his choler to rise immediately. With the practice of decades, he carefully balanced his humours.

Wulfric's armour had been torn away and discarded, scattered around the warrior's corpse. The Space Marine's throat had been ripped apart with speed and ferocity, which had prevented him from alerting his battle-brothers or calling for aid.

The thorax had been slit from neck to groin, exposing his innards. In this heat, even with the steady downpour of rain, the stink of death was strong. The fused ribcage had been shattered, leaving Wulfric's vital organs clearly visible, slick with blood and mucus. Or at least, what remained of them.

Where Wulfric's primary and secondary hearts should have been was instead a huge cavity. Gileas stared for long moments, his conditioning and training assisting his deductive capability. Whatever had attacked Wulfric had gone for the throat first, rendering his dead brother mute. It had torn through his armour like it was shoddy fabric rather than ceramite and plasteel. The assailant, or more likely the assailants, had then proceeded to shred the skin like parchment and defile Wulfric's body.

The details were incidental. One of Gileas's brothers was dead. More than that, one of his closest brothers was dead. For that, there would be hell to pay.

'Take stock,' he said to Tikaye, who whilst not an Apothecary was the squad's primary field medic. 'I want to know what has been taken.' His voice was steady and controlled, but the rumble and pitch of the words hinted strongly at the anger bubbling just under the surface.

The stoic Tikaye moved to Wulfric and began to examine the body. He murmured litanies of death fervently under his breath as he did so.

'You understand, of course,' said Gileas, his voice low and menacing, 'this means someone… or *something* is going to regret crossing my path this day.'

The falling rain, evaporating in the intense heat, caused steam to rise in ethereal tendrils from the ground. It loaned even more of a macabre aspect to the scene, and the coils partially swathed Wulfric's body as they rose. It was a cheap mockery of the tradition of lighting memorial pyres on the Silver Skulls' burial world and it did little to ease their collective grief and rage.

Staring down at their fallen brother, each murmuring his own personal litany, the remaining Silver Skulls were fierce of countenance, ready for a fight in response to this atrocity.

'Several of his implants are gone,' came Tikaye's voice from the ground. There was barely masked outrage in his tone.

'Gone? What does *gone* mean?'

'Taken, brother-sergeant. The biscopea, Larraman's organ, the secondary and primary hearts, and from what I can make out, his progenoid is gone, too. I'd suggest that whoever or whatever did this knew what they wanted and took it. It's too clean to be an arbitrary or random coincidence.'

'You said they were animals, Prognosticator.' Gileas couldn't keep the accusation out of his tone. 'That conflicts directly with what Brother Tikaye suggests. One of you is wrong.' Bhehan shook his head.

'The creature we found *was* an animal,' he countered. 'That was before I found the stone, however. It's possible that it had been wearing it as some sort of decoration. I acknowledge that may potentially suggest intelligence. I–'

'I did not ask for excuses, neither did I ask for a lecture. The runes, Prognosticator.' Gileas's voice was barbed. The sergeant had a reputation amongst the Silver Skulls as a great warrior, a man who would charge headlong into the fray without hesitation and also as a man who did not suffer fools gladly, particularly when his wrath was tested. Da'chamoren, the name he had brought with him from his tribe, translated literally as 'Son of the Waxing Moon'. Gileas's power and resilience had always seemed to grow proportionately to his rising fury.

It was a fitting name.

'Yes, sir,' Bhehan replied, suitably chastened by the change in the sergeant's attitude. Without further comment, he commenced another Sighting. He felt a moment's uncertainty, but didn't dwell on it. At first, nothing came to him and he could not help but wonder if he was going to experience what his psychic brethren termed the 'Deep Dark', a moment of complete psychic blindness. Prognosticators considered this to be a sign that they had somehow fallen from the Emperor's grace. Bhehan had tasted the sensation once before and it had left a bitter flavour of ash in his mouth. He firmly set aside all thoughts of failure and closed his eyes. The Emperor was with them, he asserted firmly. Had He not already communicated His will through His loyal servant?

Reassured, his mental equilibrium ceased its churning and settled again. Bhehan allowed the reading of the runes to draw him. The stones served well as a focus for his powers, helping him to draw in all the psychic echoes that flitted around this charnel house like ghosts. Each Prognosticator found their own focus; some, like Bhehan, chose runes whilst others divined the Emperor's will through a tarot.

'The perpetrators of this butchery… I sense that they want something from us. To learn, perhaps? To understand how we are put together.' The Prognosticator's eyes were still closed, his voice barely more than a whisper. 'Why? If they were animals, they would have just torn the flesh from his bones. They have not. They have intelligence, yes, great intelligence… or at least… no. Not all of them. Just one, perhaps? A leader of sorts?' The questioning was entirely rhetorical and nobody answered or interrupted him during the stream of consciousness. The rain drummed on their armour, creating a background rhythm of its own.

Bhehan's hand closed around the eldar stone still in his hand. To his relief, a flood of warmth suffused him, a sensation he had long equated as the prelude to a vision. No Deep Dark for him, then. His powers were intact. The feeling of relief was quickly replaced by one of intense dislike as he sensed a new presence in his mind.

*They know what you are because of us. Because of what we know. The gift unintentionally given.*

The words were perfectly sharp and audible, but the image of the being who spoke them was not. Tall and willowy, the apparition shimmered before his closed eyelids like an imprint of the sun burned onto his retina.

*They absorbed what we were, what we are. They seek to do the same to you through nothing more than a primitive urge to survive, to evolve. To change. Is this not the instinct that drives us all? Aspiration to greatness? A need to be better than we were?*

Bhehan, made rational and steady through years of training, concentrated on the image.

You are eldar. He did not speak the words aloud. There was no need to.

*I was eldar. Now I am nothing more than a ghost, a faint remnant of what once was.*

I will not speak to you, xenos.

*Such arrogance as this brought my own brothers and our glorious sister to their end. It will be your undoing, mon-keigh.*

Bhehan sensed a great sigh, like the last exhalation of a dying man, and as rapidly as the spectre had materialised inside his mind, it was gone. With a sharp intake of breath, Bhehan's eyes snapped open.

'We should not linger,' he said, slightly unfocused. 'We should take our brother and we should go.'

'Is this what the Fates suggest?'

'No,' said Bhehan, hesitating only momentarily. 'It is what *I* feel we should do.'

Gileas practically revered the majesty of the Prognosticators. Divine will or not, he would never question a Prognosticator's intuition. He nodded.

'The will of a Prognosticator and the will of the Fates are entwined as one. We will do as you say.'

Reuben stepped forwards. 'Perhaps...' he began. 'Perhaps we should not. Not yet.'

'Explain.' Gileas shot a glance at Reuben.

'We interrupted them. The aliens. We could lure them back out in the open.'

'Reuben, are you suggesting that we use our dead brother as *bait*?' Gileas didn't even bother keeping the disgust out of his tone. 'I can't believe you would even entertain such a thought.'

'Bait,' echoed Bhehan, his eyes widening. 'Bait. Yes, that's it. Bait!' He drew the force axe he wore across his back. 'That's exactly what he is.'

'Prognosticator? You surely aren't agreeing to this ridiculous scheme?'

'No! For *us*, sergeant. He's been left here to lure *us* out.'

Another echo of thunder rolled around the skies overhead in accompaniment to this grim pronouncement. The rain had slowed once again to a steady *drip-drip-drip*. It pooled briefly in the vast, scoop-like leaves of the trees and splashed to the ground, throwing up billows of dust before evaporating permanently.

None of the Reckoners other than Bhehan had psychic capability, but all of them could sense the sudden shift in the air, sense the threat hiding somewhere.

Just waiting.

'Keep your weapons primed,' snapped Gileas, his thumb hovering over the activation stud of his chainsword. 'Be ready for anything.'

'I sense three psychic patterns,' offered the Prognosticator, his hands tight around the hilt of the force axe. 'Different directions, all approaching.'

'Only three?' Gileas said. 'You are sure of this?'

'Yes.'

'Three of them, five of us. It will be a hard fight, my brothers, but we will prevail. We are the Silver Skulls.' Gileas's voice swelled with fierce pride. 'We *will* prevail.' Jalonis and Bhehan pulled their helmets back on at the sergeant's words.

With the squad at full battle readiness, Gileas turned his attentions to the reams of data which began scrolling in front of his eyes. He blink-clicked rapidly, filtering out anything not pertinent to the moment of battle, including the winking iconograph that had previously represented Wulfric's lifesigns. The brief glimpse of that particular image served as a visible reminder of the desire for requital, however, and fire-stoked battle-lust raced through the sergeant's veins.

'They are coming,' Bhehan breathed through the vox.

Gileas made a point to double-check the functionality of his jump pack at the Prognosticator's warning. He diverted his attention to the relevant streams of data that fed the device's information into his power armour, and was satisfied to note that it was at approximately seventy per cent. Certainly not representative of its full, deadly performance, but good enough for a battle of this size. He ordered the rest of the squad to do the same. If these animals were seeking a fight, then the Reckoners would willingly deliver. They would deliver a fight and they would deliver what they gave best and what had earned them their name.

A reckoning.

For most Space Marines, engaging an enemy was all about honour to the Chapter, pride in the company or loyalty to the Imperium. Sometimes, like now, it was about righteous vengeance. Occasionally, it was

simple self-defence. For Sergeant Gileas Ur'ten it was about all of these
things. Above and beyond all else, however, it was the thrill that came
with the anticipation of a fight. The burst of adrenaline and increased
blood flow as his genetically enhanced body geared up to beget the hand
of retribution that was the rightful role of all the Adeptus Astartes.

Another moment of silence followed and then a tumult of screaming
voices rose as one. It preceded the charge of a slew of enemies from the
undergrowth, each as massive as the one they had already encountered.
Gileas thumbed the activation stud of his chainsword and it roared into
deadly life, the weapon's fangs eager to feast.

The sudden appearance of so many of the xenos caused a moment's
pandemonium, but that was all it was: a single moment during which
the Assault squad formed a tight-knit, ceramite-clad wall of stoic
defence. There was vengeance to be taken and they were ready to take it.

Each of the xenos radiated a palpable desire to kill. They walked
upright, although with a certain stumbling gait that implied they may
not always have done so. It seemed probable that their hind legs hadn't
been used in this way for long. As though confirming these suspicions,
three of them dropped to all fours.

As they prowled closer to the Adeptus Astartes, their movements
became snake-like, a sinuous flow that allowed them to undulate across
the uneven ground with hypnotic ease and disconcerting speed.

The skin of one creature's mouth drew back to reveal a double set of
razor-sharp teeth. It didn't take much of a stretch of the imagination
to work out how it was that the xenos had removed internal organs so
swiftly and efficiently. Every single one of those teeth looked capable
of tearing through flesh and muscle with ease. The attackers moved as
a unit, almost as though they were as tightly trained and drilled as the
Adeptus Astartes themselves.

A rapid headcount told the Silver Skulls that there were nine of them,
and with determination every last one of the Assault squad entered the
fray. Bhehan, his force axe at the ready in his right hand, raised the
other, palm outstretched in front of him, ready to cast a psychic shield
around his battle-brothers. The crystals in the psychic hood attached to
the gorget of his armour began to pulsate as he channelled the deadly
power of the warp, ready to unleash it at a moment's notice.

Gileas and Tikaye both charged the alien on the far right with their
chainswords shrieking bloody murder. Jalonis and Reuben levelled their
bolters and began firing.

Fury descended on the previously silent jungle. Orders were shouted,
and the cries of alien life and the indignant, defensive answering retorts
of the squad's weapons flooded the surrounding area in a cacophony
of sound.

Gileas drove his chainsword deeper into the flesh of the alien he was
fighting, putting all his strength into the blow. The thing lashed out at

him, howling and chittering. Talons flashed like deadly knives before his helmet, but he ducked and weaved with easy agility, avoiding its blows. As far as he was concerned, as long as it remained affixed to the end of his chainsword, it was a suitable distance away from him and was dying at the same time. An additional bonus.

Reuben coaxed his weapon into life, discharging a hail of bolter shells at the onslaught. Beside him, Bhehan swept his hand forwards and round in a semi-circular arc, almost as though he were simply thrusting the xenos away from him. The one directly facing him stumbled backwards and howled its displeasure.

With a grunt of effort, Gileas yanked the chainsword out of the alien's flesh and swung it round, almost severing one of the wicked, scythe-like talons from its hand. He moved in harmony with the weapon as though it was merely an extension of his own body. Watching Gileas Ur'ten fight was aesthetically pleasing; even in the heavy power armour of the Adeptus Astartes he was agile, lithe and, more than that, he was a master at what he did. He enacted his deadly dance of death with practiced aplomb.

Tikaye, engaged as he was with his own opponent, did not immediately notice that another was prowling towards him. It reached out with a clawed hand and swept it towards the Space Marine. It caught him between his helmet and breastplate, and with a sudden display of strength sent him flying backwards. He landed heavily with an audible crunch of ceramite at Bhehan's feet. The Prognosticator, briefly distracted from gathering force for his next attack, glanced down at his battle-brother.

Within seconds, Tikaye was back on his feet, his weapon back in his hand, and he tore into the nearest enemy with a vengeance, letting his chainsword do the talking.

One of the three beasts that had been slithering towards the psyker leapt suddenly with a yowl of triumph. Instinctively, Bhehan trusted to the power of his force axe rather than his psychic ability and channelled his rage and righteousness into its exquisitely forged blade. The hidden runes carved deep into its metal heart kindled and throbbed with an otherworldly glow.

Years of training and dedication to the arts of war at the hands of the masters on Varsavia automatically took over and Bhehan planted his feet firmly on the ground, prepared for the moment of impact. The axe sang through the air towards its target, a low whine audibly marking its trajectory as it swept towards the enemy.

To his consternation, the force axe passed right through the alien's body. The unexpected follow-through of his own swing unbalanced him and he fell to one knee. He scrambled immediately back to his feet, ready to resume combat, only to realise that the thing was gone, utterly vanished before his very eyes. All that remained was a strange psychic

residue, streamers of barely visible non-corporeal form that were con-
signed fleetingly to the air, and then to nothing more than memory.

'Something isn't right here,' he voxed, puzzlement implicit in every
syllable.

'Really, Prognosticator? You think so?' The pithy reply from Gileas was
harsher than perhaps it might otherwise have been, but given that the
sergeant was locked in a bloody battle to the death with a creature seemingly quite capable of slicing through him like he was made of mud, it
was understandable. 'Any chance that you'd care to elaborate on this
outstanding leap of logic?'

Clenching his force axe with an iron grip, Bhehan whirled to intercept another xenos which was catapulting itself at him. He swung the
weapon again and once more his blow met with no resistance.

He had sensed three minds. No more, no less. With the two illusory
attackers dispelled, they were now facing seven.

'They are not all real, my brothers,' he stated urgently. 'Only three of
them present a real threat.'

'They feel real to me,' responded Jalonis, who had just been viciously
swept into the trunk of one of the vast trees. The armour plating across
his back was cracked. His helmet flashed loss-of-integrity warnings at
him and, ignoring them, he resumed his fighting. One of Reuben's arms
hung limp at his side as his body worked swiftly to fix the damage that
had been caused to it.

Gileas and Tikaye had fallen into battle harmony with each other and
were battering determinedly at one of the enemy. As one, they both fired
their jump packs, performing a vertical aerial leap that caused the xenos
to snap its head up sharply, its eyes fixed on the now-airborne targets.
The range of the jump packs was severely limited due to the tree cover,
but they remained aloft, well out of its reach.

It dropped its long body low, coiling like a spring and readying itself
to launch. Bhehan, thinking swiftly, took the opportunity to blast a psychic attack into the creature's mind.

It did not vanish.

'That one!' he shouted into the vox, gesticulating ferociously at the
xenos and alerting his airborne brothers. 'That one, brother-sergeant!
It's solid.'

The sergeant nodded brusquely. He had no desire to understand the
whys or hows of the situation. Bhehan's words were little more than
meaningless background noise to him at this moment. Only the solution was of importance at this stage. Only the battle mattered.

In full synchronicity, Gileas and Tikaye both bore their full weights
downwards to land on the xenos beneath them. Close-quarters combat
was one thing. During such a pitched battle, a being could fight back
and stand a chance of being a danger. Being crushed beneath the full
might of two power armour-wearing Space Marines was something else

entirely, and not something so easily eluded.

The alien, anticipating its own demise, wailed in murderous rage for a few seconds before both Space Marines plummeted solidly onto it. Bones crunched and arterial blood spurted from puncture wounds caused by the creature's exoskeleton shredding through its flesh. Crude brutality, perhaps, but effective nonetheless.

Devoid of their source, two more of the psychic projections immediately melted into the ether. Gileas and Tikaye fired their jump packs again and blasted grimly towards the rest of the fray. Bhehan, witnessing the scene, paused momentarily as realisation bloomed.

It was suddenly so clear to the Prognosticator. So very, very simple.

'They are manipulating your minds! Brother-Sergeant Ur'ten, you must listen to me! They have extremely strong psychic capability. My mind should be awash with all these things, but it is not!' The Prognosticator bit down on the excitement and forced his mind to focus. He knew he was making little sense and that was no use to anybody.

He had removed two of the illusory aliens by passing his force axe through their psychically generated forms. With the death of one of the true alien forms, two more had dispersed.

From the nine who had attacked, the Silver Skulls now faced four. If Bhehan's theory proved correct, only two of them were real. Kill those, his theory suggested, and their intangible counterparts would vanish; eliminate the phantasms and only the real xenos would remain. It seemed that whatever trick they were playing with the squad's minds meant that they were unable to tell them apart. For them, the two decoy enemies were each as solid and real as the two who were weaving the illusion. They seemed immune to all but extrasensory attack. Only he could do anything about it.

His thought processes were lightning-fast and Bhehan began to gather his psychic might once more. The most decisive way he could think of to end this situation was to crush the opposing will of the xenos with a psychic flood of the Emperor's righteous fury. Whilst the melee had been tight and kept largely confined due to the jungle's enforced restrictions, it was still a reasonably large area. The desired result would be effective, but it would tax his constitution considerably.

It did not matter. His gift might temporarily be exhausted, but he was a fully trained battle-brother. He would never be totally defenceless. With an exultant cry, he flung both hands out in front of him. His voice carrying into the jungle with strident fervour, Bhehan called forth the powers of the warp.

With a fizzing crackle, a massive burst of energy lit his hood up in a flicker of blue sparks. The resultant shock wave not only targeted the xenos, but also caused the four battling Space Marines to pause briefly as their own minds were assailed from no longer one, but two directions. For them, a mental battle for supremacy took place as the will of the

Prognosticator worked to force out the intruders.

Bhehan was trained, disciplined and strong. The aliens were clever, certainly, but they fought on instinct and did not truly know how to counter such a devastating blow to their defences. For a heartbeat, Bhehan could feel his advantage slipping as the barb of the aliens' mental hooks worked in deeper. The silent struggle continued and then abruptly, he felt the fingers of deception release their hold and fall away.

Two of the attackers instantly disappeared. One screamed with fury and began to lope away into the undergrowth. Bhehan, staggering slightly from the sheer potency of his attack, automatically reached out for its mind. Instantly, he was filled with a sense of pain and, even better as far as he was concerned, of fear. It was injured, probably dying. It was unimportant. The final alien was also mortally wounded. It would be the work of but moments to end its foul existence.

Good work, Bhehan,' said Gileas, his breathing heavy through the vox-channel.

The remaining creature slunk around the Assault squad, fluidity implicit in its every movement. Before any of them could open fire or attack, the xenos reared back, a crest-like protrusion standing up on top of its head, and emitted a screech that was staggeringly high-pitched. Had the auto-senses in the warriors' helmets not instantly reacted, it would surely have ruptured eardrums. In the event, it achieved nothing.

The xenos clamped its jaws tightly shut and stared with renewed malevolence at its enemy as it realised the futility of its last defences. Without hesitation Gileas roared the final order, his voice like the crack of doom.

'Open fire! Suffer not the alien to live!'

With resounding cries that echoed those sentiments most emphatically, bolter fire razored through the air and tore into the alien's armour-hard exterior. Every last bolt was unloaded into it, spent shells rapidly littering the ground. Blood fountained out of the wounds in the xenos's body, the sheer force of it suggesting they had successfully hit something vital, and Gileas found renewed vigour in the scent of its imminent demise. A sudden, desperate desire to eliminate this foul abomination once and for all took hold.

With a roar of determination, he took out his bolt pistol and aimed it with deadly, pinpoint accuracy between the thing's eyes. Reuben discarded his spent weapon, taking his own pistol from its holster. Falling in beside his sergeant, he stepped forwards with him as they fired together.

Every bolt that burst against the alien's skull caused its head to snap back and drew further eardrum-splitting screeches.

Bhehan responded with a psychic blow, although due to his exhaustion, the effect was greatly diminished. Heedless of this fact, he focussed all of his fury, sense of retribution and hatred, and flung it towards the xenos with a practised heft of his mental acuity. He was drained, but it provided a useful diversion. The enemy hesitated, crouching low, ready to spring at Reuben. It moved with uncanny alacrity, propelling itself with deadly grace for something that should surely have been dead by now towards the Space Marine, bearing him to the ground. It reared up, blood and saliva flying from its jaws as it prepared to strike.

'No!'

Bhehan brandished his force axe. He urged a ripple of power across its surface and bounded the short distance to his fallen brother. With an easy, accurate swing, he buried the axe deep in the alien's chest.

It stumbled back, licks of warp-lightning crackling across its carapace. It writhed on the ground in agony for a few moments and then was still.

A silence fell, disturbed only by the heavy breathing of everyone present.

Gileas lowered his pistol and nodded in grim satisfaction. 'It is done,' he said. 'Status report.'

Apart from several light wounds and Jalonis's fractured backplate, the squad had escaped almost completely unscathed from the encounter. Bhehan's weariness showed in the Prognosticator's posture and in his voice as he communicated via the vox, but he had expended a remarkable amount of energy in a very short space of time. The strength of will it must have taken for each of the xenos to maintain replicas had been quite the barrier for him to overcome. It gave him great satisfaction to acknowledge that not only had he overcome it but had also emerged triumphant.

'Are you well, Bhehan?' Gileas addressed the psyker directly, his tone brusque and formal. 'Do you require time to gather yourself?'

'No, brother! I do not "require time". I am tired, but I am not some weakling straight out of his chamber. I am fine.' The indignation in the young Prognosticator's voice put a smile on Gileas's face beneath the helmet. He might be young, but Bhehan already had the true fire of a Silver Skull with many more years of service behind him. The Emperor willing, the youth would undoubtedly go far.

'Puts you in mind of yourself, does he, brother?'

At his side, Reuben murmured the words softly enough for only the sergeant to hear. The squad commander's smile deepened.

'Just a little, aye.' Gileas leaned down slightly and wiped his bloodied chainsword on the ground. He stared up at the sky visible through the canopy. Daylight was beginning to give way to the navy-blue of what he had always known as the gloaming. The Thunderhawk would return just after dusk. For now, there was one thing only left to do.

'Brother-Prognosticator,' he said, turning to Bhehan. 'Would you do us the great honour of claiming the squad's trophy from this battle?'

Bhehan understood the largesse implicit in the gesture and was deeply flattered by the offer. He made the sign of the aquila and bowed his head in respect to the sergeant. He stepped up and raised his force axe above his head.

'The honour would be mine, brother-sergeant. In the name of the Silver Skulls, for the glory of Chapter Master Argentius and for the memory of our fallen brother, Wulfric, I claim your head as my prize. Let those who walk the halls of our forefathers gaze upon your countenance and give thanks for your end.' The axe flashed through the air and struck the neck of the dead xenos.

The moment the head and the body parted, there was a hazy shimmering and the unknown alien's body was replaced by something entirely more recognisable. Bhehan realised it first, but the others were not very far behind him.

'An illusion,' the Prognosticator breathed. 'It's woven a psychic disguise around itself!'

'No. No, that's impossible,' countered Jalonis, perturbation in his voice. 'That can't be correct. Kroot don't have psychic abilities.'

Indeed, the headless body on the ground was most definitely that of a kroot. It had the same wiry, sinewy build and avian-like features that matched every image that had ever been pict-flashed at them through doctrination tapes and training sessions. Yet despite its instantly familiar form, there were subtle differences. It varied from what was presumably the norm in a number of ways, not least of which was the most obvious which Jalonis had just voiced.

It was imbued with psychic powers. Unheard of, at least in the Silver Skulls' experience. Reports and research had never once suggested that the kroot, the fierce, mercenary warrior troops regularly employed by tau armies, were psychic. Moreover, this kroot wore no harness, carried no weapon. It was far more primitive than what they expected of such beings. An evolutionary throwback maybe, but one in possession of something perhaps far more deadly than a rifle or any other kind of physical weapon.

'A feral colony home world?' Jalonis made the suggestion first. 'A breed of kroot who have taken a different genetic path to their brethren?'

Gileas frowned. 'It is said that these things eat the flesh of their enemies, that they have the ability to assimilate their DNA. There have certainly been reports that this planet once sported animal life. It is surely not unreasonable to guess that the kroot have systematically destroyed whatever may have existed on this planet.'

He considered the dead beasts. 'These things, at least... the things that look like they did before we exposed the truth... are all we have encountered.' A thought occurred to the sergeant. 'When Reuben shot that other one in the head, it did not change its shape or form, did it?'

'The cerebral connection remained intact,' Bhehan commented absently. 'Brother Reuben obliterated its brain, yes. However, he didn't disconnect the spinal cord. Nerve impulses continued to flow after death. The mental disguise it wove remained stable until full brain death. We didn't stay there long enough to witness it change back.'

'Aye,' said Reuben, remembering the unnatural need to ignore the alien. Bhehan would have been better equipped to avoid that psychic shielding.

Something was niggling at the back of Bhehan's mind, but he couldn't quite put his finger on it. It danced tantalisingly outside his grasp and he reached out for it.

'Psychic kroot… This is a vital discovery for us. They cannot be suffered to live. This planet must be cleansed.' Tikaye offered up his opinion.

Gileas glanced up at Bhehan and remembered the deep red stone that he had found. 'Bhehan, you have a theory, I suspect. Tell me.'

Bhehan nodded slowly. 'There are, to the best of our knowledge, no psychic kroot. Not any that we've met before,' he hypothesised. 'However, what if it were to assimilate a psychic species? Say… the eldar?' He held up the red stone so that all the battle-brothers could see it. 'What would stop it from killing and eating one of the eldar? What would prevent it from the freedom to filter out the required genetic strands that would give it the most useful result?'

'Surely it must take several generations for a kroot to assimilate such powers?' The query came from Tikaye, and the others considered his words.

'We don't know what constitutes a kroot generation. We have no idea how old that ship is. We don't even know if it *is* an eldar ship. Perhaps it is a kroot vessel. Maybe they arrived before the eldar, maybe after.' Gileas's voice was grim. His patience was already strained to breaking point. 'It is without question, brothers, that both those xenos races have tainted this planet one way or the other. There are far too many unknown variables, and I have little interest in philosophical postulation about which came first.'

He put his chainsword back into its scabbard and reloaded the chamber of his pistol.

'Brother Bhehan,' he said, without another glance, 'collect the trophy. We will take Wulfric's body to the predetermined extraction coordinates and we will leave. This must be reported to Captain Meyoran. I do not presume to second-guess his actions on hearing the news, but I would not want to be on this planet when he found out.'

The Prognosticator tucked the eldar stone into the pouch with his runes and moved to the dead kroot. The very thought of such a being filled him with passionate hatred: a foul crossbreed of two xenos races with the most lethal features of both. It was an atrocity of the highest order, an abomination that had no right to exist. Yet here it was, albeit not for much longer once the Silver Skulls returned to the *Silver Arrow*.

The sudden truth of what the murderer had wanted with Wulfric's body hit the Prognosticator head-on. A kroot, with the psychic abilities and memories of an eldar, would have had some knowledge of Astartes physiology, even if only as a basic, barely recalled memory. Imagine, then, a kroot, with the psychic abilities and memories of an eldar... and the strength and resilience of a Space Marine...

Bhehan straightened his shoulders and bent down to pick up the head of the kroot. Thanks to the Reckoners, such a thing would never come to pass.

What heat remained in the day began to sap steadily as the suns continued their slow descent towards the horizon. The air was thick with heat stored by the trees and the rocks. This, coupled with residual moisture from the rainstorm, left the air feeling thick and greasy.

The squad trampled through the trees for several more minutes, all senses on full alert. They had barely arrived at the extraction point when the general vox-channel fizzed into life. The Thunderhawk would be in position in fifteen minutes.

Nocturnal life began to flood the jungle with a discordant symphony over which the approaching whine of the Thunderhawk could swiftly be heard. Once in situ, there was a hiss of servos and hydraulics and the front boarding ramp of the vessel opened, the light from within spilling out and bathing the jungle.

Gileas waited for the others to board before he joined them. He had always maintained that, as sergeant, it was his place to arrive first and leave last. He fired his jump pack, rose to the Thunderhawk and dropped to the floor with a clatter.

'All on board, Correlan. Give us a few moments to ensure that our fallen battle-brother is secure.'

'Understood. Good to have you back, sergeant.'

Gileas removed his helmet and ran his fingers through his hair. Already the words for his report to Captain Meyoran were forming clearly in his mind. They had been sent down to this planet for one thing and yet had found something entirely different and unexpected.

Bhehan remained standing at the edge of the landing ramp, staring down at the jungle. He reached into his pouch to draw a random rune and instead pulled out the eldar stone. Considering it thoughtfully, he indulged in a moment's wild curiosity as to what sort of portent the Emperor was sending him.

As his hand closed around it, he became aware of a strong push against the wards he had set in place, wards that had no doubt gone a long way towards allowing him to see through the kroot's duplicitous scheming. This mental touch was no wild and instinctual thing, though. This press against his defences was nearly as disciplined and practiced as his own. A sudden flicker of movement caught his eye.

At the jungle's edge, barely visible in the dusk and what remained of the light cast by the Thunderhawk, Bhehan saw it. A solitary figure. Tall, seemingly all whipcord muscle and sinew, the huge kroot stood boldly in direct sight of the Thunderhawk. To all intents and purposes it was little different to its kin, but it was not difficult to surmise that it was a more powerful or at least a more evolved strain of these twisted xenos. A cloak of stitched animal hide was slung around its shoulders and in one hand it held a crudely fashioned staff, from which hung feathers and trinkets of decoration. A number of stones also dangled from the staff, stones that looked remarkably like the very one in the psyker's hand.

He felt its vicious touch against his mind again and clamped the wards down tighter. The lesser kroot had been disorganised and fierce. This, though, was a calculated, scheming mind. This was a mind that would gladly extract the very soul of you and leave you to crumble to dust in its wake. It was barbed and brutal and uncannily self-aware.

The crystals on his psychic hood flickered, attracting the sergeant's attention.

'Brother-Prognosticator?' He moved to stand beside the younger Adeptus Astartes and his sharp eyes quickly made out what the psyker had seen.

'Throne of Terra!' he exclaimed and drew his pistol, ready to fire it at the alien. But by the time the weapon was out of its holster and in his hand, the kroot had gone, vanished into the jungle. Gileas lowered his weapon, his disappointment obvious.

Bhehan turned to the sergeant. His young face showed nothing of the vile revulsion he had felt at the kroot's mental challenge.

He felt one last, sickening touch on his mind and then the alpha, if indeed that had been what it was, let him go.

'This place needs to be purified,' said the psyker, fervently. 'To be cleansed of this filth.'

'It will be, brother,' acknowledged Gileas with absolute sincerity. As the gaping maw of the landing ramp finally sealed off the last sight of the Anceriosan jungle, he turned to Bhehan. 'It will be.'

# SACRIFICE

*by Ben Counter*

The warp tore at him.

The unearthly cold shot right through him.

He could see for a billion kilometres in every direction, through the angry ghosts of dead stars and the glowing cauls of nebulae, dark for aeons. Alaric fought it, tore his eyes away from the infinities unravelling around him. The psychic wards built into his armour were white hot against his skin, tattooing him with burns in the shape of their sacred spirals.

Alaric's lungs tried to draw breath, but there was no air there. He tried to move, but space and movement had no meaning here. And beyond his senses, far in the black heart of the universe, he could sense vast and god-like intelligences watching him as he flitted through their domain.

Man, he managed to think, was not meant to be teleported.

The air boomed out as Alaric emerged in real space again, several hundred kilometres from the teleporter array on the *Obsidian Sky* where he had started the journey. Even a Space Marine, even a Grey Knight, was not immune to the disorientation of being hurled through the warp to another part of space, and for a second his senses fought to make definition of reality around him.

The squad had been teleported onto the grand cruiser *Merciless*. The familiar architectures of an Imperial warship were everywhere, from the aquilae worked into the vault where the pillars met overhead to the prayer-algorithms stamped into the ironwork of the floor by Mechanicus shipwrights.

The air was a strange mix peculiar to spaceships. Oil and sweat, incense from the constant tech-rituals, propellant from the ship's guns. It was mixed with the tongue-furring ozone of the squad's sudden arrival.

Alaric took a couple of breaths, forcing out the supercooled air in his lungs. 'Brothers!' he gasped. 'Speak unto me.'

'I live, brother,' came Dvorn's reply from where he lay, a few metres away, ice flaking from his armour.

'I too,' said Haulvarn. Alaric's second in the squad leaned against a wall of the corridor. His journey had been one of intense heat instead of cold and his armour hissed and spat where it met the wall.

Brother Visical coughed violently and forced himself to his feet. In reply to Alaric, he could only meet the Justicar's eyes. Visical was inexperienced for a Grey Knight, and he had never been teleported before. It was rare enough even for a veteran like Alaric. The technology that made it possible could not be replicated, and was restricted to a handful of the oldest Imperial warships.

The whole squad had made it onto the *Merciless*. That was something to give thanks for in itself. Teleportation was not an exact science, for even the oldest machines could simply fling the occasional man into the warp to be lost forever. He could be turned inside out, merged with a wall upon re-entry or fused with one of his fellow travellers. Luckily this had not happened to any of Alaric's squad. Fate had smiled on them so far.

'We're in the lower engineering decks,' said Haulvarn, checking the data-slate built into the armour of his forearm.

'Damnation,' spat Dvorn. 'We're off course.'

'I...' spluttered Visical, still suffering from disorientation. 'I am the hammer... I am the point of His spear...'

Alaric hauled Visical to his feet. 'Our first priority is to find Hyrk,' said Alaric. 'If we can find a cogitator or take a prisoner, we can locate him.'

As if in reply, a monstrous howl echoed from further down the corridor. This part of the ship was ill-maintained and the patchy light did not reach that far down. The sound was composed of a hundred voices, all twisted beyond any human range.

'First priority is survival,' said Dvorn.

'Where is your faith, brother?' said Haulvarn with a reproachful smile. 'Faith is the shield that never falters! Bear it up, brothers! Bear it up!'

Dvorn hefted his Nemesis hammer in both hands. 'Keep the shield,' he said. 'I'll stick to this.'

Alaric kicked open one of the doors leading off from the corridor. He glimpsed dusty, endless darkness beyond, an abandoned crew deck or cargo bay. He took shelter in the doorway as the howling grew closer, accompanied by the clatter of metal-shod feet on the floor. Sounds came from the other direction, too, this time the rhythmic hammering of guns or clubs on the walls.

'Hyrk has wasted little time,' said Alaric. 'Barely a month ago, he took this ship. Already it is crewed by the less-than-human.'

'Not for long,' said Dvorn. He looked down at Visical, who was crouching in another doorway, incinerator held ready to spray fire into the darkness. 'You were saying?'

'I am the hammer!' said Visical, voice returned and competing with the growing din. 'I am the shield! I am the mail about His fist! I am the point of His spear!'

'I see them!' yelled Haulvarn.

Alaric saw them, too. They had once been the crew of the *Merciless*, servants of the Emperor aboard a loyal warship. Now nothing remained of their humanity. The first glimpse Alaric had was of asymmetrical bodies, limbs moving in impossible configurations, stretched and torn naval uniforms wrapped around random tangles of bone and sinew.

He saw the stitches and the sutures. The humans they had once been had been cut up and rearranged. A torso was no more than an anchor for a random splay of limbs. Three heads were mounted on one set of shoulders, the jaws replaced with shoulder blades and ribs to form sets of bony mandibles. A nest of razor-sharp bone scrabbled along the ceiling on dozens of hands.

'This side, too!' shouted Dvorn, who was facing the other way down the corridor.

'Greet them well!' ordered Alaric.

The Grey Knights opened fire. The air was shredded by the reports of the storm bolters mounted onto the backs of their wrists. A wave of heat from Visical's incinerator blistered the rust off the walls. Alaric's arm jarred with that familiar recoil, his shoulder hammered back into its socket.

The mutant crewmen came apart in the first volleys. The corridor was awash with blood and torn limbs. Carried forwards on the bodies, as if riding a living tide, came a thing like a serpent of sundered flesh. Torsos were stacked on top of one another, sewn crudely together at shoulder and abdomen. Its head was composed of severed hands, fastened together with wire and metal sutures into the approximation of a massive bestial skull. Its teeth were sharpened ribs and its eyes were beating hearts. The monstrous face split open in a serpentine grin.

It moved faster than even Alaric could react. Suddenly it was over him, mouth yawning wide, revealing thousands of teeth implanted in its fleshy gullet to crush and grind.

Alaric powered to his feet, slamming a shoulder up into the underside of the thing's jaw. He rammed his fist up into the meat of its neck and trusted that his storm bolter was aiming at some vital place, some brain or heart the thing could not live without.

Words of prayer flashed through his mind.

Alaric fired.

* * *

*The light was worse than the dark.*

*He was bathed in it. He felt it illuminating not just his body, but his mind. All his sins, his very fears in that moment, were laid open to be read like the illuminations of a prayer book.*

*Up above him was the dome of the cathedral. Thousands of censers hung from it, smouldering in their clouds of pungent smoke. The dome was painted with a hundred methods of torture, each one inflicted on a famous sinner from the Imperial creed. A body, broken on a wheel, had its wounds picked out in clusters of rubies. The victim of an impaling, as he slid slowly down a spear through his stomach, wept tears of gold leaf.*

*The light came not from the dome, but from below. Faith was like fire – it could warm and comfort, and it could destroy. Fire, therefore, filled the cathedral floor. Hundreds of burners emitted a constant flame, so the cathedral seemed to contain an ocean of flame. The brazen walkways over the fire, where the clergy alone were permitted to tread, were so hot they glowed red and the clergy went about armoured in shielded and cooled vestments.*

*The man who knelt at the altar was not one of the clergy. He was not shielded, and he could barely draw breath in the scalding heat. His wrists were burned where his manacles had conducted the heat. He knelt on a prayer cushion, but even so his shins and knees were red raw. He wore only a tabard of cloth-of-gold, and his head had been shaven with much ceremony that very morning.*

*A silver bowl on the metal floor in front of him was there, he knew, to catch his blood.*

*One of the cathedral's many clergy walked up to where the man knelt. His Ecclesiarchy robes almost completely concealed him, forming a shell of ermine and silk that revealed only the clergyman's eyes. His robes opened and an arm reached out. The hand, gloved in crimson satin, held a single bullet.*

*The bullet was dropped into the silver bowl. The kneeling man winced at the sound.*

*Other clergy were watching, assembled on the metal walkways, lit from beneath by the lake of fire. The reds, purples and whites of their robes flickered with the flames. Only their eyes were visible.*

*One of them, in the purple and silver of a cardinal, raised his hand.*

*'Begin,' he said, and his words were amplified through the sweltering dome of the cathedral.*

*The priest in front of the sacrificial altar drew a knife from beneath his robes. It had a blade of gold, inscribed with High Gothic prayers. The prisoner – the sacrifice – flinched as the tip of the knife touched the back of his neck.*

*The city outside was dark and cold. It was a city of secrets and dismal hope. It was a place where for a normal man – the kind of man the sacrifice had once been – to get by, rules had to be broken. In every side street and basement, there was someone who would break those rules. Fake identity papers, illicit deals and substances, even murder for the right price. Some of those criminals would open up a slit in a customer's abdomen and implant an internal pouch* where a small item could be concealed so well that even if the carrier was stripped to the waist and forced to kneel at a sacrificial altar, it would remain hidden.

The sacrifice had also paid what little he had to have one of his fingernails replaced with a miniature blade. As the priest in front of him raised the knife into the air and looked up towards the dome, the sacrifice used this tiny blade to open up the old scar in the side of his abdomen. Pinpricks of pain flared where the nerve endings had not been properly killed in that dingy basement surgery. The sacrifice's stomach lurched as his finger slipped inside the wound and along the slippery sides of the implanted pouch.

His fingers closed on the grip of the gun.

'By this blood,' intoned the priest, 'shed by this blade, shall the weapon be consecrated! Oh Emperor on high, oh Lord of Mankind, oh Father of our futures, look upon this offering!'

The sacrifice jumped to his feet, the metal scorching his soles. With his free hand he grabbed the priest's wrist and wrenched it behind his back, spinning the man around. With the other, he put the muzzle of the miniature pistol to the back of the priest's head.

A ripple of alarm ran around the cathedral. Clergy looked from the altar to one another, as if one of them would explain that this was just another variation on the ritual they had all seen hundreds of times before.

'I am walking out of here!' shouted the sacrifice. 'Do you understand? When I am free and deep in the city, I will let him go. If you try to stop me, or follow me, I will kill him. His life is worth a lot more than one sacred bullet. Don't make me a murderer.'

The assembled clergy took a collective step backwards. Only the cardinal did not move.

Even with his face hidden, the presence and authority that had made him a cardinal filled the cathedral. Vox-casters concealed in the dome sent his voice booming over the sound of the flames.

'Do not presume to know,' said the cardinal, 'what a life is worth to me. Not when I serve an Imperium where a billion brave men die every day. Not when the Emperor alone can number those who have died in His name. Do not presume to know. Be grateful, merely, that we have given you the chance to serve Him in death.'

The sacrifice forced the priest forwards a few steps, the pistol pressed against the layers of silk between it and the priest's skull. The sacrifice held the priest in front of him as if shielding himself from something the cardinal might do. 'No one needs to know you let me go,' he said. 'The priests will do whatever you say. They will hold their tongues. And I will simply disappear. No one will ever know.'

'The Emperor watches,' replied the cardinal. 'The Emperor knows.'

'Then cut a hundred men's throats on this altar to keep him happy!' retorted the sacrifice. 'A hundred killers. There are plenty of them out there. A hundred sinners. But not me. I am a good man. I do not deserve to die here!'

The cardinal held out his hands as if he was on the pulpit, encompassing a great congregation. 'That is why it has to be you,' he said. 'What worth is the blood of a sinner?'

'Then find someone else,' said the sacrifice, walking his prisoner forwards a few more paces. The main doors were beyond the cardinal, a set of massive bronze reliefs depicting the Emperor enthroned.

'Brother,' said the cardinal, his voice still calm. 'A thousand times this world blesses a bullet with the blood of a good man. A thousand other worlds pay the same tithe to our brethren in the Inquisition. Do you think you are the first sacrifice to try to escape us? The first to smuggle a weapon through the ritual cleansings? Remember your place. You are but one man. There is nothing you can do which another has not tried and failed before. You will not leave this place. You will kneel and die, and your blood will consecrate our offering.'

'This man will die,' hissed the sacrifice, 'or I will be free.'

The cardinal drew something from inside his robes. It was a simple silver chain, with a single red gemstone in its setting. It had none of the ostentatiousness of the cardinal's own diamonds and emeralds which encrusted the heavy golden chain around his neck. It looked out of place dangling from his silk-gloved fingers.

The sacrifice froze. Recognition flooded his face as his eyes focused on the necklace in the cardinal's hand.

'Talaya,' he said.

'If you do not kneel and bare your throat to the Emperor's blade,' said the cardinal, 'then she will take your place. She is a good person, is she not?'

The sacrifice stepped back from his prisoner. He did not look away from the necklace as the backs of his legs touched the scalding metal of the altar.

He threw the gun off the walkway, into the flames.

He knelt down, and bowed his head over the silver bowl with its bullet.

'Continue,' said the cardinal.

The sacrifice did not have time to cry out in pain. The sacrificial knife severed his spinal cord with a practised thrust, and opened up the veins and arteries of his throat. He just had time to see the round immersed in his dark red blood before the darkness fell.

The consecrated bolt-shell ripped up into the serpent's skull and detonated, blowing clots of a dozen brains across the ceiling.

The weight of the mutant thing fell onto Alaric's shoulders. He shrugged it off, glancing behind him to the rest of the squad. Dvorn was breaking the neck of a thing with too many limbs and Haulvarn was shredding the last of the crewmen seething down the corridor with bolter fire. Fire licked along the walls and ceiling beyond, clinging to the charred remnants of the mutants Visical had burned.

'Keep moving!' yelled Alaric. 'They know we are here!'

Alaric ran down the corridor, his armoured feet skidding on the spilt blood and crunching through corpses. Up ahead were what had once been the crew decks. Upwards of thirty thousand men had lived on the *Merciless*, their lives pledged to crewing and defending the grand cruiser. Between the mutiny and disappearance of the ship and the confirmation that Bulgor Hyrk was on board, only a few weeks had passed. That was more than enough time for Hyrk to turn every single crewman on board into something else.

Some of those transformations had taken place in the crew quarters. The walls and ceiling were blistered up into cysts of translucent veiny metal, through which could be seen the fleshy forms of incubating mutants. The crewmen had been devolved into foetal forms and then reborn as something else.

Every one would be different, obscene in its own way. Hyrk considered himself, among other things, an artist.

'Would that we could burn it all,' said Visical.

'We will,' said Dvorn. 'The fleet will. This place will all burn, once we know Hyrk is dead.'

One of the cysts near Visical split open. The thing that fell out looked like two human torsos fused together at the waist end-to-end, forming something like a serpent with a lumpily deformed head at each end. For limbs it had hands attached to the sides of its length at the wrists, fingers like the legs of a centipede.

Visical immolated the mutant in a blast of flame. It shrivelled up, mewling. 'How can honest human flesh become such a thing?' he said.

'Think not of how far a human is from these abominations,' said Alaric. 'Think how close he is. Even a Grey Knight is not so far removed from Hyrk's creations. The line is thin. Do not forget that, brother.' Alaric checked his storm bolter and reloaded. Each shell was consecrated, blessed by the Ecclesiarchy. Many, many more would be fired before Alaric saw the last of the *Merciless*.

Haulvarn had ripped a panel off the wall and was examining the wiring inside. 'The cogitator data-lines run through here,' he said. He hooked one of the lines into his data-slate. 'There is a lot of power running to the astronav dome. Far beyond normal tolerances. Whatever Hyrk's doing here, it has something to do with the dome.'

'The dome on the *Merciless* is archeotech,' said Alaric. 'It's older than anything in the fleet. It must be why Hyrk chose this ship.'

'The only thing I care about,' said Dvorn with a snarl, 'is where it is.'

The floor shook, as if the fabric of the *Merciless* was coming apart and sending quakes running through the decks. A sound ran through the ship – a howl – the sound of reality tearing. The air turned greasy and thick, and rivulets of brackish blood ran down the walls of the warped crew quarters.

'Daemons,' spat Alaric.

'Hyrk has torn the veil,' said Haulvarn.

'That is why it had to be us,' said Alaric. 'That is why no one else could kill him.'

The sound of a thousand gibbering voices filtered down from the decks above. Howling and inhuman, they were echoes of the storms that ripped through the warp. Every voice was a fragment of a god's own voice, each of the daemons now pouring into the *Merciless*.

'Upwards,' said Alaric. 'Onwards. Take the fight to them and kill every one that gets in your way! We are the tip of His spear, brothers!'

Dvorn squared up to the door at the far end of the crew quarters, hammer held ready. Though Dvorn was as skilled with the storm bolter as any Grey Knight, it was face-to-face, hammer to daemon hide, that he loved to fight. Dvorn was the strongest Adeptus Astartes Alaric had ever met. He had been born to charge through a bulkhead door and rip through whatever foe waited for him beyond.

Visical and Haulvarn stacked up against the bulkhead wall beside Dvorn.

'Now, brother!' ordered Alaric.

Dvorn kicked the bulkhead door off its hinges. The roar that replied to him was a gale, a storm of foulness that roared through the decks beyond.

Dvorn had opened the door into the wet, beating heart of the ship, a stinking mass of pulpy flesh lit by ruddy bioluminescence. Daemons, their unnatural flesh glowing, flowed along the walls and ceiling in a seething tide welling up from hell itself.

'Come closer, vomit of the warp!' yelled Dvorn. 'Let us embrace, in the fire of the Emperor's wrath!'

Knots of iridescent flesh formed a dozen new limbs and eyes every second. One-eyed, one-horned monstrosities bulged with masses of corrosive decay. Skull-faced cackling creatures with skin the colour of blood. Lithe, leaping things, with an awful seductiveness in their impossible grace.

Alaric planted his feet and braced his halberd, like a spearman ready to receive a cavalryman's charge.

The tide hit, in a storm of flesh and corruption boiling straight up from the warp.

*Xanthe knelt, as if in prayer, but she was not praying.*

*In the pitch-black hangar, she could pretend she was alone. A hundred more souls were locked in there with her, manacled to the floor or the walls, but they were silent. They had been silent for weeks now. At the start of the voyage, when they had been herded from the holding cells into the ship's hangar, they had screamed and sobbed and begged for mercy. They had learned by now that the crew did not listen. The crew, who went about the ship masked and robed, had never once spoken to any of the prisoners, no matter how the prisoners pleaded to know where they were going, or what would happen to them. Even the children had given up asking.*

*Xanthe knew why they were all there. They were witches. Some of them were wise women or medicine men, healers and sages on primitive worlds who had been rounded up and handed over to the men from the sky in return for guns, or just to make the spacecraft leave. Others were killers and spies for hire whose skills had made them valuable to noble houses and underhive gangs, but had also made them targets for the planetary authorities. Xanthe was one of them, a spy, and though she had scrupulously avoided making any deadly enemies among the cutthroat nobles of her home world, her pains had not helped her when the Arbites with their riot shields and shotguns had purged the hive of its psykers.*

*Psykers. Witches. Heretics. Just by existing, they were committing the foulest of sins. Where they were going, none of them knew, except that punishment would be waiting for them when they got there.*

*Xanthe let her mind sink down deeper. Her senses rippled out from her. She could perceive the bright minds of the other psykers in the hold. Some of them winked feebly, for they were the most dangerous ones who had been sedated for the whole trip. Others were still twinkling with hope. Most were dull with the acceptance of fate.*

*She could taste the wards built into the ship, too. They were complex geometric designs, pentagrams and interlocking spirals etched with psychoactive compounds and inked with sacred blood. They covered every surface of the hold, forming a shield blocking all psychic power. Xanthe's own powers, far greater than the ship's crew suspected, were barely a glimmer in the back of her mind.*

*On one wall was a rivulet of water, trickling down the wall. Xanthe had noticed it four months before, when the prisoners had first been shackled. Some imperfection in the wall was allowing condensation from the breathing of the prisoners to collect and pool, and then run down the wall. Over the months it had eroded the metal in a tiny channel of rust, to the naked eye little more than a reddish stain. Xanthe had not seen it – not with her normal senses – for many weeks, since the last time there had been light in the hangar.*

*The sacred oils, with which the wards had been inked, were washed away. The pattern was broken. The single rivulet had erased a channel far too small for all but the most powerful minds to exploit.*

*Xanthe's mind was very powerful indeed.*

*Xanthe let her mind slither out of her body. It was an insane risk, and in any other situation she would never have dared do it. If she was trapped outside her body she would die, with her spirit withering away and her body shutting down. If the wards were strengthened during her time outside her body, she would be cut off from her body entirely and would be at the mercy of the predators that lurked at the edges of reality waiting for unharnessed minds.*

*But these circumstances were different. It was worth the risk.*

*Xanthe's mind slipped out of her and through the tiny gap in the wards. The patterns scraped at her, lines of psychic pain across her soul. The fire passed and she was through.*

*The Black Ship stretched out around her. Impenetrable barriers were everywhere and Xanthe realised that there were many hangars, each presumably full of psykers. Thousands of them, perhaps, all alone and afraid.*

*The corridors and decks were tinged with suffering and arrogance. The crew were blank spots, their minds shielded from psychic interference so thoroughly that they were black holes in Xanthe's perceptions.*

*The Black Ship was far larger than Xanthe had expected. It stretched off into the distance in both directions, as big as a city. Xanthe stumbled blindly through the structure, slipping through walls and between decks, trying to keep moving while steering clear of the banks of wards blocking her path.*

*Cells stretched off in a long row. The minds inside them were broken and smouldering, little more than embers. The cells were drenched in pain and Xanthe had the sensation of being bathed in blood, the coppery taste and smell filling her.*

*Xanthe hurried away from the cells, but a worse sensation greeted her. A circular anatomy theatre, walls hung with diagrams of dissected brains and spinal columns, was layered in such intense pain and hate that Xanthe recoiled from it and flitted away like an insect.*

*Xanthe knew she was losing her mind. Losing it literally – the connection between her mind and the brain that still controlled it might snap and her mind would be trapped outside her, circling around the Black Ship until some anti-psychic ward snuffed it out. Perhaps there were other ghosts here, other orphaned minds wandering the decks.*

*She forced herself to concentrate. She would not end that way. In desperation she located one of the black holes, one of the mind-shielded crew, and followed it. Candles were everywhere, miniature wax-caked shrines built into every alcove and iron chandeliers hanging from every ceiling. Relics – painted icons, mouldering bones, scraps of armour, inscribed bullet casings – lay in glass-fronted cabinets to flood the ship's decks with holiness and keep the taint of the thousands of psykers out of the crew's minds.*

*They were gathering in a chapel. The holiness of it was tainted with a cynicism and cruelty that clashed with the taste of the altar, which was consecrated to the Emperor as Protector. The blank minds gathered there were kneeling in prayer, with one of them sermonising them atop a pulpit hung with manacles. More candles abounded, many of them cramped in masses of wax and wicks behind stained glass windows. Each crewman held a candle, too, and their shoulders were hunched with the symbolic weight of the light they carried.*

*Xanthe sent her mind in close to one of the crewmen. She could make out none of his features, for the cowl of his uniform contained an inhibitor unit that kept his thoughts and his face from her. But the echoes of his perception just got through, enough for Xanthe to make out the words he could hear.*

*The crewman on the pulpit was an officer. Xanthe could make out a medallion around his neck in the shape of the letter 'I'. His uniform of red and black had a collar so high he could not turn his head, and he wore ruby-studded laurels on his brow. His voice was deep and dark, enhanced by an amplifier unit in his throat.*

'And so let us pray,' he was saying, 'that our sacred duty might go unimpeded. Though we near our destination, let us not allow our attention to waver. A scant few days remain, and no doubt we give thanks that our proximity to our cargo will soon be over. Yet until the last second, we must remain vigilant! Our duty is greater than any of us. In its fulfilment, our purpose as servants of the Emperor is fulfilled. Be not content, be not lax. Be suspicious of all, at all times!'

The words continued but Xanthe let them go. She could taste the meaning of them, and they went on in the same vein. She slipped away through the chapel, following the concentrations of crewmen up through the bewildering structures of the ship's upper decks. She made out the soaring arches and sweeping stage of an opera house, a cluster of tiny buildings forming a mock village under a ceiling painted to resemble a summer sky – things that had no place on a spaceship. In her bewilderment she almost lost her way but she glimpsed a collection of black voids where more crew were gathered.

Xanthe soared along a corridor lined with statues and portraits, each one of a subject with his face covered. She emerged in a map room where several crew were gathered around an enormous map table. A servitor clung to the ceiling, scribbling annotations on a stellar map with autoquills – Xanthe could taste the tiny flicker of life inside it, for like all servitors it was controlled by a crudely reprogrammed human brain.

In the back of the room was another servitor. A holo-device, it projected a huge image that took up most of the map room, shimmering above the heads of the blank-minded crew. Xanthe perceived it through the echo of their eyes.

It was a vast furnace, its every dimension picked out in shimmering lines of light. The sight of it filled Xanthe with revulsion, turning the stomach in her body several decks below. The image was so detailed that Xanthe could shrink her perception and enter it, flitting through its vast vaulted rooms and side chapels. She was drawn to it as if by some appalling gravity of fascination. The pediments of Imperial saints and enormous pipe organ chambers enthralled her, and the yawning maw of the furnace entrance reeled her in as if hooks were latched into her soul.

The cavern of the furnace billowed around her, pure darkness harnessed in the holo-unit's bands of light. Above the furnace, suspended over the place where the flames would rage, was a circular platform on which a single suit of armour was mounted on a rack. The armour was beautiful, ornate and massive, too large for a normally-proportioned human. Cables and coils hung everywhere, and servo-skulls hovered ready to manipulate the armour as it was forged.

Xanthe withdrew her mind from the sight. She did not understand why it was at once fascinating and repellent to her. It held meaning, this place, so powerful and concentrated that it affected her even though she did not know anything about it.

The crewmen were talking. Their faces were still cowled by their psychic protection, but their words echoed. Xanthe could not help but listen, even though some cruel precognition told her that she would not like what she heard. Xanthe could not match the voices to the shadowy figures grouped around the map table, but their meaning was clear to her, as if some force wanted her to understand.

'Do they know?'

'Of course they do not.'

'What if they did? It is of no concern anyway. Without them to fuel the forge, the armour's wards will not be imbued with their power. The only concern we have is that the armour is forged and the Grey Knights receive their tithe.'

'The witches are vermin. The galaxy is better off without them.'

'It is a duty we do to mankind. That one Grey Knight fights on is worth a million of these sinners.'

Xanthe felt her stomach turn again, and her heart flutter in her chest. The link between body and mind shuddered and she was flying, hurtling backwards through the decks of the Black Ship towards where her body lay. White pain shrieked through her soul as she was torn back through the tiny gap in the hangar's wards, and she slammed into her body with such force that her first physical sensation was the metal floor cracking into her head as she fell onto her side.

Hands were on her. Gnarled and cracked, the hands of her fellow prisoners.

'Xanthe?' said one. It was the old woman, one of the few prisoners who had been willing to speak with Xanthe, for some of them suspected what she really was. 'Did you do it? Did you venture out of this place?'

'I... I did,' gasped Xanthe. She tasted blood in her mouth.

'Where are we? Where are we going?'

Xanthe opened her eyes. The other prisoners were gathered around, their eyes glinting in the only light – a flame cast from the old woman's palm. It was the only power she could manifest in the psychically dampened hangar. The old woman was powerful, too.

We are going to a furnace, *thought Xanthe.* We are going to be incinerated so that our power will be transferred into a suit of armour, that its wearer might be protected from people like us.

The faces looked at her, waiting for her answer. The children wanted to know even more than the adults.

'They are taking us to camps,' said Xanthe. 'We will be studied by their scientists. It will be a hard life, I think, and we will never go back. But we will live there, at least. We will live.'

'You have seen this?' said the old woman.

'I have,' said Xanthe. 'I saw it all.'

'Then let us place ourselves in the hand of fate,' said the old woman. She bowed her head, and the other prisoners did the same. 'Let us give thanks. Even in this place, the Emperor is with us.'

Xanthe almost choked back her lie and told the truth. But it would do no good.

She stayed silent as the old woman let the flame die out.

\* \* \*

The wards built into Alaric's armour flared white-hot as they absorbed the force of the sorcery cast at the Grey Knights. Without that armour and its coils of psychically impregnated wards he and his fellow Grey Knights would have been stripped to the bone by the purple flame that washed over them. They would have been shredded by the razor-sharp wind shrieking around the astronav dome of the *Merciless*.

Alaric crouched behind a shard of the dome, fallen from above and speared into the wind-scoured floor. The storm shrieked around him and he fought to keep from being thrown off his feet. The others of his squad were taking cover too, hammering fire up at the daemons that rode the storm overhead and left contrails of spinning knives.

Alaric could not worry about the eel-like daemons flying above him. He had to trust his squad to deal with them. His only concern was Bulgor Hyrk.

Hyrk flew on wings of steel in the centre of the astronav dome, suspended, unaffected by the storm of power around him. Hyrk had once been a man but now he looked more like a primitive vision of a god, some daemon worshipped by savages on a far-flung world. His six arms were held open in gestures of benediction and prayer. Instead of legs he had long plumes of iridescent feathers, crawling with imp-like familiars that cackled and leered. Hyrk's face was still that of a man, albeit with blank skin where his eyes should be. Those eyes had migrated to his bare chest, from which two large yellow orbs stared unblinking.

Rows of vestigial limbs ran down the sides of his abdomen, carrying scrolls with glowing letters. A crown of horns ringed his head, tipped with gold and inlaid with diamonds. The sacred implements of the rites through which he communed with his gods – chains, brass-plated skulls, sacred daggers, a lash of purple sinew – orbited around him, dripping silvery filaments of power.

'Brother,' said Hyrk, the lipless mouths in his palms speaking in unison with him. 'Grey Knight. Son of the Emperor. Child of the universe. Thank you. Thank you for being my witness. My glory is nothing without the greatest of men to behold it.'

'I spit on your glory!' shouted back Alaric, his own voice almost lost in the screaming wind.

A daemon fell from above, snaking torso torn open by bolter fire. In his peripheral vision Alaric saw Brother Visical dragging another daemon down to the floor and scorching it to corrupted bones with his incinerator.

'You do now,' replied Hyrk, his voice impossibly loud and yet possessing an awful calm and reason, for the mind had long since given up the sanity required to harbour doubt. 'But you will kneel.'

Alaric looked beyond Bulgor Hyrk. The astronav dome had shattered. Shards of its transparent dome littered what remained of the dome's holomap projectors and command pulpit. Normally, the broken dome would expose the place to hard vacuum, for the dome blistered up from the hull of the *Merciless* and looked out on the void. But nothing on the *Merciless* was obeying the rules of normality.

Through the shattered dome was a vortex of power, a vision of madness mixed with the raw stuff of reality. At its heart was a glimpse through the veil to the warp. A man without the mental training of a Grey Knight might have been transfixed by that shard of insanity, condemned to stare at it until his body gave out on, him or he was drawn by it through to the warp itself. As Alaric looked on the shard of the warp split and opened; a silvery eye looked down at him.

It was from that vortex that Hyrk drew his power. That power coalesced into sights from Hyrk's depraved life, churning randomly as the vortex echoed the seething pit of Hyrk's mind. A million bodies writhed in joy, smiles on their faces, as they were burned in the golden flame that Hyrk taught them to summon down upon themselves. The blasphemies in the Library of Absalaam tore themselves free of their pages, flocking like ravens around the figure of Hyrk. A hive city's population wept with such sorrow at the heretic's crimes that their tears rose up in a flood and drowned them.

Alaric tore his eyes away. Hyrk's many arms were making the gestures with which he channelled his own form of witchcraft. Pulses of golden fire, like miniature comets, rained down. Alaric broke cover and ran forwards, powering through the storm. Hyrk's face broke into a faint smile, as if amused by some trifle, and another gesture hurled a spear of ice into Alaric's chest. The spear splintered against his breastplate, the armour's wards discharging purple spirals of power away from the impact.

Alaric was knocked onto one knee. He forced himself another step forwards, planting the haft of his Nemesis halberd in the dome's floor to give him purchase against the storm.

'I have seen a thousand like you, Hyrk!' shouted Alaric. 'A thousand gods. A thousand vessels of the warp's glory. And I know what you cannot.'

'And what,' said Hyrk, 'is that?'

'You all die,' replied Alaric, forcing himself another step closer.

Hyrk conjured a shield of energy the colour of moonlight, covered in runes of invulnerability taught to him by his patrons in the warp. 'I am immortal,' he said simply.

'Then your masters will have forever to punish you for your failure,' said Alaric.

'You cannot hurt me,' replied Hyrk, one of his hands waving dismissively, as if he was bored of Alaric's presence at his court and was commanding him to leave.

Alaric did not reply to that.

He drew back his arm, the head of the halberd hovering beside his head. Hyrk's eyes glimmered with amusement at the motion, for he knew that even a Nemesis weapon hurled by a Grey Knight could not get through the magics he commanded.

Alaric's gaze went upwards. He focused on the eye in the heart of the vortex overhead, the eye that stared directly from the warp.

He was strong. He would have to be. It was not an easy shot.

Alaric hurled the Nemesis halberd straight up. The force of his throw kept it flying true even through the storm. It seemed to take an hour for it to spin upwards through the vortex, past the endless atrocities pulled from Hyrk's mind.

Hyrk realised, a split second before it hit, what Alaric was trying to do.

The blade of the halberd speared the eye through the centre of its pupil. The eye recoiled, folds of timespace rippling around it, and a bolt of iridescent blood squirted from the ruined pupil.

The vortex went dark. The power drained away. The daemons and the victims in Hyrk's visions dissolved away to skeletons, then darkness.

The storm died down. Alaric could hear the gunfire from his battle-brothers now, he could stand at full height without being swept aside by the storm. The gods who watched Hyrk and granted him his power were blinded for a moment, and turned away from their champion. Hyrk could not call on them now.

Hyrk was stunned. Alaric was too quick for him. Alaric dived forwards and grabbed a handful of Hyrk's feathered tail. He dragged Hyrk down to the floor, fighting against the psychic force keeping him aloft.

'I can hurt you now,' said Alaric. He wrapped an elbow around Hyrk's jaw and twisted. Bulgor Hyrk's neck snapped in his grasp.

*The first time, Thorne was ready.*

*The room into which they wheeled him was of polished steel, so harshly lit that the reflection of the glowstrips in the mirror-like walls turned it into a cube of light. Thorne was strapped into a wheelchair, for the nerve stimulation had rendered him malcoordinated and unable to walk without fear of falling. His hands shook and he sweated constantly, his body still geared up for the next tide of bafflement and pain.*

*Instructor Gravenholm sat in the room, a thick file on the table in front of him. He was haloed in the light, as if he was a bureaucrat sorting through sins and virtues in the Emperor's own court. Gravenholm was an old man, too old to live were it not for the juvenat machine sighing on the floor by his feet. Gravenholm was important enough for the Ordo Malleus to keep alive through arcane technology. Once, long ago, he had been a lowly trainee like Thorne. That was one of the thoughts that kept Thorne going.*

*'Trainee,' said Gravenholm, his words accompanied by the stuttering of the juvenat machine hooked up to his ancient lungs. 'Speak your name.'*

*'Explicator-Cadet Ascelan Thorne,' replied Thorne, forcing the strength into his voice.*

'Good,' said Gravenholm. 'What process have you just undergone?'

Thorne swallowed. 'Direct-pattern nerve stimulation.'

'Why?'

'Part of my training as an interrogator. We must resist interrogation techniques ourselves.'

'I see.' Gravenholm leafed through the file. 'Prior to this process you were given data to memorise. Describe to me the content of that data.'

'No.'

Gravenholm looked Thorne in the eye. 'Tell me, Cadet Thorne.'

'I will not do so.'

'I see. That will be all.'

The orderlies returned to the room to wheel Thorne away. 'Did I pass, sir?' he said. The words came unbidden, blurted out. In reply Gravenholm merely gave him a last look, before turning a page in the file and starting to make notes with a quill.

The second time, Thorne was not ready.

He knew there had been nerve stimulation again. But there had been more, too. He had watched pict-grabs of destruction and death, cities burning, murders and mutilations spliced with images taken of himself doing things he couldn't remember. In a dark room, men had screamed at him to confess his treachery with witches and aliens. He had woken up on an examining table with doctors describing the mutations they said he possessed. He did not know where the nerve stimulation ended and his own thoughts began.

He had seen Gravenholm many times. Perhaps it had been one of the pict-grabs, perhaps a nightmare. Perhaps he had actually been there. But now he was in the cube of light again, this time lying on a medical gurney with intravenous lines in the backs of his hands.

'What is your name?' asked Gravenholm.

Thorne coughed, and arched his back in pain. The nerve stimulation had been applied this time along his spine, and the points of pain remained where the probes had punctured between his vertebrae. 'Thorne,' he said. 'Thorne. Explicator-cadet.'

'I see. What processes have you undergone?'

'I don't... I'm not sure.'

Gravenholm made a few notes. He had not changed since the first bout of resistance training. The juvenat machine still did his breathing for him and his bald, lined face still tilted oddly so he could look over his spectacles at Thorne.

'You were given data to remember. Tell it to me.'

'No.'

Gravenholm made another note. 'If you do not, further processes will be performed on you. They will include further nerve stimulation.'

'No. I won't tell you.'

'I see.'

Thorne smiled. It was the first time he had done so in a long time. 'I did *well, right?' he said. 'I didn't break. Have I done it? Will you make me an interrogator?'*

*Gravenholm didn't bother to look up this time. He waved a hand, and the orderlies took Thorne away again.*

*The third time, Thorne barely recognised the room at all. The cube of light had been there before, but he did not know if it was in his mind or whether he had really been there. The inside of his mind was full of half-truths and random fragments. Faces loomed at him, and gloved hands holding medical implements. He saw hideous creatures, many-eyed beasts squatting in pits of rotting bodies and swarms of tiny things devouring his arms and body. He saw his hands become charred skeletal limbs and his face bloated and decaying in a mirror.*

*Maybe there had been nerve stimulation. Maybe not. Maybe a key word brought back the pain without any need for attaching the probes to his spine. It all ran together. There had been no passing of the days – just an infinite ribbon of time, a few loops illuminated in memory, most of it in darkness.*

*Thorne was again on the gurney. He had been lying on it for some time. His limbs were too weak to support him. Orderlies had to turn him onto his side so Gravenholm could speak to his face.*

*'What is your name?' said Gravenholm, the juvenat machine sighing in unison.*

*Thorne took a long time to answer.*

*'I don't know,' he said. 'Throne alive. Oh... merciful Emperor! I don't know any more...'*

*Gravenholm smiled, made a final annotation, and closed the file.*

*'Then you are ready,' he said. 'I have no use for an interrogator with his own personality. With his own name. Only when the vessel is empty can it be refilled with something the Ordo Malleus can use. Your training can begin, explicator-cadet. You shall be an interrogator.'*

Alaric watched the interrogator at work through the one-way window that looked onto the explicator suite. Like the rest of the *Obsidian Sky* it was dressed with stone, more like the inside of a sepulchre than a spacecraft. The interrogator, wearing the plain uniform of an Ordo Malleus functionary, was speaking to Bulgor Hyrk. Hyrk was bracketed to the wall of the explicator suite, with his neck braced so his head did not loll on his useless neck. His spine was severed and his body paralysed, and it had been quick work by the ship's medicae to save the heretic's life when Alaric brought the dying body back to the *Obsidian Sky*.

'Thorne is good,' said Inquisitor Nyxos. The *Obsidian Sky* was Nyxos's ship for the duration of the mission to capture Hyrk. He was an old, bleak-humoured man who seemed ancient enough to have seen everything the life of a daemon hunter could throw at him. He looked frail, but Alaric knew this was an illusion Nyxos cultivated with his bent body and ragged black robes. 'He is already getting answers from Hyrk. Hyrk thinks his gods have abandoned him so he is telling all out of spite more than anything. Much of what he has told us is rather interesting.'

'How so?' said Alaric. He had spent many hours cleaning the filth off his armour and reconsecrating it, and now it gleamed in the dim light coming through the window.

'It seems he took over the *Merciless* because he had somewhere to go in a hurry,' replied Nyxos. 'Nothing to do with the crew or the Imperial Navy. He just needed a spaceship. Everything he did to the crew was for his own amusement, as far as we can tell.'

'Where was he going?'

'To the Eye.'

Alaric shook his head. The Eye of Terror had opened and the forces of Chaos had poured through. Billions of Imperial Guardsmen and whole Chapters of Space Marines were fighting there to stem the tide, which threatened to break through into the Imperial heartlands of the Segmentum Solar. Heretics like Hyrk were flocking there, too, to pledge themselves to the cause of the Chaos lords.

'Specifically,' Nyxos was saying, 'a planet named Sarthis Majoris. A call has gone out to filth like Hyrk and Throne knows how many have answered already. It seems that Hyrk was summoned by a creature there called Duke Venalitor. I have sent to the Eye for confirmation, but either way, I intend to see your squad reinforced and sent to Sarthis Majoris as soon as we have gotten everything we can out of Hyrk.'

'I see. Could Hyrk be lying?'

'Perhaps. But as I said, Thorne is really very good.' Nyxos said this with a telling smile that told Alaric all he needed to know about what would happen to the paralysed Hyrk.

'Look at this ship,' said Alaric. 'At the crew and the resources we have spent. How much did it take to put my squad on the *Merciless*? What sacrifices are made so we can do what we must do?'

'Indeed, even I cannot count them all,' said Nyxos. 'We must take more from our Imperium than any of us can understand. This thought troubles you?'

'I can allow nothing to trouble me,' said Alaric. 'If we turn our thoughts to these things, we lose our focus. Our sense of duty is eroded. If our task is not worth sacrifice, then no task is.'

'Good.' Nyxos's face darkened. 'But speak not these thoughts too freely, Justicar. To some, they might sound like moral weakness. Like the thoughts of one who harbours doubt. Would that you were an inquisitor, Alaric, that you could speak freely and unveil the inquisitor's seal to anyone who dared question you! But you are not.'

'I know,' said Alaric. 'But someone must think of them. Otherwise, what are we? It is the Imperium we are supposed to be protecting, and yet it must suffer for our efforts to protect it. How far can we go before all become madness? Someone must watch over what we do.'

'Leave that to us. And in the meantime, prepare your men. Sarthis Majoris will not be easy, and we are thin on the ground in the Eye. You and your squad will be on your own, whatever you might encounter there.'

'I shall lead their prayers,' said Alaric.

For a while after Nyxos left, Alaric watched Thorne work. Even without eyes, the expression on Hyrk's face was that of a broken man.

It had taken untold sacrifices to break him. But Nyxos was right – that was a dangerous thing to think of. Alaric closed his eyes and meditated, and soon the thoughts were gone.

# OTHER TALES

# ECLIPSE OF HOPE

*by David Annandale*

I stand in the middle of a field of corpses.

We were summoned, and so we have come to Supplicium Secundus. We are winged salvation, but we are a terrible final salvation, and our wings embrace the horizon with fire. We are the Blood Angels. To confront us is to die, and death is my remit, my reality, my unbounded domain. I have known death and defeated it, claimed it as my own. To my cost, to my strength, death is my one gift to bestow, and I am nothing if not generous. But today, my liberality is unwanted, unneeded.

Undone.

The dead on the plain are uncountable, and not a one of them has fallen by my will. I emerged with my brothers from the drop pod to be confronted with this vista. There is, it must be said, a certain perfection to it. This is no mere slaughter or massacre. This is not a battlefield where defeat and victory have been meted out. This is death, simply death. The plain is a vast one, stretching to the distance on three sides, ending in the blurry hulk of Evensong Hive to the north. The skyline is smeared not by distance, but by smoke. It is thick, grey flecked with black, a choking pall of ash. It is the lingering memory of high explosives, incinerated architecture and immolated flesh. The fires have burned themselves out. There is a meaning to this smoke. It is the smoke of *afterwards*. It is the smoke of *finished*. It is the smoke of the only form of peace our era knows, the peace that comes when there is no one left to die.

Wind, sluggish and hot, fumbles at my cloak, breathes its last against my cheek. It pushes at the smoke, making the grey stir over the corpses like an exhausted phantom. There is no sound. There are no trees to rub leaves in a susurrus of mourning. There is no tall grass to wave a benediction. The ground has been chewed into a mulch of mud. Wreckage of weaponry and of humanity is slowly sinking into the mire. In time, all memory of the events of Supplicium Secundus will vanish. Smoke lingers. It does not last.

There is no order to the dead. There is no hint of this having been a war. There is no division between armies, no demarcating line of the clash. There is only brother at brother's throat. By bolter, by sword, by cannon, by hands, this has been the pure violence of all against all. The full panoply of Supplicium's population lies, stilled, before me. I see civilians of both genders, and of all ages. I see the uniform of Unwavering Supplicants, the local planetary defence force.

I see the proud colours of the Mordian Iron Guard, now covered in mud.

We are here because of the Iron Guard. It was their General Spira who called out to us. His message was fragmented and desperate. We have not been in contact with him since that first cry. I look at his men who have killed each other, and doubt that we shall hear from him again.

Over the vox network, reports arrive from the other landing sites. Supplicium Secundus is a compact world, dense in composition and with a handful of small habitable zones at the equator. In each of these areas, a hive has arisen, and it is just outside these hives that our strike forces have landed, a multi-pronged attack designed to inflict simultaneous punishments on the enemy. Sergeant Saleos calls from Hive Canticle, then Sergeant Andarus from Hive Oblation, then Sergeant Procellus from Hive Anthem. It is the same everywhere: endless vistas of death. We came because of heretical rebellion. We came because the Iron Guard was overmatched. We have found only silence.

Behind me, the Stormraven gunship *Bloodthorn* sits on a clear patch of land. I am in the company of Stolas, Epistolary of Fourth Company, Chaplain Dantalion, Standard Bearer Markosius and a tactical squad led by Sergeant Gamigin. Standing a few metres to my left, the sergeant scans the landscape with an auspex. Nothing. Frustration radiates from my battle-brothers. Their hunger for the bloodshed of combat eats at them. Their bolters are still raised, seeking absent targets. They are angry at the dead. Our standard rises above the plain, proud but still in the dying wind, a call to a battle that is long over.

'This is a waste of time,' says Stolas.

'Is it?' I say.

At my tone, Stolas snaps his head around. 'Lord Mephiston,' he begins, 'I–'

I cut him off. 'Do you know what has happened here?'

'No, I–'

'This is something you have seen before?'

This time, he does not try to answer. He simply shakes his head.

'Mordian has slain Mordian,' I point out. '*All* the Mordians are slain. That gives me pause.' I turn from Stolas, losing interest in the reprimand, refocusing my thoughts on the madness before me. And madness is what it is, I realise. Insanity. There is no logic, and this is the flaw in the tapestry of mortality. My eyes range over the infinity of bodies. The perfection I see is, in truth, only the perfection of abomination. 'We are not wasting our time,' I say, speaking more to myself than to Stolas. 'There is a mystery here, and it bears the mark of Chaos.'

Something flickers in my peripheral vision. I look up. Movement in the smoke. A figure approaching. A man.

His movements are jerky, random, yet purposeful in their energy. He cuts back and forth, advancing in no clear direction until he catches sight of us. Then he runs, pounding towards us over the backs of the fallen. He pistons his legs with such force that I can hear the snap of bones beneath his feet. His arms are outstretched as if he were running to embrace us. He emerges from the smoke. His teeth are bared. His face is red, his tendons popping. He is snarling with incoherent rage. What manner of man would charge, so unhesitatingly, and so completely alone, against the Adeptus Astartes? And what manner of man would do so unarmed? Only one sort: a man completely in the grip of madness.

He leaps on Sergeant Gamigin, biting and clawing and spitting. The man cannot possibly hope to break through the Blood Angel's armour. Gamigin stands there, bemused. After a minute, he hauls the man off and holds him out by the scruff of his neck. The snapping, feral creature is a Guardsman. His uniform is in tatters, but enough of it remains to identify him as a colonel.

With a sudden clench of his fist, Gamigin snaps the man's neck and hurls him to the ground. He stomps on the officer's head, smashing it to pulp. Over his helmet's vocaliser comes a growl that is growing in volume and intensity.

'Brother-sergeant?' Chaplain Dantalion asks.

Gamigin whirls on him, drawing his chainsword.

'*Sergeant*.' I use my voice as a whip. Gamigin pauses and turns his head. I step forward and hold his gaze. The lenses of his helmet are expressionless, but mine are the eyes without pity or warmth. I see the taint of the warp gathering around Gamigin like a bruise. The madness that has descended upon him is not the Red Thirst. It is not the manifestation of the Flaw, though our genetic curse may create an increased vulnerability. The tendrils of the warp bruise are deeply tangled in Gamigin's being. There is no salvation for him except what he wills himself. 'Give us space,' I tell the others. 'Take no action.' I do not draw my blade. 'Gamigin,' I say, then repeat his name twice more.

The growl stops. His breathing is heavy, laboured, but suggesting exhaustion, not frenzy. He sheaths his chainsword. 'Chief Librarian,' he says. He shakes his head. 'Forgive me. I don't understand what happened.'

'Try to describe it.'

'I felt disgust for the officer, and then a blind rage. All I wanted to do was kill everyone in sight.'

The silence that follows his statement is a heavy one. I have no need to point out the implications. The madness that killed Supplicium Secundus still lurks, seeking purchase now in our souls. I let my consciousness slip partially into contact with the everywhere non-space of the warp. I anatomise the energies that flow about me. I find the mad rage. It is a background radiation, barely detectable, but omnipresent. The planet is infected. The disease that killed its population has a pulse, an irregular beat like that of an overtaxed heart. I pull back my awareness back to the here and now, but now that I have seen the trace of the plague, I can identify its workings. It scrabbles at the back of my mind. It is an annoyance, barely there but never absent, scratch and scratch and gnaw and claw. It wants in, and it will work at us until, like wind eroding rock, it has its way. It is in no hurry. It is now as fundamental to the planet as its nickel-iron core. It has forever. If we stay here, given enough time, we will all succumb. This is not defeatism. It is realism. A Blood Angel can and must recognise inevitable doom when it is encountered. The doom we face, coded into our very genes, is just as patient, just as certain of its ultimate victory.

The difference is that we can leave Supplicium Secundus and its disease behind. I am loathe to do so without discerning a cause, however.

Then a voice sounds in my ear bead. 'Chief Librarian?' It is Castigon, captain of Fourth Company. He is aboard the strike cruiser *Crimson Exhortation*, which awaits us at high anchor.

'Yes, captain.'

'Do you concur with the other reports? There are no survivors?'

I glance at the dead colonel. 'That is now the case, yes.'

'Is it possible for you to return to the ship?' Castigon does not give me orders. He would never be so foolish. But his request is not unreasonable.

I hesitate, thinking still that perhaps some revelation might await us in the abattoir of the hive before us. 'Is this a matter of urgency?' I ask.

There is a pause. Then: 'Possibly.' I sense no deliberate vagueness on Castigon's part. He sounds genuinely puzzled. From his tone, I would say that he has chosen his answer carefully. After a moment, he speaks again. 'We have found the Mordian fleet.'

*Found.* The fleet should not have needed finding. It should have been in constant communication with us. But there was none when we arrived in the system, and no immediate sign of other ships in orbit around Secundus. 'There is an ominous ring to your words, captain,' I say.

'It is in the nature of this day, Chief Librarian.'

The Supplicium System is perched on the edge of extinction. This is nothing new. It is its very nature. There was once, against all sense, a colony on Supplicium Primus. The small planet is perilously close to the sun, but its gold deposits are vast. Its rate of rotation is the same as its revolution, and one face burns in an eternal day, while the other is forever trapped by night. Along the band of its twilight, a temperate zone permitted habitation until six centuries ago, when a solar storm of terrible magnitude stripped Primus of its atmosphere.

Secundus and Tertius, larger, more distant, and with stronger magnetic fields, weathered the storm, preserving their atmospheres and their civilisations. But here, too, humanity's grip is precarious. The orbits of the two planets are very close, but fall on either edge of the range of temperate distances from their star. Secundus is arid, Tertius frigid. But the Imperium is filled with worlds far more hostile, and they are held for the eternal glory of the Emperor. The Supplicium system has called for help. It must be heeded.

It was. Help came.

And failed.

Aboard the *Crimson Exhortation*, I stand with Castigon in the strategium. There are many tacticarium screens offering information, but our attention is focused on what we can see through the great expanse of armourglass at the front of the bridge. The hololiths and readouts render the meaning of the view clear, but there is a terrible majesty to the unfiltered, uncatalogued, raw vision before us.

The Mordians were but one system over when Supplicium Secundus cried out for help, and so they came. Now their fleet is dead. Its ships move, tumbling past each other along mindless trajectories. Some have collided. Even as we watch, a Sword-class frigate, turning end over end with slow grace, slams into the flank of the Lunar-class cruiser *Manichaean*. The smaller ship breaks in two. Its halves float away, shedding debris. The *Manichaean* has taken a solid blow amidships, but continues its sluggish momentum, its course barely altered.

There is no flare of engines anywhere in the fleet. There are no energy signatures of any kind coming from the ships. This is why the fleet was invisible to us at first. It has become, in effect, a tiny belt of iron asteroids. I look at the tacticarium screens. There is evidence of inter-ship combat. Some of the hulls show signs of torpedo hits and lance burns. Not all, though. In truth, very few. What killed the fleet took place inside the ships.

Castigon despatched squads aboard the *Crimson Exhortation*'s Thunderhawks and Stormravens with the mission to board ships, where practical. The warriors engaged in this task know what we found on the surface of Supplicium Secundus, and they know about the ongoing risk of the plague. They will steel themselves against the temptations of anger. They will hold themselves in check. As the reports come in to the strategium, however, the caution begins to seem excessive. Though the background whisper of rage is ever present, basic discipline is enough to hold it at bay because there are no triggers. The fleet is empty. No troopers have been found. The Mordian army, to a man, descended to Secundus to slaughter itself. All of the bodies on the ships belong to the naval crews, the slaves, and even the servitors. The doom is so powerful, even the mindless succumbed to killing frenzy. As below, so above. Each vessel boarded unveils another tale of mutual carnage. There is nothing left in planetary orbit but dead flesh and dead metal.

'I have never seen the like,' Castigon confesses.

'Neither have I.' The deaths of worlds and entire fleets, yes, I have seen such things. I have been instrumental in bringing about the annihilation of heretical solar systems. But this massacre is different in kind. The only weapons involved appear to have been those borne by the servants of the Imperium, who turned their arms on each other. We have not seen the smallest hint of an opposing force, which makes the enemy all the more dangerous. There *must* be an enemy. What we have seen cannot be due to chance. A warp-thing very like a disease has been spread across Supplicium Secundus and the intervention fleet. I cannot bring myself to believe that it arrived spontaneously. It was brought here. It was unleashed.

'I am recalling the reconnaissance squads,' Castigon says. I nod. He is right to do so. There is nothing more to learn here. I am now given to doubt whether there would, after all, be anything on the planet worth finding.

The question is rendered moot as the last of the gunships is docking with the *Crimson Exhortation*. There is a sudden explosion of vox traffic coming from Supplicium Tertius. The transmissions are bedlam, but the clamour of voices is clear because of the uniformity of the message. Tertius is screaming for help. The *Exhortation* receives pict feeds whose images shake, swerve and break up altogether. They are documents whose very assembly is the expression of desperation. They bear witness to riot, terror, madness. The streets of the cities are turning into massive brawls, the inhabitants swarming over each other like warring ants. Chaos – let me call it by its name – is spreading over the planet like a slick of promethium. The rapidity of the infection is remarkable. When we arrived in-system, we were in contact with the spaceport on Tertius, and there was no hint that anything was awry. Now, a day later, as we race to leave the orbit of Secundus and ride hard for Tertius, I know that we could well be too late. So does every warrior aboard this vessel. We know this, but we shall not allow it to be so. If will alone could move our ship, we would already be at anchor over the planet.

Castigon tries to hail one control node after another. Spaceports, planetary defence force bases, the lord-governor, working his way down to whatever nobles or commanding officers are mentioned in our records of Tertuis. He is forced to give up. Order is rapidly collapsing on Tertius. It occurs to me that the only minds we might save from this disaster will be our own.

The transmissions become more troubling during our journey to Tertius. Between the close orbits of the two planets and their approaching conjunction, our voyage is a short one. It is also far too long. The clamour rises to a shriek, and then the voices plummet into a far louder silence. The pict feeds vanish too. Before they do, they grace us with a mosaic of paroxysm.

As the *Crimson Exhortation* streaks towards a world now covered by an ominous calm, Castigon gathers his officers in the strategium. Stolas and the others create extra space for me around the tacticarium table. I exist, for them as for myself, in a sphere of shadow. I think of it as symbolic, but it appears to have a real force. The living, either pushed or recoiling, are distanced from the unknowable thing in their midst. I am the resurrected and the recently born. The body that was Calistarius walks. The mind that animates it is Mephiston. Calistarius was no more than than a prologue to me.

Stolas asks, 'If all communication has ceased, are we not already too late?'

Castigon does not hesitate. 'Collapse will precede extinction,' he pronounces. 'It will take some weeks for even the most determined population to kill itself. Crisis has befallen the people of Tertius under our watch, and we shall not fail them.'

He speaks for us all. We come to Tertius not as angels of death, but as salvation.

'We must destroy the obscenity,' Sergeant Gamigin says, his voice soft yet edged with righteous anger. It is the anger that will do battle with rage. He has felt the touch of the enemy, and will retaliate with a passion fuelled by justice. He, too, speaks for us all. Whatever foe is attacking Supplicium, be it xenos or daemon, we will find it, and we will exterminate it so utterly, not even its memory shall remain.

And then, in the next second, it finds us first. The collision alert sounds. Helmsman Ipos bellows orders. The ship moves ponderously to evade. We all face forwards. We witness our near destruction.

The *Crimson Exhortation* has come upon a dark ship. It is even more massive than the strike cruiser. Utterly without light, it is a deeper night against the void. It passes over us, and for minutes we are swallowed by a presence that is both shadow and mass. When this happens, when we can no longer see the stars, there is no sense of movement, no sense of the passing of this great vessel. Instead, there is only the great weight of total absence, and it is easy to believe that we have entered an eternal night. The bottom of the stranger's hull brushes the top of our spires, shearing them off. But then the ships part, ours shuddering as Ipos fights to make her angle down just a little bit faster, the other coasting on with dead serenity.

Damage is minimal. The *Exhortation* comes around, and the scanning begins. The other ship appears to be drifting. It is without power, and the

augurs find no trace any sort of radiation. 'From the Mordian fleet?' asks
Stolas. 'Perhaps the crew succumbed to the rage plague as the ship tried
to leave,' he continues.

'No,' I say. I am unsatisfied. The coincidence of our near-collision
nags at me. It is simply too improbable. In the vastness of the void, for
two specks of dust to encounter one another, something more than
chance must be at work, and this ship cannot be just another tomb of
Guardsmen.

The configuration of the ship, beyond its great size, is difficult to make
out at first. This is not just because of its darkness. Though it is solid
enough, there is a profound vagueness to the form.

'That is a battle-barge,' Ipos calls out, startled.

He is correct. He is also wrong. The shape is, it is true, based on that
of an Adeptus Astartes battle-barge. But there are insufficient details, and
much that is there seems wrong. The silhouette is distorted. The hull is
too long, the bridge superstructure too squat, the prow so pointed and
long it is a caricature. No matter how much illumination we pour onto
the ship, it defies the eye. It will not come into proper focus. 'No,' I say.
'It is not a battle-barge. It is the memory of one.' I mean what I say, even
if I am not sure how such a thing has come to be. I am not speaking
metaphorically. What drifts through space before us is a ship as it would
be imperfectly remembered.

Then a detail that is not blurred comes into view. The ship's name:
*Eclipse of Hope*.

'It's a ghost,' Dantalion says.

I frown at the terminology, not least because it seems to be accurate.
The *Eclipse of Hope* is known to me. It is known to all of us. The battle-
barge disappeared during the fifth Black Crusade. Five thousand years
ago. Worse: the ship was a Blood Angels vessel. I dislike its existence
more and more. Its presence here cannot be a coincidence. The power
necessary to orchestrate this 'chance' encounter is immense.

'Is it really the–' Gamigin begins.

'No.' I cut him off. 'That ship is destroyed.' It must be, after five millennia in the empyrean. The thing that bears the name now is a changeling,
though at a certain, dark level, it is intimately linked with the original.
Somehow, the collective memories of the *Eclipse of Hope*, or the memory of a single being of terrible power, achieved such potency that an
embodiment has occurred. Its manifest solidity is extraordinary. I have
never known a warp ghost to have so much material presence. It must
represent a concentration of psychic power such as has never been imagined. It...

I turn to Ipos. 'Can we plot the trajectory of this ship's passage through
the system?'

'A moment, Chief Librarian.' Ipos appears to slump in his throne. I
can see his consciousness slip down the mechadendrites that link his

skull to the machine-spirit and cogitators of the *Crimson Exhortation*. On the bridge, navigation servitors begin chanting numbers in answer to unheard questions. After a few moments, Ipos returns to an awareness of the rest of us. The results of his efforts appear on a tacticarium screen. If the *Eclipse of Hope* has maintained a steady course, she passed near Supplicium Secundus, and through the centre of the Mordian fleet.

'Captain,' I say to Castigon, 'that is the carrier of the rage plague. Destroy it, and perhaps there will be something to save of Supplicium Tertius.'

The phantom remains dark as the *Crimson Exhortation* manoeuvres into position for the execution. The immense shadow does not change direction. Its engines do not flare. No shields or guns flash to life. It coasts, slow leviathan, serene juggernaut, messenger of mindless destruction.

No. No, I am wrong. I am guilty of underestimating the enemy. There is nothing mindless here. The spectre of a Blood Angels battle-barge unleashes a plague whose symptoms might as well be those of the Red Thirst. There is a hand behind this. There is mockery. There is provocation that warrants a retaliation most final. But how to find the hand behind this horror?

That question must wait. The *Eclipse of Hope* is the paramount concern. It has almost destroyed an entire system through its mere presence. If its journey is not stopped, untold Imperial worlds could fall to its madness. The *Eclipse of Hope* must die a second time. Today. Now.

How, I wonder?

The *Crimson Exhortation* is in position. On Castigon's orders, Ipos has taken us some distance from the phantom. The strike cruiser is great dagger aimed at the flank of the battle-barge. Beyond the *Eclipse of Hope*, there is nothing but the void. Supplicium Tertius is still some distance away, but Ipos has placed it safely at our starboard. It is important that there be nothing for a great distance in front of us except our target. Castigon has ordered the use of the nova cannon.

'Conventional weapons will do no harm to a warp ghost,' I tell him.

'It is solid enough to have hit us,' Castigon replies. 'It broke iron and stone. It can be broken in turn.' He turns to Ipos. 'Helmsmaster, are we ready?'

'In a moment, captain.' We have never had the luxury of so passive an opponent on which to use the gun. Ipos takes the opportunity to triple-check all of his calculations and run through his instrument adjustments one more time. When he finds no errors, he signals Castigon.

I can feel the build-up in the ship's machine-spirit. It is excited to be using this weapon again. The nova cannon is a creation of absolute power, because it destroys with absolute efficiency. We are merely its acolytes, awakening it from its slumber whenever we have need of its divine wind.

'Fire,' Castigon orders.

The deck trembles. The entire ship vibrates from the forces unleashed in the firing of the nova cannon. The weapon is almost as long as the hull. The recoil jolts the frame of the *Exhortation*. The cannon is not a weapon of precision, but the shot is as close to point-blank range as is possible with the cannon without destroying ourselves in the process. The projectile flashes across the void, injuring space itself. It hits the *Eclipse of Hope* in the centre of its mass. There is a flare of blinding purity. It is at this moment that the cannon warrants its name. The explosion reaches out for the *Crimson Exhortation*, but falls short. Even so, there is another tremor as the shockwave hits us. We have hurled one of the most powerful weapons in human history at the *Eclipse of Hope*.

It doesn't notice.

The dark serenity is undisturbed. The ghost ship continues its steady drift towards Supplicium Tertius, bringing its plague of final wrath. The bridge and the strategium of the *Crimson Exhortation* are silent as we stare into a future haunted by the *Eclipse of Hope*. Within hours, one ship will have extinguished all human life in a system. It will have done so with no weapons, no struggle, no strategy. Its mere passage will have been enough. And if the phantom should reach other, more crowded systems? Or cross paths with a fleet in transit? Vectors of contagion, visions of hell: my mind is filled by the plague spreading its corroding ifluence over the entire galaxy.

The *Eclipse of Hope* must be stopped. If nothing in the *Crimson Exhortation*'s arsenal will avail, then one alternative remains.

'I will lead a boarding party,' I announce. 'The vessel must be killed from within.'

'Can you walk in a ghost?' Castigon asks.

'It is solid enough to have hit us,' I echo.

'If that is the source of the plague,' Dantalion muses, 'then entering it will be fraught with great moral peril.'

'Most especially for a Blood Angel,' I add. The Flaw will be sorely felt in this situation.

The Chaplain nods. 'The threat does seem rather precisely targeted.'

'That is no coincidence,' I say. 'It is also a risk we must run.'

Castigon nods, but his expression is doubtful. 'How do you plan to kill a ghost?' he asks.

'I will discover that in due course.' I turn to go. 'But shouldn't one revenant be able to destroy another?'

We do not use boarding torpedoes. We cannot be sure that they would be capable of drilling through the spectre's hull. Instead, the *Bloodthorn* transports my squad to the *Eclipse of Hope*. This is to be an exorcism. On board with me, then, are Epistolary Stolas, Sanguinary Priest Albinus, Chaplain Dantalion and Techmarine Phenex. Sergeant Gamigin is present, too. He was insistent upon coming, even though it seems that this mission requires a different set of skills. He has faith enough, however, and having been touched by the dread ship's influence, he is hungry for redemption.

I sit in the cockpit with pilot Orias as the *Bloodthorn* approaches the landing bay door of the battle-barge. The door does not open. This is not a surprise. What is striking is the way in which the details of the hull resolve themselves. They become clearer not because we draw nearer, but because we are looking at them. The sealed bay door has a material presence it did not a few minutes ago. I am aware, in my peripheral vision, that the surrounding hull is still blurry.

Orias has noticed the same phenomenon. 'How is this possible?' he wonders.

'It is feeding on our memories,' I answer. 'We know what a battle-barge looks like. It is supplementing itself with our own knowledge.'

I can see the anger in the set of Orias's shoulder plates. His resentment is righteous. We are witnessing a monstrous blasphemy. Still, we have also learned something. We know more about how our foe works.

Then the unexpected does occur. The door rises. The bay is a rectangular cave, dark within the dark. It awaits us. It welcomes us. We must have something it needs, then. This, too, is valuable to know. If it has needs, it has a weakness.

'This forsaken vessel mocks us,' Orias snarls.

'It is arrogant,' I reply. 'And arrogance is always a mistake.' Show me your weaknesses, I think. Show me your desire, that I might tear you in half. 'Take us in,' I tell Orias. 'Drop us and depart.'

The next few minutes have a terrible familiarity. The gunship enters the landing bay of a battle-barge. I pull back the bulkhead door. We wait a few moments, guns at the ready. Nothing materialises. We are simply staring at an empty bay.

'I do not appreciate being made a fool of,' Gamigin grumbles. His bolter tracks back and forth, aiming at air.

'Guard your temper, brother-sergeant,' I tell him. 'See with how little effort the vessel encourages us to anger.'

We disembark. The banality of our surroundings makes our every move cautious, deliberate. We trust nothing. I am first on the deck, and the fact that it does not reveal itself to be an illusion without substance is almost a surprise. The rest of the squad follows me. We step away from the gunship and form a circle, all approaches covered. The emptiness is full of silent laughter. We ignore it. Our enhanced vision pierces the darkness, and all we see is ordinary deck and walls. The known and the familiar are the danger here. Each element that is not alien is a temptation to a lowered guard. Then, as Orias pulls the *Bloodthorn* out of the bay and away from the *Eclipse*, the darkness recedes. Light blooms. It is the colour of decay.

The light does not come from biolumes, though I see their strips along the ceiling. It is not a true light. It is a phantom of light, as false as anything else about this ship, a memory plucked from our minds and layered into this construct of daemonic paradox. As we move across the bay towards its interior door, the space acquires greater solidity. The ring of our bootsteps on the decking grows louder, less muffled, more confident. Did I see rivets in the metal at first? I do now.

By the time we reach the door, the constructed memory of a battle-barge loading bay is complete. I am no longer noticing new, convincing details. So now I can see the weaknesses of the creation. The ghost has its limitations. The bay seems real, but it is also empty. There are no banks of equipment, no gunships in dock. There is only the space and its emptiness. The *Eclipse of Hope* could not make use of our full store of memories. 'I shall have your measure,' I whisper to the ship. Does it, I wonder, know what it has allowed inside. Does it feel me? Is it capable of regret? Can it know fear?

I shall ensure that it does.

As we step into the main passageway off the bay, the attack begins. It is not a physical one. There are no enemies visible. There is nothing but the empty corridor and the low, sickly grey light. But the ship embraces us now, and does more than feed off our memories. It tries to feed us, too. It feeds us poison. It feeds us our damnation. Walking down the passageway is walking into rage itself. We move against a gale-force psychic wind. It slows our progress as surely as any physical obstacle. It is like pushing against the palm of a giant hand, a hand that wraps massive, constrictor fingers around us. It squeezes. It would force self-control and sanity out. It would force uncontrollable anger in, and in, and in, until we burst, releasing the anger once more in the form of berserker violence.

I feel the anger stir in my chest, an uncoiling serpent. The bone-cold part of myself, that which I cannot in conscience call a soul, holds the serpent down. It also takes further measure of the ship. There are still limits to the precision of the attack. That is not the Black Rage that I am suppressing. It is too mundane an anger. It is potent. It is summoned by a force powerful enough to give substance to the memory of a battle-barge. But it is not yet fully aligned with the precise nature of our great Flaw. That will come, I have no doubt. But we have the discipline to defeat anger of this sort.

I glance at my brothers. Though there is tension and effort in their steps, their will is unbowed.

Stolas says, 'The light is becoming brighter.'

'It is,' I agree. Despite our resistance, the ship is growing stronger. Our mere presence is giving it life. The light, as corrupt as it was in the bay, has assumed a greater lividity. We can see more and more of the passageway. The ship cements its details with more and more confidence. The greater visibility should make our advance easier. It does not.

The phantom's mimicry is uncanny. With every incremental increase of illumination comes a further revelation of perfect recall. This is the true ghost of the *Eclipse of Hope*. We are travelling one of the main arteries, and the phantom has a complex memory to reconstruct: stone-clad walls and floor, gothic arches, vaulted bulkheads. They are all here. Even so, as accurate as the recreation is, it remains a ghost. There is something missing.

Phenex's machinic insight gives him the answer first. He raps a fist against the starboard wall. The sound of ceramite against marble is what I would expect. Yet it makes me frown.

Albinus has noticed something, too. 'That isn't right,' he says.

'There's a delay,' the Techmarine explains. 'Very slight. The sound is coming a fraction of a second later than it should.'

'The response is a conscious one,' I say. 'It is a form of illusion. That wall is not real. Your gauntlet is banging against the void, brother.'

I spot Gamigin staring at his feet, as if expecting the surface on which he walks to disintegrate without warning. If we are successful here, he may not be far wrong.

From behind his skull helm, Dantalion casts anathema on the ship. His voice vibrates with hatred.

'Save your breath,' I tell him. 'Wait until there is something to exorcise.'

'There already is,' he retorts. 'This entire ship.'

'Have you the strength to spread your will over such a large target?' I ask him. 'If so, you have my envy.'

Dantalion will not appreciate my tone. That is not my concern. What *is* my concern is that my team be as alert and focussed as possible. The ship inspires anger, and I do not think it cares in what direction that anger is expressed. Dantalion's hatred of the *Eclipse of Hope* is normal, praiseworthy, and proper. It is also feeding the vessel. Unless we find a target that we can overwhelm somehow, the Chaplain's broad, sweeping anger will do us more harm than good.

We are making our way toward the bridge. This is not the result of considered deliberation. We exchanged looks at the exit from the landing bay, and of one accord set off in this direction. There is nothing to say that we will find what we seek there, or anywhere else, for that matter, on this ship. But the bridge is the nerve centre of any vessel. We seek a mind. The bridge is the logical place to begin.

It troubles me that we are taking action based on nothing stronger than a supposition. I cannot detect any direction to the warp energies that make up the *Eclipse of Hope*. There does not seem to be any flow at all. I understand the nature of the immaterium. I know it better, perhaps, than anyone in the Imperium, save our God-Emperor. Yet the substance of the *Eclipse* defies me. It appears inert. This cannot be true, not with the intensifying light, the consolidation of the illusion, and the gnawing and scratching at our minds. There is something at work here. Perhaps I can find no current, no flow, no core because these things do not exist yet. The effects of the ship are those of a field, one that may extend the entire length and breadth of the vessel. 'It isn't strong enough yet,' I mutter.

'Chief Librarian?' Albinus asks.

'The ship is still feeding,' I say. 'We cannot be sure of its full nature until it has gorged. Perhaps then it will act.'

'Then we can kill it?' Gamigin asks.

I nod. 'Then we can kill it.'

Down the length of the battle-barge we march. We ignore the side passageways that open on either side. We stick to the direct route, always pushing against the ethereal but implacable rage. Our tempers are fraying, the effort needed to suppress flare-ups of anger becoming stronger by the hour. And there is more. There is something worse. The more I strain, the more I find traces of an intelligence. It does not drive the ship. It is the ship itself. It is as if this were truly a revenant. The knowledge is frustration, hovering at the edge of tactical usefulness, a buzzing hornet in my consciousness. If the ship is sentient, then I must cut out its mind. To do that, I must locate it. But the *Eclipse of Hope* is still too quiescent. It is a beast revelling in its dreams of rage, not yet prepared to wake. It torments us. It does not fight us.

The walk from the bay to the bridge is long. There is no incident, no attack. The march would be tedium itself, were it nor for the slow, malevolent transformation of the ship around us. We are presented with the spectacle of the familiar as evil, the recognisable as threat. The more the ship resembles what it remembers itself to be, the more we are seeing a manifestation of its power. The light is brighter yet. The growing clarity remains in the nature of a bleak epiphany. There is nothing to see but death, embodied in the form of the ship itself. Everything that presents itself to our eyes does so with a cackling malignity, pleased that it imitates reality so well. It does so only as a show of force. Everything that appears can be taken away. I am sure of this. The ship is a dragon, inhaling. The immolating exhalation is imminent.

We are one deck down, and only a few minutes away from the bridge when the dragon roars. The light dims back to the grey of a shroud. The ship now has a better use for the energy it is leaching from us. It is awake. The sudden explosion of consciousness is painful. The ghost turns its full awareness upon us.

Can a ship smile? Perhaps. I think it does, in this very second.

Can it rage?

Oh, yes.

The *Eclipse of Hope* hates, it angers, it blasts its laughing wrath upon those beings who would dare invade it, the intruders it deems little more than insects and that it lured here in its dreaming. It has fed upon us, and now would complete its feast with our final dissolution.

Dissolution comes from the walls. For a moment, they lose all definition. Chaos itself billows and writhes. And the ship can also sing. The corridor resounds with a fanfare of screaming human voices and a drum-beat that is the march of wrath itself. Then the walls give birth. Their offspring have hides the colour of blood. Their limbs are long, grasping, with muscles of steel stretched over deformed bones. Their skulls are mocking, predatory fusions of the horned goat and the armoured helm. Their eyes are blank with glowing, pus-yellow hatred. They are bloodletters, daemons of Khorne, and the sight of their arrival has condemned mortal humans beyond counting to a madness of terror.

As for my brothers and myself, at last we have a foe to fight. We form a circle of might and faith. 'Now, brothers,' Dantalion says. 'Now this vessel of the damned shows its true nature. Strike hard, steadfast in the light of Sanguinius and the Emperor!'

'These creatures, sergeant,' I tell Gamigin, 'you are at full liberty to kill.'

It takes him a moment to respond, unused to any expression of humour on my part. 'My thanks, Chief Librarian,' he says, and sets to work with a passion.

The bloodletters wield ancient swords, their blades marked by eldritch designs and obscene runes. They come at us from all sides, their snarls drowned out by the choir of the tortured and the infernal beat, beat, beat of a drum made of wrath. The music is insidious. It pounds its way deep into my mind. I know what it is trying to do. It would have us march to the same beat, meet rage with rage, crimson armour clashing with crimson flesh until, with the loss of our selves to the Flaw, there is no distinguishing Blood Angel from daemon. The bloodletters open their fanged maws wide, tongues whipping the air like snakes, tasting the rage and finding it good. They swing their swords. We meet them with our own. Power sword, glaive and chainsword counter and riposte. Blade against blade, wrath against rage, we answer the attack. Monsters fall, cut in half. The deck absorbs them, welcoming them back to non-being. And for every foul thing we despatch, two more burst from the walls.

War is feeding on war.

'This will end only one way,' Dantalion says at my side. His brings his crozius down on a daemon's skull, smashing it to mist. 'It will not be our victory.'

He is not being defeatist. He is speaking a simple truth. The corridor before us is growing crowded with the fiends. They scramble over each other in their eagerness to tear us apart. They will come at us forever, created by our very acts of destroying their brothers. Bolter fire blasts them apart. Blades cut them down. And where two stood, now there are ten.

'We cannot remain here,' says Albinus.

Even as he speaks, the ceiling unleashes a cascade of bloodletters. They fall upon us with claws and teeth, seeking to overwhelm through the weight of numbers. We throw them to the ground, trample them beneath our boots. I feel the snapping of unholy bones and know I have inflicted pain on a blasphemy before the daemon is reabsorbed.

Dantalion staggers, gurgles rasping from his vocaliser. He must have looked up at the wrong moment. A bloodletter has thrust its sword underneath his helm. With a snarl of effort, the daemon rams the blade home, piercing Dantalion's brain. Our Chaplain stiffens, then falls. Gamigin roars his outrage and obliterates the bloodletter with a single blow of his chainsword.

The rage grows. We fight for vengeance now, too. The harder we struggle, the closer we come to dooming ourselves. The onslaught of bloodletters is a storm surge, and the faster we kill them, the faster they multiply.

'To the bridge,' Gamigin calls out. 'That is our destination, and we can make a stand there for as long as it takes to exorcise this abomination.'

'No,' I answer. 'Not the bridge.' With the phantom now fully awake, I have looked at the tides of its thought. We are on the wrong path. The core of this memory-construct is not the bridge. It is, rather, a place of much knowledge. 'The librarium.'

The ship hears me. Until this moment, its strategy was one of venomous attrition, grinding us down in stages, feeding on the ferocity of our skill at destruction. Then I announce our goal, and things change. The *Eclipse of Hope* now desires our immediate deaths. To the torrent of daemons, the walls and ceiling add their own attack. The corridor distorts beyond the most delirious memory of a battle-barge interior. Hands reach for us. They are colossal, large enough to clutch and crush any of us. They are veined, the hands of a statue, and though they are stone, they seem to flow. They are not a memory; they are a creation, the spectre of art, their reality created from microsecond to microsecond. They are scaled talons, both reptile and raptor. They are clawed and hooked, with barbs on every knuckle. They are the concept of *ripping* given embodiment, but they are massive too, and what they do not tear into ribbons, they will smash.

There is a hand descending directly above me. It becomes a fist. The ship would see me pulped. It is showing me that it knows fear. It believes I can do it harm.

I shall prove it right.

The consciousness that holds the ship in this simulacrum of reality is not the only force capable of creation. The warp is mine, too. I walk in a ghost, but I am the Lord of Death. My will shapes un-matter, gives direction to the energy of madness. The air shimmers as a pane of gold flashes into being over our heads. The ceiling's hands smash into it and break apart. I pour my essence into the shield. I turn it into a dome. The daemons caught along the line of its existence are bisected. Then the dome surrounds us. Its perimeter extends a bare metre beyond our defensive circle.

I am channelling so much of my will into maintaining the shield against the hammering assaults of the bloodletters and the fists of the walls that I am barely present in my body itself. Yet I must walk. We cannot stay here. I must reach the librarium.

'Chief Librarian,' Albinus says, 'can you hear me?'

Albinus knows me best of those present. More properly, he knew Calistarius well, and seems to have taken on a quest to understand the being that rose from his friend's grave. Albinus's goal is laudable, if hopeless. Even so, there are times when he does seem to have some real insight into the realities of my being. When I nod, he says, 'We must move. Can you walk and maintain the shield?'

The blows of the enemy are torrential. Given time and strength, they will smash any barrier. The phantom is very strong. I must maintain my focus on the reality of the shield. I speak through gritted teeth: 'Barely.'

He nods. 'Then let us take our turn, brother,' the sanguinary priest says.

*Brother*. I am rarely addressed by that word. With good reason. Calistarius was a brother among others, to the degree any psyker can truly be accepted in the ranks of the Adeptus Astartes. But Calistarius is dead, and when Albinus says *brother*, he is addressing a shade, one with far less substance than the hellship in which we fight. Calistarius will not return. Mephiston walks in his stead. I am a Blood Angel. I would destroy any who would question my loyalty. But *brother*? That bespeaks a fellowship that is barred to me.

Let that pass. Albinus is correct in the matter of strategy. 'Agreed,' I manage.

'Show us our route,' he tells me.

I turn back the way we came. The effort is huge. I am holding back not just dozens of simultaneous physical attacks, but also the entire psychic pressure of the ship. Turning my body is like altering the rotation of a planet.

Albinus moves in front of me. The rest of the squad takes up a wedge formation. I relax the shield. It becomes porous, but doesn't evaporate completely. I can reinforce it at a moment's notice. The squad charges forwards to meet the rush of the bloodletters. Stolas creates his own shield. The epistolary is a powerful psyker. I have seen him devastate lines of the enemy with lightning storms worthy of myth. But he is not what I am, and though we move in an environment woven entirely of the warp, our powers are not increased. The ship is a parasite that has swallowed its host. So the shield Stolas raises slows the bloodletter horde, but cannot stop it. Our blunt spearhead collides with the foaming tide. We shove our way through the daemonic host for a dozen metres before their numbers threaten to swamp us once again. I snap the shield back to full strength, giving us space and a chance to regroup. When Albinus gives me the signal, I pull back into my physical self, and we move forwards.

This is how we advance. It is our only way, a painfully slow stutter of stops and starts. We travel thousands of metres in this manner. The tally of our slaughter lengthens with every step, and every butchered daemon, every act of wrath, is another drop of psychic plasma for the *Eclipse of*

*Hope*'s unholy engines. Our journey through the ship will be the path of our damnation if I am wrong about what I will find in the librarium.

We wend our way deep into the heart of the ship. The repository of archives, history and knowledge is not in a spire, as it is on the *Crimson Exhortation*. Rather, it waits on the lowest deck, a few hundred metres fore of the enginarium. To guide us there, I follow rip tides of the warp. The phantom is awake and blazing with power. It cannot hide the patterns of its own identity now, any more than a human could will away the whorls of fingerprints. By acting against us, the *Eclipse of Hope* exposes itself to my scrutiny and my judgement.

We reach the librarium. A massive iron door bars our passage. Its relief work is an allegory of dangerous knowledge. It announces what lies in the chambers beyond, and it warns the uninitiated away. Tormented human figures fall in worship or agony before immense tomes. Daemons are not represented in the art – no Imperial ship would sully itself with such an image. Instead, the danger is depicted as twisting vines and abstract lines that tangle and pierce the figures. The risks that lurked in the archives of the original librarium must be merely the shadows of what awaits now. On the other side of the door lies the consciousness of the ship. I can feel the pulse of its fevered thoughts beating through the walls. The rhythm matches that of the drums, still pounding and echoing through the defiled corridors. Are the thoughts the source of the daemonic march, or does the music come from a darker place and a greater master, shaping the mind of the ghost? I have no answer. All I need is the destruction of both.

Is that all I desire? No. It is not. But desire is a treacherous master.

'Albinus,' I manage, the shield still at full strength.

'Chief Librarian?'

'I will need Stolas.' The strength in that chamber will be massive. We must hit it with all the power we possess.

'We will stand and hold,' Phenex says.

'For Sanguinius and the Emperor,' Gamigin adds.

The wedge formation faces down the corridor. My fellow Blood Angels have their backs to the door. Once Stolas and I cross that threshold, their only defences will be physical. It will be enough. They will hold back the ocean of Chaos with bolter and blade for as long as Stolas and I require to triumph or fall.

I lower the shield. I grasp the ornate bronze handle of the door. When I pull, I encounter, to my surprise, no resistance. Is this surrender? I wonder. Or perhaps the ship is marshalling its resources for the true fight about to begin. No matter. Stolas and I enter the librarium. The door swings shut behind us. The boom of iron against stone has a different quality to it than the sounds in the corridor. It takes me a moment to identify what has changed. The answer comes as I take in the sights of the librarium.

*This chamber, and this chamber alone, is real.*

Stolas and I move through a vast cavern of damned scholarship. We are funnelled along a path between towering stacks of scrolls, parchments and tomes. The path takes us towards an open space at the heart of the chamber. This is not a recreated memory. This is not a product of the warp, or at least, not in the same sense as the rest of the ship. The chamber itself is of familiar construction. It could be a librarium on a true battle-barge. There is a fresco on the domed ceiling: a vision of Sanguinius, wings outstretched, sword in hand, descending in fury, bringing light and blood to the enemies of the Emperor. But the fresco has been defaced. Huge, parallel gouges, the claws of some giant fiend, cut diagonally through our primarch. Runes have been splashed in blood over the painting. I look away from the obscenity. I have no desire or need to read it.

Ah, says a whisper in the furthest recesses of my mind. *Can* you read it, then?

I sense that the stacks have changed since the ship vanished five millennia ago. They are huge. The volume of texts is astounding. The stone shelves are bursting with manuscripts. The floor is littered with lost sheets of vellum. Some curator has been at work here, accumulating works with obsession but little care. And yet there has been care enough to preserve the librarium itself after the rest of the ship has died. This space is the grain of sand around which a daemonic pearl has formed. The mind of the ship needs this core of reality in order to give a semblance of the same to the phantom. It must be the key that has allowed the *Eclipse of Hope* to escape the empyrean and spread its plague through the materium.

The centre of the librarium has become a dark shrine. There are four lecterns here. They are huge, over two metres high, created for beings larger than Space Marines. They are wrought of a fusion of iron and bone, the two elements distinguishable yet inseparable, a single substance that shrieks the obscenity of its creation. The designs are the product of nightmare: intertwining figures, human and xenos, all agonised, their mouths distorted that they might howl blasphemous curses at a contemptuous universe. Sinuous coils, both serpent and whip, scaled and barbed, weave between and around the bodies, carrying venom and pain. I think I see movement in the corner of my eye. I look at the forged souls more closely. I was not mistaken. They are moving, so slowly a year would pass while a back is being broken. But they are moving. And they are suffering.

The lecterns are coated in thick layers of dry, blackened blood. Here, too, there is movement. Slow, glistening drops work their way down the frameworks, adding to the texture of torture with the same gradual inexorability as the growth of stalactites. I raise my eyes. The blood is coming from the books.

The books. These things cannot be truly be called by that name, no more than the Archenemy can be called *human*. They are gargantuan, over a metre on each side. They rest on iron and bone, but they are bound in iron and flesh. Metal thorns pierce their spines. The sluggish gore crawls, drip by endless drip, down the pain of the lecterns. The flesh of the covers has not been tanned into leather. Rather, it is black and green and violet. It is in a state of ongoing, but never completed, decomposition. It is also not dead. There is a just-visible thrumming, as of flesh taut against the stress of torture.

Through the walls, I can make out the muffled beat of combat. There is not much time, but I must be cautious. I must be sure of my actions, or I will doom us all. I must be so very, very careful, because of the other thing in the chamber. There is a dais in the very centre of the librarium, surrounded by the four lecterns. I have avoided looking closely at it, thinking perhaps my first glance deceived me, and if I turned away, the illusion would vanish. It has not.

'Lord Mephiston...' Stolas begins. He is transfixed.

'I know,' I tell him. I turn and face what has been waiting.

Spread out on the dais is an ancient star chart. It is on fading, brittle parchment. The map is the only part of this monstrous exhibit that has always belonged to the librarium. My finger traces the name of the system depicted: Pallevon. Then I look up.

A statue sits on the dais. There is nothing grotesque about its material. It is simply bronze. It does not move. It does not cry out.

It is me.

The figure stands with weapons sheathed and holstered. Its expression is calm. It should not exist. Yet it is as real as all of the other objects in this room. It is not a ghost, but it haunts me like one.

I have been manoeuvred like a piece in a game of regicide. The ship's desire to kill me when I declared the librarium as my goal was a feint. It simply reinforced my determination to reach this point. For a moment, I am blinded by a red haze of rage. Then the cold darkness within me recognises the trap, and dampens the fire. I pull back.

'What does this mean?' Stolas asks.

'It means we were expected. It does not mean that our mission changes.'

'And this?' he points at the star chart.

'Another lure.' We must ignore it.

Stolas peers more closely at the statue. 'Look at the eyes,' he says.

I had thought the gaze was neutral. I was wrong. The eyes look just to my left. I turn in that direction to stare at one of the lecterns. I approach it. The book, immense, pulsing with the pain of its knowledge, waits for me to turn back its daemon-wrought cover.

Stolas turns around, taking in not just the four massive tomes, but the rest of the collection as well. 'So much knowledge...' he says. His vocaliser turns the whisper into a wind of static.

'Dire knowledge, all of it,' I say.

'Think of what we could do to the enemies of the Imperium with such insight,' Stolas argues.

He does not need to tempt me thus. I feel that draw on my own. I reach out to the book before me. I open it.

There is a moment. A fraction of a second so minute as to defy measure. I experience it, notwithstanding: a fragmentary impression of the being who last touched this book. A towering horned shadow. Eyes that burn crimson with malevolence and knowledge and... something else... a memory, a memory so specific that it is a weapon aimed at the soul of the Blood Angels. A memory that leads to a future that crushes our Chapter in a clawed fist.

The shard of vision vanishes. In its place is a yawning promise. The book is abyssal. It will tell me all. Whatever questions I have, they will be answered. Omniscience is within my reach. There will be no more mysteries. All of the past, all of the present, all of the future – everything will be made known to me.

My identity made clear. What is it that lies coiled in my depths? I shall know that, too.

The means to total illumination, and total power, are not complicated. I simply need to start reading.

The pull is beyond any concept of temptation. I am in the gravitational jaws of a black hole. The event horizon is long past. There is no escape, and why should I wish it?

Yet I do. I refuse. My will pushes back. It is the will that pulled me from the Black Rage, that raised me from the my tomb of rubble. It is the will that shapes the energies of the empyrean to my ends. Power? I am the Lord of Death. What is that, if not power most dread?

Is this will entirely my own? Is it entirely *me*?

No answer. No matter. I see the room with clarity again, and step back from the book.

To my right, Stolas is clutching one of the other tomes. I call to him, but it is far too late. His face is wracked by dark ecstasy. He turns his eyes my way, eyes that have become a glistening black. His body is shaking. His speech is slurred. 'Oh,' he says. 'Oh, you must know...'

'No, brother,' I tell him. 'We must not.'

The shimmering in his eyes leaks down his cheeks. The tears become tendrils. The tendrils become worms. He is lost.

Did the accursed book promise me power? Let me show it what power means. I call the warp to me. I force it to do my bidding. I accumulate the energy within me until the straining potential threatens to tear me apart. And when I am ready, as time ticks from before the act to the act itself, I know that the *Eclipse of Hope* has its own terrible moment. It senses what is about to happen. It finally does know fear.

I strike. And there is nothing but fire.

I burned the librarium to ash. I was the centre of a purging sun. When I was done, the mind of the ship was but a memory itself. Mine. Stolas, too, was gone, incinerated. Though I know his soul had already been taken, I know also that my inferno destroyed his body and his gene-seed. His trace and his legacy are gone forever, and his name, then, must be added to the register of my guilt. I left the scoured chamber to find my brothers standing in an empty, dark corridor. The bloodletters vanished when I killed the mind.

The vessel is inert once more.

But it has not vanished. Even now, after we have returned to the *Crimson Exhortation*, and nothing alive and sentient walks the halls of the *Eclipse of Hope*, the ghost ship remains intact, an apparition that will not return to the night from whence it came. The crisis on Supplicium Tertius has abated. The survivors are no longer killing each other. So the ship no longer appears to be a carrier of plague.

But we cannot destroy it. The fact of its continued existence will haunt us with the possibility of further harm. It is a memory that refuses to be forgotten. So, too, are the books. Those are my personal ghosts. I fought the temptation. I destroyed the unholy. But what might I have learned? What if I could have absorbed those teachings and stayed whole, unlike Stolas? What if the absolute self-knowledge from which I turned was the door, through darkness, to salvation?

What have I thrown away?

I will think on these things. But not now. There is something more immediate to confront. The being that launched the *Eclipse of Hope* on its voyage has not finished with us yet. We are still being moved on the regicide board. The *Exhortation* has received a message. A brother, long though lost, has returned to us.

He awaits us in the Pallevon system.

As our great ship rushes us to a destiny five thousand years in the preparation, I attune my mind to the empyrean. I am not surprised to hear, grinding over the flows of the warp, the sound of eager laughter.

# TORTURER'S THIRST

## Andy Smillie

*'I must know. I must know what lies beneath the flesh, what powers a man to draw breath when death is so much easier. I must inflict pain to level you, to strip away your falsehoods and pretences. I must show you yourself, so that I may know your secrets.'*

– Torturer's saying

Appollus echoed his jump pack's roar as it drove him downwards. He landed hard, scattering a mortar formation and crushing their spotter beneath his ceramite boots. The enemy's ribs cracked, the bone fragments spearing his innards while his organs drowned in blood. Appollus grinned. The other six members of his Death Company slammed to the earth in ordered formation around him. The backwash of their jump packs scoured the flesh from a slew of enemy warriors, filling the air with the rancid tang of burned flesh.

'Bring them death!'

Appollus opened fire with his bolt pistol, dispatching a trio of the enemy in a burst of mass-reactive rounds. The Brotherhood of Change were everywhere. A teeming mass of mauve robes and onyx masks, they pressed towards him with unrelenting fervour. Appollus thumbed the fire selector to full-auto and fired again. A swathe of Brotherhood cultists died, their bodies blown apart, pulped by the explosive rounds. Yet they did not falter. Heedless of the losses inflicted upon them, the Brotherhood lashed out at Appollus like men possessed. The tip of a barbed pole-arm cracked against his shoulder guard. He side-stepped a thrust meant to disembowel him and jammed the muzzle of his bolt pistol into his attacker's torso. A shower of limbs and flesh-chunks rained over his armour as he pressed forwards, spattering his black battle plate crimson.

The sharp tang of blood was suffocating. It was a siren's call to the killer inside him, beckoning him onwards into the press of flesh. Another blade flashed towards him. He parried the downwards stroke with his crozius, and smashed his bolt pistol into the faceplate of another of the Brotherhood. The blow caved in the side of the cultist's skull. Lines of brain-viscera clung to Appollus's bolt pistol as he swung it round and opened fire on the endless mauve horde.

The Brotherhood had been human once. Scholars from the librarium world of Onuris Siti, their counsel was sought by all who could afford it, from cardinals to Planetary Governors. But the Sitilites had turned their back on the Emperor and his Imperium. They had sworn dark oaths to darker gods, burned their librariums to the ground and denounced the teaching of the Ecclesiarchy.

Appollus snarled as he gunned down another group of attackers. He could smell the taint of the warp upon them; it saturated them, drifting from their pores like a foul poison. A warning sigil flashed on his helmet display. He was down to his last round. He blinked it away with a snarl, and blew the head from a bulbous assailant whose torso was at odds with his rawboned legs – only a raw aspirant was unable to discern his ammo count by the weight of his weapon. Appollus mag-locked the pistol to his armour, and buried his combat knife into the distended neck of the nearest cultist.

Behind them, the guns of the Cadian Eighth continued to fire in a desperate attempt to hold the line against the Brotherhood's advance. The *snap* of a hundred thousand lasguns crackled in the air like lightning, as a thousand heavy bolters continued their thunderous chatter.

Ahead of him, the Death Company were pushing forwards. Wielding their chainswords two-handed, they hacked a path through the Brotherhood's ranks. Orphaned limbs tumbled through the air like morbid hail, ripped from ruined torsos by the adamantium teeth of the Death Company's weapons. Still the enemy came, clawing and grabbing at their arms and legs. For all their rage-fuelled vigour, Appollus knew his brothers would eventually be pulled to the ground, drowned beneath the tide of flesh assailing them.

Appollus threw his arms out, his ceramite-clad limbs smashing ribs and shattering jaws. They needed to regain the initiative, to maintain momentum.

'With me!' Appollus growled over the vox.

He bent his knees, angling his jump pack towards the enemy at his rear. With a thought, he activated the booster. The cultist behind him died in a flash, incinerated in a gout of flame. Dozens more flailed around screaming, their flesh running from their bodies in a thick soup.

The raging thrusters threw Appollus forwards into a wall of enemy. He tucked his chin into his pauldron, using the shoulder guard as a battering ram. Bone broke, and necks snapped as he battered through the press of Brotherhood. A red status sigil blinked on his display – fuel zero. He pressed the release clasp and the booster fell away. Momentum carried him onwards another ten paces. He rolled, knocking over a handful of assailants, before rising to his feet to begin the slaughter anew.

'Chaplain Appollus.' Colonel Morholt's voice crackled in his ear.

He ignored it and pushed onwards. His weapons blurred around him as he hacked off limbs on instinct. His blood hummed in his veins, his twin-hearts bellowing, choirmasters propelling him through a chorus of death. This was what is was to be a Flesh Tearer. To lose oneself in the joy of slaughter. To maim. To kill. He eviscerated an enemy and tore the midriff out of another, stamping his boot down to crack the skull of a cultist whose leg he'd removed a heartbeat before. Thick gore splattered his armour, blood pooled around his gorget.

He felt lighter without the jump pack, and his progress through the forest of bodies quickened. But the Death Company were already ahead of him, churning the Brotherhood into fleshy gobbets that slid from their armour like crimson sleet.

'Chaplain, you've extended the cordon. Pull back to your sector.'

Appollus barely registered the colonel's pleas, his attention fixed on the lumbering brute that was trying to bludgeon him to death with a pair of crackling warhammers. Hemmed in on all sides by the press of enemy warriors, Appollus had no room to manoeuvre. He blocked his attacker's opening swing with his crozius, the weapons sparking off one another in a haze of blistering energy. Appollus felt his feet slide back under the force of the blow. The earth beneath his feet was slick, churned into a thick paste by constant bombardment and the hundred score warriors who had charged across it. He growled, sinking his weight through his knees to steady himself. The brute advanced on him, swinging again. Appollus stepped inside its guard and brought his head up into its jaw, grinning as he heard the sickening snap of bone. He reversed the strike, driving his forehead down into the brute's face. The blow cracked the creature's faceplate, and it cried out in pain as the obsidian fragments embedded themselves in its skin. The brute dropped its weapons, reaching up to pull the shards from its flesh.

'Die now!'

Appollus threw an uppercut into his foe's chest. It spasmed hard, blood pouring from its broken mouth as the Chaplain wrapped his fingers around its heart. Appollus squeezed the organ, grinning as it burst in his grasp. He tore his hand free, beheading another of the Brotherhood before the brute had even collapsed to the ground.

'Hold position! Emperor damn you, hold the line!'

Colonel Morholt's voice became like a persistent whine in Appollus's ear. He growled in response, deactivating his comm-feed even as he tore his crozius from another of the arch-enemy's pawns. His duty was to lead the Death Company in battle, to direct their fury to the heart of the enemy. Their rage was beyond his means to restrain, it could be sated only by blood. They had no place anywhere but at the enemy's throat. Brother Luciferus had made that plain before dispatching them to this accursed planet. Appollus grinned. Never had the Flesh Tearers' Chief Librarian spoken a greater truism. To pull back now would be to invite the Death Company's wrath upon Morholt and the rest of his regiment.

A persistent warning sigil flashed on Appollus's retinal display as his armour's auspex detected incoming artillery.

'Morholt,' Appollus snarled.

Locking his crozius to his armour, he grabbed the nearest brute by its head. The hulking traitor voiced a throttled scream as Appollus threw himself to the ground, dragging the unfortunate down on top of him. His helmet's audio dampeners activated to preserve his hearing a heartbeat before a staccato of explosions burst around him.

'I am his weapon, he is my shield!' Appollus bellowed the mantra through gritted teeth as the ground shuddered under multiple detonations.

The siege shells exploded in coarse bellows that threw dirt and malformed bodies into the air like sparks burning away from a firecracker. Flame washed over him, incinerating the screaming brute sheltering him and burning the litany parchments from his armour.

The heat liquefied the ground beneath him, his armoured bulk sinking further into the muddied earth. Biometric data scrolled across his retinal display as the bombardment ended. The concussive force of the blasts had strained his organs, but his armour had held and he was already healing.

A pair of faded ident-tags told him Urim and Rashnu had taken direct hits, blown into fleshy rain by the artillery barrage.

'Rest well, brothers.'

When the battle was over, Appollus would gather whatever fragments of their armour remained and take them to the Basilica of Remembrance. They would be mourned, as would the loss of their gene-seed.

'Cease fire!' Appollus growled into the vox.

A burst of static shot back in answer.

Snarling, he pushed himself up out of the dirt, cursing as his gauntlets slid into the earthy soup.

'Hold your fire, Morholt, or by the blood I will kill you myself!'

Appollus surveyed the destruction. The enemy dead carpeted the landscape, like purple reeds flattened by the wind. The remaining four members of his Death Company were scattered among a line of shallow craters to his left flank.

Las-fire flickered from the edge of the blast zone. The Brotherhood were starting to rally. An autocannon shell glanced his pauldron, spinning him down into the mud.

'Forwards!' Appollus roared as he regained his footing.

But the Death Company were already charging towards the Brotherhood, bolters barking in their hands as they advanced into a hail of las-fire.

'We are anger. We are death.'

Fire burned in Appollus's limbs as his legs pumped him towards the foe. Ignorant of the las-fire that licked his armour and the solid-state rounds that threw up dirt in his path, he charged towards the wall of enemy.

'Our wrath knows no succour.'

Ten more paces and he would be among them. His gauntlets would drip in entrails as he ripped apart their blasphemous forms.

'Our blades know no–'

Something unseen struck Appollus in the chest, flipping him to the ground. He landed hard, a crack snaking along his breastplate. He groaned as he lifted his head, blinking hard to clear his vision. Pain suppressors flooded his system but did nothing to quell the searing pain in his skull.

The enemy stopped firing.

Grunting with effort, Appollus got to his feet. He stumbled forwards, but the ground swung up to meet him. Blood filled his mouth as his head struck the ground. Roaring with frustration, he pushed himself onto all fours. He would crawl if he had to. Only death would stay his wrath.

Ahead the ranks of the Brotherhood stood immobile, taunting him.

Behind his skull helm, Appollus's face was set in a snarl of pure hate. He cast his eyes over the traitors, searching for sign of his Death Company. A flash of mirror-black armour among the mauve robes caught his eye. He made to look again, but in the same instant was yanked from the ground, tossed into the air and slammed back down with bone-breaking force.

Pain burned through him, as though a molten needle was being threaded into his very marrow. He couldn't move, his limbs pinned to the earth, trapped beneath a huge, invisible weight. Patches of hoarfrost rimed his armour, spitting as they cracked and reformed. The stench of sulphur choked the air around him.

*Psyker.*

The thought formed in Appollus's mind the briefest of instants before he glimpsed the mirror-black armour once more and darkness took him.

Filmy water dripped onto Appollus's face, stirring him. His head ached in a way he'd not felt since Seth had struck him in the duelling cages. Easing his eyes open, he saw thick iron chains looped around his ankles. He was naked, strung up like butchered cattle, his head a metre from the ground. His wrists were shackled too, fixed beneath him by a chain that ran through a loop set into the bare rock of the floor. Appollus strained at his bonds, his muscles rippling with effort as he tried in vain to break the irons from the floor.

'The blood grant me my vengeance,' he spat, growling with frustration.

The light in the chamber was poor, uneven. The faint smell of promethium hung in the air, drifting from oil burners. Appollus strained his eyes, snatching glimpses of his surroundings in the flickering lamplight. The chamber was perhaps five metres across, its walls pocked and irregular, hewn from solid rock by axe and pick. The air was damp, and algae and moss clung to the walls in thick patches.

There was no sign of an exit. Appollus closed his eyes, his Lyman's ear filtering out the noise of the water as it continued to drip from the ceiling. Slowing his breathing, he quietened his heart, the drumming of his warrior-pulse dropping to a whisper.

The door was to his rear. His skin tingled at the light wisps of air that pushed into the chamber through the gaps at its edges. Someone stood just beyond it. He could hear the regular exhaling and changeless heartbeat of a bored sentry. There were…

*Footsteps.*

Appollus focused on their steady rhythm as they grew closer. Judging by the gait, his visitors were human. Two men, one with a limp.

The guard's pulse quickened. Appollus smiled at his gaoler's discomfort.

The footsteps stopped outside the door, and Appollus listened as the two men spoke to the fearful sentry. The blasphemous curs spoke in the tongue of the arch-enemy. Appollus clenched his jaw. Though he couldn't discern what they were saying, he recognised the tone well enough. The visitors were the guard's superiors, his deference to them unmistakable.

The door opened inwards, the sound of its heavy latch sliding free a welcome relief from the ravaged consonants that ground from the men's throats.

Appollus tasted the familiar tang of recycled air as the door opened. The chamber was underground; a ventilation system fed air in through the corridor. He concentrated on the air as it brushed against his skin and decided that the nearest circulation shaft was perhaps ten paces beyond his cell. The door clunked as it swung closed. It was thick, but with a sufficient run-up he was confident he could fell it.

'Welcome, Chaplain.'

The speaker's voice brought Appollus's attention back into the room. The man stank of sulphur and day-old blood.

Appollus opened his eyes but remained silent. As a Chaplain, it was his duty to listen. To hear the sins of his brothers and distil their lies before they had even formed on their tongues. He had taken confession from the best of men, men of power and great strength. He had listened to the broken voices of terrible men, men whose twisted machinations had seen the end of civilisations, as they lay on his interrogation rack.

His visitor was neither.

'You hold secrets, Chaplain.' This time it was the second visitor who spoke. His voice was deeper than that of the first, and he struggled over the words as though unused to making their sounds. He bent down as he spoke, holding a long blade so that Appollus could see its blood-encrusted barbs. 'Secrets that our master would know.'

The man wore the mauve robes of the Brotherhood, though he wore no mask. Instead, the skin of his face had been dyed oil-black. Gleaming slivers of glass sat where his eyes should have been, sparkling even in the low-light of the chamber.

*Fratris Crucio.*

Appollus recognised his visitor from the numerous engagement reports and after-action accounts he'd studied. The Brotherhood's master inter-rogators were infamous throughout the Khandax warzone. Tales of their atrocities drifted from foxhole to foxhole, hushed whispers that crept along the trench line. Fratris Crucio, a byword for terror. Storm-coated officers of the Commissariat had adopted the stories as their own. It kept the men of the Imperial Guard fearful, alert. Vigilance along the watch-line absolute. To be captured by them was to suffer a fate far worse than simple death.

Appollus spat in the torturer's face.

The man tumbled back screaming, clawing at his face as the acid-saliva burned away his flesh. His companion knelt down over him but did nothing to ease his torment, simply inclining his head and watching as the acid ate into his brethren's eyes.

'Your strength will not serve you.' The torturer said finally, picking up the fallen blade and pushing it into Appollus's ribs. 'It will not last.'

The pain was excruciating but Appollus did not cry out.

It was the least of his worries. Pain was temporary, ended by absolu-tion or death; a slight inflicted upon his body and no more. But what the pain stirred in him – the anger, the bloodlust – that was terror. It thundered in his veins, threatening to drown his organs in a tide of red and rage. He would not allow himself to succumb to the curse; such a fate had no end.

Appollus closed off his mind from the pain. He pictured the High Basilica back on Cretacia, his Chapter's home world. Tens of thousands of candles burned along the stone edges of the basilica's aisles. One flick-ering memorial for each Flesh Tearer who had donned the black armour of death. The red of the candle wax was used to seal the saltires and affix the litany parchments to the armour of every new Death Company Space Marine. As a novitiate in the Chaplaincy, Appollus had spent years tending to the candles as he recited the catechism of observance; a dec-ade-long mass that armoured his mind and allowed him to walk among

830                              Space Marines

the damned of his Chapter, untouched by their madness.

He lost himself in the memory, beginning anew the observance as his torturers continued to violate his flesh.

'He has said nothing, lord. He will not speak.' The Crucio bowed as he entered the chamber, keeping his eyes fixed on the black curvature of his master's armoured feet.

Abasi Amun, encased in full battle plate, sat on an immense throne wrought from the ore-rich stone of the cavern around him. He was still, unmoving, like a sculpture stolen from the grand halls of a monarch.

'Nothing?' Abasi Amun's voice rumbled around the cavern. The metallic resonance of his helmet's vox-caster sounding machine-harsh in the enclosed space.

'He does not scream, lord.'

'Then you have failed me.' Amun said, standing.

'No, no. Perhaps...' the Crucio stammered, his mouth dry with fear.. 'Perhaps he knows nothing.'

Amun shot forwards in a heartbeat, flowing like black water across the chamber's expanse to lift the torturer by his neck. The Crucio gasped, his hands grasping in vain at Amun's gauntlet.

'He hides something, a truth.' With a flick of his wrist, Amun snapped the Crucio's neck. 'I sensed it on the battlefield, he keeps something from us,' Amun continued, talking to the limp corpse in his hand. 'I will know his secret.'

Amun brought the corpse closer and whispered. 'I will know.'

Pain. Appollus awoke with a start, expecting the sharp kiss of a blade or the cruel attentions of a neural flail. There was no trace of either. A lone figure stood before him, cloaked in shadow. The jagged light from the oil burners seemed to avoid the figure, flickering around the edges of his form but never quite illuminating him.

Appollus bared his teeth in a growl. He needn't see his enemy to know him. He could hear the figure's twin hearts thump like an indomitable engine in his chest. The shadow before him was an Adeptus Astartes. Greatest among traitors, a true pawn of the arch-enemy. A Chaos Space Marine.

Blood rushed to Appollus's muscles as he tensed against his restraints. The hatred locked into his genetic code willed him to rend the figure apart, to strike him dead. He bit down a growl. There was something else, something more. It clawed at his mind like a burrowing rodent. He could smell it. Hiding among the pungent, oleaginous balms the Traitor Marine used to maintain his armour was the foul, corrupting stench of the warp.

'Psyker,' Appollus snarled.

'You are observant, for a puppet of a false god.' The Chaos Space Marine paced forwards, throwing off the shadows the way a man might remove a cowl. 'Where you look only to the blood of your crippled father for strength, I have embraced the power of the great Changer.' The Traitor Marine flexed his arms. 'His limitless majesty feeds my veins.'

The warrior's power armour was mirror-black, its edges rounded and its surface polished to an impossible sheen. Yet it reflected nothing of the chamber. Its smooth plates were devoid of Chapter insignia and symbols of loyalty. Appollus averted his gaze. The armour was hard to look upon. It was at once dark and formless, yet as solid as the rock walls surrounding them.

Appollus looked again; he had seen its like before. 'You were there, in battle.'

The Traitor Marine dipped his head in mock deference. 'I am Abasi Amun. How should I address you, Chaplain?'

Appollus looked up at Amun's breastplate, surprised to now see his reflection staring back at him, though the tortured figure he looked upon bared little resemblance to how he had last seen himself.

The Crucio had been studious in their work.

The master torturers had administered a potent mix of toxins that had retarded his Larraman's organ and prevented his body from healing as it otherwise might. Hundreds of deep lacerations and patches of dark bruises covered his body. Several layers of skin had been shaved away from his abdomen, exposing the dermis. His face was gaunt, sapped of its chiselled sternness. Appollus met his own gaze, looked deep into his own eyes. They burned back at him with fierce intensity, reminding him of what he already knew – he would never break.

Appollus focused on the darkness of Amun's helm. 'Have you come seeking repentance, traitor?'

Amun laughed, a booming sound, incongruous with his subtle, insubstantial presence.

'My Crucio have broken many of your kind. But you, you defy me still. So close to death and yet you will part with none of your secrets.' Amun moved behind Appollus. The pressure seals around his gorget gave a popping hiss as he unclasped his helm.

'If your body will not give me the truths I seek, then I shall take them from your mind.'

Appollus snarled, his eyes fixed on the wall opposite him. 'I warn you, traitor. To know my secret, is to forfeit your life.'

Amun grabbed Appollus, his gauntleted fingers a vice around the Chaplain's throat.

'You are in no position to make threats, Chaplain.' Amun relaxed his grip. 'Save your piety. These are the final moments of your existence.' Amun removed his gauntlets as he spoke. 'I will find my answers. I will offer up your soul to my master and leave your body to rot, like the kingdom of your father.'

Amun's eyes crackled with eldritch lightning that leapt to his out-stretched palms. He curled his fingers back. The energy coalesced into a flickering ball of white fire. The temperature dropped below zero as Amun muttered a prayer in an inhuman tongue. Blood ran from Appollus's orifices as frost began to rime his limbs.

'I know... no fear.' Appollus muttered, forcing his tongue to work through the viscous fluid filling his mouth.

The fireball drifted from Amun into Appollus's torso, breaking into a fulgurant web that coursed over his flesh then vanished beneath it.

Appollus screamed.

Amun ripped into Appollus's mind. In an agonising instant, the mental barriers that had taken the Chaplain decades to erect were torn asunder. His way unbarred, Amun proceeded with more care. Haste or disregard would leave Appollus a dribbling husk, his mind ruined and his secrets lost forever.

The chains binding Appollus rattled like weapons-fire as his body jerked. His skin rippled like water as half-clotted blood slid in thick clumps from his nostrils.

Amun cut deeper. He peeled away the surface thoughts that floated in Appollus's conscious mind and prized apart the lies of memory. Blood ran from the Chaplain's lips as they gave voice to a near constant stream.

Alone in the inner reaches of Appollus's mind, Amun snarled. The Flesh Tearer was close to death, but the truth still eluded him. Abandoning his earlier care, Amun burned to the Chaplain's essence. He would know, he must.

'There...' Amun's mortal body mouthed the word as his psychic tendrils found the truth he had been searching for.

Even as he touched upon it, Amun knew he had made a mistake. The Chaplain had no knowledge of the wider Imperial forces, he knew nothing of troop dispersments or defence plans. His secret was far more potent, far deadlier. He concealed a rage, wrath in its purest form. A burning halo of fire that wrapped around his soul like a serpent. Amun tried to run, to withdraw his mind back to the safety of his body. But it was too late. The rage had found a new home, a new vessel to enact its bloody will, and it would not be denied its prize.

Abasi Amun screamed.

The door swung open. Two of the Brotherhood burst in, their lasguns trained on Appollus.

'Lord Amun...'

Abasi roared and ran at the guards, knocking them to the floor. A panicked lasgun-round scored Appollus's thigh. Another clipped his bonds, burning a deep score in the metal links.

The guards screamed in desperate horror as Amun set about them. He was a starved creature, a cornered beast hunched on all fours. He growled, low and feral as he ripped the two cultists apart with his bare hands and sank his teeth into their flesh.

'While I breathe, I am wrath.' Appollus snarled with effort as he snapped the bonds holding his wrists and swung up to break the chains around his ankles. His shoulder crunched like split kindling as he hit the ground.

Amun rounded on him, saliva and bloodied flesh-chunks dripping from his mouth.

In full battle plate, the sorcerer was more than a match for the naked and battered Appollus. But under the rage's thrall, the Traitor Marine was frenzied, uncoordinated. Appollus had fought among such warriors for longer than most men lived. He could read Amun's strikes before the warrior threw them.

Slipping a right hook, Appollus spun the lengths of loose chain dangling from his wrists around his fists, and punched Amun in the face. Blood fountained from his ruined nose, spraying Appollus's face crimson.

The Chaos Space Marine struck back with a flurry of reaching swipes. Appollus rode their momentum, absorbing their impact on his arms, though a shooting pain told of a fractured humerus. He snarled, stepping inside Amun's guard to deliver an uppercut. The sorcerer's head jerked backwards. Appollus followed it, landing two consecutive blows, before grabbing the back of Amun's head and pulling him into a headbutt.

Amun roared as he staggered backwards, lashing out with his foot at Appollus's legs.

The ceramite boot cracked Appollus's shin and knocked him to the floor. The Chaplain rolled to his feet, limping to keep the weight from his damaged leg and cursing himself for getting too close. He couldn't afford to be careless, he had to keep his own bloodlust in check.

Amun growled as he regained his footing, a stream of saliva washing from his mouth to hiss on the chamber floor. The smell of Appollus's blood was like a knife in his brain. He needed to taste it, to devour the marrow in the Chaplain's bones, to savour every last scrap of his flesh. Roaring, Amun charged.

Pain ran like molten steel in Appollus's veins as he darted forwards, turning around Amun to loop his shackles over the Chaos Space Marine's throat. The movement brought him around and onto Amun's back. He forced the chains tight, his arms burning with the effort as Amun fought to buck him.

Amun dropped to one knee, a gurgling roar dying in his throat as his wind-pipe collapsed. He thrashed at Appollus in a mix of panic and rage as the beast within him struggled against death.

'Die, traitor.' The words ground from between Appollus's bloodied teeth as he wrenched Amun's head from his shoulders.

Even in death, Amun's body continued to fight, his adrenaline-soaked limbs twitching in denial as his corpse shivered on the ground.

*'Your place is at our enemy's throat.'*

Luciferus's words resurfaced in Appollus's mind as he watched Amun grind against the stone of the floor in the last spasms of his death throes.

'Your blood be cursed,' Appollus snarled, bending to retrieve Amun's blade. He would speak with the vulpine Librarian when next they crossed paths.

Coated in blood, both the traitor's and his own, Appollus was reminded of the crimson armour he'd donned before his ordination. 'In blood we are one. Immortal, while one remains to bleed.' Using his teeth to scrape a finger clean, Appollus guided a bead of saliva around his chest, burning the toothed-blade symbol of his Chapter into his breast.

The iron lift rattled to a stop with a sharp grinding of gears. Appollus threw open the mesh door and stepped into the corridor, leaving the crumpled bodies of two Brotherhood to bleed out behind him. He felt his pulse quicken as he thought of the moment his fingers had closed around the first's aorta, and remembered the satisfying snap of the second's neck. They were the third patrol he'd come across since his escape. He hoped they would not be the last.

'His blood is strength.' Appollus mouthed the axiom as he stalked, a little unsteady on his feet, along the corridor. The exertion of his escape had forced the bulk of the Crucio's toxins from his system, adrenaline washing through him like a cleansing fire, and dark scabs of crusted blood covered his torso where his flesh had begun knitting itself back together. But he still ached to his bones, a pungent sweat clothing his body.

Appollus touched a hand to his head, rubbing his skin-starved knuckles into his temples. The psyker's touch still lingered in that pain. But pain wasn't the only thing Amun had left him with. As he fought to stave off the rage, the Chaos Space Marine had been careless. In his panic, he had let his surface thoughts spill out; a tumultuous wave of half-formed images that had bombarded Appollus's untrained mind. The psychic noise had been like harsh bursts of static filtered through a howling gale. Yet Appollus had done more than hold on to his sanity. With iron-willed devotion and unyielding resolve, he had focused on his duty, on his brothers.

Appollus stopped as he reached a bend in the corridor, recognising every glint of ore in the wall ahead. Zakiel, Xaphan, Herchel and Ziel; the four Death Company were alive. If what he'd gleaned from Amun's mind was true then they were languishing in a cell at the end of the corridor. He pressed his back against the wall, feeling his muscles tense as the sharp rock tore into his skin, and listened.

There were two of the Brotherhood patrolling the corridor. Appollus

ground his teeth, feeling his anger grow with every thump of their traitorous hearts. He listened to the fall of their booted feet, to the clack
of their weapons as they swung loose on straps. His pulse raced as the
stink of their unwashed flesh drifted to his nostrils. A red mist mustered
behind his eyes. A tremor passed through his hands, forcing his fists into
balls of sinew. The urge to kill was great. He looked down at the Chapter
symbol on his breast as he waited and let out a slow breath of calm. Rage
was not yet his master.

He waited. He counted. Focusing on the guards' footsteps, he waited
until the distance was right.

'I am death!' Appollus rounded the corner and threw his knife into
the chest of the nearest of them. Running, he caught the body on his
shoulder before it fell, and charged towards the second. The man spun
round, startled, sweeping up his lasgun and opening fire. Appollus felt
his corpse-shield shudder as a half dozen rounds cut into it, and snarled
as a round sliced the flesh from his bicep. A second later he barrelled into
the guard, tackling him to the ground. Appollus recovered first, pinning
the cultist beneath him and thundering a fist into his face. He hit him
again and again, deaf to the cracking of bone and ignorant of the visceral
lumps of brain matter that dripped from under the cultist's mask. Only
when his fist struck rock, did Appollus stop.

The reek of torture greeted Appollus as he entered the cell, hitting
him as surely as any blow. He snarled in disgust, craving the air-filter-
ing properties of his battle helm. The four Death Company hung from
the ceiling, chained in the same manner as he had been. He growled,
angered by the extent the Crucio had violated their bodies. Ziel was in
the worst state, the skin of his left forearm peeled back to reveal bone.
Their eyes widened as he approached. They wanted to kill. Even over the
stench he could smell their bloodlust. He wouldn't keep them waiting.
Raising the lasgun he'd stripped from the Brotherhood guards, he shot
through their bonds.

'Brothers.' Appollus spread his arms. 'I feel your thirst.' He thrust an
arm out, jabbing his blade towards the door, 'The enemy are many, but
they are flesh. We, are immortal lords of battle. We are wrath. We are
death.'

The Death Company growled, shaking their limbs loose, their fists
opening and closing as they sought to rend.

'Kill until killed. Leave none alive.'

Appollus watched them go, surprised by how much effort it took not
to follow them. He ached to join the Death Company in slaughter. The
Brotherhood had wrought a terrible injustice upon him, and he vowed
he would see it drowned from his memory by a river of their blood. But
he had gleaned more than his brothers' location from Amun's mind, and
he had another task to attend to first.

* * *

The cavern was immense. The largest by far that Appollus had encountered. Banks of luminators hung on racks of chain, suspended from
the ore-rich rock of the ceiling. Plasteel panels had been bolted down
over the rock of the floor to create something resembling a functioning
hangar. Rusted supply crates were heaped in small clusters around the
walls. At the far end of the chamber, an antiquated Stormbird drop-ship
sat locked to the deck. Its oil-black flanks were polished clean of insignia. The armour on one of its wings had been peeled back, exposing
the plasteel frame beneath. Fuel cables and pressure hoses hugged its
sides like creeper-vines. Beyond it, a flickering energy shield kept out
the infinite void.

Appollus stared through the electro-haze of the shield. The surface of
the asteroid stretched as far as he could see, a pitted landscape of undulating rock and trenched gullies. If what he'd learned from Amun was
correct, the damaged Stormbird was the only transport off this rock.

Shouldering his stolen lasgun, he moved towards the drop-ship. The
weapon was lighter than he was used to, like a child's toy compared to
the reassuring weight of his bolter. The lasgun followed his eyes as he
scanned for targets. A trio of Brotherhood cultists rounded the Stormbird. Appollus fired, killing them without breaking stride. He ground his
teeth. He missed the reassuring bark of his boltgun; the clinical snap of
the lasgun was far removed from the visceral booming of mass-reactive
rounds.

Klaxons screamed from what sounded like every surface. Strobing red
light filled the cavern and cast wicked shadows among the rock. The
resounding thud of booted feet warned Appollus of threats to his left
and rear. The Brotherhood were spilling into the chamber from every
angle.

He snarled as weapons-fire began competing with the klaxons,
las-rounds cutting the air around him. Firing in blazing streams on
full-auto, Appollus cut down the forerunners. He grinned darkly as the
familiar tang of blood filled the air, and continued moving towards the
drop-ship. The remaining Brotherhood approached with more caution,
ducking back behind what little cover they could find. He counted at
least sixty of them as he panned his weapon around, slamming in a spare
powercell as the charge counter flashed empty.

To his left, an arm reached up to throw a grenade. He shot it off at the
elbow. Its owner cried out an instant before the explosive detonated.
Gobbets of flesh and bloodied robe fountained into the air. *Fifty-seven.*
Appollus updated his mental tally as he ducked under the tangle of fuel
feeds.

The Brotherhood stopped firing.

Appollus used the moment's respite to assess his options. The Brotherhood had formed a firing perimeter. A few had unsheathed blades and
were edging towards him. He smiled. They were waiting for him to break

for the Stormbird, but he had never had any intention of boarding the vessel.

Appollus opened the intake valve in the nearest fuel hose and lifted the locking catch. Choking promethium vapour wafted out, forcing a cough from his lungs. Appollus ejected the powercell from his lasgun and struck it hard with the hilt of his knife.

'He is my shield.'

Appollus dropped the sparking energy cell into the fuel pipe and ran. He ran with all the speed his enhanced physiology could muster. He ran like a man racing to the side of imperilled loved ones. He ran in the only direction the Brotherhood hadn't refused him. He ran towards the energy barrier.

Shutting his eyes to protect them from the shield's glare, Appollus threw himself through the barrier and out into the void.

Less than a heartbeat later, the Stormbird detonated, the promethium in its fuel tanks exploding outwards in a halo of fire.

Too late, the Brotherhood realised what Appollus had done.

The nearest of them were incinerated in the initial blast, vaporised where they stood. The others fled as best they could. Flaming shrapnel chased them across the chamber, tearing through flesh and bone with all the care of a maddened butcher.

Appollus watched as the rolling carpet of flame pushed out through the energy shield and vanished, its ire stolen by the airless void. He followed the fire's retreat, diving back through the barrier and rolling to his feet.

Shards of burning metal littered the chamber. The broken and torn corpses of dozens of Brotherhood cultists were strewn about like discarded dolls. Some of the traitors were still screaming, thrashing around as their faceplates seared their skin, the thin metal super-heated by the blast. The smell of cooked blood hung in the air, as tangible as the ground beneath Appollus's feet.

Fire and the flickering, red light conspired to recreate the Hell described in ancient Terran myth. Appollus smiled as he strode through the carnage: that made him the Daevil.

The remaining Brotherhood staggered from cover, their robes singed and ragged. They moved without purpose, staring at the smouldering wreck of the drop-ship, gripped by disbelief at what had transpired. Appollus paced towards them. Smoke drifted in wistful columns from his limbs, his void-frozen skin singed by the heat of the energy shield.

A bleeding Crucio, his face knotted in confusion, glared at Appollus. 'Fool. That was the only ship.' The Crucio indicated a smouldering crater filled with tangled ceramite and plasteel plating. 'You are trapped here with us.' He spread his arms to indicate the rest of the Brotherhood who had recovered enough to ready their weapons. 'When I'm done with you, all the pain you have suffered thus far in your miserable life will seem like an eternity of ecstasy. On your flesh I shall redefine the art of my sect. I will hear you beg for death, *Chaplain*.'

'No, heretic.' Appollus stopped ten paces from the nearest cultist. He took a breath and looked down at the knife in his hand. Pulling back his broad shoulders, he straightened to his full height and raised his knife towards the Crucio. 'You are mistaken.'

At the rear of the chamber, a lift rattled and bucked to a stop, its iron grate swinging open.

'It is you who are trapped here with us.'

The Crucio looked over his shoulder.

Behind him, Zakiel, Xaphan, Herchel and Ziel paced into the cavern, bloodied blades grasped white-knuckle tight in their murderous hands.

Appollus smelled the torturer's fear and smiled.

'Fear not, *torturer*,' Appollus snarled. 'You will not have time to beg.'

# TOWER OF BLOOD

*Tony Ballantyne*

The ceiling was dripping blood.

It dripped on the bald head of Goedendag Morningstar, Adeptus Astartes of the Iron Knights Chapter, and the Space Marine made no move to wipe it away.

'How many floors lie above us?' he asked.

Though the Imperial Guard trooper was a big woman, she would still have been dwarfed by Goedendag even had he not been wearing his power armour.

'One hundred and forty-three floors,' she managed to say, awestruck by this post-human demigod. She straightened up, despite her exhaustion. 'Eight hundred and sixty-five lie below us. We met the horde in battle at the nine hundredth floor. They pushed us back to here. Many lives were lost in action, many more civilians were evacuated.'

'But not all,' said Ortrud. The Iron Knights had completed their survey of the eight hundred and fifty-sixth floor; now they clustered around their commander.

'Not all,' agreed the Guard, looking around the seven men now towering over her in their gunmetal and black armour, streaked red with dripping blood. Their unhelmed heads seemed so small, lost in the heart of the powerful machinery of their suits. 'By no means all. There are thousands still trapped above us, all at the mercy of the warp fiends.'

'The warp fiends do not understand the meaning of mercy,' said Fastlinger. 'Commander, may we now don our helmets?' He drew his hand across his face.

'No,' said Goedendag. 'We fight unhelmed. We do not want to lead civilians into areas where we are safe and they are not. What if we led them into a vacuum?' He noticed the way the Imperial Guardswoman was looking at him. 'Do you have a question?' he asked.

'I'm sorry,' she said. 'I was just wondering, why do you wear two morning stars on your back?'

Goedendag smiled.

'For weapons.'

'You seem different to other Space Marines.'

'Have you met many?' asked Fastlinger.

Goedendag flashed him a warning look. The Imperial Guard were an honoured force; they did not deserve to be ridiculed.

'The Iron Knights are siege specialists,' said Goedendag. 'The warp fiends have sealed off the top floors and surrounded this tower with a warp instability that is spreading across the sky, threatening the neighbouring hives. This siege needs to be broken *now*.'

The Guardswoman was torn between exhaustion and awe. Still, something caused her to speak.

'Are you going to wait for the Ordo Malleus?'

'The inquisition's daemonhunters are not here,' interrupted Telramund. 'Goedendag, I grow weary. Let us join the fight!'

'Peace, Telramund! This soldier stands alone in a room with seven Iron Knights in full armour–'

'Save for their helms,' muttered Fastlinger.

'If things had been otherwise, we would have found nought here but corpses. She is brave indeed.' Goedendag looked down at her. 'What's your name?'

'Kelra.'

'Then listen to me, Kelra. You and your troops have done well to hold back the daemons, but now it is our turn.'

He waved a hand around the floor. It was empty save for the four lift shafts that ran to the top of the hive building. All the internal walls, all the possessions of those who had once lived here were vaporised, smashed, shattered, destroyed by the weapons of the Imperial Guard as they had fought to hold their ground. The wide, low space was filled with darkness, the stench of battle, the drip of blood. Even the stairs had broken away. The stairs; the last route of escape for those lucky civilians who had not taken the lifts. The shafts still creaked with the agony of those caught within.

'Kelra, before we leave, you mentioned something about the origin of the warp rift?'

Kelra nodded, pleased to help.

'I have heard something. Escaping civilians have spoken about a Gutor Invareln who lived on the nine hundred and ninety-second floor. He was a bitter man, an outcast. He claimed he was a latent psyker, that he had been ignored by the Imperium. His neighbours laughed, they thought he was seeking attention. The children mocked him, asked him why he had not been taken to Terra, but Invareln would scowl in answer that he was deliberately forgotten.'

'He *was* a psyker,' said Franosch, concentrating. 'His mind is now possessed by a daemon. A greater daemon. He is the portal by which the lesser daemons are entering this world.'

Kelra's eyes widened as she looked to Franosch.

'He's a psyker too?' she asked.

'Gamma level at best,' answered Franosch. He turned to Goedendag. 'Commander, there are daemonettes above us. Many, many daemonettes.'

'Enough talk,' said Telramund. 'The instability is spreading.'

Goedendag looked up at the ceiling, watched the clotting drops forming stalactites.

'So much blood,' he said. 'Telramund is right. We move out. Draw your chainswords.'

Telramund was already holding his meltagun. 'This weapon will suit me fine, commander.'

'And what of the civilians who stand above us? No meltaguns, no flamers, no frag grenades…'

'How about missile launchers?' said Fastlinger, innocently.

'How about you take point, Fastlinger?' replied Goedendag. He noted the look of disappointment on Telramund's face. 'Telramund, you accompany him.'

Telramund smiled as he holstered his meltagun and drew his chainsword. An angry buzzing noise sounded as he set it in motion, a buzz that was immediately answered by Fastlinger's weapon.

The Iron Knights began to move apart, assuming combat positions.

'Gottfried. The battle cry.'

Gottfried looked down at the floor and clasped his hands together. In a low voice, he intoned the words: 'Strike, death, as silent as the swan.'

The rest of the group repeated the words.

Now the other chainswords powered up, the angry screeching made all the louder as it echoed from the low ceiling. Low ceilings, the better to cram in more humans, ready to work on this manufactory world.

The time for joking had passed, and Fastlinger looked to his comrades and saw they were all ready. He looked to Goedendag last. The commander nodded and Fastlinger raised his sword to the ceiling, the angry buzz rising to a scream as it cut through the thin metal. Immediately, there was a convulsive eruption of blood, dark blood rupturing through the widening crack. It spilled down over Fastlinger's cutting arm and shoulder, running down the blue gunmetal and black of his powered armour. He shifted his position and his feet slipped on the pools that congealed around his feet. Retractable spikes sprang forth from the soles of his power armour, holding him in place.

Kelra, the Imperial Guard trooper, backed away, dodging a second burst of blood as Telramund too began to cut into the ceiling. The tide of blood widened with the hole, and now smooth yellow shapes slipped through amongst the liquid. Rounded and polished, they splashed and knocked on the floor.

'That's a skull,' said Kelra. Still, she stood her ground, noted Goedendag. Not for nothing had the Imperial Guard gained the respect of humanity.

Goedendag gestured Franosch forward, and the psyker stood at the edge of the widening waterfall of blood.

'They know we're here,' he said. 'They are eager to meet us.'

'Who? The daemonettes?'

'Oh yes. They are filled with the bitter joy of battle, and yet… something is holding them back.'

'What?'

'I don't know. Something at the top of the tower.'

'Will this tide never end?' called Telramund impatiently. He was itching to fight.

'Surely this is more blood than all the humans of the hive would hold?' said Kelra.

'Some of it spills from the portal,' said Franosch.

'Enough of this,' said Goedendag. 'The gap is wide enough! Through it! Go!'

Fastlinger crouched and then jumped upwards on leg muscles massively expanded by the biscopea implanted in his chest. He soared through the gap above him in a spray of ruby, followed closely by Telramund.

Now Goedendag stepped forward. Despite the fact that he heard the buzzing of chainswords above him, the innate courtesy of the Iron Knights caused him to pause for a moment and turn to Kelra.

'Thank you for your help,' he said.

'I'll be waiting here for your return.'

Drips of blood bouncing from his bald head and matting his long white beard, Goedendag Morningstar jumped up into the space above.

He landed on the eight hundred and fifty-seventh floor, his balance thrown by the tide of blood swirling into the hole. Something white came flashing in at his side; something sharp was pricking towards his eye. He swung his chainsword, shearing through the crab claw of the daemonette who bore down upon him. The white skinned woman hissed at him, her rusty hair plastered by blood to her bare shoulders.

'*Goolvar h'nurrgh!*' she spat, and made to draw something from behind her back. It was a feint! As Goedendag brought his chainsword up to parry the attack, she kicked out at him, a three-toed foot tipped in razor-sharp claws scratching across the armour on his sword arm. Goedendag made to chop at her leg, but she gripped him with her foot and held on, twisting the chainsword upwards.

Now the daemonette smiled at him, her sweet, seductive body undulating as she brought the snake-fiend from behind her back. She hissed, and lashed the fiend forwards like a whip. Its eyes blazed, its mouth, surrounded by a ring of venom pierced needles, snapping towards Goedendag's face. His chainsword-wielding hand was trapped by the daemonette's foot.

The betcher's glands in Goedendag's mouth had been working overtime, and he spat corrosive acid into the eyes of the lashing snake-fiend. The creature screamed and drew back in pain. Goedendag flicked the chainsword to his left hand, then brought the weapon up as if to parry *quinte*, slicing through the snake-fiend's body. He carried on with the movement, circling down to cut through the daemonette's leg. She screamed and jumped forward, needle teeth moving within her mouth, but Goedendag's right hand now reached to his shoulder and took hold of one of the morning stars there. He brought the weapon forward in a circle, cracking it down on the daemonette's skull as, simultaneously, his sword thrust into her body.

She thrashed as she died, her bitter scream rippling the pools of blood gathered on the floor.

'You took your time on that one,' said Fastlinger, standing coolly nearby over the bodies of two more dead daemonettes. 'And we saved her especially for you, too.'

'You talk too much,' said Telramund, three daemonettes to his credit.

The other members of the squad were now entering the room, jumping up from below.

'One hundred and forty-two floors to go,' announced Ortrud, looking at the dead daemonettes.

'There are many more above us,' said Franosch, looking to the dripping ceiling, 'yet still they hold back.' He looked at Goedendag. 'Do you think they know it is us? Are they waiting for us?'

'Who cares?' said Telramund. 'We shall meet them soon enough.'

The daemonettes had been fought to a standstill here as they descended the tower from the warp portal. As they had fought, they had ripped apart the thin walls that partitioned the human apartments crowded into the hive block. The ceiling above had been punctured in many places, and Goedendag and the other Iron Knights could now look up through several floors.

Ortrud waded through ankle-deep blood, kicking aside yellow skulls, the flesh recently ripped from the bone.

'They sealed this floor to keep the blood in,' he said.

'There is blood still dripping down upon us,' said Telramund, ever impatient.

Franosch was frowning, straining to understand.

'They carry some of the living through the warp portal,' he says. 'I hear their screams. But the daemonettes grow bored. They torture and kill those who remain.'

'Then let us make speed to meet them,' said Telramund.

'Telramund speaks well,' said Goedendag. 'Franosch, I see the stairs resume undamaged on the next floor. Is it meet that we should take them?'

'For the moment.'

They advanced in turns, running in pairs up flights of stairs whilst those behind covered them. As they climbed through the floors, the damage inflicted by the holding action lessened. The internal walls of the hive tower reasserted themselves, and Goedendag and the rest began to make out the tiny apartment spaces in which the civilians had lived.

'What do they make here?' asked Gottfried.

'On Minea? Phosgene gas, mainly. They also export Banedox ore.'

'Look,' said Gottfried.

Goedendag looked to the floor. A child's toy lay there, a model Space Marine.

'There were children here,' said Fastlinger. 'What did they do with them?'

'Next floor up,' said Ortrud. 'You'll see.'

They climbed the stairs to the next level.

'Nine hundredth floor,' said Gottfried.

'They sealed the stairwell above,' said Telramund, looking up.

'Then we cut through with chainswords,' said Goedendag.

'We won't need chainswords,' replied Telramund bitterly.

Goedendag moved forward to get a better look. A patchwork had been stitched over the stairwell. Shapes of brown, pink and yellow. Blood seeped through the stitches.

'That's children's skin,' said Goedendag.

'That's daemonettes amusing themselves, killing time,' said Telramund.

'It's a warning line,' said Franosch. 'It will summon trouble.'

'Then I will invite trouble to join me,' said Goedendag, cutting through the patchwork of flesh with a knife. Blood spurted through, and amongst the curling currents and eddies slipped the writhing bodies of snake-fiends, pouring through the gaps, wriggling as they sought out their human prey. Chainswords buzzed into life once more, and the warriors began to swing at the prickling creatures.

'They cannot penetrate our armour!' shouted Fastlinger, cutting a snake-fiend in two in a spray of green ichor that steamed and sizzled on contact with the clotting blood.

'They're not trying to penetrate,' called Ortrud. 'They seek to entangle us.'

As he spoke, a bundle of snake-fiends whipped their way out of the bloody stream and corkscrewed their way towards Goedendag's sword arm, seeking to wrap it to his body. Goedendag feinted to the side and then brought his chainsword down on the mass of bodies, their scales dark and shining. The scream of the sword joined the splashing of blood and the hiss of ichor. Through the mass of moist movement he saw the white bodies of the daemonettes of Slaanesh dropping down to join the melee.

'Too much blood,' gasped Franosch, launching a *coulé* attack on a snake-fiend, grazing the chainsword down the side of its body before neatly flicking back to sever the head.

'Less technique, Franosch,' called Ortrud, 'More slashing!'

'There is too much blood,' repeated Franosch, stamping down on a bundle of snake-fiends with his spiked boots. 'Still it pours from the warp.'

"Ware the daemonettes!' called Gottfried, launching a *fleche* attack at the closest enemy. A white female staggered towards him, seemingly drunk on blood. Goedendag brought his chainsword up beneath Gottfried's strike, parrying it.

'Hold,' called Goedendag, seeing the look of betrayal in his comrade's eyes. 'She's human.'

The Space Marines halted as one, the mocking laughter of daemonettes filling their ears. They took a moment to discern the situation: the followers of Slaanesh stood at the far side of the wide room, bending, taunting, snapping their crab-like claws at the Space Marines. Now Goedendag's men realised just what the daemonettes had pushed towards them: human women, stripped naked and daubed with white paint, their hair tied up and stained with blood. Prisoners, sent forward to die on the Space Marine's blades, for was it not a fact that the followers of Slaanesh delighted in killing their opponents in the most vile and tormenting ways?

'More snake-fiends!' called Goedendag, as the writhing creatures rose out of the rising tide of blood, circlets of needle teeth glistening with poison, redoubling their attack, this time on the human women as well as the Space Marines themselves.

It was left to Gottfried and Hellstedt to dispatch the snake-fiends. Ortrud and Fastlinger launched themselves at the daemonettes screaming with insane laughter at the other side of the room. They waited a moment as the Space Marines advanced and then retreated at a sedate pace back up the stairs to the next level, wriggling their bodies in an alluring fashion as they did so, taunting their pursuers.

'Leave them,' called Goedendag. 'Look to the women first.'Reluctantly, Ortrud and Fastlinger returned to his side.

The unceasing flow of blood continued from above, though the tide was diminishing. It swirled in whirlpools around the stairwells leading further down the tower. Seven human women stood weakly, buffeted by the dying tide. And now Goedendag saw why they had remained silent throughout their torment: their mouths had been sewn shut with thick, red thread. He took a knife from his combat armour and cut through the thread sealing the first woman's mouth.

'There are more of them above,' she shouted, red thread piercing her lips in a grotesque moustache. 'Hundreds, thousands. They're waiting for you.'

'Peace,' said Goedendag Morningstar. 'We have the advantage.'

The woman's eyes widened.

'No! There are only seven of you. You have no advantage. They make ambushes, deadfalls.'

'Yes,' said Goedendag. 'But they must fight us one floor at a time.'

The other women now had their mouths cut free. Goedendag was impressed to see how they held themselves. Frightened, hurt, it was true, but they had not broken down. He remembered Kelra, the Imperial Guardswoman, and he realised that they bred them tough on Minea.

Franosch stepped forward.

'There is a warp portal near the top floor,' he said. 'Have you seen it?'

'No,' said the women in unison, but one of them stepped forward. She was rubbing white ichor from her body as she did so, exposing the dark skin underneath.

'I have not seen the warp portal, but I have heard from one who has. One who fled down the stairs while the lift shafts filled with fire. He told me there is a daemon up there, a greater daemon.'

'I knew it!' exclaimed Franosch.

'Yet why does it not attack?' said Ortrud. 'Why does its horde remain at the top of the tower?'

'They're waiting for something. It's part of the deal.'

'What deal?'

'Gutor Invareln,' said the woman. 'There was a phosgene leak, his body was badly scarred. He was a bitter enough man before his injuries, afterwards he blamed the world for his troubles. He turned upon all his fellow humans; he claimed he was a latent psyker and that he would have his revenge on us all.'

'Surely this would have brought the Inquisition down upon him,' called Franosch. 'Most latents try to avoid their attention.'

'None of us thought anything of his words. Gutor had always sought any attention to make himself seem more important. To him, even the inquisition would have been welcome.'

'You believe that Gutor made a deal with a daemon?' said Goedendag.

'Yes. He wanted to live to see the destruction of all those who lived around him. Only after that would he surrender to death and allow the portal to fully open! And after that…'

'After the portal is fully open there will be daemons enough for all of Minea,' said Franosch.

'Then we must hurry to make the greater daemon's acquaintance,' said Goedendag.

'Meltaguns?' said Fastlinger.

'What about the humans?' said Ortrud.

'Use them,' said one of the women. 'Better a quick death than what *they* plan.'

'Chainswords,' said Goedendag. 'Telramund. Less than one hundred floors to go. Move out!'

They splashed up the stairs of the tower. Globs of blood gathered in clumps on their boot spikes. They had to pause to shake them free.

The corridors they passed through were empty; they looked into empty rooms where humans had once lived and saw signs of fighting – overturned chairs, broken tables, even food scattered across the pooled blood on the floor – but of bodies, living or dead, there was no sign.

'Carried away,' said Franosch. 'Sport for now or later.'

They passed floor nine hundred and ten, then nine hundred and twenty.

'What's that?' asked Ortrud. The noise came again, a shrieking sound as of many voices crying in agony.

'It's coming from the elevator shaft,' said Goedendag.

The black metal wall of the elevator shafts was their only constant as they climbed, that and the never ending flow of blood. Each set of doors had buckled and melted shut. Once more, the metal of the shafts seemed to hum with an unearthly music.

'Like a trumpet call, blown from the warp,' said Ortrud, darkly.

'The bodies of those who fled,' said Franosch. 'Trapped, still living, in the shafts. Boiled in blood and feasted on by snake-fiends.'

On they climbed. On the nine hundred and twenty-seventh floor, the rooms were filled with human feet. On floor nine hundred and twenty-nine, glistening hearts lay in pools, still beating. They pumped blood from pool to pool, from room to room.

'This is sick even by Slaaneshi standards,' said Fastlinger. Goedendag said nothing.

Still they climbed.

Franosch concentrated.

'Next floor,' he said. 'Daemonettes. Hundreds of them. The humans lie beyond them. And then...'

He paused, pushing his meagre psychic ability to its limit.

'...and then nothing again. Nothing until the top of the building, and whatever awaits us there.'

'It's an invitation,' said Goedendag, calmly. 'Whatever is at the top is waiting for us. Waiting for me.'

The Space Marines looked at each other. Each felt the guilt of their Chapter, each felt the determination to atone for the sins of their fellow Iron Knights.

'Tell us what to do, Goedendag.'

Goedendag looked at his chainsword. His lyman's ear was attuned to the noises from above now, the pitiful cries of the tortured.

'We've climbed nine hundred and forty floors in search of a fight,' said Goedendag. 'Now we'll have one. I have a plan.' He smiled slowly. 'And Fastlinger, it's time for you to sheathe your chainsword for a while...'

They fixed melta bombs to the ceiling, retreated to the floor below and waited for the explosion.

Ortrud was an expert at demolition. The bombs broke the ceiling and nothing more. Or rather, he broke more than the ceiling, for the ceiling was a floor as well, and as the ground beneath their birdlike feet gave way, the daemonettes of Slaanesh found themselves falling, falling down in a rain of blood, of thrashing limbs, of dust and screams and noise, falling towards floor nine hundred and forty, falling in a tangled mass. And erupting from the centre of this confusion came Goedendag and his Iron Knights.

Chainswords buzzed as they chopped at limbs and clove heads in two.

The daemonettes recovered quickly, righting themselves and lunging towards the Space Marines, slashing their crab-like claws and kicking with taloned feet. The Iron Knights formed a circle; seven chainswords thrust, cut and parried with elegant precision. More daemonettes dropped down from the floors above and Goedendag withdrew to the centre of the circle, the better to take on this new attack. One daemonette dropped headfirst towards him, one clawed arm stretched out, pointing at his face. He sidestepped, took her arm and rammed the claw straight down into the floor, piercing the metal there. He pushed her forward, breaking her arm, but at that moment a second daemonette fell on his back and he felt the eldritch power of her claw pierce the shell of his armour, the shrieking pain transmitted to his body through his black carapace. He reached for one of the two morning stars strapped to his back and pulled it free, the spiked head of the ball scraping across the face of the daemonette. Now he swung the ball around, as if to hit his own back. He heard the sickening crunch as her body was crushed between the ball of the morning star and the ceramite of his suit.

Still more daemonettes dropped into the room. The space was filled with white flesh, the slash of claws and the buzz and shriek of chainswords. Above him, Goedendag saw a space leading to the nine hundred and forty-second floor, two floors up.

'Telramund, you're in charge,' he called. Summoning all of his enhanced strength, he leapt upwards, catching hold of the bottom-most step.

A claw slashed down and he caught it, pulling the daemonette down to join her sisters below. Quickly, he scrambled up to the next floor.

Daemonettes crowded towards him. Goedendag took a last look at his fellows fighting below, and then he raised his chainsword and charged forward, cutting his way through to the stairs.

He fought his way upwards against the tide of daemonettes, against the tide of blood. All the while, he had the impression that they were playing with him, that they were allowing him to pass, allowing him to climb higher. The waves of daemonettes diminished, though one or two of them still launched themselves at his chainsword.

Now he passed through the floors where the humans lay prisoner. Some were bound, some crawled on their knees, lacking feet, some lay half eviscerated, their shouts of pain weak in their throats, their tormentors called away to fight the Iron Knights.

The humans called out to him for succour. Goedendag ignored them. He could better aid them by confronting whatever lay at the top of this tower.

He pounded on up the flights of stairs, his anger acting as a buffer, pushing away all those that came before him. Now the daemonettes hung back as he passed; now they stood and watched as he climbed, or they turned and headed downwards to the fray with the remaining Iron Knights.

Now he was certain something was waiting for him at the top of the tower. As he climbed higher, a feeling of anxiety prickled at his heels, and he began to understand the nature of what lay ahead.

The sound of fighting faded to leave an eerie emptiness, a weariness that weighed down on his very soul.

He reached the nine hundred and ninetieth floor, and glimpsed an open space above him.

On floor nine hundred and ninety-two, he stepped out into a vast cavern. The last eight floors had been removed to leave a huge space at the very top of the hive tower. A nascent warp portal hung in the middle of the space, silver and black roiling in a halo on the boundary between this reality and the dreadful void of the otherworld. Blood flowed through the warp portal in a thin stream, splashing onto the mound of dead bodies below that lay folded up to look like pebbles. A mound of pink and brown and yellow pebbles, bound in red cord. And there, standing at the summit, surrounded by the dark halo of the nascent warp, bathed in the blood that ran from it, a shape within a shape.

Goedendag climbed the pile of the dead, and finally he came face to face with Gutor Invareln, latent psyker, the cause of all the horror.

Around the human, Goedendag could see the outline of the creature that had possessed him. Huge and powerful, with a bovine face, one female breast and four arms. Two of them ended in human-like hands, two of them in crab-like claws.

A greater daemon of Slaanesh. A Keeper of Secrets.

The daemon had not achieved full corporeality; it seemed to be still existing in some halfway state as it entered this universe. The psyker was completely possessed, looking out from the translucent form of the demon that surrounded him, eyes vacant, an idiot grin on his face.

The daemon giggled at the sight of Goedendag.

'How appropriate,' said the daemon. 'For the Iron Knights have their secrets, do they not?'

'And you are a Keeper of Secrets,' replied Goedendag.

'What is your name?'

'Goedendag Morningstar.'

There was silence, broken only by the ever present dripping of blood.

'Don't you wish to know my name?' asked the daemon.

'No.'

A look of petulance crossed the daemon's face, like that of a small child denied a toy. It quickly passed.

'And yet I believe I do hold a secret you wish to know. Do you wish to know the location of your brethren?'

'I don't know what you're talking about.'

The daemon laughed.

'I *know* that you are lying. Everyone knows of the penitence of the Iron Knights. Few outside the order know the reason. I am one of them. I am a Keeper of Secrets, and I know the location of your traitor brethren. It lies beyond the portal, Goedendag Morningstar, but I think you know that already. Why else would you have come here?'

'To kill you, of course.'

The daemon looked beyond Goedendag's shoulder. Goedendag did not turn. He could hear the skittering, giggling sound made by the daemonettes who filed into the room behind him.

'My daughters are here. It would appear the comrades you left behind on the floor below have fallen, Goedendag Morningstar.'

'It is no disgrace to die in battle.'

'The traitors you seek thought otherwise, Goedendag Morningstar. They chose Chaos, Goedendag Morningstar. And you nearly chose the same!'

Goedendag said nothing, for to speak with a daemon was to be drawn into an argument with a daemon.

'I will take your silence as agreement.' The half seen features of the daemon looked down. Within its form, the psyker beamed with happy idiocy. 'There is no need for you to lie, Goedendag Morningstar. I can sense the shame within you. It is the only thing that you have that outshines the temptation you feel, for you are full of lust for the pleasures of life. The pleasures denied to a Space Marine.'

Still Goedendag was silent.

'And I should know. Isn't that what I am about? The Keeper of Secrets? What secrets could be greater than those *we do not want to know about ourselves*?'

'What secrets, indeed?' said Goedendag tightly.

'See? You speak! You should not be ashamed, Goedendag Morningstar. Your behaviour does not surprise me. Who is more zealous in following a path than one who has almost fallen from it? A man who was never tempted would not have half your ferocity. Look, it brought you to the top of this tower!'

'I came to destroy you.'

'So you say. Come, Goedendag Morningstar. Soon the portal will open fully. Why not pass beyond it? Join your dark brethren. Join the Iron Knights that you call traitors.'

'Enough talk, daemon. It is time to fight.'

The daemon laughed.

'Fight? It is all that you can do to stand, Goedendag Morningstar. Look at you. My very presence induces anguish and ecstasy within you.'

Goedendag looked down at the floor, focused on the corporeal feet of the psyker that stood within the outline of the daemon, and he tried to concentrate on the reality of the situation. In truth, he felt a savage joy within him that he usually knew best from battle, but this time it was mixed with something more innocent, something that rang with the purity of childhood, but a tainted purity, something polluted by blood and perverted in daemonic fashion. He felt the excitement that he had known when, as an aspirant, he had first begun the transition to Space Marine, when the gene-seed had been implanted and he had begun the long process of modification. Except now he felt something that he hadn't known at the time. A deep anguish, a total certainty that the procedure would fail, that his body would reject the process and he would be branded a failure, that he would let down those who had come to depend upon him.

'You're strong, daemon' admitted Goedendag. 'You are affecting even me.'

'This human is strong,' said the daemon, indicating the psyker within himself. 'Strong enough to offer himself in sacrifice in order to open the portal.'

'He was a weak man!' shouted Goedendag.

'He was a bitter man. Bitter that his powers were overlooked by the Imperium.'

'He should have been executed as a danger to all.' Goedendag felt his willpower draining away.

'Lucky for us that he was not. You know what price he asked in order to sacrifice himself to the portal? Only that he lived long enough to see us succeed. That was one bargain that we were happy to keep.'

Goedendag felt the chainsword getting heavier in his hands.

'You're getting weaker,' said the daemon, as the chainsword slipped though Goedendag's fingers and clattered to the floor.

'I can still fight.'

'I don't think so. And so, Goedendag, before you die, I have one final question to ask you. Goedendag means Morningstar, does it not?'

'It does. This is the last question you wish to ask me?'

'No, you interrupt me. Your name, therefore, is Morningstar Morning-star. Why is that?'

'Because of this,' said Goedendag. And he crossed his hands over his chest and, gripping the two morning star handles that were fastened on his back, he swung them up and around, through the translucent outline of the daemon and brought them together, crushing the psyker's head. There was a crunch of bone, grey matter exploding in a disk between the spikes of the two balls.

The daemon shrieked, and immediately Goedendag felt the sense of anguish and ecstasy decrease.

'The portal is closing,' said the daemon. 'But I will make my mark in this world first!'

Goedendag stooped and scooped the chainsword from the floor. The daemon saw what he was doing and laughed.

'That will not harm me in this form!'

'I am not aiming for you,' replied Goedendag coolly as he triggered the chainsword and used it to cut through the dead psyker's neck. 'Remov-ing the head will speed the closing of the rift.' He straightened up and moved around so that his back was to the shrinking portal.

'And now,' he said. 'What will your daemonettes do? Will they attempt to pass me as they flee for the closing warp?'

The daemon laughed.

'One man against the force of the daemonettes? I only wish I could sustain corporeality enough to watch you die under their onslaught! As it is, I will take comfort in the fact the location of your Iron Brethren will remain my secret!'

'Daemon, when I have disposed of your daughters, I will come looking for you. You have my word on that.'

The daemon laughed louder.

'You say that when you fight only with a chainsword? And listen! My sisters approach now!'

It was true. Goedendag heard the skittering of claws on blood and iron.

'Only a chainsword, you say,' said Goedendag, smiling grimly. 'You forget my morning stars.'

'And will that be enough?' laughed the daemon.

'Let us see,' said Goedendag, and he triggered the chainsword. The angry buzzing was an invitation to the approaching daemons. He stepped forward and raised his sword.

Simultaneously, eight white-bodied daemons leapt at him, scream-ing in unison. They raised their crab-like claws and plunged towards Goedendag, teeth bared. Eight more leapt up behind them.

'Goodbye,' said the daemon, and Goedendag stepped forward to meet the lithe attackers. The first lunged forward with one snapping claw. Goedendag swung his chainsword in a tight circle that sliced through the claw and into the side of the daemonette that followed. A clawed foot lashed out and took hold of his armoured boot. Goedendag ignored it and slashed at another attacker.

'Come on!' he called. 'Come on, all of you!'

White bodies advanced on all sides. Claws, screaming, blood, ichor. Goedendag stood at the top of a mound of naked, bound bodies, bathed in blood, and he fought like a daemon himself. But there were too many of them. The sheer weight of numbers began to overwhelm him.

And then he heard a shout. There, in the distance, he saw Telramund, armour half broken, bathed in blood and ichor. And behind him, Fastlinger, and then Franosch.

The shout came again.

'The humans are clear.'

Tired though he was, Goedendag smiled.

'Now,' he said, holstering his chainsword. 'Now it is time for meltaguns!'

The Iron Knights looked at the bodies of the fallen. Goedendag and Franosch watched the shrinking remnants of the closing portal.

'Anything?' asked Goedendag.

Franosch shook his head.

'Sorry. Nothing.' He wiped his forehead, removing a splash of blood. 'Did it occur to you that the daemon could be lying?'

Goedendag looked thoughtful.

'I don't think so,' he said. 'It knew too much.'

'Then the Iron Brethren exist somewhere in the warp. The story is true.'

'Perhaps...' He placed a warning hand on Franosch's arm. Kelra, the Imperial Guardswoman, had entered the room.

'So, Goedendag,' she said, 'you succeeded. The tower is secure. The civilians are safe. Thank you.'

'We don't do this for gratitude,' said Goedendag. 'Don your helmets, brothers. It's time to leave.'

'But–' called Kelra.

'Thank you, sister,' said Goedendag. 'We'll see ourselves out.'

# LAST MAN STANDING

WRITTEN by DAN ABNETT
DRAWN by MIKE PERKINS
LETTERED by KID ROBSON

"MY NAME IS FERON.

"SPACE MARINE SCOUT, IMPERIAL FISTS CHAPTER.

"THE OLD CHARTS CALL THIS PLANET KOLKUN.

"HERE, IN THE PUMICE OCEANS OF THE SOUTHERN HEMISPHERE, THE FISTS HAVE SPENT SIX MONTHS HOLDING THE LINE AGAINST AN ENEMY INCURSION.

"IN THE MIDDLE OF THIS CARNAGE, I AM A FLEETING SHADOW, WHO OBSERVES AND LEARNS AND INFORMS.

"THAT IS MY ALLOTTED ROLE."

"MY MISSION TODAY, TO SURVEY THE *ORK* GUNNERY POSITIONS ALONG THE WESTERN EDGE OF THE *TARKOOM FLATS.*

"TOMORROW, A MAJOR OFFENSIVE WILL *LIVE OR DIE* ON THE ACCURACY OF MY DATA-GATHERING. I—

"SOMETHING FLICKERS, FLASHES, *BURNS...*

"THE SKY LIGHTS UP, TWO MILES TO THE EAST, SOME GREAT DRAMA IS PLAYED OUT.

"I HEAR BOLTERS COUGHING, CHAINSWORDS SHRIEKING.

"COMM-LINK TRAFFIC ERUPTS. FAST-CUT STACCATO EXCHANGES ON THE ENCRYPTED BEAM.

"IT'S A SQUAD OF FISTS. PINNED DOWN. *DYING.*

"GLORY WALK WITH YOU, BROTHERS.

"WHAT HELP I CAN OFFER IS YOURS.

"WEAPONS TO STANDBY. MOVE OUT.

"*GET A FIX! GET A FIX!*"

"THERE...A SOLID RETURN!

"BLOOD OF THE EMPEROR, THEY'RE BEING SLAUGHTERED! LIFE SIGNALS ARE DISAPPEARING FROM MY TRACER AS I WATCH!"

"IF I CAN ONLY—

KXAP!!

KXAP!!

"HELL'S TEETH!"

"I'M SUDDENLY FAR TOO AWARE THAT I'M JUST A SOLO SCOUT, STRAYING BLINDLY FROM HIS ASSIGNED AREA, RUNNING INTO THE JAWS OF DEATH.

"STILL...I THUMB OFF THE SAFETY ON MY INFERNUS 5...

"...AND I LET DEATH KNOW I'M HERE!"

BTAMM! BTAMM! BTAMMM!

FTUMP!

KWATCHH!

WHUMPA WHUMPA WHUMPA WHUMPA?

WHERE HUMAN RUNT?

MUCH DEATH-KILL.

MUST BE DEAD. KILL HIM *GOOD*.

WHAT THIS STRING DO?

BRAINLESS F—

"MY SERGEANT ALWAYS SAID THE SIMPLE IDEAS ARE THE BEST."

"EIGHT FRAG GRENADES TIED TO A TRIP-LINE, BURIED IN THE DUST. CURIOSITY DOES THE REST."

"COMM-TRAFFIC BLURTS AGAIN—"

ALL FIELD UNITS WITHDRAW FROM GRID NINE NINETY EIGHT. OPPOSITION TOO INTENSE. LOSSES GREAT, REPEAT...

"NO!"

"THERE'S STILL **ONE** LIFE SIGNAL LEFT. WEAK, BUT THERE. THEY'VE GOT A **PRISONER.**

"SIGNAL IDENT SHOWS IT TO BE THE APOTHECARY. I'D NOT WISH TO LEAVE **ANY MAN** BEHIND, BUT OF THEM ALL, HE IS THE MOST PRECIOUS..."

"EVEN IF IT MEANS WALKING ON INTO THOSE JAWS OF DEATH."

# THE CHOSEN

I TELL YOU THIS: WE ARE THE CHOSEN.

WE GATHER TODAY TO HEAR OUR STORY, OF HOW WE WERE FAVOURED.

LISTEN! I TELL THE TALE OF A THOUSAND SUMMERS PAST.

' IN THE LAND OF THE WESTERN JUNGLE LAY THE VALLEY OF THE DEAD.

' THE KING OF KINGS DECRIED, IN THE STAR EMPEROR'S NAME, THAT NONE SHOULD TRESPASS.

' AND NONE DID. UNTIL THE MAN CAME. THE GREEDY MAN.

' HE IGNORED THE COMMANDMENT OF THE KING OF KINGS AND WENT UNTO THE TEMPLES.

' HE WENT SEEKING TREASURE.

' SEEKING POWER.

' BUT HE FOUND ONLY DEATH WEARING A METAL MASK. '

STORY: KIERON GILLEN • ART: STEVE PUGH • LETTERS: FIONA STEPHENSON

' THE WARRIORS BORE THE MARK OF THE SALAMANDER WHICH WAS HOLY TO THEM.

' AND IN THEIR HANDS THEY CARRIED SWORDS OF THE STARS AND SPEARS OF THE HEARTH.

' THEY STRUCK WITH FIRE HOT ENOUGH TO SEAR EVEN THE COLD FLESH OF THE METAL DAEMONS.

' THE SUN DID RISE AND FALL IN THE SKY, SEVEN TIMES OVER.

' AND STILL THE BATTLE RAGED.

' FOR EVERY DAEMON STRUCK DOWN WOULD BE REPLACED BY ONE OF ITS DARK KIN ARRIVING...

'...OR RISE AGAIN FROM THE EDGE OF THE GRAVE TO PRESS ITS ATTACK. '

END

STORY: JAMES PEATY · ART: SHAUN THOMAS · LETTERS: FIONA STEPHENSON

AS A YOUNG WARRIOR I WAS PART OF A PILGRIMAGE TO THE PYRE-TOMBS OF KHUM KARTA.

OF THOSE WHO JOURNEYED TO THE FINAL RESTING PLACE OF OUR HEROES...

WHITE SCARS!

KCHINK-

KCHINK-
KCHINK-

...ONLY I RETURNED.

'...AND ONE DAY TAKE YOUR PLACE THERE.'

AT THE TIME, I LAUGHED AT THE OLD MAN.

BOOOOM!

KA-BOOM!

KREEEAKK!

BUT IN MY HEART...

KILL HIM!

BLAM! BLAM!

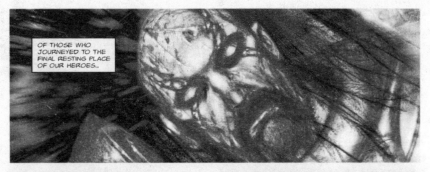

OF THOSE WHO JOURNEYED TO THE FINAL RESTING PLACE OF OUR HEROES...

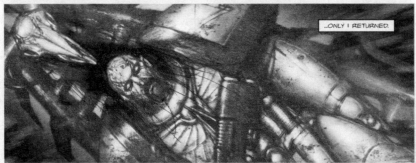

...ONLY I RETURNED.

FOR THE KHAN...

...AND THE EMPEROR

END

For biographies of the authors in this volume
visit *www.blacklibrary.com*

# READ IT FIRST
EXCLUSIVE PRODUCTS | EARLY RELEASES | FREE DELIVERY
### blacklibrary.com

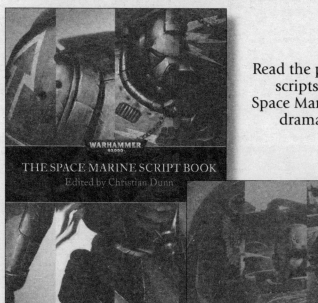

Read the production
scripts for the
Space Marines audio
drama range

WARHAMMER
40000

THE SPACE MARINE SCRIPT BOOK
Edited by Christian Dunn

WARHAMMER
40000

THE SPACE MARINE SCRIPT BOOK TWO
Edited by Graeme Lyon

Exclusively available from
*blacklibrary.com*